To

Onkel Eddy,

" Merry Christmas "

1992

Love

Laurier

James Herbert

Moon

Shrine

The Dark

Fluke

CHANCELLOR

PRESS

Moon first published in Great Britain in 1985 by New English Library
Shrine first published in Great Britain in 1983 by New English Library
The Dark first published in Great Britain in 1980 by New English Library
Fluke first published in Great Britain in 1977 by New English Library

This collected volume first published in Great Britain in 1990
by Reed International Books Ltd

This edition published in 1992 by Chancellor Press
an imprint of Reed International Books Ltd
Michelin House
81 Fulham Road
London SW3 6RB

ISBN 1 85152 239 5

Printed and bound in the United Kingdom by The Bath Press

Contents

Moon

Before

The boy had stopped crying.

He lay in his narrow bed, eyes closed, his face an alabaster mask in the moonlight. Occasionally a tremor would run the length of his body.

He clutched the bedsheets, pulling them tight under his chin. A dreadful heaviness inside weighed his body down, a feeling that his blood had turned to liquid lead: the burden was loss, and it had left him exhausted and weak.

The boy had rested there a long time – how many hours he had no way of knowing, for all of the last three days had been a timeless eternity – but his father had forbidden him to move from the bed again. So he lay there, enduring the loss, frightened by the new loneliness.

Until something caused him to open his red-rimmed eyes once more.

The figure stood near the end of the bed and she smiled at him. He felt her warmth, the momentary shedding of bereavement. But it was impossible. His father had told him it was impossible.

'You . . . can't . . . be . . .' he said, his small voice a shivery intrusion on the night. 'He . . . says . . . you can't . . . you can't . . . be . . .'

The sense of loss was renewed, for now it was also within her.

And then the startled boy looked elsewhere in the room, gazing upwards into a far corner as if suddenly aware of yet another presence, of someone else watching him, someone he could not see. The moment vanished when footsteps were heard along the corridor and he looked away, for the first time real fear in his eyes. The woman was gone.

In the doorway stood the swaying shadow of a man.

The boy's father stumbled towards the bed, the familiar reek of alcohol as much a part of him as the perpetual sullenness of his features.

'I told you,' the man said, and there seemed to be guilt mixed with anger in the harsh words. 'No more! No more . . .' His fist was raised as he approached and the boy cowered beneath the bedsheets.

Outside, the full moon was clear-edged and pure against the deep blackness of the night.

At last she was dead.

Where there had been terror, there was now only emptiness.

Dead eyes. Those of a fish on an iced slab.

Her body dormant, the final spasm exhausted, the final gasp silenced. Her last expression dissolved.

Clawed fingers still held the shape above her, one thumb curled inside its mouth as though she had tried to rip away the smile.

The shape rose, releasing its grip from her throat; its breath was barely laboured, even though the woman beneath had struggled for a long time.

It pulled the thumb from its mocking lips and the corpse's hand fell away, smacking against bare flesh.

It paused, studying the victim. Smiling all the while.

It reached for the lifeless hands, gripping their wrists, lifting them. It ran the cracked nails downs its own face, drawing the shock-stiffened fingers around its throat as if taunting them, tempting revenge. A low chuckle derided their inertia.

It trailed the hands across its exposed body straddled over the corpse, moving them down so that they touched everywhere, caressed every part. The deathly soft stroking incited further sensations.

The figure busied itself upon the woman's slowly cooling body.

After a while it rose from the bed, a light sheen of perspiration coating its skin. Not yet was it satiated.

Cold drizzle spattered the window in a sudden gust as if protesting against the cruelty inside. Faded curtains, closed against daylight, muffled the sound.

A bag in the corner of the dingy room was snapped open, a black package removed. The package was unrolled on the bed, close to the corpse, and the gleam of metal instruments was only slightly dulled by the poor light. Each one was lifted, examined, held close to the eyes whose gleam could not be subdued. The first was chosen.

The body, cooling to room temperature, was sliced from sternum to pubic symphysis, then from hip to hip. Blood quickly seeped though the deep cross.

The flaps were separated then pulled back. Fingers, already crimson, delved inside.

It removed the organs, cutting where necessary, and placed them on the bed covers where they glistened and steamed. The heart, reached for last and wrenched free, was tossed onto the heap. It slithered down the slippery mound and plopped to the floor. The sickly odour pervaded the room.

A receptacle made, it was soon filled.

The figure searched the room for small objects, but only after the dead woman's own appendages had been used.

When at last it was satisfied, it drew needle and thread from the wrapping on the bed.

It began to sew the flaps together again, piercing the flesh with large, crude stitchwork, smiling all the while. The smile broadening to a grin as it thought of the last object placed inside the body.

He finned over the green-hued rocks, movement leisurely, relaxed, hands used only occasionally to change direction, careful to avoid barnacles that could cut deep into water-softened skin. His legs flexed slowly, moving from the hips with long, graceful strokes, semi-hard fins propelling him easily through the currents.

Coral weed waved ghostly patterns at him, and startled fish jack-knifed away from his stealthy intrusion; snakelocks anemone seemed to beckon silently. Daylight filtered through from above, its rays dissipated, the seabed sanctum muted and secretive. Childes could hear only the ponderous, dull sounds of his own actions.

A tiny undulation, a scurry of sand, caught his eye and he cautiously approached, gently placing his hands on an outcrop of rock, bringing himself to an easy, swaying halt.

Below him, a starfish had attached itself to a cockle, pinning it down and prising the two shell valves apart with tube feet. The starfish worked patiently, its five tentacles used in relays, tiring its prey, resolutely widening the gap to expose the cockle's body tissues. Childes watched with mild but fascinated revulsion as the hunter eventually extruded its own stomach and sank it into the opening to suck out the fleshy substance beneath.

A subtle displacement among the ridges and caverns of barnacled stone close by diverted the diver's attention. Puzzled, he studied the craggy relief for a few moments before a further shifting directed his gaze. The spiny spider crab skited across the rock face, its shell and claws sprouting green algae, a natural and effective camouflage in both the shallows and the deeper waters. When still, it was virtually invisible.

Childes followed the crab's progress, admiring its agility and speed, the little multi-legged creature enlarged and brought much closer by the magnification of his diving mask's glass faceplate and the seawater itself. The spider crab stopped as if suddenly aware of being stalked; he used a probing finger to galvanize another spurt.

The diver's smile at the sudden panicked flurry was distorted by the snorkel wedged into his teeth and gums, and he was abruptly aware that his lungs were almost exhausted of air. Unhurried, he prepared to skim back to the surface.

The sighting came without warning. Just as other sightings had in the past.

Yet he hardly knew what he saw, for it was in his mind, not his vision; a confused jumble of colours, of smells. His hands tingled in the water. There was something long and shiny, coiled, red and gleaming wet. Now metal, keen-edged steel against a mushy softness. Swimming in blood. He was swimming in blood. Nausea hit him and he drew in salt water.

His body curled up painfully and bile mixed with seawater exploded from his throat, clogging the snorkel pipe. The mouthpiece shot free of his lips and more water rushed in. Childes cried out involuntarily, the sound a muffled, gurgling croak, and he kicked down, arms reaching for the surface. Wildly escaping bubbles matched the crazy disorder behind his eyes. The light-spread ceiling above seemed a long way off.

Another vision stabbed into his nightmare. Hands, cruel, blunt fingers, moving in rhythm. An insane thought-sight. They were sewing.

Childes' body doubled up once more.

He instinctively tried to close his mouth, no clear direction in his head any more, but it continued to drink in great gulps of salt water as though conspiring with the sea against him. His senses began to dim, his arms and legs felt feeble. So quickly, he thought. They warned how quick drowning could be. Yet ridiculously, he was aware of the J-shaped snorkel, tucked into the retaining band of his diving mask, scratching loosely against his cheek. He struggled, feeling himself drifting, sinking.

A slender arm slid beneath his shoulder, gripping tight. A hugging body against his back. Rising. Slowly, controlled. He tried to help, but an opaque mantle was descending.

Bursting through the surface as though shot from a black stifling embrace, life painfully thrust back into him rather than gently returned.

His stomach and chest heaved, jetting liquid; he choked, spluttered, threatened to drag them both down again. He vaguely heard a soothing voice and tried to heed the words, forcing himself to relax, commanding his lungs to take in air cautiously, gasp by gasp, spitting out residue, coughing out the last of the bile.

She towed him back to the shoreline, holding his arms above the elbows, his head cradled against one of her own arms. She swam on her back by his side, fins driving them easily through the small waves. His breathing was still laboured, but soon he was able to help by flexing his own legs, keeping in time with hers.

They reached the shallower water and the girl hauled him to his feet. She pulled the mask from his face and put an arm around his hunched shoulders, hitting his back when he coughed more sea, bending with him, her young face etched with concern. Kneeling, she drew off his flippers, then removed her own. His shoulders still jerked with the effort of breathing as he stood half-crouched, hands on his knees; gradually he recovered, the shudders merging into a shivering. The girl waited patiently, her own diving mask raised high over her forehead, her blonde hair worked loose, darkened by the water and hanging in dripping trails over her shoulders. She didn't speak, knowing it would be pointless just yet.

Eventually it was the man who gasped, 'Amy . . .'

'It's all right, let's get to shore.'

They left the water, lurching slightly as they went, her arm beneath his shoulders, supporting. Childes slumped onto the shingle, feeling relieved, shocked, sickened – all these emotions. She sat next to him, sweeping hair from his eyes, gently massaging his back.

They were alone in the small, remote bay, the steep climb through the rock-eroded cleft too daunting for many, a chill south-easterly breeze deterring others. Lush vegetation spilled over the clifftops, flowing down the steep slopes, stemmed only by an uncompromising stone face near the base, a granite fringe washed clean by thunderous tides. Early May flowers littered the upper reaches, speckling the verdure with blue, white and yellow. A miniature waterfall gushed close by, its stream winding through the pebbles and rocks to join the sea. Further out, little fishing boats, dinghies mainly, bobbed easily on the slate sea, their mooring lines stretching like grey thread to a quay on the far side of the inlet. Access to the quay was by a narrow track, a jumble of boulders separating it from the beach itself. The girl noticed one or two faces peering in their direction from the quayside wall, obviously concerned over the incident; she signalled that all was well and they turned away.

Childes pushed himself into a sitting position, wrists over his raised knees, head slumped forward. He was still shivering.

'You scared me, Jon,' the girl said, kneeling before him.

He looked at her and his face was pale. He brushed a hand across his eyes as if trying to dismiss a memory.

'Thanks for dragging me out,' he said at last.

She leaned forward and kissed his cheek, then his shoulder. Her eyes were curious. 'What happened out there?'

His body juddered and she realized how cold he was. 'I'll fetch the blanket,' she said, standing.

Her bare feet ignored the hard shingle as she skipped over to their pile of clothing and bags lying on a flat slab further up the beach. Childes watched her lithe figures as she snatched a blanket from a hold-all and was grateful for her presence – not just because she had pulled him from the sea, but because she was with him. He shifted his gaze back to the lapping water, a white band on the horizon, harbinger of the coming storm.

His eyes closed and he tasted salt in his throat. He cast his head downwards and moaned quietly.

Why now, after so long?

The weight of the blanket over his shoulders drew him back.

'Drink,' Amy said, holding a thin silver flask under his nose.

The brandy loosened the salt inside and he relished the sudden inner warmth. He raised one arm and she joined him beneath the blanket.

'You okay?' she asked, snuggling close.

He nodded, but the shivering had not yet ceased.

'I brought your glasses over.'

He took them from her, put them on. The focused world was no more real. When he spoke, his voice was shaky.

'It's happening again,' he said.

'Tomorrow?' he asked.

Amy shook her head. 'Daddy has guests – all day.' She rolled her eyes. 'I'm on duty.'

'Business?'

'Uh-huh. Potential investors from Lyon. He invited them for the weekend, but thank God they could only make it for Sunday. They fly back Monday afternoon, after they've visited the company. He's disappointed – he wanted to show off the island as well.'

Paul Sebire, Amy's father, was chief executive of Jacarte International, a powerful financial investment company based in the offshore island, itself a low-tax haven for those on the Continent as well as on the mainland. Although predominantly British, the island was physically closer to France.

'Pity,' Childes said.

'I'm sorry, Jon.' She leaned back into the car to kiss him, her hair, now tied back into a tail, twisting around her neck to brush against his chest.

He returned her kiss, relishing the smell of sea on her, tasting the salt on her lips.

'Doesn't he ever relax?' he asked.

'It is relaxation for him. I'd have swung you an invite, but I didn't think you'd enjoy yourself.'

'You know me so well.' He prepared to drive away. 'Give your father my love.'

She mock-scowled. 'I doubt he'll reciprocate. Jon, about earlier . . .'

'Thanks again for dragging me out.'

'I didn't mean that.'

'What I saw?'

She nodded. 'It's been so long.'

He looked straight ahead, but his gaze was inward. After a while, he replied, 'I never really thought it was over.'

'But almost three years. Why should it start again now?'

Childes shrugged. 'Maybe it's a freak. Could be it won't happen again. It may just have been my own imagination playing tricks.' He closed his eyes momentarily, knowing it wasn't, but unwilling to discuss it just then. Leaning across the steering wheel, he touched her neck. 'Hey, c'mon, stop looking so anxious. You have a good time tomorrow and I'll see you in school Monday. We'll talk more then.'

Amy took her hold-all from the back seat, Childes helping her to lift it over. 'Will you call me tonight?'

'I thought you'd planned to mark papers.'

'I don't have much choice, with Sunday so busy. I'll have earned a few minutes break, though.'

He forced a light tone. 'Okay, Teach. Don't be too hard on the kids.'

Depends on what they've written. I'm not sure which is more difficult: teaching them French or decent English. At least with computers your own machines can correct their mistakes.'

He huffed, smiling. 'I wish it were that simple.' He kissed her cheek once more before she straightened. The first raindrops stippled the windscreen.

Take care, Jon,' she said, wanting to say more, needing to, but sensing his resistance. Getting to know Childes had taken a long, long time and even now she was aware there were places – dark places – inside him she would never reach. She wondered if his ex-wife had ever tried.

Amy watched the little black Mini pull away, frowning as she gave a single wave. She turned and hurried through the open iron gates, running down the short drive to the house before the rain began in earnest.

Childes soon turned off the main highway, steering into the narrow lanes which spread through the island like veins from primary arteries, occasionally slowing and squeezing close to hedges and walls to ease past oncoming vehicles, whose drivers adopted the same tactics. He clutched the wheel too tightly, his knuckles white ridges, driving by reflex rather than consideration; his mind, now that he was alone, was preoccupied with other thoughts. By the time he reached the cottage he was trembling once more and the sour taste of bile was back in his throat.

He swung the Mini into the narrow opening before the old stone cottage, a patch he had cleared of weeds and brambles when he had first arrived, and switched off the engine. He left the bag containing his swimming gear in the car, jumping out and fumbling for the front-door key. The key resisted his first attempts to insert it in the lock. At last successful, he thrust open the door and rushed down the short corridor, just making it to the tiny bathroom as the bottom of his stomach rose like an express elevator. He retched over the toilet bowl, shedding, it seemed, only a small portion of the substance clogging the insides. He blew his nose on tissue, flushing the toilet and watching the soft paper swirl round until it was gulped away. Removing his brown-rimmed glasses, he washed his face in cold water, keeping his hands over his eyes for several moments, cooling them.

Childes regarded himself in the cabinet mirror as he dried his face and his reflection was pallid; he wasn't sure if his own imagination was creating the shadows under his eyes. Stretching his fingers before him, he tried to keep them still; he couldn't.

Childes replaced his glasses and went through to the sitting room, ducking his head slightly as he entered the door; he wasn't especially tall, but the building was old, the ceilings low, the door frames lower. The room lacked space, but then Childes had not packed too much into it: a faded and lumpy sofa, portable TV, square coffee table; low bookcases flanked the brick fireplace on either side, their shelves crammed. On top of one, by a lamp, was a small cluster of bottles and glasses. He went over and poured himself a stiff measure of Scotch.

Outside, the rain had become a steady downpour and he stood by the window overlooking his diminutive rear garden, broodingly watching. The cottage, among a row of others, all detached, but only just, backed on to open fields. At one time the houses had all been field-hand's tied homes, but the estate had been divided up long since, land and properties sold off. Childes had been fortunate to rent one when he had come to the island over two, almost three, years before, for empty property was scarce here, and it was the school's principal, Estelle Piprelly, eager for his computer skills, who had directed him towards the place. Her considerable influence had also helped him obtain the lease.

In the far distance, on the peninsula, he could just make out the college itself, an odd assortment of buildings, expanding over the years in various, unbalanced styles. The predominant structure, with its tower, was white. From that far away, it was no more than a rain-blurred greyish projecton, the sky behind gloomed with rolling clouds.

When Childes had fled the mainland, away from pernicious publicity, the curious stares, not just of friends and colleagues, but of complete strangers who had seen his face on TV or in the newspapers, the island had provided a halcyon refuge. Here was a tight community existing within itself, the mainland and its complexities held at arm's length. Yet, close-knit though their society was, it had proved relatively easy for him to be absorbed into the population of over fifty thousand. Morbid interest and – he clenched the glass hard – and *accusations* had been left behind. He wanted it to stay that way.

Childes drained the Scotch and poured another; like the brandy earlier, it helped purge the foul taste that lingered in his mouth. He returned to the window and this time saw only the ghost of his own reflection. The day outside had considerably darkened.

Was it the same? Had the images his mind had seen beneath the sea anything to do with those terrible, nightmare, visions which had haunted him so long ago? He couldn't tell: nearly drowning had altered the sensation. For a moment, though, during and shortly after, when he had lain gasping on the beach, he had been *sure*, certain the sightings had returned.

Dread filled him.

He was cold, yet perspiration dampened his brow. Apprehension gripped him, and then a fresh anxiety homed in.

He went out into the hallway and picked up the phone, dialled.

After a while, a breathless voice answered.

'Fran?' he said, eyes on the wall but seeing her face.

'Who else? That you, Jon?'

'Yeah.'

A long pause, then his ex-wife said, 'You called me. Did you have something to say?'

'Where's, uh, how's Gabby?'

'She's fine, considering. She's next door with Annabel playing at who can create most havoc. I think Melanie planned to banish them to the garden for the afternoon, but the weather won't allow. How's it over there? – it's piddling here.'

'Yeah, the same. I think it's working its way up to a storm.'

Another silence.

'I'm kinda busy, Jonathan. I have to be in town by four.'

'You working on a Saturday?'

'Sort of. A new author's arriving in London today and the publisher wants me to cosy him, give him a prelim on his tour next week.'

'Couldn't Ashby have handled it?'

Her tone was sharp. 'We run the agency on a partnership basis – I carry my load. Anyway, what do you expect of a born-again career woman?'

The barely veiled accusation stung and, not for the first time, he wondered if she would ever come to terms with his walking out. Walking out is how she would have put it.

'Who's taking care of Gabby?'

'She'll have dinner at Melanie's and Janet'll collect her later.' Janet was the young girl his former wife had hired as a daily nanny. 'She'll stay with Gabby until I get home. Is that good enough for you?'

'Fran, I didn't mean –'

'You didn't have to go, Jon. Nobody pushed you out.'

'You didn't have to stay there,' he replied quietly.

'You wanted me to give up too much.'

'The agency was only part-time then.'

'But it was *important* to me. Now it's even more so – it has to be. And there were other reasons. Our life here.'

'It'd become unbearable.'

'Whose fault was that?' Her voice softened, as though she regretted her words. 'All right, I know things happened, ran out of control; I tried to understand, to cope. But you were the one who wanted to run.'

'There was more to it, you know that.'

'I know it would have died down eventually. *Everything.*' They both knew what she meant.

'You can't be sure.'

'Look, I don't have time for this now, I have to get moving. I'll give your kisses to Gabby and maybe she'll call you tomorrow.'

'I'd like to see her soon.'

'I . . . I don't know. Perhaps at half term. We'll see.'

'Do one thing for me, Fran.'

She sighed, anger gone. 'Ask me.'

'Check on Gabby before you leave. Just pop in, say hello. Make sure she's okay.'

'What is this, Jon? I'd have done that anyway, but what are you saying?'

'It's nothing. I guess this empty house is getting to me. You worry, y'know?'

'You sound . . . funny. Are you really that down?'

'It'll pass. Sorry I held you up.'

'I'll get there. Do you need anything, Jon, can I send anything over?'

Gabby. You can send over my daughter. 'No, I don't need anything, everything's fine. Thanks anyway.'

'Okay. Gotta run now.'

'Good luck with your author.'

'With business the way it is, we take anything we can get. He'll get a good promo. See you.'

The connection was broken.

Childes returned to the sitting room and slumped onto the sofa, deciding he didn't want another drink. He removed his spectacles and rubbed his eyes with stiffened fingers, his daughter's image swimming before him. Gabriel had been four when he'd left them. He hoped one day she would understand.

He rested there for a long time, head against the sofa back, legs stretched out onto the small patterned rug on the polished wood floor, glasses propped in one hand on his chest, sometimes staring at the ceiling, sometimes closing his eyes, trying to remember what he had seen.

For some reason, all he could visualize was the colour red. A thick, glutinous red. He thought he could even scent the blood.

The first nightmare visited him that night.

He awoke afraid and rigid. Alone.

The after-vision of the dream was still with him, yet it resisted focus. He could sense only a white, shimmering thing, a taunting spectre. It faded, gradually overwhelmed by the moonlight flooding the room.

Childes pushed himself upright in the bed, resting his back against the cool wall behind. He was frozen, fear caressing him with wintry touches. And he did not know why, could find no reason.

Outside, in the bleak stillness of the silver night, a solitary gull wailed a haunted cry.

'No, Jeanette, you'll have to go back and check. Remember, the computer hasn't got a mind of its own – it relies totally on yours. One wrong instruction from you and it doesn't just get confused – it sulks. It won't give you what you want.'

Childes smiled down at the girl, a little weary of her regular basic errors, but well aware that not *every* youngster's brain was tuned into the rapidly advancing technological era, despite what the newspapers and Sunday colour supps informed their parents. No longer in the commercial world of computers, he had had to adjust himself to slow-down, to pace himself with the children he taught. Some had the knack, others didn't, and he had to ease the latter through their frustration.

'Okay, back to **RETURN** and go through each stage slowly this time, step by step. You can't go wrong if you think about each move.'

Her frown told him she wasn't convinced. Neither was he.

He left Jeanette biting her lower lip and pressing each key with exaggerated deliberation as though it was a battle of wills between girl and machine.

'Hey, Kelly, that's good.'

The fourteen-year-old glanced at him and beamed, her eyes touching his just a little too deeply. He peered at the screen, impressed.

'Is that your own spreadsheet?' he asked.

She nodded, her gaze now back on the visual display.

'Looks like you won't get through the year on those expenses.'

'I will when I send the printout home. Dad'll pay up when he sees the evidence.'

Childes laughed: Kelly had soon discovered the potential of microelectronics. There were seven such machines on benches around the classroom, itself an annexe to the science department, and it seemed all were in constant demand even when he was not there to supervise. He had been fortunate when he had come – *fled* – to the island, for the colleges there, so many of them private concerns, were keen to embrace the computer age, well aware that fee-paying parents regarded such knowledge as an essential part of their children's education. Until his arrival, Childes had been employed on a freelance basis by a company specializing in aiding commercial enterprises, both large and small, to set up computer systems tailored to their particular needs, advising on layout and suitable software, devising appropriate programs, often installing the machinery itself and running crash courses on their functions. One of his usual tasks was to smooth out the kinks in the system, to solve problems that invariably arose in initial operation, and his flair – *intuition*, some called it – for cutting through the intricacies of any system to find a specific fault was uncanny. He had been highly skilled, highly paid, and highly respected by his colleagues; yet his departure had come as a relief to many of them.

Kelly was smiling at him. 'I need a new program to work on,' she said.

Childes checked his watch. 'Bit late to start one now. I'll set you something more difficult next time.'

'I could stay.'

One of the other girls giggled and, despite himself, Childes felt a sudden, ridiculous flush. Fourteen years old, for Chrissake!

'Maybe you could. Not me, though. Just tidy your bench until the bell goes. Better still, run through Jeanette's program with her – she seems to be having difficulties.'

A mild irritation flickered in her eyes, but the smile did not change. 'Yes sir.' A little too brisk.

She sidled rather than walked over to Jeanette's monitor and he mentally shook his head at her poise, her body movement too knowing for her years. Even her close-cropped sandy hair and pert nose failed to assert her true age, and eagerly budding breasts easily defeated any youthful image presented by the school uniform of blue skirt, plain white shirt and striped tie. By comparison, Jeanette appeared every inch the young schoolgirl, with womanhood not yet even peeking over the horizon. It seemed aptitude was not confined just to learning.

He shifted along the benches, leaning forward here and there to give instructions to the other girls, some of whom were sharing machines, soon enthused by their enthusiasm, helping to spot their own 'bugs', showing them the correct procedures. The bell surprised him even though he knew it was imminent.

He straightened, noticing Kelly and Jeanette were not enjoying each other's company. 'Switch off your machines,' he told the class. 'Let's see, when do I take you again . . .?'

'Thursday,' they replied in unison.

'All right, I think we'll cover the various types of computers then, and future developments. Hope you'll have some good questions for me.'

Someone groaned.

'Problem?'

'When do we get on to graphics, sir?' the girl asked. Her plump, almost cherubic, face was puckered with disappointment.

'Soonish, Isobel. When you're ready. Off you go and don't leave anything behind; I'm locking up when I leave.'

The concerted break for the door was not as orderly as the principal of La Roche Ladies College would have wished for, but Childes considered himself neither teacher nor disciplinarian, merely a computer consultant to this school and to two others on the island. So long as the kids did not get out of hand and appeared to absorb much of what he showed them, he liked to keep a relaxed atmosphere in the classroom; he didn't want them wary of the machines and an informal atmosphere helped in that respect. In fact, he found the pupils in all three schools remarkably well-behaved, even those in the boys college.

His eyes itched, irritated by the soft contact lenses he wore. He considered changing them for his glasses lying ready for emergencies at the bottom of his briefcase, but decided it was too much trouble. The irritation would pass.

'Knock, knock.'

He looked around to see Amy standing in the open doorway.

'Is sir coming out to play?' she asked.

'You asking me to?'

'Who am I to be proud?' Amy strolled into the classroom, her hair tied back into a tight bun in an attempt to render her schoolmarmish. To Childes, it only heightened her sensuality, as did her light-green, high-buttoned dress, for he knew beyond the disguise. 'Your eyes look sore,' she remarked, quickly looking back at the open doorway, then pecking his cheek when she saw it was clear.

He resisted the urge to pull her tight. 'How was your day?'

'Don't ask. I took drama.' She shuddered. 'D'you know what play they want to put on for end-of-term?'

He dropped papers into his briefcase and snapped it shut. 'Tell me.'

'Dracula. Can you imagine Miss Piprelly allowing it? I'm frightened even to put forward the suggestion.'

He chuckled. 'Sounds like a good idea. Beats the hell out of Nicholas Nickleby again.'

'Fine, I'll tell her Dracula has your support.'

'I'm just an outsider, not a full member of staff. My opinion doesn't count.'

'You think mine does? Our headmistress may not be the Ayatollah in person, but I'm certain there's a family connection somewhere.'

He shook his head, smiling. 'She's not so bad. A little over-anxious about the school's image, maybe, but it's understandable. For such a small island, you're kind of heavy on private schools.'

'That comes with being a tax haven. You're right, though: competition is fierce, and the college's governing body never lets us forget it. I do have some sympathy for her, even though . . .'

They were suddenly aware of the figure in the doorway.

'Did you forget something, Jeanette?' Childes asked, wondering how long she had been standing there.

The girl looked shyly at him. 'Sorry, sir. I think I left my fountain pen on the bench.'

'All right, go ahead and look.'

Head bowed, Jeanette walked into the room with short, quick steps. A sallow-complexioned girl with dark eyes, who one day might be pretty, Jeanette was petite for her age; her hair was straggly long, not yet teased into any semblance of style. The jacket of her blue uniform was one size too large, shrinking her body even more, and there was a timidity about her that Childes found disarming and sometimes faintly exasperating.

She searched around the computer she had been using, Amy watching with a trace of a smile, while Childes set about unplugging the machines from the mains. Jeanette appeared to be having no luck and finally stared forlornly at the computer as though it had mysteriously swallowed up the missing article.

'No joy?' Childes asked, approaching her section of the bench and stooping to reach the plug beneath.

'No, sir.'

'Ah, I'm not surprised. It's on the floor here.' Kneeling, he offered up the wayward pen.

Solemnly, and avoiding his eyes, Jeanette took it from him. 'Thank you,' she said, and Childes was surprised to see her blush. She hurried from the room.

He pulled the plug and stood. 'What are you smiling about?' he asked Amy.

'The poor girl's got a crush on you.'

'Jeanette? She's just a kid.'

'In a girls-only school, many of them fulltime boarders, any halfway decent-looking male is bound to receive some attention. You haven't noticed?'

He shrugged. 'Maybe one or two have given me some funny looks, but I – what d'you mean *halfway* decent-looking?'

Smiling, Amy grabbed his arm and led him towards the door. 'Come on, school's out and I could use some relaxation. A short drive and a long gin and tonic with lots of ice before I go home for dinner.'

'More guests?'

'No, just family for a change. Which reminds me: you're invited to dinner this weekend.'

He raised his eyebrows. 'Daddy had a change of heart?'

'Uh-uh, he still despises you. Let's call it Mother's influence.'

'That's pretty heartwarming.'

She looked up at him and pulled a face, squeezing his arm before releasing it as they went out into the corridor. On the stairway to the lower floor she was aware of surreptitious appraisal by several pupils, a few nudged elbows here and there. She and Jon were strictly formal with each other in the presence of others on school grounds, but a shared car was enough to set tongues wagging.

They reached the large glass entrance doors of the building, a comparatively new extension housing the science laboratories, music and language rooms, and separated from the main college by a circular driveway with a lawned centre. In the middle, a statue of La Roche's founder stared stoically at the principal white building as if counting every head that entered its portals. Girls hurried across the open space, either towards the carpark at the rear of the college where parents waited, or to dormitories and rest-rooms in the south wing, their chatter unleashed after such a long restraint. The salt tang of sea air breezing over the clifftops was a welcome relief from the shared atmosphere of the classroom and Childes inhaled deeply as he and Amy descended the short flight of concrete steps leading from the annexe.

'Mr Childes! Can you spare a moment?'

They both groaned inwardly when they saw the headmistress waving at them from across the driveway.

'I'll catch up with you,' he murmured to Amy, acknowledging Miss Piprelly with a barely-raised hand.

'I'll wait by the tennis courts. Remember, you're bigger than her.'

'Oh yeah, who says?'

They parted, Childes taking a direct path over the round lawn towards the waiting headmistress, her frown informing him that he really should have walked around. Childes could only describe Miss Piprelly as a literally 'straight' woman: she stood *erect*, rarely relaxed, and her features were peculiarly angular, softening curves hardly in evidence. Even her short, greying hair was rigidly swept back in perfect parallel to the ground, and her lips had a thinness to them that wasn't exactly mean, but looked as if all humour had been ironed from them long ago. The square frames of her spectacles were in resolute harmony with her physical linearity. Even her breasts refused to rebel against the general pattern and Childes had sometimes wondered if they were battened down by artificial means. In darker moments, the thought crossed his mind that there were none.

It hadn't taken long, in fact, to find that Estelle Piprelly, MA (Cantab), MEd, ABPsS, was not as severe as the caricature suggested, although she had her moments.

'What can I do for you, Miss Piprelly?' he asked, standing beside her on the entrance step.

'I know it may seem premature to you, Mr Childes, but I'm trying to organize next term's curriculum. I'm afraid it's necessary for parents of prospective pupils, and our governing body insists that it's finalized well before the summer break. Now, I wondered if you could spare us more of your time in the autumn term. It appears that computer studies – mistakenly to my way of thinking – have become something of a priority nowadays.'

'That could be a little awkward. You know I have the other colleges, Kingsley and de Montfort.'

'Yes, but I also know you still have a certain amount of free time available. Surely you could fit in just a few more hours a week for us?'

How did you explain to someone like Miss Piprelly, who lived and breathed her chosen profession, that the work ethic was not high on his priorities? Not any more. Things had changed within him. Life had changed.

'An extra afternoon, Mr Childes. Could we say Tuesdays?' Her stern gaze defied refusal.

'Let me give it some thought,' he replied, and sensed her inner bristling.

'Very well, but I really must have the first draft curriculum completed by the end of the week.'

'I'll let you know on Thursday.' He tried a smile, but was annoyed at the apology in his own voice.

Her short sigh was one of exasperation and sounded like a huff. 'On Thursday then.'

He was dismissed. No more words, no 'Good day'. He just wasn't there any more. Miss Piprelly was calling to a group of girls who had made the mistake of following his route across the hallowed lawn. He turned away, feeling somehow as though he was sloping off, and had to make an effort to put some briskness into his stride.

Estelle Piprelly, having reproved the errant girls (a task that for her needed very few words and a barely-raised voice), returned her attention to the retreating figure of the peripatetic teacher. He walked with shoulders slightly hunched forward, studying the ground before him as if planning each footfall, a youngish man who sometimes seemed unusually wearied. No, wearied was the wrong word. There was sometimes a shadow behind his eyes that was haunted, an occasional glimpse of some latent anxiety.

Her brow furrowed – more parallel lines – and her fingers plucked unconsciously at a loose thread on her sleeve.

Childes disturbed her and she could not reason why. His work was excellent, meticulous, and he appeared to be popular with the pupils, if not a trace *too* popular with some. His specialist knowledge was a useful addition to the prospectus and without doubt he relieved a partial burden from her overloaded science teachers. Yet, although she had requested extra lessons of him because of the governing body's dictum, something in his presence made her uneasy.

A long, *long*, time ago, when she herself had been no more than a child and the German forces had occupied the island as a spearhead for their attack on the mainland of England, she had felt a pervading air of destruction around her. Not uncommon in those tragic warring times, but years later she realized that she possessed a higher degree of awareness than most. Nothing dramatic, nothing mediumistic or clairvoyant, just an acute sensing. It had become subdued yet never relinquished with the passing of time, the pragmatism of her chosen career, but in those early days she had seen death in the faces of many of those German soldiers, an unnatural foreboding in their countenance, in their mood.

In a more confusing way, she sensed it in Childes. Although he was now gone from view, Miss Piprelly shivered.

As he returned from the hotel bar with the drinks, weaving his way round the garden tables and chairs, Amy was releasing her hair at the back so that if fell into a ponytail, an old style transformed through her into something chic. There was a subtle elegance to Amy that was inborn rather than studied and, not for the first time, Childes thought she looked anything *but* a schoolteacher – at least not the type who had ever taught him.

Her skin appeared almost golden in the shadow of the table's canopy, her pale green eyes and lighter wisps of hair curling over her ears heightening the effect. As usual, she wore the minimum of make-up, a proclivity that often made her resemble some of the girls she instructed, her small breasts, just delicate swellings, hardly spoiling the illusion. Yet at twenty-three, eleven years younger than himself, she possessed a quiet maturity that he was in just a little wonder of; it was not always evident, for there was also a tantalizing innocence about her that enhanced the pubescent impression even more. The combination was often confusing, for she was unaware of her own qualities and the moods could quickly change.

Amy's slender and mockingly desperate fingers reached for the glass as he approached and early-evening sunlight struck her hand, making it glow a lighter gold.

'If only Miss Piprelly knew she had a lush on her staff,' he remarked, passing the gin and tonic to her.

She allowed the glass to tremble in her grasp as she brought it to her lips. 'If only Pip knew half her staff were inebriates. And she's the cause.'

Childes sat opposite so that he could watch her, sacrificing closeness for the pleasure of eye contact. 'Our headmistress wants me to put in more time at the school,' he said, and Amy's sudden smile warmed him.

'Jon, that would be lovely.'

'I'm not so sure. I mean, yes, great to see more of you, but when I came here I was opting out of the rat race, remember?'

'It's hardly that. This is a different civilization to the one you were used to.'

'Yeah, another planet. But I've got used to the easy pace, afternoons when I can go walking, or diving, or just plain snoozing on the beach. As last I've found time to think.'

'Sometimes you do too much thinking.'

The mood changed.

He looked away. 'I said I'd let her know.'

Humour came back to Amy's voice. 'Coward.'

Childes shook his head. 'She makes me feel like a ten-year-old.'

'Her bark isn't as bad as her bite. I'd do as she asks.'

'Some help you are.'

She placed her glass between them. 'I'd like to think I am. I know you spend too much time on your own and perhaps a bigger commitment to the college might be what you need.'

'You know how I feel about commitments.'

A look passed between them.

'You have one to your daughter.'

He sipped his beer.

'Let's lighten up,' he said, after a while. 'It's been a long day.'

Amy smiled, but her eyes were still troubled. She reached for his hand and stroked his fingers, masking more serious thoughts with bright banter. 'I think Pip would consider it quite a coup to have you on the staff full-time.'

'She only wants me for an extra afternoon.'

'Two and half days of your time now, tomorrow your soul.'

'You were supposed to be encouraging me.'

Her expression was mischievous. 'Just letting you know it's useless to resist. Others have tried,' she added, her voice deepening ominously, making him grin. 'Strangely enough, she has been giving me some peculiar looks lately.'

'Working her voodoo.'

He relaxed back in the chair. A few more people were wandering out into the hotel's beer garden, drinks in hand, taking advantage of a welcome relief from the preceding weeks of cold drizzle. A huge, furry bee hovered over nearby azaleas, its drone giving notice of the warmer months to come. Until recently, he had felt close to finding his peace on the island. The easy-going lifestyle, the pleasant nature of the island itself, Amy – beautiful Amy –, his own self-imposed occasional solitude, had brought a balance to his existence, a steadiness far removed from the frenetic pace of the constantly changing microchip world, a career in and around the madding city, a wife who had once loved him, but who had later been in fear of . . . of what? Something neither of them understood.

Psychic power. An inconsistent curse.

'Who's serious now?'

He stared blankly at Amy, her question breaking into his thoughts.

'You had that faraway look, the kind I should be getting used to by now,' she said. 'You weren't just day-dreaming.'

'No, just thinking back.'

'It's in the past and best kept that way, Jon.'

He nodded, unable to explain it to himself. Unsure of the creeping uneasiness he had felt since the nightmare two weeks ago.

She rested her folded arms on the table. 'Hey, you haven't given me an answer yet.' She frowned at his puzzled expression. 'My dinner invitation: you haven't said you'll come.'

'Do I have a choice?' For the moment the bad thoughts had retreated, vanquished by Amy's wickedly innocent smile.

'Of course. You can either accept or be deported. Daddy hates bad manners.'

'And we all know his influence in the States' affairs.'

'Precisely.'

'Then I'll come.'

'How sensible.'

'How much coaxing did your mother have to do?'

'Not much. She relied on threats.'

'Hard to imagine your father being afraid of anybody.'

'You don't know Mother. She may seem all sweetness and light on the surface, but there's a hidden streak of steel underneath it all that frightens even me sometimes.'

'At least it's nice to know *she* likes me.'

'Oh, I wouldn't go that far. Let's just say she's not totally against you.'

He laughed quietly. 'I'm really looking forward to the evening.'

'You know, I think she's quite intrigued by you. A darkly attractive man with a shady past, and all that.'

For a moment, Childes looked down into his beer. 'Is that how she sees my past?' he asked.

'She thinks you're mysterious and she likes that.'

'And dear Daddy?'

'You're not good enough for his daughter, that's all.'

'You sure?'

'No, but it's not important. He respects my feelings, though, and I haven't diguised how I feel about you. Pig-headed as he is sometimes, he would never hurt me by going against you.'

Childes wished he could be sure. The financier's hostility on the few occasions they had met was barely masked. Perhaps he didn't like divorcés; or perhaps he distrusted anyone who did not conform to his own standards, his perception of 'normality'.

In danger of becoming too serious again, Childes asked with a grin, 'Do I need a dinner suit?'

'Well, one or two of his business associates have been invited – and that includes a member of La Roche's governing body and his wife, incidentally – so nothing too informal. A tie would be nice.'

'And I thought the *soirée* was for my benefit.'

'Your being there is for *my* benefit.' She looked intently at him. 'It may seem a trivial thing, but it means a lot to have you with me. I don't know why there's this antagonism between you and my father, Jon, but it's unnecessary and destructive.'

'There's no animosity from me, Amy.'

'I know that. And I'm not asking you to bend his way. I just want him to see us together at a normal gathering, to let him see how well we go together.'

He could not help chuckling and she gave him a reproving look. 'I know what you're thinking and I didn't mean that. I'm still his little girl, remember.'

'He'd never understand how much of a woman you are.'

'He doesn't have to. I'm sure he doesn't imagine I'm still as pure as driven snow, though.'

'I wouldn't be too sure. Such things are hard for any doting father to face.'

The intimacy of their conversation charged his body with a flush of pleasure and he felt good with her, warm in her presence. It was the same for Amy, for her smile was different, not secretive but knowing, and her pale green eyes were lit with an inner sharing. She looked away and gently whirled the melting ice in her glass, watching the clear, rounded cubes as if they held some meaning. Conversations from other tables drifted in the air, occasionally punctuated by soft laughter. An aircraft banked around the western tip of the island, already over the sea just seconds after take-off from the tiny airport, its wings catching the reddening sun. A slight evening breeze stirred a lock of hair against Amy's cheek.

'I should be going,' she said after a while.

Both were aware of what they really wanted.

Childes said, 'I'll take you back to La Roche for your car.'

They finished their drinks and stood together. As they walked through the garden towards the white gate leading to the carpark, she slipped her hand into his. He squeezed her fingers and she returned the pressure.

Inside the car, Amy leaned across and kissed his lips, and his desire was tempered and yet inflamed by her tenderness. The sensation for them was as paradoxical as the kiss: both weakening and strengthening at the same time. When they parted, breathless, wanting, his fingertips gently touched a trail along her cheek, brushing her lips and becoming moist from them. He realized that recently their relationship had unexpectedly, and bewilderingly, reached a new peak. It had been slow in developing, gradual in its emergence, each always slightly wary of the other, he afraid to give too much, she cautious of him as a stranger, unlike any other man she had known. It now seemed that they had just passed a point from which there could only be a lingeringly painful return, and both recognized the inexorable yet purely sensory truth of it.

He turned away, unprepared for this new, plunging shift of emotions, unsure of why, *how*, it had happened so swiftly. Turning on the ignition and engaging gear, Childes drove into the land leading away from the hotel.

Childes pushed open the front door of the cottage and briefly stood in the small hallway, collecting his thoughts, catching his breath. He closed the door.

Amy's presence was still with him, floating intangibly in the air, and again he wondered at the startling new pace of their feelings for one another. He had held his emotions in check for so long, enjoying her company, taking pleasure in all her aspects, her maturity, her innocence, not least her physical beauty, aware that their relationship was more than friendship, but always in control, unwilling to let go, to succumb to anything deeper. Wounds from his broken marriage were not yet entirely healed, a bitterness still lingered.

He could not help but smile wryly. He felt as if he had been zapped by some invisible force.

The ringing phone made him start. Childes moved away from the door and picked up the receiver.

'Jon?' She sounded breathless.

'Yes, Amy.'

'What happened?'

He paused before answering. 'You too?'

'I feel wonderful and terrible at the same time. It's like an exciting ache.'

He laughed at her description, realizing its aptness. 'I should say the feeling will pass, but I don't want it to.'

'It's scary. And I love it.'

He could sense her uncertainty and her voice was quiet when she added: 'I don't want to be hurt.'

Closing his eyes and leaning back against the wall, Childes struggled with his own emotions. 'Let's give each other time to think.'

'I don't want to.'

'It might be better for us both.'

'Why? Is there anything more to know about each other? I mean, anything important? We've talked, you've told me about yourself, your past, how you feel: is there any more that I should know?'

'No, no dark secrets, Amy. You know all that's happened to me. More, much more, than anyone else.'

'Then why are you afraid of what's happening to us?'

'I thought *you* were.'

'Not in that way. I'm only scared of being so vulnerable.'

'That's the answer, don't you see?'

'You think I would do anything to hurt you?'

'Things can happen that we have no control over.'

'I thought they already had.'

'I didn't mean that. Events can somehow interfere, can change feelings. It's happened to me before.'

'You told me your marriage was shaky before these dreadful things happened, that they just widened the gulf between you and Fran. Don't run away, Jon, not like . . .'

She stopped and Childes finished for her. 'Not like before.'

'I'm sorry, I didn't mean it that way. I know circumstances had become intolerable.' Amy sighed miserably. 'Oh, Jon, why has this conversation turned out like this? I was so happy, I needed to talk to you. I *missed* you.'

His tenseness loosened. Yet a gnawing, subconscious disquiet remained. How could he explain his own almost subliminal unrest? 'Amy, I'm sorry too. I'm being stupid. I suppose I'm still masochistically licking ancient wounds.'

'Bad past experiences can sometimes distort the new.'

'Very profound.'

She was relieved the humour was back in his voice, yet could not help but feel a little deflated. 'I'll try and keep a tighter grip on myself,' she said.

'Hey, c'mon. Don't mind an old man's self-pity. So you missed me? I only left you ten minutes ago.'

'I got home from school and felt so . . . so, I don't know – flushed. Happy. Mixed-up. Sick. I wanted you here.'

'Sounds like a bad case.'

'It is, God help me.'

'I've got it too.'

'But you –'

'I told you: pay no attention. I get moody sometimes.'

'Don't I know it. Can I buy you lunch tomorrow?'

'Creep.'

'I don't care.' The warmth was quickly returning.

'Tell you what,' he said. 'If you can stand it, I'll cook you lunch here.'

'We'll only have an hour.'

'I'll prepare it tonight. Nothing fancy; freezer stuff.'

'I love freezer stuff.'

'I love you.' He'd finally said the words.

'Jon . . .'

'I'll see you in school, Amy.'

Her voice was hushed. 'Yes.'

He said goodbye and barely heard her response. The line clicked dead. Cradling the receiver, his hand still resting on the smooth plastic, Childes stared thoughtfully at the wall. He hadn't meant to let the words slip out, hadn't wanted to breach the final barrier with an admission he knew they both felt. Why did it matter when it was the truth? Just what was he afraid of? It wasn't hard to reason.

The bizarre vision followed by the nightmare a fortnight before had left him with a dispiriting and familiar apprehension, a rekindling of the dread that had once nearly broken him. It had ruined his life with Fran and Gabby; he didn't want it to hurt Amy. He prayed that he was wrong, that it wasn't happening all over again, his imagination was running loose.

Childes rubbed a hand over his eyes, aware of how sore they had become. Drawing in a deep breath, then releasing the air as if ridding himself of festering notions, he went into the tiny, ground-floor bathroom and opened the medicine cabinet. After taking out a small plastic bottle and his lens case, he closed the cabinet door to be confronted by his own image, reflected in the mirror. His eyes were bloodshot and he thought there was an unnatural pallor to his skin. Imagination again, he told himself. He was foolishly allowing the morbid introspection to build, to become something other than it was. Which was a throwback, a long-delayed reaction to something past, and that was all. When he had nearly drowned it was probably because he had stayed too long beneath the water, not noticing his lungs had used up precious air, lack of oxygen bringing on the confused images. The nightmare later was . . . was just a nightmare, with no particular significance. He was attributing too much to an unpleasant but unimportant experience, and perhaps it was understandable with past memories to goad his thoughts. Forget it. Things had changed, his life was different.

Peering close to the mirror, Childes gently squeezed the soft lens from his right eye, cleansed it in the palm of his hand with the fluid, and dropped it into its liquid-filled container. He repeated the procedure with the left lens.

Outside in the hallway, he dipped into his briefcase and withdrew his spectacles, his eyes already feeling relief from the irritation. He was about to go through into the kitchen to discover what he could come up with for lunch the following day when a soft thud from upstairs stopped him. He held his breath and gazed up the narrow stairway, seeing only as far as the bend. He waited, going through that peculiar middle-of-the-night sensation of not wanting to hear again a mysterious, intrusive noise yet seeking confirmation that one had been heard. There was no further sound.

Childes mounted the creaky, wooden stairs, unreasonably nervous. He rounded the bend and saw that his bedroom door was open. Nothing wrong in that: he had left it open that morning – he always did. Climbing the rest of the stairway, he walked the few feet along the landing and pushed the bedroom door open wider.

The room was empty and he admonished himself for behaving like a timorous maiden-aunt. Two windows faced each other across the room and something small and delicate was clinging to the outside of one. He went over, feeling the bare, wooden floorboards giving slightly beneath his weight, and clucked his tongue when he saw the shivering flotsam was no more than a feather stuck to the glass, either a gull's or a pigeon's, he couldn't be sure which. It had happened before: the birds saw sky in the window on the other side of the room and tried to fly through, striking the window-pane on that side but rarely doing more damage than giving themselves a shock and probably a severe headache, leaving a plume or two on the glass. Even as he watched, the breeze caught the feather and whisked it away.

Childes was about to turn around when he caught sight of the distant school. His heart stopped momentarily and his hands gripped the sill when he saw the fiery glow. His relief was instant when he quickly realized the white building was merely reflecting the setting sun's rubescent rays.

But the image remained in his mind, and when he sat down on the bed his hands were trembling.

It watched from beneath a tree, the cheerfully sunny day giving the lie to the misery witnessed in the cemetery.

The mourners were grouped around the open grave, dark clothes struck grey by the sunlight. Stained white crosses, slabs, and smiling cracked angels were dispassionate observers in the field of sunken bones. The mushy cadence of traffic could be heard in the distance; somewhere a radio was snapped off, the graveyard worker realizing a ceremony was in progress. The priest's voice carried as a muffled intonation to the low knoll where the figure waited in the yew's shadow.

When the tiny coffin was lowered, a woman staggered forward as if to forbid the final violation of her dead child. A man at her side held the woman firm, supporting her weight as she sagged. Others in the group bowed their heads or looked away, the mothers agony was unbearable as the untimely death itself. Hands were raised to faces, tissues dampened against cheeks. The features of the men were frozen, pale plastic moulds.

It watched from the hiding place and smiled secretly.

The little casket disappeared from view, swallowed by the dank soil, green-edged lips eagerly wide. The father threw something in after the coffin, a bright-coloured object – a toy, a doll, something that had once been precious to the child – before earth was scattered into the grave.

Reluctantly, yet with private relief, the bereaved group began to drift away. The mother had to be gently led, supported between two others, her head constantly turning as if the dead infant were calling her back, pleading with her not to leave it there, lonely and cold and corrupting. The grief overwhelmed and the mother had to be half-carried to the waiting funeral cars.

The figure beneath the tree stayed while the grave was filled.

To return again later that night.

'Thank you, Helen, I think you can clear away now.' Vivienne Sebire noted with manifest satisfaction that the meal she had so carefully and lovingly prepared earlier that afternoon, salmon mousse followed by apple and cherry duckling, served with *mangetouts* and broccoli, had been devoured with relish and much voiced praise. She observed, however, that Jonathan Childes had not eaten as heartily as the rest of their guests.

Grace Duxbury, sitting close to the host, Paul Sebire, who was at the head of the table, trilled, 'Marvellous, Vivienne. Now I want to know the secret of that mousse before I leave this house tonight.'

'Yes,' agreed her husband. 'Excellent first course. Why is it, Grace, that yours rarely venture beyond avocado with prawns unless we've got the caterers in?'

A remark that would be paid for later if she knew Grace, thought Vivienne, smiling at them both. 'Ah, the secret's in just how much anchovy essence you add. A little more than is recommended, but not too much.'

'Delicious,' reaffirmed George Duxbury.

Helen, a short, stoutish woman with a cheerful smile and eyebrows that tended to converge to a point above her nose, and who was the Sebires' housekeeper-cum-maid, began collecting dishes while her mistress preened herself on more praise. Amy, sitting opposite and slightly to the right of Childes, rose from her seat. 'I'll give you a hand,' she said to Helen, making eye-contact with Childes, a covert smile passing between them.

'What I'd like to know, Paul, is how a reprobate like you manages to have a beautiful and brilliant cook for a wife and an absolute charmer for a daughter?' The good-humoured jibe was delivered by Victor Platnauer, a *conseiller* of the island and a member of La Roche Ladies College's governing board. His wife, Tilly, seated next to Childes, tutted reproachfully, although allowing herself to join in the chuckles of her fellow-guests.

'Quite simple, Victor,' Sebire riposted in his usual crisp manner. 'It was my darling wife's culinary expertise that coaxed me to marry her and my genes that produced our beautiful Aimée.' He always insisted on calling his daughter by her correct name.

'No, no,' Platnauer insisted. 'Amy inherits her looks from her mother, not her father. Isn't that correct, Mr Childes – er, Jonathan?'

'She has both her parents' finer points,' Childes managed to say diplomatically, dabbing his lips with a napkin.

Score one, thought Amy, halfway through the door to the kitchen, as someone clapped and proclaimed, 'Bravo!' So far, so good. She had observed her father discreetly studying Jon throughout the evening, knowing so well the calculating appraisal usually reserved for prospective clients, colleagues or rivals. Nevertheless, he had played the perfect host, courteous and suitably inquisitive of his guest, allowing Jon as much attention as any of the others, including a business associate from Marseilles. Amy suspected that Edouard Vigiers had been invited not just because he happened to be on the island that week to discuss certain financial arrangements, but because he was young, successful, yet still thrusting, and *very* eligible. An ideal son-in-law in Paul Sebire's eyes. She was beginning to wonder if her father's sole motive in inviting Jon was so that she, Amy, would be presented with a direct comparison between the two, Edouard and Jon, the contrast undeniable.

She had to admit that the Frenchman was attractive as well as bright and amusing, but her father was wrong, as usual, in judging by such obvious and superficial standards. She knew Paul Sebire to be a kind man with a generous heart, despite his cutting ruthlessness in business affairs and thorniness over certain matters, and she loved him as much as any daughter could love a father; unfortunately, his self-concealed possessiveness dictated that if he were to surrender his daughter to another, then it would be someone in his own image, of his own kind, if not a younger version of himself. It was a transparently clumsy ploy, although her father probably deemed it subtle, as usual underestimating others, particularly his only child.

Amy thought dreamily of her lunch with Jon earlier that week, their first confrontation alone in his cottage after having realized just how far their relationship had journeyed, how much more deeply they cared for each other than either had understood before. There had been little time for intimacies that day, but touching, holding, caressing had been filled with a new potency, a new tenderness.

'I'd like those plates, Miss Amy, when you've finished listening at the door.' Helen's amused voice had broken into the reverie. She stood, one hand on the sink, the other clenched on her hip.

'Oh.' Amy smiled sheepishly. She carried the dishes over to the draining board. 'I wasn't eavesdropping, Helen, only daydreaming. Just lost somewhere.'

Victor Platnauer was leaning forward over the table, looking directly at Childes. In his early sixties, Platnauer was still a well-proportioned man, with a hard ruddiness to his features and large hands that was common to many of the native islanders; there was a gravelly tone to his voice, a bluffness in his manner. By contrast, his wife Tilly was soft-spoken, almost demure, similar in appearance and demeanour to Vivienne Sebire.

'I'm pleased to hear you're to give La Roche a little more of your time,' Platnauer said.

'Only an extra afternoon,' Childes replied. 'I agreed earlier this week.'

'Yes, so Miss Piprelly informed me. Well, that's good news, but perhaps we can persuade you to spend even more time at the college. I'm aware that you also teach at Kingsley and de Montfort, but it's important to us that we extend this particular area of our curriculum. It isn't only a parental demand – I'm told the pupils have shown great keenness for computer sciences.'

'That's not true of all of them, unfortunately,' said Childes. 'The children, I mean. I think we're fooling ourselves if we imagine every kid has a natural aptitude for electronic calculation and compilation.'

Tilly Platnauer looked surprised. 'I thought we were well into the Star Wars era, with every boy and girl a microchip genius compared to their elders.'

Childes smiled. 'We're just at the beginning. And electronic games are not quite the same as the practical application of computers, although I'll admit they're a start. You see, the computer process is totally logical, but not every child has total logic.'

'Neither do many of us grown-ups,' Victor Platnauer commented drily.

'It's a double-edged sword, in a way,' Childes went on. 'The leisure industry has encouraged the consumer to think that computers are fun, and that's okay, it creates interest; it's when the public, or the kids in our case, discover hard work is involved before enjoyment through understanding begins, that the big turn-off comes.'

'Surely then, the answer is to begin teaching at the earliest age, so it will become an everyday part of the child's life.' It was Edouard Vigiers who had spoken, his accent softening rather than distorting his words.

'Yep, you're right. But you're talking of an ideal situation where the computer is a normal household item, a regular piece of furniture like the TV or stereo unit. We're a long way off from that situation.'

'All the more reason for schools to introduce our children to the technology while their minds are still young and pliable, wouldn't you say?' asked Platnauer.

'Ideally, yes,' agreed Childes. 'But you have to understand it isn't a science that's within everbody's grasp. The unfortunate side is that microtechnology *will* become a way of life within the next couple of decades and a hell of a lot of companies and individuals are going to feel left behind.'

'Then we must ensure that the children of this island don't fall by the wayside,' stated Paul Sebire to Platnauer's nodded approval.

Childes hid his exasperation that his point had been missed, or at least gone unheeded: technical knowledge could be spoon- or force-fed, but it was not so easily digested if the inclination was not there.

Vigiers changed the conversation's direction. 'Do you also teach science at La Roche and these other schools, Jon?'

Sebire unexpectedly answered for him. 'Not at all. Mr Childes is a computer specialist, Edouard, something of a technical wizard, I gather.'

Childes looked sharply at Sebire and wondered how he had 'gathered'. Amy?

'Ah,' said Vigiers. 'Then I am curious to know what made you turn to the teaching of children. Isn't this a, let me see, er . . . a slow down? Is that correct? I am sorry if my question appears impertinent, but an abrupt change of lifesyle – *un brusque changement de vie* we would say – is always interesting, do you not agree?' He smiled charmingly and Childes was suddenly wary.

'Sometimes you discover running on a constant treadmill isn't all it's cracked up to be.' he replied.

Vivienne Sebire enjoyed the response and added, 'Well who could resist the peacefulness of the island, despite how much you money-men try to disrupt it?' She looked meaningfully at her husband.

The door leading to the kitchen opened and Amy and Helen came through carrying the dessert on silver trays.

'More delights!' enthused George Duxbury. 'What are you tempting us with now, Vivienne?'

'There's a choice,' she told them as the sweets were placed in the centre of the table. 'The apricot and chocolate dessert is mine and the raspberry soufflé omelet is a speciality of Amy's. You can, of course, have both if you've room.'

'I'll make room,' Duxbury assured her.

'My nutritionist would throw a fit if she could see me now.' His wife was already offering up her plate to the amusement of all. 'Apricot and chocolate, please, but *don't* ask me if I want cream.'

Amy sat while Helen served. Vigiers, seated next to her, leaned close and spoke confidentially. 'I shall most certainly try the soufflé; it looks delicious.'

She smiled to herself. Edouard had the kind of low voice that could sell liqueurs on television. 'Oh, Mother is a far superior chef. I only dabble, I'm afraid.'

'I am sure that whatever you do, it is well. Your father tells me you also teach at La Roche.'

'Yes, French and English. I also help out with Speech and Drama.'

'So you are fluent in my language? Your name implies that you are of French descent, yes? And if I may be permitted to say, you have a certain ambience that has an affinity with the women of my country.'

'Your own Victor Hugo once wrote that these islands were fragments of France picked up by England. And as we were once part of the Duchy of Normandy, many of us have French forbears. The *patois* is still spoken by a few of our older residents here, and I'm sure you've noticed we retain many of the ancient placenames.'

Grace Duxbury had overheard their conversation. 'We've always been a prized possession, Monsieur Vigiers, for more than one nation.'

'I hope my country has never caused you distress,' he responded, humour in his eyes.

'Distress?' laughed Paul Sebire. 'You've tried to invade us more than once, and your pirates never left us alone in the old days. Even Napoleon had a crack at us in later times, but I'm afraid he got a bloody nose.'

Vigiers sipped his wine, obviously amused.

'We've always appreciated our French origins, though,' Sebire continued, 'and I'm pleased to say our associations have never been relinquished.'

'I gather you do not have the same warm feelings towards the Germans.'

'Ah, different thing entirely,' Platnauer voiced gruffly. 'Their wartime occupation is recent history and with their pillboxes and damn coastal fortresses all over the place, it's hard to forget. Having said that, there's no real animosity between us now; in fact, many veterans of the occupying forces return as tourists nowadays.'

'It's rather strange how attractive this island has been to man from far, far back,' said Sebire, indicating his preference for the soufflé, too. 'In Neolithic times, he made his way here to bury his dead and worship the gods. Massive granite tombs still survive and the land is practically littered with megaliths and menhirs, those standing stones they paid homage to. Aimée, why don't you show Edouard around the island tomorrow? He returns to Marseilles on Monday and hasn't had a chance to take a really good look at the place since he's been here. What do you think, Edouard?'

'I should like that very much,' replied the Frenchman.

'Unfortunately Jon and I have made plans for tomorrow.' Amy smiled, but there was a coolness in the look she flashed her father.

'Nonsense,' Sebire persisted, conscious of her annoyance, but undeterred. 'You see each other all the time at the college, and most evenings, it seems nowadays. I'm sure Jonathan wouldn't mind releasing you for a few hours considering how little time our guest has left.' He looked amiably along the table at Childes, who had been engaged in conversation with Vivienne Sebire, but whose attention had been drawn at the mention of his name.

'I, uh, I guess it's up to Amy,' he said uncertainly.

'There you are,' Sebire said, smiling at his daughter. 'No problem.'

Embarrassed, Vigiers started to say. 'It really does not matter. If –'

'That's quite alright, Edouard,' Sebire cut in. 'Aimée is well-used to helping entertain my business visitors. I often wish she had chosen my profession rather than teaching; she would have been a remarkable asset to the company, I'm sure of that.'

'You know I have no interest in corporate finance,' said Amy, disguising her chagrin at having little choice but to accept her imposed role as tourist guide. Jon, why didn't you help me? 'I enjoy children, I enjoy doing something useful. I'm not criticizing, but your way of making money wouldn't be fulfilling enough for me. I need to see some tangible evidence of success for my efforts, not just figures on balance sheets.'

'And you find this with your students?' asked Vigiers.

'Why, yes, with many.'

'I'm sure with most, with you as their tutor,' Sebire put forward.

'Daddy, you're being patronising,' she warned menacingly.

The two men laughed together and Grace Duxbury said, 'Pay them no mind, Amy dear. They're both obviously of that near-extinct breed who imagine that men still rule the world. Tell me, Monsieur Vigiers, have you tried many of our restaurants during your stay? Tell me how you found them compared to some of the excellent cuisines of your own country.'

While the conversation went on, Amy glanced over at Childes. She tried to convey apology for the next day in her expression and he understood, shaking his head imperceptibly. He raised his wine glass, tilting it slightly in her direction before drinking; lifting her own glass, Amy returned the toast.

Helen had returned to the kitchen and was already loading the dishwasher with plates and cutlery from the sink. She was pleased for her mistress that the dinner party appeared to be going so well. Miss Amy was lucky to have two men in attendance and Helen wondered how she could resist the smooth, cultured Frenchman, with his French ways and his French looks and his French voice . . . irresistible.

She shivered and reached over the work surface near the sink to close the window. The night had turned chilly. And it was black out there, the moon but a thin sliver. Helen pulled the window shut.

There was laughter around the dining table as Duxbury who, as well as being a commodity importer to the island, supplying local companies with office furniture, equipment and generally whatever else they needed, also arranged sales conferences for outside organizations, regaled his fellow-guests with one of his long-winded but generally funny conference-mishap stories.

Childes took a spoonful of the soufflé and made an appreciative face at Amy. She mouthed a discreet kiss in return. He had felt on edge at the beginning of the evening, unsure of Paul Sebire, aware that he would be put through some devious kind of test by him, a judgment of character and perhaps of his worth now that it was evident Amy was becoming emotionally tied. Yet the financier had been more than cordial throughout, the curtness of previous meetings gone or at least held in check. Still Childes had not relaxed, gradually becoming aware that the younger Frenchman was not just another dinner guest, but introduced by Sebire as a potential rival; the Sebire-inspired outing for Amy and Vigiers the following day had confirmed his suspicions. It was both obvious and disingenuous but Childes had to admit he did look a little shabby against Vigiers.

On the other hand, Vivienne Sebire had been gracious and attentive, genuinely welcoming him and, like the perfect hostess, making him feel a valued guest. She was the ideal counter to her husband's general brusqueness.

He joined in the laughter as Duxbury reached the climax of his story, the importer barely giving them all time to recover before launching into another. Childes reached for his wine, and as he brought it towards him, he thought he caught a glimmering in the glass. He blinked, then peered into the light liquid. He had been mistaken: it must have been a reflection. Childes sipped and was about to place the wine glass back on the table when something seemed to stir within him. He looked again, bemused rather than concerned.

No, just wine inside, nothing else, nothing that could . . . nothing that . . .

An image. But not in the glass. In his mind.

Suppressed chuckling as Duxbury continued his yarn.

The image was unreal, unfocused, *like the nightmare*, a shimmering blur. Childes set the wine glass down, aware that his hand was shaking. A peculiar sensation had gripped the back of his neck, like a hand, a frigid hand, clasped there. He stared into the liquid.

Amy giggled, suspecting Duxbury's story was building up to a somewhat risqué ending.

The image had become images. They were slowly swimming into focus. The warmth of the room had become suffocating. Childes' other hand unconsciously went to his shirt collar as if to loosen it.

Grace Duxbury, having heard her husband's story on numerous other occasions in different company, and knowing the punchline, was already twittering with embarrassment.

Childe's vision had shifted inwards; he viewed a scenario inside his mind, an event that was beyond the confines of the room, yet within himself. He seemed to be moving closer to the ethereal activity, becoming integrated with it, a participant; but still he was only watching. Soft earth was being disturbed.

Victor Platnauer's rasping chuckle, a low rumble about to erupt, was infectious, and Vivienne Sebire found herself laughing even before the story was concluded.

Blunt, stubby fingers, covered in damp soil. Scraping against wood. The effort renewed, frantic. The wood cleared of earth so that its shape was revealed. Narrow. Rectangular. Small. Childes shuddered, spilling wine.

Vigiers had noticed, was staring across the table at Childes.

The coffin lid was smashed, splinters bursting outwards under the axe blows. Jagged segments were ripped away, the hole enlarged. The tiny body was exposed, its features unclear in the dismal light. Childes' hands tightened on the glass. The room was shifting; he could barely breathe. The invisible pressure on the nape of his neck increased, squeezing like a vice.

For a moment, the hands, seen by Childes almost as his own, paused as if the defiler had sensed something, had become aware of being observed. Sensed Childes, himself. Something deep inside his mind was coldly touched. The moment had passed.

Tilly Platnauer knew she should not be enjoying the tale, but Duxbury's bluff rendition was compelling. Her shoulders were already beginning to judder with mirth.

The little corpse was torn free from the silk-lined casket and now Childes could see the tiny open eyes that had no depth, no life-force. The boy was laid on the grass beside the pit, where the night breeze ruffled his hair, blowing wisps across his pale, unlined forehead, giving an illusion of vitality. His clothes were cut free and pulled aside so that the body was naked to the night, white marble in colour and stillness.

Metal glinted in the thin moonlight. Plunging downward. Entering.

Slicing.

The glass shattered, wine mixed with blood spilling on the lace tablecloth. Someone had screamed. Childes had risen, knocking over his chair, was standing over them, swaying, his eyes staring towards the ceiling, a glistening wetness to his lips, a light sheen moistening his skin.

His body shook, went rigid, even his hair appeared brittle. With a desolate cry he fell forward onto the table.

Gloatingly, it bit into the heart of the dead child.

Amy clenched her fists and closed her eyes against the reflection of her father.

They were in her bedroom, she white-faced with eyes tear-puffed and red, sitting miserably at her dressing table, Paul Sebire agitated, angrily pacing the room behind her. She could not clear from her mind the sight of Jon when he had been led away from the house by Platnauer, the *conseiller* helping him into his own car, refusing to allow him to drive himself home, despite his protests: Jon's face had been so taut, so stricken.

He had refused a doctor, had insisted that he was okay, that he had just suffered a blackout, that the heat of the dining room had overcome him. They knew that the night was cool, that the house was merely warm, not too hot, but hadn't argued. He would be fine as soon as he could lie down, he had told them, as soon as he could rest; he strenuously declined Amy's and Vivienne's offer of a bed for the night, saying he just needed to be on his own for a while. His distant gaze had frightened her as much of his ashen face, but it was useless to argue.

She had held him before he left, feeling his inner trembling, wishing she could soothe it away. His cut hand had been treated and bandaged, and Amy had brought it to her lips before letting him go, kissing the fingertips, careful not to hold on too tightly. Childes hadn't allowed her to go with him.

Paul Sebire stopped pacing. 'Aimée,' he said, putting his hand on her shoulder. 'I don't want you to be angry, I just want you to listen to me and to be rational.'

He stroked her hair, then let his hand fall back onto her shoulder.

'I'd like you to end this relationship with Childes.' He waited for the outburst which never came. Amy was merely staring coldly at his reflection in the mirror and, in a way, that was more unsettling. He went on, his tone cautious: 'I believe the man is unstable. At first I thought tonight he was suffering from an epileptic fit of some kind, but soon realized the symptoms were not the same. Aimée, I think the man is heading for a mental breakdown.'

'He's not unstable,' Amy said calmly. 'He's not neurotic and he's not heading for a breakdown. You don't know him, Daddy, you don't know what he's been through.'

'But I do, Aimée. I just wonder if you're fully aware of his background.'

'What do you mean?' She had turned towards Sebire, his hand sliding from her shoulder with the movement.

'Something rang a bell for me a long time ago when you first started mentioning his name; I couldn't put my finger on it, although I was bothered for quite some time. More recently, when I began to suspect you were becoming seriously involved with him, I did some checking.' He raised a defensive hand. 'Now don't look at me like that, Aimée. You're my only daughter, and I care more about you than anything in the world, so do you really think I wouldn't pursue a troublesome matter which concerned you?'

'Wouldn't it have been possible to ask me about Jon?'

'Ask you what? I had a feeling, that was all, a nagging doubt. And I couldn't be sure of how much you yourself knew about Childes.'

'And what did you discover?' she asked caustically.

'Well, I knew roughly when he had come over from the mainland and that he had a career in the computer industry before. I asked Victor Platnauer, as a member of the Island Police Committee, to make a discreet – I promise you it was discreet – investigation into Childes' background, whether he had any dealings with the police in the past, that sort of thing.'

'Do you imagine he would have been employed by any of the colleges if he had some kind of criminal record?'

'Of course not. I was looking for something else. I told you, his name was somehow familiar to me and I didn't know why.'

'So you found out what drove him away from England, why he was forced to leave his family.'

'You made no secret of his divorce, so that didn't come as a surprise. But what did was the fact that he had been under suspicion for murder.'

'Daddy, if you had him thoroughly investigated you must be aware of all the facts. Jon helped *solve* those crimes. The penalty he paid was false accusations and relentless hounding by the media, even for long afterwards.'

'Officially, the murders were never solved.'

She groaned aloud, half in despair, half in anger.

Sebire was undaunted. 'There was a series of three murders and the evidence indicated the killer was the same person. All the victims were children.'

'And Jon was able to give the police vital clues.'

'He led them to where the last two were buried, that's true enough. But everyone wanted to know *how*. Aimée, that's what caused the outcry.'

'He told them, he explained.'

'He said he witnessed the killings. Not physically, he hadn't actually been there when the crimes had been committed, but he had "seen" them happen. Can you blame the police, the public, for wondering?'

'He has . . . had a . . . kind of second-sight. It's not unusual, Daddy, it's happened to others. Police have often used psychics to help them solve crimes.'

'Whenever a particularly gruesome series of murders is reported, any number of crackpots always contact the police saying the spirits have told them what the murderer looks like or where he'll strike next. It's common and pathetic, and a total waste of police time.'

'Not always, it isn't always. Crimes have been solved by such people many times in the past.'

'And you're telling me Childes is one of these gifted persons.'

Sebire made the word 'gifted' sound like a sneer. 'That's what the newspapers reported at the time.'

'That's just the point: he isn't. He's not clairvoyant, he's not psychic in the usual sense. Jon had never experienced such an insight before, not in that way. He was just as mystified and confused as anyone else. And frightened.'

'The police held him on suspicion.'

'They were staggered by what he knew. Of course they suspected him at first, but he had too many witnesses testifying he was elsewhere at the time of the murders.'

'It was still felt he was involved in some way. He was too accurate with his information.'

'They eventually traced the murderer and proved that Jon had no connection with him.'

'I'm sorry, but that's not on record. The killings were never solved.'

'Check with your sources, Daddy. You'll find that they were – unofficially. The madman cut his own throat. The case was never officially closed because he left no suicide note, nothing to admit he had murdered the children. All the authorities had was very strong circumstantial – no, conclusive – evidence against him. They hinted as much at the time, and so did the newspapers, but now one could officially announce the fact; the law, itself, prevented them from doing so. But the murderer killed himself because he knew they were closing in; Jon had given the police enough information for them to pinpoint their man, someone who was known to them as a child-molester, who had spent time in prison because of it. The killings stopped when he took his own life.'

'Then why did Childes run away?' Sebire was pacing the room again, determined not to leave until he had made his daughter see sense. 'He deserted his wife and child to come here. What could make him do such a thing?'

'He didn't desert them, not in the way you're suggesting.' Amy's voice had risen in pitch. 'Jon begged his wife to come with him, but she refused. The pressure had been too much for her as well. She didn't want either herself or Gabriel, their daughter, to be subjected to any more innuendo, phone calls from cranks, the media at first pointing the finger of suspicion and later trying to build Jon into some kind of super-freak! She knew there'd be no peace for them . . .'

'Even so, to leave them . . .'

'Their marriage was in trouble before that. Jon's wife was a career woman when they were first married. When their daughter came along she took up all her time; Fran became sick of being a housewife, always living in his shadow. She wanted her own life before these incidents took place.'

'And the child? How could –?'

Amy's voice lowered. 'He loves Gabriel. It nearly broke him to leave her, but he knew if he stayed the tension would destroy them all. There was nothing he could offer his daughter on his own; he didn't know at that stage how he would live, what he would do. My God, he'd thrown away a brilliant career, was leaving his wife everything they possessed and almost all their savings. How could he take care of a four-year-old daughter?'

'Why here of all places? Why did he come to this island?' Sebire had once more stopped his pacing and was now hovering over Amy, his own anger building.

'Because it's close to home, don't you see? It's far enough away for him to have been a stranger when he arrived, yet easy for him to return, to keep in touch with his family. Jon hasn't walked out, he hasn't turned his back on them. He was devastated when he discovered his wife had sued for divorce – perhaps he imagined one day they'd patch things up for the sake of Gabriel, that they'd come to live with him here, I don't know. He may even have had plans for returning to England in a few years time when he would be long forgotten by the public. All that changed when he received the divorce papers.'

'Okay, Aimée, given all that, accepting there was no complicity on his part in those brutal killings and that he was not totally to blame for the break-up of his marriage –'

Amy opened her mouth to speak, her pale eyes blazing, but Sebire stopped her.

'Hear me out.' His manner was firm, allowing no dissension. 'The fact remains that the man is *not* normal. How do you explain these – I don't know what you'd call them, I'm not familiar with psychic mumbo-jumbo – let's just say "intuitions"? Why on earth did they happen to him?'

'Nobody knows, least of all Jon himself. No one can explain them. Why are you blaming him?'

'I am not blaming him for anything. I'm merely pointing out that there's something odd about that man. Can you tell me exactly what happened here tonight, what caused his so-called blackout? Has this sort of thing ever occurred before? Good God, Aimée, what if he'd been driving a car, perhaps with you in it?'

'I don't *know* what happened to him, and neither does he. And as far as I know, he's never suffered anything similar.'

'But he refuses to even consult a doctor.'

'He will; I'll make him.'

'You will stay away from him.'

Amy smiled disbelievingly. 'Do you really think I'm still a child to be told what I can and cannot do? Do you honestly imagine you can forbid me to see him again?' She laughed, but the sound was brittle, without humour. 'Wake up to the twentieth century, Daddy.'

'I shouldn't think Victor Platnauer is too keen on having a tutor in his school who is susceptible to fainting spells.'

Her breath escaped her. 'Are you serious?'

'Absolutely.'

She shook her head and stared at him with a simmering anger. 'He wasn't well, it could have happened to anybody.'

'Perhaps. With anyone else it would soon be forgotten though.'

'And you won't forget this?'

'That's hardly the point.'

'Tell me what is.'

'He worries me. I'm afraid for you.'

'He's a kind, gentle man.'

'I don't want you involved with him.'

'I already am. Very.'

Sebire visibly flinched. He strode to the door and stopped, looking back at her. She knew her father so well, knew his ruthlessness when opposed. His words were controlled, but there was seething intensity in his eyes.

'I think it's time others were made aware of Childes' dubious past,' he said, before leaving the room and firmly closing the door behind him.

Perspiration flowed from him, literally trickling in smooth rivulets onto the sheets of the bed. He turned onto his side, damp bedclothes clinging, his own dank smell unpleasant.

The vision, the sighting, was still fresh in Childes' mind, for it had been so real, its horror so tangible, so palpable. It filled him now. Potent. Vigorous.

His presence had been in the graveyard, so close to the little corpse, almost *feeling* its cold, clammy touch. For a few brief moments he had existed *inside* the other being, this thing that had defiled the dead child. Had felt its obscene glory.

Yet had been apart from it, an observer with no influence, a watcher of no power.

Still the thoughts persisted and with them, sneaking through like an insidious informant, came a new dread, an unspeakable notion that caused him to moan aloud. The thought was too distressing to contemplate, yet would not go away. Surely he would have known, would have been aware in some way, no matter how deeply hidden his conscious mind had kept the secret? But hadn't he felt at one stage, when those monstrous hands had raised the lifeless body from the grave, that they were his own, that those hands belonged to him?

Was the vision merely a released memory? Was he, himself, the desecrator? No, that couldn't be, it couldn't be!

Childes stared at the closed window and listened to the night.

It sat in the shadows watching the slender crescent of light that was the moon through the grimy window, and it grinned, thoughts dwelling on the ceremony it had carried out in the burial ground earlier that night.

It relived the exquisite moment of opening the body, of scattering the contents, and relished the memory.

A tongue slid across parted lips. The silent heart had tasted good.

But now a frown changed its countenance.

In the cemetery, for one brief moment as it had drawn out the dead child, a sensation had stayed the movement, a feeling of being watched. The graveyard had been deserted, though, that was certain, only headstones and frozen angels the nocturnal spectators.

Yet there had been contact with something, with someone. A touching of spirits. Who?

And how was it possible?

The figure stirred in the chair as a cloud engulfed the moon; its breathing was shallow and harsh until the feeble light returned. It considered the possibility that someone was aware of its existence, and stretched its mind, seeking the interloper, searching but not fading. Not yet.

But in time. In time.

'You look a little pale,' Estelle Piprelly remarked as Childes entered the study and took a chair facing her on the other side of the broad desk.

'I'm fine,' he responded.

'You've hurt yourself.'

He raised the bandaged hand in a deprecative gesture. 'I broke a glass. Nothing serious, just a few minor cuts.'

The ceiling was high, the walls half-panelled in light oak, the upper portions a restful pastel green, except one wall which was covered from floor to ceiling with crowded bookshelves. A portrait of La Roche's founder dominated the wall to Childes' right, undoubtedly an accurate facsimile but one that revealed little of the sitter's true character, so typical of many Victorian studies. Beside the door, an ancient clock loudly ticked away the seconds as if each one was an announcement in itself. Childes looked past La Roche's principal, bright sunlight from the huge windows behind her blazing her grey hair silver. Outside were the school gardens, green lawns bordered with awakening flowers and shrubs, the slanted roof of a white-framed summerhouse dazzlingly mirroring the sun's rays. Beyond were the clifftops, rugged and decaying, slowly eroding bastions against the sea. The darker blue of the horizon indicated the clear divide between sea and sky, a distinct edge to the calm affinity between both elements. Although the room itself was spacious and its tones soothing, Childes suddenly felt confined, as if the walls were restraining an energy emanating from within himself, a force that the bounds of his own physical body could not contain. He knew that the sensation was simple claustrophobia, nothing more, and much of it was due to the impending confrontation with the headmistress.

'I had a call from Victor Platnauer this morning,' Miss Piprelly began, confirming his expectation. 'I believe you met on a social basis last Saturday evening.'

Childes nodded.

'He told me of your, er, unfortunate accident,' the principal went on. 'He said that you had fainted during dinner.'

'No, dinner was just about over.'

She eyed him coolly, 'He was concerned over your state of health. There is, after all, a huge responsibility on your shoulders when teaching youngsters, and such an occurrence in the classroom could cause some distress among the girls. As one of our governors, *Conseiller* Platnauer was seeking some assurance that you were not prone to such collapses. I think that's reasonable, don't you?'

'It's the first time ever for me. Really.'

'Any idea as to why it happened? Have you consulted a doctor yet?'

He hesitated before answering. 'No to both questions. I'm okay now, I don't need a doctor.'

'Nonsense. If you fainted, there must be a reason for it.'

'Maybe I was a little tensed up on Saturday. A personal thing.'

'Enough to make you black out?' she scoffed mildly.

'I can only tell you it's not a regular occurrence with me. I feel healthy nowadays, probably healthier than I've felt in a long time. Life on the island has meant a big change for me, a different style of living, away from the pressure of my last job, out of a rat-race profession. And I don't mind admitting there was a considerable strain on my marriage for several years. Things have changed since I came here: I'm more relaxed, I'd even say more content.'

'Yes, I can believe that. But as I said when you came in, you look a trifle peaky.'

'What happened shook me as well as the other dinner guests,' he said testily.

He felt uncomfortable under her gaze and looked away, brushing an imaginary speck of dust from his cords. For a moment it had seemed she had looked into the very core of him.

'All right, Mr Childes, I don't intend to pursue that particular matter any further. However, I do suggest you consult a doctor at the earliest opportunity; your fainting spell may well be a symptom of some hidden illness.'

He was relieved, but said nothing.

Miss Piprelly lightly tapped the blunt end of a fountain pen on the desktop as if it were a gavel. 'Victor Platnauer also brought something else to my attention, something, I'm afraid, to do with your past history, Mr Childes, and of which you have omitted to inform me.'

He straightened in his seat, body tensed, hands clasping his knees, knowing what was coming.

'I refer, of course, to the unhappy dealings you had with the police before you came to the island.'

He should have realized it would not be forgotten so easily, that England was too close, too accessible, for such news not to have travelled, and to have been remembered by some. Had Platnauer always known? No, it would have been mentioned long before. Someone had told him very recently, and Childes smiled to himself, for it was so obvious: Paul Sebire had 'looked into' his background – either that, or Amy had told her father – and passed on the interesting information to the school governor. In a funny way, he was glad the secret was out, even though he considered it to be nobody's business but his own. Suppression leads to depression, right? he told himself.

'Right,' he answered.

'I beg your pardon?' The headmistress looked surprised.

'My "dealings with the police" as you put it, were purely as a source of information. I helped, in the true sense, with their investigations.'

'So I gather. Although your method was rather peculiar, wouldn't you say that?'

'Yes, I would say that. In fact, the idea still astounds me. As to my not having informed you when you hired me, I hardly thought it necessary. I wasn't criminally involved.'

'Quite so. And I'm not making an issue of it now.'

It was Childes' turn to be surprised. 'My, uh, standing here isn't affected in any way?'

The ticking clock timed the pause. Six seconds.

'I think it only fair that I tell you I've asked our police department to supply me with more information on the matter. You should appreciate my reasons for doing so.'

'You're not going to fire me?'

She didn't smile and her manner had its usual brusqueness, but he regarded her with new interest when she said: 'I see no reason for doing so; not at this stage, at any rate. Unless you have anything further to tell me right now, anything that I'll probably find out anyway?'

He shook his head. 'I've got nothing to hide, Miss Piprelly, I promise you that.'

'Very well. We have a particular need for your special abilities, otherwise I wouldn't have asked you to spare La Roche more of your time, and that I've explained to Victor Platnauer. I must admit he was reluctant to see my point of view at first, but he's a fair-minded man. He will, however, be keeping a close eye on you, Mr Childes, as I shall. We've agreed to keep the whole affair strictly to ourselves: La Roche would find any such publicity regarding yourself totally unacceptable. We have a long-established reputation to protect.'

Estelle Piprelly sat back in her chair and, even though her body was still ramrod straight, the position seemed almost relaxed for her. She continued to study Childes with that unsettling, penetrating gaze and the fountain pen stood stiffly between her fingers, base resting on the desktop, like a tiny immovable post. He wondered about her, wondered about her sudden frown, what she was reading in his expression. Was there just a hint of alarm behind the thick lenses of her spectacles?

She quickly recovered, leaving him unsure that he had seen any change at all in her demeanour.

'I won't keep you any longer,' Miss Piprelly said curtly. 'I'm sure we both have lots to do.'

I want him out of the room, she thought. I want him out *now*. It wasn't his fault, he wasn't to blame for this outrageous extra sense he possessed, just as she was not responsible for her own strange faculty. She could not get rid of the man on that basis; it would have been too hypocritical, too cruel. *But she wanted his presence away from her, now, that instant.* For a moment she had thought he'd seen through her own rigid mask, had sensed the ability in her, an unwelcome gift that was as unacceptable to her as adverse publicity was unacceptable to the school. Her secret, her *affliction*, was not to be shared; it had been too closely guarded for too many years. She would take the chance of keeping him on – he was owed that much – but she would keep away from him, avoid unnecessary contact. Miss Piprelly would not give Childes the opportunity to recognize their similarity. That would be too foolhardy, too much to give after so long. Dangerous even, for someone in her position.

'I'm sorry, Mr Childes, is there something you wanted to say?' She deliberately quelled her impatience, years of self-discipline coming to her aid.

'Only thanks. I appreciate your trust.'

'That has nothing whatsoever to do with it. If I thought you untrustworthy I wouldn't have employed you in the first place. Let's just say I value your expertise.'

He rose, managed to smile. Estelle Piprelly was an enigma to him. He started to say something, then thought better of it. He left the room.

The principal closed her eyes and let her head rest against the high-backed chair, the sun on her shoulders unable to dispense the chill.

Outside in the corridor, Childes began to shake. Earlier that morning he had assumed he was in control, that much of the anguish had been purged the day before, literally walked from his system, so exhausting him that when he returned home sleep would overwhelm him. And it had. There had been no dreams, no restless turning in the bed, no sweat-soaked sheets, just several hours of oblivion. That morning he had awoken feeling refreshed, the sighted images of Saturday evening a contained memory, still disturbing but at least uneasily settled in a compartment of his mind. Subconscious reflex, self-protecting mental conditioning; there had to be a legitimate medical term with which to label the reaction.

The morning newspaper had easily shattered that temporary defence.

Still he had gone through the motions of everyday living, unnerved but determined to get through the day. Halfway there and then his meeting with Miss Piprelly. Now he was shaking.

'Jon?'

He turned, startled, and Amy saw his fear. She hurried to him.

'Jon, what's wrong? You look awful.'

Childes clung to her briefly. 'Let's get out of here,' he said. 'Can you get away for a while?'

'It's still lunchbreak. I've got at least half an hour before my next lesson.'

'A short drive then, to somewhere quiet.'

They parted when footsteps echoed along the corridor, and turned towards the stairs leading to the main entrance, saying nothing until they were outside, the sun warming them after the coolness of the school's interior.

'Where were you yesterday?' Amy asked. 'I tried to reach you throughout the day.'

'I thought you were showing Edouard Vigiers around the island.' There was no criticism in his response.

'I did for a hour or so. He understood my concern for you, though, and suggested we cut it short. I wasn't terribly good company, I'm afraid.' They walked towards the carpark. 'I came by the cottage, but there was no sign of you. I was so worried.'

'I'm sorry, Amy, I should have realized. I just had to get away, I couldn't stay inside.'

'Because of what happened at dinner?'

He nodded. 'I hardly ingratiated myself with your father.'

'That's not important. I want to know the cause, Jon.' She took his arm.

'It's starting all over again, Amy. I knew it that time on the beach; the feeling was the same, like being somewhere else, watching, seeing an action taking place and having no control over it.'

They had reached his car and she noticed his hands were trembling as he fumbled with the keys. 'It might be a good idea if I did the driving,' she suggested.

He opened the car door and handed Amy the keys without argument. They headed away from the school, taking a nearby winding lane that led to the coast. She occasionally glanced at him while she drove and his tenseness was soon passed on to her. They parked in a clearing overlooking a small bay, the sea below a sparkling blue, hued green in parts, lighter in the shallows. Through the open windows of the car they could hear the surf softly lapping at the shingle beach. In the far distance, a ferry trundled through the calm waters towards the main harbour on the eastern side of the island.

Childes watched its slow progress, his mind elsewhere, and Amy had to reach and turn his face towards her. 'We're here to talk, remember,' she said. 'Please tell me what was wrong with you on Saturday.' She leaned forward to kiss him and was relieved that his trembling had lessened.

'I can do better than that,' he told her. 'I can show you.' He reached over to the back seat and unfolded the newspaper before her. 'Take a look,' he said, pointing a finger.

'"INFANT'S GRAVE DESECRATED",' she said aloud, but the rest was read silently, disbelievingly. 'Oh, Jon, this is horrible. Who could do such a thing? To dismember a child's corpse, to . . .' She shuddered and jerked her head away from the open page. 'It's so vile.'

'It's what I saw, Amy.'

She stared incredulously at him, her yellow hair curling softly over one shoulder.

'I was there at the grave-side. I saw the body being torn open. I was part of it somehow.'

'No, you couldn't have . . .'

He gripped her arm. 'I saw it. I touched the mind of the person who did this.'

'How?' The question was left hanging in the air.

'Like before. Just like before. A feeling of being inside the person, seeing everything through their eyes. But I'm not involved, I've got no control. I can't stop what's happening!'

Amy was shocked by his sudden abject terror. She clung to him, speaking soothingly. 'It's all right, Jon, you can't be harmed. You're *not* part of it, what's happened has nothing to do with you.'

'I had my doubts on that score the other night,' he said, drawing away. 'I wondered if I were only recalling violence I'd committed myself, certain acts my own mind had blanked out.' He indicated the newspaper. 'This occurred on the mainland on the night I was at your home. At least that fact came as a relief.'

'If only I could have been with you yesterday to knock that silly idea out of your head.'

'No, I needed to be alone. Talking wouldn't have helped.'

'Sharing the problem would have.'

He tapped his forehead. 'The problem's inside here.'

'You're not mad.'

He smiled grimly. 'I know that. But will I stay sane if the visions keep coming at me? You have to know what it's like, Amy, to understand how scary it becomes. I'm left ragged when it's over, as if a portion of my brain has been eaten away.'

'Is that how you felt last time? In England, I mean.'

'Yeah. Maybe it was worse then; it was a totally new experience for me.'

'When they found the man responsible for those killings, what then?'

'Relief. Incredible relief. It was as though a huge black awareness had been released, something like, I'd imagine, when someone suffering from over-sensitive hearing suddenly finds the overload has been blocked out, that their ear-drums have finally managed the correct balance. But strangely, the release came before they tracked the man down; you see, somehow I knew the exact moment he committed suicide, because that was when my mind was set free. His death let me go.'

'Why him; why that particular murderer, and why only him? Have you ever wondered about that?'

'I've wondered, and I've never reached a satisfactory conclusion. I've sensed things before, but nothing startling, nothing you could describe as precognition or ESP, anything like that. They've always been mundane, ordinary stuff that I suppose most people sense: when the phone rings you guess who's at the other end even before you pick it up, or when you're lost, guessing the right turn to make. Simple, everyday matters, nothing dramatic.' He shifted in the car seat, eyes watching a swooping gull. 'Psychics say our minds are like radio receivers, tuning into other wavelengths all the time, picking up different frequencies: well, maybe he was transmitting on a particular frequency that only I could receive, the excitement he felt at the kill boosting the output, making it powerful enough to reach me.' The gull was soaring upwards once more, its wings brilliant in the sun's rays.

Childes twisted round to face Amy. 'It's a stupid theory, I know, but I can't think of any other explanation,' he said.

'It isn't stupid at all; it makes a weird kind of sense. Strong emotions, a sudden shock, can induce a strong telepathic connection between certain people, and that's well known. But why now? What's triggered off these psychic messages this time?'

Childes folded the newspaper and tossed it onto the back seat. 'The same as before. I've picked up another frequency.'

'You have to go to the police.'

'You've got to be kidding! That kind of publicity finished off my marriage and sent me scuttling for cover last time. Do you really imagine I'd bring it all down on myself again?'

'There's no alternative.'

'Sure there is. I can keep quiet and pray that it'll go away.'

'It didn't last time.'

'As far as I know, nobody's been murdered yet.'

'As far as you know. What happened the other week, when you saw something that shook you so much you nearly drowned?'

'Just a confused jumble, impossible to tell what was going on.'

'Perhaps it was a killing.'

'I can't ruin everything again by going to the law. What chance would I have at La Roche or the other schools if word got around that there was some kind of psychic freak teaching kids on the island? Victor Platnauer's already gunning for me and I'd hate to gift-wrap more ammunition for him.'

'Platnauer?'

He quickly summarised his meeting with Estelle Piprelly.

'I think Daddy had a hand in this,' she said when he had concluded.

'And did you tell your father about me? I'm sorry, I didn't mean that harshly – there's no reason for you to keep secrets from your family, so I wouldn't blame you if you had.'

'He got the local police to look into your history. I had nothing to do with it.' Childes sighed. 'I should have known. Anything to break us up, right?'

'No, Jon, he's just concerned about who I get involved with,' she half-lied.

'I can't blame him for getting upset.'

'Acting the wimp doesn't suit you.' She touched his lapel, her fingers running along its edge, a frown hardening her expression. 'I still think you should inform the police. You proved last time you weren't a crank.'

He held her moving fingers. 'Let's just give it a bit more time, huh? These . . . these visions might just amount to nothing, might fade away.'

Amy turned from him and switched on the ignition. 'We have to get back,' she said. Then: 'What if they don't? What if they get worse? Jon, what if someone is murdered?'

He found he had nothing to say.

Childes assumed his mock-official tone when he heard Gabby's squeaky 'Hello?'

'To whom am I speaking to?' he asked, for the moment pushing aside troubled thoughts.

'*Daddy*,' she warned lowly, used to the game. 'Guess what happened in school today, Daddy.'

'Let me see.' He pondered. 'You shot your teacher?'

'No!'

'The teacher shot you lot.'

'Be *serious*!'

He grinned at her frustration, imagining her standing by the phone, receiver pressed to her ear as if glued, her glasses slipped to the end of her nose in their usual fashion.

'Okay, you tell me, Squirt,' he said.

'Well, first we brought our projects in and Miss Hart held mine up to the class and told everyone it was really good.'

'Was that the one on wild flowers?'

'Yes, I told you last week,' she replied indignantly.

'Oh yeah, it slipped my mind. Hey, that's great. She really liked it, eh?'

'Yes. Annabel's was nearly as good, but I think she copied me a little bit. I got a gold star for mine and Annabel got a yellow one, which is very good really.'

He chuckled. 'I think it's marvellous.'

'Then Miss Hart told us we were all going to Friends Park next Tuesday on a big coach where they've got monkeys in cages, and a big lake with boats, and slides and things.'

'They've got monkeys on a coach?'

'No, at Friends Park, silly! Mummy said she'd give me some money to spend and make me up a picnic.'

'That sounds lovely. Isn't she going with you?'

'No, it's just school. Do you think the weather will be sunny?'

'I should think so, it's pretty warm now.'

'I hope it will, so does Annabel. Are you coming to see me soon?'

As usual, she threw in the question with innocent abandon, not knowing the tiny stab wound it caused.

'I'll try, darling. Maybe at half-term. Mummy might let you come over here to see me.'

'On a plane? I don't like the boat, it's too long. It makes my tummy feel sick.'

'Yes, on a plane. You could stay with me for a few days until term begins again.'

'Can I bring Miss Puddles? She'd be very lonely without me.' Miss Puddles was Gabby's cat, a black cat bought for her on her third birthday. The cat's development had easily out-paced his daughter's, kittenish behaviour giving way to imperious coolness long before Childes had left the household.

'No, that wouldn't be a good idea. Mummy will need someone to keep her company, won't she?' He hadn't seen his daughter for almost six months and he wondered how tall she'd grown. Gabby seemed to grow in sudden leaps, taking him by surprise each time he saw her.

'I suppose so,' she said. 'Did you want to speak to Mummy?'

'Yes, please.'

'She isn't here. Janet's looking after me.'

'Oh. All right, let me have a world with Janet.'

'I'll go and fetch her. Oh, Daddy, I sprinkled glitterdust all over Miss Puddles yesterday to make her sparkly.'

'I bet she liked that,' he said, shaking his head and grinning.

'She didn't. She got really sulky. Mummy says we'll never get it out and Miss Puddles keeps sneezing.'

'Get Janet to run the vacuum attachment over her. That should shift some of it if you can keep the cat still for long enough.'

Gabby giggled. 'She's going to get cross. I'll tell Janet you want to speak to her, all right?'

'Good girl.'

'Love you, Daddy, 'bye.' As abrupt as that.

'I love you,' he returned, hearing the phone clunk down before he'd completed the sentence. Running footsteps echoed away; her squeaky little voice called in the distance.

More footsteps along the hall, heavier, and the receiver was picked up.

'Mr Childes?'

'How're things, Janet?'

'Okay, I guess. Fran's working late at the office this evening, so I'm staying until she gets home. I brought Gabby home from school as usual.'

'Any luck with a job yet?'

'Not yet. I've got a couple of interviews next week so I'm keeping my fingers crossed. Neither are really what I wanted, but anything's better than nothing.'

He sympathized. Janet was a bright teenager, although with few qualifications: with fulltime employment so difficult to come by for the young and inexperienced, she had quite a struggle on her hands.

'Did you want to leave a message, Mr Childes?' Janet asked.

'Uh, no, it's okay, I'll probably call again tomorrow. I just wanted to chat with Gabby.'

'I'll tell Fran you rang.'

'Thanks. Good luck for next week.'

'I'll need it. 'Bye for now, Mr Childes.'

The link was severed and he was alone again in his cottage. At such times there was a brutal finality in the replacing of a receiver. His injured hand throbbed dully and there was an unnatural dryness at the back of his throat. He stood by the telephone for some time, his thoughts slowly drifting away from his daughter and settling on the memory of the police detective who had been involved in the child-slaying case years before, someone whom he'd helped to track down the maniac killer. His fingers rested on the still-warm plastic, but he could not make them grip the receiver. Amy was wrong: there was no point in going to the police. What could he tell them? He couldn't identify the person who had dug up the dead boy, could give them no clues as to the desecrator's whereabouts. Until he had seen the morning paper, he'd had no idea even that the offence had taken place in England; he had assumed, if the sighting was a true one and not merely a fantasised image, that it had happened closer, somewhere on the island. There was nothing to say to the police, nothing at all. He took his hand away from the phone.

Gabby's birth had been difficult, a breech.

She had come from the womb feet first and a purplish shade of blue, almost causing Childes, who had stayed by Fran's side throughout, to collapse with fear. He had felt that nothing looking like that, so shrivelled and frail, so darkly-coloured, could possible live. The obstetrician had tilted the baby, drawing mucus from her mouth, having no time to reassure the parents, anxious only for the life of the child. He had cleared the blockage and blown hard against her slippery little chest to encourage breathing. The first cry, no more than a quietly-pitched whimper and hardly heard, sent relief surging through them all, doctor, nurse and parents alike. She had been wrapped and placed on Fran's breast, the umbilical cord deftly cut and Childes, as exhausted mentally as Fran was physically, had viewed them both with a spreading glow which transformed his weariness into a relaxed tiredness.

Fran, her features wan and aged after the ordeal; the baby, still wet and bloodied, her face screwed up and wrinkled like an ancient's; both so peaceful in the struggle's aftermath. He had leaned over them, careful not to crush, yet needing to be as close as possible, the sterile hospital smell mixing with the sweat odour of battle, and had thought then that nothing could ever disrupt their unity, nothing could make them part.

In the ensuing weeks it was as though Gabby was slowly emerging from a deep and terrible trauma, as indeed she was – the transition between mere existence and dawning awareness. He had begun to understand the shock creation brought with it.

Sleep laid claim to most of her life in those days, releasing her in gentle episodes to absorb and learn, to sustain herself, and the transformation was fascinating to see. Her growing was a marvel to him and he spent hours just observing, watching her develop, become a little girl who toddled on unsteady legs and who had a great affection for her own thumb and a ragged piece of material that had once been her blanket. Her first word had delighted him, even though it hadn't been 'Dadda', and her unbounded reliance on him and Fran and her uncomplicated love had drawn from him a new tenderness that was reflected in other areas of his life. Gabby had made him understand the vulnerability of every living person and creature; a time-consuming career involved in machines and abstractions had tended to blunt that perception.

The newfounded compassion had nearly destroyed him when he had mind-witnessed the indecent destruction of the children.

Three years later the thoughts still haunted him, and just lately, their power to do so was greater than ever.

Childes had spent the evening preparing exercises for the next day's lessons, the Tuesday afternoon he had promised to Miss Piprelly and which had already come into practice. Examinations for the girls would soon be upon them and Computer Sciences would be one. He was irritated that his thoughts had kept wandering throughout the evening, thinking of Gabby, the years of happiness they had shared as a family, even though Fran had never completely laid to rest the ghost of her PR career. So much had happened to spoil that in such a short time, and the intervening years could not quite dispel the anguish of it all.

He stared unseeingly at the papers spread before him, the shielded desk-lamp casting deep shadows around the small living room. Was Gabby asleep by now, glasses folded next to her pillow for security? He glanced at his watch: nearly half-past nine. She had better be. Did Fran still read her a bedtime story, or was she too busy nowadays, too exhausted when she got home? Childes shuffled the papers together, dismayed that some of the girls he had tested today with quick-fire questions still did not know the difference between analog and digital computers, or that they could be combined in a hybrid. Simple, basic stuff that shouldn't have been a problem. He dreaded the exam results, hoping practice would prove more fruitful than theory.

He ran a hand across weary eyes, his contact lenses feeling like soft grit against his pupils. Food, he thought. Ought to eat, they say it's good for you. So tired, though. Maybe a sandwich, a glass of milk. A stiff drink might be more beneficial.

He was about to rise when something cold, numbing, stabbed at his mind.

Childes put both hands to his temples, confused by the unexpected sensation. Blinking his eyes, he tried to rid himself of the coldness. It persisted.

Outside he could hear the night breeze stirring the trees. A floorboard cracked somewhere inside the house, a timber settling after the warmth of the day.

The numbness faded and he shook his head as if dizzy. Too much paperwork, he told himself, too much concentration far into the night. Concentration disturbed by thoughts of Gabby. And other things.

That drink might relax him. He rose, pressing down on the desk top to heave himself up. The icicle touched nerves once more and he swayed, hands gipping the sides of the desk to steady himself.

His thoughts were jumbled, tumbling over each other in his head, the iciness now like probing fingers pushing through those thoughts, taking them and somehow . . . somehow . . . feeding upon them. His shoulders hunched and his head bowed. His lips drew back as though he were in pain, yet there was no hurt, just the spreading numbness and the mental chaos. A groan escaped him.

And then his mind began to clear. He remained standing, leaning over the desk, breathing heavily, allowing the sensation to subside. It seemed to take a long while, but Childes knew it was no more than seconds. He waited until his quivering nerves had settled before crossing the room and pouring himself a drink. Strangely, the whisky was almost tasteless.

He choked on the next swallow as the burning flavour came back at him at full strength. Spluttering, he wiped the back of his arm against his lips. What the hell was happening to him? He tasted the drink again, this time more carefully, sipping slowly. He was warmed.

Childes looked around the room uneasily, not sure of what he was searching for, merely feeling another presence. Foolish. Apart from him, the room was empty, nobody had crept in while he had been hunched over paperwork.

The shadows thrown by the metal desk-lamp made him uncomfortable and he went to the switch by the door, bandaged hand outstretched to turn on the overhead light. He stopped before touching the switch and stared at his fingers, surprised by the sudden tingling in them, as if they had received a mild electric shock. They had not touched the light-switch. He glanced down when the peculiar tingling began in the hand clutching the whisky glass and it seemed as though the glass itself was vibrating.

The unseen, insidious fingers probed again.

His body sagged and he quickly sank onto the nearby sofa, pushing into its softness as if trying to evade a pressing weight. The glass fell to the floor, the rug soaking up its spilled contents. Childes's eyes closed as the sense of intrusion became intense. Images whirled inside his head, computer matrixes, faces, the room he was in now, numbers, symbols, floating in and out, something white, shimmering, past events, his own face, his own self, his fears, dreams long-forgotten recalled and pried into.

He moaned, pushing away the delving ice tentacles, forcing a calmness in his mind, willing the confusion to stop.

Childes' muscles relaxed a little when the cold probing faded once again, his chest rising and falling in exaggerated motion. He stared blankly at the shadows cast against the opposite wall. Something was attempting to reach him, something – *somebody* – was trying to *know* him.

With scarcely any relief, the creeping sensation came back, tautening his body, infiltrating his consciousness. No! his mind screamed. And '*No!*' he cried aloud. But it was there, inside, searching, sucking at his thoughts. He could feel its existence, delving into him like some psychic thief. It invaded him and dwelt on thoughts of the island, the schools he taught in, thoughts of Amy, of Fran, of . . . Gabby. Of GABBY! It seemed to linger.

Childes forced himself off the sofa, struggling against the extraneous consciousness, painfully dislodging each numbing tentacle as though they were physical entities. He felt there grip loosen and the effort sent him to his knees. He made himself think only of a white mist, nothing else, nothing to distract him nor give substance to the intruder, and soon his head began to clear.

But before relief came fully, leaving him crouched and shivering on the floor, he heard a sound so real it caused him to twist his head and search the dark corners of the room.

He was alone. But the low snickering seemed close.

Jeanette was late. The other girls from her dormitory had already gone down and she was still in her dressing gown, furiously brushing her teeth.

Today of all days! Exams! Maths! *Aargh, maths!* Jeanette sometimes wondered if she were a bonehead as far as figures were concerned.

Morning sunlight poured into the washroom, reflecting off the rows of porcelain basins, making them gleam; water gathered in small pools on the tiled floor, liquid debris from the girls' washing rituals. She was alone and preferred to be: the others often embarrassed her by comparing breast sizes and shapes, all of them eager competitors in the development race. Jeanette was a long way behind most of the other thirteen- and fourteen-year-olds in her class and did not care much for the comparisons. To add to her feelings of inadequacy, her periods had not even started yet.

Jeanette rinsed her mouth, spat into the basin, dabbed her lips with a face-cloth, and dumped her toiletries into her pink plastic washbag. She padded to the door, bare feet nearly slipping on the wet tiles, then hurried along the gloomy corridor, leaving damp footprints on the polished floorboards in her wake. Bare feet were forbidden inside the school, but she had not had time to rummage beneath her bed for skulking slippers, and besides, everyone, staff included, would be downstairs by now tucking into breakfast.

It was shivery in the dormitory she shared with five other girls, despite the bright sun outside, and Jeanette quickly laid out her underwear, plain regulation navy-blue panties and white vest, on the narrow, rumpled bed. Shrugging off her quilted dressing gown, she pulled her pyjama top off over her head without undoing the buttons and threw it onto the bed alongside the underwear. She briskly rubbed at the sudden goose-pimples on her arms as if to brush them off, then reached for the vest. Before pulling on the garment, she paused to examine her chest and sighed at its complacency. The nipples were longish, erect now because of the chill, but the tiny mounds they thrust from were, as usual, a disappointment. She tweaked the nipples to make them harder and tugged at the soft bumps to encourage growth. A delicate flush of pleasure warmed her and she imagined her breasts had swelled a little more. She sat on the bed, still in her pyjama bottoms, and cupped a mound in each hand. It felt pleasant and she wondered what it would be like if . . . No, no time for that – she was late enough already!

She stripped off the pyjama legs and swiftly donned vest, panties, and white socks retrieved from the bottom drawer of her bedside locker. Since the weather had changed for the better, La Roche girls were allowed their light blue, short-sleeved summer dresses and Jeanette shrugged on hers, shoes, badly in need of polish, following. She tidied the bed, hiding her nightwear beneath the sheets, then grabbed a brush and attacked her long, tangled hair, wincing at her efforts. The small blue-rimmed mirror, a china butterfly frozen on one top corner, standing on top of the locker, reflected the results, which were not pleasing. In spite of her haste Jeanette leaned close and examined her face for overnight blemishes. She had almost entirely cut out chocolate and did her utmost, puke-making though it was, to finish off all the green vegetables on her dinner plate, but the spots came up with predictable regularity, and nearly always on special occasions. But there – today wasn't special, only rotten exams, and her skin was clear! She bet that on her wedding day there would be at least five zits to every square inch of flesh on her face and she'd have to wear a veil all through the ceremony and she'd be afraid to lift it afterwards for her husband's kiss and when she eventually did she would look like an ice-cream topped with raspberry pips.

Jeanette moved even closer to the blue-rimmed mirror, looking deep into her own dark eyes, dreamily wondering if she could see the future there. She had been scolded enough by her parents and tutors alike for spending too much time day-dreaming and not enough time *thinking*, and she had tried to concentrate her mind on more serious things, but after a few minutes her mind always drifted inwards and became lost in her own fantasies. She tried, she *tried*, but it seemed her thoughts had a separate will. To look through a window at the sky meant seeing herself soar over tree tops, swooping down into valleys, skimming over white-crested oceans, not as a bird but as her own free spirit. The sun warming her face would evoke fiery deserts, golden beaches, sultry days spent with – a keen-edged excitement with the word – her future *lover*. To catch a flower's fragrance initiated thoughts on the existence of all things, large or small, animate or inanimate, and her part in such order. To see the moon –

A shadow passed behind her.

She turned and there was no one there; save for her, the dormitory was empty.

Posters and cut-outs of pop stars, movie starts, tennis stars, hair styles, fashion styles, *crazee* styles, covered the walls in carefully assembled groups. One or two raggedy teddy-bears and dolls, kept now as mascots rather than the cuddly, loved companions they once were, watched with dead eyes. Colourful mobiles over beds stirred gently as if touched by a breeze.

There was no one there; yet Jeanette felt there was.

The goose-bumps had returned to tickle her bare arms. The sun did not seem as bright. She moved away from the locker, treading warily into the centre aisle between two equal rows of beds, examining the shadows beneath each one before passing, almost as if she expected a hand to emerge and snatch her ankle. Her pace increased as she neared the doorway.

Then, with a rush, she was through, looking back and seeing only an empty dormitory, bright with posters, motionless mobiles and coloured quilts, the sun streaming in to warm and to disperse shadows.

There was no one else there. Nonetheless she hurried away.

She stood over him and vigorously shook her head, showering him with sea-water. He opened one eye, shielding it from the sun's rays which were still strong even though it was late afternoon, appreciating the cool droplets on his chest.

'How is it?' Childes asked.

'Cold,' Amy replied, dropping to her knees beside him and briskly rubbing her hair with a thick towel, 'but lovely. Why don't you come in for a while?'

He closed his eye again and answered lazily, 'Too much trouble to take out my lenses.' He did not mention he had not swum since his unfortunate experience of nearly a month before, when they had been snorkling; the near-drowning had left him feeling just a little too vulnerable in deep water.

'Ah, come on, it'll refresh you.' She placed a flat, damp hand on his tummy and giggled as the muscles there quickly retracted.

He pulled her down to him, enjoying her wetness, her salty, sea smell. 'I need rest,' he told her, 'not exertion.'

'Rest? This is exam week; you've never had it so easy.'

'That's right, and I intend to keep it that way for as long as possible.'

Amy draped the towel around her head and shoulders, creating a shade over both of them. She crossed her hands on his chest, supporting herself, and pecked at his lips with her own.

'Nice taste,' Childes remarked. 'Like kissing an oyster.'

'I'm not sure if that's a compliment or not, so I'll let it go.' Her damp, tangled hair trailed across his cheek and he raised his head slightly to lick moisture from her chin.

There were few people on the beach at that time of day, tourists from the mainland and the Continent not yet having descended upon the island in force, and most of the island's working inhabitants being still trapped inside places of employment. The cove held a wide stretch of sand, one end guarded by a triple-level German bunker, a huge granite monolith facing the sea, and a grim reminder of recent history. Jagged rocks, as if freshly tumbled from the cliffs, blocked the opposite end.

'You made it up with Daddy yet?' asked Childes.

Amy knew his use of the word 'Daddy' was only slightly mocking, a faint jibe that she was still her father's little girl and still using the world herself, and she had long since given up taking offence. 'Oh, he's still huffy with me and I'm still huffy with him, but I think he'll eventually come to accept the situation.'

'I don't think I quite believe that.'

'He's not an ogre, Jon, he doesn't wish you any harm.'

'That wasn't the case a couple of weeks ago when he primed Victor Platnauer to complain to Miss Piprelly about me.'

'Pip's nobody's stooge; she makes up her own mind about things. In fairness to Daddy though – and I don't condone for a minute what he did – your past is a tiny bit disconcerting.'

He could not help but smile as he curled clogged strands of her hair around his finger. 'Does it still bother you?'

'How can it not, Jon? Especially after recent events. You know how much I care for you, so how can you expect me to put aside everything that's happened?'

'Nothing's happened since, Amy, not after the dinner party. I don't feel so uneasy any more, I'm not jumping at shadows. I can't explain it, but I feel as though a huge pressure has been lifted from me. At least for the moment.' He hadn't told her of the night alone in his cottage when the strange tension in his mind had brought him to his knees. In the following days, the sense of foreboding had slowly dissipated as though he were being released from an outside force, a debilitating spell lifted. He felt the threat had somehow passed him by. And yet that malignant snicker of laughter still echoed inside his head.

'I hope so, Jon,' Amy said, her soft voice dismissing the final dregs of doubt. 'I like the old you better, the one I first met. Quiet, easy-going, sometimes amusing . . .' he tugged her hair '. . . sometimes sexy . . .'

He drew her down so that her lips pressed against his. Their kiss, at first soft, soon hardened, became almost fierce, their tongues tasting each other's warm moistness. Her body pushed firmly against his, one slim leg parting his knees.

'Hey, take it easy,' he said breathlessly after a few moments. 'I'm only wearing swimming trunks, remember, and this is a public place.'

'Nobody's watching.' She nuzzled his neck and her thigh was strong against his.

'This is no way for a schoolmarm to behave.'

'School's out.'

'And so will I be if you carry on.'

'Oh, is it peeping over the top?'

'Amy,' he warned.

She chuckled and drew away. 'What a prude,' she said, sitting up and continuing to dry her hair.

He sat up too, drawing up his legs and resting his arms over his knees for the sake of modesty.

'Shame,' she mocked.

'I've got an idea,' he said brightly.

'Oh yeah?' she replied, still mocking, but her voice deeper, a huskiness to it.

'Why don't you dry off properly back at my place. Unless you've got to get home for some reason?'

'As a matter of fact, I said I wouldn't be home for dinner tonight.'

'Is that right? You had plans, huh?'

'No, but I thought you might.'

'Some ideas are coming to mind . . .'

They drove to the cottage, not bothering to change back into their clothes, semi-nude figures driving cars being a common feature of the island when the weather was warm, and they were soon inside the small, grey-stone house.

Amy shivered as Childes closed the front door. 'It's cooler in here,' she said.

'I'll get you my robe and fix you a drink.'

'I'd like to soak off this salt.'

'I'll get you my robe, fix you a drink and run the bath.'

Her arms went around his neck and she kissed his nose. 'You just do the drinks.'

He gripped her waist, hugging her close, his lips seeking hers.

Amy returned his kiss with equal fervour, feeling him hard against her stomach, but she pulled away when things began to get out of control. 'Let me get cleaned up first,' she said, slightly out of breath.

'You've just come out of the sea – you're clean enough.'

She broke free. 'Do the drinks and read your mail. I won't be long.' She disappeared into the bathroom before he could protest further, leaving him to retrieve the letters lying on the doormat. The pink envelope with Snoopy in one corner caught his eye and he grinned, recognizing the childish scrawl. Pulling on his shirt which had been tossed over the stair banister with his other clothing, Childes strolled into the sitting room, throwing the other two brown envelopes which were the bills onto the desk. He crossed the room, opening the pink envelope as he went. Gabby wrote to him at least once a week, sometimes the letters long and informative, other times, like today's, only a few scribbled lines, her way of keeping open the link despite the miles between them. Miss Puddles still had glittering hi-lites, Annabel had CHICKEN SPOKS, and Mummy had promised to show her how to make fairy cakes next weekend. Childes touched his lips to the row of XXXXXXs, his and Gabby's shared secret that all written kisses were sealed by a real one.

The sound of running water came from the bathroom and he returned the letter to its envelope, placing it on one side. He poured a Scotch for himself and a dry Martini for Amy, then went through to the kitchen for ice. She was just stepping into the bath, the water still running, when he brought the Martini in to her. He watched from the doorway, admiring her lightly browned skin, the slimness of her legs and body, the long, delicate fingers gripping the edge of the tub. Her hair, still darkly wet from the sea, hung in tangled strands around her face and over her shoulders. Her pale green eyes closed as she sank further into the water and she sighed, a quiet moan of pleasure, as the warmth flooded her. The nipples of her small breasts rose above the waterline.

Childes turned off the taps and handed her the drink. Her eyes opened as she took the glass and the smile in them was his thank-you. They clinked glasses and sipped, Childes trailing one hand in the water, brushing the smoothness of her skin, running his fingers down so that they entwined in the fine hair between her legs.

Amy drew in a short breath and her teeth pressed gently against her lower lip. 'Feels good,' she murmured as his hand lingered. He leaned over and kissed an erect nipple as she lightly stroked his hair, sliding her fingers into its dark thickness, following the flow to where it lapped over his shirt collar, sinking her hand beneath the material so that she touched his spine. She kneaded the flesh there, soothingly, without hurry, and it was his turn to murmur pleasure. His lips moved to her shoulder and he nipped the skin, not enough to hurt, before moving on, his mouth finding certain nerves in her neck where it loitered, drawing softly on them so that her head twisted to one side in sensuous delight.

He relaxed, not wanting to take the love-making too far, not yet. She turned her head back to look at him, and there was a shine in her eyes. 'I love you,' she said simply.

He kissed her again, just lightly, and his hand brushed a lank hair from her cheek. 'There's a comfortable bed waiting upstairs,' he whispered.

Amy lowered her eyes, as if suddenly timid. 'And I love being with you.' She sipped her Martini, content in the soothing liquid warmth. He helped her massage shampoo into her hair, rinsing it with his own empty whisky glass, using a cloth on her back, all movement slow, languid, no vigour and no haste used. Eventually he drew her from the water and she stood before him, a golden, lissom figures, so sensually innocent in her nakedness, so knowing in her smile. Childes towelled her dry, using a restrained, patting movement as though her skin would break if touched too hard. He reached her legs and they parted a little as he dabbed at them; he paused to kiss her tummy, her hips, the top of her thighs. She was very damp there and it was not just water.

'Jon,' she said, and there was a mild urgency in her tone. 'Can we go upstairs now?'

He rose and reached for the dark blue bathrobe hanging behind the door, wrapping it around her shoulders and tying the belt at the front for her, her arms trapped inside. 'You go ahead, I'll pour us another drink.'

Back in the sitting room, he heard her bare footsteps overhead, the bed creaking as she lay down. He quickly replenished their glasses and climbed the short stairway, forgetting about ice. Amy, still in the bathrobe, was lying on top of the bedclothes, waiting. One leg was provocatively exposed to the thigh, while the robe was loose enough around her neck to reveal the delicate curves of her breasts.

Childes took in the sight before moving into the room. He put their drinks on a bedside cabinet and sat on the bed close to her. Neither of them spoke, but they watched each other, enjoying what they saw, both relishing the waiting.

Finally, Amy drew him down, easing off his shirt as he sank. His hands went inside the robe, reaching round to her back, pressing her flesh, pulling her close. They kissed and there was no control, their mouths open to each other's, their lips crushing. Her relentless hands caressed his sides, his back, his hips, squeezing, scratching, inciting. He fondled her breasts and they were soft and malleable, only their centres resisting, the hardened tips thrusting themselves at the moving palms of his hands.

She kissed his chest, causing pleasurable tension there, her tongue heightening that sensation.

His hand slid towards her thigh, delving beneath the rough material of the robe to feel the roundness of her buttocks, pressing them in a circular motion, his fingers probing the end of her spine. Amy moaned aloud and collapsed onto her back, one leg raised over his. His searching hand came back to find her warm moistness and a small cry welcomed his approach. He touched, lingered, entered when her risen hips urged him. She opened to him and his fingers pierced, his thumb caressing her sensitive outer regions, using soft, smooth friction to make her gasp, to clutch him tightly, to grip his body with all her limbs.

Amy's breath was fast, shallow, and she groaned in disappointment when he released her, craving more, more touching, more feeling, but he needed her, wanted to be engulfed by her. She realized his intent and helped him free himself from his remaining clothing, reaching for him when the swimming trunks were gone and guiding him down to her.

He entered and there was no hindrance, the journey into her liquid-smooth, and the motion causing them both to murmur. Childes forced himself to stop, wishing to see her face, her love, to show his. They kissed once more and the tenderness was soon overtaken by driving need.

He felt the hot, pliant softness of her thigh around his own and he ducked low to kiss her breasts, their taste a bitter stimulant; he supported himself on his elbows so that their stomachs parted while their bodies remained locked together, with no intention of separating. The sight of her beneath him was exquisite and his thrusting became hurried, Amy soon matching him. He collapsed onto her, his chin pressing into the side of her neck, and she revelled in his strength, holding him to her, their bodies moving against each other's, their gasps filling the room, her appreciative whimpers driving him on, their final cries resounding off the walls, their slow, sinking sighs whispering their contentment.

After a while they drew apart, kissing as they did so. They lay on their backs, both allowing the excitement to ebb away, each catching their breath. Childes' chest heaved with the exertion and there was a faint shine on his dampened skin. Amy recovered more quickly and turned to him, a hand draping loosely over his waist. She studied his profile, loving the roughness of his chin, the slight bump on the bridge of his nose. She traced a finger across his open lips and he bit softly, his breathing slowing down.

'Seconds?' she asked mischievously.

He groaned and slid an arm beneath her shoulders. Amy settled against his chest.

'Sometimes, you know,' he said, 'you look about fifteen.'

'Now?'

He nodded. 'And a few minutes ago.'

'Does it put you off?'

'Far from it, because I know different. I know the woman inside.'

'The whore in me?'

'No, the *woman*.'

She nipped his skin. 'I'm glad it pleases you.'

'You've made an old man very happy.'

'Thirty-four isn't exactly ancient.'

'I've got eleven years on you.'

'H'mn, on consideration maybe that is a little old. I may have to rethink my plans.'

'You've made plans?'

'Let's say I have intentions.'

'Care to tell me what they are?'

'Not at the moment. You're not ready to hear them.'

'I wonder if your father would approve.'

'Why does he always have to come into it.'

'He's an important element in your life and I don't think you enjoy his disapproval.'

'Of course I don't, but I have my own life to live, my own mind to make up.'

'Your own mistakes to make?'

'Those too. But why are you such a pessimist? Do you think we're a mistake.'

Childes propped himself up on one elbow and looked down at her. 'Oh no, Amy, I don't think that at all. It's so good between us lately that sometimes it frightens me – I get scared I'm going to lose you.'

Her arm tightened around him. 'You were the one who put up barriers that had to be broken down.'

'We both held back part of ourselves for a long time.'

'You were a married man when I first met you at the school, even though you were separated from your wife and daughter. And you were something of a mystery, but maybe that aspect attracted me initially.'

'It took me a year to ask you out,' he said.

'I asked you, don't you remember? The beach barbecue one Sunday? You said maybe you'd turn up.'

He smiled. 'Oh yeah. I was keeping pretty much to myself those days.'

'You still are.'

'Not as far as you're concerned.'

She frowned. 'I'm not so sure. There's a corner of you I've never managed to reach.'

'Amy, without sounding too self-absorbed, I often feel there's a point inside me that even *I* can't reach. There's an element in me – I don't know what the hell it is – that I can't explain, a factor that's tucked away in the shadows, something dormant, sleeping. Sometimes it feels like a monster waiting to pounce. It's a weird and uncomfortable sensation, and it makes me wonder if I'm not just a little crazy.'

'We all have areas inside that we're not certain of. That's what makes humans so unpredictable.'

'No, this is different. This is like . . . like . . .' His body, having become tensed seemed to deflate. 'I can't explain,' he said at last. 'The nearest I can get is to say it's like some eerie, hidden power – maybe that's too strong a word, too definite. It's so insubstantial, so unreal, it could be my imagination. I just sense there's something there that's never been explored. Perhaps that's common to all of us, though.'

She was watching him intently. 'In some ways, yes. But has the feeling got anything to do with these "sightings", as you call them?'

He thought for a few moments before answering. 'The awareness seems stronger then, I must admit.'

'Haven't you ever looked into it further?'

'How? Who do I go to? A doctor, a shrink?'

'A parapsychologist?'

'Oh no, no way would I jump on that particular roundabout.'

'Jon, you're obviously psychic, so why not contact someone who knows about these things?'

'If you had any idea of the crank calls and letters from so-called "psychics", not to mention those who turned up on the doorstep to torment my family three years ago, you wouldn't say that.'

'I didn't mean those kind of people. I meant a genuine parapsychologist, someone who makes a serious study of such phenomena.'

'No.'

She was surprised by the firmness in his voice.

He lay back looking at the ceiling. 'I don't want to be investigated, I don't want to probe any deeper. I want it left alone, Amy, so maybe the feelings will fade, die away.'

'Why are you so afraid?'

His tone was sombre and his eyes closed when he replied. 'Because I've got a peculiar dread – call it a sense of foreboding, if you like – that if this unknown . . . power . . . really is discovered in me, is aroused, then something terrible will happen.' His eyes opened once more, but he did not look at her. 'Something terrible and unthinkable,' he added.

Amy silently stared at him.

Later that evening, Amy cooked supper while Childes restlessly mooched around from sitting room to kitchen. The mood had changed with their earlier talk although the closeness between them remained. She was both puzzled and anxious over his remarks, but decided not to press him further. Jonathan had his problems, but Amy was confident enough in their relationship to know that when the time was right, he would unburden himself to her. In a way, she was sorry the conversation had taken place, for he had become introspective, pensive even. When they ate supper, it was she who did most of the chatting.

They made love again before she left, this time downstairs on the sofa, and with more ease, less hurriedly, both prolonging their release, savouring every moment of their shared pleasure. The bond between them had become strong and there was no element of doubt in their feelings for each other. He was tender and caring, his mood eventually reverting to its earlier relaxed state, and he loved her in a way that made her quietly weep. She told him it was joy, not sadness, that caused the tears, and he held her so tightly, so firmly, that she feared her bones might break.

When he finally drove Amy home it was in the late hours and both felt as if a warm mantle of euphoria had been drawn over them, joining, combining their spirits.

She lingeringly kissed him goodnight in the car, then left him sitting there, having to wrench herself away. He waited until she reached the front door before turning out from the drive; only when the red tail-lights disappeared did she insert the doorkey.

Before entering the house, Amy took one last look at the night, the landscape somehow magical under the flooding light of the full moon.

The old man heard the door open, but kept his eyes closed tight, pretending to be asleep. Footsteps came into the room, that curiously lumbering shuffle he had come to hate, causing him to stiffen against the restraining straps of the narrow cot. The odious smell confirmed his suspicions and he gave the game away, unable to keep his tongue still.

'Come to torment me again, have you?' he rasped. 'Can't leave me alone, can you? Can't leave me in peace.'

There was no reply.

The old man strained his neck to get a clear view. The overhead bulb, protected by a tough wire covering, burned low and was no more than a dimmed nightlight, but he could see the dark form waiting by the door.

'Ha! I knew it was you!' cried the recumbent man. 'What d'you want this time, heh? Couldn't you sleep? No, you couldn't, that's what they say about you, did you know that? Never sleeps, prowls all night. They don't like you, you know, none of them do. I don't. As a matter of fact, I detest you. But then, you've always known that!' The old man's laugh was a dry cackle.

'Why are you standing there? I don't like being stared at. That's right, close the door so no one can hear you torment me. Wouldn't want to wake the other loonies, would we? I've

informed the doctors, you can be sure of that. I've told them what you do to me when we're alone. They said they'd have words with you.' He sniggered. 'No doubt you'll be got rid of, and pretty soon, I should think.'

The figures moved away from the door, towards the cot.

'Bet you thought they wouldn't listen to me,' the old man prattled. 'But they know all the lunatics aren't locked away at night. There's them that roam the corridors when others sleep, them that pretend sweetness and kindness in the day. Them whose brains are as crazy as the maniacs they guard.'

It stood over him, blocking out the dim light. It carried a bag in one hand.

'Brought me something, have you?' said the old man, squinting his eyes in an attempt to discern features in the blackness hovering over him. 'More of your nasty little tricks. You left marks on me last time. The doctors saw them.' He chuckled triumphantly. 'They believe me now! Couldn't say I hurt myself this time!' Spittle crept from the edge of his mouth, slithering down the cracked parchment of his cheek. He felt the weight of the bag on his frail chest, heard the metal clasp snapped open. Large hands delved inside.

What's that you've got there?' the old man demanded. 'It's shiny. I like shiny things. I like them sharp. Is that sharp? Yes it is, I can see it is. I didn't really tell the doctors, you know. I only pretended just now to upset you. I wouldn't, no, I really wouldn't tell them about you. I don't mind you . . .' the words came out like short gasps 'hurting . . . me. We . . . have . . . fun . . .'

He twisted against the stout straps, his wasted muscles having no effect. Strangely, the terror in his eyes gave him an expression of clarity of, saneness.

'Tell me what that is you're holding.' His words were fast now, almost strung together, rising in a whine. His shoulders and chest heaved painfully against the binding leather. The figure bent low and he could see its features. 'Please, please don't look at me like that. I hate it when you smile at me that way. No . . . don't put that across my . . . across my . . . forehead. Don't. It's . . . it's hurting. I know if I scream no one will hear me, but I'm . . . going to scream . . . any . . . anyway. Is that blood? It's in my eyes. Please, I can't see . . . please don't do that . . . it's hurting . . . it's cutting . . . I'm . . . going . . . to . . . scream . . . now . . . it's going . . . too . . . deep . . .'

The scream was just a gurgling retch, for one of the old man's bedsocks, lying close by, had been stuffed into his open mouth.

The figure crouched over the cot, its patient sawing motion regular and smooth, while both inmates and staff of the asylum slept on undisturbed.

The nightmare came to Childes that night, but he was not sleeping. It hit him as he drove towards home.

A feeling of cloying heat gripped him at first, the atmosphere becoming heavy as if thick with unpleasant fumes. His hands tightened on the steering wheel and, although clammy with dampness, the fingertips seemed to tingle. He concentrated on the moonlit road ahead, trying to ignore the building pressure inside his head. The pressure increased, a cloudy substance expanding in his brain, and his neck muscles stiffened, his arms became laden.

The first vision flashed before him, dispersing the pressure for an instant. He could not be certain of what he had seen, the moment too soon gone, the dark heaviness quickly crowding back, causing him to swerve the car, bushes and brambles on the roadside tearing and scratching at the windows as if attempting to break in. Childes slowed down but did not stop.

He thought the vision had been of hands. Large hands. Strong.

His head now felt as if it were filled with twisting cotton wool that was steadily pushing aside his own consciousness as it grew in ill-defined shape. There was not far to go to reach home and Childes forced himself to keep a constant though reduced speed, using the centre of the narrow road, knowing there would be little other traffic that late at night. His mind saw the sharp instrument weilded by the big hands, a brilliant vision that struck like lightening and excluded all else.

He fought to keep the car straight as the manifestation just as abruptly vanished. The heaviness was less dense when it returned, although the tingling sensation in his fingers had travelled along his arms.

Not far to go now, the road leading to the cottages was just ahead. Childes eased his foot from the accelerator and began to brake. A sweat droplet from his soaked forehead trickled down to the corner of one eye and he used the back of his hand to clear his sight. The movement was slow and deliberate, almost difficult. He turned the wheel, the Mini's headlights revealing the row of small houses in the near-distance. He was aware of what was happening to him and dreaded what images were to be further unveiled. He experienced a desperate need to be safe inside his home, feeling terribly exposed, vulnerable to the luminescent night, the moon's stark glare causing the surroundings to appear frozen, the trees oddly flat as if cut from cardboard, the shadows deep and clear-edged.

Nearly there, a few more yards. Keep it steady. The car pulled up in the space before the cottage and Childes cut the engine, sagging forwards, his wrists resting over the steering wheel. He drew in deep breaths, the pressure at his temples immense. Pulling the keys from the ignition, he staggered from the Mini, moonlight bathing his head and shoulders silvery white. He fumbled with the lock, finally managed to turn the key and push open the door, falling to his knees in the hallway when the full force of the vision poured into his mind.

The old man's terror-stricken features were vivid, the horror clear in his eyes. His thin, cracked lips babbled words that Childes could not hear, and spittle dribbled from the corner of his mouth as he struggled against the straps that restrained him on the narrow bed. The tendons of his scrawny neck stretched loose skin taut as he twisted his head, and the exaggerated bump of his thyroid cartilage constantly moved up and down as if it were swallowing air. His pupils were large against their aged, creamy surrounds, and Childes saw a reflection in them, an indefinable shape that grew in size as someone moved closer to the old man.

Childes slumped back against the wall as a metal object was placed across the frightened man's forehead, and he cried out when the sawing motion began, bringing his hands up to his own eyes as if to block out the vision. Blood oozed from the wound, flowing thickly down the victim's head, washing his sparse white hair red, blinding his eyes against the horror.

Movement stopped for a moment, save for the quivering of the old man's frail body, the surgeon's small saw fixed firmly into the bone. Recognition streamed through Childes, a touching of minds; but it was the perpetrator who identified *him*.

And welcomed him.

'Overoy?'

'Detective Inspector Overoy, yes.'

'It's Jonathan Childes here.'

'Childes?' A few moments pause. 'Oh yes, Jonathan Childes. It's been a long time.'

'Three years.'

'Is it? Yes, of course. What can I do for you, Mr Childes?'

'It's . . . it's difficult. I don't quite know how to begin.'

Overoy pushed his chair back, propping a foot up against the edge of his desk. With one hand he shook a cigarette free of its pack and grasped it with his lips. He flicked a cheap lighter and lit up, giving Childes time to find the words.

'You remember the murders?' Childes said finally

Overoy exhaled a long stream of smoke. 'You mean the kids? How could I forget? You were a great help to us then.'

And I paid the price, Childes thought but did not say. 'I think it's happening to me again.'

'Sorry?'

Overoy was not making matters any easier for him. 'I said I think it's happening to me again. The sightings, the precognitions.'

'Wait a minute. Are you saying you've discovered more bodies?'

'No. This time I seem to be witnessing the crimes themselves.'

Overoy's foot left the desk and he pulled himself forward, reaching for a pen. If it had been anyone else on the end of the line, the policeman would have dismissed them as a crank, but he had come to take Childes' statements seriously, despite a hard-bitten reluctance to do so in earlier times. 'Tell me exactly what it is you've, er, "seen", Mr Childes.'

'First I want an understanding between us.'

Overoy looked at the receiver as if it were Childes himself. 'I'm listening,' he said.

I want whatever I tell you kept strictly between ourselves, no leaks to the media. Nothing like last time.'

'Look, that wasn't entirely my fault. The Press have a nose for anything unusual, always will have. I tried to keep them off you, but once they caught the scent it was impossible.'

'I want your guarantee, Overoy. I can't take the chance of being hounded again – it did enough damage last time. Besides, what I have to tell you may mean nothing at all.'

'I can only say I'll do my best.'

'Not good enough.'

'What d'you expect from me?'

'An assurance, for the moment at least, that you'll keep whatever I tell you between ourselves. Only if you find some verification will you take matters further, and then only to your superiors or whoever's directly involved in the particular cases.'

'Which cases are you talking about?'

'Just one for now. Another's possible.'

'I'd like to hear more.'

'Do I have your word?'

Overoy scribbled Childes' name on a piece of paper, underlining it twice. 'Since I don't have any idea of what you're talking about, fine, you've got my word.'

Still the other man hesitated, as if not trusting the detective. Overoy waited patiently.

'The boy whose grave was torn open, his body mutilated: have your investigations come up with anything yet?'

Overoy's eyebrows rose in surprise. 'As far as I know, not a thing. Do you have information?'

'I saw it happen.'

'You mean, like before? You dreamt it?'

'I wasn't physically there, but I didn't dream it, either.'

'Sorry, wrong word. You saw what happened in your mind.'

'The coffin was smashed open by a small axe of some kind, the body laid on the grass beside the grave.'

There was another silence at the end of the line. 'Go on,' Overoy said eventually.

'The corpse was split open with a knife and the organs torn out.'

'Mr Childes, I'm not saying I don't believe you, but those details were in most of the nationals. I know you had a difficult job convincing me before – I admit I thought you were just another nutter at first – but you managed to in the end. Even I couldn't dispute the facts when you showed us where the second body was. But, I need a little more to go on, you understand?'

Childes' tone was flat, without expression. 'One thing the newspapers didn't mention – certainly not the one I read anyway. The boy's heart was eaten.'

The pen Overoy had been restlessly twirling in his fingers came to a stop. 'Overoy? Did you hear me?'

'Yes, I heard. The heart wasn't actually eaten, but it had been torn open; the pathologist found teethmarks. There were other bits on the body also.'

'What manner of creature . . .?'

'We'd like to find out. What else can you tell me, Mr Childes?'

'About that – nothing. I saw what happened, but I can't describe the person who did it. It was as if I were seeing the mutilation through the eyes of whoever was responsible.'

Overoy cleared his throat. 'I understand you went to the Channel Islands after the last, er, business. Is that where you're calling from now?'

'Yes.'

'Could you let me have your address and phone number?'

'You mean you don't have it on file?'

'You'll save me time looking it up.'

Childes gave the information and then asked, 'So you're taking what I've told you seriously.'

'I did last time, didn't I?'

'Yeah, eventually.'

'Just one routine question, Mr Childes, and I think you'll appreciate my reason for asking. Can I take it you were still in the Channel Islands on the night the boy's grave was desecrated?'

There was a weariness to the reply. 'Yes, I was here and I'll give you the names of witnesses who'll verify.'

Overoy's pen scribbled on paper again. 'Sorry about that,' the policeman apologized, 'but it's better to get these things out of the way right at the outset.'

'I should be used to it after last time.'

'The circumstances were somewhat unusual, I think you'd admit. Now are you sure there's nothing more you can tell me about this particular incident?'

'I'm afraid not.'

The detective dropped his pen and retrieved his cigarette from the ashtray. Ash fell onto his notes. 'This happened a couple of weeks ago, so I'm surprised you didn't call earlier.'

'At the time I thought it might have been a one-off, an isolated sighting, and in any case there wasn't much I could tell you.'

'What's changed your mind since?'

Childes' voice faltered. 'I . . . I had another vision last night.'

The pen was picked up once again.

'It's all a bit confused now, like . . . like a dream remembered. I was driving home quite late when an image jumped into my mind, a sensing so strong I nearly crashed my car. I barely made it to my house and when I did manage to get inside, I collapsed. It felt like my mind had gone to another place.'

'Tell me what you saw.' Overoy was tensed, expectant.

'I was in a room – I couldn't see too much of the place, but it seemed stark somehow, bare – and I was looking down at an old man. He was afraid, terribly afraid, and trying to avoid something that was approaching him. That something – that *someone* – was me, and yet it wasn't. I was seeing everything from someone else's point of view. There was something abhorrent about this . . . this monster –'

'Monster?'

'That's how I felt. It was sick, depraved; I know because I was inside that mind for a while.'

'Any clue as to identity?'

'No, no, it was like before, three years ago. Wait – I remember large hands. Yes, it had large, brutal hands. And they carried a bag . . . there were instruments inside.'

'Cutting instruments,' said Overoy, not as a question.

'I didn't see them at all, but I *felt* that's what they were.'

'Did the old man call out anything, perhaps the other person's name?'

'I couldn't hear, everything was silent to me.'

'Was the old man trying to get away?'

'He couldn't. He was struggling, trying to escape, but he couldn't move from the bed. That was another thing that was so strange: he was lying on a narrow bed, like a bunk, and he was held there by straps of some kind, I think. He fought, but he was pinned to the bed. He couldn't get away!'

'Okay, take it easy, Mr Childes. Just tell me what happened.'

'The hands, those big hands, took a small saw from the bag, began to cut into the old man's head . . .'

Overoy could sense the anguish in the silence that followed. He waited several seconds before asking, 'Do you have any idea where this took place, any clue at all?'

'I'm sorry, but no. Not much help, is it. But you see, the reason I decided to call you was because I'm sure the person who did this to the old man is the same one who mutilated the boy's corpse.'

Overoy swore under his breath. 'How can you be so certain? You said yourself you didn't see whoever committed these acts.'

'I . . . I just know. You have to take my word. For a few moments I was inside this creature's mind, sharing its thoughts. I *know* it's the same person.'

'Did you say this happened last night?'

'Yes. It was late, after eleven, maybe around twelve, I'm not sure. I looked through this morning's newspapers and thought perhaps the story was too late to catch the early editions. There was no mention on the radio, either.'

'As far as I know, nothing like that has happened within the last twenty-four hours. I can check with Central, but cases like this tend to get circulated pretty fast.' Cigarette replaced pen once more and the detective inhaled deeply. 'Tell me,' he said through a cloud of smoke, 'are these the only two incidents you've seen recently?' Such a question would never have been asked so naturally a few years before.

'Why do you ask?'

'Well . . .' the word was drawn out as if the policeman were reluctant to divulge too much. He came to a conclusion. 'A prostitute was murdered a month or so ago and we believe there's a connection with that crime and the opening of the kid's grave.'

'The same person?'

'There are more than strong indications. The same kind of mutilations, the body torn open, insides removed, indents in the flesh that proved teethmarks, certain –'

'A month ago?'

The sharpness in Childes' question brought Overoy to a halt. 'Roughly, yes. Does that mean something to you?'

'The first sighting . . . I was swimming . . . I saw blood . . . organs . . .'

'Round about that time?' the detective interrupted.

'Yes. But nothing was clear, I didn't realize what I'd seen. You're certain it was the same person?'

'Very certain. We matched saliva left on both bodies as well as wax dental impressions: there's little doubt. As for motive, well, the insane need no such thing. The prostitute was sexually abused and we believe that took place *after* her death – no living woman, no matter how far down the road she was, would have allowed such abuse. As far as forensic could tell, no penetration took place – there were no semen traces – but objects had been forced into the vagina, so maybe the killer was frustrated by his own inadequacy. We know he had to be immensely powerful, because the prostitute had been strangled with bare hands, and she was no lightweight. Far from it, in fact: she had a record for violence herself, particularly against men.'

Overoy drew on the cigarette. 'There was one other thing that makes the connection conclusive. I want you to think, though: did you "see" anything else, anything unusual, something you could identify?'

'I told you, there was nothing.'

'Just take time to think about it.' Overoy stared down at his notepad and waited. After a while, he heard Childes' voice again.

'I'm sorry, there's nothing more. When I concentrate, it only becomes more hazy. Can you tell me what you had in mind?'

'Not right now. I'll tell you what I'm going to do, Mr Childes. First I'll check out this old-man business, see if anything's come in yet. Then I'll contact the officer in charge of the prostitute murder and the violation of the dead boy's corpse. I'll try and get back to you after that, okay?'

'And you'll keep this strictly between you and me?'

'For the moment, yes. There really isn't much for me to tell anybody, is there? And despite getting a result last time, I'm still the butt of jokes around this department for involving myself with you in the first place, so I've got precious little inclination to revive the whole matter again. Sorry to be so frank, but that's how things are.'

'That's all right, I feel the same way.'

'I'll call you if I learn anything definite, then. It may be a while.'

When Overoy replaced the receiver he stared down at his notepad for some time. Childes was sincere, he was sure of that. A bit weird, perhaps, but that was hardly surprising with the extra sense he possessed. And then again, it was really the gift that was strange, not Childes himself.

The policeman stubbed out his cigarette and examined his fingers, frowning at the nicotine stains between them. He lit another cigarette, then reached for the pumice stone which doubled as a paper weight and began rubbing it vigorously against the stained skin. Childes had been right about the dead boy, yet had needed prompting over the prostitute, and even then had been vague. So what was he, a so-called hard-bitten, cynical police detective, to make of it? Maybe nothing. Maybe something. He scanned his notes again. This grisly business of the old man – what the hell was that all about? Overoy dropped the pumice stone and circled one word with his pen.

Straps. Childes had said the old man had been strapped to a narrow bed. And the room had been sparsely furnished – how had he put it? Stark, that was it. What kind of place . . .?

Overoy stared hard at the circled word, then looked blankly at the wall opposite. He could see movement in the outer office through the frosted glass, hear typewriters, telephones ringing, voices, but none of that registered. There *was* something, a tragic incident the previous night. Could there possibly be a connection?

Uncertain, but more than curious, Overoy picked up the phone.

The policeman waited by the arrivals gate, conspicuous in his uniform of light-blue epauletted shirt and dark trousers. His height made him even more noticeable, and one or two of the passengers who had just alighted from the Shorts SD330 from Gatwick and were approaching the Customs desk eyed him nervously.

The small airport was crowded with seasonal tourists and businessmen. Outside, the sun blazed with a summer intensity, any lingering chill in the air fiercely shrugged off by now. A constant stream of vehicles prowled the non-parking zone, spilling passengers and their luggage, swallowing up arrivals. Inside, the rows of seats were full with travellers, bored, scampering children tripping over stretched legs, weary mothers pretending not to notice, groups of healthy-looking holidaymakers laughing and joking, determined to enjoy even the last few minutes of their vacations.

Inspector Robillard grinned when he spotted the familiar figure striding along the arrivals corridor. At first glance, Ken Overoy didn't appear to have changed much over the years, but as he drew closer, the thinning, sandy-coloured hair and the slight bulge of his waistline became even more apparent.

'Hello, Geoff,' said Overoy, switching his overnight bag into his left hand and extending his right. He ignored two Customs officers waiting by their desk. 'Good of you to meet me.'

'No problem,' said Robillard. 'You're looking well, Ken.'

'Yeah, who you kidding? Island life looks good on you, though.'

'Put it down to weekend sailing. It's great to see you after all this time.' The two police officers had met while Robillard was on a CID training course at New Scotland Yard and later when both were attending an Inspectors course in West Yorkshire. Robillard had kept in contact with Overoy through the years, always seeking him out whenever excursions took him to England, enjoying the stories of intrigues that inevitably went with policing the nation's capital, so different from law enforcement on the island – although Robillard had to admit they had their share of skulduggery. On this occasion, he took pleasure in being of assistance to the London detective.

He led Overoy from the air terminal to the waiting vehicle outside, a white Ford, the island's crest on its sides, a blue light mounted on the roof.

'How's crime here?' asked Overoy, as he tossed his bag onto the back seat.

'Increasing rapidly with the start of the tourist season. Wish you'd keep your tearaways over there where they belong.'

The other man laughed. 'Even villains need a break.'

Robillard switched on the ignition and turned to face his companion who was settling into the passenger seat and lighting a cigarette. 'Where to first?' he enquired.

Overoy consulted his watch. 'It's just after three, so where's he likely to be at this time of day? In school?'

The inspector nodded. 'Let's see, it's Tuesday, so he'll be at La Roche.'

'La Roche it is them – I'll catch him when he comes out.'

'You'll have a wait.'

'Doesn't matter, I've got plenty of time. Maybe I could check into a hotel first, though.'

'No way. Wendy would never forgive me if I didn't insist you stay with us overnight.'

'I don't want to put –'

'You won't. We'd be glad of your company, Ken, and you can fill us in on crime in the wicked city. Wendy'll love it.'

Already beginning to relax, Overoy smiled. 'Okay. Let's talk on the way to the school, shall we?'

Robillard soon forsook the busy main road for the quieter shaded lanes leading to the coast. The brilliant colours of the hedgerows and the sea-freshness of the air served to relax Overoy even more. He dropped the half-smoked cigarette from the moving car and took in a deep breath through the open window.

'What d'you know of Jonathan Childes?' he asked, keeping an eye on the narrow road ahead.

Robillard slowed the car, to allow an oncoming vehicle to squeeze past. 'Not too much, only what we sent you in our report. He's lived here alone for nearly three years, appears to take life fairly easily even though he's employed by more than one college. Keeps a low profile, generally. Funny enough, we asked the Met. for information on him ourselves just a few weeks back.'

Overoy regarded him with curiosity. 'Oh? Why was that?'

'A *conseiller* here who happened to be a member of our Police Committee asked us to look into Childes' background. Name of Platnauer. He also serves on the governing board for La Roche, so presumably that's why he was checking.'

'But why now? Childes has taught at the school for some time, hasn't he?'

'Couple of years or so. I have to admit to being puzzled myself by the sudden interest in the chap. What's he been up to, Ken?'

'Don't worry, he's clean. Certain incidents have occurred that he might be able to give us a lead on, that's all.'

'Now I'm really curious. The information, such as it was, was given to *Conseiller* Platnauer who passed it on the Miss Piprelly, headmistress of La Roche, and we've heard nothing since. Childes' assistance in police investigations three years ago on the mainland was documented well enough, but that was his only involvement with the law. As you were on that case, I'm surprised you weren't contacted personally.'

'There wouldn't be any need; it's all on record.'

'So come on, tell me what this is about.'

'Sorry, Geoff, can't at the moment. It could amount to nothing and I'd hate to cause Childes any further embarrassment – I caused him enough last time.' Overoy took out another cigarette. 'I blew too much to the Press and they were on him like vultures on a fresh carcase.'

'What is he, this feller? Some kind of clairvoyant?'

'Not exactly. He's psychic, that much we know. But he doesn't have premonitions, or hear spirits of the dead – that sort of thing. He mentally saw where the bodies of those kids were buried three years ago and gave us enough clues about the killer for us to find him. Unfortunately, we were too late – already topped himself by the time we reached him.'

'But how –?'

'I've no idea; I don't even pretend to understand these things. Call it telepathy, if you like. All I know is that Childes isn't a kook of any kind – in fact, he seems to be more upset by what he can do than anyone else.'

Overoy saw the girls college before his companion pointed it out to him. The main building, white and imposing, loomed up before them over the treetops as the police car rounded the bend, the sun striking its walls to dazzling effect. They drew up before the gates and the detective whistled as he looked down the long drive.

'That's some setting,' he commented. Behind the tall building and its various annexes was the sea, a sparkling cobalt blue that challenged the sky itself for dominance. The lush greenery of the clifftops and surrounding woodlands provided a pleasing variation in tones, the colours of sky, sea and land blending rather than contrasting. Close to where they were parked were tennis courts fringed by lawns and flowerbeds; even the mechanical colours in the nearby carpark failed to intrude.

'I could happily go back to learning if it were in this place,' said Overoy, waving cigarette smoke from his face.

'You'd have to change sex first,' Robillard replied.

'I'd even do that.'

The inspector chuckled. 'D'you want me to take you right up to the school itself?'

Overoy shook his head. 'I'll wait for Childes on the bench over there by the courts; no need to draw attention.'

'Up to you. His car's a black Mini.' He withdrew a slip of paper from his shirt pocket. 'Registrations 27292 – I checked before I picked you up. Let's just make sure he's there before I leave you.' He smoothly eased the police car through the iron gates and drew up near the carpark. 'There she is,' he said, pointing, 'so he's still inside the school.'

Overoy pushed open the passenger door and reached for his overnight bag lying on the back seat.

'You can leave that there, if you like,' Robillard told him. 'I'll have to pick you up later, anyway.'

'Just need something,' replied the detective, unzipping a sidepocket and delving in. He took out a plain brown envelope. 'No need to collect me, Geoff. Hopefully Childes will invite me back to his place so we can talk and I'll call a cab from there.'

'You know our address.'

'Yeah, got it.' Overoy stood outside the car, squinting against the sunshine. He leaned back through the open window for a moment. 'Oh, and Geoff,' he said. 'I'd appreciate it if you kept quiet about all this back at the station. I promised Childes I'd play it low-key.'

'What would I tell anyone?' Robillard returned, smiling. 'Catch you later.'

He reversed the Ford through the main gates and gave Overoy a wave as he drove off. The detective stretched his back, then tucked the envelope into the inside pocket of his jacket. He wandered towards a bench, bemoaning both the fact that he had neglected to bring sunglasses and that none of the older girls were playing tennis.

Cars were pulling into a road on the other side of the courts and Overoy assumed the drivers were parents arriving to collect their day-girl daughters from a separate carpark near the rear of the buildings. He glanced at his watch: Childes would be out soon.

The detective's jacket lay on the seat beside him and his shirtsleeves were rolled up to his elbows, tie loosened around his neck. It had been peaceful to sit there in the sun with time to think for a change, and in many ways he envied his friend Robillard for the congenial atmosphere he operated in. Overoy knew, however, that attractive though the conditions appeared, they would soon frustrate someone used to city life with all its corruption, seediness and villainy. Someone like him, who, at thirty-eight, revelled in the faster pace of city policing. Josie would love it, though, he thought, picturing his wife glorying in the relaxed way of life, the beaches, the barbecues, the freshness of the air – the fewer late-night calls for himself and less overtime. How bleak was it here in winter, though? There was the rub.

A distant bell sounded within the college and soon girls began drifting from the various buildings, their chatter disturbing the previous quiet. It was still some time before he noticed Childes strolling towards him accompanied by a slim blonde girl in a yellow summer dress. As they walked, the girl reached around and did something at the back of her head, releasing her hair so that it swung loose in a tail. Overoy studied her as they approached: young, lightly tanned and *very* pretty. He wondered if there was a relationship between her and Childes and the briefest touch of her fingers to the man's arm confirmed that indeed there was. Overoy stood as they drew near, swinging his jacket over one shoulder and sliding his other hand into his trouser pocket.

Childes was about the enter the carpark when he caught sight of the detective. He became still and the girl looked up at him in surprise. She followed his gaze and saw Overoy as the policeman started forward.

'Hello, Mr Childes,' he said. 'You recognize me?'

'You're hard to forget,' came the reply and Overoy understood the rancour behind it. The two men shook hands, Childes reluctantly.

'Sorry to surprise you like this,' apologized the detective, 'but I've been looking into the, uh, situation we discussed over the phone a week or so ago and thought it might be appropriate to see you in person.' He nodded at the girl, noticing her pale green eyes; close up, she was more than just *very* pretty.

'Amy, this is Detective Inspector Overoy,' Childes said. 'He's the policeman I told you about.'

Amy shook Overoy's hand and now there was suspicion in those eyes.

'Can we talk privately?' the detective asked, switching his attention to Childes.

Amy immediately said, 'I'll call you later, Jon,' and turned to walk away.

'There's no need –'

'It's all right,' she assured him. 'I've got things to do, so let's talk later. Goodbye, Inspector.' She hesitated before moving off, as if to say more, but changed her mind. She went to a red MG and glanced back at Childes with apparent concern before getting in. Childes waited until she had driven through the gates before rounding on the detective.

'Surely you could have taken care of this by phone?' he said, unable to disguise his anger.

'Not really,' Overoy replied easily. 'You'll understand after we've spoken. Could we go to your home?'

Childes shrugged. 'All right. Have you been assigned to this case?' he asked as the policeman followed him to his car.

'Not entirely. Let's just say I happen to be dealing with one particular aspect of it because I'm acquainted with you.'

'Then there is a connection.'

'Maybe.'

'But a man was murdered in the circumstances I described to you?'

'We'll talk back at your place.'

They drove from La Roche and Overoy was surprised how quickly they reached the narrow lane in which Childes' house stood; but then, he reasoned, the island was not many miles in length and width. The house, no more than a cottage, stood at the end of a row, and he appreciated even more Childes' resentment at the intrusion on his domicile. The cottages had great old-world charm, the type the wealthy on the mainland paid and arm and a leg for as a second-home country retreat.

The air was cool inside, much to Overoy's relief, and he settled into a sofa as Childes removed his own jacket and hung it in the small hallway.

'Can I get you something to drink?' Childes asked, his tone less hostile. 'Tea, coffee?'

'Uh, a beer would be great.'

'Beer it is.'

Childes disappeared into the kitchen and soon returned carrying a six-pack and two glasses. He broke off a can and passed it and a glass to Overoy, who relished its chill after the heat of the day. He poured the beer and raised his glass to Childes in a gesture of friendliness. Childes sat in a chair opposite without acknowledging the gesture.

'What do you have to tell me?' he asked, pouring his own beer, the cans placed on a low coffee table between them as if in a neutral zone.

'You may have been right about the old man,' Overoy said, and Childes leaned forward in his seat.

'You found the body?'

The detective took a long swallow of beer, then shook his head. 'When you told me he was strapped down to a bed – a narrow bed, if I remember correctly – and the room itself was bare of other furniture, it rang a bell with me. A report had come in that morning concerning the burning down of part of a psychiatric hospital.'

Childes was staring across the room at him, glass poised halfway to his lips. 'That's it,' he said quietly.

'Well, we can't be sure. Twenty-five people were killed in the fire, staff among them, and several were elderly male patients, mostly senile, others more seriously disturbed. One of them could have been your man, but nearly all the bodies had been so badly burned it was impossible to tell if any had been mutilated beforehand.'

'How did the fire –'

'It was no accident, because the experts are certain it was started in two places, somewhere on the upper floors *and* in the basement. Empty petrol cans were found in both locations. We've no idea who the arsonist was, though, but it's generally considered that one of the inmates had been wandering around loose in the night and had discovered the cans of petrol in the basement. Those in charge of the investigation suspect the arsonist might also have perished in the blaze.'

'How can they be so sure?'

'They can't. But patients and staff who survived have been questioned all this week and there's no reason to believe any are responsible. Of course, as quite a few of the patients are total lunatics, it's impossible to be a hundred per cent certain. Then again, it could just as easily have been an outsider.'

Childes rested back in his chair and drank his beer, thoughts directed inwards. Overoy waited, in no rush. The distant drone of an aeroplane could be heard passing overhead.

'What happens now?' Childes said after a time.

'Obviously, if there is a connection between all these crimes, then we'll need any scrap of information we can gather to build up a picture of the madman involved. At the moment, I should tell you, nobody's seriously considering a tie-in with the arson attack – nobody except me, that is – but there is evidence regarding the other two suggesting a link. D'you mind if I smoke?'

Childes shook his head and Overoy took cigarettes from his jacket and lit one, using the empty beer can as an ashtray.

'What kind of evidence do you have?' asked Childes.

'The similar mutilation of the prostitute and the boy's corpse, for a start. They had all the hallmarks of a ritual defilement: organs severed and removed, the heart torn out, foreign objects placed inside the open body – in the case of the woman, junk from the room she lived in; for the boy it was mostly dirt and grass, dead flowers even. The wound itself stitched up again. Acts of a lunatic, of course, but with some crazy method.'

'Then maybe it was more than one person, a sect of some kind.'

'Fingerprints of only one person were found at both scenes of crime: on the boy's coffin and on objects taken from inside the prostitute, and whoever it was didn't give a damn about leaving prints. Naturally, with the near-gutting of the mental home no evidence was left.'

'No fingerprints on the petrol cans?'

'Too badly charred themselves. Tell me about the incident with the old man: what more did you see?'

Childes looked pale. 'I'm afraid I blacked out fairly quickly. The image was so intense, the torture . . . I couldn't take too much.'

'That's understandable. But you're convinced the other person was the same as before?'

'Absolutely, but it's difficult to explain why. When you're in someone else's mind the recognition is as easy as seeing them physically, maybe even easier – there can be no disguising.'

'You mentioned you saw a large pair of hands.'

'Yes, I was looking down at them as if they belonged to the person whose mind I'd reached. They were big, rough like a workman's. Strong hands.'

'Was there jewellery of any kind? Rings, a chain, a watch?'

'No, nothing like that.'

Overoy had been appraising the other man while they were talking, noting the weariness in his face, the tension in his movements. If he had found his peace in his years on the island, it was no longer in evidence. Overoy felt pity for Childes, but he also knew he had no choice but to press him further. The detective spoke almost soothingly. 'Do you remember last time, how we finally traced the killer?'

'He left something at the scene of the last murder.'

'That's right, a note. A note saying he would murder another child, he couldn't help himself. A psychiatrist said at the time that the man wanted to be caught, to be stopped from committing those acts, that he'd written begging us to do just that. When we showed you that note you were able to describe the killer and give us a general idea of where he lived, how he was employed. All we had to do was check our records for known sex offenders in that area who matched the description.'

'I still don't understand how I knew.'

'That's because you ran away from it.'

'Plenty of people contacted me to explain what had happened and they couldn't understand why I wasn't interested. The Institute for Psychical Research wanted to publish a paper on me; one or two American universities invited me to give lectures, and God knows how many people wanted me to find missing relatives for them. I didn't know what the hell was going on inside my head and truthfully I had no desire to know. All I wanted was to be left in peace, but unfortunately it wasn't meant to be. Have you any idea what I felt like?'

'Yeah, the Elephant Man. I think you let yourself take things too seriously.'

'You may be right, but I was shaken, scared. You can't imagine what I had to witness because of this freak in me.'

'But you contacted me last week, despite all that attention before.'

Childes opened another can of beer, his glass still half-full. He filled it to the brim and drank. 'I had to,' he said at last. 'Whoever is doing this now has to be stopped. I'm praying the fire did just that.'

'Apart from waiting for another incident, there may be a way of finding out.'

Childes eyed him suspiciously. 'How?'

The detective placed his glass on the coffee table and reached for his jacket, taking the brown envelope from the inside pocket. 'I told you we have evidence of a connection between the first two and that there was something almost ritualistic in both.' He held the envelope up to Childes and said, 'Inside is an object, identical to another which is still with forensic. Both were taken from the scenes of crime, one from inside the body of the prostitute, the other from inside the boy. It took some doing, but I managed to get permission to bring one to show you.'

Childes stared at the envelope, unwilling to touch it.

'Take it,' urged the detective.

Childes' hand was unsteady as he reached forward. He let the hand drop. 'I don't think I want to do this,' he said.

Overoy rose and carried the package with him. 'This mental torment only stopped for you last time when we found the killer.'

'No, when he killed himself. I knew it had ended at that precise moment.'

'What do you feel now? Did this maniac die in the fire?'

'I . . . I don't think so.'

'Then take the envelope, hold what's inside.'

Tentatively, Childes took the brown envelope from Overoy.

He flinched as if touched by a low charge of electricity. There was hardly any weight to the object.

He opened the envelope and probed inside with thumb and forefinger. He felt something smooth, round. Something small.

Childes withdrew the clear, oval stone. And as he held it in the palm of his hand, he saw the iridescent flash of blue inside its silvery shape, a blue fire contained within the stone's own shimmering body.

Childes swayed and Overoy grabbed his shoulder, immediately letting go as if he had received a shock. The detective took a step backwards and saw movement in Childes' hair, ripples, as if static were running through.

The tingling swept through Childes, clenching his body tight, yet seeming to expand his nerve cells. He felt his body quivering and had no control. A stab of cold lightning touched his mind. He felt surprise, not just his, but from another. Something putrid seemed to crawl inside his head. Eyes watched him, but from within. His hand closed around the stone, fingernails piercing his own skin.

He sensed It . . .

. . . It sensed him . . .

'It was a moonstone,' Childes told Amy. 'A tiny moonstone that had been left inside the body of the prostitute. Overoy said their pathologist had discovered another inside the boy's corpse.'

Amy sat on the floor at Childes' feet, one arm resting over his knee, her face staring anxiously into his. He leaned back on the sofa, whisky glass in his lap. He had continued drinking after the policeman's departure two hours before, the alcohol having little effect, causing him to wonder if his brain was already too numbed by his experience earlier.

'But one wasn't found at the hospital after the fire?' asked Amy.

'There was too much damage to find anything so small.'

'Yet this man Overoy believed you when you told him the same person had done all this.'

'He learned to trust me before, difficult though it was for him.'

Chides sipped the whisky, the taste bitter in his mouth, but the fiery liquid helping to drive out some of the coldness he felt inside. 'It's the image I've been catching glimpses of all along, Amy, a shimmering whiteness, like the moon seen through thin clouds. It was even there in a nightmare I had.'

'You've no idea of its meaning.'

'None at all.'

'The moonstone caused a strong reaction in you.'

His smile held no humour. 'I scared the hell out of Overoy. And myself. This creature, whoever, whatever, it is, knows me. It was here, in this room, *inside* my head, Amy, feeding off my mind like some crawling parasite. I tried to resist, to keep my mind clear, but it was too strong. The same thing happened before, but not so overwhelmingly.'

'You didn't tell me.'

'What could I say? I thought maybe I was going crazy, and then it eased off for a while, I felt okay, not threatened. Today it came back with a vengeance.'

'I still don't understand why *you*, Jon. You don't claim to be psychic except on these few occasions, and you're not even interested in the subject – quite the reverse, in fact. You shun the subject of the paranormal as if it's taboo.'

'We've discussed what happened to me before.'

'I didn't mean that. I meant in general terms, the occult, the supernatural, the kind of things people like to talk openly about nowadays. You've always shied away whenever I've happened to mention anything to do with spiritualism or ghosts or vampires.'

'That's all kids' stuff.'

'There you are, dismissing the subject out of hand. Almost as if you're scared to talk about it.'

'That's nonsense.'

'Is it? Jon, why have you never really spoken to me about your parents?'

'What kind of question is that?'

'Answer me.'

'They're both dead, you know that.'

'Yes, but why don't you ever tell me about them?'

'I hardly remember my mother. She died when I was very young.'

'When you were seven years old, and she died of cancer. What of your father? Why don't you ever speak of him?'

Childes lips tightened. 'Amy, I've been through enough for one day without an inquisition from you. What are you getting at? You think I'm the seventh son of a seventh son, some kind of mystic? You know how ridiculous that is?'

'Of course! I'm only trying to make you open up, Jon, to delve a bit deeper into holding yourself. Ever since I've known you I've sensed you've been holding something back, not just from me, but more importantly, from yourself!' Amy was angry and it was his blind stubborness that caused the feeling. And she could tell by his eyes that she had hit a nerve, and there was truth in what she told him.

'All right, your so eager to hear, I'll tell you. My father was a rational, pragmatic man who worked for twenty-six years as a wages clerk for the same company and who was a lay preacher in his spare time –'

'You've told me that much.'

'– and who died of alcoholism.'

She stopped, taken aback, but anger still rising in her. 'There's more, I know there's more to it.'

'For God's sake, Amy, what do you want from me?'

'Just the truth.'

'My past has got nothing to do with what's happening now.'

'How do you know?'

'He hated anything to do with mysticism or the supernatural. After my mother died he wouldn't mention the dead. I couldn't even visit her grave!'

'And he was a lay preacher?' she said disbelievingly.

'*He was a drunkard.* He choked on his own vomit when I was seventeen! And d'you know something? I was relieved. I was glad to be rid of him! Now what do you think of me?'

She knelt and her arms went around his shoulders. She felt him stiffen, try to pull away, but she held him there. Gradually the tension seemed to drain from him.

'You're spilling my drink,' he said quietly. Amy squeezed him harder until he said, 'Hey.'

She eased off and sat beside him, her body at an angle so that she could see his face. 'Were you so guilt-ridden all this time that you couldn't tell me? Didn't you know it wouldn't have made any difference to us?'

'Amy, let me tell you something. I don't feel guilty at all over my father. Saddened, maybe, but not guilty. He killed himself.'

'He missed your mother.'

'Yes, he did. But he had another obligation, a son to look after. He did that to some degree, but there were other things I could forgive him for.'

'Was he cruel?'

'Not to his way of thinking.'

'He beat you.'

A shadow passed across Childes' face. 'He raised me after his own fashion. Let's drop the subject now, Amy, I don't have any more energy.' He noticed her eyes were moist and leaned forward to kiss her. He said, 'You wanted to help me, but this hasn't really got us anywhere, has it?'

'Who can tell? At least I know you a little more.'

'Some achievement!'

'It helps me understand.'

'What?'

'Some of your reserve. Why you keep certain things to yourself. I think your emotions were repressed after your mother died. You didn't have a father you could fully love and a moment ago you called him rational, a pragmatist, strange words for the only person you had to turn to.'

'That's how he was.'

'And some of it rubbed off on you.'

He raised his eyebrows.

'You never realized how totally logical you often are, how boringly-down-to-earth? No wonder you were so traumatized by your first psychic experience.'

'I've never disbelieved in the paranormal.'

'Neither have you embraced such ideas.'

'Why so hostile, Amy?'

The question shook her. 'Oh, Jon, I didn't mean to sound that way. I just want to help, to get you to explore yourself. There must be a link between you and this person, something that's drawing your mind to his.'

'Or vice versa.'

'Whichever. Perhaps it's a two-way thing.'

The notion sent a shudder through him. 'It's not . . . it's not a person, Amy. It's a creature, a malevolent, corrupted being.'

She took his hand. 'After all I've said this evening, now I want you to be logical. This killer is human, Jon, someone who is immensely strong according to your detective friend, but a *person* with a particularly warped mind.'

'No, I've seen into that mind, I've witnessed the horror there.'

'Then why can't you see who he is?'

'He . . . it's . . . too strong, its pressure too overwhelming. I feel as though my own mind has been scoured, ravaged, as if this *thing* is eating away at my psyche, stealing my thoughts. And I see these gross acts because it allows me to, it wants me to see. This creature is mocking me, Amy.'

She took the glass and placed it on the floor, clasping her hands over his. 'I want to stay with you tonight,' she said.

It was his turn to be surprised. 'Your father . . .'

Despite the seriousness of their mood, Amy could not help but laugh. 'Good God, Jon, I'm twenty-three years old! I'll ring Mother and let her know I won't be home.' She made as if to rise and he grabbed her arm.

'I'm not sure it's such a good idea.'

'You don't have to be. I'm staying.'

His tension eased slightly. 'I don't want your father on my doorstep with a loaded shotgun. I don't think I could handle that tonight.'

'I'll tell Mother to hide the cartridges.' She got to her feet and touched his face for a lingering moment before going into the hallway. Childes listened to her muffled voice, finishing the Scotch in one last gulp. He closed his eyes, resting his neck over the back of the sofa, and wondered if Amy knew how relieved he was that he would not be alone that night.

His murmuring woke her. She lay there beside him in the darkness and listened. He was asleep and the sounds he made were dreamwords.

'. . . you're not there . . . he says no . . . he says . . . you can't be . . .

he . . .'

Amy did not wake him. She tried to understand the meaning of his words repeated over and over again.

'. . . you can't *be* . . .'

It had searched the man's mind, puzzled at first but excited by the contact made between them. Who was he? What was his power? And could he be dangerous?

It smiled. It enjoyed the game.

So many images had flowed between them, at times their force and swiftness perturbing, but soon accepted and pleasured in. It had probed, searched, unleashed its own consciousness to find this frightened person, not always successfully; yet the intangible sensory link was becoming stronger. It had sensed and absorbed and had felt his panic. And even memories had been unable to hide.

The past killings, the murders of the infants, locked away in the deeper recesses of the man's mind, had been uncovered and viewed with surprise and soon with sadistic pleasure. More than observed, for visual manifestation did not apply in the literal sense, they were perceived – experienced. Revelled in. And it understood this man's association with these murders.

There were many other sensory evocations in this person to contemplate, for there was enjoyment for it here, a new torment to be exploited. He could be discovered, for his past was still present in his thoughts, much of it acutely so, and though his physical image could not be perceived, those he knew could be tenuously glimpsed. The moonstone, mysterious though it was that the gem should be in his possession, had been the catalyst to their mind's congress, the breakthrough sudden and almost overwhelming where before it had been tentative and probing. When the infant-killings had been unveiled, the connection with the stone and the police had been established and the man's gift of psychometry comprehended. Those previous murders held the key.

Records of them were easy to find, for the newspapers at the time had gloried in the atrocities and their bizarre conclusion; library microfilm provided the answers it needed.

A week had passed and now it dialled the next number on the list, all others bearing the same area code, those above already crossed through with a felt-tip pen.

It grinned when the receiver at the other end was lifted and a small voice said, 'Hello?'

The sun reclaimed them like returning prodigals as they stepped from the air-conditioned coolness of the Rothschild building, the warmth wrapping itself around their bodies in welcoming embrace. The girls, twelve of them, dressed in La Roche's summer blue, chattered incessantly, enjoying every free moment from the college. They gathered on the pavement outside the modern office block while Childes counted heads, making sure no pupil in his charge had gone astray. He felt the visit to the financial company's large computer room had been well worthwhile, even if most of his pupils had been baffled by the operator's highly technical explanation of the machines and their facilities (Childes had smiled to himself as the inevitable glazed looks had come into the girls' eyes). Nevertheless, they now had a glimmering of how computers helped such international corporates to function.

All present and correct, no heads lost, no bodies missing. It had been a good morning. Childes consulted his wristwatch: 11.47.

From where they stood, the wide thoroughfare swept down and around the harbour, the congregated yacht masts stirring lazily as if gently beckoning.

'We've a while before we have to get back for lunch,' he told the girls, 'so why don't we take a break down by the harbour?'

They squealed delight and quickly fell into an orderly double-line. Childes led them away after suggesting they keep the gabble down to a minimum. For the first time that week he felt some kind of mental equilibrium returning, the bright sunshine, the girls' chatter, the normality of their surroundings having their effect. Not only had the experience with the moonstone left him with a peculiar sense of futility, but his conversation with Amy afterwards had dredged up memories that were better left dormant. During the days that followed, the darker strictures of his upbringing had returned to haunt him, although he realized he no longer hated his father; he had long since learned to repress such emotions along with certain others. And oddly, it was his father who had forced such self-subjugation upon him. That was how he was coping now, with resilience born of his own intrinsic suppression; both the recent macabre events and his own disquieting retrospection could be resisted when sunshine and normality lent their support. Only the dark night hours were allies to dread.

Childes spotted an empty bench overlooking one of the marinas and six of the girls quickly laid claim when he pointed it out to them, squeezing themselves into the limited space with much giggling and groaning. The others leaned against the rail opposite.

The harbour was bustling with tourists and residents alike, cars and white buses making slow progress around its perimeter, the wharves themselves tight with parked vehicles. The two marinas, enclosed by granite arms, were filled with yachts and motorboats of all sizes and descriptions, the island's fishing boats having separate berthing in a quieter section further along the port. A lighthouse rose up at the end of one curved pier while a fort stood watch on its twin, ancient guide and guard. Shops and bistros faced the sea, bright façades, old and new, edging the concrete haven with postcard colours. Here and there steps cut through the terraces in steeply-rising alleyways, the gloomy passages invitingly cool and mysterious, their destination the narrow upper reaches of the town itself.

'Two of you are about to do your day's good deed for the elderly,' Childes told the seated girls as he belatedly approached. They looked up curiously and he jerked a thumb. 'Let teacher have a seat.'

'Does Isobel count as two, sir?' Kelly asked with a cheeky grin, pointing to her plump schoolmate on the other end of the bench, instigating more laughter and one loud protest.

'I think I'll take your place, Kelly,' he said, 'while you perform yet another good deed.'

She rose, no malice in her smirk, but her eyes, as ever, challenging. 'Whatever you say, sir.'

He reached for his wallet. 'You girls have a choice: vanilla or strawberry. No Tutti-Fruities, no Super-Dupe Chocolate with Almonds, no Three-layer Mango, Tangerine and Passion Fruit Delights – nothing to complicate life, okay? And two more volunteers to go get 'em with Kelly.'

Eyes gleaming and with indecent haste, Isobel rose while the others were still exclaiming their pleasure. 'I'll help, sir,' she offered brightly.

'Oh no,' someone moaned. 'There'll be none left by the time she gets back.' More laughter from the others and a miffed stare from the plump girl.

'All right,' said Childes, sitting in the place vacated by Kelly and removing two notes from his wallet. 'How about you going with them, Jeanette?' He smiled at the small girl leaning against the railings, who immediately stiffened to attention. 'I think I can trust you with the loot.' She reached for the money almost timidly, avoiding his eyes. 'You take the orders, Einstein,' he said to Kelly, 'and make mine vanilla. And the three of you watch that road – Miss Piprelly would never forgive me if I returned without the full company.'

They set off, Kelly and Isobel sharing some secret joke, Jeanette lagging behind. Childes kept an eye on them until they were safely across the busy road, then turned his attention back to the harbour to watch the mainland ferry ponderously approaching the docking quay near the end of the north pier. Further out, white sails specked the sea's calm surface like tiny upturned paper cones, while overhead a yellow Trislander, a twelve-seater aircraft used almost as a regular bus service between islands, began its descent, the muted engine sound as much a part of the island's ambience as the summer bee's droning. He reassured himself that the hubbub around him, the constant hum of traffic and passing conversations, was merely a seasonal interruption of the rest of the year's peacefulness, and even so, just gazing out at the sea, with its soft-rippling textures and gracefully swooping gulls, induced a calming effect.

Relaxed himself, he was also pleased that the girls appeared at ease in his presence, obviously enjoying their outing as much as he had enjoyed escorting them. He began asking questions concerning the Rothschild's computer room to discover just how much they had absorbed, but their conversation soon developed beyond mere educational studies; he found the girl's remarks interesting and sometimes amusing, and was reminded that such excursions often led to a more knowing tutor/pupil relationship. Childes planned a similar field-trip with a class from Kingsley but did not anticipate such a pleasurable morning, for it would require a more disciplinarian approach to keep the boys' natural raucousness in order.

Kelly, Isobel and Jeanette returned laden with ice-cream cones to the cheered approval of their classmates who quickly relieved them of their burdens. Childes smiled at Jeanette when she dug a hand into her dress pocket and drew out his change.

'Thank you,' he said.

'Thank *you*, Mr Childes,' she responded, smiling back, some of her timidity having evaporated.

'Did much of what you saw this morning make sense?' he asked her.

'Oh yes, I think so.' She paused. 'Well . . . a lot of it did.'

'It's not half so scary once you begin to understand, you know. You'll find it all begin to click when you've got the basics under control. You'll see,' he added reassuringly, then looked around at the others. 'Hey, who's got mine?'

'Whoops, sorry,' said Kelly, giggling. 'I wasn't going to eat it, I promise.'

The ice-cream cone was already beginning to melt, white streams oozing down the cone and over her fingers. Kelly's own, which was clutched in her other hand and already half-consumed, was dwarfed by the one she held out to Childes.

He took the ice-cream from her and her hand immediately rose to her lips to lick the white stickiness from them.

As she did so, the smell of burning came to him. A peculiar smell. Like meat being cooked. Only worse, far worse. Like flesh being incinerated.

He stared at Kelly, and the hand she held to her mouth was blackened, merely gristled tattered skin clinging to white bone. Her hand was a malformed, charred claw.

He heard laughter around him and the sound came from a long way off, even though it was the laughter of his pupils. He felt the cold stickiness on his thigh, glanced down in reaction, saw the white blob of melted ice-cream sluggishly sliding over his leg.

When he looked back, Kelly was laughing with the others while she licked clean the hand that was now unblemished.

The road was wide and quiet, traffic sparse.

All the houses were detached, with their own garages and small well-kept front gardens. The rear gardens were no doubt ample, for it was that type of neighbourhood, affluent without being wealthy. The car moved along slowly, the driver searching for a particular number, a particular house.

The vehicle drew to a smooth halt and its occupant watched that particular house.

It knew he would not be there: the little girl with the funny squeaky voice of the very young had said on the telephone that Daddy didn't live there any more, that he had moved away to an island. Of course she could remember the island's name, the squeaky voice had insisted, she was seven-and-a-half years old, wasn't she?

It waited in the car, observing and unobserved, for it was early Saturday morning, a time for the dwellings' occupants to relax from the usual weekly haste. Now that the house had been located, the driver would come back when night fell and darkness could assist.

The observer became more alert, though, when a small girl ran from behind the house chasing a black cat. A tingling thrill ran through its gross body.

The cat leapt onto the low wall bordering the garden and froze on seeing the shadowy form huddled inside the parked car. The animal's fur bristled, its tail stiffened, its yellow eyes glared. Then the cat was gone, intimidated into flight.

A little girl's face appeared in its place, peering curiously over the wall.

The figure inside the car watched for a moment longer. Then opened the car door.

Fran stretched her limbs, her mouth agape in a huge yawn. She settled back into the bed, enjoying the langour of sleep's after-moments, her appreciation voiced in a blissful moan. She turned onto her side, auburn hair spilling over her face to flood the pillow.

A weekend to herself for a change, no commitments, no client pandering-to, no meetings, no phone calls. No cajoling journalists or radio and TV producers for interviews with clients who were just as likely to veto such hard-earned concessions on a personal whim. No fending off grubby-minded business associates (or even clients – no, *especially* clients) who considered any healthy-looking divorcée fair game. A chance to spend time with little neglected Gabby, the greatest kid in the world. Oh God, give me the energy to go down and cook her a decent breakfast for a change. Allow me ten minutes in bed first, though.

Gabby had already crept in earlier to kiss her good morning and to sneak a warm, snuggly cuddle beneath the bedsheets. After promising a nice cup of tea to revive her weary Mummy, Gabby had left the bedroom, her high-pitched trilling broken only by calls for Miss Puddles.

Fran was relieved that Douglas hadn't stayed the night – not that there had been much chance anyway, with the way he protected his own marriage. Douglas Ashby was a sound business partner and a splendid, inventive lover; unfortunately for Fran, he was also a considerate husband (apart from one infidelity – herself) and never stayed away from home longer than was necessary. Well, maybe that was okay: one serious man in her life had already proved too much. She knew Gabby desperately missed Jonathan, and there had been times over the past couple of years when Fran had regretted her own uncompromising attitude towards him, but enough had been enough. They had both been forced to face up to the truth of the situation: they were not good for one another.

But oh, it would be nice to have a male body next to her right now. Funny how a glorious love-making session the night before always left her wanting more the following morning. Her muffled moan this time contained a hint of frustration. Tea, Gabby, tea. Save your mother from self-abuse.

Fran pushed herself upright, fluffing up the pillows behind her and leaning back against them. She appraised her image in the dressing-table mirror on the opposite side of the room. Still good, she told herself. Breasts firm and not too many spare inches on her body to pinch. Hair long and lush, its sheen not yet from a bottle. Mercifully her reflection was too far away to discern perfidious lines around eyes and neck. She lifted the sheet to examine her stomach. H'mn, could do with some tummy exercises before 'loose' became 'flab'. No problem with thighs, though: slim and as nicely-shaped as ever. Pity such a well-toned body was so under-used. Fran allowed the sheet to drop.

Her neck arched back and she studied the stippled ceiling. Must do something with Gabby today, she thought. A trip to the shops to stock up, then lunch out somewhere. She'd like that. Perhaps a movie tonight, invite Annabel along – Gabby would like that, too. Got to spend more time with Gabby, to hell with her job. Her daughter was quickly growing mature beyond her age, becoming a little too responsible for one so young. The innocent years were too precious to be brushed aside so easily. And it was surprising, considering how rare and brief were the times she spent with her father, how like Jonathan she was becoming. Not only were they both short-sighted, but their resemblance went beyond mere physical characteristics.

Fran heard a car outside pull away, the noise of its engine fading in the distance.

She closed her eyes, but it was useless: tired though she was, sleep had absconded, her head, as usual, buzzing with thoughts, most of them trivial. Why, oh why, when she had time to relax, would her brain never let her do so? And where was Gabby with that blessed tea?

Throwing back the sheet, Fran rose from the bed and snatched her flimsy nightgown from the back of a chair; slipping it on, she made for the door. Leaning over the rail at the top of the stairs she called down.

'Gabby, I'm dying of thirst up here. How's the tea coming along?'

There was no reply.

She stirred and Childes remained still, not wishing to wake her.

One breast lay exposed, delicate curves a temptation to touch. He resisted.

But her lips, slightly parted in sleep, were too compelling not to taste.

He kissed them and Amy's eyelids fluttered open.

She smiled.

He kissed her again and this time she responded, one arm sliding around his shoulders to hold him tight. Although their lips eventually parted, their bodies clung together, each enjoying the other's warmth, the comfort of filling closeness. Her legs parted as his thigh gently pushed between them and the soft pressure caused her to sigh. She ran her fingertips slowly down the ridges of his spine.

They shifted position so that they lay side by side, each wanting to see the other's face, he fondling her nipples which stood so proud from their small, fleshy mounds, she reaching down to caress him with firm but tender motion. Their lovemaking was slow and easy, neither wishing to rush, all frenzy spent the night before: now was a time for leisure, a relaxed joining, a steady exhilaration.

He moistened her with his own tongue and she fought to control her rising excitement, the exquisitely sensuous stabbing movement dangerously irresistible; sensing the ebbing of her resolve he quickly entered her, the penetration so glidingly smooth that she was full with him before realizing he had changed position. Her thighs rose around him and she pulled at his lower back.

It did not take long for the tension to break, an intoxicating warmth shuddering through them in waves, only gradually depleting in strength to leave them panting breathlessly. They stayed locked together until their senses became placid once more.

Eventually they parted, both taking pleasure even in that movement, to lie side by side, waiting for their breathing to steady.

'Did you sleep last night?' Amy asked him.

'I didn't expect to, but, yes, soundly,' he replied.

'No dreams?'

'None that I can remember.'

She touched his face and he could smell their bodies on her fingertips. 'You looked so terrible yesterday,' she said.

'I was scared, Amy. I'm scared now. Why did I see Kelly's hand mutilated like that? Thank God the girls were laughing so much they didn't notice how frightened I was.' He gripped her arm. 'What if it was some kind of premonition?'

'You've told me before you're not precognitive.'

'Something's changing inside me, I can feel it happening.'

'No, Jon, you're confused and upset by this business with the moonstone. Someone's playing tricks with your mind, deliberately tormenting you – you've said as much yourself.'

'Putting these thoughts into my head?'

'Perhaps.'

'No, no, that's nonsense. Things like that don't really happen.'

'Christ!' she exploded. 'How can you say that? Why do you keep avoiding the reality of the situation?'

'You call this real?'

'It's happening, isn't it? You've got to come to terms with yourself, Jon, stop resisting something that's unnatural to others but natural to you. Accept whatever extra sense you have so that you can learn to control it! You've already admitted that some outside influence is encroaching on your thoughts, so try to understand your own power in order to defend yourself.'

'It's not that simple . . .'

'I never said it would be. But surely nobody else can determine what you choose to think or see?'

'I know you're right and I wish I could get a grip on myself, but it seems whenever I'm over one shock nowadays, another comes along to knock me rigid again. It's getting tedious. I need to think, Amy. Something you said recently had bothered me since and I need to brood on it a little while longer. There's a door waiting to be unlocked – all I need is the key.'

'Can't we work on it together?'

'Not just yet. I'm sure there's something which only I can resolve, so be patient for a bit longer.'

'If you promise not to hide any answers from either me or yourself.'

'That's an easy promise to keep.'

'We'll see.'

'You hungry?'

'You change the subject so well.'

'Is there any more to say?'

'Lots.'

'Later. What can I get you for breakfast?'

'If you don't have a horse, coffee and toast will be fine.'

'If you're that hungry I can do better than coffee and toast.'

'I'll leave it to you, but wouldn't you rather I cooked?'

'You're my guest.'

'Then I hope I haven't outstayed my welcome these last couple of days.'

'No fear of that. How's Daddy taking it?'

'Stone-faced. I need a bath, Jon.'

'Okay. You bath while I cook.'

'Prude.'

'After the last few nights?'

'Maybe not. Your tub's too small anyway.'

He left the bed and grabbed his bathrobe. 'Give me a couple of minutes,' he called over his shoulder as he descended the stairs.

Amy closed her eyes and soon a frown lined the softness of her features.

Downstairs, Childes quickly electric-shaved and washed, first turning on the bathtaps for Amy. He opened the bathroom cabinet and removed his contact lens case, inserting the soft lenses into his eyes before the mirror steamed up. He ran back up the stairs two at a time and donned faded jeans, tan sneakers and a grey sweater while Amy watched from the bed.

'You need fattening up,' she remarked.

'For which slaughter?' he answered and neither found any humour in the response.

'Your bath's about ready,' he said, running fingers through his dark tousled hair.

'I feel like a kept woman.'

'So do I once in a while, but they're hard to come by.'

'You're cheerful again.'

'It's a habit.' He realized there was a certain truth in his reply: suppression of the unfaceable, he reminded himself.

'A kiss will get me out of bed,' Amy said.

'Yeah? What will get you downstairs?'

'Come and find out.'

'The water will run over.'

'You're no fun at all sometimes.'

'And you're no schoolmarm.' He threw her a robe. 'Food in ten minutes.' Childes couldn't help moving to the bed, though, and kissing her lips, neck and breasts, before going down to the kitchen.

Later, when Amy sat opposite him at the tiny kitchen table, her wringing wet hair and his blue bathrobe transforming her from schoolteacher to schoolgirl once again, they discussed their plans for the day.

'I'll have to go home and collect some things,' she told him, tucking into bacon, eggs and grilled tomatoes with undisguised enthusiasm.

'Want me to come with you?' He grinned at her appetite, no longer surprised that her trim figure was never affected by the amount of food she consumed. He bit into his toast, all that was on the plate before him.

Amy shook her head. 'Might be better if I went alone.'

'We'll have to have some kind of showdown sooner or later,' he said, referring to Paul Sebire.

'Later's better than sooner. You've got enough to contend with for now.'

'I'm getting used to having you around.'

She stopped eating for a moment. 'Feels sort of . . . okay, doesn't it?'

'Sort of.'

She screwed up her face and continued eating. 'I mean, it feels right, doesn't it? Comfortable. But exciting, too.'

'I think so.'

'You only think so,' she said flatly while chewing.

'Sure so. I could even grow to like it eventually.'

'Should I move in permanently?'

He was taken aback, but she did not appear to notice.

'We could give it a try,' she went on, not even looking at him, 'see how it goes.'

'If you won't think of your father, consider how Miss Piprelly would take to the idea of two of her teachers living in sin together.'

'At least we're male and female – that must be in our favour. Anyhow, Pip need never know.'

'When if someone sneezes at one end of an island this size people at the other end catch a cold? You've got to be kidding. She probably knows what's going on between us right now.'

'No problem then.'

He sighed good-humouredly. 'There is a difference, you know.'

Amy laid down her knife and fork. 'Are you trying to talk your way out of this?'

He laughed. 'Sounds like a great proposition to me. But –'

He stopped. He looked at her, but did not see. His eyes were wide.

'Jon . . .?' She reached across the cluttered table and touched his hand.

The coffee percolator bubbled in the corner of the kitchen. A fly buzzed against a window frame. Dust motes floated in the rays from the sun. Yet everything seemed still.

'What is it?' Amy asked nervously.

Childes blinked. He began to rise. Stopped halfway. 'Oh no . . .' he moaned, '. . . not that . . .'

His knuckles were white against the table-top and his shoulders suddenly hunched, his head bowing.

Amy shivered when he raised his head once more and she saw the shocked anguish.

Jon!' she shouted as he lurched for the door, knocking his empty coffee mug from the table, the handle breaking off as it hit the floor.

Amy pushed back her chair and followed him into the hallway. He was standing by the phone, one trembling finger attempting to dial a number. It was no use, he was shaking too much. He looked at her beseechingly.

She reached him and grasped him by the shoulder. 'Tell me what you've seen,' she implored.

'Help me, Amy. Please help me.'

She was stunned to see his eyes glistening with tears. 'Who, Jon, who do you want to ring?'

'Fran. Quickly! Something's happened to Gabby!'

Her heart juddered as if from a blow, but she took the receiver from him, forcing herself to keep her own nerves under control. She asked him to tell her the number and at first, ridiculously, perversely, he could not remember. Then the figures came in a rush and he had to repeat them slowly for her.

'It's ringing,' she said, handing back the receiver and moving closer to him. She could feel the quivering of his body.

The phone at the other end was lifted and she heard the distant voice.

'Fran . . .?'

'Is that you, Jonathan? Oh God, I'm glad you rang!' There was a terrible distressed brittleness in her voice and Childes sagged, the dread almost overpowering.

'Is Gabby . . .?' he began to say.

'Something terrible's happened, Jon, something awful.'

'Fran . . .' His tears were blinding him now.

'It's Gabby's friend, Annabel. She's missing, Jon. She came over earlier to play with Gabby, but she never came in. The police are next door with Melanie and Tony right now, and Melanie's almost hysterical with worry. Nobody's seen Annabel since, she's just vanished into thin air. Gabby's distraught and won't stop crying. Jonathan, can you hear me . . .?'

Only Amy's support kept Childes from collapsing to the floor.

Amy drove Childes to the airport, casting frequent anxious looks at his pallid face. He said nothing at all during the short journey.

His relief was mixed with sorrow for the missing girl, for he knew Annabel's fate. *It* had made a mistake, he was sure of that; his daughter was meant to have been the victim. *It* would know by now.

Amy parked the MG while Childes checked in at the flight desk. She joined him in the lounge bar where they waited, neither one saying much, until his flight was called. She walked with him to the departure gate, an arm around his waist, his around her shoulders.

Amy kissed Childes tenderly before he went through, holding him tight for a few seconds. 'Ring me if you get a chance, Jon,' she told him.

He nodded, his face gaunt. Then he was gone, disappearing through the departure gate with the other passengers for Gatwick, his overnight bag slung over one shoulder.

Amy left the terminal and sat in her car until she saw the aircraft rise into the clear sky. She was weeping.

Childes rang the doorbell and saw movement behind the panes of reeded glass almost immediately. The door opened and Fran stood there, a mixture of gladness and misery on her face.

'Jonathan,' she said, stepping forward as if to embrace him; she hesitated on seeing the figure standing behind Childes and the moment was gone.

'Hello, Fran,' Childes said, and half-turned towards his companion. 'You probably remember Detective Inspector Overoy.'

Confusion, then hostility, altered her features as she looked over his shoulder. 'Yes, how could I forget?' She frowned at her ex-husband, questioning him with her eyes.

'I'll explain inside,' Childes told her.

She stood aside to let them through and Overoy bade her good evening as he passed, eliciting little response.

'Let's go into the sitting room,' Fran said, but they heard the scampering of footsteps on the landing above before they could do as she suggested.

'*Daddy, Daddy!*' came Gabby's excited cry and then she was hurtling down the stairs, leaping the last three into Childes' outstretched arms as he went to meet her. She hugged him close, dampening his cheeks with her kisses and tears, her glasses pushed sideways on her face. He closed his eyes and held her tight.

She was sobbing as she blurted out, 'Daddy, they've taken Annabel away.'

'I know, Gabby, I know.'

'But why, Daddy? Did a nasty man take her?'

'We don't know. The policeman will find out.'

'Why won't he let her go? Her mummy misses her, and so do I – she's my best friend.' Her face was blotchy from crying, her eyes puffed up behind the lenses of her spectacles.

He eased his daughter down and sat next to her on the stairs, taking a handkerchief from his pocket to mop away the wetness on her cheeks. He removed her glasses and polished them, talking softly to her as he did so. Her fingers clutched his wrist all the while.

Overoy interrupted. 'I think I'll call next door and have a word with Mr and Mrs, er . . .'

'Berridge,' Fran finished for him.

'You go ahead,' said Childes, putting an arm around Gabby's hunched shoulders. 'We'll talk when you're through.'

With a brief nod towards Fran, Overoy left, closing the front door behind him. She immediately locked it.

'What the hell is he doing here?' she demanded to know.

'I rang him before I left,' Childes explained. 'He picked me up at Gatwick and drove me over.'

'Yes, but what's he got to do with this?'

Childes stroked his daughter's hair and Gabby looked from him to her mother, revealing a new anxiety. He didn't want an argument in front of her.

'Gabby, look, you run upstairs and I'll be up to see you soon. Mummy and I have to talk.'

'You won't shout at each other, will you?'

She still remembered.

'No, of course not. We just have to discuss something privately.'

"Bout Annabel?'

'Yes.'

'But she's my friend. I want to talk about her too.'

'When I come up to you can talk all you want.'

She rose, standing on the first step. Her arms went around his neck. 'Promise me you won't be long.'

'I promise.'

'I miss you, Daddy.'

'You too, Pickle.'

She climbed the stairs, turning and waving from the top before running along the landing to her room.

'Gabriel,' Fran called after her. 'I think it's time you got yourself ready for bed. Pink nightie's in your top drawer.'

They heard a sound that could have been a protest, but nothing more.

'It's been a bad day for her,' Fran remarked as Childes stood once more.

'Looks as though it's been tough on you as well,' he said.

'Imagine the hell Tony and Melanie have been through.' She kept her distance for just one moment longer, watching him uncertainly; and then she was in his arms, her head resting on his shoulder, hair soft against his cheek. 'Oh, Jon, it's so bloody awful.'

He soothed her as with his daughter, by stroking her hair.

'It could so easily have been Gabby,' she said.

He did not reply.

'It's funny,' she said, 'but I felt something was wrong this morning. Gabby was downstairs making tea and I got up to see why she was taking so long.' Fran gave a small, tired laugh. 'Would you believe she'd spilt the sugar and was patiently sweeping up every last grain so I wouldn't find out? Annabel must have come through the garden to play with her around that time. Perhaps she went out onto the main road – nobody knows, nobody saw her. Except the person who took her. Oh God, Gabby and Annabel have been warned so many times about going outside the gate!'

'We could both do with a drink,' he suggested.

'I was afraid to start – didn't know if I'd be able to stop. I'd be no help to Melanie if I'd got plastered. I suppose it's okay now that you're here, though. You were always good at controlling my drinking.'

They went through to the sitting room, holding each other as though still lovers. Everything was so comfortably familiar to Childes despite the odd pieces of furniture collected after he had gone, five years of living in the house were difficult to forget; yet it was all so remote, no longer a part of him, of his life. It was an odd sensation, and not pleasant.

'You sit down,' he said. 'I'll fix the drinks. Gin and tonic still?'

Fran nodded. 'Still. Make mine a large one.' She slumped on to a sofa, kicking off her shoes and curling her legs beneath her, watching him all the time. 'Jonathan, when you phoned this morning I didn't give you the chance to say much, but I realized afterwards you were already distraught before I spoke. I don't know, there was something anxious just in the way you said my name.'

'D'you want ice?'

'Doesn't matter, just give me the drink. *Were* you upset when you rang?'

He poured a good measure of gin and reached for a tonic inside the glass cabinet. 'I thought something had happened to Gabby,' he replied.

'To Gabby? Why, what . . .?' Her voice trailed off, and then she closed her eyes. 'Oh no, not again,' she murmured softly.

He brought her gin and tonic over and her gaze never left his as he handed her the glass. 'Tell me,' she said, almost as a plea.

Childes poured himself a Scotch, then returned to the sofa, sitting close to her. 'The sightings are happening again.'

'Jon . . .'

'This morning I had an overpowering feeling that Gabby was in danger.' Could he tell her yet that he had *known* their daughter was in danger, that Annabel had been taken by mistake? Throughout the day he had been taunted by this other, perverted mind, received glimpses of the prolonged atrocity, the creature, whoever and whatever it was, tormenting him, searching out his mind to inflict painful visions. And oddly, after a while Childes had learned to inure himself to the sightings, for he had become aware that the worst had already happened, that Annabel could no longer feel the torture. She hadn't from almost the beginning. He had to tell Fran that much at least.

'But it wasn't Gabby, it was her friend, Annabel,' his ex-wife had already said.

'Yes, somehow I got things wrong in my mind.' It was the coward's way, but she would have to face another shock before the whole truth could be told. Take it slowly, he said to himself, one bit at a time. 'Fran, there's something you've got to know.'

She took a large swallow of gin as if steeling herself, aware that his 'intuitions' were always bad, never good. She said it for him, unable to stop herself. 'Annabel's dead, isn't she?'

He bowed his head, avoiding her eyes.

Fran's face crumpled, the drink spilling over onto her trembling hand. Childes took the glass from her, leaning over to place it on the occasional table beside the sofa. He slid an arm around her shoulders and pulled her against his chest.

'It's so vile, so wicked,' she moaned. 'Oh dear God, what will we tell Tony and Melanie? *How* can we tell them?'

'No, Fran, we can't say anything yet. That'll be up to the police when . . . when they find the body.'

'But how can I face Melanie, how can I help her when I know? Are you sure, Jon, are you absolutely certain?'

'It's like before.'

'You were never wrong.'

'No.'

He felt her body stiffen. 'Why did you think Gabby had been taken?' She pulled away so that she could look into his face. Fran had never been a fool.

'I'm not sure. I suppose I was confused because it happened so close to home.'

She frowned disbelievingly and was about to say more when they heard the doorbell.

'That's Overoy,' Childes said, relieved. 'I'll let him in.'

The detective's expression was sombre when he followed Childes into the sitting room. 'They're taking it badly,' he said.

'What would you expect?' Fran countered with a sharpness that surprised both men.

'Sorry, that was pretty trite,' Overoy apologized. He nodded as Childes showed him the whisky bottle from across the room. 'Can I ask you the same question I asked Annabel's parents, Mrs Childes? Er, it is still *Childes*, isn't it?'

'Childes sounds better on a letter-heading than my maiden name so I never bothered to revert. It's less confusing for Gabriel, too. As for your first question, it's one I've been asked several times today by your colleagues and the answer remains the same: I've noticed no one who could be described as suspicious within the last week or so, or even the last few months. Now let me ask you two a question.'

Overoy took the whisky glass from Childes and their eyes met for a brief moment.

'Take a seat, Inspector, you look uncomfortable standing there.' Fran reached for her gin and tonic, noting her hand was still shaky as she picked up the glass. But she was curious too, a new suspicion forming in her mind. Childes came over and sat next to her.

'It seems peculiar to me that Jonathan should immediately contact you just because he's had another of his famous sightings, and that you should take the trouble of picking him up at the airport and bringing him here. I mean, why you when he hasn't seen you for – what, nearly three years?'

'I'm familiar with his background, Mrs Childes, his special ability.'

'Yes, I know you've come to believe in it. But to drop everything just to meet him? I wonder if you were even on duty today? It is a Saturday, after all.'

Childes answered this time. 'As a matter of fact I contacted Inspector Overoy at home.'

'Ah, you had his private number.'

'We didn't intend to keep anything from you, Fran. It's just that we thought – *I* thought – that you might be upset enough over Annabel's disappearance without giving you more to worry about.'

A fresh fear was in her eyes. She used both hands to raise the gin to her lips, sipped, then slowly lowered the glass so that it rested in her lap. Her back was rigid and her voice unsteady when she said: 'I think it's time you told me everything.'

The hour was late.

Childes and his ex-wife sat alone at a table in the kitchen, the remains of an unenthusiastically cooked meal before them, the food itself eaten with even less enthusiasm. All was quiet in Gabby's bedroom.

'I should see how Melanie is.' Fran bit into her lower lip, an anxiety habit that he had often chided her over during their marriage.

'It's well after ten, Fran – I shouldn't disturb her now. Besides, Melanie's doctor may have sedated her, so she could be sleeping.'

Fran's shoulders slumped. 'What would I say to her anyway, knowing what you've told me? Can you really be so positive?'

He knew what she referred to. 'I wish I could have some doubt.'

'No, as I said before, you were never wrong about . . . about those things.' There was no jibe in her remarks, only an immense sadness. 'But there is something different going on this time, isn't there? This isn't like those other incidents years ago.'

He sipped lukewarm coffee before answering. 'I've got no explanation. Somehow this monster knows me, can penetrate my mind: how and why is a mystery.'

'Perhaps he's accidentally stumbled upon your access code.'

He regarded her with surprise. 'I don't follow.'

Fran pushed her plate to one side and leaned her elbows on the table. 'Look at it this way, using your beloved computers as an analogy. When you want to gain access to another system, you need that system's special code to open the door, don't you? Once you have that code, you can get inside the other machine's memory bank. In fact, you have dialogue between both computers, right? Well, maybe this other mind got hold of your access code by accident or other means. Or perhaps subconsciously, you have his.'

'I didn't realize you were interested in such things.'

'I'm not as a rule, but what happened to us last time left me a little curious. I did some research – not much, just enough to try and understand. A lot still doesn't make much sense to me, but at least I know something of the various theories on psychic phenomena. Admittedly most appear to be ridiculous, though there is a certain pleasing logic to some. I'm only surprised you never investigated further yourself.'

He became uncomfortable. 'I wanted to forget everything that happened, not pursue it.'

'Strange.'

'What is?'

'Oh, it doesn't matter.' She smiled distantly. 'I remember you never liked ghost stories. I always put it down to your microchip disposition; you've no room in that technological brain of yours for such romanticisms. How ironic that someone like you should have received psychic messages; it might even have been funny if they hadn't been so horrendous.'

'I've changed at least in some ways.'

'I'd be interested to hear.'

'Computers have taken a back seat. They're just a job, and only part time at that.'

'Then you really have changed. Any other miracles?'

'Different lifestyle, more easy-going I guess you could say, more time spent relaxing, enjoying the things around me.'

'You weren't some kind of work ogre when you were here, Jon, although you did put in too many hours. You made time for me and Gabby when you could.'

'I realize now it was never enough.'

'I was at fault too, I had my own unfair demands. But it's old territory now, there's no point in re-exploring.'

'No, as you say: old territory.' He placed the coffee mug back on the table. 'Fran, I'm worried about you both staying here on your own.'

'Then you really do think this monster meant to snatch Gabby?'

'It wanted to get at me through her.'

'How do you know it's the same person?' Her voice rose in anger. 'And why do you refer to him as *it*? My God, he's a ghoul, but of a human kind.'

'I just can't think of it as a man. The feeling of total malevolence is too overpowering, too *in*human. When its thoughts force their way into mine I can almost smell the corruption, I can almost *see* its depravity.'

'God, you have changed.'

He shook his head wearily. 'I'm trying to describe the impression I'm left with, the sense of festering malignancy it imposes upon me. The feeling is ugly, Fran, and terrifying.'

'I can see. Jonathan, I don't doubt these visions, that you actually *suffer* these awful things, but are you sure you're not losing control of you own mind?'

He tried to smile. 'You never were one for holding back. You mean am I going mad?'

'No, I don't mean that. But could these terrible experiences cause you to hallucinate as well? Let's face it, there's precious little that anybody knows about the million functions of the mind, so who can tell what it takes to throw it slightly out of sync?'

'You have to take my word for it: the person, if that's what you want to call this creature, who murdered the prostitute and the old man, and who mutilated the dead boy, is the same one who mistakenly took away Annabel. It knows me and wants to hurt me. That's why you and Gabby have to be protected.'

'But how could he know where we lived? Did he read the address from your mind, too? The whole thing's crazy, Jonathan!'

'I can't hide my past from it, Fran, don't you see?'

'No, I bloody don't.'

'Like the computer, it's all in my memory bank and, as you said, access is easy once you have the code. Maybe it discovered what happened to me before, how I saw those other murders.' A thought occurred to him. 'Fran, did you have this number put back in the phone directory?'

'Not the old one, not after all those crank calls we used to receive. I couldn't stay ex-directory, not in my line of work, so I had a new number listed.'

Childes slumped back in his chair. 'Then that's probably the answer.'

'Oh, it's not human, but it can look up telephone numbers.' She tapped her foot impatiently.

'I've tried to explain. It's a person, but something inside isn't human. This thing's intelligent, otherwise the police would have caught it by now, and it's perceptive.'

'Not perceptive enough to kidnap the right little girl,' she snapped.

'No, thank . . .' He stopped himself from finishing the sentence and that moment of guilt between them somehow eased the tension. 'The point is,' Childes went on more gently, 'it will soon realize the mistake – if it doesn't know through Annabel.'

'The newspapers.'

'All the media.'

Her eyes widened. 'Jon, if they make the connection . . .'

He studied the table top. 'We'll have to go through the whole business all over again. It's too much of a coincidence for another child to be kidnapped right next door to the man who assisted police investigations last time through psychic detection.'

'I couldn't face that again.'

'Another reason for you to move out for a while. Overoy's arranged for someone to watch the house for your protection, but they can't keep reporters away. As it is, the pretext is that the police are keeping an eye on Tony and Melanie, but that won't fool any journalist for long. They're going to have a field-day when they learn the truth.' He was cautious with his next suggestion. 'I think it would be a good idea if you both came back with me for a while.'

'There's no way I could do that, Jon,' she responded immediately. 'I've got my job, remember? And Gabby has school.'

'A couple of weeks off for her wouldn't hurt, and you must be due for some leave.'

She shook her head. 'Uh huh, the agency's too busy right at this moment and we can't afford to turn away clients. Besides, Gabby and I would have to come back eventually, so what would happen then?'

'Hopefully this killer will have been caught.'

'I'd like to know how. Your idea's impractical, Jon, but there is a compromise: I could stay with my mother. She'd love to have Gabby in her clutches and she's not too far out of town, so travelling in to work would be easy for me.'

'Why not let Gabby return with me on her own?'

His ex-wife's reply was sharp and unequivocal. 'The court gave me custody.'

'I didn't contest.'

'You were wise not to. Anyway, hasn't it occurred to you that you're the danger point in this situation? Haven't you wondered if your so-called tormentor didn't come to this house looking for you?'

That possibility had been discussed between Overoy and himself during the drive from the airport. 'You may be right, Fran, there's no way of being sure; but that would prove it doesn't know where I live now.'

'The more delving into your mind he does, the more he'll discover about you.' She persisted in not referring to Annabel's kidnapper as 'it'.

'The power doesn't work that way, the thoughts aren't that definitive. It will have some idea of surroundings, but not location. Don't you recall how I could describe only the area where the murdered children were to be found?'

'You were pretty accurate but, all right, I take your point. You're still a danger, though.'

He had to concede. 'You'll have to be guarded if you do go to your mother's.'

'She'll adore the excitement, you know what she's like.'

'Yeah, I do. You'll keep Gabby away from school?'

'If you think that's best. Maybe we'll find another close to Mother's.'

'Better still.'

'Okay, I agree.' Fran ran a hand through her auburn hair and seemed to relax a little. 'Would you like more coffee?'

'No, I'm sinking fast. Is it okay if I stay the night?'

'I was assuming you would. Despite everything that's happened between us in the past, you know you're always welcome here.' She touched his hand across the table, the gesture only slightly awkward, and he responded by squeezing her fingers, then letting go. 'We may not have made each other very happy in the long run, but we did have a certain something going for us, didn't we?'

Tired though he was, Childes managed to smile back. 'They were good years, Fran.'

'To begin with.'

'We changed in ourselves, became unfamiliar to each other.'

'When –' she began to say, but he interrupted.

'Old territory, Fran.'

She lowered her gaze. 'I'll fix up the bed in the spare room for you. If that's where you want to sleep . . .' The words were deliberately left hanging in the air.

He was tempted. Fran was no less desirable than she had ever been and the emotions wrung out by a fraught day had left them both in need of physical comforting. Moments went by before he answered.

'I've got kind of close to someone,' he said.

There was a trace of resentment in Fran's question. 'A certain fellow-teacher?'

'How did you know?' Childes was surprised.

'Gabby was full of the nice lady teacher she met last time she came back from visiting you. It's been going on for quite a while, hasn't it? Don't worry, you can speak freely; I'm long past jealousy, not that I have that particular right any more so far as you're concerned.'

'Her name is Aimée Sebire.'

'French?'

'Just the name. I've known her for more than two years now.'

'Sounds serious.'

He did not reply.

'I just get involved with married men,' Fran sighed. 'I suppose I never did choose very well.'

'You're still beautiful, Fran.'

'But resistible.'

'Under different circumstances, I –'

'It's okay, I'm deliberately making you squirm. Independence for a woman isn't all it's cracked up to be, even in this day and age; a warm body to cuddle up with, a strong male shoulder to fall asleep on, can still be a necessity for us liberated ladies.' She rose slowly from the table and for the first time he noticed the shadows beneath her eyes. 'I'll get the bedclothes. You haven't told me yet what you and Inspector Overoy plan to do about our friend the ogre.' She waited by the kitchen chair for his reply.

He twisted in his chair to face Fran and the tone of his words and their implications chilled her. 'So far it's been searchng for me, probing my mind. Overoy thinks it's time I tried to reverse the situation.'

He awoke and sensed someone else was in the room with him. For a few brief seconds he was disorientated, the dim light unfamiliar, subdued shapes unidentifiable. The events of the day crowded back in on him. He was home. No, not home. Temporarily back in his old house with Fran and Gabby. The light was from the streetlamp outside.

A shadow was moving closer.

Childes sat up, the movement sharp and rigid, stiffness caused by sudden fear.

A weight on the bed, and then Fran's quietened voice.

'I'm sorry, Jon. I can't sleep alone, not tonight. Please don't be angry.'

He raised the covers and she slid in beside him, pushing close. Her nightdress was soft against his skin.

'We don't have to make love,' she whispered. 'I'm not here for that. Just put your arms around me and hold me for a while.'

He did so. And they did make love.

He awoke again in the night, much later, when sleep had a firmer hold.

A hand gripped his shoulder: Fran had been roused too. 'What is it?' she hissed.

'I don't –'

The sound came again.

'Gabby!' they both said together.

Childes scrambled from the bed, Fran following, and made for the door, the coldness of terror abruptly roughening the skin of his naked body with tiny bumps. He fumbled for the light-switch in the hallway, giddy for a moment, the light hurting his eyes.

They saw the black cat standing outside Gabby's open bedroom door, back arched, a million needles bristling. Miss Puddles glared ahead, eyes venomous, jaw wide in an angry, pointed-tooth grin.

Gabby's cry again, calling piercingly.

The cat's stiffened hairs ruffled as if disturbed by a draught. She disappeared down the staircase.

They rushed along the landing and when they entered their daughter's room, Gabby was sitting bolt upright in the bed. She was staring into a far corner by the doorway, the weak glow from the nightlight casting deep shadows across her features.

She did not look at them when they ran to the bed, but kept watching the darkened corner, seeing something there. Something that was not visible to her mother and father.

When Fran hugged her close, she blinked rapidly as if emerging from a dream. Childes looked on with concern as Gabby pulled away and scrabbled around her bedside cabinet for something; she found her glasses and quickly put them on. Once more she peered into the shadowy corner.

'Where is she?' Gabby's words were tearful.

'Who, darling, who?' asked Fran, holding her comfortingly.

'Has she gone away again, Mummy? She looked so sad.'

Childes felt the hair on the back of his neck prickle. His forehead and the palms of his hands were clammy with cold sweat.

'Tell me who, Gabriel,' said her mother, 'tell me who you saw.'

'She touched me and she was so cold, Mummy, so *freezing*. Annabel looked so sad.'

Deep within Childes, a long-forgotten memory stirred.

The package arrived by first post Monday morning and it was addressed to JONATHAN CHILDES. Both the name and his ex-wife's address were hand-written in small, neat, capital letters. The brown envelope was a standard ten-by-seven size.

Inside was a narrow, four-inch square box.

Inside the box was crumpled tissue paper.

Wrapped in the tissue were six objects.

Five were tiny fingers and thumb.

The last was a smooth, white moonstone.

Life went on; it always does.

Childes returned to the island after two days of intensive questioning by the police and having seen his ex-wife and daughter safely away to Fran's mother, who lived in a quiet village not many miles from London. He had not accompanied them, wanting no impressions of the journey imprinted on his mind.

Although there had been no more help he could give the investigating officers, he suspected that only Detective Inspector Overoy's assurances had persuaded them to allow his departure. Neither the postmark (a suburb of the city) nor the neat handwriting of the address on the macabre package provided any useful clues. There had been no saliva traces on the gummed envelope flap, for it was of the self-adhesive kind, and no clear fingerprints could be established on the paper or on the box inside. Mention of the semi-precious stone found among the mutilated human fingers had been kept from the media: copycat crimes were never encouraged by the police. That there was a 'probable' connection between the kidnapping and possibly three other crimes already under investigation could not be withheld, but the authorities declined to say why they believed there was a link.

Childes benefited from their discretion and had managed to leave the mainland before conclusions could be drawn by outsiders. His psychic contact with the killer had remained a closely guarded secret. The pathologist's report stated that the fingers had been severed from a victim already dead. There was mercy in that alone.

Annabel's body was not recovered and no vision of its whereabouts came to Childes. He tried earnestly to probe with his mind but to no avail.

Nothing more was to happen until a few weeks later.

In the dream he watched the dark-haired boy and knew the boy was himself.

He sat upright in the narrow bed, sheets bunched around him, and he was young, very young. He was speaking, the same words repeated over and over again like a senseless litany.

'. . . you . . . can't . . . be . . .'

The figure of a woman stood at the end of the bed, an ivory statue, unmoving in the moonlight, watching as did he, the dreamer. A terrible sorrow ebbed from her and, just as the sleeping observer knew that the boy was his younger self, he knew that the woman was his mother. But she was dead.

'. . . he . . . says . . . you can't . . . you can't . . . be . . .' mumbled the boy, and the sadness between woman and child, mother and son, became immense.

And the son then became aware of the observer, his startled eyes looking upwards, into the darkest corner of the room. He looked directly at himself.

But the moment was gone as heavy, lumbering footsteps sounded along the corridor outside. So, too, was gone the spectral vision of his mother.

The dark shadow of a man stood swaying in the doorway and Childes, the onlooker, was almost overwhelmed by the wretched anger exuding from his father in threatening waves, a guilt-ridden fury that charged the atmosphere. Childes cringed, as did his younger self, the boy, when the drunken man lurched forward, his fists raised.

'I told you,' the father shouted. 'No more! No more . . .' The boy screamed from beneath the bedclothes as the blows fell.

Childes tried to call out, to warn his father to leave the boy alone, that he could not help seeing his mother's ghost-spirit, that she had returned to reassure him, to let him know that her love had not perished with her cancer-riddled body, that love always continued, the grave was no captor or gaoler or executioner, that she would ever love him and he could know through his special gift which allowed him to see . . . But his father would not listen, did not hear, his wrath over-riding all other senses and emotions. He had told his son there was no life after death, the dead could never come back to torment, that his mother had died full of hate and had deserved the suffering because God willed such upon those whose hearts were corrupted with hatred, and she could not rise again to talk of love when she was filled with an odious loathing of him, her husband, the boy's father, and there were no such things as spirits or ghosts or hauntings because even the Church denied them, and there was nothing like that, nothing at all, *nothing* . . . !

The boy's screams had sunk to sobs and the beating this time was worse than any of the others. Soon his consciousness began to fade as he closed his mind, deliberately rejecting what was happening, what *had* happened. And Childes, the man, the dreaming witness, was aware that the boy's mind had closed against what *would* happen.

He awoke whimpering, as he had all those years ago when only a boy.

'Jon, are you all right?'

Amy was leaning over him, her hair brushing his cheek. 'You were having a nightmare, like before, saying the same words, and then yelling at someone, screaming for them to stop.'

His breath was shallow, fast, his chest rising in sharp movements. She had turned on the bedside lamp and her sweet face, anxious though it was, was a relief from the nightmare.

'He . . . he made me . . .' he whispered.

'Who, Jon? And what?'

Alertness was swiftly returning. Childes lay there for a few more seconds, gathering his thoughts, then pushed himself up so that his back was against the wall. Amy half-knelt beside him, shadows accentuating the soft curves of her body as the bedsheet fell around her waist. She smoothed away dark hair that hung over his forehead.

'What did I say in my sleep?' he asked her.

'You mumbled, but it sounded like: "It can't –" no, "– *you* can't be". You kept saying the same thing over and over again and then you started shouting.'

Although the hour was late, there was no chill in the air; not even a breeze came through the open window.

'Oh, Amy, Amy, I think I'm beginning to understand,' he said, and the words were almost a moan.

Her arm went around his body and she rested her head against his shoulder. 'You frighten me so much,' she said. 'Talk to me now, Jon, tell me what you think it is you understand. Please don't hide anything away from me.'

He caressed her back, absorbing the warmth that was more than physical through sensitive fingertips. He began to talk, speaking in a soft, low voice, hesitant at first, the words as much for himself as for her.

'When Gabby . . . when she saw . . . when she thought she saw Annabel that night . . . after Annabel had been . . . taken . . . something was revived in me, a thought, a feeling, a memory. Something kept hidden away for a long, long time. It's complex, and I know I won't be able to explain it all, but I'll try, if only for my own sake.'

Amy eased away so that her weight was not on him.

'I suppose no one really wants to hate their father,' he went on, 'and remember, for so many years he was my only parent, so that guilt may have played some small part in my refusal to admit certain facts about myself. I can't be sure, I'm just searching, Amy, trying to come up with some answers, a *rationale*, if you like.'

He fell silent, as though searching his own thoughts, attempting to bring some order to them, and Amy tried helping. 'Your dream, Jon. Perhaps you should start there.'

Childes' fingers pressed against his closed eyelids. 'Yes,' he said after a while, 'the dream, that's the key. Only I'm not sure it was just a dream, Amy.' Reaching for her hand, he held it in his lap and looked towards the window on the far side of the room. 'I saw myself as a boy – about Gabby's age, I think – and I seemed to be looking down at him – at *myself* – as if hovering over his bedroom. The boy was sitting up in bed, afraid, yet somehow I felt there was a kind of happiness about him. Someone else was in the room, standing in the moonlight, watching the boy as I was. A woman. I know it was my mother.'

Childes breathed in deeply while Amy quietly waited. His face was drawn and the glistening in his eyes indicated both sadness and the subdued excitement of discovery. She tensed when he said, 'But my mother had been dead for over a week.'

'Jon –'

'No, just listen, Amy. Gabby wasn't dreaming when she saw Annabel that night. Don't you see? She has my gift, she's psychic, mediumistic – I don't know what term you'd use because it's a subject I've evaded most of my life. Gabby and I are the same, she's inherited the power from me. But my father, God help him, beat such notions out of my head; he refused to acknowledge such a power and wouldn't let me *accept* it! In my dream I watched him come into the room and beat the boy – beat me! – until I lost consciousness. And that hadn't been the first time, and I don't think it was the last. He made me reject this ability, this extra-sensing, forced me to black the power from my mind.'

'But why should he –?'

'I don't know! I had a feeling from him, though, in the dream. He was confused and angry – and God, yes, he was frightened – but there was guilt also! He may have blamed himself in some way for her death, or . . .' he squeezed his eyes shut to concentrate, to remember '. . . or maybe for the way he couldn't cope with her last weeks of dying. He was a drunkard, a selfish man who could never face up to his own responsibilities. I don't think he could take her suffering, he wasn't able to help her through the pain. He may even have treated her badly and later was ashamed. My father wanted to shut out her memory totally, but my visions, my "sightings", wouldn't allow that. I was destroying the barrier he'd erected around his own emotions.'

He paused, to regain his breath, for the words had been an unleashed torrent. 'I don't think I'll ever know the whole truth, Amy; I can only tell you what I've sensed. Consciously I've spurned anything to do with the supernatural, as any kid who has been constantly taught that something is wrong or unnatural might eventually, yet the power has always stayed locked away inside me. Can you imagine the conflict that must have gone on inside my young mind? I loved and missed my mother, wanted her comfort, yet my father forced me to reject her, and with her, my own special perception. I suppose the conscious side of my mind finally won the battle, but it wasn't a victory that could be maintained for ever.'

Amy took her hand from his so that she could touch his face. 'It could explain so much about you,' she said, and smiled. 'Perhaps even why you chose such an ultimately logical career. The only wonder is that you're not full of neuroses.'

'Who says I'm not?' He shifted in the bed, aware of his own tenseness. 'But why now, Amy? Why has all this bubbled to the surface, now?'

'It hasn't just happened, don't you see? The process began three years ago.'

'The murders of those children?'

'Isn't that when the extra sense began to surface again? But who knows what else you perceived in this special way that you put down to mere intuition?'

He was thoughtful, then said slowly. 'Maybe it took another mind to trigger it off.' He added more quietly, 'Somebody may have found my code.'

'What?'

'Something Fran said to me, equating minds with computers and access codes. The comparison isn't important, but the principle could be.' He suddenly raised his knees and leaned forward. 'Another point I've remembered about my dream tonight, if that's what it can be called. The boy saw me. He was aware of me.'

She shook her head. 'I don't understand.'

'He looked up at me from his bed. I looked up at *myself*, Amy! No, I didn't dream tonight; it was a memory, a recall. I remember my mother's spirit coming to me, showing me her love, telling me that death wasn't final; and I remember a different pair of eyes watching me that particular night – *I swear to you I remember that night from the boy's point of view* – and those eyes belonged to someone who cared, like my mother, someone who was concerned for me. Amy, do you understand now? I had the power then to see my future-self! Am I insane, Amy, or is that the truth of it? I had the power to see my future-self and tonight I had the power to go back and see my *past*-self!'

He shuddered and she clung to him. 'It's strong in me,' he told her. 'God, I can feel the power so strong in me. And . . . and . . .'

The glow was before him, a vaporous shimmering, yet he knew the image was inside his head, not there in the room. Small to begin with, gradually growing solid, becoming rounded, taking form.

A moonstone.

But no. Still growing, altering in shape, in texture. Not a moonstone any longer.

Fissures and craters scarred its surface. Mountain ranges shadowed its whiteness.

He saw the moon itself.

And with the image came a dreadful, stomach-wrenching foreboding.

Jeanette sprinted across the circular lawn, heading for the science department and praying that no staff member would catch her trespassing on hallowed ground. She skirted around the statue of the school's founder, dark hair flailing loosely behind, books for the next lesson tucked tightly beneath one arm. Fortunately, the lesson was Computer Studies and Mr Childes seldom got really cross, although occasionally he could get quite stern if the girls misbehaved *too* much.

She was relieved to be off the lawn and on the gravel turning circle for visitors' cars. Taking the stone steps two at a time, Jeanette pushed through the glass entrance doors and pounded up more stairs to the computer room which was on the first floor with the science laboratory, spilling her books near the top so that she had to pound down again to gather them up. Once more she made the ascent.

Outside the computer room she paused in order to compose herself. Three deep breaths, a swift combing of hair with clawed fingers, and she entered.

'Hello, Jeanette,' Childes greeted her with a trace of a frown. 'You're a little late.'

'I know, sir, I'm sorry,' she said, still breathless despite her efforts to steady herself. 'I left my program sheet in the dormitory this morning and didn't have the chance to fetch it between lessons.' She regarded him apprehensively and he smiled.

'That's okay,' he told her. 'Let's see, you'll have to share with Nicola and Isobel, then take your turn with the screen when they're finished. Hope you worked out a decent program to try.'

'A spelling test, sir.'

Somebody giggled.

'Well, that's a little basic, Jeanette, but it'll be fine,' said Childes, then added for the benefit of the rest of the class: 'Everybody has to find their own way with computers, there are no short cuts to begin with. Takes a while for the sheer logic of it all to sink in, but once it has, you'll be up and running.'

Jeanette pulled up a chair behind Nicola and Isobel and looked over their shoulders at the monitor screen they were using. She saw they were playing an anagram game.

Childes went from machine to machine, offering advice and suggestions as to how his pupils could increase the information in their programs and make them more interesting.

He lingered behind Kelly and nodded with pleasure. She was devising sailing times from and into the local marina, assuming she had a yacht or motorboat moored there, having taken the trouble to visit the harbour master for detailed information on traffic flow and regulations. Kelly became aware of his interest and glanced round at him, a smile on her upturned face.

As usual, he thought, you're just a trifle too smug, Kelly, but there's no denying you're my brightest. He said, 'That's a good exercise, Kelly. Looking towards the future?'

'Yes, Mr Childes, the very-near future. But my yacht's more likely to be in the Bahamas.'

He held back the grin. 'I don't doubt it.'

She turned back to the machine and he watched her deft fingers tap decisively at the keyboard. The only blemish on her hand was an ink stain and he wondered, not for the first time, what had caused him to see the limb so horribly burned those few weeks ago. Premonitions were not part of the strange ability he possessed. Yet, as a boy, hadn't he seen his future-self? He was confused and afraid, but no longer willing to be a compliant victim of this terrible curse, nor of the monster who had taunted him through his own mind. Childes had finally began to probe himself, a tactic he had agreed with Overoy to try, searching for the perverted psyche of his tormentor. The burning down of the psychiatric hospital had still not officially been attributed to any particular person, but neither he himself, nor Overoy, had any doubt it was the same one who had mutilated and murdered before. He supposed he ought to have been grateful for the detective's belief in him, and Overoy had certainly worked hard behind the scenes to prevent Childes' name being linked with Annabel's disappearance. Overoy was making amends for mishandling the publicity surrounding their past association, yet Childes could not find the willingness to fully trust the man. The last time they had spoken, just three days before, Overoy had told him that he was now the chief liason officer in charge of investigations into all four crimes, his involvement with Childes being the prime factor in the appointment; unfortunately, there had been no solid leads as yet to follow up. Was there any more information Childes could give him to save him from looking a total jackass? None at all, Childes had replied, then, almost, apologetically, he had mentioned the curious vision of the moonstone which had gradually changed into the moon itself. What did it mean? Who the hell knew? And no, there still had not been any contact with the other mind. In fact, after finally accepting he possessed an extra-sensory ability, Childes now wondered if the power had left him, like some spectre that vanished when focused upon.

He wondered: Is it all over? Had the creature, like the child-murderer before, ceased to exist, become its own executioner? Had the terrible visions and the nightmares ended?

'Sir. Sir?'

Kelly's voice had broken into his thoughts. He quickly glanced up to find she had twisted towards him once more, this time with a look of consternation on her face.

'What is it, Kelly?' he asked, rising from the desk.

'Something's going wrong with my computer.' She turned back to the screen and stabbed at the keyboard below.

'Whoa!' he said, going over. 'Don't take it out on the machine. Let's just go through the thing logically.'

He leaned over her and froze, further words locked in his throat. His hand gripped the back of her chair as a soft pressure nudged at his mind.

'What made you write this on the display, Kelly?' he forced himself to say calmly.

'*I* didn't do it,' she retorted indignantly. 'It just appeared and everything else went off.'

'You know that's impossible.'

'Honest, sir, I didn't do anything.'

'Okay, clear the screen and start again.'

The girl touched the **RETURN** key. Nothing happened.

Childes, not sure if she were playing stupid games with him, impatiently leaned forward and pressed the same key. It had no effect.

'Kelly, have you –?'

'How could I? There's no way I could make the computer do that.'

'All right, let me take your seat.'

She stood and Childes eased himself into the chair, watching the monitor warily as if disbelieving his own eyes. His hands hovered nervously over the keyboard. Other girls in the classroom were looking round curiously at them.

'We'll try **RESET**.' Childes murmured, keeping his voice steady, disguising the panic bubbling inside. He could not hide the beads of perspiration that had rapidly formed on his forehead, though.

He fingered the key.

The screen went blank and he sighed with relief.

The single word appeared again.

'Why's the computer doing that, sir?' Kelly asked close to his shoulder, both astonished and fascinated by the phenomenon.

'I've no idea,' he replied. 'It shouldn't happen, it should be impossible for it to happen. Could be an outsider's somehow tapped into your circuit.' Extremely unlikely, he thought and then remembered Fran's computer/mind analogy. Nonsense, that had nothing to do with this! He pressed **RESET** again.

The word disappeared. Then reappeared.

'I don't want to lose your program,' Childes told Kelly, his voice more even than the turmoil inside his head should have allowed, 'but I'm afraid I'll have to.'

'This time he tapped **HOME**.

The screen went blank, became a dark void. He rested back in the chair.

And sat rigid when the word shone from the blackness yet again.

He stared transfixed at the screen, his eyes wide, the green glowing word reflected in his contact lenses. The small, computer-typed word said:

ΠΟΟΠ

Some of the other girls had gathered round, but sudden cries came from those who had remained at their machines. Childes pushed his chair back and went to each one. The same single world was impossibly displayed on every monitor.

In a desperation that alarmed the girls, he reached underneath the benches and yanked out all the plugs, cutting off the power supply to each computer so that the screens blinked to a lifeless grey. He waited in the centre of the classroom, his chest heaving, the girls beginning to huddle together as if he were mad.

Cautiously he approached the computer which Kelly had been operating. He knelt, picking up the power plug again, and slid it into the socket.

The computer screen came to life, but now the word that had frightened him so much was missing.

He found Amy after the lesson had finished, having barely managed to show his pupils a calm face throughout the rest of the period, explaining that what had occurred was due to some peculiar malfunction or the intrusion of another computer. The explanation was hardly feasible, but the girls appeared to accept his word.

Childes drove Amy away from school, grateful that the lesson had preceded the lunch break, giving them the opportunity to be alone. He did not stop until they had found a remote point on the clifftops.

He switched off the engine and looked out to sea. Only after a few more moments when his breathing had steadied did he turn to her and say: 'It's here, Amy. It's here on the island.'

The day was perfect. Only a few small clouds clung to the sky like glued cotton-wool buds, seemingly stuck fast to a vividly blue board, unable to drift, with no breeze even in the upper reaches. The sun, a brilliant fireball, gloried in its dominance. A faint low mist spread over the sea, and other islands were merely hazy smudges in the distance.

Scores of small motor-boats left short white plumes in their wakes, while yachts searched in vain for the slightest wind that would allow the use of canvas. Further in, closer to the shore, wind-surfers drifted astride their boards, colourful sails resting flatly beside them in the water. Sandy beaches were full, only the less accessible coves and inlets still quiet and uncrowded, refuges for those who valued their peace enough to undertake arduous climbs.

On the clifftop overlooking one such secluded bay, stood La Roche Ladies College, its white main structure a beacon lit by the sun.

A perfect Saturday for Open Day, when staff and girls and classrooms preened themselves under inspection. An important day for the school: prize-giving, awards and certificates for excellence (or even plain usefulness), and general school or house achievements throughout the year; speeches by the principal, Miss Estelle Piprelly, and a member of the governing board, *Conseiller* Victor Platnauer; a recitation by La Roche's head girl of the year's events within the school related in obligatory (by tradition) rhyming verse, a test of nerve and ingenuity (and often of perseverance by the assembled guests); the luring of more fee-paying parents. A fun day for the school: various raffles, a lottery, games, a second-hand uniform sale; a strawberry-and-cream stall, a jam, sweets and cake stall, a hot-dog stall and barbecue, a wine and orange-squash stall, a gymnastic display, light choral singing, country dancing; and all to be enjoyed on the lawns

A day for things *not* to go wrong.

Milling parents, arriving vehicles jostling for space in the over-crowded carpark and driveway, schoolgirls excited and pretending not to be, giggling though under threat to be on best behaviour. Childes had left the computer classroom when the mandatory parent/teacher discussion period was over. Now he watched the activity with restless attention. He tried not to let his close scrutiny of each passing face appear too obvious, but more than one parent was made to feel uncomfortable under his gaze.

And after a while he, too, had the feeling of being studied. He turned quickly and found Miss Piprelly, only yards away and supposedly in conversation with a group of parents and staff, staring intently at him. Their eyes met and a curious recognition passed between them, a *knowing* that had never been present before. An anxiety shadowed the principal's features and Childes watched as she said something to those around her, then broke away from them, striding in her stiff-backed manner towards him.

She acknowledged greetings from other visitors she passed with a brief smile that was polite yet rebuffed conversation, and then she was before him, looking up into his face. He blinked, for he had seen the energy glowing from her, an aura of vitality that was of many subtle colours. The phenomenon was extraordinary and something he had witnessed more than just once recently, the radiance like a gentle many-hued flame that flared briefly to fade when concentrated upon, leaving him perplexed and slightly spellbound. The unusual effect vanished when Miss Piprelly spoke and his attention was diverted.

'I'd rather you didn't stand there inspecting everybody with quite such intensity, Mr Childes. Perhaps you could tell me if there is something wrong?'

That uncanny *awareness* in her eyes. He was slowly beginning to view the school's principal in a different light, catching glimpses of deeper sensitivities beneath the somewhat brittle exterior. Yet their relationship had not changed. He wondered if these fresh insights into the woman were due to the confusing developments within himself.

'Mr Childes?' She was waiting for an answer.

The urge to tell her everything was almost overwhelming, but how could she believe him? Estelle Piprelly was a rational, no-nonsense headmistress, energetic and diligent in her pursuit of educational excellence. Yet what was it in her that puzzled him so, what elusive – or camouflaged – quality did she possess that belied her image?

She sighed impatiently. 'Mr Childes?'

'I'm sorry, I was miles away.'

'Yes, I could see that. If you'll forgive me for saying so, you seem unwell. You've looked haggard for a while now, since your few days absence, in fact.'

A minor illness, a summer cold, had been how he had accounted for his time spent on the mainland after Annabel's disappearance. 'Oh.' He shrugged. 'Well, summer term's nearly over, so I'll have plenty of time to rest up.'

'I wouldn't have thought your curriculum is exactly full, Mr Chides.'

'Perhaps not.'

'*Is* there something on your mind?'

He faltered, but it was neither the time nor the place to be frank with her. She would have probably ordered him off the premises if he had, anyway.

'No, I was, uh, interested in the parents, trying to associate them with their offspring. Just a little game I like to play. Have you ever noticed how like their mothers or fathers some of the girls are, while others are total opposites? Incredible, really.'

She was not satisfied, but she was far too busy to indulge him. 'No, I don't find it incredible at all. Now I suggest you forget your "game" and mingle a little more with our guests.' Miss Piprelly began to turn away, but paused. 'You know, Mr Childes, if there is some kind of problem, my door is always open to you.'

He avoided her stare, feeling uncomfortable, for there was more in her remark than a casual invitation. Just how much did she really know about him?

'I'll remember,' he told her, then watched her walk away.

Amy spotted Overoy endeavouring to resemble a visiting parent but succeeding only in looking like a plain-clothes policeman on the lookout for pickpockets, his intent look and alert stance the give-away. She could not help smiling: maybe he only looked like that to her because she knew who he was and why he was there. She resisted the mischievous urge to wave and call out, 'Inspector!' Instead, she said to the two thirteen-year-old girls helping her on the strawberries-and-cream stall, 'Take over for a while and make sure you give the correct change. And only *four* strawberries to a basket otherwise we'll run out too fast and without even showing a profit.'

'Yes, Miss Sebire,' they replied in unison, delighted to be in charge.

Amy made her way from behind the stall, exchanging hellos with any parent she recognized. Overoy was standing beneath a tree, sipping wine from a plastic cup, shirtsleeves rolled to the elbows and jacket hanging over one arm.

'You look hot, Inspector,' Amy said when she drew near.

He turned in her direction, surprised for a moment. 'Hello, Miss Sebire. You seemed busy on your stall.'

'Strawberries and cream are in great demand on a day like today. Would you like me to bring you some?'

'That's very kind, but no, thank you.'

'They would add to your disguise.'

He grinned at the mild leg-pulling. 'I stick out that much, do I?'

'Probably only because I know who you are and what you're doing here. At least your numbers are discreet.'

He gave a wry shake of his head. 'Yes, I know. I'm sorry about that, but as it is, I'm on my own time. Difficult to convince my governors that an undercover team was needed for this little exercise – not that we have any jurisdiction on the island anyway. Fortunately Inspector Robillard is an old friend, so I'm here on a weekend social as his guest.'

'I thought I'd seen him wandering around with his wife.'

'Like me, he's on unofficial duty, keeping an eye on things.'

'Looking for our monster?'

'Yeah, a bit difficult when you don't know what he looks like, though.'

'"It", you mean: Jon refuses to accept the killer as human.'

'I'd noticed.' Uncomfortable, Overoy scratched his cheek with a nicotine-stained finger, careful not to spill the wine. 'Mr Childes is, er, a strange man in some ways, Miss Sebire,' he said.

Amy smiled sweetly. 'Wouldn't you be if you'd been through what he has, Inspector?'

'No, I'd be worse: I'd be out of my brain by now.'

A quick frown replaced the smile. 'You can be sure he's not.'

He held up the plastic cup between them as if a shield. 'I'm not suggesting anything, Miss Sebire. In fact, I find him a remarkably down-to-earth character, considering. I just mean this ESP business is a bit odd, that's all.'

'I thought you'd be used to it by now.'

'He isn't, nor am I.'

'Jon is beginning to accept the ability.'

'I accepted that in him a long time ago, but that doesn't mean I'm used to it.'

A passing group of parents waved to Amy and she called out a hello in return. She faced the policeman again. 'Do you really think this person could have come to the island?'

Overoy sipped the wine before answering. 'He knows Childes is here, so it's possible. I'm afraid this business may have turned into a personal vendetta against Childes.'

'But you really think he could read Jon's mind in that way?'

'To find his location, you mean? Oh, no, he didn't need to. Childes' daughter, Gabriel took a funny phone call a day or two before her friend was abducted – she couldn't remember exactly when – and we're assuming it was from the kidnapper.'

'Jon mentioned that to me.'

'We didn't find out for some time after, when we questioned Gabriel again and specifically asked her if she or Annabel had spoken to any strangers in the days or weeks before Annabel was taken. She remembered the call then.' His eyes ranged over the crowds, but he was recalling something unpleasant. 'Gabriel couldn't describe the voice, so she did an impression for us. It made my flesh creep just to listen.' He finished off the wine and looked around for somewhere to dispose of the plastic cup. Amy took it from him.

'Please go on,' she said.

'The voice was weird, a kind of low growling. Rough, but with no particular accent, nothing for us to latch on to. Of course, she's just a kid and anyway the caller could have been deliberately assuming a different voice to normal, so even that doesn't help us much. Unfortunately, when he asked to speak to her father, Gabriel said he didn't live there any more, that he was here, on the island.'

'Then when he went to the house . . .'

'He specifically went there for Gabriel, or at least to do some mischief. We haven't mentioned our notion to Annabel's parents – it would be heartless and at this stage, there'd be no point – but we believe he mistook Annabel for Childes daughter. She'd told her mother she was off to play with Gabriel, so we reckon she was in the Childes' garden when she was abducted.'

'You still haven't found her body?'

Overoy shook his head. 'Not a trace,' he said dismally. 'But then the killer doesn't need her body to be found: he's already presented us with the moonstone, along with the girl's fingers.'

Despite the heat of the day, Amy shuddered. 'Why should he do such a thing?'

'The moonstone? Or do you mean why the mutilations? Well, the desecration of the bodies has all the hallmarks of ritual, and the moonstone could play some part in that.'

'Did Jon tell you about his dream?'

'The moonstone changing into the moon? Yeah, he told me, but what does it mean? And why did the word "moon" appear on the computer screens in his classroom? And was it *really* there?'

Amy was startled. 'I don't know what you mean.'

'The mind is a funny thing, and Childes' apparently, is a little different from most. What if he *imagined* he saw the word on the monitor screens?'

'But the girls in his class saw it too.'

'Pubescent girls at their most sensitive age, minds open to suggestion. I'm talking about a form of mass hypnosis or collective hallucination. Such things aren't rare, Miss Sebire.'

'The circumstances weren't like –'

He held up a hand. 'It's merely a consideration we have to keep our *own* minds open to. I wouldn't be here if I thought Childes was making the whole thing up, and I'm working on one particular theory that might throw some light, but I need to do more research.'

'Couldn't Moon be somebody's name?'

'First thing that occurred to me, so I checked whether the prostitute who was murdered had any associate or regular clients by that name. So far, nothing. I also did a run-through of the list of staff and inmates at the hospital, but drew a blank there, too. Something's bound to turn up sooner or later, though – it's the natural order of events in most criminal investigations.'

'Is there any way in which I can help?' Amy offered.

'I wish there were – we need all the help we can get. Just keep an eye out for anyone acting suspiciously around Childes. And for that matter, around yourself. Remember, the killer tried to get at him through his daughter; next time it could be you.'

'Do you . . . do you think this person is here today?'

He sighed, still looking around. 'Hard to say. After all, what do we have? A word on a computer screen? Doesn't tell us much, does it? But if he is here, he'll know where Childes lives – all he had to do is look in the phone book and find there's only one Childes listed.'

'But surely you're keeping a watch on the cottage,' said Amy, alarmed.

'I've got no authority here, Miss Sebire.'

'Inspector Robillard . . .'

'What can he do? I've had a hard enough job getting my own people to listen, so what can Inspector Robillard, who thinks I'm slightly out of my head anyway, tell his superiors?'

'But that leaves Jon so vulnerable.'

'We may come up with something today. Childes has one of his feelings about the safety of the girls, that's why I'm here and why I've persuaded Geoff Robillard to give me a hand. Not much of a task force, I admit, but under the circumstances, all you're going to get. It had crossed our minds to let the principal in on our little secret, but what sane reason could we give for our presence? You know, I'm not at all sure of this myself, but I'd hate anything to happen here without at least taking a few precautions.'

Amy had been quietly appraising Overoy while he spoke. 'I think Jon has been fortunate to find an ally in you,' she said. 'It's hard to imagine any other policeman taking him too seriously.'

Overoy glanced away, embarrassed. 'I owe him,' he said. 'Besides, he's a definite link – why else would this lunatic send him a moonstone? Frankly, Miss Sebire, Jonathan Childes is all we've got to go on.' He continued to search among the strolling people, looking for a certain indefinable something, a guarded look in someone's eyes, an awkwardness of movement betraying an unnatural self-consciousness – any small nuance that would make an individual subtly conspicuous to the trained eye. So far, all appeared normal; but the day was still young.

Amy was about to walk away when Overoy said, 'Did he tell you about his daughter's dream?'

She stopped. 'When Gabby saw Annabel after she'd been taken?'

He nodded.

'Yes, he did.'

'It wasn't just a dream, was it?'

'Jon's already told you.'

'He was vague. He said that he and Mrs Childes heard Gabby call out in the middle of the night from another room along the hallway and when they got to her she was sitting up in bed, very upset and claiming to have dreamt about Annabel. Those were his words. I'd like to know if she really had been dreaming. It's not important, Miss Sebire; I'm just curious. Does Gabby have the same gift as her father?' He failed to notice that something he had said had shaken Amy.

'Jon doesn't believe it was a dream,' she said distractedly. 'He may have told you that to protect her –'

'From me?'

'You let matters get out of control last time; he wouldn't want Gabby to go through what he had to. I'm surprised he even mentioned it to you.'

'He didn't. Mrs Childes told me and later he explained it as a sort of nightmare.'

'Perhaps I shouldn't have said otherwise.'

This time he was aware that her initial cheerfulness had been dampened and, mistakenly, he assumed she regretted her disclosure. 'Like I said, it's not important, so let's leave the matter there. I'm sorry he still doesn't have confidence in me, though. I'd hate to think Childes would keep anything important from me.'

'I'm sure he wouldn't, Inspector. Jon is a very frightened man at the moment.'

'To be honest, he's not the only one: I've seen the forensic photographs of what this maniac can do.'

'I don't think I want to know more than I do already.' Amy looked over at the strawberries-and-cream stall. 'I'll have to get back and help the girls; they're being swamped with customers.'

'You'll see me and Inspector Robillard wandering around throughout the afternoon, so let either one of us know if anything suspicious catches your eye. I don't think anything's going to happen with all these people around, but you never know. Oh, and Miss Sebire,' he added as she turned away, 'if you do casually bump into me again, try not to call me Inspector.' He smiled, but her mind was obviously now on other things, for she did not respond in kind.

'I'll remember,' was all she said, and then she disappeared into the throng milling around the stall.

He checked his wristwatch: soon it would be time for the gymnastics and dancing to begin.

Childes kept careful watch as visitors and staff began drifting towards the main lawn at the rear of the school. He continued to feel uneasy, even though nothing had occurred as yet to give him cause for concern. He had come across nobody who appeared in the least bit out of place, no one who made his spine stiffen or the skin on the back of his neck crawl, a reaction he instinctively knew he would have once he set eyes on the person – creature – he sought. *The creature who sought him.* Could he have been wrong? Was the idea that it was on the island a misguided assumption? He did not think so, for the feeling was too strong, too intense.

Childes followed the visitors, spotting the island policeman, Robillard, among them; Overoy would not be far away.

Lively chattering around him, smiling faces, movement of bright colours and the buzz of activity – all conspirators to the air of normality. Why did he doubt so? There had been no warnings, no sensing of overt danger; only a trembling within, a creeping unease, a certain tenseness. No recognition, but a heavy, shadowy awareness without definition, without clarity. He felt eyes upon him and was suddenly afraid to turn. He forced himself to.

Paul Sebire stood three yards away, supposedly in conversation with Victor Platnauer, but his gaze boring into Childes. The financier abruptly excused himself and strode towards him.

'I don't intend to create a scene here, Childes, but I think it's about time you and I had a serious talk,' Sebire said gruffly when he reached the teacher.

For a moment, Childes forgot his main concern. 'I'm ready to discuss Amy at any time,' he replied with a calmness he scarcely felt.

'It's *you* I want to discuss, not my daughter.'

They stood facing one another, the crowd flowing around them like a river around boulders.

'I've discovered certain things about you,' Sebire went on, 'that were rather alarming.'

'Yes, I guessed it was you who initiated the investigation into my background. It must have come as some surprise to learn that Amy knew all about my past.'

'Whether or not you'd already informed her doesn't concern me. What does is the fact that you've been under police investigation.'

Childes sighed wearily. 'You know what that was all about; I don't have to explain myself.'

'Yes, I grant that you were cleared of any suspicion, but I have to say one thing, Childes: I don't believe you to be a very stable man. You revealed that when you were my dinner guest.'

'Look, I'm not going to argue with you. You can think what you like about me, but the truth is, I love you daughter and it should be fairly obvious even to you that she returns that love.'

'She's blinded by you for the moment, though God knows why. Do you realize I haven't seen Aimée since she moved in with you?'

'That's between you and her, Mr Sebire; I certainly haven't kept her away from you.'

'She's not for someone like you.' His voice had risen a tone and passers-by looked in their direction.

'That's for Amy to decide.'

'No, no it isn't −'

'Don't be ridiculous.'

'How dare −'

Another figure smoothly interposed itself between the two men. 'Paul, I think we should make our way to the main lawn,' Victor Platnauer said soothingly. 'The performances are about to begin and I'm afraid I have my usual speech to make.' He gave a short laugh. 'I'll try not to bore you too much this year, you gave me enough stick after last time. Please excuse us, Mr Childes. Now there's a point I want to raise about . . .' He gently led the financier away, continuing to speak placatingly, obviously anxious to avoid any upset to the day's proceedings.

Childes watched them go, regretting the brief but vitriolic exchange with Sebire, yet dissatisfied that nothing had been resolved. He hadn't meant to fall so deeply in love with Amy − what man or woman consciously rendered themselves so vulnerable? − but since he had, he would do his utmost to keep her. Though arguing with her father in public was hardly going to help matters. Come to that, nor was sleeping with Fran. He pushed the thought away, but guilt was a lingering reprover.

There were not too many people left around him by now, most having made their way to the rear of the college. Instead of following, Childes took the long way round, checking the quieter areas of the school grounds, keeping a wary eye on the bordering shrubbery and woodland, peering into the recessed doorways and shadowed corners of the building itself and the annexes.

Gulls wheeled lazily above, suddenly swooping out of sight as they dived below the nearby clifftops; the sound of surf breaking on the rocks came to him when he stopped for a few seconds and listened intently. A huge, furry bumble bee staggered sluggishly across the path before him, unable to fly, victim of premature summer mating. The sun beat down relentlessly, causing a shimmer above the ground in the near-distance.

Childes walked on, carefully stepping over the stumbling insect. A slight rustling somewhere to his left brought him to a halt once again until he saw, with relief, that the bushes from where the noise had come were low, incapable of concealing anything other than a smallish animal or bird. He resumed walking.

The hubbub of voices hit him as soon as he rounded the corner, the bustling panorama in sharp contrast to the quiet emptiness behind. Benches and chairs were laid out in long lines facing the building, leaving a wide expanse of green between them and the terrace to accommodate the display which was to be followed by speeches and prize-giving. Visitors and schoolgirls filled the benches, presenting a vibrant mixture of restless colours across the clear sweep of lawn. A yellow island-hopper plane flew low overhead, while a backdrop of trees behind the assemblage stood lush against the strikingly blue sky.

Childes made his way along the gravel path fringing the lawn and, seeing all the seats allocated to staff and guest dignitaries had been taken, moved on towards the back rows. Finding an empty place, he sat and waited for the activities to begin.

On the terrace, Miss Piprelly was seated alongside members of the governing board, representatives of the parents' association and chosen teachers, before a long table containing trophies, rolled certificates, raffle prizes and a somewhat ancient-looking microphone. A short, wide flight of stone steps led up to the terrace, and the old grey stone building which housed classrooms and dormitories loomed up darkly behind, while the white tower of the more recent building, which housed the assembly hall and gymnasium, reigned over all.

The crowd settled as La Roche's principal rose to speak and Childes, with the warmth of the sun on his back, seriously began to doubt his earlier misgivings.

Jeanette lay on her bed, head propped up by the pillows and cushions, knees raised high with the hem of her light blue dress stretched over them, white-stockinged feet digging into the quilt beneath her. A less than immaculate black-and-white Pierrot doll sat on her stomach, back resting against her thighs, wide stiffened ruff framing its smooth face with its tearfully sad expression. She despondently picked at the cotton buttons of the doll's tunic.

Jeanette should have been outside with the other girls in her class, but had sneaked away, wanting only to be alone. *They* all had their parents and brothers and sisters with them, while she had no one, and to be among them only made her miss her own parents more. Besides, she hadn't been chosen for the dancing display and certainly had no gymnastics prowess, and knew there would be no awards or certificates waiting on the prize table for *her*. There never were! Oh yes, once she'd won a merit badge for embroidery, but the earth had hardly moved for that. Perhaps it was just as well that her parents hadn't flown all the way from South Africa just to sit with her on the sidelines and watch her friends collecting their prizes. Her father was an engineer of some kind – she never quite understood *exactly* what he did – and used the island as a base for his various journeys to other parts and different jobs, her mother often accompanying him. They'd be away for eighteen months this time – *eighteen months*! – but at least she would stay with them for two months as soon as the summer term was over. She missed them terribly, but didn't know if they missed her. They said they did, but then they would, wouldn't they? Of course we love you and miss you, darling, but it just isn't practical for you to be dragged halfway around the world and have your education broken up in such a way. Of course we want you with us, but learning must come first. Jeanette allowed Pierrot to tumble off her body and slide from the bed onto the floor. His woebegone expression had been making her miserable.

She closed her eyes for a few minutes, face pointed towards the ceiling, her single plait of hair (she told herself it was in the style of Miss Sebire) spread on the pillow. If anyone caught her in the dormitory she'd be in trouble; fortunately all the teachers would be too busy toadying up to fee-paying parents to patrol the school's upper floors, otherwise she would never have risked being there. She liked occasional solitude, but found the only trouble with being alone was that it got lonely.

Jeanette sighed, pictured Kelly confidently marching forward to receive her trophies – best debater, highest grade in maths and physics, special award for progress in computer studies, etc,. etc., etc. – and wished she could be like her. Kelly was *so* pretty, too. It was wrong to be jealous, Jeanette knew that, but sometimes, *oh, sometimes*, she wished she were like her classmate. She never would be, though, Jeanette had to accept that, but everybody had to have at least *one* quality, something that made them as good as the rest; it was just a little bit difficult to discover what hers was. Someday it would shine through, though. Perhaps soon. And perhaps when her periods started her spots would disappear and her breasts start to grow. And her head would be less dreamy all the time and she might even grow taller and –

– And the mobiles were beginning to move.

Of course, windows were open on the upper floors on such a brill day, so a draught was moving them. Jeanette was annoyed at herself. The other girls often accused her of being frightened of her own shadow and sometimes she was forced to agree with them. She didn't like dark corners, didn't like scary movies – *hated* crawly things – didn't like the creaking of the old building or the rattling of windows when she lay awake in the middle of the night while others around her slept. And shadows did frighten her, especially those under beds.

Jeanette sat up, but did not immediately swing her legs to the floor. She crouched forward and peered under the bed first.

Satisfied no beast was lying in wait to reach out and pull her into its dark lair, Jeanette allowed her stockinged feet to touch the floor. She remained on the edge of the bed for a little while, listening intently and not quite sure what she was listening for. Perhaps the crack of floorboards in another room, a mysterious scratching that might or might not be a tiny mouse, the slithering of some loathsome slime-covered creature that wandered empty corridors, or a huge cloaked figure lurking just beyond the doorway, waiting for her to come out, clawed, scabby fingers with long curling nails waiting to –

Stoppit! She was frightening herself again. Sometimes Jeanette hated her own stupid imagination for conjuring up such self-inflicted spectres. It was broad daylight, the school grounds were full of people, and she was deliberately teasing herself with scary thoughts. Jeanette reached for her shoes, deciding it was time to join the rest of the world.

Her toes had wriggled into one shoe, two fingers hooked into the heel, when she heard the footsteps approaching. She watched curiously as the fine hairs on the back of her bare arm stiffened and began to rise. The crawling sensation on her flesh reached the sharp ridge of her spine.

Jeanette straightened. Listened. Looked towards the dormitory's open doorway.

The footsteps were heavy, almost lumbering. Drawing closer. The sound mesmerising.

Her heart seemed to be beating unusually loudly.

The footsteps stopped and, for a moment, she thought that so, too, had her heart.

Could she really hear the sound of breathing beyond the doorway?

Jeanette slowly rose, the shoe slipping off her foot. She stood by the edge of the bed, barely able to breathe, Pierrot staring blankly up at her, still frozenly weeping.

She did not want to walk towards the doorway; something – perhaps confrontation with her own silly fears – compelled her to. Her stockinged feet were silent on the polished floorboards as she stealthily crept forward, and her hands were clenched into tight fists.

She hesitated just before she reached the open door, suddenly more afraid than she had ever been in her life.

Beyond the opening, something waited.

The dancing and gymnastics display was over. Miss Piprelly had given her usual incisive and succinct oration before introducing *Conseiller* Victor Platnauer, whose discourse was more leisurely and contained at least a modicum of humour. Nevertheless, Childes found it difficult to concentrate on either speech, for he constantly searched the crowd in front of him for some telltale sign, the slightest indication that one person amongst the guests was not quite what he seemed.

He not only observed nothing out of the ordinary, but *felt* nothing that gave cause for concern. All was as it should have been: attentive spectators, splendid weather, although perhaps a trifle too warm, fine exhibitions by the pupils themselves, and adequate speeches.

Prize-giving had just begun when a movement caught his attention. He blinked, not sure it had only been a trick of the light, a reflection in one of the windows across the lawn. Yet something in his vision was not quite as before and that change was sensed rather than seen. His eyes were drawn towards on particular spot high in the building opposite.

A face was at an upstairs window.

Blurred, too far away to be indentifed, but he instinctively knew whose face it was.

His very blood was suddenly chilled.

Stunned, Childes could only sit there, a burdensome dread pinning his body to the seat. His mouth opened to speak, to cry out, but it was as if a fist, a cold, steel, clenched fist, had blocked his throat.

The face was still, and it seemed that its eyes were on him alone.

Then the whitish blur was gone.

Childes staggered to his feet, his limbs feeling almost too heavy to move; somehow he managed to step over the back of the bench. He looked around for Overoy, the semi-paralysis of shock beginning to fade, but failed to locate him in the crowd. He couldn't wait. Something was wrong inside the school, something awful that sent a sharp terror knifing through him.

He skirted the rows of seating and hurried back along the gravel path towards the school building. Applause broke out behind as a pupil went up to receive her prize. Only a few people noticed his rushing figure, one being Overoy, who had been loitering beneath a tree at the edge of the gardens, a position that had provided a good view of the proceedings. Unfortunately, he was on the far side of the lawns and some distance away from the path Childes had taken; the detective decided it would be easier if he went in his own direction and met Childes on the other side of the building. Overoy slipped on his jacket and briskly strode towards the front of the school.

Childes entered the first door he came to, shivering involuntarily as he stepped into the cooler atmosphere. He took a short flight of stairs and found himself in the main building running centrally along the length of the building. The face had been at a window on the third floor where the older girls' dormitories were; he ran down the hallway in the direction of the main stairway, footsteps echoing off the half-panelled walls around him.

He passed the library, the staffroom and parents' waiting room, before reaching the wide stairway where he paused, craning his neck to look into the upper reaches as if expecting to find someone peering down. The stairs were deserted.

Not giving in to his trepidation, Childes began the ascent.

Overoy cursed himself. He had forgotten that the college's layout was not conventional for various wings and annexes had been added over the years. The detective had found himself cut off from Childes by the white structure with its high tower, attached to the older section at right angles. He could either go around and join up with Childes on the other side, or go through. He found the nearest door and went through.

First floor. Childes scanned the corridor leading off in both directions. Empty. But a sound from above.

He leaned over the balustrade. Sharp sounds, scuffling. He looked up.

'*No!*' he shouted. '*No, don't!*'

He ran, mounting the stairs three at a time, using the handrail to pull himself up with each step, not even the exertion overcoming the sudden pallor of his features.

Second floor. The noise from above had ceased. He kept climbing. A kicking sound.

As he went higher, he heard a strangulated wheezing.

Nearly on the third floor and a shadow – an ungainly, lumbering shadow – seemed to dissolve away at the top of the stairs. He thought he heard footsteps, but his attention was on the small thrashing figure dangling over the empty space of the stairwell.

As she swung in his direction, he saw her face was already turning a mottled bluey-purple. Her eyes bulged wildly as she tried to tear at the coloured noose around her neck. The girl's stockinged feet kicked out at the air.

'*Jeanette!*' Childes cried.

He was almost at the top when he tripped, skidding onto the landing and instantly rolling over ignoring the wrenching pain as his knee grazed against wood. He did not even try to rise, but scrabbled on all fours to the balustrade, reaching through, grabbing at the twisting body below, finding her arms, gripping them tightly and supporting her weight.

He thought he sensed movement behind but concentrated on holding the hanging girl. He pulled, but his position was awkward. He could only lie there, sprawled and gasping, straining to maintain his grip.

He could feel her beginning to slip.

'Don't struggle, Jeanette. Just try to keep still . . . please . . . don't fight against me!'

But she could not help herself. Her choking became a wheezing sibilance. Her fingers clawed at her own neck, drawing speckles of blood.

Childes felt the girl slipping from him.

Running footsteps on the stairway. Overoy staring up at them, not breaking his stride, tearing up the stairs with all the speed and strength he possessed.

Childes clung to Jeanette, his legs spreadeagled behind, body flat against the floor and face pressed against the metal struts of the balustrade. As he willed himself not to let go, the struggle slowly becoming too much, an object lying close to the edge of the landing caught his eye.

It was tiny. It was round. It was a moonstone.

Traffic was heavy going through the island's main port-town, and Childes forced himself to drive with extra care, his nerves still ragged and hands less than steady. Beside him, Amy was pensive, obviously shaken by what had happened, yet strangely reserved.

He stopped the Mini at traffic lights on a junction overlooking the harbour. Tourists strolled in the comfortable warmth of early evening, while in the marina yacht crews relaxed on deck, sipping wine and discussing the day's unfortunate lack of sailing breeze. Day-trippers returning from one of the other islands disembarked from a hydrofoil docked at the far end of the long, curving pier. Light green cranes used for loading and unloading cargoes stood along the quaysides near the harbour entrance, jibs leaning at odd angles as if in conversation with each other.

He glanced at Amy. 'You okay?'

'I'm frightened, Jon.' She turned to him briefly, then looked away again.

'You and me both. At least there'll be closer police surveillance here from now on.'

'Poor little Jeanette.'

'She'll recover. Her throat was bruised and her larynx and windpipe badly compressed by the school tie this maniac found to use as a noose, but she'll mend.'

'I'm thinking of the damage to her mind. Will she ever get over such an ordeal.'

The lights changed and Childes took his foot from the brake pedal to ease down on the accelerator, swinging the wheel right to drive along the harbour front.

'She's young, Amy, and time dulls even mental trauma.'

'I hope so, for her sake.'

'Just thank God Overoy got to us – I couldn't have held on much longer.'

'He didn't see . . . anyone else?'

'No. But then he had Jeanette and me to think about. The police think the fire stairs were used as an escape route, and from their exit it would have been easy enough to slip through the school grounds into the woods. La Roche isn't exactly a secure property.'

Past the harbour, the road began to slope upwards into a steep winding hill; soon they were beyond the outskirts of the town.

'I wish your detective had see him,' Amy said abruptly.

Childes cast a quick surprised look at her.

'Did you notice how some of the police were watching you when they were asking you questions?' she went on.

'Yeah, suspiciously. I've come to expect that. No one else caught even a glimpse of this lunatic, least of all Jeanette herself. From what we can gather – and remember, she's still in a state of shock and her throat injuries make talking difficult for her – she came out of the girls' dormitory and someone grabbed her from behind, throwing the tie around her neck before she could cry out. She fought as hard as she could, but was forced along the corridor and tossed over the stairway and left to hang there while her attacker tied her to the balustrade. Can you imagine the strength it would take to do that? I know Jeanette is small for her age, but it would require considerable power to carry out such a feat. If anyone other than Overoy had discovered us, they couldn't be blamed for assuming I was the one trying to hang Jeanette, but even they'd have to admit I don't have the kind of physique to manage anything like that.'

He turned off into the narrower country lanes which would eventually lead them to his cottage. Tall hedges and old walls screened off the countryside around them.

'Why should he come here?' Amy had shifted in her seat now, and her expression was earnest. 'And why pick on the children?'

'To torment me,' he replied grimly. 'It's playing a game, knowing it'll be caught sooner or later, especially now it's trapped on the island, and I don't think it cares one way or the other. But until that happens, there's fun to be had with me.'

'But what *is* the connection? Why you?' She sounded desperate.

'God help me, Amy, I don't know. Our minds have met and that seems to be enough. Maybe I represent a challenge, someone to show off to as well as taunt.'

'You need protection. They've got to keep a watch on you.'

'Overoy might be able to persuade them, but I doubt I'll get anything more than an occasional patrol car passing by the cottage. I think the Island Police will be more concerned with guarding La Roche until the end of term.'

Trees formed a canopy over the roadway, darkening the car's interior. Childes rubbed his temple with one hand, as if to soothe a headache.

'Surely Inspector Overoy will insist you have proper protection.' Shifting light speckles, the evening sun's rays diffused by overhead leaves, patterned Amy's face as they sped along the lane.

'I'm sure he'll do his best, but Robillard told me at the hospital that his force is stretched to the limit because of the tourist season. You know how sharply the crime rate rises during the summer months.'

She became quiet again.

Childes pulled into the side of the road as another car approached from the opposite direction. The driver waved an acknowledgement as he eased past; the Mini picked up speed again.

Amy broke her silence. 'I spoke to Overoy earlier this afternoon, before the speeches: he wondered if Gabby might be like you, Jon – psychic.'

'I've wondered myself. Of course Gabby may have been so overwrought she only *thought* she saw Annabel, although she was adamant when we got to her.'

'When you and Fran got to her?'

'Yes.'

'Where were you both when you heard Gabby call out, Jon?' Her voice was steady, her eyes on the road ahead, but Childes sensed the intent behind the question. 'We've not discussed that particular point before, have we? But you and Fran arrived in Gabby's bedroom together, from what I can gather.'

'Amy . . .'

'I need to know.'

He pulled at the wheel to avoid a branch extending dangerously from a hedge. 'I was sleeping on my own that night in the spare room.' Easier, so much easier, to lie. But he couldn't, not to Amy. 'Fran was upset, she came to me.'

'And you slept with her?'

'It just happened, Amy. I didn't mean it to, I didn't want it to. Believe me, it just happened.'

'Because she was upset?'

'Fran needed comforting. She'd been through an awful lot that day.'

He stole a glance at Amy. She was weeping. Childes reached for her hand. 'There was no meaning to any of it, Amy, just a comforting, nothing more.'

'So, you imagine that makes things okay?'

'No, I was wrong and I'm sorry. I don't want you to think I was involved –'

'I don't know what to think any more. In a way I suppose I understand – you were married to her for a long time. But that doesn't lessen the hurt.' She moved her hand from his. 'I thought you loved me, Jon.'

'You know I do.' There was a gradually expanding pressure inside his head that had nothing to do with the conversation with Amy. 'I . . . I just couldn't turn her away that night.'

'Like doing an old friend a favour?'

'That isn't far from the truth.'

'I hope Fran didn't realize.'

The road dipped, became more gloomy.

'Don't let what happened ruin what there is between us.'

'Can we be the same?'

A crawling sensation at the back of his neck, similar to the feeling earlier in the afternoon when he had looked up to see his face at the window.

'It . . . it wasn't im-important . . .' he stammered, his fingers beginning to tingle on the steering wheel. He felt his shoulder-blades contracting inwards.

'I don't know, Jon. Perhaps if you'd told me before . . .'

'How . . . how could I? How could I have explained?' A heavy cold hand reached from the gloom of the back seats and was resting on his shoulder. But when he looked, there was nothing there.

'Amy . . .'

He saw the eyes peering at him from the rear-view mirror. Wicked, malevolent eyes. Darkly gloating.

Amy looked at him, feeling his tension, seeing the horror on his face. 'Jon, what's –?'

She turned to the empty back seats.

Childes saw the eyes glow larger in the mirror, as the thing – the grinning thing – in the back was leaning forward, was reaching out for him, numbing fingers touching his neck, nails pressing into his skin . . .

The car veered to one side, scraping the hedge.

'*Jon!*' Amy screamed.

The gloating eyes. Steely fingers clamped around his throat. Fetid breath on his cheek. He pulled at the hand and touched only his neck.

The car swerved to the right, hit a low stone wall on that side. Sparks flew off metal as the Mini sheered along the wall's rough face. Bushes and branches lashed at the windows.

Amy grabbed the steering wheel, tried to wrench it to the left, but Childes' grip was solid, frozen. The rending of the metal screeched in her ears.

He could hardly breathe, so constricted was his throat. His right foot was hard against the accelerator as he tried to flee from the snickering thing behind. But how could he escape when it was in the car with him? The road curved. He pulled at the wheel, turned it slightly, just enough to swerve the car, not enough to carry it through the bend. He jammed his foot on the brake pedal, but too late. The car skidded, the wall seemed to rise up and throw itself at them.

They crashed at an angle, the vehicle brought to a shattering halt, Childes thrust against the steering wheel, his arms reflexively bearing his weight, softening the blow.

But Amy had nothing to cling to.

She hurtled forward, the windscreen exploding around her, screaming as she pitched over the car's bonnet to land writhing and bloody beyond the wall.

Childes leaned forward and rested his head in his hands, the dull throbbing inside making him nauseous. There was an aching in his chest, too, and he knew it had been bruised by the steering wheel. But he had been lucky. Amy hadn't.

A double-door swung open at the end of the long corridor and a figure in a white coat came through. The doctor spotted Childes waiting on the cushioned bench and strode briskly towards him, stopping to speak to a passing nurse on the way. The nurse hurried on, disappearing through the same doors from which the doctor had emerged. Childes began to rise.

'Stay there, Mr Childes,' Dr Poulain, called out and, on reaching him, said, 'I could do with a sit-down myself – it's been that kind of day.' He sat, giving a grateful sigh. 'And, it would seem, an eventful day for you.' He scrutinized Childes with a professional eye. 'Time to have a look at you,' he said.

'Tell me how she is, Doctor.'

Poulain ran his fingers through tousled prematurely-grey hair and blinked at the other man through gold-rimmed spectacles.

'Miss Sebire has extensive lacerations to her face, neck and arms, one or two of which I'm afraid will leave small but permanent scars. I had to remove some glass fragment from one of her eyes – no don't be alarmed: they had hardly penetrated the sclerotic coating and were nowhere near the iris or pupil, so her vision shouldn't be affected; the damage there was purely superficial.'

'Thank God.'

'Yes. He is to be thanked. I wish the State government would follow the mainland's example and declare it unlawful not to wear seat-belts in cars, but I'm sure they'll continue to dither for years to come.' He clucked his tongue once and gave a shake of his head. 'Miss Sebire also sustained a fractured wrist as well as severe bruising and lesions to her ribs and her legs. Nevertheless I'd say she's a very lucky girl, Mr Childes.'

Childes released a long-held breath and rested his head in his hands once more. 'Can I see her?' he asked, looking back at the doctor.

'I'm afraid not. I want her to rest so I've given her a sedative; she'll be sleeping by now, I should think. She did ask for you, by the way, and I told her all was well. Miss Sebire seemed happy about that.'

At once Childes felt totally and utterly exhausted. He watched his hands shaking uncontrollably before him.

'I'd like to take you down to an examination cubicle,' Dr Poulain urged. 'You may have been injured more than you know. There's a rather nasty bruise developing on your cheekbone and one side of your lower lip is swelling considerably.'

Childes touched his face and winced when his fingers found the bruising there. 'I must have turned my head when I hit the steering wheel,' he said, gingerly probing the puffed lip.

'Take a deep breath and tell me if it hurts,' Poulain told him.

Childes complied. 'Feels stiff, nothing more,' he said after releasing the air.

'H'mn. No sharp pain?'

'No.'

'Still needs checking.'

'I'm alright. A little shaky, maybe.'

The doctor gave a short laugh. 'More than just a little; your nerves have been shot to pieces. This afternoon, when you came in with the schoolgirl – what was her name? Jeanette, yes Jeanette – I recommended a mild sedative for you, but you refused. Well now I want to suggest something stronger, something you can take when you get home and which will make you sleep soundly.'

'I think I'll sleep okay without any help.'

'Don't be too sure.'

'How long will Amy have to stay here?'

'Much depends on how her eye looks tomorrow. She'll need a couple of days under observation even if all's well in that department.'

'You said –'

'And I meant it. I'm almost positive her eye hasn't been seriously damaged, but naturally we have to take precautions. Incidentally you haven't explained how this accident occurred.' He frowned at the fear that abruptly changed the other man's countenance.

'I can't tell you,' Childes said slowly, avoiding the doctor's gaze. 'Everything happened so fast. I must have been distracted for a moment just as we hit the curve.' What could he say that Poulain would believe? That he had seen eyes reflected in the rear-view mirror, staring eyes that were somehow obscenely evil and which were watching him? That he'd seen someone in the back of the car who wasn't there at all?

'By what?'

Childes looked at the doctor questioningly.

'You were distracted by what?' Dr Poulain persisted.

'I . . . I don't remember. Maybe you were right – my nerves were shot to pieces.'

'That's now. Earlier today you were most definitely shaken up, but not quite that badly. Forgive my curiosity, Mr Childes, but I've known the Sebire family for a number of years and Amy since she was a child, so it goes beyond mere professional interest for me. Had you been quarrelling with her?'

Childes could not answer immediately.

Dr Poulain went on. 'You see, I think you might have to explain to the police the other marks that are beginning to show around your throat. A discoloration that looks to have been caused by a hand – the pressure points are quite clear.'

A wild, momentary panic seized Childes. Could there be such power? Was it possible? He had *felt* the hand, the tightening fingers; yet no one other than Amy had been with him in the car. He forced the panic away: no one – *nothing* – could physically mark another by thought alone. Unless the victim was a helpless accomplice and the injury self-induced.

There was no time for further speculation on his part, or more questions from the doctor, for the lift doors along the corridor opened and Paul Sebire and his wife stepped out. Childes had rung the Sebire home soon after arrival at the hospital and had spoken to Vivienne Sebire, telling her of the accident. Paul Sebire's concern instantly turned to anger when he saw Childes who, with the doctor, had risen from the bench.

'Where is my daughter?' the financier asked Poulain, ignoring Childes.

'Resting,' the doctor replied, then quickly informed them of Amy's condition. Sebire's expression was grim when Poulain had finished. 'We want to see her.'

'I don't think that's wise at the moment, Paul,' the doctor said. 'She'll be asleep and you might be more upset than necessary. In this kind of accident injuries often look much worse than they are. I've just advised Mr Childes here that she shouldn't be disturbed.'

Pure hatred shone from Sebire as he turned to the younger man. Vivienne quickly reached for Childes' arm. 'Are you all right, Jonathan? You didn't say too much on the telephone.'

'I'm fine. It's Amy I'm worried about.'

'This would never have happened if she hadn't been such a fool over you,' snapped Sebire. 'I warned her you were nothing but trouble.'

His wife interposed once more. 'Not now, Paul. I think Jonathan has been through enough for one day. Now Dr Poulain has assured us that Amy will recover without permanent injury –'

'She may have been scarred for life, Vivienne! Isn't that permanent enough?'

Poulain spoke. 'The scarring will be minimal, nothing that minor plastic surgery won't easily repair.'

Childes rubbed at the back of his neck, the movement awkward because of the painful stiffness in his chest. 'Mr Sebire, I want to say how sorry I am.'

'You're sorry. You really think that's good enough?'

'It was an accident that could have . . .' *Happened to anyone?* It was a sentence Childes could not complete.

'Just stay away from my daughter! Leave her alone now before you cause her more harm.'

'Paul,' Vivienne warned, catching her husband's sleeve as he moved towards Childes.

'Please, Paul,' said Dr Poulain, 'there are patients on this floor to consider.'

'This man isn't what he seems.' Sebire stabbed a finger at Childes. 'I sensed it from the very start. You only have to look at what happened this afternoon at the school to realize that.'

'How can you say that?' his wife protested. 'He saved the little girl's life.'

'Did he? Did anyone else see exactly what happened? Perhaps it was the other way round and *he* was attempting to murder her.'

The last remark was finally too much for Childes. 'Sebire, you're being your usual kind of fool,' he said in a low voice.

'Am I? You're under suspicion, Childes, not just from me but from the police as well. I don't think you'll be returning to La Roche or any other school on the island where you can hurt helpless children!'

Childes wanted to lash out at the financier, to vent his frustration on someone, anyone – Sebire would be ideal – to strike back in any way he could. But he didn't have the energy. Instead he turned to walk away.

Sebire clutched his arm, swung him around. 'Did you hear me, Childes? You're finished here on this island, so my advice to you is to get out, leave while you're still able to.'

Childes wearily pulled his arm away. 'You can go to hell,' he said.

Sebire's fist struck his already bruised cheek and he staggered back, caught by surprise, going down on one knee. He heard a jumble of sounds before his head fully cleared – footsteps, raised voices – and regaining his feet seemed an unusually slow and difficult procedure. Someone else's hand under his shoulder helped. Once up, he felt unsteady, but the person by his side supported his weight. He realized it was Overoy who held him and that Inspector Robillard was restraining Sebire from attacking him further.

'I'd have hated to have read your horoscope this morning,' Overoy said close to his ear.

Childes managed to stand alone, although he had to resist the urge to slump onto the nearby bench. His limbs felt sluggish, as if their blood flow had thickened, become viscid. Vivienne Sebire was pale beside her husband, her eyes full of apology. Sebire himself still struggled against restraint, but his efforts were slack, without vigour, the thrust of his anger dissipated in that one blow. Perhaps there was even an element of shame behind the rage.

'Come on, Jon,' Overoy said, using Childes' Christian name for the first time. 'Let's get you out of here. You look as if you could use a good stiff drink and I'm buying.'

'Mr Childes hasn't been examined yet,' the doctor quickly said.

'He looks okay to me,' Overoy replied, gently tugging at Childes' elbow. 'A little battered maybe, but he'll survive. I can always bring him back later if need be.'

'As you wish.' Poulain then spoke to Sebire in an attempt to diffuse the situation. 'Perhaps it would be all right for you to look in on Amy, as long as you're quiet and she isn't disturbed.'

The financier blinked once, twice, his face still a patchy red from fading anger, then finally tore his gaze from Childes. He nodded and Robillard released him.

'Let's go,' Overoy said to Childes, who hesitated, opened his mouth to say something to Amy's mother, but then could not find the words. He walked away, the detective at his side.

Inside the lift, Overoy pressed the G button and said, 'The officer keeping watch on the schoolgirl got word to us that you were back at the hospital. You must like the place.'

Childes leaned back against the panelled wall, his eyes closed.

'We heard you ran off the road.'

'That's right,' was all that Childes would say.

The lift glided to a stop, its door sliding open to admit a porter pushing a wheelchaired patient, a grey-haired woman who gloomily surveyed the arthritically-deformed knuckles of her hands folded in her lap and who barely noticed the men, so quietly immersed in her own infirmity was she. Nobody spoke until the doors opened again at ground level. The porter backed out the wheelchair and whisked away his sombre patient, whistling cheerfully as he went.

'I've hired a car for the weekend so I'll drive us somewhere quiet where we can talk,' said Overoy, holding the doors before they could close on them. 'Even if your car were still driveable, I don't think your capable. Hey, we're here, ground floor.'

Childes was startled. 'What?'

'This is as far as we go.'

'Sorry.'

'You sure you're okay?'

'Just tired.'

'What condition did you leave your car in?'

'Terminal?'

'They'll mend it eventually.'

'So like I said, we'll take mine.'

'Can you get me home?'

'Sure. We need to talk, though.'

'We'll talk.'

They left the hospital building and found Overoy's hire-car parked in a doctor-reserved bay. They climbed in, Childes relieved to sink back into the cushioned passenger seat. Before switching on the engine, the detective said, 'You know I have to leave tomorrow evening?'

Childes nodded, his eyes closed once more.

'So if you've anything more to tell me . . .?'

'It made me crash my car.'

'How do you mean?'

'I saw it looking at me, Overoy. I saw it in the back seat. Only it wasn't really there!'

'Easy now. You thought you saw someone in the back of your car and that's what caused you to crash?'

'It was there. It tried to choke me.'

'Miss Sebire can verify this? She saw this person?'

'I don't know. No, she couldn't have, it was in my own mind. *But I felt its hands choking me!*'

'That isn't possible.'

'I can show you the marks. Dr Poulain noticed them.' He pulled at his shirt collar and Overoy flicked on the interior light.

'Can you see them?' asked Childes, almost eagerly.

'No, Jon. No scratches, no bruising.'

Childes swivelled the rear-view mirror in his direction, stretching his neck towards the glass. The detective was right: his skin was unmarked.

'Get me home,' he said wearily. 'Let's do that talking.'

It stood inside the blackness of the ancient and solitary tower, perfectly still, perfectly silent, relishing the void. The dark oblivion.

The sound of waves crashing against the lower cliffs drifted through openings, echoing around the Martello's circular walls like many whispers. The thing in the dark imagined they were the hushed voices of those lost to the sea, forever mourning in their starless limbo. The thought was amusing.

Strong stenches hung in the air inside the crumbling tower – urine, faeces, decay – the abuse of those who cared little for monuments and even less for their history; but these odours did not offend the figure lurking in the comforting blackness. The corruption was enjoyed.

Somewhere in the night a tiny creature screamed, prey to another more swift and more deadly.

It smiled.

The forces were building. The man was part of that building. Yet he did not know. He would. Before very long.

And for him, it would be too late.

Estelle Piprelly searched the darkness, the incomplete moon consumed by thick clouds so that little was visible below her window. The lawns were still there, the trees were still there – and the sea still battered the lower cliff faces – but for all she knew there might be no existence beyond the confines of her room. So acute was her aloneness that life itself could well have been an illusion, a fantasy invented by her own mind.

Yet that could easily be borne, for loneliness was nothing new to her, despite crowded days, duty-filled hours; it was this new, threatening emptiness arousing a deeper, soul-touched, apprehension that was hard to bear. For the night's mood presaged menace.

She turned away, leaving the soft ghost of her reflection, a slight bending of her famously ramrod-straight spine appearing to change her character, render her frail. There was an aimlessness to her step as she paced the room which was part of her living quarters in the college, a listlessness in her movement. Lines frowned her face and her hands curled into tight balls inside the long, knitted cardigan she wore. Her lips were less firm, less severe than usual.

It was not just the sable bleakness of the night that haunted La Roche's principal, nor the unsettling quietness of late hours: Death had bid her a mocking hello that day. And its unholy visage had been present in the faces of a certain number of her girls. Just as many years before, when a mere child who could not understand but who could be *aware* had observed the imminent mortality of certain of the island's occupying forces, she had now discerned the death masks of her own pupils.

The disquiet weakened her, forcing her to sit. On the mantleshelf over an unlit fire, a dome-shaped clock, its face set in lacquered wood, counted away the moments as if they were the beats of an expiring heart. She pulled the cardigan tight around her, clutching the wool to her throat, the chill from inside her rather than the air around.

Miss Piprelly, swiftly aged and almost tremulous, pushed her thoughts outwards, wanting to – desperate to – perceive, but knowing ultimately that the strength was not within her, the faculty not that great. By no means comparable to Jonathan Childes'. How strange that he himself did not know his own potential.

The enigma of the man frightened her.

She turned as a breeze brushed against the window. Had she expected Death himself to be peering in?

Miss Piprelly wondered how secure the school was. True enough, a policeman guarded the main gate, frequently leaving his vehicle to prowl the grounds, checking doors, windows, shining his torch into surrounding shrubbery. But could a solitary policeman prevent somebody from entering one of the buildings, with their numerous access points, the irregularity of the complex itself making surveillance difficult and providing easy concealment for skulking figures. She had spoken with Inspector Robillard that very afternoon, voicing her concern (and, of course, unable to explain the reason) and he had assured her that the area in and around the college was regularly patrolled, had been since the attempt on Jeanette's life. He understood her anxiety perfectly well, yet felt it was misplaced: he doubted the attacker would return to La Roche now that the police had been alerted. The principal wished with all her heart that she could accept the policeman's calm assurances.

Her thoughts dwelt on Jonathan Childes once more – as they often had over the past few days. Reluctantly, Miss Piprelly had asked him to stay away from the college – no, she had insisted, he was not on suspension, neither was he under suspicion; but his presence at La Roche appeared to have put her girls at risk, and their welfare must always be her prime concern. She, Victor Platnauer, and several other members of the governing board had discussed the matter with Inspector Robillard and it was deemed wise, for the time being, that Childes should be kept away from the school (she had not mentioned that Victor Platnauer had insisted Childes be instantly dismissed). As there were less than two weeks left of summer term, it did not seem unreasonable that Childes should accede to their request. He had. And without hesitation.

When she had called him to her study that Monday morning, just three days ago, his intensity had been disconcerting. He had hardly seemed to hear her words, yet had not been inattentive. His mind was grappling with inner confusions, while still acutely aware of everything around him. Of course he was distressed not only by Jeanette's terrible ordeal, but also by the injuries to Miss Sebire in the car crash on the same day; however, she felt his inward preoccupation had little to do with shock. The man was seeking – she had *felt* his probing inside her own head – but his searches were random, speculative. He had recognized the gift in her, although he had not yet spoken of it. At times she sensed a vibration all around his form, a psychic field constantly expanding and contracting. Its fluctuating levels disconcerted her, yet he appeared unaware of these invisible emanations.

Her body juddered as the terrible violence to come, a jagged cutting thought only, pierced her brain like a heated knife. Her mind no longer lingered on the days past. Now was the real nightmare.

Some alien presence was inside the school.

With the notion, the shadows of the room pressed in closer, the ticking of the clock grew louder, both seeking to intimidate, to influence reason.

Miss Piprelly's initial reaction was to call the island's police headquarters and she actually pushed herself from the chair – *pushed herself because the pressure from the enclosing shadows and the thunderous ticking of the clock sought to smother all movement* – and walked – *staggered?* – over to the telephone. But her hand stayed on the receiver, did not lift it.

What could she tell them? *Please come, I'm alone and frightened and somebody is with me here in the school, someone who wishes us harm, and my girls are sleeping and I've seen death in their faces and they're so young, so unknowing, their lives unlived, and they have no idea of the danger . . .!* Could she tell the police that?

Had she heard a break-in? they would ask. Their man had reported nothing unusual, but they would radio through, ask him to check the grounds, more closely, report back to them. No need to worry, Miss Piprelly (an old spinster grown frightened of her own shadow), all was well, their man was on duty, call again later if you're still anxious.

She could lie, *pretend* to have heard noises. And if they arrived in force to find no sign of an intruder, what then? Raised eyebrows, condescending smiles? Mocking chuckles on the return journey?

That consideration straightened her back, set her face into firmer lines once more. She would not be belittled by the apprehensions of one night. Miss Piprelly headed for the door. She would look for herself and on finding the *slightest* evidence that all really was not well, she would contact police headquarters. The barest indication . . .

But her resolve faltered for an instant when she opened the door and fear touched her like a skeletal hand from the darkness.

Childes awoke.

There had been no nightmare, no chasing demons, no horror to jolt him from sleep. His eyes had merely opened and he was awake.

He lay in the darkness and listened to the night. Nothing there to disturb him. Only the wind, a breeze, a guileless whispering of air.

But still he rose from the bed, naked and quickly chilled, to sit there on the edge, unsure, uncertain of the tingling expectation that gnawed at him. The outline of the nearest window was a grey patch among the black. Mellowed patterns of ragged cloud edges shifted in the frame.

After fumbling at the bedside table for glasses, Childes slid them on and went to the window.

His hands clutched at the sill as something cold and vicious inside his chest clamped hard.

In the distance, near the clifftops, La Roche glowed red.

Unlike before, there was no setting sun to flush the school's buildings. This time, flames coloured the walls as they fluttered upwards from windows to lick at the clouded sky.

As Estelle Piprelly descended, her footsteps unusually loud in the emptiness of the corridors and stairway, an unexpected smell wafted upwards to meet her. A smell unfamiliar only because it was not in context with the school's normal odours of age-mellowed wood, polish, and the constant but subtle taint of transient human bodies. Life itself.

This was not part of that common texture.

She paused, one hand on the thick stair-rail. Listened to a silence that was more ominous than peaceful. The aroma, still mild because its origin was not close, was faintly cloying and reminded her of an outhouse in the school grounds where garden machinery was stored. A small, ramshackle brick building full of tools, lawn-mowers, hedge cutters and the like, which always reeked of earth, oil and . . . petrol.

Now that she knew the source her disquiet increased tenfold, for the malodorous scent was a precursor, an indication that perhaps her own intuitive dread was not unjustified. The prevailing urge was to retrace her steps, climb the stairway to the top floor where her charges slept, rouse the girls and lead them from this unsafe place. But another impulse weighed against that course of action. An irrestible force lured her downwards.

Curiosity, argued her own rationalising thoughts. A need to substantiate her suspicions so that she would not be accused of crying 'wolf'. But a tiny voice, a whisper almost, tucked somewhere deep in her consciousness, hinted otherwise. This voice alluded to a morbid compulsion to confront the ghost that had constantly haunted her in the unknowing faces of those soon to die.

She descended further.

On the last step, the hallway widening, corridors stretching from right to left, Miss Piprelly lingered once more, sniffing the air and wrinkling her nose at the now powerful fumes. The floorboards were damp with sleek liquid. Light came from the stairway behind, so that the farther reaches of the corridors were but gloomy tunnels. The large double-door entrance to the school building was directly opposite the stairway, a distance of perhaps thirty feet. A bank of light-switches was on the wall next to those doors.

Thirty feet was not too far. So why did the expanse appear so formidable? And why the graduating blackness so menacing?

Because she had become a silly old maid who would soon begin looking beneath the bed each night, she scolded herself, but knowing that was not the reason. The darkness *was* menacing, the distance from there to the doors *was* immense.

And she had no alternative but to cross. Returning upstairs would mean the spilled petrol would be lit. Turning on the lights might possibly flush out the intruder, hopefully frighten him off. At least the lights would attract the policeman on watch.

One brown, chunky-heeled shoe touched the floor. The other followed. Miss Piprelly began the long journey across the hallway.

Again, only halfway there, she halted. Had she heard something, or had she *felt* it? Was there someone in the corridor to her left? Was there a shadow moving among the other shadows? Miss Piprelly journeyed on, the thin layer of inflammable liquid spread over the floorboards sucking at her feet. Her pace quickened as she neared the doors.

There was someone lurking in the covering gloom, someone who wished ill on her and her school. The sense of it was overwhelming, tightening her chest so that her breaths came in short gasps. Her heart raced with her legs, her hands stretched outwards long before she was in the proximity of the switches. The *presence* was closer, drawing near, still unseen but undoubtedly reaching for her, soon to touch, soon to feel.

She had to get out!

She would find the policeman, call him to her, inform him of the intruder inside. He would know what to do, he would prevent the petrol from being lit! He would save her!

She was at the doors, almost crashing into them, scrabbling hurriedly for the handles, the lock, sobbing now with relief that she was there, soon to be free from the impending threat behind.

She knew it was close, but would not turn to look, sure that the prickling of her neck was due to this intruder's cold breath.

A vague wondering at why the doors were already unlocked, and then she was twisting the handles, a small cry of triumph mixed with fright escaping her. She pulled the doors inwards. Chilled air ruffled in.

And the shape, a dark blankness against the night, was standing before her on the porch steps *outside*, unmoving and impassable.

Miss Piprelly's legs buckled and her voice was merely a sighing moan as the shape reached for her.

Childes brought the hire-car to a lurching halt outside the tall open gates of La Roche, hands locked tight on the wheel and foot hard on the brake pedal. Despite the steadying grip, his body shot forward with a jolt, then rocked backwards with the motion of the vehicle.

His eyes widened as he stared down the long driveway, lit by the Renault's headlamps, at the college buildings.

They were darkened and impassive, the whiteness of the main building reduced to a heavy grey by the cloud dense sky. No flames leapt from the windows, no redness scorched the interiors. There was fire.

He hadn't heard sirens during the brief, frantic journey from his home to the school, hadn't met any other vehicles similary racing to La Roche. The roads were deserted. And why should they be otherwise at this late hour when there really wasn't any blaze?

He shook his head, bewildered. Then saw the patrol car waiting just inside the gateway, lights and engine switched off. Childes shifted into first and gentled the Renault through the gates as if the police vehicle were some slumbering animal he had no wish to disturb. He pulled up alongside. The car was empty.

Wasn't it?

Then why the compulsion to leave his own car and look through the window of the other? And why the counter-compulsion to turn the hire-car around and flee from these forbidding, ill-defined grounds, their mooonlight mastered by massed, scarcely-moving clouds?

Why indeed? spoke a low, mocking voice somewhere outside his own dimension.

The silvery patterns of cloud edges streaked the black sky like stilled lighting; a lively breeze swept in from the sea to unsettle leaves and branches; the headlights beamed a vignetted tunnel towards the tall, weighty buildings. Beyond any doubt, Childes knew he would look inside the patrol car, then drive up to the school itself, as though the rules had already been laid down for him, the pattern already set. His will was still his own, and he could deviate from the course at any time he chose, but a certain destiny had been predetermined. He would follow it through, but would not succumb. He prayed he would not succumb.

Childes left the Renault and walked round its bonnet to the other vehicle. He peered through the open window.

The policeman had slid down in his seat, his knees high behind the steering wheel. For one hysterically funny moment, Childes thought the man had fallen asleep, but the black stain spreading from his throat like an infant's bib onto his light-coloured shirt told otherwise. Even so, he reached in and nudged the policeman, careful not to touch the slick mess that was still seeping outwards. There was no response to the touch, as he knew there wouldn't be. He pulled at the handle and opened the door a fraction, just enough for the interior light to come on.

The uniformed man's chin rested on his chest so that the neck wound could not be seen. He was plump for a policeman, the overhead light throwing a shiny highlight on his balding head. His eyes were partially closed as though he were looking down, contemplating the inky crimson spoiling his shirt. Hands resting placidly at his sides, fingers unclawed, relaxed, they looked as if death had arrived too quickly for combat. He appeared in repose, unmindful of his fate.

Childes closed the door, its soft *clunk* the sound of a coffin lid falling into place. He leaned against the roof of the car, head bowed onto forearms. The victim, unaware, extreme violence rare in his career on the island, had been watching the school, the car's side-window open so that any inconsistent sounds could be heard. Probably his attention had been focused upon the complex of buildings ahead, or/as well as the shrubbery surrounding them, not – for a few moments, at least – on the roadway behind. A knife, a razor – a sharp steel blade of some kind – had quietly thrust through the opening to slice his throat, deep and neat, the movement taking no more than two, perhaps three seconds. Had the policeman cried out, the noise would have been no more than a throttled gurgling, all that the wound would have allowed.

It was here, in the school. The thing he knew only as Moon.

The notion curdled inside his lower stomach and the walls of his lungs became hardened, stiff, barely able to pump air. He raised his forehead from his arms and looked down the long drive, gravelly surface traced by the light beams, towards the buildings that now stood gaunt and sullen. Overcast.

The agonized moan was inside his head but did not come from him. It belonged to someone behind the doors of the tallest, grey building. Someone beyond those stout walls was in mortal terror.

And something *in there was enjoying that terror.*

Now, in the lower-floor windows of La Roche's main building, Childes saw a rapidly spreading orange glow, the fire no longer a precognitive vision of his mind, but there in reality before him.

Miss Piprelly lay on the floor, unable to move, her head twisted at a grotesquely odd angle.

She was conscious and she was terribly afraid. And she was aware in a strangely detached fashion – for there was no pain, only paralysis – that her neck was broken, the bones snapped easily by rough, powerful hands that had reached for her from the darkness outside as her legs had given way. In that one terrifying instant of confrontation, the principal had realized that the intruder had hidden outside the doors at the sound of her approach.

Miss Piprelly had not seen her assailant, had perceived only an image of bulk, *black, unremitting bulk*, that shuffled forward to ensnare. Stale, noxious breath. A raspy, grunting satisfaction. The twisting – *the snapping* – of her own neck column when her head, viced between palms as hard and grazing as rock, was sharply turned sideways. The ungainly moving away of the raven form, *clump, clump*, on bare floorboards. Its return. The splashing of liquid over her clothes, her body, smooth coldness running through her hair; shutting her eyes against the wetness.

Lying there, limbs useless, her voice only a weakened garbling. The stinging of her eyes, as fluid drained from her forehead into them. Blinking – at least she could blink her eyelids – clearing her sight, but the burning sensation still there, impeding her vision.

Then just able to see the lumbering shape at the end of the corridor, and crying out in dread, the sound inside her own head, unable to be released.

The distant flare that was a match being struck. Its slow, plunging fall to the floor, the bright effulgence as the petrol exploded into flame.

The creature lit by the fire, smiling . . . grinning . . . grinning at her!

The flame snaking fast – so very, very fast – along the corridor towards her own soaked, unmoving body . . .

The fire was all but consuming the ground floor, the conflagration widening before Childes' eyes as he raced towards the buildings, flames eager to gorge themselves on the old, dry timber inside. Window after window became a fierce reddish orange. At the blaze's core glass had already began to burst outwards with the heat. As he drew near he saw the shimmering glow was quickly moving upwards to the first floor. Ringing of alarm bells, set off by smoke sensors, came faintly to him.

His footing almost skidded away as the surface beneath changed from gravel to night-damp grass; he recovered, scarcely breaking stride, and pounded across the circular lawn of the school's turnaround drive. La Roche's sculptured founder impassively watched the burning, his countenance taking on a ruddy glow.

Childes leapt the few steps to the main entrance, expecting the double-doors to be locked, yet, because they were the easiest access to the stairway, having to try that way first. He pushed at a metal handle and to his surprise one half of the doors swung inwards. A scorching blast of heat sent him spinning sideways, his back coming to rest against the closed section.

Shielding his eyes against the searing glare, his brown-rimmed glasses also acting as a thin barrier, Childes took a fast look back inside, skin on his hands and face immediately scalded by the exposure, breath torn, it seemed, from his throat by molten fingers. He staggered away again, varnish on the wood he had rested against beginning to bubble and crack, the door ready to ignite.

The stairway was ablaze. And closer, near to the entrance and within the flames, something black sizzled. Only briefly did he wonder whose body it was.

Childes wanted to run, to leave the grounds, to get away from there; afraid for himself, yet aware of the danger for those on the upper floors, the boarders and few members of staff who lodged at La Roche. The alarm bells would have roused them by now and they would be confused, panic-striken, their first thought to escape by the easily-accessible main stairway, not knowing its lower reaches were already destroyed, perhaps fright and haste overcoming the carefully indoctrinated fire-drill they had rehearsed so often.

Before running to the rear of the building where the fire-exit was located, Childes reached into the inferno with one hand and grasped the door's handle, shouting out in pain at the touch of scorched metal. Forcing himself to maintain a grip, he banged the door shut, knowing it was a small gesture to prevent a draught being sucked in to aid the flames in their journey up the staircase, but hoping the action might make some difference. The door bounced against its partner, the wood already warped from its original shape. Childes left it and jumped down the steps, running alongside the school, passing dazzling windows, ducking as glass shattered.

Turning the corner, coolness hit him like air from an opened freezer door, changing perspiration on his face into cold liquid drops. He was in darkness, no fire-glow on that side – *yet*. Areas of reflected light began appearing on the lawn as lights were switched on in dormitories and corridors. Feeling the wall to his left for guidance, Childes hurried forwards, turning a corner again, soon reaching the fire-door itself. Finding it already open, a glass pane smashed at waist level where a hand could be put through to pressure the lock bar inside.

Childes wasted no time pondering the who or the wherefore: he pushed his way in, reaching for the light-switch he knew to be nearby.

Acrid smoke had searched out that part of the building although, as yet, the swirling clouds were thin and nebulous. The alarms, so much louder inside, served to stoke his fear with their incessant shrill, but he forced himself onto the stone steps, taking them three at a time, jangled nerves reminding him a similar upward flight only a few days before. This time, though, there was more than one life at stake.

Smoke grew thicker as he went and the crackling rumble of the fire itself could be heard. Then voices, footsteps descending, growing louder. More light from above, glimpses of movement on the stairs. Thank God, they were on their way down!

He paused on the first floor, both hands resting on the iron stair-rail, and scanned the corridor running off from that landing. The far end was an inferno, rolling flames filling the space from floor to ceiling. Sweltering heat roared from the passageway to wash over him.

Onwards. Foolish to stop, even for a second. Foolish to take time to consider the danger.

The voices were near, now perhaps only one flight above, and Childes continued to climb, smoke beginning to sting his eyes, the air itself becoming parched, somehow burnt dry, even though the heart of the blaze was some distance away. It made him wonder how much ground the fire had gained below. The first stumbling figures appeared above and he quickly covered the distance between them.

A girl of no more than ten or eleven tumbled into his arms, her face streaked with tears, the hem of her nightdress flapping loosely over bare ankles and feet.

'You're safe,' he told her, looking over her head towards the other girls crowding behind. 'You'll soon be outside.'

'Mr Childes, Mr Childes, is that you?' came a breathless voice from somewhere in their midst.

A figure, taller than most of the girls, worked her way through. Like the pupils, she was in night attire and she clutched her dressing gown around her as if for protection against the mounting heat. Incongruously, she wore normal flat-heeled walking shoes. For a moment, he thought it might have been La Roches's principal, but he quickly recognized Harriet Vallois, history tutor and one of the house-mistresses.

'Are all the girls out of their dormitories?' he asked, shouting over the noise of the alarms and frightened girls; some of the girls were coughing into cupped hands because of the worsening atmosphere.

'Matron and Miss Todd are checking,' the teacher replied, a quivering of her lips suggesting that she, too, was close to tears. 'They sent me with this group.'

He clasped her shoulder, more to steady her than to comfort. 'Is Miss Piprelly with them?'

'N-no. I passed her rooms and knocked at her door, but there was no reply. I assumed she would have gone straight up to the dormitories, but ... there was no sign of her!'

The burning thing in the hallway!

Childes shuddered. The body might well have been that of the arsonist, destroyed by its own intent, caught in its own trap. He couldn't *really* be sure that it had been Estelle Piprelly lying there, a frizzling lump of blackened meat; he couldn't really be sure, yet somehow he was, somehow he had no doubts.

Harriet Vallois was looking back up the stairway, her eyes wild, desperate.

'Get the girls out!' he snapped, sharply increasing his grip on her arm. The sudden pain made her spin round towards him once more.

'Get them out!' he repeated, pulling her forward and handing over the girl still clinging to him. 'Keep them all together and don't stop for anything.' Then, closer to her ear, 'You haven't got much time.'

Her alarm increased. 'Won't you help me?' she pleaded.

Oh yes, he would love to help by leading her and the girls away from that place of impending death in which a body lay crisped and inhuman in the main hallway, where God-only-knows-what might still be roaming the corridors and where ravenous flames ate away the very innards of the building.

'You'll be okay,' he reasoned with her, 'there isn't much further to go. I've got to try and help those still left upstairs.'

He gave her a firm but gentle shove downwards and reached for the nearest girls, encouraging them to follow. The rest quickly fell into step and he urged them to take care not to lose their footing, reassuring each one as they went by. He estimated that at least thirty had passed him and more were continuing to trickle down. Childes had no idea how many of La Roches's three hundred pupils were boarders, but a calculated guess put the figure at sixty or so. Apart from Estelle Piprelly, only two staff members and the matron were in charge of the girls at night. His pace quickened even though the effort of climbing was becoming harder, the air more difficult to breathe. The higher he went, the more dense the rolling smoke became. The soot-filled fumes were like some insidious scout, exploring and seeking out, giving gleeful warning of its master's seething approach. Louder, also, was the grumbling resonance of the fire itself, with timbers cracking somewhere deep within the furnace like rifle shots. And overall were the stridulous alarms inciting their own special panic.

Beginning to choke, he drew out a handkerchief and held it to his mouth. More girls appeared, their spluttering cries preceding them.

'Keep going!' he shouted to them, though they did not need his bidding. Two older girls were supporting another whose hysteria had virtually rendered her helpless. Childes was tempted to lift the screeching girl and carry her down himself, but realized that despite their difficulties the trio would make it to the exit.

Someone staggered into him and he held out his arms to prevent the figure from falling.

'Eloise!' he said, recognizing the other teacher who lodged at the school.

Miss Todd gaped at him, bewildered, unsure, her plump chest rasping noisily as she sucked in spoilt air.

'How many are left up there?' he yelled close to her face.

She shook her head, impatient to be away.

'*For God's sake, try to think!*'

'Let me go,' she begged. 'There's nothing we can do!'

'How many?' he insisted, gripping her flailing arms tightly.

'We looked, we searched! Some were so frightened they were hiding in the bathrooms. Others were screaming from the windows.'

'Did you get them all out?'

'*Oh let me go let me go!*'

He held her rigid. 'Did you get them all out?'

Girls pushed past, all of them clinging to the stair-rail for guidance, shoulders jerking and eyes streaming tears. Their screams had merged into a kind of wailing. The teacher broke away from Childes and joined them in their flight, her arms going round the shivering shoulders of one, giving comfort in spite of her own desperate fear.

She turned to call back to him. 'Some of the girls went in the other direction, towards the main staircase! Matron went after them!' Then she hurried away, pushed on by those behind.

Childes wasted no more time. Covering his mouth with the handkerchief, he mounted the remaining flights, passing no one else on the way. He had lost count, but he suspected that most of the boarders were on their way down.

He arrived at the top floor where the smoke was almost overpowering. His eyes were blurred, his throat painfully dry. With dismay he saw that the flames had reached that level, for there was a glow from further down the corridor he now faced. It was considerably softened by the whirling haze, but he was sure its source was the other stairway.

Bending low to avoid the worst of the smoke, Childes ran along the passageway, looking into dormitories as he passed.

A bout of coughing made him clutch his chest and sink to his knees. Realizing he was near one of the washrooms, he crawled inside to find the air much clearer. He staggered to a basin and turned on a tap, removing his spectacles and splashing water on his face. He grabbed a towel, throwing it into the basin to soak, then wrapped it around his neck like a scarf, pulling the sodden material up over his nose and chin.

First checking the toilet cubicles and bathrooms, he went back out into the corridor, the wet towel serving as a mask against the fumes. The fire's sound had become a low roar and the heat was stifling as he drew near the main stairwell. He was about the enter another dormitory when a different noise caught his attention, faint under the mêlée of alarm bells and burning, splintering wood, but distinct from them. The screaming seemed to come from the heart of the blaze itself.

Pulling the towel over his head and holding one end across most of his face, Childes moved along, touching the wall on that side for support as much as guidance.

Sparks leapt upwards from the stairwell, shooting into the air like volcanic debris, while writhing flames were consuming tongues, licking at walls, woodwork, rolling in white-hot balls towards the ceiling. The landing was not yet ablaze, but the flooring was beginning to smoulder, smoke rising like steam.

Childes went to the rail, quickly pulling back his hand when he touched the peeling wood.

The girls were bunched in a corner just below, opposite where he stood, the stairs ahead of them in flames. As were the stairs behind. They had attempted to leave that way and had been stopped by a rapidly advancing wall of fire. When they had rushed back up, they had found their line of retreat cut off by flames that had leapt ahead of them, currents of displaced, turmoiled air sweeping them upwards.

Several of the girls appeared to be unconscious, while the rest huddled or pushed against each other, hands and arms covering their faces from the approaching heat. There were six or seven girls down there (they were grouped so closely, it was impossible to count) and the matron was with them, her back to the fire, arms stretched out as if to protect her charges.

Childes moved around to the edge of the stairs, descending a little way, but the heat soon drove him back. A blazing impenetrable wall blocked the wide staircase. Maybe he could leap through the flames onto the landing below where the girls crouched, but what good would that do him? *What good would that do the girls?* He hurried back to balcony.

'Matron!' he called. 'Mrs Bates, up here!'

He saw the matron raise her head and he yelled again.

Her face turned in his direction, looked up. She saw him. Childes thought there was a sudden look of hope in her expression, but shimmering heat distorted everything.

The matron left the girls, advancing only a few feet to the edge of the landing. 'Is – is that you, Mr Childes? Oh, thank God! Please help us, Mr Childes, please get us away from here!'

Several of the night-clad girls were staring up at him now, although they still cowered back in the corner.

Help them, yes; but how? *But how?* He couldn't get down to them, and they couldn't reach him.

The matron was bent over, retching and choking, the air itself boiling. She stumbled back, away from the inferno. A sudden flare-up of yellow-white light sent Childes reeling back, too. Flames shot towards the ceiling, biting into the rafters there. They just as quickly diminished, disappearing back into the well to become part of the broiling mass. The rafters, however, had not been left unscathed; they had begun to burn fiercely. There was very little time left.

A ladder might have helped, angled between the balcony and the landing below. But there was no time to go back down and find one. A rope, then. They could loop one end beneath their arms and he could pull them up, one by one. How many could he save before his strength gave out, though? And where the hell would he find a rope in the dormitories.

'*Help us!*' came the cry again. The girls, too, had begun to call out to him.

'Keep away from the stairs!' he shouted, seeing that some of them had ventured forward to stand by the matron. Childes recognized Kelly among the group, her face darkened with smoke-grime, tear trails descending through the dirt on her cheeks. She stretched out a beseeching hand towards him, a vulnerable weeping child, and the memory of a charred and gristled arm hit him, freezing his movement, shocking him rigid.

He moaned, swaying there, the towel – now almost dry, its moisture sucked by the heat – falling limply around his shoulders. Thick, choking smoke weaved and dodged around him, tufts of fire sprang up between the floorboards. Shrieks brought him to his senses and a splintering crashing of wood made him peer over the balustrade again.

A section of stairway had fallen inwards, leaving a deep, seething chasm before the landing on which the group sheltered. The girls and the matron had retreated into the corner once more, where they huddled together, those on the outside beating at the air with clawed fingers as if they could push back the terrible engulfing heat. More had slumped against the companions.

'I'm going to get something to lower down to you!' he yelled. 'I'll be back soon!' He did not know if they even heard. And would it be a useless gesture anyway? Could he really haul every one of them across that inferno? Childes pushed the begging questions from his mind.

He could feel the scorching heat of the floor through the soles of his shoes as he scrambled away. A thick swirling fug filled the corridor. He sensed the building pressure – like steam trapped inside a boiler because of a faulty valve-release –

the atmosphere itself seeming to become combustible, ready to explode into one huge incandescent fireball. He sucked in oxygen-starved air and was instantly seized by a choking fit. His lungs felt scorched dry.

Childes did not stop. On hands and knees, chest and shoulders heaving, he crawled onwards, his palms tender against the hot timber, until he found an open doorway. He scrambled through, kicking the door shut behind, rolling onto his back, allowing himself the briefest, gasping respite. The haze was not as thick inside the dormitory, although the rows of beds were seen through a swift-curling fog. Pushing himself to his knees, he reached for the nearest bed and pulled off sheets.

Still crouched, he tied two sheets together, scrambled to another bed and tore off more, refusing to accept the hopelessness of his efforts.

It was when he was tying one of these to the two already joined, his eyes blurred, a pain in his chest as if a knife was lodged sideways there, that Childes heard the muffled sobbing.

He looked around, unsure of the source. He heard only the crackling rumble of the fire. Bending low to the floor, he searched beneath the beds and found no crouched figures. He completed knotting the sheets, then stumbled towards the closed door.

The sobbing again.

He whirled, his back slamming against the door, and scanned the room, eyes skimming over rumpled bedclothes, discarded dolls, past crazily whirling mobiles, over posters that were beginning to curl downwards from their corners. His glasses were grimed with soot and his own perspiration; using a corner of sheeting, he wiped them clean, still listening for the sobbing as he did so. The sound was soft, quiet, but had become more distinct from the other noises. His gaze came to rest on a store cupboard set in the wall at the far end of the room.

No time. There was no time to look. He had to get back to the girls on the landing.

Nevertheless, dropping the sheets, he ran the length of the dormitory.

He pulled open to cupboard doors and the two whimpering, sobbing girls, crouched there in the darkness among hockey sticks and tennis rackets, hanging raincoats draped over their heads and shoulders, screamed and cowered away from him.

Childes reached in and the girl whose shoulder he touched flinched and screamed even louder, forcing herself deeper into the recess. He took her arm and pulled her away from her companion, using his other hand to bring her face round towards him. He just had time to see she was one of the juniors when the lights went out.

He lost her in the darkness and screams pierced all sides. Childes dropped to his knees and groped forward, finding their shivering bodies and encompassing them with his arms.

'Don't be frightened,' he said as soothingly as possible, conscious of the tightness in his own voice. 'The fire's burnt into wires downstairs, that's why the lights have gone out.' Still they pulled away from him. 'Come on now, you know me. It's Mr Childes. I'm going to take you out of here, okay?' He tugged at them, but still they resisted. 'All your friends are waiting outside for you. They'll be getting anxious by now, won't they?' *The others on the landing – Oh God, he had to get back to them before it was too late!* 'Come on, we'll just go right downstairs, then you can tell your friends how exciting it was. Just a quick walk downstairs and we'll be out.'

The scared little voice fought hard to stem the sobs. 'The . . . the . . . stairs are all on . . . f-fire.'

He stroked her hair, pressing close. 'We'll use the other staircase. Don't you remember fire-drill and the stone steps that lead out of the building? They can't burn, so there's nothing to be frightened of there. And you remember me, don't you? Mr Childes? I bet you've come into my computer classroom at some time to have a look, haven't you?'

As if by silent mutual consent, they threw themselves into his arms and he held their small, trembling bodies close, feeling the dampness of their tears on his neck, against his chest. Without further words, he lifted the two girls and made his way back between the short rows of beds, carrying them on either arm, their combined weight hardly encumbering him for those few moments. He stumbled once, twice, using a red-glowing line he knew to be from beneath the closed door as a guide.

Yet another sound now mingled with the general muffled roar, this one distant, beyond the school itself, and growing louder with each passing second. Approaching sirens.

The two schoolgirls, one in pyjamas, the other in an ankle-length nightie, buried their faces against him, bouts of coughing jerking their bodies.

'Try not to breathe in too deeply,' he told them, swallowing with some difficulty to relieve his own parched throat. The towel had fallen from his shoulders and become lost.

When they were at the door, Childes put down the girls and fumbled around the floor for the discarded bedsheets. His fingers closed around the material and he drew it up, remaining on one knee, the two frightened girls staying close.

He forced himself to speak easily, discarding any hint of panic.

'I know you both, I'm sure, but for the life of me I can't remember your names. So how about telling me, eh?'

'Sandy,' a quivery voice said close to his ear.

'That's nice. And what about you?' he asked, pulling the other to him. 'Aren't you going to tell me yours?'

'R – Rachel,' came the stuttered reply.

'Good girl. Now listen, Sandy and Rachel: I'm going to open this door and go outside, but I want you to wait here for me.'

The fingers dug into him.

'I promise it'll be alright. I'll only be gone for a short while.'

'*Please don't leave us here!*'

He couldn't tell which one had cried out. 'I've got to help some of the others, some of the older girls. They're not far away, but they're in trouble. I've got to go and fetch them.' He pulled their arms free, hating what he was doing, but having no choice. They struggled to keep hold of him, but he stood, the sheets over one shoulder, and felt for the door knob. Was it warmth from his own hand, or was the metal really hot? He yanked open the door.

To squint against the torrid glare, his skin contracting against the harsh blast of heat that swept in.

Shielding his eyes, he peered into the corridor and was dismayed at how much more the fire had spread.

The awful, splintering roar came just as he stepped out from the dormitory. No shrieks and no cries for help accompanied that sound – at least, none that he heard – but he knew its source, he *knew exactly* what had happened.

Yet he had to make sure. He had to be certain. If there was the slightest chance –

'*Stay there!*' he screamed at the two clutching, terrified ten-year-olds. He ran, crouching low, ignoring the peeling sensation of his skin, knowing it was only drawing tight around his bones, not really breaking, that it only felt that way. He bumped off the wall as he ran, the tied sheets trailing behind.

Childes reached the wider area overlooking the main staircase, only a few areas of unburnt flooring left. Overhead, curious rolling waves of fire swept the ceiling.

He could no longer touch the balustrade that was part of the balcony over the stairs, for the wooden beam was engulfed, a burning log amidst a greater fire. But he could see sections of the stairway through occasional gaps in the flames.

Only there was no stairway any more, just bits of burning timber protruding from the walls. And there was no longer any landing below. Everything had collapsed into the screeching volcanic pit.

Childes returned to the dormitory, too numbed for emotional tears, his blurred vision caused by stinging smoke-whirls. The three tied bedsheets lay further back along the corridor where he had dropped them and were already beginning to flame. He staggered, an arm resting against the wall, but kept moving, knowing it would be fatal to stop. His pace quickened when he saw that the two girls were no longer by the doorway. He prayed that they had obeyed him, had not run off in the opposite direction, away from the oncoming fire. If they got lost in the thickening smoke . . .

The door was still ajar and he pushed it back so that the wood smacked against a bedside cupboard behind. His shadow was black against a yellow-red patch of shifting, soft-edged light and Sandy and Rachel, cuddled together on the nearest bed, watched him with wide fearful eyes.

'Come on,' he said, and they both felt the deadness in his voice. 'I'm taking you out.'

They ran to him and he scooped them up, one in each arm. Now they were heavy, but he would manage. Whatever it took, he would at least save these two. Childes backed out and headed down the long corridor, away from the worst of the flames, everything around them – walls, ceiling, floorboards – sizzling, ready to ignite, to explode into one huge conflagration. He could barely see and there was a steady growing numbness inside his head, a constricting of his throat. Flames shot out from the floor near a wall, forcing him to turn his back and face the opposite wall to squeeze by. There wasn't a murmur from either of the girls. Their arms were around his neck and they kept perfectly still, terribly afraid yet trusting. Perhaps they had sobbed out the worst of their terror inside the cupboard.

They were in semi-darkness for a while, smoke obscuring even the light at their backs, but another soft-hued glimmer soon came into sight ahead. Although this flickering glow acted as a beacon, it was unwelcome; he had hoped that the fire stairs were far enough away to be still untouched by the fire below.

After groping his way along, almost blind, sliding his back along the wall at one side, they finally reached the stone landing over the stairway. Childes all but collapsed onto hands and knees. Sandy and Rachel squatted by his side, waiting for his coughing fit to ease, they themselves choking into open palms.

Recovering enough to pull himself up by the metal railings of the stairs, Childes looked over the top. The stairway acted as a chimney, smoke pouring upwards to swill into the corridor they had just left. Through the sweltering clouds he could see several fires emerging from corridors below.

There was still a chance to get out – if they didn't choke to death on the way down.

He gathered the two girls to him, kneeling so that his face was on a level with theirs. 'We're going to be fine,' he said, his voice dry and strained. 'We're walking down the stairs and we'll be outside within minutes. The stairs are concrete, as I told you, so they can't catch fire, but we'll have to keep away from the corridors.' He reached into his pocket. 'Rachel, you keep this hanky over your mouth and nose.'

Obediently, she took the handkerchief from him and pressed it to her face.

'Sandy, I'm afraid we'll have to spoil your nightie.' He reached for the hem and tore off a long strip of material, then tied it around her neck so that the lower half of her face, was masked. He stood, but still crouched low. 'Okay, here we go,' he said.

Childes took their hands and led them down the first flight of stairs, keeping to the wall and away from the rising fumes.

The deeper they went, the fiercer the heat became.

Sandy and Rachel hung back and Childes had to tug at them to keep them moving. Reaching a corner between first and second floors, he closed them in, protecting their bodies with his own. Rachel's knees were sagging as she leaned into the corner and he could see in the red light that she would never make it all the way down. He shrugged off his jacket and draped it over her head, then lifted her. She slumped against him, only half-conscious. Maybe that was just as well; she'd be easier to handle. He took Sandy's hand once more and continued the descent, shielding her as best he could.

'Not far now!' he said loudly to encourage her.

In response, her other hand curled around his upper arm, holding tight. For an instant, Gabby's bespectacled face swam before him and he almost cried out her name. It was he who faltered, sliding down the wall to sit on the steps, Rachel cradled in his lap, completely covered by his jacket and almost oblivious to what was going on. And it was Sandy who tugged at his shoulder, who worried him into rising again, refusing to let him rest for even a moment.

He looked into her upturned, dirt-streaked face, flickering shadows playing over her features, and she repeated his own words: 'Not far now.'

Not far, he kept telling himself, not far now, soon be on the last flight of stairs. But his strength was fading fast, was really leaving him this time, the last reserves expelled with his now ceaseless dry-retch coughing, each lungful of air taken in filled with asphyxiating fumes; and he could hardly see where to place his next step, so full were his eyes with running, stinging tears which made the rims of his eyelids so sore that it hurt even to squeeze them shut . . .

. . . and Sandy was pulling him down, her exhausted little body unable to cope any more, her bare legs giving way so that she began to sink lower and lower until he was finally dragging her down the stone steps by her arm . . .

. . . and his senses were reeling, full of images of moonstones and Gabby's face and torn mutilated bodies and piercing malevolent eyes that leered mockingly through flames, and Amy, cut and bleeding and writhing, and the glistening white and smooth moon shining through the whirling smoke layers, its lower curvature seeping dark blood . . .

. . . and he was fading, slowly sinking with each blundering step downwards, losing his grip on Sandy, his hand touching warm concrete, taking his own weight so that he could gently lower himself, let his body fold up to rest, succumbing to the choking heat, even though there was only a short way to go, just one more flight, one more –

A tiny part of his flagging senses revived a fraction, became alert to something that was happening below. His length sprawled on the stairs, he raised himself on one elbow.

Voices. He could hear voices. Shouting. Dark silhouettes against flames that billowed from a corridor on the ground floor. Figures on the stairs. Coming towards him . . .

```
MOONSTONE
(potassium aluminium silicate KA 1Si₃O₈)
Density:  2.57
Hardness:  6
Indices of refraction:  1.519 - 1.526 (low)
A variety of orthoclase feldspar, moonstone
exhibits a faint but characteristic
fluorescence when subjected to X-ray
radiation.
Moonstone, so called because when held to
light, presents silvery play of colour
not unlike that of the moon.  Colour,
usually white, known to mineralogists
as schillerisation, from German word
'schiller' meaning iridescence.  Found in
Sri Lanka, Madagascar and Burma.
```

Overoy stubbed out the remains of his cigarette, rubbing his tired eyes with thumb and forefinger of his other hand. He sat at the dining-table, a light hanging so low over the smoked-glass surface that the room around him was cast in shadows. The living area was beyond a squared archway, two small rooms made into one large, an alteration he had tackled himself when he and Josie had moved nine years before, a distant time when he possessed energy for both career and domestic enterprises. Only a single lamp shone in that room, the television in grey suspension, curtains closed against the summer's night.

Nothing. He looked down at his notes and said the word: 'Nothing.'

The tiny gem was no more than some kind of kinky calling-card. But calling-cards were a reference.

So why a moonstone?

A reference to the moon?

With one hand he spread the notes before him, sweeping them in an arc like a winning hand of cards.

Amy Sebire had suggested that Moon was a name. Yet Childes had psychically seen the moon as a symbol.

A symbol representing a name?

Overoy reached for the cigarette pack, found it empty, tossed the carton towards the end of the table. He stood, stretching his arms out behind his back, taking a short walk around the table. He sat once more and ran his hands over his face and around to the back of his neck, entwining his fingers there.

How was Childes coping? he wondered. Against all the rules, Overoy had left scene-of-crime evidence with him. A tiny piece of evidence, the moonstone itself. Childes had wanted the gem. So why not? It was useless to the police. But the stone had some significance for the killer. Checking jewellers in and around the London area had yielded nothing so far, even though the gem on its own wasn't a usual item for sale. The person they were looking for was obviously shopping around, never using the same place twice.

His weary eyes ranged over the pile of books heaped on the dark glass, most of them unhelpful, the information he needed sifted only from a few. That information was all to do with the moon; or more precisely, the mystical aspect of the moon.

Moon-madness, Josie had scolded him before leaving him in the gloom for their bed.

Not my moon-madness, Josie; someone's else's.

Ask any policeman how the crime rate, usually with violence, inexplicably increased during the full moon. Even headshrinks believed a full moon tended to bring out the loonies. Overoy had underlined a note he had made: *If the moon has an effect on the earth's water masses, then why not also on the brain, which is semi-liquid pulp?* It was a thought.

And two *new* moons in one single month was said to be calamitous by those who believed in such things. There had been two new moons in May when the Moonstone atrocities had begun. That point had been underscored in his notes as well.

Another common belief among many people was that the moon's maleficent character (despite his weariness he smiled at himself, thinking of the old Man in the Moon and his cranky ways) could be manifested here on earth as a baleful emanation by those who had occult powers. Interesting but not a point to put before the commissioner.

He picked up a red felt-tip and circled the capital-letter word MUTILATIONS, then drew a line from it to another: RITUAL. Close to that he now wrote: SACRIFICE?? Perhaps a better word was OFFERING.

Offering to what? The moon? No, there had to be some kind of reasoning, even if only a crazy man's reasoning. To a moon god then? Goddesses seemed to dominate that area of worship, so let's make it moon goddess. Oh boy, if the boys in blue could see him now.

All right. There were a few moon goddesses to ponder on. Let's run through the list again:

DIANA
ARTEMIS
SELENE

Then three who were the same:

AGRIOPE - Greek   ⎫
SHEOL - Hebrew   ⎬   HECATE
NEPHYS - Egyptian   ⎭

Hecate. Why did that one ring a bell, albeit a very distant bell? Coming across that name in his researches had prompted further investigation into moon worship and the relevant gods and goddesses. (She seemed to be the most popular, but why should that mean anything? Let's have a look at her.)

Hecate. Goddess of the dead. Necromantic rituals devoted to her. Daughter of the Titan Perses and of Asteria. Protector and teacher of sorceresses. (Was he really taking all this seriously?)

Hecate. Keyholder of Hell, dispatcher of phantoms from the underworld. At night she would leave Hades and roam on earth accompanied by hounds and the souls of the dead, her hair like bristling snakes and her voice like a howling dog. Her favourite nocturnal retreat was near a lake called Armarantiam Phasis, 'the lake of murders'. (Nice lady.)

Hecate. Possessor of all the great dark knowledges, mother of witches. (What was it about the name?)

Hecate. Like the moon she was fickle and inconsistent of character. At times benign and motherly, acting as midwife, nurse and foster-mother, watching over crops and flocks. But the other side of her nature, the dark side, gradually superseded her kinder side. She had become an infernal diety, a snake goddess with three heads – a dog's, a horse's, a lion's. (Real Edgar Allan. Hell, he couldn't believe he'd written it all down. At least he'd been wise enough to carry out his research at home.)

Overoy reached for the half-drunk mug of coffee lurking behind the pile of books, his lips curling back in disgust on tasting the tepid dregs. He put down the mug again and relaxed back in the chair. Where was he getting with all this? Was the research mere timewasting or did it really have some relevance? They were dealing with someone who had a sick, deranged mind, someone who desecrated the dead, mutilated murdered victims. Someone who left a moonstone as a calling-card, and someone who got a kick out of psychological torment. Not a pleasant person. But a moon-worshipper? Or, more accurately, a moon-goddess worshipper?

Nah, no sense to it.

But their quarry was demented anyway.

Why had Hecate stuck in his mind? What was familiar about that name? Something he'd seen somewhere . . .

He groaned. No good, he was too tired to think any more. Everything was buzzing around inside his head and none of it settling. Bed. Sleep on it. Talk with Josie – whoops, was that the time? Talk to her in the morning; she always helped clear his thoughts. Maybe he'd got it all wrong anyway. Moon-goddesses, moon-worshippers, moonstones. Psychics. Life was simpler on the beat.

Overoy rose from the dining-table and, hands tucked into trouser pockets, took one last look at his spread notes.

Finally shrugging, he turned off the light and went up to bed . . .

. . . And awoke at dawn, the answer there before him like a faint neon sign seen through fog. Not much, no big deal, but a glimmer.

All grogginess instantly gone, he scrambled out of bed.

Full moon . . .

'To whom am I speaking to?'
  'Hello, Daddy!'
  'Hi, Pickle.'
  'Daddy, I've started a new school.'
  'Yes, I know, Mummy just told me. Have you made any new friends yet?'
  'We-ll, one. Two really, but I'm not sure of Lucy yet. Do I have to stay at this school, Daddy? I miss my proper one.'
  'Only for a little while, Gabby, just until summer holidays begin.'
  'Then will we go home to our own house?'
  'Don't you like it there at Nanny's?'
  'Ooh yes, but home is nicer. Nanny spoils me, she thinks I'm still a baby.'
  'She doesn't realize you're a big girl now?'
  'No. But it's not her fault, she has good pretensions.'
  He chuckled. 'Make the most of it, kiddo, you're a long time old.'
  'All grups say that.' 'Grups' was their special world for grown-ups. 'Are you coming to see me soon, Daddy? I've done some pictures for you, I did them with finger-paints. Nanny's cross about the walls, but she didn't smack me, she never does. *Are* you coming to see me, Daddy?'
  Childes hesitated. 'I'm not sure, Gabby. You know I want to, don't you?'
  'Are you too busy at your schools? I told my new friends you were a teacher, but Lucy didn't believe me. She said teachers didn't teach video games. I tried to explain, Daddy, but you know how thicko some children can be. When it's holiday time, can I come and see you?'
  So many uncertainties in his mind, but he told her yes, anyway.
  'But I don't want to go on a boat this time, Daddy,' she said after her initial pleasure, her voice becoming low.
  'No, you'll come by plane.'
  'I mean there – I don't want to go on a boat like last time.'
  'When we cruised round the island on that little motorboat, when we went to all those sandy beaches? I thought you enjoyed that.'
  'I don't like water any more.'

That was all she would say.

'Why not, Gabby? You used to.'

Silence for a while. Then: 'Can Mummy come too?'

'Yes, of course, if she'd like to. Maybe Mummy'll let you stay on for a month or so.' Forget those black uncertainties, he told himself. Let these promises bring you out on the other side. Think of them as weapons against . . . whatever was about to happen.

'Really? D'you really mean it? I can stay with you for more than two weeks?'

'It's up to your mother.'

'Will you ask her now – *please?*'

'Uh, no, Gabby, not just yet. I've got something that needs . . . well, it needs clearing up first. Then I'll know everything for certain.'

'But you won't forget you promised?'

'I won't forget.'

'Okay, Daddy. Miss Puddles is here and she wants to say hello.'

'Tell her *meow* from me.'

'She says *meow* back. Not really, but I can tell she's thinking it. Nanny's bought a basket for her, but she likes sleeping on top of the fridge.'

'Nanny does?'

'Silly. D'you want to speak to Mummy again? She's going to read me a story in bed.'

No, he wanted to ask her about the water. Small children often developed sudden and irrational fears that bothered them for a while, then disappeared just as quickly, but Childes had been disconcerted by what Gabby had said. Perhaps she'd seen a bad TV movie, or one of the other kids had told her a drowning story. No matter; he hadn't been keen on water himself for some time.

'Yes,' he said, 'find Mummy for me. Listen, I'll speak to you soon, all right?'

'Yes. Lubboo, Daddy!'

For a fleeting, terrifying moment, Childes felt he might never hear his daughter say that to him again. The feeling passed, a cold breeze rustling through a tree.

'I love you, too, Gabby.'

She mouthed six rapid kisses down the phone and he returned one big one.

Just before Gabby rested the receiver, she said. 'Oh and Daddy, tell Annabel I miss her and tell her about my new school.'

He heard the *clunk* as the phone was laid down and Gabby's voice growing fainter as she went looking for her mother.

'Gabby –'

She was gone.

Had he misheard? More probably, Gabby had meant to say Amy. Tell Amy I miss her . . . Her little friend Annabel was dead, Gabby knew that by now. Fran had explained that Annabel wouldn't be coming back.

'Me again, Jon.' Fran's voice sounded rushed as usual.

Childes gave his head a little shake – or was it a shudder? – to clear his thoughts. 'Fran, has Gabby been acting okay lately?'

'Hardly. The move's upset her more than she let's on and starting a new school is always a mite traumatic anyway.' Her tone changed. 'I get a weird feeling when you start asking about Gabby nowadays.'

'No premonitions, Fran. Honest. Has she mentioned Annabel to you?'

'Several times. But she's not as distressed as you'd have thought. What makes you ask?'

'I just get the impression she believes her friend is still alive.'

Fran did not answer immediately. Eventually she said, 'Gabby's been dreaming a lot recently. Not particularly bad dreams, nightmares, anything like that; she's taken to talking in her sleep a lot.'

'Does she mention Annabel's name?'

'She did once or twice at first; not any more, though. I think she's accepted she'll never see her again.'

Why is she suddenly afraid of water?'

'What?'

'She seems to have gone off boats and water.'

'That's a new one to me. Fire I could understand, after what you've been through. But water? That I can't figure.'

'You told her about La Roche?'

'Sure. Her daddy's a hero; she's entitled to know.'

'Hardly a hero.'

'Modest, too.'

'A few over here would like to know how I got to the school so fast, even before the Fire Department had been alerted.'

'The police surely don't suspect you?'

'I wouldn't put it that strongly, but let's say nobody's clapped me on the back yet.'

'Oh, Jon, I can't believe this. They can't be that stupid! You barely got out of there alive yourself. And you rescued those two little —'

'I left seven others to die.'

'You *tried* to save them, you did your best. You told me that, Jon.'

'What happened was because of me.'

'Stop being such a bloody martyr and start talking sense. Just because some psychopath has chosen you for a crazy personal vendetta, it doesn't mean you're to blame. None of what's happened has been within your control. Now tell me what these hick policemen are up to.'

'You have to see things from their point of view.'

'Like hell I do?'

'They wanted to know what had made me go to the school *before* the fire started.'

'That must have been difficult to explain. Explain it to me again.'

'I've told you, Fran; let's not do a re-run. Anyway, their questions came thick and fast even while I was still in a hospital bed having oxygen pumped into me.'

'The ungrateful —'

'They had a burnt-out school, lives lost, a murdered policeman – what would you expect? That's twice I was ahead of anyone else at the scene of a crime.'

'So they suspect you of arson and murder. That's terrific. Jon, why the hell don't you get back over here, right now, take a late plane or the first one in the morning? Why put up with all this?'

'I don't think they'd like that.'

'They can't hold you there.'

'Maybe they can. I'm not leaving, Fran. Not yet.'

Her exasperation bordered on raw anger. '*Why?*'

'Because *it's* here. And while that's so, you and Gabby are safe, don't you understand that?'

She did. She said so. Quietly.

Childes went through into the sitting room, heading for the small array of drinks kept on the bookshelf opposite the door. He lifted the whisky bottle, twisted the top. And stopped. That's not going to help, he told himself. Not tonight.

He returned the bottle.

The room was shaded only a table lamp providing light. The curtains were drawn back at both ends of the sitting room, open to the night, and he saw the sky was sheened an eerie metallic blue. Childes closed the curtains nearest to him, those at the front of the cottage, then walked the length of the room to the other window. Outside, the moon, white and only faintly smudged, not yet high in its cloudless territory, resembled a communion wafer, flat and delicately tissue thin. He drew the curtains against the night.

Hands tucked deep into the pockets of his cord jeans, Childes went to the coffee table near the room's centre, his movement slow, almost sauntering (except there was nothing casual in his demeanour). A two-day stubble darkened his chin and there was an intensity to his fixed gaze that was oddly both weary and alert as he stood over the low table, looking down. In his eyes, too, was a steady resoluteness.

He lowered himself onto the edge of the sofa facing the coffee table, leaning forward, elbows on knees, observing the tiny round object on the smooth wooden surface.

The lamp's reflection infused a hint of warmth into the moonstone's transluscent coldness, while liquid blue, toned to indigo, shimmered a wintry variegation.

He stared into the moonstone's depths, like some old-fashioned clairvoyant gazing into a crystal ball, as though fascinated by the subtle shades; in truth, he looked beyond that interior, seeking perhaps the inmost part of his own self. But searching for something else as well: grasping for a link, a connection, *an access code*.

All he found was names. And unearthly faces. Kelly, Patricia, Adele, Caroline, Isobel, Sarah-Jane. And Kathryn Bates, Matron. All dead. Ashes. Estelle Piprelly. Ashes. .

Annabel. Dead.

But: Jeanette, alive. Amy, sweet Amy. Alive. And Gabby. Alive.

Strangely, these last three were not as strong in his vision as the others; thoughts of them were shallow, somehow irrelevant, not part of this new thing.

His thoughts lingered with the dead.

Even those he had not known.

The prostitute. The boy, violated in his grave. The old man with the top of his head sawn off. Others in the asylum. He did not want to envisage them, nor hear their voices, for he sought something—someone—else; but their images and sounds pulsated before him, throbbed inside his mind . . . palpitating . . . growing, fading . . . growing, fading . . . expanding, contracting . . . a swelling, deflating, incorporeal balloon . . . a misty white ball . . . a moon – He gasped, his hand jumping to his forehead, the pain sudden and sharp, cutting through the dull ache that had troubled him throughout the day. He slumped back on the sofa.

His mind had almost touched . . .

'Vivienne?'

'Yes?'

'It's Jonathan Childes. I'm sorry to bother you this late.'

The silence at the other end of the phone lasted for a while. 'Just closing the door,' Vivienne said. Childes imagined Paul Sebire was on the other side of that door. 'How are you, Jonathan? Have you recovered from that dreadful experience?'

'I'm okay,' he replied. Physically, at least, he added to himself.

'Amy's very proud of what you did. So am I.'

'I wish –'

'I know. You wish you could have saved those other girls, too. But you did all you could, you must realize that. I just hope they soon catch the madman responsible. Now, I don't suppose you want to waste time chatting to me. Amy's resting in her room, but I can put you through to her. I know she isn't sleeping because I've only just left her – we were discussing you, as a matter of fact. She'll be glad you called.'

'You're sure it's okay?'

Vivienne laughed quietly. 'Positive. Um . . . I'll have to sneak upstairs and tell her rather than call up.'

'Her father?'

'Her father. He's not as bad as you might think, Jonathan, he just likes to give that impression. He'll come round eventually, you'll see. I'll put the phone down now, and go up to Amy.'

He waited, his head still aching, the dull throb of before. A click, then Amy was on the line.

'Jon? Is anything wrong?'

'No, Amy. I wanted to hear your voice, that's all. I suddenly felt the need.'

'I'm glad you rang.'

'How're you feeling?'

'Same as when you called this afternoon. Sleepy, but that's the pills I'm taking. No problems. The doctor called earlier this evening and he says the cuts aren't half as bad as he at first thought. "Healing nicely", to use his words. I can get up and out tomorrow, so guess where I'm heading.'

'No, Amy, not here. Not just yet.'

'I *know* where I want to be, Jon, and who I want to be with. It's useless arguing. I've had time to think over the past few days and I think I can put any jealousy I have over you and Fran to one side. Not easily, I admit. But I can do it.'

'Amy, you have to stay away.'

'Tell me why.'

'You know the reason.'

'You think you're a danger to me.'

'I'm a danger to anyone at the moment. I even had to consider the risk when I phoned Gabby tonight. I'm frightened to *think* about her in case this monster discovers where she is through me.'

'The police will find him soon. There's no way he can get off the island.'

'I don't think it cares about that any longer.'

A sharp, probing pain again. Childes drew in a quick breath.

'Jon?'

'I'll let you rest now, Amy.'

'I've had plenty of rest. I'd rather talk.'

'Tomorrow.'

There was an uncomfortable vagueness in the word.

'Is there something going on that you won't tell me about?' she asked almost cautiously.

'No,' he lied. 'I guess I'm just tired of standing on the sidelines while this mayhem goes on.'

'There's nothing you can do. It's for the police to bring it to an end.'

'Maybe.'

Again she didn't enjoy his tone. For all its solemnity, there was an anger there, a contained but inwardly seething rage; she had felt its potency when she had picked up the phone, incredibly even before he had spoken, as if beams of furious energy were coursing through the lines. She was thinking the impossible, and Amy knew that; yet why did she feel so ill at ease, so weakened by this – imagined? – force?

'Sleep now, Amy,' he said. 'Rest.'

And she suddenly felt so tired, almost as if he'd given an order that her body dare not disobey. She was *unbelievably* tired.

'Jon . . .'

'Tomorrow, Amy.'

His voice was hollow, the tail end of an echo. The receiver felt awkwardly heavy in her hand.

'Yes, tomorrow, then,' she said slowly, her eyelids ridiculously weighty. *What is this – hypnosis by phone?* 'Jon . . .' she began to protest, but somehow not having the energy left to complete the sentence.

'I love you more than you know, Amy.'

'I do know . . .'

The phone clicked, the connection was dead. The sudden deep sense of loss almost roused her again. But he had told her to rest, to sleep . . .

The receiver slipped from her fingers.

Childes put down the phone and wondered if the pills Amy was taking were making her so tired. They probably contained a sedative as well as a painkiller. He went into the bathroom to douse his face, also feeling weary – but paradoxically, also acutely aware. Filling the basin with cold water, he bent low and splashed his face, holding his wet fingers against his closed eyelids for several moments each time. Eventually, he straightened, confronting himself in the cabinet mirror; he stared into his own eyes, noticing the bloodshot coronas around the soft contact lenses he wore.

And if mirrors had reflected auras, he might also have observed short dancing white-to-violet rays of ethereal energy dazzling from his own body.

Childes wiped his face and hands dry, then went back into the low-lit sitting room. Once more he sank into the sofa near the coffee table, and once more he resisted the urge to pour himself a large whisky. He wanted his senses clear, would risk nothing that might dull them. The moonstone seemed brighter, the bluish flare inside diminished.

Pain in his head again, tiny repeated knife jabs this time. But he would not desist. Only the sudden urgent need to speak to Amy had interrupted the long, long process – and before that, the urgent need to hear Gabby's voice – and now there could be no more intrusions, for Amy and Gabby were safe, away from harm. He could concentrate his mind. It hurt, though; God, how it hurt. He closed his eyes and still saw the stone.

He opened them when he heard whispers.

Childes looked around. The whispering stopped. He was the room's only occupant. He shut his eyes once again.

And again heard the hushed whispers.

He allowed his mind to go with the sounds, to absorb them and be absorbed by them, and it all came so fast (so fast after hours of probing, sending out his thoughts, seeking) like tumbling into a snowy pit, the sliding plummet soft and smooth, landing with scarcely a jar, sinking into cushioned earth.

Whispers.

Voices.

Some he recognized. Some belonged to girls from La Roche Ladies College, those who had been fused into one melting mass of flesh when they had plunged together into the fiery maelstrom, incinerated into ashes, cremated into no more than a collective powdery heap.

Others.

A small squeaky voice, like Gabby's, but not Gabby's.

Others.

Demented even in death.

He could almost *feel* their presence.

Voices warning him.

Voices welcoming him.

His head reeled with them. And the moonstone that was now the moon throbbed and pulsated, grew large, encompassing . . . threatening . . .

. . . And this time he touched wholly the malignant and diseased other mind . . .

If Police Constable Donnelly had not considered all life sacred – even that of rabbits who squatted, paralysed by headlamps, in the middle of the road late at night – then probably he would never have lost the car he was supposed to be following.

As it was, he had watched Childes leave his cottage from the darkness of his patrol car, the teacher easily visible under the moonlight glare, observed him climb into the hired Renault and drive off into the deeply-shadowed lanes. After first radioing HQ to let them know their target was loose, the policeman had followed, keeping a safe but reasonable distance between himself and his quarry.

The rabbit (or had it been a hare? They said hares had a special affinity with the full moon and would run senseless before it) had appeared near a bend in the road and Donnelly had braked only just in time – in fact swerving to the left a little to avoid the stupid animal, the patrol car brushing the hedge on that side.

The rabbit (or hare – he could never quite remember the difference) had stayed crouching there on the road, directly in his path, stunned and shivery, one black and glistening eye watching with dumb blankness, and the agitated policeman had had to leave his car and actually shoo the silly creature away.

When PC Donnelly had finally resumed his journey and rounded the bend, the Renault's red tail-lights were nowhere to be seen.

It was as if the car, driver and all, had been swallowed up by the moon-bleached landscape.

First the ringing doorbell disturbed Amy's sleep, then the sound of voices roused her into wakefulness. One of the voices was unmistakably her father's, and it was angry. She pulled back the bedclothes, wincing slightly at the effort, and went to the bedroom door, limping only slightly, opening it just enough to listen.

The voices were still muffled, but her father was evidently complaining about the lateness of the hour. She thought she recognized both the other speakers. Amy joined her mother who was in her dressing gown on the landing, peering over the balustrade at the three men grouped in the downstairs hallway. One was Paul Sebire, fully clothed, obviously having been working late. The two other men were Inspector Robillard and Overoy. Amy wondered what Overoy was doing back on the island. She stood beside her mother and listened.

'This is ridiculous, Robillard,' Paul Sebire was saying. 'Why on earth should we know where he is? Frankly, it would suit me fine if I never laid eyes on the man again.'

It was Overoy who replied. 'We need to know if Miss Sebire has heard from him.'

'I believe he may have telephoned my daughter occasionally over the last few days, but I'm sure Aimée would have no idea of his whereabouts tonight.'

Amy and her mother exchanged glances.

'Find your dressing gown and come down,' Vivienne quietly told her daughter, moving round to the head of the stairs.

'Inspector,' Vivienne said, descending. 'Amy did receive a call from Jonathan earlier tonight.'

Paul Sebire looked up at his wife in surprise and then annoyance.

'Ah,' said Overoy and waited for her to reach the hallway. 'Would it be possible, then, to have a word with Miss Sebire? It *is* a matter of urgency.'

'Look here,' interjected Paul Sebire, 'my daughter is sleeping and shouldn't be disturbed. She still hasn't recovered from her accident.'

'It's all right,' came Amy's voice.

Sebire turned to see that now his daughter was coming down the stairs. Amy hardly gave him a glance – indeed, she had hardly spoken to him since she had learned he had struck Childes at the hospital.

Overoy frowned at Amy's bandaged eye and plaster-cast from hand to elbow on her left arm. She walked with an awkward stiffness, limping a little. Healing cuts on her face and hands marred the smooth, light-tanned skin that he remembered so well from their previous meetings; he sincerly hoped none would leave permanent marks.

'We're sorry to disturb you at this hour, Miss Sebire,' apologized Robillard, looking distinctly uncomfortable standing there in the open hallway, the front door still open behind him, 'but as we've already explained to Mr Sebire, the matter is rather important.'

'That's quite all right, Inspector,' Amy replied. 'If it concerns Jon, I'm only too willing to help. Is there something wrong?'

'You should be resting, Amy,' Paul Sebire remarked rather than rebuked.

'Nonsense. You know the doctor said I could be up and about tomorrow.'

Overoy spoke up: 'I was sorry to hear of your accident. Jon told me about your injuries. Er, your eye. . . .?'

Although impatient to learn of the reason for their visit, Amy managed a flicker of a smile. 'Apparently there is no serious damage, my sight won't be impaired. The bandage is really only there to prevent infection and to force me to rest the eye. Now you must tell me what this is all about. Please.'

Vivienne moved closer to her daughter and slipped an arm around her waist, drawing her close.

'Mr Childes disappeared from his home earlier tonight,' Inspector Robillard said. Over his shoulder and through the door, Amy could see that more than one police car was parked in the drive. She felt a tightness in the back of her throat. 'One of our patrolmen,' the inspector went on, 'who was, uh, on watch, lost his car in the lanes, I'm afraid.'

She gave a small shake of her head, not understanding.

'We wondered if Jonathan might have phoned to let you know where he was going,' said Overoy, a nicotine-stained finger scratching his temple.

Amy looked from one policeman to the other. 'Yes. Yes, he did call, but he didn't mention anything about going out. If anything, he sounded tired. But why do you want to know? Surely he's not under suspicion?'

'He never has been as far as I'm concerned, Miss Sebire,' replied Overoy, eyeing his colleague with mild but apparent disdain. 'No, I caught the last flight over here tonight because I wanted to talk to him. I also hope to help the Island Police make an arrest.'

He paused to take in a breath, looking at each of them in turn. 'You see, we've discovered the identity of the person responsible for this madness. Someone we've checked on and know is still here on the island. Someone who might get to Jonathan Childes before we do.'

Childes sat in the Renault for a while, suddenly terribly afraid.

It had drawn him here to this place, inducing an image of a large moonlit-smooth lake. Yet no lake of that immensity existed on the island. But there was one such vast area of water, a valley that had been flooded a long time before, covering trees and the deserted houses alike to form a reservoir, a great concrete dam built across that valley to prevent its rivers from reaching the sea.

A voice – no, less than that: a thought – had enticed, had *lured*, him there with a promise.

The thought's instigator had no shape, no substance. When Childes concentrated, his own consciousness drew its periphery inwards to almost a defined line of thought, only a soft-brimmed radiancy formed at a point behind his eyes, a moon-shape that shimmered hugely on the wall of his mind and excluded all other images and all other rationality.

It wanted him here, and Childes had not resisted.

The promise? The incentive?

An end to the killings. An end to torment. An answer, perhaps, to Childes' own mystery.

The notion made him push open the car door, just as it had impelled him to drive through empty lanes to reach this point. He had felt sure he was being followed when he had left his cottage – presumably by a police control car, for he assumed he was now under observation night and day – but the lights of the vehicle behind had soon disappeared, the other driver having turned off somewhere along the way. Maybe he, Childes, had finally become paranoid: and who could blame him?

The night was chilly despite the season, cool air breezing in off the sea to soothe the land after the heat of the day. Sweater and cord jeans could not prevent that chill from causing a back-juddering shiver; he pulled up the collar of his jacket, closing the lapels around his throat. The full moon was still unsullied by clouds and bathed the countryside in a stark luminescence, rendering it peculiarly flat, while shadows were deep and uncompromisingly black. So brightened was the sky by its round hanging lamp that stars, untold millions of them, were visible only beyond the far-reaching canescence. As Childes walked towards the dam, it seemed that the landscape was frozen beneath the eerie gleam.

His senses were alert and acutely clear, his eyes ceaselessly searching the area around him, well aware that any inert creature would easily blend in with the surroundings, so dark were they in places, so oddly-shaped in others. Here, a lone bush might be a crouching animal; there, a tree stump with thick roots stretched outwards could be a sitting man; a clump of trees to his left might easily hide a lurking figure, while a spread of undergrowth ahead could provide a concealing canopy for some waiting predator.

He wondered now if he wasn't disappointed that he had not been followed by a patrol car. Perhaps he should have rung Robillard before he left the cottage. But then, how would he have explained to the police inspector, who was sceptical to say the least, that earlier that evening his mind had finally fused with another's? The difference this time was that the fusion had been whole, with Childes on the offensive, seeking out and delving, surprising the other with his strength at first, then becoming absorbed by it.

By It!

Explain the silent, tortuous mental battle that had followed as the creature taunted him with horrors that had come to pass, revealing the deaths to him again like some edited movie rough-cuts, with each frame containing feelings, smells, the pain and fear of the real event, a new stupendous dimension in cinematography. 4D. All in random order:

The old man feebly protesting against the saw edge cutting into his brow.

Jeanette's abject terror as she dangled over the stairway, hung there and choked by a knotted tie, to be saved but not spared the ordeal of near-death.

The prostitute, whose torn innards Childes had sighted at the beginning, not knowing then it was the first in a stream of macabre visions, the return of an old nightmare.

Kelly's charred and withered hand.

The school alight before the fire had been lit.

The dead boy, defiled and torn, his putrefying organs spread over the grass around the graveside.

Annabel. Poor little Annabel, mistaken for Gabby, her tiny dismembered fingers wrapped in a package.

And he had witnessed for the first time Estelle Piprelly's horrendous death, lying helpless on the floor, her neck broken, a trail of fire snaking towards her.

Explain that macabre run-through to a pragmatic, not to say dogmatic, Officer of the Law. Explain how he knew where *It* would be waiting for him, that the vision of a huge moon-silvered lake had unfurled inside his head like a fast-running tide, and that it was here that everything would be resolved. Such matters could not be explained or logicized: they could only be sensed, or believed in faith. Not many had that kind of faith. Certainly, for most of his life, Childes hadn't.

By now he had crossed the rough-hewn parking area, a patch scoured of shrubbery and trees, set back from the narrow road which circumscribed the reservoir to descend into the valley below the dam. He mounted the slabs that were broad steps leading onto the dam, pausing there to study the long, narrow concrete walkway with its thick, waist-high parapets on either side. The middle section was raised, low arches out of sight beneath to allow for overspill should the reservoir become too glutted with rainfall; stout concrete posts reinforced the parapets at regular intervals and grafitti etched the walls where tourists had marked their visit; dark grass fringes sprang up through wide-spaced parallel joins in the walkway's surface. Beyond the raised section loomed a water tower, octagonally shaped and set into the dam as part of its structure, where water was syphoned down to the pumping station at the base of the giant barrier.

Childes started forward, a breeze ruffling his hair. He felt exposed out there on the dam and constantly scanned the path ahead, natural moonlight somehow soaking everything unnaturally, so that the effect was surreal and colourless. The lake could have been a gently rippled aluminium sheet so smoothly solid did it appear; yet the power of the massive volume of water beneath the light-reflecting skin was ominously present, concealed but nevertheless threatening. Falling would mean being sucked down into a pitched black nether-world to be crushed rather than drowned.

He counted the narrow steps, seven in all, as he climbed to the bridge formation over the outlet arches. In the centre he waited, alone and afraid, yet determined.

Childes could hear the sea from his high position, could even make out the thin whitish plume as wave after wave broke against the distant shoreline, so clear was the night. Keen air wafted against his face as he peered over the parapet on the unflooded side. The wall below sloped outwards, a concrete basin to contain overflow at the base, a conduit leading from that underground, taking surplus water beneath the valley to the sea. Not far from the basin was the white pumping station and behind another shiny flat area, the processing plant's sludge lagoon. Occasional lights shone further out in the valley, glowing from homes whose inhabitants kept late hours: he envied their unknowing snugness.

A creature winged darkly across his vision, too swiftly erratic to be a disturbed bird; a bat, then, in accord with the night, abruptly disappearing into covering shadows. The soft beating of its wings had resembled the uneven fluttering of a frightened heart.

As Childes lingered, his face a pale unlined mask under the moonlight's glare, the visions plagued his mind once more, assailing him with fresh intensity; not for the first time he wondered at the malignancy governing their perpetrator. Childes' last few days had been filled with outward mental probing, only a growing acceptance of his own unique powers giving strength to those endeavours. He no longer resisted what he had subconsciously known but rejected for so many years, that personal acknowledgement flushing his senses, lending vigour to his mysterious faculty.

He had remembered other times, insights that he had dismissed as chance, as coincidence, suppressing that psychic seepage, even the memory of such incidents rebuffed until now.

He had remembered the boyhood friend whom he knew would die beneath the wheels of a hit-and-run, the accident happening weeks later. A seldom-seen uncle whom he realized would be cut down by a diseased heart after their last meeting, that same uncle paralysed by coronary sclerosis months later. *The death of his own mother, envisaged long before cancer had ravaged her body.*

His father had treated him cruelly for that weeping revelation, just as he had savagely beaten him afterwards when his mother's spirit had come to him, the boy. Beaten him, Childes remembered, because his father had blamed the boy's precognition for *causing* his mother's death, for *initiating* her awful ending. Punishing him so badly that his nose and three ribs had been broken. And forcing him to agree through fear and, even then, loyalty, when his father had told the ambulance men and subsequent doctors that the boy, distressed by the loss of his mother, had fallen down a flight of stairs in the home.

Worst of all, in the feverish days that followed, the boy himself had come to *believe* his father's reason for mercilessly beating him, had *believed* that his premonitions really had caused his mother's death as though it were some evil witch's curse; and with the recognition had also come the belief that he was responsible for his friend's car accident, that he had instigated the disease inside his uncle's heart.

His guilt far outweighed the agony of broken bones and bruised flesh and soon, when the fever that was the result of uncontrollable remorse more than injury, had broken, his mind had erected within itself a protective wall, acceptance of his psychic faculty expelled along with his own guilt, for they went hand in hand, had become part of the same.

And the infant-murderer three years ago had somehow loosened the hold inside Childes' mind, had set the precognitive process in motion once more.

Now this killer had broken through the mental wall, turned a leak into an unsteady stream.

Childes' subconscious had even sent him back to witness his own boyhood misery, a long-hidden part of him yearning for answers. And such was the power within the boy that he had observed his older self return. The mature Childes had been the presence watching from the corner of the boy's room.

The answers, of course, provoked other mysteries, but these were of the human psyche, secrets that might never be unravelled for they involved secrets of life and the mind itself.

These thoughts coursed through him as he waited high on the dam, arousing a tantalizing yet wary exhilaration, as though he were on some kind of sensory threshold. As he gazed upwards, he saw that even the moon's glacial radiance was extraordinarily puissant, dominating the night sky with a peculiar flooding vitality. Tension shook Childes' body.

He sensed that he was no longer alone.

He looked behind, in the direction he had come.

Nothing there moved.

He looked ahead, towards the other end of the dam where there were more dark trees and thick undergrowth, another path from the winding road.

Something there did move.

It had watched him from the cloaking darkness and had smiled an ungodly smile.
So. At last he was here.
That was good, for their time had come. Now, under the full moon. Which was appropriate.
It moved from the trees towards the dam.

If fear had bounds, then Chides considered he had reached the outer limits. He found he had to lean against a parapet to support himself, so weak did his legs suddenly become. His insides were full of wildly floating feathers, the rigid tightness in his chest disallowing their escape; even his arms were useless, their muscles somehow wasted.

It was on the dam, a black, lumbering shape in the moonlight, coming towards him, the wide, squat body rocking slightly from side to side, an awkward trundling motion that lacked any fluidity.

And as the figure approached, Childes could *hear* the sniggering laughter in its mind. A mocking laughter that iced him, imprisoned him.

Childes leaned more heavily into the parapet. *Oh dear God, its mind is in mine, stronger than ever before!*

Soon he was able to perceive moon-cast outlines in its form, reflecting off immense sloping shoulders, jumbled in the texture of curled and matted hair. The shape of a nose, a chin. The planes of forehead and cheeks. The dark slash that was a wide, grinning mouth.

It drew nearer, passing the water tower, much of its ungainly body becoming lost from view behind the steps of the raised section on which Childes stood. For a moment, only the head and shoulders could be seen.

Its eyes were still shadowed, black pits that were as deep and as full of foreboding as the lake below.

It mounted the steps, its body rising as if from a tomb, broad, wild-haired head grinning, eyes unseen, coming closer, moving nearer, its thoughts stretching forward, reaching for him. And there was something else that was disturbing about this almost shapeless mass which seemed to shuffle rather than walk, something that was slowly – ever so slowly – becoming evident as it advanced, drew closer and closer, to stop when it was no more than three yards away.

It was only then, when he was able to look into that broad, moonlit face and see the gimlet eyes, small and black, that realization pounced, for when she spoke her voice betrayed nothing of her gender, the sound so low, so rasping.

'I've . . . enjoyed . . . the . . . game,' she said, each word slow and singular.

Her low chuckling laughter was as unpleasant as her voice and punched into him like physical blows. He clutched at the parapet more tightly.

The woman shuffled a yard closer and he noticed that her ankles, revealed beneath a long, voluminous skirt, were swollen, flowing over the laced shoes she wore as though her flesh were melting. An outsized anorak was spread over her upper body in untidy folds.

Childes forced himself to stand erect. His head was buzzing with confused thoughts, nausea clogging his throat. *He could smell this woman. He could scent her madness!* He swallowed hard, desperate to regather his failing strength.

All he could think of to say was: 'Why?'

The word was nothing more than a croaking sound, but she understood. He sensed, he *felt*, her shift of emotions: amusement had scuttled away.

'For her,' she said in that low, ungendered rasp, arching her neck so that her face was lifted towards the moon. 'My Lady.'

She gaped her mouth and he saw crooked, disfigured teeth. She drew in a deep scratchy breath as though inhaling the moonlight itself and when her head lowered, for one fleeting, unnerving moment, the moon reflected in those dark, cruel eyes, and it seemed as if the shine came from within, that the moon was inside filling her body, the eyes merely windows. The illusion was transient, but the vision lingered.

'Tell me . . . tell me who you are,' Childes uttered, uncertain of his *own* sanity.

The grossly-shaped woman regarded him for some time before speaking again, the brightness gone from her eyes, but replaced with a different kind of gleaming. 'Don't you know?' she asked, her words slow, but less so than before. 'Didn't you learn anything from me? There was so much that I got from you, my lovely.'

He no longer leaned so dependently against the ledge. 'I don't understand,' he managed to say, striving to keep a steady tone, willing his legs to stop their incessant trembling. *She's only a woman*, he told himself, *not an 'It'. Just a woman!* But a madwoman, a small chuckling voice in his head whispered. An incredibly *strong* madwoman, it taunted. And she knows you're terribly afraid, my lovely.

'I stole the girl from you.' The woman sniggered. Her mood had changed yet again, that shift sweeping through Childes himself, as though his senses were an integral part of hers.

'Not *your* girl . . .' she said slyly, '. . . unfortunately. The other little girl. How the little dear wriggled, how she squirmed.'

The beginnings of anger flared inside him, a tiny flame struck in the darkness of fear. The flame expanded, forcing back some of that darkness.

'You . . . killed . . . Annabel,' he said flatly.

'And those others.' Her voice was a low growl – a good-humoured growl. 'Don't forget all those others. Those girls were for my Lady too.'

The breeze sweeping over the dam was stronger, colder, flicking at his upturned lapels. It carried the salt smell of the sea.

'You murdered them,' he said.

'Fire murdered them, my lovely. And the woman who tried to stop me. Fire murdered the retards in the home, too. Oh how I enjoyed *that* place.' Her massive bulk edged closer and she leaned her head forward in a conspiratorial manner, silvery light haloing the matted curls of her hair. Once more her eyes lay hidden in black pits. 'Oh, how I enjoyed that place,' she repeated in a whisper. 'My asylum. Nobody believed those lunatics, not their snivelling tittle-tattle. Who in their right mind *would* believe what I did to them when I got them alone? Such a pity it had to end, but you were coming closer, weren't you, my lovely? And you would have given me away. That made my Lady very cross.'

Now only one of Childes' hands rested against the concrete ledge. 'I still don't understand. What lady?'

She leered at him – at least he imagined it was some form of grotesque leer. 'Don't you know? Haven't you felt her divine force inside you? The power of the moon goddess that waxes and wanes with the moon's cycle. Can't you feel her strength in our minds? You have the gift too, my lovely, don't you see?'

'The sightings . . .?'

She became impatient, her irritation rumbling through his own senses. 'Whatever you care to call it – none of that matters. When we share that gift, when our minds are together – *like now!* – its strength is so powerful . . . so beautifully . . . powerful.' The thought had made her breathless. Her body swayed from side to side, her face upwards again.

Her smell of insanity was rancid.

She became motionless and her head lowered. 'Don't you remember what we did with your machines? Our little game?'

'The computers?' He shook his head in bewilderment. 'You made the word "MOON" appear on the screens.'

She laughed, and the sound was threatening. '*You* made the word appear in their *minds!* Not on the machines, my lovely fool! We did it together, you and me, we made your precious girls see what we wanted them to see! And you saw what I wanted you to!'

Illusion. Everything was illusion; and perhaps it made more sense that way, knowing none of it was real.

'But why,' he pleaded, 'for God's sake why did they have to die?'

'Not for God's, but for our goddess's. Sacrificial lambs, lovely. And for their spiritual energy, feeble though it was in most. Interestingly strong in the woman, though, the one whose neck I broke inside the school.'

'Miss Piprelly?'

A shrug of those immense sloping shoulders. 'If that's who she was. You understand the energy I mean, don't you? I think you'd call it psychic force or some such fancy name. That energy tucked up inside here.'

A stubby finger tapped her temple and Childes shuddered inwardly when he saw how large her hands were. Powerful hands, swollen, like her body.

'But the woman's was nothing like yours, my lovely. Oh no, yours is special. I've searched inside you, I've touched your spirit. Such force, and held back for so long! It belongs to me now, though.'

She grinned and shuffled closer.

'All those others,' Childes said quickly, needing time for his anger to surge through him, to lend its vigour. 'Why did you mutilate them?'

'I tasted their souls through their inner flesh. That was the way, d'you see, my lovely? I emptied them and filled them again, but not with their own organs – oh no, their organs couldn't be returned, or they would have tried to reclaim their souls. And their souls belonged to our goddess. But I left them the stone, her physical presence here on earth. You've witnessed her earthly spirit inside the moonstone, haven't you, that tiny blue-glowing spark that's her essence? My gift to those unfortunates who had to die for her.'

Mad. She was totally mad. And she had moved very close now.

Dread, icy and clutching, held him there as she stretched one of those big hands towards him. The fingers slowly uncurled, the palm upwards, so that moonlight struck the fleshy surface.

'I've got one for you,' she whispered, smiling at all that her offer implied.

A tiny round stone lay in the outstretched palm and it might only have been the madwoman's disrupted and disruptive mind working on his, implanting the thought, the illusion – for she did have the ability; despite her madness, she did possess unbelievable psychic power – but there was an effulgence inside the gem, a bluish phosphorescence heightened by moonshine. In that glimmer he saw all the deaths.

With a gasping cry of fear and rage, Childes slapped at the hand so that the moonstone flew into the air, a minute shooting star snuffed out almost immediately as it arched down into the void that was the dam's valley.

The demented woman, who held within her an uncanny force, stood silently before him, her hand still outstretched, her face, with its shadowed eyes, inscrutable. Childes, too, was transfixed, the air between them somehow dangerously charged, an insidiously creeping current thrumming around his body so that each hair stiffened on its own little island.

A thought burst into his mind, causing him to stagger.

Amy, sprawled writhing beyond the low wall by the roadside, her face a pincushion of glass shards, her neck unnaturally twisted against the base of a tree trunk, her mouth open with blood dribbling out.

'*No!*' he shouted.

The thought was gone.

And the shadowed gash on the woman's face was a grin.

He ducked his head into a hand as another image struck.

Jeanette, dangling over the stairway, her neck squeezed tight by the noose that was a tie, flesh puckered and swollen over its edges. Her bloated tongue slowly oozing between her lips, growing in length like some emerging purple worm, crawling down her chin to quiver over the throat that was drawn so tight. Her eyes bulging against their sockets, first one and the other plopping loose to swing against her cheeks. A trickling of clear yellowish liquid from between her legs, soaking into the white sock on one leg, falling in a broken stream into the well of the stairs.

'*It isn't real!*' he cried.

Gabby in repose, little white body unclothed and unmoving, as still and quiet as death. Her stomach cut open, sticky sweaty organs breaking free, throbbing as they wriggled forth like slimy parasites. Her mouth beginning to open while these slithering things that were her existence escaped. Her fingers missing. Her feet blunted, each toe gone. She was calling for him, calling for *Daddee . . . Daddee . . . DaddeeEEE!*

'*Illusion!*' he screamed.

But the thing facing him on the dam only laughed, a deep, gutteral noise that was as evil as her deranged mind.

His head shot sideways as an invisible force swiped at him. He touched his stinging cheek, feeling the hotness there. Yet she had not moved. Her snickering taunted him as cold, iron fingers jabbed at his lower body, clamping his testicles, excrutiating pain doubling him over.

'Illusion, my lovely?' came her voice.

He shrieked and fell to his knees as the unseen hand turned to fire and thrust up inside his anus, piercing through, singeing the passage, reaching for his innards to melt and pulp them in its flaming grip.

'*ILLUSION?*' she demanded.

And although the agony was beyond belief, a white searing brand risen high inside him, an intense hurting that clawed his fingers and bowed his head against the concrete, Childes understood it was not real, the appalling severity driving off fear itself, and with the fear her intimidating control of his thoughts.

The pain ceased immediately with the realization. But he was left weakened and slumped against the parapet wall. He stared up at the black looming shape that had not moved.

'Illusion,' he affirmed breathlessly.

Her anger rushed out at him like a wind squall, pressing him to the stone. A sharp scratching against his pupils blurred his sight and his fingers reached for the shrivelled contact lenses, tearing them from his eyes. He dropped the crinkled plastic onto the walkway and struggled to regain his feet, blinking away tears.

An unknown pressure tried to force him down, but Childes resisted, his hand reaching for the ledge above to pull himself up. *Not real*, he kept telling himself, *not real, not real!* Tentatively he struck out at the monstrosity in front of him. Not with his body. Not with his fists. With his mind. He aimed a blow at her with his mind.

He was surprised to see her shudder.

She came back at him and Childes reeled, his lower spine jarring against the top of the parapet. But this time the mental strike was softer, had less effect.

He heard voices, distant and somehow hollow, non-existent. They were inside his head and as unreal as the brutal thoughts she sent him. Childes pushed at her mind again and felt her flinch. It was impossible – he *knew* it was impossible – but he was hurting her.

The voices grew louder, but still they were from within and had nothing to do with the night.

It seemed as though she were listening too, but again she endeavoured to wound him with her own secret torture. Cruel clawing fingers that weren't really there dug into his face, drawing down, jagged nails raking his skin. He felt their pressure, but not the pain. A curious vibration had begun to hum through his body as though flowing through arteries and nerves, and the voices dipped and dived inside his head.

'No more,' came her rasping growl. 'Game's over for you, my lovely!'

She lumbered forward and her hands were like huge crane claws reaching out for him.

Outrage helped. Childes aimed for that wide fleshy face, his fist balled into a weapon. It struck the blob of her nose, but she turned her head, lessening the damage. Blood smeared her upper lip.

One big hand swatted his away and then she was upon him, crushing his body against the low wall with her bulky weight. The breath rattled wheezingly in her throat. A rough hand went beneath his chin, lifting, pushing back his jaw so that he was sure the bones in his neck would snap. His fingers encircled that fat wrist and he tried to wrench it away, but she was too strong, too incredibly strong. He struck at her face and she merely shrugged off the blows. His back stretched over the ledge and Childes could sense the empty space behind him.

His feet left the concrete floor and kicked uselessly at the obese body that held him there.

His mind went cold.

He was going to die.

Oddly, he was aware of the breeze brushing against his cheeks. And he was aware of the abyss behind. His blurred eyes were filled with the roundness of the full moon, its edges hazy to him now, as it watched impassively, lighting his upturned face with an umblemished radiance. He smelled her foul breath, harsh and heated with her exertions, as well as her body odour, stale with sweat and uncleanliness. So keenly acute were his senses that his thoughts mingled with hers, their separate psyches almost merging so that he knew her, touched the craziness that was inside, flinched back when it spasmed as if to seize. And as his mind retreated from hers, he was aware that she also heard the screeching voices, for they were within both their minds.

His balance had gone, his weight pivoted over the ledge; she held him their as though prolonging the moment.

But she was looking around, searching for the voices. She stopped. She looked towards the end of the dam, its granite structure softened by moonlight.

Childes managed to pull himself back a little while her attention was diverted. He swivelled his head, followed her gaze.

Saw the misty shapes drifting towards them.

They came from the night like wisps of curling vapour, nebulous and vague, a gauzy shifting of air, thin ethereal shapes that had little form and no substance.

Yet theirs were the voices that wailed inside Childes' consciousness.

At first they seemed almost as one, a delicate cloud bank slowly moving along the top of the dam, but they had soon begun to separate, unthread into individual plasmic patterns, becoming different entities. Evolving into definite forms.

The woman's grip on him loosened as she straightened, an expression of bewilderment on her puffy, moonlit face. There was something more than simply uneasy surprise in her reaction, but this Childes sensed through her mind: it was an inner tremor, a flickering of fear. He eased himself from her grasp and slipped back onto the walkway, wrist muscles quivering with the effort of hauling his body over; he sank to the concrete floor, his shoulders resting against the parapet wall.

She had hardly noticed his movement, so intent were her shadowed eyes on the drifting spectres. Her brow was furrowed into deep shaded ruts and her big killer's hands were clenched before her as though Childes were still in their grip. She took a step backwards, obese body at an angle to the approaching mists, only her head turned in their direction.

Closer they came.

Childes was weakened, as if these immaterial bodies were drawing off his strength, using his energy; but the madwoman's body sagged also, for they sucked at her spirit just as they fed off his.

He began to understand what she meant when she had spoken of the gift they shared and how strong and how *beautifully* powerful it was. But had she really known how powerful the gift could be? For it was gradually becoming evident what these slow-twisting apparitions were. Electric shivers ran through Childes and he cowered back against the wall.

The woman – *It* – the creature – the killer – was now standing in the centre of the walkway like some squat monolith as flat white light from above eerily revealed the advancing forms, their shapes becoming less firm, less incorporeal affording only occasional glimpses of the terrain beyond their discarnate bodies.

The first was small and no more than a boy. A very young boy. A very pale boy. A boy whose flesh held no blood, whose eyes held no life, and who shivered in his nakedness. A young boy whose stomach had been gouged out, shreds of skin flapping loosely over his emptiness. His mouth had opened and there were earth things inside, tiny crawling pallid grubs that always fed from graves. His decomposed lips moved and although he uttered no sounds, his words could be heard.

'*Iv i mack,*' the boy said, and those words in both Childes' and the woman's minds were slurred and ill-formed, as though the gluttonous worms feeding on his tongue also interfered with is ghostly thoughts.

'*Iv i mack.*'

('Give it back.')

'*I ont i mack.*'

('I want it back.')

His skeletal hand reached out for the heart that had been stolen from him. The woman lurched and this time it was she who clung to the parapet.

Another immaterial figure came from behind the boy, this one, Childes discerned, a female; lipstick was smeared across her face as though a violent hand – or perhaps lips just as ferocious – had spread the redness. Mascara had run from her eyelashes in thick sooty rivers, giving her the painted mask of a demented clown, sick make-up to frighten small children. Like the boy, she was naked, her torso slit from breastbone (except there were no breasts, only runny wounds were breasts should have been) to pubic hair. Crude stitch-work had burst and objects protruded and fell from that crossed gash, hilariously funny objects, although no one was laughing, no one found them amusing: a hairbrush, an alarm-clock, a hand mirror - even a small transistor radio. She pulled at the edges of the wound like a woman closing a cardigan, afraid to lose any more items, as if those foreign objects were actually her lifeforce, her internal organs. There was a baleful hatred in her smudged eyes for the woman who had so ravaged her body and had not even paid for the privilege.

That woman, dressed in her oversized anorak, put up a fat, ugly hand to ward them off.

But an old man had slipped between the grotesquely painted prostitute and the shivering boy, a lewd, ridiculous grin on his wizened face. Pyjamas hung loosely over his emaciated frame and the moon struck his eyes to give them vitality, a reflected gleam that was full of lunacy. Dried, caked blood darkened his pallid features in parts, and his head ended an inch or so above his eyebrows, sheered flat, more squirming things sucking at the protruding mushy pulp. He gibbered uncontrollably (again the sound only in their minds) as if cold air and gorging parasites were doing funny things to his exposed brain.

The woman shrieked, the cry as manic as the old man's gibbering, and

Childes cringed back, refusing to believe but knowing it was happening.

Now it was the woman's turn to cry: '*It's not real!*'

The shifting figures crowded around her, pulling and snatching at her clothes, raking her face with their hands. The boy stood on tiptoe to reach into one black pit hoping to pluck out an eye.

She pushed him away, but he came back, and he was laughing at the game. She was dragged to her knees – or perhaps she fell in terror – and she thrashed her arms, all the while shouting, '*Not real, you're not real!*'

They became still and looked down at her gross, huddled bulk, the old man sniggering, the prostitute holding her stomach with cupped hands, the boy pleading for the return of his heart.

'Illusion,' Childes whispered and the woman, the she-thing – *It* – screamed at him.

'*Make them go away, make them go away!*'

And for a moment, as his thoughts wavered between reality and illusion, it seemed their forms did partially fade, did become insubstantial mists again. Did become nothing more than thought projections.

Until a diminutive figure pushed her way through the fluctuating images to confront the obesity huddled on hands and knees.

The little girl wore a thin cotton dress and there were no shoes or socks on her feet, no jumper or cardigan to keep off the chill night air. One side of her hair was braided into a plait and tied with a ribbon; the other side was loose and straggly, the ribbon gone. Her cheeks glistened like damp marble and a tiny hand sought to rub away tears. But the hand had no fingers; it ended in five blood-clotted stumps.

'Annabel,' said Childes in an awed breath.

'I want to go home now,' she said to the quivering woman, her voice small and squeaky, reminding Childes of Gabby's.

The woman raised her head and howled, a long wailing cry of anguish that was amplified over the reservoir's watery acres, swelling to become hollow and plaintive.

The boy plunged in his hand, sinking it into the woman's eye socket almost up to the thin wrist – at least it looked as if it were so to Childes. *Impossible*, Childes insisted to himself, *a nightmare only!* But when the skeletal fingers were suckingly withdrawn, dark fluid gushing in their wake, they held something round and glistening, something that was restrained by a thin stretching tendril which eventually snapped, a thread left dangling in the oozing liquid.

The woman rose, clutching at the gushing hole in her face to stem the blood flow. She shrieked and wailed and screamed and begged to be left alone.

But they would *not* leave her alone: instead they pushed forward and reached for her.

She tore herself free, striking out, unbalancing the old man so that the pulpy substance and its feeding parasites inside the open container of his skull spilled out like contents from a weird Toby jug. He bent over, still grinning, still inanely sniggering, and picked up the liquefying brain from the concrete, replacing it inside the jug of his skull as easily as someone donning a hat; in truth, the gesture had all the ludicrousness of a geriatric replacing a wind-blown hairpiece.

Childes wondered if it was he, himself, who had finally gone mad.

The woman was backing away, tripping over Childes' sprawled legs as she retreated and grabbing at the parapet ledge to maintain her balance, moving towards the other end of the dam, towards the water tower, towards an escape into the trees and undergrowth where she had skulked earlier. The moonlit shapes drifted after her, arms still reaching, lustreless eyes intent on her. They followed, wandering past Childes as though *he* were the ghost, unnoticed, unperceived.

Only the small figure who had been Annabel stopped to linger by him.

Childes watched the stumbling woman retreat, despising her for the atrocities her perverted yet extraordinary mind had allowed, but taking no pleasure from this macabre retribution. One of her hands pressed against her eye socket, the fingers inky with leaking substance, but she never ceased moving backwards, shuffling away from those stalking spectres. Finally she turned her back on them, her stumbling pace increasing, nightmarish terror forcing her thick legs with their overflowing ankles into a staggering lope.

She soon came to a halt. She began to back away from the steps that she herself had risen from earlier like a ghoul from a dank tomb.

She reversed into the eagerly waiting arms of those who had followed.

Beyond her, Childes saw what had brought her to a stop, for more ethereal figures were mounting the steps, their heads coming into view first, then their shoulders, their chests, their waists, and they were not wearing their night-clothes in which they had burned to death, but their school uniforms, the La Roche colours monochromed in the moonlight, unsoiled and uncharred by flames, although their bodies were blackened and gristled, their hair gone, skulls darkened and mangled, with exposed lipless teeth set in hideous grins and flesh hanging in rotted slivers, and Kelly pointing with a burnt and withered arm at the lumbering hulk of the woman, while her companions giggled as if Kelly had whispered some risqué joke . . .

. . . And Miss Piprelly leading them, her charcoaled head resting on one shoulder, perched uneasily there as if about to topple, her oddly tilted eyes blazing whitely from blackened bones and skin, yet full of infinite sadness, full of weeping . . .

. . . And Matron following up from behind, herding her girls, checking that none had strayed, none were lost, and all were sound and the scars and melted tissue did not hurt, that there was no longer any searing pain, not for the girls and not for her . . .

Everything was blurred to Childes now that he no longer had his contact lenses, yet somehow everything was crystal clear inside his head. Clear even when tears crept into his eyes as the crocodile file of girls, led by their principal and tailed by their ever-watchful matron, became momentarily whole again, their unmarked flesh glowing with life, Miss Piprelly's head erect and body ramrod proud, Kelly bubbling and impudent as ever, her pointing hand smooth and slender, with only their eyes still dead things. The change was fleeting. By the time they had all climbed the steps and were on a level with the transfixed woman, they were charred and disfigured corpses once more.

The woman's screams were piercingly shrill as the drifting figures converged on her, discarnate bodies hemming her in, clutching and tearing, beating her, raining blows that should have no effect, yet which somehow drew blood, somehow caused the woman, the *beast*, to fall back. One thick arm was raised to protect her face while her other hand still covered her gouged eyes. Childes became aware that in the background and more hazily vague, observing rather than participating, was the figure of a uniformed man, the blood-seeping slash at his throat matching the tight-lipped smile on his wan face. Childes thought of the policeman he had found slumped in his patrol car at La Roche. Other shapes moved in the background, but these had no definite form, could indeed have been nothing more than mist drifting in from the lake. But there was laughter and moaning and wailing among those vapours.

Still sprawled against the wall, Childes watched on, horrified and unable to move, unable even to call out. The silent figure of Annabel stood nearby.

The woman was leaning back against the parapet, her huge sloping shoulders stretching over the ledge in an effort to keep away from those grasping spectral hands. She twisted to protect her face and a stream of blood ran through the fingers to splatter against the dam's massive wall, where the flow continued to trickle down, a dark leak on a vast concrete expanse.

The next thing to happen was so fast that Childes was unsure of what he had seen – or what he had perceived, for his brain still insisted that none of this was true, that it wasn't taking place at all.

She might have attempted to climb onto the parapet to escape them.

In her wretched pain and craziness, she might even have decided to jump.

Or the figures that surrounded her might have really lifted those huge tree-trunk legs and pushed her over.

Whichever, Childes saw her huge bulk disappear and heard her scream rip through the night.

He closed his eyes, shutting out the madness, retreating into a blankness that unfortunately hid nothing. Everything was still there before him inside his besieged mind.

'Oh God . . .' he moaned. And opened his eyes.

The shapes were less defined, had become vaporous and uncertain once more. They grouped on the walkway, forms indiscernible and undulating as if disturbed by the breeze. He was dimly aware of other sounds and lights in the distance. Annabel had not moved, was near him, sad and small, her face a fading image of haunting loneliness.

Childes exhaled a sighing breath, air held so long that it had become stale in his lungs. He sagged, his head sinking onto raised knees, arms hanging limply by his sides, hands resting against the concrete like two dead animals who had rolled over and died, his clawed, upturned fingers tiny legs frozen in the air. It was over, and exhaustion claimed him as he wondered if he would ever comprehend the true and intrinsic nature of this woman who had been a devious tormenting abstraction – an *It* – to him for so long: Maniacal, certainly, a monster, too; but possessing such a strange power, a psychic force that was nothing less than demonic. He prayed that the power had been forever laid to rest.

And felt the cold insidious prickling ruffle his skin again.

Childes raised his head and looked towards the weaving mists, to where the woman had fallen. His mouth slowly dropped open, his eyelids stretched wide, and a trembling shook him as it had before.

For, even though his vision was poor, he could make out the shape of the big hand whose stubby fingers curled over the ledge like a fleshy clamp. Holding her there.

'No,' he murmured, a mere whisper to himself. 'Oh no.'

Was there a flicker of pleading in Annabel's otherwise lustreless eyes?

Childes twisted onto his knees, groped a shaking hand towards the ledge above, and pulled himself up. It seemed at first that his legs would not bear his weight, but strength returned like blood flowing into a limb that had gone to sleep, the process almost as painful.

He leaned heavily against the ledge for a brief time, then stumbled towards the clutching hand. The mists appeared to reassemble as he approached, again taking on separate forms. His legs were unsteady and he had become curiously numbed by all that had happened. When he drew near, the wispy figures parted.

They watched him, remote and impassive. The grinning old man whose skull lay open to the sky. The naked boy who held something white and bloody in his frail fist, something he tried to push into the deep wound in his body as if to replace his lost heart. The bizarrely painted woman whose breasts were missing and whose belly bulged with small lumps as she pulled the sliced skin together. The schoolgirls and the matron, grisly, charred figures whose bones shone dully through gaping and mangled flesh. The uniformed man with two tight smiles, one above his chin, the other below. Estalle Piprelly, for a moment whole, unmarked, and who looked deep into Childes' eyes, an emotion passing between them.

They watched Childes and they waited.

He reached the spot where the hand spread over the ledge to grip the inner side, the fingers seeming to oscillate with the tension of bearing the woman's full weight. He saw the fleshy wrist, the sleeve of the anorak stretched tight over the edge, disappearing at the elbow in the void. Childes leaned over the parapet.

Her round moonlit face was just below him, slick dark liquid that reflected light shading her jaw and cheeks. One eye and a deep black leaking socket stared back at him, her other arm hanging loosely beside her as though useless.

'Help . . . me . . .' she said in her low rasping voice, and there was no entreaty in her tone.

As he looked down into her wide, upturned face, her silver hair sprayed out behind in wild tangles, he touched her madness once more, felt the crawling sickness that went beyond the iniquitous and corrupted mind which worshipped a mythical moon-goddess in insane justification for the evil she herself perpetrated; this sickness sprung from a cruel and degenerate soul, a spirit that was itself malign and rancorous. He felt and *saw* her warped essence not in that one eye that stared up at him so balefully, but in the other deep black oozing pit that watched him with equal malevolence! And the words *help . . . me . . .* were full of taunting, alive with mocking. Childes felt and saw these things because she was in him and he was in her, and she filled him with images, for still she enjoyed the game between them. Her game. Her torture.

But a new sensation passed through that depraved mind when his hand closed over the fat, stubby hand.

Fear stabbed those tormenting thoughts like a blade piercing a pus-filled wound when he lifted her first finger.

A frightened moan as he prised loose the second.

A despairing, outraged shriek as he pushed at the last two fingers and she plummeted down, down, *down*, into the valley, her body bouncing off the sloping dam wall.

Childes heard the squelching breaking thud when she hit the concrete basin below. He slid to the floor of the walkway. And even before he had settled, an overwhelming relief swept through him, his being liberated from a black turbulent pressure, a confused boiling rage. He was too numbed for tears, too wearied for elation. He could only watch as the mists swirled and gradually dispersed.

Although one lingered.

Annabel leaned forward and touched his face with cold little fingers, fingers that had not been there before. Light from the far end of the dam shone through her and she became no more than a floating haze. Then she was gone, had become nothing.

'Illusion,' he said softly to himself.

The lights came from headlamps and torches that shone at the end of the walkway. Childes looked into the glare, shading his eyes with a raised hand. He heard car doors slamming, voices, saw silhouettes appear against the brightness. He was mildly curious to know how they had found him, but not surprised: nothing more could surprise him that night.

Childes no longer wanted to stay there on the dam, even though the illusory mists had dispersed completely and no hand clutched grotesquely at the parapet ledge. The night had presented too much, and now he had to find refuge, his own peace. His head felt light from released pressure and, although he was confused, bewildered, his senses were flushed with a quiet euphoria. He needed time to think, a period for consideration, but acceptance of his sensory ability was complete and calmly acknowledged. For he was sure it could be controlled, used with restraint and intention – *she* had shown him this, although her purpose was unequivocally evil and her deranged mind had exercised a different kind of control. He rose to his feet and looked out, not into the valley, but across the reservoir itself, the moonlight glimmering off the water's placid surface, no longer sinister but with a luminous purity. Childes breathed in crisp nocturnal air, tasting the sea's faint brine, brought inland by the breeze; the air was cleansing and seemed to rid his inner self of skulking shadows. He turned and walked towards the lights.

Overoy was the first to reach him at the foot of the steps, Robillard and two other uniformed policemen close behind.

'Jon,' Overoy said. 'Are you okay? We saw what happened.' He held Childes by the arm.

Childes blinked at the lights.

'Turn those torches away,' Overoy ordered.

The two officers following Robillard went by them, the beams from their torches sweeping towards the centre of the dam's walkway. Robillard signalled for the police car's headlamps to be switched off. The relief was instant, a heavy shade drawn against a blinding sun.

'You saw?' Childes uttered.

'Not clearly,' Robillard said. 'A fogbank had drifted off the reservoir and obscured our view somewhat.'

A fogbank? Childes said nothing.

Overoy spoke quickly, as if anxious to forestall Robillard. 'I saw you trying to save the other person, Jon.' He looked squarely into Childes' eyes and though his gaze appeared expressionless, it barred any dissension. Childes was grateful, while Robillard looked doubtfully at his colleague but made no comment.

Unabashed, Overoy went on: 'I assume she was trying to kill you before she fell. Pity for her she was too heavy for you to hold.' The words were chosen carefully, almost as a statement that should be memorized.

'You knew it was a woman?' said Childes quietly.

Overoy nodded. 'We traced her lodgings back on the mainland. I rang you a couple of times earlier in this evening to let you know, but your line was busy. I was lucky to get the last plane out tonight.'

The two policemen were shining their flashlights over the side of the dam, spotlighting the crumpled shape below.

'What we found at her home wasn't very pleasant – in fact, it was pretty grisly – but at least it proved conclusively that the woman was the killer we were looking for,' Overoy said grimly. 'The girl's body – Annabel's – was hidden under floorboards. To put her there was crazy because eventually the smell of decomposition would have given the woman away; other lodgers would have soon complained. But maybe she didn't care, maybe she already knew the game was up when she fled here. She must have been totally mad, and that's an irony in itself.'

Childes looked at the detective quizzically.

'It's how I got on to her,' Overoy explained. 'Her name was on our list of staff and patients at the psychiatric hospital. She was a nurse, and obviously as lunatic as those in her charge. Christ, you should have seen the junk at her lodgings – occult stuff, books on mythology, emblems, symbols. Oh yeah, and a small collection of moonstones, which must have cost her quite a bit. If each one was for a new victim . . .' Overoy suggested.

'She said she worshipped –'

'The moon? Yeah, she did, one moon-goddess in particular. It was all there in her books, in her ornaments. Crazy, crazy stuff.'

Other figures were on the dam coming towards them.

Robillard spoke. 'When Inspector Overoy gave us the woman's identity, we were easily able to verify that she'd arrived on one of the ferries. She's been here for a couple of weeks, as a matter of fact. After that it was easy to locate her whereabouts on the island. She'd been staying at a guesthouse tucked away inland, far from the coast and main centres. She hadn't been seen all day, but we searched her room. Evidently, you've been lucky tonight, Mr Childes: she left her "tools of the trade", as it were, behind in the guesthouse. We found a small black bag containing surgical instruments. She obviously felt confident enough to do away with you with her bare hands.'

'She was strong enough,' remarked Overoy, 'so we learned from her employers at the hospital. They used her, apparently, to restrain their most violent patients and, according to the doctors and nurses there, she never had much trouble doing just that.'

'Didn't they wonder why she'd disappeared after the fire?'

'She didn't. She was interviewed by the police – she was on our list with the rest of the staff, remember? She took her normal annual vacation after most of the fuss had died down. She was insane, but not stupid.'

Maybe it would all sink in later; for the moment, though, none of what they had told him had much meaning to Childes. He stirred when he heard another voice, one so familiar and so welcome.

'Jon,' Amy called.

He looked past the two detectives and saw her only a few yards away, Paul Sebire holding her arm to support her. There was anxiety on Sebire's face, and it was directed at him.

Childes went to Amy and she raised her hands, the cast on her injured arm reflecting whitely in the moonlight. He hugged her close, loving her and wanting to weep at the sight of her bandaged face. She winced as he held her tight.

He relaxed his grip, afraid to hurt her more.

'It's okay, Jon.' She was laughing and there was a dampness on one cheek. 'It's okay. I was so afraid for you.'

Over her shoulder, he saw Paul Sebire frowning. The older man said nothing as he turned and walked back to the cars parked at the end of the dam.

Childes stroked her hair, kissed the tears from her cheek. 'How did you know where to find me?' he asked.

Amy was smiling and returning his kisses. Somehow she sensed the change in him, the dark cloud that had shadowed him for so long now swept away. It was as though his very thoughts transmitted that change to her.

'We found out from Gabby,' she told him.

'From Gabby?'

Overoy had joined them, and it was he who said, 'We went to Miss Sebire's home tonight looking for you after the patrolman watching your place lost you. She didn't know where you were –'

'But I remembered you said you'd spoken to Gabby earlier,' Amy interrupted. 'It was only an idea, but I thought you might have mentioned to Fran where you were going tonight. Inspector Overoy considered it worth a try, anyway, so he rang Fran at her mother's number. She was having problems with Gabby.'

'Your daughter was in hysterics because of a nightmare she'd had,' Overoy continued. 'She'd dreamt you were by a huge lake and there was a monster-lady trying to drag you down. Your wife told us Gabby was inconsolable.'

'You knew where I was from that?' Childes asked incredulously.

'Well, I'm used to *your* precognition by now, so why shouldn't I believe your daughter?'

Gabby too? Childes was stunned. He remembered she had asked him to tell Annabel she missed her.

Amy broke into his shocked thoughts. 'There are no "huge" lakes on the island, Jon. Only the reservoir.'

'We had nothing to lose,' added Overoy with a grin.

'No, just me to convince,' commented Robillard. 'But what the hell? None of this business has made much sense to me, so why should I mind tearing across the countryside in the middle of the night up to the reservoir.' He shook his head in perplexity. 'As it happens, they were right. My only regret is that we didn't get here sooner. You've been through quite an ordeal.'

'Is it over, Jon?' implored Amy, her hand reaching up to touch his face. 'Is it really over now?'

He nodded, but the moon shone from behind him so she could not see his face. He turned to look at Overoy.

'Who was she?' he asked the detective. 'What's was her name?'

'She had an assumed name, we discovered, one she'd been using for years. She called herself Heckatty.' For some reason, there was a certain satisfaction in Overoy's tone.

Heckatty. The name meant nothing to Childes. And he hadn't expected it to. He wasn't even sure of what had taken place that night. Had their spirits really returned to haunt the creature whose very name was so ordinary, so meaningless? Or had the fusion between their minds, his violent psychic contact with this madwoman, brought forth imaginations that were merely, in essence, visions and fragments of disrupted minds.

'Illusions,' he said quietly to himself yet again, and Amy looked up at him, puzzled.

'Oh my God,' came a voice from near the centre of the walkway.

They turned in the direction of the two policemen who were crouched on the bridge section of the dam and shining torches on an object lying between them. One officer was taking something from his tunic pocket to push it beneath whatever was lying there. He rose and made his way back to the watching group, gingerly carrying the object down the steps of the bridge, his companion following.

Of course all their faces were colourless under the moonlight, but there was a tightness to this officer's features that suggested he had become physically pallid.

'I don't think you want to see this, Miss,' he said to Amy, shielding the item he held so carefully on the small plastic bag taken from his pocket.

Curious, Overoy and Robillard moved closer to look.

'Oh . . .' murmured Robillard.

Childes moved away from Amy. The other policeman was shining his torch at his colleague's cupped hands. Overoy had turned away, his face wrinkled in disgust.

'Some struggle you had,' he said sympathetically to Childes, who stared down at what the officers had found.

The bloodstained eye looked too ridiculously large to have been contained in a face. Dripping tendrils hung loosely over the side of the plastic bag and, as Childes looked down and the policeman's hands turned slightly, moonlight struck the eye's pupil. For a moment – just for a *fleeting* moment – a glint, almost like a tiny life-force, was reflected in there, and to Childes it had resembled the bluish phosphorescence that shone from within a moonstone.

Childes shivered as he turned away, and breathed in deeply, as he had only a short time before, dispersing shadows.

He slipped an arm around Amy's waist, pulling her gently to him, and they left that haunted, silver lake.

And Childes wondered where this newly-accepted power would lead him . . .

Shrine

Red blood out and black blood in,
My Nannie says I'm a child of sin.
How did I choose me my witchcraft kin?
Know I as soon as dark's dreams begin
Snared is my heart in a nightmare's gin;
Never from terror I out may win;
So dawn and dusk I pine, peak, thin,
Scarcely knowing t'other from which –
My grandma – She was a Witch.

THE LITTLE CREATURE:
Walter de la Mare

PART ONE

Alice! a childish story take,
  And with a childish hand
Lay it where Childhood's dreams are twined
  In memory's mystic band,
Like pilgrim's wither'd wreath of flowers
  Plucked in a far-off land.

ALICE'S ADVENTURES IN WONDERLAND:
Lewis Carroll

ONE

Down with the lambs,
Up with the lark,
Run to bed children
Before it gets dark.

OLD NURSERY RHYME

The small mounds of dark earth scattered around the graveyard looked as though the dead were pushing their way back into the living world. The girl smiled nervously at the thought as she hurried from grave to grave. They were molehills. Moles were difficult to get rid of; poison one, another moved into its lodgings. She had often watched the molecacher, a round man with a pointed face, and thought he looked like a mole. He grinned as he delicately dipped stubby fingers into his baked beans tin and plucked out a strychnine-coated worm from its wriggling friends and relatives. He always grinned when she watched. And chuckled when he held it towards her and she jumped away with a silent shriek. His lips, ever wet, like his dosed worms, moved but she heard nothing. She hadn't for as long as she remembered. A shudder as the molecatcher mimed eating the writhing pink meat, but she always stayed to watch him push his metal rod into the earth then poke the worm into the hole he had created. She imagined the mole down there, snuffling its way through solid darkness, hunting food, searching for its own death. Digging its own grave. She giggled and couldn't hear her giggle.

Alice stooped and took withered flowers from a mud-soiled vase. The headstone against which the flowers had rested was fairly new, its inscription not yet filled with dirt nor blurred by weather. She had known the old lady – was she just bones now? – and had found the living corpse more frightening than the dead one. Could you be alive at ninety-two? You could move, but could you live? The time-span was incomprehensible to Alice, who was just eleven years old. It was hard to imagine your own flesh dried and wrinkled, your brain shrunken by years of use so that instead of becoming wise and all-knowing you became a baby. A hunched, brittle-stick baby.

She dumped the dead flowers into the red plastic bucket she carried and moved on, her eyes scanning the untidy rows of headstones for more. It was a weekly task for her: while her mother scrubbed, dusted and polished the church, Alice removed the drooping tributes left by relatives who thought those they had lost would appreciate the gesture. The flowers would be emptied into the groundsman's tip of rotting branches and leaves, there to be ritually burnt once a month. When this chore was completed, Alice would hurry back into the church and join her mother. Inside she would find fresh flowers ready to adorn the altar for the following day's Sunday services and, while her mother scrubbed, she would arrange the glass vases. Afterwards, she would dust down the benches, skimming along each row, down one, up the next, holding her breath, seeing how far she could get before her lungs exploded. Alice enjoyed the work if she could make it a game.

Once this was accomplished, and provided her mother had no other tasks for her, she would head for her favourite spot: the end of the front pew at the right-hand side of the altar.

Beneath the statue. *Her* statue.

More fading colours caught her eye and she skipped across a low mound – this one body length and not mole-built – to gather up the dying flowers. Tiny puffs of steam escaped her mouth and she told herself they were the ghosts of words that lay dead inside her, words that had never themselves escaped.

It was cold, although it was sunny. The trees were mostly bare, their naked branches seen for the twisted and tortured things they really were. Sheep, their bellies swollen with slow-stirring foetuses, grazed in the fields just beyond the stone wall surrounding the churchyard. Across the fields were heavy woods, sombre and greeny brown, uninviting; and behind the woods were low-lying hills, hills that were lost completely on misty days. Alice stared into the field, watching the sheep. She frowned, then turned away.

More flowers to collect before she could go inside where the air was not quite as biting. Cold – the church was always cold – but winter's teeth were less sharp inside the old building. She wandered through the graveyard, the tilted headstones no bother to her, the decomposed corpses hidden beneath her feet causing no concern.

The sodden leaves and branches were piled high, higher than her, and the girl had to swoop the plastic bucket back and swiftly forward for its wasted contents to reach the top. She reached for stems that fell back down and tossed them once more, satisfied only when they settled on the heap's summit. Alice smacked her hands together to dislodge the grime on her palms, feeling the sting, but not hearing the sound. She could once, but that was long ago. When she listened intently and there were no distractions, she thought she could hear the wind; but then Alice thought that even when no breeze brushed her cheeks or ruffled her yellow hair.

The small, thin girl turned and began to walk towards the ancient church, the empty bucket swinging easily by her side. Back, forwards, back, forwards, gleaming red in the cold sunlight. Back, forwards, back – and she looked behind her.

The plastic bucket slipped from her fingers and clattered to the ground, rolling in a tight semi-circle until it came to rest against a stained green headstone. Alice cocked her head to one side as though listening. There was a puzzlement in her eyes and she half-smiled.

She stood still for several seconds before allowing her body to turn fully, staying in that frozen position for several more long seconds. Her half-smile faded and her face became anxious. She moved slowly at first, making for the rough stone wall at the rear of the churchyard, then broke into a run.

Something tripped her – probably the corner of a flattened gravestone – and she tumbled forward, her knees smearing green and brown from the soft earth. She cried out, but there was no sound, and quickly regained her feet, eager to reach the wall and not knowing why. She kept to the narrow path leading through the cluttered graveyard and stopped only when she had reached the wall. Alice peered over, the highest stone on a level with her chest. The pregnant sheep were no longer munching grass; all heads were raised and looking in the same direction.

They did not move even when Alice clambered over the wall and ran among them.

Her footsteps slowed, her shoes and socks soaked by the long grass. She seemed confused and swivelled her head from left to right. Her small hands were clenched tight.

She looked directly ahead once more and the half-smile returned, gradually broadening until her face showed only rapturous wonder.

A solitary tree stood in the centre of the field, an oak, centuries old, its body thick and gnarled, its stout lower branches sweeping outwards, their furthest points striving to touch the ground again. Alice walked towards the tree, her steps slow but not hesitant, and fell to her knees when she was ten yards away.

Her mouth opened wide, and her eyes narrowed, the pupils squeezing down to tiny apertures. She raised a hand to protect them from the blinding light that shimmered from the base of the tree.

Then her smile returned as the light dazzled into a brilliant sun, an unblemished whiteness. A holy radiance.

TWO

Another Maiden like herself,
Translucent, lovely, shining clear,
Threefold each in the other clos'd –
O, What a pleasant trembling fear!

THE CRYSTAL CABINET
William Blake

The white van slid to an abrupt halt and the driver's head came uncomfortably close to the windscreen. Cursing, he pushed himself back off the steering wheel and smacked the hardened plastic as though it were the hand of an errant child.

The van's headlights lit up the trees on the other side of the T-junction and the driver peered left and right, grumbling to himself as he tried to penetrate the surrounding darkness.

'Should be right, got to be right.'

There was no one else in the van to hear, but that didn't bother him: he was used to talking to himself. 'Right it is.'

He shoved the gear lever into first and winced at the grinding sound. The van lurched forward and he swung the wheel to the right. Gerry Fenn was tired, angry, and a little drunk. The public meeting he had attended earlier that evening had been dull to say the least, dreary to say the most. Who gave a shit whether or not the more remote houses in the locale went on to main drainage? Not the occupiers, that was for sure; a link-up with the sewage system meant higher rates for them. Nearly two hours to decide nobody wanted drains. They preferred their cesspits. As usual, Rent-a-Left had prolonged proceedings. A totalitarian sewer network was good for the cause, Fenn supposed. He hadn't intended to stay that long, hadn't even needed to. The fact was, he had fallen asleep at the back of the hall and only the noisy conclusion to the meeting had aroused him. The agitators were angry that the motion for had been defeated – good headline in that: 'LOCAL SEWER MOTION DEFEATED'. Too pithy for the *Courier*, though. Pithy. That wasn't bad either. He nodded his head in appreciation of his own wit.

Gerry Fenn had been with the *Brighton Evening Courier* for more than five years now – man and boy, he told himself – and was still waiting for the big one, the story that would make world headlines, the scoop that would transport him from the seaside town's local rag to the heart of the journalistic world: FLEET STREET! Kermit applause for FLEET STREET! YEEAAAY! Three years indenture at Eastbourne, five on the *Courier*. Next step: leader of the *Insight* team on the *Sunday Times*. Failing that, *News of the World* would do. Plenty of human interest there. Dig up the dirt, dole out the trash. File the writs.

He had phoned the newsdesk after the meeting, telling the night news editor (who hadn't been amused by Fenn's instruction to HOLD THE FRONT PAGE!) that the meeting had ended in near-riot and he had barely escaped with his vitals intact let alone his notebook. When the news editor had informed him that the office junior had just resigned because of an emotional crisis in his sixteen-year-old life, so the vacancy was available, Fenn had modified his story, explaining that the meeting really had been lively and maybe he should have left sooner but when the wild-eyed Leftie had rushed the platform and tried to stuff a turd (it looked like a dog's, obviously just used for effect) into the nostrils of a surprised lady councillor, he figured . . . Fenn held the phone away, almost seeing the spit spluttering from the earpiece. Excited pips brought the tirade to an end, and a fresh coin renewed the connection. The news editor had gained control by then, but only just. Since Fenn enjoyed the country route so much, there were a couple of little items he could cover in that area. Fenn groaned, the news editor went on. A trip to the local cop shop: find out if the boy scout impersonators (bob-a-job, once inside, pension books, loose money, small valuables, gone) were still impersonating boy scouts. Pop into the local flea-pit: were feminists still daubing the sexy posters outside with anti-rape graffiti and chucking runny tomatoes at the screen inside? On the way back visit the caravan site at Partridge Green: see if they've got their power yet (the *Courier* had run a small campaign for the residents encouraging Seeboard to connect the site to the grid – so far it had taken six months). Fenn asked if the news editor knew what the bloody time was and was assured of course he bloody did and was Fenn aware that all his night shift had produced for tomorrow's editions was one RTA (Road Traffic Accident) and one diabetic poodle who went for check-ups in a bloody Rolls-Royce? And the RTA wasn't even fatal.

Fenn got mad and advised the news editor of his agitated state and informed him that when he returned to the office he would show the news editor just how mad he really was by shoving his copy spike right up his tiny arse, wooden end first, and by stuffing the nearest typewriter into the fat mouth which was always full of shit but never kind shit, then brain-drain the *Courier* totally by handing in his resignation. He told the news editor good, but made sure the receiver was resting on its cradle before he did so.

His next call was to Sue to tell her to expect him when he got there, but there was no reply from his flat. Then none from hers. He wished for Chrissakes she would move in with him permanently; it was a pain never knowing where she was likely to be.

Thoroughly morose, he did what he was paid for. The boy scout impersonators were now impersonating jumble-sale collectors (one old lady had even lost her false teeth – she'd left them on the kitchen table – but was understandably reluctant to talk about it). The flea-pit had been running *Bambi* for the past fortnight (expected trouble next week when *Teenage Goddesses of Love* and *Sex in the Swamps* was playing). He drove to Partridge Green and saw only candlelight through the caravan windows (he knocked on one door and was told to piss off so didn't bother with any more).

He scraped in to the nearest pub just five minutes before closing time and fortunately the landlord wasn't adverse to afters once the main crowd – two domino players and a woman with a cat in a wooden cage – was cleared. Fenn let it slip that he was from the *Brighton Evening Courier*, an admission that could have got him shown the door pretty promptly, or engaged in an informative after-hours drink. Landlords generally sought the good will of the local press (even the most drab were contenders for the Pub of the Year Award) unless they had some private reason for feeling bitter towards journalists (exposed marital upsets, too many voluptuous barmaids in the business, or reported unhygienic kitchens was usually the cause for their distrust). This one was okay; he even allowed Fenn to buy him a rum and pep, a gesture that had the reporter mentally scratching his head – shouldn't the landlord be cosying up to him, not the other way round? He wasn't in to investigative journalism tonight – Fleet Street and the world's wire services would have to wait until he was in the mood – so why the hell was he treating the landlord? Oh yeah, so he could drink after time, that was it. Fenn was tired.

Three pints and forty minutes of unexciting conversation later, Fenn found himself outside in the cold night air, bolts snapping behind telling him the drawbridge was up, the public house was no longer a refuge but a stronghold, built to resist the strongest invaders. He kicked the side of the white van before throwing himself into the driver's seat.

The vehicle was an embarrassment. It carried his newspaper's name, white lettering in a brilliant red flash, on both sides. Very discreet. Very undercover. The *Courier* had fallen out with their usual fleet hire company and now the journalists had either to use their own cars, for which there was no petrol allowance, or the one and only spare delivery van. Great for tailing suspected arsonists or dope peddlers. Great for keeping an eye on illicit rendezvous between well-knowns who should well-know better. Ideal for secret meetings with your favourite grass. Would Woodstock and Bernstein have met 'Deep Throat' in a fucking white van with *Washington Post* emblazoned on its sides?

The headlights barely pierced the darkness ahead and Fenn shook his head in further disgust. Bloody things were never cleaned. Christ, what a night. Sometimes the late shift could be good. A nice rape or mugging. The occasional murder. Brighton was full of weirdos nowadays. And Arabs. And antique dealers. Funny things happened when they all got together. Trouble was, many of the best stories never got into print. Or if they did, they were toned down. It wasn't the *Courier*'s policy to denigrate the seaside town's image. Bad for business. Great for family trade, Brighton. Mustn't scare off the punters. Unfortunately his earlier routine calls had produced nothing of interest. He always made the standard calls when he came on duty: police, hospitals, undertakers and fire stations were all on his regular list. Even the clergy merited a bell. Nothing much doing with any of them. The newspaper's *Diary*, listing events of the day (and night) which had to be covered, offered little to excite. If it had, he could have probably ducked out of tonight's council meeting; as it was, there wasn't much else to do.

Lights ahead. What town was that? Must be Banfield. He'd passed it on the way out. Not a bad little place. Two pubs on the High Street. What more could anyone ask? If the weather was nice on Sunday he might bring Sue out for a drink. She liked country pubs. More atmosphere. Real ale. Usually a fair selection of gumboots, polonecks, and tweeds. With the odd diddicoi thrown in to lower the tone.

He squinted his eyes. Bend ahead. So bloody dark. Whoops. Brake. Downhill.

The van levelled out at the bottom of the hill and Fenn eased his foot off the pedal. Sure these brakes are going, he told himself. Sometimes he suspected the delivery men sabotaged the vehicle as a mild protest against it being used by journalists. One day, someone was – *Christ, what was that?*

He jammed his foot down and pulled the wheel to the left. The van skidded, turning almost a full circle, front end coming to rest on the grass verge by the side of the road.

Fenn pushed the gear into neutral and briefly rested against the steering wheel. A sharp, quavering sigh later, his head jerked up and he swiftly wound down the window. He poked his head out into the cold night air.

'What the bloody hell was it?' he asked himself aloud.

Something had run out from the darkness straight across his path. Something white. Small, but too big to be an animal. He'd almost hit it. Missed by a couple of inches. His hands were trembling.

He saw movement, a greyish blur.

'Hey!' he shouted.

The blur dissolved.

Fenn pushed the car door open and stepped out onto the damp grass. 'Hold up!' he called out.

Scuffling sounds came his way. Feet on gravel.

He ran across the road and was confronted by a low gate, one side open wide. His eyes were swiftly adapting to the poor light, and the half-moon emerging from slow-moving clouds helped his vision even more. He saw the tiny figure again.

It was running away from him along a path that was lined with trees. He could just make out some kind of building at the end of the path. He shivered. The whole thing was spooky.

It had to be a kid. Or a midget. Fenn tried not to think of Du Maurier's dwarf in *Don't Look Now*. He wanted to get back into the van. His jiggling sphincter muscle could lead to an embarrassment. But if it was a kid, what was it doing out at this hour? It would freeze to death in this weather.

'Hey, come on, stop! I want to talk to you!'

No reply, just slapping feet.

Fenn stepped inside the gate, called out once more, then began to run after the diminishing shape. As he pounded down the path and the building ahead grew larger and more visible, he realized he was in the grounds of a church. What was a kid running into a church for at this time of night?

But the figure, still just in sight, wasn't going to the church. It veered off to the left just as it reached the big cavern doors and disappeared around the corner of the building. Fenn followed, his breath becoming laboured. He almost slipped, for the path was muddy now, and narrower. He recovered and kept going until he reached the back of the church. There he came to an abrupt halt and wished he'd stayed in the van.

A dark playground of silent, still, greyish shapes spread out before him. Oh, Jesus, a graveyard!

The blur was skipping among them, the only moving thing.

The moon decided it had had enough. It pulled a cloud over its eyes like a blanket.

Fenn leaned against the side of the church, its flint brickwork rough against his moist hands. He was following a bloody ghost. It would roll into a grave at any moment. His instinct was to tiptoe quietly back to the van and go on his uninquisitive way, but his nose which, after all, was a newspaperman's nose, persuaded otherwise. There are no such things as ghosts, only good ghost stories. Walk away from this and you'll always wonder what you missed. Tell your friends (not to mention your pal the editor) you flunked out and they'll never buy you another drink. Go to it, Ace. His nose told him, not his brain, nor his heart.

'Hey!' the shout cracked in the middle and the H was over-pronounced.

He pushed himself away from the wall and strode boldly in among the grey sentinels. He blinked hard when he saw the conical-shaped mounds of dark earth at his feet. *They're making a break for it!*

He forced the explanation from himself. They're molehills, you silly bastard. His weak smile of self-contempt was perfunctory. Fenn caught sight of the wispy figure flitting through the gravestones once more. It appeared to be making its way towards the back of the churchyard where large squarish shapes seemed to be lurking. Oh my God, they're tombs! It's a vampire, a midget vampire, going home to bed! Fenn didn't find himself too amusing.

He crouched, suddenly afraid to be seen. The moon was no friend; it came out for another peep.

Fenn ducked behind a tilting headstone and cautiously peered over the top. The figure was clambering over a low wall. Then it was gone.

Cold night air touched his face and he imagined lonely souls were trying to gain his attention. He didn't want to move, and he didn't want to stay. He didn't want to look over that wall either. But he knew he was going to.

The reporter crept forward, his knee joints already stiff from the cold. Dodging around the graves, doing his best not to disturb the 'not-dead-but-resting', he made for the back of the churchyard, towards the tombs standing like ancient, cracked supermarket freezers, their contents allowed to putrefy. He noticed the lid of one was askew and tried not to see the imaginary hand clawing its way out, skin green with age, nails scraped away, bones glistening through corrupt flesh. Cut it out, Fenn!

He reached the wall and knelt there, not overly-anxious to see what lay beyond. He was shivering, out of breath (kept forgetting to breathe in) and scared stiff. But he was also curious. Fenn raised himself so that his shoulders were level with the top of the wall, head projecting like a coconut waiting to be shied.

There was a field, slate grey and flat in the timid moonlight, and near the middle, some distances away, stood a contorted black spectre. Its multitudinous twisted arms reached skywards while the thicker lower limbs were bent in an effort to reach the ground from which it had sprung. The isolated tree provided a demonic relief in an otherwise dull landscape. Fenn's eyes narrowed as he searched for the little figure. Something was moving. Yes, there it was. Walking directly towards the tree. It stopped. Then walked on. Then – oh Christ, it was sinking into the ground! No, it was on its knees. It didn't move. Nor did the tree.

Fenn waited and grew impatient. The beer he had consumed pressed against his bladder. He continued to wait.

At last he decided if he didn't make something happen, nothing would happen. He climbed over the wall and waited.

Nothing happened.

He walked towards the figure.

As he drew near, he saw that it wasn't a midget.

It was a girl.

A little girl.

And she was staring at the tree.

And she was smiling.

And when he touched her shoulder, she said, 'She's so beautiful.'

Then her eyes rolled upwards and she toppled forward.

And didn't move again.

THREE

'Who are you?' he said at last in a half-hearted whisper. 'Are you a ghost?'
'No, I am not,' Mary answered, her own whisper half-frightened. 'Are you one?'

THE SECRET GARDEN
Frances Hodgson Burnett

Father Hagan lay there in the darkness, forcing his senses to break away from sleep's gooey embrace. His eyes flickered, then snapped open. He could just make out the thin glimmer of night through the almost closed curtains. What had disturbed him?

The priest reached for the lamp on the bedside table and fumbled for the switch. His pupils stung with the sudden light, and it was several seconds before he could open his lids again. He looked at the small clock, his eyes narrowing to a short-sighted squint, and saw it was past midnight. Had he heard something outside? Or inside the house? Or had his own dream disturbed him? He lay back and stared at the ceiling.

Father Andrew Hagan was forty-six years old and had been part of the Church for nearly nineteen of those years. The turning point for him had been two days after his twenty-seventh birthday when a mild heart attack had left him dazed, frightened and exhausted. He had been losing God, allowing the materialism of a chaotic world to confine his spiritual self, to subdue it to a point where only he was aware that it existed. Four years teaching History and Divinity in a Catholic grammar school in London, then three years in a madhouse comprehensive in the suburbs had slowly corroded the outer core of his faith and was chewing on the innermost part, the very centre of his belief which had no answers but merely KNEW. He had to retrieve himself. The closeness of death was like a prodding mother who would not allow her offspring to stay under the bedclothes for one moment longer.

He no longer taught Divinity in the comprehensive school, just History, and occasionally he took an English class; religion in that particular school was almost defunct. Humanity had replaced the subject and the young teacher of

Humanity had been sacked in his second term for blacking the headmaster's eye. English had soon become Hagan's second subject. No longer able to discuss his faith every day with curious, albeit often bored, young minds, his thoughts of God had become more and more introverted, restrained by shackles of self-consciousness. The heart attack, mild though it was, had halted the gradual but seemingly irrevocable slide. Suddenly he was aware of what he had been losing. He wanted to be among others who believed as he, for their belief would strengthen his, their faith would enhance his own. Within a year he was in Rome studying for the priesthood. And now he wondered if the earlier corrosion had not left a seeping residue.

A noise. Outside. Movement. Father Hagan sat upright.

He jumped when someone pounded on the door below.

The priest reached for his spectacles lying on the bedside table and leapt from the bed; he went to the window. He drew the curtains apart, but hesitated before opening the window. More banging encouraged him to do so.

'Who's there?' Cold air settled around his shoulders and made him shudder.

'Just us spooks!' came the reply. 'Will you get down here and open up!'

Hagan leaned out the window and tried to see into the porch below. A figure stepped into view, but was indistinct.

'I've got a problem – *you've* got a problem – here!' the voice said. The man appeared to be carrying something in his arms.

The priest withdrew and quickly pulled on a dressing gown over his pyjamas. He forgot about slippers and padded downstairs in cold, bare feet. Switching on the hall light, he stood behind the front door for a few moments, reluctant to open it. Although the village was close, his church and presbytery were isolated. Fields and woods surrounded him on three sides, the main road at the front being the link with his parishioners. Father Hagan was not a timorous man, but living over a graveyard had to have some effect. A fist thumping against wood aroused him once more.

He switched on the outside porch light before opening the door.

The man who stood there looked frightened, although he was making an attempt to grin. His face was drawn, white. 'Found this wandering around outside,' the man explained.

He moved the bundle in his arms towards the priest, indicating with a nod of his head at the same time. Hagan recognized the frail little body in the nightdress without seeing her face.

'Bring her in quickly,' he said, making way.

He closed the front door and told the man to follow him. He turned on the sitting-room light and made for the electric fire, switching it on.

'Put her on the settee,' he said. 'I'll fetch a blanket. She must be frozen.'

The man grunted as he placed the girl on the soft cushions. He knelt beside her and brushed her long yellow hair away from her face. The priest returned and carefully wrapped a blanket around the still form. Father Hagan studied the girl's peaceful face for several moments before turning back to the man who had brought her to his house.

'Tell me what happened,' he said.

The man shrugged. He was in his late twenties or early thirties, needed a shave, and wore a heavy thigh-length corduroy jacket, its collar turned up against the cold, over dark blue trousers or jeans. His light brown hair was a tangled mess, but not too long. 'She ran across my path – I just braked in time. Thought I was going to hit her.' He paused to look down at the girl. 'Is she asleep?'

The priest lifted one of her eyelids. The pupil gazed back at him without flinching. 'I don't think so. She seems to be . . .' He left the sentence unfinished.

'She didn't stop when I called out to her, so I followed her,' the man went on. 'She ran straight up to the church, then round the back. Into the graveyard out there. It scared the bloody hell out of me.' He shook his head and shrugged again as if to relieve tension. 'Any idea who she is?'

'Her name is Alice,' the priest said quietly.

'Why did she run in here? Where's she from?'

Father Hagan ignored his questions. 'Did she . . . did she climb over the wall at the back of the churchyard?'

The man nodded. 'Uh huh. She ran into the field. How did you know?'

'Tell me exactly what happened.'

The man looked around. 'D'you mind if I sit down for a minute – my legs are kind of shaky.'

'I'm sorry. You must have had a nasty shock, her running out at you like that.'

'It was the bloody graveyard that shook me up.' He sank gratefully into an armchair and let out a long sigh. Then his face became alert again. 'Look, hadn't you better get a doctor? The kid looks done in.'

'Yes, I'll call one soon. First tell me what happened when she went into the field.'

The man looked puzzled. 'Are you her father?' he asked, keen blue eyes looking directly into the priest's.

'I'm a father, but not hers. The church is Catholic, I'm its priest, Father Hagan.'

The man opened his mouth, then nodded in understanding. 'Of course,' he said, managing a brief grin. 'I should've known.'

'And you're Mister . . .?'

'Gerry Fenn.' He decided not to tell the priest that he was from the *Courier* for the moment. 'You live here alone?'

'I have a housekeeper who comes in during the day. Otherwise, yes, I live here alone.'

'Creepy.'

'You were going to tell me . . .'

'Oh yeah. The field. Well, that was weird. I followed her in and found her just kneeling in the grass. She wasn't even shivering, just staring ahead, smiling.'

'Smiling?'

'Yeah, she had a big beam on her face. Like she was watching something, you know? Something that was pleasing her. But all she was looking at was a big old tree.'

'The oak.'

'Hmn? Yeah, I think so. It was too dark to see.'

'The oak is the only tree in that field.'

'Then I guess it was the oak.'

'What happened?'

'Then came the strange part. Well, it was all bloody – sorry, Father – it was all strange, but this was the ringer. I thought she might have been sleep-walking – or sleep-running to be more precise – so I touched her shoulder. Just gentle, you know? I didn't want to frighten her. She just went on smiling and said, "She's so beautiful," like she could see something there by the tree.'

The priest had stiffened and was looking at Fenn so intently that the reporter stopped speaking. He raised his eyebrows. 'Something I said?' he ased.

'You said the girl spoke. Alice spoke to you?'

Fenn was puzzled by the priest's attitude. He shuffled uncomfortably in the seat. 'She didn't actually speak to me. More like to herself. Is there something wrong, Father?'

The priest looked down at the girl and gently brushed her cheek with the palm of his hand. 'Alice is a deaf mute, Mr Fenn. She cannot speak, and she cannot hear.'

Fenn's gaze turned from the priest's face to the girl's. She lay there pale, unmoving, a rumpled frail figure, small and so very vulnerable.

FOUR

'But I don't want to go among mad people,' Alice remarked.
'Oh, you can't help that,' said the Cat: 'We're all mad here. I'm mad. You're mad.'

ALICE'S ADVENTURES IN WONDERLAND
Lewis Carroll

A hand lightly cuffed Fenn's shoulder.

'Hi, Gerry. Thought you had the graveyard shift this week.'

He glanced up to see Morris, one of the *Courier*'s thirteen sub-editors, moving past him, his body half-turned in Fenn's direction but his stride hardly broken as he made for his desk.

'What? Yeah, you don't know the truth of it,' Fenn answered without elaborating. He turned his attention back to the typewriter, quickly reading through the last line he had just two-finger typed. He grunted in satisfaction and his index fingers rapidly stabbed at the machine once more. He ignored the apparent chaos around him: the clatter of other over-used and badly-kept typewriters, the occasional curse or even less occasional burst of raucous laughter, the hum of voices, machines and odours. The hubbub would grow steadily through the day, building to a restrained frenzy which broke without fuss when the evening edition was finally put to bed at 3.45 p.m. Every trainee reporter soon learned the art of closing out the din, their thoughts, hands and black type on paper spinning their own frail cocoon of insularity.

Fenn's right index finger punched a last full-point and he ripped the paper with its three blacks from the machine. He read through it quickly, his smile turning into a broad grin. Shit-hot. Figure appearing like a white banshee in the night. Running out in front of the van. Chasing the apparition. Through the graveyard (could be a little bit more creepy, but let's not overkill). The girl kneeling in the field, staring at the tree. She's small, dressed in white nightgown. Alone. She speaks. Our intrepid reporter later finds out that she is – or was – a deaf mute. Terrific!

Fenn marched between crammed desks, his gleaming eyes on the news editor. He stood over the hunched figure and resisted the urge to tap a finger on the enticing bald dome before him.

'Leave it there, I'll get to it,' the news editor growled.

'I think you ought to read it, Frank.'

Frank Aitken looked up. 'I thought you were on the midnight shift, Hemingway.'

'Yeah, I am. Just a little special for you.' Fenn jiggled the copy in his hand.

'Show it to the sub.' The bald man returned to his pencilling out.

'Uh, just look through it, Frank. I think you'll like the story.'

Aitken wearily laid the pencil down and studied Fenn's smiling face for several moments. 'Tucker tells me you didn't produce last night.' Tucker was the night newsdesk editor.

'I came in with a couple of things, Frank, but not much happened last night. Except for this.'

The copy was snatched from him.

Fenn stuck his hands into his pockets and waited impatiently while Aitken skimmed through the story. He whistled an almost soundless, self-satisfied tune. Aitken didn't look up until he had read every word and when he did there was a look of disbelief on his face.

'What is this shit?' he said.

The grin disappeared from Fenn's face. 'Hey, did you like it or not?'

'You've got to be kidding.'

Fenn leaned on the news editor's desk, his face anxious, his voice beginning to rise. 'It's all true, Frank.' He stabbed at the paper. 'That actually happened to me last night!'

'So what?' Aitken tossed the typed sheet across the desk. 'What's it prove? The kid had a nightmare, went sleep-walking. So what? It's no big deal.'

'But she was deaf and dumb and she spoke to me.'

'Did she say anything to anyone else? I mean, after, when you took her into the priest's house?'

'No, but –'

'When the doctor got there? Did she say anything to him?'

'No –'

'Her parents?'

Fenn stood up straight. 'The quack brought her round to examine her while the priest fetched her parents. By the time they got there, the kid was asleep again. The doctor told them there was nothing wrong with her – slight temperature, that was all.'

The news editor leaned his elbows on the desk and said with belaboured patience: 'Okay, so she spoke to you. Three words wasn't it? Were those words normal or slurred?'

'What d'you mean?'

'I mean if the kid was a deaf mute, she wouldn't know how to pronounce words too well. They'd be distorted, if not incomprehensible, because she would never have heard them spoken before.'

'They were perfect. But she hadn't always been a deaf mute. The priest told me she'd only been that way since she was four years old.'

'And she's what now?' Aitken looked at the typed copy. 'Eleven? Seven years is a long time, Gerry.'

'But I know what I heard,' Fenn insisted.

'It was pretty late, you'd had a shock.' The news editor looked at him suspiciously. 'And probably a drink or two.'

'Not enough to make me hear things.'

'Yeah, yeah, so *you* say.'

'It's gospel!'

'So what d'you want me to do with it?' He held up the copy.

Fenn looked surprised. 'Print it.'

'Get outa here.' Aitken screwed the sheet of paper into a ball and dropped it into a bin by his feet.

The reporter opened his mouth to protest, but Aitken raised a hand.

'Listen, Gerry. There's no story. You're big and ugly enough to understand that. All we have is your say-so that the girl, after seven years of being deaf and dumb, spoke. Three words, kiddo, three fucking words, and nobody else heard them. Only you. Our star reporter, well-known for his vivid imagination, renowned for his satire on local council meetings . . .'

'Ah, Frank, that was just a joke.'

'A joke? Oh yeah, there's been a few little jokes in the past. The hang-glider who loved to jump off the Downs and float around stark naked.'

'I didn't know he was wearing a skin-tight pink outfit. It looked pretty realistic to . . .'

'Yeah, so did the photograph. The police weren't too happy when they tore around the countryside waiting for him to land the next time he was spotted.'

'It was an easy mistake to make.'

'Sure. Like the poltergeists of Kemptown?'

'Christ, I didn't know that old lady had a neurotic cat.'

'Because you didn't bother to check, Gerry, that's why. The clairvoyant we hired sold his story to the *Argus*. And you can't blame them for going to town on the joke – they're our biggest bloody rivals.'

Certain reporters in the near vicinity had grins on their faces, although none looked up from their typewriters.

'There's more, but I don't have time to go through the list.' Aitken picked up his pencil and pointed it in the general direction of the office windows. 'Now will you get out there and come back when your shift begins.' He hunched down to his pencilling and his shiny bald pate defied Fenn to argue.

'Can I follow it up?'

'Not on the *Courier*'s time,' came the brusque reply.

For the benefit of his eavesdropping colleagues, Fenn waggled his tongue in the air and tweaked his ears at the preoccupied editor, then turned and walked back scowling to his desk. Jesus, Aitken wouldn't recognize a good story if it walked up to him and spat in his eye. The girl had spoken. After five years of silence, she'd said three words! He slumped into his seat. *Three words*. But what had she meant? Who was beautiful? He chewed his lip and stared unseeingly at his typewriter.

After a while he shrugged his shoulders and reached for his phone. He dialled the local radio station's number and asked for Sue Gates.

'Where the hell were you last night?' he said as soon as she came on.

'Get off it, Gerry. We've got no fixed arrangement.'

'Okay, but you could have let me know.'

He heard the long sigh. 'Okay, okay,' he said quickly. 'Can you make lunch?'

'Of course. Where?'

'Your place.'

'Uh uh.' Negative. 'I've got work to do this afternoon. It'll have to be a short lunch.'

'The Stag, then. In ten minutes?'

'Make it twenty.'

'Deal. See you there.'

He rang off, thought for a few moments, and went to the office telephone directory. He flicked through the pages, then ran a finger down a list of names, stopping when he found the number he was looking for. He soundlessly repeated it as he hurried back to his desk, where he dialled. No reply. He tried again. No reply. The priest must be out on his rounds or whatever priests did during the day. Housekeeper wasn't there either. St Joseph's seemed like a lonely place.

Fenn stood and pulled his jacket from the back of his chair, glancing towards the windows which ran along the whole length of the large office. It was a sunny day of a mild winter. He made for the door and almost bumped into the sports editor coming in.

'How goes it, Ace?' the editor said cheerily and was surprised at the low-growled response.

Sue Gates was late but, he had to admit, she was worth waiting for. At thirty-three, fours years older than Fenn, she still had the trim figure of a girl in her twenties. Her dark hair was long, fluffed away from her face in loose curls, and her deep brown eyes could gain a man's attention across any crowded room on any enchanted evening. She was wearing tight jeans, loose sweater and a short, navy blue, seaman's topcoat. She waved when she saw him and pushed her way through the crowded bar. He stood and kissed her when she reached him, relishing her lips' moist softness.

'Hi, kid,' he said lightly, enjoying the spreading glow which swiftly ran through him and came to rest around the region of his groin.

'Hi, yourself,' she said, squeezing into the seat next to him. He pushed the already ordered lager in front of her and she reached for it gratefully, taking a long appreciative swallow.

'You eating today?' Fenn asked her. Sue often went a couple of days without touching a scrap of food.

She shook her head. 'I'll catch something tonight.'

'Going fishing?'

'Idiot.'

He popped the last of his cheese and pickle into his mouth and grinned through bulging cheeks.

Placing a hand over his she said, 'Sorry I missed you last night.'

Fenn had to gulp down the food before he could reply. 'I'm sorry I was ratty on the phone,' he counter-apologized.

'Forget it. I did ring the *Courier*, by the way, just to let you know I wouldn't be there. They told me you were out on an assignment.'

'I rang your place, too.'

'I was out . . .'

'I know.'

'Reg took me to dinner.'

'Oh, yeah.' His voice was casual. 'Good old Reg.'

'Hey, come on. Reg is my boss – you know there's nothing in it.'

'Course I know. Does Reg?'

Sue laughed. 'He's as thin as a drainpipe, wears glasses that look like the ends of milk bottles, is losing his hair and has a disgusting habit of picking his nose with his little finger.'

'It's the last bit that makes him irresistible.'

'On top of that he's married with three kids.'

'I told you he was irresistible.' Fenn drained his glass. 'I'll get you another while I'm up there.'

'No, let me get you one,' she insisted. 'You can reflect on what a wimp you're being while I'm at the bar.' She reached for his glass. 'Another bitter?'

'Bloody Mary,' he said smugly.

He watched her weave through the crowd to the bar and told himself how much he admired her independence – he'd told himself, *and* her, many times – and wished he was convinced of his own admiration. Sue had been married and divorced before she was twenty-six, her ex being an advertising man in London – high-powered, high-living, hi, girls! – something on the creative side of the business. After just one-too-many indiscretions on his part, Sue had sought a divorce. She'd had a good position with a film production company – she and her husband had met when her company was hired to make a TV commercial for his agency – but after her divorce came through, she decided she had had enough of advertising people, enough of London, and enough of men.

The big problem was that the marriage had produced a child, a son named Ben. He had been the reason for moving down to the south coast. Her parents lived in Hove, which was the other half (some said the better half) of Brighton, and they had agreed to become semi-permanent baby minders. Ben stayed with his grandparents most of the time, but Sue made sure they got together nearly every day and he moved in with her on most weekends. Fenn knew that she missed having the boy around all of the time, but she had to make a living (her fierce independence meant refusal of any maintenance, even for Ben, from the errant husband. Half the money from the sale of their Islington house was all she had demanded). She managed to get herself a job with Radio Brighton and had soon become a producer. But it took up a lot of her time and she was seeing less and less of Ben, which worried her. And she was seeing too much of Fenn, which worried her almost as much. She hadn't wanted to become entangled with another man; casual acquaintanceships were all she would allow, necessary only for those odd times when a weak body needed something more than a pillow to cling to. Those odd times had become more frequent since she had met Fenn.

He had urged her to give up her flat, to move in with him. It was ridiculous that they should feel so close and live so far apart (three blocks away, to be precise). But she had resisted, and still did; Sue had vowed never to become totally dependent on one single person again. Ever. Sometimes, and secretly, it was a relief to Fenn, for it gave him his own independence. Guilt hit him occasionally (the bargain seemed to be *too* much in his favour) but when voiced, she always assured him that the boot was on the other foot and it was she who was getting the better deal. A man to lean on when the going got rough, a body to comfort her when the nights were lonely, and a friend to have fun with when things were going right. A shoulder to cry on, a lover to spy on, and a wallet to rely on. And solitude when it was needed most. What more could any woman ask for? Plenty, Fenn thought, but he wasn't going to prompt her.

She was back, handing him the thick red cocktail with an expression of mild disapproval on her face. He sipped the Bloody Mary and winced: Sue had told the barman to go *heavy* on the Tabasco. He noticed she was trying hard not to smirk.

'What are you doing here today, Woodstein?' she asked. 'I thought you'd still be tucked up in bed after your late shift.'

'I ran into a good story last night. Well, it kind of ran into me. I thought it might make the late edition but the Ayatollah had other ideas.'

'Aitken didn't like it?'

Fenn shook his head. 'Like it? He didn't even believe it.'

'Try me. I know you only lie when it's to your advantage.'

He briefly told her what had happened the previous night, and she smiled at the excitement that gradually began to blaze in his eyes as the story went on. At one point, when he was describing how he'd found the little girl kneeling in the field, cold fingers had touched her spine, making her shiver. Fenn went on to tell her about the priest, the doctor, then the arrival of the distraught parents.

'How old was the girl?' Sue asked.

'The priest said eleven. She looked younger to me.'

'And she was just staring at the tree?'

'She was just staring *towards* it. I got the impression she was looking at something else.'

'Something else?'

'Yeah, it's kind of hard to explain. She was smiling, you know, like something was making her very happy. Rapturous, almost. It was as if she were seeing a vision.'

'Oh, Gerry . . .'

'No, that's it! That's just what it was like. The kid was seeing a vision.'

'She was having a dream, Gerry. Don't exaggerate the whole thing.'

'How d'you explain her talking to me then?'

'Maybe you were dreaming too.'

'Ah, Sue. . . . Come on, I'm being serious.'

She laughed and linked his arm. 'I'm sorry, lover, but you get so het up when you think you're sniffing out a good story.'

He grunted. 'Maybe you're right. Maybe I did imagine that part of it. The strange thing was, I got the impression it wasn't the first time. When the girl's parents arrived, I heard the mother mumble something about Alice – that's the kid's name – going to the same place before. The priest nodded, but his eyes seemed to be warning her not to say too much in front of me. It was all kinda cagey.'

'Did he know you were a reporter.'

Fenn shook his head. 'He didn't ask, so I didn't tell him.' He sipped his drink thoughtfully. 'He wanted me out of the way, though. Couldn't wait to get rid of me once the mother and father got there. I petended to be more shaken up than I really was, so he let me rest a while. Then, just before the parents took Alice away, he went through some ritual with her. Mumbled something or other and made the sign of the cross.'

'He blessed her.'

He looked at Sue quizzically. 'If you say so.'

'No. That's what you're saying. He must have blessed her.'

'Why would he do that?'

'A priest will bless a house, a holy medal, a statue. Even your car if you ask him nicely. Why not a child?'

'Yeah, why not? Hey, how do you know all that?'

'I'm a Catholic – at least I used to be. I'm not sure if I still am; the Catholic Church doesn't actually approve of divorce.'

'You never told me.'

'It was never important. I don't go to church any more, only at Christmas, and that's mainly for Ben's sake. He likes the ceremony.'

Fenn nodded knowingly. 'So that's why you're so wild in bed.'

'Creep.'

'Uh huh. That's why you're into flagellation!'

'Will you stop. The day I let you beat me –'

'Yeah, that's why I have to undress in the dark . . .'

She groaned and pinched his thigh under the table. Fenn yelped, almost spilling his drink. 'Okay, okay, I lied, you're normal. It's a pity, but it's the truth.'

'Just you remember it.'

He squeezed her thigh in return, but his touch was gentle as well as higher and further in. 'You're saying, then, that it would have been standard practice for him to bless the girl?'

'Oh, no, it sounds unusual to me under those circumstances. But not especially so. It may have been to reassure the parents more than anything else.'

'Yeah, could be.'

Sue studied his profile, and was aware that she loved him some days more than others. Today was a more day. She remembered when they had first met, over three years ago. It was at a party given by the radio station for one of their announcers, who was leaving to join the mother ship, Great Auntie BBC, in London. Some of the friendlier Press had been invited; Gerry Fenn was considered aggressive but friendly enough.

'You look familiar,' she had told him when he skilfully got around to introducing himself. She had caught him looking her way several times before he edged his way round the room so that he could deliberately bump into her.

'Yeah?' he had said, eyebrows raised.

'Yes, you remind me of an actor . . .'

'Right. Who?' He was grinning broadly.

'Oh, what's his name. Richard . . .'

'Eastwood. Richard Eastwood?'

'No, no. He was in that space thing . . .'

'Richard Redford?'

'No, silly.'

'Richard Newman?'

'Dreyfuss, that's who. Richard Dreyfuss.'

His smile disappeared and his lips formed an O. 'Oh, yeah. Him.' He beamed again. 'Yeah, he's okay.'

They had talked, and he had made her laugh with his swift changes of mood, his sudden intensity broken by a wicked grin that would leave her wondering if he were not joking when he looked so serious. That was three years ago and she was still never sure.

He turned to face her, that same wicked grin on his face. 'You busy this weekend?'

'Not especially. I'll be seeing Ben, of course.'

'Could you keep Sunday morning free?'

'Sure. Any particular reason.'

His grin broadened.

'How would you like to go to Mass with me on Sunday?'

FIVE

'Well I don't,' said the mother. 'I've got forebodings like there was going to be an almighty thunderstorm.'

THE JUNIPER TREE
The Brothers Grimm

Molly Pagett listened from the bottom of the stairs. It was a small, red-brick house, identical to all the others on Banfield's council estate, and movement in any of its rooms could be clearly heard from the bottom of the stairs. The familiar *bip bip* of Alice's Galaxy Invader came to her ears; her daughter spent hours playing the battery-operated game, shooting down the descending green aliens with an unerring skill that both baffled and impressed Molly. She went into the kitchen and filled the kettle.

At least Alice had put away her crayons for a while.

Molly sat at the fold-away table, her face, already thin, even more gaunt because of the increased anxieties of the past two weeks. Alice had been a constant source of concern for Molly Pagett since the usual children's illness at four years of age had left her daughter its unusual legacy; the effects of mumps had turned Alice into a deaf mute. Molly drummed her fingers on the table and resisted the urge to light a cigarette. Five-a-day was her maximum: one first thing in the morning, one halfway through the morning, one just before Len, her husband, arrived back from work, and two later in the evening while watching telly. Five-a-day was the most she could afford, but sometimes she smoked ten. Other times she smoked twenty. It depended on Len. He could be such a bastard.

Molly quickly crossed herself, an appeasement to God for the profanity, but not for the thought; that was well-founded.

Her frown increased when she remembered the night before. The priest had frightened her and Len, knocking on their door in the middle of the night, then standing in their hallway, his face white and anxious, a black-garbed messenger of bad tidings. Nonsense, she'd told him when he said Alice was up at the presbytery, a doctor taking care of her. Alice is safe in bed, Molly had insisted. She's been there since seven. Wanted to go up early because she was feeling tired.

Father Hagan had just shaken his head and urged them to get dressed and come with him; but Molly had run into Alice's room, knowing the priest wouldn't lie, just sure he was making a mistake. Her bed had been empty, covers thrown back, her doll hanging halfway out of the bed staring lifelessly at the floor. Len and the priest had followed and it was Father Hagan, not her husband, who tried to calm her. Alice was all right as far as the doctor could tell. She had probably been sleep-walking, that was all.

All the way to the bloody church? Len had asked, not caring that he was talking to a priest.

Father Hagan had told them to find warm clothing for their daughter; she was only wearing a thin nightie. By the time they had both hurriedly dressed, Len's mood had turned into one of anger for, being an atheist, he kept clear of churches (although he enjoyed the occasional funeral, which he regarded as a social event) and to be dragged out to one in the middle of the night – and a bloody cold night, too! – was not much to his liking.

Alice had looked so pale when they arrived there. Even Len stopped his sullen muttering. Yet she looked so peaceful.

The doctor told them he had found nothing wrong with her, but to keep her home for a day or two, make sure she got plenty of rest. If she acted strangely, or appeared not to be her usual self, give him a ring and he would pop round. He was sure there was nothing to worry about, though. Young children often went for midnight jaunts, whether asleep or otherwise; Alice had just jaunted a little farther than most.

Molly was still frightened. Why had Alice gone to the tree again? She had been frantic when her daughter had gone missing two weeks before. She had searched the church and its grounds, twice running down to the road to make sure Alice wasn't out there. In a panic she had run to Father Hagan's house and he had helped search the grounds again. It was the priest who spotted her daughter in the field kneeling before the tree. Alice had been smiling when they went to her, a smile that had vanished when she became aware of their approach. Then she had become confused, disorientated. They had led her back and, in sign language, Molly had asked her why she had gone into the field. Alice had merely looked puzzled, as if she didn't understand. She had seemed fine after that (perhaps a little distant, but that wasn't too unusual for Alice; it was easy to get lost in a world of silence) and Molly had tried to forget the incident.

Now, because of the previous night, the anxiety was back with a vengeance. And the fear was mixed with something else. What was it? Apprehension? More. Something more. The faint glimmer of hope. . . . No, it was impossible. The man had been mistaken. He had seemed so certain, though.

She couldn't remember his name, the young man who had nearly run down Alice. He had been sitting in an armchair looking a little worse for wear when she and Len had arrived. The familiar stink of booze permeated the air around him (familiar to her because that same unpleasant odour was so much a part of her husband), although he didn't appear to be drunk. He said Alice had spoken to him.

The kettle changed its hissing tone and steam billowed out across the kitchen. Molly switched the gas jet off and dropped a tea bag into an empty cup on the draining board. She poured undiluted lemon squash into another cup for Alice and filled both with boiling water. Molly stood looking down at the swirling yellow-green liquid, thinking of her daughter, her only child, thinking that miracles never happened. Not to the Molly and Alice Pagetts of the world, anyway.

She put the cup and two biscuits into a saucer and made her way from the kitchen. As she mounted the stairs, her mind ran through a quick, silent prayer; but she dare not let herself hope. Alice would soon be back at the special school for the deaf in Hove, and Molly, herself, would be back at her part-time job as a home-help, and Len would be his usual disagreeable self, and everything would be normal again in the Pagett household. She prayed it would be so, yet she prayed also for something better.

Alice did not look up when Molly entered the bedroom. Even though she couldn't hear, her daughter could always sense when someone had entered a room, but this time she was intent on her drawing. The Galaxy Invader now lay on the floor beside the bed and her crayons were near at hand in a box on the bedside cabinet. Molly stood over her with the hot lemon drink and still Alice did not look up from the sketchbook.

Molly frowned when she saw the picture. It was the same one. The same one she had drawn day after day for two weeks. Molly had shown them to Father Hagan, who had dropped in earlier that morning and he, too, had made no sense of them.

Molly placed the cup and saucer beside the crayons and sat on the edge of the bed. Alice looked surprised when the yellow crayon was removed from her hand. For an instant, it was as though she did not recognize her mother. Then she smiled.

The rain was like tiny ice pellets striking at Father Hagan's face. He stood at the wall, looking into the field, watching the tree; the sky, after a bright start to the day, was now dark overhead, a thin haze of silver between the distant horizon and the brooding clouds.

Nothing happened. Nor did he expect it to. The tree was just a tree. A tired old oak. A silent witness to passing time. He could see the sheep grazing in a far corner of the field, their bodies yellowy-grey and bloated, concerned only for the next mouthful of grass and the growing heaviness in their pregnant bellies.

The priest shivered and pulled the collar of his dark blue raincoat tight around his neck. His black hair was damp, his glasses speckled; he had been standing there for five minutes paying no heed to the freezing rain. There was a feeling inside him that he could not grasp, a sense of unease that he could not define. He had not slept well the night before, after the doctor had left with the Pagetts and Alice, and the man called Fenn had gone. A peculiar loneliness had descended afterwards, leaving him feeling vulnerable, isolated. In his years as a priest, loneliness had become an acquaintance, and rarely an enemy. But last night, the solitude was total, his room a cell surrounded by impenetrable blackness, devoid of life, a deathly vacuity separating him from the rest of humanity. He had the terrifying feeling that if he left his bedroom and walked out into that darkness he would never reach its edge, that he would walk and walk and become lost in it, never to find even his room again. The sensation was suffocating and he was afraid.

He had prayed and prayer slowly forced back the contracting walls of fear. His sleep had been restless, more exhausting than if he had stayed awake, and the barest glimmer of morning had been welcomed with immense gratitude. He had shivered alone in his church, his early-morning devotions fervent, intense, and later, at morning Mass shared with four of his flock, he had begun to shake off the nagging unrest. But not completely; it still lingered through the day like an elusive tormentor, refusing to be identified, content to stab then hide.

The tree was withered; the years had made it a twisted thing. It dominated that part of the field, a gargantuan guardian, innumerable arms thrown outwards to warn off intruders. A grotesque shape disrobed of summer leaves, intimidating in its ugliness. Yet, he told himself, it was just a centuries-old oak, its lower branches bowed, bark scarred and dry, its vitality patiently stolen by time. But why did the girl kneel before it?

The Pagetts had always lived in the parish, Molly Pagett a staunch, if quiet, member of the Catholic community. She was paid for the work she did keeping the church clean, but the wages were minimal; she would have probably worked for nothing if Father Hagan had asked her to. He had not met Leonard Pagett often, and he had reluctantly to admit that he cared little for the man. Pagett's atheism and ill-disguised dislike of the Church and churchmen had nothing to do with his feelings towards him, for the priest knew and respected many such people. No, there was something, well, not good about the man. On the rare occasions when Father Hagan had called at their home, Pagett had always appeared sullen, uncomfortable in the presence of the priest. And in turn, the priest felt uncomfortable in the presence of Pagett. He was glad Alice's father had been absent when he called in to see her that morning.

Alice. A good child, a curious child. Her disability had made her a solitary one. She was frail, yet seemed to carry an inner strength within that small body. She was happy at the church, helpful to her mother, respectful of her surroundings. Alice didn't appear to have many friends but, of course, her silence was frustrating to other children who had little pity for such things. She appeared to be as intelligent as any other child of her age despite the cruel affliction, although she was often lost in her own world, in her own dreams, an obvious result of her disability. That morning she had seemed almost completely lost in that private domain, absorbed in her confused scribblings.

It was the memory of Alice's drawings that turned him back towards the church.

He walked through the bleak graveyard, his shoulders hunched against the stinging rain, his footsteps hurried. Molly Pagett had shown him more pictures drawn by the child over the past two weeks, and they had all looked similar to each other, mostly in yellow and grey, some with added touches of blue. Strangely, only one was different, although not in style; the colour had changed. It was in red and black. All had looked vaguely familiar.

Alice was no artist, but her illustrations endeavoured to portray a figure, a person dressed in white, the blue used infrequently, red just once. The figure was surrounded by yellow and it had no face. It appeared to be a woman, though the overall shape was not clear.

He entered the church porch, relieved to be out of the rain. He fumbled for the key to open the big oak doors, for the church was always kept locked nowadays because of increasing vandalism and theft. The holy sanctuary was only available to those in need at appointed times. The long key clicked in the lock and he swung one side of the double-doors open, stepping inside and closing it again. The thud echoed around the walls of the gloomy church and his footsteps were unusually loud as he walked to a side aisle after genuflecting and blessing himself.

He paused before beginning the journey to the front of the church, gazing at the distant frozen figure against a wall to one side of the altar. Could it be? Father Hagan became more certain as he approached the statue: the outstretched arms, the head slightly bowed to gaze at whoever knelt, sat or stood before it. The drawings made more sense when the image they represented was viewed.

Alice often sat here. Curiously, it came as no relief to identify the object of her obsessive drawings. Instead, it was a mildly unsettling sensation.

The priest stared up at the compassionate but stone face of the Blessed Virgin and wondered at the acute sense of despair he suddenly felt.

SIX

*'I say, how do you do it?' asked John, rubbing his knee. He was quite a
practical boy.*
  *'You just think lovely wonderful thoughts,' Peter explained, 'and they lift you
up in the air.'*

PETER PAN

J. M. Barrie

Sunday. Morning. Sunny. But cold.

Fenn pulled his Mini in behind a long line of cars, most of which were settled
halfway on the grass verge beside the road.

'It's gone 9.30, Gerry. We're going to be late.' Sue sat in the passenger seat,
making no attempt to get out of the car.

Fenn grinned. 'They don't make you wear sackcloth any more, do they?' He
turned off the engine.

'I'm not sure I want to do this.' Sue's teeth chewed anxiously on her lower lip.
'I mean, it's a bit hypocritical, isn't it?'

'Why?' Fenn looked surprised, although his eyes were still smiling. 'Prodigals
always get a good reception.'

'Cut it out, it's not funny.'

Fenn changed his tone. 'Ah, come on, Sue, you don't have to become a Born
Again Catholic. I'd feel a bit lost if I went in there alone; I wouldn't know what
the hell to do.'

'Admit it: you're bloody scared. What do you think Catholics do to agnostics?
Burn them at the stake? And what makes you think you'd be noticed anyway?'

Fenn squirmed uncomfortably. 'I guess I do feel like a trespasser.'

'A spy, don't you mean? And how do you think I'm going to feel?'

He leaned forward and put a hand around her neck, gently tugging her
towards him. 'I need you with me, Sue.'

She looked into his face, about to rebuke him for his blatant small-boy
expression; instead she groaned, and pushed her way out of the car, slamming
the door behind her.

Fenn winced but couldn't repress the chuckle. He locked the car and hurried
after Sue, who was stamping along the tree-lined path leading to the church
entrance. A few other late arrivals hurried along with them, the sound of organ
music speeding their footsteps.

'The things I do for you, Fenn,' Sue muttered from the corner of her mouth as
they entered the porch.

'Yeah, but they're not all bad,' he whispered back, a sharp elbow making his
grin disappear.

The church was full and Fenn was surprised; he thought clerics were
complaining about the fast-diminishing number of churchgoers. There were

plenty here. Too many, in fact; he and the other latecomers would have to stand at the back. He watched as Sue dipped her hand into the font at the top of the centre aisle and admired her legs as she quickly genuflected. Remember where you are, Fenn, he told himself. He decided he would feel too self-conscious to follow her act and discovered he felt self-conscious not following it. Shuffling to one side, trying too look as unobtrusive as possible, he glanced around the church interior. The congregation ranged over all ages and all shapes and sizes. Plenty of kids, some with adults, others just with brothers and sisters or friends; plenty of women, mostly middle-aged or older, a few teenage girls here and there; and a good sprinkling of men, most of them family types, one or two groups of teenage boys among them. A hymn was being sung and mouths opened and closed, many not forming words – just opening and closing. The tune wasn't bad, though, and the overall effect of all the voices banded together by the rich strains of the wheezing organ was not unpleasant. Fenn hummed along with them.

The hymn finished and there was the rustle of closing books and shifting bodies, a muffled sound like a wave soaking the shore. The congregation knelt and he wondered what to do – the stone floor looked unreasonably hard. He snatched a look at Sue for guidance and was relieved to see her merely bow her head slightly. He did the same, but his eyes looked upwards, roaming over the heads of the people in front.

The priest's monotone litany drew his attention towards the altar and he barely recognized the man in his dazzling uniform of office, a white cassock and bright green and yellow vestment. Father Hagan had changed identity; he bore little resemblance in both character and appearance to the confused and anxious man in dressing gown and bare feet of a few nights ago. The transition was as dramatic as Clark Kent changing into Superman. Or Popeye after spinach. He wore his robes like a suit of holy armour and it afforded him a calm strength. Fenn was just a little impressed, but cynically reminded himself that fancy dress was the most camouflaging disguise of all.

Father Hagan's face was expressionless, his eyes cast down, almost shut, as he quickly went through the opening prayers. The congregation responded to his solemn supplications in an almost incoherent drone. Then both priest and worshippers prayed as one; and as they did so, Fenn noticed the priest's eyes were fully open, his head no longer bowed. He kept glancing to his left as though watching someone kneeling on that side of the church. Fenn followed his gaze but could only see rows of bowed heads. He shifted his position to get a clear view down the side aisle; still he saw nothing unusual. He turned his attention back to the Mass, interested in the service, but deriving no sense of well-being from it, no spiritual uplift. Soon he became aware of a growing frustration, a slight resentment.

Maybe he just didn't like being part of the gathering, part of a crowd that seemed – to him – to be mindlessly repeating words as though they were a magic formula, a collective petition of adoration. It began to unnerve him. Fenn neither believed nor disbelieved in the existence of God: either way, it meant little to him. Find your own morality, your own code; then stick with it. So long as nobody else got hurt (too badly) you were doing okay. If there was a God, He was big enough to understand that. It was man, mortal bloody man, who created the myths. What Supreme Being could encourage let alone appreciate this dogmatic repetitive ritual? What Almighty Power would encourage His own creation (whom, so the rumour went, He had created in His own image) to toady up to Him so they could have a slice of the heavenly action when their number was called? It didn't make sense.

Fenn glared defiantly towards the altar. There were lots of other things to toss in for debate. Like idolatry, theological misinterpretation, and naïve symbolism. Like birth control, confession and penance and absolution. Like bigotry (who says you have to be a Catholic to get a foot in the gate?), ceremony, solemnization, and in-bloody-fallibility. Original Sin, for Christ's sake! And not to mention the Church's view on fornication.

He began to smile at his own indignation. Nothing like a good church service to stir the emotions, for or agin.

As Father Hagan read from the Gospel, Fenn looked at Sue and surreptitiously reached for her hand, squeezing it softly; she ignored him, intent on the priest's words. He let his hand drop away, surprised.

The sermon began and Fenn paid scant attention, although he studied Hagan with interest. It was strange: the priest didn't look so invincible now. His face looked strained and he still glanced towards the side, at someone sitting in the front pew. Once again, the reporter tried to see for himself, and this time he could just make out the back of a woman's head between the shoulders of a man and woman sitting in the second row.

She was wearing a bright pink scarf. Maybe the priest didn't like pink.

Fenn shifted his feet, becoming restless. If he were a smoker, he'd be dying for a cigarette. Was it sacrilege to chew gum in church? He decided it probably was.

The priest's words seemed hesitant, as though even he were not convinced. But as he spoke and developed his theme, his words became stronger and Fenn could almost feel the sense of relief that passed through the congregation; they obviously preferred their sermons hard and unrelenting. Father Hagan's voice subtly rose in pitch, at one moment accusing and the next coaxing, then reassuring, returning to a more reproachful tone when things were getting too cosy. Fenn enjoyed his technique.

The service went on (to Fenn, on and on . . .) and he regretted having arrived for the full Mass. His idea was to soak up the atmosphere of the Sunday service, maybe chat to some of the people afterwards; but the prime purpose was to get to the priest. He intended to have a long talk with him when Mass was over, wanting to find out how the little girl was. Had she returned to the church? Had she spoken again? Now he wondered if he wasn't suffering too much for the sake of his craft.

He sneaked another sideways peek at Sue, feeling a trifle embarrassed by her obvious reverence towards the surroundings. Once a Catholic, always a Catholic. He hoped it didn't mean she was going to kick him out of her bed that night.

The church became particularly hushed. Father Hagan was doing something with a highly polished chalice, breaking what looked like a white wafer into it. The Communion, that was it. Drinking of wine, breaking of bread. Christ's blood and body. What did they call it . . .? The Eucharist.

All heads were bowed and the people standing around him sank to their knees as a tinkling bell rang out. He looked down at Sue in alarm and she motioned with her eyes for him to get down beside her. The stone floor hurt his knees.

He kept his head low, afraid to offend anyone – particularly HE WHO SEES ALL – until he heard movement around him. Looking up, he saw that people were stepping into the aisles and forming a double-line queue leading up to the altar rail where the priest waited with silver cup and Communion wafers. An older man wearing a white cassock attended him at one side. The procession of people shuffled forward and the organ wheezed into life once again.

Several people were sitting now and a few of those at the back of the church had risen to their feet, not prepared to suffer bruised knees any longer. Fenn considered their judgement to be sound and rose himself; Sue remained kneeling.

Singing began and the congregation moved down and around, approaching the altar from the centre aisle, returning to their places by the side aisles. Fenn saw the pink scarf moving along the bench towards the centre and instantly recognized its wearer as the woman who had come with her husband to collect the little deaf and dumb girl from the priest's house a few nights before. The priest had been looking towards Alice's mother throughout the service.

The pink scarf joined the other bowed heads in the slow-paced procession and disappeared completely from view when the woman knelt to receive the host from the priest.

It was then that a small figure rose from the spot where the woman had been sitting throughout the Mass. She stepped into the side aisle and looked up at a statue before her; then she turned and walked towards the back of the church. Fenn recognized Alice. Her yellow hair was parted in the centre, two long plaits resting over her shoulders; she wore a maroon raincoat, a size too big for her, and long white socks. Her hands were clasped together tightly, fingers intertwined, and her eyes looked straight ahead and at nothing in particular.

Fenn stared, aware that something was wrong. Her face was pale, her knuckles white. He realized the priest had been watching *her*, not her mother.

And Father Hagan was watching her now.

The Communion wafer hovered tantalisingly above a gaping mouth, the receiver's tongue, draped over a lower lip, beginning to twitch. Alice's mother, kneeling beside her fellow-communicant, was too lost in her own devotional prayers to notice the delay in proceedings.

The priest looked as though he was about to call out and Fenn saw him visibly restrain himself. A few other heads were turning to see what was provoking such riveted attention from their priest, but all they saw was little Alice Pagett, the deaf mute, walking towards the back of the church, presumably to join the queue for Holy Communion. Father Hagan realized he was delaying the Mass and resumed the ceremony, but his eyes worriedly followed the girl's progress.

Fenn was curious. He thought of stepping forward to block her way but knew that would be stupid: she might just be feeling unwell and in need of fresh air. Yet, although she was pale, there was a look of happiness on her face, a faraway joy in those vivid blue eyes. She seemed to see nothing, only what was beyond her physical vision, and the notion disturbed Fenn. Could she be in a trance? She bumped into no one, nor were her footsteps slow or dream-like. He looked down at her as she passed, and half-smiled, not knowing why.

The organ played on and voices rose in communal worship, emotions high at this particular point in the Mass.

No one seemed to notice the other children leaving the pews.

Fenn looked from left to right in surprise. The kids – some no more than six years old, others up to twelve or thirteen – were slipping away from their elders and making their way towards the church exit, the infant exodus largely unnoticed because of the throng of people in the centre aisle.

Unlike Alice, there was nothing trance-like about these children. They were excited, some giggling, as they skipped after the deaf and dumb girl.

A mother realized her offspring was trying to make an escape (a common enough occurrence with this one) and swiftly caught him. His howl of rage and struggles to get free shocked the mother. People around her, other parents, began to realize what was happening. They were startled at first, then confused. Then just a little angry. One father forgot himself and called out after his departing boy.

Father Hagan heard the shout and looked up. He was just in time to see the small girl in her maroon raincoat and long plaits pull open the church door and disappear into the bright sunlight. Other children rushed after her.

The voices grew weaker as people became aware that something was amiss. Soon only the plump nun at the organ, lost in her own rapturous praising of God's benevolence towards mankind, was singing.

Fenn suddenly became alert. Christ, he had almost been in a trance himself; it had taken an effort of will to snap out of it. He moved swiftly to the door and pushed one side open. The light stung his eyes for several moments, but a few rapid blinks allowed him to see clearly once more.

The children were running through the graveyard towards the low grey-stone wall at the back.

Fenn stepped from the porch and followed, his footsteps quickening when he saw Alice clamber over the wall. The other children began climbing over too, the smaller ones helped by their bigger companions.

A hand grabbed the reporter's arm.

'Gerry, what's going on?' Sue stared after the children, then at him as if he would know.

'No idea,' he told her. 'They're chasing after the little deaf and dumb girl. And I think I know where she's going.' He broke away, running now, anxious to get to the wall.

Sue was too surprised to move. Voices from behind caused her to turn her head; bewildered parents were emerging from the church, looking around anxiously for their missing children. The priest pushed his way into the crowd, saw Sue standing on the path leading through the graveyard, then looked beyond at Fenn's retreating figure.

The reporter skipped over fresh molehills, stumbling once but managing to keep his feet. He practically fell against the wall, his hands smacking its rough top. There he stood, drawing sharp breaths into his belaboured lungs, his eyes widening.

The girl, Alice, was kneeling before the crooked oak, just as she had on that dark chilly night less than a week ago. The other children were spread out behind her, some kneeling as she was, others just staring. Several of the younger ones were pointing at the tree, laughing, jumping little steps of delight.

Fenn's eyes narrowed as he studied the object of their attention. There was nothing else there! Just an old tree! It wasn't even beautiful; in fact, it was bloody awful. What was the fascination?

Someone bumped into him and he looked round to see Sue had caught up with him once more.

'Gerry . . .?' The question froze on her lips as she saw the children.

Hurried footsteps behind them, other bodies brought to a halt by the low wall. Fenn and Sue were jostled as parents pushed to see what had become of their offspring. A mild shock ran through the gathering crowd. Then a hushed silence. Even the organ had stopped playing.

Fenn became aware that the priest was standing beside him. They regarded each other for several moments and the reporter thought he detected a touch of hostility in Hagan's gaze, almost as if he suspected Fenn of having something to do with the phenomenon.

Fenn looked away, more interested in the children than the priest. He reached into his pocket and drew out a cheap, pocket-size camera; he clicked off four rapid shots, then leapt over the wall.

Sue, irrationally, tried to call him back; for some reason she was afraid, or perhaps just shocked, and it was the sense of fear that kept her quiet. The people around her grew restless when they saw him enter the field, and they seemed reluctant to follow. Scared, like her, or perplexed. Perhaps both.

He approached the first child, a boy of eleven or twelve in duffle coat and jeans. The boy was smiling, just as Alice had smiled that first night. He appeared to be unaware of Fenn, and the reporter waved a hand before the boy's eyes. A brief frown crossed the boy's features and he jerked his head aside, trying to get a clear view of the tree.

Fenn left him, went on to another child. A girl this time, squatting in the damp grass, a look of bliss on her face. He crouched beside her, touching her shoulder.

'What is it?' he asked softly. 'What can you see?'

The girl ignored him.

He moved on and watched a five-year-old clap his hands together and sink to his haunches with glee; two girls, twins, holding hands, both smiling; a boy of about thirteen, on his knees, hands held together before his nose, palms flat against each other, lips moving in silent prayer.

Another boy, this one in short trousers, his knees smeared with mud from where he had obviously fallen, stood hugging himself, shoulders hunched, a wide grin on his face. Fenn stood in front of him, deliberately obscuring his view. The boy stepped sideways, still grinning.

Fenn bent down so that his face was level with the boy's. 'Tell me what you see,' he said.

One thing was sure: he didn't see Fenn. Nor did he hear him.

The reporter straightened and shook his head in frustration. The little faces around him were all smiling. Some wept, but they still smiled.

He noticed the priest was climbing over the wall, others following his example. Fenn turned and walked swiftly towards the girl in the maroon coat, the deaf and dumb child, who knelt some yards before the other children, close to the oak tree. He moved in front of her, but to one side so that he did not block her vision of the tree. Crouching slightly, he aimed the camera and shot two more frames. Straightening, he photographed the rest of the children.

Then he turned and photographed the tree.

The parents and guardians were among the children, claiming their charges, taking them up in their arms or hugging them close. A girl, not six yards away from Fenn, swayed, then fell into a heap on the soft ground before her distraught mother could reach her. Another younger girl followed suit. Then a boy. The five-year-old who had been clapping earlier broke into hysterical tears as his mother and father approached him. Many of the children began to weep, worried voices dispelling the uncanny silence that had prevailed as the adults tried to comfort them.

Fenn's eyes shone with bemused wonder; he had a story, a *great* story. He was witnessing the same kind of hysteria that had swept through a crowd of over three hundred children in Mansfield a few years before; there had been a mass collapse at the Marching Bands Festival. This wasn't on the same grand scale, but the events bore some similarity. These kids were being affected by whatever was going on inside Alice Pagett's mind. Somehow she was transmitting her own hypnotic state to them, making them behave in the same way! Jesus, some kind of telepathy! It was the only explanation. But what had induced *her* delirium – if delirium it be?

Father Hagan strode through the concerned families and swooning children, making straight for Fenn.

The reporter was tempted to snap off a quick picture, but decided it wouldn't be the right moment; there was something daunting about the priest, despite his worried manner. He slipped the camera back into his pocket.

The clergyman disregarded Fenn and knelt beside Alice Pagett. He put an arm around her, his hand covering one shoulder completely. He spoke to her, knowing she could not hear, but hoping she would sense the kindness in his words.

'Everything's all right, Alice,' he said. 'Your mother is coming, you're going to be fine.'

'I don't think you should move her, Father,' Fenn interrupted, crouching low again so he could look into Alice's eyes.

The priest looked at him in a strange way. 'Weren't you the man who brought her to me the other night? Fenn, isn't it?'

The reporter nodded, still watching the girl.

'What's your game, Mr Fenn?' Hagan's voice was brusque. He rose, pulling Alice up with him. 'What have you got to do with this business?'

Fenn looked up in surprise, then stood himself. 'Now look . . .' he began to say when another voice spoke.

'She wants us to come again.'

Both men were shocked into silence. They stared down at Alice.

She smiled and said, 'The lady in white wants us to come again. She says she's got a message, Father. A message for all of us.'

Fenn and the priest were not aware that the crowd was hushed again, that everyone had heard Alice's soft-spoken words even though it should have been impossible over the frantic hubbub of anxious voices.

The priest was the first to speak, his words hesitant. 'Who, Alice?' Could she hear him? She had spoken, but could she hear? 'Who . . . who told you this?'

Alice pointed towards the oak. 'The lady, Father. The lady in white told me.'

'But there's . . . no one there, Alice.'

The girl's smile wavered for a moment, then returned, but was less strong. 'No, she's gone now.'

'Did she say who she was?' The priest still spoke slowly, keeping his voice low, gentle.

Alice nodded, then frowned in concentration, as though trying to remember the exact words. 'She said she was the Immaculate Conception.'

The priest stiffened, blood draining from his face.

It was at that moment that Alice's mother, her bright pink scarf hanging loose at the back of her head, rushed forward and threw herself on her knees, pulling Alice to her and hugging her tight. Molly Pagett's eyes were closed, but tears poured from them to dampen her daughter's face and hair.

WILKES

So the mother took the little lad and chopped him up in pieces, threw him in the pot and cooked him in the stew.

THE JUNIPER TREE
The Brothers Grimm

He closed the door, not forgetting to lock it. Then he switched on the light. It took no longer than two seconds to cross the small room and slump onto the narrow bed.

Kicking his shoes off, he laid his hands across his chest and stared at the ceiling.

'Fucking people,' he said aloud. *Treating me like scum*, he added silently.

His job as busboy in a trendy Covent Garden restaurant had not gone too well that day. He had spilt coffee, returned to tables with wrong orders, rowed with the barman – *who was a fucking poof, anyway!* – and locked himself in the staff toilet for twenty minutes, refusing to come out until he had finished weeping. The manager had warned him for the last time – *any more scenes and you're out! –* and the joint owners – *two fucking ex-advertising men not that much older than himself!* – had agreed.

Well he wouldn't go back! Let's see how they get on without me tomorrow! Bastards.

He picked his nose and wiped his finger under the bed. He tried to calm himself, repeating his mantra over and over in his mind; but it had little effect. Visions of his mother (as always, whenever he was angry) flashed into his mind, rudely elbowing his chosen soothe-word aside. It was because that cow had thrown him out that he'd had to accept such menial labour. If he had still lived at home he could have afforded to live on the dole like the other three million or so unemployed.

After a while he got up and went to a white-painted chest of drawers on the other side of the bedsit. Opening the bottom drawer he took out a scrapbook and carried it back to the bed. He turned the pages and, although it did not relax him, a different mood descended. He liked reading about them. Even now, nobody really knew why they had done it. The fact was: THEY JUST BLOODYWELL HAD!

He studied their newsprint faces, an impatient hand brushing away the thick lock of blond hair that fell over his eyes. He thought that one of them even looked like him. He grinned, pleased.

All you needed was the right person, that was all. It was easy if you found the right one. Someone famous, that's all it took.

He lay back on the hard, narrow bed and, as he considered the possibilities, his hand crept to his lap where he fondled his own body.

SEVEN

How cheerfully he seems to grin,
How neatly spread his claws,
And welcome little fishes in
With gently smiling jaws!

ALICE'S ADVENTURES IN WONDERLAND
Lewis Carroll

Monday, late afternoon

Tucker used to love Monday stocktaking. Every empty shelf meant money in the bank. Every empty carton meant his bills could be met. Every empty freezer meant his smile was a little broader. But shelves, cartons and freezers were never so empty nowadays. Recession didn't stop people eating and drinking – they just didn't do it so well; the punters became careful with their money and particular in their choice. The profit margin on a tin of asparagus was higher than on a tin of peas, but the peasants were more interested in substantiality than taste. He understood their problem, for he was marking up new, dearer prices on virtually every product each week, but it didn't mean he sympathized. He had to eat, too, and when his customers ate less well, then so did he. Maybe not yet, but eventually he would have to.

However, there was still one small joy left to Monday stock-taking, and that was Paula. Paula of the lovey bum and thrusty tits. The face was a bit too fleshy, but when you poke the fire you don't look at the mantelpiece he always told himself, the old adage a serious consideration to him, never an excuse or a witticism.

Rodney Tucker owned the one and only supermarket in Banfield's High Street, a smallish store compared to the usual chain supermarket, but then Banfield was a smallish town. Or village, as they liked to call it. He had moved there from Croydon eleven years before, his grocery shop having been forced out of business by the big combine superstores of the area. Not only had he learned from the experience, but the money he had made by selling the premises had enabled him to join the competition. Banfield was ripe for exploitation just then; too small for the big chains, but just right for the big individual (he had always considered himself a *big* individual). The two grocery stores in the town had suffered in the way he had suffered, although not as badly – only one had been forced to close down. Strangely enough, that particular shop had been turned into a laundromat, as had his own shop in Croydon. Recently, he had driven past his old premises and had noted that it had now become a porn video centre; would that happen in Banfield now that washing machines were as common as toasters? He doubted it, somehow; the planning committees of such places were notoriously hard to impress with the changes in twentieth-century retailing requirements. Streuth, it had been hard enough getting planning permission for his supermarket eleven years ago! Such towns and villages had their own way of carrying on. Even having lived in the area all these years, he was still considered an outsider. He knew most of the important men of Banfield, having dined with them, played golf with them, flirted with their wives – no matter how ugly – but still he wasn't accepted. You didn't just have to be born and bred in the area to be considered one of them: your father and *his* father had to be born there! It wouldn't matter one iota to him, except that he would like to have been elected to the parish council. Oh, yes, that would be nice. Lots of land going spare around Banfield, and he had many contacts in the building trade. They'd be very grateful to any council member in favour of giving certain plots over to development. Very grateful.

One hand rubbed his bulging stomach as though his thoughts were food set before him.

'*Running low on grapefruit segments, Mr Tucker!*'

He winced at the shrillness of Paula's voice. Add fifteen years and another four stone and Paula would be a replica of Marcia, his wife. It would have been nice to imagine that his attraction towards Paula was because she reminded him of his wife when she was younger, before years of marriage had exaggerated the weakness rather then realized the promise. Nice, but not true. Fat, thin, buxom, titless – it made no difference to Tucker. Pretty (he should be so lucky), plain, experienced, virginal (he could never be *that* lucky) – Tucker would take them all. Age? He drew the line at eighty-three.

Most of the bits he pursued had one thing in common with Marcia, though. They were all fucking dumb. It wasn't a qualification he demanded, far from it; it just helped his bargaining position. He was realistic enough to know that physically he didn't have a lot to offer: his girth was broadening by the month (despite lack of sales), and his hair, it seemed, was thinning by the minute (his parting was now just above his left ear, ginger strands of hair, some nine inches long, swept over and plastered down onto his skull). But: he had a quick mind, a quick wit, and the eyes of Paul Newman (a bloated Paul Newman, granted). Most of all, and an attraction he had to admire himself, he had a few bob. And it was an attraction he was never modest about. Expensive suits, made-to-measure shirts, Italian shoes, and a change of socks every day. Chunky gold jewellery on his fingers and wrist, chunky gold fillings in his teeth. A flash bright yellow XJS Jag to drive, a beautiful mock-Tudor house to live in. A fifteen-year-old daughter who won rosettes for horse riding and certificates for swimming; and a wife – well, forget the wife. He had a bit of cash and it showed. He made sure it showed.

Tucker knew how to give the women in his life a good time (forget the wife again) and because they were all fucking dumb, that was all they wanted. He could spot a schemer a mile off and had sense enough to stay well clear: no way did he want his comfortable boat rocked.

The dummies were just right: give them a good time in Brighton – a tasty meal, a spot of gambling in a casino or the dogs, disco afterwards – and round off the evening in his favourite motel on the Brighton road. If they were worth it, a trip up to London would be in order; but they really did have to be worth it. Paula merited two stays in the motel so far, but not a trip up to town. Shame about the face.

'*Stacks of cannelloni!*'

The voice didn't help, either.

Tucker sauntered down the rows of shelves, the smell of cardboard and plastic bags strong in his nostrils. Paula was on a small stepladder, clipboard in one hand, her other hand reaching up to examine the contents of a carton. The fashionable split at the rear of her tight skirt revealed the backs of her knees, not always the most sensual of sights, but on a late, wet, Monday afternoon, enough to tug a nerve in the shadowy regions below the overhang of his belly.

Sidling up to her, he placed a chubby hand against her calf muscle. His fingers slid upwards and she stiffened, annoyed because his heavy gold bracelet had snagged her tights.

'*Rodney!*'

He pulled the bracelet free and let his hand travel upwards once more. He stopped where the tights joined in the middle, forming, in collaboration with her panties underneath, an unbreakable seal, a nylon scab over a soft, permanently moist wound. The man who invented tights should have been strangled with his own creation, Tucker thought soberly. His fingers played with the round buttocks.

'Rod, someone might come in!' Paula pushed at his hand beneath the skirt.

'They won't, love. They know better than to interrupt while I'm stocktaking.' His voice still held faint strains of a northern whine, hinting at his origins before Banfield, before Croydon, and before London.

'No, Rod, we can't. Not here.' Paula began to descend the ladder, her lips pursued with resolution.

'It's never bothered you before.' He snatched his hand away lest his finger got crushed in the vice between her thighs.

'Well, it's a bit tacky, isn't it?' She turned away from him, clutching the clipboard to her breasts like a chastity shield and looking thoughtfully at the shelves around her as though concentration, too, was a protective force-field.

'Tacky?' He looked at her in surprise. 'What's that bloody mean?'

'You know perfectly well.' She moved away, ticking off items on the clipboard.

Paula was Tucker's secretary-cum-supervisor-cum-easy-lay-ever-since-the-Christmas-Eve-after-the-store-closed-party. He'd taken her on three months before because she could type, add up without using her fingers, organize staff (she had worked one season for Butlin's as assistant to the entertainments manager) and had thrusty tits and looked knockout against the three spotty-faced youths and one failed double-glazing representative who had applied for the position. Paula was twenty-eight, lived with her widowed, arthritic mother, had a few boyfriends but no steady, and wasn't bad at her job. Since the Christmas-Eve-after-the-store-closed-party, their relationship had been highly pleasurable: drinks after work, a few nights in Brighton, a couple in the motel, swift titillating gropes whenever the occasion allowed. Like Monday stocktaking. What the fuck was the matter with her today?

'Paula, what the fuck is the matter with you today?' His words were whispered so that the cashiers in the shop could not hear, but his exasperation raised the tone to a squeal.

'There's no need for that kind of language, Mr Tucker,' came the stiff reply.

'Mr Tucker?' He touched his chest pointing at himself in disbelief. 'What's all this Mr Tucker? What happened to Rod?'

She whirled on him and the disdain in her eyes was intimidating. 'I think, *Mr Tucker*, we should keep our relationship on a strictly business basis.'

'Why, for f–? Why, Paula? What's happened? We've had fun together, haven't we?'

Her voice softened, but he noticed her eyes didn't. 'Yes, we've had a lot of fun together, Rodney. But . . . is that enough?'

Alarm bells began to clang in his head. 'How d'you mean exactly?' he asked cautiously.

'I mean perhaps I think more of you than you do of me. Perhaps I'm just a good screw to you.'

Oh yes, he thought, here we go. She's building up to something. 'Of course you're not, love. I mean, you are, but I think more of you than just that.'

'Do you? You never show me!?'

He raised his hands, palms downwards. 'Keep it quiet, lovey. We don't want the whole shop to know our business, do we?'

'You may not; I'm not particularly bothered who knows. I wouldn't even care if your bloody wife found out!'

Tucker sucked in his breath and felt his heart go *thump*. Oh no, he may have misjudged Paula. Maybe she wasn't so dumb. 'We could have a night up in London, if you like,' he said.

She looked at him as though he had slapped her face. Then she threw the clipboard at him.

He was more concerned with the clatter as it bounced off and then fell to the floor than any injury to himself. He bent to retrieve it, one hand flapping at her in a 'keep the noise down' gesture. A silent grope was one thing, an hysterical row that could be heard outside was another: it could demean his position as owner/manager – and word could also get back to Marcia.

He staggered against the shelves as Paula pushed by. 'You can finish the bloody stocktaking yourself!' she told him as she marched towards the door leading into the main shopping area. She paused at the door as if to adjust her emotions before stepping through. As she looked back at him he was sure there was calculation in those tear-blurred eyes, just behind the distress. 'You'd better think about our situation, Rodney. You'd better decide what you're going to do about it.'

She disappeared through the door leaving it open wide.

Tucker groaned inwardly as he straightened. He'd misjudged her. She wasn't so dumb. Her next ploy would be conciliation, get him panting again; then *wham!* – more histrionics, only more so. Something to really frighten him. Bitch! He knew the name of the game – he'd played it once before – but not whether the blackmail would be emotional or financial. He hoped it wouldn't be financial.

He emerged from the stockroom an hour later and his mood was even blacker than before. He had already known the weekend take was bad, but the untouched cartons piled high on the shelves always mocked him with the fact. Not much to re-order this week and the way things were going, there wouldn't be much the following week, nor the one after that. Streuth, Monday, bloody Monday!

The sight of his customerless shop and his three cashiers huddled together at one checkout increased his gloom. His shelf-loader was sitting in a corner reading a comic, index finger lost up to its first joint in his nose. Tucker turned away in disgust, too gloomy even to shout at the boy. He looked up at the office and saw through the long plate-glass window that it was empty; Paula had obviously gone for the day. Just as well. He was in no mood.

'Come on, ladies,' he said loudly, forcing himself to walk briskly towards the cashiers. 'Back to our tills, get ready for the rush.'

The three women in their green overalls looked up with a start. Hubble bubble, toil and trouble, he thought as he approached them. God, there were some ugly women in this village!

'Ten minutes to closing time, ladies. Word might get around there's threepence off the double-pack Kleenex this week, so be prepared for the stampede.'

They giggled self-consciously at his oft-repeated joke – he changed the product from time to time to keep the humour fresh – and one of the cashiers held something up in the air. 'Have you seen the early *Courier*, Mr Tucker?'

He stopped before them. 'No, Mrs Williams, I haven't. Been far too busy to read newspapers, as you well know.'

'We've made the big time, Mr Tucker,' another cashier said enthusiastically, causing her companions to giggle like croaky schoolgirls.

'Your syndicate's come up on the Pools, has it? I hope this doesn't mean you're going to leave the security of a good job just because you've become millionaires.'

'No, Mr Tucker,' Mrs Williams chided. 'It's about Banfield. We're on the map now.'

He looked at her questioningly and took the newspaper. His lips moved as he silently read the main story.

'It's the church just up the road, Mr Tucker. Didn't you hear about it yesterday? My sister's boy was there, you know. I don't go to church much myself, nowadays, but my –'

'You've seen the little girl, Mr Tucker. Alice Pagett. She's often in here with her mother doing the weekly shop. Deaf and dumb, she is . . .'

'Used to be deaf and dumb, Mr Tucker. They *say* she can talk and hear now. Some kind of miracle, they reckon . . .'

He walked away from them, quickly scanning the columns. It was a good story, although the reporter had obviously got carried away with himself. But it claimed to be an eyewitness account, that the reporter was present when it happened. 'MIRACLE CURE BANFIELD GIRL' the headline screamed. And underneath, the subhead asked: 'Did Alice Pagett see vision of Our Lady?'

He climbed the three steps to his office, studying the article, and closed the door behind him. He was still re-reading the story when the three cashiers and the shelf-loader left.

Finally he reached into his desk, took a cigar from its pack, lit it, and stared thoughtfully at the exhaled smoke. His gaze returned to the paragraph which compared the alleged 'miracle' cure to the 'miracle' cures of Lourdes in the French Pyrenees. Tucker wasn't a Catholic, but he knew about the holy shrine of Lourdes. A gleam came into his eyes and, for the first time that day, excitement pierced his gloom like a laser through fog.

He reached for the phone.

Monday, early evening

The priest left the Renault and walked back to the white swing-gate he had just driven through. He pushed it shut, gravel crunching beneath his feet, wind, spiked with drops of rain, whipping at his face. He stepped back into the car and drove slowly up to the presbytery, eyes constantly flicking towards the grey-stone church on his right. The drive ran parallel to the church path, trees, shrubbery and a small expanse of lawn between them. It seemed appropriate that there should be a division between the two, one path leading directly to the House of God, the other leading to the house of His servant. Father Hagan sometimes wondered if his gate should bear a TRADESMEN ONLY sign.

He stopped the car and cut the engine. The church was just over a hundred yards away and its stout, weathered walls looked bleak, so very bleak, in the grey weather. Its image was mirrored in the newspaper lying on the passenger seat. It was a bad reproduction, blurred at the edges, a hurriedly-taken photograph blown up as if to emphasize the photographer's ineptitude. Below it was an even fuzzier shot of Alice Pagett kneeling in the grass.

Father Hagan looked away from the church and down at the *Courier*. He didn't need to read the article again, for it seemed engrained on his mind. The story, so coldly objective in its telling, seemed wrong, distorted; yet it reported exactly what had happened yesterday. Perhaps sensationalism substituting for passion confused its truth. Had there been a vision? Had everyone gathered at the church witnessed a miracle? *Was* Alice Pagett really cured?

He smiled, but it was a guarded smile. Of the last question there was no doubt: Alice was no longer a deaf mute.

Hagan had just driven back from the Sussex Hospital in Brighton where the girl was still undergoing tests. Alice's sudden ability to both speak and hear had elevated her from being an interesting case to an extraordinarily interesting case. Years before, specialists, unable to find any physical malformation in Alice's ears or throat, had informed her parents that they believed the girl's condition was purely psychosomatic – her mind told her body she could neither hear nor speak, therefore she neither heard nor spoke. Now her mind was telling her she could. So, to the medical profession, there had been no miracle; just a change of mind. If there had been a 'miracle' – and there had been cynical smiles when the word was mentioned to the bewildered parents – then it was whatever had caused the change of mind. Even though the remark was flippant, it was something Father Hagan could accept.

The newspaper article had likened Alice Pagett's experience to that of a young French girl, Bernadette Soubirous, who claimed to have had a series of visions of the Blessed Virgin in 1858. The grotto, just on the outskirts of the small town of Lourdes, where the visions had allegedly taken place, had become a place of worship with four or five million pilgrims visiting the shrine each year. Many suffered from illnesses or disabilities and journeyed there in the hope of being cured, while others went to re-affirm their faith or merely pay homage. Of the former, more than five thousand cures had been recorded, although, after stringent investigations by the Catholic Church's own Medical Bureau, only sixty-four had been proclaimed as miraculous. But so many other pilgrims, not just the sick, were blessed by another kind of miracle, one ignored by medical recorders, but noted by the Church itself: these people received a renewal of faith, a calming acceptance of what was to be, an inner peace which enabled them to cope with either their own disability or that of loved ones. That was the true miracle of Lourdes. Intangible, because it was an intimate, spiritual realization, an enlightenment that could have no meaning to clinical registers, to medical 'score-sheets'.

Alice Pagett had undoubtedly undergone a profound emotional, *perhaps* spiritual, experience which had caused repressed senses to function normally once more. That, in itself, was the miracle. The real question for Father Hagan was whether or not it was self or divinely induced; no one was more wary than the Church itself of so-called 'holy' miracles.

He folded the newspaper under his arm and left the car. The evening sky had grown considerably darker in the last few minutes, as if the night was in a rude hurry to stake its claim; or had he sat in the car for longer then he imagined? His verger would be arriving soon to light the church for evening service and the priest would welcome the company. He let himself into the presbytery and went straight through to the kitchen. If he had been a drinking man – and he knew many priests who were – a large Scotch would have been very welcome; as it was, a hot cup of tea would do.

He flicked on the kitchen light, filled the kettle, then stood watching it on the gas ring, only vaguely aware that the longer he watched the longer the water would take to boil. His thoughts were of Alice.

Her mother was thrilled and tearful over the incredible recovery, her father still in a state of disbelief. Not only could Alice speak and hear perfectly, but there was a special radiance about her that was due to something more than just her physical mending.

Father Hagan needed to speak with the girl privately, to question her closely on her vision, to gain her confidence so that there would be no invention in her story; but privacy had been impossible that day. The local doctor had whisked the Pagett family off to hospital late Sunday afternoon. So stunned was he at the abrupt change in her condition that he insisted on an immediate examination by specialists. Alice had been kept overnight for observation and further examinations had been carried out all through the next day.

For someone who had been given back the power of speech, Alice wasn't saying much. When the doctors questioned her on the lady in white she professed to have seen, her happy face became serene and she repeated what she had told the priest.

– The lady in white said she was the Immaculate Conception (the difficult title had become easier for Alice to pronounce) –

– What did she look like? –

– White, shiny white. Like the statue in St Joseph's, but sort of glowing, sort of . . . of sparkling –

– You mean shimmering? –

– Shimmering? –

– Like the sun does sometimes when it's a hazy day –

– Yes, that's it. Shimmering –

– And what else did she say to you, Alice? –

– She told me to come to her again –

– Did she say why? –

– A message. She has a message –

– A message for you? –

– No. No, for everyone –

– When must you go back? –

– I don't know –

– She didn't tell you? –

– I'll know –

– How? –

– I just will –

– Why did she cure you? –

– Cure me? –

– Yes. You couldn't speak or hear before. Don't you remember? –

– Of course I remember –

– Then why did she help you to? –

– She just did –

A pause then, thoughtful, bemused, but good-willed. The medical staff were obviously pleased for Alice, but something more was affecting them. Her quiet serenity was infectious. A psychologist, familiar with Alice's case, broke the silence.

– Did you like the lady, Alice? –

– Oh yes, yes. I love the lady –

Alice had wept then.

Father Hagan left the hospital, confused, hardly touched by the elation around him. By that time the story had broken and he was stunned when he saw the banner headline in the *Courier*. It wasn't just the attention his parish church would now undoubtedly receive that worried him so much, nor the publicity that would pursue Alice – it was a small price for her to pay weighed against the loss of her affliction – but it was the comparison with the miracle cures of Lourdes. Hagan dreaded the circus such news would create. And there was something more. A sense of foreboding. He was afraid and did not know why.

The kettle was steaming when he left the kitchen and went to the phone in the hallway.

Monday, late evening.

'How was the lamb, Mr Fenn?'

Fenn raised his wine glass towards the restaurateur. '*Carré d'agneau* at its best, Bernard.'

Bernard beamed.

'And yours, Madam?'

Sue made approving noises through the *Crêpe Suzette* in her mouth and Bernard nodded in agreement. 'And a brandy with your coffee, Mr Fenn?'

Normally he allowed his clients plenty of time to relax between courses, but by now he knew Gerry Fenn could never relax until the whole meal was over and a large brandy was placed before him.

'Armagnac, Sue?' the reporter asked.

'No, I don't think so.'

'Come on. We're celebrating remember?'

'Okay. Er, Drambuie, then.'

'Very good,' said Bernard. He was a small, neat man, who took a genuine interest in his customers. 'You're celebrating?'

Fenn nodded. 'Haven't you seen the evening edition?'

The restaurateur knew that Fenn was referring to the *Courier*, for the reporter had written a small piece in the newspaper on his restaurant, The French Connection, a few years before when he and his business partner (who was also the chef) had first opened in Brighton. It had provided a good boost for business at that time, for the seaside town was saturated with restaurants and pubs, and from that time on the reporter had become a favoured client. 'I haven't had a chance to look at the papers today,' he said apologetically.

'What?' Fenn feigned surprised horror. 'You've missed my big scoop? Shame on you, Bernard.'

'I'll catch it later.' The restaurateur smiled, then disappeared upstairs to ground level where the small bar was. Almost as if they were working on pulleys, a waiter descended to the basement area to clear away the dessert plates.

The restaurant was on three floors, sandwiched between a picture framer's and a public house, such a narrow building that it looked as if it had been hammered into the position it occupied. To Fenn it was the best restaurant in town, to be used only on special occasions.

'You're looking pretty smug, Gerry,' Sue said, one finger running around the rim of her wine glass.

'Yep,' he acknowledged with a grin. The grin disappeared when he saw she was frowning. 'Hey, it was a good story.'

'Yes, it was. A little over the top, though.'

'Over the – ! Christ, what happened was over the top!'

'I know, Gerry, I know. I'm sorry, I'm not getting at you. It's just that, well, I can see the whole thing getting blown up out of all proportion.'

'What do you expect? I mean, that was a weird thing that happened out there. A deaf mute suddenly cured, claiming she had a vision of the Immaculate Conception. Some of the other kids say they saw something too, when I spoke to them afterwards. That is, the ones I could get to – their parents scooted them away so fast I had a hard job catching any of them.'

'I was there, remember?'

'Yeah, I do. You didn't look too clever, either.'

Sue toyed with the napkin in her lap. 'I had the strangest feeling, Gerry. It was . . . I don't know . . . dreamy. Almost hypnotic.'

'Hysteria. Didn't you notice it was flying around yesterday? The kids picked it up from the girl. Do you remember that story a few years back? The Marching Bands Festival in Mansfield? Three hundred kids collapsed together in a field while they were waiting to take part in the contest; after a pretty thorough investigation the authorities put it down to mass hysteria.'

'One or two of the investigating doctors disagreed. They said the children could have been suffering from organic poisoning. And traces of malathion were found in the soil.'

'Not enough to cause that kind of result, but okay, let's call that an open-ended conclusion. Anyway, there are plenty of other cases of crowd hysteria to prove it happens, right?'

She nodded, then said, 'So you think that's what this is all about. Mass hysteria.'

'Probably.'

'That didn't come over too strongly in your story.'

'No, it was more implied. Look, people want to read about the paranormal nowadays. They're sick of wars, politics and the failing economy. They want something more to think about, something that goes beyond mundane human activities.'

'And it sells more copies.'

Fenn was prevented from voicing a sharp retort by the return of Bernard.

'Armagnac for Sir, Drambuie for Madame.' Bernard's smile wavered as he sensed the sudden icy atmosphere.

'Thanks, Bernard,' Fenn said, his eyes not leaving Sue's.

Bernard melted away to inquire how things were on the next table.

'Sorry again, Gerry,' Sue said before Fenn could form his reply. 'I don't mean to pick a fight.'

Easily appeased, Fenn reached across the table for her hand. 'What is it, Sue?'

She shrugged, but her fingers entwined in his. After a few moments, she said, 'I think it's that I don't want the whole thing cheapened. Something wonderful happened out there yesterday. Whether or not it was some kind of miracle isn't important; it was just something good. Didn't you feel that? Didn't you feel something warm, something peaceful washing over you?'

'Are you serious?'

Anger blazed in her eyes. 'Yes, damn it, I am!'

Fenn gripped her hand more tightly. 'Hold it, Sue, don't get upset. You saw I was busy; I didn't get the chance to feel anything. I noticed one thing, though: one or two of the people – those not worried about their kids – were pretty cheerful over what had happened. They were grinning all over their faces, but at the time I thought it was just general amusement at the kids skipping Mass. They weren't laughing or joking, though, just standing around looking happy. Maybe they felt what you did.'

'Hysteria again?'

'I'm not ruling it out.'

'You don't suppose this little girl, Alice, really did witness a visitation?'

'A visitation?' The word startled Fenn momentarily. He shifted uncomfortably in his seat, then reached for the brandy. He sipped it and allowed the liquid to singe the back of his throat. 'I'm not a Catholic, Sue. When it comes down to it, I guess I'm not anything religious-wise. I'm not even sure there's a God. If there is, He must be tuned to another channel. Now, can you really expect me to believe the girl saw God's mother?'

'Christ's mother.'

'Same thing to Catholics, isn't it?'

Sue let it go, not wanting to confuse the debate. 'How do you explain Alice's words? The Immaculate Conception. Not many kids could pull that one together, particularly if they'd been deaf for most of their lives.'

'She shouldn't have been able to pronounce anything coherently after all those years, but that's another argument. She could have picked up that label in any religious textbook.'

'And the drawings. In the paper, you say that Alice's mother had told you her daughter had been drawing pictures of Our Lady over and over again since her previous vision.'

'Yeah, she said that. That was about all I got out of her before the priest interfered. He whisked them away before I could get much more. But that doesn't prove anything, Sue, except that Alice was obsessed by the image. And *that* she could get from any book on Catholicism. There's even a statue of Mary in the church itself.' Fenn paused, drinking his brandy as the waiter poured coffee.

When they were alone again, Fenn said, 'The point is this: Alice had a vision, to her it was real; but that doesn't make it real for everyone else. My personal view is that she's a suitable case for a psychiatrist.'

'Oh, Gerry . . .'

'Wait a minute! For her to speak so clearly and so well after all these years, she must have been hearing words, sounds, for most of the time.'

'Unless she remembered them.'

'She was four years old when she was struck deaf and dumb, for Christ's sake! There's no way she could have remembered.'

Diners on the next table were looking their way, so he leaned forward and lowered his voice. 'Look, Sue, I'm not trying to knock your religion – although I didn't know you cared so much until now – but have you any idea of how many cases there are each year of people claiming they've seen God, angels or saints? Yeah, and even the Blessed Virgin. Any idea?'

She shook her head.

'No, neither have I.' He grinned. 'But I know it's on a par with UFO's. And there are plenty of murderers who commit the act because "God told them to". Look at Sutcliffe, the Yorkshire Ripper. It's a common enough phenomenon.'

'Then why are you building it up to be something else?'

He flushed. 'That's journalism, babe.'

'It's sickening.'

'You're in the media business too.'

'Yes, and sometimes I'm ashamed. I want to go home now.'

'Ah come on, Sue, this is getting out of hand.'

'I mean it, Gerry. I want to leave.'

'What's got into you? I'm sorry I took you to the bloody church now; you're going holy on me.'

She glared at him and for one gulp-making moment, he thought she was going to hurl her glass at him. Instead she wiped her lips with her napkin and stood. 'I'll see myself home.'

'Hey, Sue, cut it out. I thought you were staying with me tonight.'

'You must be joking.'

Fenn looked at her, amazed. 'I don't believe this. What's got into you?'

'Maybe I'm just seeing you for what you really are.'

'You're being bloody ridiculous.'

'Am I? Perhaps you're right, but it's how I feel at the moment.'

'I'll get the bill.' Fenn drained the brandy, then began to rise from the table.

'I'd rather see myself home.' With that she pushed her way past the table and clumped up the stairs.

Fenn sat, too confused to protest any more. He reached across the table for the untouched Drambuie, raised it towards the other diners who obviously found him fascinating, and drained it in two swift gulps.

Footsteps on the stairs made him turn in the hope that Sue had relented.

'Everything all right, Mr Fenn?' Bernard asked anxiously.

'Terrific.'

Monday night

He puffed his way up the hill, occasionally muttering to himself about the perplexing instability of the female character. His 'celebration' dinner had started out well enough, but the more he discussed the Alice Pagett story with Sue, the quieter she had become. She had a changeable temperament, volatile at one moment, tranquil, or even indifferent, the next. The trick was to predict her moods (and he cared enough to make the effort) and bend with them. Tonight, though, he had been unprepared for her attack. Unprepared and still mystified.

Why the hell had she been so offended? Had going to Mass on that particular Sunday morning brought about the resurgence of her past religious ideals? Why should it? She took Ben to Mass at Christmas, and there were never any sudden religious metamorphosis then. So why now? It had to be because of the kids; may-be she just didn't want to see them exploited. And maybe she was right.

But it was his job to report news, right? And Jesus Christ, that *was* news. Even the Nationals wanted it. There was no question: the story would be his ticket to Fleet Street.

With relief he finally stopped outside one of the street's rising (or descending – it depended on which way you were going) terraced houses, a two-storey, excluding basement, Regency house, walls painted flaky white, window frames and door flaky black.

Fenn inserted the key, his hand shaking slightly from pent-up frustration rather than the few pints he had consumed in the pub next door to The French Connection. He closed the door behind him and trudged up the staircase to his first-floor flat, hoping that Sue would be waiting for him, more than sure that she wouldn't.

The ringing phone hurried his steps.

EIGHT

'Will you, won't you, will you, won't you,
will you join the dance?
Will you, won't you, will you, won't you,
won't you join the dance?'

ALICE'S ADVENTURES IN WONDERLAND
Lewis Carroll

The size of the Crown Hotel was in keeping with the village itself: small, intimate, the kind favoured by weekend lovers. The plaque on the Reception wall told Fenn it was once a sixteenth-century coaching inn which had been extensively refurbished in 1953 when additional bedrooms were added. The oak-beamed dining room comfortably seated fifty people and the hotel's sixteen bedrooms were all well appointed, some with private bathrooms and all with television and radio. The sign also informed Fenn that the management knew he would enjoy the good food and friendly service and had great pleasure in welcoming him to the Crown Hotel. Thank you, he acknowledged silently, but I don't think I'll be here that long.

He noticed the bar to his left was open and decided that 10.35 was a little too early for a beer. The smell of morning coffee wafted through and the occasional elderly couple wandered in from the street and disappeared into the bar, the aroma a subliminal siren's song for geriatrics.

'Mr Fenn?'

Fenn turned to see a grey-haired but youngish-faced man smiling at him from a doorway further down the hall.

'Mr Southworth?'

'I am indeed.' The grey-haired man stepped into full view, one arm raised towards the open doorway as an invitation for the reporter to join him within. Fenn gave an appreciative nod towards the pretty receptionist who had summoned the hotel manager for him, considering a wink a little too frisky in full view of her employer.

'Very good of you to come, Mr Fenn.' Southworth offered a firm hand to the reporter which he shook briefly before entering the room. Another man rose from his seat and stuck out his hand towards Fenn's midriff. He shook the chubby hand and resisted wiping the transferred dampness against his trouser leg.

The hotel manager quietly closed the door, walked around a large, leather-topped desk, and sat. He wore a black suit with a light grey waistcoat and grey silk tie; on closer inspection his face did not look so young, although the skin was smooth save for giveaway line-clusters around his eyes and the corners of his mouth. Fenn and the second man sat on two straight-backed chairs facing the desk.

'This is Mr Tucker,' Southworth said.

Mr Tucker nodded and for one uncomfortable moment Fenn thought he would have to shake the sweaty hand again; but the paunchy man merely nodded in his direction, his smile having little affiliation with the gimlet eyes shrewdly sizing up Fenn.

Southworth continued the introduction: 'Mr Tucker has been a resident of Banfield for . . . what, Rodney . . . ten years now?'

'Eleven,' Tucker corrected.

'Yes, eleven years. A very highly regarded member of the community, if I may say so.'

Tucker preened and Fenn secretly winced at the ingratiating smile on the blubbery lips. He noted the heavy gold chain on the thick wrists, the rings, one a sovereign, on the fleshy fingers, and wondered how many extra pounds they added to the already overweight load.

'Very nice of you to say so, George.' There were the barest traces of a northern accent in Tucker's voice. He turned to the reporter. 'I own the local supermarket.'

'That's wonderful,' Fenn replied.

Tucker eyed him for a moment, not quite sure how to take the appreciation. He decided the reporter was sincere. 'I read your marvellous story in the *Courier* last night, Mr Fenn. First-rate bit of journalism.'

'Obviously that's why you wanted to see me this morning.'

'Yes, quite.' Southworth said. 'As you can imagine, the news was all around town by Sunday evening, but it was your report which has given the news a greater prominence in the region. For that, we are grateful.'

'That may be premature.'

'I'm sorry?'

'You may find a lot of unwelcome visitors to the town in the next few weeks now that the Nationals have got hold of the story too.'

Fenn noticed the look that passed between the two men. Tucker's eyes gleamed briefly, but Southworth's remained impassive.

'Weeks, Mr Fenn,' the hotel manager said, 'but unfortunately, not months.'

'Unfortunately?'

Southworth leaned back in his chair and picked up a fountain pen lying on the desk top; he coolly appraised the reporter while he toyed with the pen. 'Let me be perfectly frank with you, Mr Fenn. I had heard of what took place up at St Joseph's, of course, but had not given the story much credence, or even, I'm afraid, too much attention. I had, naturally enough, assumed that the story was wildly exaggerated or just – to put it bluntly – misinformed. But when Mr Tucker rang me yesterday evening and I took the opportunity to read your account of the occurrence, I must admit to giving the matter further thought. In the subsequent meeting with Mr Tucker, I became convinced that this event might well develop into major proportions.'

'Give it a couple of weeks, as I said, and it'll blow over. The public are pretty fickle when it comes to news; they like it fresh.'

'That's precisely the point.'

Fenn raised his eyebrows.

Southworth leaned forward, his elbows resting on the desk, the pen still held between the fingers of both hands like a delicately poised bridge across a ravine. His words were slow, measured, as though it were important that their meaning be received in the correct spirit. 'The world, I need hardly tell you, is in grave recession. Economic problems are not just confined to individual countries any more; the concern is global. But it's individual *people* who are suffering, Mr Fenn, not continents, nor countries. The common man has to bear the brunt of world management failure.'

Fenn shifted in his seat. 'Er, I don't see the connection . . .'

'Of course not, Mr Fenn. I do apologize. Let me be more direct. We are a small town – a village, really – in a small country, and it's we, the small villages and towns, that suffer under unfortunate government economic policies. Nobody subsidizes our local industries or businesses because, individually, their loss is insignificant when compared to the big combines or Nationalized Industries. Our local businesses are dying, Mr Fenn. Banfield itself is slowly dying.'

'It can't be that bad.'

'No, I may be over-emphasizing to make my point. It isn't that bad, but, given a few years, it will be. Unless the decay is stopped.'

'I still don't see what this has to do with what happened on Sunday.' But Fenn had begun to; the idea was just starting to glimmer through.

Tucker moved his bulky frame around in his seat and drew in a deep breath as though about to speak. Southworth hastily cut in, as though fearing his colleague's expression of their thoughts.

'You may have seen enough of Banfield by now to have formed some opinion of the place, Mr Fenn.'

'I can't say that I have. I've driven through it once or twice before, but until a week or so ago when I almost ran down the Pagett girl, I hadn't really given it a second thought.'

'And now?'

'It's a nice enough place. Quite pretty . . .'

'But unexciting.'

'Yeah, you could say that. There are plenty of other towns and villages in the south that are prettier, more traditional.'

'And more attractive to the tourist trade?'

Fenn nodded.

'That's exactly it. We, as a community, really don't have too much to offer. In summertime this hotel is quite a busy place, but my guests use it only as a base for travelling around the Sussex countryside or visiting Brighton and the other south-coastal resorts. The benefit to Banfield is minimal. Yet, I personally, would be willing to invest more money in the village if I thought it would yield a reasonable return. I know Mr Tucker feels the same way, but is also reluctant to throw away good money.'

'It's not just us, Mr Fenn,' Tucker spoke up at last. 'There are plenty of other businessmen around here looking for a good investment.'

'I'm sorry, I'm not with you. What kind of investment are you talking about?'

'For myself,' said Southworth, 'I would very much like to open a new hotel. A modern one, with more amenities than the Crown can offer. Perhaps even a motel on the outskirts; that would be most suitable for the amount of passing trade we receive.'

'And I'd like to open more shops,' said Tucker enthusiastically, 'maybe a couple of restaurants – you know, the cheaper kind where parents on a day-trip can afford to take their kids.'

'And there is plenty of local land waiting to be developed,' said Southworth. 'The village could grow, spread outwards, become a real town.'

And make you and your friends some money in the process, Fenn thought ruefully. 'Okay,' he said, 'I see what you're getting at. I'm still not sure what all this has to do with me, though. When my news editor rang me last night he said you, Mr Southworth, wanted to see me personally, that you had more information on the Banfield "miracle" – your words, I believe, not his. As you wouldn't pass anything on to him, he decided it might be important for me to turn up this morning. Was he right?'

Again, a look passed between the two men; this time it was cautious.

'We found your account of what happened at St Joseph's a first-rate piece of journalism, Mr Fenn. Accurate in detail, and imaginative in the quetions it posed.'

Tucker made agreeing noises.

Oh yeah, Fenn thought. 'What questions?'

'Well, comparisons really. It was that which caused Mr Tucker to contact me in my role as chairman of the parish council. You compared Banfield to Lourdes. In fact, you posed the question: Could Banfield be another Lourdes?' He placed the pen on the desk top and smiled sweetly at the reporter.

'I admit I got a little carried away.'

'Not at all, Mr Fenn. On the contrary, we feel it was a very perceptive remark.'

The metaphorical light bulb above Fenn's head flashed brightly. He could see where it was all leading, but wondered what part he was to play. 'There's been more than one so-called miracle at Lourdes, Mr Southworth. In all seriousness, I hardly think Banfield qualifies, do you?'

'Oh I think it does. Look at Walsingham and Aylesford, both towns in England. They have become shrines to many thousands of pilgrims each year. As for Aylesford, nobody is quite sure whether or not a visitation from the Blessed Virgin ever took place there at all; many believed it happened in France. Also, there have never been any spectacular miracles in either of these towns, yet the mystique is there, the people flock to them in the true belief that they are holy places. At least we have evidence that something quite extraordinary happened at St Joseph's, something that enabled a little girl to hear and speak after years of silence.'

'Extraordinary, yes, but not necessarily a miracle,' Fenn broke in.

'Do you know one of the best definitions of a miracle: "A divinely ordained exception." I think that's rather appropriate in this case.'

'"Divinely ordained"? Don't you need some evidence of that?'

'The Church does, of course. But the girl claimed she saw the Immaculate Conception; why should she lie?'

'And why should you believe her?' Fenn came back quickly.

'I think it's irrelevant whether we do or do not. Perhaps as a Catholic myself, I'm more ready to believe than Mr Tucker here is, but as I say, that's besides the point. The fact is, many thousands – who knows, perhaps millions if the story is circulated wide enough – will believe. And they'll want to visit St Joseph's.'

'Giving a dying village a new life.'

'Is that so wrong?'

Fenn paused before he answered. 'No, it may not be wrong. But you'll forgive me if I say it sounds a little cynical on your part.'

Tucker could contain himself no longer. 'This is the real world we're living in,

Mr Fenn. Opportunities come along, you have to grab at them.'

Southworth looked embarrassed. 'Come now, Rodney, it isn't quite so black and white as that. I deeply believe, Mr Fenn, that something – I hesitate to use the word, but I feel it's necessary – something *divine* has taken place at the church. Something ordained by God. And if that is so, there has to be a reason. Perhaps the real miracle is that Banfield has been given the chance of a rebirth, an opportunity to save itself from oblivion. And a chance for the people themselves to regain their beliefs. It was Shaw who wrote, "A miracle is an event which creates faith"; why shouldn't faith be created or renewed here?'

Fenn was confused. Southworth appeared to be sincere, yet openly admitted he would benefit financially if Banfield became revitalized. The fat man, Tucker, made no bones about his motives: he was in it for the money. But what, exactly, did they want of him?

'I appreciate your frankness, Mr Southworth, but I'm still not sure why you're telling me all this.'

'Because we would like you to write more on what will become known as the Banfield Miracle.' Southworth's eyes fixed on Fenn's and his expression was serious, almost grave. 'Your story has already created enormous interest. I don't know if you've had a chance to visit St Joseph's this morning . . .?'

Fenn shook his head.

'I went to see Father Hagan myself earlier,' Southworth continued. 'He wasn't there, but his house was under siege from a small army of your journalist colleagues.'

'From the Nationals?'

'I believe so. I spoke to them but, unfortunately, I'm very much in the dark about this incredible event. There wasn't too much I could tell them.'

I'll bet you managed somehow, Fenn mused to himself. 'Well, you can be sure the "Banfield Miracle" will get good coverage now. Maybe too much.' He was a trifle aggrieved that the big boys were muscling in on what he regarded as his scoop, but knew – and had known – it was inevitable.

'I'm sure it will – for a day or so. As you say, the public is fickle when it comes to news, and so is the Press itself.'

Tucker broke in once more: 'This is too wonderful a story to be allowed to die in a couple of days, Mr Fenn.'

The reporter shrugged. 'There's nothing you can do about it. Unless, of course, something else happens . . .'

Unless something happens, unless something happens! What was wrong with this idiot? Tucker's left heel did an impatient jiggle on the red patterned carpet. He had tried to persuade Southworth to deal with the biggies, not mess around with the local rag. The Nationals could give maximum publicity *now*, when it was hot; Southworth was *too* worried about declining interest afterwards, when nothing more happened up at the church. He'd insisted that a steadily built and maintained awareness would give more sustenance to a long-term plan, whereas massive, sensationalist coverage would only benefit in the short term. By patronizing the *Courier* they would, hopefully, ensure that sustained interest. The newspaper was, after all, a reflection of local affairs: it had a duty towards its audience (and to itself in terms of circulation figures) to consistently report (and, of course provide) any such newsworthy stories that would generate interest (and trade) in the area. But was this man Fenn taking the bait or was he too pea-brained to see the possibilities?

'There's the problem,' Southworth was saying. 'There is no guarantee that anything else *will* happen at St Joseph's. Which is why we felt the *Courier* will give the incident and its consequence more coverage than any of the other media. We can promise you, personally, Mr Fenn, every cooperation, any assistance, you might need.'

Fenn was silent.

'We do realize,' said Tucker, 'that your paper probably isn't over-generous with your expenses, so we would expect to help you out . . .'

His words trailed off at the icy glares he received from both the reporter and the hotel owner.

'I'm sorry, Mr Fenn,' Southworth said quickly. 'What Rodney is trying rather clumsily to say is that we would not want you to be out of pocket on this matter. Indeed, as a member of the parish council, I shall propose the setting up of a special fund to cover any expenses on the development of this, um, project. It could cover initial promotional material, personal expenses incurred by council members, and any extra miscellaneous costs.'

'And I'd come under any "extra miscellaneous" costs?' asked Fenn.

Southworth smiled. 'Precisely.'

To Fenn, it didn't smell any sweeter than the way the fat man had put it. He leaned forward, elbows on knees.

'Look, Mr Southworth, Mr Tucker, I work for the *Courier*, it pays my salary, and my news editor tells me what stories to cover. If he wants me to write obits for a month, that's what I'll do. If he wants me to cover garden fêtes for the next month, I'll do that, too. If he wants me to spend time delving into the strange happenings at the local church of a little country village, I'll be only too happy.' He took a deep breath. 'What I'm saying is, my editor calls the tune. He pipes, I dance. I'm independent to a degree – and that's a small degree – but there's no way he'll let me waste time on a story he considers to be defunct. Now, like I said, if something more happens, then I'll be back like a shot.'

Southworth nodded. 'We appreciate your position. However –'

'There are no howevers to it. That's it, that's the way it is.'

'I was merely going to say that the girl, this Alice Pagett, mentioned that the figure she allegedly saw has asked her to return.'

'She didn't say when.'

'But if she has another . . . another visitation, you would consider that newsworthy.'

'I'm not sure. A prepubescent girl's hallucinations don't warrant too much attention.'

'After what happened on Sunday?'

'That was Sunday. Today's Tuesday. Tomorrow will be Wednesday. Things move on, Mr Southworth, and we live in an apathetic age. What you need is another miracle, then maybe you've got a continuation of the story. For the next few days Banfield will get all the attention it needs, so my advice to you is to make the most of it now. Next week, it will be dead news.'

Fenn rose to his feet and Southworth rose with him. Tucker remained sitting, a mixture of disappointment and ill-disguised contempt on his face.

Southworth walked to the door and opened it for the reporter. 'Thank you for coming by, Mr Fenn, and thank you for being so frank.'

'Right. Look, if anything does happen, I'd like to know.'

'Of course. Will you be going up to the church?'

Fenn nodded. 'And I'll have a look around the village, get some reactions from the people.'

'Very good. Well, I hope we'll see you again.'

'Right.'

Fenn left the room.

Southworth closed the door and turned to face the fat man.

'So much for involving the bloody local Press,' Tucker said scornfully.

Southworth crossed the room and sat at his desk once more. 'It was worth a try. I'm afraid he got the impression we were trying to bribe him into writing the story.'

'Weren't we?'

'Not in the true sense of the word. We were just offering financial assistance.'

Tucker grunted. 'What now?'

'We – I – make sure the parish council becomes interested in our scheme. If not, all we can do is hope – as Mr Fenn put it – something else happens.'

'And if it doesn't?'

The sun shone through the window in dusty rays, highlighting one side of Southworth's face in a golden hue. 'Let's just pray it does,' he said simply.

NINE

And see ye not that braid braid road,
That lies across that lily leven?
That is the Path of Wickedness,
Tho' some call it the Road to Heaven.

THOMAS THE RHYMER
Anon

Bishop Caines regarded the priest with concerned eyes. 'I have grave misgivings about this whole matter, Andrew,' he said.

The priest found it difficult to look directly into his bishop's face, as though his gaze would see what lay beyond his own eyes. 'I'm worried too, Bishop. And I'm confused.'

'Confused? Tell me why confused.'

It was dark in the bishop's study, for the two windows which overlooked the tiny garden faced away from the morning sun. The deep wood panelling of the walls added to the room's sombreness and even the glow from the fire seemed muted.

'If –' he struggled with his own words, '– if the girl really did . . . really did see . . .'

'The Blessed Virgin?' The bishop frowned at the priest.

Father Hagan looked up briefly and said, 'Yes. If she did and was cured because of it, then why? Why Alice, and why at my church?'

Bishop Caines' tone was clipped, impatient. 'There is no evidence, Andrew, none at all.'

'The other children – they saw something.'

'No evidence,' the bishop repeated slowly, and his fingertips pressed against the polished surface of the desk. He forced himself to relax, aware that the parish priest somehow irritated him, and was even more vexed, not contrite, because of it. 'The Church must tread warily in such matters.'

'I know, Bishop, that's why I was so reluctant to bring it to your attention. When I read the newspaper report yesterday I knew I had no choice. Foolishly, I had imagined that the incident would be contained.'

'You should have contacted me immediately.' The bishop strived to keep the harshness from his rebuke, but did not succeed.

'I phoned you as soon as I saw the *Courier*'s article. It seemed so exaggerated.'

'Was it? The girl was cured, wasn't she?'

'Yes, yes, but surely not miraculously?' The priest looked at his superior in anxious surprise.

'How do you know that, Andrew?' The bishop's words had softened, for he had no desire for the man before him to be afraid. 'The child claimed to have seen the Blessed Virgin after which an incredible transformation took place. The girl could speak and hear.'

'But you said that was no evidence of a miracle.' The priest looked away again.

'Of course it isn't. But while we have to reject the proposition as we see it now, we must not close our minds to the faint possibility. Do you understand that, Father?' He didn't wait for a reply. 'It has to be looked into thoroughly before a judgement can be made. There are strict guidelines for such matters, as you well know.' The bishop smiled thinly. 'Some say our guidelines are too strict, that we eliminate all aspects of faith. But that isn't entirely true; we endeavour to eliminate doubts. The rules we follow for the discernment of a miracle date back to the eighteenth century, and they were laid down by Pope Benedict XIV, a man who had many progressive interests. He realized the jeopardy in which the Catholic Church could place itself by proclaiming miracles that later could be proved false by scientific means. In an age such as ours, where technological advancement is continually explaining "phenomena" in rational, scientific terms, the need to follow those rules is even greater.'

The priest's eyes were too intense and Bishop Caines wondered why. There was something wrong with the man, something – what? Unbalanced, perhaps? No, too strong a word. Father Hagan was disturbed by the peculiar happening in his parish, on his own church's doorstep, no less. And he was – yes, just a little frightened. The bishop forced a smile, an encouragement for his priest to open his heart.

'Would these rules apply to Alice Pagett?' Hagan asked.

'They would have to, should we decide to take the matter further,' Bishop Caines replied, maintaining the smile.

'Please tell me what they are, Bishop.'

'I don't think it's necessary at this stage. This whole matter will be forgotten within a month, I can assure you.'

'You're probably right, but I'd like to know.'

Bishop Caines curbed his impatience, then sighed. His eyes searched the ceiling as though scanning the corners of his own memory. 'The affliction or illness has to be very serious, impossible or extremely difficult to cure,' he began. 'The health of the person concerned should not be improving, nor should the nature of the illness be one that might improve by itself. No medication should have been given. At least, if it has, its inefficacy must be clearly established. The cure has to be instantaneous, not a gradual improvement.' His eyes dropped towards the priest again. 'The cure shouldn't correspond to a crisis in the illness brought about by natural causes. And, of course, the cure should be complete;

there should be no recurrence of that particular illness.' He stopped speaking and Father Hagan nodded his head.

'It would seem almost impossible to establish a miracle,' the priest said.

'Yes, it would, but I have to admit the rules have been stretched just a little in the past. Generally though, they are adhered to.' He smiled again, and this time his warmth was genuine. 'That's why some of our best miracles get away.'

The priest did not respond to the humour. 'Then it would be too soon to make any judgement on the child?'

'Much too soon, and very unwise. Father, I'm a little perturbed by your seriousness. Is there something else troubling you?'

The priest straightened in the chair as though surprised by the question. He did not answer straight away. He shook his head, then said, 'It's just the change in Alice herself. Not the fact that she can now hear and speak, but in her manner, her disposition. Her personality has changed.'

'And so it should after such a wonderful cure.'

'Yes, yes, I know. It's something more, though, something . . .' His words trailed off.

'Something you can't define?'

Father Hagan's body seemed to slump into itself. 'Yes. It's more than just elation. She's serene – as though she really had seen the Mother of God.'

'It's not an uncommon apparition, Andrew. Many have claimed to have seen Our Lady and, of course, there is a great cult of Mariologists. But psychologists say that children can often see what is not there. I believe the term is "eidetic imagery".'

'You're convinced she was hallucinating?'

'At the moment I'm not convinced of anything, although I tend to lean towards that theory. You say the girl's favourite statue in your church was that of Mary. If her affliction truly was psychosomatic, then perhaps it was an hallucinatory vision which effected her cure. Even the Church cannot deny the power of our own minds.'

Bishop Caines glanced at his wristwatch and pushed his chair back, his portly shape making the action an effort. 'You'll have to excuse me now, Father; I have to attend a meeting with our financial committee. It's the time of month I dread.' He gave a short laugh. 'It's a pity the Roman Catholic Church cannot run on faith alone.'

Father Hagan stared up at the bulky figure, aware for the first time that black cloth hardly symbolized holiness. He was embarrassed by the thought: he knew his superior was a good man, infinitely better than he, himself. Why then, had the thought jumped into his head? Was it just part of his own self-doubt, the unease that was insidiously gnawing on his beliefs? His head ached, buzzed with thoughts that were unformed, fleeting – attacking. The urge to lie down and cover his eyes was almost overwhelming. What in God's name was happening to him?

'Andrew?'

The voice was soft, tender almost.

'Are you all right, Father Hagan?'

The priest blinked, seemed bewildered for a moment. 'Yes. I'm sorry, Bishop, my thoughts were miles away.' He stood as Bishop Caines approached around the desk. 'Are you not well, Andrew?'

The priest tried to calm himself. 'I may be coming down with a cold, Bishop, that's all. The weather is so changeable.'

Bishop Caines nodded understandingly and led the way to the door. 'You're not too worried over this matter?'

'I'm concerned, naturally; but no, I think it's just a chill.' Or a sense of foreboding. 'Nothing to worry over.' He stopped before going through the open door into the outer office and faced his bishop. 'What shall I do, Bishop? About the girl?'

'Nothing. Absolutely nothing.' Bishop Caines attempted to look reassuring. 'Keep me informed of developments, watch over the situation carefully. But have no part in the hysteria that may well arise during the next few days. And keep away from the Press – they'll exploit the situation to the full without your help. I'll need a full report for the Conference of Bishops which will be held within the next two months, but only as a matter of record. I'm sure it will all have been long forgotten by then.'

He patted the priest's arm with an affection he hardly felt. 'Now you take care, Andrew, and remember to keep me informed. God bless you.'

He watched the priest walk through into the outer office and ignore the secretary who bade him good-bye. He waited for the other door to close before he said, 'Judith, would you be a dear and find me Father Hagan's file. And then let the finance committee know I'll be five minutes late.'

Judith, his secretary, a quiet but capable woman in her early fifties, was not even curious about the request. She never questioned anything her beloved Bishop Caines asked of her.

The bishop sat at his desk again, fingers drumming on the desk top. Was it all nonsense? Had Father Hagan exaggerated the situation? The priest had joined the diocese thirteen years before as an assistant priest in Lewes, and then on to Worthing as active assistant priest. Banfield was his first parish as senior priest. Was it proving too much? His work had been exemplary, and while his devotion to the Church was not remarkable among his peers, his conscientiousness was; where every secular priest would try if possible to visit at least four or five parishioners during the day, and spend ten or fifteen minutes with each, Father Hagan would visit the same number, but spend at least a half-hour with them; he taught for two mornings at the local convent school; he joined in with many local organizations such as the Self Help Group, the Liturgy Group, the Youth Group, as well as attending the monthly fraternal meetings of all the Banfield ministers – the Baptists, Anglican, Evangelical Free Church, and the Christian Fellowship (quite a few for such a small place). And these were just fringe activities outside his normal duties. Perhaps it *was* too much for a man with a weak heart.

A light tap on the door, and Judith was placing a buff file on the desk before him. He smiled his thanks and waited until she had left the room before opening the file. Not that there were any guarded secrets contained within; it was just that peering into a man's background was like peering into his soul, and both should be done in private.

There was nothing surprising, nor anything he'd forgotten in the file. The schools he had taught at, six years in Rome studying for the priesthood after his heart attack, ordained in Rome, returned to England. Then Lewes, Worthing, Banfield. But wait – there *was* something he had forgotten. Father Hagan had spent six months in a parish near Maidstone on his return from Rome. His first assignment, as it were. Six months as assistant priest in Hollingbourne. Only six, then moved on. It wasn't significant; young priests made frequent shifts to where they were most needed at any particular time. Why did it concern him now? Had he already begun to lose confidence in his priest's ability to cope with a difficult situation, one which could so easily escalate into a major phenomenon

. . . if handled correctly? A miracle cure in his diocese. Something extraordinary, proven beyond all doubt. Bishop Caines was a pragmatist; the Holy Roman Catholic Church would not be harmed by such a miracle in these cynical and anti-religious times. The Holy Roman Catholic Church would benefit by it.

Imagine: a holy shrine in his diocese . . .

He pushed the thought away, ashamed of his own vanity. But it lingered. And soon he knew what he had to do. Just in case . . . just in case it really had been a miracle . . .

TEN

Once he was across the water he found himself at the gates of Hell. It was all black and sooty in there and the Devil wasn't at home, but his grandmother was sitting there in a big armchair.

THE THREE GOLDEN HAIRS OF THE DEVIL
The Brothers Grimm

Bip bip bid-dip . . .

Molly Pagett's eyes flickered. Opened. What was the sound?

Her thin body lay stiff in the bed, her husband sprawled leadenly beside her. She held her breath, listening, wanting to hear the sound again, but dreading hearing it.

. . . *bip bip bip bid-dip bip* . . .

It was faint. And familiar.

She drew the covers back, careful not to wake Len. Her dressing gown was laid across the end of the bed and she drew it across her shoulders to keep away the chill of the night. Len grunted, turned over.

. . . *bid-dip* . . .

The sound, the familiar sound, was coming from Alice's room. Molly sat on the edge of the bed for a few moments, collecting her thoughts, shooing away the remaining dregs of a restless sleep. The day had been long, a confusing mixture of joy and anxiety. They had wanted to keep Alice overnight in the hospital again, but Molly would not consent to it. Somehow she felt their tampering, their tests, their probing – their endless questions – would undo the miracle.

. . . *bip bip* . . .

And miracle it was. There was no doubt in her mind. The Blessed Virgin Mary had smiled on their child.

. . . *bip* . . .

Molly rose from the bed, pulling the dressing gown tight around her. Quietly padding to the open door, fearful of waking Len, she stepped into the hallway. She left the door open just in case Alice cried out in the night – the *joy* of having Alice cry out in the night! It was a sound Molly had not heard since her daughter was very small. How she had listened in those early days, alert for the slightest whimper, the beginnings of a cry. Molly would scamper up the stairs, or rush along the hallway, in a panic which her husband could only scoff at. But then he had never appreciated just how much the new baby had meant to Molly. Alice had filled a barren, empty life, an answer to years of prayer. God, through the divine intercession of Mary, Mother of Jesus, to whom Molly had fervently prayed, had blessed her with marriage and child.

How cruel, then, to smite the child so young. (And how disappointing the marriage.)

. . . *bip bid-dip* . . .

Now once again, Our Lady had intervened. The affliction had gone, just as suddenly as it had come. Molly's faith in the Blessed Virgin had not wilted during the years of trial, and she had encouraged Alice to worship Mary as she did. If anything, her daughter's adoration for Christ's Mother was even greater. And the years of devotion had been rewarded.

Molly stood outside Alice's door. Silence for a while then – . . . *bid-dip bid-dip bip bip* . . .

The excitement of the last two days had been too much for Alice: it was the middle of the night and she could not sleep. She loved to watch the luminous green invaders descending the black screen of the microchip toy, destroying them with a quick stab at the red button, flicking a switch with the other hand so that her spaceship scuttled from side to side, dodging the invaders' deadly bombs. Now she could hear the machine, hear the computered pipes of victory when the last invader had been vanquished from dark plastic space. It must seem like a new toy again to her.

. . . *bip bip* . . .

But she had to sleep. The doctors had insisted that she rested. And Molly did not want a relapse. That would be too harsh of God . . .

. . . *bip* . . .

She pushed open the door.

. . . *bi –*

Molly was not sure that she had seen the small green light vanish on the far side of the room. It had been just a flicker in the corner of her eye, and it could have been nothing at all. She looked towards Alice's bed, expecting to see her daughter sitting up, eyes wide and happy, Galaxy Invaders in her hands. All she saw in the street light shining through the curtains was the little shape beneath the bedclothes.

'Alice?' Molly realized how naturally she had called her name, how swift was the acceptance of her daughter's returned senses, as though she had never really accepted their loss. 'Alice, are you awake?'

There was no sound. Nothing from the child, nothing from the machine.

Molly smiled in the gloom and moved towards the bed. Little faker, she scolded silently, teasing your mum.

She bent over her daughter, ready to tickle her nose and end the pretence. She stayed her hand. Alice really was asleep. Her breathing was too deep and her face too much in repose for her to be faking.

'Alice,' Molly said again, softly, touching her shoulder. The child did not stir.

Molly lifted the covers, searching for the electronic toy, expecting it to be cuddled in Alice's arms. It wasn't there. And it wasn't on the floor beside the bed. But it had to be nearby; Alice couldn't have scooted across the room to get back into bed before she had entered. It wasn't possible.

Molly knelt and ducked her head to floor level, peering beneath the bed. No plastic shape lurked there.

She remembered the green fading light.

No, that was ridiculous. Just not possible.

But she looked anyway.

The electronic game was lying on the small dressing table on the other side of the room, its switch in the OFF position, its screen black and lifeless.

Molly knew she hadn't imagined the familiar sound. She also knew it could not have been in her daughter's hands. And there was no one else in the room. Just shadows and the sound of Alice's steady breathing.

ELEVEN

'Could you keep a secret, if I told you one? It's a great secret, I don't know what I should do if anyone found it out. I believe I should die!'

THE SECRET GARDEN
Frances Hodgson Burnett

Fenn rolled over in the bed and his own groan brought him awake. His head seemed to continue rolling.

'Oh, Jes . . .' he winced, one hand fumbling towards the throbbing lump that common sense told him really was his forehead. His fingers hardly eased the pain at all.

Turning onto his back, a hand over his closed eyes, he endeavoured to control the spinning sensation. Another groan developed into a low, self-pitying hum, a sound which was in perfect harmony with the higher-pitched hum melodying around inside his head. A full minute later, the cadence began to ease and slowly, experimentally, he eased back the shutters over his eyes. It was another half-minute before he lifted his hand.

The ceiling settled down when he stopped blinking and he considered sitting up in the bed. Consideration over, he lay there and groped a hand towards the bedside table, careful not to lift his head from the pillow, nor turn it in any direction. The searching fingers could not find his wristwatch and he cursed his necessary habit of keeping the alarm clock as far away from the bed as possible (necessary because it was much too easy to turn off the bell and go back to sleep; he found the distance covered to find the bastard was enough to arouse him from his usual morning-zombie state). Where the hell was his watch? He couldn't have been that drunk last night. On the other hand, he could well have been.

Fenn sighed, screwed up his courage, and let his head slide towards the edge of the bed. Head hanging over, blood beginning to pound at the slab of concrete inside like waves against a sea wall, he stared at the floor. No watch there. But one arm was hanging over the edge too, hand bent back limply against the floor.

'Stupid, stupid,' he muttered when he spied the leather strap around his wrist. He twisted his arm and squinted at the watch-face. Six minutes past eleven. It had to be morning; that was light coming through the closed curtains.

He drew himself back towards the centre of the bed, resisting the urge to lie down again. Head resting against the headboard, back propped up by the pillow, he tried to remember how he had come to this state. Beer and brandy was the answer.

He scratched his chest and mentally – the physical act would have been too painful – shook his head at himself. You gotta cut it out, Fenn. A young drunkard could be fun, an old one just a bloody bore; and you're not getting younger. Journalists had the reputation of being big drinkers, and it wasn't true. They were *enormous* drinkers. Not all of them, of course; just those he knew personally.

Fenn tentatively pushed himself further up in the bed. He called this slow method of reclaiming the day 'gradual resurrection'.

Memories of the night before came filtering through and he grinned once or twice, but ended up frowning and lifting the bedclothes to inspect his lower body as though suspecting something might be missing. He grunted with relief; still there although it was making no big thing of it. What the hell was the girl's name. Boz, Roz, something like that. Or it might have been Julia. He shrugged, not really caring. So long as I'm not pregnant, he told himself.

He eased the covers away, using his feet to kick them towards the end of the bed. Then slowly, and ever so carefully, he teased his body from the bed. His head weighed more than the rest of him and the trick was to keep it balanced on his shoulders as he made towards the window. He drew the curtains, sensible enough to keep his eyes closed against the glare which he knew would hit the room; the sun was especially partial to his bedroom at that time of day. He stood there, allowing the rays to warm his body, the worst of the day's coldness blocked by the glass. When he finally opened his eyes he saw a woman trudging up the hill outside, pushing a supermarket trolley laden with shopping before her, staring up open-mouthed at his naked body. Her stride did not break, although her progress was slow, and her head swivelled round in an almost *Exorcist* turn. Fenn faded back into the room, smiling sheepishly and giving the shopper a friendly little wave to show there was no menace in him. He hoped her head would not lock into its unnatural position.

Once out of the sunlight, coldness staked its claim with tiny, itchy goose-pimples, and Fenn grabbed his dressing gown from the end of the bed. It was short and loose, ending well above his knees, and looked much better on Sue. It had looked pretty good on Boz, Roz – or was it Anthea? – last night, too, but not as good as on Sue. Even that drunk he had noticed and noted.

He went into the kitchen and filled the kettle, staring at the running water as though fascinated, but not really seeing it. He switched the kettle on and then ran both hands through his rumpled hair. I need a cigarette, he told himself, and was relieved he didn't smoke. The note was propped up against the cornflakes packet and he pulled out a chair and studied the message for a few seconds without touching it. It was a telephone number and signed 'Pam'. Oh yeah, *that* was her name. He briefly wondered whether she had tried to wake him before leaving the flat. Probably had, not knowing it would take a major earthquake to rouse him after a drunken binge. Only Sue could do it with sneaky groping hands, but then she had a technique all her own. He laid Pam's note down on the table and tried to remember what she looked like. He remembered remarking to Eddy, his drinking-buddy from the sports page of the *Courier*, 'nice face, shame about the legs,' when they saw her and a friend in the club, but couldn't recapture her image. The legs, though. Yeah, they were coming back. They'll crush your little head, Eddy had warned him; and Eddy hadn't been far wrong he now recalled. He gingerly touched his ears and wondered if they were as red as they felt. Could ears bruise? He went into the bathroom to check.

When Fenn returned to the kitchen, satisfied at least that his ears had not been pressed flat against the sides of his head, but not too pleased with the bleary-eyed reflection that had sneered at him from the bathroom mirror, the room was filled with steam. He had taken time to ease the punishment on his bladder, senses suddenly sharp for any strange tingling sensation as the liquid flowed; you could never be too sure with girls you didn't know. And some that you thought you did.

Jesus, he missed Sue.

He poured the boiling water into a cup, only remembering to add coffee when he was settled down at the kitchen table again. It burnt his lips when he sipped, but at least it was a clean, stinging pain, not like the droning ache in his head. He dipped his hand into the cornflakes packet and ate some, reflecting sombrely that it was just as well he was working the night shift; he was in no fit state this morning.

He looked around the small kitchen and shuddered. He would have to make an effort today; he couldn't go on living in such a pig-sty. Maybe he was a little untidy, but this mess was ridiculous. Time to get yourself back together, Fenn. No woman was worth it. Are you kidding? he answered himself. Every one was worth it – well, maybe with just a few exceptions.

Fifteen minutes later he was still brooding over his third cup of coffee when the doorbell rang.

He leaned out of the kitchen window and saw Sue standing in the street below. Either his hangover cleared instantly or racing emotions swamped the ill-effects. She looked up and waved.

He found it difficult to speak for a few moments, then stuttered, 'Use your . . . your key, Sue.'

'I didn't like to,' she called up.

She fumbled in her shoulder-bag, then stuck the key into the lock. Fenn drew his head back inside, scraping the hair on the back of his head painfully against the frame. He rubbed the skin and couldn't stop smiling. He hadn't seen her for nearly three weeks, not since she'd walked out of the restaurant. They'd had several strained telephone conversations, but that was all. It had taken her absence to make him realize how hooked he was on her. He leaned against the cooker, still smiling, relieved, expectant.

'Oh, shit!' The smile vanished.

Fenn scooped up the note still lying on the kitchen table and considered swallowing it; he shoved it into his pocket instead. Running into the lounge, he did a quick survey of the room. No incriminating evidence there. Then into the bedroom, lunging at the bed, scouring it for fallen hairgrips, strands of hair coloured differently to his own, smudges of lipstick or eyeshadow on the pillows. He made sure there were no other stains either. Sighing with relief, he allowed himself a few moments to collect his thoughts. Then: Christ, did she smoke? He couldn't remember. No ashtray beside the bed. The lounge! There'd be cigarette butts smudged with lipstick in the lounge! He ran back in just as Sue opened the flat door.

'Sue,' he said, sniffing the air for the stale aroma of cigarettes. The air seemed to be okay if just a little alcoholic.

'Hello, Gerry.' Her smile was not a full one.

'You look terrific,' he said.

'You look awful.'

He rubbed his unshaven chin, feeling awkward. 'How've you been?'

'Fine. You?'

'Pretty good.'

He stuck his hands into the pockets of the robe. 'Why the hell didn't you return my calls?' He tried to keep his voice level, but the last word was on the ascendant. 'For Christ's sake, three weeks!'

'Not quite. And I've spoken to you a couple of times.'

'Yeah, you just haven't said anything.'

'I haven't come to argue with you, Gerry.'

He stopped himself from a retort, then said quietly: 'You wanna coffee?'

'I haven't got long. I'm on my way to the university to tape some interviews.'

'A quick one.' He went into the kitchen and reboiled the kettle. He was fortunate to find one cup that was clean at the back of the cupboard.

Her voice came through from the lounge. 'This place is a mess.'

'The maid's day off,' he called back.

When he returned she was sitting on the settee, calmly watching him. He felt a tightness in his chest; she looked good. He placed the two cups on the glass coffee-table, then eased himself down into the other end of the small sofa. A two-foot gap separated them.

'I called round once or twice,' he told her.

'I've been spending a lot more time at my parents with Ben.'

He nodded. 'How is he?'

'Boisterous as ever.' She sipped and pulled a face. 'Your coffee hasn't improved.'

'Nor has my disposition. No shit, Sue, I've missed you.'

She stared into her cup. 'I needed a break from you. You were becoming . . . a little too much.'

'Yeah, I know. It's a habit of mine.'

'I needed a breather.'

'You said. Nothing personal, right?'

'Stop it, Gerry.'

He chewed on his lip.

'And maybe you needed a break from me, too,' she said.

'No, babe, I didn't.'

She couldn't help asking. 'Have you been seeing anyone?'

He looked squarely into her eyes. 'No. I haven't wanted to.' His ears tingled sorely for a few guilty seconds. He cleared his throat and said, 'How about you?'

Sue shook her head. 'I told you, I've been busy with Ben.' She sipped her coffee again and he moved closer. He took the cup from her hand and placed it back on the saucer. His fingers travelled to her neck, beneath her hair. He kissed her cheek, then turned her head with his other hand to reach her lips.

She was soft, yielding against him, returning his kiss with an emotion that matched his; but then she was pulling away, one hand held against his shoulder.

'Please don't. That's not why I'm here.' She seemed to have difficulty in breathing.

He ignored her and tried again, a feeling that was more than just desire strong within him.

'No, Gerry!' This time there was anger.

He stopped, having problems with his own breathing. 'Sue . . .'

Her glare stopped his words. And further action. Fenn struggled to contain his own anger. 'Okay, okay.' He turned away from her in a heavy sulk. 'What the hell have you come for, Sue? Just to collect some of your things?'

He heard her sigh. 'Not to upset you, Gerry. I didn't want that,' she said.

'Who's upset? I'm not upset. I may break out in pimples any moment now, but that's just late puberty. Christ, how could you upset me?'

'You're such a bloody baby!'

'Go ahead, turn on your charm.'

She had to smile, despite herself. 'Gerry, I came to tell you about the church. The church at Banfield.'

He looked at her curiously.

'I've been back. I've taken Ben there on Sundays.'

He opened his mouth to speak, but couldn't find anything to say.

'It's wonderful, Gerry.' Now her smile was full, and her eyes were shining with excitement. The transition was so swift it took Fenn by surprise.

'So many people are flocking to St Joseph's,' Sue went on. 'People are bringing their children, their sick, their handicapped. It's almost like a pilgrimage to them. And the happiness – it seems to hit you before you even reach the church grounds. It's unbelievable, Gerry.'

'Hey now, wait a minute. I thought it had all died down. I've rung the priest there – this Father Hagan – and he told me nothing more has happened. No more miracles, no more apparitions. Certainly nothing newsworthy or the Nationals would have been swarming over it like flies over a shit heap.'

'You have to be there to see it! Of course there's no more physical miracles, but the miracle is the atmosphere itself. That's why I came today, Gerry. I want you to see it for yourself. I want you to experience it.'

He frowned. 'But I'm not a Catholic, Sue.'

'You don't have to be, that's the joy of it. You only have to *feel* to know it's a holy place.'

'But why should the priest lie to me?'

'He didn't lie. Nothing is happening in the material sense; he told you the truth. He doesn't want the situation exploited, can't you see that?'

'And do you?'

'Of course not.'

'Then why are you telling me?'

She took his hand and clasped it tightly in both of hers. 'Because I want some of that cynicism knocked out of that silly head of yours. If you could just see for yourself the effect the place has on people, I know you'll begin to have some beliefs yourself.'

'Wait a minute. You're beginning to sound like a religious freak. You're not trying to convert me, are you?'

She surprised him by laughing. 'I don't think the Holy Ghost Himself could do that. No, I just want you to bear witness –'

'Oh, definitely a religious –'

'Just see for yourself.' Her voice had become quiet.

He drew in a deep breath and sank back against the sofa. 'What about the girl, Alice? Is she still going to the church?'

'That's the other thing you have to see.'

'What do you mean?'

'It's hard to say.' Her words were slow, deliberate, as though her thoughts were deep. 'She seems to have changed.'

'In what way?'

'It's difficult to describe. She seems – I don't know – older, more mature. There's a special kind of aura around her. Some people weep when they see her.'

'Ah come on, Sue. It's just some kind of hysteria. They've heard the story – their minds are doing the rest.'

'See for yourself.'

'Maybe I should.' He had to admit, he was becoming curious about the whole affair once more. The contact with Sue might bring them back together again, too. 'I could go there this afternoon,' he said.

'No. Wait 'til Sunday.'

He looked questioningly at her.

'Come to the Mass with me, when the crowds will be there.'

'You know it could have fizzled out by then. The place might be empty.'

'I doubt it. But there's another reason I want you to come on Sunday.' She got to her feet, looking at her watch. 'I've got to go or I'll be in trouble.'

'What? What are you talking about? You can't just leave.'

Sue walked to the door. 'I'm sorry, Gerry, I really do have to go. Pick me up on Sunday morning at my place. Ben will be staying with me so we can all go together.' She opened the door.

'But what was the other reason?' he asked, still sitting perplexed on the sofa.

'There's a rumour that Alice has told the priest and her mother that the Lady wants to see her again. On the 28th. That's this Sunday.'

Sue closed the door quietly behind her.

TWELVE

You parents all that children have,
And you that have got none,
If you would have them safe abroad,
Pray keep them safe at home.

OLD NURSERY RHYME

This Sunday was different. It was cold, drizzling, and miserable. But Fenn's senses keened to the excitement in the air as a rat's nose twitches at the scent of distant blood.

Sue had been right: it hit you before you reached the church grounds. The first signs came as he drove through the village High Street: there was a bustling activity that was unusual for a Sunday morning in any town, village or city, particularly on a cold and damp one. And most of the people were heading in the same direction. Traffic, too, was far heavier than normal.

Ben, in the back seat, had become quiet, which was a relief at any time. His arms were resting against the back of the front passenger seat, his face close to his mother's. Fenn quickly glanced at the eight-year-old boy and saw an expectant look in those large brown eyes; Ben's mouth was open and half-smiling as he stared ahead through the windscreen.

'Are you beginning to feel the atmosphere, Gerry?' Sue asked, looking past her son's head at the reporter.

Fenn muttered non-committally. He wasn't prepared to admit anything yet. He slowed the car as they approached a zebra crossing and the gathering on the pavement waved acknowledgements as they scurried across. Small children clutched their parents' hands, the elderly hung on to sturdier companions. A middle-aged man in a wheelchair came last, pushed by a younger man: their similarity in appearance indicated they were father and son. The cripple smiled at Fenn, then looked over his shoulder at his son, urging him to push faster.

Once the road was clear, Fenn eased his foot down on the accelerator, aware that traffic had built up behind him. The traffic moved off in convoy, Fenn's Mini at its head.

He glanced into his rearview mirror, surprised at the swift build-up he had caused. 'I hope we're not all going to the same place,' he commented.

'I think you're in for a surprise,' Sue replied.

He was passing groups of people along the roadside now, the houses on either side becoming fewer until there were only fields and trees. Even the steady drizzle could not dampen the cheerfulness that seemed to exude from the walkers.

Soon there were cars parked by the roadside, all driven half onto the grass verge.

'I don't believe this,' Fenn said as they were forced to drive past the church entrance.

'I said you'd be surprised.' There was no hint of smugness in Sue's voice.

He scanned each side of the road, looking for a space. 'Has it been like this every Sunday since?'

'No. It's been crowded, but not like this. The rumour has obviously spread.'

'You didn't tell me how *you* heard about it.' He swerved the Mini to avoid an opening door. Two metal sticks stretched out from the other vehicle's interior, followed by two ill-controlled legs. The driver was just emerging to assist his invalid passenger as Fenn's car passed.

'I was here at the evening service last Wednesday. I overheard some parishioners talking.'

Fenn risked a quick look at her. 'You were at evening service? In the week?'

'That's right, Gerry.'

'Right.'

He pulled in behind the last vehicle in the line. 'I guess this'll do,' he said ironically. The Mini bumped onto the verge and another car pulled up in front almost immediately. 'Okay, Ben, time to get wet.'

The boy was already pushing at the back of his mother's seat, eager to get going. Sue stepped out and pulled the passenger seat forward, allowing Ben to scramble through. Fenn slammed his door shut and pulled up the collar of his raincoat. 'Fine day for a bloody carnival,' he muttered under his breath. He tucked his hands into the coat's large pockets, conscious of the bulky object in one: this time, after moans from the *Courier*'s picture editor, who hadn't liked his last pocket-camera efforts, he had borrowed an Olympus. *If* (and it was a big *if*) anything happened, he was going to be prepared. In his other pocket he carried a micro-cassette recorder, a Christmas gift from Sue. They set off towards the church, Sue's arm linked through his, Ben racing ahead.

More vehicles were slowing, then stopping just beyond his. The gate to the pathway leading up to the church was crammed with people and Sue had to grab Ben, holding him close to prevent him from being jostled. Fenn stared around at the eager throng, bemused and becoming excited himself with their mood. Even if nothing spectacular happened – and he was sure it wouldn't – he now had a nice follow-up story to the previous one. It might take a little exaggeration on his part to say that St Joseph's was being besieged by pilgrims, believers and the just-plain-curious, but it wasn't too far from the truth. He

James Herbert

shook his head in wonder: what the hell did they all expect to see? Another miracle? He suppressed a chuckle, delighted now that Sue had persuaded him to come. It wasn't going to be a complete waste of time.

The three of them, Fenn, Sue and Ben, squeezed through the open gateway, bunched together by the shuffling crowd. Fenn noticed that a young girl on his left, no more than fifteen or sixteen, was trembling visibly, then quickly realized her spasmodic movements were something more than just excitement. The tight drooping of one side of her mouth gave him a hint, for he had seen the disorder before. Her movements were clumsy, her hands and arms twitching uncontrollably; she was flanked on either side by a man and a woman, presumably her parents. If he was right, the girl was suffering from a form of chorea, most probably St Vitus's Dance, for he had seen exactly the same symptoms in a young woman he'd interviewed in a Brighton hospital when covering the story of the hospital's imminent closure because of government cuts. It was an assignment he hadn't enjoyed, for the sick always made him feel unhealthy, but at least his article, with its many poignant interviews from the patients, had helped cause a stay of execution for the hospital. Its future was still uncertain, but that was better than positively no future at all.

He stood aside, allowing the small group more room for manoeuvring, and the father smiled gratefully. Once through the gate, the queue thinned out, although the line stretched up to the church doorway itself. There were several among the throng who, like the young girl, were helped along by others. They passed a small, emaciated-looking boy in a wheelchair, chattering happily to his surrounding family, his eyes, large and bulging, shining with some inner exhilaration. Fenn saw the smiling sadness in the face of the boy's mother; and there was hope in her expression, too, a desperate hope. It made Fenn feel uncomfortable, as if he were a voyeur into the private misery of others. Not just that, though: he was about to be a witness to their disappointment. He could sympathize with their desperation, but could not understand their gullibility. What had happened to little Alice Pagett had been a fluke of nature, an accidental triggering off of something in her brain that had over-ridden other, disobedient nerves, returning senses that she had never really lost physically; these people now thought the same chance process could happen again to themselves or those in their care. It was, he had to admit, strangely moving. And he began to feel anger, for he resented having his protective wall of cynicism breached by such blatant stupidity, and that anger was turned towards the Church which nourished and encouraged such ignorance. His rancour had become seething indignation by the time they reached the porch.

Inside the church it was crowded, the rows of pews full to capacity. Fenn had expected it to be so because of the activity outside, but was nevertheless surprized by the size of the congregation. And the noise, the steady murmur of whispered conversations. A peaceful silence, he had always assumed, was the prerequisite of any church when not responding to the service taking place, but it seemed today the collective tenseness was difficult to contain.

Looking at his watch he saw that it was still sixteen minutes before the start of the Mass. If they had come any later, they would never have got inside the door.

Sue dipped her fingers into the font, making the Sign of the Cross in a quick, fluid movement and encouraging Ben to follow suit. The boy reached into the receptacle, but his ritual was slower, more solemn. One of the men obviously designated as ushers to control the inflowing crowd, politely gestured for the three of them to move to the left of the church towards a side aisle where those unable to find seats were standing. Fenn resisted, for he already knew from which vantage point he wished to view the proceedings. He took Sue's elbow and guided her towards the right. The usher opened his mouth to protest and decided it really wasn't worth it.

Sue looked at Fenn in surprise as he urged her towards the spot they had occupied on his previous visit. There were a few disapproving stares as they jostled their way through, Ben anxiously clinging to his mother's coat, but they reached the right-hand aisle without hindrance. She was puzzled as Fenn stood on tiptoe, craning his neck towards the front of the church, then realized he was looking for Alice Pagett, whom he no doubt assumed would be sitting beneath the statue of Our Lady again. There was no way of telling if she was there, for the aisle was too full. Sue noticed there were more wheelchairs alongside the benches and emotion swept through her, feelings aroused in her that had been held in check for many years. Those emotions had been growing over the last three weeks and now she felt them unleashed, flowing through her and outwards, joining with others, uniting. She wasn't sure what these feelings were, but they had much to do with compassion, love for others. She felt like crying and knew she was not alone in that feeling. There was an anticipation inside her that exulted yet frightened her.

Even now, she was still uncertain as to whether or not Alice's cure had been miraculous, although she wanted to believe with all her heart. After years in a spiritual wilderness, clinging by only a thin thread to her religion, something had happened here at this church which had drawn her back, the absorption gradual at first, the link still tenuous, until her own will had strengthened the renewed acceptance. She had witnessed something extraordinary, be it a miracle or not, and that impression had rekindled her trust. And *that* was the feeling she shared with so many others gathered in St Joseph's church. *Trust.* It pervaded the air like the accompanying smell of incense.

She hugged Ben close and tenderly touched Fenn's arm, loving them both and wanting their love.

Fenn turned and winked and a small unpleasant shock made her hand drop away. The rushing compassion coursing through her almost stumbled to a halt, tripped by his wink of reality. No, not *her* reality, but *his*. His insensitivity, his mocking attitude. His only reason for being here was because there might be a story in it, a sequel to a feature that had enhanced his journalistic reputation. She thought he had come because he loved her and wanted to please; she had persuaded him because of her feelings towards him, wanting him to share her own acceptance. That one small gesture of his had dispelled her sentiment, made her realize they were two very different people, for it had contained the destructive contempt, no matter how lightly or how humourously disguised, of the detractor, the person who would never believe – never *trust* – because to do so would influence their own self-seeking opportunism. At that moment – and this was why her emotions had stumbled – she despised him.

He frowned as she stared at him, recognizing the sudden hostility in her eyes and confused by it. Sue averted her gaze, leaving him wondering.

More people were crowding in from behind, forcing them to move further down the aisle. Fenn tried once more to see the front bench, but there were still too many heads blocking his view. His initial excitement was now beginning to fade, the waiting and the claustrophobic atmosphere of the packed church taking effect. The tension was still around him, but he no longer shared it, or at least, not its particular brand of tension; his feelings were more of sharp curiosity. He examined the faces of those sitting in the benches. Were they all from the village or had word spread further afield? He recognized some, for he had spoken to them before on the day Alice had been cured. His gaze stopped on a particularly familiar face, this one seen only in half-profile, for the figure sat on the other side of the centre aisle, near the front. It was Southworth, the hotel owner. Well, Mr Southworth, it seemed he had been wrong: interest hadn't completely died away. Maybe it would after today, though. The punters were expecting too much, and they could only be disappointed. In fact, he wouldn't be at all surprised if there were some angry scenes after the service.

Fenn looked for the fat man, Tucker, whom he had met with Southworth at the hotel, but he was either hidden from view or not present. A disturbance at the back of the church drew his attention.

The doors were being closed, much to the annoyance of those still outside. Heads were turning as the dispute grew louder and a dark-suited man, wearing the unobtrusive collar of the modern-day cleric, rose from the front bench and strode purposely up the centre aisle towards the source of the trouble. He was tall, well over six feet Fenn estimated, even though his shoulders were stooped, and he was painfully thin. Yet his face, with its high forehead and prominent nose, showed strength, a fact further confirmed by his vigorous stride. The priest's cheeks were sunken, his cheekbones high ridges on shadowed valleys, and his skin had a jaundiced look that betrayed a past illness; yet even that failed to detract from the strength.

When he reached the end of the aisle, he raised a hand as if to gently scythe a way through the crowd gathered there, and Fenn was surprised at its size; from where the reporter stood, it looked as though the priest's fingers could easily wrap themselves around a football. It may have been an exaggeration in Fenn's mind, but the congregation back there seemed to agree, for they parted before the advancing limb like the sea heeding Moses. He followed the tall man's progress, for he was easily seen above the heads of others, and wondered who he was and why he was there. Within seconds, the priest was walking back down the aisle, the disturbance behind having settled, the doors of the church left open wide, despite the chill, and Fenn had a chance to study the man's face in more detail.

His eyes were cast downwards, the lids heavy, giving the appearance of being completely closed. His jaw was firm, though not prominently so, and the upper lip slightly protruding, spoiling what otherwise would have been dauntingly strong features. His brow was furrowed in deep lines, and further wrinkles were etched sharply around his eyes, curling both upwards and downwards like the splayed ends of a wire brush. His eyebrows were grey and full, like his hair, shadowing his eye-sockets. His stoop was more than fatigue or negligent posture; the spine was curved unnaturally, though not badly. The priest genuflected, then took his seat once more. Fenn had the distinct feeling of just having witnessed a magnetic storm in human form. He realized, too, that the buzz of hushed conversation had come to an abrupt halt while the priest was on the move. The whispers began again now that the intimidating figure had disappeared from view.

The crowd at the rear swelled into the centre channel and the three ushers forced their way through to form a human barrier, preventing the overflow from filling the aisle completely. Fenn was intrigued by everything that was happening and already regretting not having followed up his story in the ensuing weeks. Evidently an undercurrent of interest and speculation had developed in the area, culminating in today's little turnout. They wanted to see the trick done again. Maybe a bit more this time, though. We've had the triple somersault, now let's see the quadruple. That was why they had brought their sick along. Great trick last time, but what's in it for me? Or: Sorry, missed the last show – can we have a repeat?

His story, the angle, the view it would take, was already forming in his mind and it had much to do with gullibility, superstition, avarice – and, yes, maybe even duplicity. The meeting with Southworth and Tucker, whose motives leaned more than overtly towards exploitation, gave a good indication of what could be behind the spreading rumours. They had tried to recruit him into their campaign and had been disappointed but probably not discouraged. And how culpable was the Catholic Church itself? Just how much had they done to dispel the story of a miracle? Or had they encouraged it? Fenn felt grimly satisfied: there was the makings of some nice investigative journalism here. Not enough to set the world on fire, but controversial enough to sell a few extra copies in the southern counties. Then he glanced at Sue and fingers of guilt pushed at his thoughts.

Her head was bowed, her hands clasped tightly on Ben's shoulders. She was praying silently, a small frown of concentration on her forehead. Even Ben was still, lost in his own thoughts.

Fenn was perplexed. Sue was no fool and certainly not naïve as far as religion was concerned. At least, not since he had known her. So why this change? What had happened to bring her back to the Church so swiftly and with such conviction? And how would she react to the exposé he was already planning? He tried to shrug off the uncomfortable guilt: perhaps his story would bring her to her senses. He hoped so, because there was no way he could back off now he'd bitten the bait.

The tinkling of a bell startled him and a general movement swept through the church as those in the congregation lucky enough to have seats stood, and those already standing came to reverential attention. A door to the left side of the altar had opened and Fenn could just see movement between the heads of those standing at the front. The organ sounded its first chords, a brief clue as to which key the hymn was to be sung in, and throats were cleared and breaths drawn in. The start of the hymn was ragged, but quickly gained a unified momentum.

The priest mounted the two steps to the altar and turned to face the congregation. Fenn was surprized and a little shocked by the change in Father Hagan's appearance. The man seemed to have aged, to have become almost bowed. His eyes had the strange luminous quality of someone who was near death through hunger, and his skin had become sallow, stretched across his cheekbones. His tongue flicked across his lips in a nervous gesture and Fenn noticed that the priest's eyes flitted around the church in swift movements as though the very size of the congregation was unsettling to him. Hagan's vestments were no longer a shield; they merely emphasized the frailty beneath them.

Fenn leaned closer to Sue to make a comment on the disturbing change in the priest, but realized she was too absorbed in the service itself to notice.

Throughout the long Mass – drearily long, to him – he studied Father Hagan, gradually becoming aware that the man's deterioration was not as drastic as he had first supposed (or it could have been that the priest was regaining more of his previous stature as the Mass continued). It might also have been the fact that Fenn had not seen him for some time, and the sudden confrontation had heightened the aspects of change.

At the sign of peace, when everybody present shook their neighbour's hand and bade them, 'Peace be with you,' Fenn offered his hand to Sue. She looked at him coldly before taking it and her grip had no firmness. When she released him, he held on, squeezing her palm in an effort to make some mental contact. Her eyes dropped downwards and it seemed as though a shadow crossed her features. Fenn could only stare until a tiny hand tugged at his raincoat and he looked down to see Ben thrusting his hand upwards, waiting to shake.

'Peace be with you, Ben,' Fenn whispered, glancing again at Sue. She was watching the priest on the altar.

The Mass continued and, after the Eucharist Prayer, Fenn's interest switched to the congregation itself. Those wishing to receive Communion surged forward with undignified (and perhaps unholy) haste, causing a bustling bottleneck in the centre aisle. Invalids in wheelchairs, others on crutches, came forward, and Fenn could not help but feel sorry for them. Their desperation was obvious and it renewed his anger to see them exploited so. There were children in the queue, none younger than seven years old, but several not far past that age. They were eager and wide-eyed, probably not understanding exactly what was going on, but caught up in the excitement of it all. A youth of seventeen or more was being led towards the altar as if he was a five-year-old, and his shuffling gait explained why. The boy was severely retarded and Fenn could see the brimming hope on his mother's face.

Father Hagan's expression was one of anguish as he surveyed the long treble line of worshippers and the reporter grudgingly sympathized. He felt sure that none of it was the priest's doing and that Hagan was just as appalled as he, himself.

There were several nuns among the slow-moving procession, their heads bowed, hands clasped tightly together. The hymn being sung reached its conclusion, the verses running out long before the queue, leaving only the noise of scuffling feet and echoing coughs. Returning communicants were pushing their way alongside aisles to their seats, causing those standing to crush against their neighbours to allow them through. A small figure suddenly appeared before Fenn, and the reporter winced when he saw the boy's hands were covered in unsightly verrucas. In the centre aisle another child, this one a boy also, was being carried towards the priest, his legs wrapped in a heavy blanket. It was the same child whom Fenn had seen in the wheelchair on the path leading to the church. The boy, coaxed by the man holding him, opened his mouth to receive the Host and the priest's eyes were filled with fresh sadness.

The procession went on, a constant human stream that seemed to have no end, and twice there was a delay while Father Hagan prepared more wafers. Finally, his reserves were depleted and the priest was forced to announce the fact to those still waiting.

Fenn took grim amusement in their disappointment as the remains of the queue shuffled mournfully back to their places. It was like a bloody pub with no beer, he told himself.

The Mass ended soon after and the congregation looked around at each other as if expecting more. The priest and his white-frocked entourage disappeared into the sacristy, and the sense of anticlimax was almost tangible. Murmurs ran around the church and heads peered towards the right-hand side of the altar, to the pew beneath the statue of Our Lady. The whispers came back over the rows of seats: the little girl wasn't there. Alice Pagett had not attended Mass that morning. There were a few audible moans, a few muttered complaints, but because they were in the House of God, most of the congregation kept their grievances to themselves. They left the church, clearly feeling they had been let down, but having no recourse to take (which increased their frustration).

People were pushing against Fenn, and Sue looked up at him questioningly, ready, herself, to leave the church.

'Take Ben out with you, Sue, and I'll meet you back at the car,' he told her.

'What are you going to do?' she asked as she was jostled from behind.

'I just want to have a few words with the priest.'

'You can't go into the sacristy, Gerry.' She was almost forbidding him to.

'They gonna burn me in oil? Don't worry, I won't be long.'

Before she could protest further, he eased past her into the advancing crowd.

It was hard going, but churchgoers were not generally arrogant as a crowd and they made way for him where they could. The benches were emptying and he used one as a channel to reach the centre aisle. He stopped briefly to catch a closer look at the statue of the Madonna, the stone image that had fascinated Alice Pagett so, and briefly considered taking a quick photograph. Deciding it might be better to snap a few later when the church was empty – he didn't want to upset anyone present, especially the clergy – Fenn resumed his journey.

Once in the main aisle, the going was easier, for the crowd was more concentrated towards the church exit by now. He crossed the front of the altar, heading for the door at its side, finding it slightly ajar. He hesitated before entering. There were voices coming from inside.

'. . . why, Monsignor, why do they listen to these rumours? What have they expected – '

'Calm yourself, Father. You must behave as on any normal Sunday by going to the door of your church and conversing with your parishioners. If you wish to discourage them from such idle wishful-thinking, then show them that everything is normal.' The second voice was deep, commanding.

Fenn pushed open the door, deciding not to knock first. Father Hagan's back was to him, but the other cleric, the tall dark-suited man with the hunched shoulders, was facing the doorway. He stopped in mid-sentence, staring at the journalist over the smaller priest's shoulder. Hagan turned and his features stiffened when he saw Fenn.

'What do you want?' he asked, the hostility evident in his voice.

Not one to be easily intimidated, Fenn stepped inside. He smiled in pretended apology and said, 'I wondered if I could have a few words, Father.'

'I'm sorry, but you're not allowed in here,' the priest snapped back.

The altar-servers, three boys and a man, who had been busy removing their cassocks, stopped and looked at the priest in surprise, his sharpness alien to his normally mild temperament.

Fenn held his ground. 'It won't take a minute.'

'I want you to leave right now.'

The reporter's smile dropped away as he returned the priest's icy glare. It was the older priest, the tall one, who quickly stepped in to break the deadlock. 'I'm Monsignor Delgard,' he said. 'Is there something we can help you with?'

'He's a reporter,' Hagan interrupted as Fenn began to reply. 'It's largely due to him that this fuss has been created.'

The older priest nodded and said pleasantly, 'You are Mr Fenn? The man who found Alice in the church grounds when this affair began? I'm very pleased to meet you, young man.' He offered his huge hand, which the reporter took cautiously. In fact, the cleric's grip was firm but surprisingly gentle.

'I didn't mean to barge in . . .' Fenn said and the priest smiled at the lie.

'I'm afraid we are rather busy at the moment, Mr Fenn, but if we could be of some assistance later?'

'Could you tell me why you're here at St Joseph's today?'

'Merely to assist Father Hagan. And to observe, of course.'

'Observe what, exactly?'

'You saw how many people attended Mass today. It would be silly for the Church to pretend the congregation has not placed some special significance on this particular Sunday.'

'But have you, Monsignor?' The tape recorder in Fenn's pocket was running, flicked on by his thumb.

The priest hesitated, but he was still smiling. 'Let me just say we did not expect any phenomenon to occur. We are more concerned with our parishioners –'

'There's more than parishioners outside,' Fenn broke in. 'I'd say they've come from a larger area than Banfield.'

'Yes, I'm sure that's the case,' Hagan said coldly, 'but that's because your newspaper ran a grossly exaggerated story which played on the public's susceptibility.'

'I only reported what happened,' Fenn retorted.

'With some of your own speculation. And I might add, speculation that barely hid the cynicism behind it.'

'I'm not a Catholic, Father. You can't expect –'

'Please.' Monsignor Delgard stood firmly between the two protagonists, his big hands held at chest level as if to hold back their remarks. His voice was not raised, its tones barely hardened, but it was a voice to take notice of. 'I'm sure this discussion should continue – you must have your questions answered, Mr Fenn, and you, Father, may benefit from listening to a more objective view of this whole affair – but now is neither the time nor the place. I suggest you leave, Mr Fenn, and return some time later today.'

It was hardly a suggestion, more of a command, and one which the reporter reluctantly decided to obey. It would be better for the sake of his story to have Hagan's cooperation rather than his antagonism, and their conversation at this point was going nowhere useful. However, always one to turn a situation to his advantage, no matter how small, Fenn said, 'If I come back this evening, will you give me an hour of your time?'

Father Hagan opened his mouth to protest, but Monsignor Delgard spoke quickly. 'As long as you like, Mr Fenn. We won't restrict your time.'

Fenn was taken aback. He'd expected half-an-hour, maybe twenty minutes. 'It's a deal,' he said with a grin, then pulled open the door.

The church was almost empty and it seemed much darker. He realized that the rainclouds had become heavier, the light outside shining through the stained-glass windows poor and diffused, having no thrust. He closed the sacristy door and crossed the front of the altar towards the statue of the Madonna. The pupil-less eyes of the white statue gazed sightlessly down on him, its stone lips bearing the slightest traces of a benevolent smile. The sculptured hands stretched downwards, palms outwards, symbol of the Madonna's acceptance of all who stood before her.

It was just a block of stone to Fenn, a skilful effigy but one that had no meaning for him. The blank eyes were disturbing because they were blind; the look of compassion was meaningless because it was hand-made, not heart-felt.

He narrowed his eyes. And the statue was flawed. There was just the faintest hairline crack barely visible in the poor light, running from beneath the chin down one side of the neck. Nobody's perfect, he silently told the Madonna.

He was reaching inside his raincoat pocket for the camera, having decided it was as good an opportunity as any to photograph the statue, when running footsteps made him turn. A young boy of fifteen or sixteen was hurrying down the centre aisle, making for the altar. He did not seem to notice Fenn as he swung around the front bench and headed for the sacristy door. He thumped against the door with the flat of his hand, then burst in.

Fenn quickly hurried over and was just in time to hear the youth breathlessly say: 'It's Alice Pagett, Father. She's here.'

'But I instructed her mother to keep her away today,' came Father Hagan's voice.

'But she's here, Father. In the field, by the tree! And everybody's following her. They're all going into the field!'

THIRTEEN

'The Magic is in me – the Magic is in me. It's in every one of us.'

THE SECRET GARDEN
Frances Hodgson Burnett

When Fenn entered the sacristy he caught just a glimpse of the two priests and the boy departing through another door leading to the outside. The altar-boys and the older altar-server were still too surprised to move. The reporter ran through the room, following the three who had just left. Outside he found himself in the section of graveyard at the back of St Joseph's; the two priests and the youth were hurrying along a narrow path between the graves towards the low wall dividing the church grounds and the field beyond. He hurried to catch up, the eager gleam back in his eyes.

He veered off when he saw that the wall was crowded with people, many of whom were anxious to see into the field, but reluctant, for reasons of their own, to enter it. A section of wall towards the corner of the graveyard was clear, and it was this he made for. The two priests were trying to push through the jostling onlookers, but were having difficulty in reaching the wall. Fenn scuffed the top of a molehill with his shoe as he raced towards his chosen spot. The grass was damp and slippery and twice his feet nearly slid from under him. He was soon at the wall, leaning over it, catching his breath. Then he was on the wall, balancing on its rough, uneven top, fumbling for the camera in his pocket, fingers trembling.

Alice, wearing a blue plastic raincoat, was standing before the tree, staring up at its twisted branches, the light rain spattering against her upturned face. The clouds were dark and heavy, their full load having not yet been shed; the horizon was silvery white in contrast. The others stood further back from the girl as though afraid to approach her, afraid to go too near the oak. They stood in small groups, silent, watching. More were climbing over the wall, cautiously moving forward, but never beyond the groups behind the girl. Fenn saw the crippled boy, the one who had received Holy Communion earlier, being lifted over the wall, then carried through the waiting people towards the little girl. Just five yards from her, his father knelt and gently laid the boy on the ground, adjusting the blanket around the frail body to keep out the dampness.

A young girl was led forward and Fenn recognized her from her clothes: she was the same girl he'd made way for at the church gate, the one suffering from chorea.

Others were pushing their way through, bringing children with them, or supporting adults. Soon the groups were less obvious as the space around them filled, and the sick were laid on the grass, no one caring about the ground's wetness, or the chill in the air.

Fenn estimated there had to be at least three hundred people present, many now in the field itself, the rest still nervously lingering behind the wall as though it were a shield. All were hushed.

He could feel the tension and almost wanted to shout against it. It was building, passing from person to person, group to group, a rising hysteria that would reach a peak before breaking. He shivered, for it was uncanny, eerie.

He focused the camera, trying to keep his hand steady. His vantage point on the wall gave him a good overall view and he hoped he had chosen the correct aperture for the dim light. The Olympus had a built-in flash unit, but he was reluctant to use it: he felt that the sudden light might somehow upset the mood of the crowd, might break the spell they appeared to be under. Spell? Get a hold of yourself, Fenn. It was no more than the atmosphere created at football matches or pop concerts. Just quieter, that was all, and that was what made it so spooky.

He clicked the button, first photographing Alice and the tree. Then her and the crowd behind. The people at the wall next. Good shot, you could see the apprehension on their faces. And something more. Fear. Fear yet . . . longing. Christ, they were *yearning* for something to happen.

He saw the two priests climbing over and took a quick shot. The picture could be great when blown up and cropped in around Father Hagan's head, for he had rarely seen such an expression of pure anguish on another man's face before.

The priests moved through the gathering, but even they did not go beyond the fringe of people forming a ragged semi-circle around the girl. Fenn jumped to the ground and made his own way towards the oak tree, approaching from the side, affording himself a good view of what was taking place. His shoes and the ends of his trouser legs were soaked by the time he reached the edge of the crowd, yet he did not feel the discomfort. He, like the others, was too fascinated by the diminutive figure standing perfectly still, gazing up at the tree. From his position he could see Alice's profile and her expression was one of sheer happiness. Many of the children were smiling too, their joy not altogether shared by the adults with them, although even they were not showing the same fearful apprehension of moments earlier. At least, those nearest the girl were not. Fenn caught sight of Alice's mother kneeling close to the group who had brought the crippled boy into the field and wasn't sure if it was just rain on her face or if she was crying. Her eyes were closed and her hands were gripped tightly together in a gesture of prayer. The scarf she wore had fallen back onto her shoulders and her hair hung damply over her forehead. Silent words formed on her lips.

And then everything became unnaturally still.

Only the falling rain convinced Fenn that the world had not ground to a stop.

There were not even any sounds. No birds, no bleating of sheep on the far side of the field, no traffic noise from the nearby road. A vacuum.

Until the breeze ruffled the grass.

Fenn shivered, for the sudden draught of air was more chilly than the drizzle. He pulled his raincoat collar tight around his neck and nervously looked around, the feeling of some unseen presence unreasonably strong. There was nothing there of course, just the field and its bordering hedge. To his left was the crowd, the wall, the church; to his right the tree . . . the tree. . . . Beyond . . . the tree. . . . He could not focus beyond the tree.

The wind – for it was no longer a breeze – was rustling through the bare branches, stirring the deformed limbs, making them sway as though they were slumbering tentacles suddenly come to life. The rustling became a low howling as the grotesque limbs shifted.

The onlookers' clothes were whipped by the wind and they clung to each other or held up their arms against it. Several began to back away, plainly frightened, while others stood their ground, also afraid yet curious – and for some, desperate – enough to stay. Many dropped to their knees and bowed their heads.

Strangely, Fenn felt his own legs grow weak and it became an effort to keep himself erect. He saw Father Hagan begin to stumble forward in an attempt to reach the girl, but the other priest caught his arm and held him back. Words passed between the two clerics, but they were too far away and the wind was too loud for the reporter to hear. He lurched, feeling as though something had pushed him from behind. He could feel muscles in his back stiffening and his windblown hair had become brittle.

But it passed. The low howling ceased, the wind died. The rain continued its drizzle, no longer blown off course.

The people looked relieved, several blessing themselves. They looked around at their neighbours, each seeking comfort from the presence of others, turning to their parish priest for reassurance. Father Hagan could offer none. His skin looked even more pallid as he stared at Alice Pagett.

Her arms were stretched outwards towards the now still oak and she was speaking, although no one present could catch the words. She was laughing too, joy almost visibly radiating from her small body. Yet there was nothing at the tree, no form, no movement, nothing at all. A gasp ran through the onlookers, a gasp that became a moan.

Alice's feet were no longer on the ground. She hovered two or three inches above the tallest blade of grass.

Fenn blinked, not believing what he was seeing. It just wasn't possible. Levitation was just a trick performed by conjurers under contrived conditions. But there were no such conditions here, just an open field. And no conjurer, just an eleven-year-old girl. Jesus Christ, what was going on?

He felt an electricity running through him, a sharp, tingling flush that somehow jumped from his body to others, linking them all in a binding blanket of static. He was mesmerized by the girl, not sure if he were hallucinating, still refusing to accept the evidence before his eyes. Vaguely, somewhere in the more sane region of his mind, he was reminded of the camera in his pocket; but he could not find the strength nor, more importantly, the desire, to reach for it. He shook his head, partly to clear it, partly to feel some physical sensation. The dream, the hallucination, the telepathic illusion, was still there in front of him, refusing to obey that part of his brain that insisted it was all unreal. Alice Pagett was standing above the ground and the grass was gently swaying beneath the soles of her feet.

Minutes passed and nobody dared move or speak. There was an aura around Alice that, although it could not be seen, could be felt. A radiance that, if it *were* visible, would be brilliantly white, golden-hued at its periphery. Her position did not fluctuate; she neither rose nor descended. And her body was immobile, arms still outstretched, only her lips moving.

Not many of those gathered there remained standing. Fenn's legs began to give way completely and it was not reverence for what was taking place that caused him to sink to the ground. It was weakness, a peculiar tiredness that assailed him; it was as though his body were being drained of energy. He felt so numb, so cold.

He crouched on one knee, a hand resting on the earth to keep himself balanced. The priests were still standing, although the monsignor had Father Hagan's arm tightly gripped as if supporting him. They appeared confused, bewildered by the incredible spectacle and, Fenn thought with some grim satisfaction, they too now looked afraid.

He turned his head to look at Alice once more and saw that she was sinking, slowly, slowly descending, grass blades bending beneath her feet, a pliant cushion before she touched earth. She was down and she turned to look at her audience, a rapturous smile on her face.

At which point the miracles began.

A tiny boy ran forward, his outstretched hands a mass of grey-black lumps. He fell at Alice's feet, holding his hands aloft so that those watching from behind could see their ugliness. His tearful mother tried to join him, but her husband held her back, not knowing what was going to happen, just praying that it would be good for his son.

The girl smiled down at the boy and the blackish verrucas, with their edges of grey, began to fade.

The mother screamed and broke free, rushing to her son and hugging him close, tears streaming from her eyes to mingle with the rain in the boy's hair.

A cry from the crowd and all eyes turned in the direction of the teenage girl whose facial muscles could not be controlled, whose limbs twitched spasmodically and incessantly. She had been kneeling with her family group, but now was on her feet, her expression serene. Although she moved cautiously, there was no trembling, no twitching; she stared down at herself, examining her hands, her legs. The girl came forward, slowly but surely, her chest beginning to heave with her joy. She knelt at the feet of Alice Pagett and wept.

A man stumbled forward, pushing through the kneeling people, his eyes clouded with cataracts. They cleared a path for him, guiding him forward with gentle pressure on his arms, urging him on, praying for him.

He fell before he reached the girl and lay sobbing, his face wretched with longing. The opacity in his eyes began to clear. For the first time in five years he began to see colour. He began to see shapes. He began to see the world again, only his tears now blurring his vision.

A young girl, who attended the same hospital as Alice and whose parents had been given new hope ever since the latter's sudden cure, asked her mother why the man on the ground was crying. The words were not too clear, but the girl's mother understood them. To her they were the most beautifully formed words she had ever heard, for her daughter had not spoken in all the seven years of her short life.

Many in the crowd were collapsing, sprawling on the ground, or falling against those nearest to them, like marionettes whose strings had been cut. Fenn was forced to sit, his supporting knee giving way. His eyes were wild, looking from the girl to the crowd, the girl to the crowd, the girl . . . to the tree . . .

Another cry, becoming a wail, from among the rain-soaked people. A woman's moan of anguish.

Fenn's eyes scanned the crouched bodies and came to rest on the blanket-wrapped bundle lying on the fringe of the semi-circle. The boy was sitting upright; his eyes shining with some new-found understanding. He pushed the blanket aside and hands reached to help him. He didn't need their help though. He was rising, his movements stiffly awkward like a newborn lamb's. He was on his feet and the hands steadied him. He moved forward, ill-balanced but coping, staggering and eager to reach the girl. His father and another man quickly stood beside him, taking his arms. He walked, using the adults for support, but the motion coming from his own legs. They helped him forward and it was not until he was within touching distance of Alice Pagett that he allowed himself to sink to the ground. He half-sat half-lay there, his knees together, thin legs almost hidden in the grass, his upper body upright, his father holding onto his shoulders.

They gazed at the girl with adoration on their faces.

Fenn was stunned. His strength was returning although he did not yet feel steady enough to stand. Jesus Christ, what happened here? *It just wasn't possible!*

He looked towards the two priests, one dressed totally in black, the other in the robes of the Sunday service, green and yellow, white beneath. Father Hagan had already fallen to his knees, and the tall priest, the monsignor, was slowly collapsing beside him. Fenn could not be sure if they were suffering the same debilitating weakness that had assailed his own body, or if their gesture was one of homage. Father Hagan bowed his head into his hands and rocked backwards and forwards. Monsignor Delgard could only stare wide-eyed at the girl standing in the field, her small body so vulnerable beneath the black twisted tree that towered over her.

FOURTEEN

'She's as tender and sweet as a fat little lamb. Yum, yum!
She'll make a tasty dinner!' She drew out a bright sharp knife,
which glittered quite dreadfully.

THE SNOW QUEEN
Hans Andersen

Riordan wearily shook his head. *It made no sense.* In his thirty-eight years as a farmer, nothing like this had ever happened before. Not to his livestock. He motioned the lorry to back further into the field, then nodded to his farm labourers to get busy with their shovels.

The vet came over and stood by him, saying nothing, his face haggard. The call from Riordan had come in the early hours of the morning and when he, the vet, had arrived he knew there was only so much he could do. Even those he had cut from their mother's stomachs, those he believed were well-formed enough to cope with premature birth, had not survived. It was inexplicable. Why should it happen to all of them at the same time? There had been a disturbance in the field the day before – an incredible event from all the confused accounts he had heard

– but the pregnant sheep had been far away from it all, in a different section of the field. He sighed and wiped a hand over his tired eyes as the labourers scooped up the tiny glistening corpses on the shovels and tossed them into the back of the lorry. The sheep, the mothers the vet had not been able to save, were picked up by stiffened legs and swung onto the waiting vehicle.

Riordan looked at the grey church in the distance and wondered how people could worship such an ill-natured God. Farming was a hard life: you expected failures, mishaps – even tragedies. Crops could be ruined, animals could, and always did, have accidents or illnesses from which they perished. It happened to farm workers, too. But you never expected, could never be prepared for, something like this. There was just no sense to it.

He turned his back on the field and watched the heavily-laden lorry pull away.

PART TWO

'I wonder if I've changed in the night? Let me think: was I the same when I got up this morning? I almost think I can remember feeling a little different. But if I'm not the same, the question is, Who in the world am I? Ah, that's the great puzzle!'

ALICE'S ADVENTURES IN WONDERLAND
Lewis Carroll

FIFTEEN

'When I used to read fairy-tales, I fancied that kind of thing never happened, and now here I am in the middle of one!'

ALICE'S ADVENTURES IN WONDERLAND
Lewis Carroll

'Good Lord, are you unwell, Andrew?'

Bishop Caines stared at the priest, shocked by the change in the man. He had looked ill when the bishop had spoken to him just a few weeks before, but now his physical appearance had deteriorated alarmingly. Bishop Caines moved forward and took the priest's hand, then indicated towards an armchair opposite his desk. He looked questioningly at Monsignor Delgard, but the tall priest's expression remained impassive.

'I think perhaps a small brandy might do you some good.'

'No, no, I'm fine, really,' Father Hagan protested.

'Nonsense. It'll give you back some colour. Peter, the same for you?'

Delgard shook his head. 'Perhaps some tea?' he said, looking directly at the bishop's secretary who had shown them into the study.

'Yes, of course,' said Bishop Caines, returning to his seat behind the desk. 'Both for me, I think, Judith. I may need it.' He smiled at his secretary and she left the room. The smile dropped as soon as the door closed.

'I'm extremely disturbed, gentlemen. I would have preferred that you came to me yesterday.'

Monsignor Delgard had walked to the study's leaded window overlooking the secluded garden. The weak, late-February sunlight settled into the far side of the neat, partly-shadowed lawn, unable to draw the moisture from it, sparkling off the dew. It had rained heavily during the night and throughout the preceding afternoon; the sun had looked as though it were still recovering from the soaking. He turned towards the portly bishop.

'I'm afraid that was not possible.' His voice was low, but the words filled the dark, wood-panelled study. 'We couldn't leave the church, Bishop, not after what had taken place. There was too much hysteria.'

Bishop Caines said nothing. He had assigned Monsignor Delgard to watch over the younger priest and his church, to control any situation that might arise over this girl and her apparitions; his role was to observe, influence and report. Peter Delgard was a priest not unused to incidents of the alleged paranormal or supernatural, his reputation for bringing sanity to insane situations renowned in ecclesiastical circles. He was a quiet, remote man, sometimes intimidating in his intensity; yet one knew instantly that he was a man of compassion, someone who shared the suffering of others as if the burden were his own. His authoritative quietness did little to reveal this side of his nature, but it was present in his aura as clearly as it must have been in Christ's. The bishop trusted Monsignor Delgard, respected his judgement, acknowledged his wisdom in matters that were often too bizarre for his own sensibilities to accept; and he was a little afraid of the tall priest.

Delgard was looking out of the window again. 'I thought, too, that Father Hagan needed some rest,' he said.

Bishop Caines studied the priest in the armchair. Yes, he could see that: Father Hagan looked as though the shock had been too much. His flesh was greyer than the last time; his eyes were dark, a look of desperation in them.

'Father, you look drained. Is it because of what happened yesterday?', he asked.

'I don't know, Bishop,' the priest answered, his voice almost a whisper. 'I haven't been sleeping too well over the past few weeks. Last night I hardly slept at all.'

'I'm not surprised. But there's no need for it to cause you such anxiety. Indeed, there may be much to celebrate.'

The bishop became aware of Delgard watching him. 'Don't you agree, Peter?'

A brooding silence, then, 'It's too soon to know.' The monsignor's stoop seemed more pronounced as he slowly strode from the window and sat in the study's other armchair. He regarded Bishop Caines with eyes that saw too much. 'What took place is quite inexplicable, beyond anything I've ever witnessed before. Five people were cured, Bishop, four of them no more than children. It's somewhat early to say how complete were their cures, but as from two hours ago, when I checked with each one, there had been no relapses.'

'Of course, we cannot accept these cures as miraculous until the medical authorities have made a thorough examination of those involved,' Bishop Caines said, and there was a carefully subdued eagerness in his tone.

'It will be a long time before the Church can even accept them as cures, let alone "miraculous",' Delgard replied. 'The procedure before such a proclamation is made is lengthy to say the least.'

'Quite so,' the bishop agreed. 'And properly so.' He found Delgard's stare disconcerting. 'I managed to reach the Cardinal Archbishop last night after you telephoned me. He has reiterated my own feelings that we must tread warily: he has no desire for the Roman Catholic Church in England to look foolish. He wants a full report before anything is announced to the media, and any statements must come directly from his offices.'

Hagan was shaking his head. 'I'm afraid it's beyond our control, Bishop. The reporter, Gerry Fenn, was there again yesterday. We haven't yet seen the early edition of the *Courier*, but you can be sure the event will receive full coverage.'

'He was there? Good Lord, the man's intuition must be incredible.'

'I think not,' Delgard put in. 'Apparently the rumour that Alice was to receive another "visitation" was spread around Banfield long before Sunday.'

'I forbade her mother to bring her,' Hagan said just as the door opened and Judith entered with a tray of drinks.

'I think that was unwise.' Bishop Caines nodded for his secretary to leave the tray on a small table at the side of the room. He waited for her to leave before he spoke again. 'Most unwise. You cannot forbid people to come to church, Father.'

'I thought it best that Alice stay away for a while.'

'Best for whom?'

'For Alice, of course.'

Delgard cleared his throat. 'I think Father Hagan was concerned over the traumatic effect the child's obsession was having on her.'

'Yes, that was one reason. The other is that I don't want St Joseph's turned into a fairground!' His voice had become strained, almost strident, and his two colleagues looked at him in surprise. Delgard appraised him with troubled eyes.

Bishop Caines rose with an audible sigh and went to the tray of drinks. He handed the brandy to the pale priest. 'It's a little early for this kind of beverage, I know, but it will do you good, Andrew.' He noticed the priest's hand was trembling as he took the drink and quickly looked across at Delgard. The monsignor's face was impassive, although he, too, was watching Father Hagan.

Bishop Caines turned back to the small side table. 'No sugar for you, Peter? No, I remember.' He gave the tea to Delgard, then placed his own and the brandy on the desk. 'Tell me more about this reporter,' he said as he took his seat once again. 'Just how much did he see?'

Hagan sipped his drink, hating the taste and the burning it caused to his throat. 'He saw everything. He was there from the beginning.'

'Well, no matter. The news would have soon got out. What we must consider now is how we should proceed. Where is the girl, this Alice Pagett?'

Delgard spoke. 'I thought it best that she and her mother should move into the convent in the village for a few days; there she cannot be bothered by the Press.'

'Her mother agreed?'

'She's a devout Catholic and willing to follow our guidance. Her husband, I'm afraid, is another matter. I doubt he'll let us keep Alice there for long.'

'He's not Catholic?'

Father Hagan managed to smile. 'Most definitely not. An atheist.'

'Hmm, that's a pity.'

Delgard wondered at the meaning behind the bishop's remark: was it a pity that the man did not believe in God, or that as a non-Catholic he could not be so easily manipulated by the Church? Delgard did not enjoy having such suspicions about Bishop Caines' motives, but he knew the man was ambitious. Even men of the cloth were not without that stain.

'I think perhaps I should see the child and her mother,' the bishop said, sipping his brandy thoughtfully. 'If Alice really has been blessed, there could be certain consequences to the Church in England.'

'An upsurge of religious fervour?' Delgard said bluntly.

'A return to the Faith for thousands,' replied the bishop.

Father Hagan looked quickly from one man to the other. 'You mean St Joseph's could become a shrine?'

'Surely you realized that?' said Bishop Caines. 'If this girl really did have a vision of the Blessed Virgin, then pilgrimages will be made from all over the world to worship at the place of the Visitation. It would be a most wonderful thing.'

'Yes, it would,' said Delgard. 'But as I said earlier, there is a long and extremely thorough process to be gone through before any such declaration can be made.'

'I'm well aware of that, Peter. The first thing I must do is bring forward the Conference of Bishops and place all the information we have before them. I shall ask for the Apostolic Delegate to be present so that the matter can be brought to the Pope's attention without delay and perhaps discussed at the next Synod in Rome.'

'With due respect, Bishop, I feel we may be moving too fast,' said Hagan, clenching his brandy glass tightly. 'We have no proof at all that Alice really saw Our Lady, or that the cures were miraculous.'

'That is what has to be ascertained,' the bishop quickly replied. 'Whether we like it or not, the news will spread rapidly. I dread to think of the sensation this man, Fenn, will make of it. Five cures, Andrew, *five*. Six counting Alice Pagett's own recovery. Do you not realize the excitement it will cause, not just among Catholics but in the hearts of all people who believe in the Divine Power? Whether or not St Joseph's is declared a holy shrine will be quite irrelevant; people will flock to the site in thousands out of sheer curiosity. That is why the Catholic Church must control the situation from the beginning.'

Father Hagan seemed to shrink into himself, but the bishop would not relent. 'There are many precedents,' he continued, 'the most famous being Lourdes. There was tremendous resistance by the Church authorities in accepting that Bernadette Soubirous had truly seen the Immaculate Conception, and it wasn't just the overwhelming evidence of miraculous cures and Bernadette's obvious integrity that influenced their final judgement: it was public opinion itself. The Church could not disregard the situation because the people – and they were not just local people – would not allow it. Do you realize how many thousands flock to the shrine to Our Lady in Aylesford each year? And there is no evidence at all that an apparition of the Virgin Mary appeared there. In fact, the Church authorities do not even suggest it. Yet pilgrims visit every year from all over the world. The same applies to the other shrine at Walsingham. If people want to believe, then no edict from the Church will persuade them otherwise.'

'Are you saying we should acknowledge Alice's story?' asked Hagan.

'Absolutely not. The whole matter will be carefully looked into before any official statement is made. What I am saying is that we must act swiftly to govern whatever else happens at St Joseph's. Don't you agree, Peter?' He glanced at the tall priest whose eyes were downcast.

He spoke slowly, his words measured. 'I agree that the situation will develop of its own accord. We have already had experience of that with the large crowd that gathered at the church yesterday. Even this morning, before the news has broken in the Press, and on a working day, there was a large gathering. In a way, it's a relief to be here away from them. Nevertheless, I feel we must not yet offer any encouragement.'

'No, no, of course not.'

'We must first interview each one of the persons apparently cured yesterday. Their individual doctors must also be approached for permission to examine their medical records. I think we will easily gain permission from the patients themselves, so the doctors in question should have no objection. I propose the immediate formation of a Medical Commission, one that is independent of the Catholic Church, which can investigate fully the medical histories of these six fortunate people – I include Alice, of course. With the enormous interest that will generate from yesterday's spectacular . . .' a wry smile '. . . I see no problem in that respect. Indeed, I imagine an inquiry would be instigated without our bidding.'

Bishop Caines nodded and avoided looking directly into the monsignor's penetrating eyes.

'Also,' Delgard went on, 'if we are to follow the example of Lourdes, I feel we must consider organizing our own Medical Bureau on the site of the shrine.'

Bishop Caines could no longer contain his eagerness. 'Yes, that would be sensible. So many alleged miracles have been dismissed in the past because of lack of scientific or medical data.'

'We must be fully aware, Bishop, that therein lies the danger to the Church itself. It could leave us open to ridicule if logical and sound reasons are found for what happened. At this very moment one of the Catholic Church's greatest mysteries may well be explained away by science, and the beliefs of millions will suffer because of it.'

'You mean the Shroud?'

'Yes, the Turin Shroud. Thermographic investigation, infra-red spectroscopy, radiography, electronic microscopy and chemical analysis – all these scientific means have been used to prove or disprove that the image on the length of linen discovered in 1356 is that of Christ. As yet, nothing conclusive has emerged from any of those tests. Needless to say, the Church is regarded with some suspicion for not allowing a further vital – according to the scientists – test. I refer to carbon dating.'

'But that would require destroying a fairly large section of cloth,' Bishop Caines protested. 'We could never allow that.'

'Methods of testing have been considerably improved since permission was last sought. No more than 25mg. of material would be needed. Yet still we say "no" and the public wonders just what it is that we're afraid of.'

'All the more reason we should not suppress our findings on this matter. I think we have nothing to fear, although I'm in full agreement about proceeding cautiously.'

'I . . . I think we're making a grave mistake.'

The two clerics turned towards Father Hagan. He was leaning forward in his seat, hands clasped tightly together.

Bishop Caines was alarmed at the distress on the priest's face. 'Why do you say that, Andrew? What is it that's troubling you?'

The priest rubbed a hand against his temple. 'It's just a feeling, Bishop. I don't know why, or what it is, but I feel things are not right. There's an atmosphere about the church . . .'

'Do you feel this . . . this atmosphere, Peter?' the bishop asked.

Delgard paused before answering. 'No, I'm afraid I don't. At least not the kind that Father Hagan is evidently referring to. Yesterday there was a tension in the air that was almost tangible, but it was caused by the congregation itself. I've experienced mass hysteria before, but cannot positively say it was the same. I'm sure scientists will theorize on mass hypnosis, collective hysteria, mass suggestion, and they may well prove to be correct. I know I fell to my knees to worship what was before me.'

'The child?'

'What she represented. Or appeared to represent.'

'Then you felt her holiness?'

'I can't be sure. A weakness seemed to overcome the whole crowd, not just Father Hagan and myself, but I just cannot remember my emotions. I can only remember the weakness, the incredibility of what had just taken place. Perhaps a psychologist could explain the phenomenon. Or a parapsychologist.'

'I meant the atmosphere at St Joseph's,' said Father Hagan quietly. 'It feels so cold.'

The bishop gave a little laugh. 'It is winter, you know. The church is bound to feel cold.'

'No, it's not just a physical coldness. And it isn't confined to just the church; it's in the grounds, in the presbytery.'

'You appeared to be under some strain the last time I saw you, Andrew,' Bishop Caines said not unkindly. 'It was one of the reasons I asked Monsignor Delgard to help you – that, and because of his experience in such extraordinary matters. Frankly, your health seems to have suffered considerably since last we met. Are you sure your general disposition does not account for these strange feelings you have?'

'I'm sure. I admit I haven't been in the best of health lately, but I think that, in itself, may be due to present circumstances.'

'I don't see how, unless it's the publicity that's upsetting you. If that is the case –'

'No!'

The bishop blinked in surprise.

'I'm sorry, Bishop,' the priest apologized. 'I didn't mean to raise my voice. Please forgive me. But there is something more, something happening that I don't understand.'

'We are all aware of that, Father,' said Bishop Caines, keeping the irritation from his voice.

'I don't just mean with Alice Pagett. There is something more . . .'

'Yes, yes, you have already said that. Can you explain exactly what you mean?'

The priest slumped back in his seat and closed his eyes. 'I wish I knew,' he said after a while.

'Then I think it best –' A gentle rapping on the door interrupted his words.

'Yes, Judith?' the bishop called out.

The secretary peered around the door. 'A call from London, Bishop. It's the *Daily Mail*, I'm afraid. They say they would like a statement from you on the incident at St Joseph's in Banfield yesterday.'

'Well, gentlemen,' the bishop said, 'it seems the story has broken nationally. Put the call through, my dear, then contact His Eminence for me when I've finished.'

He lifted the receiver and Delgard was not sure if his smile was one of resignation or anticipation. As the bishop began to speak, Delgard noticed that Father Hagan's hands were clenched around the arms of his chair. Clenched so tightly that the knuckles showed gleaming white through the pallid skin.

SIXTEEN

'I can't explain myself, I'm afraid, sir,' said Alice, 'because I'm not myself, you see.'

ALICE'S ADVENTURES IN WONDERLAND
Lewis Carroll

Tuesday, mid-morning

Southworth smiled as he poured himself a sherry. He filled the glass almost to the top. Normally a half-glass was adequate, a private mid-morning treat he occasionally allowed himself; but today there was something to celebrate.

An emergency meeting of the parish council had been called the previous evening because of the new 'Banfield Miracles', the astonishing cures that had taken place at St Joseph's on Sunday. And not just cures: many claimed they had seen Alice Pagett levitate. Southworth, who had also been there, wasn't certain of that aspect, for his view had been somewhat restricted by those in front of him, but he was ready to believe almost anything after the breath-taking cures. The child's levitation could have been imagined, such was the intense feeling running through the crowd, but there was no imagining the healing of the invalids. Even now, even though he was an eye-witness, it was difficult to accept.

Fortunately, there was no question of fraudulence. The five who had been cured had genuine illnesses, all confirmed by their own doctors, and further guaranteed by the medical records from the hospitals they had attended. Those illnesses and debilities had disappeared completely in all but two cases: the man whose cataracts had cleared still did not have perfect vision, although the morning report was that his sight was steadily improving; the crippled boy still had difficulty in walking unassisted, but this could hardly be otherwise with his wasted leg muscles – his condition was expected to improve as his legs grew stronger.

Southworth sipped the dry sherry and glanced over the newspapers spread before him on his desk. The story was now worldwide news. Banfield was literally crawling with media people. Press, television, magazines – all wanted the story. The village was bustling in a way it never had before, nor had ever expected to. It was alive! The residents were bewildered, but the world knew of their existence! And they, the villagers, were responding to the sudden attention. Not just responding, but thriving on it! Of course, there were those who found the publicity unwelcome, those who preferred their cosy, stagnating privacy, but they were in the minority. An indication of the high excitement generating through Banfield was conveyed at the council meeting on Monday evening. Never had he seen his fellow-members so active! And so willing to listen to plans of expansion.

There was no question but that St Joseph's would become a shrine after last night's news broadcast and this morning's headlines, even if the Catholic Church refused to proclaim it as such. The publicity alone would undoubtedly attract pilgrims, tourists and thrill-seekers to the area in their thousands (one councillor, the manager of one of Banfield's two national banks, was carried away with the whole idea enough to estimate the number in millions, a reckoning that drew guffaws from his fellow-members, although secretly not entirely rejected by them). Southworth ventured that the Church would be forced into making concessions and might even relish the situation. What more could any religion ask for than a present-day miracle to perpetuate the Faith? He knew the bishop of the diocese, Bishop Caines, personally, and would arrange for a meeting to discuss recent events. He would also broach the subject of how they could combine forces to meet the human deluge that must surely descend upon the area.

Southworth had spoken with the bishop that morning and had been surprised at the eminent cleric's general receptiveness to the council's proposition. Yes, he understood absolutely the need for agreement between the parish council and the Church in the coming months, and he would endeavour to cooperate fully with any plans put forward by them provided they did not entail cheap exploitation or pertain to any activities which would infringe on the dignity of the Catholic Church itself. Southworth was more than pleased with the statement, albeit somewhat pompous, and assured Bishop Caines that the council had no intention of commercializing what must be considered a most holy event. The bishop warned him without hesitation that it could not yet, and perhaps never would, be proclaimed a 'holy' event. Indeed, the whole matter would require lengthy examination to determine the validity of Alice Pagett's vision and the cures that had ensued within a religious context. His Eminence, the Cardinal Archbishop, had expressed deep concern and urged caution.

Bishop Caines went on to suggest that a meeting between members of the council, Monsignor Delgard, whom the bishop had appointed overseer at St Joseph's, and Father Hagan might prove fruitful at this early stage. They would report back to him and he in turn would report to the Conference of Bishops.

Southworth had thought that to be an excellent idea. In fact he would stage two meetings: one informal, between him and the two clergymen in which he could appraise their attitudes (and perhaps he would invite the reporter, Fenn, along too); another, larger meeting involving the rest of the council. In that way he could smooth the path first – certain colleagues on the council were a little too earnest with their ideas. Like Rodney Tucker, they were non-Catholics and inclined to forget the sensitivities of the religious. Most of the councillors were long-standing members of the community, their family histories, as did his, tracing back through the centuries to the beginnings of the village itself, somewhere in the fourteenth century. It had been known as *Banefeld* then, a community formed by those who had fled the horrors of the Black Death, which had become rife in the more densely populated towns. Those early settlers had thrived on the rich agricultural land of the area and had stayed, content to ignore the changing face of England, like so many other small communes. Nothing world-shattering had ever happened in Banfield; perhaps a few minor misdeeds through the centuries, but nothing of any great consequence. But now the village had the opportunity to rise from obscurity, a chance to save itself from the oblivion it was slowly and surely sinking into. And the council members knew it – even the old 'keep-the-world-away-from-our-door' diehards were aware. Those with family names entwined with Banfield's inglorious and uneventful past saw the chance, not just to revive the mouldering corpse, but to inject it with a life far more brilliant than it had ever experienced, and so to re-establish their own history.

And all were excited by the prosperity this dramatic and awesome incident could bring them.

Southworth smiled again. It was difficult not to.

Wednesday, early evening

She pulled the covers up to her neck and lay there staring at the ceiling, waiting for him to come out of the bathroom. That was one of Rodney's good points: he was clean. He always washed himself before and after. His *mind* wasn't as clean, but that didn't bother Paula too much; her own thoughts could be just as raunchy.

She rubbed her hands over her stomach, the feeling sensuous, almost as enjoyable as if it were another's fingers probing the flesh. Paula, still single, knew well the pleasures of her own body. She checked her nipples to see if they were erect, wanting to be at her most desirable for her employer, tweaking them both for full projection. The toilet flushed and she became a little impatient with Rodney's ritual. Keep cool, Paula, she told herself, tonight wasn't the night for upsetting him. Tonight was progress night. She'd given him enough to worry about over the past few weeks, now was the time for a little mercy, a little loving, a little giving on her part. It was a fine balance, keeping him anxious and keeping him interested.

He was in a buoyant mood, for his plans were going well. The village was stirring, at last awakening to the big world beyond its semi-rural confines. Things were moving and Tucker was moving with them.

Paula's fingers probed lower, sliding their way through tough dark hair like snakes through undergrowth, middle finger, the leader of the pack, finding the dip below. She opened herself, knowing Rodney liked to find her wet and waiting, and caught her breath at the stab of pleasure. There was something sordidly exciting about making love in a motel bedroom, the kind of self-abasement that went with self-abuse, and Paula was partial to both. She would have preferred a candlelight dinner for two, followed by a night of love in a plush hotel suite, energy and ideas sustained by an ice-bucket containing Dom Perignon (there were several things she could do with a linen towel packed with ice). But failing that, a gin and tonic and a motel fuck had some merit.

She heard Rodney splashing at the bathroom sink and worked a little more vigorously at herself, only too aware that her employer was not the most lingering of lovers. Too many times she had lost the climax race to him; nowadays she made sure she had a head start. She moaned a little and closed her eyes.

Tucker watched her from the open doorway, enjoying the view. He loved her to do it to herself, so long as she held back on the best bit for him. It saved him a lot of preliminary work.

Paula confused him, for her moods seemed to change from day to day. It was worrying, too: on her really bad days there was more than just a hint of hysteria in her actions. When she shouted at him she didn't seem to care who heard and twice she had suggested that it might be better in the long run if Marcia found out about their affair. She was fed up with being treated like a trollop.

But today and yesterday she had been all sweetness and light and genuinely pleased at his personal good fortune (or imminent good fortune). Maybe she had just caught the village's carnival atmosphere. Or maybe she wanted a part in his new schemes.

Tucker's freshly washed penis indicated its impatience by pressing uncomfortably against his underpants. Never one to keep a personal friend waiting, he made for the bed where Paula's movements were becoming a little too frantic. She opened her eyes and smiled lasciviously at him, her hand slowing to walking pace.

'Enjoying yourself?' he said, unbuttoning his shirt and placing it neatly over his trousers draped on the back of a nearby chair. The ginger hair on his floppy chest stuck through his string vest like stuffing from an old sofa.

'Just waiting for you, lover,' she replied and slowly drew back the covers for him. She allowed him a titillating glance at her naked body, then let them fall back over her. 'Take your vest off, lovey,' she said as he clambered in next to her. Paula didn't relish having the criss-cross pattern all over her breasts and stomach.

He squatted in the bed and struggled out of his vest, the released blubber swimming around the waistline of his underpants for a second before finding its level. My God, Paula thought, it was like being fucked by a whale.

Switching off the wall-light on his side of the bed, but leaving hers on, he wriggled down under the blankets. Without preamble a cold hand closed around her right breast like a metal claw in an amusement arcade's lucky dip.

'Wait, Rod,' she said pleadingly, 'there's no rush'. Paula squirmed against him to make sure he realized there was no rebuke or rejection in her words. 'Besides . . .' she giggled '. . . I've got a little treat for you.'

Tucker's ears pricked up and his penis took a new interest. Paula's 'little treats' were usually worth delaying the action for.

Her hand roamed around his chest, over his belly, then round to his fleshy back. Delicate fingers surfed through the tidal wave of fat to swoop down beneath the stretched elastic of his underpants and splay out over his buttocks. He nuzzled her neck in appreciation.

She murmured something and he said, 'What?'

'I said, did you see Southworth this morning?' Her teeth chewed his nipple.

He grunted and she took it as an affirmative.

Paula drew away when he said nothing more and looked into his face.

'Well?' she said.

'Well what?'

'What happened at the council meeting? What was decided?'

'Oh bloody hell, I don't want to talk about that now.' He yelped when she dug in her long fingernails.

'You know I'm interested in your affairs, Rodney.'

'You *are* my affair, precious.'

He yelped again.

'You know what I mean,' she scolded. 'You've got ideas, Rod. You could do things in this town.'

'That's true enough. Anyway, I think it's all set.' He turned onto his back, sex forgotten for the moment, ambitions elbowing the physical need aside.

'They've given the go-ahead for another shop?'

'No, no, they don't move that fast. But they're listening to Southworth now; he's shifting them off their backsides. And the way it's going, my lovely, it might mean more than just another shop. It might mean a bloody big supermarket, bigger than the one I've already got.' He chuckled and she joined in.

'So you'd probably need me to run this one on my own, then, so you could get on with organizing everything,' she said slyly.

'Uh. Well, yes . . . I suppose I would. It's early days though, pet. You know, anything might happen.' She couldn't see the frown on his face.

Too bloody right it could, Paula thought. Tourism was going to hit the town in a big way if this shrine business came off, and a lot of money was going to be made. She knew Tucker well enough to realize he would be at the front of the queue, arms spread wide to receive the benefit. And she intended to be there right alongside him, Marcia Tucker or no Marcia Tucker.

His frown was replaced by a smile as he went over the meeting with Southworth in his mind. The hotel owner wasn't one for over-exuberance, but even he couldn't contain his delight. New development plans would be pushed forward to the Horsham District Council over the next few months with an incautious speed that had never before been allowed. Expansion – rapid expansion – was a necessity. The village was already jammed solid with sightseers and even if another 'miracle' never occurred again, the legend was already born. The incredible amount of worldwide publicity had seen to that.

He chuckled again. It was only because the motel manager knew Tucker would not require the room all night that he had kept it free for him. The motel was packed, almost every room taken by media people, the rest by tourists, and he and Paula had to be out by ten so that a camera crew from Holland could move in.

'What are you laughing at?' Paula asked, giggling herself.

'Just the thought of glories to come, my darling. Banfield won't know what's hit it.'

She wasn't cold, but Paula shivered. It was almost as if something icy had touched her. She shrugged off the peculiar feeling.

'You won't be too busy for me, will you, Rod?' Her voice was wheedling again and her hand was tugging at his underpants.

'You, my love?' 'No way. I'll always have time for you.' He moaned as she yanked the pants down and lifted his fat bottom so that they would go all the way. Physical need was back on top again. 'Hey, what's my special treat?' he reminded her.

Paula sat up, her thrusting breasts bouncing together with the sudden movement. Tucker couldn't resist nipping at her well-rounded bottom as she turned from him and stretched down beside the bed. She gave a little screech and wriggled her rump; he kissed it better, wondering what she was reaching for.

She came up with a paper-wrapped bottle and he guessed its contents immediately. He couldn't stop grinning as Paula unwrapped the Freezomint. 'Have you been raiding the store again?' he asked without malice.

'I know you don't mind me helping myself to this, Rodney. Not when it's for your benefit.'

She unscrewed the top and took a deep swig of the *crème de menthe*, gargling it around her mouth and throat until they were coated with the green liquid. She swallowed, then drank again, her tongue burning as she wriggled it in the cold, stinging liquid. Her eyes were seductively half-closed when she placed the bottle on the bedside unit and Tucker's were wide open in anticipation.

His penis, short but stocky, was already tingling, but he knew it was nothing like the shocking tingling it would feel when her lips and tongue closed around it.

He was smiling again, as she lowered her head towards his body. All in all, it had been a good day.

Thursday, early morning

Alice stood in her nightdress staring out of the window. The sun hurt her eyes although there was little warmth from it. Behind her, the bedclothes on the nun's cot were rumpled as though her sleep had not been easy. As yet, there were no other sounds in the convent, for the sun had not long risen. Soon though, the nuns would be gathered for prayer in the room used as a chapel, and Alice's mother would be among them, thanking God for the honour He had bestowed upon her and her daughter.

There was no expression on Alice's face.

Only twelve nuns lived in the convent, for it was merely a large house, acquired ten years before from a retired theatre actor who had moved abroad to sunnier climes. Its walls were painted cream, doors and window frames white. A high brick wall kept the nuns their privacy and beyond the heavy black gates, which were as high as the wall itself, was a spacious yard where they parked their Morris 1100 and minibus. The minibus was used during the week to collect the village children who attended the Catholic school four miles away and in which the nuns taught.

The high gates, solidly forbidding, and the surrounding wall had been a formidable defence against the hordes of reporters that had descended upon Banfield during the past week, for it had soon become known that little Alice Pagett was being kept at the convent for her own privacy and protection.

The convent was situated at the southern end of the town, close to a sharp bend where the main road turned left for Brighton and another, minor road continued straight on into the Downs. A garage was on the bend itself and the nuns knew the proprietor was hiring out the offices above to camera crews and photographers so they could film over the convent wall. There was little the nuns could do about the situation but pray that Alice's mind would not be too disturbed by the frantic attention.

Alice's spartan room overlooked the courtyard at the front of the convent. Apart from the small bed, it contained only a chair, a straw rug, and a small sink in the corner. A plain wooden crucifix hung on the wall. Two of Alice's favourite dolls shared her bed at night, but each morning her mother found them thrown into the far corner of the room.

Molly Pagett slept next door, close to her daughter, and had spent most nights since moving in with the Sisters lying awake mumbling prayers and listening for any disturbance in Alice's room. Her eyes were red-rimmed through lack of sleep and her face and stance seemed to have aged ten years since the miracles had began. A woman always devoted to the Church, it had now become her obsession.

Alice did not appear to feel the chill as she stood at the window, nor did the birds that swooped into the courtyard interest her.

She hated the convent, hated its sparseness, its lack of comfort. And she disliked the dull greyness of the nuns' habits. She was frightened of the doctors who tested and probed her, who examined her body and asked her questions, questions, questions. And she was tired of the questions from the priests, from the nuns, from . . . from . . . just about everybody who spoke to her.

She wanted to leave this place.

She wanted to go back to the church.

She wanted to see the tree.

A movement below caught her attention. The cat had leapt from the high wall into an empty flower bed at the courtyard's side. It stalked lazily across the damp cobbles, the birds having already flown. It stopped. Looked up. Saw the small figure in white watching it.

It sat and gazed upwards.

For the first time in days Alice smiled. Her hand unconsciously touched her side and rubbed at the small lump six inches below her heart. The doctors had shown great interest in the strange protruberance at first and her mother had explained it had always been there, although very tiny, and nothing to worry about so her local doctor had said. They had agreed it was nothing to worry about and did not mention nor probe it again.

But it itched now and was bigger, though not much, than before. Alice rubbed at it as she watched the cat and her smile did not seem that of an eleven-year-old.

SEVENTEEN

A slumber did my spirit seal;
I had no human fears:
She seemed a thing that could not feel
The touch of earthly years.

William Wordsworth

'Hey, come on, Sue, open up!'

Fenn put his head against the door and listened. He knew she had to be in there because he had run from the call box on the corner just a few minutes earlier and put down the phone as she'd answered. Twice that week Sue had hung up on him and twice she had been out when he'd gone to her flat. It had given him no satisfaction to hang up on her in return, but he wanted to see her. It was time to stop frigging around. If she really wanted to end it, fine – but she would have to tell him to his face.

It had been a heavy, glorious week. The *Courier* had syndicated his personal story of the 'Banfield Miracles' to most of the Nationals both in Britain and abroad, while magazines, periodicals and television companies were offering substantial amounts for follow-up stories and interviews. In just four days he had become what could only be termed as a 'media figure', the Alice Pagett phenomena inextricably linked with his own name, for it had been his first-hand coverage of both extraordinary events – the first vision and miracle experienced by Alice herself, and the subsequent five miracles on the second Sunday – that had caught the attention of millions around the world. He was riding high and enjoying the journey.

There was movement inside.

'It's me, Sue.'

Only silence.

'Come on, Sue, I only want to talk.'

The door-chain being slid back, the latch being turned. Sue peering through a six-inch gap.

'There's nothing much to say, Gerry.'

'Oh yeah? That's your considered opinion?'

'Have you been drinking?'

'Sure.'

It looked as if she was going to close the door again, so he put his hand against it.

'Sue, let's just talk a little. I promise to leave within ten minutes if you want me to.'

For a moment she was undecided and he lifted his eyebrows in a silent 'please?' Sue disappeared from view and with relief he pushed open the door. He followed her down the short hallway into the lounge. As always the room was comfortably neat, lit by a small lamp which cast intimate shadows. He saw she was in her dressing gown.

'Bed so early?' he asked. 'It's only just gone ten.'

'It's late to call on someone,' she replied, sitting in an armchair. He realized she had carefully avoided the sofa. He was about to sit on the arm of her chair when she shook her head and pointed at the sofa opposite. With a sigh, he obeyed.

Neither one spoke for several moments, then Sue said, 'You're making quite a name for yourself.'

He cleared his throat, hating the awkwardness. 'I was lucky enough to be on the spot. It's a reporter's dream.'

'I'm glad you're reaping the benefit.'

'We went through this before, Sue. It's my job.'

'I'm not being sarcastic, Gerry. I really am pleased for you. And I like the way you've written your features; they've been factual, no gloss, no exaggeration. Not like your first story.'

'There was no need for exaggeration. The truth was spectacular enough.' He leaned forward, resisting the urge to kneel at her feet. 'So what is it, Sue? Why haven't you wanted to see me, to speak to me? What the hell have I done?'

She looked into her hands. 'I'm not sure if it's you or just me. I've found my faith again, Gerry, and I don't have time for anything else.'

'You mean being a Catholic excludes being in love with someone.'

'Of course not. I just think you're probably not the right one.'

'Oh terrific. Excuse my wicked ways, but we seemed to get along pretty fine until you started with this church business.'

'That's just the point! I've changed. But you haven't.'

'Why the hell should I? I'm not a bloody Catholic!'

'You were witness to one of the most shattering and marvellous things that could happen on this earth. Why hasn't it meant anything to you?'

'How d'you know it hasn't. You haven't seen me all week. Today's Thursday; I could have sent in my convert's application forms since Sunday!'

'Stop joking, Gerry. I read your articles, I know nothing's changed.'

'You said you liked them.'

'Yes, and I said they were factual. *Cold* and factual, an impartial observer's account.'

'What did you expect?'

'I expected you to be moved by what you saw! I expected you to be spiritually moved!'

Fenn's eyes widened in surprise. He shook his head. 'I don't get it.'

Her voice softened. 'That's just it. You really don't understand, do you?'

He remained silent.

'Everyone else present that day underwent some deep, emotional experience; I know, I've spoken with many of them since. They believe they witnessed a divine act of God, healing miracles that proved His existence beyond any doubt, and their lives have taken on a new order because of it. Yet you feel nothing. You can't deny what took place, but it has no effect on you. What's wrong with you, Gerry? What makes you so . . . so unreachable?'

'I'm not so sure it's just me. I haven't had a chance to get near Father Hagan during the last few days – he's avoided all contact with the Press – but he doesn't look too happy.'

'Couldn't you see the poor man was overwhelmed by it all? Six wonderful miracles. The levitation of a young child who saw the Blessed Virgin. In his parish! Have you any idea at all of the magnitude of what's happened? Father

Hagan is still in a state of shock and his own humility will see he stays that way for some time to come. So don't compare his reaction to yours – because with you there's been no reaction at all except to seize the opportunity to make a name for yourself.'

'That's unfair.'

'I know it's unfair and I'm not blaming you for that. I just wish there was something more, some indication that your cynicism had been, if not broken, then at least pierced.' She was weeping freely and he felt a flush of irrational guilt.

He went to her, kneeling on the floor, gently taking her wrists and pulling her hands away from her face. She looked at him and there was sheer misery behind the tears.

'Oh, Gerry . . .' she said, and then was in his arms, head buried against his shoulders, her body shaking.

His throat felt sticky and there was a heaviness dragging at his chest. Sometimes a woman's crying could make him cold, could numb his emotions so that he was accused of having no feelings, an accusation that was often true but only in relation to that particular woman or situation. Fenn had learned to guard himself, to protect his own sensitivities against the demands of others, past hurts, rejections, perhaps forgotten but their marks indelibly made. With Sue there was no such protection. He hugged her tight, close to tears himself.

'I'm sorry,' was all he could think of to say.

'It's not your fault, Gerry,' she said softly. 'You can't help the way you are. Maybe I'm wrong in wanting you to be different.'

'I love you, Sue.'

'I know you do, and I wish you didn't.'

'It's impossible not to.'

'Have you tried?'

'All the time. It's no good, though, I'm hooked.'

She pulled away slightly. 'Gerry, I'm not sure any more how I feel about you.'

That hurt. God, it hurt. He hugged her back to him. 'It's because of everything that's happening, Sue. Things're moving too fast, it's confusing. Just don't make me into the anti-Christ, eh?'

'It's just that I'm seeing you differently. Oh, I've known your failings –'

'Failings? Me?'

'I've known them and chosen to ignore them. Now, though, we seem to be in conflict with each other . . .'

'Not me with you, babe.'

'Then why can't you feel the same way? Why is it just a launching pad for your own career, a way to make money?'

This time it was Fenn who pulled away. 'Let me tell you something,' he said. 'I'll agree I'm taking full advantage of a fantastic story that just happened to fall smack into my lap. Any reporter worth his salt would do the same. But there are others using the Banfield Miracles for their own purposes too. You know, after Alice saw her first vision and I wrote the feature, a guy called Southworth contacted me. He's the owner of the Crown Hotel in Banfield, a councillor and, from what I can gather, owns quite a lot of property in the area. He and someone called Tucker – another of Banfield's fat cats – wanted to hire me to exploit the situation with follow-up articles, keeping the place in the public eye, drumming up more interest than was warranted at that time. Oh, they were a little more subtle with their proposition than that, but that was the strength of it! They wanted to start the carnival there and then.'

He rested back on his heels. 'You might be pleased to know I turned them down.'

'It doesn't mean anything. Two men out of a –'

'Have you been into the village lately?'

'Of course. I've been to St Joseph's –'

'No, not the church. The village itself. All the merchants can talk about is the money that's going to come pouring in. A lot of the property-owners are applying for planning permission to turn their premises into souvenir shops, tea-shops, restaurants, bed-and-breakfast – anything that will bring in money from the tourists that are already flocking in.'

'Now you are exaggerating.'

'Am I? You should take a close look. A kind of insanity has hit Banfield and it's easy to see why. For the first time in its history, the village is the focus of world attention. Maybe it's because we're all sick of hearing nothing but violence, wars and depravity, maybe it's because when something good happens, something that restores our faith in goodness itself, we go overboard. Everybody loves a miracle because it transcends this rotten stinking world we live in. Don't forget this is the age of science, where everything is becoming explainable. Religion is nothing but wish-fulfilling stories for the masses, love is only body chemistry, art is a surge of conditioned reflexes. And now we've got something that really is inexplicable. Something today, in this time!'

'But you're saying the village only wants to make money from it.'

'Sure it does. It doesn't mean they don't believe in the miracles.'

'But they can't all be thinking that way.'

'In cash terms? No, of course not. There are plenty who love what's happening for its own sake, who feel proud their Banfield's been chosen to play host to the Madonna.'

She listened closely for a hint of sarcasm, but found none.

'Yeah, they're happy and more than over-awed. Stunned – and grateful. There'll be the few who'll want nothing to do with it, maybe some who'll move away, but they'll be in the minority. The rest, I figure, will wallow in the glory.'

'There's nothing wrong in that.'

He shook his head. 'No. But wait and see the competition to tell the media their own personal stories. How they've known Alice Pagett since she was a baby, how she came to their shop once a week for sweets, how they're distant cousins twice-removed, how their piles miraculously cleared up one day when they passed St Joseph's, how their migraine disappeared when Alice smiled at them. You may think cheque-book journalism is an overworked phrase, but wait and see just how many personal accounts of the Banfield Miracles are sold to the newspapers. And wait and see how many "close" friends the Pagett family are going to have, all with intimate details of their private lives. The whole personality of the village is going to change, Sue, as well as its appearance.'

She was staring at him, for the first time realizing the commercial aspect of the mystical experience. For someone whose profession was journalism, she had been remarkably naïve; or perhaps too spiritually involved.

Fenn hated to disillusion her further, but went on, anxious to vindicate his own motives. 'Pretty soon, you won't be able to get near the church without being bombarded with religious junk. Madonnas in snow storms, Madonnas that light up, Cindy Doll Madonnas, rosaries by the thousands,s postcards, crucifixes, medallions . . . you name it, it'll be on sale.'

'The Church wouldn't allow it –'

'Huh! The Church will be part of it.'

'That's not true.'

'Do you really think the Catholic Church, with its steady loss of followers and general disenchantment among its worshippers, can afford not to take advantage of something like this? Young priests are leaving, some to get married, women are demanding to be allowed into the priesthood, the Vatican itself is criticized for hoarding its vast wealth and not using it to feed the starving, to help the underprivileged, criticized for not condemning the violence in Northern Ireland more strongly, openly mocked for its out-dated views on birth control, divorce, and plenty of other topics which seem to have no relevance to today's society. The Church needs its miracles to bloody survive!'

Sue flinched and he checked his growing anger. 'Look, when Pope John Paul was shot in '81 – shot six times, mind, an old man pumped with bullets – Catholics by the millions turned back to their faith. Even non-believers felt grief. When he lived, when he *miraculously* recovered, everyone – everyone who was not insane or just plain evil – had a new respect for the Papacy. The world was reminded of the ultimate triumph of good. Well now the Church has got something even more grand: six cures, all witnessed, a possible levitation, and a Visitation. There's no way they won't take advantage of it.'

'Father Hagan won't allow it to be exploited.'

'Father Hagan will be over-ruled. I don't know too much about Bishop Caines, who's the governor of the diocese, but from what information I've managed to gather this week he appears to be an ambitious man. Oh yeah, they have that kind in the Church hierarchy, you know. Apparently he's already sought authorization to buy the field next to the church and the farmer who owns it is willing to sell. Seems he's been down on his luck lately.'

'It makes sense to make the field where Alice had the vision part of St Joseph's.'

'Yeah, makes perfect sense. Church ownership of the field will be necessary to accommodate all the visitors who're going to flood the place. I'll bet you the bishop will be accommodating in other ways, too, as this thing snowballs. He's already arranged a Press conference for tomorrow.'

'That's hardly surprising with all the public interest.'

'Well, we'll wait and see how he handles it. How much he refutes, how much he evades and how much he encourages. It should be pretty telling.'

'You'll be there?'

'Would I miss it?'

She sighed and lay back in the chair, wiping at her damp face with the back of her hand. He straightened his legs and leaned over her, conscious of her knees against his groin. 'Sorry for the diatribe, babe, but I wanted you to understand that I'm not the sole passenger on this particular bandwagon.'

Her hand cupped his cheek. 'I still don't trust you, Gerry.'

He groaned aloud.

'Perhaps the miracles have changed us,' she said. 'Brought out the worst in some, the best in others.'

'Maybe some are more gullible than others.'

Her hand froze on his face. 'Meaning?'

He shrugged. 'Maybe some have been taken in by a phenomenon that has no mystical basis whatsoever.'

'"The Power of the Human Mind" theory again?'

'Could be. Who's to say otherwise?'

'Your ten minutes are up.'

'There you go again, not prepared to listen to any other argument. Does all that's happened suddenly make me an enemy, Sue, a child of Satan you have to close your ears to? We used to have long, rational debates at one time, for Christ's sake. With all this deep, religious feeling you're going through, shouldn't you love me even more?'

She didn't answer.

'Okay, let's forget the other alternative for now and accept that the so-called "miracles" have a religious context. Seems to me that Jesus Christ hired twelve pretty good PR guys to spread the Word, four of whom wrote a worldwide best seller. His life story. I guess you couldn't call me a twentieth-century disciple, but isn't there some kind of saying in the Good Book about using the best tools available? Could be I'm one of the tools.' He raised his eyebrows.

Sue was frowning, but Fenn knew he'd scored a point. After a while she pulled his head down towards her and he was grinning against her chest.

'I'm confused, Gerry, still confused. But maybe I've had my head in the sand. It could be that our beliefs are not allowed to be insulated or introspective any more.' She kissed his hair. 'Your cynicism might even be a healthy thing, who knows? It's so easy to get carried away with it all.'

He held his tongue, not wanting to spoil the mood. Raising his head to look into her eyes, he said, 'All I ask is that you don't lock me out. You might not approve of my approach to the subject, or my appraisal of it, but you can be sure it's honest. And I think that's something you can at least respect.' He kissed her chin. 'Right?'

She nodded, then kissed his lips and he was acutely aware that her abstinence had made her very, very hungry.

It was dark, the curtains drawn.

Fenn lay there, puzzled for a few seconds. Where the hell was he? Then he remembered and relaxed. He smiled in the darkness, remembering their love-making. Christ, Sue had been almost frightening in her intensity. Her physical need for him had seemed to surprise even herself. He wasn't complaining, though; exhausted, but not complaining. He felt her moving in the bed.

Had she disturbed him with her restlessness? He moved towards her, touched her back, and was alarmed at how hot she felt. He pushed close, his arm going around her and becoming damp with her stickiness. Her body jerked and her head twisted into the pillow.

'Sue?' he whispered.

She murmured something, but did not waken. Her limbs were trembling.

Fenn gently shook her shoulder, wanting to wake her from the nightmare, but not wanting to frighten her.

She twisted towards him, still asleep, her breathing rapid, shallow. 'It isn't . . .' she murmured.

'Sue, wake up.' He felt her face, her neck and her breast. She was soaking.

He quickly reached over and switched on the bedside lamp. She pulled her head away from the light, still murmuring. He could hardly hear the words, but it sounded like, 'it isn't . . . her . . . isn't . . . isn't . . .'

'Sue, wake up!' He shook her more fiercely and suddenly her eyes were wide open. Staring.

The fear in them was alarming.

Abruptly, they seemed to cloud over and she blinked several times. She recognized him. 'Gerry, what's wrong?'

He breathed a sigh of relief. 'Nothing, babe,' he said. 'You just had a bad dream.'

He switched off the light and settled down again, holding her in his arms. She was asleep almost instantly.

But he stayed awake for quite some time.

EIGHTEEN

'The devil told you that! The devil told you that,' shrieked the little man, and in his fury he stamped his right foot into the ground, right up to his waist, then, foaming at the mouth, he grabbed his left foot in both hands and tore himself apart right down the middle.

RUMPELSTILTSKIN
The Brothers Grimm

DAILY MAIL:	Has the Vatican an 'official' statement concerning the Banfield Miracles?
BISHOP CAINES:	The only 'official' statement we can issue at this very early stage is that the Holy Roman Catholic Church acknowledges that a series of what can best be described as, extraordinary cures, have taken place in the grounds of St Joseph's –
DAILY MAIL:	Forgive me for interrupting, Bishop, but you just said in the grounds of St Joseph's. Surely it was in the field next to the church?
BISHOP CAINES:	That's quite correct, but in such close proximity that it could be considered within the church property. I should perhaps inform you that agreement for the purchase of the land by the Church has already been reached and that the necessary documents will be signed within the next day or two. However, to return to your original question: The six extraordinary cures – alleged cures, I should say – which have occurred at St Joseph's will be scrupulously examined by a specially-formed Medical Bureau and their findings passed on to the International Medical Committee. No announcement, proclamation, and no assertions will be forthcoming until the International Committee is satisfied that every aspect of the six individual cases has been fully investigated.
REUTERS:	Will the International Committee you refer to be the same committee that examines the cures at Lourdes?
BISHOP CAINES:	Yes.
CATHOLIC HERALD:	But the Committee can only recommend that the cures be declared miraculous.
BISHOP CAINES:	That's correct. As bishop of the diocese in which the

                                cures took place, the final decision as to whether or not
                                the cures are declared miraculous is mine alone.

THE TIMES: Have you a view right now?

BISHOP CAINES: I have not.

THE TIMES: None at all? Even after having talked with Alice Pagett
                                and the others most closely concerned – your own parish
                                priest, for instance?

BISHOP CAINES: I find the whole matter intriguing, to say the least, but I
                                cannot possibly make any judgement at this stage.

WASHINGTON POST: What would, then, Bishop Caines, constitute a miracle
                                in the eyes of the Church?

BISHOP CAINES: A cure that is medically inexplicable in the present state
                                of science.

DAILY EXPRESS: When will the Medical Bureau be organized?

BISHOP CAINES: It's being organized right now.

DAILY EXPRESS: And how will it operate?

BISHOP CAINES: Well, it will consist of at least twelve medical men –

JOURNAL DE GENEVA: All Roman Catholics?

BISHOP CAINES: No, most certainly not.

DAILY EXPRESS: But will it be an independent body?

BISHOP CAINES: Absolutely, although the director of the Bureau and
                                several members will be employed by the Church.
                                Others will be gathered from interested medical and
                                scientific research units. Medical records of each cured
                                person will be examined and the individual's own GP
                                and the hospital under which they are receiving treat-
                                ment will be consulted. They will, naturally, undertake
                                their own thorough medical examination of each cured
                                person and a dossier will be kept. Their findings will
                                eventually be passed on to the International Commit-
                                tee, who will make the final recommendation.

ASSOCIATED PRESS: What will be the criteria? For a miracle, I mean.

BISHOP CAINES: Perhaps Monsignor Delgard would like to answer that?

MONSIGNOR DELGARD: I think it should be clearly stated: the Medical Bureau
                                and the International Committee will only be con-
                                cerned with whether or not the cure is inexplicable, not
                                if it's a miracle.

ASSOCIATED PRESS: Is there a difference?

MONSIGNOR DELGARD: Bishop Caines said earlier that the cure must be
                                medically inexplicable in the present state of science.
                                The Committee will decide upon that aspect, not
                                whether the cures had a religious or mystical connota-
                                tion. What is considered medically inexplicable today
                                might be perfectly logical a few years hence. It is the
                                bishop and his advisors who must examine the spiritual
                                aspects of the cures and decide if divine intervention is
                                the cause of the recoveries.

                                The Bureau and the International Committee have
                                to satisfy themselves on the following points:

                                Was the cure sudden, unexpected and without
                                convalescence?

                                Is it complete?

Is it lasting? That, ladies and gentlemen, means a certain amount of time – say three or four years – must elapse before the cure can be confirmed.

How serious was the illness?

Was it due to a specific disease? Infirmity due to a mental disorder, for instance, would rule out any acceptance of a miracle cure.

Had the illness been objectively proved by tests, X-rays, or biopsies?

And was the medical treatment previously given responsible in any way, even if in part only, for the cure?

These are the criteria on which the Bureau and the International Committee must be satisfied. There are others, more technical, but I think those I've listed will give you the general idea.

PSYCHIC NEWS: Can you tell us, Monsignor Delgard, just what is your involvement in this matter?

BISHOP CAINES: Perhaps I should answer that. At the time of the first cure – when, in fact, Alice Pagett was able to hear and talk again after seven years of being unable to do so – an enormous amount of public interest was created. I felt then that Father Hagan would need some support and guidance in dealing with the crowds who would inevitably descend upon St Joseph's.

PSYCHIC NEWS: But you've been involved in certain cases of unusual phenomena in the past, Monsignor Delgard?

MONSIGNOR DELGARD: Yes, that's correct.

PSYCHIC NEWS: Would you describe them as paranormal.

MONSIGNOR DELGARD: (*Pause.*) They could be termed as such, I suppose.

PSYCHIC NEWS: In fact, haven't you performed several exorcisms?

MONSIGNOR DELGARD: Yes.

PSYCHIC NEWS: Did you and do you now suspect that Alice Pagett might be possessed?

(*Laughter.*)

MONSIGNOR DELGARD: By the Devil?

(*Laughter.*)

PSYCHIC NEWS: Or evil spirits.

MONSIGNOR DELGARD: I would think that's most unlikely. The child seems well-balanced enough to me.

PSYCHIC NEWS: Then why –

BISHOP CAINES: I've already explained why Monsignor Delgard was temporarily appointed to St Joseph's. While it's true to say he has investigated many strange incidents over the years for the Church and has made a study of psychic phenomena, Monsignor Delgard's role usually has been – if I might use the term – devil's advocate rather than devil seeker.

(*Laughter.*)

You see, the Catholic Church often has to undertake the examination of unusual incidents on behalf of concerned parishioners and clergy. We live in a peculiar world, you know, where human logic is not always

applicable to certain events. Monsignor Delgard looks
at both aspects of such happenings – natural and
unnatural – and usually manages to provide the correct
balance. At St Joseph's we have circumstances that are,
without doubt, unnatural, so it's perfectly sensible to ask
for the assistance and advice of someone who has had
experience in such matters, and who can also provide a
more material assistance in dealing with the public
interest. The fact that Monsignor Delgard has performed exorcisms is quite irrelevant in this case.

May we have another question?

DAILY TELEGRAPH: It's rumoured that Alice Pagett's illness could have been
psychosomatic. Is it true?

BISHOP CAINES: That's for the medical authorities and the Bureau to
decide. But, of course, it's doubtful that all five of the
other illnesses were due to psychosomatic causes.

LE MONDE: What is the Catholic Church's opinion on faith healing?

BISHOP CAINES: Jesus Christ was the greatest faith healer of all time.
(*Laughter.*)

GAZETTE (Kent): I have a question for Father Hagan. Some years ago you
were assistant priest near Maidstone.

FATHER HAGAN: (*Pause.*) Yes, in a place called Hollingbourne.

GAZETTE (Kent): You weren't there for very long, were you, Father?

FATHER HAGAN: About six months, I think.

GAZETTE (Kent): You left rather suddenly. Could I ask the reason why?

FATHER HAGAN: (*Pause.*) As assistant priest I went where I was needed
most. Often the need was urgent and my departure from
one parish to another could be abrupt.

GAZETTE (Kent): There was no other reason, then, for you to leave
Hollingbourne, apart from being required elsewhere?

FATHER HAGAN: As far as I can remember the parish priest of St Mark's in
Lewes had fallen ill and assistance was badly needed.

GAZETTE (Kent): No other reason?

BISHOP CAINES Father Hagan has answered your question. May we
move on to the next?

DAILY TELEGRAPH: Could this whole business of the miracle cures be a hoax?

BISHOP CAINES: A rather elaborate one, don't you think? And for what
purpose?

DAILY TELEGRAPHY: Isn't Banfield liable to make a considerable amount of
money from tourism?

BISHOP CAINES: Yes, I suppose it's conceivable. The village is already the
focus of world attention and I suppose sightseers will
flock to St Joseph's even before the results of our
investigations are made known. But unless you believe
that all the children and the one adult involved in these
cures are swindlers and liars – not to mention marvellous
actors –
(*Laughter.*)
– then I hardly think your suggestion has any merit.
And, of course, the children's parents and their general
practitioners would also have to be involved in the
fraud.

L'ADIGE:	Alice Pagett claims to have seen a vision of the Madonna. Can you comment on this, please?
BISHOP CAINES:	Not at this time.
NEW YORK TIMES:	Did anyone else see anything? Father Hagan, you were present on two occasions when the child claimed she saw the Virgin Mary – did you see nothing at all?
FATHER HAGAN:	I . . . no, no, I can't say that I did.
NEW YORK TIMES:	But did you sense anything strange going on?
FATHER HAGAN:	There was certainly atmosphere, yes, a highly-charged atmosphere, but I can't account for it.
OBSERVER:	Surely it would have had something to do with the mood of the crowd, wouldn't it?
FATHER HAGAN:	Yes, I suppose so.
OBSERVER:	Sorry, Father, I didn't catch that.
FATHER HAGAN:	I said I suppose so. Certainly on the last occasion. Several of the other children present seemed entranced in the same way that Alice was, but they could remember nothing when questioned later.
DAILY MIRROR:	What steps are the Church taking to ensure the situation isn't exploited?
BISHOP CAINES:	Exploited?
DAILY MIRROR:	Commercially exploited.
BISHOP CAINES:	I believe we dealt with that in a previous question. There is very little the Church can do to prevent local traders and businessmen from, shall we say, taking full advantage of the situation. But that is hardly our province and we can only hope that proper restraint and discretion is used.
MORNING STAR:	But won't the Catholic Church itself exploit the situation?
BISHOP CAINES:	Why should we do that?
MORNING STAR:	For publicity.
BISHOP CAINES:	I hardly think God needs publicity. (*Laughter.*)
STANDARD:	But it wouldn't harm the Church.
BISHOP CAINES:	On the contrary, such publicity could be most damaging. Many churchgoers might have their illusions shattered if what they believe to be genuine miracles performed at St Joseph's are later proved by the medical authorities to be nothing of the sort. That is one of the reasons the Catholic Church is extremely cautious in such matters.
ASSOCIATED PRESS:	Almost to the extent that miracles are harder to prove to the Church than to the layman?
BISHOP CAINES:	Yes, in most cases that's true. In fact, the Medical Bureau at Lourdes dismisses nearly all Lourdes cures as non-miraculous. I believe there have been only sixty or so miraculous cures officially recognized at Lourdes since 1858.
OBSERVER:	Many people claim they saw Alice levitate last Sunday. Could I ask Father Hagan and Monsignor Delgard if it really did happen?

MONSIGNOR DELGARD:	I can't be sure. I wasn't as close to Alice as some of the others. To be perfectly honest, I have no clear recollection.
OBSERVER:	Father Hagan?
	(*Silence.*)
MONSIGNOR DELGARD:	Father Hagan and I were standing together, so we both had the same view. I don't . . .
FATHER HAGAN:	I think Alice did levitate.
	(*Disordered questioning.*)
ECHO DE LA BOURSE:	You actually witnessed this?
FATHER HAGAN:	I can only say I think that's what happened. The grass in the field is long – perhaps she was merely standing on tiptoe. I just can't be sure.
OBSERVER:	But other witnesses say her feet actually left the ground.
FATHER HAGAN:	It's possible. I can't be sure, though.
	(*General conversation.*)
STANDARD:	If it is proved that the cures were miraculous and that Alice Pagett really saw the, er, Virgin Mary, will the girl be proclaimed a saint?
BISHOP CAINES:	How do you prove such a thing? And before someone can be considered for canonization they have to be dead for some time.
	(*Laughter.*)
BRIGHTON EVENING COURIER:	Why is Alice Pagett being kept hidden away?
BISHOP CAINES:	Ah, it's Mr Fenn, isn't it? Well, Alice isn't being kept 'hidden away' as you put it. Judging by the amount of media people surrounding the Our Lady of Sion convent in Banfield I certainly wouldn't have said her whereabouts are secret.
	Alice is resting. She has been through an extraordinary experience and, as you can imagine, is quite exhausted both physically and emotionally. She needs peace and quiet – her own doctor is adamant that she receives just that. And, of course, she's there with the full agreement of her parents. Alice is a delicate child, and until recently, classed as an invalid. She has to be treated with great care.
BRIGHTON EVENING COURIER:	Is she undergoing medical tests?
BISHOP CAINES:	Yes, very stringent tests.
BRIGHTON EVENING COURIER:	And interrogation by the Church authorities?
BISHOP CAINES:	Interrogation is far too strong a word. Obviously she is being questioned, but I promise you she is under no pressure. I think her only danger at the moment is that she might be smothered by kindness.
	(*Laughter.*)
BRIGHTON EVENING COURIER:	How long will Alice be kept at the convent?
BISHOP CAINES:	She is under no detention order, Mr Fenn. She is at perfect liberty to leave when her parents want her to and

	when her doctor thinks it will be in her own interest.
CATHOLIC HERALD:	Has Alice had any more visions since last Sunday?
BISHOP CAINES	She hasn't spoken of any.
DAILY MAIL:	Will she attend Mass this Sunday? At St Joseph's, I mean.
MONSIGNOR DELGARD:	(*Pause.*) Alice has expressed a desire to. We must consider the consequence to herself, however. We're rather worried that with all the publicity these, er, incidents have been given, St Joseph's will be swamped with sightseers – and obviously the media itself. As Bishop Caines has just said, Alice is a fragile child and the continued excitement might be too much for her. She has to be protected.
INTERNATIONAL HERALD TRIBUNE:	But she'll have to face the public sooner or later.
BISHOP CAINES:	That's true, but I suppose that at this stage the medical team studying her case, her own doctor and the Church, would rather it were later. However, nothing yet has been decided regarding this coming Sunday.
BRIGHTON EVENING COURIER:	But Alice does want to go to Mass this Sunday?
BISHOP CAINES:	Alice is somewhat confused at the moment. I think that's quite understandable.
BRIGHTON EVENING COURIER:	But she does want to.
BISHOP CAINES	As the monsignor said, she has expressed a desire to.
BRIGHTON EVENING COURIER:	So it's a strong possibility?
BISHOP CAINES:	I believe I've already answered that question. (*Disordered questioning.*)
BISHOP CAINES:	I'm afraid we must bring this Press conference to a close, gentlemen. Thank you for your questions and I hope we've been able to clarify a few points. I'm sorry, no more questions. Our schedule is tight and we now have television and radio interviews to do. Thank you for your time, ladies and gentlemen. (*Press conference ends.*)

WILKES

'If thy mother only knew,
Her heart would surely break in two.'

THE GOOSE-GIRL
The Brothers Grimm

He couldn't sleep.

His hair itched, the sheets on the narrow bed felt soiled, stiff and unwashed. He wasn't hungry, he wasn't thirsty; he certainly wasn't tired. It was his own fault for staying in bed most of the day. He should have gone to the Job Centre, but what the fuck? They would only have offered him some poxy job waiting on tables like his last one, or digging bloody holes in roads, or working some machine in a factory. Or worse, Community fucking Service! Sod em! He'd have to blag the old lady for money tomorrow. Christ, how he hated going back there! *Look at you! Why don't you get your hair cut. You'll never get a decent job like that. And look at your clothes. When was the last time that shirt was ironed? And can't you at least polish your shoes?*

Worst of all: *When was the last time you went to church? What would your poor father say if he were still alive?*

Shit on her! If he didn't need the bread he would never go back.

He turned in the bed, a crease in his vest irritating his skin.

He stared out the window into the dark night. Christ, if only he could get a bird up here; that would warm him up, all right! They didn't want to know, though. If you didn't have money, then they just weren't interested. If you were a nobody you were bloody nobody! He turned again and thumped the lumps from the pillow with an angry fist. He'd had a guy up there once, but that hadn't been too good. The jerking off was okay, but all that fucking kissing had made him want to puke.

He stared at the ceiling and pulled the end of the vest over his bare stomach.

It was all a big bucket of shit. You fell into it and the bastards wouldn't let you climb out. You just went round and round in the slime until you had to eat it to stop drowning. And then it poisoned you and killed you dead anyway.

But at least *they* had kicked back! Those three had swallowed the shit and spewed it right back into the onlookers' faces. *They* had found a way, and that was all it took.

He grinned in the darkness. Yeah, they had found a way.

He yanked back the covers and padded over to the wardrobe in stockinged feet. Standing on tiptoe, he reached up to the top of the wardrobe and found the box he was looking for. He brought it down, then took a small key from his jacket hanging over the back of the room's only chair.

Climbing back into the bed he inserted the key and opened the lid. He took a dark object out and pressed it to his cheek, smiling in the darkness. He placed the open box on the floor and covered himself.

Lying there in the darkness, he pushed the object beneath the bedclothes so that its cold metal lay between his inner thighs. He sighed as he felt himself grow hard.

NINETEEN

Here lies the Devil — ask no other name.
Well — but you mean Lord —? Hush! we mean the same.

ON A LORD
Samuel Taylor Coleridge

Fenn yawned and checked his watch at the same time. 7.45. Jesus, so this was what the dawn was like.

Another car was approaching him from the opposite direction and he gave the driver a tired wave as though they were both members of the same exclusive club. The other driver looked at him as if he were mad. Fenn hummed a tuneless tune, only the fact that he was tone deaf making the noise bearable to himself.

He glanced at the South Downs to his left; the clouds were heavy over them, soft woolly bottoms scraping against the hilltops. It was going to be another cold, overcast day, the kind that dragged at the keenest optimism, muffled the most ardent enthusiasm. The kind of day to stay in bed until positive night-time darkness over-rode the negative dullness.

The houses on either side of the road were few and far between, mostly big and set back with high hedges or walls protecting them from unsolicited attention. The road was normally quite busy as one of the main routes from the coast to the larger Sussex towns, scything through country villages like wire through cheese; but on a chilly damp Sunday morning – a chilly damp, *early* Sunday morning – birds and rabbits were a more common sight than motorists.

Fenn's humming droned to a stop when he saw the outskirts of Banfield ahead and the dregs of tiredness evaporated as if hoovered from his head. He grinned, ready to enjoy the special privilege he had been allowed and to forget about the warm bed he had just left. It was regrettable that Sue's naked body had not been in that bed (even though it would have been even harder to leave), but they were still not the close lovers that they had been. When they had slept together just three nights before, Fenn had imagined their relationship would be back on the same footing and had been disappointed to find on the following morning her new aloofness had only suffered a slight relapse. While not as cold as before, and certainly not as contemptuous, she had made it plain that she needed more time to think. She loved him, of that there was no doubt, but the confusion was still there and their love-making had not cleared it. Okay, it's down to you, Sue. You know my number.

Fenn was angry and frustrated at her change of moods, particularly at a time when things were happening for him, when he shouldn't have had such distractions. He cursed himself for not being able to cut her from his mind. Christ, he was buying his ticket to Fleet Street and she acted as though he had forged the money! The invitation for that Sunday morning was an indication of just how far he had advanced in prestige in a matter of a few short weeks. Only he and five other reporters shared the privilege, his colleagues chosen from the cream to represent the media world. So maybe he was over-rating his own importance a little, but the position he now found himself in was no mean thing.

He eased off the accelerator as he entered the speed restricted zone. The road swung sharply to the right, joined by another minor road from the left, the round white bump of a tiny 'mickey mouse' roundabout helping (or hindering) the merger. The Convent of Our Lady of Sion was almost opposite, just to the left, and Fenn brought his Mini to a halt, checking that the roundabout was clear. From his position he could see the upper windows of the large cream-coloured house and for one brief moment thought he caught a small pale face peering down at him. Then it was gone and he wasn't sure that it had been there.

A lone policeman stood outside the gates, his panda parked half on the kerb further down the road. To one side was a group of reporters, damp and miserable looking. They eyed Fenn's car suspiciously as he drove over the circle in the road. Fenn pulled into a nearby empty garage forecourt and parked. The garage was closed and, as it was Sunday, he guessed it wouldn't be open at all that day. He left the car and walked back to the convent.

The journalists and cameramen, pasty-faced, shoulders hunched, feet stamping the pavement, made ready to receive him into their midst, any newcomer welcome to break the monotony of their cold vigil.

'Morning, hacks,' he said, grinning and winking as he strode past them. He ignored their muttered replies as he walked up to the gates. The policeman on duty raised a hand.

'I'm Fenn, *Brighton Courier*.'

The uniformed man produced a folded piece of paper from his tunic pocket and quickly scanned the list of names.

'Okay, in you go.' The policeman pushed open one half of the gates just enough for Fenn to slip through. He chuckled at the indignant voices and groans of the other reporters.

Across the courtyard and at the top of three broad steps was a black door, open and somehow forbidding. Fenn crossed the yard and took the first two steps in one. He stepped into a dark hallway and a hooded shape loomed up from the shadows.

'You are Mr . . .?' the nun asked.

'Gerry Fenn,' he told her, his heart skipping just a little, either from the leap up the stairs or her sudden appearance. *'Brighton Evening Courier.'*

'Ah, yes. Mr Fenn. Shall I take your coat?'

He slipped off his raincoat and handed it to her. 'There's no money in the pockets,' he said.

She looked at him, startled, then returned his smile. 'If you'd like to go through, you'll find nearly everyone has arrived.' She pointed to a door near the end of the hallway.

He thanked her and walked down the hall, his steps sharp against the shiny bare floorboards. The room beyond the door was large and on a sunny day would have been light and airy; today its natural brightness was muted grey. It was filled with people and hushed voices.

'Mr Fenn, glad you could come.'

He turned to find George Southworth approaching him.

'Glad I was invited,' Fenn responded.

'Your other colleagues have already arrived.'

'Oh?'

'A rather small selection of élite journalists. You're the sixth.'

Fenn enjoyed being among the 'élite'.

'*Associated Press, Washington Post, The Times* – that sort of thing. I'm sure you know them all.'

'Oh yeah, sure.' Fenn shook his head. 'I'm puzzled, Mr Southworth. Why me?'

Southworth smiled disarmingly and patted Fenn's arm. 'Mustn't be so modest, Mr Fenn. You've covered this story from the start. More than that, you brought it to the attention of the world. We could hardly have excluded you.'

'Hardly.'

'Quite. Would you like some tea?'

'No thanks.'

'I'm sure you'll appreciate our reluctance in allowing young Alice to attend Mass at St Joseph's this –'

'Your reluctance?'

'Well, to be honest, Bishop Caines' reluctance. And the doctors, of course – they feel the hullabaloo might prove too much for her. The cameras, the television, the crowds, people wanting to get near her, to touch her – that sort of thing.'

Fenn nodded. 'So you decided on a private service, without the fuss.'

'Precisely.'

'A lot of people are going to be disappointed.'

'I'm sure. Frankly, if I had had my way, I would have let Alice go to the church today as she wanted. But her well-being must come first.'

'She wanted to go to St Joseph's?'

'Apparently so.' Southworth lowered his voice. 'I heard she became quite upset when Reverend Mother told her she couldn't. Still, I'm sure it's for the best.'

'So you just invited certain members of the, er . . .' he scanned the room '. . . public and the media here.'

'Yes. My idea, actually. And the Bishop concurred. We're well aware, you see, that the public has to know what's going on. That's their right. This way, they'll see that Alice is being properly cared for.'

'And they'll know the Catholic Church isn't locking her away, and that she's not going through some modern-day Grand Inquisition.'

Southworth chuckled. 'That's very astute of you, Mr Fenn. In fact, that was my argument to the churchmen. With the chosen few here, representatives of the people, as it were, and an excellent cross-section of the world media, public interest can be catered for without unnecessary but inevitable pandemonium.'

And without loss of maximum publicity, Fenn guessed. It seemed that Southworth (and Fenn was sure other local businessmen were involved) had to walk the tightrope between exploitation (and so risk the resulting criticism), and ensuring that Alice Pagett was sheltered from the public eye (and making sure they were seen to be doing so). He, Fenn, was necessary to the idea not because he was a brilliant journalist, but because as instigator of the story, his articles were followed more closely than any other reporter's. He was also 'local', therefore perhaps more in tune with local opinion. Well, don't knock it, Fenn. It made sense. And it had got him here today.

'In a moment,' Southworth was saying, 'I'll introduce you to a few people.

Your colleagues are already well into them, but I'm sure they will want to speak to you as the man who was "on the spot". Mass will begin at 8.30, so you'll have just . . .' he checked his watch '. . . just under half-an-hour to interview.'

'Will I get to talk to Alice?'

'We plan to have a brief question and answer session after Mass. Only twenty minutes, I'm afraid, and only if Alice feels up to it. I'm sure she will.' He moved closer to Fenn and said in a conspiratorial whisper: 'I'd like to invite you to dinner tomorrow evening. I think you'd be most interested in coming along.'

Fenn raised his eyebrows.

'I still haven't forgotten our little chat at the beginning of all this business, Mr Fenn. By the way, it's Gerry, isn't it? Do you mind if I call you that? It's far less formal. I think at the time you said the story would probably die out.'

Fenn grinned wryly. 'Someone once said that about Lennon and McCartney.'

'I think your opinion was very fair. But you remember my offer? Yes, well, I think you may have suspected my motives at that time. You can see now that the publicity machine is in motion of its own accord and needs absolutely no impetus from myself, or the parish council. It may need just a little steering from the inside, though, and I think you could be helpful in that respect.'

'I don't understand.'

'We have enough confidence in you, having read all your articles in the *Courier*, to invite you to write the complete story of the Banfield Miracles.'

'For my newspaper?'

'For any newspaper you care to work for. Or for a book. We would make you privy to all council meetings and any other decisions, discussions and plans concerning this whole affair.'

Fenn's eyes gleamed. It was too good to be true. The *authorized* chronicler of the Banfield Miracles. Any newspaper editor would jump at serialization rights and any publisher would give his right arm (or his marketing manager's right arm) for the rights to the book. There had to be a snag. 'Why me?' he asked.

'I believe you asked that question before, or something like it. The answer's simple: because you were there at the beginning. You already have more inside knowledge than anyone else in this matter apart from the clergy. And even they – Father Hagan and Monsignor Delgard – were not there at the very beginning.'

'Would the priests be agreeable?'

'I've already broached the subject to Bishop Caines. He's interested but wary.'

'Oh?'

'He's pragmatic enough to realize the story has become almost exclusive to you. However, he is not altogether sure that, to use an old-fashioned phrase, your "intentions are honourable".'

'Are his?'

'I beg your pardon?'

'It doesn't matter.'

'That's the reason for my invitation to dine with us tomorrow evening.'

'Bishop Caines will be there?'

'Yes, along with Father Hagan and Monsignor Delgard. Our meeting initially is to talk about the development of a shrine at St Joseph's and Banfield's part in it. Bishop Caines is insistent that there should be full cooperation and liaison between the parish council and the Church.'

'It's moving things pretty fast for them, isn't it. I thought it took years for the

Church to allow a shrine to be authorized.'

'Normally it would. Fortunately or unfortunately, whichever way you care to look at it, the pilgrims are going to come and nothing will stop them. The bishop wants to be prepared. Officially, the Church cannot declare St Joseph's a shrine, but that won't prevent the public from regarding it as such.'

'Do the two priests know I've been invited?'

'Yes. Bishop Caines, himself, told them.'

'And they agreed?'

'Reluctantly. I suppose you could say the Bishop gave them little choice. I hope, after all this, you *are* interested?'

'What do you think? Where and when?'

'My hotel, 8.30.'

'I'll be there.'

'Fine. Now, let me introduce you to a few people.'

Fenn spent the next twenty minutes talking to assorted 'guests', among them the local Tory MP, who was not himself a Catholic but professed a deep interest in all religions, several members of the clergy, whose titles he instantly forgot, certain leading members of the local community, the Reverend Mother of the convent and, most interestingly of all, the Apostolic Delegate to Great Britain and Gibraltar. Fenn understood that this clergyman was the official 'go-between' for the Catholic Church in Britain and the Vatican. A quietly-spoken, unassuming man, he seemed genuinely pleased to be introduced to Fenn, and gently led him to one side so that he could question him on the articles he had written and what he had personally witnessed. Soon the reporter began to feel like the interviewee, but he enjoyed the priest's frank questioning and the deference with which his answers were treated.

When the audience was over, for that was what it felt like, Fenn realized he had asked hardly any questions himself. He was puzzled by the priest's accent and one of the grey-garbed nuns who was flitting through the crowded room urging more tea or coffee on the assemblage provided the answer: The Most Reverend Pierre Melsak was from Belgium. Fenn accepted a coffee from the sister and wished he'd declined the ginger biscuit which resisted all attempts to be bitten. He left it on the saucer, his teeth groaning after the battle, and was sipping the lukewarm coffee when a husky voice said, 'Hi.'

He turned to see a dark-haired woman smiling at him; at least her lips were smiling – the eyes were too calculating to be easily happy.

'Shelbeck, *Washington Post*,' she told him.

'Yeah, somebody already pointed you out to me. How's Woodward?'

'Redford was better. You're Gerry Fenn, aren't you?'

He nodded.

'I liked your copy. Maybe we can get together later?'

'That'd be nice. What for?'

'Compare notes?' Her accent was pure New York.

'I'm ahead.'

'You could benefit.'

'How?'

'Financially, how else?' The smile had finally reached her eyes.

'Okay . . .'

The buzz of conversation stopped as sliding doors covering one side of the room were drawn back. Another room, white-walled and low-ceilinged, lay beyond. Fenn guessed it had once been a double-garage attached to the house that the Sisters of Our Lady of Sion had had converted into a small chapel. The altar was simple, no more than a rectangular table covered in a spotlessly white cloth on which stood a crucifix. Small benches stood before it, enough to accommodate the nuns who lived in the convent.

'If you would please take your places,' Bishop Caines told the select group, 'the Mass will begin in a few moments. I'm afraid there isn't room for everybody to sit, even though our kind sisters have volunteered to stand throughout the service, so could the male journalists please take a position at the back of the chapel.'

People began to move into the next room and Shelbeck winked at Fenn. 'I'll talk to you after the show,' she whispered. 'The name's Nancy, by the way.'

He watched her push her way into the chapel, heading for a seat near the front. Her age could have been anywhere between thirty and forty, though he guessed it was at the higher end, say thirty-six or seven. She wore a sensible grey tweed suit, the kind native New Yorkers managed to make look business-like yet attractive. Her figure was slim and, from the back, her legs were good (which was the real test for legs). At a quick appraisal, she was abrasive, brittle and more than a little shrewd, the kind of woman who could intimidate the more easily intimidated of the male species (which was most of them). She could prove interesting.

'Um, could we leave the front bench free for myself, Reverend Mother, Alice and Mr and Mrs Pagett?' Bishop Caines said, a beaming smile on his face. 'Monsignor Melsak, would you please join us at the front?'

The small Belgian priest did as requested and the bishop turned his attention back to the rest of the congregation. 'Alice will join us presently. The service will be kept short and she will be the first to take Communion. May I ask our friends from the media to refrain from asking any questions of the child when she enters the chapel. I promise you'll have the opportunity as soon as the Mass is finished. Only twenty minutes, of course, but you must remember she is under considerable strain.' He tried a disarming smile. 'I need hardly add that no pictures will be allowed and members of the Press have been invited on that understanding. So if any of you have cameras hidden about your person, please keep them that way – hidden and unused.'

Soft chuckles greeted his last remark and there were one or two embarrassed smiles among the Pressmen.

Everyone soon became settled and Fenn found himself standing to one side of the room at the back. He was above the congregation, for three steps led down from the general room into the chapel itself. He thought the drawn doors might be a good spot to lean against if the service wasn't as short as the bishop had declared. There was an air of expectancy, the same excitement present at St Joseph's on the previous Sunday. The nuns of the covent knelt around the side walls, heads bowed, rosaries entwined between fingers. The politician and some of the other dignitaries looked uncomfortable, not sure of the ceremony, anxious not to offend. He caught a glimpse of Nancy Shelbeck as she turned her head to study, and no doubt to make note of, her surroundings. Whispered conversation faded and the congregation settled into an uneasy silence.

Fenn turned as a door behind him opened. A man walked awkwardly into the room and Fenn quickly recognized him as Len Pagett, Alice's father. He wore an ill-fitting suit, one that had seen better days, its obviously recent dry-clean giving it a short-term smartness. He looked with trepidation across the room into the chapel and Fenn could see resentment in his eyes. He stood back from the door, revealing the small figure of Alice. She emerged from the darkness of the hallway, a nervous, doe-like creature, her face pale, eyes wide and darting.

She wore a pale blue dress and her blonde hair was tied back at one side with a white bow. Her father muttered something and she moved more quickly into the room. Her glance went immediately to the large patio windows overlooking the convent's garden and Fenn felt she was like a young caged animal, yearning to be on the outside, away from the smothering kindness of captivity.

Immediately behind came Molly Pagett, an uncertain smile on her face as she urged Alice onwards into the chapel. A nun was the last to enter; she turned to close the door, then stood with her back to it as though a guard.

All heads turned as Alice approached the steps; she stopped for a moment to take in the scene before her. She seemed even younger than her eleven years, yet there was a subtle change in her features, a look that made her less of a child than before. Fenn could not define the change. Maybe it was in the eyes . . .

She turned towards him as though suddenly aware that he, in particular, was watching her. For a brief moment, something chilled him. Then it was gone, had passed, and he was only looking into the face of a small, timid child. Something lingered with him, though, and it was a feeling he could not understand.

Alice stepped down into the chapel as Bishop Caines beckoned her forward. She genuflected before the altar, then disappeared from view as she sat with her parents on the front bench.

Once again, the door behind Fenn opened, the nun who had been standing in front of it quickly stepping to one side as the handle turned. Father Hagan entered, dressed in the bright robes of the Mass, followed by Monsignor Delgard, who wore his customary black garb. The first priest carried a covered chalice as he swept through the room into the chapel, his eyes downcast. Monsignor Delgard gave Fenn a brief nod of recognition as he passed.

Both men made their way to the altar and stood behind it, facing the congregation. Fenn assumed Delgard was there to assist Father Hagan in the absence of altar-servers. Again, the expression on another's face disturbed the reporter, for Hagan looked desperately tired and unwell. He placed the chalice on the altar and, even from where Fenn stood, his unsteadiness was evident. Still leaning forward over the altar, the priest's attention was taken by someone seated in the front row. Fenn knew that Father Hagan was staring into the face of Alice Pagett.

The priest became still for several seconds, then appeared to remember where he was and the service began.

Fenn was getting used to the Mass by now and was relieved it was to be a short one. Short though it was, he was soon looking around, totally unmoved by the service itself. Daylight, grey and depressing on such a morning, flooded the small chapel through a broad skylight, presumably built into the roof when the garage had been converted. The walls themselves were still of rough brick but painted gleaming white, and the floor was carpet-tiled. There were no windows, just a heavy, locked door leading out into the courtyard. The congregation, led by the nuns and the invited clergy, responded to the priest's intonations and Fenn tried to follow the proceedings in the Mass Book handed to him by the same sister who had served him coffee. He lost his place several times and eventually gave up. He found it difficult to understand the appeal of such a weekly ritual to someone like Sue, who was a level-headed, sensitive and capable woman. She was also pretty smart, certainly nobody's fool. So how come she was hooked on all this?

Something caught his eye. A sudden movement above. He looked towards the skylight and smiled. The shadowy form of a cat was moving across the slanted, frosted glass. It stopped and the ghostly head grew larger as the cat tried to peer through the unclear glass. It rested its front paws against the pane, head weaving from side to side as if frustrated. Its body appeared to stiffen, then it eased back down the slope and sat, only the shadow of its upper body visible.

Fenn and the other reporters knelt when the rest of the congregation knelt, stiffened to attention when those seated stood, and generally responded to the service in a superficial way. He realized it wasn't out of reverence, but more out of respect for the sweet-looking nuns whom he felt might have been upset if the correct movements were not adhered to. A tiny bell rang and heads bowed. Fenn, kneeling uncomfortably, knew it was almost time for Holy Communion. He eased himself upright, sure that he wouldn't be noticed at this crucial point. The silence in the room was disconcerting. In a church, atmospherics, and general rustling of restless bodies, moaning children and muffled coughs were enough to combat any true silence, but here in the little chapel, even a rumbling stomach had no camouflage.

Father Hagan stood before the altar, the chalice and Communion wafer in his hand. His eyes were almost closed.

Fenn saw Bishop Caines lean over and whisper something to Alice. For a moment she did not move and he had to whisper again. She stood, her hair bright yellow, the white bow like a butterfly nestling in wheat. She looked frail, too small, and Fenn found himself concerned, caring about her. She had been through so much, this little squirt, and he wondered how she had remained so calm throughout.

She was looking at the priest, still not moving.

Her mother touched her arm, but Alice did not look at her. Eventually it was the Reverend Mother who rose and led Alice towards Father Hagan. The priest looked down at the little figure and his eyes widened. His hand was visibly trembling when he held the Host forward.

Fenn frowned, aware of the tension in the priest. My God, he thought, he's frightened. Something's scaring him bloody silly.

Alice's head tilted backwards slightly, as though she were offering her tongue to take the Communion wafer. The priest hesitated, then seemed to resolve something in his own mind. He placed the wafer on Alice's tongue.

Her head bowed and for a moment both she and the priest were still.

Then her small body began to shudder. Alice fell to her knees as the retching sound screeched from her. Vomit splattered onto the floor. Onto the shoes of the priest. Onto his white robes.

TWENTY

Then out has she ta'en a silver wand,
  An' she's turned her three times roun' and roun';
She mutter'd sic words till my strength it fail'd,
  An' I fell down senseless upon the groun'.

ALISON GROSS
Anon

'Father, you've hardly touched your soup. Is there something wrong with it?'

The priest looked up, startled. 'I, uh, no, of course not. I'm afraid I'm just not very happy.' Southworth looked relieved.

Bishop Caines laughed jovially. 'I swear you're wasting away before my eyes, Andrew. Come on, man, you must eat, especially if you're going to cope over the next few months.'

Father Hagan picked up his spoon once more and dipped it into the mushroom soup, his movements slow, distracted. Bishop Caines and Monsignor Delgard exchanged concerned glances.

'Are you still unwell?' Delgard asked quietly. The others on the table were watching the priest with interest. The man's decline in health had spanned the past few weeks, but the overnight change had been more dramatic.

Father Hagan sipped from the spoon. 'It's just a chill, I think,' he said unconvincingly.

'Would you like me to take you home?'

'No. Our discussion tonight is important.'

Bishop Caines dabbed at his lips with a serviette. 'Not important enough to keep you from a nice warm bed. I'm sure that's where you'd be better off, Andrew.'

'I'd rather stay.'

'So be it. But I insist you see a doctor tomorrow without fail.'

'There's no need –'

'Without fail,' the bishop repeated.

Father Hagan nodded, then laid down his spoon. He sat back in his chair, feeling strangely detached from his surroundings. Occasionally it was like viewing the scene through the wrong end of a telescope. Even the conversation sounded distant.

He looked across at the reporter who was sitting on the opposite side of the round dinner table, between the hotelier and Bishop Caines, and again he asked himself the silent question: why had they involved this man? Fenn wasn't a Catholic and didn't appear to have any sympathy at all towards the Catholic religion. Objectivity, Bishop Caines had said. They needed someone like Fenn, an agnostic, to write objectively on the Banfield Miracles, someone without bias who would be more credible because of it. He would report the untainted facts and, after all, that was all that was necessary here, for the facts alone would convince and perhaps convert.

Would the young reporter listen to him? Would he want to hear? And what could he, Hagan, really tell him? That he was afraid? Afraid of a child? Afraid of . . .? What? Nothing. There was nothing to fear. Nothing at all . . .

'. . . Alice is fine.' Bishop Caines was speaking. 'I'm afraid all the excitement yesterday was a little too much for her. Her own doctor gave her a thorough check-up and said there was nothing to worry over. She had a slight temperature, but that was all. A few more days of peace and quiet is all she needs.'

'I'm pleased to hear it,' Southworth said. 'She had us all worried yesterday. Mercifully it didn't happen up at St Joseph's in full view of the crowds. Very wise of you, if I may say so, Bishop, to keep the child at the convent.'

'Yes, much as I understand the need for people to see Alice, her own best interests must be considered.'

'Does that mean you won't let her return to the church for some time?' asked Fenn.

'Oh, no, no. It would be quite wrong to keep Alice from her beloved St Joseph's. She's known the church all her young life, Mr Fenn; it's a second home to her. In fact, you could say she was practically born there.'

'You mean she was baptized –'

'I think it would be wise to keep Alice away from St Joseph's permanently.'

The interruption surprised everyone sitting at the table. Bishop Caines studied his parish priest with evident impatience.

'Now, Andrew, you know that would be impossible. Reverend Mother tells me she has found the child weeping in her room because she misses the church so much. We can't keep her locked away forever.' He quickly looked at Fenn. 'Not that we are keeping her locked up, you understand. Alice is free to leave at any time her parents wish her to.'

'But she wants to leave,' Fenn said.

'Of course it's no fun for a little girl to be shut away in a convent, Mr Fenn. Naturally she would like to be seeing her friends, playing with them, carrying on with all the usual activities young children indulge in. And she will, before very long.'

'Don't let her come back to the church. Not yet.'

'Andrew, I cannot understand your attitude in this matter.' The soothing amiability had left the bishop's tone, although his words were still softly spoken. 'Just what is it that disturbs you about the girl?'

Fenn leaned forward, elbows on the table, interested in the priest's reply.

Father Hagan looked uncertainly around at the dinner guests. 'I . . . I'm not sure. It just . . . doesn't . . .'

'Come now, Father,' said Bishop Caines. 'I think it's time you shared your unwillingness to accept these rather wondrous events with us. Don't worry about our Mr Fenn here – we will have no secrets from the Press. If you have doubts, please voice them so that they can be discussed.'

The door opened and the head waiter unobtrusively entered the room. He quickly surveyed the dinner table, then nodded at someone just outside the door. A waitress hurried through and began to gather up the used dishes.

'Oh, I'm sorry, Father,' she said, about to take the priest's soup bowl.

'It's all right, I've finished.'

The dish was taken away. Nobody spoke until the waitress had left and the head waiter had closed the door, abruptly cutting off the noise from the public restaurant and bar below. Southworth had deemed it wise to hold the dinner in a private banqueting room on the first floor, away from the hotel's other guests, who that week were mainly visiting journalists.

'Andrew?' the bishop prompted.

'It's difficult, Bishop,' the priest said quietly.

'I beg your pardon?'

'I said it's difficult. Difficult to put my feelings into words.'

'Do try.' It was said kindly.

'Something . . . something is wrong. I can't say what it is, but something doesn't feel right. The church . . . St Joseph's . . . somehow seems . . . empty.'

'Empty? I don't understand.'

'I think I know what Father Hagan means,' said Monsignor Delgard. All eyes turned towards him. 'I've been concerned over the atmosphere inside St Joseph's for a few days now and I believe I understand what Father Hagan is trying to say.'

'Then perhaps you'd enlighten us,' said Bishop Caines.

'It seems to me the church has become spiritually devoid.'

'I'm very surprised at you, Monsignor,' the bishop said coldly. 'That remark could be regarded as sacrilegious. The House of God can never be spiritually devoid – it's impossible, contrary to all our beliefs to hold such a view.'

'A church is just a building made of stone, Bishop,' the monsignor replied calmly.

Bishop Caines' face reddened and Fenn hid his smile behind his wine glass.

'It might be better to confine our discussion tonight to the more, er, "material" aspects of the situation,' Southworth cut in. 'Don't you agree, Gerry?'

'Well, no. I –'

'Yes, you're absolutely right,' Bishop Caines said, not wishing to hold a theological debate now in front of the reporter who could so easily misinterpret everything. 'We can talk of this later.' He looked meaningfully at the two clergymen.

'As you wish,' Delgard responded stiffly.

Father Hagan opened his mouth to say more but, on seeing the stern expression on his bishop's face, he refrained.

Fenn was disappointed.

Southworth allowed no respite. 'One thing I'm sure the media will want, Bishop, is a statement on Alice's health at this present moment . . .'

'Haven't I already told you?' The bishop was still watching his two priests, but he turned to give Southworth a warm smile.

'Yes, but I meant her state of health generally. Yesterday was an exception.'

'Yes, that it was. A culmination of events, if you like. It had to catch up with the child sooner or later. The monsignor has the latest information from the medical team.'

'A medical report is generally private to the individual,' said Delgard. He nodded towards Fenn. 'Why should it be made public by the Press?'

'We have an understanding with Mr Fenn,' Southworth said.

Fenn looked at him in surprise. 'Now wait a minute. The only understanding that we have is that I'll write the truth.' Then he added, 'As I see it.'

'Naturally, Mr Fenn,' Bishop Caines assured him. 'We would not expect otherwise. However we would expect, er, *discreet* journalism.'

'Oh, I can be discreet. It's secrets I can't keep.'

He caught the glance that passed between the bishop and Southworth.

'Okay,' he said, raising a hand, 'I understand your dilemma. You want the story told without frills, without exaggeration, and truthfully. That's good, that's what I want to do. On the other hand, you want personal privacy respected and anything that could cause embarrassment smoothed over, if not scrubbed out.' He paused to take a breath. 'I'll go along with you on the first count. No exaggeration, no exploitation. As for personal privacy, I'm afraid that went out the window when Alice saw her first vision. Not just for her. For you. And for the whole of Banfield. On the third count – revealing anything that could cause embarrassment – well, you have to leave that to me.'

'I'm not sure that's good enough,' said the bishop.

'It'll have to be.' Fenn grinned. 'Look, I know Alice's father is a drunken old sot, but at this stage, I don't think it's essential to the story. It's not exactly a state secret, but I don't intend to make anything of it. Discretion, right?'

'Yes, Mr Fenn, but not much of a concession on your part.'

'True enough. But it's all I can offer.'

It was Southworth who saved the situation. 'Why don't we rely on that good old journalistic standby, "off the record"? That way you can be intimate with the situation as a whole, but professionally bound to keep certain items to yourself.'

It's either that, or be blown out entirely, Fenn told himself. 'Okay, so long as there aren't too many "off the records",' he said.

'Agreed, Bishop?' Southworth asked.

Bishop Caines was thoughtful. 'You understand, Mr Fenn, that we do not want to veil anything. The Church doesn't work that way.'

Oh no? Fenn said silently. Get the Pope to tell the world the third secret of Fatima. Or disclose all the Church's financial assets, exactly what companies and properties they're into. And any other items of world interest that the Catholic Church is keeping to itself.

'We want only the truth to be written,' Bishop Caines continued, 'but we do not wish any person to be harmed by it. If you take our view, then I'm sure there will be no problems between us. I'm sure there are many other journalists who would be only too pleased to understand.'

You wily old bastard. You know I can't refuse. 'All right. But one proviso: if I really believe you're holding back on something that needs to be told – I mean, if I think it morally wrong not to publish – then I go ahead and do so.'

'Are you suggesting we would lie?'

'Not at all. But you might want to withhold information that doesn't suit the Church's image.'

'Then we'll let you be our conscience, Mr Fenn.'

'Okay.'

Southworth breathed a sigh of relief as Bishop Caines and the reporter relaxed in their chairs. 'You were going to tell us the medical team's findings to date,' he urged the monsignor.

'Their report is very detailed and extremely technical in parts, so I'll try to break it down as concisely and simply as possible. If you require the full text, Mr Fenn, I can obtain a copy for you.' He sipped his wine, then set it to one side. 'First let me deal with the findings on Alice's previous infirmity. There has been no physical change in the organs of her ears and throat, which consolidates the long-standing opinion that her handicap had psychological origins. There never had been any discernible damage to the auditory nerves, no apparent disorder to the ossicles, cochlea or eardrums of either ear. There may well have been some infection due to her illness seven years ago, but there were certainly no signs that it had lingered. There had been no hardenings or formation of bones in the inner ear, no inflammation of the membranes. Mastoiditis, otitis media – I'm sorry, that's middle ear infection – had been discounted long ago. As for her vocal cords, there was no damage or disease to the laryngeal nerve. Her condition was always thought to be a result of hysteria.'

'You're saying Alice was just suffering from prolonged hysteria all these years?' Fenn asked incedulously.

'It's not quite that simple, nor is it as unusual as your tone suggests. There may very well have been other infections present that were not detected by her family doctor when Alice suffered mumps at four years of age, infections that could have been the root cause of her condition. The doctor considered it to be a routine childhood illness and looked no further in the early stages. Test came later when the disastrous consequences became evident. I should add that there is no criticism levelled at the GP in the medical report – at the moment we're dealing purely with conjecture.'

'Has the family doctor seen this report?' Fenn asked.

'No. And, of course, he would undoubtedly deny any suggestion of negligence on his part. But I would hate you to draw any hasty conclusions – this is partly theory now, just an attempt to offer reasons.'

'May I remind you of our discussion a short while ago,' Bishop Caines said, looking directly at the reporter. '"Discretion" was the favoured word, I believe.'

'Don't worry, I've no intention of getting into a lawsuit with an aggrieved general practitioner over something that couldn't possibly be proved after all these years. Anyway, the medical team could be entirely wrong.'

'Yes, they could well be,' said Monsignor Delgard. 'The point they are trying to make, however, is that the shock of being unable to hear or speak was sustained psychologically by Alice in her own mind. The more afraid she was of her handicap, the worse her mental block became. Medical records are full of similar case histories: fears growing into phobias, phobias into physical infirmity. The subconscious mind has its own peculiar logic. It took an altogether different kind of shock to break down the mental block Alice had imposed on herself. The vision – be it imaginary or real – released Alice from her self-inflicted illness.'

'You're saying categorically, then, that there was no miracle cure in Alice's case?' said Fenn.

'After seven years of silence she can speak, she can hear. Whether or not her disability was due to a mental or physical disorder, the result is still the same . . .'

. . . the church . . . the church . . . everything that happened to Alice was centred around the church . . .

Father Hagan put a soothing hand to his temple, pressing the thin flesh there, gently rubbing. The voices sounded distant again, somehow hollow, as if they were all in a vast cavern, the others far away on the other side. Or in a church . . . a vast, dark church. He was beginning to hate . . . the church.

No! The church was the House of God! No one could hate it! Especially not a priest . . .

'. . . general health?' Bishop Caines was speaking. 'How is she?'

'It can be summed up very simply and without any medical jargon,' Delgard replied. 'Alice is a perfectly normal, healthy child. A little tired perhaps, and somewhat withdrawn, but that's to be expected after all she's been through. There is one small abnormality, however, but it's something she's had since she was a baby according to her own doctor.'

Fenn, wine glass halfway from the table to his lips, asked, 'What's that?'

Delgard hesitated, regarding the reporter warily. 'This has to be off the record. It's not very important, but it could cause the child some personal embarrassment. I promise you it has nothing to do with her cure.'

Fenn considered for no more than a second. 'I wouldn't want to hurt the kid.'

'Very well. Alice has a small growth on her body. It's on the left side of her body, a few inches below her heart.'

'A growth? Good Lord . . .' Bishop Caines began to say.

'Don't worry, it's nothing serious,' Delgard reassured them. 'It's what's known as a supernumerary nipple . . .'

. . . Supernumerary nipple . . . a third nipple . . . he knew something about that . . . had read something somewhere . . . oh God, what was it . . .?

'. . . nothing at all to worry about. It has increased a little in size since her doctor examined her last, but then her body is developing naturally. There's no reason to believe that it will grow any larger.' Monsignor Delgard sipped his wine once more. 'And there you have it. Alice Pagett appears to be healthy in every way, except for this slight, er, blemish.'

'That's very good news indeed,' asserted Bishop Caines. 'Thank you for your lucid report, Monsignor. Do you have any questions, Mr Fenn?'

At that point the door opened and two waitresses entered laden with dishes.

'Ah, our main course,' said Southworth. 'The hotel is rather busy tonight, gentlemen, hence the slight delay. A foretaste of the coming months, I believe,' he said, beaming happily. And hopefully, the coming years, he thought.

The conversation concerned itself with generalities as the food was served and Fenn found himself looking into the haunted eyes of Father Hagan. The priest averted his gaze and Fenn was puzzled. It was obvious that the priest was ill: there was a light sheen of perspiration on his sallow face, his eyes were dark and shadowy; there was something brittle in the movement of his long, delicate fingers. Bishop Caines should make the man take a rest. What was it they went into? Retreat. That's what he needed, a complete break away from all this. And the going was only going to get worse once the publicity machine was rolling. *That*, he understood from Southworth when he had spoken to him earlier that evening, was going to be one of the items on the agenda. Fenn smiled down at the medallions of veal in herb sauce placed before him and sipped his wine while waiting for the vegetables to be served.

He listened to Southworth as the hotelier tentatively broached the subject of publicity.

'I'm sure we all realize by now, Bishop, that we have a situation here that private entrepreneurs from all over the country will endeavour to make money from. I really do think it's time for us to seriously consider the setting up of an official publicity machine to monitor . . .'

'. . . somewhat premature . . .'

'. . . no, not at all. We must plan . . .'

'. . . Lourdes is not the best example to follow, George . . .'

. . . I can't eat. The bishop shouldn't have insisted . . .

'. . . hired for the papal visit to England in '82 . . .'

'. . . but, goodness, that organization took something like twenty percent of profits . . .'

'. . . worth every penny . . .'

. . . each night, the feeling gets worse . . . even with the monsignor nearby . . . the feeling of being alone . . . empty . . . yet there is something there!

'. . . statues, T-shirts, records of the services . . .'

'Andrew, you must try to eat. It will do you good.'

'What? Yes, Bishop . . .'

'Entrecôte steak Roquefort is one of the chef's specialities, Father. I'm sure you'll enjoy it.'

'Of course . . .'

'. . . we cannot be seen . . .'

'. . . I understand your feelings, Bishop, but the Church has to keep a shrewd eye on the commercial world . . . as it has always done in the past . . .'

. . . her eyes . . . why did she look at me in that way . . . why was the Host unacceptable to her . . .?

'. . . findings from the Institute for the Works of Religion, the Vatican itself, Bishop . . .'

'. . . think not . . .'

'. . . bank itself . . . I'm sure they'll accept a modest collateral from the Roman Catholic Church . . . already spoken with the manager . . . member of the parish council . . .'

. . . meat . . . no taste . . . must eat, Bishop says must eat . . . her eyes . . . she knew . . . what are they saying . . .? Must stop them . . .

'. . . design a centre-piece, something like the one designed for the papal visit to Phoenix Park in Ireland. . . . stunning simplicity . . .'

. . . can't swallow . . . the meat . . . can't swallow . . . oh, my God . . . it's growing . . . the meat is growing . . . in . . . my . . .

'Father!'

Delgard rose from his seat, the chair clattering backwards onto the floor. He reached for the choking priest, alarmed at the bluey-redness of the man's face, the wheezing breath squeezed from his open mouth.

Fenn ran round to the other side of the table. 'He's choking!' he cried. 'For Christ's sake, he's choking on something!'

. . . filling me . . . can't breathe . . . growing, growing . . .!

Father Hagan twisted in his chair, hands tearing at his throat. He tried to speak, tried to scream, but his words were blocked by the meat that was expanding in his gullet. He fell forward on the table, his wine glass tipping, cutlery jumping with the impact. His dinner plate crashed to the floor as his upper body straightened and fell back into his chair, a terrible, anguished rasping sound coming from his throat as he tried to suck in air.

'He's having a heart attack!' Bishop Caines cried. 'His heart is weak. Quickly, he must have his pills on him!'

'No, he's choking!' Fenn insisted. 'Get him forward so I can reach his back.'

Delgard held onto the squirming priest and Fenn brought his fist smashing down between the priest's shoulder blades. Father Hagan jerked with the force. Only a retching sound came from him. Fenn hit him again.

'It's no use, it won't shift!' said Delgard.

'I'll get an ambulance.' Southworth ran from the room, glad to be away from the priest's agony.

'It's a heart attack, I tell you,' said Bishop Caines.

'Okay, let's get him back and his mouth open.' Fenn reached for the priest's forehead and hauled him back into the chair. Monsignor Delgard cupped a hand beneath his colleague's chin and held his mouth open. The priest tried to twist away, the pain, the yearning to draw air into his starved lungs, unbearable.

Fenn looked into the open mouth, down into the darkness of the throat. 'There's something there, I can see it!'

He stuck his fingers into the priest's mouth, probing deep, desperate to reach the object lodged there. It took all his and Delgard's strength to keep Hagan from rolling to the floor.

'I can't reach it! Christ, I can't reach it!'

. . . hands . . . hands on me . . . can't . . . can't breathe . . . help me, God . . . eyes, her eyes . . .

His throat muscles were jerking spasmodically, but still the lump of meat would not dislodge. Instead it sank deeper. And grew larger inside him.

His body arched in a paroxysm of fear and pain and choking. He fell to the floor, taking the two men who were trying to save his life with him.

'Get his head down! Maybe we can dislodge it that way!'

. . . no good . . . it was too late . . . oh, God, the pain . . . in my chest . . . in my arms . . . oh, Jesus, they should be told . . .

'I've got it, I've got it! Hold him, I can . . .'

The priest screamed and the sound was just an agonized gurgling, a clogged scream of mortal dread. His body threshed wildly, his face took on a bluish tinge . . .

. . . into They hands . . .

. . . his eyes reflected the fear of approaching death . . .

. . . I commend . . .

. . . the noise from his throat was continuous, a wet, rattling sound . . .

. . . my spirit . . .

. . . that died just seconds after he died . . .

. . . forgive me . . .

TWENTY-ONE

And did the Countenance Divine
Shine forth upon our clouded hills?
And was Jerusalem builded here
Among these dark Satanic Mills?

JERUSALEM
William Blake

Cold. Bloody balls-chilling cold.

Fenn locked the car door and pulled the lapels of his dark overcoat tight around his neck. Vapour from his mouth spread a small round mist over the side window as he stopped to insert the key into the lock. He straightened and looked towards the church.

For once the entrance to the grounds wasn't crowded with Pressmen. Probably yesterday's funeral had satiated their appetites for a while.

He trudged towards the gate, the earth verge beside the road, long since trampled of its grass, hard and brittle. Jagged ridges crumbled beneath his boots. A solitary figure watched him warily as he approached.

'Cold morning,' Fenn called out.

The man nodded.

'I'm Fenn, *Brighton Evening Courier*,' the reporter said when he reached the gate.

'I know you,' replied the man, a volunteer helper to St Joseph's, 'but I'd better see your Press card.'

Fenn fumbled for his wallet, his fingers already stiff with the chill. He flicked it open and produced his identity card. The man grunted, satisfied.

'I've come to see Monsignor Delgard.'

The man opened the gate. 'Yes, he left word.'

Fenn stepped through. 'Not so busy this morning.'

The man carefully closed the gate, then looked at the reporter. 'They'll show up later. Most are down at the convent.'

He pulled out a handkerchief and blew his nose.

'I've just passed it. There's a few there, not many.'

'I suppose they had their fill yesterday. Leeches.' He stared at Fenn, no apology in his gaze.

'Did you know Father Hagan well?' the reporter asked, ignoring the slight.

'He was a good man. A good, hard-working man. This was all too much for him, I suppose, with his weak heart. We'll miss him.'

Fenn moved on leaving the man shaking his head, blowing his nose.

He went to the house and the door was opened by a young priest, one that the reporter either hadn't seen or hadn't noticed before. There were several at St Joseph's now, acting as clerks, secretaries – crowd controllers.

The priest smiled and said in a soft, Irish accent, 'Mr Fenn? Ah yes, Monsignor Delgard is at the church. Will I fetch him for you?'

'It's okay, I'll go over.'

Fenn turned away and the priest watched him walk towards St Joseph's for several moments before quietly closing the door.

The reporter shivered. There was a faint mist rising up against the old building and swirling around the scattered green-stained headstones. He knew the freshly-dug plot was on the other side, a secluded place in the graveyard close to the boundary wall, and felt no desire to see it. Watching Father Hagan's coffin lowered into its frigid pit had disturbed him as much as when his parents, both dying within weeks of each other, one of cancer and the other, like the priest, of heart disease, were buried. It was as though the covering of earth were really the final and irrevocable consummation of life, the moment of death itself just the first phase. He had known others whose deaths were premature (didn't death always seem premature, even among the aged – not many were ever quite ready) but none had affected him in this way. It had been understandable with his mother and father, for they had died when he was still in his teens and their mutual parents/son affection had not had time to sour; but the priest had been almost a stranger, had even seemed to dislike Fenn. Perhaps it was because he had tried, and failed, to save the priest's life, that he felt the loss so much. But then there was little he could have done anyway, for the post-mortem had revealed that Hagan had died of a heart attack; the meat he had swallowed may have started the priest's initial panic, but it was hardly big enough to have choked him. So why his own guilt which compounded the sense of loss? It was a question to which Fenn had no answer.

The church doors were closed and he twisted the heavy black metal ring to open one side. It was bitterly cold outside, but the church interior had a special chill to it. He closed the door and walked towards the altar, towards the black figure sitting near the front.

Monsignor Delgard did not turn around at the reporter's approach; his eyes studied the stained-glass window above the altar-piece, but his gaze was inwards.

Fenn sat next to the priest. 'Monsignor Delgard?'

The priest continued to stare. 'What is happening here?' he said, and the words were not directed at the reporter.

'Sorry, what was that?'

The priest blinked and said, 'I don't understand what is happening to this church, Mr Fenn. I don't understand why Father Hagan died, why he was so afraid.'

'Was he afraid?'

'Oh yes. He was in mortal fear.'

'He was ill.'

'Yes, he was ill. But something more. Something else took his strength.'

'I'm not following you.'

The priest sighed and lowered his face. He turned to the reporter. 'Do you believe in God, Mr Fenn?' he asked.

Fenn was surprised at the question and a little embarrassed by it. 'I think so. I'm not sure. Guess I haven't given it enough thought.'

'Everybody gives it enough thought, Mr Fenn. Are you reluctant to offend me because I'm a priest?'

'No, it isn't that. I'm really not sure, that's all. I can't believe in this great Father-figure in the sky, if that's what you mean.'

'There's no need to. In fact, it would be rather naïve to think of Him as such. Let me ask you this, then: are you afraid *not* to believe?'

'I suppose most people are.'

'But you?'

'Count me in with the crowd.'

'Do you fear death because of past transgressions?'

'No. I just hope when I get up there, He'll accept my apology. Look, what's all this got to do with Father Hagan?'

The monsignor returned his gaze to the altar. 'He was a devout priest, a truly good man; yet he was afraid of dying.'

'Maybe he had secrets you didn't know of.'

'Yes, we all have our secret shames. They're usually trivial; important – shameful – only to ourselves. Strangely, I heard Father Hagan's confession just the night before he died and I know he had nothing to fear.'

Fenn shrugged. 'Just death alone is enough. It's a big leap and no guarantee of a soft landing. Or any landing at all. It doesn't matter how strong your beliefs are, how deeply religious you may be, there's no guarantee been given, right?'

'Not quite true, Mr Fenn, but I take your point.'

'So when it came to it, Father Hagan was no different from the rest of us – scared of the pain and a little apprehensive of the Great Moment of Truth.'

'Father Hagan was afraid of what he would leave behind.'

Fenn looked puzzled.

'He was afraid of what was happening to his church.' The big priest turned to face the reporter once again, leaning one elbow on the backrest of the bench, his long fingers clasped together. 'You know, he hardly slept at all after the first so-called miracle. For some reason he no longer felt secure in his own church grounds.'

'I noticed his appearance was getting worse each time I saw him; I put it down to general ill-health, though.'

'You met him for the first time when you found the child in the field, didn't you?'

'Yeah. And he didn't look the picture of health then. But like I say, he grew worse each time I saw him. I thought it was all the pressure that'd been laid on him.'

'He was undergoing great mental stress long before that, I'm afraid. During my stay here we had lengthy discussions about St Joseph's, the child, Alice Pagett, and her visions. And about Father Hagan himself. He was a troubled man.'

'Did his, er, assignment in Hollingbourne have anything to do with his troubles?'

Delgard's features sharpened. 'Who told you of that?'

'Nobody. I just remembered the uncomfortable silence at the Press conference when a reporter from that area asked him about it. What was the problem, or is it still a big secret?'

The priest sighed. 'With your tenacity I'm sure you would find out sooner or later. It's all in the past and really not very important.'

'So if it isn't, tell me.'

'On the understanding it will go no further?'

'Absolutely.'

Delgard was satisfied. If he refused to tell, Fenn would be even more interested and would dig around until he raked up something; this way he was sworn to secrecy because of their 'off the record' agreement a few nights before.

'Father Hagan was young, a novice, when he was sent to Hollingbourne,' he began. 'He was uncertain of himself, but hard-working, eager to learn. And he was vulnerable.' Delgard fell silent and Fenn grew impatient.

'Are you trying to tell me he had an affair with one of the parishioners?'

'Not exactly. Not exactly an affair and not with one of his parishioners.' Delgard shook his head sadly. 'He . . . he formed an attachment towards his senior priest.'

'Oh, Jes –'

'There was no sexual involvement, let me make that quite clear. If that had been the case, then neither one would still be in the priesthood.'

'Then why –?'

'Rumours spread. A small place where things are noticed. Affection – deep affection – couldn't go unnoticed. It came to the attention of the bishop of that particular diocese and he quickly stepped in, fortunately before the situation could develop.'

'Forgive me for asking, but just how do you know it hadn't?'

'Both priests would have confessed the moment they were confronted.'

'You've got a high opinion of human character.'

'They wouldn't have lied.'

'So Father Hagan was assigned elsewhere.'

'Yes. The other priest – his name isn't important – left the parish some time later. I know what happened had tortured Father Hagan throughout his ecclesiastical career, and I also know such temptation was never succumbed to again. He buried himself in work and prayer.'

'But the guilt was always there?'

'He was a sensitive man. I don't believe he ever purged himself of the guilt.'

'That's something your religion dotes on, isn't it?' It was difficult to keep the rancour from his voice.

'An unkind remark, Mr Fenn and not true. However, a debate on the theosophical ideals of the Roman Catholic Church would be rather pointless at this moment. Let's confine ourselves to the topic of Father Hagan and his fears for this church.'

'That's something that's been puzzling me since the night he died. He said there was something wrong with St Joseph's and you seemed to be in agreement.'

'Look around you, Mr Fenn. Does it seem dark in here to you?'

'Well . . . yeah. But it's misty outside, the light's pretty poor.'

'Now close your eyes, tell me what you feel.'

Fenn closed his eyes.

'What do you feel?'

'Stupid.'

'Don't. Just think of the church, think of where you are.'

He didn't like it. He didn't like having his eyes closed inside the church.

'No!'

His eyes snapped open and he looked at the priest in surprise. 'I'm sorry,' he said. 'I don't know what made me shout.' He shivered. 'I . . . I don't know what happened.'

'Did you feel an atmosphere?' Delgard prodded gently.

'No, I felt nothing.' He frowned. 'Christ, that was it! I felt nothing. It's empty in here. I don't mean it's empty of people . . . but what was it you said the other night. Something about the church being spiritually devoid . . .'

'That's exactly what I said. You felt it too.'

'I . . . I don't know. It's cold, and it's creepy, let's face it. But there's something creepy about any empty church.'

'Not to a man of the cloth. A priest finds only tranquillity in an empty church, a place to pray, to meditate. There is no such peace here, just a sense of desolation.' Delgard shifted from his position, sliding forward to the edge of his seat and resting his clasped hands over the seat in front. Fenn studied the man's profile, the high-bridged nose, the firm chin, the deep furrows on his brow. Only one heavy-lidded eye was visible from that angle and there was a sadness in its gaze, a weariness reflected from within. When the priest spoke again, his voice was strong, deep, but the inner sorrow was somehow contained in its timbre.

'If Alice truly had a Visitation, then the presence of the Holy Spirit would be overwhelming inside this place.'

'You said yourself a church is just a building made of stone,' Fenn said.

'I meant that it was a physical container that could be drained of its contents just like any other container. Bishop Caines should have understood that. This church has been drained.'

'I don't get it. How can you tell?'

'You only have to feel. Just as you did a few moments ago. Father Hagan had been going through the same trauma for many weeks, only his perception was greater, his feelings stronger. You noticed yourself how he was changing physically, how his vitality was being sapped.'

'The man was ill. His heart . . .'

'No. His life-force was being drained just as the spiritual essence of his church was being drained. I should have been aware sooner, I should have realized what was happening when he told me of his doubts. He didn't believe the cures were miraculous, Mr Fenn. Nor did he believe Alice saw the Blessed Virgin. At first he wasn't sure. Alice had always been such a good child, an innocent who liked nothing better than to help her mother in her work at St Joseph's. He'd known her since she was a baby –'

'Before she was struck deaf and dumb?'

'Oh yes. He arrived in the parish just before she was born. He watched her grow, gave her her First Communion, encouraged her to play with the other children despite the disability. Yet, towards the end . . . these last few weeks . . . he was afraid of her.'

'Afraid of an eleven-year-old kid?'

'You were there at the convent last Sunday.'

'Sure. She was sick.'

'Before that. The way Father Hagan looked at her.'

'You're right, he was scared. With everything that's happened since, I'd forgotten. He looked terrified.' Fenn tapped thoughtfully on the bench. 'But he was cracking up,' he said. 'Sorry, Monsignor Delgard, I don't mean to be disrespectful to him. But you know yourself his hinges were loosening. He was just about ready to fall apart.'

'That may be so, but for good reason. The stress he was suffering would have been too much for any man.'

'You mean the publicity –'

'I mean nothing of the sort. That was only part of it. I'm talking of the mental anguish he was going through, knowing his church was being raped, knowing a child was being used –'

'Hey, wait a minute. This is all getting a little far-fetched, isn't it?'

The priest smiled, but it was a grim smile. 'Yes, Mr Fenn. Yes, you would think so, and I can't say that I blame you. You're a born cynic and I think it's probably the cynics who suffer least in this world.' He regarded the reporter with eyes that held pity in them. 'Or perhaps they suffer most, who can say?'

Fenn swung round in the seat, facing the altar, away from the priest's gaze.

'It's your very cynicism that may help in this matter, Mr Fenn,' he heard Delgard say.

He slowly turned his head to look at the priest again.

'You're not a great believer in anything, are you?' Delgard said. 'You've no deep religious beliefs, you have no family, no wife –'

'How do you know that? You don't know anything about me.'

'Oh, but I do. I've had a long discussion about you with Miss Gates, you see.'

'Sue? She wouldn't . . .' His words trailed off as the priest nodded.

'Susan is a regular visitor to the church nowadays. I'm afraid she's very confused about you at the moment, Mr Fenn.'

'Yeah, I'd noticed. But why should she tell you about me?'

'Because I asked.' Delgard's voice became brisk. 'I need your help. I found out as much as possible about you – firstly, because of the association you now have with the Church under Bishop Caines' edict, and secondly, because I think you may be able to help in other ways.'

'You're losing me again.'

'Your employer tells me you're a good journalist. A troublesome one, but basically sound. Apparently you have an inquiring mind or, as your news editor puts it, a snooper's nose. He wasn't very complimentary about other aspects of your character, unfortunately, but that does not concern me greatly.'

'I can imagine what he said.'

'Good. So you and I are both aware of your faults.'

'I didn't –'

'It was Susan who told me you had a clinical, open mind towards most things, especially where your work was concerned. I must admit, having read your first article on Alice and St Joseph's, I thought you rather too emotional, hardly objective at all. But she explained that to me, in fact made me realize just how objective you could be. It was somewhat perverse, but I suppose I should respect your opportunism in some way. You didn't *believe* in what you wrote, although you wanted your readers to believe. You very skilfully sensationalized the story without giving any clear credence to what happened. It's only on second reading and with some knowledge of the author that one can detect the deliberate ambiguity of your statement. That was your objectivity: you wrote a crude, yet on the surface, sincere piece of journalism to promote your own interests. In other words, you wanted a scoop. And that you surely got.'

'Maybe you're giving me more credit than I deserve. That's if you are giving me credit . . . I'm kinda confused.'

'You have a sharp mind, Mr Fenn. And that's what I want. I need your objectivity also.'

'Can you get to the point of all this?'

'The fact that you're cynical about the Church could mean you're also cynical about its opposite. It could give you an advantage.'

'Over what?'

'Over the evil that's surrounding us now.'

Fenn grinned. 'Oh yeah?'

'You see, if you don't believe, then you won't be so afraid. Evil is a parasite that breeds on people's beliefs.'

'I thought it bred on ignorance.'

'It's often the ignorant who have unreasonable beliefs. But yours is not that kind of ignorance. You would believe something if it was proved conclusively to you and, furthermore, you would seek that proof; the ignorant would not. And that's what I want you to do, Mr Fenn. I want you to seek.'

Fenn tucked his hands into his overcoat pocket. He wasn't sure if it was the conversation or the church itself that made him feel so cold. 'Just what is it you want me to seek, Monsignor Delgard?'

'I want you to find out about this church.'

Fenn looked at him in surprise. 'Surely that'd be easier for you to do.'

'Objectivity, Mr Fenn, and practicality. I shall be too busy in the next few months organizing St Joseph's itself, preparing for pilgrims, supervising the building work that will have to be carried out. As for objectivity, I'm too ensconced in the dreadful atmosphere of this place, too involved with the tragedy of Father Hagan, to see anything in a pure, objective light. More than that, I want you to find out about the village. It needs a researcher's eye, someone who can dig deep, find answers. You've already reached an agreement with Bishop Caines and George Southworth; this would merely be part of that work. All I ask is that you look for something more, something that could have happened here in the past.'

'Like what?'

'I don't know. That's for you to find out.'

Fenn shrugged. 'Okay. As you say, it would be part of the job anyway.'

'And one more thing: I want you to find out more about Alice Pagett. And her parents. There's something missing and I've no idea what it is. I only know we must find out.'

'I think you may be coming a little unhinged yourself, Monsignor.'

Delgard studied him coldly for a moment, then said, 'That's good. I want you to think that way. But before you leave, I want to show you something.' He rose from the bench and Fenn quickly followed suit, stepping into the aisle so the priest could get through.

Delgard genuflected before the altar, then walked towards the right-hand side of the church. He turned back towards Fenn when he was below the statue of Our Lady.

'Would you please come here?' he said.

Fenn, hands still tucked into his pockets followed. He looked curiously into the face of the tall priest who indicated the statue with a nod of his head. 'Father Hagan told me Alice loves this statue, that she used to spend long periods sitting before it. You could say it was almost an obsession. *If* her visions were merely the hallucinations of a disturbed mind, it's not improbable that they would take the form of something she was fascinated by. Take a good look at the statue.'

He remembered studying the statue just two weeks before, on the Sunday of the miracles. He had noticed a flaw then, the faintest crack running from beneath the chin down one side of the neck.

Now the effigy was a mass of black lines, a crazy network of thin jagged veins that covered almost every inch of white stone. Cracks running from the corners of the Madonna's lips gave her a grotesque smile, an obscene leer. Even her sightless eyes were cruelly scarred.

Instead of a finely sculptured and compassionate image of the Madonna, it seemed that a hideously wrinkled harridan stared down upon the two men, her ravaged palms a mocking gesture of supplication.

Fenn stepped away, as if fearing the stone figure might reach down and touch him.

TWENTY-TWO

Dame, dame! the watch is set:
Quickly come, we are all met.
From the lakes and from the fens,
From the rocks and from the dens,
From the woods and from the caves,
From the churchyards, from the graves,
From the dungeon, from the tree,
That they die on, here are we!
  Comes she not yet?
  Strike another heat!

THREE WITCHES' CHARMS:
Ben Jonson

He walked down the gravel path towards the gate. Overhead the branches of the leafless trees joined, forming a web-like canopy. Thin, winter-brittle branches snapped against each other, the cold breeze that shifted the mist causing their movement. His footsteps were unnaturally loud, as they had been inside the church, but now there was no echo, no hollow sound to reflect the emptiness of the sanctum. It was dark beneath the trees, almost as dark as inside the church.

The whole business was crazy! Bloody stupid crazy! What was Delgard trying to pin on the kid? An eleven-year-old, for Christ's sake! How the hell could she cause any harm? And why should she? Was he implying she was in some way responsible for Hagan's death? She hadn't even been there!

He stopped for a moment, breathing fiercely.

Delgard was becoming as neurotic – as paranoid – as Father Hagan! He just couldn't be serious! He had almost begun to believe the priest. Christ, he was nearly as crazy as the two of them!

He continued walking, shoving his hands deep into his overcoat pockets.

But the statue. What the fuck had happened to the statue? A flaw in the stone? Huh! That was a new one! Running cracks like ladders in tights. Maybe someone had been secretly pounding away at it. No way. It would have been chipped. The statue had scared him. It was somehow . . . repulsive! Jesus, Delgard was to blame. He was the one making him jittery.

He jumped when something stepped out of the shadows.

'All finished, Mr Fenn?'

'Jes – . You gave me a fright.'

The man chuckled as he opened the gate for the reporter. 'Sorry about that. I was just keeping out of the breeze. Bit chilly.'

'Yeah.' Fenn stepped through the gate, glad to be outside the church grounds.

'Hey, Fenn,' a familiar husky voice called out. He turned to see the journalist from the *Washington Post* approaching. 'What gives?' she said. 'You look white as a ghost.'

'It's the weather,' he replied, heading for his car.

'Funny. I usually get a red nose.' She kept pace with him.

There were one or two cameramen loitering by the side of the road, but they lost interest when they saw it was only a fellow-journalist who had emerged from St Joseph's.

'I saw you drive past me in the village,' the woman at his side told him. 'Figured you were on your way up here. How about a lift back to the hotel?'

He opened the car door, then straightened. 'It's Nancy, isn't it?'

'Yup. Shelbeck. We met last Sunday.'

He nodded. 'Jump in.'

With no further heeding, she ran round to the other side of the car. Fenn climbed in and opened the passenger door. She joined him inside and smiled her thanks.

'You're right,' he said. 'You do get a red nose.' He started the engine.

She waited until he had pulled out into the road, reversed back, then headed the Mini in the direction of the village, before asking, 'How come you get into St Joseph's when nobody else can?'

'You could have got in through the field next door.'

'You wanna bet? They've got a couple of priests posted out there.'

He took a quick glance at her. Even though her nose *was* red, she was an attractive woman. He noticed she had green eyes.

'So you were going to tell me?' she said.

'Tell you what?'

'Why you were allowed in.'

'The Pope's my uncle.'

'Come on, Fenn, give.'

'You could say I'm there by, er, papal appointment. I've been officially authorized to write the story of St Joseph's and the Holy Miracles.'

'Shit, how did you manage that?'

'They know an ace when they see one.'

'Forgive me for saying so, but you don't seem so happy about it. Money not too good?'

He laughed humourlessly. 'D'you know, I forgot to mention money.'

'How remiss. I'm sure you'll make it in other ways, though.'

'I'll do my best.'

'As a matter of fact, that's what I wanted to talk to you about. Remember I mentioned it last Sunday.'

'You said something about comparing notes.'

'Uh huh. Look, why don't we stop and have a drink?'

'At this time of the morning?'

'It's gone ten. Nearly half-past, actually. Your country pubs open early here. Come on, you look as if you need a snort.'

'You don't know how right you are,' he said, shaking his head.

They had almost reached the edge of Banfield where the first of the village's two public houses stood. He indicated left and pulled into its courtyard. There were several other vehicles already parked even at that early hour, but he knew many of the locals used the pubs as coffee shops that early in the morning, as they did the Crown Hotel further along the High Street.

The White Hart had just one L-shaped bar; polished brasses and hunting horns adorned the walls, and the heavy beams set in the low ceiling gave the interior a feeling of ancient solidity. A freshly-lit fire blazed in the huge inglenook fireplace. There were no more than a dozen people drinking, some of whom were vaguely familiar to Fenn. He recognized them as Pressmen.

'What d'you want to drink?' he asked the *Washington Post* reporter.

'No, let me. It was my invitation.'

Fenn acquiesced. 'Make mine a Scotch, no ice, no water.'

He found a seat by a window while she ordered the drinks from a tall, bearded and bespectacled barman, and settled into it with a silent sigh. Jesus, his legs felt weak. The statue . . . it was hard to clear the hideous image from his mind. How could something like that happen? He could understand the stonework cracking into such a fine network over the years – and it would take a good many years for such results – but to reach that state in just under two weeks? It was impossible! And what was Delgard insinuating? What was –?

'I got you a double. You could use it.'

He stared blankly at the woman, then at the glass she was offering.

'Thanks,' he said, taking the whisky and drinking half in one gulp.

'I was right,' she observed. She sat next to him and sipped her drink from a half-pint glass.

'Bitter?' he asked in surprise.

'Sure. I like to try your beer. Want to tell me what's on your mind?'

Fenn studied her closely, taking in more than he had on their first meeting. Her dark hair had a reddish tinge to it, not one that came from a bottle, though (at least, not obviously so). It was still difficult to determine her age, for she was one of those women who could be either younger than she looked or older, but never guessed exactly. Her eyes, which were alert, watchful, said older – maybe approaching forty – but her skin, which was pale and smooth, and her lips, which were not full but were well defined, said younger. Her nose was a little too straight to make her pretty, but it gave her an appearance of attractive strength. She had removed her topcoat and her figure was trim, if not particularly shapely, beneath the roll-topped sweater and straight-legged trousers. He had noticed the high-heeled boots she wore earlier and they were of thin burgundy leather, stylishly cut.

'I feel as though I'm under a microscope,' she said.

'I was just thinking,' he said. 'You fit the image.'

'Hmn?'

'The hard-bitten New York reporter-lady.'

'Thanks. You must have a way with women.'

He laughed. 'Sorry, I didn't mean that nastily. As a matter of fact, it was a kind of compliment.'

'Yeah? I'd hate to hear your snipes.' She sipped her bitter again, then reached inside her bag for cigarettes. She offered him one first and he shook his head. She lit her own with a slim Dunhill lighter. 'What's the problem, Fenn?' she said, blowing blue smoke across the small table.

'My name's Gerry,' he said evenly.

She smiled. 'I think I prefer Fenn.'

He returned her smile, beginning to enjoy her company. 'I think I do too.'

'Is it the death of the priest, this Father Hagan, that's upsetting you? I understand you were actually there when he had his heart attack.'

He nodded. 'The post-mortem said it was a heart attack, but I was sure he was choking. I tried to save him.' He took another long swallow of Scotch. 'I'm certain I saw the meat in his throat. Christ, I even tried to yank it out.'

'But the coroner would have known if it was asphyxiation.'

'Maybe it was both, I don't know. Maybe he just imagined he was choking. The priest was in a pretty hysterical state towards the end.'

'That's likely when your heart is seizing up.'

'No, I didn't mean then. He was in a highly-strung state for weeks before.'

She was thoughtful for a moment. 'I noticed there was something peculiar about him that Sunday at the convent. Are you saying, in your sweet way, that he was bananas?'

'No . . . just, well, neurotic. He was upset by what was happening at the church.'

'But that had to be fantastic for any priest. He actually witnessed the miracles himself. What was it he didn't like? The publicity?'

Fenn realized he was saying too much. As a reporter himself, he should have known better. He quickly changed the subject. 'Have you got a deal to offer me?'

She raised her eyebrows. 'Where's your British reserve? Okay, to business. How'd you like to form a partnership with me in this little enterprise. We work together, you supply the information, I write the story for my paper, I get you a fat fee. I also get you your name alongside mine.'

'Are you kidding? Why the hell do I need you?'

'Because I'm a better writer.'

He put his empty glass down. 'I need another drink.'

'At this hour of the morning? Hey, wait a minute, don't get sore. Look, you're good, but I hate to say it – you're provincial. Come on, don't get up, just listen. You haven't had the experience of working on a National yet. I know, I've checked. You haven't the experience of working under a good editor, I mean, someone who's going to kick your butt 'til you get it right, someone who's going to *show* you how to get it right –'

'My butt's been kicked plenty of times,' he said in weak defence.

'Yeah, but there's different ways to kick different asses. All I'm saying is that you haven't had the right guidance yet. Sure, you're good to a degree, and okay, you're going to get a lot of offers; but I can make whatever you do with this thing better. Believe me, much, much better. And if you want to get down to figures –'

Fenn was no longer paying attention. He was looking towards the door, which had just opened. A figure stood there, staring around the pub as if looking for someone. Two men immediately rose from their seats at the bar and hurried towards the man.

'That's Len Pagett,' Fenn said, more to himself than to the woman.

'Pagett? Oh, yeah, Alice's father.'

Fenn was already out of his seat, quickly making towards the three men, who were now shaking hands. Nancy Shelbeck soon followed.

'Mr Pagett?' Fenn said, barging into the group and offering an outstretched hand. 'You've met me before. I'm Gerry Fenn, *Brighton Evening Courier*.'

One of the other men quickly stepped in between Fenn and Pagett. 'On your bike, Fenn,' the man said, his voice almost a snarl. 'Mr Pagett's ours. We've made an arrangement.'

'Who're you?' Fenn asked, but he had already guessed. He now recognized one of the men as a reporter from one of the heavies.

'He's signing an exclusive contract with the *Express*,' the other man, who was just as belligerent, told him. 'And that means he doesn't talk to any other papers.'

'Don't be bloody silly. You can't –'

'Piss off.' A hand shoved him, and the first man took Pagett by the arm. 'Let's go somewhere quiet, Mr Pagett, where we can talk. We've got the contract ready for you.'

Pagett looked confused. 'Can't I have a drink first?'

'We've got plenty where we're going,' the first reporter assured him. 'It's not far.' He guided him towards the door.

The few other journalists in the bar who had been taking a sneaky morning nip (purely to keep out the cold for when they took up their vigils outside the church and the convent) were converging on the shuffling group.

'What's going on, Fenn?' Nancy asked when she reached his side.

'These bastards have done a deal with Alice's father. They won't let him talk to anyone.'

The second *Express* reporter blocked the doorway. 'That's right, he belongs to us now.'

'Wait a minute,' the New Yorker said. 'Has he signed any agreement yet?'

'That's none of your business.'

Fenn smiled thinly. 'I just heard you say you had the contract ready. That means he hasn't signed.'

The *Express* reporter wasted no more time with words. He whipped open the door and sped through, slamming it hard behind him.

'What's going on here?' The tall, bearded barman blinked through his glasses as the crowd barged through the doorway in pursuit. He welcomed the business, but wasn't too keen on the rowdiness of the journalists.

Outside in the carpark, a silver-grey Capri was revving up its engine and the *Express* reporter was running towards it. He pulled open the passenger door as the car moved off and jumped in.

Fenn and those who had followed him from the pub had to step back to avoid being hit.

'Where're they taking Pagett?' Nancy Shelbeck yelled.

'Probably to some nearby hotel. They'll keep him locked away for a few days where no one can find him.'

'That can't be legal.'

'It is if he agrees to it.' Fenn broke away, heading for his Mini. He climbed in, thankful that he hadn't locked the doors. Through the windscreen he saw the other journalists scurrying for their own vehicles. The Capri was disappearing into the High Street. His passenger door swung open as he started the engine.

'This is ridiculous,' Nancy said, and she was laughing. 'It's like the goddam Keystone Cops!'

Fenn didn't have time to enjoy the humour, nor to tell her to get out of his car. He shoved it into first and roared across the carpark, swinging left into the High Street, barely looking to see if the coast was clear. He was in luck: the Capri carrying Len Pagett and the two journalists had been forced to stop at a zebra crossing while two old ladies, lost in conversation, ambled across.

He slapped the steering wheel in triumph. 'Got the bastards! They won't lose me now.'

Nancy laughed aloud. 'I don't believe this!'

Tyres burnt the road as the Capri screeched off. Heads turned as Fenn pushed his foot down and followed suit.

'Take it easy, Fenn. It isn't worth getting killed for!'

Both cars roared down the High Street as others, driven by the slower journalists, began to emerge from the carpark. Vehicles were parked on both sides of the road, making its centre a narrow channel and forcing the two cars to slow down when they met others coming from the opposite direction. Fenn was aware that it would be tougher to keep up once they were through the village and out on the open road, but he had an advantage: he knew the roads. He guessed they were heading for Brighton, using one of the many hotels there as a hideaway, and cursed them (although he didn't blame them) for their opportunism. Somehow, because of his involvement, he felt proprietor of this story and that the other newspapers were infringing on his territory. From what he had learned of Len Pagett, and from what he had surmised of the man himself, he wasn't surprised he had sold out to 'cheque-book journalism'. No one had to be famous any more to make money from selling their own personal story; they just had to know somebody who was.

The Capri was fifty yards ahead, approaching the end of the village. Fenn could see the road junction in the distance, the small roundabout, the garage next to it, the convent. Clear of parked vehicles, he increased his speed, desperate to keep up with the Capri, guessing it would turn left at the roundabout, keeping to the main road rather than carrying straight on into the minor one. The High Street was busy with shoppers, many of whom shook their heads in disgust at the racing cars, perhaps resigning themselves to the advance symptoms of what their once peaceful village was about to become.

Next to him, Nancy Shelbeck bit into her lip, amused by the chase but a little alarmed also.

They were nearing the roundabout. Shoppers were hurrying in and out of a grocery shop on the left, bags full, purses not so full. A huge yellow and green tanker stood in the garage forecourt on the right, shedding its load into the tanks beneath the pumps. Fresh virgin cars gleamed in the large showroom windows by the side of the service bay. A green, single-decker bus negotiated the tiny roundabout, rolling over the white-painted bump in the road as it headed into the village. The driver was accelerating as his bus straightened up.

The Capri barely slowed as it approached the roundabout.

Fenn did not know why he glanced ahead at the cream walls of the convent; the compulsion was just there.

He saw the small white face at the window, blackness behind giving it prominence. Instinctively he knew it was Alice. Watching the High Street.

Looking at the cars.

Too late he saw the car in front weaving from side to side as though the diver had no control. He was almost upon it. Nancy was screaming. He was trying to turn the wheel, trying to avoid crashing into the erratic Capri. But the wheel had no say in what direction the vehicle took. It moved in its own wild direction.

He jabbed hard on the footbrake, but it was too hard, too panicked. The wheels locked, the car skidded.

The green bus, horrified faces peering from its windows like a row of peas in a split pod, turned to avoid the wildly-spinning Capri, but there was only one direction the driver could take. Into the garage forecourt. Where the tanker was emptying its contents.

The Capri smashed into the front corner of the bus, its bonnet buckling instantly, its engine rising up and sheering through its own windscreen into the screaming faces of the two men in front. The bus driver went forward with the impact, through the large front glass of his cab, hurtling beneath the tanker a split second before his bus hit it. Mercifully he was dead before he could realize what was going to happen.

As the long tube pumping fuel into the underground petrol tanks was sheered by screeching metal, sparks flew in all directions showering into the spilling volatile liquid.

Fenn saw the crash and cried out as his own car smashed through the showroom window. He was only vaguely aware of the blinding flash and the thunderous whoosh as the petrol tanker exploded.

TWENTY-THREE

'Your life is finished,' and he threw her down, dragged her into the room by her hair, struck off her head on the block and chopped her into pieces so that her blood streamed all over the floor. Then he threw her into the basin with all the others.

FITCHER'S BIRD
The Brothers Grimm

Someone was shaking him. He groaned, but the effort to open his eyes was too much. His cheek rested against something hard.

A single voice began to filter through the cacophony of sounds, sounds which he wasn't sure were inside or outside his head. He groaned. Christ, his head hurt!

Tentatively he forced his eyes open, the effort exhausting, like trying to will himself awake from a nightmare. A face was nearby, a woman's face, someone he vaguely recognized.

'Fenn, are you all right?'

He wasn't ready to reply.

Hands reached around his shoulders and he was pulled off the steering wheel back into his seat. He felt his jaw clutched and his head shaken. He opened his eyes again and this time it was hardly any effort at all. There was something wrong with Nancy's face, but he couldn't figure what. It was smeared red; thick cherry juice, dark red ink. No, blood. Her face was bleeding. He struggled to sit upright.

'Thank God,' he heard her say.

'What happened?' he managed to gasp, and it all flooded into his head before she replied. The careering Capri, the green bus, the petrol tanker – oh Jesus, all those people. His mind snapped into instant attention.

The Mini's windscreen was a spider's silver web of shattered glass, but through the side windows he could see the gleaming bodywork of that year's models. Yet there was a darkness out there that puzzled him until he realized it was swirling black smoke. A figure rushed by the window, arms waving, shouting incoherently. Fenn turned to the woman next to him.

'You okay? Your face . . .'

'It's okay. I hit the windscreen when we went through the showroom window.' She put a hand to her forehead and brought it away smeared with blood. 'It doesn't hurt; I think it's just a gash.' She clutched his arm. 'We've got to get out of here, Fenn. The tanker . . . the tanker out there exploded. The whole place is going up in flames . . .'

He pushed open the driver's door and the heat hit him immediately, even though the car showroom was partially shielded by a side wall. The smoke was growing thicker by the second and he began to cough as the acrid fumes poured into his nose and throat.

'Come on, quick!' he urged her.

'My door's stuck! It's jammed up against a car you hit!'

He pushed his own door open as far as it would go, denting the side panel of the new Rover standing next to the crashed Mini. He jumped out, then reached back inside to help her across. Nancy came scuttling through, almost throwing herself into the open. Fenn held her steady and quickly took in his surroundings.

Not much was left of the showroom window his car had smashed through; huge, lethal-looking shards of glass hung from the top like transparent stalactites. Smoke poured through the opening, filling the area with its choking denseness, and fire was already spreading across the width of the broken window. Flames filled the glass doorway by the side of the window and this suddenly exploded inwards with the heat. Fenn realized burning petrol must have spread all over the garage forecourt and was attacking anything flammable.

He pulled Nancy back, closing the door of the Mini so they could squeeze through the cars towards the rear of the showroom. 'Keep low!' he yelled at her. 'Try to keep under the smoke!'

To the rear of the display area was a glass partitioned office and he quickly ascertained that there was no back exit from it. The office was empty of people, the figure he had seen rushing by moments before obviously the salesman or manager who had occupied the room. Nancy doubled over, her body wracked by choking coughs.

Holding her tightly, giving her support, Fenn looked around for some other means of escape. He thanked God when he saw the door to his left.

Nancy almost collapsed to her knees when he tried to drag her towards the door. He allowed her to sag for a few moments, kneeling beside her, waiting for her coughing spasm to cease. Her eyes were streaming tears and her face was now a red mask from smeared blood.

'There's a way out, just over there!' he shouted over the rumbling, burning sound and the splintering of glass, the cracking of burning wood.

'Okay,' she gasped, at last controlling the seizure. 'I'll be okay! Just get me out of here!'

Fenn half-lifted her to her feet and she leaned against him as they made for the door. Such was their momentum that they stumbled against it and Fenn pushed out a hand to cushion the impact. He quickly pulled his hand away. The wood was scorching hot.

He pulled Nancy to one side, his back against the wall beside the doorframe. She looked at him questioningly, but all he said was, 'Keep back!'

Crouching, he reached for the door handle. It, too, was hot and he ignored the pain as he gave it a twist and flicked the door open.

Nancy screamed as flames roared through, bursting into the showroom as though exhaled from the jaws of a dragon. They both fell back to escape the intense heat and lay panting on the floor in a tangled heap as the fire withdrew to lap around the edges of the opening. Within seconds the door itself was blazing.

They rose and staggered away, collapsing against the bonnet of a Maxi. Both were retching now, their vision blurred by smoke-caused tears. Fenn tore off his overcoat and pulled it over their heads as they lay half-across the bonnet.

'We'll have to go out the front way – through the window!' he yelled.

'It's too hot there! We'll never make it!'

'We've got no choice! There's no other way!'

But by now, even that choice was not open to them.

They raised their heads from the overcoat and stared in disbelief at the wide showroom windows. The broken one, the window Fenn's Mini had smashed through, was totally filled with yellow-red churning flames, tongues of fire licking inwards to scorch the ceiling. A thick column of concrete separated it from the adjacent window, where the glass was already beginning to crack with the heat. The fire had spread across at least half its surface, the ground outside molten hot as the petrol gushed forth and flowed burning across the concourse outside.

'Oh my God, we're trapped,' Nancy moaned.

Fenn looked around wildly. There had to be another way out! The ceiling, a skylight. Through the billowing smoke he could tell the ceiling was solid as he realized there were offices above, not a roof. A stairway then, there had to be a way up. No stairway. It had to be through the doorway behind him, which was now no more than an opening into the furnace beyond. The fire was moving in, greedily pouncing on the hard plastic tiles of the showroom, creating fumes that were more choking and more lethal than the smoke above.

The display windows were the only way out.

He pulled the reporter upright and bent close to her ear. 'We're going out the front way!'

She shook her head. 'We'll never make it!'

Fenn wiped his sleeve across his eyes, then reached for a handkerchief, spreading it across his mouth and nose. He tugged at her roll-neck sweater, unfolding the material at the neck so it covered her lower face. Yanking her off the bonnet and holding the overcoat before them as a shield, he led her towards the front of the showroom in a stumbling run. He left her crouched between his own Mini and the Rover parked next to it and raced towards the still unbroken window. He ducked as a long jagged crack appeared in the glass and a sound like a gunshot rang out. For one long, dreadful moment he thought the window would shatter inwards to flail his body with shards of dagger-like glass, but the huge panes held. He went forward again, one arm holding his coat out to protect himself from the terrible heat. The display windows were the type that slid back into each other, depending on which side the salesman wanted to drive a car through, and Fenn went to the far corner, to the side that had been furthest from the fire; only now the scene outside was almost obliterated by the spreading flames.

He pulled at the handle and cried out as the red hot metal burned his fingers. Using the material of the overcoat to protect his hands, he tried again, but to no avail: the window was either locked, or the metal frame had swollen with the heat, jamming it solid within its housing. He swore, more of a scream of frustration than a curse.

The heat and fear of the glass exploding inwards forced him back. He returned to his companion who was slumped against the door of the Rover.

'It's no good! The window won't open!'

She looked at him fearfully, then yelled, 'Shit!' She grabbed his lapel and pulled him down to her. 'Can't you break the goddam window?'

'Even if I could the fire out there would roast . . .' he broke off. 'Prick!' he called himself.

He shoved her away from the car door and swung it open, groaning with disappointment when he discovered there were no keys in the ignition. Quickly he stood, then rolled over the Rover's bonnet to the Marina standing next to it. He yanked open the door and was once again thwarted: no keys. He went back over the bonnet and landed next to the woman.

'The keys must be in the office!' he shouted. 'You wait here!'

Then he was running back, crouching low behind a car as he passed the open doorway where the fire raged, noticing the floor around it was now blazing. Coughing and spluttering into the handkerchief, Fenn reached the rear office. He hurriedly pulled open drawers, spilling their contents onto the floor in his haste. No keys, no keys, no bloody keys! He looked around wildly, desperately. Where the fuck . . .? He groaned aloud when he saw the hooks in a cork notice board on the wall; labelled keys were hanging from each hook. He rushed to them, examined the labels, found two tagged 'Rover'. Taking both sets he dashed back into the showroom.

The suffocating heat hit once more and he knew that soon the whole area would be in flames. His breathing was laboured, drawn in in short, sharp gasps. The oxygen was being eaten by the heat and what remained was smoke-filled. He was staggering by the time he reached the woman.

He climbed into the Rover, Nancy crouching at the open door beside him. 'There won't be any gas in it!' she shouted.

'Course there bloody will! How d'you think they get them in here?' He jabbed in the first key, praying it would be the right one. It was. The engine roared into life. 'Jump in the back and keep down!' he screamed at her over the noise.

Without further bidding, she slammed his door shut, opened the one behind, and leapt in. The car was moving forward before she had slumped into the back seat. She tucked in her legs just as the Rover's momentum swung the passenger door shut.

Tyres screeched against the plastic floor as he stuck his foot down hard on the accelerator. The car zoomed towards the window and Fenn raised his arm to protect his face, hoping nothing solid was just beyond the flames outside.

Nancy screamed as the Rover burst through the huge panes of glass.

Shards flew back at the windscreen, but it withstood their onslaught. The car was engulfed by the fire and Fenn kept his foot down, holding the steering wheel straight, expecting the vehicle to explode into flames at any moment.

It could have been little more than two seconds before they broke free of the fire, but for both of them it seemed like an eternity. The smell, the heat – the fear – was overpowering, and the sight of blinding, twisting flames all around was a nightmare that they would never forget. Self-preservation rather than coolness kept Fenn's foot down.

He yelled in triumph as they emerged from the inferno, the cry turning into one of panic as he saw the stationary car immediately in his path. He swung the wheel hard to his right and the Rover went into a curving skid, smashing sideways on into the other vehicle. His body bounced off the driver's door to be thrown across the passenger seat. Crushed metal made fierce rending sounds and the car jerked violently as its engine cut out. One of Fenn's hands was still on the steering wheel and he used it to pull himself upright. Without thinking he switched off the ignition.

He drew in deep mouthfuls of air, the burning stench still present but not to the same overwhelming degree. His eyes widened as he stared at the carnage before him.

Balls of flame were rolling upwards into the smoke-filled air, their very brightness, let alone the heat, stinging his eyes. The tanker itself was completely engulfed in fire, only brief glimpses of its shape visible as the flames shifted and weaved; most of the garage forecourt was alight, the burning liquid still spreading, still greedily devouring anything in its path. The car showroom was totally hidden behind a blazing wall, the top part of the building, where the offices were, already scorched black. There were faces at the open windows, terrified, screaming faces, with eyes that beseeched the people below to help them, *please, please help!*

The very ground shimmered with the heat and there were people crawling, dragging themselves away from the devastation. The green bus was imbedded in the side of the petrol tanker, half its length a mass of flames; most of the windows were shattered and there were still some passengers left, those who had not been instantly burned to death or made incapable of moving by the initial blast, struggling through the flames, bodies cut by remaining glass fragments, flesh seared by the intense heat. The silver-grey Capri was several yards away from the two burning vehicles as though it had rebounded on impact, but there were flames all around, licking at the metal body, melting the glass of its windows.

Fenn blinked his eyes against the glare. Had he seen something move in the back of the car?

Everywhere there were people running, staggering away from the destruction, but one or two moving towards it as if fascinated by the danger, the mayhem. Those who were paralysed by fear crouched against walls, or cowered behind cars.

A face was suddenly next to his, a tear-streaked, blood-smeared image that for a moment, through shock, he failed to recognize.

'You did it, Fenn!' Nancy shouted, her voice cracked and almost tearful. Her arm went around his neck and she pressed her cheek against his in a hug that made him wince. It also helped bring him to his senses. He pulled himself free and reached for the doorhandle. 'We've got to get away!' he shouted back at her. 'There'll be other petrol tanks below ground that the fire hasn't touched yet! When the heat reaches them . . .' He left the sentence unfinished, but Nancy understood the implication.

The dry, scorched air hit them like a blast from an open furnace as they emerged from the car and both put up their arms to protect themselves. It was difficult to breathe, for the atmosphere was filled with choking fumes. Fenn turned his head away from the scene in a reflex action and immediately wished he hadn't.

The village grocery was to his left and its huge, plate-glass windows had shattered inwards. Bodies of women who had been thrown against the windows by the blast lay scattered among the wreckage inside, tins and packaged goods littered around them like fallen pieces of masonry. Some lay still, others squirmed in pain. He wondered why the legs of one woman failed to move in conjunction with her twisting torso, then realized they had been almost severed at the thighs by the shattered glass. Another woman, young and who would have been pretty were her face not contorted in agony, sat upright before the window, back resting against the wall below the frame, her hands clutching a wide rent in her throat, desperately trying to squeeze the sides together to prevent her life's blood from gushing out. Red liquid began to pump between her fingers as he watched.

The noise, the confusion – the screams for help – battered against his reeling brain. He put a hand against the Rover to steady himself and the metal was hot.

A hand tugged at his shoulder and Nancy was shouting, 'Fenn, there's someone moving in the other car!'

He turned, shielding his eyes, looking over at the burning wrecks. She was right, and he had been right a moment or two before: there was someone moving in the back of the Capri, a pair of hands beating at the rear window.

'Oh Christ, it's Pagett.' It came out as a low moan, for the knowledge struck a new fear into Fenn. Nancy was staring at him and he knew what she was going to say.

'You've got to help him!'

'It's no good! I'll never get near it!'

'You can't just let him burn!'

'What can I do?' He was shouting at her, almost screaming. What the hell did she want of him?

'Something! Just do something!'

'There's a woman over there!' He pointed desperately towards the supermarket window. 'She's bleeding to death!'

'I'll take care of her!' Nancy pushed him roughly away from the Rover. 'Please try, Fenn!' she pleaded.

'So much for Woman's fucking Lib!' he yelled at her, then was running towards the fire, angry at her and shit-scared for himself.

As he drew closer to the burning vehicles, an even more intense wall of heat hit him, forcing him to whip off his jacket and hold it in front of him. He thought he could smell singeing material. Fenn moved in, feeling stifled, his skin dry and hot. Breathing was difficult, walking was agony. Not just his legs felt on fire, but so did his lungs. He lowered the guard just enough to steal a glance at the Capri.

Pagett's face was pressed against the rear window, his features flattened, the palms of his hands white against the glass. He was trying to push himself through the tailgate which was obviously locked, his mouth open to suck in scant oxygen, his eyes bulging with terror.

Fenn was forced to bring his jacket up over his head, but even that made little difference. He felt hot air rushing round him, then he was in darkness as heavy black smoke swilled down to cover the forecourt in a dense fume-filled fog. Even the winter wind was playing its part in the havoc.

He stumbled, his eyes streaming tears, his lungs heaving as they expelled the poisonous smoke. He fell and his back was scorched as he rolled over on the ground, exposing it to the worst of the heat. The skin of his face and hands felt incredibly tight as if it were shrivelling in on itself. He had to get away. It was no use. He couldn't get any closer. He would be roasted alive if he tried.

He pushed himself back, digging his heels against the concrete, using an elbow that was quickly rubbed raw to gain momentum. The jacket was held before him to protect his face, but it was smouldering fiercely as though about to burst into flames. After a few feet he raised himself to one knee and risked another look at the burning Capri. What he saw was so horrific he forgot about his own searing pain.

He only caught brief glimpses through patches of swirling smoke and at first he could not understand what was happening. A strange, unclear shape was emerging from the back window of the Capri. It seemed to be blurred as though its form were distorted by Fenn's own tears. He blinked his eyes and realized they were already dry from the scorching heat. Then he understood.

Pagett was pushing his way out of the car, but the glass had not broken. It was melting, clinging to his face and hands like thick, viscous liquid, burning and mouldering itself into his flesh, becoming a part of him. Pagett had become a writhing, ill-formed monster, a human larva prematurely struggling free from its shiny, clinging chrysalis, demented in his agony and that madness driving him on. His head twisted and his eyes were looking towards Fenn, but they saw nothing for the liquid glass had already burned its way through to the retinas. Part of his face and nose was still flattened, moulded into that shape and transfixed by the sticky covering. As he slowly, twistingly, emerged, the glass stretched, becoming thin, beginning to tear. A gaping rent appeared near his neck and shoulder, and smouldering smoke from his clothes mingled with steam from his body. He was screaming, but the sound was muted by the soft transparent screen covering his mouth.

It wasn't just the heat that made Fenn cover his eyes.

He tried to rise, but was too giddy and too weak to gain his feet. He began to crawl away, choking and sobbing as he did so. He had to get away from the horrible, dying creature in the car.

It was too much; the heat was drowning him. His hands gave way beneath him and he rolled onto his back.

Pagett was ablaze now. His arms thrashed in the air, one hand banging against the Capri's boot as though in frustrated anger. His hair burned and the glass on his face was running down his skin in red-glowing rivulets into flames from his clothes. He fell forward and was still moving, climbing from the window, an automated, charcoaled figure that had no reason, no clear driving force any more, just movement caused by pain.

The petrol tank of the Capri exploded and the hideous sight was no more.

The fresh wave of torrid air flattened Fenn and he quickly rolled onto one side, pushing with his legs in a frantic pedalling motion, expecting to burst into flames himself. There were others around him, those who had leapt from the bus windows, those who had been caught walking near the garage, those who had come too near the fire to help others. All were crawling or staggering away, all trying to reach some safe point where the heat could not touch them, where they could breathe fresh, moist air. But the fire was not diminishing. It had found fresh sustenance, more material to burn, more inflammable liquid to reinforce its energy. Vehicles within the garage itself began to explode; cans of oil and petrol flared into incandescent balls of fire. The heat in the remaining tanks below ground was building up to the point where combustion was inevitable.

Fenn cursed himself for not having run away, for not ducking into cover until the danger was over. He pushed feebly against the ground.

The cold air hit him and seemed to close every pore on his body. The heat was gone from his skin, the stinging from his eyes. He raised his shoulders from the ground, turned over onto one elbow to see what was happening, looking back at the flames, not believing what he saw.

Smoke swirled down and across the scene, forced by the wind, obscuring everything one moment, lifting to reveal all the next. The flames were dying. They seemed to be shrinking, becoming small patches of fire, losing their strength by the second. Wavering. Disappearing. The wrecked vehicles were just burnt-out, smouldering shells, the petrol station a blackened, smoking ruin.

And through the swirling smoke came a tiny figure, a small girl with blonde hair who walked slowly, unafraid, through the carnage. Her yellow dress was ruffled by the wind as she held out her hands, and what was left of the flames cooled and died completely.

PART THREE

Come, hearken then, ere voice of dread,
With bitter tidings laden,
Shall summon to unwelcome bed
A melancholy maiden!
We are but older children, dear.
Who fret to find our bedtime near.

THROUGH THE LOOKING GLASS
Lewis Carroll

TWENTY-FOUR

And like a ravenous beast which sees
The hunter's icy eye,
So did this wretch in wrath confess
Sweet Jesu's mastery.

THE OGRE
Walter de la Mare

Television broadcast from ITN, all regions, early Sunday evening:

'. . . the once peaceful village of Banfield in West Sussex today. Thousands gathered at the Roman Catholic Church of St Joseph's, hoping to catch a glimpse of Alice Pagett, the eleven-year-old schoolgirl who has been proclaimed a miracle worker. There was a two-mile-long queue of cars and coaches from both directions into the village and extra police had to be called in from the surrounding area to control the crowds. For an on-the-spot report we go over now to Hugh Sinclaire, who has been at the church since this morning . . .

HUGH SINCLAIRE: The scenes here today have been quite extraordinary. People began to gather outside St Joseph's in the early morning hours – devout Catholics, many, but others who were just sightseers, curious to catch a glimpse of this little girl whom, it's claimed, can perform miracles. And perhaps they expected to see more miracles today.

Alice Pagett came to world attention just a few weeks . . .'

Television broadcast from BBC 1, late Sunday evening:

'. . . cured five people who were suffering from various illnesses. Three were said by the medical profession to be incurable. Alice herself was deaf and dumb until – she claims – she saw a vision of the Immaculate Conception. Although there has been much scepticism over her claim, particularly from the Catholic Church itself, the fact that she and five others have been cured cannot be denied.

It's estimated that at least two thousand people went to St Joseph's this morning and that the numbers doubled throughout the day. Trevor Greaves is still in the village of Banfield tonight . . .

TREVOR GREAVES: Although the crowds have thinned considerably, there is still a vigil being kept around the old church of St Joseph's tonight. It's as though the crowds were waiting for the same apparition that Alice Pagett alleges to have seen. Earlier today the atmosphere among the many pilgrims could only have been described as electric. There was no mass hysteria – something the authorities feared among such a gathering – but there was much fainting, much weeping and much praying.

When Alice arrived for the Sunday service at 9.20 this morning, accompanied by her mother and a bodyguard of priests and policemen, she found it difficult to get anywhere near the church, let alone inside. The Mass was delayed for forty-five minutes as her protectors struggled to get this diminutive child, pale-faced and dressed in white, obviously distressed by the loss of her father, so tragically killed last Thursday . . .'

Radio broadcast from LBC, after midnight:

'. . . further interest in Alice Pagett was aroused only last Thursday when eyewitnesses say she quelled a fire which threatened to devastate a large part of Banfield village. The fire was started when a car in which Alice's own father was passenger collided with a bus and a petrol tanker. The fire was spreading, fuelled by escaping petrol from the damaged tanker. The tanker itself had been refilling tanks beneath a garage's pumps, and the danger was that the fuel below would ignite too, when Alice appeared and, eyewitnesses say, put out the fire. Ironically, Leonard Pagett was killed before his daughter arrived on the scene.

How Alice Pagett could have stopped the fire nobody knows, but those who were there claim that the flames just seemed to extinguish themselves as soon as she appeared. Accident and Fire Prevention officers who have made a thorough examination of the wreckage maintain there is no logical explanation for the incident. There was little rain that day, although it was bitterly cold. Apart from the initial explosion when the petrol tanker was hit, there were no others big enough to have "blown out" the fire. The investigation officers found half-burnt timber which should have been totally charred had the fire followed a natural course, and petrol still awash on the ground which had not burned. Only small, scattered and relatively harmless fires were still alight when the local fire brigade arrived. A fuller report is expected within the next day or so but, for the moment, the experts are saying very little.

Yesterday I spoke with people who had travelled from all over the country to St Joseph's in Banfield, many of whom were infirm themselves, or had brought along sick relatives or friends to the place they now consider to be a holy shrine . . .'

Extracts from interviews on Today, BBC Radio 4, UK, early Monday morning:

'. . . we couldn't get near the place. Somebody said the girl was there, but we didn't see her . . .'

'. . . yes, we were inside the church. There weren't supposed to be cameras in there, but there were, going off all the time. The priests couldn't control the newsmen, so I suppose they gave up in the end . . .'

'. . . she's a saint. I saw her. She looks like an angel. I suffer from chronic arthritis, but as soon as I saw her I felt better. It's her, I know it's her. She did it, no question . . .'

'. . . well, we got into the field by the side of the church. We weren't supposed to be there, the priests were trying to turn people back, but there were too many, you know? I carried my sister, I wanted to get her inside the church. She's crippled. We couldn't get anywhere near, though. Even the graveyard was swamped with people . . .'

'. . . oh, no, I'm not a Catholic. No, I just wanted to see what all the fuss was about. I saw her in the car going up to the church, but that was all. Just a flash as she went by. Still it was a day out, the kids enjoyed it . . .'

'. . . The village is chock-a-block. I couldn't even get out of my shop doorway earlier for people. Business was good. As a newsagent I was open 'til lunchtime. Had to close up long before, though – ran out of stock. I think the other traders were upset. Couldn't open up, you see, not licensed to. All the same, business should be good for the rest of the week . . .'

'. . . I camped out all night. Myself and a few hundred others. We all wanted to get into the Sunday service. I managed to, me and the wife. Yes, we saw Alice. She's got an aura about her, you know, like a saint . . .'

'. . . she's a holy child, you can tell just by looking at her. She smiled, even though she must have been dreadfully unhappy over her father. I'm sure she smiled directly at me. I felt her love go right through me, it seemed to fill every part . . .'

'. . . I'm still blind . . .'

Extracts from interviews on World at One, BBC Radio 4, UK, Monday lunchtime:

'. . . people were pushing, shoving. A girl in front of me fainted. It was terrible. Just like the Beatles all over again . . .'

'. . . everyone felt peaceful, everyone was serene. It was wonderful, like a wave of love flowing over us all . . .'

'. . . somebody stood on my foot. I think a toe's broken . . .'

'. . . we didn't want to leave. We just wanted to stay there and pray. Even though we didn't get inside the church we could feel the Holy Spirit's presence . . .'

'. . . I brought my father down from Scotland. The journey was terrible for him – he's got cancer. We only caught a glimpse of Alice, but father says he feels better, better than he has for months . . .'

'. . . everyone – well, nearly everyone – in the home wanted to come. They insisted. As it's a private nursing home, they paid for the trip. Three coaches in all. Only those who didn't want to come and those too ill to be moved were left behind . . .'

'. . . she was only tiny, but somehow, somehow she stood above us all. She seemed to shine with an inner radiance . . .'

'. . . we were packed solid lunchtime and the evening trade is just as bad – just as good, I should say. Look around, you can see for yourself. I hear all the pubs in the area are just as busy . . .'

'. . . perhaps people will now understand there is only one true faith. Alice is showing them the way . . .'

Standard, Tuesday, late edition:

MIRACLE GIRL'S FATHER BURIED

The funeral of Leonard William Pagett, father of Alice Pagett, the proclaimed 'Miracle Worker of Banfield', was held today. He was not a Roman Catholic and so was buried in a public graveyard just on the outskirts of the village. Pagett, 47, was killed in a car crash on Thursday of last week. His widow, Molly Pagett, 44, was visibly distressed, not just over the tragic loss of her husband, but over the hordes of onlookers and Pressmen who besieged the cemetery. Alice stood silently by the graveside, seemingly oblivious to the crowds and obviously shocked by the second tragedy in her short life within a week – a few days before her father's death, her parish priest, Father Andrew Hagan, to whom she was very close, died of a heart attack . . .

Transcript of interview on Nationwide, BBC 1, all regions, Tuesday, early evening:

Q:　Surely, Canon Burnes, after what happened last week, the Catholic Church cannot deny there is something rather extraordinary about the child?

A:　I wasn't there, so I can't verify what took place.

Q:　Yes, but there were many witnesses who say Alice Pagett stopped the fire. Some even say she walked through the flames.

A:　The reports are confusing, to say the least. Different witnesses claim to have seen different things. Some say she appeared to walk through the flames while others say the flames died out as she approached them. And there are a few who say that Alice didn't appear until the fire was almost extinguished.

Q:　Nevertheless, she does seem to have an extraordinary effect, wouldn't you say?

A:　It would be hard to deny.

Q:　And has the Church now reached any conclusions over the miracles Alice performed?

A:　The "alleged" miracles. They are still under investigation.

Q:　Well, do you think the Church is the correct body to carry out such an investigation?

A:　I'm sorry, I don't follow.

Q:　Perhaps parapsychologists should be looking into the matter. Or at least there should be one or two included on your committee of inquiry.

A:　We have several members of the medical profession –

Q:　That's hardly the same thing.

A:　Our findings will be open to scrutiny from any recognized scientific institution that may be interested.

Q:　But not to parapsychologists?

A:　We would not wish to exclude any respectable organization. For the moment, however, we prefer to deal with the matter on a more rational basis.

Q:　Why do you think there were no more miracles last Sunday?

A:　I haven't acknowledged that there have been any miracles at any time. Unfortunately, the media is creating a huge burden for this poor child. It's they who are creating this image of a thaumaturge.

Q:　A thaumaturge?

A:　A miracle worker. People have come to expect it of her.

Q:　Indeed, it seems St Joseph's has become a holy shrine to many. But that's hardly the fault of the media – we can only report on events that have happened.

A:　And speculate.

Q:　It's certainly a matter for speculation. How will you cope with the thousands that are bound to visit the church after all this publicity? I gather there was a near-riot on Sunday.

A: That's nonsense. The crowd was very well behaved, even though many must have been disappointed that they didn't actually see Alice.

Q: Are you expecting a larger gathering this Sunday? And if so, will you be better prepared this time?

A: I think I must emphasize to the public that it would be quite pointless to travel to St Joseph's. There really will be nothing to see.

Q: But it's true that there is construction work in progress at this very moment.

A: Yes, yes, that is true. Although we are asking the public to stay away, we must be ready for any contingency.

Q: Then you are preparing for – forgive me – a siege?

A: I hope not a siege. But yes, we are making preparations for a large number of visitors, although we are doing our utmost to discourage them from coming.

Q: Thank you for answering my question. Can you tell us the kind of, uh, preparations you're making?

A: We're simply constructing an altar-piece in the field adjacent to St Joseph's –

Q: Where Alice claims to have seen the Blessed Virgin?

A: Er, yes. Seating for as many as possible will be arranged around a central altar, but I'm afraid many will have to stand and endure the muddiness of the field itself. The Sunday service will take place there instead of inside the church.

Q: And one last question, Canon Burnes: will Alice Pagett attend Mass this Sunday?

A: That I can't say.

Conversation between building contractor and Monsignor Delgard, Wednesday morning:

'Does the tree stay, Monsignor? Shall we cut it down?'

'No. You mustn't destroy anything in this field. You have the plans. Build the platform around the tree.'

Telephone conversation between Frank Aitken, Editor of the Brighton Evening Courier, *and Head Office, London, Wednesday morning:*

AITKEN: 'I don't know where the hell Fenn is. He rang in last Friday, said he'd been burned slightly in the fire at Banfield the day before. Yeah, he saw the whole bloody thing – he was there, for Chrissakes! No, I don't know why he didn't bring in the story. I told you that last week. He said he had some leave coming, so he's decided to take it. Bloody minded? Sure it is. You want me to fire him, I'll do it gladly. You don't want me to fire him? Didn't think you would. No, I've tried his home. No reply. I even sent someone round there. No one home. No, not since Friday. Hospitals? He wasn't that badly burned, but yeah, we checked. He's just disappeared, gone, vanished. Maybe he's moon-lighting on an offer he couldn't refuse. Sure I raised his salary, soon as the story got big. I guess it wasn't enough. Christ, I've had to instruct our switchboard to politely tell all our "friends" in the business trying to contact him to go to hell. No, Fenn didn't say how long, but I'll break his bloody legs when I see him. No, Mr Winters, I won't break his bloody legs when I see him. Yes, sir, I'll kiss his arse. Thank you. I'll let you know soon as I hear.'

Extract from LBC interview, Brian Hayes Phone-In, London area, Thursday morning, with T. D. Radley, Professor of Eastern Religions and Ethics, University of Oxford:

'. . . of course, western religions emphasize God's uniqueness and regard him as a supernatural Being. Miracles can be worked by Him alone, although mere mortals may entreat Him by prayer to perform them on their behalf. Usually this is done through the personages of saints or mystics. Now, the eastern religions generally dismiss miracles altogether and this is because they tend to draw the same distinction between God and mankind. To them, such happenings are all part of the total reality and obey a kind of cosmic law. But, of course, that cosmic law is outside the material order. Although the – let's call them miracles, then – are exceptions to *our* laws of logic, our nature, if you like, their source is from Beyond and of course, the logic of Beyond is not of our understanding, but nevertheless logical in itself . . .'

Extract from article in the Guardian, *Thursday morning, VISIONARY, FRAUD, OR SELF-DELUDED by Nicola Hynek, author of Bernadette Soubirous:* The Facts Behind The Fallacy *(Hodder & Stoughton, 1968):*

. . . in his book *Vraies et Fausses dans L'Église,* Dom Bernard Billet gives a complete list of Marian visions reported to have taken place around the world between March 1928 and June 1975. There were 232 in all, two of which were in England (Stockport, 1947 and Newcastle, 1954) . . .

From the Universe, *Friday:*

BISHOPS TO DISCUSS BANFIELD MIRACLE GIRL

The curious events surrounding the 11-year-old schoolgirl, Alice Pagett, will be discussed by cardinals and bishops in Rome next month. With unprecedented swiftness the Holy See has decided the conference must take place before completion of the Church Committee's special inquiry. It is thought that there is some apprehension over the hysteria being caused by the girl's claim to have received a Visitation, and her alleged ability to perform miracles.

Several high-ranking members of the clergy have stressed the urgency for such a conference, among them the controversial Cardinal Lupecci, a prefect of the Congregation for Doctrine, who issued a statement yesterday in Rome: 'In an age where religious values are under constant attack, the Roman Catholic Church must take a firm lead in maintaining, or restoring, the beliefs of its followers. The Church must constantly seek divine guidance, and will ignore any sign or portent from God at its own peril. To disregard the latter, or to fail to determine whether or not they are genuinely God sent would be to put the Holy Church, itself, at risk.'

Extract from Psychic News *leader, Friday, IS IT REALLY EVOLUTION?:*

. . . many prominent geneticists believe that we have now developed the biological capacity to carry ourselves forward to the next level of evolutionary achievement, and that Alice Pagett is merely a forerunner, an advance representation of that progress. Their contention is that genetically conditioned educability, which has always been mankind's most consistently favoured quality in the process of natural selection, is now our most effective biological adaptation to our culture.

In a rapidly changing environment where cultures can adapt within a generation, whereas biological changes require thousands of years, man's psychic senses are developing in a rapidly proportionate degree, conferring upon us such mental powers as witnessed in Banfield over the past few weeks. It should be clearly stated that Alice Pagett is not exceptional, or will not be thought to be so within the next generation or two. There have been thousands of other authenticated cases of mental phenomena involving psychokinesis, paradiagnostics, psychophotography, psychometry; and, of course, faith healing and levitation have been with us through the centuries. Her experiences have been cunningly presented in a religious context, to which those disillusioned with the overwhelming materialistic aspects of today's society and the spiritually deflating discoveries of modern-day science have clung to . . .

Extract from conversation heard in The Punch Tavern, Fleet Street, Friday, early evening:

'. . . it's all a load of shit . . .'

TWENTY-FIVE

'I thought you were a ghost or a dream,' he said. 'You can't bite a ghost or a dream, and if you scream they don't care.'

THE SECRET GARDEN
Frances Hodgson Burnett

It was paper. Rough-edged, yellow parchment, the leaves filled with faded script. They were everywhere, floating in the air, scattered on the floor, filling his vision, everywhere, everywhere . . .

It's okay, he told himself. I'm dreaming. I can stop this. I only have to wake.

But the ancient pages were beginning to curl, the edges beginning to smoulder. Brown stains caused by small flames crept inwards.

Wake up.

It was dark in there. Tomb dark. But the flames were growing higher, throwing light, casting dancing shadows. He turned, fell. Smooth stone bruised his knees. He reached out and his hand touched rough-grained wood. He pulled himself up, half-sitting on the bench that he had grabbed. In the flickering light he saw other benches, plain wood, functional, no elaboration. He saw the altar and he shuddered.

Wake up, Fenn!

The flames grew larger, snatching at the old manuscripts in bursts of fire. The church was St Joseph's ... yet, it wasn't St Joseph's. It was somehow different... smaller . . . newer . . . but older . . .

He had to get out! He had to wake up! He was conscious of the dream, so he had to be awake! But the flames were beginning to burn him and the smoke was filling his head. His outstretched foot was being singed.

He pushed himself erect and the fire rose with him. He backed away towards the altar and, as he did so, he looked down at the burning paper. One sheet lay at his feet, as yet untouched by the flames, although it was beginning to curl inwards. There were no lines of ancient script on its surface, just one word, written boldly, without embellishment. It said:

MARY

And the letters were being eaten by the flames and he saw that all around the other sheets of parchment bore the same inscription and these, too, were burning and the flames were ecstatic with their consummation.

Wake up!

But he couldn't because he knew he wasn't dreaming. He looked beyond the flames, down the aisle of the church that was St Joseph's yet wasn't, towards the door that was slowly opening. His skin was beginning to blister with the heat, but he could not move; he was locked into his fear. He knew he was burning, but he could only stare at the small white figure that had stepped through the door, watch her as she approached, her face passive, her eyes closed. She walked through the flames and they did not harm her.

And now her lips were smiling and her eyes were smiling. And she was looking at him and it wasn't Alice, it was –

'FOR CHRIST'S SAKE, FENN, WAKE UP!'

He wasn't sure if he screamed in the dream, or screamed when he awoke. A face was peering down at him, long, dark hair resting over naked shoulders.

'Jesus, Fenn. I thought I'd never wake you. Sorry for the shock, but I don't believe in letting people sleep out their nightmares.'

'Sue?'

'Oh, shit, you're terrific.' Nancy rolled away from him and reached for cigarettes lying on the bedside table.

Fenn blinked his eyes and focussed on the ceiling, the dream fading rapidly. He turned his head apprehensively towards the sudden flare as a match was lit.

'Hi, Nancy,' he said.

She blew a stream of smoke as she shook out the match. 'Yeah, hi,' she said moodily.

Fenn's body felt sticky with perspiration and his bladder ached. He sat up and rubbed a hand over his neck and then his face. The stubble on his chin made a scratching sound. Lifting the covers, he swung his legs out onto the floor, then sat for a moment on the edge of the bed. He squeezed his eyelids tight and opened them again.

'Excuse me,' he said, almost to himself, then stumbled off into the bathroom.

Nancy puffed on the cigarette while she waited for him to return, the bedside lamp bathing her naked arms and breasts in a soft glow. What the hell was wrong with him? This was the second time that week she'd had to pull him out of a nightmare. Had the fire in Banfield frightened him that much? And what the hell had he been doing all that week, disappearing during the day, not letting her know where he was going, turning up late each night, half-drunk? She had let him move into her rented Brighton apartment because he wanted to get away from other newsmen – particularly from his own newspaper – to work on something special, something to do with the miracles in Banfield; but he wasn't letting her in on the act. Sure, he was paying his way, but she had hoped they would be sharing the project by now. When she mentioned teamwork, he would just shake his head and say, 'Not yet, babe.' She was being used and that was all wrong; *she* should be using him.

The toilet flushed and after a few seconds he appeared in the doorway, scratching at an itch just below his armpit. She sighed and flicked ash into the ashtray beside the bed. He flopped down next to her and groaned.

'Want to tell me about it?' she asked, no softness in her voice.

'Uh?'

'Your dream? Was it the same as before?'

He raised himself on his elbows and studied his pillow. 'It was something to do with fire again, I know that. It's a bit fuzzy now. Oh yeah, there were lots of manuscripts –'

'Manuscripts?'

He realized his mistake. She was staring curiously at him, the cigarette poised a few inches from her lips. Fenn cleared his throat, wishing his head could be cleared as easily. His mouth felt like something rancid had curled up inside and he silently cursed the demon booze. He made a quick decision, aware that Nancy was the kind of woman who would allow herself to be left out in the cold for only so long before snapping. He was sure she tried his briefcase every night (a case with a combination lock that he'd bought for the specific purpose of keeping snoopers out) when he was asleep, wondering what he had been up to during the day and just what was so precious that it had to be kept locked away. Well, the truth was, after a week of tedious research, there *was* nothing precious to be locked away. It was time to come clean with her, an easy decision because there was nothing to give away.

He sat up, resting his back against the headboard, pulling the covers over his naked stomach and legs. 'Do you want to get my briefcase?'

'Oh, you mean your portable wall safe?' she replied, confirming his suspicions.

Nancy jumped out of bed without further bidding and padded over to the briefcase leaning against a compact working desk. The apartment was really a holiday studio/flat, one of the countless off-season empty apartments that winter months bestowed upon the seaside resort, and ideal for the likes of Nancy whose stay in the country was to be fairly brief, but too long to make a hotel financially viable.

She came back to the bed and he winced as she dumped the case on his belly. She squashed out the cigarette and jumped in beside him, the pointed brown nipples of her small breasts as eager as the expression on her face. 'I knew you'd level with me sooner or later,' she said, smiling.

He grunted, working the dials of the briefcase locks with his thumbs. When the six-digit combination showed, he flicked back the locks and opened the lid. The inside of the case brimmed with pencil-scribbled notes.

Nancy reached in and took out a handful, turning back to the light with them.

'What the hell is this, Fenn?' She saw dates, names, short notes.

'That's the fruits of one week's solid research. And partly the cause of the nightmares.'

'How d'you mean?' she asked, sifting through the notes and reaching for more.

'When I was a student, I worked one summer in a restaurant. In a fairly high-class tearoom, to be exact; you know, the kind matrons and aunts go to for afternoon tea and scones. It was a busy place and the work was pretty new to me. In the first couple of weeks, all I could dream of at night was silver teapots and scalded fingers. This week I've been dreaming of old parchment papers. Tonight – and the other night – a little extra was thrown in.'

'But what's it all for. You writing the history of Banfield?'

'Not quite. I'm looking into it, though. You know the Church is paying me to write about the Banfield miracles –'

'That doesn't mean you can't write for us as well.'

'We've been through all that, Nancy. It doesn't exclude me from writing for anybody, but for now, I want to get the whole story straight in my own head.'

'You've been acting kinda strange since the fire.' She touched the discoloration on his forehead; the swelling was gone but the mark was still ugly. 'You sure the damage wasn't permanent?'

He took her hand away. 'You want to listen or not? I needed to get the whole historical background on Banfield –'

'Come on, Fenn. I don't buy that. You could get all the background from the local library. That's what I did, and so did the other reporters.'

'I wanted some in-depth material.'

'Okay, treat me like a hick, I'll go along with you for now.'

He sighed in exasperation. 'Just listen, will you?'

'Sure.'

'The local library was the first place I went to. It doesn't have too much – just a book written by a guy who used to be the vicar to the village in the thirties, and a couple of volumes on the history of Sussex.'

'Yeah, no meat.'

'So I went to the village hall, the public records office. The Parish Clerk was helpful, but their records only went back to the 1960s. From there I went to the county records office in Chichester and that's where I've spent the past week. I think the archivist who helped me is sick of the sight of me by now. I've been through every piece of paper on Banfield from the eighth century onwards – not that I understood much of the earlier stuff. Most of it was either illegible or written in Latin. Even the later scripts were difficult, all those "f"s instead of "s"s, you know the kind of thing.'

'What were you digging for?'

He looked away. 'I can't tell you.'

'Why not? What's the big secret?'

'There is no big secret.'

'Then why are you in such a state?'

He turned to her once more. 'What?'

'Have you seen how you look?' She brushed her hand roughly against his chin. 'Aren't you aware of how you've been acting? Getting back here each evening juiced up, keeping your goddam papers locked away like they were state secrets, your nightmares, mumbling in your sleep – screwing me like you were a goddam zombie!'

'You don't like my technique?'

'Shaddup! What d'you think when we're in the sack, that you're just paying your dues on the use of this pad? What the hell d'you think I am?'

He put a hand to her shoulder, but she slapped it away. 'I thought maybe we could get together on this thing,' she said angrily. 'I've stood back and let you get on, waiting for the time you'd open up to me. Just now you could've, but you chose different. Okay, my friend, since we have no deal, it's time for you to scoot.'

'Hey, there's no need –'

'Get out!'

'It's . . . it's . . .' he scrabbled for his wristwatch lying beneath his pillow. '. . . it's after three . . .'

'Tough shit! Get moving.'

'I can improve my style,' he said, brushing his palm against her nipple.

'I'm not kidding, Fenn. Out!'

His hand slid beneath the covers and around her waist. 'I'll shave.'

She pushed against his chest. 'Get lost.'

He gently ran his hand down her thigh.

She punched his shoulder. 'I mean it, you fucker.'

He rolled on top of her and her legs clamped tight together.

'You think,' she hissed, 'you're suddenly a hot lover? You think I'm going to swoon away, you little shit?'

He slumped against her, defeated, then rolled over onto his back and stared at the ceiling. 'Jesus,' he breathed, 'you're rough.'

Nancy sat up and looked down at him. 'I'm rough and I mean it. You've used me, Fenn, and given me nothing in return –'

'Okay, okay, you're right.'

'I guess it's your style using people, situations. But not with this lady.'

'Aren't you the same, Nancy?' he said quietly. 'Aren't you the same kind of animal?'

She hesitated. 'Sure, it takes one to know one. That's why I'm wise to you. That's why I know I'm not getting anywhere –'

'Hold it. I said you're right and maybe I'm beginning to feel guilty. I've felt strange this week, almost . . . well, almost obsessed with this kid Alice. Ever since the fire, ever since she came through those flames . . .'

Nancy was silent, fuming still, and he looked at her as though seeking an answer. Her body was thin, her breasts not as firm as they probably once had been, faint lines around her neck betraying the passing years. The hardness in her face was softened by the dim light, but the fierceness in her eyes could not be muted. Even when she was younger he felt sure she had never been classed as beautiful, yet she had the attractiveness that any woman would envy, that would make most men want her (maybe just for one night, perhaps two – she would prove too hard to handle for much longer).

'I was there, too, you know,' she said, disturbed by his gaze. 'Alice didn't have the same effect on me.'

Fenn lifted himself up on one elbow so that his face was closer to hers. 'Tell me what effect she did have on you.'

'Wha – ? Hey, you're sneaking out of this, you're changing the subject.'

'No, tell me. I promise I'll come straight with you after you tell me.'

She looked at him doubtfully, then shrugged. 'What the hell do I have to lose?' She thought for a few seconds, thinking back to the Thursday of the fire. 'Okay. She had absolutely no effect on me at all. Nothing. Zilch. I didn't believe what was happening and I still don't.'

'But you saw it.'

'Yep. And I still don't believe it.'

'That's crazy.'

'Sure. I saw her arrive on the scene, I saw the fire die out. But something in here . . .' she tapped her temple '. . . won't, or can't, put the two together.'

He shook his head. 'And how about Alice herself? Do you have any feelings about her?'

'She's just a kid. A skinny, undersized kid. Quite pretty, but nothing special.'

'A lot of people say she has a radiance about her, a kind of holiness.'

'Maybe to some she has; not to me, though. In fact, if I have to be perfectly honest, she leaves me a little cold.'

'Why?'

'Well, I guess it's because she doesn't seem to sparkle like other kids. I know she's been through a lot, but there's something . . . I don't know . . . something flat about her. It's as if her emotions are locked away somewhere deep inside. She was obviously upset by the death of her father, but I didn't see her shed a tear at his funeral. Maybe she cried herself out in private.'

He sank back down in the bed. 'Lately I've had the same feeling about her. When I first saw her, the very first night I chased her into the field, she was just a scared, vulnerable little girl. Now . . . now she seems different. She probably saved me getting badly burned last week, yet I can't seem to find any gratitude towards her. And . . . oh, Christ, I remember now! I saw her just before the car crashed! I'm sure it was her.' He was sitting up again, arms over his raised knees. 'She was standing in the window of the convent, watching. Just before the cars went . . . out . . . of . . . control . . .'

'What are you saying, Fenn?'

'The cars. Don't you remember? The Capri in front went out of control, then so did mine. The steering just went.'

'I don't remember. I thought the Capri went into a skid and you tried to avoid it.'

'That's what I thought – until now. It just came back to me, Nancy. I couldn't control the bloody car. And she was watching all the time.'

'I don't get you. What the hell are you trying to say? That she was responsible?'

He nodded slowly. 'Maybe that's exactly what I'm saying.'

'You're insane.' She reached for her cigarettes again, lit one.

'If she can control a fire she can interfere with a car's steering.'

Nancy opened her mouth to speak, then just shook her head.

'Strange things have been happening around her,' Fenn insisted.

'Shit, that's an understatement. But there could be other factors involved, psychological reasons for these so-called miracles. And besides, her father died in that fire. The kid wouldn't have had anything to do with that.'

He rubbed a thumb across his lower lip. 'No,' he said slowly. 'No, of course not.' He became lost in his own thoughts.

Nancy ran a hand up his back towards his shoulder. 'You were going to level with me.'

Fenn relaxed against the headboard and Nancy withdrew her hand, letting it rest on his thigh.

'Simply, it's this,' Fenn said. 'Monsignor Delgard is seriously concerned over what's happening at the church –'

'That's hardly surprising.'

'Let me finish. He feels something wrong is going on there –'

'With all those miracles? He should be jumping for joy.'

'Perhaps he should be, but he isn't. He's worried about Father Hagan's death –'

'That was a plain old coronary.'

'Will you shut up and listen. He's also worried about the atmosphere of the church. He feels it's – to put it in his own words – "spiritually devoid".'

'What does *that* mean?'

'I suppose it means the sanctity has disappeared.'

'You can't be serious. You're not trying to tell me the place is possessed by demons?' She gave a short laugh.

'No. St Joseph's is empty. There's nothing there at all. Father Hagan felt the same before he died.'

'Hey, I can't write this kind of junk.'

'For Christ's sake, I don't want you to write about it! I'm telling you in confidence, because you wanted to know. You've baled me out this week, you've helped me stay away from the scavengers so I could get on with all this. I'm returning the favour by letting you know what I'm up to, but I don't want it broadcast to the bloody nation!'

'Don't worry, that won't happen. My chief would bury me. Now if you're saying there's some kind of fraud going on, then I'm with you all the way.'

'Yeah, maybe it is all some elaborate fraud, who knows?'

'Why go into this, uh, "spiritually devoid" shit, then? You're spoiling the chance of a good story, Fenn, probably the biggest that'll ever come your way, by going off on that tack.'

'It's hard to explain, but I feel there's something wrong, too.'

'You're a cynic. It's natural for you.'

'Thanks, but I mean *deeply* wrong. Like you, I think there's something strange about Alice.'

'I only said she didn't have much personality.'

'You implied more.'

'All right, you and the priest think something wicked this way comes. So what's the point of all this research? Where's it going to get you?'

'Probably nowhere, but I might uncover something in the church's history that could shed some light.'

'You mean root out some dark secret from St Joseph's past. Fenn, I don't believe this of you. I thought your flat feet were firmly on the ground and your grubby little fingers always ready to grab the golden egg. I'm not knocking you. From me it's a compliment, it's how I operate myself. But now you're beginning to disappoint.'

'Monsignor Delgard sees me the same way – that's why he hired me.'

'Oh yeah, that makes sense.'

'It does in a crazy way. He wanted someone to look at the whole business coolly and logically, someone who wasn't wrapped up in religion and someone who would scoff at bad vibrations.'

'Until a few moments ago I would have said he'd chosen the right boy. Now I'm not so sure.'

Fenn sighed and his body sank lower against the headboard. A smile slowly formed on his lips. 'Yeah,' he said, 'could be I was getting carried away. The crash, the fire – maybe it just scared the shit out of me, enough to make me think too much, anyway. I could have panicked and imagined the car's steering had gone. There may have been oil on the road – that would account for the other car losing control. Anyway . . .' he emptied the suitcase full of notes onto the floor

'. . . I found nothing nasty in the history of Banfield or St Joseph's. Nothing, at least, that hasn't happened in every other village, town or city in England over the past hundred years. I guess it should be a relief.'

Nancy looked down at the scattered paper. 'D'you mind if I go through your notes sometime?'

'Help yourself, there's nothing there that'll interest you.'

She settled down closer to him and her hand moved towards his inner thigh. 'What about us, Fenn?'

'Us?'

'Working together.'

'I thought you wanted me to leave.'

'That was before. Now you've told me what you've been up to.'

'There wasn't much to tell, was there?'

'No, but at least you confided in me. What about our deal?'

'I'm working for the Church, Nancy.'

'Come on, Fenn. You're working for yourself – you're *using* the Church. It's a way of being right up there in front and getting all the inside information you need. Whatever they're paying you, you'll make treble, probably quadruple, from other sources when your job for the Church is done. Isn't that why you accepted in the first place?'

His smile was slow to surface, and when it did it was strained. After a while, he said, 'I won't work with you, Nancy, but I'll pass on information, try to get you a ringside seat for any special occasions, and generally help in any way I can.'

'Up to a point, right?'

'Yeah, up to a point.'

She groaned, giving up the fight. 'I guess it's gonna have to do. I think you're a fool, though – I could have improved anything you wrote, given it style. I mean it, I could have. And I could have gotten you a good deal from the *Post*.'

He reached over and kissed her neck, the pressure of her hand having some effect. 'When do you have to get back to the States?' he asked.

'Soon as I figure I've got all I'm going to get on this miracle thing. I can't stay forever, that's for sure. Maybe a coupla weeks; unless, of course, even bigger things break.'

'It's hard to imagine anything more mind-blowing happening.' He wondered, though. Just a few weeks ago he had been saying the whole affair would fizzle out and Banfield would sink back into anonymity once more. For his own personal motives, he didn't want that to happen, but some small instinct which became elusive when he tried to focus upon it warned him that it might have been for the best.

Nancy nuzzled her cheek against his forehead. 'What I'm saying, Fenn, is if you're going to help me, it's gotta be soon. No keeping it to yourself. Okay?'

'Sure,' he agreed, not believing himself. He'd help her but, as he had already said, up to a point. Newsmen were generally selfish creatures where their work was concerned and he was no exception to the rule. Her hand had moved upwards and her fingers began to close around his stiffening penis. For the first time that week (and much to his own relief) his desire became much more than just the need to fulfil a bodily function. He squirmed when her movement gained a pleasurable rhythm.

He kissed her lips, turning towards her to press close, but she did not relinquish her possession, nor break the rhythm. Her palm, her fingers, were soft, knowing just the right pressure, knowing when to tighten, when to release. His kiss became hard, his lips moist. She bit down on his lower lip, gently, just enough to excite and not enough to hurt. Her tongue sought his and his whole body became tensed, the area of excitement spreading from his loins to his arms, his thighs, the muscles of his buttocks, his nipples. His own fingers slid over his hips, reaching for her breasts, caressing them, each one in turn, pressing and pulling at the erect nipples, flattening his hand to encompass every part, squeezing hard one moment, fondling tenderly the next.

She could feel his passion and it was unlike any of the other times during the week. It was as if he had finally roused himself from a semi-drugged state. She smiled inwardly. Or she had roused him from that state.

Nancy pushed him onto his back, using her shoulder to do so, not wanting to release him yet. She kept her fingers there, stroking, moving the soft skin against its rigid core in a steady motion, occasionally increasing the pace to heighten his excitement, then slowing the movement before it became too late for them both.

His hand slid down to her stomach, the muscles there quivering, then tightening, at his touch, but she pushed it away when it sought to reach lower. She raised herself to her knees, releasing his penis so that her hand could explore more of his body. Both hands felt their way across his stomach, moving upwards in small circular motions, gently kneading his skin, the pressure spread with open palms and outstretched fingers. She ran them across his chest, spending a little time around his nipples, bending to kiss, to suck, to make them wet, gently blowing on them before moving onwards, her hands smoothing themselves over his shoulders, around his neck, touching the backs of his ears with her thumbs.

He was smiling and she kissed his smile, shifting her body so that it was over him. She stretched herself down, resting her body against his, their skin touching and moulding together in a fusion that was comforting as well as exquisite, as though the pores of their flesh were opening themselves to each other, drinking in each other's juices. Nancy writhed against his hard body, her own pleasure beginning to rise, feeling the sensation deep between her thighs, the moisture there beginning to flow. Her legs opened, her thighs spreading around him. His penis was against her stomach and he shifted his hips so that it moved against her. She took his hands that were clasped around the small of her back and pulled his arms upward, fingers curling through his, holding tight, pushing his hands over his head, pressing them into the pillow, pinning his body down with her own. She moved herself upwards so that her opening rested against his testicles, the risen root of her own pleasure pressing hard against the swollen base of his rod. She moaned as she squirmed and he used his body to give her more pleasure.

She brought up her knees as the sensation grew, but still crouched over him, still pinned his arms back. She stroked her vagina, so moist, so alive, along the length of his penis, then down again, her whole body shivering with its sensuality. She moved upwards again until his tip touched hers, and there she lingered, bringing on her own excitement, the tremor quickly becoming unbearable, but too good to release.

Her fingers untwined from his and reached down. She raised her body, touched his penis more firmly against herself, one hand pushing his protective skin down and up in the coaxing, teasing – exhilarating – movement of moments before; she teased herself with him, allowing his body only partial entry, using him to titillate the outer lips of her vagina.

He groaned, pushing himself upwards, but she went with him, a deep-throated chuckle that was almost a moan escaping her. She allowed him more, her own wetness making the entry smooth, no pain involved, only pleasure. Inner muscles tightened, closing around him, holding him there, her hand still fondling the rest of him, touching between his legs, curling around his testicles and gently squeezing. Her hips moved in a circular motion and his hands clutched at her thighs, spreading around them, reaching upwards, along her body, touching her breasts, holding them together, releasing them, running back down, touching the top of her opening with his thumb, teasing her, but pleasing her as she teased and pleased him.

It was too much for her. She sank lower and he rose into her, every part of his erection surrounded by warmth, by wetness, by muscles that sucked at the juices within him, drawing them out, skilful contractions that needed little movement from the rest of their bodies.

They were both covered in a light sheen of perspiration, Nancy's hair hanging limply over her forehead. Her eyes were half-closed, the pupils rolled upwards, and her lips parted just enough to show her teeth, her smile almost a grimace of agony.

Fenn looked at her and the sight increased his own sensations. He moved against her, but she controlled everything; the final pleasure would not be his until she was ready, until her own climax was ready to be fulfilled. And that would be soon.

She gasped, the sound almost a tiny scream. Her whole body was moving now, pushing him into her, as much as she could take, which was all. He helped her movements, hands around her hips. He lifted her from the bed, his heels digging into the sheets, and she moaned sharply, wanting more, more. Her hands closed around his sides and pulled him upwards.

He felt the juices deep within begin their turmoil, erupting, pressure building for the moment they would break free.

She felt the change in him, the even stronger stiffening, his whole body becoming more forceful, more rigid, more intense. And she was ready for it. The tumult inside was ready to explode.

Her body tightened as though every sinew, every nerve, had drawn itself inwards. She could no longer draw in breath and her heart was straining with the exertion, it's pace matching the rhythm of her own movements. And then the peak was reached and she was floating and soaring, reaching one great height and then another, the climax not just a single, exquisite burst, but a series of senses-reeling eruptions, the first two or three expanding her mind so that it touched all of her, making each nerve part of the whiteness, part of her mind, it's intensity diminishing slowly, leaving her panting, sensuously drained.

Her shoulders slumped forward, her arms bent, barely supporting her, long dark hair hanging down into her face. She gave a low, smiling sigh as the pleasure ebbed away until it was replaced by a deep satisfaction.

She slowly pulled herself free and lay down beside him, his fluid seeping from her to rest on her inner thigh. 'That was better,' she sighed.

'You did all the work,' he told her, wiping clinging strands of hair away from her damp brow.

'Yeah, but your cooperation this time helped.'

They were silent for a while, their bodies relaxing, their thoughts beginning to drift. Nancy heard Fenn's breathing become deeper, more regular, and she knew he was sleeping. She carefully eased herself from his arms and went to the bathroom, walking lightly, not wanting to disturb him. She washed herself and put on a bathrobe, then poured herself a glass of cold milk in the kitchen. Returning to the bedroom she gathered up Fenn's fallen notes, taking them through to the lounge and placing them on the room's sofa. She switched on a lamp, then went back into the bedroom to retrieve her cigarettes.

Nancy settled down on the sofa, lit a cigarette, shuffled the notes into three neat piles beside her, and began to read.

TWENTY-SIX

There was a little girl, and she wore a
little curl
    Right down the middle of her forehead
When she was good, she was very, very,
good,
    But when she was bad, she was horrid.

JEMIMA
Anon

Monsignor Delgard's stride had lost much of its briskness and his tall figure was more stooped than usual. The High Street was dark and quiet, the two public houses not having yet regurgitated their Saturday night trade onto the pavements; his footsteps sounded harsh and lonely along the concrete. Not many shop windows were lit, the lights from the few lamp-posts along the roadside feeble, creating shadows that were more menacing than natural darkness. It was bitterly cold again, no significant change in climate noticed as the borderline between February and March fast approached. The priest hugged the lapels of his overcoat tight around his neck, wondering if it was more then just age that allowed the night chill to penetrate his bones. He shuddered, feeling cold fingertips touch his nerves.

He could see the lights of the convent ahead, his eyes, beneath their heavy lids, usually keen, still having a clear vision that only disturbed thoughts of aching temples could sometimes blur. His head ached, the cool air no panacea, and his thoughts, too, were disturbed. The lights of the convent shone like a beacon, as though guiding him towards a friendly refuge, a place of Retreat, away from the brooding church. But was it a false refuge? What did he fear within its sanctuary? He shrugged off the doubts. There was only a child safely lodged within those walls, a frightened, bewildered child. But perhaps a child that was being used . . .

Delgard had encountered the phenomenon termed as 'possession' many times in the past, had helped victims conquer the evil inside themselves, had helped their minds break free of schizophrenic emotions which chained and tormented. In later years, the effort of such psychological battles had been almost too much for his drained body, his mind (or soul) taking longer each time to recuperate. But then it took broken bones longer to heal as age crept into them. He suddenly turned his head as though a disembodied finger had tapped his shoulder.

An empty street. The sightseers had left for the day and the reporters and cameramen had retired for the night, eager for tomorrow, Sunday, a day of labour. He looked towards the convent once more, his pace becoming faster, refusing to accept he was fleeing from a frightening uncertainty behind to a disturbing uncertainty ahead.

He passed the burned-out shell of the garage and thought of Gerry Fenn. Delgard had received one agitated phone call from the reporter the day after the terrible accident, telling him what had happened, what Fenn had witnessed, then . . . nothing. The reporter had disappeared, informing no one, not even his editor, not even Susan Gates, of where he could be reached, what he was up to. Delgard was concerned for the reporter; had he led the man into something he could not comprehend and so could not regard with the respect (and fear) it demanded? The man was no fool and his very cynicism afforded him some protection. But only up to a point. Beyond that point he was as vulnerable as anybody else. Delgard breathed in the frosty air and expelled a white mist as if it were an escaping soul.

The panda car was parked half on the kerb outside the convent and the policeman inside watched the tall priest as he approached the gate. Headlights dazzled Delgard, freezing him in their glare like a paralysed rabbit.

'Sorry,' a voice said from the window. 'It's Monsignor Delgard, isn't it?' The headlights died, leaving the priest sightless for a few moments. He heard a car door open and could just make out a dark shape as the policeman approached him. 'Didn't expect any visitors this time of night,' the voice said. The convent gate was pushed open and the policeman stood to one side to let the priest through.

'Thank you,' Delgard said as he entered the courtyard. 'No journalists tonight?'

The policeman chuckled. 'No chance. It's Saturday. They're either in the local pubs getting stoned or tucked up in bed waiting for the big day tomorrow. The former mostly, I'd say, knowing that crew.'

Delgard nodded and crossed the courtyard, mounting the three steps to the main door as the gate scraped closed behind him. He rang the doorbell and waited.

It seemed like a long time before the door was opened, the coldness reaching into him with deliberate intensity, punishing him because he dared to be still when only movement could keep the chill at bay. The nun peered out at him, her face barely discernible because of the light behind, her attitude cautious.

'Oh, Monsignor,' she said with relief. The door swung wide.

'Reverend Mother is expecting me,' he told her, stepping into the hallway.

'Yes, of course. Let me show you into –'

'I'm glad you could come, Monsignor Delgard,' said a voice from the other end of the hallway. Mother Marie-Clare, the Reverend Mother of the convent as well as Head Mistress of the convent school, walked towards them, the silver cross she wore outside her grey tunic briefly flashing as it caught the light from overhead. She was a small woman, thin, and vulnerable in the way most nuns, even the more robust, seemed to be. Light-framed spectacles perched on a narrow nose and her unplucked eyebrows gave her a severity that Delgard knew was not in her nature. Her hands were clasped low before her as they always seemed to be; it was as if she were constantly praying, and he thought that that probably was the case. She stopped before him and he could see her anxiety behind the thin lenses.

'I'm sorry I'm so late, Reverend Mother,' he said. 'There was much to do in preparation for tomorrow.'

'I understand, Monsignor. It was good of you to come at this hour.'

'Is she in her room?'

'Yes, but not sleeping. She appears desperate to see you.'

'Then she knew I would come?'

Mother Marie-Claire nodded. 'May I offer you something hot to drink before you see her. You must be frozen.'

'No, thank you. I'm all right. I think I'll go straight up.'

'You wouldn't rather see her down here? In my study, perhaps?'

Delgard smiled. 'No, she may feel inclined to speak more freely in the privacy of her own room, temporary though it may be.'

'As you wish, Monsignor. I'll take you up.'

He raised a hand. 'I know where her room is, Reverend Mother. Please don't trouble yourself.' He made for the stairs, unbuttoning his overcoat as he went and handing it to the sister who had opened the door.

'Monsignor?'

He paused and turned back to the nun.

'Do you think it wise to allow Alice to attend Mass tomorrow?'

'It's what she wishes, Reverend Mother. She insists upon it.'

'She's just a child . . .' The nun let the words trail off.

'One who must be treated with great care,' Delgard said kindly.

'But the crowds. So many . . .'

'We cannot keep her locked away. The public would believe some sinister motive, I'm afraid.'

'But for her own good.'

'How upset she gets when we try to keep her away from the church. I'm of the same mind as you, Reverend Mother, but this matter is not entirely in my hands.'

'Surely Bishop Caines –'

'No, it isn't just the bishop who wishes Alice's exposure to the public. None of these decisions are made by one man any more. Please, don't concern yourself for her safety; she'll be well protected.'

'It's her peace of mind I'm concerned with, Monsignor.' There was no criticism, nor harshness, in her tone, just a caring sadness.

'We all are, Reverend Mother. I promise you, we all are.' He began to climb the stairs, his footsteps slow, almost as though he were reluctant to reach the upper floor.

Mother Marie-Claire unconsciously fingered the silver cross dangling from the chain around her neck, then walked back towards the tiny chapel beyond the hallway where she had been deep in prayer before the priest arrived. The nun who had opened the door to Monsignor Delgard now locked it and followed her superior down the hallway, stopping on the way to hang the priest's overcoat on a coathook beneath the stairs. She glanced up at the tall, ascending figure before it disappeared into the gloom of the upper level, then returned to her duties in the convent's kitchen.

Delgard paused at the top of the stairs, allowing his eyes to adjust to the poor light. There were doorways on either side of the corridor, each one a nun's private, sparse cell. The room he sought was halfway down, to his right. He wondered why it was so urgent for her to see him that night and told himself he would soon know. He walked towards the door and tapped lightly on it.

There was no sound for a moment or two, but then a voice said: 'Who's there?'

'It's Monsignor Delgard,' he replied, his voice soft, not wanting to disturb those sleeping.

The door opened almost immediately and the pale, tired face of Molly Pagett was peering out at him. 'Thank you so much for coming,' she said, and there was a tremor to her voice.

'Mother Marie-Claire said you needed –'

'Yes, yes, I needed to see you. I'm sorry you've had to come out so late. Please come in.'

The room contained a single cot bed, a sink, a hard-back, uncomfortable-looking chair, a tiny wardrobe, and no other comforts, except a black crucifix on the wall. After the gloom of the corridor, the single ceiling light was harsh, ugly. Molly Pagett sat on the edge of the bed, her hands clasped together in her lap, and Delgard took the chair from its position by the wall, placing it near to her. He sat, allowing himself a small groan of pleasure, pretending his bones ached more than they actually did, knowing she had some fear of him and wanting to appear less daunting.

'I'm afraid the cold weather stiffens these old joints of mine,' he told her, smiling.

She returned the smile, but it was short-lived, nervous.

He felt too tired for preamble, yet felt her need to put at ease. 'How are they treating you here at the convent, Molly? Not very comfortable by the looks of it.'

She looked down at her hands and he saw they were clenched tight. 'They're very good to us here, Father . . . I'm sorry, Monsignor.'

He reached forward and patted her troubled hands, his own large hand covering hers completely. 'It's all right. There's no real difference between a monsignor and a priest; one's just a fancier title, that's all. You look tired. Molly. Haven't you been sleeping?'

'Not very well, Monsignor.'

'Well, that's understandable; you've been through so much. Hasn't your doctor prescribed something for you? Something to relax you, help you sleep.'

'Yes, yes, he gave me some pills. I don't like to take them, though.'

'I'm sure they wouldn't do you any harm. Your doctor would only give you something if he thought it was for the best.'

'No, it's not that,' she said quickly. 'It's Alice, you see. She might need me in the night. She might call out.'

'I'm sure one of the nuns would tend to her.'

'She'd want her mother. If she woke up in the middle of the night, she'd be frightened. She'd want her mother . . .'

He saw the tears beginning to well in her eyes before she bowed her head.

'Don't upset yourself, Molly,' he said kindly. 'I know there's a huge burden on you at the moment, but I promise you it will ease. The loss of your dear husband, this strange thing that's happening to Alice . . .'

She looked up and her eyes were shining through the unshed tears, an inner glory that she could not, nor tried to, conceal. 'It's a wonderful, holy thing, Monsignor. Leonard . . . Leonard . . . he couldn't understand it, couldn't appreciate what's happening to my Alice. He didn't believe in God, Monsignor, so it had no meaning for him.'

He was shocked by the distaste in her voice when she spoke of her late husband.

'He just thought he could make money out of it, did you know that, Monsignor?' She shook her head as though disbelieving her own statement. 'He wanted to make money out of my little girl.'

'I'm sure he was as concerned for her welfare as you are, Molly. I don't think he would have exploited her.'

'You didn't know him the way I did. He hated everything that was happening at first, scolded her, as if it were her fault. He didn't want us in this convent, didn't want us surrounded by these good sisters. Then he realized little Alice could make him money. Everybody else was cashing in, he said, so why shouldn't he, her own father? He was going to tell everything to the newspapers, to the highest bidder, everything about Alice, everything about me and him. He was wicked, Monsignor, wicked!'

'Please calm yourself, Molly.' His voice had become firm, but was still low. 'You've been through too much, you don't know what you're saying.'

'I'm so sorry, I didn't mean . . .' Her body rocked back and forth on the bed and now the tears fell onto her lap.

'Would you like me to fetch you some tea, some water?'

She shook her head and continued to look down, her rocking motion slowly becoming more steady.

Delgard was annoyed at himself for allowing her to become upset, the exact reverse of his intentions, but the outburst had been so sudden, so unexpected. He decided there was little point in attempting to redeem the situation. 'Why did you want to see me, Molly? Was it about Alice?'

Her body seemed to hunch into itself and she did not answer immediately. Finally she pulled a crumpled handkerchief from the sleeve of her woolly cardigan and dabbed at her eyes before looking up. 'It's more to do with me and Len,' she said, her voice unsteady.

He leaned forward in the chair. 'What is it that's troubling you?'

'I . . . I never even told Father Hagan. In all those years I never confessed to him. Now it's too late.'

'You can make your confession to me, Molly. You know whatever you tell me will be between ourselves and God.'

'I was always too ashamed to tell him, Monsignor.'

'I'm sure Father Hagan would have understood. He wouldn't have judged you, Molly.'

'I just couldn't . . .' A shudder went through her, but she seemed to make an effort to gain control.

'What couldn't you tell your parish priest?' Delgard quietly urged.

She would not look at him and her words faltered as she spoke. 'He . . . Father Hagan knew I was pregnant when he married Len and me. I told him that, I confessed that . . .'

Delgard remained silent, his own large hands clasped together.

'But I didn't tell him everything.' The words came in a rush, and none followed.

'What did you omit to tell your priest?' Delgard was forced to ask. 'You know there can be no complete forgiveness if you have not confessed everything.'

Molly gave a small moan. 'I know, I know, but I couldn't say it, I couldn't tell him!'

'You can tell me now, Molly. There's no need to punish yourself further.'

She sniffed and raised her head slightly, but her eyes were still downcast. 'It's . . . it's just that the field . . . the field next to St Joseph's . . . it's become sacred ground, Monsignor. It's a holy shrine.'

Delgard waited patiently.

'Len . . . Leonard used to wait for me outside the church before we were married. He wouldn't come inside, said he didn't feel right there. I didn't realize then just how much he hated religion. Perhaps I would never've married him if

I'd known.' She dabbed at her damp cheeks with the handkerchief. 'I used to work for the church even in those days, Monsignor. I loved the place, just as . . . just as Alice loves it. And Len . . . he'd wait for me, like I said.'

She took a deep breath, as though resigning herself to the confession. 'One day he was there, just beyond the wall, watching me – I was collecting the dead flowers from the graves. He called me over. We'd been going out together for a couple of months by then, but . . . but nothing had really happened between us. You know what I mean, nothing . . . nothing *really* serious . . .'

Delgard nodded slowly.

'But that day . . . that day, I don't know what got into us both. It was evening – dusk really – and it was in the summer. Warm, the end of a fine day. We kissed across the wall, sure no one could see us. And then he lifted me over. He was so . . . so strong, so demanding. And I couldn't resist, Monsignor, I couldn't help myself.' Her breasts rose and fell almost in a panting movement, as if the memory of her passion was still alive inside her. She flushed red, embarrassed by her own emotions. 'We lay down by the side of the wall, in that field, in that sacred ground, and we made love. I don't know what possessed me! I'd never gone that far with anyone before, please believe me, but that day I was helpless, I was swept away. We both were. It was as though we were different people, almost strangers to each other. There didn't even seem to be any love involved, just . . . just passion, just lust! Oh God, can I ever be forgiven?'

His hunched shoulders seemed even more pronounced as he spoke. 'Of course you are forgiven. You've been foolish to hold onto this unreasonable guilt all these years. If you feel you need Absolution, I –'

'Alice was conceived in that field, Monsignor, don't you see? And now there's a shrine to the Blessed Virgin . . .'

He suddenly felt nauseous. But it was ridiculous! Such a sin so long ago had no bearing on what was happening today! Yet his head reeled with the notion. He fought to conceal his dismay. 'You . . . you confessed your sin to Father Hagan all those years ago.'

'He was new to the parish. I was too timid to tell him where it had happened, so near the church and all.'

'That wasn't important.'

'But it was on sacred ground.'

'No, Molly, it was beyond the church boundary. And even now, even now a service is to be held in the field tomorrow, the land hasn't been consecrated. There is no need for your confession.' He searched for the right words, needing to be sure, but aware of her distress. There was no delicate way to ask, though. 'Why . . . why are you so sure Alice was conceived there? Were there no other occasions –'

'No, no, Monsignor. It was just that time. I felt so ashamed afterwards, so very ashamed. And I was pregnant, I knew almost right away. Don't ask me how I knew – I just did. I never allowed Leonard to touch me after that, not till after we were married. But I was happy to be pregnant. I wanted my child. Despite our sin. I felt my baby was a gift from God. And she was, she is, don't you see? I wasn't young, Monsignor, I could have remained a spinster.' She gave a choked laugh. 'I'd almost resigned myself to that. Spinster of the parish! Perhaps that's why I devoted so much time to the church. It had become my life. But God gave me something for myself, something to cherish in the way I cherished the church. But that can't be right, can it, Monsignor? My sin shouldn't have provided such a gift, should it? God doesn't reward sinners.'

Delgard sighed inwardly, saddened by the woman's confusion, depressed by his own. If only there were simple answers. A priest had to conceal his own doubts, his own confusions; he had to appear strong in his beliefs, convinced that God's way was always right, never allowing the perplexity of those ways to infringe on his own faith. How to reassure this woman when her question pricked his own uncertainty? And when her words caused a peculiar revulsion within him. The revelation could have no special significance, yet why did it distress him so?

'You were blessed with a child,' Delgard found himself saying, 'and for that you must be grateful. You need not look beyond that.' It was inadequate, but what more could he have said? 'Don't concern yourself with what happened all those years ago. You raised a fine child in the ways of the Church, as God knew you would. Be content, Molly, look no further. God can reward now for what will come to pass later.'

She smiled, tears still sparkling in her eyes. 'I think I can understand what you're saying, Monsignor. Yes, Alice is a very special gift; He chose me to be the mother of . . . of . . .'

'Hush now. The miracles have still not been proven. You must not be so convinced, not yet.'

Her smile broadened, telling him *she* was sure, *she* knew. Her face clouded for an instant. 'Then . . . then there was no desecration of hallowed ground?'

'How could there be? It was more than eleven years ago, long before the field was thought of . . .' he paused '. . . as sacred. Your sin was one of passion, not irreverence, and for that you've already been forgiven.'

A weight seemed to have been lifted from her. 'Thank you, Monsignor. I'm sorry if you think I'm foolish.'

He patted her hands. 'Not foolish, Molly. Recent events have put concerns into your mind that are not so important as you may think. I can only urge you to put such worries behind you; the coming weeks, months, will impose their own new burdens. Would you like to say a short prayer with me?'

'A penance?'

'No, not a penance. I told you that the sin you spoke of has long since been forgiven. Let's both pray for strength to sustain us in whatever the future may bring.'

Delgard bowed his head and for a few quiet minutes they prayed together. He made the Sign of the Cross before her, then rose to his feet. She smiled up at him, and he could see there was still ill-concealed anxiety in her eyes. 'Thank you, Monsignor,' she said.

'Peace be with you.' He turned back to her before opening the door, not sure what prompted the question. 'Is there anything you'd like to tell me about Alice?'

Molly looked startled. 'Alice? What do you mean, Monsignor?'

He stared at her for several seconds before turning away again. 'It doesn't matter, Molly.' He opened the door. 'But if you ever need to speak to me, if anything at all about your daughter gives you cause for concern, please don't hesitate to tell me.' He closed the door behind him and stood in the dark hallway for several moments, collecting his thoughts. Alice, conceived in the field where she now saw the visions! It could have no meaning. Surely it could have no meaning? Her illness, when she had been struck deaf and dumb – had she been in the field then? No, no, that had nothing to do with it. It had just been a perverse legacy from a child's normal illness. There could not possibly be any connection. Why the unease in his mind? Why did what Molly Pagett had just revealed trouble him so? His fingers went to his brow, moving to a point below, between his eyes, squeezing the bone there to relieve the pain. He had never been so unsure. In all the days of his ecclesiastical career he had never been quite as uncertain as now. Perhaps the sudden death of Father Hagan had unsettled him more than he knew. He began to walk quietly down the corridor towards the stairs, still careful not to wake those sleeping beyond the doors on either side. Father Hagan had seemed so –

He stopped abruptly, a rush of blood causing his heart to beat rapidly. A dark shadow moved from the other shadows towards him.

'Who –?'

'It's me, Monsignor Delgard, Mother Marie-Claire. I'm sorry if I alarmed you.'

Delgard let his breath go. 'Reverend Mother, a man of my years shouldn't be subjected to such frights.' He endeavoured to keep his voice light. 'A tired old heart doesn't enjoy the shock.'

'Forgive me, but I want you to hear something.' Her words were whispered.

'What is it, Reverend Mother?' he asked, immediately concerned.

She drew him back along the corridor. 'Every night since Alice has been with us I, or one of the sisters, have stopped by her room to see if she is sleeping soundly. On two separate occasions I've heard her voice beyond the door. Sister Theodore has also heard her.'

'Is Alice having difficulty in sleeping? Many children talk to themselves when they're alone.'

'Oh no, Monsignor, she has no problem in sleeping. In fact, I would say the child sleeps too much and too often. However, the doctor thinks it's just as well considering the stress she's under.'

'You mean she's talking in her sleep?' His voice was too loud and he adjusted it as he said, 'It's nothing to be alarmed over, Reverend Mother. It's just a symptom of the turmoil she is going through. The loss of her father –'

'It's the words she says that concern me, Monsignor. They're . . . strange, unchildlike.'

Intrigued, Delgard moved closer to the door beyond which he knew Alice slept. 'What kind of words?' he whispered. 'What does she say?'

'Hear them yourself, Monsignor.' The nun turned the handle quietly and slowly opened the door a few inches. They listened. Delgard looked at Mother Marie-Claire quizzically and, although she could not see his face in the gloom, she sensed his puzzlement. 'She was speaking just a few moments –' Her voice broke off when they heard the murmurs from the bed. The nun pushed the door open further and slipped through, Delgard following close behind. A nightlight on a small table standing against the wall threw a dim glow around the sparse room, revealing the small, white-sheeted bed, the bundle lying beneath the covers. The figure stirred and the priest and the nun held their breath.

'O, do not deny me, sweet . . .'

Delgard tensed. It was Alice's voice, soft-spoken, mumbled almost, but there was a difference to it. He strained to hear the words.

'. . . let thy passion fill me . . .'

The voice was heavily accented, the vowels broadened, almost coarse.

'. . . mad, exceeding mad . . .'

Almost unintelligible, sometimes too soft to hear, sometimes too . . . too strange to comprehend.

'. . . have used me unmannerly . . .'

It wasn't a foreign accent, but one of an English county that he could not quite place. West Country, yet not quite. Too thick, too heavy. . . . She said a name, but Delgard did not catch it.

'. . . passion that flails my body . . .'

He made as if to move towards the bed and felt his arm held lightly by Mother Marie-Claire. 'Best not to disturb her, Monsignor Delgard,' the nun whispered.

He hesitated, wanting to hear more. But Alice's voice had deteriorated into a droning mumble, the words slurred and joined almost into one continuous sound. Even as he watched, she seemed to drift off into a deeper sleep and soon there were no more words, just a regular deep breathing.

The nun beckoned him to follow her from the room and, reluctantly, he did so. She closed the door quietly. 'What manner of speech is that, Reverend Mother?' Delgard asked, remembering to keep his voice low. 'Is it the same each time?'

'It seems to be, Monsignor,' she replied. 'Please come with me – there is something more I'd like to show you.'

Delgard glanced once more at the door before following the dark shape down the corridor. As they descended the stairs, the nun said, 'It's hard to understand what it is she is saying. At first I thought it might be an impediment of speech working subconsciously in her sleep. All those years of deafness – it would have had to have had some effect.'

'No, I'm sure that would be impossible. If the situation were reversed, if she spoke with an impediment while conscious and perfectly when asleep, there might be some sense to it. Not this way, though.'

'I agree, Monsignor. It was just a silly first thought, and quickly dismissed. Besides, I believe the words are well-formed, though strange to our ears.'

'Are they a dialect?'

'I believe them to be so, but one I can't place.'

'Nor me. Cornish, perhaps, but not quite.'

'No, not quite. Unfortunately, Alice talks in her sleep only in brief snatches, never enough to identify the source of her accent, or the meaning of her words.'

They reached the bottom of the stairs and Mother Marie-Claire crossed the hallway and opened the door to her private study. She indicated a chair for the priest to sit in. 'May I offer you a hot drink now, Monsignor Delgard?'

He shook his head. 'No, no. Perhaps in a moment. You said you had something to show me.'

She turned away and went to a chest of drawers. Before opening the top drawer, she said, 'Alice has been forced to spend a lot of time alone in her room. Perhaps too much time for one so young. There isn't much the convent can provide to keep her occupied, but she appears to enjoy working with paints and crayons.' She opened the drawer and drew out a folder. 'I've kept her discarded work since she's been with us.'

She returned to her desk and laid the folder on the top. 'Her fascination is for one subject alone.'

'Ah yes,' Delgard said, leaning forward. 'Father Hagan showed me some of her pictures before he died. Her mother had allowed him to take them from the house. They were all of one person, a person we surmised to be the Blessed Virgin.'

'Yes, Monsignor, that's right. Alice has no real skill as an artist, but she has a certain . . . enthusiasm for her subject. To the point of obsession, I would say.'

'The child worships Mary.' He allowed himself a smile. 'I think that's obvious to all. I think her devotion may . . .'

'Devotion? Is that what you think, Monsignor?' Mother Marie-Claire opened the folder and held the first sheet towards him. He took it and the sheet trembled in his grip.

'It can't . . .'

'The same figure throughout, Monsignor.' The nun spread other sheets of paper from the folder on the table. All bore the same crude workmanship, the same garish colours, the same broad, slashing strokes of the paintbrush.

Even the painted-in obscenities were the same, although an erect phallus in one might be different in size and colour from the next, the shape of the breasts different in shape from another, the grinning red mouth more distorted than the one next to it.

TWENTY-SEVEN

Their belief in the Magic was an abiding thing.

THE SECRET GARDEN
Frances Hodgson Burnett

Ben scooted along the rows of benches, Indiana Jones fleeing from hundreds – no, *thousands* – of screaming Arabs, ready to turn and whip swords from the hands of any who got too close, his imaginary bull-whip settled comfortably over his left shoulder and no weight at all. Up one row, down the next, slipping once on the damp grass, but up in a flash, pausing only to gun down the seven-foot-tall, black-clothed assassin brandishing a long, curved sword, laughing at his scream of surprise, speeding on in his race to find the Lost Ark before the dirty Nazis got to it and used its power to win the world. Indiana Jones was better than Han Solo (even if it was the same man) and Han Solo was better than Luke Skywalker. Run, out of breath, mustn't stop, mustn't catch me, out of breath, got to keep going, mustn't – somebody's foot!

He sprawled on the ground and hands reached down to pick him up. It hadn't hurt, just jarred his knee. He rubbed at the earth on his jeans and a voice said, 'Careful, son, you're going to hurt yourself if you tear around like that.'

He said nothing, remembering he was still Indy, a man of few words. The hands released him and with one bound he was free.

The field was fast filling up with people, the benches nearer to the scaffolded centre-piece – not those specially roped off for particular Church and non-Church dignitaries, nor those reserved for certain religious associations – becoming more and more full, the crowd spreading outwards like a blossoming flower. It was still early, two hours before the Mass was due to begin, but already the people were pushing through the newly constructed entrance gate to the field, eager to find a seat near the altar, many wanting just to see the Miracle Girl, others wanting to be close so that her holiness would wash over them, fearful that it wouldn't stretch too far back.

The sun was just a dull glow in the hazy sky and there was a harshness in the air that was particularly unkind to the invalids in the crowd. The buzz of conversation, of excitement, and of a certain fear, increased as the numbers swelled; the well-organized stewards, ushers, the young priests called in to help marshal the expected huge congregation, could not help but feel a trembling of their own senses as the intoxicating atmosphere spread. Voices were hushed, reverential, as though the gathering were inside a cathedral, only their multiplicity giving them an overall loudness. Wheelchairs, their passage through the field not easy because the soft earth had been churned up by too many feet, were already beginning to obstruct the aisles and the ushers made mental notes that an area would have to be sectioned off for such invalids on future occasions.

Ben ran on, this time careful to avoid booby-trap feet, keeping to the less occupied benches, a seven-year-old enjoying his game, oblivious to the gathering tension, lost in the excitement of his own mind's creation. A truck-load of dirty Nazis was tearing down on him and he rolled over the bench to his right, shooting the driver in the face as he went by. Then he was up again, running on, fearless and to be feared. He was dimly aware that the game would have to end soon, that his mother had made him promise to return to the church before the field became too full. If she wasn't there, she would be in the priest's house. It wasn't too full yet, there were plenty of empty benches, plenty of dark, Arab alleyways, plenty of –

The man had just entered that particular row and Ben's hurtling body caught him momentarily off-balance, knocking him onto the bench on which he was about to sit. He held the boy's shoulders to steady him and Ben, startled and breathless, looked up into his face. The man cringed inside when he saw the boy's eyes widen in shock, his mouth drop open, his body become rigid. The man could only smile to reassure him, but even that made his physical mask more grotesque.

He released his grip and the boy slowly shrank away, never taking his eyes off the man's ulcerated mouth and nose, the terrible disfigurement of facial tuberculosis. He lifted the silk scarf, dislodged when the boy had cannoned into him, to his face again, the mask natural enough on such a cold day. He shouldn't have been here, not with this terrible affliction; people were afraid of him, friends, so-called loved ones, afraid his disease was contagious. In the old days *lupus vulgaris* was known as 'dog's muzzle' and the description was appropriate; sometimes they treated him warily, like a crazy dog, afraid he would bite them and they would become as he. The skin disease was rare, but that gave him no feeling of distinction, just a sense of hopelessness, a feeling of impotent fury that he should be chosen to bear the hideous brand which, for *him*, no antibiotics could clear. One last hope. Today, one last hope. If not, if he could never again feel another's lips against his, never look into another's eyes without seeing the barely-hidden revulsion therein – never hold a child without feeling their muscles tense to run away – then there was no point to it all, no reason to go on. What was so precious about life that you felt obliged to live it? Better cold, senseless oblivion than a scorned existence. He watched the boy run from him and tried to retain the numbness in his mind, his only barrier against the seeping self-pity.

Ben ran on, afraid now of this big field, these people pouring in, all strangers, all suddenly a threat. Time to find mummy; Indiana Jones had faded without final credits.

'You'll have to move on. Nowhere to park here.'

'Press.' Fenn leaned across and flashed his card at the constable.

'Yeah, you and eight thousand others. Keep moving.'

Fenn forced his car back into the slow-moving traffic. 'Bloody carnival day again,' he muttered.

'What?' Nancy asked.

'It's amazing how many'll turn up for a free show, isn't it?'

'I think a lot of them have stronger motives for coming than that, Fenn.'

'Maybe.'

They were nearing the drive to the priest's house and Fenn saw even that was blocked with vehicles, presumably those of visiting clergy and helpers. He swore. 'I should have cleared it with Delgard to get parking space. I'm supposed to be "official".'

'I guess we should have gotten here earlier.' Nancy studied the shuffling people, the queue spilling into the road, police and stewards at various points endeavouring to keep some kind of order, preventing the thoroughfare itself from being swamped. The coach in front of Fenn's hired car came to a halt and he reluctantly eased his foot down on the brake pedal. Nancy poked her head out the window on her side to see what was causing the hold-up.

'There's an ambulance up ahead – by the entrance to the field, I think,' she told him. 'Yeah, it's unloading. Jesus, coupla stretcher cases.'

'Doesn't surprise me. They'll be bringing their dead along next.'

Nancy rummaged in her bag for cigarettes. 'I'm not sure why you're still so cynical,' she said as she lit up. 'You gotta face it, there's been results.'

'I know, but look, look over there.' He indicated to the opposite side of the road where makeshift stalls were set up on the grass verge. Through the gaps in the crowds around the stalls they could see small statues and holy trinkets hung from wire frames, while flimsy posters of the Virgin Mother, the Virgin and the Christ-baby, the Virgin at the Crucifixion, hung limply from long strings tied to the branches of trees behind the stalls. They caught a glimpse of a poster of the Pope in a cowboy hat, another blurred one of him being shot. The traders looked sullen, even though business appeared to be brisk. A Mr Whippy van looked busiest of all, and Fenn wondered if Madonna ice-lollies were on sale.

'I'm surprised your police allow it.'

'Probably too busy keeping the crowds under control to worry about unlicensed traders,' Fenn replied, moving the car on again as the coach in front advanced.

'Looks like nobody's getting into St Joseph's today,' Nancy said as they approached the church gate.

He saw the policemen moving the queue along past the locked gate, patiently explaining to the more insistent that the service was to take place in the field today, not the church. 'They don't look too happy about it.'

'I'm not surprised – it's goddamned cold outside.'

'It's not going to do some of those invalids much good.' Fenn shook his head. 'I can't understand their doctors allowing it.'

'You can't stop human nature, Fenn. If they think they're going to get cured, nothing'll keep them away. How would you feel, say, if you had an incurable disease, or a terminal illness? Wouldn't you take one last desperate chance, even if you thought the possibility of being cured was a thousand – or even a million – to one?'

He shrugged. 'Who knows?'

'You'd have nothing to lose.'

'Except to feel pretty stupid.'

'What's stupid against a chance to live again?'

He remained silent, accepting the point. Then he said, 'There's the entrance to the field. Look, it's jammed solid.'

They could now see that the queue converged on the gate from both directions, forming an untidy mass at the entrance.

'If only I were selling tickets,' Fenn muttered.

They drove on, the journey slow, cars, vans and coaches now parked bumper to bumper along the roadside, only the immediate area around the church and field entrance kept clear by the police. 'You want to jump out here while I find somewhere to park?' Fenn suggested.

'You're going to see Delgard, aren't you?'

He nodded.

'Then I'll stick with you.'

'Suit yourself.'

'Like glue.'

'Okay.'

Ahead, he saw the driver of a coach parked half on the grass verge having a heated argument with a policeman. Guessing what the dispute was over, Fenn swung in towards the vehicle's rear tyre and stopped. Angry blasts from horns behind greeted the manoeuvre as other drivers were forced to swing around and squeeze through the gap between his hired Fiesta and approaching traffic.

'What the hell are you doing, Fenn?'

'The road isn't wide enough for coach parking so the driver's being moved on now that his passengers are unloaded.'

'It doesn't look like he's moving to me.'

'He will be.'

Fenn was right. With a last gesture of disgust the driver disappeared back inside and the coach throttled into life. He pulled out into the traffic without signalling and without waiting for space. Fenn whipped in quickly, two cars behind following his strategy. 'There you go,' he said triumphantly as he pulled on the handbrake.

They left the car and began the walk back to St Joseph's, keeping to the opposite side of the road from the shuffling queue. 'There's gotta be thousands upon thousands here today,' Nancy remarked, pulling her scarf around her throat to keep out the cold.

'There were thousands last week.'

'Yeah, but not this many. Even the Pope couldn't haul in these kind of numbers.'

Soon they were forced into the roadway to avoid the people clustered around the traders' stalls. They stopped for a closer inspection of the wares. 'Unbelieveable,' Fenn said, shaking his head and smiling at the same time. 'Look, over there.' He pointed. 'Flasks containing Holy Soil from the field of the Madonna. Jesus wept!'

Nancy picked up a small dome-shaped transparent container filled with water in which an ill-defined plastic version of Mary stood. She shook it and snowflakes almost obliterated the image.

Fenn shook his head again in amused dismay when he saw a seven-inch shrine, again made of plastic, small red candles in holders on either side of an inset photograph of Alice which had obviously hastily replaced another kind of holy picture. The black and white shot had been reproduced from a newspaper, for the blow-up revealed the fine print dots to a crude degree.

Nancy pointed out a white-painted grotto whose lights flashed on intermittently to reveal a Madonna and what could only have been Bernadette of Lourdes.

They watched as a pilgrim picked up a tiny doll which bore the faintest resemblance to Alice Pagett, and a mechanical parody of a child's voice said, 'Hail Mary, full of grace, the Lord is . . .'

'I don't believe it,' Fenn said. 'How can they manufacture these things so fast.'

'They call it enterprise,' Nancy said, not amused by any of the trivia on display. 'They're just quick and simple adaptations of junk that's been selling for years. I'll bet under some of those labels saying "Alice, the Miracle Worker" or "Our Lady of Banfield" you'll find others referring to something totally different.'

They moved on, passing medallions of all shapes and sizes, crucifixes plain and gaudy, chinaware, handbags, even umbrellas, somehow alluding to the fact that they were all touched by holiness. They were approached by a man selling postcards of Sussex villages, Banfield itself not among them. Fenn declined the offer to buy with a bemused wave of his hand.

They crossed the road when they were opposite the gate leading to St Joseph's, dodging between the slow-moving cars and plunging into the queue. The policeman they had spotted earlier directing the crowd barred their way.

Fenn took out his Press card. 'Monsignor Delgard is expecting me.'

The policeman turned towards a steward who was lurking beyond the entrance. 'D'you know anything about a Mr Gerald Fenn?'

The small man, who had spoken with Fenn on a previous occasion, nodded his head. 'He's okay, you can let him through.'

The gate swung open and Nancy made as if to follow her companion.

'Sorry, miss, Mr Fenn only.'

'But I'm with him.' Nancy opened her bag and took out her card. 'Look, I'm Press too.'

'Miss, er, Shelbeck?' The policeman had scrutinized the card and turned towards the other man again.

'No, don't know anything about her.'

'Sorry, miss, you'll have to use the other entrance further down. Only authorized persons allowed through here.'

'But I told you, I'm with *him*.' She pointed at Fenn who was trying not to grin.

'I'd like to oblige you, miss, but I'm afraid I can't.'

'Fenn, will you speak to this guy?'

'Sorry, Nancy. I guess orders is orders.'

'You bastard! You knew this would happen.'

Fenn held out his hands in mock denial. 'How could I?'

Nancy's mouth became a straight line across her face. 'Now, look, officer, I'm from the *Washington Post*. I'm here to cover this –'

'I'm sure you are,' came the polite but firm reply, 'but if you'll just join the queue. You can go straight to the front, just show your Press card.'

'But –' she saw there was no point in arguing. 'I'll see you later,' she snapped at Fenn before shoving her way back into the crowd.

Fenn passed through the gate, the grin broad on his face. It slowly faded as he walked along the shadowed path towards the church. He felt uncomfortable, as though the old building itself were watching him, the black open doorway waiting to devour his soul. If there was such a thing as a soul. He wasn't sure (he'd reached no definite conclusions – and how could anyone?), but he thought he believed in the 'spark' of life, an essence inside which gave man his drive, generating energy as well as thoughts, through chemically derived impulses. A tiny pilot light, if you like, that was necessary to set everything else in motion. So what was God? A bigger spark? Were his and all the others just offshoots from the big one? Or was God everything the different religions wanted Him to be?

And did it really matter? Not to Fenn. And maybe not even to God.

But the church puzzled him. There was a coldness to it that seemed to be more noticeable each time he visited – unless he, himself, was absorbing the fears of first Hagan, and now Delgard. 'Spiritually devoid' was a strange expression to anyone who had no particular beliefs in that direction, so why did it seem so apt to him? He had been disappointed that his week's research had uncovered no deep mysteries or scurrilous activities surrounding St Joseph's or the village, but only because it would have provided an interesting, perhaps intriguing, storyline. Yet had he been that cynical when he had first undertaken the research, or was it just rationalization after discovering no hidden skeletons? He remembered that his attack on the archives had been almost obsessive. The fire, the deaths of the priest and Alice's father, the strangeness of Alice herself, and the veiled insinuations of Monsignor Delgard, had instilled doubts and suspicions in his own mind, had kindled a peculiar fear within himself, one that he had not understood and could not ignore. Perhaps the week of relentless research had purged the fear from him, the multitude of mundane historical facts and dates overwhelming the real purpose of his searches.

He stood outside the worn building and gazed up at the small tower. Its origins dated from way back – no one was sure just how far back its history went – and he wondered at how much the ancient stones must have witnessed, how times had changed beneath its spire, those changes escalating with each passing century. It had stood, or parts of it had stood, from pre-mediaeval England to the era of microchips and space rockets, through sorcery and superstition into the age of the realist. If the church were human, if stone and mortar were flesh and blood, the window its eyes, the altar its brain, how would it absorb those vast changes, what effect would they have on its living being? And would its spiritual aura survive the debasing onslaught of materialism? Or would the wisdom-giving years pass on a new perception that far surpassed the achievements of scientific knowledge?

He shook himself. Jesus, Fenn, a philosopher yet. It was just a pile of stones standing before him, with no feelings, no brain, and no soul. Man-made, stamped and packaged by the Roman Catholic Church. End of profound philosophical contemplation. Footsteps made him turn sharply.

'Can I help you?' It was a different priest to the young Irishman that Fenn had spoken to in the church house more than a week before.

'Ah, yeah. My name's Fenn. I'm looking for Monsignor Delgard.'

'Oh yes, Mr Fenn, I've heard all about you. I've just left the Monsignor up at the presbytery.'

'Thanks.' The reporter turned in that direction.

'He's rather busy now, preparing for Mass.'

'I won't take up much of his time,' Fenn replied over his shoulder.

The priest went into the church.

As he walked, Fenn could see the gathering in the field just beyond the graveyard. He paused and squinted his eyes, looking towards the distant oak tree, noticing with interest the platform built before it, the raised altar. 'Showtime,' he muttered and went on.

He knocked on the door of the presbytery, then rang the doorbell too, his usual method of announcing his arrival when given two options, and raised his eyebrows in surprise when Sue answered.

'Hi,' he said.

'Hello, Gerry.'

'You on the team now?'

'Just helping. So much is going on.' She stood aside so that he could enter. 'Did you want to see Monsignor Delgard?' Sue asked, then added pointlessly, 'Of course you did.'

'It's good to see you.' And it was, even though she looked tired, dark shadows under her eyes, hair not as springy and vibrant as usual. 'You been losing sleep, Sue?'

'What?' She brushed a wisp of hair away from her face and looked away as though embarrassed. 'Oh, no, no, I'm fine,' she said with false lightness. 'Working too hard, I suppose.'

He moved closer. 'Doing two jobs: the radio station and the church.'

'St Joseph's doesn't take up too much time, not really.'

'What do you do here?'

'It's not just me, there's a few women from the village who come in to help. We clean the church, the house. Buy food in for the monsignor – he's terribly busy, you know. This morning I've been answering the phone for him – it seems to have been ringing non-stop.'

'And answering the door?'

'Yes, that too.'

'Is Ben with you?'

'He's around somewhere, in the field, I think. I tried to call you lots of times this – last – week.' She looked at him with concern.

He smiled, pleased that she had. 'I got snowed under. Thought I needed to keep away from people for a while.'

'You weren't at the *Courier*.'

'No, I was doing some digging for Monsignor Delgard. Sorry you couldn't reach me, but then I didn't think you wanted to.'

'After the accident last week, the fire? You didn't think I'd care? I heard you were involved, heard it from others.' Her eyes glistened softly.

'Oh, Chri . . . ! I really am sorry, Sue, but you know you've been kinda funny towards me. I didn't even know if you wanted to see me again.' He reached out and put a hand on her arm.

She looked down and was about to say something when the phone, nearby in the hallway, rang. 'I'll have to get that.' She turned away from him and picked up the receiver. 'Oh, Bishop. Yes, did you want the monsignor? No, I haven't been out there myself for a while, but one of the priests told me it's getting very crowded . . .'

Delgard emerged from a door just off the hallway. He smiled and gave a small wave when he saw Fenn. Sue handed him the receiver and whispered, 'It's Bishop Caines, wants to know how everything's going.'

Delgard nodded and took the phone. Sue came back to Fenn. 'It's pretty hectic just now,' she said, speaking quietly so that the priest would not be interrupted.

'Can I see you later?' Fenn asked, feeling slightly ridiculous having to ask.

'Do you really want to?'

'What kind of question is that?'

'Where were you last week? I mean, where did you stay?'

The lie came easily. Only he decided not to tell it. 'We'll talk about it later.' He was surprised himself that he had not immediately told her he had stayed in a Chichester hotel, near to John Dene House where the historical records of Sussex were kept.

'You're not keeping something from me?'

He decided honesty couldn't run too deep. 'Nothing.' he replied.

Delgard had replaced the receiver and was coming towards them. 'Gerry, I'm certainly glad to see you again. I thought perhaps I'd frightened you away.'

Sue looked at the priest sharply, but said nothing.

'You don't know how much you got me to chew off,' Fenn said. 'I haven't crammed so much since I left school.' He added as an afterthought, 'Although I didn't cram too much then.'

'You can tell me on the way over to the church. I have to get into my vestments for the Mass.'

'You're taking it?'

'I seem to have inherited a parish, at least temporarily. Susan, will you look after Alice and her mother while we go to the vestry?'

'Alice is here? In the house?' Fenn's voice rose in surprise.

'I thought it best we install her in here early. That way she won't have to fight her way through all the people who have come to see her. We'll just go through the churchyard into the field.'

'Seems like a good idea. Could I see her?'

'I really must make ready for the service now and I'm anxious to hear what you've uncovered. I'd rather you came over to the church with me.'

'Sure. Maybe later?'

The priest did not answer, but glanced at his watch and said to Sue, 'Bishop Caines is on his way from Worthing, he should be here in twenty minutes or so, unless the traffic holds him up. Will you wait here with Alice and the Reverend Mother until he arrives, then take them to their places five minutes before Mass begins?'

She nodded.

'I think the bishop may arrive with an entourage.'

'I'll take care of them, Monsignor.'

He smiled his thanks and led Fenn outside. As they walked back towards the church, he said, 'You look tired, Gerry.'

'You know, I was just about to say the same thing to you. And so does Sue. I think she's taken on too much.'

'Perhaps we all have.' He turned his head to study the reporter's face. 'She's a good woman, very able, very sincere. She told me her faith had wandered for a while, but now it seems to have returned with a renewed vigour.'

'Because of Alice?'

'They say the true miracle of Lourdes is not the sick that are cured, but the replenishing, the strengthening, and even the beginning, of faith for the pilgrims.'

'Sue appears to have caught the bug.'

The priest laughed. 'I think that's an appropriate description. It is rather like catching a bug, although there are no ill-effects, just good ones.'

'That's a matter of opinion.'

'Ah yes, I understand your relationship is under some stress. But do you really blame Susan for that, Gerry?'

'Not entirely.'

Delgard thought it best to leave the subject alone; there were far more important issues to concern himself with at that time. Fenn was an impulsive, and certainly selfish, young man. Some aspects of his scepticism were healthy and clearly intrinsic in the profession he'd chosen, while others were somewhat destructive. He had an air of ruthlessness about him, although it was often disguised beneath an apparent nonchalant attitude; yet Delgard suspected the reporter was a compassionate man, again that sensitivity concealed beneath an indifferent exterior. It was the priest's understanding of the human character through years of listening, delving, consoling, that allowed his harsh assessment – not judgement – of Fenn to be tempered by more kindly impressions. The man was complex but ultimately likable, someone whose faults could irritate but could be soon forgotten.

'Have you discovered anything of interest, Gerry?' Delgard asked.

Fenn took a deep breath. 'Nothing that relates to our – your – particular problem. I'll type out my notes for you in some kind of order, giving correct dates and names, but I can give you a brief run-down now.'

Then had reached the church door and Fenn shivered when they entered the gloomy interior. 'It's cold.'

'Yes,' was all the priest said.

The church was empty, the priest that Fenn had passed earlier either in the vestry or having left to join the congregation in the field.

'Let's sit here.' Delgard pointed to a bench.

'I thought you were in a hurry.'

'There's time to talk. Please proceed.'

They sat, Fenn on one bench, Delgard in front, his body twisted to face the reporter, his back to the altar.

'Okay, here goes,' Fenn said, taking out a notebook from his pocket. 'I'm afraid this place isn't famous for much. I'll amend that: it isn't famous for anything. It gets its first official mention as far back as 770 AD when the Saxons had a castle nearby at Stretham. The Lord of the Manor was granted a charter by Osmund, the King of the West Saxons, to assign fifteen hides of land to endow the church in Banefelde. Presumably it was this one, St Joseph's, since there's no record of any other churches existing at that time. The village seems to have had a variation in spelling over the years, by the way. Banefelde, Banedryll, Banefeld without the "e" on the end, Banfield got to be the final handle.

'Before the coming of the Saxons, prehistoric men had a track right across the county, east to west, and it went right through the settlement which eventually became this village. You've got to remember this part of the country was nearly all forest-land; the settlement was probably just a clearing in the forest.

'Its second earliest official mention was in the Domesday Survey in 1085 when William wanted to know just how much the kingdoms were worth and who exactly was in them. Not much seems to have happened since. A little excitement around Reformation time and the Civil War in the following century. Sixty-two villagers died of the plague in the seventeenth century. Not much of any importance until it became a staging post on the London to Brighton turnpike in the eighteenth. Oh yeah, that's when it got its own workhouse, too, for the parish destitutes. The villagers also got their own railway line around 1880 and kept it until the cuts a hundred years later. It could be the line will be re-established with all the attention Banfield's getting now.

'A few familiar names keep cropping up over the years, some going right back to the thirteenth and fourteenth centuries. Southworth's one of them. Two others, Backshield and Oswold, are with him on the parish council today. There's a Smythe who gets several mentions, Breedehame, Woolgar, Adams and a Charles Dunning who seems to have been of some note. He was knighted in the time of Henry VIII. Most were independent landowners or farmers. There was conflict between some of the families during the Civil War – some supported Charles I, others hung in with Cromwell. Knowing village feuds, they probably resent each other to this day. A few of the villagers have been involved in smuggling. I suppose it was an open road from the coast with plenty of places to hide along the way. That was about all the skulduggery that went on, or at least was recorded.' He smiled at the priest.

Delgard waited for him to continue and frowned when he didn't. 'That's it?' he asked in surprise.

'That's the bones of it. You'll get the details in my typed notes. Sorry I couldn't provide you with murders, pagan sacrifices or witch-burning, but they're just not there.'

'It's something of an anticlimax.'

'Especially when you've been through just about everything written on the place since Saxon times. Dead-ends are never fun.'

'The church itself. There must be more on the church.'

'There is. Not much though. In England, Sussex was one of the last pagan strongholds. It was cut off from the north by forests, on the east and west by marshes, and the south by sea. Augustine and his Christian followers from Rome got short shrift from the natives at that time. It took a bishop called Wilfred, who was driven onto the Sussex coast by rough seas, to make the breakthrough. He was appalled by the barbarism and resolved to come back and convert the savages. He did, twenty years later, and got his way. The story goes that Banfield, or Banefelde as it was known, was one of the last settlements to hold out. The interesting thing is that the first Christian church – and we can only assume it was St Joseph's – was built over the pagan's place of worship. And their burial grounds.'

There was an iciness in Delgard's stare that was a reflection of inner thoughts and not directed at Fenn. He said, 'That's probably not significant; many churches have been built over pagan altars as a firm and symbolic rebuttal of what previously took place. And burial grounds have always been sacred in the minds of men, Christian or pagan.'

'Sure. It's just a statement of fact from me, not an insinuation.'

The priest nodded. 'Please go on.'

'The first curate to get a mention here was . . .' he consulted his notebook '. . . a John Fletcher. That was in 1205. The church records, by the way, only go back as far as 1565, and they deal solely with marriages and deaths. I got the information on Fletcher from a book on the village.'

'Are you sure?'

'Yeah. But I discovered something else that I'll get to in a minute. As I said before, Banfield was particularly resistant to Bishop Wilfred and his followers when they began converting the Sussex people. A lot of blood was spilt. Once the church was established, though, there were no more problems – at least, none that have been recorded. Some trouble with Charles II – the minister here was a Royalist and was involved in sneaking the king across the Downs to the coast where he took a boat to France. Cromwell had the priest executed. Apart from that, the clergy have kept a low profile in Banfield; no scandals, no misuse of church funds, and no anarchy.

'But the records only date to the late sixteenth century. We don't know how this church was affected with the spreading of Lutheranism in England. Those were troubled times for Catholics.'

'The Reformation brought change and problems to all the churches in this country, but I couldn't find anything specific to St Joseph's. One or two dignitaries in the area got into heavy trouble when they wouldn't swear allegiance to Henry VIII as head of the English Church, but most decided to go along with the idea for the sake of peace. Besides, many were benefitting from the transformation; Henry was selling off the lands available with the dissolution of the monasteries, and the gentry were the recipients.'

Something was nagging at the back of Delgard's mind, a teasing, darting thought that dissolved like a disturbed dream each time he tried to focus on it.

'There were opposing factions in Banfield,' Fenn continued, 'and the controversy was probably used to continue feuds that had been going on for some time. Anyhow, there are no church records touching that period in the archives. And that leads to the matter I mentioned earlier.'

Delgard leaned towards the reporter, as though hearing his confession.

'Is there an old chest somewhere in the church?' Fenn asked.

The priest looked at him in surprise.

'An old chest made of thick elm or oak?' Fenn went on. 'It's held together by bands of Sussex iron. And, oh yeah, it has three locks.'

The priest shook his head slowly. 'I don't know of any such chest. I haven't seen it.'

'Could it be stored away somewhere?'

'There's only the vestry and the crypt. I'm sure it isn't in either.'

'In the house? The attic?'

'What size is it?'

'I'm not sure. Something like five feet by two. It's ancient, dates back to the fourteenth century.'

'No, it's not in the presbytery. Why is it important?'

'Because that's where old documents, church valuables, books and records were kept. I found mention of it in the archives. Henry VIII ordered that every church had a strong coffer, paid for by the parish, in which records were to be kept. That was in fifteen-something-or-other but, according to the archives, Banfield already had its own chest dating back two centuries before. We may be able to find more about St Joseph's from it.'

It was important. Somehow Delgard knew the chest was important. It tied up with the elusive thought he had had moments before. 'I can check the crypt later, after Mass.'

'I can do it now.'

Delgard hesitated, looked at his watch, and said, 'Very well. Come with me into the vestry and I'll give you the key; the entrance to the crypt is outside.'

He rose, a tall, dark-clothed man, his eyes in shadows. Fenn, still sitting, looked up at him and remembered how indomitable the priest had appeared when he had first laid eyes on him; now some of that strength seemed to have waned as though Delgard were drawing into himself, his vibrancy not gone but diminished. Although the change was barely discernible, Fenn was sure it wasn't just in his own imagination.

'Is something wrong?' the priest asked.

Fenn pulled himself together. 'Uh, no, just thinking. Let's get the key.'

As they walked towards the vestry, footsteps unnaturally loud in the empty church, Fenn glanced over at the statue of the Madonna. There was no whiteness left to it.

TWENTY-EIGHT

Then a child's puzzled voice was clearly heard. 'He's got nothing on!'

THE EMPEROR'S NEW CLOTHES
Hans Christian Andersen

Ben jigged his buttocks on the hard wooden bench, one cheek to the other, hands jammed beneath his legs. His mother sat beside him, eyes closed, oblivious to the noise around her.

Ben was over his earlier fright, having seen a lot more worse sights than the man with the funny face: men with no legs, children with heads too big and silly wobbly eyes, women with lumps and bumps and jelly limbs; and nervous eyes peering out of rag bundles in wheelchairs.

'I'm cold, Mummy,' he complained.

'Hush,' Sue told him. 'Mass'll be starting soon.' She looked around, amazed at the vast numbers. Here and there banners waved above the sea of pink faces, proclaiming districts and religious associations. Many in the row she sat in wore small badges denoting the wearers as pilgrims to Lourdes. A smart young man directly behind her bore a plastic identity card boasting that he was Anthony Roberts of St Peter's Tours. Others around him sported different coloured badges than those on the bench. A leaflet lay in the churned earth at her feet, discarded with some disgust by a pilgrim further along who had received it from a young girl as he had entered the grounds; it asked for contributions towards the following of the Rev. Sun Myung Moon in order that the Unification Church might become an important economic force. A muddy heelmark had sullied the moon-face of the man beaming from the leaflet, reducing the image to that of a soiled oriental Mr Happy. A contingent of white-robed figures sitting a few rows back had puzzled her at first, their bright ribbons and cloaks unfamiliar to any ecclesiastical order that she knew of, until the woman sitting next to her had noticed her gaze and given her a nudge. 'They're just a lay society,' the pilgrim had confided. 'Knights of the Holy Sepulchre they call themselves. We often see them at Lourdes.'

She and Ben were fortunate enough to be seated close to the recently erected altar-piece, its platform raised five feet above the ground so that all the congregation could witness the ceremony; a young priest, acting as usher and who knew Sue as a voluntary helper, had made the pilgrims shuffle along the bench until there was room for her and her son. The only reserved area was the benches in front of her and that was now filled with a mixture of clergy, nuns and 'civilians', some of whom in the latter group she recognized. The man called Southworth was one and she could see him chatting and laughing quietly with Bishop Caines, giving the impression that they were waiting for an open-air concert to begin rather than a holy service.

Across the centre aisle from her a wide area had been left clear for stretchers and wheelchairs; members of the St John's Ambulance Brigade, crisply-dressed young women who were obviously private nurses, and relatives of the invalids, sat on benches directly behind them. The Press had been given no special privileges, apart from being allowed early entry, and most had managed to find places near the front where they grouped together, some with notebooks poised, others who had seen it all before (though nothing *quite* like this, they had to admit) passing wry comments and wondering if it would be sacrilege to smoke. Cameramen were squeezed onto ends of benches, and many squatted on the grass in the central aisle, having already been moved back from directly beneath the altar. Television cameras had not been allowed inside the grounds, but cranes leered over the tall hedge along the roadside, zoom-lenses focused on the twisted oak tree and the simply decorated rostrum before it.

From certain sections of the congregation voices raised in gentle hymn could be heard; the chanting drone of prayers came from other groups.

Sue was tense and she sensed the people around her felt the same. If anything, the excitement that Sunday was at a higher pitch than on the previous week. The expectancy had somehow increased. Even Ben's eyes were shining, his usual boredom with just 'hanging around' not voiced, nor even hinted at. He was cold, but she felt his shivering was more akin to hers than to the chill; it was pure exhilaration, a feeling shared with everyone present. There was a sudden hush, and then a low, wondrous moan rippled through the crowd. Alice had been seen emerging through a newly-created opening in the church's boundary wall.

Molly Pagett held her daughter's hand and the Reverend Mother from the convent led the way to the seats in front of the altar. There was white apprehension on Molly's face, yet Alice was expressionless, her gaze only on the tree, not once looking at the crowds who watched her with reverent awe. Total silence descended.

Ben jumped to his feet, anxious to see what the grown-ups could see, but was too small to get a clear look over the heads and shoulders in front. Before his mother could stop him he clambered onto the bench. He saw Alice and was unimpressed.

Fenn descended the short flight of steps, careful not to slip on the moss-slimed surfaces, and inserted the long key into the door's rusted lock. Surprisingly, the key turned easily. He pushed open the door and stood there for a few seconds, allowing his eyes to become accustomed to the gloom inside, remembering the old TV programme he used to watch as a very young kid. 'Inner Sanctum' it had been called, and the credits each week always began with an old crypt door slowly swinging open, the creaking sound classically drawn out. He'd had bad dreams about that door and the unknown thing that lay beyond, but morning had always brushed the memory aside like a hand sweeping back a drape. Only now it was morning and this wasn't a dream. A damp, musty smell lurched out to greet him.

He smiled at his own nervousness. Delgard had assured him that St Joseph's no longer kept its dead below stairs.

His hand groped around the wall just inside the door, feeling for the light switch. He found it, clicked it down.

'Wonderful,' he muttered. The poor light barely reached the chamber's four walls.

He moved in and felt a fresh – no, a dank – coldness creeping under his skin. Something scuttled away into some dark recess. Cardboard boxes littered the floor. An old table with heavy Michelin legs and battered surface stood in the centre, a wooden, paint-blotched ladder leaning like an inebriate against it. Other grey shapes loitered just beyond the circle of light.

Fenn looked around, hoping to find the chest without searching. A low, squarish object covered by a dust sheet caught his eye and he cautiously headed towards it. The floor was uneven and his shoes became wet as he walked through puddles that had formed in the dips. He squatted and reached towards the mildewy cover.

Monsignor Delgard turned to the congregation, his large hands resting on either side of the lectern, eyes looking into the expanse of expectant faces rather than the missal before him. He drew in a sharp breath, his stooped shoulders almost straightening.

Dear God, there are thousands, *thousands*.

Why have they come here? What do they want of the child?

His heart grieved for the sick among them, the cripples and invalids who regarded him with shining eyes, with lips that were parted, smiles of anticipation lightening their haunted features. Oh dear Lord, please help them in their faith; don't let disappointment taint it. What happened before with the child cannot be repeated, they must realise that. Let today be the end of all this! Show them there are no miracles here.

The two microphones skilfully fitted into the lectern whined disconcertingly for a few moments.

A small breeze licked at the pages of the missal.

The emotions of the congregation seemed to sweep over him in euphoric waves and his head felt light with its directed energy. Flushed faces spread out before him, pink pebbles on an undulating beach, reaching back, beyond the point where there were no more benches, the change in level resembling a tide-caused step, stretching to the entrance of the field, the high hedges that bordered the road a green, containing sea wall. It's madness, he told himself. A foolish delusion in which the Catholic Church should take no part. Bishop Caines was smiling encouragingly below him. Southworth had his head turned, watching the crowds. There were many other priests out there, their presence giving credence to the deception. But no, there was no deception! Alice Pagett was a sincere child! There could be no deep, grievous sin on her young soul. Perhaps it was he, the priest, who was in sin with this doubt, this refusal to accept that which he himself had witnessed. Perhaps he lacked the humility to believe that a child could evoke such spiritual power. Perhaps . . .

He raised his hands to shoulder level, palms outwards, and began the service. Alice was watching him intently, her eyes staring yet somehow glazed, expressionless, looking right through him . . . looking . . . looking not at him . . . but at the tree . . .

The cover felt clammy to his touch and Fenn had to force himself to grip the material and pull it away. A wooden box lay beneath and tiny black things fled across its surface from the exposing light. He knew immediately that it wasn't the chest he sought – it was too small and not ancient enough – but decided to open it anyway; the relevant documents might well have been transferred to it some time in the past. There was no lock; he lifted the lid.

Swirling dust particles caused him to sneeze and he looked down at the old books and papers with watery eyes. The lid fell backwards as he reached inside and grabbed a book. It was a well-worn Parish Mass Book, the words inside in Latin. Dead. Defunct. Only to be used by religious die-hards since the Vatican had decided that modern-day native language was flavour-of-the-month. The book beneath was the same, the one below the one beneath also the same; the box was full of them. The papers were yellowing hymn sheets, nothing more. He closed the lid, disappointed. That would have been *too* easy.

Fenn stood and, hands on hips, scanned the underground chamber once more. Christ, it was cold! He moved to the centre, the light bulb, with its heavy metal shade, just six inches above his head and casting black shadows beneath his brow and nose. Two insects flickered around the light, unknowingly seeking death in their personal sun.

How many ancient bones were beneath this floor? Fenn wondered. Pagan bones, heathen remains. Did their spirits linger when their bodies were done? He realized he was spooking himself unnecessarily and mentally kicked his own shin. Get on with it, Fenn, and then get out!

He followed his own advice and strode over to a pile of boxes behind a stack of chairs in one corner of the crypt, whistling tunelessly as he began pulling at them. A quick look-through should suffice, no need to examine anything too closely, it was an old chest he was after, quite big, too big to hide itself away easily. A discarded radiator, disturbed by his searching, began to slither down the wall it had been leaning against; it crashed to the floor with a thunderous clang, the noise echoing off the damp stone walls.

Fenn froze, shoulders hunched, until the reverberations died away. Sorry, he apologized to the ghosts, then continued looking.

He went over to the grey shapes that had been silently watching throughout. They stood like stunted spectres, and he winced at their disfigurements as he drew close. There were four of them and two still had some faded colour left in their chipped plaster clothes; the other two had begun life as white, but now were almost as black as the darkness around them. You've got a pal upstairs who'll be joining you soon, he silently told them, thinking of the crazy-paved Madonna. The nearest was a noseless/chinless Christ, who appeared to be holding something in one curled arm; its other arm was broken off at the elbow. Fenn bent slightly, curious to see what was the strange looking object he held. 'Nice,' he murmured when he discovered it was a stone heart with a little cross protruding from the top like a faded strawberry stalk.

The statue behind was taller, its surface discoloured and grimy. This one was presumably a sculpture of Jesus too, although, without a head and just part of a beard above a ravaged neck, it was hard to tell. The next was as small as the first and its form was slightly bent, the man depicted carrying a child on his shoulders. The staff was missing and both faces, the child's and the bearer's, had been mutilated, but Fenn easily guessed it was St Christopher and the Christ-boy.

He turned quickly towards the light as it dimmed momentarily. 'Don't you bloody dare,' he snapped. It grew bright instantly.

Fenn returned his attention to the damaged statues. There was something familiar about the one at the very back. He narrowed his eyes, wishing the light were stronger; the metal lampshade cutting out half its beam didn't help much either. Squeezing past the first statue, he peered between the two blocking his way. The face that stared back sightlessly was the same as the face upstairs in the church. It was Mary and she looked serene.

He frowned in puzzlement. From across the chamber, this figure had looked in as bad shape as the others, soiled, cracked and parts missing; it must just have been the poor light throwing deceptive shadows, for no mutilations or grime were evident that close. He tried to get nearer; there was something about the blind staring eyes . . .

Resting one hand on the headless statue to his right, he leaned forward. The white face was smiling. And he had the uncanny feeling that the eyes could see him. His other hand touched the St Christopher and the child-burdened figure wobbled dangerously. He steadied the statue and eased his body closer to the shadowy Virgin. It had to be a trick of the light: the smile on the stone lips seemed to have broadened. He blinked. They seemed to have parted, too.

There was a numbness in his mind as though pain freezer had been sprayed onto certain brain cells. The pupil-less eyes were mesmerizing. Fenn's breathing was shallow, but he hardly noticed. He had to get closer, had to touch the statue, had to touch those parted lips.

The light was dimming. Or did it appear to be, because he could only focus on those moist lips, those piercing eyes? There was a faint sputtering noise behind, but he barely registered the sound or noticed the flicker.

He was only a foot, perhaps just inches away, and he could get no further; the other two statues held him in check. He stretched forward, craning his neck towards the soft lips, the two guardians beginning to tilt.

He could not move any nearer, but just before the light disappeared, the statue of Mary moved towards him.

Priest: *My brothers and sisters,*
            to prepare ourselves to celebrate the sacred mysteries
            let us call to mind our sins.

The wind stirred headscarves and banners and ruffled the hair on uncovered heads. People coughed above the silence. Somewhere a baby howled.

Priest: *Lord, we have sinned against you:*
            Lord have mercy.
Response: *Lord, have mercy.*

On top of a crane overlooking the field, a cameraman looked quizzically at his machine.

'Hey, what's going on down there?' he shouted, heedless of the Mass in progress. 'The power's fluctuating. Do something before the whole thing's messed up!'

Priest: *Lord, show us your mercy and love.*
Response: *And grant us your salvation.*

A press cameraman quietly cursed the motor on his Nikon. 'What a bloody time to pack up.' He didn't notice that several of his colleagues were having the same problem.

Priest: *May almighty God have mercy on us,*
            forgive us our sins,
            and bring us to everlasting life.
Response: *Amen.*

A woman reporter who had been quietly talking into her micro-cassette recorder shook it impatiently when the cogs slowly stopped turning. 'Fuck,' she cursed, keeping her voice low, and smacking the machine against the palm of her hand.

Priest:	*Lord, have mercy.*
Response:	*Lord, have mercy.*
Priest:	*Christ, have mercy.*
Response:	*Christ, have mercy.*
Priest:	*Lord, have –*

Monsignor Delgard clapped his hands to his ears as the microphones shrieked violently, then went dead.

Through half-closed eyes he saw Alice rise from the bench and come towards him.

The statues on either side of Fenn crashed to the floor and he fell with them. He cried out, suddenly aware he was in total darkness, the smashing of stone joining the cry. Something crushed his fingers, but the pain was hardly felt. A heavy weight fell on his shoulders, bearing him down, stunning him with the blow. Instinctively he tried to roll away and something to his right prevented him. He thrashed out, terribly afraid, remembering the Madonna statue, how it had moved, how it had wanted him . . . the desire in her eyes . . .

'No!' he shouted, his voice ringing around the corrupt-smelling chamber, and the sound increased his panic. He kicked out, pushed, shoved, heaved. The statue was unreasonably heavy, pressing hard against him. He managed to half-turn and his hand grasped at the cold stone. It was wet with slime and his fingers slid along its surface; at points his hand ran into what could only have been lichen but which felt like soft, rotting flesh.

He could almost feel hot, fetid breath warming his skin.

Fenn managed to pass an arm beneath the cumbersome weight and roared as he pushed. The statue slowly slithered off his body; a grating noise as it hit the floor. He turned, elbows beneath him, gasping in the foul air, his chest heaving. He had to get out, the very darkness was closing in! Reason told him the cellar was filled with dead, inanimate things; imagination insisted they could move, could breathe, could see. Could touch.

His feet slipped in wetness as he scrabbled to rise. He blinked against the blackness, afraid he would be smothered by it. The doorway, there was grey daylight coming from the doorway. He had to reach it.

He began to crawl, over dead, mutilated figures, through the sticky puddles formed on the uneven floor like stagnant underground lakes, knocking aside boxes, anything that got in his way, trying to gain his feet but still too unsteady, desperate to reach the light, desperate to get away from cold, lifeless fingers that stretched towards him from the darkness . . .

Only the light could return those fingers to stone. But now there was a shadow in that grey rectangle of open doorway, a mass of blackness that devoured the light as it moved closer to Fenn. As it reached out for him.

There were no more sounds from the crowd; no more coughs, no more children wailing, no more mumbled prayers. It was as if the thousands present were holding their breath as one. Even though only those nearest the raised platform could see what was happening, some mass-consciousness sent the tension eddying around the congregation like widening ripples on a disturbed pond. They held their breath and looked towards the centre-piece.

Then a hushed coalescent 'aaaah' escaped them as the tiny figure of the child mounted the steps to the altar. Wonder and excitement brimmed in their eyes. The television cameramen, on top of their cranes, could only groan with frustration at the untimely breakdown of their generator, none of them aware that their rivals were experiencing the same problem. A policeman outside the gate, and oblivious to what was taking place inside, could only frown at the static from his hand-radio as he tried to call in reinforcements. The crowds were fast becoming uncontrollable as they tried to push their way through the jammed entrance to the field.

Delgard felt his legs trembling as the rapturous little face approached him up the steps. She was so tiny and so frail, and her eyes saw something that was visible to no one else. Alice passed him and his body drained of vitality as though she were a strange spiritual magnet attracting energy. He swayed and had to reach for the lectern to steady himself. The oak tree rose up behind the altar, a black twisted giant, a looming creature that seemed to beckon the child.

Alice's eyes half-closed when she stood before the tree, white slits only showing between the lids. Her face slowly tilted upwards as if she were looking into the upper branches and a smile drew back over white teeth. Her yellow hair fell low between her shoulders and her hands rose away from her sides, ready to embrace. Her breathing came in short, sharp gasps, quickening so that her chest moved rapidly, gradually slowing, becoming even, deep, steady. Stopping.

The air shimmered around her and the clouds seemed blacker overhead. But then the sun broke through and the field, the altar, the tree, was bathed in a pure light.

Alice slowly turned to face her spellbound audience, her small body trembling, shivering with some inner ecstasy which the onlookers could feel growing within themselves.

Alice suddenly gasped as though an invisible blade had pricked her flesh; the smile remained, though, and became even more serene. And now the crowd gasped as she began to rise into the air.

'Fenn, what the hell is the matter with you?'

He stopped struggling, stopped trying to kick himself away from the figure stooping over him. His mind began to clear, although the panic still remained. 'Who . . . who is it?' he asked, voice shaking.

'Who the shit do you think it is, you idiot? It's me, Nancy.' She reached down for him again and this time her hand wasn't slapped away.

'Nancy?'

'Yeah, remember? The *friend* you unloaded at the church gate.'

He scrabbled to his feet and she had to hold him back as he tried to break for the door.

'Take it easy,' she snapped. 'There's a lot of junk lying around here – you'll break your goddam neck.' Nancy kept her arm through his, restraining him as they made for the open door. The last few steps were too much for him; he tore himself loose and rushed through. She found him leaning against the church wall outside, a stream of saliva running from his mouth as though he had just been retching.

She gave him a few more moments to recover, then said, 'You gonna tell me what happened down there?'

His shoulders heaved as he tried to regain his breath.

'I was on the other side of the wall,' Nancy said, concerned at his condition. 'I just caught a glimpse of you through the graveyard going down the steps to the door back there. It took me a little time to sneak over without the holy mafia stopping me.' Her voice softened. 'What happened, Fenn? You look as though you've seen the proverbial ghost.'

He let out a long sigh and turned to her. His eyes were watery. He said breathlessly, 'I . . . I . . . think I may have.'

Nancy chuckled and, now that he was outside in the daylight, in the open air, it seemed almost ridiculous to himself. Only *he* had been there; *he* had seen it. 'There . . . there was a figure . . .'

'You mean a statue. I heard the crash when you knocked it over, only it sounded like more than one.'

'There were four of them. But one . . . one at the back, the one of Mary wasn't. It wasn't a statue. It moved.'

'Hey, Fenn, are you serious? You just bumped into it and it toppled. I saw you from the doorway scrabbling around like a maniac. Why were you stumbling around in the dark anyway?'

'There was a light. It must have blown.'

'Yeah, scaring you to death when it did. That must have been when you tripped and knocked over the statues.' She chuckled again. 'Nice going.'

He shook his head; it all seemed so unreal.

'What were you looking for?' Her eyes were sharp, the amusement gone.

'Uh? Oh, a chest, an old chest we thought might be down there. It could have some early church records inside.'

'Let's go back and see if we can find it.'

She turned away and Fenn grabbed her arm. 'No, it's not there, I would have seen it.'

'Sure you're not just chicken?'

'I would have seen it!'

'Okay, okay, I believe you. Look, the service has already started, so let's get over there before we miss too much. You never know, it might just be another miracle day.' She took his hand and pulled him away from the wall. 'You're shaking,' she said in surprise, stopping to face him squarely. 'Jesus, you were really frightened.'

'I'll be okay in a minute.' But would he be okay when it was time to close his eyes and sleep?

'Sure.' Nancy touched fingertips to his cheek. 'Take it easy for a moment. We'll take a slow walk to the field.' She led him away from the church, away from the black hole in its side that was the crypt. Every so often, she sneaked a look at his face and frowned. She could understand his fright, his crashing around down there in the dark; it had scared *her*, for Chrissakes, just hearing the racket! Tripping through the graveyard with its crusty old tombs and tippling slabs had made her uneasy even though it was broad daylight. The little mountains of earth scattered around didn't lighten the atmosphere, either. By the time she'd reached the steps leading down into what looked like a murky pit, she was more than a little edgy! It was only because she thought Fenn had fallen and hurt himself that she had ventured inside. Still, scary or not, he was panicked to a ridiculous degree. Strange, he hadn't seemed the type to be scared of bogeymen.

Something felt wrong as they neared the recently-created gap in the low boundary wall, and Nancy couldn't quite figure just what. Fenn was too preoccupied with his own thoughts to notice. It dawned on her slowly as they drew nearer to the field. It was the silence. In a nine or ten acre plot crammed full with people, there was total, blanket silence.

She came to a halt and Fenn looked up in surprise. He, too, finally noticed the absence of sound. When they looked towards the raised altar they understood.

Monsignor Delgard sank to his knees, one hand still grasping the top of the lectern. Those watching, those who could tear their eyes off the child hovering five feet in the air, would have thought it was a gesture of homage and not just a sapping weakness in the priest's limbs. The altar-servers, who had been kneeling just moments before, were now half-sitting, half-lying on the platform, arms and elbows outstretched to support them.

Delgard's eyes felt misted; it was like watching the girl through a fine veil. He wiped his free hand across his brow, his arm leaden with its own weight, and told himself that what he saw was impossible. He wasn't dreaming, though; she was there above him, her face still tilted towards the sky, her arms slightly outstretched, the breeze ruffling her skirt. His lips moved in silent prayer.

One by one, the momentum gathering, people began to slip from their seats onto their knees, their action one of worship and not involuntary. Soon it was like a vast moving wave as the reaction spread, the shuffling sound curiously muted. There were tears on the faces of many, smiling adoration on the faces of others; some had to close their eyes against the glare that emanated from the girl, while others only saw a tiny, still form that appeared to glimmer and fade in their vision. All were humbled by the miracle child.

Delgard tried to rise and the strength just wasn't there. He watched open-mouthed as Alice bowed her head and her eyes, her gloriously blue eyes, opened fully. She smiled. And slowly, singularly, many of those who had been lying on stretchers on the ground or who had sat helplessly in wheelchairs, raised themselves to stagger and limp towards the altar. They gathered there, supporting each other, faces looking upwards, their eyes beseeching, a growing cluster of shattered, shrivelled bodies. Quiet, throaty murmurs came from them as they praised the child and the Madonna for what they felt was happening to them.

There was a sudden cry as a man with a hideously swollen and marked face pushed his way through the throng of invalids and collapsed on the steps leading up to the altar.

He stretched out a wavering arm and implored, 'Help me! Help meeeeee . . .' the sound dying in a high-pitched moan. His uplifted hand shot to his face and he screamed; when he took his hand away, bubbles of pus were bursting from his cheeks, mouth and chin.

Only Ben, who could see clearly, for he stood while others knelt, could not understand what was happening.

TWENTY-NINE

'How do you do?' she chirped. *'I'm so glad it isn't yesterday, aren't you?'*

POLLYANNA
Eleanor H. Porter

Riordon carefully closed the door to the cowshed, not wanting to disturb the creatures inside; they were tetchy enough already. He crossed the yard, making for the back door of the farmhouse, lights from the windows guiding him towards the warmth within. He shook his head and mumbled something under his breath. Times were hard enough without livestock playing up. He stopped for a moment, listening, coldness clamping tightly around him like a blood-pressure cuff around an arm. That bloody dog was howling again like a banshee in the night. It was the usual mutt, old Fairman's, starting it all off. His own, Biddy, would be next, then the Rixby's in the house further down the road. Three nights they'd been at it and there wasn't even a full moon for them to be making a fuss of! As if on cue, his labrador, Biddy, began to whine and then to howl from inside the house.

Mebbe it was that floodlight they kept on all night in the field yonder. It looked eerie enough, the way it lit up that blasted oak; mebbe Fairman's animal could see the glare from its kennel, the light being unfamiliar en'all. Riordon had never liked the tree when he had owned the field it stood in, although he had never understood why – it was just ugly, he supposed – but the field was only used for grazing so the oak was doing no harm, wasn't worth bothering with. Still, the land belonged to the Church now, and a nice price they'd paid for it. Why they thought a dead oak was special just because a little girl was doing some peculiar things in front of it, he couldn't fathom. But it was a bloody nuisance having it lit up like that, scaring the dogs.

He heard his wife cursing Biddy inside the house, shouting for the animal to keep quiet. Some chance once she'd started.

And it was a bloody nuisance having all those people clomping through the field on Sundays! That's what his cattle were afeared of; they kept well away from that area, cowering at the far side of their own field as if they thought the crowd might harm them, rolling their eyes at him when he came to herd them in, trembling as though there was thunder in the air.

He stood in the middle of his yard looking back past the covered silage pit and machinery store, studying the beam of light cutting through the indigo blue sky two fields away. Somehow it made even him feel uncomfortable. It was a silvery intruder, unfamiliar and unwelcome, disturbing the stability of the country night. He looked up at the stars, the sky clear, no clouds to smother the shimmering clusters; yet there *was* thunder in the air, an electricity that made his senses tingle. It was unearthly and he didn't like it, not one little bit. When dogs howled at night it was usually a forewarning of death; tonight, standing there alone in the yard, coldness and darkness embracing him like sisters of oppression, he felt the howling was a warning of something more. Much more.

Oh bloody hell, not more trouble! He studiously finished filling the pint glass, ignoring the raucous voices from the other end of the bar for the moment. He took the money for the round, rang it up, then casually sauntered towards the source of trouble, sighing wearily when he saw it was three locals who were causing the disturbance.

He was a big man, though not a rough one, and his mere arrival on the scene of trouble was usually enough to pacify even the most belligerent of customers. He'd had to make his presence felt twice the night before, and once (unfortunately to no avail) the night before that. While he appreciated the extra trade all the publicity had brought in, the aggravation that came with it wasn't so welcome. The White Hart had always been a peaceful pub – at least, relatively so – and he intended to keep it that way.

'All right, lads, keep it down now.'

They regarded him resentfully but, he thought, respectfully. The glass that whistled past his head had no respect at all. He could only stare after the three figures, stunned, as they pushed their way through the crowded bar and disappeared outside, an obscenity their goodnight bidding.

All conversation had ceased when the glass shattered against the optics behind the bar, and now the customers stood watching the tall barman, as surprised as he. A barmaid rushed forward to mop up the spilt beer and pick up the broken glass; the barman could only shake his head in bewilderment.

'What's got into everybody?' he said and his customers could only shake their heads in sympathy. Conversation returned, a trickle breaking into a flood, and the barman turned his back on the bar and poured himself a double scotch, breaking his own rule never to drink before ten o'clock. Those three are barred, he told himself sullenly. He had never known them to cause trouble before, but he was sure as hell they would never cause trouble in there again. What was Banfield coming to? It had been alive, buoyant, over the past few weeks, but the mood seemed to be changing. At night there seemed to be a heaviness hanging over the village, like in summer when broody black clouds lay low and threatening; yet the air outside was oddly crisp and there were no clouds.

He gulped the scotch, pulling a face, but grateful for the sudden rush of warmth.

'You promised, you bastard!'

Tucker put up a stubby hand as if to soothe her temper, his eyes staying on the road ahead.

'It's early days yet, Paula,' he said placatingly. 'I don't know if the plans are going to go through yet.'

'You know, you bastard. Everything's going through now! Everything!'

'No, no, we have to wait for the District Council to give the go-ahead and you know how slow they are. And even if they granted planning permission, it'd take another year to have a supermarket built, maybe more.'

'You said you were going to buy out a couple of shops in the High Street and knock them into one.'

'I would have, but no one's selling now there's likely to be a boom on.' That wasn't true, for he'd put in tentative offers for two shops side-by-side, the owners ageing and fearful of extra trade rather than eager for it. No point in mentioning it to Paula until the sale was a certainty. What a pain in the bloody arse she was becoming!

'Even so, even if you build a new supermarket, why can't you say yes to me running the old one? At least I'll know where I stand.'

'Paula, there's a lot more to running –'

'You promised!'

The XJS swerved as she punched his arm.

'For fuck's sake, Paula, what's wrong with you? You'll have us off the road.' He squealed as she lunged for the wheel. 'Paula!' Pushing her back with one hand and steering the car with the other, he silently cursed the day he had got involved with her. He'd misjudged Paula, he realized. She was dumb, but she was conniving, too. The Jaguar slowed down and he pulled off the main highway into a side road. He stopped the car, switched off the engine and lights. 'Now look, pet –' he began to say.

'You don't care about me! You just want me for one thing!'

True enough, he thought. 'Don't be daft. You know how much I think of you.'

'You don't care! What have you ever given me?'

'There were those ear-rings at Christmas –'

'Bastard! You don't even know what I'm talking about.'

Although the car was stationary, his hands still gripped the wheel and his eyes still watched the road ahead. A frantic bird or bat fluttered darkly across the windscreen. His grip stiffened and his words came out through tight lips. 'Just tell me what you *are* talking about, Paula.'

'I'm talking about my life! Me! My future! I've helped you – your business and *you*. I've worked for you night and day, never complained . . .'

His eyes rolled upwards.

'. . . always been there when you needed me. I've always been available, for business or pleasure. I've given up so much for you.'

'What are you bloody talking about? I've given you a bloody good job, I've given you presents, I've taken you out –'

'To a sodding motel! That's just about your mark! And you give better presents to your wife! I've seen her parading round the village in her stinking fur coat and jewellery!'

'You want a fur coat, I'll give you a fur coat!'

'I don't want a fucking fur coat! I want something more!'

'Just tell me what!'

'I want the supermarket!'

There was an astonished silence in the car for a few moments. Then he said disbelievingly, 'You want the supermarket.'

She turned her head away.

'You want the bloody supermarket?' His voice had risen several octaves. 'You're fucking mad!'

'I don't want all of it, just part. I want to be a partner.' Her voice had sunk several octaves.

Tucker was just as incredulous. 'And how d'you suppose I'd explain that away to Marcia?'

'You could tell her you need a partner for business.'

'Need a partner? You? You must be fucking joking!' He tried to laugh, but it came out as a dry, rasping sound in his throat. 'You're a good screw, Paula, and not bad with figures and ordering stock. But running a business – actually running a business – and being a partner? I love your snatch, darling, but I don't worship it. You can take a running fucking jump!'

She was on him, scratching, slapping, punching, grabbing his hair, spitting on him, screaming at him. Tucker tried to grab her wrists, but her arms flailed at him viciously, hysterically.

'Paula!'

The car was rocking with her strength.

'Paula!'

'*I'll tell her, you bastard! I'll tell her everything! You're not treating me like a piece of dirt! She's going to know everything, you bastard!*'

'Paula!'

His hands found her throat and the fit was snug, pleasing. He squeezed.

'*You bastard, I'm going to –*'

Oh, that was good! That was keeping her quiet! Her neck was soft, mushy. He could feel the beginnings of an erection. Yes, that *was* good!

'*You . . . you . . .*'

It was dark, but he could see the whiteness of her eyes, and he could smell her fear. Try to blackmail him, would she? Thought I was that stupid, did she? Stupid of her, fat slug of a cow! Muscles in her neck were trying to resist the pressure and that felt good too; he wanted it to take time.

Her hands were on his chest, squeezing the fat there, and even that wasn't unpleasant. In fact it was rather nice.

He could see her tongue beginning to protrude from the whiteness of her face, like a beak hatching from an eggshell. Now a funny sound was coming from her, a whining, gurgling noise. That's better, you bitch, that's better than all those nasty, blackmailing words. That was a much sweeter sound. He increased the pressure. Funny how small a neck can become when you squeeze hard enough. Probably one hand could go round it at the death . . .

. . . at the death . . .

Oh my God, what am I doing?

'Paula!'

He released her throat and she fell away like a rag doll.

'Paula, I'm sorry, I'm sorry . . .'

Her eyes were staring at him and there were still gurgling noises coming from her.

He leaned towards her. 'I didn't mean . . .'

She cried out, but the sound was still strange, as though still squeezed from a flattened aperture. He touched her arm and she flinched violently. What had he been trying to do, what had come over him?

He tried to touch her again and this time she thrashed out wildly. Tucker jumped back, fingernails raking his cheek before he was out of reach. She was scrabbling around, searching for the door-lock. She found it, pushed the door open, the light exposing rounded buttocks as she tumbled from the car. She lay in the road, the squealing sounds still coming from her and he reached over the automatic column shift, his own eyes now wide with fear.

'Paula!' he said yet again.

She was on her knees, tights torn by rough concrete. She staggered to her feet, was running, stumbling, gasping for breath.

'Paula!' he called after her. 'Don't tell anyone . . .'

She was gone, swallowed by the night, and he sat there for a long time afterwards, door closed, in his own cocoon of darkness, wondering what had come over him, why he had tried to strangle her. It just wasn't like him.

Southworth closed the accounts book, a smile of satisfaction twisting his lips. He flexed his narrow shoulders and placed his elbows on the desk, steepled fingers resting against his chin. Then his smile broadened and he relaxed back into the chair.

Everything was going well, marvellously well. Banfield had changed almost overnight, the merchants flushed with new trade as tourists poured in, the pubs and restaurants packed tight each day and night. And his hotel had been over-booked since the miracles had begun. Morale in the village was high, the excitement sending waves of adrenalin coursing through its inhabitants, bringing them alert again, the sluggish burden of decline thrown off. All this achieved in just under two months, an incredible escalation of events, miraculous in that context alone.

In the coming months, when the clerics had stopped their predictable dithering and the shrine had become truly established, trade would increase tenfold, for pilgrims would journey from all over the world to see the scene of the Visitation. Southworth was already negotiating with the village's only travel agent, a small concern whose revenue had been slowly sinking with the country's economy, to form a new partnership. 'St Joseph's Tours' was to be the title of their joint venture, Southworth himself supplying the capital (his credit was particularly good with the bank these days) to buy a fleet of coaches which would cover the British Isles, the agent's connections abroad helping to form alliances with other, foreign, travel companies. Such a partnership, apart from the obvious financial gain in the tourist business itself, would prove extremely beneficial to his own hotel trade.

Soon work would begin on a new hotel, one that was more modern, easier to run and geared for a fast turnover. There were other properties, also, that he secretly owned in Banfield, shops that he had acquired cheaply over the years when their owners had given up trying to make a decent living in the lack-lustre village, bought by him under a company name, his solicitor handling all negotiations so that no one else knew who the true purchaser was, not even – *especially* not even – his fellow members of the parish council. The tenants he leased the properties out to would have something of a shock when their rents were doubled, probably trebled, within the next few months. They could hardly appeal, not with the way business would be booming, and if they refused to pay, well then, there would be plenty of others eager to move in. And their rents would be even higher.

Southworth rose from the desk and walked to the drinks cabinet. He reached for the sherry bottle, then changed his mind and took out the brandy. The brandy glass chimed pleasantly as the bottle touched its lip. He sipped slowly, pleased with himself, pleased he had been the first to see the opportunity and seize upon it.

Father Hagan had been a problem, the bishop much more susceptible to Southworth's persuasion; but then Bishop Caines had his own private ambitions. Of course, Southworth regretted the priest's untimely death, but it had meant the removal of what could have proved to be a minor stumbling block. Yet would he really have? Bishop Caines, a shrewd politician as well as a respected man of the cloth, would surely have stepped in and gently eased the doubting priest from the situation. In fact, in his many private discussions with Southworth, the bishop had hinted that Father Hagan might soon need a long rest, the fuss much too draining for a man of such ill-health. Monsignor Delgard, a priest who had much experience of what might be termed as 'phenomena', would have acted as both investigator and overseer. Southworth knew the bishop had no other choice but to send in a man with such unique qualifications and he wondered how skilfully he had balanced his briefing to Delgard.

Scepticism well to the fore, no doubt, but with enough receptiveness for a message from God to keep Delgard's mind open. And now nobody, *nobody* could deny the miracles.

On Sunday, before thousands and thousands (*eight to ten thousand*, it had been estimated, had travelled to St Joseph's, most of whom had not been able to get into the field for the service) more miracles had been performed. None could yet be confirmed, of course, for they could have just been temporary improvements, the sufferers deluded by their own hysteria: the boy whose condition was known as post-encephalitic dementia (brain damage caused by a virus infection) could just be experiencing a brief spell of normality; the young girl whose asthma was an almost constant companion and whose attacks could send her close to death, might find it returned within a week or two; the man whose multiple sclerosis confined him to a wheelchair might find that nerve tissues had not been impossibly regenerated and he would soon need his wheelchair again. There were others, many others, some trivial, some literally deadly serious, the victims claiming they 'felt better' or that they felt 'uplifted'. There was one case, though, that was indisputable.

A certain man had come alone to the field next to St Joseph's, a man who, through shame, had kept his face hidden from the crowd. His lower jaw, lips and nose had been infested with open sores and scabs, much of the flesh eaten away. Lupus was the medical term for the condition; tuberculosis of the face. Standing below Alice, whose small body had risen into the air (there were those among the vast congregation who swore they had *not* seen her rise, but these were far away, some near the back, and their view would have been impaired) the man's face had suddenly began to blister, the scabs falling away and the sores closing upon themselves. His face had healed in full view of all those present, for he had turned to the crowd so that they could witness the miracle. By the end of the service (completed with such incredible emotion, the child taking her place back among the congregation, her face white, skin taut) the deep pits in the man's flesh were being covered by rapidly-growing skin. The most cynical of men could not repudiate what had physically happened in front of thousands.

Even Monsignor Delgard could not reject such an astounding thing.

Southworth returned to his desk, taking the brandy with him. He sat, his mind alive with the new prospects that the Miracle Girl had opened up for him. That was *his* miracle: the revitalization of his own expectations. The Southworth name would not sink with Banfield into the mire of obscurity but, like the village, would again become a name to be noted, would enhance its centuries-old heritage. The village would grow, and he, his name, his wealth, would grow with it.

He raised the glass to lips and wondered why an awful instinctive fear had began to nag at these happy thoughts.

The priest rose wearily from his kneeling position by the bed, his compline, the last prayer of the day, completed. His knee-joints cracked with the effort and he stretched his stiff back, feeling old, spent. He turned and sat on the edge of the bed, too tired for the moment to go through the before-bed toiletries. A hand that trembled slightly brushed against his forehead as if it could wipe away the weariness. There had not been many times in his life that he had felt this depleted; usually it had followed particularly wearing exorcisms – rare occasions but not as rare as some people might think – and times when he had witnessed the world at its most dreadful – Biafra, Bangladesh, Ethiopia. At the age of twenty-one he had helped in the aftermath of Nagasaki, and perhaps that was worst of all; the nuclear weapon exemplified man at his most potent and most loathsome. It was at those times that his spiritual being had sagged, then plummeted to despairing depths awash with hopelessness; but the human spirit had a buoyancy of its own. On each occasion, though, the upward journey took longer, the years and events making the burden more cumbersome. But why the spiritual fatigue now?

Father Hagan had not needed to speak of it before he died; it was evident in his appearance, the weariness of his soul reflected in his lustreless eyes. Why was this depression hovering over the church, over the house? Why, when the sick were being miraculously cured, when a dramatic religious interest, perhaps even revival, was spreading throughout the country and, it was reported, throughout the world, was he so afraid? The Episcopal Council had convened that very day to question Alice further and the child had remained calmly resolute in her conviction that she had conversed with Mary. Why the miracles? they had asked. And why did the Mother of God choose to appear to *her*, a mere child? What had Alice done to receive such grace? And what was the purpose of the Visitations? Alice had just one answer to all the questions: the Lady would reveal the purpose in time; now was too soon to know.

It was an unsatisfactory reply.

The bishops had been divided, some believing the child really had received a divine vision, others claiming there was no evidence at all that the visions had been divine. It was still too early for the cures to be claimed miraculous and, as for the levitation, it was an illusion that could be seen in theatres all over the world. When it was argued that Alice could not possibly have used trickery in front of so many people and in such an open setting, it was counter-argued that Indian fakirs also performed such feats in similar circumstances with the use of mass hypnosis. To strengthen their claim, those churchmen who were anti, stressed that not everyone present *had* seen Alice levitate, and furthermore, not one television or still camera had recorded the phenomenon. It seemed their mechanisms had been mysteriously interfered with; only blank film had emerged. That in itself, those 'pro' claimed, was evidence of paranormal influences at work. Quite, the others scoffed, but that did not deem it holy. The debate had gone on late into the evening with no conclusions drawn. The bishops would reconvene tomorrow, in London, and the inquiry would continue until some kind of official proclamation could be given to an impatient world, although it would be a carefully-worded avoidance of any specific acknowledgement by the Church.

Delgard was puzzled by the failure of the cameras and the lectern microphones, wondering if it was linked in some way with his own sapping of energy that Sunday. He had fallen to his knees with the weakness that had come over him and those in near proximity had done the same, although they might now claim they were merely paying homage. Could there be some strange parasitical force at work which drained energy from the body and power from man-made machinery? It didn't seem possible; but then, neither did levitation nor miracle cures. Yet levitation and miracle cures were not unknown. The Catholic Church had its own levitators such as St Thomas Aquinas, St Teresa of Avila, St John of the Cross, and St Joseph of Cupertino, as well as many blessed with the miracle of stigmatism, the appearance of bleeding wounds on the hands, feet and side, resembling the wounds of Christ on the Cross. Some even bled from the head as if a crown of thorns had been placed there. And miracle cures had become almost religious lore. As well as that, perhaps the most stunning miracle of all had been at Fatima, in Portugal, when nearly seventy thousand onlookers had witnessed the sun spiral in the sky and descend towards the earth. Mass hallucination? Was that the explanation for Fatima and for what had happened in England on that Sunday? It was a logical man's reasoning, a scientist's smug answer. But even so, what had caused the hallucination? Alice was just a child.

Delgard walked to the window and gazed out into the night sky. He could see the bright floodlight in the field beyond, accentuating the twisted form of the oak tree. Its visibility disturbed him; he would rather it were hidden by the darkness. Vandals – perhaps just worshippers who cherished what the tree represented, in the same way that the Church cherished the wood of the Cross – had begun to strip the bark, wanting the aged wood for souvenirs or their own personal sacred relic, and now the tree had to be guarded, the light itself acting as a deterrent. The tree dominated the field as it had never before.

He drew the curtains together, the sight somehow distasteful to him; but when he was undressed and in bed, his eyes unable to close against the shadows around him, the light still glowed through the material, reminding him the tree was still there, a sinister sentinel. Waiting.

Alice's head twisted from side to side, slamming into the pillow with a force that would have stunned had it connected with anything solid. Her lips moved constantly and her pale body was damp with perspiration, even though the room was winter cold. The words she whispered, anguished, tormented, were said in a voice which scarcely resembled that of an eleven-year-old child.

The bedclothes lay loose and rumpled around her ankles, and her thin legs were stretched and trembling.

'. . . *aye, good Thomas, fill me with thy seed . . .*'

Her pelvis jerked spasmodically, her cotton nightdress thrown high upon her chest.

'. . . *so dear in heart, of such good strength . . .*'

Her small chest sank and heaved with her dream.

'. . . *disperse thyself into me . . .*'

She moaned, a long, howling moan, but there was an ecstasy in the sigh that followed. For a moment, her body became still and her eyelids fluttered but did not open. She moaned again and this time the sound was languid.

'. . . *more filling than e'er it was . . .*'

The moaning became deep breaths of pleasure, sighs that exalted the joy to her senses. Something small and black moved against her white stomach.

Outside, in the hallway leading to the nuns' cells, a dark-clad figure stood listening, breath held, tensed fingers on the door handle.

'. . . *allay their tongues, my priest . . .*'

Alice's eyes snapped open, but her body had not woken from the dream.

'. . . *cursed Mary . . . cursed MARY . . .*'

The nun's eyes widened in shock, her grip tightening on the door handle.

'. . . *CURSED MARY . . .*'

Alice's body stretched upwards, her heels and shoulders digging into the bed. The black creature on her stomach was almost dislodged and the girl cried out in pain as sharp needles pierced her tender flesh. But she did not wake.

She fell back to the bed and lay still, no longer making any sound.

The nun, Mother Marie-Claire, Reverend Mother of the convent, one hand unconsciously clutching the crucifix that lay against her chest, pushed the door open, slowly, quietly, as if afraid for herself. The beam of light from the hallway broadened as the door opened wider, the nun's shadow an elongated spectre on the room's floor. Coldness flew out at her and it was unnatural, almost painful.

She moved in, footsteps slow and soft. 'Alice?' she whispered, reluctant to wake the child but not sure if she slept. There was no reply from Alice, but another sound came to the nun's ears, a strange yet not unfamiliar noise. It was vaguely repellent, a sucking sound. The nun's forehead creased into a puzzled frown. She approached the bed and looked down at the near-naked form lying there.

Saw the small, bristling shape hunched on the child's stomach.

Raised the crucifix to her lips in horror when she discovered it was a cat.

Felt nauseous when she realized it was suckling at Alice's third nipple.

THIRTY

Look out! Look out, boys! Clear the track!
The witches are here! They've all come back!
They hanged them high – No use! No use!
What cares a witch for the hangman's noose?
They buried them deep, but they wouldn't lie still,
For cats and witches are hard to kill;
They swore they shouldn't and wouldn't die –
Books said they did, but they lie! they lie!

LOOK OUT BOYS
Oliver Wendell Holmes

The two men emerged from the crypt into the daylight, the shorter one leading, bounding up the stone steps as if relieved to be away from the musty chamber. Fenn stood in the graveyard, hands in his topcoat pockets, and waited for the priest to join him.

Delgard's progress was slower, his legs moving as though they were tied with weights, his shoulders more hunched than usual. Fenn was concerned for the priest: his pallor and demeanour were similar to Father Hagan's before he had died.

The priest reached him and they walked through the gravestones towards the boundary wall.

'That's that, then,' the reporter said, deliberately scuffing the top off a molehill as they passed. 'No chest, no information on the church's history.'

They had searched through the underground chamber with a fine toothcomb, Fenn's nerves jangling every moment they were down there, only the tall priest's presence keeping him from running out into the open. The light bulb had been working, even though Fenn had insisted it had blown the previous Sunday; nevertheless, both men were armed with torches just in case the power failed again.

'That may not be so.' Delgard's voice was heavy, his eyes focused on the ground before him. 'The chest wouldn't have been lost, not if it contained documents referring to St Joseph's earliest days. It must be elsewhere.'

Fenn shrugged. 'It could have been stolen or destroyed.'

'Possibly.'

'Well, where else can we look?'

They had reached the wall and both men looked towards the centre-piece in the field.

'That tree gives me the shudders, d'you know that?' Fenn said, not waiting for a reply to his previous question.

Monsignor Delgard smiled grimly. 'I can appreciate your feeling.'

'You too, huh? It's hard to reconcile it with a place of worship.'

'You think this ground is sacred?' the priest asked, nodding towards the field.

'You're the priest: shouldn't you be telling me it's so?'

The priest gave no answer.

Workmen in the field were carrying in benches, the rows of seating spreading outward, as yet barely covering half the field. Refinements to the centre-piece were in progress, the makeshift altar of the previous Sunday replaced by a large and more ornamental carved-wood version; close by was a small uncovered credence table. Posts which would eventually carry banners were being put up along the aisles and a low rail had been erected around the raised platform for the congregation to kneel at while the priest or priests administered Communion. The activity gave a normality to the scene which belied the extraordinary events that had taken place there just a few days before.

Delgard thought of Molly Pagett and the irony of the less-than-immaculate conception that had happened here. His conversation with Mother Marie-Claire earlier that morning made him wonder just what the illicit coupling nearly twelve years before had spawned.

'I feel it's vital that we locate the church chest, Gerry,' he said, his hands resting on the cold stone of the wall.

'I'm not so sure; what could it tell us? It's probably filled with old Mass books and hymn sheets, like the box in the crypt.' His flesh seemed to tighten around his bones when he thought of the underground chamber.

'No, I'm sure it's important.'

'How can you be? I think we're clutching at straws.'

'It's just a feeling – a very strong feeling. The other records you found go back to the late sixteenth century; why not before that, why should it begin there?'

'Who knows? Maybe that was the first time they thought of keeping any documentation.'

'No, the idea of keeping records goes way beyond that period. It could be that they've been purposely hidden.'

'I think you're guessing. I can't believe –'

'Still disbelieving, Gerry? Last Sunday you believed a statue of the Virgin Mary – a white unblemished statue – moved towards you. You said its lips and eyes were alive, that they even tried to seduce you. And today? What do you believe today?'

'I don't know what happened!'

'But a few moments ago in the crypt. There was no such statue, just a broken and old stone carving, almost unrecognizable as the Virgin, lying behind three other equally disfigured statues.'

'I fell against it, knocked it over.'

'The breaks were grimy with age, not fresh at all. And there was no face on the Virgin.' Delgard's voice was reasoning, no hint of criticism in it. 'Can't you believe something happened there that you cannot logically explain?'

It was Fenn's turn to remain silent. Eventually he said, 'What makes you so certain the answer's in past records?'

'I'm not sure, not at all. But the Reverend Mother of the convent came to me this morning. I'm afraid she was a little agitated.' That was an understatement: the nun had been frantic with worry. 'Alice has been speaking in her sleep again. Last night, Mother Marie-Claire listened outside her door as I had just a few days ago. She couldn't catch much of what Alice said, but it was in the same form as we had both heard before. She recalled some of the words, one or two of the phrases. "Fill me with thy seed" was one, "Allay their tongues" was another. Mother Marie-Claire also heard the word "priest".'

'Old language. Sounds like Shakespeare.'

'That's precisely what it is. It was the peculiar accent that puzzled me before; it made Alice's words sound garbled, nonsensical. Today I remembered a new treatment of Shakespeare's plays at the National I saw several years ago. I should say an "old" treatment; all the actors spoke in Elizabethan English, but not just using Elizabethan dialogue. An authority on the subject had tutored them in the accent used at that time. It was quite different, not just in form, to the language we speak today. It was the same language used by Alice as she slept.'

'She was quoting Shakespeare in her sleep?'

Delgard smiled patiently. 'She was speaking the language of that period, possibly before that time, in its correct idiom.'

Fenn raised his eyebrows. 'You can't be sure of that.'

'I'm not. However it gives us a basis to work from. How can a child of Alice's years – and remember, one who has been profoundly deaf for most of those years – know of a language she has never heard or probably even read before?'

'What are you getting at? Possession? Demonic possession? Speaking in tongues?'

'I wish it were that simple. Perhaps we could call it retrogression.'

'You mean reliving a past life? I thought Catholics didn't go in for reincarnation.'

'Nobody has ever proved that retrogression has anything to do with reincarnation. Who knows how much race memory is retained within our genes?'

Fenn turned to sit on the wall, his hands still tucked deep into his pockets. A light drizzle had started while they were talking. 'No wonder you're anxious to see what records are in that old chest. You know, a coupla weeks back I would have laughed at all this. Now all I can manage is a half-hearted chuckle.'

'There's more, Gerry. Something else I should have remembered before.' The priest squeezed his temples with thumb and fingers of one hand as if trying to press away a headache. 'The night Father Hagan died, the night we had dinner at the Crown Hotel.'

Fenn nodded, urging Delgard on.

'Remember I was talking of Alice's general state of health at that time? I said she was fine except for feeling tired and being a little withdrawn.'

'Yeah, I remember.'

'I also said the doctors had noticed a small growth in her side, beneath her heart.'

'You said it was a – what was it? – an extra nipple of some kind, nothing to worry about.'

'A supernumerary. I happened to be watching Father Hagan when I mentioned that and noticed he became even more agitated than he had been earlier during the evening. It slipped my mind because of the tragedy that followed. I think it struck a chord somewhere in him, something that was in the back of his mind and which he could not bring to the fore. I was a fool not to have known myself.'

'Forgive my impatience, Monsignor, but I'm getting wet. Are you going to tell me what it is you've remembered?'

Delgard pushed himself away from the wall and looked back towards the church. The light rain had created small speckles of dew on his face. 'Reverend Mother told me she had found a cat in Alice's room last night. It was resting on her sleeping body and it was drinking from her.'

Fenn's head, kept tucked in against the drizzle, snapped up. 'What the hell are you talking about?'

'The cat was suckling at Alice's supernumerary nipple.'

Fenn's face crinkled in disgust. 'She was sure? She actually saw it?'

'Oh yes, Mother Marie-Claire was certain. When she told me I realized what I had previously forgotten.' He looked away from the church and directly at the tree in the field beyond the wall. 'I remembered the ancient folklore concerning witches. It was generally believed that such women bore a mark on their bodies. It could be a blue or red spot, the flesh sunken, hollow; it was known as the Devil's Mark. Naturally enough, in such superstitious times, scars, moles, warts, or any natural excrescences on the body of a suspected witch could be given diabolical significance, but there was another protruberance or swelling which established the guilt of any person bearing the deformity beyond question.'

'The supernumerary nipple?'

Delgard nodded, his eyes still on the tree. He asked. 'Do you know what is meant by a witch's familiar?'

'I'm not sure. Isn't it something to do with a guide from the spirit world?'

'Not exactly. You're thinking of a spiritualist's familiar, a spirit who helps the medium contact souls on the other side. A witch's familiar is alleged to be a gift from the Devil, a spirit-beast which helped in divination and image. Usually it was a small animal, anything from a weasel, rabbit, dog, toad, or even a mole.'

'But more often a cat, right? I've read the fairy stories.'

'Don't dismiss such stories out-of-hand; they're often based on folklore passed down through the centuries and can contain some element of truth. The point is this: such spirit-beasts were sent on mischievous and often malicious errands by the witch and rewarded with drops of the witch's own blood. Or they were fed from the witch's supernumerary nipple.'

The reporter was too stunned to scoff. 'You're talking about witchcraft, here, now, in the twentieth century?'

Delgard smiled thinly and finally tore his eyes away from the oak. 'It's by no means unusual nowadays; there are many witches' covens throughout the British Isles. But I believe I'm speaking of something much more. You associated witchcraft with fairy tales. What if such myths were based on a reality, something which the people of that time could not understand, could only perceive in terms of sorcery? Witchcraft would have been something they could not understand, but could accept. We laugh at such ideas today because it's comfortable for us to do so, and our scientific technology precludes such notions.'

'You're losing me. Are you saying little Alice Pagett is a witch, or that she's not? Or that she's the reincarnation of some ancient sorceress?'

'I'm saying none of those things. But I think we must delve into the past for some link with what is happening here today. This force must emanate from somewhere.'

'What force is that?'

'The force of evil. Can't you feel it around us? You, yourself, experienced it last Sunday in the crypt. The same force weakened, then destroyed, Father Hagan.' He did not add that he felt that same pressure bearing down on himself.

'There's nothing evil about the miracles,' Fenn said.

'That,' Delgard replied, 'we do not yet know. We don't know where or what all this is leading to. We must keep searching, Gerry. We must find clues. We have to find the answer before it's too late, while there's still a chance to combat this force.'

Fenn let out a long sigh. 'You better tell me where else I can look for the chest,' he said.

Fenn was a dumbhead. He should have seen the connection. Maybe all the research he had been doing had addled his brain. Guess it was easy to be objective when all the work had been done and you only had to read through the notes. But still, she could be wrong: it might not be here at all.

Nancy stood before the heavy-looking door inside the porch, its wood painted and marked with time, wondering if it would be locked. She twisted the metal handle and her eyes glinted with satisfaction when it turned and the door opened easily. No reason for it to be locked in such an isolated place.

It was when Fenn had told her that the old church chest he was looking for wasn't at St Joseph's that she realized the possibility. If he hadn't played so cagey with her, she'd have told him. That's what you get, Fenn, for trying to cut me out.

She pushed the door open wider and stepped in from the porch. The light inside was dull, diffused by the thick, leaded windows.

The chest dated back to the fourteenth or fifteenth century and must have disappeared some time during the sixteenth, for that was as far back as the records Fenn had found went. That had been her clue.

The door made a low growling noise as she closed it, a muffled thump disturbing the stillness inside when it shut completely. Nancy looked around the miniature church, loving its quaintness, impressed by its tradition. A leaden font stood before her, the dark, letter-ornamented metal speaking of another time, a different era. Nearly all the pews were boxed in, the panels chest-height, narrow doors allowing entry. Whole families probably sat in each one, Nancy assumed, cut off from their neighbours, enclosed in their own small islands of worship. The wood panelling was stripped of any varnish, its bareness somehow complementing the character of the chapel itself. No more than thirty to forty feet away, at the head of the narrow aisle, was the tiny altar.

So this was where the lord of the manor came to pray, Nancy mused. Cute.

She moved around the font into the chapel and at once gave a small cry of triumph. There it was. It had to be the one!

The chest stood against a wall to her right, immediately below a large polished-wood board, the names of all the clerics who had served the church from 1158 to the present day inscribed on its surface in gold. She stared at the long, low chest, scarcely believing her eyes, but almost certain it was the one Fenn had been searching for. It matched the description in his notes perfectly: made from planks of thick elm or oak, bound together with metal bands, the wood battered and marked, an indication of its antiquity; and there were three unusual looking padlocks on its facing side.

Nancy squatted beside it, still smiling in triumph, and handled all three locks. 'Great!' she said aloud. 'Now all I need is the goddam keys.'

She pushed herself erect and looked around. Where would the priest be? He obviously wouldn't be resident, there was no house, only the large mansion some distance away. The board in front of her said that the priest since 1976 was a Father Patrick Conroy of Storrington. Ah, that was it. The priest obviously bussed in from the neighbouring parish to run the show here. She would have to go to the town or village of Storrington to locate him. But then, would he allow her access to the chest? Probably – no, definitely – not. Fenn might get permission, though, with his church connections. Shit, she would have to tell him.

Unless.

Unless the keys were kept in the church. Improbable, but worth a look. Maybe in the vestry.

She strode down the aisle towards the front of the nave, her footsteps brisk. Shadows of light passed across the high windows, heavy, low clouds moving by outside. The sound of wind whistling through a gap somewhere in the church roof. A small scratching sound, a mouse working at wood somewhere in the shadows.

Her footsteps faltered as some subliminal change in her awareness told her she was not alone in the church.

She stopped for a moment and listened. The scratching had stopped as though the mouse also knew there was an extra presence nearby. The clouds outside thickened, the light diminishing.

Her footsteps were slower, more cautious, when she moved on. She peered over the tops of the high box pews, almost expecting to find someone praying in one. To her right, by the side of the altar she could see the closed vestry door. To her left was a corner, the interior flanking out in that direction possibly to form a side chapel. Yet the unvarnished wood panelling indicated it had to be another pew, this one set apart from the rest. This would be where the lord of the manor sat with his family, she reasoned.

No sound came from that direction, but apprehension stabbed at her chest like a thin, sharp icicle.

Get a hold of yourself, asshole. There could be someone there, but why not? It *was* a church, for Chrissake! She coughed, loudly, hoping for some reaction if there was somebody praying in there. A shuffling of knees, or a returned cough would do. Anything to show that whoever it was wasn't skulking. There was no other sound.

It would be stupid to leave, Nancy told herself. Stupid and childish. She walked on, her footsteps deliberately loud on the stone floor.

The first thing she saw when she drew level with the chest-high partition was a picture on the far wall. It was a painting of the Madonna and Child in the style of Perugino, and it hung above a fireplace. The recess, in fact, was a small room, obviously built for the comfort of the squire and his family from the huge Tudor manor house which shred the estate with the tiny church. She moved closer. The door in the panelling was open.

A figure sat on one of the benches inside, a small, dark-clad figure.

Nancy almost whistled with relief when she saw it was a nun.

But the habit was strange. It wasn't the two-toned grey she had seen the nuns in the village wearing, and the skirt was longer. The black hood was pulled forward, well over the face.

She was sitting sideways to Nancy, her back hunched over, hands hidden deep within her lap, the loose black material flowing around her.

'Excuse me,' Nancy said quietly, tentatively, standing in the doorway of the pew, one hand on top of the panelling, fingers curled around it.

The nun did not move.

'I . . . I'm sorry to bother . . .' Nancy's words trailed away. There was something wrong. Oh God, there was something wrong. She moved as if to back away, not knowing why she was afraid, only aware that she was irrationally, inexplicably, in mortal dread of this thing sitting there; but her limbs would not react, would not take her away from the dark, hidden figure.

Her legs sagged and a small trickle of urine dampened her inner thighs as the nun slowly turned to face her.

THIRTY-ONE

'Who knocks?' 'I, who was beautiful,
  Beyond all dreams to restore.
I, from the roots of the dark thorn am hither.
  And knock on the door.'

THE GHOST
Walter de la Mare

Rain spattered against the windscreen as Fenn drove through the tall iron gates. He slowed the car, expecting to be challenged, but there was no one on duty. Must be out of season, he explained to himself. The estate was probably closed to the public until the spring. He picked up speed, ignoring the sign indicating that 10 mph was the approved pace.

Outside the clouds were low and dark, overloaded with rain, the speckles on the windows just the appetizer for what was soon to come. Trees rushed by on either side, their barren branches like petrified arms thrown out in alarm. A flicker of movement to the left caught his eye and abruptly he was braking as a deer bounded across the narrow road. He watched it disappear into the trees, a fleeting light-brown spectre, and envied its skittish grace. It was gone from view within seconds, swallowed up by the stark arboreal sanctuary.

The hired car resumed its journey, slowing again when it reached an open gate, rattling its way across the deer grid. He frowned at the dullness in the air, the dismal weather making the late afternoon seem like evening. Winter in England could be bearable if only it didn't drag itself through eight or nine months of the year. The road curved, emerging from the trees to be confronted by a sweeping panorama of lush green fields, the misty South Downs in the distance a rolling backdrop merging into the grey puffy sky.

The drive dipped easily, then separated, the main arm going onwards towards the grey-stone manor house, the other, narrower, arm branching off to the left, towards a levelled compound behind a group of elms, a non-obtrusive carpark for sightseers to the estate. Beyond the carpark, no more than a quarter of a mile away, stood a small church.

Stapley Park, Barham. The big Tudor house was Stapley Manor. The little twelfth-century church was St Peter's.

Fenn silently swore at himself for being such a jerk; he really should have made the connection. It was all laid out for him, all there in the notes he'd taken from the archives. The trouble was he'd become too swamped in the history to give full attention to details that had not seemed relevant. Well, it didn't matter that much now; he was pretty sure the chest in the little church was the one he had been searching for. Earlier that day, after leaving Delgard, and on the monsignor's advice, he had gone to the cathedral at Arundel hoping to find further documents concerning St Joseph's, and it was there that he had learned of St Peter's at Stapley, and of Stapley Manor itself.

The Catholic Church had owned the Stapley Estate, in whose ground St Peter's stood, before being dispossessed of such lands and properties at the time of the Reformation in England.

In 1540, with the Dissolution of the Monasteries, when the lands and properties of the Church were being 'legally' acquired by the Crown, Henry VIII granted the manor house at Stapley and its entire estate to Richard Staffon, a mercer of London. He lived there with his family until the counter-Reformation under the new Catholic queen began its short-lived but fearsome reign of terror. Staffon was fortunate: he and his family were driven into exile with many fellow Protestants, whereas almost three hundred others were burnt at the stake as heretics.

By devious means, the estate was passed on to Sir John Woolgar as a reward for his loyalty to the Catholic Church in Henry's time. Woolgar was a wealthy Sussex businessman whose only son was the priest at St Joseph's in Banfield.

Fenn had stopped the car and was surveying the panorama, allowing the information to assemble itself in his mind. He had learned of the connection between Stapley Manor and Banfield from his research into the Sussex records, the warden at Arundel merely prompting the recall; the further information concerning the Reformation had been added by the priest he had just left at Storrington.

The priest, a Father Conroy, as well as serving his own parish at Storrington, also served weekly Mass at St Peter's in Stapley Park; apparently it was a duty handed down to each new priest to that particular parish. He had confirmed that there was, indeed, a large ancient chest in St Peter's, the description matching Fenn's, and a phone call to Monsignor Delgard (for whom Father Conroy had undisguised respect) gave him the authority to hand over the keys to the reporter. Fenn also gained permission to take away any documents he might find useful, provided he made a complete list, signed it, and allowed Conroy to examine those he had taken. The priest would have accompanied him to St Peter's himself, but various duties dictated otherwise. That suited Fenn fine: he preferred to snoop alone.

The priest had filled in other details concerning the Stapley Park Estate and St Peter's. There had originally been a small village around the church, but it had become regarded as a source of infection after a mysterious plague had broken out in the early 1400s killing off most of the villagers; subsequently, the houses around the church had been destroyed. Much alteration and restoration had taken place over the years, each new lord of the manor contributing financially to the work, whether they were Catholic or not, for, like the mansion itself, St Peter's was of historic importance and an attraction for the many tourists who flocked to the estate during the summer months. Father Conroy recalled reading somewhere that the chest had been taken to St Peter's from Banfield in token acknowledgement of a stained-glass window that Sir John

Woolgar had donated to St Joseph's.

A crow landed in the roadway, twenty yards ahead of the car, and seemed to challenge its further progress. It was a breed of bird Fenn found hard to admire; too big, too black. He allowed the car to move slowly forward, the tyres crunching against the gravel road. The bird calmly walked to the side and watched Fenn with one eye as he drove past.

The vehicle gained momentum as the road dipped. Herds of black-backed deer, settled in the grass beneath trees, gazed on with stiff-necked curiosity as he approached, the stags among them, antlers high and menacing, glaring as if daring him to come closer. He drove into the branch-off, making for the empty grass carpark, and the deer in that area rose as one to move away, their flight unhurried, cautious but unafraid.

The grass in the compound was cut short, the parking areas neatly marked by straight, narrow lines of soil, unobtrusive and neatly patterned. Bullocks in a field nearby bawled at him, the sound echoing around the trees, as if they, too, did not welcome his presence.

Fenn grabbed a hold-all from the passenger seat and pushed open the door. The wind tore into him as he stepped from the car; it swept over the Downs from the sea, carrying with it a damp chill and an unrestrained force. Pulling his coat-collar tight around his neck and blinking against the wind-driven rain, he set off for the church, the strap of the hold-all over one shoulder.

A long, straight path led from the carpark to the mediaeval church; to the right, about a quarter of a mile away, stood the daunting manor house, an impressive structure of Tudor design, yet curiously empty-looking, lifeless. Indeed, it probably was at that time, for Fenn had learned earlier that the owner had died some years before and his family only stayed at the house for certain months of the year, preferring sunnier climes in the winter months.

As he trod the narrow path, the church loomed up like an image framed in a slow-moving zoom lens, and he began to feel very lonely and very isolated. Like the manor house in the distance, St Peter's was constructed of grey stone, green-stained with age; one section of the roof was covered with large moss-covered slates, the rest with red tiles; the windows were leaded, the glass thick and smoothly rippled as though each pane had been placed in its frame still hot and melting. He saw now how oddly-shaped the building was and could imagine the various segments being added at various times through the centuries, each portion reflecting its own period. The path led past the church, presumably to where the entrance had to be, for he could see no doors as he approached. The expanse he had just crossed had been bare; now there were trees, mostly oak, around the church, and the wind rustled through the empty branches, an urgent, rushing sound that increased his sense of isolation. Small branches broke away and scuttled in the air before reaching the earth; stouter branches lay scattered, victims of previous, stronger gusts, resembling twisted human limbs. The horizon, just above the distant Downs, now glowed silver in a strip that was held level by the dark, laden clouds above. The contrast between broody clouds and condensed sky was startling.

Fenn stepped off the path into rough grass to get near one of the church windows and, cupping a hand between brow and glass, peered in. There was an unappealing gloom inside and he could just make out the empty pews enclosed by wood panelling. At first glance it reminded him of a holy cattleshed. He took his hand away and twisted his neck, nose almost pressed against the glass, in an effort to see more. There were other windows opposite that threw little light into the interior, but he could just make out the shape of a font and more enclosed benches nearby. A movement caught his eye and it was so sudden that he drew back a few inches. Then he realized, the blood vessels in his throat seeming to constrict, that the action was not inside the church, but was a reflection in the glass.

He turned quickly and saw there was nothing there. Just a swaying branch. Creepy, he told himself. Creepy, creepy, creepy.

Hoisting the hold-all back onto his shoulder, he rejoined the path and headed for the front of the church. When he reached the corner the wind tore into him with fresh force, driving the rain into his face like ice pellets. A square tower rose above him, too short and stubby to be majestic, reaching no more than forty feet into the air, its rampart top almost as grey as the clouds above it. A matt, rust-coloured door stood beneath the tower, the shade drab and unimaginative, paying no dues to the history it guarded. An unlocked iron gate protected the door, only inches away from the wood surface like some early misconceived idea of double glazing.

Before entering the church, Fenn took a walk to the other side. Beyond a flint wall was a small graveyard, the gravestones crammed in as though the corpses had been buried standing up. Here and there were more spacious plots and some headstones that appeared to have been regularly scrubbed clean; there were also one or two rotting wooden crosses laid in the grass, marking the resting places of those who could not afford better. Opposite the church was a two-strutted fence, beyond that, waist-high undergrowth, beyond that – nothing, it seemed. The land obviously dropped steeply away into a small valley, woodland rising up on the other side towards the slopes of the Downs.

Fenn turned back to the doorway, his hair flat and wet against his forehead. He opened the iron gate, then the heavy door, and stepped into the church, glad to be away from the hostile weather. The door closed behind him and the wind outside became just a muted breathing.

As in all churches he had visited, which wasn't many, he felt uncomfortable and intrusive, as though his presence showed a lack of respect rather than a mark of it. The interior was certainly unusual with its enclosed pews, low barrel ceiling, and tiny altar. A raised pulpit stood near the altar, behind it a door he assumed led to the vestry. Would the chest be in there? The priest at Storrington had omitted to say.

Then he saw it, no more than five feet away to his right. His eyes lit up and he smiled ruefully. You better be worth it, you bugger, he said to himself, remembering the experience of searching the crypt at St Joseph's. Above it was a plaque of highly-polished wood, names and dates inscribed on its surface. He took a closer look, realizing it was a list of clerics who had served at St Peter's. He found one that was familiar:

REV. THOMAS WOOLGAR 1525–1560

Thomas would be Sir John's son, the priest from Banfield. Presumably he arrived after his father had been granted the estate, so if he had died in 1560, the service had been only for a few years. He quickly worked out the priest's age at the time of death: thirty-five; young by today's standards, but reasonable for that period.

Rain lashed at the windows with a new intensity, beating at the thick glass as though demanding entry.

Fenn rummaged in his pocket for the keys that would open the three locks. He hesitated before inserting the first one. Maybe this is crazy, he told himself. How could something that had happened – *if* anything significant happened – over four hundred years ago have any relevance to what was happening at St Joseph's today? Just because a kid used an old, outdated language in her sleep and had a blemish on her body that used to be thought of as a witch-sign, it didn't mean the answer lay somewhere in history. Was Delgard truly convinced of it, or was he just desperate? Alice, the Miracle Worker, was a modern-day phenomenon; why should the past play any part?

The wind outside became louder as it battered against the old church walls; a fresh squall of rain threw itself at the windows like thousands of tiny shrapnel pieces.

A noise somewhere near the front of the church made Fenn turn his head.

He straightened, uneasy.

The noise came again.

'Someone there?' he called out.

No reply and no more noise. Just the wind and rain outside.

He walked to the centre of the aisle and waited. The sound again. A small scraping sound.

Could be anything, he reassured himself. A mouse, a trapped bird. Then why was he so sure that there was someone else in the church? He felt he was being watched and automatically his eyes went to the pulpit. It was empty.

The sound again. Someone or something near the front of the church.

'Hey, come on, who's there?' he called out with forced bravado.

He began to walk towards the altar, refraining from whistling a happy tune, eyes searching left to right at every pew he passed. All were empty, but the last one disappeared around a corner, the building jutting out in that direction. He was certain that was where the sound had come from. He reached the corner and stopped, for some reason reluctant to go further. He had the distinct feeling that he really did not want to see whatever was lurking there. The noise came again, louder this time, startling him.

He took several quick paces forward and peered over the enclosure.

Empty.

Fenn breathed a sigh of relief.

It was a strange room, a fireplace at the far end, a picture of the Virgin and Child hanging above the mantel. Cushioned benches stretched the full length on either side. He heard the sound again and saw the tree branch outside, buffeted by the wind, scraping at a window. He was too relieved to even smile at himself.

Going back to the chest, he knelt and turned the first key. When nothing happened he remembered the short metal rod Father Conroy had given him. As instructed, he inserted it into a small hole at the side of the padlock, pressed a lever, then twisted the key again. The padlock came away in two parts.

He repeated the procedure twice more and laid the separate sections on the stone floor. His tongue flicked nervously across dry lips as he prepared to open the lid.

The porch door rattled as though someone were banging their fists against it. It was the wind, he told himself, just the wind.

The lid was heavy and at first resisted his efforts. Then it came slowly up, hinges groaning at the unfamiliar movement. Fenn swung the lid right back so that it rested against the wall behind. He looked down into its depths, a musty odour leaping out at him like a released animal.

Old vestments lay scattered on top, their colours faded, the material no longer springy soft. He pulled the clothing out, draping them over the side of the chest. Beneath lay sheaves of yellowed paper and various books, worn and wrinkled with age. He took the latter out one by one, quickly leafing through the pages, placing them on the floor when he discovered they did not date back far enough. He felt some of the various papers would have proved interesting to a historian, but to him they were useless. Next he drew out several loosely-bound books, the covers in hide of some sort, the paper inside thin and rough-edged. He opened one and saw it was a form of ledger, an accounts book for St Peter's. In neat script it listed payments made to workmen for tasks carried out for the church. The first page gave the year: 1697. The other books dated back further, but none to the century he sought.

There were more scattered papers, several Latin Mass books, and then he found what he had been looking for. There were three of them, each book roughly measuring twelve by eight inches; the covers were of stiff, yellow vellum, the inside leaves bound together by twisted vellum tackets, braided through hide strengthening pieces. The writing on the pages was forceful in style, each letter precisely angled, the ink brown and, unfortunately, very faded. Even more unfortunate was that it was all in Latin. But the date said 1556.

Eagerly he looked at the other two, and the dates ran in consecutive years. As he handled the third book, a sheaf of loose leaves fell from the back into the chest. He reached for one and noticed it was undated. The writing was in the same brown ink and although similar in style to the previous handwriting, it was scrawled, less tidy, the lettering spidery and undisciplined. It, too, was in Latin. Fenn gathered up the other scattered pages, quickly scanning them for a date, smiling when he found one.

The roof groaned loudly as the wind pounded on it; something broke away, probably a slate, and slid down, its fall muffled by the soft earth around the church. Fenn looked up anxiously and assured himself that the church had stood up to such battering for centuries and was unlikely to collapse around him now. Nevertheless, he quickly opened the hold-all and put the three vellum-covered documents inside, first placing the loose leaves in the back of the book they had fallen from.

The church door was rattling insanely and nothing could be seen through the windows, so fierce was the rain. He began stuffing the other books, sheets and vestments back into the chest, unwilling to search any further, the urge to be away from the church too great. He had the same sense of black oppression that he'd experienced in the crypt of St Joseph's. The lid closed with a heavy thump and Fenn stood, relieved that it was done. Back to the car now, away from this godawful place, with its tearing wind and dark, dark church. . . . He hadn't noticed before just how dark it had become.

He stepped into the aisle, averting his eyes from the altar. The howling wind outside sounded like the wailing of lost souls. The door before him shook violently and something made him back away. The lift bar above the lock jiggled up and down as if some neurotic hand outside were playing with it. The wood trembled within its frame and he could sense the pressure behind it, the gale screeching for entry.

An awareness crept upon him with dank, scaly fingers. Something else, not just the wind, wanted to get into the church. *Something* wanted to reach him.

He was still backing away, his eyes on the agitated porch door, drawing closer to the altar, passing pews one by one, the partitions screens behind which things could hide. The pulpit came into the periphery of his vision, rising over him like a tensed predator. To his right was the strange segregated room, with its empty fireplace, its picture of the woman and the Christ-child, with its window, the branch tapping and scrapping at the glass like a hand begging for admission . . .

with its dark-clad figure sitting by the empty grate . . .

He stood, his legs paralysed, his throat constricted.

The figure was hooded, the head crouched low over its knees. It began to straighten, to turn towards Fenn.

And the porch door burst open with a force that shook everything inside the church.

THIRTY-TWO

There never more she walks her ways
by sun or moon or stars;
she dwells below where neither days
nor any nights there are.

SHADOW-BRIDE
J. R. R. Tolkien

Fenn was thrown backwards, more by shock than force. He stumbled, fell. The floor was hard against his back, but he felt no pain, only a jolting numbness.

The wind howled around the church, a banshee let loose, so that even the leaden font seemed to tremble against its wrath. Fenn's clothes were buffeted by the wind, his hair swept back, coat collar flapping against his cheek. He was forced to turn his head aside from the initial onslaught, his eyes squeezed tight against the blast. Rain was carried in, dampening the walls, the pews, an ally to the whirlwind. The roar of air was amplified by the tight confines of the stone building, assaulting his ears with its frenzied screaming.

Something was moving to his right, something black, small, rising from the seat in the side room, standing in the opening. Bending to touch him.

He dared not look. He sensed its presence, glimpsed the dark shape only on the edge of his vision. He did not want to see.

Fenn scrambled to his knees, swayed there for a few moments, the circling wind rocking his body. He tried to rise, found his legs were not strong enough to support him, even though the gale was not as fierce, its force deflected by the walls into confused and separate currents. He began to move forward, dragging the hold-all along the floor with him, fearful of the storm bursting through the open doorway, but more fearful of the hooded figure that watched him.

He flinched as though he had been touched, but reason told him he was not within reach of the thing that stood there. It seemed that cruel fingers had raked his arm, leaving the flesh beneath his clothes torn and branded. The same sensation clawed at his cheek and he gasped, the pain searing, yet unreal. More heat – for that was what it felt like, raw, white heat against his skin – touched his outstretched hand and when he glanced down he saw the red weals already beginning to rise. His head was snapped upwards as though long fingers had tangled themselves in his hair and pulled. His body arched as jagged nails scored bloody tracks down his back.

Yet the figure was still beyond touching distance.

He staggered to his feet, fear lending him strength, and stumbled along the aisle, fighting the wind as a drowning man fights an undertow, forcing himself towards the grey light of the doorway, collapsing against a partition, clasping its ridge, pushing himself away, feeling malignant eyes on the back of his neck. He fell again, the wind shoving him with giant, unseen hands, knocking him to the floor.

The large wooden door swung on its hinges, banging into the wall, cracking the plastered stone. Outside, the driven rain had turned the landscape into a hazy, moving pattern of muted greens.

Fenn was still afraid to look back, not understanding where the dark-cloaked figure had come from, only knowing it was there, an unearthly presence that burned with malevolence. He crawled again and something tugged at his ankle. He screamed as the scorching grip tightened and dragged his leg backwards.

His hand reached for the corner of a pew, the other scrabbling at the cracks in the uneven floor. His heart felt it would come loose in his body, so wildly was it beating. He was shouting now, ranting at the thing that drew him back, tendons in his wrists high and rigid against the flesh as he struggled to pull himself free. Then he was kicking, frightened yet enraged, eyes blurred with the tears of his own anger and frustration. Kicking, kicking, his knees scraping raw against the stone, globules of blood collecting beneath the fingernails of the hand that scratched at the rough floor, kicking, kicking, eyes closed with the effort but mouth open to force out the shouts.

He was suddenly free, thrusting at empty air. He found himself moving forward once more, the wind still pressing against his shoulders, whipping his face with rain icicles. He was on his feet, staggering towards the door, still refusing to look over his shoulder, hot, corrupted breath warming the back of his neck. His footsteps slowed . . . slowed . . . slowed . . . the compulsion behind dragging at him, creating the nightmare of legs in quagmire . . . the childhood dreams of . . .

. . . the Frankenstein monster ploddingly catching up, arms outstretched to grab, huge club-foot boots shuddering the ground . . .

. . . the grinning Fe-Fi-Fo-Fum giant swinging his axe . . .

. . . the slush-slurp of the Creature emerging from the Black Lagoon . . .

. . . the dead son returning from the grave, thumping against the other side of the bolted door for his mother, who clasped the monkey's paw, to let him in . . .

. . . the thing that was always waiting in the dark at the bottom of the cellar stairs . . .

. . . the green-faced bogeyman tapping at the bedroom window in the middle of the night . . .

. . . Norman Bates, dressed as Mother, behind the shower curtain . . .

. . . the white shape at the foot of the bed, who would not let him wake from the nightmare until it had dissolved back into the night . . .

. . . the hand that would coldly curl around his ankle should he let it slip from beneath the bedsheets . . .

. . . all the nightmare companions of his childhood were gathered there behind him in the church, every late-night dread creeping up on him, their images the tentacles that bound him . . .

And like a nightmare, it had to break when the terror became too much.

The release was like being blasted from a cannon. He burst through the doorway, skidding and falling heavily onto the path outside the church. He rolled over, resting on one elbow, and the rain beat against his upturned face with such force he was sure it would leave indentations on his face. The arched door loomed over him, the interior a murky cavern of gargoyles; the stunted tower rose above and for one brief moment he imagined he was looking down from the ramparts at his own prone figure lying on the path. He blinked his eyes against the rain and against the confusion.

He began to push himself away from the threatening doorway, using heels and elbows, his clothes and skin already soaked, the hold-all dragged across the path with him. Chill softness brushed his back as he slid into the rough grass. He stared back at the ancient church, his eyes wide and face deathly pale. His brain screamed at him to get up and run. As he pushed himself upright he saw a fleeting figure just on the other side of the perimeter fence.

It had risen from the sea of green like a swimmer breaking surface, and then it was running, pushing a path through the foliage, heading away from Fenn, away from the church.

The figure looked familiar, but his thinking was too haywire to allow recognition for a moment or two. When he finally realized who it was he was even more bewildered. Grabbing the hold-all and tucking it under his arm, he ran to the fence, used one hand to leap untidily over, and fell into the foliage on the other side. The figure had disappeared by the time he regained his feet.

A low gust tore across the undergrowth creating a sweeping ripple that reached him and made him unsteady.

'Nancy!' he called out, but the storm smothered any reply. He pushed through the foliage, gathering speed as he went, shouting her name. He wasn't just afraid for her; he needed her. He was frightened for himself.

Fenn ran on through the rain, the wind, almost blinded, recklessly crashing through the undergrowth. Then he was falling, slipping, tumbling over and over, rolling into an abyss he hadn't realized was there. Stalks and brambles snapped at his face and hands, and he thought the slide would never end, that the world would never re-stabilize itself. He came to a cushioned halt at the bottom of the slope and leaves closed over his eyes like mischievous hands.

He sat up and tried to shake the dizziness from his head. The movement only made it worse and the world continued to tumble for long seconds after. When the spinning finally settled, he searched for her running figure. He was in a narrow valley, woodland rising up on the opposite side. A rough, earth roadway led through the valley, disappearing in the distance round a jutting slope. Directly in front, no more than two hundred yards away, was a barn, the likes of which he had never before seen. It was very old and obviously no longer used, such was its disrepair; immediately below a thatched roof supported by stout beams, were openings, the covered sides of the barn itself reaching only to a certain level. The wood was faded and weather-worn, the thatch still thick but dark with age.

Fenn knew she would be in there.

He got to his feet and picked up the bag. Then, hunching his shoulders against the pounding rain, he lurched towards the barn. The wind in the bottom of the dip was weakened, its rushing sound softened. He turned quickly to look back up the hill and saw that St Peter's was out of view, not even the tower showing above the false horizon; the foliage at the top of the slope swayed back and forth, bowed but resilient to the elements.

There was no door to the barn, just a vast opening running half the length of its side, a post from floor to roof dividing the entrance. From where he stood he could see the interior was crammed with old logs, wood planking, and some rusted machinery. He had no desire to enter, for it looked even darker and just as foreboding as the church. Only the whimpers above the noise of the muted wind urged him in.

He found her crouched behind a pile of wood at the back of the barn, her frightened sobbing guiding him to her. Her head was buried into her knees, arms clenched tightly around herself, and she shuddered violently when he touched her shoulder.

'Nancy, it's me, Gerry,' he said softly, but she would not look at him.

He knelt beside her and tried to take her in his arms; with an animal yelp she pushed against the side of the musty barn, scrabbling to get away from him.

'For Christ's sake, Nancy, calm down. It's me.' He gently pulled her back to him and rocked her in his arms. 'It's me,' he kept telling her, his voice falsely soothing, for the hysteria was not far from his own mind.

It took some time before he could lift her head and force her to look at him. And when he did the expression in her eyes frightened him almost as much as the thing inside the church.

THIRTY-THREE

Wake all the dead! What ho! What ho!
How soundly they sleep whose pillows lie low,
They mind not poor lovers who walk above
On the decks of the world in storms of love.
   No whisper now, nor glance can pass
   Through wickets or through panes of glass;
For our windows and doors are shut and barred
Lie close in the church, and in the churchyard.
   In every grave make room, make room!
   The world's at an end, and we come, we come.

WAKE ALL THE DEAD! WHAT HO! WHAT HO!
                     Sir William Davenant

Delgard pushed the reading glasses up from the bridge of his nose and rubbed at the corners of his weary eyes. The reflection from the ultra-violet light cast a bluish-white tinge over his features, the stark, artificial glare ruthlessly exposing lines of fatigue. The faded papers lay spread on the table before him, parchment edges rough and flaky through time; to one side was a thick, heavily-bound book, an aid to the translation of the ancient but enduring language on the parchments. He clicked off the fluorescent tube, no longer needing its peculiar light to enhance the faded script, and quickly scribbled more notes onto his writing pad. Then he laid the pen down, held his spectacles with one hand and massaged his forehead with the other. His shoulders appeared even more hunched, his chest even more sunken.

When he took his hand away, his eyes were haunted, filled with disbelief. It couldn't be true, the papers had to be a madman's dream, the guilt-ridden imaginings of a man born nearly five hundred years before.

Delgard's mouth felt dry and he flicked his tongue uselessly across brittle lips. There was a tightness to his skin, a stiffness to his joints, the tension of the last few hours the cause. He craned his neck towards the reporter, who lay slumped in a nearby armchair, and imagined he could feel his own bones grind against one another as he turned. Fenn was fast asleep, exhaustion, and perhaps even boredom, stealing him from the late-night vigil with the priest.

He should rouse the reporter, tell him what he had learned, but for the moment Delgard felt a stronger need. A need to cleanse himself, to pray for spiritual strength and guidance. And to pray for the defiled soul of one who had perished centuries before.

Delgard rose and his large frame was unsteady. He had to rest his hands on the desk for several moments before he felt able to stand fully erect. The room settled around him once more, but his strength and vitality were still fading. He pushed back the chair and walked to the door, pausing to look back at Fenn before going through.

'Gerry,' he said, but not loudly enough.

The reporter slept on and it was hardly surprising; his mind was taking refuge from the terrors of the day. When Fenn had brought the old manuscripts to the priest's house earlier that evening, his whole demeanour had been one of bewildered nervousness. A cynic who did not believe in ghosts believed – *knew* – he had now seen such an apparition. It had taken two hastily swallowed whiskies before he was calm enough to tell the story coherently.

Delgard regretted having let the reporter go to the church at Barham alone; he should have realised the danger sooner.

After the incident at St Peter's – an incident which Fenn had described in great detail, as though needing to rationalize it with the spoken word – he had found the American reporter, Nancy Shelbeck, hiding nearby. She had refused to be taken to a hospital where Fenn hoped she might be treated for the obvious shock she was in, and he had been too afraid to leave her alone in his or her own apartment. So he had taken her to Sue Gates, in whose flat she had fallen into a dazed sleep.

Sleep. The tiredness was upon him, too. It was as though the unseen presence, the presence that had emanated *here*, in these church grounds, was parasitical, taking its strength from the human psyche. The weakness he had felt at the onset of the miracles, the interference with electrically operated machinery, the strange atmosphere, the vibrancy in the air itself, all suggested a reaction was taking place, perhaps a sapping of existing energy to create a new form. And, he now felt sure, the catalyst, both physical and spiritual, was Alice Pagett.

He glanced back at the faded manuscript papers. The answer lay there, written in Latin, the ancient language common to priests since the Christian religion began. It was incredible, but then he had witnessed the unbelievable as reality many times before. The link, centuries old, was in those papers, the tortured, quirky handwriting giving evidence of the tormented, even demented, man who had written the shame-filled words. And that man had been a priest, a sixteenth-century cleric, who had sinned not just against his faith, but against humanity itself.

And what made the priest's iniquity even more unforgivable was that he had the gleamings of understanding in an age of superstition and ignorance. He had been aware of parapsychological forces, had been capable of differentiating them from misguided concepts of sorcery; yet he had encouraged and used his fellow-man's false perceptions for his own purposes and, in so doing, had invoked a far worse power against himself. The people of that time believed they had destroyed a witch under the authority and incitement of their ruler, a queen called Mary. *Mary Tudor.* But they had destroyed something more than a mythical invention: they had destroyed someone whose extraordinary mental powers could transcend her own death. And eventually, when certain psychical elements came together, could possibly recreate her own physical being.

Witchcraft, the name of *Mary*, the mental energy released by religious fervour: these were the strange, intrinsic ingredients. The latter-day priest who had sinned, the child who had been conceived in sin: these were the catalysts. And it was Alice who played the most important part in the metamorphosis, *for she had been created in the same field where the nun had been butchered then burnt to death almost five hundred years before.*

Delgard leaned against the door, incredible, insane theories rushing into his head.

Could a centuries-late metempsychosis, the migration of a soul at death into another body, have taken place? Had Alice been taken at the very spark of her existence? She had grown into a child, guided by her mother, devoted to the church, worshipping the name of Mary, becoming severely handicapped at the age of four, an infirmity her doctors could not satisfactorily explain, to be inexplicably released from that disability seven years later. Miraculously. The cures to others had appeared miraculous, too. But were they really psychically induced?

He shook his head against the jumble of thoughts.

Alice had spoken in a tongue alien to her own, the voice mature, the words old-English, the content . . . disturbed, lustful. Had she been possessed? Or . . . or was she a reincarnation? As a Catholic priest, the idea should have had no validity to him, but it was a nagging thought he found impossible to push away.

Yet even this was quelled by the question that over-rode all others: what was the purpose of it all?

Foreboding dragged at him with such intensity that his body sagged and he was forced to cling to the door for support. The premonition of disaster was nothing new – the feeling of dread had been with him for weeks – but now he knew it was imminent. The brief insight was like a physical blow, striking at him and vanishing instantly, so that all he was left with was a feeling of total desolation, a distressing cognisance of . . . nothing. A void, absolute in its emptiness. It was the most frightening thing he had ever perceived.

The need to be on hallowed ground sent Delgard staggering from the room. He had to pray, had to seek spiritual guidance to combat the impending evil.

He threw open the front door and outside the night seemed as black as the void he had just briefly borne witness to.

A cold draught of air found its way down the hallway and into the open room where the reporter slept. Fenn changed position restlessly as the drop in temperature touched him, but he slumbered on, his dreams no refuge, merely extensions of the daytime nightmare. The corners of the faded papers on the small desk stirred with the chill breeze.

Sue glanced at her watch. Nearly eleven. What was taking Gerry so long? Was he going to leave Nancy Shelbeck here all night? He said he'd get back.

She stirred the coffee and took it from the kitchen into the lounge. The door to her bedroom was slightly ajar and she stopped to listen for a few seconds. Nancy's breathing seemed more regulated, deeper, the earlier disturbed panting having faded to small childlike whimpers before a more natural sleep had taken over. Sue went to the sofa and sat, placing the steaming mug of coffee on the coffee table before her. She sank into the soft cushions and closed her eyes.

Abruptly she opened them and stood up; she walked to the window and drew the curtains together. For some reason she had felt the night intrusive. She returned to the sofa and absently stirred the coffee.

What had happened to make them both so frightened? Earlier that evening Gerry had garbled something about finding the American at a church in Barham, in a state of shock, then pleaded with her to take care of the woman until he got back. He had hurried out, clutching his bag as if it contained his year's salary, telling her he had to see Monsignor Delgard, that he had something important to show him. What could have been so important? Why had he and this woman gone to the church at Barham in the first place? And what were they so afraid of?

Sue tapped at her chin in frustration. Why bring her here of all places? Was he so insensitive to the situation? It was obvious that something was going on between them. Yet Sue knew that Gerry's insensitivity was often a put-on, that he was fully aware of the emotions he aroused in others, that he preferred reaction to inertia. But this time there was a desperation in him that dismissed any notion of lovers' games; he needed Sue's help and that it involved another woman with whom he had a relationship had no relevance.

She sipped the coffee. Damn him! She had tried to fall out of love with him, had even tried to despise him for a while, but it had been no use. Her religion, the work at the church, the time spent with Ben, had all contrived to compensate, but the fulfilment had been short-lived and, if she were to be completely honest with herself, never entirely realised. She had found renewed spiritual awareness, but still it could not fill her emotional needs, could not replace or dispose of a different kind of love, the love of one person for another. At first, just weeks before, she had thought such physical love unnecessary; its traumas, the dependence on another (particularly when the other person wasn't so dependable) the jealousies, the *responsibility*, was a trial she would be better off without; but it had gradually dawned on her that to love and be loved on equal terms, with all its hang-ups, was essential. For her, anyway.

Sue frowned as she held the mug in both hands, her elbows resting on her knees. She had been trying to escape, thinking she had found another refuge, an alternative, only to discover that both were equally important. The realization had been there for the last few days, but it had taken their meeting earlier that evening for the fact to hit home. Perhaps it was his new vulnerability that had moved her. Or perhaps it was the thought that this other woman might mean something to him. The fear of losing had always been a prime motivator.

Just what was she to . . .

The scream caused her to spill the coffee over her hands. Quickly Sue slammed the mug onto the coffee table and ran for the bedroom. She fumbled for the light switch, flicked it on, and stared aghast at the woman who was trying to bury her head into the pillow. Sue went to the bed, 'It's okay, you're safe, there's nothing to worry –'

Nancy thrashed out, pushing her hands away.

'Nancy! Stop! You're all right now.' Sue's voice was firm as she tried to pull the American around to face her.

'Don't, don't . . .' Nancy's eyes were unfocused as she struggled away from Sue.

Sue grabbed her wrists as long nails tried to lash her face. 'Calm down, Nancy! It's me, Sue Gates. Don't you remember? Gerry brought you here.'

'Oh God, don't touch me!'

Sue pinned the frightened woman's arms to her chest and leaned heavily on her. 'Calm down. Nothing's going to harm you. You were dreaming.' She spoke steadily, repeating the words, and eventually, Nancy's struggles became weaker. Her eyes began to lose their glazed look and came to rest on Sue's face. 'Oh noooo!' Nancy moaned, and then she was weeping, her thin body wracked by the sobs.

'It's all right, Nancy. You're perfectly safe.'

Nancy threw her arms around Sue and clung to her as an upset child would cling to its mother. Sue soothed her, stroking her hair, feeling awkward, but compassionate enough not to pull away. Laughter drifted up from the street below, late-night revellers returning to their homes. The bedside clock ticked away the minutes.

It was some time before Nancy's sobs ceased and her hands relaxed their tight grip around her comforter's shoulders. Her body trembled as she mumbled something.

'What?' She pulled away slightly. 'I didn't hear you.'

Nancy drew in a shuddering breath. 'I need a drink,' she said.

'I think I've got some brandy. Or gin. Would you prefer that?'

'Anything.'

Sue left her and went into the kitchen, opening the larder where she kept her meagre supply of alcohol. She took out the squat bottle of brandy, then reached into another cupboard for a glass. On reflection, she brought down two glasses. Her nerves were jumpy too.

She took the two brandies into the bedroom and found the American sitting upright against the headboard. Her face was white, its paleness made grotesque by the streaks of running mascara. She was staring blankly at the wall opposite, her hands twisting the edge of the bedsheets into a crumpled roll.

Sue handed her one of the glasses which she grabbed with both hands. The amber liquid almost spilled over the sides as she raised the glass to her lips. Nancy drank and began to cough, holding the brandy away from her. Sue took the glass from her and waited for the choking to subside.

'Try it more slowly this time,' she said when Nancy reached out again. The reporter followed her advice and Sue sipped at her own drink.

'Th – thanks,' Nancy finally gasped. 'You don't . . . you don't have a cigarette, do you?'

'Sorry.'

'It's okay. There's some in my bag.'

'I'm afraid you didn't have a bag with you when Gerry brought you here. You must have left it in his car.'

'Oh, shit, no. It's back there at the church, probably somewhere in the undergrowth.'

'What happened? Why did you leave it there?'

Nancy looked at Sue. 'Didn't Fenn tell you?'

'He didn't take time to. He said something about St Peter's at Barham, asked me to take care of you, then dashed out. What were you doing at the church?'

Nancy took a swallow of the brandy and leaned her head back against the wall, closing her eyes. 'I was searching for something. I assume he came looking for the same thing.' She told Sue about the chest and the historical records they had hoped to find inside. Her voice still shook with tension.

'That's what he must have had in his bag,' Sue said.

Nancy's head came away from the wall. 'He found them?'

'I think so. He said he had to take something to Monsignor Delgard.'

'Is that where he's gone – to Delgard, to St Joseph's?'

Sue nodded.

'I know this sounds odd,' Nancy said, clutching Sue's arm, 'but what did I tell him? I . . . I just can't remember anything after running from that goddamned church.'

'I don't know. You were in a state of shock.'

'Yeah, I must have been.' Her whole body shuddered. 'My God, I think I saw some kind of ghost.'

Sue looked at her in surprise. 'You don't look the type.'

'Uh-huh, that's what I thought. But something scared the shit out of me inside that church.' She closed her eyes once more, trying to relive the memory. Her eyes snapped open as the image came to her. 'Oh no,' she said, then wailed, 'Oh no!'

Sue shook her gently. 'Take it easy. Whatever it was, you're safe now.'

'Safe? That was a fucking dead thing I saw back there! How can you be safe from something like that?'

Sue was stunned. 'You must have imagined it. You couldn't possibly have –'

'Don't tell me that! I know what I saw!'

'Don't get upset again.'

'Upset? I got a right to get fucking upset. I'm telling you, I saw something that's never gonna leave me, something I'm never gonna forget.' The tears were flowing again and the brandy glass clattered against her teeth as she attempted to drink. Sue steadied her hand for her.

'Thanks,' Nancy said when she had managed to swallow more of the alcohol. 'I didn't mean to yell. It's just . . . you don't know what the hell it was like.'

'Do you want to tell me?'

'No, I don't want to tell you, I want to erase it from my mind. But I know I never will.'

'Please, it might help you.'

'Do I get another drink?'

'Take mine.' They exchanged glasses. It took two more sips – but at least they were just sips – for Nancy to speak again. Her words were slow, as though she were trying to control them, to rationalize them in her own mind.

'I was inside the church – St Peter's on the Stapley Estate. D'you know it?'

'I've heard of it. I've never been there.'

'Give it a miss. I'd found the chest –'

'You said you were looking for some historical records.'

'Right. Fenn said a certain part of St Joseph's history was missing. We tracked down the chest they might have been kept in. It was at St Peter's.'

'You went there together?'

'No, separately. Fenn didn't want me in on the deal. You know how he is.'

Sue said nothing.

'I'd found the chest – I was sure it was the right one. Then I heard – maybe I just felt – someone else in the church. I walked down towards the altar to take a look. There was someone sitting behind a kind of alcove, in a closed-in pew affair. It looked . . . it looked like a nun.'

She gulped back more brandy.

'Only it wasn't a nun,' she continued. 'It wasn't a nun . . .' Her voice trailed off.

'Tell me, Nancy,' Sue urged quietly.

'She was wearing one of those hooded cloak affairs, a habit of some kind, but not like those you see nowadays. It was old, I'm sure it was goddamned old. I couldn't see her face at first.' She was trembling again. 'But she . . . it . . . turned towards me. Oh God, oh God, that face!'

Sue could feel the bristling of her own hairs on the back of her neck, the sudden rising of goose-pimples down her spine and arms. 'Tell me,' she said again, horrified but peculiarly fascinated.

'It was just a charred, cindered mess. The eyes were black, just slits with burnt gristle poking through. The lips and nose had been scorched away, the teeth were just burned-out stumps. There was nothing left to it, no features, nothing human! And I could smell the burning, I could smell roasting flesh. And she began to move. She was dead but she began to move, to rise, to come towards me. She touched me! She touched my face with her burned stubble of a hand! And she tried to hold me there. She breathed onto my face! I could feel it, I could smell it! Her fingers, just withered stumps, touched my eyes! And she was laughing, oh God, she was laughing! *But she was still burning! Do you understand? She was still burning!*'

THIRTY-FOUR

And sleep shall obey me,
And visit thee never,
And the curse shall be on thee
For ever and ever.

KEHAMA'S CURSE
Robert Southey

When Fenn awoke he was shivering. He rubbed at his eyes, then peered around the room.

'Delgard?' he called out. The door was open, cold air sweeping into the room. He wearily pushed himself from the armchair and crossed the floor. Peering into the dark passageway, he called the priest's name again. There was no answer. Fenn noticed the front door was open. Had Delgard gone over to the church? He stepped back into the room and checked his watch. Jesus! Nearly one in the morning!

His eyes fell on the small writing desk and the scattered papers on its surface. With a final glance into the hall, he closed the door and went to the desk. He picked up a few sheets of the old parchment paper, realizing they were the same papers that had fallen from the vellum manuscript inside the church on the Stapley Estate. He studied them for a few seconds as though the words would translate themselves, then returned them to the desk. The top pages of Delgard's notebook were folded over as if the draught had disturbed them. He flicked them back and scanned the lines on the first page. He slowly sat, his eyes never leaving the words before him.

Leafing through the pages, he saw that the monsignor had translated most, if not all, of the ancient papers, adding and initialling his own notes as he went along. His tiredness quickly dispersed as he read Delgard's first note:

(The script is unclear in parts, much of the writing almost illegible. The handwriting is erratic, scrawled, unlike the neat hand of the manuscript these papers were found in, even though author seems to be same. Translation will be as close to the original as possible, but own interpretation and meaning will have to be used to make sense of certain sections of text. Also, Latin is not correct in parts – may be due to disturbed mind of writer. D.)

Fenn picked up a single sheet of parchment once more and frowned at the scrawl. A disturbed mind, or a frightened one?

He looked over at the door and wondered if he should find Delgard. How long the priest had been gone, he had no way of knowing, but the translation must have taken hours judging by the amount of notes. Fenn was annoyed at himself for having fallen asleep. It was a strange time for Delgard to have gone into the church, but then he, Fenn, knew little of the lives of such men: perhaps it was normal for him to make his devotions at such a late hour. On the other hand, Delgard may have just gone out to check on the two young priests whose duty it was to keep an all-night vigil in the next-door field. With some of the crazy people around it would have made more sense to bring in Securicor but, he supposed, the Church had its own way of doing things.

It was still cold in the room, even though the door was now closed. He noticed the fire was low, almost out, the burnt logs charcoaled with patches of white ash breaking the blackness. He went to the fireplace and threw on two more logs, cinders briefly flaring as they landed. He rubbed his hands together to clear the wood-dust and willed the logs to ignite, the chill beginning to sink into his bones.

The wood sizzled as gas escaped and small flames began to lick at the underneath. He grunted with satisfaction and turned towards the desk. For some reason his eyes were drawn towards the window and at the long narrow gap between the curtains; he drew them tightly closed as if the night outside were a sinister voyeur. He sat once more and pulled Delgard's large notebook towards him. He began to read, and he was still cold.

Seventeenth Day of October in the year 1560

She is dead yet dwells not in the underworld. At night I see her before me, a vile thing from Hell that cannot rest, nor yet let me be, a rotting creature of the grave that once I cherished. But then, her beauty was unspoiled. Now sweet, Damnable, Elnor will not leave, not until she has me with her amongst her corrupted brood. 'Tis true I deserve such fate, for my Sins cry out and are not to be forgiven by Our God in Heaven. Mayhap my madness is an earthly Penance and this makes better choice than the Hell to which she draws me. But she has bid me, and she, my Elnor, will surely take me.

(Script impossible   *My hand trembles for she is here! Her corpse's presence surrounds*
to read here and no   *me and makes foul the air!*
meaning can be
guessed at.   D.)   *My father, that noble Lord, forbids that I confess to my Bishop, for*
he sees only madness in my eyes and would mute my madman's utterings. Thus he keeps me prisoner in this mean Chapel where only the servants and landsmen bear witness to my decline. No longer am I a freeman, for I have fallen in his eyes and no blame to

him for that. Yet how long must I hear his Chaucer jibe:
> *'That if gold rust, what then will iron do?*
> *For if a Priest be foul in trust*
> *No wonder that a common man should rust!'*

For all his scorn, still I know he understands not the depths of my Sin. Haste now! Though my brow be fevered and my hand trembles as if with ague, this must be set down that others may read of she whose vengeance is boundless nor leashed by earthly time. Give me strength, Dear Lord, and deny me not the courage to carry out this duty, that others shall know her vileness and be warned. My guilt lies open in these my words. You who read them

(Scrawled lines at this point and many deletions. As if writer cannot put his thoughts on paper. D.)

dismiss them not as a madman's ravings. But keep close hold of the vision of Our Saviour that is within you, lest your Soul be tainted by this Confession.

I served long years at the Church of St Joseph's in Banefeld and there I knew joy. The village was my house, the villagers my trusting children. Disputes I settled and they had Faith in my Word for they believed it the Word of God. The womenfolk unburdened their worries upon my shoulders and I was pleased to give counsel to these simple people, for it gave purpose to my life and Grace to my Soul. The children had some small fear of me for my countenance is not pleasing. Yet fear of God's Servant on Earth is proper to the young. My Holiness was revered and the True Faith was kept in my Parish throughout all those troubled Heretical times.

(He refers to the Reformation and the Establishment of the Church of England during the reign of Henry VIII. D.)

No man betrayed my trust, though Evil entered my Soul and yet holds sway.

It was the Prioress who brought Elnor to me, unknowing that she did the Devil's work. Elnor, this Cursed Nun, was fair and gentle to look upon; a child, an innocent, whose treachery to God and Mankind I did not perceive. Blacker than jet was her Soul, her mind full of guile and her personage well-armed with deceit. Her mistress considered her spirited, but her own cheveril conscience could not perceive Elnor's subtle wickedness.

She was to be of help in the Church, an aid much needed, for my duties were plenty. Then was I stirred by carnal desires, urgings of the flesh that could not be subdued, unholy dreams that betrayed my Chastity. And it was as though straightway she had Knowledge of my hidden Sinfulness, for her eyes saw clearly into my very Soul. Such was her Mystery. Too soon I knew that Elnor was as no other woman and that her Holy Vocation was but the aberration of a perverse mind. Yet it was her mind that first distracted me from my duties. My studies have encompassed astronomy, medicine, physics and even the ancient esoteric craft of alchemy; and of medicine and alchemy her knowledge was by far the greater.

(As the son of a wealthy nobleman, his learning may well have included such diverse subjects. But how could this nun know of such things? D.)

I was soon to become fascinated by her Knowledge and thus captivated.

From the beginning, she was like no other Religious of my acquaintance; in truth, like no other woman. Elnor fulfilled her duties pleasingly well, but always there was the smile that held

(A person's body was conceived of being composed of the four elements: Earth, Water, Air and Fire. Earth – cold and dry; Water – cold and moist; Air – hot and moist; Fire – hot and dry. Sickness was an inbalance of these qualities.   D.)

(Effigies.   D.)

(More incoherent writing here, much of it indecipherable. Although Priest has stated he will not detail his indecencies with this woman, it appears he has done so to a certain extent. Unclear whether it is guilt that has subconsciously made writing almost illegible, fear, or his own reawakened excitement. Much sacrilege and the use of holy objects seems to be involved. Names here and there, but can make no sense of them.   D.)

some veiled secret, the gaze that lingered too long on my own. I was soon Bewitched and was later to deem that term rightly used. In those first days I saw only guileless innocence, not the true self which made fool of me. We prayed together and her adoration inclined most towards the Blessed Mother of Christ, daughter of St Anna. There was at this time a sickness in the village, no plague this, but illness that sent many to their beds. Two children died, yet these were frail from birth, so God was praised for His Mercy and for sending so skilled a mortal in the tending of the sick. For her powers of medicine were soon made manifest and even our physician, a pompous though well-meaning fellow, ventured his admiration. Two other young Holy Sisters joined us in our work. Novices these, whose names were Agnes and Rosemund, and they remained at the Church when the sickness was passed. It was said that a Divine Hand guided hers, that by gazing upon a man, be he reeve or hayward, she could tell if he were dry or cold, moist or hot. Thus would she administer her restorative simples and cures. She also used images
to be worn about the neck when the planets were favourably inclined; energies descended into the image with great benefit to the dependent. I had cause to scold Elnor for such practices, but she would smile and say it was Faith that offered the cure and nothing more. If I found this sacrilegious, I would keep my peace because of the deep interest it aroused in me. Such then was my initial Enchantment with Elnor that I did not consider to consult with the Prioress. It was when a mysterious malady struck down my own body that pending illfortune had its consummation. Elnor was sent by her Prioress to tend me and, in my delirium, I felt her hands upon my body, soothing my pains, bathing away fever's moisture; and kindling a desire that had been smouldering. Perchance it was her own potions which aroused my passion. Thus ensnared was I, and once so, became her willing captive. My abandonment was complete, my taste for her delights insatiable. I am too shamefaced to relate all that took place in our sinful fornication; suffice to say that our carnal acts plunged into bestiality of such low nature that I fear my Soul is perished, never more to be reborn in God's light.

As Elnor opened her flesh to me, so too did she open her mind. She spoke of things ancient and of matters not yet of this Earth. She spoke of voices that were from the dead, and of forces that rode the air like silent thunderstorms; forces perceived only by the Chosen. She likened these incorporeal powers to great unsighted tidal waves that sought entry into the shallow world of men, Furies that if unleashed would destroy and recreate in their own image. I would ask her if it was the Devil's power she spoke of and she would mock me and tell me there was no greater power than the Will of Man. I cowered at such blasphemy and believed her to be a sorceress; but in the passage of time I learned that she was much more. To her, magic was but a product of the Will, and potions, poisons and transmuters the tools of alchemists and physicians, not of the sorceress.

I was irrevocably lost in her; this wretched Nun dominated my existence. My frail body, so exquisitely scourged by her instruments, lived only to gratify itself with her pleasures. As well I sought her Knowledge; yet still am I mystified.

From whence does your Evil come? I would ask of her. And from where your Goodness? For still she cured the sick. Why do you venerate the Holy Name of the Sacred Virgin, yet blaspheme her presence by fornication before her Image? Why choose the righteous path of handmaiden of Christ when your secret deeds are not to His Way? And why have you made prisoner of this poor Soul? These questions I asked many times, but she answered them not until one year had gone by and, I think, until she was sure that the invisible chains which girdled my Will could not be loosed. She cured the sick that her name should be exalted as was the name of Mary; and she exalted Mary's name that she, Elnor, be as the Virgin Mother, an intermediary of power, though not yet fully tested. I am a Nun, Elnor told me, because I seek position over others, that I may be revered and obeyed. As Prioress, I shall gain that trust and 'tis you, sweet Thomas, who will help me in this, for has not your noble father great influence with the Church?

As I write the Chapel goes colder, swift dissolving breath clouds falling to the page below. The wind shakes windows and doors, and Demons seek me out. Stay away Elnor! This ground is Sacred, its Sanctity inviolate. Still my fingers grow numb with the freeze and become brittle as if fit to snap. O God have Mercy on this miserable creature and allow my Chronicle to be written.

Methinks I hear a voice that calls my name from without. Would that it were the mewlings of some night animal, but I fear 'tis the voice of my dead mistress. The Chapel is dim and the lamp cannot light up the dark places. There is no peace for me here, nor will be until she is laid to rest. But who will do that deed? Not I, that I know.

In truth then I knew Elnor, but still could not resist her Will. She laughed at my words and scorned my horror. She spoke of poison for the Prioress: Orpiment or Realgar would be the insiduous assassin.

(Trisulphide of arsenic and disulphide of arsenic. D.)

The poisoning would be slow that no suspicion would arise. The Prioress would suffer a long and wasting sickness and it would be seen that even the skilful and tender administrations of Sister Elnor would not prevent the aged Nun's death. O cunning Witch! Yet Witch you are not. No sorceress you, sweet, Damned Elnor; something more, something much more.

Too late I learned of these ambitions, poor debauched fool that I was. Weak, lecherous disciple of Sin! Help me God before my dying comes.

Yet so lost to her own lust was Elnor that her downfall was of her own doing. And Blessed be to Jesu for that. My people revered her for they considered her pure of heart and she had cured many an ailment. They brought to her gifts, some mere trinkets and others of value. The latter kind she stored secretly in the Crypt of St Joseph's lest the Prioress discover them, and those of little value she gave to the Priory. And all thought her most fair and generous.

The children flocked to Sister Elnor, this vile creature of depravity, adoring her, beseeching her Blessing, for they knew from their elders that here walked a Saint on Earth; and her black heart welcomed them, for they were as lambs to a wolf. What makes a Soul thus? There is no answer in this World, but lies in a place of darkness, where shadowed spirits conspire with devils to destroy Mankind's peace.

In Church she prayed long hours, her body prostrate before the altar, that all might witness her devotion. At night, when observers were none, then would she defile that same altar in practices that now cause sickness in my throat, for I was her willing accomplice. Still I know not what led me to this disgrace, what Spirit released this carnal lust in me. I reason that her Will governed mine, her thoughts controlled my own; but in my heart I know the Will had first to come from me. Her temptations were so cursedly sweet, the torture upon my body so cursedly glorious! Her child's face, her white flesh, that Devil's gateway between her thighs from which she bade me drink, these were too wondrous to forswear.

Yet I wander, my thoughts no longer gathered. My father, that steadfast patron of the Church, thinks me mad; and perhaps 'tis so. Still I have not the madman's escape into delirium and there is no comfort in my dreams.

But in the second year of my Knowledge of Elnor, suspicions were whispered abroad. My demeanour had changed. I had never been a robust man, but there was a weakness upon me, a stoop to my stature that was plain to see. My obsession with the young Nun would no longer be disguised. Worse yet was the disappearance of the children, lost over several months in the nearby forests, never to be seen again. Three children in all, whose names I have already set down.

(Set down?   D.)

(The names must be those mentioned in the earlier unclear passage. The priest and the nun killed the children!   D.)

How these simple peasant children had believed in sweet Sister Elnor, and how I had to stifle their screams when her punishment was visited upon their small bodies. Dear God, there can be no forgiveness for my part in these foul deeds. I could not even pray over their hidden graves.

The Prioress had become weakened, her life's Spirit ebbing more each day. Stealthy was her demise, for Elnor would not allow that any should say the hand of another played part in the old nun's death. Bolder became this Devil's Daughter and more demanding in her excesses. My endeavours were no longer sufficient for her lusts and less often could my tortures satiate her appetite. As well, it had become dangerous to take more children from the district. Her appetites were turned upon the two young novices who came daily to St Joseph's. One accepted her debasement willingly, for her heart was already lost to Elnor; the other submitted but fled shamefaced afterwards. This novice took her own life in remorse, but first Confessed her Mortal Sin to the ailing Prioress.

Outrage gave the Mother Superior a newfound strength. But so too was she cunning, for my father's coffers were ever open to the Church. His loyalty to our Holy Roman Pope had not wavered during the Heretical time of Henry's Lutherism, nor during the confused reign of the young Edward. Now my father was favoured by good Queen Mary and justly rewarded for his fortitude and loyalty. To have him as enemy would not have been wise for the Prioress, who had oft times benefitted from his generosity.

This wise woman sent for me and, knowing all was lost, I threw myself on her mercy. The blame lay all with the vile temptress, Sister Elnor, whose magic potions had robbed me of my reason. I wept and scourged myself before the Prioress; I confessed my most grave and sinful fornication with Elnor and begged forgiveness. But I did not tell all, for I was afraid for my life.

Though she looked upon me with loathing in her eyes, the Prioress gave me her forgiveness. Elnor's Spirit was darkened by spectres who rejected the Christian Path. She was a child of Satan whose sorcery had overcome my Will. A mere mortal, I could offer scant resistance to the leeching of my strength and the magic potions she fed my body. I eagerly accepted these Judgements, well knowing they were my Salvation, willing to believe I was but helpless victim to Entrancement. That day we discussed the punishment of Sister Elnor.

The Prioress doubted not that Elnor was Witch and Profaner and, 'though I knew she was more, I readily agreed. Good Queen Mary had decreed that both Witch and Dissenter should be driven from her Realm and from this Mortal World. Rumour had it that two hundred and more Heretics had already been burnt at the stake, and the County of Sussex had played part in many of these burnings. I myself had witnessed two in nearby Lewes. The Summoner was sent for and I denounced Sister Elnor as Heretic and Witch. The Prioress was well pleased with this and seemed satisfied with my Contrition. When the Summoner had left us to make arrangements for Elnor's confinement, she bade me warn my congregation of the Nun's evil-doings lest more suffering ensued. There was a gleam to her eyes when she hinted that Elnor might lie too well at her trial, and my own person would be brought to book. I well knew that the truth would indeed bring this about, and I suspect that Prioress, my new found guardian, knew this too. I journied back to Banefeld with much haste, my brow as fevered as when the true fever had been upon me. I was mindful of my own safety and wished to protect the good name of my father. In the village I quickly told certain members of my Congregation of what the Prioress and I had discovered of Elnor, and word spread like flames in a forest fire. These good people were full of wrath, for to have their Faith abused and in such a manner was more than they could bear. Those whose children had been lost screamed for vengeance and their cry was taken up, along with sticks and cudgels, by their fellows. They hastened to the Church of St Joseph's, a vehement, threatening mob, and I followed, spurring them on, enlivened with their passion, for had I not been unwittingly Seduced into her Wickedness? There were children amongst us, those who had once revered this Holy Nun and who now despised her. So sudden was our descent upon the Church that Elnor was found by the altar, beneath the statue of Our Lord's

(Summoner: someone paid to bring sinners to trial before an ecclesiastical court. D.)

blissful Mother, there embraced in the arms of the novice, Rosemund, who had so easily succumbed to her wiles. As had I. Elnor was dragged screaming from the Church, her protesting companion in desire thrown to one side. O how I cowered when Elnor's eyes met mine; it seemed poison-tipped daggers had plunged into my heart. She knew at once that I was her betrayer and such was the malevolence in her eyes that I fell to the ground. My flock believed me Spellbound and tore at her eyes with fingers and sticks. Even when she wailed piteously, sightlessly, they gave no mercy but flailed her for her witchcraft. She cried out that I, their spiritual leader, was partner to her iniquity, and I denied her charges most absolutely, bidding them pay no heed to the Heretic's lies, urging them to look for the Devil's Mark about her person, for secretly I knew that upon her body was a third nipple, an aberration that the ignorant believed to be a suckling breast for a witch's Familiar.

(Alice!   D.)

They stripped her of her Nun's robes and found the Accursed Mark. Their rage all but consumed them. The menfolk beat her relentlessly, their women and children urging them on, until her naked body ran with blood. And all the while they beseeched her to Confess to witchcraft. But still she did not; curses were her only words. They pulled hair, greased with her own blood, from her body, until she was an obscene, hairless figure; yet still she would not admit to sorcery. O the torture they inflicted upon her! And yet my pleas for the punishment to end were feeble and went unheard. They broke her limbs, these Christian men, and dragged her through the mire as the children and women stabbed at her with pointed sticks. I could not stop them and I no longer tried.

Elnor implored mercy but still did not Confess to the crime of which she was accused. So angered were they that they dragged her to a nearby ditch, the river too far from their seething passion. The water ran scarlet when they put her to the Test and her tortured body gave way at last to the agony. She Confessed to witchcraft, and such was my own fear and need for vengeance that I almost believed this to be true. May He that Harrowed Hell forgive me, but this I wanted to be true.

They carried Elnor to a young oak nearby and there they tied a rope about her neck and hoisted her aloft. Still she screamed, and those screams filled my head until I felt my skull must needs burst. And when they lit the fire beneath her naked, dangling feet, it seemed her agony consumed my own flesh. Those bloodfilled sockets, once the holders of the softest of eyes, stared at me through the mob each time her twisting body turned in my direction, and her broken lips poured Curses upon my head, and upon all those present, each man, woman and child, and their descendants. And she cursed the name of Mary. I knew not whether she meant Christ's Holy Mother, or our own Good Queen Mary, and I wonder if by then this demented creature knew herself. Even when the carpenter, a strong man this with no weak stomach, cut into her bowels and drew down her organs so that they sizzled and roasted upon the fire below, her Curses still filled our heads.

At her death I knew that this woman was indeed more than Witch,

*for the sky darkened and the ground trembled beneath our feet.
Those that could ran, whilst others cowered in the mud. I thought
my Church nearby would topple, but its sturdy build held fast,
though several stones fell. So afraid was this poor Mortal Soul
that I believed I saw spectres rising from the graveyard. I know
not what foul force from Hell had been released by Elnor's death.
The very earth appeared to open beneath my feet and I stared into a
Black Pit and there I saw the twisted creatures of the lower world,
wretched Lost Souls, whose sins so foul were irredeemable, whose
anguished moans rose up in torment to pervade the darkened
landscape. What manner of creature she to invoke such horrors!
Now fallen, crawling on my belly like a worm, I turned my head
from this Hellish sight and looked upon the black-charred carcase
of she who once had been my sweet, wicked mistress.*

*The rope from which she hung broke and its gruesome burden
dropped into the fire below where it did seethe and hiss until it was
as charcoaled wood. I thought that I heard from this blackened
thing one last howling screech, but this could only have been my
own tortured imaginings for, in surety, there was nothing human
left of that once fair body.*

*It became as night, though day was not spent, darkness falling
upon darkness, and I ran from that Infernal Place, the vile stench
and inhuman cries rising from the Black Pit to assail my senses. I
fled, unsteady on my feet, for the ground still shook, and beseeched
the Lord Christ to save me from Satan's Anger. The Church
Crypt was my refuge, my Sanctuary, and I covered my eyes against
the demons that rose and beckoned me from their disturbed resting
places. Three days I hid in that tomb of darkness, curled in the
blackest corner, my head covered by coarse sacking, my eyes closed
tight against the shadows. Mayhap the time spent in that lonely
dungeon loosed my reason completely, for when my father's
servants found me at last, no words of meaning came from my lips.
They took me from there and my eyes were blinded by the light of
day. It was well, for I had no desire to look upon that ravaged
scene again. I was locked in a room in my father's house and
physicians endeavoured to soothe my ramblings with medicines
and kind words. When at last my ravings had calmed, my Bishop
came and spoke quietly with me, my father at his side, a staunch
rock of reality. They told me that the people of Banefeld, the
landsmen, their womenfolk, their children, would not speak of
that Evil day but to say that Elnor had Confessed to witchcraft
and the slaughter of three children, and had Cursed them in her
dying breath. A thunderstorm had shaken the land and dark clouds
had gathered low overhead, though no rain had fallen. But they
did not tell of rising demons, nor black openings to Hell. I
implored my father and the Bishop to believe me, but their reply
was gentle admonishment: Elnor had poisoned my mind with her
drugs and I had seen that which was not, had lived only in the
realm of my own thoughts. At this I further ranted and two
servants were summoned to strap me to my bed.*

*Weeks passed, though I know not how many, and in that time it
was decided between my father and the Bishop that my health, by*

which they meant the condition of my mind, might be better served
if I stayed away from St Joseph's and Banefeld. I suspect the
hand of the Prioress was in this, for while she would not condemn
me before my father, her Conscience would not allow my tainted
person within her Province. Thus my days would be spent at the
small Church of St Peter's, on my father's estate, where my
babblings would be ignored by his servants and the tenants. I
would serve as Pastor. Here I would stay safe, locked in my own
cell of madness. Money was given to St Joseph's by my father for
repairs to fallen stonework – ha! Struck by lightning they said,
and a new stained glass window was set into the south wall. He
brought to me several items from my old Parish, vestments and
such like. The Church chest was also carried to St Peter's and I
believe it was of this he was most mindful. Methinks private
words had passed between my father and that wily Sister of the
Cloth, the Prioress, for he seemed eager to obtain this chest in
which were kept all records of St Joseph's and the parish of
Banefeld. He need not have been thus concerned, for I had not been
foolish enough to set down my carnal acts with Sister Elnor, nor
any statement which would speak foul of her. How he must have
pored over these letters and scripts, searching for that which would
bring down shame on the Woolgar crest, and how he must have
sighed when none was found. How then would he view this paper
that I now scribe for future reading, which will remain well-hid
until God deigns it shall be found? Not well, I am sure.
Hark now! The door rattles once more, but already she is within.
Her stench grows stronger and I will not look at the dark shadow
that lingers at the edge of my vision. My body is stiff with cold
and the quill with which I write scratches deep into the page. Yet
my fear will not let me rest! I must finish this task quickly lest my
courage fail and others be not warned! I have served my days here
with diligence and with Godliness, knowing my Soul is forever
Damned. After a while, many months to be sure, I learned to keep
dread contained within me, giving vent only when alone to the
anguish and remorse that tortured me. They thought me still mad
and their gaze avoided mine. But no longer were they burdened
with my rantings, my impassioned pleas against unseed forces.
Once more our Holy Pope in Rome is denied now that Elizabeth
has come to the throne, but that concerns me little, for I am left
alone in peace here. In peace! What insanities I write! Yet would
I gladly exchange persecution from our new Queen for the vile
pursuance of this soul-less spirit. I have not seen the Prioress since
I was ensconced here and she ignores the messages I send through
my father's servants (it may be that he intercepts them). His reeve
had told me that Sister Rosemund was cast out of the Priory after
Elnor's death and took to living in the forests near the village.
This may well be true; I care not. My pity is for myself alone.
None is to spare for that unfortunate. Elnor breathes upon me and
it is the fetid breath of Death! She wills me look into those
bloodfilled eyes, to fall into her lover's embrace. A withered hand
touches my shoulder and still I will not look! Not yet, dear Elnor.
Not 'til this task be done, these words set down that others may

learn. Doubt not these words, reader; denounce them not as the ravings of a madman, but pay them heed! Her Evil is not yet done and her maligned Spirit is not yet at rest.

The door is opened and the howling wind enters the church. It shrieks at these papers, seeking to tear them from my hand. But I will resist. She shall not have them. They will be well kept, hidden away, and then shall I turn to my Elnor. And I shall embrace her as I have embraced her in dreams of late, for my desires are still of her. I see only her beauty, not this scarred, blackened creature who stands over me, whose lipless mouth stays close to my cheek, whose

Enough of this! She has me, for there are no lies between us now. I still fornicate with her in my thoughts and it is my Sinful lust that binds us forever. I leave this warning for those who seek it. She touches me and I am hers once more!

Guard your soul. With this script I may find some Redemption. Guard your Soul and Pray for one who is already lost.

(End of document. Beyond doubt Thomas Woolgar, priest of St Joseph's, Banfield, and latterly of St Peter's, Barham, son of Sir Henry Woolgar, is author.   D.)

Questions:
1. *Was* Thomas Woolgar insane?
2. What did he mean: Elnor more than just a witch?
3. Is curse coming true??
4. Father Hagan/Molly Pagett: catalysts?
5. IS ALICE ELNOR?!!!

D.

Fenn sat back in the chair, his eyes never leaving the papers. He let out a long sighed breath. Jesus Christ! Was it possible? Were these words just the rantings of a madman, or were they the truth? Could this event, this terrible, misguided witch-burning that happened nearly five hundred years ago be the cause of everything that was happening at St Joseph's today? No, it *had* to be superstitious mumbo-jumbo! Witches were from fairy tales, folklore, legends that parents loved to tell their kids around a cheery fire on a dark night. But then Woolgar wasn't claiming that Elnor was a witch. In fact, he *disclaimed* it. But was the supernatural any more real than fairy tales or folklore? Even though he, Fenn, had witnessed events in Banfield that could only be called paranormal, his logical mind found it difficult to accept such a term as fact. But how could he dismiss what had happened to him that very day? There had been something in that church with him, something that threw out a malignant aura of evil. It had scared Nancy half to death and loosened his own bowels somewhat. So what the hell was it? The ghost of poor Sister Elnor?

'Aaah,' he said aloud in disgust. It just couldn't be. There were no such things. 'Keep telling yourself that, Fenn,' he muttered. He studied his hand and there were no weal marks on it, no demon marks on the skin. Yet there had been inside the church, for he had seen them appear. And there were no other marks on his body save where the foliage had lashed him during his tumble down the slope.

He wondered what Delgard's opinion would be. As a priest, the supernatural was part of his dogma, and the concept of life after death was the basis of his religion. But the manifestation of an evil woman's curse from another era? How would that grab him? If he believed in all this, maybe he'd gone over to the church to pray for help!

Fenn shook his head. It was all too incredible. And yet it was happening.

He pushed back the chair and stood, suddenly realizing how stiff and cold he was again. The fire had burned low once more. He reached for his topcoat and shrugged it on, pulling the zipper all the way up to the neck. Better find Delgard, talk it out with him. The priest was no fool, despite his vocation; if he felt there was some relevance to the document, then there sure-as-hell was. And if that was the case, the problem would be what to do about it.

Fenn left the room, pulling the neck of his coat tight around his cheeks, not sure whether it was the coldness of the night that made him shiver, or the faded script lying on the desk top.

He closed the door and walked the length of the hallway, an icy draught greeting him from the doorway ahead. He stepped out into the night and automatically looked up at the sky: it was clear, as if freshly scrubbed of clouds by the winds of the day, its blueness deep, almost black, the star clusters sharp, vivid. There was a light showing dimly through the windows of the church and Fenn walked briskly along the path towards it. His pace quickened until he was almost running. There was something strange about St Joseph's, something he could not understand. It seemed totally black, darker than the night around it, no starlight reflected from the flint walls, no relief in its shape, no shades of grey. Unnaturally black, just a dim light glowing from its windows. He could feel his heart pounding and suddenly he did not want to reach the church; he wanted to turn away, to run from the grounds, away from this malevolent place. He felt as he had at St Peter's earlier in the day: afraid and bewildered.

But he knew Delgard would be in there, alone, unguarded, unaware of the transformation that had occurred. Fenn had to warn the priest, to get him away from there, for he suddenly understood that St Joseph's was no longer the house of God, but the sanctum of something unholy.

When he touched the door, it felt repellent to him, as though the wood, itself, were unclean. He was badly frightened, but he forced himself to push the door open.

THIRTY-FIVE

'But I want my payment too,' said the witch, 'and it's not a small one either . . .'

THE LITTLE MERMAID
Hans Christian Andersen

Monsignor Delgard's wrists rested against the low altar rail and his head was bowed into his chest, his back arched into an unpleasant shape. His lips moved silently in litany, yet there was an immobility about his face, as though his features had been carved from grey stone. He had no idea of how long he had prayed at the altar in St Joseph's; an hour, perhaps less. His fear and confusion had not yet subsided, nor had any solutions to the imminent problem presented themselves. He had no doubts that the ancient words he had translated had been written in truth and he was equally sure that the curse was coming true. He believed that the power of the human mind had no limits on this earth, and neither did the human psyche. Elnor had possessed a power far beyond the knowledge or understanding of her fellow-men; she was of a breed that was rare, unique, a development in genetic terms that most men could barely perceive let alone strive to attain. She had had the ability to draw the wills of others, their energies, their beliefs, into a collective power that could transcend mere human forces. She had not cured the sick; they had cured themselves. Elnor's role had been one of psychic 'director'. That power was now acting through Alice and in a more potent way than in the nun's own lifetime. Had death, that entry into the spiritualistic world where no physical restrictions controlled the mind's energy, enabled her power to increase to this awesome degree? Something more had occurred to Delgard. He had reasoned that Father Hagan and Molly Pagett might have been the catalysts for unleashing these terrors: now he also wondered if it had taken Elnor's spirit this long to develop her strange powers in the 'other' world (what were a few centuries to infinity itself?). And it was this thought that frightened him most for, if Elnor really had returned, how strong would her psychical forces be, and to what purpose would she put them?

He felt inadequate and defenceless. How could he combat something he could not even fully comprehend? Through his bishop he must seek the help of those skilled in such matters, layment some, while others were men of his own calling; perhaps together they could control this evil. But mostly, he would seek God's help, for only the omnific could truly vanquish such a creation.

A sharp sound made him raise his head. He looked around and the church interior was dim, the lights fading. He could see no one else in the church. His attention turned back to the crucifix on the altar and his heavy eyelids closed as he resumed his prayers. His joints felt brittle and once more, as it had frequently over the past few weeks, his body reminded him that age and weariness of mankind's ills were taking their inevitable toll. Perhaps, when all this was done, he would seek his own peace, a retreat into –

The sound again! A sharp, cracking noise. It had come from his right.

He looked over at the disfigured replica of the Virgin Mary and his lips moved, this time caused by an old man's trembling rather than prayer.

Delgard pushed himself upright, the effort seeming to take more than it should have. His footsteps were slow, almost a shuffle. He approached the statue and stood beneath it, looking up with curious eyes at the grotesquely cracked face. The Virgin Mother's hands were spread slightly outwards as if to welcome him, but her smile was no longer the tender expression of maternal love: the cracked stone had distorted it into a sinister leer.

His eyes widened as the once-beatific face seemed to change expression and he quickly realized that the cracks were deepening, running into longer jagged lines. Several pieces of stone dropped away, falling to the floor to crumble into dust. The smile became broader, malevolent. Its lower lip fell and it was as though the mouth had opened to silently laugh. The surface plaster began to move, currents moving through it, and Delgard tried to back away, but found himself transfixed, fascinated by the change in its structure.

He stared up into the statue's eyes and powdered dust slid from them so that they became hollow, empty.

His mouth opened in horror and he began to raise a trembling hand to protect himself, as if suddenly aware of what was going to happen.

Fenn stumbled into the church and immediately saw the tall priest at the far end, near the altar. Delgard was looking up at the statue of the Madonna, one hand half-raised.

And there was something else in the church. A small hooded figure, sitting in one of the pews just a few rows behind the priest.

The dark coldness that enveloped Fenn was now a familiar sensation. He felt his stomach muscles grip together and his hair stiffened. He tried to call out to the monsignor, but just a hissing sound escaped his lips. He began to move forward, but was already too late.

The statue exploded and thunder roared through the church. Thousands of stone pieces tore through Delgard's exposed body like metal shrapnel, lacerating his flesh, cutting through his face, chest, hands, groin, throwing him backwards so that he fell over the first bench into the next row, fragments that had found entry through his eyes already lodged deep in his brain, destroying cells so that the incredible pain was only momentary. His body, now unfeeling, twisted and twitched in the narrow confines between the benches, and one large torn hand raised itself as if pleading with something unseen. It gripped the back of the bench and tightened, closing around the wood in death's grip, a last contact with the material world.

Fenn ran towards the fallen priest. He stopped in the aisle, his hands on the backs of benches, looking down at the bloody, twisted figure, Delgard's face ripped open, his white collar stained crimson. He screamed Delgard's name, even though he knew the priest would not hear, nor ever hear again.

With eyes filled with enraged tears, he looked towards the small black-garbed figure. But there was nothing there. The church was empty. Apart from himself and the dead priest.

WILKES

'But is there nothing I can do to get an immortal soul?' asked the little mermaid.

THE LITTLE MERMAID
Hans Christian Andersen

He locked the box, testing the lid to make sure it was secure. Satisfied, he picked it up from the table and crossed the tiny room to the wardrobe, taking no more than three paces; stretching his body, he placed the box on top of the wardrobe, and shoved it hard so that it slid to the back out of sight. He presumed his snooping landlady had already discovered it, but saw no reason to re-arouse her curiosity by letting her eyes fall on it each time she inspected the room. He smiled, imagining what her reaction would be if she ever discovered its contents. But that was *his* secret. He was sure even his mother did not know it was missing; or, if she did, had not reported the loss to the police, for it was, after all, an illegal possession.

He sat on the narrow, single bed, brushing away the blond hair that fell over his eyes. The newspaper lay spread on the floor at his feet and once more he quickly scanned the article he had been reading. A local Sussex reporter had tried to discredit the little saint, had maintained that the priest had not been killed by a bomb planted by some fanatical anti-religious movement, had made himself a laughing-stock by denouncing all that had happened at Banfield as some crazy witch's curse!

He looked thoughtful, nodding his head several times as he read the article. A bishop, in turn, had denounced the reporter as a sensation-monger who was trying to make as much mileage out of the story for his own financial gain. Although the Church could not yet acknowledge the St Joseph's cures as miraculous, they could most certainly issue a firm rebuttal to the idea that they were the work of some ludicrous 'fairy-tale witch'.

He smiled.

Furthermore, the little saint had asked that a special service should be held for the murdered monsignor and the parish priest who had died earlier. She had told the Church authorities that the Lady of the Vision had asked for a candlelight procession through the village in memory of the good priest, and that a Revelation was to follow. The Church was to comply with her wishes, for it was felt that, while they did not expect to receive any such Revelation, the priests, one of whom had been a courageous victim of those who denied Christ's work here on earth, merited such a tribute.

He was not smiling now.

He lay back on the bed, his head and shoulders resting against the wall behind, his teeth chewing at a thumb-nail that had already been bitten to the quick. Three faces, cut from old newspapers and sellotaped to the wardrobe door, stared back at him. Pasted across the dot-printed photographs was the name of each man. Soon he would take the images down and put them back among the other newspaper articles he had kept in a scrapbook dedicated to them.

But for now he silently mouthed the three names, his faraway smile returning:

CHAPMAN
AGCA
HINCKLEY

THIRTY-SIX

The Hag is astride
This night for to ride;
The Devil and she together:
Through thick, and through thin,
Now out, and then in,
Though ne'er so foul be the weather.

The storm will arise,
And trouble the skies;
This night, and more for the wonder,
The ghost from the Tomb
Affrighted shall come,
Called out by the clap of the Thunder.

THE HAG
Robert Herrick

It was madness. Sheer bloody madness.

Fenn brought the Mini to a halt and wound down the window. 'What's the hold-up?' he called out, gesturing towards the snarled traffic ahead.

The policeman, who was trying to bring some order to the chaos, strolled over, the slow walk a disguise for his agitation.

'You won't get through the village,' he said brusquely. 'Not for some time, at any rate.'

'What's the problem?'

'The High Street's chock-a-block. The procession starts from there.'

'It's only seven; I thought it didn't start 'til eight.'

'They've been arriving since six o'clock this morning and pouring in all day. God knows how many there are in the village by now, but it's a good few thousand, that's for sure.'

'Look, I'm from the *Courier*. I need to get through to the church.'

'Yeah, well we all have our problems, don't we?' The policeman scowled at the cars that had stopped behind Fenn's, several further back tooting their horns. His arm lifted towards them like a conductor's baton bidding silence. 'You could try the back roads. Go around through Flackstone; it'll get you nearer at least.'

Fenn immediately put the car in reverse and backed as far as he could go towards the vehicle behind. When he felt the gentle touch of bumpers he pushed into first and eased the wheel around. It took four backward/forward shuttles, even though he used the grass verges on either side of the road, but eventually he was pointed away from Banfield and heading into the dazzling lights of oncoming traffic.

He should have realized it would be this bad; the media had been full of the story over the last few days. Why hadn't the bloody fool of a bishop listened to him? Fenn banged the steering wheel with the flat of his hand, his anger boiling over.

He soon reached the sign pointing towards Flackstone and swung into the unlit country lane. It was a winding road, few houses on either side until he reached the hamlet itself; even here there were just one or two country cottages and flintstone houses set on a blind bend. To his left, he could see a strange glow in the sky and he knew it was from Banfield, the village lit up as it had never been before. He swore under his breath. And then aloud.

Fenn reached another main road shortly after and groaned when he saw the amount of traffic all headed in the same direction. He made a quick decision and pulled over onto the grass verge. He locked the car and started walking, knowing that the traffic moving slowly past him would soon be brought to a halt. It was at least a mile to the church, but walking was the only way to get there before everything, even pedestrians, came to a standstill.

Madness, he kept repeating to himself as a rhythm to his walking. They've all gone bloody crazy.

A strong white light shone high into the night, a beam that was separate from the diffused glowing of the village. It was the main searchlight of the shrine itself and it seemed to him like a siren beacon luring wayfarers to some devious destruction. The eerie whiteness made him shiver. There were heavy rolling clouds above, their fringes occasionally caught by silver moonlight, briefly accentuating their ragged and turbulent form.

The pilgrims he passed, in their coaches, mini-buses, cars – and even on motorbikes and bicycles – all seemed in good humour despite the long delays in any kind of forward movement. Hymns of praise came from many vehicles, the low intonations of prayer from others. Yet it soon became obvious that there were groups among them whose journey derived from curiosity only, those seeking thrills, the unusual, the inexplicable. And there were others who had made the trip because there was nothing much on telly.

Again, as Fenn drew nearer to St Joseph's, he felt the peculiar vibrancy in the air. It was akin to the atmosphere in London in the summer of '81, on the day of the Royal Wedding, or Pope John Paul's visit the following year. Yet the coming together of this conscious energy had a peculiar potency of its own, a heady surging of impulses that he knew would find its peak in the area around the shrine. He knew now that this was Alice's source of power, just as it had been Elnor's so many years before. He knew this as surely as if dead men had whispered the secret to him. The omnipotent mind-energy that transcended the physical, which allowed disabilities in the physical form to be overcome in those who would allow the scavenging of their own psyche. In those who *truly* believed. And that, he was convinced, was the gift of all faith healers: the ability to direct the psychic energies of others. The words of the wretched sixteenth-century priest had provided the key; the dream-whispers of latter-day priests who, like their early predecessor, no longer lived, had provided the answer. But Bishop Caines had not listened to Fenn. A sensationalist reporter's beleaguered dreams had meant nothing to the clergyman. Proof, Fenn, it was proof that was needed.

Where was the manuscript he spoke of?

Dust on the floor of the priest's house.

Where was the late monsignor's translation?

Dust on the floor of the priest's house.

Where, then, was the proof?

Dust, like the statue of the Virgin Mary inside the church.

Fenn's shoulders were stooped, his eyes pouched through nights of disturbed sleep. He had known when trying to convince the bishop that his intensity was near-demented and his words frantic, too emotive for Caines to regard him seriously; but in truth, he had felt a shade too close to insanity for his *own* liking. He had even less luck with Southworth, the businessman behind the scenes, whose greed had skilfully engineered the commercial aspect of the shrine. And no luck at all with the head of the Catholic Church in England. It was hardly the eminent cardinal's fault, he knew, for Bishop Caines' warning of a lunatic reporter on the loose had preceded his own attempts to reach the Cardinal Archbishop. His alternative was to turn to his own profession and it, too, had shunned him. Even the *Courier*, still miffed that he had turned his back on the newspaper but desperate for his story anyway, had baulked at his revelation. They had compromised with an interview, a piece written by one of his colleagues with the same scepticism he would have allowed himself just a few weeks before had he been the interviewer. It was a come-uppance that was hard to take; and yet he could see the ironic humour of the situation. The cynic was being paid for his past cynicism; the sensationalist was disbelieved because of his past sensationalism.

Fenn could almost smile at himself. Except it hurt when he tried.

A car's horn made him jump and he realized he had wandered into the path of a slow-moving vehicle. He kept to the side of the road, his breathing heavy now, but his pace fasther than the traffic travelling alongside him.

He reached a T-junction and there was the church further down to his left. The main road was jammed with people and vehicles, the hubbub tremendous. There were more stalls than ever by the roadside, selling food, drinks and all kinds of trinkets, as well as the usual religious paraphernalia; the police were obviously having enough trouble coping with the crowds to deal with the flagrant infringement of trading laws.

He pushed his way into the shuffling mob, heading for the side entrance to the church, and it took a good twenty minutes to cover no more than five hundred yards. He reached the gate, now brightly lit, and attempted to push it open.

'One moment,' a voice said from inside.

He recognized the man whose whole life seemed to be devoted to guarding the church entrance. This time he was flanked by two priests and a constable.

'It's okay,' Fenn told him. 'It's me, Gerry Fenn. I think you know me by now.'

The man looked embarrassed. 'Yes I do, sir. But I'm afraid you can't use this entrance.'

'You're kidding.' Fenn showed his Press pass. 'I'm working for the Church on this.'

'Er, that's not what I've been informed. You'll have to use the other entrance.'

Fenn stared at him. 'I get it. *Persona non grata*, right? I must have really pissed off the bishop.'

'There is a special Press entrance now, Mr Fenn. It's just further along.'

'Yeah, I passed it. Looks like I'm no longer among the privileged.'

'I'm just following instructions.'

'Sure, forget it.' Fenn moved off, knowing there was no point in arguing.

He made his way back to the small entrance marked PRESS, which had been cut through the hedge surrounding the field, and was relieved when his pass got him through without further hitch; he wouldn't have been at all surprised if the ban had extended to all entrances, including the public one. He stopped just inside and his tired eyes widened.

Jesus, he thought, the beavers've been busy.

A network of benches all but covered the field like a carefully constructed spider's web, at its centre the spider itself. The twisted oak may have been inanimate but, to Fenn, it now had all the sinister predatory aspects of the creature he had likened it to. The altar-piece below the tree was more ornate than before, although there were no statues, no images of Christ and His Mother that would mean the Catholic Church was fully committed to the popular belief that this was hallowed ground. The religious authorities had been subtle: there were no extravagant displays of crucifixes, save for the solitary cross on the altar itself, but there were many such symbolisms woven in the cloths that covered certain sections on and around the main platform. The centre-piece itself had been broadened to allow for more seating above congregation level, with a deep-red canopy on either side to protect the worshippers from the more inclement weather; a special tiered section had been constructed to the left to contain, he guessed, a choir. Banners were rooted at intervals along the side aisles, their bright reds, greens and golds giving a rich, though dignified, cast to the vast arena. He noted PA systems at strategic points in the field so that no one should miss the words of the service. And the cameras were no longer confined to the outer limits, for platforms had been erected inside the boundary hedges where a congregational view could be taken of the proceedings.

The overall lighting was dim, enhancing the startling vividness of the centre-piece with its bank of floodlights and dramatic single searchlight, which gave the tree and its upper branches a peculiar flatness against the night sky. This central blaze of luminescence dominated the field, a focal point to which every worshipping mind would be drawn.

As he watched, two figures in white cassocks mounted the platform and began to light rows of tall devotional candles that had been placed behind the altar. The question struck him again, as it had repeatedly over the past few days: why had the Church acquiesced to Alice's strange request for a candlelight procession through the village of Banfield? She had told them that the Lady had asked for this to be done in memory of Father Hagan and Monsignor Delgard, and that a divine revelation was soon to come. Bishop Caines had been restrained in his announcement that a procession was to take place, playing his now-familiar public role of reluctant advocate. He had stressed that the ceremony was more in the way of a tribute to two fine priests, one of whom had been assassinated by what would appear to be an anti-religious fanatic's bomb, than compliance with the wishes of a young girl who may or may not have had a vision of the Sacred Virgin. But why had the bishop been so vehement in his attack on Fenn when the reporter had tried to persuade him that there was no goodness in what was happening, only evil? Ambition – for oneself, for one's cause – could be a great blinker to truth, and a formidable dismisser of argument – religions and ideals had succumbed to its influence throughout time – yet he had expected more of this Church representative. He, the unbeliever, wanted more from those who professed to believe. At any time, the disillusionment would have been bitter, but could have been accepted with a cynic's shrug; now it provoked a deeper resentment, a desperate anger whose root cause was fear.

He moved down the aisle as if attracted by the bright light, the soft layer of churned mud beneath his feet sucking weakly at each step.

The field was filling up fast and he vaguely wondered how so many people – those in the vehicles that he had passed, those who were to walk in the procession, and those still milling around the entrance, eager for a ringside seat – were to be accommodated. And where would they all run to?

'Fenn!'

He stopped and looked around.

'Over here.'

Nancy Shelbeck was rising from a bench in a section marked PRESS.

'I didn't expect to see you here,' Fenn said as she approached.

'I wouldn't have missed it.' There was an excitement in her eyes, although trepidation was just behind it.

'After what happened to you? Didn't it scare you off?'

'Sure, I got spooked. I still have to make a living though. Can you imagine what my chief would say if I flew back without a report on the main event?'

'The main event?'

'Can't you feel it? The tension? The air's thick with it. It's like everybody knows something big's gonna happen.'

Fenn's voice was low. 'Yeah, I can feel it.' He suddenly clasped her arm. 'Nancy, what did you see in the church the other day?'

They were jostled as people pushed by, eager for seats near the front.

'Didn't Sue tell you?'

'I haven't seen her since I took you to her flat. I've been pretty busy the last few days.'

'She tried to reach you – we both did. No reply to our phone calls, no one there when we went to your place. Just what have you been up to?'

'I've been trying to get this show called off. Now answer my question.'

She told him and was surprised he wasn't shocked. 'Is that what you saw, too, in St Peter's?' Nancy asked when she had finished.

'I guess so. To tell the truth, I didn't take too close a look. But it all fits.'

'Fits into what?'

'It's too complicated to explain now.' He looked around and was surprised to see just how full the field had become in the few moments he had been speaking to the American. 'Is Sue here?' he asked her.

'I saw her just a little while ago. She had her kid with her. They're somewhere near the front, I think.' She pulled his face around towards her. 'Hey, are you okay? You look kinda rough.'

He managed to smile. 'A couple of restless nights, a few bad dreams. I've got to find Sue and Ben.'

She held onto him. 'I had a long chat with Sue, Gerry; she knows about us.'

'It's not important.'

'Thanks.'

'I didn't mean it –'

'That's okay, I know what you mean. She wants you, schmucko, you know that? I think she's reached some kinda decision about you.'

'It's taken a long time.'

'It would have taken me longer. And then I think I'd have dumped you.'

'You trying to make me feel good again?'

'I figure it'd have been hard to live with you; we'd be a bad combination.'

He shrugged. 'I'm relieved I didn't ask you to.'

'I'm not saying I couldn't change my mind, you understand?'

He held her and kissed her cheek. 'Take care of yourself, Nancy.'

'I always do.' She returned his kiss, but on the lips.

Fenn broke away and she watched him disappear into the crowd. The tension showed in her face once again. She was frightened, badly frightened, and only her professionalism had brought her back here. She knew that she would never have returned to the other church, St Peter's, not for a million bucks or her own network chat-show. For those around her, the atmosphere must have been vastly different; their faces revealed only shining expectancy, a willingness to believe that the Holy Virgin had blessed this field with her presence and that, if they wished it enough, she would appear again. Or, at least, the child would perform more miracles.

Nancy stood aside to let an old woman, assisted by a younger one, both bearing a vague resemblance to each other – mother and daughter perhaps – shuffle by. The reporter turned away, desperate for a cigarette but not sure it was proper in such a place, and made her way back to the Press section. To hell with it: Alice had given these people a new hope in a sick world where optimism was considered banal, trust in a higher goodness misguided. While it was true that the shrine had proved a rewarding commercial venture for opportunists, it had also succoured the faith of thousands – maybe even millions throughout the world. But the nagging doubt persisted: should the word have been *suckered*? Nancy sat in the reporters' bench and pulled her coat tight around her; the desire for a smoke took second place to her yearning for a stiff bourbon on the rocks.

Paula helped her mother down the aisle, hoping to get her as close to the altar-piece as possible. She had been told at the gate that spaces had been provided beneath the central platform only for the very sick, those brought on stretchers and in wheelchairs; those who could walk, whether assisted or not, had to take their place among the other members of the congregation. An arthritic hip and hypertension were not considered severe enough ailments, even as a combination, so her mother could be given no special treatment. Having seen the number of walking wounded that had turned up, Paula was hardly surprised. God, it made a person feel ill just to look at them all.

'Not far to go, Mother,' she coaxed her burden. 'We're quite near the front row now.'

'What's all the bright lights?' came the querulous response. 'Hurts my eyes.'

'It's just the altar. They've lit it all up with floodlights and candles. It looks lovely.'

Her mother tutted. 'Can't we sit down now? I'm tired, dear.'

'Nearly there.'

'I want to see the girl.'

'She'll be here soon.'

'I've suffered enough.'

'Yes, Mother. But don't expect too much.'

'Why not? She's cured all them others; what's she got against me?'

'She doesn't even know you.'

'Did she know them others?'

Paula groaned inwardly. 'This'll do, Mother. We can sit on the end of this bench if this gentleman will kindly move up a bit.'

The gentleman seemed reluctant, but the squinty stare of Paula's mother encouraged him to do so.

The old lady groaned aloud as she sat, assuring those in close proximity of her disability. 'This cold weather isn't going to do my hip any good, is it? When's it all start, when's it all over?'

Paula was about to give an impatient reply when a familiar face caught her attention. Tucker was standing by a bench just a dozen or so rows ahead and he was calling to someone. Paula's eyes narrowed when she saw a plump hand tugging at his elbow, obviously urging him to sit down. She half-lifted herself from the seat to peer over the heads of those in front, and her eyes frosted when she recognized the bulky fur-coated shape next to Tucker. So the fat slug had brought the fat she-slug along with him. Dear, pampered Marcia. Trust her not to want to miss anything! Well maybe tonight she'd learn something new about the pig she was married to. A little confrontation between them, mistress and wife, might offer some compensation for the scare she, Paula, had suffered under Tucker's podgy hands! She hadn't been into the supermarket since – hadn't even sent in a sick note – and her boss was too much of a coward to ring and find out how she was. Well tonight, in front of Miss Piggy's ugly sister, she would tell him exactly how she was! Let's see how he coped with that.

Paula's mother was muttering something about the dampness from the ground creeping into her boots and the man beside her hadn't moved up far enough and she was being squashed and wasn't that Mrs Fenteman in front who never went to church except at Christmas and Easter and wasn't she carrying on with the man in the hardware shop?

Paula did not even look at her mother. She said slowly and evenly: 'Just . . . shut . . . up.'

Tucker ignored his wife's tugging and pushed his way past knees to reach the side. 'What are you doing here, Fenn?' he said loudly when he reached open space.

Fenn turned back and recognized the fat man. 'My job,' he said, ready to walk on.

'You're not working for the Church any more, I hear.'

'No, but I'm still working for the *Courier*.'

'You sure of that?' The question was accompanied by a sneering smile.

'Nobody's told me otherwise.'

'Well you're not very welcome here with all the lies you've been spreading.'

Fenn moved nearer to him. 'What're you talking about?'

'You know very well. George Southworth gave me a personal account.'

'Yeah, Southworth and the bishop must have had a good laugh between them.'

'We all did, Fenn. Pretty lunatic, wasn't it? Witchcraft, nuns coming back from the dead. Did you expect anyone to believe it?'

Fenn waved his hand towards the altar. 'Do you believe all this?'

'It makes more sense that what you've been saying lately.'

'Financial sense, don't you mean?'

'So some of us are making a nice profit. It's good for the village and good for the Church.'

'But particularly good for you and Southworth.'

'Not just us. There are plenty of others who're reaping the benefit.' Tucker's sneer became more pronounced. 'You haven't done so badly yourself, have you?'

The reporter could think of no adequate reply. He turned away, forcing himself to ignore the chuckle of derision from behind.

He drew nearer to the centre-piece, the bright lights causing his eyes to narrow. A broad section before the platform had been kept clear and stewards were directing stretcher bearers and those pushing wheelchairs into it. He stopped beneath a squat, scaffold tower where a cameraman was aiming his television camera into the invalid section. Fenn was jostled from behind and he reached out towards the metal scaffolding to keep his balance. He quickly withdrew his hand as a tiny static shock tingled his fingers. He frowned and, as an experiment, touched the metal frame of a passing wheelchair. Again, a tiny shock crackled at his fingers. He knew that every possible safety precaution would have been taken with all the electronic machinery in the field, particularly bearing in mind the damp soil that the insulated cables would be buried beneath. He looked up into the night sky, at the dark, thunderous clouds, now so low and menacing. A storm was in the air, its charge already in the atmosphere. Sudden feedback from several of the amplifiers spread around the field made the gathering congregation gasp and good-humouredly rub their ears, laughing and smiling at their neighbours.

Fenn could see no humour in it at all; in fact, the peculiarities in atmospherics inceased his dread. He looked ahead at the tree, the twisting of its gnarled limbs accentuated in the glaring light, and remembered the first time, just a few weeks before (it seemed a lifetime), when patchy moonlight had exposed its grotesqueness, hovering over the kneeling child like a monstrous angel of death. The sight of the oak had frightened him then and it frightened him even more at this moment.

He eased his way through the long line of invalids until his path was blocked by a man wearing a steward's armband.

'Can't go through this section, sir,' he was told. 'Invalids only.'

'Who are those benches for?' Fenn asked, pointing at the rows behind the open space.

'They're reserved for special people. Can you move back please; you're blocking the way.'

Fenn spotted Sue sitting on the end of one of the privileged benches, the small figure of Ben next to her. He produced his Press card. 'I just need to speak to someone in there – can I go through?'

'I'm afraid not. You reporters have got your own section back there.'

'Just two minutes, that's all I need.'

'You'll have me shot.'

'Two minutes. I promise I'll come back then.'

The steward grunted. 'Make it quick, mate. I'll be watching you.'

Fenn was through before the man could change his mind.

'Sue!'

She spun round and he saw relief flush across her face. 'Where've you been, Gerry? My God, I've been so worried.'

She reached out for him and Fenn quickly kissed her cheek.

'Hi, Uncle Gerry,' Ben greeted him cheerfully.

'Hi, kiddo. Good to see you.' He tweaked the boy's nose as he squatted down by Sue. The rest of the bench was occupied by nuns from the convent and they looked down at him disapprovingly. He drew Sue close and kept his voice low.

'I want you to leave,' he said. 'Take Ben and get out.'

Sue shook her head, consternation in her eyes. 'But why? What's wrong, Gerry?'

'I don't know, Sue. I can only tell you something bad is going to happen.

Something nasty. I just don't want you two around when it does.'

'You've got to tell me more than that.'

His grip tightened on her arm. 'All these things, Sue, these strange events, there's something evil behind them. Father Hagan's death, the fire in the village, these miracles. Alice isn't what she seems. She caused Monsignor Delgard's death . . .'

'There was an explosion . . .'

'She caused that explosion.'

'She's a child. She couldn't possibly –'

'Alice is more than just a child. Delgard knew; that's why he had to die.'

'It's impossible, Gerry.'

'For God's sake, all this is impossible!'

The nuns began to whisper among themselves, gesturing towards him. Several began to look around for a steward. He glanced at them and tried to keep his voice calm.

'Sue, please trust me.'

'Why didn't you come to me? Why didn't you ring?'

He shook his head. 'I just didn't have time. I've been too busy trying to stop this thing.'

'And I've been bloody frantic! I've been so worried . . .'

'Yeah, I know, I know.' His hand brushed her cheek.

'Nancy told me what had happened at Barham. That wasn't true, was it, Gerry? It couldn't have been.'

'It was true. She saw something there – we both did. It's all connected with the past; this whole business is the result of something that happened centuries ago.'

'How can I believe you? It just doesn't make any sense. You say something evil is happening, but look around you. Can't you see how good these people are, how much they believe in Alice? All the good she's done?'

He held both of her hands in his. 'We found an old Latin manuscript in the church on the Stapley Estate. Delgard translated it and found the answer. That's why he was killed, don't you see?'

'I don't see anything. Nothing you say makes sense.'

'Then just trust me, Sue.'

She raised her eyes slowly and looked deeply into his. 'Is there any reason why I should? Are you really that trustworthy?'

He knew what she was referring to and became silent. Then he said, 'If you love me, Sue, if you really love me, you'll do as I ask.'

She jerked her head away angrily. 'Why now? Why have you left it so late?'

'I told you: for the last couple of days I've been running around like a lunatic trying to get this whole thing stopped. I didn't get home till early this morning, and then I just slept and slept. And the dreams were clearer than ever.'

'What dreams?' she asked wearily, wanting to believe in him again, wanting to forget his opportunism, his unreliability, his infidelity, but telling herself she would be a fool to.

'The priests, Hagan and Delgard, spoke to me. I saw them in my sleep. They warned me about this place.'

'Oh, Gerry, can't you see you're deluding yourself? You've become so wrapped up in this thing that you don't know what you're doing, what you're saying.'

'Okay, so I'm going nuts. Humour me.'

'I can't leave . . .'

'Just this once, Sue. Just do as I ask.'

She studied him for long seconds, then grabbed Ben's hand. 'Come on, Ben, we're going home.'

Her son looked up at her in surprise and Fenn's head slumped with relief. He kissed her hands and when he lifted his head again his eyes were sparkling with unshed tears.

Fenn stood and pulled her up with him. It was at that very moment that a hush fell over the crowd. The voices became whispers, the whispers fading, the settling of a breeze. Everybody was listening intently.

Voices could be heard in the distance. Voices singing in praise of God and the Virgin Mary. The strangely haunting sound grew in strength as the procession from the village approached.

Fenn looked back at the oak and he closed his eyes as though in anguish. His lips moved in silent prayer.

THIRTY-SEVEN

But the old woman was only pretending to be friendly. She was really an evil witch.

HANSEL AND GRETEL
The Brothers Grimm

'Okay Camera 1, let's get a nice close-up. Slow zoom in on Alice. That's good. Keep it slow. We'll cut to 2 in a moment for the overall shot. Keep the CU coming, 2. Good, it's a good one of the girl – what's happening, 1? Picture's breaking up. Oh for Christ's sake, cut to 2. That's better, keep on that. What's happening, Camera 1? Where's the interference coming from? Okay, sort it out. Stay on 2. We'll cue Richard in five. Camera 3, that's good on Richard. Slow pull-back to show congregation in field as soon as he starts speaking. I want a good shot of the altar and that bloody tree in the background. Okay, Richard – 4 – 3 – 2 – Camera 3.'

'As the procession approaches the field, now called by many "The Field of the Holy Virgin", the lights around are dimmed. Soon, the procession will enter this, what has become, open-air temple, led by the Bishop of Arundel, the Right Reverend Bishop Caines, followed by priests, nuns and of course, little Alice Pagett herself. It seems that thousands have joined this holy march, many from the village of Banfield, while others have journeyed from far and wide to be here today. Not all have held deeply religious beliefs before; indeed, when I spoke to many of them earlier in the day, they told me (static) in this small Sussex vill – Banfield that has made – realise a deeper truth –'

'What's happening with sound out there. John, we're losing Richard's voice. Keep talking, Richard, we're having problems, but still receiving.'

'Perhaps then, this vast gathering this evening is a symbolic gesture of people's faith in a world – turmoil (static) – (static) prevails –'

'Oh God, we're losing picture now!'

'. . . in memory (static) priest who was cruelly struck down – Thursday by (static) explosion – the perpetrators of such – (static) – knows, but –'

'Jesus bloody Christ! Everything's gone!'

Fenn turned with the rest of the congregation as the leaders of the procession entered the field. Flashlights were popping from all points, casting strobe effects on the chanting leaders. Even from that distance he recognized Bishop Caines, who was flanked by robed priests on either side. The first candles were thick and high, held by young altar-servers, their small flames flickering with the breeze. The singing grew louder and the people already in the field joined in. Voices broke off as Alice entered and the worshippers and the curious alike rose to catch a glimpse of her. Fenn stood with them trying to peer over their heads. It was no use: all he could see were the raised candles and banners carried by the marchers. Sue stood by his side and Ben clambered onto the bench for a better view.

The emotions of the crowd seemed to swell like an ocean tide as the singing grew louder and the four lines of marchers drew deeper into the field, the bobbing candles a dazzling display of warm light. Fenn scanned the faces around him: even in the darkness he could see their eyes shining, their lips smiling in some deep-felt rapture. The same expression was on Sue's face. He touched her hand and flinched as another tiny spark snapped at him. Staring at his fingers, he thought: *The whole bloody field's alive.* He shook her gently, this time touching only the cloth of her coat.

'Sue,' he said quietly. 'We've got to leave *now*.'

She looked at him blankly, then turned away.

Ben stifled a yawn.

Fenn tugged at her arm once more.

'No, Gerry,' she said without turning, 'it's too wonderful.'

The head of the procession had reached the centre-piece and Bishop Caines was mounting the steps, smiling down at the invalids spread out on blankets and in wheelchairs below. Alice Pagett followed him, her mother close behind, hands clasped tight together, head bowed in prayer.

Voices all around rose in a crescendo of sound, the hymn soaring into the sky as if to push back the low, brooding clouds. Fenn thought he heard the rumble of distant thunder, but couldn't be certain. Bishop Caines took his seat by the side of the altar and beckoned Alice and her mother to sit next to him as priests and servers filed onto the platform. The benches in front of Fenn began to fill and many of the faces were familiar to him. Some were those cured by Alice in previous weeks, while others were local dignitaries and clergymen. He watched as Southworth took his place and saw the hotelier cast a long sweeping look around the congregation; his smile seemed to be one of satisfaction rather than blissful worship.

A movement on Fenn's bench caught his attention: one of the nuns had fainted and her companions were gently lifting her onto her seat. He felt Sue beside him sway and he held her steady. Others here and there in the congregation were silently collapsing, their neighbours catching them before they could harm themselves.

Fenn drew in a breath. Hysteria was in the air like a rampant germ hopping from person to person.

The hymn singing reached its height, the voices ecstatically unified in the repetitive refrain. He felt strange: there was a lightness in his head, an unsettling in his stomach. This time it was he who felt dizzy and he clutched at Sue. She almost fell, but instead they both sank to the bench.

Ben knelt on the seat and put his arms around his mother's shoulders, one outstretched hand brushing Fenn's cheek. Immediately, the dizziness left the reporter; it was as though the uncomfortable weakness had been discharged into the boy. Yet there were no visible signs of distress in Ben.

The hymn came to its end and the sudden quiet was almost stunning in its effect. The silence was soon broken as the congregation sat, but it returned once they had settled. There were no coughs, no whispers, no shuffling of bodies. Just a hushed, reverential quiet.

The young priest who was to take the service stepped forward to the lectern with its array of microphones. He raised his arms towards the congregation, then made the Sign of the Cross in the air.

'Peace be with you,' he said and the vast crowd responded as one. The priest spoke for a few moments of Father Hagan and Monsignor Delgard, dedicating the special Mass to the two late priests, paying homage to the exemplary work they had carried out in the name of the Holy Catholic Church. He was forced to stop several times when the microphones whined and hummed, and seemed relieved when the preliminaries had been completed. He nodded towards the choir, which had taken its position in the specially erected tiers, and a fresh hymn began.

Candles all around the field were lit, creating a myriad star cluster around an effulgence that resembled the sun.

In the village of Banfield, less than a mile away from the church of St Joseph's, an old man stumbled along the kerbside. It had been a long walk for him, ten miles or more, but he was determined to reach the shrine before the service was over. Although walking had been his sole occupation for the past fifteen years – tramping the quieter roads of Southern England, surviving on the kindness of others, embittered by the non-caring of yet others – his feet were sore and blistered, his breathing laboured. Brighton was his base, for there were enough churches and charitable organizations in the seaside town to keep his belly fed and his body warm on the coldest of nights. Never too well fed, never too warm; enough to keep him alive, though. What had brought him to this level of existence was not important – not to him, anyway. At that moment, he was what he was; dwelling on the past would not make him or his circumstances different. On the other hand, dwelling on the future might do so.

The belief that he was not completely irredeemable had come to him only that morning when the word had spread along the reprobate grapevine, the efficient word-of-mouth communications system of his kind that never failed to report 'easy pickings'. He had been told of the little miracle girl, of the service that night where thousands were expected to turn up, people of good will who would not reject the entreaties of those less fortunate than themselves. But curiously, it was the miracles of this child that the old man was interested in, not the chance to beg from others.

He had knocked on the door of a priest, a man of God who knew him, who had always shown kindness without reprimand towards him. The priest had told him it was true, that there was a young girl in Banfield who had performed certain acts that could be described as miracles, and that tonight there was to be a candlelight procession through the village. The old man had resolved that he would be there, that he would see this child for himself. He knew, as any man who was dying instinctively knew, that his death was not far away; yet he did not want the miracle of further life. He craved salvation. One last chance to witness something that was beyond this mortal and despicable world. A chance to believe once again, a positive sign that atonement would not be in vain.

Like thousands of others who flocked to the shrine, he sought the means of his own redemption, a physical symbol of the immaterial. A living saint who disproved omnipotent evil.

But would he get there in time to see her?

He leaned against a shop window, a hand resting against the cold glass. The High Street of the village was dimly lit, but there was a beacon in the distance, a bright light that pierced the sky, striking out from a suffused glow around its base. He knew that this was his first glimpse of the shrine, a brightness in the night that called him to observe the greater goodness.

And as he leaned there against the window, gathering his strength, a new gleam in his rheumy old eyes, something touched his soul and passed on. Something cold. Something that produced a shudder in his brittle bones. Something that made him sink to his knees, leaving him bowed. Something whose destination was his own. Had been his own.

His head sank to the pavement and he wept. It was some time before he crept into a dark doorway and curled up into a foetal position. He closed his eyes and waited.

The tall, bearded barman of the White Hart blinked glumly at his only customer. He sighed as he leaned on the bar. A bloody pint of mild and a packet of pork scratchings would last the old trouper all night. Two barmaids stood idly chatting at the far end of the bar, enjoying the quietness of the usually busy Sunday evening.

Still, the barman thought, the service can't go on all night. They'll be piling in here in an hour or so, desperate for a drink, and he certainly couldn't complain about the recent trade: his turnover had not just doubled – it had trebled! If he had had a bigger pub it would have quadrupled! The brewery could hardly refuse to put up the money for an extension at the back now. What a great little miracle worker that kid was.

He wiped the bar for the eleventh time with a damp cloth, then poured himself a bitter lemon. Cheers, he saluted the absent crowds. Don't stay away too long.

Lifting the bar-flap, he crossed the floor and retrieved two glasses left by earlier customers.

'Judy,' he called to one of the barmaids, placing the glasses on the counter. Let the lazy cow do something for her money, he thought. He turned and, hands in pockets, strolled to the door. Standing in the opening, one foot jammed against the door, he surveyed the High Street. Empty. Not a blessed soul where, less than an hour before, it had been packed with marchers. Banfield was like a ghost town, nearly all its residents gone to the shrine. The village was empty without them, all right, he thought, then chuckled at his own irrefutable logic.

The chuckle ceased and the smile froze as something cold passed by him. It was like standing in a chilly draught, except that it seemed to cling to his body, searching out hidden crevices, covering every part of him like cold water before being sucked away, journeying onwards to who-knew-what destination. The lights in the pub behind him seemed to flicker momentarily, then gain their normal brightness.

He looked down the road towards the church and saw the sudden breeze as a shadow creeping towards the light.

The tall man shivered and quickly went back inside. He resisted the urge to lock the door behind him.

To the north of St Joseph's, little more than a mile away, a motorist kicked at the deflated rear tyre of his Allegro. Nearly there and this had to happen, he complained bitterly to himself.

'Is it flat?' a woman's voice asked from the passenger window.

'Aye, it's a bloody flat. All the way from Manchester and we get a blow-out now. The place must be just down t'road.'

'Well you'd better just get crackin then. Our Annie's fallin asleep already.'

'Better that she is. It's been a long journey for her. I just hope it's worthwhile.'

'Our John travelled to Lourdes with cancer.'

'Yes, an a lot of bloody good it did im,' the woman's husband muttered quietly.

'What did you say, Larry?'

'I said he didn't last long afterwards, did he?'

'That's not the point; he made the effort.'

Aye, an it finished im off a lot bloody sooner, the man thought. 'Bring the flashlight out, will yuh?' he said aloud.

His wife rummaged around the glove compartment and found the torch.

'What's wrong, Mummy,' a voice came from the back seat.

'You just hush now, pet, and go back to sleep. We've got a puncture and your father's going t'fix it.'

'I'm thirsty.'

'I know. We'll be there soon, never fear.'

'Will I see Alice?'

'Course you will, pet. An she'll see you and make you better.'

'An I won't need sticks no more?'

'That's right, pet. You'll be runnin like t'others.'

Their daughter smiled and snuggled back down beneath the blanket. She pulled Tina Marie's plastic cheek close to her own and she was smiling as her eyes closed.

The wife left the car, guiding the flashlight towards her husband as he opened the boot and reached inside for the jack.

The errant wheel was off the ground when the light beam began to fade. 'Hold bloody light steady,' he told her.

'It's not me,' she replied testily. 'Batteries must be going.'

'Eh? They're fresh uns in.'

'Bulb, then.'

'Aye, appen. Get a bit closer, will yuh?'

She bent towards him and he searched for a spanner in the car's tool kit. Suddenly she dropped the torch.

'Aw, flamin eck!' he groaned.

Her hand clasped his shoulder. 'Larry, did you feel that? Larry? Larry!' She could feel him trembling.

At last, he said, 'Aye, I felt it. It must have been the wind.'

'No, it wasn't the wind, Larry. It went straight through me. Right through me bones.'

His reply was slow in coming. 'It's gone,' he said, looking towards the glow in the sky just about a mile away.

'What was it?'

'I don't know, lass. But it felt like someone walking over me grave.'

From the car came the whimpers of their daughter.

In the Riordon farmhouse, on the land adjoining the field in which the night-time service was taking place, a dog yelped and ran helplessly around the kitchen. At the end of each circuit, Biddy would hurl herself at the door, desperate to get out into the open. Her owners had left her to guard the place – 'too many strange people wandering around the area because of that blessed shrine' – while they, themselves, took part in the Mass – 'better than going to the pictures' – and now the dog sensed the agitation from the cows in their stalls. Sensed and heard, for they were frantically kicking in an effort to break free, and their piteous bellowing was driving the dog into a frenzied fit.

Biddy scratched at the door, raking the paintwork with her claws, howling with the outside ululations, matching their pitch. Around the kitchen the dog ran, back to the door, jump, scratch, push, bark, yelp, howl, around the kitchen once more. Round and around, and round and –

The commotion had stopped. Had stopped more suddenly then it had started.

The dog stood in the centre of the darkened room, one ear cocked, head to one side. She listened. There were no more sounds. She sniffed the air. There were no strangers outside.

She began to whine.

Something was moving through the farmyard, quietly, stealthily, something that had no smell, that made no sound, that had no shape. The dog's tail dropped and her legs bent, her back bowed. Biddy whimpered. She whined. She shook. The dog crawled beneath the kitchen table.

And one eye watched the kitchen door, fearful of what was out there.

It crept through the night, unseen, intangible, a thing of no substance, which existed, but only in the deep corridors of the mind. Now it was drawn inwards, focusing towards a centre induced by a kindred power, slithering through the darkness like an eager reptile towards a helpless insect, guided by someone, something, that had transcended the natural.

It was sucked into the vortex to be absorbed and used.

But evil belongs to the individual and, as any one marching soldier can upset a platoon's rhythm, so individual evil can disrupt the purpose of the whole.

WILKES

'I did it,' he said, reflecting. 'When ladies used to come to me in dreams, I said, "Pretty mother, pretty mother". But when at last she really came, I shot her.'

PETER PAN

J. M. Barrie

The third hymn was drawing to its close and he tucked his hands between his thighs so that those around him would not see how much they trembled. His head was bowed, lank, yellow hair falling across his forehead, curling inwards and almost touching the tip of his nose. He stared into his lap and there was a shiny brightness to his eyes that was not akin to the brightness in the eyes of other worshippers. His vision was not focused on his own body; it was focused on the future. Pictures of his own destiny flashed before him: he saw his name written in large, black headlines, his face, smiling, flashed on screens all over the world, his life, his motive, discussed, dissected and wondered at by knowledgeable persons, by eminent persons, by . . . *everybody*!

He could hardly contain the shuddering expansion of his inner self, the blinding whiteness that pushed outwards against his chest. The sensation left him so weak he could hardly breathe.

He had travelled down the night before, sleeping rough inside a bus shelter near the village, feeling certain he would freeze to death with the cold, only the thought of what was to come sustaining him, giving him comfort. He had hardly slept, his brief dozes fitful and full of bad images.

He had been dismayed at the size of the gathering outside the church of St Joseph's next morning, thinking he would be first there, wanting to find a prime position on the benches inside the field. To his further dismay, no one was allowed into the shrine that early; work was still in progress to accommodate the expected crowds, and entrance would not be permitted until early evening. So he had queued with the rest of them, joking with his fellow pilgrims, playing the good guy, pretending interest in boring stories of their little lives, feigning devotion to the Church and all its works, secretly laughing at these insignificant fools who had no idea who they were standing next to.

At last they were granted entry and he faced what he imagined might be the severest test. But, although bags and containers of any kind were glanced into for security purposes, no body searches were made; so the object tucked into his underpants and taped against his groin, and which caused a semi-erection whenever he was conscious of its weight (which was most of the time), was not found nor even suspected. Even if they had asked him to unbutton his old grey overcoat, the shirt he wore outside his trousers would have covered any unnatural (or unseemly) bulge around his fly area.

Although it was hours before the benches were filled and the procession started, he was not bored with the wait; too many visions screamed into his mind for that.

Like everybody else, he craned his neck to see the girl when she arrived with the procession and, because he had chosen a seat right on the centre aisle, as near to the altar as possible, Alice passed within feet of him. The urge to do it there and then – no one could have stopped him – was almost overwhelming, but he knew it would be better, more spectacular, to wait. He wanted them all to see.

And now the third hymn was almost over. He had watched her at the beginning of the service, had soon found he could not study her small, enraptured face for too long; her goodness, her divinity, seemed to spread outwards and it made him uncomfortable. The words of the Mass were just a mumble in the back of his chaotic thoughts and, although he stood when the congregation stood, knelt when they knelt, sat when they sat, he did it in automated fashion, a robot response to the activity around him. And all the while he kept his head bowed.

The singing suddenly began to fade, taking a short while to die completely, for not everyone saw Alice rise to her feet and walk to the centre of the platform at the same time.

He looked up, puzzled by the interruption to the background wall of noise, and he saw the little girl in the middle of the stage, her face pointed upwards, her glazed eyes looking at something no one else could see. Behind her was the altar and, behind that, the brilliantly illuminated and grotesquely twisted oak tree.

The field was quiet, all eyes on the small figure in white, breaths held in excited anticipation. There was fear also in their expectancy, for the unknown always generates such emotion.

Alice lowered her head and looked down at the crowd, scanning the multitude of adoring, fearing faces. She smiled and to most it was enigmatic.

In the distance, thunder rumbled.

She spread her arms outwards and began to rise into the air.

He left the bench and nobody saw him unbutton his coat, lift his shirt and reach into his trousers, for everyone was transfixed by the small figure in white rising above them.

He strode down the aisle to the altar, the German Luger, the *Pistole '38*, a relic of the last big war when half the world had gone mad with bloodlust, held down by his side, barrel pointed towards the churned earth.

When he was directly below the platform and just a few feet away from the girl in white who hovered at least eighteen inches in the air, and before anyone could realize what he was about to do, Wilkes raised the gun and fired point-blank into Alice's young body.

He kept firing until the fifth of the Luger's eight bullets jammed between chamber and magazine.

THIRTY-EIGHT

And it was only a moment before she opened her eyes, raised up the lid of the coffin, and sat up alive again.

LITTLE SNOW-WHITE
The Brothers Grimm

It was a scene from a nightmare, a sluggishly unfolding drama of horror.

Fenn saw but could not understand.

Alice had walked to the centre of the platform and the hymn had faltered, then died on the people's lips. Her face had been beatific – even *he*, knowing what he did – had been enchanted. She had looked skywards and then slowly down, scanning the crowd; and that was when he had shuddered. She had smiled. And it seemed that her eyes had found his. He saw her smile as a rictus grin, wide, malevolent and somehow, greedy. It mocked him personally and sneered at the crowd generally.

Yet it was just a child's sweet smile.

The crowd was mesmerized and, to him, it was the fascination of a fear-paralysed rabbit staring into the deadly eyes of a snake.

Yet it was just a child standing there.

He felt weak once more, his vitality drawn from him and those around him, drawn into this malignant thing standing in a blaze of light.

Yet she was just a child too young to know evil.

The lights had flickered, dimmed, and then Alice was moving upwards, rising above them in a slow but steady ascent, her arms stretched outwards as though beseeching their love. Their trust.

The crowd moaned as if in rapture, and there were gasps and cries from different parts of the field. Fenn felt his throat constricting and dizziness invaded him once more. It was difficult to breathe, difficult to keep on his feet.

He was only vaguely conscious of the thin, blond person striding down the aisle towards the altar and did not understand when that person raised his arm and pointed something at the small figure floating above him.

He did not even hear the gunfire – at least, the four sharp reports did not register in his brain; but he saw the blood spurt from four points in Alice's chest, gushing out in separate fountains to fall back onto the whiteness of her dress, a crimson dye scattered on a field of snow.

There was shock, disbelief, and finally pain in her small face, before she fell to the platform to lie in a crumpled heap. The blood spread outwards, finding the edge of the platform, flowing over in two sickeningly plentiful streams.

There was no sound among the crowd. The pilgrims, the sightseers, the believers, the unbelievers, all stood in total, uncomprehending silence.

Until thunder roared directly overhead, and pandemonium erupted in the field.

Fenn caught Sue as she slumped against him.

The rush of noise was terrifying, a chaotic babble of screams and shouts that soon became a wailing lamentation, the anguish affecting groups, individuals, in different ways: many – men as well as women – were reduced to hysterics, while others merely wept quietly; some just stood in numbed silence, too shocked to do or say anything; the anguish of others quickly turned to rage, shouts of vilification against the assassin passing from person to person, joining in a vehement chant for revenge. There were yet others among them who had not seen the brutal act and who pulled at their neighbours, demanding to be told what had happened.

Ben was frightened and grabbed at his mother's limp body. Fenn put a protective arm around him while still holding Sue upright.

Figures broke from the mass to rush at the blond man who had shot Alice Pagett and who still held the German pistol at his side. He went down under a tumult of bodies and screamed as he was flailed by fists and feet. Sharp fingernails raked his face, a lower eyelid was pulled down and torn, bones in the bridge of his nose were crushed and he felt the crushed fragments pour from his nostrils with the blood. The gun was torn from his grasp and the fingers on that hand were caught awkwardly beneath someone's weight. The snapping sound was lost in the cries of the mob, but the sharpness of the pain could not be lost to his own consciousness.

He shrieked as his limbs were pulled and joints were stretched free of their sockets. His tears ran into his own blood as impossible, suffocating, weight pushed against his chest. Something was giving way there and he could not quite reason what. The bones in his chest slowly caved in, pressing against his heart and lungs, restricting the pumping organ and squeezing life-giving air from the delicate sacs. It slowly dawned on him that perhaps he had made a mistake.

Nearby, a young girl who had come to the shrine to pay homage to the little miracle worker for the gift she had bestowed on her, stared at the still, blood-stained bundle before the altar. The girl's face suddenly twitched. One side of her mouth moved downwards, grotesquely twisting into a gargoyle's grimace. An eyelid flickered once, twice, and then would not stop. Her arm jerked, then shuddered; it began to move spasmodically. Then her leg joined in the unsightly and uncontrolled dance, the girl screamed and collapsed to the ground.

– As did the boy in another part of the field, who had come back to the shrine in adoration of the child called Alice, the living saint who had restored the use of his legs. Their strength was gone and he floundered between the benches, calling out in frustration, afraid to be a cripple once more –

– Elsewhere, a man's vision rapidly began to fade, the blaze of light in the middle of the field becoming a hazy cloud, the cataracts which the child had caused to clear returning with a speed that was unnatural and inexplicable – just as their disappearance had been. He cupped his hands to his face and slowly sat down on a bench, a low moaning sound coming from him –

– While in a different part of the field a young girl found once more that sounds emitted from her throat could not be formed into words and that her distressed mother did not understand her when she asked what was happening –

– And a boy in the crowd whose hands had began to fill with ugly verrucas could only wail and beat his fists against the bench in front –

– A bench where, further along, a man felt his face exploding into open sores, his skin cracking like parched earth. He gasped, not just because the opening wounds hurt, but because he knew he was becoming a freak once more, a man wearing a dog's muzzle of hideous lacerations and dripping ulcers.

From all over the field came such moans and cries of piteous despair, for there were others who fell to the ground, others whose limbs became useless, others whose afflictions suddenly and cruelly returned to dominate their lives. They had thought, had prayed, that their cures were permanent, that Alice Pagett had granted them a new and lasting hope, a divine manifestation of God's caring that would not be erased with time. Now they were betrayed, lost. Defeated.

Fenn no longer felt weakened, and the dizziness had left him. His nerves were taut, tightened, so that his actions were swift, his senses aware. He huddled Sue and Ben close to him, protecting them from the confusion all around. Sue began to revive and her legs took her own weight.

'Gerry?' she said, still dazed.

'It's okay, Sue,' he replied, his head nestling hers. 'I'm here; so's Ben.'

'Is she . . . is she dead?'

He closed his eyes for a second. 'I think so. She must be.'

'Oh, Gerry, how could it happen?' She was sobbing. 'How could someone do that to her?'

Ben clutched at his mother, wanting to comfort her, upset but still not understanding everything that was happening. 'Let's go home, Mummy. I don't like it here any more. Please let's go home.'

Fenn looked over the sea of moving heads towards the altar. 'Christ,' he said, 'nobody's gone to her yet. They're all to shocked.' And he knew that they were all too afraid, even her own mother, to approach the inert body. Afraid, possibly, to discover that Alice really was dead.

'I've got to get up there,' he said.

Sue's grip tightened on him. 'No, Gerry. Let's just get away from here. There's nothing we can do.'

He looked down at her. 'I've got to make sure . . .' He could only shake hs head. 'You wait here with Ben; you'll be okay.'

'Gerry, it's not safe. I can feel it's not safe.'

'Sit here.' He gently lowered her to the bench. 'Ben, keep hold of your mother; don't let go.' He knelt beside them both, oblivious to the chaos around them. 'Stay here and wait for me. Just don't move from this spot.'

She opened her mouth to protest, but he quickly kissed her forehead and then was gone, climbing over benches, pushing his way through the disoriented crowd.

Fenn found himself in the clearing before the platform, the ground littered with beseeching invalids, a battleground after the war had passed. To his right was a mob of shouting, tearing people, and he knew what lay beneath their stomping feet, sure that the man with the gun could no longer be alive. They had always been impotent over past publicity-blazed assassinations and assassination attempts, forced to contain their anger, their spite, against the perpetrators, frustrated in their grief, despising those who mocked and flaunted the very rules of civilization. But now the aggressor was within their reach, one of the Devil's legion lay beneath their feet; for once the people had the power to take revenge.

He kept clear of them, making for the stairs at the side of the platform. A man, visibly distressed and wearing a steward's armband, made a half-hearted attempt to bar his way, but the reporter easily brushed him aside. Fenn was almost at the top of the steps when he stopped.

Most of the altar-servers were weeping; some were on their knees praying, their faces wet with tears, while others could only rock their bodies to and fro, heads buried in their hands. The priest who had been conducting the service, ashen-faced, his lips moving in silent prayer, supported Molly Pagett; she was obviously in a state of extreme shock, for her eyes were wide, her mouth open and her movements stiff. Bishop Caines, in all his finery, had the same unsteady awkwardness, the blood drained from his face.

Fenn shared their grief and wondered if he had been wrong about her. It was impossible to believe that evil could exist in that tiny, prone body, in a child that had brought so much happiness and renewed faith.

He climbed another step and the lights – even the candles – began to dim.

He fell to one knee, a hand dropping to the platform to steady himself. Giddiness struck him once again and he fought against nausea. He was faintly conscious of the lightning flash, followed by rolling thunder.

He shook his head and looked towards the group on the stage. Bishop Caines, the priest, and others around them, were sinking to their knees. Only Molly Pagett stood transfixed, one hand outstretched towards the bloodied bundle that had been her daughter.

The bundle that was beginning to stir, beginning to sit up. The daughter who had been shot four times and who was rising slowly to her feet.

The daughter whose face no longer resembled any earthly child's, who looked around with malevolent intent and smiled. And grinned. And chuckled.

THIRTY-NINE

We spelled our loves until close of day.
I wished her good-night and walked away,
But she put out a tongue that was long and red
And swallowed me down like a crumb of bread.

THE TWO WITCHES
Robert Graves

Fenn slumped against the steps, one elbow supporting his upper body, a hand still on the platform itself. He wanted to run; if not to run, then at least to slither down the steps and crawl away from this monstrosity that stood in the centre of the sanctified stage. But there was little strength in him. He could hardly move. He could only watch.

Her head was turning in his direction and every nerve in his body tensed; it seemed as though a deeply cold shock were running through him, paralysing his muscles, scraping the *inside* of his skin, working its way into his bloodstream so that even his life's fluid was almost frozen, moving slowly, nearly stopping. He tried to draw in breath, but his lungs would hardly stretch, would hardly expand to take in air.

Her eyes found him. But there were no eyes, just deep, black holes. Her flesh was burnt, charred, her body misshapen. Her head was at a strange angle, almost resting against one shoulder, and her neck was scarred, a tight restricting band of indented flesh cutting across her windpipe. Thick oozing blood still poured from the wounds in her body and the child's dress was no longer white: it was a red, blood-smeared rag. And then the hideous doll-like figure was smouldering, curls of smoke rising from the cloth and flesh. Her face began to blister, the skin began to tear. Her skin turned black.

And she was Alice once again.

Confused, lost, a small child who had experienced death's advent and could not understand why she did not lie dying.

'Alice, Alice!'

The girl turned, her eyes wide, afraid, to face her mother.

'Oh God,' Fenn moaned softly as he saw her features change once more. Her voice was low, rasping. 'Rosemund.'

Molly Pagett, who had found strength to move towards her daughter, stopped and her mouth opened in a scream that tried to deny the sudden perception. 'No, no!' Molly fell, yet her eyes would not leave the little figure standing before her. 'No!' she screamed, 'I'm not Rosemund! Not her!'

The steps on which Fenn lay seemed to reverberate with the thunderclap, but the trembling did not stop. He clung to the wooden stairs as they shook, the agitation becoming more jarring, more violent.

An explosion to his left as a floodlight popped, sparks leaping outwards like dragon's breath. A fluctuation of light as other lamps dimmed, became bright, exploded. Cries of panic from the crowd as an earth tremor ran beneath their feet. The ruffling of his hair and clothes as a wind swept across the platform, bending the candle flames before extinguishing them, A crash as the crucifix on the altar fell to the carpeted boards.

Sue and Ben huddled together as panic-stricken people rushed by. The nuns, with whom they had shared the bench, were filing into the centre aisle, the vibrations from the ground causing them to lurch from side to side. They held onto each other as though they were a blind group being led to safety.

Others of the crowd were clambering across the benches, shoving their way through fellow worshippers who were too shocked to move, or who could not flee fast enough. Those who had brought along invalid relatives or friends struggled with them through the thronging mass, desperately trying to keep up with the human tide, falling with their charges when the merciless crush became too much, pleading for help, protecting their sick with their own bodies, disappearing under a welter of thrashing arms and legs.

The bench on which Sue and Ben clung to each other was toppled over and they found themselves on the shuddering ground, the narrow crevasse between fallen bench and the one behind affording them some protection against the frenzied mob. Sue pulled the boy close, a hand against his cheek, an arm around his shoulders, while he closed his eyes against the terror and tried to shut out the noise, the screams, the cries, the low rumbling that came from underground.

Television and film cameramen were leaping from their perches into the throng, their machines and the very platforms they were mounted on live with dangerous power, the current running through the technicians' bodies in swift waves, not strong enough to kill or maim, but enough to shock their systems rigid. Photographers, many who had steadfastly continued to shoot the bizarre scene on the central platform despite the panic around them, were forced to drop their instruments as the metal casing scorched their fingers.

The congregation which had come to worship, to idolize, to witness, fled towards the field's three exits, converging on these points to form their own human blockade. Many were squashed against the tall locked gates that had been erected at one side of the field, a wide entrance meant for lorries bringing in construction materials and film equipment, before the heavy lock gave way under the strain. As they burst open, those people pressed against them fell and others fell on top, and still more fell onto the scrambling heap.

Police at the central entrance gate tried to control the fleeing mobs, but were swept away with them. Children were held high by their parents and many suddenly felt themselves adrift on moving waves of heads and shoulders. The less fortunate slipped into the smallest openings to be drowned in the pulverizing human current. Those who managed to escape the field, bruised, battered and almost demented, fled into the road, many running towards the lights of the village, others just fleeing in all directions, into the darkness of opposite fields, along the road heading towards open country, dragging helpless companions with them, thanking God that they were safely away from the dreadful place, that ground they had thought to be hallowed, sacred. And they thanked God that the earth no longer shook beneath them.

The Press entrance was too narrow to take the deluge; it was totally blocked. The pile of crushed bodies grew higher as more and more people tried to scramble over and became entangled themselves in the mass of writhing bodies. Others were lacerated as they attempted to force themselves through the tough bramble hedges surrounding the field, the natural barrier acting as hundreds of barbed-wire coils.

Those who had been outside the shrine throughout the service – the stallholders, the police, the pilgrims and sightseers who had arrived too late to be allowed entry into the already overcrowded compound – could only stare aghast. They had heard the rumbling thunder overhead and had glanced anxiously at the troubled clouds, somehow aware that the atmosphere had changed, that there was danger close by. They could not explain the feeling and had looked at one another with uncertainty; something had seemed to pass through them, a frigid coldness, a nerve-tingling iciness, and their apprehension became an overt fear. Many of the stallholders had began to pack away their goods, all good-natured bantering between them gone. Disappointed worshippers and tourists suddenly felt relieved that they had not gained access; they began to hurry back to their vehicles, not sure of their feelings, but wanting to be away from this place. Their anxiety increased when the engines of their cars, vans and mini-buses whined and refused to start. The police and officials outside the grounds were alarmed and a uniformed sergeant tried to radio through to his chief-inspector who was inside the field keeping an eye on proceedings. The sergeant received only static on the handset.

Despite their concern, nothing untoward had occurred until the third hymn was drawing to a close. There had been a long silence, then four unmistakable gunshots had rung out, followed by pandemonium. Even though they had heard the clamour from within, they did not realize the extent of the panic until the congregation had come pouring out, sweeping over the uniformed men who stood in their way.

But not everyone inside had tried to escape. Certain individuals fell to their knees and clasped their hands together in prayer, their eyes raised upwards to the turbulent skies; some were collected in groups, quavery voices raised in hymn, afraid but stalwart; others cowered on the shaking ground, clutching grass and mud as though afraid they would slide off the face of the earth. And yet others lay there never to move again, life pressed from them by trampling feet.

Paula was pulling her gibbering mother to her feet, for they had both fallen in the initial rush. Bewildered, she looked around; everything was in gloom, confused, chaotic. She could hear singing above the cries for help, but it was faraway, remote. Brittle, claw-like fingers scratched at her throat and her mother's fear-struck, tremulous pleading filtered through to her. She pulled the feeble hands away and tried to see more clearly.

The only light came from the altar, the bright beacon still shining high into the sky, lighting the misshapen tree whose branches quivered and oscillated as though it was a living creature. There were silhouettes in front of the light, a black drama acted out on the stage. She understood, even in her confused state, that the fear stemmed from that centre-piece: the people were not just running because the ground shook beneath them, but because they were repelled by the abhorrent thing that stood before the altar and which had looked at each one of them personally and mockingly invaded the intimacy of their very souls. It had scorned and reviled each man, woman and child, and had *known* each one's cruelness, every sin and iniquitous desire they held. It knew them and made them recognize themselves.

Paula put her arms around the frail shoulders of her mother and led her unsteadily along the row towards the centre aisle. They staggered and nearly went down several times as the ground lurched; it was exhausting, dragging her mother along, pushing her way through those who had become paralysed with terror, fighting off others who were desperate to get by. They made it to the end of the bench and paused, gathering strength to join the mainstream of struggling people.

Somebody collapsed against them and they fell, rolling over the bench behind to crash into soft earth. Paula scrabbled onto hands and knees, feeling for her mother, a moving jungle of legs passing within inches of her face. She touched her mother's body and tugged at it, but it did not move. Her fluttering hands moved along the shape towards her mother's face: they found it and the mouth was gaping open, the eyes closed.

'Mother!' she screamed and the tremoring earth became still. The surrounding cries of terror quietened with the stillness of the earth. People stopped and looked around. Whimpers came from everywhere, but they were soft, the moans of animals after a harsh beating. Even the hymn singing had stopped. Even the praying.

On the altar, something burned.

Paul knew instinctively that her mother was dead, even though she pushed a hand beneath the old woman's coat to feel her chest. The heart was as still as the air around them. She felt no grief, only a numbness. And in a way, a release.

But the numbness dissipated when she saw Rodney Tucker collapsed against a bench nearby. Hatred seethed within her, a fury that quickly devoured the numbness and sent emotion soaring through her.

And then, just as an uneasy calmness began to settle over everyone, the earth opened.

George Southworth had fled towards the church wall, all dignity shed, naked terror revealed.

Everything had gone so well, his dreams easily within his grasp. The shrine – *his project* – had become a huge success, a fantastic money-spinner. He, and others in the area, those with the foresight to invest, to deal themselves in at the very beginning, were about to see their shrewd business acumen rewarded. Indeed, the rewards had already been made apparent; now they could only increase. The village of Banfield was no longer dying; it flourished and would continue to do so, just as had the French village of Lourdes, now a bustling town, a thriving community that was known worldwide.

But she, that thing, that bloodied monster who had impossibly risen from the dead, had looked at him, just him, and seen the greed in his heart. And she had laughed at it, and had welcomed it, for it was part of the evil that gave her existence.

He was running even before the earth had began to tremble. Those around him were too blind to see, too horror-struck to realize the meaning of this unholy resurrection. He knew, but did not understand how he knew, that this creature was the manifestation of their own evil, that she existed on the power she drew from their own blackened souls. The awareness had struck him because she willed it so. That instigation was this creature's torment: the realization of one's own infinite vileness. The guilt that the Church taught all men to suffer was founded on actuality: the culpability was real because the wickedness had always been there in each and every person. Even in the innocent, the children. Children like Alice.

He brushed by those who could only gaze up at the altar and he fought the weakness and dizziness that assailed him, knowing that catastrophe was to follow this new, obscene miracle.

Vaguely, somewhere in the far distance, he heard the hunched thing speak, one word, perhaps a name, and the echo in his mind was drowned by thunder, a sound so loud, so shattering, *so near*, it seemed to rip into his heart. But he was still moving, staggering among the invalids stretched out on the ground.

Then there were others fleeing with him, screams breaking loose from terrified souls, entreaties from those too crippled to move. A hand grabbed at his leg and he looked down to see a wasted, skeletal man wrapped in a heavy red blanket, begging him with wide, frightened eyes to carry him away from the disorder. He knocked the yellow, withered hand away and staggered onwards, the ground vibrating beneath him, the low rumble seeming to rise up through the soles of his feet to shake him like a rag doll.

It was an eternity before he reached the low wall surrounding the church grounds, and the oscillation had grown more violent. There were others with him, those who realized the exits would be blocked, and they, too, climbed the wall, leaping into the graveyard beyond.

He fell heavily and lay panting in the rough grass, hands clenched into the earth. He was kicked as others scrambled over and a blow caught him on the temple, sending him reeling. Southworth pushed himself back, rolling close to the wall and lying there gasping for breath, cautiously waiting like a dislodged jockey under a jump.

High-heeled boots scraped off his shoulder and he vaguely recognized the American journalist who had been at the convent when Alice's stomach had refused the Communion wafer. He called after her fleeing figure, needing help, too dazed to move; but she was gone, disappearing between the gravestones.

He had no record of time, no knowledge of how long he lay there, for his senses were jumbled, both fear and the knock he had received combining to confuse. He became aware that the ground was no longer trembling and that a quietness had descended. He wiped a palm across his face and found it came away wet; he hadn't realized he had been weeping.

Southworth groaned as the pandemonium broke loose again. The tearing, wrenching sound felt as if the very earth was erupting. Everything shook: the trees, the ground, the gravestones. Lush, fresh soil trickled in rivulets down the tiny pyramid molehills. As he watched, a grey slab no more than eight feet away tilted, then fell. The stone lids on the tombs reverberated; one was jolted in quick shuddering movements so that it slid from its perch, breaking into fragments when it landed, leaving the tomb gaping open.

He had to reach the church. There he would find sanctuary from this bedlam. He tried to rise, but the quaking of the earth would not allow it; he staggered forward, bent, sometimes on all fours like an animal, sometimes flat on the ground, propelling himself with arms and legs.

Figures around him stumbled through the graveyard, falling against the headstones, leaning on trembling tombs for support.

Occasionally, the rolling clouds allowed a glimpse of moonlight, its brightness sparing and soon gone.

A mound of earth near Southworth moved and he stared spellbound, telling himself it was the earth tremors causing the disturbance to the grave. But the soil was being pushed upwards, from within, as though something beneath it wanted to breathe the air of the living once more.

More shifting of soil nearby. An urn containing fresh flowers tipped over. Earth beneath it began to bulge, began to break.

A trickle of soil touched his outstretched fingers and he pulled his hand away, tucking it beneath his chest. He saw the small grave nearby, a child's grave – or perhaps a dwarf's. A tiny hillock was forming, rising from the flatness around it and, before the moonlight was swallowed by the heavy, thunderous clouds again, little white things pushed through the soil. Little white things that could have been worms. Worms that were stiffened, upright. Five of them. Joined by five more.

Southworth screamed and staggered to his feet. He ran, stumbled, crawled, to the door of St Joseph's, aware of the moving shapes in the ground around him.

He slammed into the old wood, whimpering, his legs drenched and stained with his own excrement, his eyes blurred by tears. He scratched at the wood as if to claw his way through, scrabbled for the metal ring at waist level, twisted it, once, twice, pushed the door open and stumbled inside. He slammed it shut and stood there in the dark church, his back against the door, his chest heaving, gasping for breath.

Until he froze, his lungs half-filled.

And listened to the scratching against the wood outside.

FORTY

Where have the dead gone?
Where do they live now?
Not in the grave, they say,
Then where now?

GRAVE BY A HOLM-OAK
Stevie Smith

Fenn raised his head from the platform's surface and tried to take in a deep breath. The air was fetid, though, full of corruption and the stink of burning; he choked, his stomach heaving in short gut-wrenching spasms.

He was vaguely aware of the turmoil below, the panic-stricken people staggering towards the exits, earth tremors causing many to fall to the ground where they lay and were trampled. But it was dark out there and virtually impossible to make out more than a confused mêlée of struggling bodies; it was the screams and piteous wails that revealed the true horror.

Somewhere in the channels of his fuddled mind, reason told him he had to get away, that he had to go back and find Sue and Ben and lead them away from the danger, for this abhorrence meant to destroy, to devastate. He had no strength; his muscles felt sluggish even though his nerves were tautly stretched. He wanted to look away from the smouldering, bloody monstrosity, but the vision held his gaze, held his debilitated body, held him there as if chains restrained any action.

He heard her speak and there were other voices inside his head that told him he must resist her power. Her strength was *his* strength, was the strength of all those present, was accumulative potency drawn from the evil of others, the negative force torn from the positive, creating an imbalance over them all. But resist. *Resist!* The voices repeated the word and they were the same voices and the same words as in his dreams. Elnor could only exist through the kinetic energy of those living. *Resist her!* She could not govern those who opposed.

Was it mere self-delusion that the voices in his mind and dreams were those of the two dead priests?

Fenn moaned and he tried to *resist*, but the effort was too much. He could not even look away from the disfigured creature. In the church at Barham he had run from his nightmares, refusing to confront them, denying their reality; now he had no option in the confrontation. His will was too weak to leave.

Every person on the stage around the altar was in a state of near-collapse. Bishop Caines was on his knees, one hand against the flooring, the other waving feebly in the air in an uncoordinated movement that vaguely resembled the Sign of the Cross. His lips moved ceaselessly, and spittle drooled from them to glisten against his chin. The words were almost inaudible, but they were clear in Fenn's mind:

'*. . . Holy Lord, Almighty Father, Everlasting God and Father of our Lord Jesus Christ. Who once and for all consigned that fallen tyrant . . .*'

The priest who had been conducting the service lay prostrate on the floor, his arms outstretched as if in supplication. He was motionless and Fenn could see his eyes were rolled back into his head, only whiteness showing; the priest's mouth was open but there was no indication that he was breathing.

'*. . . to the flames of Hell. Who sent your only begotten Son into the world to crush that roaring lion; hasten to our call . . .*'

Some of the altar-servers were crouched over, their knees drawn up, foreheads pressed against the rich carpet of the centre-piece, hands tucked around their heads as if to shut away the evil that had manifested itself; others swayed as they knelt, white, draining horror in their expressions, but eyes riveted on the small, unclean figure.

'*. . . for help and snatch from ruination and from the clutches of the noonday Devil this human being made in Your image . . .*'

Only Molly Pagett stood.

Yet even she was sinking, her arm still raised towards her daughter.

'Aliiiiiicccce!' she moaned.

And the malevolent voice hissed back: 'Your daughter is in death, sweet Rosemund. She, our Devil's spawn, is between this place and the underworld, her service to me almost complete. None can save her. Nor save you.' The scarred, bent creature turned her head towards the blackness. 'Nor those who slew me and denied my right.'

'*. . . and likeness. Strike terror, Lord, into the beast now laying waste Your vineyard. Let Your mighty . . .*'

'Noooooo!' Molly Pagett stumbled forward, sinking to the floor, moving towards the smouldering thing, both hands reaching out.

And the creature who was Alice, who was Elnor, laughed, and Fenn saw a shape hanging from a lower branch of the tree, and it was burning and twisting, and its neck was stretched, its feet twitching and turning black, and substance was dripping from its body to fall steaming onto the altar below, and its head was aflame and its flesh burnt, and as it turned it was Alice.

'*. . . hand cast him out, so he . . . he . . . she . . . may no longer hold captive this person . . .*'

With a screech of sheer despair, Molly Pagett lunged forward and touched the charred and rotted body of Elnor, then screamed in pain as rivulets of fire ran along her fingers, along her arms, engulfing her head and shoulders.

There was a silence. A silence that was as terrifying as the clamour preceding it.

Bishop Caines became quiet.

Molly Pagett blazed but did not move.

Fenn felt his senses beginning to fade.

And the image-corpse of the sixteenth-century nun chuckled as thunder suddenly roared and the field began to open.

Paula let go of her mother's dead body.

The deep rumbling noise reverberated in her head as the earth wrenched itself apart, the cacophony of screams and shouts beginning anew. She watched mesmerized as a gaping wound appeared in the soil; it widened, ran jagged along the centre aisle, sending the petrified crowd clambering back into the rows of benches.

The ground yawned open and Paula saw the blackness down there, so deep, bottomless, an infinity of darkness. Yet, as moonlight fought its way through the massed clouds and cast its glow into the chasm, she saw movement, hands reaching upwards, limbs clinging to the soft, rent earth. Shapes climbing from the depths, figures that were twisted, that moaned and stared open-mouthed at the sky above, tormented souls that yearned for the world above.

Paula closed her eyes, telling herself it couldn't be true, that this was not really happening. She opened them again and saw it was true, it *was* happening.

There were figures on the edge of the opening chasm, backing away, pushing each other to keep clear of the widening gap. Even in her own terror, Paula recognized two of them.

Tucker was struggling away from the pit, hindered by his wife, who had slipped, one leg over the edge, disappearing into the blackness. She scrabbled at his clothes, desperately trying to cling to him, but he pulled her hands away, afraid she'd take him with her, knowing he could not drag her weight clear. She screamed at him, imploring him to save her, but he shouted back at her, shrieked for her to let go, slapped at her face, prised at her fingers. She held on with one hand, the other grabbing at the soil beneath her, one knee on the very lip of the chasm. The earth crumbled beneath her heavy body and the material of his coat tore as she fell screaming.

Tucker stumbled back, then righted himself. He stood with hands against his thighs, struggling to recover his strength, soon realizing he had to keep moving back, that the opening was still widening.

He turned just as Paula rushed at him.

Hatred drove her forward, loathing for a fat bastard who had betrayed her, used her, abused her body, and lied, lied, *lied*! Beneath the ground was where he belonged, to wriggle and squirm with the slugs and worms and underground creatures that he was akin to.

She slammed into him and he caught her. But her impetus was too forceful: he could not keep his balance. He toppled backwards and clutched at her, taking her with him.

Together, locked in screaming embrace, they plunged.

Southworth ran from the door.

He touched every pew with his left hand as he passed, like a child touching every spoke in a railing, an action that had no logic, panic its prompter.

He reached the low rail in front of the altar and slumped against it, whining against the solitude of the church, afraid of the frozen corpses outside seeking entry.

The church began to vibrate. Statues around its walls moved, shifted by the tremor. The rail he clung to became impossible to grip. The cracking of ancient stone rang out like a report from a cannon, jerking his head in the direction of the sound. He watched in fascinated horror as the jagged line ripped across a wall. More ear-splitting sounds and more lines joining the first. Now from the other side of the church. Now from the roof.

Pieces of masonry began to clatter onto the stone floor. Powdered concrete descended as white dust, and the dim lights of the church began to falter, flickering as if candlelight caught by the wind. On – off – on – off. Then, just very low.

His hands were at his mouth, stifling the cries that nobody would have heard over the tearing of old stone. Behind him, candlesticks toppled from the altar; the tabernacle door swung open, revealing the white silk emptiness inside; the huge stained glass window, donated to St Joseph's by a sixteenth-century nobleman flew inwards, sending shards of coloured glass spearing through the air.

He gasped as several pieces struck his head, scything through his hair and scalp, leaving fine cuts that quickly oozed with blood. He was fortunate that the rail he clung to protected most of his face and neck.

The turbulence became more intense, the cracking and rumbling sounds deafening. A long, jagged line appeared in the stone floor, running beneath the pews and across the aisle. A gap began to open, a scissure so black it seemed painted. Pews shifted, fell against one another as the cleft became a fissure, the fissure a wide split.

The knuckles of his hands began to bleed as he bit hard; he watched slime-covered fingers appear over the edge of the hole. He bit down until his teeth were grinding against bare bone.

Hands, then arms, filthy with earth and mould appeared. Small black things scuttled out, disappearing into darker corners; something long slithered across the floor and curled itself around the base of a statue. More fingers slid over the edge, more arms reached into the air. More hands and naked, death-discoloured shoulders began to appear.

The door at the far end of the church began to splinter, pressure from the breaking stone around it forcing it from the frame. It burst open and the dead creatures entered.

Sue felt strangely calm.

'What's happening, Mummy? Why are all the people screaming?'

Sue held Ben tightly, one hand against the back of his neck, his head tucked against her chest.

'It's all right,' she soothed, stroking his hair. 'Don't be frightened.'

He pushed his head away from her, looking round to see what was going on. 'I'm not afraid,' he said seriously, eyes widening at the spectacle.

Someone hurtled over them, tripping on their recumbent bodies. The figure scrabbled to his or her feet – there was no way of telling whether it was man or woman in the poor light – and rushed on.

Ben sat up again. 'I can see Uncle Gerry,' he said, pointing towards the altar.

Sue pushed herself up, using the overturned bench next to her for support. The ground was still trembling, although not quite as violently as before, and the rumbling sound was now deep down as if in the bowels of the earth. For some reason people were fleeing from the centre aisle, but it was impossible to see why. She followed Ben's pointing finger and gasped when she saw the scene on the altar.

There were bodies dressed in the robes of the Mass littered all over the platform. She recognized the portly figure of Bishop Caines, his sparse, grey hair flat against his forehead, dampened with perspiration; his hand waved uselessly in the air. Not more than two yards from him something was bright with flame. It was a figure, a kneeling figure that did not move, nor squirm, in its agony. Only the head, arms and shoulders were burning, the hands outstretched towards someone who stood just beyond the light thrown from the one remaining lamp. It was just a small black silhouette, a child's figure, standing before the gruesome display, watching, perfectly still, smoke eddies from burst lights swirling around the altar. And dominating everything, towering over the shrine, was the oak tree, its stout lower branches twisted downwards like arms about to scoop up the fallen bodies.

She saw Fenn lying on the steps of the platform. He looked so helpless and afraid.

She stood, bringing Ben up with her.

'Where are we going?' he asked.

'Away from here,' she replied. 'But we have to get Uncle Gerry first.'

'Sure!' he shouted and scampered over the bench.

At once, Sue felt nauseous and dizzy. Her knees began to sag.

'Ben!' she cried out and he was back with her, arms wrapped around her waist, little face peering anxiously up at her.

The dizziness vanished. She swallowed and the sickness was gone. Sue looked curiously down at her son.

She bent close. 'Don't leave me, Ben. Don't let go of me.'

He took her hand and together they climbed over the benches towards the altar.

Sue forced herself to ignore the pitiful cries for help coming from the invalids scattered on the stretch of ground between the front benches and the altar-piece, knowing she could not go to their aid, that she had to reach Fenn, then perhaps together they could carry just one or two away from there. She clutched Ben's hand tightly, not understanding why her strength, her calmness derived from him, just aware that it was so.

She tried not to look at the burning figure and saw that Ben had become fascinated by it. She pulled his head against her hip, a hand covering his face to shield him from the sight, but he pulled her fingers open and peeped between them.

They reached the foot of the steps and began to climb.

'Gerry?' Sue was beside him, peering anxiously into his face. He blinked his eyes, seeming not to recognize her at first.

'Sue,' he said softly and she breathed a sigh of relief. Fenn suddenly grabbed her arm. 'Sue, you've got to get away from here! Now, right away! Where's Ben?'

'It's all right. He's here. Come on, you're coming with us.'

His head sank against the step. 'No, I can't move. I'm too weak. You've got to go without me.'

She pulled her son up the steps. 'Touch him, Gerry. Hold his hand,' she urged.

Fenn looked at her uncomprehendingly. 'Just get away, Sue. Just go!'

She put her son's hand into his and Fenn looked from her to the boy; then down at their joined hands. His sapped vitality began to return.

Shrieks of agony made all three look towards the altar.

Molly Pagett was slowly rising from her knees, beating at her enflamed hair with hands that were also alight. The sound of her screams struck into them, chilling them.

'Oh God, I've got to help her.' Fenn tore off his coat and climbed the rest of the steps onto the platform. He stumbled forward, coat held before him, ready to be thrown over the burning woman's head and shoulders.

But Molly Pagett was beyond help.

With one last piercing scream she lunged at the dark figure standing just beyond the light. The figure did not appear to move, yet the burning woman's arms did not strike it. Molly plunged off the platform, falling into the darkness to lay writhing in the field below, a fiery rag, the agonized shrieks slowly becoming weak, fading, stopping abruptly when her life was spent.

Fenn groaned and slumped to the floor, rocking back on his heels, his eyes closed, coat held uselessly in his lap.

The small figure stepped forward into the arena of light and stood before the altar, looking up at the tree. Then it turned its gaze on Fenn.

Lightning flashed, freezing the shrine, the field, the church in the distance, in its silvery light. Fenn, whose eyes had opened, felt he was not part of the scene, but hovering somewhere above, viewing from a great height and having no involvement. The jostling, tearing worshippers, the sick left behind, arms upraised beseechingly; the huge black abyss from which crawling things emerged; the church, its tower beginning to crumble, the opening graves; the shrine, the slumped bodies before the altar, the fallen crucifix, the hideous, mis-shapen tree. The creature who watched him.

The lightning flash expired, a two-second exposure that ingrained an indelible monochrome vision of Hell's chaos on Fenn's mind.

Thunder boomed, a deafening sound that overwhelmed all others and he clapped his hands to his ears in reflex.

Ben tugged at his mother and said: 'There's blood all over Alice's dress, Mummy.'

Fenn stared back into Elnor's knowing eyes and found himself sinking into their softness, a peaceful vortex that drew him inwards to be exquisitely drowned in their depths. He was aware of her delicately beautiful features, the whiteness of her skin, the moist, natural redness of her lips, even though he looked only into her eyes. He sensed the pleasing suppleness of her body, its litheness, its vitality, and the firmness of young breasts which the nun's simple costume could not disguise.

Elnor smiled and his head reeled.

When she spoke, he barely understood her words, so strange was her accent and so low, rasping, was her voice.

'Witness my vengeance,' she said. 'And be, thyself, part.'

And her eyes were no longer soft and brown, but were darkly hollow, deep pits that held him fascinated. Her skin was no longer soft and white, but was charred and torn, the lips burnt away to reveal stumps of blackened teeth and weeping gums. Her body was no longer supple and straight, but was twisted, bent, a warped scarred figure that in some curious way resembled the malformed tree which towered over her. Her stench clawed at him in putrefying waves. He raised a hand against her, falling backwards, pushing himself away.

Her laughter was insidious, a sly creeping chuckle.

'Why is Alice standing there?' Ben asked his mother.

The laughter grew, filled Fenn's head, swamped his mind. *Must get away*, he told himself. *Must get free of her. O God, Jesus Christ, please help me!*

The platform began to vibrate. His hands were forced from its surface, his body rolling backwards. He turned, tried to get his knees beneath him, toppling over, the splintering of wood sharp against the rumbling noise. The long black rent in the field was widening, the gash growing longer, flowing like a dark river towards the raised altar, stretching towards the shrine.

The nun's clothes were smouldering as she approached Fenn, and her skin was blistering once more. Yet still she chuckled and her lipless mouth mocked him. Broken charred fingers were reaching for him. A streak of lightning cut its jagged way through the sky.

Elnor was almost upon him and her breath was as foul as her body.

He screamed, unable to move.

And she grinned her death's grin.

But then she had stopped. Was looking back towards the tree. Was moaning, a low, piteous wail. She straightened and her broken hands clenched tightly at her breasts. Her moans became louder.

Fenn followed her sightless gaze and saw nothing. Then a shimmering.

A glow.

At the base of the tree.

He felt renewed fear, but this was of another kind. The glow became stronger, became bright, like a newborn sun. His hand tried to shade his eyes, but the radiance was too great, too blinding. Yet there was something in its centre. Something standing within its incandescent core.

And in his mind he could hear the voices of the two priests. *Pray*, they urged him. *Pray*.

He blinked. He closed his eyes. He prayed.

Lightning struck the tree and his eyes shot open.

The hunched creature was moving away, shuffling backwards, arms stretched towards the splintered oak. She screamed, cursed, her guttural voice rising in pitch.

The upper branches of the tree were in flame, its trunk torn open, tiny creatures pouring out, maggots, lice, glistening wood leeches. The tree was rotted, dead inside, a nesting place for parasites that fed on dead things.

Thunder, and, almost at once, forked lightning. It struck the tree and every branch became alive with blue dancing flashes, energy pouring through the contorted limbs, seeking earth. The whole of the oak burst into flames and a tearing rending sound split the air. The tree began to topple.

Hands tugged at Fenn's shoulders. A woman's hands and a child's.

Sue and Ben pulled at Fenn until he was moving with them, running from the platform, away from the screaming creature, away from the falling tree. Hand in hand they jumped from the shrine into the night.

They landed heavily, but the muddy earth was soft, yielding. Fenn, winded, his ankles jolted by the fall, turned to see the small girl standing beneath the descending, screeching inferno, the child who was already dead, slain by a madman, Alice, who now raised her arms as if to ward off the fiery nemesis, yet no longer the child as the flames engulfed her, once again the black, hunched creature who could not defy the greater power. Fenn believed he heard Elnor cry out as the burning tree crushed then incinerated her corrupt and unearthly body.

The centre-piece collapsed, all those sprawled on its surface falling inwards towards the heart of the fire. Soon the whole structure was burning.

Only the crackle of flames could be heard and the weeping of those still left in the field. The earth tremors had stopped. There was no more screaming.

Fenn reached for Sue and Ben, their distraught faces bathed in the warm glow of the fire. He pulled them to him and they huddled together, moving only when the flames of the burning platform came too near.

And then the rain gently began to fall.

FORTY-ONE

'Round and round the circle
Completing the charm
So the knot be unknotted
The cross uncrossed
The crooked be made straight
And the curse be ended.'

'... THE CURSE BE ENDED'
T. S. Eliot

'Come in with us.'

Fenn smiled at Sue, who was peering in the open car door, and gently shook his head. 'You go with Ben,' he said. 'I'll pick you up later.'

The boy scrambled from the back seat out onto the kerb. Sue leant back into the Mini, one knee on the passenger seat, and stretched across to kiss Fenn's cheek. She tenderly hugged him and then was gone.

He watched as they walked down the long path towards the church entrance, Sue's hair caught by the sun, made golden at its edges, Ben holding her hand, skipping alongside her.

It was Sunday morning, a bright fresh day, the smell of the sea strong in the air. The church was of contemporary design, elegantly simple, its structure rejecting any solemnity or oppressiveness. More inviting than a couple of churches I could think of, Fenn thought grimly. Few people strolled the streets in that part of the seaside town for, although it was a bright, sunny morning, winter's chill still clung; only those with dogs to be exercised, those who were too lonely to stay indoors, and those attending Sunday services at the many and various Brighton temples and chapels, had left the warmth of their homes. One such person, a dog-stroller, passed by on the opposite side of the road and Fenn caught a word of the front-page headline in the newspaper the man was avidly reading.

It said 'SHRINE' and Fenn turned his head away.

He was tired of their theories, their conjectures, their desperate need for a rationale. The current favourite was that an electrical storm had centred on the field, its lightning destroying the altar-piece, causing the tree to burn and fall, even striking the ground to send shock currents running through the earth. Film, radio and television technicians present complained that electrical interference had jammed their equipment. Even the film in the cameras of the Press photographers had been blanked out, although nobody could quite explain how an electro-magnetic storm could have that effect. The police, receiving severe criticism for not having controlled the panic, had limply claimed that their own communications system had been disrupted by the storm. The shock-waves had caused mass hysteria among the already highly-charged, emotional crowd, causing hallucinations, breakdowns and panic. That was the Number One, highly-rated conclusion. Others were even more fanciful but nevertheless not totally rejected: Alice Pagett had acquired some unknown paranormal mental powers and, having no control over them, had upset nature's delicate balance; an underground eruption had shaken the area, frightening the whole assemblage into hysteria (unfortunately no seismographic evidence substantiated the idea); an anti-religious organization had planted a bomb beneath the shrine (probably the same group that had killed the monsignor). More and more solutions, more and more confusion.

Over twenty thousand pilgrims had arrived at the shrine on that black Sunday and, if there had been any miracle to that day, it was that only one hundred and fifty-eight had been killed in the panic. Many had been crushed to death beneath the trampling feet of their fellow-worshippers; some had suffered heart seizures or fatal fits; others, those on the central altar-piece, or close by, had been burned to death; still others had died in accidents as they had fled the field. Many, many more had been seriously injured and maimed, while the condition of a number of the invalids present had deteriorated to an alarming degree. Strangely, those whom Alice Pagett had cured at other times at the shrine found their illnesses and infirmities had returned, as though the child's death had cancelled the miracles.

Scores of the unfortunate worshippers, clerics and nuns among them, claimed they had witnessed the ground tear itself open. But these people were confused, even weeks later, and their mental state could at best be described as 'unstable'. It was a fact that hundreds, possibly thousands, had blanked the incident from their minds completely; all they could remember was the fierce storm and running from the field.

Speculation in the media was rife, swinging from the wild sensationalism of the so-called popular Press (as if the incident needed any sensationalizing) to the deliberately underplayed scientific and psychological views of the more conservative. Fenn was no longer a part of that particular circus. He had resigned from the *Courier* and refused offers of employment with the large Nationals. He had even refused to answer questions concerning the events of that night. Maybe one day, when his head was clear and his nerves more controlled, he would sit down and write a definitive book on the Banfield shrine. But it would have to be marketed as fiction, for who would believe the facts?

He smiled as he remembered Nancy's frantic phone call from the States. Her bosses wanted him over there, were offering him a job on the *Post* – 'name your own figure' – in return for the full story of the shrine. He declined the offer and Nancy had fumed and ranted on the other end of the line. She had been one of the first to flee as soon as she realized 'something bad was going down', mindful and still fearful of what had happened to her at St Peter's. So scared had she been that the slightest hint of trouble had sent her scampering. Unlike most of the panicked people, she had headed directly towards the church grounds, knowing that all exits would be swamped, and had followed a man she thought was Southworth, the hotelier in the village, losing sight of him somewhere in the graveyard. She had used the entrance to St Joseph's as her escape route and had missed the finale. That was why she was so chagrined. Happy to be alive, of course, but pissed that she hadn't witnessed the grand slam. Nancy had urged, begged, threatened, but he refused to join her. She was still in a rage at the end of their conversation, but managed to growl, 'I love you, you fink,' before her receiver clunked down.

He rubbed his temples with stiffened fingers and thought of those who had died in the field. The fat businessman, Tucker, found lying in the mud, his face purplish blue from a heart attack. His chief assistant, a woman whose name Fenn could not remember, lay on top of him as though trying to protect his gross body from the crushing feet of others. She was in a state of shock. Ironically, her mother was found dead nearby, she too having suffered heart failure. Employer and mother, both lost at the same time with the same cause. No wonder she was still in shock. Tucker's wife, also found nearby, could remember nothing, only that she had fainted while trying to escape the field.

Bishop Caines had died, along with other clerics and altar-servers, in the fire. Crushed by the tree, burned by the flames.

George Southworth had been more fortunate, although some might reason otherwise. He had been discovered hiding in St Joseph's, a shivering, slavering wreck of a man. They had to drag him screaming from the church, for he refused to walk down the aisle to the broken doorway. Apart from the cracked door and a shattered stained-glass window (both struck by lightning, it was thought) there was no other damage to the church, even though Southworth insisted it lay in ruins around him.

Then there was Molly Pagett.

He closed his eyes, but the vision of her enflamed body was even sharper. That poor, poor woman. How she had suffered in the final minutes of her life, seeing her daughter shot, resurrected, changed into something unspeakable, then dying in agony. Perhaps it was better she had died, no matter how terribly, for the memory would have killed her just as surely, only death would have been slow and more cruel in its claiming.

Why had Alice – no, *Elnor*! – called her 'Rosemund'? One of the two nuns mentioned in the sixteenth-century priest's chronicle had been named Rosemund. She had been one of the young novices whom Elnor had seduced, one that had been cast out from the church and was said to be living in the forests around the village. Could Molly Pagett possibly have been a descendant of that girl? Or was the creature Elnor, this resurrection, this reincarnation, confused by its own hatred? He would never know, for there were no clear answers.

There was not even a clear answer as to why the young man had shot Alice. His dead body had been found among the others, battered and crushed; nobody would even suggest that he had been torn apart by the mob. The German gun was found nearby, its barrel jammed. His name was Wilkes, and the only abnormality of his typically middle-class background was that he appeared to have, judging by the collected newspaper clippings found in his bedsit, a fascination for the assassin of John Lennon, and the would-be assassins of Pope John Paul and Ronald Reagan. If he had been a little older, then perhaps his heroes would have been Oswald, Ray, and Sirhan.

Whatever his twisted reasons were, a trigger-squeeze to fame, a rejection of what *he* believed to be total good, Alice was dead. Perhaps evil had defeated evil.

Elnor had sought her revenge and had claimed much of it. Only the child's unpredicted death had thwarted its completeness, and the shrine had been destroyed as surely as if the hand of . . . Fenn could not accept it. It was too unclear in his mind. He could have imagined he'd seen . . . everything was so confused . . .

Alice's body – what was left of it – had been found beneath the charred remnants of the tree. She had been buried, along with the remains of her mother, in the graveyard of St Joseph's nearby. Curiously, when the site of the shrine had been excavated a week later, the remains of another body had been found buried beneath the roots of the fallen oak.

But this one was centuries old, just a twisted skeleton. It appeared to be that of a small person, many of its bones broken at the time of death. Burned black, also.

The remains had been taken away to be studied by experts who would decide on the date of its origins. Eventually the bones would go to the British Museum where they would be displayed in a glass case for tourists and those interested in mankind's evolution could come and smile at the grinning skull.

Fenn looked up and Sue and Ben were nearly at the church door. Ben had been distracted and was squatting by the edge of the path, watching something on the ground, perhaps an insect of some kind. Sue was speaking to him, obviously telling him they would be late for the Mass.

What strange power did Ben have? Was it his total innocence that had protected him, that had not let him see what others *thought* they saw, not let him hear what others *thought* they heard.

He had never witnessed Alice's radiance, had never witnessed her levitate. *And he had not seen Elnor.* Nor felt the earth shake, nor watched the ground open. And he was not alone, for other children in the field that night had not shared their parents' and guardians' terror. Yet there were other young ones who had.

Fenn had felt his strength return when he touched the boy; so had Sue. It was as though their weakness had passed through him, the boy acting as a human conductor, and dissipating their weakness into the ground. Was innocence so powerful against such evil?

Whoever said that questions were more important than answers was a fool. Unanswered questions could drive you to insanity.

He forced himself to relax. Outside the windscreen, the sky was a clear Disney blue, the sun hazy, soft-edged. Even though there was no strength to its glow, it was painful to look at, and he shielded his eyes, resting his elbow on the windowsill. He was reminded of the glow he had seen at the shrine, the glimmering shining at the base of the tree; the one sight more than any other on that terrible night that constantly haunted him. Yet it was not an unpleasant haunting. Somehow it gave him courage. Something more. . . . Faith?

His hand scraped against his chin and he shifted in the seat in agitation.

Why did it disturb him so? Why, out of everything else that had happened, should this drive him to such distraction? Why had the thing called Elnor been so afraid when it, too, had seen the glow?

And had he really glimpsed the shadowy figure of a white-gowned woman within that radiance?

It couldn't be! He had suffered too many delusions that night! His mind had been filled with too many terrors! His own survival mechanism had suddenly worked against them, creating a different kind of illusion, one that spread calmness, peace, a vision that exuded a quiescent tranquillity.

Yet why had Ben, who had *not* seen the other horrors, asked later who the lovely lady in white was standing by the tree that night when everybody was screaming and the altar burned down?

Who was she?

Who was she?

What was she?

His eyes were closed, his hand covering them. He opened them, looked towards the church. Sue was leading Ben up the short flight of steps to the open doorway.

He clenched his fist and rapped his knuckles against his teeth. He opened the car door and strode towards the church gate. He hesitated.

Sue turned and saw him. She smiled.

And he strode up the path to join them. Together they went into the church of Our Lady of the Assumption.

> *Little Alice, sweet and pure*
> *Come see her if you need a cure*
> *She'll stop your boils and clear your head*
> *And smile sweetly when you're dead.*

NEW NURSERY RHYME

ACKNOWLEDGEMENTS

The Author and Publishers gratefully acknowledge permission to include the following extracts:

From 'The Little Creature', 'The Ogre', and 'The Ghost' by Walter de la Mare, by permission of the Literary Trustees of Walter de la Mare and the Society of Authors as their representative.

From *Alice's Adventures in Wonderland and Through the Looking Glass* by Lewis Carroll, published by Macmillan Ltd.

Old Nursery Rhymes in *The Oxford Nursery Rhyme Book*, published by Oxford University Press.

From 'The Crystal Cabinet' by William Blake, 'A Slumber did my Spirit Seal' by William Wordsworth, 'Wake all the Dead!' by Sir William Davenant, 'The Hag' by Robert Herrick and 'Alison Gross' and 'Jemima' in *The Faber Book of Children's Verse*, published by Faber and Faber.

From *The Secret Garden* by Frances Hodgson Burnett, published by Frederick Warne Publishers Ltd.

From 'The Juniper Tree', 'The Three Golden Hairs of the Devil', 'Rumpelstiltskin', 'The Goose Girl', 'Fitcher's Bird', 'Hansel and Gretel', and 'Little Snow White', in *The Brothers Grimm: Popular Folk Tales*, translated by Brian Alderson, by permission of Victor Gollancz Ltd.

From *Peter Pan* by J. M. Barrie, by permission of Hodder and Stoughton Children's Books, copyright © Great Ormond Street Hospital.

From 'The Little Mermaid', 'The Emperor's New Clothes' and 'The Snow Queen' by Hans Andersen in *Hans Andersen's Fairy Tales*, chosen by Naomi Lewis published by Puffin Books, copyright © 1981 Naomi Lewis.

From 'On a Lord' by Samuel Taylor Coleridge, 'Three Witches' Charms' by Ben Jonson, 'Look Out, Boys' by Oliver Wendell Holmes and 'Kehama's Curse' by Robert Southey in *The Beaver Book of Creepy Verse* chosen by Ian and Zinka Woodward, published by Hamlyn Paperbacks.

From *Pollyanna* by Eleanor H. Porter, by permission of Harrap Ltd.

From 'Shadow Bride' in *Adventures of Tom Bombadil* by J. R. R. Tolkien, by permission of George Allen & Unwin.

From 'The Two Witches' by Robert Graves in *Collected Poems* published by Cassell Ltd, by permission of Robert Graves.

From 'Grave by a Holm-oak' by Stevie Smith in *Collected Poems of Stevie Smith*, published by Allen Lane, by permission of James McGibbon, the executor of Stevie Smith, and the Publishers.

From 'The Curse be Ended' in *The Family Reunion* by T. S. Eliot by permission of Faber and Faber Ltd.

The Dark

PART ONE

. . . And God saw that the light was good; and God separated the light from the darkness . . .

Genesis 1:4
(R.S.V.)

It was a bright, sunny hot day. Not, you might have thought, the sort of day for hunting ghosts. Nor was the house the kind of house you might expect to be haunted. But then psychic phenomena pay scant attention to time, place, or weather.

It was a nice road, but ordinary, with that mid-morning, suburban quietness that areas only minutes away from high streets have. The houses themselves were an odd mixture of semis and detached buildings; bright new town houses sparkled at the far end, as yet undaunted by the daily grime.

I drove slowly down the road, looking for the right house, and drew into the kerb when I saw the sign. 'Beechwood'. Unimpressive.

This was one of the detached buildings, tall, grey-bricked, Victorian. I took off my driving glasses and slipped them into the glove compartment; then I rubbed my eyes and settled back to study the house for a few moments.

The small area in front, which obviously had been a garden at one time, had been concreted over to provide an off-the-road parking space for cars; but there were no cars there. I had been told the house would be empty. The windows were opaque from the glare of the sun and for a brief, uneasy moment, it seemed the house itself was staring out at me through mirror sunglasses.

I quickly shrugged off the feeling — imagination could sometimes be a hindrance in my job — and reached over to the back seat. The black case was neither large nor heavy, but it contained most of the equipment I would need. The air had a deceptive edge to it when I stepped out on to the pavement, a hint that winter would soon have its turn. A woman whose small child preferred to skip rather than walk gave me a curious look as they passed by, as though my presence in her road had broken a routine. I nodded but the contact made her lose interest.

After locking my car, I crossed the concrete area and climbed the five stone steps leading to the front door. There I paused, placing the case by my feet, and searched for the key. I found it and dropped it. The attached faded address card flapped loosely in the air when I retrieved the key and inserted it into the lock. For some reason I stopped and listened before I pushed the heavy door open, peering uselessly through the leaded glass of its top section. There were no sounds and no moving shadows.

I wasn't nervous, nor even apprehensive, for I saw no reason to be. I suppose my initial hesitation was simply due to caution. Empty houses had always made me so. The door swung open and, picking up my case, I stepped inside. I closed the door behind me.

The rays of the sun shone brilliantly through the leaded glass of the door and windows on either side, casting my own shadow deeply and well-defined along the hallway. A broad staircase, its ascent beginning only five feet from where I stood, disappeared into the upper portion of the house, and near the top, from the overhang of the first floor, there dangled a pair of legs.

One shoe — a man's — had fallen off and lay on its side halfway down the stairs; I could see the heel of the man's sock was worn, the pink flesh almost visible through the punctured material. The wall beside the hanging legs was scuffed and blackened as though it had been marked by the man's death-throes. I remember dropping my case and walking slowly down the hall, craning my head upwards, not wishing to mount the stairs, but strangely curious to see the rest of the corpse. I remember peering into the gloom of the stairwell and seeing the bloated face above the grotesquely stretched neck, the ridiculously small loop of plastic flex, no more than three inches in diameter, biting into his flesh as though someone had tugged at his legs to pull it tight. I remember the smell of death coming to me, subtle yet cloying, elusive but all around. It was fresh, unlike the heavy, pungent odour of stale corpses.

I backed away and stopped when I came into contact with the edge of the open doorway opposite the staircase. I turned in surprise and looked into the room; the others were in there, some lying on the floor, some sprawled in armchairs, some upright, staring, as though watching me. But they were all dead. I knew it was not just from the smell, the unseeing eyes, the mutilated bodies. I knew it from the stagnant atmosphere, the stillness of the room itself.

I pushed myself away from the door, sliding my body along the wall for support, my legs suddenly weak. A movement ahead made me stop and I saw there was a small door beneath the staircase. I could only go forward towards the sun-filled front door, not daring to rush back into the depths of the house. The door under the stairs moved again, only slightly, and I realized a draught was disturbing it. I moved closer, keeping my back pressed hard against the wall, and soon I was level with the small opening, sliding past, going beyond it. And then, for some reason still unknown to me, I reached out and pulled the door open, its back slamming against the rising staircase, rebounding so it half closed again. I thought I saw movement but perhaps it was only the shadows receding from the sudden light.

There were stairs leading down to what must have been the cellar. All I could see was the blackness down there, a deep, almost solid darkness. And it was the darkness more than the corpses that made me flee from the house . . .

ONE

She sat at the kitchen table, lonely, brooding. She knew she had to face up to it: their life together was no good, it never would be. The idea of moving into the new town house seemed fine at the time; she thought a real home of their own would change his attitude. No more drab flats where everything mended, everything painted, was for the benefit of the landlord. A chance to build something solid, a foundation for their relationship. Marriage didn't matter to her, she'd never pressure him. But the house was right for children . . .

They had snapped up the chance of buying the place, for property prices were constantly soaring, reaching an unbelievable level, settling for a few months, then continuing their relentless upward flight. They had been hesitant about asking the agent to repeat the purchase price again, almost afraid he would realize his mistake and add on an extra three or four thousand. He had confirmed the original cost.

Richard had been a little suspicious and she had stepped in quickly with a firm offer. Whatever unseen drawbacks there might be, this was at least a new start for them. Besides, it was mostly her savings that would pay the ten per cent demanded by the building society towards the cost of the property. The existing owners had already moved out – 'Gone abroad,' said the agent – so within a month they had settled themselves in. It wasn't long before the rumours reached them.

She looked down at the empty Diazepan container before her on the table, picking it up and twisting the plastic tube between her fingers. There had been seven left that morning. She had steadily cut down the valium tablets, making progress, moving away from her breakdown of six months ago, suppressing the memory, coping. But Richard hadn't changed. Her near self-destruction had only stemmed the flow briefly; his old ways had soon come slinking back. His excuse was the house now, the road, the other houses. The place made him uneasy, people were unfriendly. Others were moving away – at least three families in the two months they had lived there. There was something wrong with the road.

She had felt it too, almost as soon as they had moved in, but her uneasiness had been quelled by her new hope. Things were meant to change, to become better; instead they had become worse. His drinking had always been hard to take, but bearable – his job as a rep for a finished-art studio demanded he drank with clients, anyway. The women he occasionally slept with didn't matter to her anymore – knowing his inadequacy, she doubted he even enjoyed himself. It was his resentment that had become impossible to live with.

He resented being trapped by the responsibility of owning a home, resented being in debt to a building society, resented her demands, both physical and mental, on him. He resented being the cause of her breakdown.

Now that she had finally come to bear the physical marks of his bitterness – bruising, scratchmarks – she knew it had to end, it was pointless going on. Even though they were not married, the house was in their joint names. But who would be the one to go? Would she come out with nothing after four years of torment? If he insisted, she knew she couldn't stand up to him. She smashed the empty tube down on to the kitchen table. The pills hadn't helped at all.

She stood, her chair scraping harshly against the tiled kitchen floor, and strode towards the sink. She filled the kettle, water splashing fiercely off the metal side, soaking her blouse. She swore, dumping the kettle on the gas ring. After switching on the gas she reached for her cigarettes, the packet lying open on the breadboard. She snatched one out and thrust the end into the gas flame, then quickly into her mouth, drawing her breath in sharply to make it light. Her fingers drummed against the aluminium draining-board, becoming more rigid as she tapped until it was her fist beating down, harder and harder, the sound echoing around the small kitchen. It stopped when a tear slid from her face on to her thinly covered breast, the single damp sensation more disturbing than the overall tap splatter of a few moments earlier. But one tear was all she would allow herself. She rubbed a hand roughly against her eyes, then drew in deeply on the cigarette, looking out through the window into the street below, the lights casting isolated silver pools along its length. Would he come home tonight? She was no longer sure if she even cared. She would have her coffee and go to bed; there she would decide what to do.

She lit another cigarette – the last one, she noticed with annoyance – before carrying the coffee through the kitchen towards the stairs leading to the bedroom. The town house consisted of three floors, the ground being the garage and back workroom, the second level the kitchen and lounge-dining area, the third the two bedrooms and bathroom. She paused at the top of the stairs descending to the front door: should she lock him out? Steam rose in spiralling wisps from the coffee as she pondered. Abruptly she stepped on to the top stair, her mind made up and, just as abruptly, her hand grasped tightly around the balustrade. It was dark down there.

Normally light shone in from the outside street-lamp through the reeded glass door, bathing the tiny hallway in its diffused light. Now she could only see a heavy blackness. Strange, she hadn't noticed the street-light not working from the kitchen. Twisting her body, she flicked on the switch controlling the downstairs light. Nothing happened, but sudden movement caused hot coffee to spill over on to her fingers. She gasped with shock and quickly changed the mug over to her other hand, sticking her burnt fingers into her mouth to lick the offending liquid off. The pain served to remind her of the pain she might receive if she did lock Richard out. She stepped back on to the landing and walked down the hallway, her troubled mind not noticing the bright artificial light shining through the hall window from the street-lamp outside.

Pinky Burton was still angry. The boys in the house opposite had no right to call him such names. They were nothing more than pimply-faced louts, yobbos. He couldn't understand why he had even bothered to be friendly with the younger one, the one with the long, golden locks. Golden when he bothered to wash his unruly mop, that is. Neither had any respect for their elders, not even their father. Father? God, it was little wonder the boys were so offensive with a big abrasive man like that as a father. It was hardly surprising the brute's wife had run off years ago. She obviously couldn't stand any of them.

It used to be a nice respectable road at one time, before the riff-raff moved in. He could remember when one had to have wealth to live in this road, and every family was respectable. And respected. These two gutter-snipes certainly had no respect for him. It was nonsense to suggest he would take the time and trouble to spy on them. Perhaps he had watched them sometimes as they had worked, stripped to the waist, on the older one's motor-cycle. What of it? He was interested in machinery, always had been since his RAF days. The younger one wasn't so bad at first – at least one could have a conversation with him – but the other yobbo, the sneery one, had obviously influenced his brother. How dare they suggest . . . just because a man . . . *how did they find out about that, anyway?*

Pinky turned over in bed and pulled the covers up over his ears. The road was full of nastiness. Never used to be. Nasty modern boxes they called town houses at one end, the old, bigger houses becoming dilapidated, allowed to run down; and greasy-haired louts like those two roaring up and down all night on motorbikes. Well, perhaps they were the only two, and they had one machine between them, but they still made enough noise for a dozen or more. And then there was the house further down, the big detached one – what on earth could have caused something like that? Totally unbelievable. Totally insane. Sign of the times. New – worse – atrocities every day. Made one wonder if there was any goodness at all left in the world. But nothing could match the inhumanity he had found in . . . Pinky still found it hard to form the word in his mind. Why had they sent him there? Hadn't he done enough for his country in the last war? Had it been necessary to punish him so harshly for one misdemeanour? The child had suffered no real harm. All right, so there had been other minor offences to take into account. But they *were* minor, small lapses on his part. It wasn't as if he had ever actually hurt anyone. The degradation inside that . . . place. The degenerates. The vicious, mean bullyboys. To put a man like him alongside such animals. And when he had been released after months that seemed like a thousand years, his position at the club had gone. None of the members had rallied round to support him as their bar manager. No, it was the cold shoulder, them and their bloody tweeds and afternoon golf, their bloody cocker spaniels and crusty-fannied wives. People he had known for years saying nasty, spiteful things. Thank God mother had left the house – thank God she was long dead before it all came out. The shock would have killed her. He would never have been able to afford the place on the measly sum he earned as a part-time barman. And it was humiliating to be on a 'suspect list' of sex offenders. When any crime was committed in the area that had any sexual connotations he could be sure of a police visit. Routine inquiries they always said. Well it wasn't bloody routine to him!

He turned over restlessly on to his back and stared hatefully at the light patterns on the ceiling. The nebulous shapes shivered as a breeze disturbed the leaves on the tree outside, giving the reflected light from the street-lamp a living, embryonic quality. Pinky swore at the ceiling.

The jeers, the sly insinuations, from the two louts over the road had cut deep that day. His other neighbours had always treated him with respect, had always politely acknowledged his greetings, had never pried into his affairs. But these . . . these scumbags had shouted out their obscenities for the whole world to hear, had laughed at him when his own temper had forced him to run back indoors. He did not know what he might have done if he hadn't. Well, tomorrow the police would be informed of the racket they made with their infernal machine. He was still a citizen and, as such, entitled to his rights. Just because he had made a mistake once, it didn't mean he had lost his civil rights! He bit into his lip and choked back a sob. He knew he would never venture into a police station again, not of his own volition. Those bastards, those dirty, little, long-haired bastards!

Pinky closed his eyes tightly and when he opened them, wondered why it had become so dark, why the patterns on the ceiling had disappeared.

She knelt on the bed, a small, huddled form. Susie was small for an eleven-year-old, but her eyes sometimes had a knowing look of someone way beyond her years. At other times they were completely blank. She pulled methodically at the hair of her Cindy doll, the silver strands falling on to her lap. Glass-mounted pictures of Beatrix Potter animals gazed down impassively at her from the blue walls of her little bedroom, oblivious of the sharp snap as a plastic arm was wrenched from the doll's body. The tiny limb bounced off Peter Rabbit and clattered to the floor. Susie pulled at the other arm and threw this, too, across the room, towards the closed window. It fell on to her toy chest beneath the window and lay there, the hand bent back supplicatingly on its swivel-joint.

'Naughty girl, Cindy,' Susie scolded in hushed anger. 'You mustn't stare when you're at the dinner table! Mummy doesn't like it!'

The doll's expression did not change as her leg was pulled back and tugged. 'I've told you time and time again, You mustn't smirk when Uncle Jeremy tells you off! He doesn't like it – it makes him angry. It makes Mummy angry, too!' The leg came away with a sucking sound and was tossed towards the door. 'Uncle Jeremy will go away and leave Mummy if he gets cross. Then Mummy will send me away. She'll tell the doctors I've been acting bad again.' Susie drew in a deep breath at the effort of tearing the last limb free, her small body sagging into a relaxed position when her exertions were rewarded.

'There! Now you can't run away and you can't get into mischief.' Susie smiled triumphantly, but her happiness lasted only seconds. 'I hate that place, Cindy! It's nasty. And the doctors and the nurses are nasty. I don't want to go there again.' Her eyes became tearful, then her face suddenly screwed itself up into an expression of spiteful anger. 'He's not my uncle, anyway. He just wants cuddles from Mummy. He hates me and he hates my Dad! Why doesn't Daddy come back, Cindy? Why does he hate me too? I wouldn't touch matches ever again if he came back, Cindy, I promise I wouldn't.'

She fiercely hugged the limbless doll and rocked to and fro on her knees. 'You know I wouldn't don't you, Cindy? You know I wouldn't.' There was no reply from the doll and Susie thrust it away from her in disgust. 'You never answer me, you naughty girl! You never show you love me!'

She pulled at the pretty plastic head, her arms quivering with the effort, a scream building up in her throat. She suppressed her cry as the head popped free and laughed when she threw it at the stars outside the window. Her body went rigid as the doll's head rebounded off the pane and rolled to the floor. She dared not breathe for a few moments as she listened for footsteps to come thumping along the corridor. She sighed with relief when no such sounds came. They were both asleep. Him, with her, in Daddy's bed. The thought made her angry again. It wasn't just cuddles he wanted. He did other things. She knew, she'd heard, she'd watched.

Susie sprang from the bed and padded towards the window, careful not to disturb the toys lying scattered in the dark on the bedroom floor. She examined the pane of glass which had been struck by the doll's head, looking for a crack to show up against the stars outside. It would mean more misery for her if the glass had been broken. She grinned when she saw there was no damage.

Pressing her face to the window she tried to pierce the gloom of the garden below. She spent most of the summer days there when she wasn't at the special

school; a prisoner, not allowed to go out on her own. Susie could just make out
the shape of the rabbit hutch, weather-beaten and empty, not understanding
why they had taken the rabbits away. The baby ones had been gorgeous, lovely
to hold, to squeeze. Perhaps if she hadn't squeezed so hard they would have let
her keep them.

She returned to the bed and squatted on it, ankles crossed, her arms hugged
around her raised knees. The blankets lay rumpled around her. If Uncle Jeremy
went away, perhaps Daddy would come back. They could all live together again
and be happy, like before. Like before the time she'd been *really* naughty. Before
the trouble.

Susie lay back in the bed, pulling the clothes up around her. She gripped the
silky edge of the blanket and brushed it rhythmically against her cheek, staring
out into the deep blue night framed by the window's edges. One by one she
began to count the stars, determined this time to number every one in the
rectangle before falling asleep. And one by one, as she silently counted, the stars
went out, until only blackness filled the window-frame.

TWO

Bishop glanced discreetly at his watch and was relieved that the two-hour
lecture was nearly up. Usual mixed bunch, he thought wryly. Most of them
deadly serious, several just curious, one – maybe two – sceptics. And, of course,
the token headcase. He smiled generally at the gathering in the small lecture
hall.

'So you can see by my list of equipment on the blackboard, parapsychology –
the study of paraphysical phenomena – uses technology rather than the more
unreliable and, if I may say so, the dubious spiritualistic methods. Graph paper
will usually tell you more about strange disturbances in a house than self-
imposed mental trances.'

A nervous hand fluttered in the air from the second row. Bishop noticed the
man wore a clerical collar. 'May I, er, ask a question?' the equally nervous voice
said. All eyes turned to look at the cleric who steadfastly kept his eyes riveted on
Bishop's as if embarrassed by his own presence.

'Please do,' Bishop encouraged. 'In fact, we'll spend the last ten minutes
discussing any points you might want to raise.'

'Well, it was just that for someone whose profession is the investigation of the
paranormal or paraphysical . . .'

'Call it ghost-hunting – it's simpler,' said Bishop.

'Yes, ghost-hunting. Well, it hasn't really been made clear by you whether or
not you actually believe in ghosts.'

Bishop smiled. 'The truth of the matter is, having been involved in the study of
parapsychology for some years, I'm still unsure. Certainly I've come up against
the inexplicable time and time again, but every day science is uncovering new
facts about our own powers. Somebody once said that mysticism is just
tomorrow's science dreamed today. I think I'd go along with that. For instance,

we know concentrated thought, or often unconscious thought, can physically move objects. Scientists throughout the world, particularly in Russia, are now studying the psychokinetic power. Years ago it would have been called witchcraft.'

'But how does that explain spirit sightings?' A middle-aged woman, plump and pleasant looking, had asked the question. 'There are so many cases of hauntings you hear about practically every day.'

'Perhaps not every day, but there are between two and three hundred sightings each year, and probably just as many not publicised. One of the many theories is that ghosts are caused by someone under stress, their minds giving out electrical impulses in the way the heart does, and these impulses are picked up later in particular circumstances.'

The puzzled frown on the woman's face and on the faces of several others in his audience told Bishop he wasn't making himself clear. 'It's rather like a mental picture being transmitted by one individual to be picked up later by someone else who acts as a kind of receiver. Like a television set. This could explain why apparitions are often misty, faded or why sometimes only faces or hands appear: the pictures, or transmissions, if you like, are wearing out, fading until there's nothing left.'

'What about places that have been haunted for centuries, then?' said a young, bearded man in the front row, who was leaning forward antagonistically. 'Why haven't they just faded away?'

'It could be explained by regeneration: the transmission, or apparition, draws on energy from electrical impulses that surround us all. This could account for the appearance of a ghost. A spirit can "live" on indefinitely as long as its image can be seen by others: the ghost is actually telepathic waves, the image created in the mind of a living person years, days, perhaps centuries before and transmitted into the mind or minds of others living today.'

Bishop sighed inwardly: he could see he was losing them. They hadn't expected him to explain ghosts as a scientific phenomenon. They wanted the subject romanticized, the mystic aspect heightened. Even the sceptics among them looked disappointed.

'You're putting it down to electricity, then?' The bearded man in the front row sat back and folded his arms, the slightest indication of smugness in his smile.

'No, not exactly. But an electrical charge given to the nerve tissues of the brain can make a subject see flashes or hear noises. It would seem that a charge given to the appropriate receptive area of the brain can create a phantom image. Remember, the brain functions through electrical impulses and we're also surrounded by them. Impulses picked out of the air by our senses – that's us acting as receivers – isn't a difficult concept to understand. You may have heard of crisis apparitions, where someone sees an image of a friend or relative who is going through some traumatic experience, perhaps dying, many miles away. A voice may even be heard at the same time.'

A few heads nodded appreciatively.

'This can be explained by the person who is undergoing that extreme moment of stress thinking of the person closest to him, perhaps calling out to them. At such times, brain-waves are extremely active – this has been proved by the use of electro-encephalograph machines. When they reach a certain pitch a telepathic image can often be transmitted either to a recipient or into the atmosphere. New factors concerning our own brain power are being brought to light by science at an ever-increasing rate. My guess is that by the end of the century, mysticism and technology will be one. There really will be no such thing as "ghosts".'

A low murmur ran through the gathering as they looked around at each other with various expressions of bemusement, disappointment, or satisfaction.

'Mr Bishop?' The woman's voice came from the back row and Bishop squinted his eyes to see her more clearly. 'Mr Bishop, you term yourself as a ghost-hunter. Can you tell us, then, why you've spent so many years hunting electrical impulses?'

A small ripple of laughter ran through the audience and Bishop smiled with them. He decided to use his reply as a closing statement for the lecture.

'I'm involved in the investigation of hauntings because I believe they have special significance. All phenomena have some rational explanation – it's just that we are not yet advanced enough to perceive that explanation. Any useful information we can gain towards those ends must have value. Mankind is at an exciting stage of development where science and the paranormal are heading towards a meeting point. We have reached the time where parapsychology has to be taken seriously and studied logically with all the advanced technology we have at hand. We can no longer afford to tolerate the fools, the romantics, the misguided; even less can we tolerate the charlatans, the professional ghost-seers, or the mediums who live off the ignorance and distress of others. The breakthrough is nearly here and cannot be allowed hindrance by these people.'

His last words induced a smattering of polite applause from the audience. He held up a hand to let them know he had not quite finished.

'There's one other point. Many people have been emotionally disturbed or frightened by evidence of the paranormal, by "ghostly" appearances: if I can help them understand such occurrences and not to fear them, then that alone justifies my work. Now, I have a list of organizations dealing in physical research, paraphysical studies, metaphysical and ESP research groups and plain old ghost-hunting organizations. There's also a couple of addresses where you can find your own ghost-hunting equipment. Please help yourself to a copy before you leave.'

He turned his back on them, shuffled his lecture notes together and placed them in his briefcase. As usual, his throat was dry after the two-hour talk, and his thoughts now were only of the tall glass of beer that would soothe it. He hardly knew this town, but he hoped the pubs were decent. First, though, he had the gauntlet to run, for there were always those eager to continue the debate on a more personal level long after the allotted time was up. The chief librarian, who had arranged the series of talks in the town library's lecture hall, was the first to come forward.

'Most interesting, Mr Bishop. I'm sure next week's attendance figure will be even higher once word gets around.'

Bishop smiled cynically. He wondered if there would be half as many judging by the disappointment on some of the faces.

'I'm afraid they didn't hear quite what they expected to,' he said without apology.

'Oh no, on the contrary, I think many now realize just what a serious subject the whole matter is.' The librarian rubbed his hands together as if in glee. 'I must say, you've certainly whet my appetite. Let me tell you of the strange experience I had just a few years ago . . .'

Bishop listened politely, knowing he would have to hear several 'strange experiences' from the others in the hall before he could take his leave. As an authority on the subject, he was constantly used as a kind of father confessor by the many who had witnessed real or imaginary phenomena. A small group had soon gathered round and he answered their questions, encouraging them to make a serious study of the paranormal themselves. He also reminded them to keep an open mind and to maintain a careful balance between belief and scepticism. One or two expressed their surprise at his own reservations and he informed them his researches had always been more clinical than biased. The fact that a few years ago an American university had offered £80,000 to anyone who could prove conclusively that there was life after death and as yet the amount was still unclaimed had to have some significance. There was much evidence but still no substantial proof and, although he believed in the continuance of life after death *in some form*, he was still unsure there was a spirit world in the sense of latter- and present-day concepts. While he spoke, he saw the woman who had asked the final question of the lecture period sitting alone at the back of the hall. He wondered why she hadn't joined the group. Eventually, Bishop was able to disengage himself from his inquisitors, mumbling that he had some distance to travel that night and further questions could be asked during the course of the following lectures. Briefcase in hand, he strode briskly down the centre aisle towards the exit. The woman's eyes gazed at him fixedly and when he drew near, she rose from her seat. 'Could I talk to you for just a moment, Mr Bishop?'

He glanced down at his watch as though worried about a pending appointment. 'I really haven't the time now. Perhaps next week . . .?'

'My name is Jessica Kulek. My father, Jacob Kulek, is . . .'

'Is founder and president of the Research Institute of Parapsychological Study.' Bishop had stopped and was looking at the woman curiously as she made her way from her seat towards him.

'You've heard of him?' she said.

'Who in the field of psychical research hasn't? He was one of the men who helped Professor Dean to persuade the American Association for the Advancement of Science to finally accept parapsychologists as members. It was a giant step in forcing scientists throughout the world to take the paranormal seriously. It gave the whole business credibility.'

She gave him the briefest of smiles and he realized she was younger and more attractive than he had at first thought from a distance. Her hair, neither dark nor fair, was short and tucked in closely to the nape of her neck, her fringe cropped high and neatly across her forehead. The tweed suit she wore was stylishly cut and emphasized her slim figure, perhaps too much so – she seemed too slender, frail even. Her eyes were made to look larger by the thinness of her face and her lips were small but finely drawn, like a child's. She seemed hesitant, almost nervous now, yet he felt there was a determination about her that was belied by her appearance.

'I hope my comment didn't offend you,' she said, an earnestness in her expression.

'Hunting electrical impulses? No, I'm not offended. In a way you're right: I am hunting electrical impulses half the time. The other half is spent searching for draughts, land subsidence and water seepages.'

'Could we talk privately for a few moments? Are you staying here tonight? Perhaps your hotel?'

He grinned. 'I'm afraid my talks don't pay well enough for me to stay overnight in hotels. I'd have nothing left over from the evening's work if I did. No, I'll have to drive back home tonight.'

'It's really very important. My father asked me to see you.'

Bishop paused before answering. Finally, he said, 'Can you tell me what it's about?'

'Not here.'

He made up his mind. 'Okay. I'd intended to have a drink before I hit the road, so why not join me? We'd better make our exit fast, though, before the throng back there catches us up.' He pointed over his shoulder at the remaining group of chattering people who were gradually edging their way down the aisle. Bishop took her arm and guided her towards the door.

'You're a little cynical about your profession, aren't you?' she said as they descended the library steps, the cold night drizzle dampening their faces.

'Yes,' he answered brusquely.

'Can you tell me why?'

'Look, let's find a pub and get out of the rain. Then I'll answer your question.'

They walked for five minutes in silence before finding a welcoming pub sign. He led her inside and found a quiet corner table.

'What would you like?' he asked.

'Just orange juice, please.' There was a slight hostility in her tone.

He returned with the drinks, placing the orange juice on the table before her, sinking into the chair opposite with a grateful sigh. He took a long, satisfying swallow of beer before looking across at her.

'Are you involved in your father's research?' he asked.

'Yes, I work with him. You were going to answer my question.'

He was irritated by her persistence. 'Is it important? Has it anything to do with your father asking you to see me?'

'No, I'm just curious, that's all.'

'I'm not cynical about my job – I'm just cynical about the people I come in contact with. Most of them are either fools or publicity seekers. I don't know who are the worse.'

'But you have a good reputation as a psychic investigator. Your two books on the subject are standard reading for any student of the paranormal. How can you deride others who follow the same pursuits as yourself.'

'I don't. It's the fanatics, the idiots steeped in mumbo-jumbo mysticism, and the fools who turn the whole thing into a religion that I despise. The people they prey on, I just feel sorry for. If you've read my books you'll know they're directed towards realism and away from mysticism. For Christ's sake, I've just spent two hours talking about that very thing!'

She flinched at his raised voice and he immediately regretted his impatience. But she came back at him, her lips tight with her own suppressed anger.

'Then why don't you do something more constructive about it? The Society for Psychical Research and other organizations wanted you as a member. Your work could have been invaluable to them. As a ghost-hunter, as you like to call yourself, you're one of the foremost in your field, your services are in great demand. So why do you disassociate yourself from others in your profession, others who could help you?'

Bishop leaned back in his seat. 'You've been checking up on me,' he said simply.

'Yes, my father asked me to. I'm sorry, Mr Bishop, we didn't mean to pry. We just wanted to find out more about your background.'

'Isn't it time you told me why you came here tonight? What does Jacob Kulek want with me?'

'Your help.'

'My help? Jacob Kulek wants *my* help?'

The girl nodded and Bishop laughed aloud.

'I'm truly flattered, Miss Kulek, but I don't think there's much about psychic phenomena that I could tell your father.'

'He doesn't expect you to. It's a different kind of information he wants. I promise you, it's important.'

'Not important enough for him to come himself.'

She looked down into her glass. 'It's not easy for him nowadays. He would have come, but I convinced him I could persuade you to see him.'

'It's all right,' Bishop conceded. 'I realize he must be a busy man . . .'

'Oh no, it isn't that. He's blind, you see. I don't like him to travel unless it's absolutely necessary.'

'I didn't know. I'm sorry, Miss Kulek. I didn't mean to be so blunt. How long . . .?'

'Six years. Chronic glaucoma. The nerve structure was already severely damaged before they diagnosed the disease. He'd left it too late before consulting a specialist – he put his blurred vision down to old age and hard work. By the time they realized the real cause, the optic nerves were too far gone.' She sipped her orange juice, then looked at him defiantly. 'He still goes on lecture tours both here and in America and, as head of the Institute, with its growing membership, his days are even more active than before.'

'But if he knows I want nothing to do with organizations such as yours, what makes him think I'd want to help?'

'Because your thinking is not that much different from his. He was once an important member of the Society for Psychical Research until he felt their ideas were at variance with his own. He rejected them too, Mr Bishop, to form his own organization, the Research Institute of Parapsychological Study. He wanted to research phenomena such as telepathy and clairvoyance to find out if the mind can gain knowledge by means other than the normal perceptual processes. It has nothing to do with ghosts and goblins.'

'All right, so what information does he want from me?'

'He wants you to tell him exactly what you found in Beechwood.'

Bishop's face paled and he quickly reached for his beer. The girl watched him as he drained the glass.

'That was nearly a year ago,' he said carefully placing the empty glass back on the table. 'I thought it had been forgotten by now.'

'The memory has been revived, Mr Bishop. Have you seen today's papers?'

'No, I've been travelling most of the day. I haven't had a chance to.'

She reached for her shoulder-bag which was propped up against a table leg and drew out a folded newspaper. Opening it, she pointed to the main news item on an inside page. He quickly scanned the bold headline: 'TRIPLE TRAGEDY IN HORROR ROAD'.

He looked inquiringly at the girl.

'Willow Road, Mr Bishop. Where the Beechwood house is.' His eyes returned to the open newspaper, but she told him the details of the story herself.

'Two teenage brothers were blasted by a shotgun last night while they slept. One died instantly, the other is now in hospital in a critical condition. His father is there with him, half his face blown away when he attacked the assailant. He is not expected to live. The madman who did it is in police custody but as yet no statement has been released.

'A fire, which started in the kitchen of a house nearby, burnt through the floor of the bedroom above. The two sleeping people, presumably husband and wife, fell through when the floor collapsed and were burnt to death. Firemen found a little girl in the garden outside watching the flames, petrified with shock. It's not yet known how the fire started.

'In another house, near the end of Willow Road, a woman knifed her common-law husband to death. She then cut her own throat. Their milkman apparently saw the bodies lying on the hall stairs through the glass front door. The report says the woman was in her nightclothes and the man was fully dressed as though he had just come home when she attacked him.'

She paused as if to let the related events sink in. 'All this in one night, Mr Bishop, and all in Willow Road.'

'But it can't have anything to do with the other business. Christ, that was a year ago!'

'Nine months to be exact.'

'So how can there be any connection?'

'My father believes there is. That's why he wants you to tell him everything about the day you went to Beechwood.'

Just the name made him feel uncomfortable. The memory was still too fresh in his mind, the terrible sight he'd witnessed inside the old house still filling his vision like a suddenly projected film slide. 'I told the police everything that happened that day, why I was there, who had hired me. Everything I saw. There's nothing new I can tell your father.'

'He thinks there might be. There has to be something, some explanation. There has to be a reason for thirty-seven people committing mass suicide in one house. And *why* that house, Mr Bishop.'

He could only look down at his empty glass, suddenly feeling the need for something much stronger than beer.

THREE

Jacob Kulek was tall even though stooped, his head thrust forward as if in a constantly inquiring gesture. The ill-fitting suit he wore seemed to hang from his thin frame in draped folds, his shirt collar and tie joining loosely at the very base of his neck. He rose when his daughter showed Bishop into the small room he used as a private study at the Research Institute, the building itself almost anonymous in the medical and financial ghetto of Wimpole Street.

'Thank you for coming to see me, Mr Bishop,' he said, extending a hand.

Bishop was surprised at the firmness of his grip. A muted voice – he realized it was Jessica Kulek's – came from a pocket-size cassette-recorder lying on a low coffee table beside Kulek's easychair. The tall man reached down and switched off the machine, his fingers finding the stop button without fumbling.

'Jessica spends an hour each evening recording for me,' he explained, looking directly into Bishop's eyes as if scrutinizing him. It was hard to believe he could not see. 'New research information, business correspondence – general matters that fail to receive my attention during the day. Jessica unselfishly shares her vision with me.' He smiled at his daughter, instinctively knowing where she stood.

'Please seat yourself, Mr Bishop,' Jessica said, motioning towards another easychair facing her father's across the coffee table. 'Would you like some coffee – tea?'

He shook his head. 'No, I'm fine, thanks.' As he sat, Bishop glanced around the room; nearly every inch of space on the walls was taken up by volumes of books. It seemed ironic that a man with a mind like Kulek's should surround himself with what must have been the greatest source of frustration imposed by his infirmity.

As if reading his thoughts, Kulek waved a hand generally towards the book-covered walls. 'I know every work in this room, Mr Bishop. Even its position on the shelves. *Masonic, Hermetic, Quabbalistic and Rosicrucian Symbolic Philosophy* – middle bookcase of right-hand wall, third shelf up, seventh or eighth book along. *The Golden Bough* – end bookcase by the door, top shelf, somewhere in the centre. Every book here is important to me, every one taken from those shelves many times before my blindness. It seems that without vision, the mind is more free to turn inwards, to examine more closely one's memory. There are compensations for everything.'

'Your blindness doesn't seem to have affected your work,' Bishop said.

Kulek gave a short laugh. 'I'm afraid it is a hindrance. There are so many new concepts, so many old theories abandoned – Jessica and our little machine have to keep me aware of the changes in thought. My legs are not as strong as they used to be, either. My trusty cane serves both as a guide and a crutch.' He patted the stout walking-stick leaning against the chair almost as though it were a pet animal. 'I have reluctantly cut down on my lecture tours at my daughter's insistence. She likes to have me where she can keep an eye on me.' He smiled reprovingly at his daughter and Bishop felt the closeness between them. The girl had seated herself in a high-backed chair near one of the two windows in the small study as if she were to be an observer only of the conversation about to take place.

'My father would work twenty-two hours a day if I allowed him,' she said. 'The other two he would spend talking about the next day's work.'

Kulek chuckled. 'She is probably right. However, Mr Bishop, to the matter at hand.' His forehead creased into deep lines of concern and his shoulders became even more stooped as he leaned forward. Again, Bishop had to remind himself of Kulek's blindness as his eyes bore into him.

'I believe Jessica showed you the news item on Willow Road last night.'

Bishop nodded, then remembered to voice his affirmation.

'And have you seen this morning's papers?'

'Yes. The man who shot the boys and their father apparently refuses to speak to anyone. The little girl whose parents – no, it turned out to be the mother and her boyfriend – died in the fire is still in a state of shock. The woman who knifed her lover committed suicide, of course, so it can only be assumed that the motive was jealousy or a dispute between them.'

'Ah yes, motive,' said Kulek. 'So it would seem the police have not established a clear motive for each case.'

'There wouldn't be one for all of them. Don't forget, the mother and her boyfriend were killed in the fire. The girl was lucky to get out alive. There's no mention of arson.'

Kulek was silent for a few moments, then he said. 'Don't you think it's rather strange for these three bizarre events to happen on the same night and in the same road?'

'Of course it is. It would be strange if two murders happened over the course of several years in the same road, let alone on the same night. But how could there possibly be a connection between them?'

'On the surface, I agree, there seems to be none other than the time and location. And, of course, the fact that mass self-destruction took place in that same place only months ago. Why were you asked to investigate Beechwood?'

The abruptness of the question startled Bishop. 'Mr Kulek, don't you think you should tell me why you're so interested in the events of Willow Road?'

Kulek smiled disarmingly. 'You're quite right, I have no right to question you without giving you some explanation. Let me just say I have reason to believe the incidents in Willow Road and the suicides of nine months ago have some connection. Have you heard of the name Boris Pryszlak?'

'Pryszlak? Yes, he was one of the men who killed himself in Beechwood. Wasn't he a scientist?'

'Scientist, industrialist – he was an unusual combination of both. He had two main interests in life: making money and the study of energy. A dedicated man in both pursuits. He was an innovator, Mr Bishop, and a man who could turn his scientific achievements into hard cash. A rare man indeed.'

Kulek paused, a curious, hard smile on his lips as if he had a mental picture of the man he spoke of and the memory was unpleasant. 'We met in England in 1946, just before the Communist regime was established in Poland, our homeland. We were refugees: we had realized what was about to happen to our ravaged country. Even then, I could not say he was the kind of man I would choose as a friend, but . . .' he shrugged his shoulders. '. . . we were fellow countrymen and homeless. The situation itself formed our relationship.'

Bishop found it difficult to return Kulek's stare, for the sightless eyes were unwavering. He felt a little unnerved by them. He glanced across at the girl, and she smiled encouragingly, understanding his discomfort.

'One of the other factors that drew us together was our shared interest in the occult.'

Bishop's eyes quickly went back to Kulek. 'Pryszlak, a scientist, believed in the occult?'

'As I said, Mr Bishop, he was a most unusual man. We were friends for a few years – no, perhaps acquaintances would be a better word – then, because our ideas on so many matters differed, we went our separate ways. I settled in this country for a while, married Jessica's late mother, and eventually went to the United States where I joined the Philosophical Research Society under the leadership of Manly Palmer Hall. I heard nothing from or of Pryszlak during those years. Nothing, in fact, until after I returned to England ten years ago. He came to me with a man called Kirkhope and invited me to join their very private organization. I'm afraid I neither agreed with the direction in which their research was taking them, nor had any sympathy for it.'

'You said the other man's name was Kirkhope. Would that be Dominic Kirkhope?'

Kulek nodded. 'Yes, Mr Bishop. The man who used Beechwood for his occult activities.'

'You know Kirkhope was indirectly one of the reasons I went to the house?'

'I suspected it. His family hired you?'

'No, it was done entirely through the estate agents. Apparently Beechwood has been in the Kirkhope family for years, but never used by them. It was always rented out along with other properties they owned. It seems in the 1930s some strange practices went on there – the estate agents were not allowed to disclose exactly what kind of practices to me – and Dominic Kirkhope became involved. The goings-on were so bad that the Kirkhopes – Dominic's parents, that is – had the tenants forcibly removed. New families moved in but they never stayed long – they complained the house "wasn't right". Naturally, over the years the house gained a reputation for being haunted and eventually it just remained unoccupied. Because of Dominic Kirkhope's past association with Beechwood, it became a kind of bugbear to the family, a blemish on their good name. It was neglected for a long time, until just over a year ago they decided to try and rid themselves of the place once and for all. But still it didn't sell. There were continuous reports of an "atmosphere". I think sheer desperation made them decide to hire a psychic investigator to try and root out the problem. That's where I came in.'

Kulek and his daughter were silent, waiting for Bishop to continue. They suddenly realized his reluctance to do so.

'I'm sorry,' Kulek said. 'I know the memory is unpleasant for you . . .'

'Unpleasant? My God, if you'd seen what they had done to each other in that house. The mutilation . . .'

'Perhaps we shouldn't have asked Mr Bishop to relive his terrible experience, Father,' Jessica said quietly from her position near the window.

'We must. It's important.'

Bishop was surprised at the sharpness in the old man's voice.

'I'm sorry, Mr Bishop, but it's vital that I know exactly what you found.'

'Dead bodies, that's *all* I found! Torn, cut, dismembered. They'd done things to each other that were sickening!'

'Yes, yes, but what else was there? What did you *feel?*'

'I felt bloody sick. What the hell do you think?'

'No, not within yourself. I meant what did you feel in the house? *Was there anything else there, Mr Bishop?*'

Bishop's mouth opened as if he were about to say something more, then it closed and he slumped back in his chair. Jessica rose and went to him; the old man leaned further forward in his seat, puzzlement on his face, not sure what had happened.

'Are you all right?' There was concern in Jessica's eyes as she touched Bishop's shoulder.

He looked at her, his face blank for a few moments, then recognition came filtering through. 'I'm sorry. I was trying to think back to that day, but my mind just seemed to close down. I don't remember what happened, how I got out.'

'You were found in the road outside the house,' Kulek said gently. 'You were lying half-collapsed against your car. Residents reported you to the police and when they arrived, you couldn't speak, you could only stare at Beechwood. That much I found in the official police report. At first they thought you were involved in some way, then your story checked out with the estate agent's. Have you no memory at all of what else happened in that house?'

'I got out, that's all I know.' Bishop pressed his fingers against his eyes as if to squeeze the memory from them. 'I've tried to think back over these past few months, but nothing happens; I see those grotesque corpses, nothing more. I don't even remember leaving the house.' He let out a deep breath, his face becoming more composed. Kulek seemed disappointed.

'Can you tell me now why this is of so much interest to you?' Bishop asked. 'Apart from Pryszlak being involved, I can't see why this business should involve you.'

'I'm not sure that I can be specific.' Kulek rose from his seat and surprised Bishop by walking to the window and gazing out as if he could see into the street beyond. He inclined his head towards the investigator and smiled. 'I'm sorry, my behaviour as a blind man must seem idiosyncratic to you. It's the rectangle of light from the window, you see. It's all my eyes can perceive. I'm afraid it attracts me rather like a moth to a flame.'

'Father, we do owe him an explanation of some kind,' the girl prompted.

'Yes, we do. But what can I really tell our friend? Would he understand my fears. Would he understand, or would he sneer?'

'I'd like the chance to do either,' Bishop said firmly.

'Very well.' Kulek's thin frame swung round to face Bishop. 'I mentioned earlier that Pryszlak wanted me to join his own organization, but that I did not approve of the direction in which his research was leading. I even tried to dissuade him and this man, Kirkhope, from continuing their dubious pursuits. They knew of my own beliefs relating to the psychic linkage between man and the collective unconsciousness; they thought I would ally myself with their particular cause.'

'But what were they looking for? What were their beliefs?'

'Evil, Mr Bishop. They believed in evil as a power in itself, a power derived from man alone.'

FOUR

The two policemen began to wonder why they both felt so tense. Their night shift should have been an easy number for them; boring, but easy. The main duty that night was to keep an eye on the road, to report anything suspicious and let their presence be known to the residents by occasionally cruising the road's length in the Panda. Two hours so far, two hours of tedium. Yet their nervousness had grown by the minute.

'This is fucking ridiculous,' the slightly heavier of the two men finally said.

His companion looked across at him. 'What's that?' he asked.

'Sitting here all night just to keep the bleedin neighbours happy.'

'S'pect they're a bit worried, Les.'

'Worried? Murder, manslaughter, bloody house burning down – all in one night? It'll be another hundred years before anything else happens down this road, mate. They've had their lot all in one night.'

'You can't blame them, though. I mean, it's not Coronation Street, is it?' Les looked out of his side window in disgust. 'Bleedin right it isn't.'

'We'll have another ride down there in a minute. Let's have a smoke first.'

They lit their cigarettes, hands curled round the match flame to cover the sudden flare. Les wound down his window a little to toss the match out, leaving the gap open so the smoke could escape. 'I dunno, Bob. What do you put it down to, then?' He drew in deeply on the cigarette.

'One of them things. Normal road, normal people – on the surface, anyway. Just happens sometimes. Something snaps.'

'Yeah, well it fuckin snapped last year, didn't it? Thirty-seven people bumpin themselves off? Nah, there's something wrong with this road, mate.'

Bob grinned at him in the dark. 'What, touch of the old supernatural? Leave it out, Les.'

'You can laugh,' Les said indignantly. 'Stands to reason something's not right down here, though. I mean, did you see the nutter who blasted those two kids and their old man? Right round the twist, he is. I had a look at him down the cells. Sittin there like a fuckin zombie. Won't do nothin unless somebody makes him. He's an old pouf, you know.'

'Eh?'

'Yeah, got a record. Been done a couple of times.'

'Well how come he had a gun, then? There's no way he'd have a licence, so where would he get a gun from?'

'Wasn't his gun, was it? It was the old man's, the bleedin kids' father. That's the joke of it. This nutter, Burton, broke into the house and found the gun. I reckon he knew they had it. He found the cartridges, the lot. Even reloaded it to do the old man in after he'd got the boys. Then, so the Sarge was sayin, he tried to turn it on himself. Barrel's too fuckin long on a shotgun, though. Couldn't even part his hair with it. Bloody funny, trying to get it up his nose and he can't even get it past his forehead.'

'Yeah, bloody hilarious.' Bob sometimes wondered if his partner would have been happier as a villain.

There was a silence between them for a few moments and once again the feeling of unease began to build up.

'Come on,' said Bob abruptly, reaching forward to switch on the ignition, 'let's take a ride.'

'Hold it a minute.' Les had raised a hand and was peering intently through the windscreen.

'What's up?' Bob tried to see what his companion was looking at.

'Over there.' The bigger policeman pointed and Bob frowned in irritation.

'Where, Les? You're pointing at the whole bloody road.'

'No, it's nothing. I thought I saw something moving along the pavement, but it's only the street lights flickering.'

'Must be, I can't see anyone. They should all be tucked up in bed, anyway, this time of night. Come on, we'll have a closer look just to be sure.'

The police car slowly crept away from the kerb and crawled quietly down the road. Bob flicked on his headlights. 'Might as well let anyone who's interested know we're here,' he said. 'They'll sleep more easily.'

They had travelled the length of the road three times before Les pointed again. 'Over there, Bob. There's somethin movin around in there.'

Bob brought the Panda to a smooth halt. 'But that's the house that had the fire the other night,' he said.

'Yeah, so why should anyone be in there now? I'm goin to have a look.'

The burly policeman clambered from the car while his companion radioed in a brief message to their station. He reached back inside and grabbed the torch in the glove compartment. 'Bloody dark in there,' he muttered.

The gate was already open, but Les gave it a brisk kick as he went by; he sometimes liked to warn anyone who might be lurking in the shadows of his approach and give them the chance to get away – confrontations with villains wasn't one of his bigger joys in life. He stopped for a moment, giving Bob a chance to catch up, and shone the powerful torch towards the house. Although the damage to the front, apart from the empty, hollow-eyed windows, was not too bad, the building had a shattered, humbled look, no longer a home. He knew the worst of the damage was at the back, for the fire had started in the kitchen. He swung the light to the attached next-door house. They were bloody lucky, he thought. They could have gone up with this one.

'See anything, Les?' He glanced angrily towards Bob who had crept stealthily up the front path.

'Don't creep about like that, will you?' he whispered. 'Frightened the fuckin life out of me.'

Bob grinned. 'Sorry,' he said in a pleased way.

'I thought I saw someone climbin through a window when we were in the car. Might just have been a shadow from the headlights.'

'Let's have a look while we're here. Bloody stinks still, don't it? Is there anyone still next door?' Bob was moving towards the house and Les hurried to keep up with him.

'Yeah, I think so. Their place wasn't touched.'

Bob left the path and crossed the tiny front garden to reach the glassless downstairs window. 'Bring the torch over, Les. Shine it in.'

Les complied and they both peered into the shattered room beyond the window-frame. 'Bit of a mess,' Les observed.

Bob did not bother to agree. 'Come on, let's have a look inside.'

They walked back to the open front door and the bigger policeman shone the torch along the length of the hall.

'After you, Les.'

'It might not be safe. Those floorboards might have been burned through.'

'No, the carpet's only been scorched. The firemen got here before there was too much damage done to this part of the house. Go on, get in there.'

Les entered the house, gingerly testing each footstep as though expecting to go crashing through the floorboards at any moment. He was halfway down the corridor when a strange thing happened.

The broad, undefined circle of light at the end of the torch beam began to dim as though it had run into a thick blanket of smoke. Except there were no swirling eddies, no grey reflected light. It was as if the beam had met something solid, something that was devouring its brightness. Something dark.

Bob blinked rapidly. It had to be his imagination. There was a movement coming towards them, but there was no shape, no substance. The end wall seemed to be closing in on them. No, it had to be the torch batteries; they were dying, the light becoming dim. But there was still a bright beam along its length, only fading towards the very end.

Les was backing away into him, forcing him to go backwards too. Almost as one, they retreated down the narrow corridor towards the open front door, the torch beam growing shorter as they went until it reached no more than twelve feet ahead of them. Inexplicably, they were afraid to turn their backs on the approaching darkness, fearing that to do so would leave them vulnerable, unprotected.

They had reached the doorway when the torch beam grew strong again and began to force back the gloom. They felt as if an oppression had left them, a fear had been abruptly removed.

'What was it?' Bob said, his voice as well as his legs trembling.

'I don't know.' Les was leaning against the door-frame holding the torch in both hands to control the shaky beam. 'I couldn't make anything out. It was just like a bloody great black wall coming at us. I'll tell you something – I'm not going back in. Let's get some back-up down here.'

'Oh yeah. And tell them what? We got chased out by a shadow?'

The sudden scream made both men jump. Les dropped the torch and it clattered on to the doorstep, its beam dying instantly.

'Oh my Gawd, what was that?' the big policeman said, his legs growing even weaker.

The scream came again and this time both men realized it wasn't human.

'It's coming from next door,' Bob said, a brittleness in his voice. 'Come on!' He ran across the small garden and leapt over the low fence dividing the two properties. Les trundled after him. Bob was pounding on the door by the time the bigger policeman reached him. Inside they could hear a terrible, agonized howling, then another sharp scream sent a coldness running through them.

'Kick it in, Bob! Kick the door in.' Les was already standing back, bringing his foot up high and crashing it against the door lock. The small frosted-glass panel above the letter-box became illuminated and both men stood back in surprise. A faint buzzing noise came to their ears.

Bob thrust his face up to the letter-box and pushed open the flap. His body went rigid and Les could see his eyes widening in shock in the light shining through the letter-box.

'What is it, Bob? What's going on in there?' He had to push his partner aside when he got no reply. He bent down and stared through the rectangular opening. His thumb released the flap as if his own body were rebelling against the sight and refusing to let his eyes see any more. But the sight was already ingrained in his mind. The howling dog pushing its way along the corridor towards him, its back legs slithering frantically in the trail of blood it left behind. Its progress was slow, no more than a panic-stricken shuffle, for it had no front legs, just stumps oozing blood. Behind it, staring down and smiling, stood a man, in his hands a machine of some kind. A machine that whirred, its blades moving faster than the eye could see. He was walking towards the front door as the policeman's thumb had let the letter-box flap drop.

FIVE

He was beneath the ocean, swimming downwards, deeper and deeper, away from the silvery light of the sea's calm surface, into the depths where it was dark, the blackness waiting for him, welcoming him. His lungs were bursting, the last bubble of air having escaped an eternity before, yet his body glowed in some strange ecstasy, the pain having no meaning as he reached for the sublimity waiting within that dark, cavernous womb. He entered and swiftly it closed around him, clawing at his limbs, clogging his orifices, choking him as he realized the deception. He gasped for air and the darkness filled him. He floated downwards, arms and legs no longer flailing, his body spinning in a tight circle, faster, faster. Deeper. Then the faint glow, the small shape growing larger, rising to meet him, black waters giving way to its progress. He recognized her face and tried to call her name, but the ocean smothered his cry. She smiled, eyes sparkling in her small, child's face, and reached for him, a plump little hand appearing from the gloom. She still smiled when the other face appeared by her side, her mother's face, the eyes wild, angry, the venom in them meant for him. They began to recede, to grow dim, and he called out for them not to leave him, to help him escape the terrible crushing darkness. They grew smaller, the girl still smiling, the woman's face becoming blank, her eyes lifeless; they disappeared, two tiny wavering flames extinguished, only the total blackness remaining. He screamed and the gurgling became a ringing sound which forced its way into the nightmare, drawing him out, dragging his bedraggled senses back to the surface and reality.

Bishop lay staring at the white ceiling, his body damp with perspiration. The telephone in the hall downstairs refused him time to think of the dream, its shrill cry insistent, demanding to be answered. He threw back the bedclothes and scooped up the dressing-gown lying on the floor by the bed. Slipping it on, he padded down the stairs to the hall, his mind still reeling from the nightmare. He had learned to control the memory, its harshness softened by constancy, but every so often it tore into him mercilessly, shattering the protective wall he had built around his emotions.

'Bishop,' he said into the receiver, his voice dull with fatigue.

'It's Jessica Kulek.'

'Hello, Jessica. Sorry I took so long . . .'

'There was another incident last night,' she interrupted.

His fingers curled tightly around the phone. 'Willow Road?'

'Yes. It's in the morning editions. Haven't you seen them yet?'

'What? Oh, no. I've only just woken up. I had to drive back from Nottingham last night.'

'Can I come over and see you?'

'Look, I told you last week . . .'

'Please, Mr Bishop, we have to put a stop to this.'

'I don't see what we can do.'

'Just let me talk to you. Ten minutes of your time.'

'With your father?'

'He's at a conference this morning. I can come over right away.'

Bishop leaned against the wall and sighed. 'Okay. But I don't think I'll change my mind. Have you got my address?'

'Yes, I have. I'll be there in twenty minutes.'

He replaced the receiver and stared down at it, his hand still resting on the black surface. Snapping himself out of his brooding thoughts, he walked to the front door and pulled the newspaper from the letter-box. The headline sent the remaining nightmare fragments scurrying away.

He was washed, shaved, dressed and drinking coffee by the time he heard her car pull up outside.

'I'm sorry, it took a little longer than I thought,' she apologized when he opened the door. 'The traffic across the bridge was terrible.'

'That's the trouble with being south of the river. You wait till you try to get back.'

He showed her into the small sitting-room. 'Join me in breakfast – coffee?' he said.

'Black, one sugar.' She took off her fawn-coloured topcoat and draped it over the back of an armchair. The slim legged jeans and loose crew-neck sweater she wore combined with her short hair and small breasts to make her look boyish.

'Take a seat. Be with you in a minute,' Bishop told her.

He went back into the kitchen and poured her a coffee, topping up his own. Her voice made him jump, for she had followed him out.

'You live here alone?'

He turned to see her in the doorway. 'Yes,' he answered.

'You're not married?' She seemed surprised.

'Yes, I'm married.'

'I'm sorry, I didn't mean to pry.'

'Lynn is . . . away. Hospital.'

She seemed genuinely concerned. 'I hope she isn't . . .'

'She's in a mental institution. Has been for three years. Shall we go through into the sitting-room?' He picked up the two cups of coffee and waited for her to move from the door. She turned and led the way.

'I didn't know, Mr Bishop,' she said, seating herself and taking the coffee from him.

'It's all right, no reason why you should. And my name is Chris, by the way.'

She sipped her coffee and once again he was bemused by her. One minute she seemed tough, almost brittle, the next, young and timid. An unsettling mixture.

'Did you get a chance to see today's newspaper?' she asked.

'I read the headline, glanced at the story. "More Madness in Horror Road". I'm surprised the Residents Association doesn't take it up.'

'Please, Mr Bishop . . .'

'Chris.'

'Please, the situation is more serious than you think.'

'Okay, I shouldn't be flippant. I agree, a man cutting his sleeping wife's throat with an electric hedge-trimmer, then cutting the legs off his dog isn't a joke. Running out of cable before he could attack two policemen outside is mildly funny, though.'

'I'm glad you think so. You read he turned the machine on himself, didn't you? He severed the main artery in his thigh and died from loss of blood before they could get him to a hospital.'

Bishop nodded. 'Maybe that was his intention from the start, kill his wife, pet dog, then kill himself. He wanted to share his death wish with them.' Bishop held a hand up to ward off her protests. 'I'm not joking now. It's common enough for a suicide to take his loved ones with him.'

'Suicide or not, it was still an act of madness. And why did the other two kill themselves?'

'The other two?'

'The woman who killed her lover and the man who shot the two boys and their father.'

'But he didn't die.'

'He did, last night. My father and I went to the police station where he was being held – we hoped to be allowed to question him. He was dead when we arrived. He was left alone in a cell and he cracked his skull open against the wall. He ran at it, Mr Bishop. From one end to the other, a matter of only eight feet, but enough to split open his head. They said he must have run at the wall twice to cause such damage.'

Bishop winced at the thought. 'The girl. The little girl . . .?'

'They're keeping a very close watch on her. The police are now wondering about the cause of the fire; they seemed to think it may have been deliberately started.'

'Surely they don't imagine the kid set fire to her own home?'

'She has been under psychiatric care for some time.'

'You think that's the link. Everyone in Willow Road is going mad?'

'No, not at all. We've done some checking since we saw you last and discovered that the three people involved in last week's slayings . . .'

'There's no evidence against the child,' Bishop was quick to point out.

'I said the police think the fire may have been deliberately started. There were no electrical appliances switched on, no gas leaks, no fireplace in the kitchen, and they haven't as yet discovered any faulty wiring. What they are reasonably sure of is that the kitchen curtains went up first. A burned-out box of matches was found on the sill. They're now wondering just how the girl got out when the couple in the room next to hers couldn't. Maybe they're wrong in their suspicions, Mr Bishop . . . Chris . . . but the fact that she has needed psychiatric help in the past, that the fire was no accident, and that she got out completely unscathed – and unmarked by smoke – well, it all seems to point in her direction.'

Bishop sighed. 'Okay, so maybe she did cause the fire. What was your point?'

'The woman and the girl were mentally unstable. The woman tried to commit suicide six months ago. The man with the shotgun had been convicted for child molesting. He'd lost his job, had become a social outcast, and the neighbours say the two boys he shot had derided him. It could have been enough to tip him over the edge.'

'You're saying all three were mad?'

'Most people who kill have reached a point of madness. I'm saying something in Willow Road acted as a catalyst.'

'To make them insane?'

She shook her head. 'To direct their instability.'

'Towards murder.'

'Towards an evil act. I don't think it necessarily has to be murder.'

'And you think this is all tied up with the mass-suicide last year?'

Jessica nodded. 'We believe there was a reason for the suicides. Pryszlak, Kirkhope and all those others had a motive.'

Bishop placed the coffee at his feet and stood up. Thrusting his hands deep into his pockets, he walked thoughtfully towards the fireplace. He gazed down at the empty grate for a few moments before turning to her again.

'It's all a bit fantastic, isn't it?' he said mildly. 'I mean, there can only ever be one basic reason for suicide. Escape. That's what it finally comes down to.'

'Release might be another word.'

'Well, yes, release. It's the same thing.'

'No, not quite. Escape means running away. Release is a freedom, something you can embrace. The thirty-seven people who killed themselves in Beechwood were not being persecuted in any way. Not one note was left from any of them to say why they were committing such an act and no individual reasons could be found. There had to be some point in their self-destruction.'

'And you and your father think the events of last week have something to do with it?'

'We're not certain. But we know of the ideals of Pryszlak and his sect. My father told you they wanted his help.'

'He told me they believed in the power of evil. I wasn't quite sure what he meant by "power".'

'He meant evil as a physical entity, a solid force. Something to be used as a weapon could be used. Pryszlak believed this not only as an occultist, but as a scientist, too. He endeavoured to use his knowledge of both to harness that power.'

'But he killed himself before he met with success.'

'I wish we could be sure of that.'

'Oh, come on. At least the man and his lunatic cronies are out of the way. If there is such a power – which I seriously doubt – none of them seems to be around to use it.'

'Unless their very deaths played some part in their search.'

Bishop looked at her in dismay. 'You're not being logical. What good would the knowledge be if they weren't around to use it?'

Jessica's face took on the determined look he had come to recognize. She reached down for her bag and drew out cigarettes. Her hand was trembling slightly when she lit one. She blew out a puff of smoke and regarded him coldly through the sudden haze. 'Then why these sudden acts of violence? Why this sudden madness, Mr Bishop?'

'Chris.'

'Why then?'

He shrugged. 'Who the hell knows? I'm not sure I even care.'

'You're a psychic researcher. You're supposed to have an interest in the paranormal.'

'Sure, but I like to keep my feet planted firmly on the ground. You're flying high.'

'When I first came to you, you seemed to express some respect for my father.'

'I respect his work and his opinions in many things.'

'Then why not in this?'

He turned away from her, resting an elbow on the mantelpiece, his other hand still tucked into a pocket. A small, framed face smiled up at him, the photograph taken when she was only four. A year before she died. Christ, he thought, the bitterness still strong enough to tighten the muscles in his chest, she would have been nearly thirteen now. Even then they could tell she would be the image of her mother.

'Chris?'

He shut the thoughts from his mind. 'It's too implausible, Jessica. And it's all speculation.'

'Isn't all investigation into the paranormal speculation to begin with? You said in your lecture the other night it was your belief that man's natural evolution was reaching the point of breakthrough, that science and parapsychology were converging to become one and the same thing. Is it beyond you to accept that a man like Pryszlak had already reached that point, had made the breakthrough? At least keep an open mind to it. Isn't that what you tell your students? Isn't that the whole point of your books – openmindedness, with a little realistic scepticism?'

Jessica was on her feet now, her head jutting forward like her father's. 'Or are you too wrapped up in your own personal cynicism? Psychic research needs clear-minded people, Mr Bishop, not cynics, nor fanatics. People who are willing to accept facts and people who are willing to uncover those facts.'

She stabbed her cigarette towards him. 'You're a paid ghost-hunter. All right, we'll hire you. We'll pay for your services. We'll pay you to finish the job you started nine months ago. We want you to investigate that house in Willow Road. Maybe *you* can come up with an answer.'

SIX

Bishop brought the car to a halt, relishing the satisfying sound of crunching gravel. He looked out at the tall, red-bricked, Queen Anne building and said, 'Looks like she's worth a few bob.'

Jessica followed his gaze. 'The Kirkhopes are a great tradition in the shipping industry. At least, they were in the thirties and forties when Dominic Kirkhope's father was alive, but his offspring have had problems now that the shipping boom is over.'

'And she's all that's left?' He tucked his glasses into his breast pocket.

'Agnes Kirkhope is the last of the direct descendants. She and her brother took over when their father died, but, from what I can gather, Dominic played little part in the running of the business.'

'Do you think she'll talk about him. Families are generally reticent about their black sheep.'

'I suppose it depends on our questions. She may not like us digging too deep.'

'When the estate agents hired me to investigate Beechwood I asked to see the owners of the property, but they wouldn't let me. They felt it was unnecessary. In a strict sense they were right – but I usually like to know a house's history. I let it go then because it was just another routine job to me. This time I want to know as much as possible before I set foot in there again.'

'First we have to get her permission to carry out another investigation.'

'Correction: an investigation. The last one wasn't even started.' He switched off the engine and reached for the door-handle on his side. Jessica placed a hand on his other arm.

'Chris,' she said. 'You really think this is for the best?'

He paused before opening the door wide. 'If we tell her the whole story she'll run a mile. Do you really think she'd want her brother's bizarre suicide dredged up again and, even worse, linked with these recent deaths. Let's stick to the story I told her over the phone. She was reluctant enough to see me anyway without giving her further cause for alarm.'

They walked across the drive towards the large main door which opened at their approach.

'Mr Bishop?' a plump, dark-skinned woman inquired.

'And Miss Kulek,' he replied. 'Miss Kirkhope is expecting us.'

The maid nodded, grinning in agreement. 'You come in, Miss Kirkhope is expecting you.'

She busily ushered them into a large, high-ceilinged room off the wide hallway. Pictures of sea-going vessels, from ancient clippers to modern liners, adorned the walls and several detailed models of ships were encased in glass cabinets at various points.

'You wait, please. Miss Kirkhope will be down. She is expecting you.'

The maid left the room, still grinning enthusiastically as though their presence had made her day worthwhile. Bishop ran his eyes around the room while Jessica took a seat on an old Chesterfield, its dark brown bulkiness enhancing the maritime surroundings.

'Business can't be that bad,' he mused.

'It isn't that bad, Mr Bishop, but it lacks the impetus of a few decades ago.'

Agnes Kirkhope's sudden appearance in the doorway startled them both.

'I'm sorry, I didn't mean to be rude,' Bishop apologized.

'That's quite all right, quite all right,' she said striding briskly into the room, her eyes alive with some private amusement. 'I must say this is my most impressive room, though. That's why I receive visitors here.'

She was a small woman, her body thin but ramrod straight, an alertness about her that defied the passage of years. Her hair was pure white but still had a wavy softness to it. She sat at the opposite end of the Chesterfield, her body at an angle so she could still face Jessica, and peered at them through tiny, gold-rimmed spectacles. There was still amusement in her eyes for the embarrassment she had caused Bishop when she spoke.

'I didn't expect two visitors.'

'No, I'm sorry, I should have said on the phone. This is Miss Kulek.'

The old lady smiled at Jessica. 'And *who* is Miss Kulek.'

'Jessica works for the Research Institute of Parapsychological Study.'

'Really.' Miss Kirkhope frowned. 'And what exactly is that?'

'We study the paranormal,' Jessica answered.

The old lady's frown increased. 'For any particular reason?'

Bishop grinned.

'To find out more about ourselves, Miss Kirkhope,' Jessica answered.

Miss Kirkhope sniffed as if to dismiss the subject. 'Can I offer you both a sherry? I like to indulge myself at least once a day. Anna! The sherry please!' The maid appeared as though she had been hovering outside the door waiting for the command. She beamed at them all.

'And I think the Cyprus,' Miss Kirkhope added, 'not the Spanish.'

Bishop and Jessica glanced at each other, sharing their own amusement at the slight. They restrained their smiles when the old lady turned her attention back to them.

'Now, Mr Bishop, you said on the telephone you would like to resume your investigation of Beechwood. Hasn't your dreadful experience last time put you off?'

'On the contrary,' Bishop lied, 'it's given me even more reason to investigate the property.'

'Why, exactly? And please do be seated.' She flapped a hand towards an armchair.

He sat on the edge of the seat, resting his forearms on his knees. 'There has to be some explanation as to why all those people killed themselves. There may well be some psychic forces at work in the house.'

'Really, Mr Bishop. The agents told me you were a most practical man despite your profession. You were hired originally to find more material reasons for Beechwood's disturbing atmosphere.'

'Yes, and I still hope to. But we can't just ignore what happened, we have to look for other . . . elements. That's why I'd like to take along Miss Kulek and her father, who is President of the Research Institute. They may discover more than I can on my own.'

The sherry arrived and was distributed by Anna who treated the amber liquid as if it was holy wine and left the room in a fluster of smiles.

'She's new,' Miss Kirkhope explained crisply. She raised her glass. 'Your very good health, my dears.'

They sipped their drinks, Bishop wincing at the sweetness.

'And what has suddenly encouraged you to resume your investigation, Mr Bishop? I wonder if the other recent happenings in Willow Road have rekindled your interest?'

He almost choked on his sherry.

'I ran my father's shipping business practically single-handed for years after his death, with precious little help from dear brother Dominic.' She nodded towards a framed photograph standing on a nearby sideboard; the picture showed a pudgy-faced young man with curly black hair. The resemblance to Miss Kirkhope was minimal. 'True, we eventually went into decline, but that was the case of shipping in general, so please don't take me for a fool just because I'm an old woman. I follow the news and Willow Road is a name I'm hardly likely to forget.'

Jessica spoke up. 'We're very sorry, Miss Kirkhope, I hope we haven't offended you. Chris had no intention of going back to that house until I persuaded him.'

'If we're going to be frank, let's go all the way,' said Bishop. 'Jacob Kulek is hiring me to investigate Beechwood – that is, if I get your permission. We don't want to drag up old memories for you, but Jessica and her father feel there is a link between Beechwood and the recent deaths in Willow Road.'

'Do you feel there is?'

Bishop hesitated before he answered. 'No, I don't. But . . .' he looked across at Jessica '. . . I think it's worth looking into. Jacob Kulek is a renowned figure in his field of work, so any opinion he has on this subject has to be respected. He knew your brother, by the way, and a man named Pryszlak, who was a colleague of your brother's.' He saw the old woman flinch at the mention of Pryszlak's name.

'I warned Dominic about that man.' Her lips were a thin line. 'My brother was a fool, little more than a buffoon, but Pryszlak was evil. I knew it as soon as I set eyes on him. A son of the Devil.'

Both Jessica and Bishop were astonished at the outburst. Just as suddenly, the tension left the old woman's body. She smiled at them, almost mischievously.

'I try not to let things bother me nowadays, my dears, but sometimes memories intrude. Now, assuming I gave you permission to enter Beechwood, what would your plan of action be?'

'You'd have no objections?' Bishop asked, surprised.

'I haven't said that yet,' came the curt reply.

'Well, first I'd like some background history on the house. I'd like to know about the activities that took place there in the 1930s. I'd like to know what your brother was involved in, Miss Kirkhope.'

'And if I decide not to give you any information?'

'Then as far as I'm concerned, the matter is ended. I won't investigate the house.'

Silence descended on the room. Bishop and Jessica studied Miss Kirkhope as she sipped her sherry thoughtfully. She stared down at the floor for a long time and there was a sadness in her voice when she finally spoke. 'Beechwood has been part of my family's history for many, many years. Dominic was born there, you know. An accident really. It was a country house for my parents, you see, built at a time when it really was open country in those parts, long, long before it became a residential area. My father sent my mother and me there for the weekend; he wanted her to rest. He was busy, so very busy, and mother was seven months pregnant. He thought the change would be good for her.' She gave a bitter laugh. 'She had no rest that weekend. Dominic was premature; it was just like him to rush foolishly into the world before his time.'

Her eyes took on a faraway look as though she were studying an image in her mind. 'I was only seven at the time, and I was the one who found her at the foot of the cellar stairs. Why she went down there in the first place nobody ever found out. Mother certainly couldn't remember after the pain she suffered giving birth to Dominic. My God, how she screamed that night. I remember lying in bed listening, praying to God to let the baby die so it couldn't hurt mother any more. She hadn't wanted to be moved, she would have had Dominic right there in the cellar if the servants hadn't ignored her pleas. I can still hear her screams of agony to this day as they dragged her up those steps. He came in the early hours of the following morning and I heard one of the servants say she wondered what all the earlier fuss was about because of the way he finally just plopped out on to the sheets.

'I don't think Mother ever really recovered from that dreadful night. She always seemed to be frail after that, always sickening for something or other. She loved Dominic, though. Oh, how she doted on that boy! She would never go back to Beechwood after his birth, so father began renting it out rather than let it go empty. It had become too modest for folk as grand as us, anyway! Our fortunes were rising rapidly, you see. I haven't seen the place myself since, had no wish to. But Dominic went back – he must have been twenty-five, twenty-six, I can't remember how old exactly. He was inspecting several properties we owned at that time, doing his duty as father's son, you see. But Beechwood held some strange fascination for him; I suppose it was because he was born there.'

Miss Kirkhope paused to sip her sherry, then suddenly looked up at the other two occupants of the room as if remembering they were still present and that her reminiscences were for their benefit. 'That was the real turning-point for Dominic, I think. Up until then he had certainly been wayward, but that was only the robustness of youth. He returned many times to Beechwood and we naturally assumed he enjoyed the company of the people who occupied the house. There seemed to be no harm in it although my father did warn him it wasn't wise for landlords to become too friendly with their tenants. The area was becoming more populated then and Beechwood was soon surrounded by other properties; it was still an impressive house, perhaps not the most elegant, but firm, solid, a house that would last forever. Dominic became rather an elusive character – we never seemed to see much of him. It was only years later when the police informed my father that they had received complaints about the activities of Beechwood's occupants that we became alarmed. I think my father had already lost hope of Dominic following in his footsteps by that time and, in fact, I myself was fulfilling that role. I was, as they say, on the shelf – I don't know why, I don't think I was unattractive in those days; possibly the shipping business interested me more than men. I think it was a relief to my father that he had at least someone to rely on, someone he could trust to help him in his business ventures. I'm afraid mother had become progressively more fragile over the years and, God bless her, she wasn't much use to anybody. She only seemed to come alive in Dominic's presence which, of course, wasn't very often. Mr Bishop, you've hardly touched your drink. Perhaps you'd like something stronger?'

'Uh, no, it's fine. Thanks.'

'Then perhaps you'd be kind enough to refill my glass. Miss Kulek, another for you?'

Jessica declined and Bishop took the thin glass from the old lady to the silver tray resting on a small, ornately carved table. As he poured he prompted Miss

Kirkhope. 'What exactly was going on in Beechwood?'

Anxiety deepened the many lines already ingrained on the old woman's face. 'Some new kind of religious sect was using the house as their church – The Temple of the Golden Consciousness, I believe they called it. Something silly like that. There seemed to be so many ridiculous societies around in those days.' Her anxiety had given way to disdain.

'Unfortunately there still are,' Jessica said.

'Had your brother joined this religious sect, Miss Kirkhope?' Bishop asked as he handed her the sherry.

'Oh yes, he belonged to it. A full, practising member by that time. My father kept the more sordid details from my mother and me, but I gather sexual orgies played a large part in their worship. I suppose they could have got away with that but for the terrible row they made. The neighbours objected. Father cancelled the lease on Beechwood right away, of course, and ordered the tenants and their strange friends out. Dominic wouldn't come anywhere near us; he hid himself away somewhere. Suffering from shame, no doubt.'

'Who were these tenants?' Jessica asked gently.

'Oh, I can't remember their names, it was too long ago. A man and his wife or mistress – I can't be sure now. They must have been insane, anyway.'

'What makes you say that?' said Bishop.

'They refused to leave. Nothing odd in that, I know, but when they were informed they would be forcibly evicted, they took a rather extreme stand.'

'What did they do? Barricade themselves in?'

'No,' Miss Kirkhope replied mildly, 'they killed themselves.'

Bishop felt his muscles tense and he knew by the expression on Jessica's face she had been startled too.

'For some reason,' the old lady continued, 'nobody seemed to settle in Beechwood after that. Stories, silly rumours spread by neighbours, saw to it. People would move in, stay perhaps a few months, then leave. I think a year was the longest anyone ever stayed in that house. My mother died, my father's health became poor, and I became even more involved in his business activities, so Beechwood was rather lost in the background of things. We had agents who looked after our various properties and they rarely bothered us unless a specific problem arose. I must admit I didn't give much thought to Beechwood over the years.'

'What of your brother?' Jessica inquired. 'Did he ever return to the house? Apart from the . . . last time, that is.'

'I don't know. Possibly. Probably. As I said, Beechwood held a special fascination for him. The only time I had any real contact with Dominic after the earlier scandal was when father died. Let me see, that would be . . . 1948. He came for his share of the inheritance. He gladly relinquished any rights in the family business, but was rather chagrined at being left out on the property. Father, rather wisely, left it all to me, you see. I remember my brother wanted to buy Beechwood from me, but I refused, having recalled what went on there in the past. Quite enraged, he was, like a naughty little boy who couldn't have his way.' She smiled but it was only a sad memory.

'I didn't see much of him after that, nor did I want to. I didn't like what he'd become.'

'What was that, Miss Kirkhope?'

She looked steadily at Bishop, the smile still on her face. 'That is my secret, Mr Bishop. I only heard stories from other people and I had no proof that they were true; but whether they were or not, I've no wish to discuss it.' Her thin, white hands curled around her glass, the fingers locking together. 'The house remained empty for many years, until I decided to put it on the market along with the other properties I owned. I was no longer able to carry on with the business in an efficient manner and I placed responsibility in more capable hands. I still have a nominal place on the board, but hardly any influence in how the company is run. I sold the properties at a time when the company needed a swift injection of ready cash, but the respite, I'm afraid, was only brief. Still, I'm comfortable enough. There's not much financially that can touch me in my last years. That's one of the nice things about old age – you have less of a future to worry about.'

'But you didn't sell Beechwood.'

'Couldn't, Mr Bishop, *couldn't*. That was the irony of it – the one property I wanted to be rid of, no one would buy!' She shook her head in amusement. 'The Kirkhope Folly you might call it. Or the Kirkhope Curse. I even went to the lengths of having it completely renovated, but still nobody wanted it. The agents blamed it on "bad atmosphere". Apparently it happens occasionally in the property market. That's why your services were called upon, Mr Bishop, to officially "cleanse" the house, if you like.'

'I told the agent at the time I was no exorcist.'

'Nor did you have any belief in ghosts as such. That was why they chose you in particular. The estate agents informed me that unexplained disturbances in a place could often be due to nothing more than an underground stream running beneath the house, land subsidence or even shrinkage.'

'A great many strange happenings can be explained by a detailed site examination, Miss Kirkhope. Rappings, doors opening for no reason, creaks, groans, sudden pools of water, cold spots – there's usually a logical explanation for them all.'

'Well, the agents felt sure you would uncover the cause.'

'Unfortunately, I didn't get the chance to.'

'No. But now you want another crack at it.'

He nodded. 'With your permission.'

'But your motives are not quite the same as Miss Kulek's and her father's.'

'No. Jacob Kulek and Jessica believe there is something sinister in Beechwood. I'd like to prove them wrong.'

'And I thought you were doing it for money,' Jessica said, the sarcasm heavy in her voice.

'There's that too.'

Agnes Kirkhope ignored the sudden antagonism between her visitors. 'Don't you think there has been enough publicity concerning Willow Road? Do you really think it's necessary to drag up the whole terrible affair of Beechwood again?'

'I told you earlier that Jacob Kulek's opinion is highly regarded in the field of psychical research. From what I know of him he's not a man to make rash judgements or speculate wildly. He thinks I may remember something more about the day I went to Beechwood. For my part, I'd just like to finish the job I started and, for reasons of my own, I'd like to prove him wrong about the house.'

'I promise you the investigation would be discreet,' Jessica said earnestly. 'We would report our findings to you before taking any other action.'

'And if you did, and I asked you not to take the matter any further, would you comply?'

'I can't say, Miss Kirkhope. That would depend.'

'On what you discovered?'

'Yes.'

With a loud sigh and a shrug of her shoulders, Agnes Kirkhope surprised them both again by saying, 'Very well. There's very little to interest an old woman like me nowadays. Perhaps this will throw some light into my rather dull life. I take it, then, that you will pay Mr Bishop's fee?'

'Yes, of course,' said Jessica.

'I think I would like to know why Dominic killed himself.'

'There's no way we'll find that out,' Bishop said quickly.

'Probably not. But perhaps I believe more in the mysteries of life than you do, Mr Bishop, despite your profession. We shall see.'

'Then we can go ahead?' asked Jessica.

'Yes, my dear, you can go ahead. There is just one thing.'

Bishop and Jessica leaned forward as one.

'You have a very short time in which to complete your investigation. In four days from now, Beechwood will be demolished.'

SEVEN

Night fell with little preamble and the residents of Willow Road nervously drew their curtains against it as if the darkness was a seeing thing. It was quiet out there now, the journalists and TV men having long since departed, their notebooks and cameras crammed with the opinions and fears of the road's inhabitants. Even the sightseers had left, finding nothing in the ordinary, rather drab, road to fuel their curiosity. Two constables strolled the pavements, up the left hand side, down the right, conversing in low tones, their roving eyes studying each house they walked by. At the passing of every twenty minutes, one would speak into his small hand-radio, reporting back to their station that all was quiet. The street-lights were inadequate, the gloom between them somehow threatening, each entry the policemen made into the shadowed areas briefly and secretly considered first.

At No 9, Dennis Brewer switched on the television set, telling his wife to come away from the window where she stood peeking through the curtains. Their three children, a boy of six and a girl of seven sitting on the carpet in front of the television screen, an eleven-year-old boy struggling with his homework on the living-room table, stared curiously at their mother.

'Just checking to see if those policemen are still there,' she said, letting the curtains drop into their closed position.

'Nothing else is going to happen, Ellen,' her irritated husband said. 'Bloody hell, there's not much more that *can* happen.'

Ellen sat on the sofa beside him, her eyes on the over-colourful shapes on the screen. 'I don't know, it's not natural. I don't like this road any more, Dennis.'

'We've been through all that. There's nothing for us to worry about – all those other silly sods were round the twist. Thank God they've all been sorted out in one go, is what I say. Now we can have a bit of peace and quiet.'

'They can't all have been lunatics, Dennis. It doesn't make sense.'

'What does nowadays?' For a second his eyes flickered away from the screen to find the children watching them with rapt attention. 'Look what you've done,' he complained. 'You've frightened the kids.' Disguising his annoyance, he smiled reassuringly at them, then allowed his thoughts to return to the programme.

At No 18, Harry Skeates was just closing the front door behind him.

'Jill, I'm home!' he called out.

His wife came hurriedly from the kitchen. 'You're late,' she said and he was alarmed by her anxious tone.

'Yeah, had a drink with Geoff at the station. You all right?'

'Oh, I'm a bit nervous, I suppose.'

He kissed her on the cheek. 'There's nothing to be nervous about, silly. You've got the law walking up and down outside.'

She took his overcoat from him and hung it in a cupboard under the stairs. 'I'm okay when you're around. It's just when I'm on my own. This road's become a bit frightening.'

Harry laughed. 'Old Geoff was full of it. Wants to know who's going to be bumped off next.'

'It's not funny, Harry. I didn't know the others very well, but Mrs Rowlands was very nice the times I spoke to her.'

Harry shoved his dropped briefcase to the side of the hall with his foot and made his way into the kitchen. 'Yeah, what a way to go. Throat cut by a hedge-trimmer. He had to be potty, that bloke.'

Jill switched on the electric kettle. 'I didn't like him very much. I don't think she did either, the way she spoke about him. She said he hated her dog.'

'Well I don't like poodles much.'

'Yes, but to do that to the poor creature.'

'Forget about it now, love. It's all over and done with.'

'You said that last week.'

He shook his head. 'I know, but who'd have thought anything else would have happened after that. It's beyond all reason. Anyway, I'm sure that's the last of it. Let's have that cup of tea, eh?'

She turned away, reaching into the kitchen cabinet and wishing she felt as confident.

At No. 27, the elderly man lay in his bed and spoke to the nurse in a quavery voice.

'Are they still there, Julie?'

The nurse re-drew the curtains and turned to look down at the old man. 'Yes, Benjamin, they've just passed by.'

'All the years I've lived here, we've never had to have police patrols before.'

She walked over to the bed, the table-lamp by its side casting her giant shadow against a corner of the room, creating a deep black void. 'Would you like some milk now?' she asked quietly.

He smiled up at her, his wizened old face parchment yellow in the poor light. 'Yes, I think so, just a little. You will sit with me tonight, won't you, Julie?'

She leaned over him, her full breasts pressing against the high-necked, starched dress she wore in place of a uniform, and straightened the bedclothes around his shoulders. 'Yes, of course I will. I promised, didn't I?'

'Yes, you promised.'

He reached for her plump, but firm hand. 'You're good to me, Julie,' he said.

She patted his hand, then tucked it back inside the blankets, rearranging them again around his frail old body.

'You will sit with me, won't you?' he said.

'I just told you I would,' she answered patiently.

He settled back into the bed, shuffling his shoulders more comfortably into the sheets. 'I think I'll have that hot milk now,' he sighed.

The nurse rose from the bed, tiny beads of perspiration glinting in the fine hairs above her upper lip. She crossed the room and quietly closed the door behind her.

At No. 33, Felicity Kimble glared angrily at her father.

'But why can't I go out, Dad? It's not fair!'

'I told you, I don't want you out of the house tonight,' Jack Kimble said wearily. 'I don't want you stopping out late while all this business is going on.'

'But I'm fifteen, Dad. I'm old enough to look after myself.'

'Nobody's old enough to look after themselves these days. I'm not telling you again – you're not going out.'

'Mum!' she whined.

'Your Dad's right, Felice,' her mother said in a softer voice than her husband's. 'You don't know what sort of people all these goings-on have attracted to the neighbourhood.'

'But what could possibly happen? We've got the Fuzz on the doorstep.'

'The police, Felice,' her mother corrected.

'Anyway, Jimmy can bring me home.'

'Yes,' her father said, rumpling his newspaper, 'and that's another reason for not going out.'

Felicity looked at them both, her mouth a tight line across her face. Without a further word, she marched from the room, 'accidentally' kicking over her younger brother's Lego tower as she went.

'Perhaps we should have let her go, Jack,' her mother said as she helped her wailing son reassemble the plastic bricks.

'Oh don't you start,' Jack said, dropping his newspaper on to his lap. 'She can go out as much as she likes when things quieten down a bit. Providing she comes home at a reasonable hour, that is.'

'It's not the same for kids today, Jack. They're more independent.'

'Too bloody independent, if you ask me.'

Upstairs in her room, Felicity flicked on the light and flounced on to her narrow bed. 'Silly old twits,' she said aloud. They treated her like a ten-year-old. She only wanted to go down the club for a couple of hours. Jimmy would be waiting. She'd had enough of it, treated like a kid at school, treated like a kid at home. She was a woman now! She looked down at her ample swellings to reassure herself she was. Satisfied, she turned over on the bed and thumped the pillow with a clenched fist. Bloody silly street, people bumping each other off all the time! She thought a little wistfully of the two brothers who had lived further down the road, both blasted by a shotgun; the younger of the two had been nice looking, she quite fancied him. Not that Dad had a good word to say about either of them. Still, they were both dead now, the younger one having died of his injuries only the day before. He and his father had died within minutes of each other. What a waste! Felicity jumped up from the bed and went to her portable cassette player. She rewound the tape already settled in its deck, then pressed the 'play' button. A soft, slow number began, the kind she preferred, the rhythm emphasized rather than exaggerated. She moved in time with it, lost in the meaning of the words, her resentment towards her parents forgotten for the moment. Her movements led her unconsciously towards the window where her own reflection against the black backdrop made her stop. She pressed her face against the glass, cupping her hands between its surface and her eyes, providing a dark tunnel for her to see through. The two policemen passing below glanced up and continued walking. Felicity watched their progress for a few moments until they disappeared into shadow beyond the street-light. She drew the curtains, her expression thoughtful.

Across the road at No. 32, Eric Channing grunted in disappointment. A rectangle of muted light was all he could see of the window opposite. The girl usually left her curtains half-drawn, seemingly unaware that she could be seen from the bedroom across the road. Eric had spent many lonely vigils in his bedroom over the past year, his wife downstairs imagining he was in the small room next door tinkering with his hand-built railway set. He knew Veronica felt his trains were a childish pastime for a man of thirty-eight but, as she often said in company, it kept him out of mischief. It had often been a tricky business, his eyes glued to the window, ears pinned to the stairs, listening for her footfalls. He would rush silently on to the landing as though he had just emerged from the loo when he heard the living-room door open. She would give him hell if she ever found out. He had often sat there for hours in the cold while the miniature train next door whirred round and round on its tireless journey, scrutinizing the ten to eighteen inches – depending on how wide she had left the curtains drawn – of bright light across the road, tensing at the flicker of movement, heart almost stopping when she came into view. On a bonus night, she would suddenly appear wearing only a bra and panties. Once, and only once, on a super-bonus night, she had taken off her bra in front of the window! Occasionally he wondered if she really was unconscious of the interest her lush young body caused, or whether she secretly knew he was crouching in the dark as she flaunted herself.

Eric sat there for another ten minutes, his face only inches away from the parted curtains, where the light from the street could not shine directly on to him. He knew from experience that tonight was a minus night: there would be nothing more to see. He would pop up now and again to make sure a gap hadn't appeared in his absence, but he felt certain the evening's performance was over. He had jumped back further into the shadows when she had suddenly appeared at the window. His heart pounding wildly, he realized she was only watching the two policemen below. They must have been the reason for her closing the curtains. Interfering bastards! He reluctantly tore his eyes from the window and slunk dolefully from the room. Sometimes he wished he was Clark Kent and had X-ray vision. Or the Invisible Man and then he could actually be in the room with her.

His wife looked away from the television screen and her knitting stopped momentarily when he opened the door. 'Not playing with your trains tonight, darling?' she said.

'No,' he replied mournfully, 'I'm not very interested tonight, dearest.'

In the street outside, the two policemen strolled in step with each other.

'Bleedin cold tonight, Del,' one said, blowing into his gloved hands.

'Yeah, don't know why they didn't put another Panda on.'

'Can't waste a car on one street every night, can they? We haven't got enough to cover the whole patch anyway.'

'Plenny of helmets, though.'

'Eh?'

'Not enough patrol cars but plenty of helmets. I've had three new ones this year. Keep getting them dented at the matches.'

'Go on.'

'Every time I'm on duty. It's about time they slung those little bastards inside for a couple of weeks instead of lettin them off with piddlin fines.'

'Yeah, I used to enjoy the old football duty. So you've had three helmets then?'

'And a new radio. One of the bastards ran off with the last one. Crowd opened up in front of him like the partin of the Red Sea. Soon came tumblin down on top of me when I went after him, though.'

They walked on in silence for a few moments, their own unisoned footsteps a comfort to them in the quietness of the road.

'Yeah, plenny of em,' Del observed.

'What, helmets?'

'Yeah. Not enough recruits coming into the force, you see. Lots of helmets to go round. And radios.'

'Not enough patrol cars.'

'No. Not enough of them. Beats the old whistles.'

'What does?'

'Radios.'

'Oh yeah. Bit before my time, whistles, Del.'

'Yeah, s'pose it would be. Still handy to have them on us though. You never know when your radio's going to pack in.' They walked in silence for a few steps. 'Too many, you know.'

'What, helmets?'

'No, you silly bastard. Soccer hooligans. Too many of them, not enough of us. We can't control em any more. There used to be just a few troublemakers at a match, now it's most of em. Too many for us to handle.'

'Yeah, nutters, the lot of em.'

'No, most just go along with the ringleaders. They get carried away with the atmosphere.'

'I know what I'd like to do with em.'

Del tutted. 'You're not allowed to, son. They're only victims of their environment.'

'Environment? I've never seen one of em with rickets yet. A bloody good hidin would do em a lot of good.'

'Now, now, that's not the attitude. Mustn't upset our friendly neighbourhood social worker.'

The younger policeman's sneer of derision was hidden in the shadows as they passed beyond the feeble circle of light. He glanced to his left, squinting at the huge, detached building looming up from the general gloom.

'Gives me the creeps, that place,' he remarked.

'Yeah, I don't care for it much, either.'

'Another bunch of lunatics.'

Del nodded in agreement. 'This road seems to have its share.'

The younger policeman looked back down the road. 'I wonder whose turn it is tonight?'

Del grinned. 'No, it's due for a bit of peace and quiet, this road. It's had its share of troubles. I don't think there's any more murderers left in those houses.'

'Let's hope you're right,' the younger one said as they continued their watchful journey, the sound of their footsteps fading as they srolled beyond the house called Beechwood.

Julie poured the lukewarm milk into the cup, then drank a little to test it. She wouldn't mind if it burnt the old bastard's throat except it would mean a night of whining. And she wasn't sure she could stand much more of that.

Six years she had been with him: six years of fetching and carrying, nursing, placating, cleaning up his filth, and . . . the other thing. How much longer could he last? When she had first arrived from the private nursing agency, she had expected him to survive for two or three more years at the most. But he had fooled her. Six years! The temptation to slip something into his soup or milk was almost irresistible, but she knew she had to be careful. The circumstances would be too suspicious. His Will would immediately point the finger of suspicion directly at her; there was no one else it could be pointed at. And no one else he could leave his money to. He wasn't wealthy, she knew, but he had enough to pay her salary all these years without any visible means of income, and he owned the property they lived in. Christ, when he went, she would turn it into a glorious house. Perhaps a small residential nursing-home for the elderly. It was certainly big enough. There were a few other similar properties in Willow Road – old Victorian houses that had seen better, grander days, but they, too, had become immersed in the general drabness around them. Yes, it would make a fine nursing-home. Just five or six old people, none with complicated illnesses – that would be too much trouble. And a small staff to do the work. No more skivvying for her! She would merely supervise the running of the place. How much money did the old man have? Her eyes glinted greedily in the dim kitchen light. He'd hinted often enough about his 'little nest egg' that he was saving just for her. She had tried to find out – surreptitiously, of course – just how much that 'little nest egg' amounted to, but the old fool would only grin slyly at her and touch a withered finger to his nose. Cunning old bastard.

She placed the mug of milk on a tray that already held his medicine bottle, spoon, and an assortment of pills. God, he would rattle if she ever picked him up and shook him – and that would be difficult to do with her size and him being nothing more than skin and bones. Half the pills he didn't really need, but they gave him the impression he was being looked after. They were harmless enough. How much longer, though? How much longer would the stubborn old fool live, and how much longer could she stand being around him? Patience, Julie, she told herself. It will be worth waiting for. Christ, she'd dance on his fucking grave, all right. Maybe the winter would finish him off. The mean old skinflint didn't believe in central heating and the single-bar electric fire he had in his room just about heated the piece of carpet in front of it. She had left his bedroom window open often enough when she went out shopping as well as creeping in to open it in the middle of the night when he was asleep, always closing it first thing the following morning before he woke. If he didn't catch pneumonia before this winter was out, then he was never going to die, he would go on forever. But she had to be careful: sometimes she thought he wasn't as senile as he pretended.

She carried the tray from the kitchen and began to climb the stairs to the bedroom. She almost missed her footing on the gloomy stairway, the milk slurping over on to the tray, and she silently cursed his meanness. The whole house was dismally lit because of his insistence on low wattage light bulbs. Even when one expired it was difficult to get his permission to buy a new one. He scrutinized every bill she presented him with, his whole body suddenly becoming alert, helplessness mysteriously disappearing; it was as though he suspected her of swindling him, that the weekly shopping bill was a concoction of her own making. Crafty old bugger! The only thing he didn't mind paying for was the medicines and pills she fed into him. He regarded this as the mortgage on his life.

Benjamin's rheumy old eyes watched her from over the top of the bedclothes as she entered the room. He pulled the blankets down under his chin and smiled toothlessly at her.

'Bless you, Julie,' he said as she used her broad rump to close the door behind her. 'You're a good girl.'

She brought the tray over to the bed and moved the lamp on the small bedside table back against the wall to make room for it. The shadows in the room adjusted themselves to the change.

'There now,' she said, sitting heavily on the side of the bed. 'Medicine first, then your pills. You can take them with your milk.'

'Help me sit up, Julie,' he said, putting on his weak voice.

Julie groaned inwardly, knowing full well he was capable of propping himself up. She stood and reached under his armpits, heaving his light frame into a sitting position, fluffing up the pillows behind him. He sat grinning at her, yellow, wrinkled and gummy. She turned her head away.

'Medicine,' he said.

She shook the bottle then poured some of its contents on to the spoon. Benjamin opened his mouth wide and she was reminded of a baby gannet waiting to have a worm dropped into its beak. Julie pushed the spoon in, resisting the urge to shove the whole thing down his scrawny throat, and he sucked noisily at the sticky liquid.

'One more, there's a good boy,' she forced herself to say.

He put on a childish mock grimace, then dropped open his lower jaw.

When he had swallowed the second dose, she scraped the spoon up his grizzled chin, shovelling the dribbles back into his mouth. The pills came next, delivered on to his glistening wavering tongue like communion wafers, and washed down with the warm milk. She patted his mouth with a Kleenex tissue and he sank back down into the bed, his head still propped up by the pillows, a smile of contentment on his face.

'You promised to sit with me,' he said slyly.

She nodded, knowing what he meant. It was a small price to pay for the old bastard's money, she supposed wearily.

'You're good to me, Julie. All these years, you're the only one who's cared for me. You're all I've got in my last years, dear. But you won't be sorry, I promise you that, you won't be sorry. You'll be well taken care of when I pass on.'

She patted his hand. 'Now you mustn't talk like that. You've years ahead of you. You'll probably last me out.' She was only thirty-nine, so there was no bloody chance of that, she thought.

'You'll be well taken care of, Julie,' he repeated. 'Untie your hair, dear. You know how I love to see it.'

Julie reached up behind her head and with a few swift tugs, her lush, dark brown hair cascaded down on to her broad shoulders. It was long and when she tossed her head it fell beyond her shoulders to settle almost to the bottom of her back.

He reached up a trembling hand. 'Let me feel it, dear, I love to touch it.'

She leaned forward so her glistening mane was within reach. He ran a gnarled hand through it, relishing its rich texture. 'Beautiful,' he murmured. 'So thick, so strong. You really have been blessed, Julie.'

She smiled despite herself. Yes, her hair was her greatest attribute. She knew her body was heavy, although her well-rounded curves were not unattractive – Rubenesque would be way to describe them; and her face, too, was a little plump, but then again, not unattractive. Her hair, though – as her drunken old father in Ireland used to tell her – was a 'gift from the gods'. She became coy, playing the game the way he liked it.

'Come on, Julie dear,' he said in mock pleading, 'let me see you.'

'You know I shouldn't, Benjamin.'

'There's no harm in it. Come on now,' he coaxed.

'It might over-excite your heart, Benjamin.' She hoped one day it would.

'My heart is already excited, dear. Won't you give me some reward for the reward I'll be leaving you.'

'I told you not to talk like that. Besides, my reward is taking care of you.'

'Then take care of me now, Julie dear.'

She stood, knowing he would become impatient if the game went on too long. Reaching behind her back, Julie unhooked the clasp at her neck, popping the descending buttons open so the stiff dress hung loose around her shoulders. She shrugged herself free of the top and stood there before him in a fake poise of modesty, her breasts hanging heavily inside her bra.

His mouth opened as he gazed up at her, the corners wet with saliva. He nodded his head in quick jerky movements, encouragement for her to go on. Julie undid the bow that secured her white nurse's apron to her waist, letting it fall to the floor. The rest of the dress was pushed, not without effort, over her hips, and the starched material crackled as she slid it down her legs. The elastic in her dark tights was tucked inside a deep crease around her middle and she dug her thumbs into her flesh to find it. Benjamin groaned when these were pulled from her firm legs and she stood over him, a mountain of white flesh contained only by bra and panties.

'Lovely,' he said, 'so very lovely.' His hands disappeared beneath the covers to scurry around in search of his shrunken member. 'The rest, Julie dear. Now the rest.'

She unhooked the bra, her great mounds spilling free and resting sullenly on the rise of her belly. The bra was dropped on to the pile of clothes at her feet and she ran her big hands over her breasts, squashing them flat and teasing the two pink buttons at their centres until they rose like blunted antennae. She allowed her fingers to run down her large expanse of tummy, hooking her thumbs into the top of her panties and slowly drawing them down over her thighs. He moaned aloud and craned his neck forward off the pillow to see her dark, bushy triangle more clearly.

Completely naked, she placed her hands on her hips and stood before him.

'Yes, yes, Julie. You know what to do now.'

She did. She danced.

Her gross shadow matched her movements around the room, sometimes stretching over the ceiling as she drew near to the lamp, hovering darkly over them both. She weaved and turned, crouched and leapt, flinging her arms high in the air, giving him the chance to see every inch of her fleshy body. She finished with a pirouette, crudely performed and grotesque to see, but he cried, 'Encore!' his eyes alight with the thrill.

Julie slumped breathlessly into a wicker chair standing in one shadowy corner of the room, the wooden struts uncomfortable under her bare skin. But this was where he liked her to sit for stage two of the game.

He watched her expectantly, waiting for her to catch her breath, his own breathing sharp and fast with excitement. If only she knew the money was nearly all gone. Paying her for her services all these years had drained it; there was just enough to last another year, a year-and-a-half at the most, then there would be nothing left. But she had been worth it! By God, she had! He knew as soon as Julie had walked in the door that she would be the one. Everything about her had been sensual: her robust figure, the way she moved, those starchy, high-buttoned nursing frocks she wore. Even her voice with its bare traces of an Irish lilt. And when he had first seen the full glory of her wonderful hair flowing over her shoulders like a soft, umber waterfall! Bliss! She was the one! The others had done their job well enough, but they cared little for him and his needs. It hadn't taken long to convince Julie her future was with him and not with the nursing agency. Of course, a little deception had been necessary. But after all he had provided for her all these years. It was a shame it had to end, but the money he would get for the house would pay for his last years in a comfortable nursing-home. He would give her a couple of hundred pounds from the proceeds, maybe even three hundred; she had been very obliging. That should keep her happy! Oh yes, Julie, now, do it now!

Julie's legs were stretched wide and her hand was travelling down between her thighs. Her fingers cut a path through her triangle of hair and found the fleshy lips lurking beneath. She moaned, not just for his pleasure, but because her own passion was beginning to awaken. Self-abuse was her greatest pleasure nowadays. Men, on the rare occasions she had found one to smuggle in, were seldom strong enough for her demands. Her teeth bit down on to her lower lip and her face became moist with perspiration as her middle finger forced entry. Her hand moved in a soft, languid motion, but gradually the strokes increased in both speed and firmness as the muscles in her stomach tautened.

Benjamin's hand movements beneath the bedclothes had increased also, but to no avail. 'Julie,' he called out, 'over here now, please, over here.'

He blinked his eyes as her white, mountainous shape seemed to dim in the poor light. The bulb in the lamp must be dying, he thought, unless his vision was failing along with certain other parts of his tired old body. The shadows in the room became darker and he could hardly see her now, just the ends of her legs from the knees down sticking out of the black patch in the corner, her large feet jerking spasmodically.

'Julie! Please come into bed now,' he pleaded. 'I need you, my dear.'

Her great flabby shape emerged from the shadows and she padded over to the bed. He grinned in welcome as she threw the covers back, and held his limp member upright for her to see. She climbed in next to him and he shivered as her cold feet touched his legs.

'Good girl, Julie. That's my girl,' he murmured as she smothered his thin body with her own oozing flesh.

'Careful now,' he gasped as her weight bore down on him, forcing the air from his lungs. She rolled off and her hand grabbed down at him, brushing his own hands away. He winced at the rough treatment she gave to his half-erect penis, pulling and kneading it as though to mould it into a firmer shape.

'Do be careful, Julie,' he complained, 'you're being rather rough.' He could feel her hot breath panting in his ear and his skinny old hands grabbed her wobbling breasts, squashing the two points together, holding them out for his gummy lips to close in on. He sucked at the nipples making baby-like gurgling sounds, then yelped as her arm went beneath him and pulled his body on top of hers with a great heave.

'Come on, you old bastard, give it to me,' she whispered.

'Julie, what . . .'

His words were cut off as she spread her legs and tried to pull him into her. She had to stuff his flaccid organ in with her fingers and it was like dough being forced into an open purse. Her great hands clasped around his fleshless buttocks and she heaved him in, her own hips rising up from the bed to meet him.

'Julie!' he screamed. 'Stop this at once!' He felt as if his lower body was being crushed, his bones ground to powder.

'Come on, you old bastard! Fuck me!' Tears of frustration ran from the corners of Julie's eyes, running into her ears, filling the wells. She rose and pulled, writhed and jerked, but there was nothing of substance inside her. 'Fuck me!' she screamed, and the shadows closed in around them until there was a barely audible fizzing sound as the light bulb splattered into lifelessness and the darkness engulfed them like a black tide.

He was wailing now, hurt in the struggle, desperate to be free. But she would not release him. She held him against her with one hand, her knees rising up on either side of him, her ankles hooked over his reedlike legs. Locking him there. Her hand reached behind her lifted head, gathering up the hair that billowed out on to the pillow. She worked it into one long, thick length and wound it round his scrawny neck.

'Julie, what are you doing? Please stop this! I don't want to play any . . .'

His words were choked off as she began to pull on the hair, tightening it, using her other hand to hold the roots firmly against her head. She pulled harder, tighter, his face twisted to one side, his eyes wide in terror, his mouth spitting small white specks.

'All these years,' she hissed between clenched teeth. 'All these years . . .' Her tears were now because of her own pain, the roots screaming against her scalp. But still she pulled, his gurgling sounds music in her ears. 'All these years . . .'

The darkness in the room became even denser until there was not even light shining through the cracks of the curtains. She could not see anything at all in the blackness. She could only hear his gurgling chokes. And that was enough.

EIGHT

He sat in the car, watching the house, afraid. Although the engine was switched off, his hands were gripped tightly around the steering-wheel as though whether to stay or drive off was still unresolved in his mind. The sun was hidden behind troubled clouds this time and the windows were black and secretive. Beechwood was no longer an ordinary house.

Bishop drew in a deep breath and released the wheel, one hand whipping off his glasses and tossing them on to the passenger seat, then reaching back for his case. He strode briskly across the paved area, knowing if he hesitated any longer he would never enter the house. He knew his fear was irrational, but that did not make it any less real. The door opened as he mounted the steps and Jessica smiled down at him. As he drew nearer, he saw the smile was restrained; a nervousness was in her eyes. He understood that nervousness.

'We thought you might not come,' she said.

'You're paying me, remember?' he replied and instantly regretted his harshness.

Jessica looked away and closed the door behind him. 'They're waiting for you.' She pointed to the first door on his left, the one opposite the stairs. For a moment he couldn't move, almost expecting to see the legs still dangling over the stairway, the fallen shoe lying on its side beneath them. They were gone, of course, but the scuff marks on the wall remained.

He felt the gentle pressure of Jessica's hand on his arm and shook the thoughts from his mind. Almost. He walked down the gloomy corridor and entered the room she had indicated. A woman was waiting with Kulek and she rose as Bishop walked in.

'I'm glad you came, Chris,' Kulek said from the armchair he occupied, one hand curled around the top of his walking-stick. 'This is Mrs Edith Metlock. She is here to help.'

Bishop shook her hand and tried to remember where he had heard the name before. She was short and stout, almost matronly in appearance. Grey streaks broke up the blackness of her tightly curled hair and her cheeks bulged ruddily when she smiled. He realized she must have been rather beautiful in her younger days, but plumpness and time had concealed most of that beauty now. Like Jessica, her pale eyes held a nervousness in them. Her grip was firm but, despite the coldness of the room, the palm of her hand was moist.

'Please call me Edith,' she told Bishop, curiosity now mingled with her unease.

'In what way are you going to help . . .?' He stopped in mid-sentence. 'Edith Metlock. Yes, I thought I knew the name. You're a medium, aren't you?' He felt his anger rising.

'I'm a sensitive, yes.' She let go of his hand, recognizing the aggression, knowing the scepticism that would follow.

Bishop turned to Kulek. 'You didn't tell me. There's no need for this.'

'It was only decided at the last moment, Chris,' Kulek said placatingly. 'If the house is soon to be demolished, then we do not have too much time. Edith is here to observe. She will assist only if necessary.'

'How? By calling up the ghosts of the people who died here?'

'No, nothing like that. Edith will tell us of the atmosphere of the house, the feelings she receives. She will help you remember.'

'I thought we were going to investigate this house by more scientific means.'

'And so we shall. Edith will be an extra method of investigation if we fail with your, shall we say, more material approach.

'But you still think there's something I've forgotten from my last visit here. What the hell makes you so sure?'

'I am not sure. But several moments have been lost to you. You found yourself outside the house without knowing how you got there.'

'It's not unusual when someone panics.'

'No, but we *are* talking of an unusual event.'

'May I interrupt?' Edith Metlock said, looking from one to the other. Without waiting for a reply, she asked Bishop: 'Why are you so afraid?'

'Afraid? What makes you say that?'

'Your whole manner, Mr Bishop. The uneasy way you entered this room . . .'

'My God, if you'd seen . . .'

'Your resistance to Jacob Kulek's efforts to discover the secret of this house . . .'

'That's nonsense . . .'

Bishop's protests faded and he stared down at the medium, his face grim. 'Yes, I object to your presence. I've heard you have an excellent reputation as a medium; unfortunately I don't have the same high regard for your kind.'

'My kind?' She smiled at him. 'I have heard of you also, Mr Bishop. You have a reputation for taking great delight in exposing the mistakes of my "kind".'

'Not the mistakes, Mrs Metlock. I'd rather call them the deceptions.'

There was concern on Jacob Kulek's face. 'Chris, please. Edith is here at my invitation.'

She walked over to Kulek and patted his hand. 'That's all right, Jacob. Mr Bishop is entitled to his views. I'm sure he has his own reasons for his attitude. Perhaps he will tell us?'

'I think we've wasted enough time,' Bishop said angrily. 'By all means stay. But please don't try to interfere with my work here.'

Jessica came forward and stood beside the investigator. 'Chris is right. We *are* wasting time. Let's get on with ths business, Father.'

'I'll stay out of your way, Mr Bishop,' Edith Metlock said. 'I'll keep to this room while you go about your investigation. If you should need me . . .'

'I won't. But maybe you can help me, Jessica?'

'Of course.'

'What do you intend to do, Chris?' inquired Kulek.

'First I want to take the temperature of each room. I don't know if any of you have noticed, but it's freezing in here, much colder than it is outside.'

'Yes,' said Jessica, 'it was the first thing I noticed when I came in. I thought it was just the fact that the house had been unoccupied for so long.'

'It probably is the reason. It'll be interesting to see if every room is the same, though.' He ignored the faint smile on the face of the medium. 'Miss Kirkhope's agent has managed to supply me with a geological map of the area as well as a two-and-a-half inch scale survey map. One will tell us the type of soil the house is standing on and the general structure of the land around it; the other will show if there are any streams or wells near the property. Tunnels or underground streams beneath the house could cause the chill – or perhaps you would call it "atmosphere", Mrs Metlock.'

'I most certainly would,' the medium said, still smiling. 'I felt it immediately I entered. But I hope you do find some physical reason for it, Mr Bishop.'

'Then I want to test the structure of the house itself. No plans of the building are in existence, unfortunately, but I'll do my own survey. I want to know the materials used in its construction, test the walls for damp, look for shrinkage of any kind.'

'It seems you need a more practical knowledge for your work than just experience of the paranormal,' Kulek remarked.

'Practical knowledge outweighs any other as far as I'm concerned. I used to be a planning surveyor before I took up chasing ghosts, and I needed to know just how houses got themselves built for that.'

'And when you have done all this?' Kulek asked.

'Then I want to set up some equipment to be left here overnight.'

'Equipment?'

'I want to know if there's any activity in this place when it's supposedly empty. I intend to set up a camera connected to a tape-recorder, linked up to photo-electric cells and a sound and vibration detector. If anything moves or makes a noise in this house tonight, we'll know.'

'But you can only set this up in one room,' said Jessica.

Bishop nodded. 'This will be the room. For the others I'll have to rely on powder and black cotton. If we find traces of disturbance in any other room, we'll move the electrical equipment into there for the following night.'

'Have you considered staying overnight in Beechwood yourself?' It was the medium who posed the question.

'Sure. And my considered reply to myself was "no".'

'But I thought you didn't believe in ghosts.'

'I don't believe in being uncomfortable.' He turned to the girl. 'Jessica, I've brought along two thermometers, the greenhouse kind. It would save time if you tested one room while I did the same in another.'

'All right, shall we start down here?'

'No, upstairs. I want to get an idea of the general layout first. Jacob, do you want to come with us?'

'I'll stay and keep Edith company. I'm afraid I wouldn't be much help to you.' He smiled encouragingly at his daughter and Bishop.

Bishop picked up his case and told Jessica to follow him. He paused at the foot of the stairway, looking up into the sombre greyness of the landing above.

'I suppose there's no electricity?'

'No, we tested the lights when we came in,' Jessica said.

Bishop shrugged. 'I didn't really think there would be.'

He climbed the stairs, taking two at a time, his strides swift, leaving the girl hurrying to keep up. He stopped at the top and waited for her.

'That's where I found the first body,' he said, nodding towards the balustrade. 'It was hanging from there.' He saw her shiver.

'Did you come up here, to any of these rooms?'

'No. Just into the main room downstairs. That was enough.' He walked to the end of the landing and drew back the curtains. Light sprang in but made little progress along the hallway.

'Come on,' he called to her and she joined him at the foot of another staircase.

'Two upper floors,' he commented, reaching into his case and producing a torch. 'The principal bedrooms will be on this floor and upstairs will probably be what was once the servants' quarters. There's enough light to see by, but we'll need the torch for looking into cupboards and suchlike.'

His progress up the second staircase was slower and Jessica was able to keep close behind him. There were four doors on the landing above, all closed. Once again he walked to the window and drew back the curtains, a strong musty smell from the material irritating his nasal passages. The daylight revealed the hatchway in the ceiling and he flicked on the torch, shining its beam upwards.

'I'll have a look in the loft later,' he said.

Jessica tried the handle of the door nearest to her. It turned easily and she gave the door a gentle push. The small room was devoid of any furniture, the floorboards bare, dark with age. A tiny, iron-framed fireplace faced her. Bishop pushed past her and walked over to it, crouching and shining the torch up the chimney. He withdrew his head and said, 'Can't see too much. I can't tell if it's blocked or not.'

'Is it important?'

'I need to know where any draughts come from. Or if there are any birds nesting in the chimneys. Our feathered friends are often the cause of "ghostly flutterings".' He took a thermometer mounted on a thin block of wood from his case and looked around for a suitable peg to hang it on. He settled for resting it on top of the small mantelshelf above the fireplace, placing it in an upright position, top resting against the wall. Then he produced a ten-by-eight sketchbook and a felt-tipped pen. There were no curtains at the window, so the light was adequate for his purposes.

'I'm going to make a plan of each room,' he explained, 'then an overall plan of the house. I'll mark on it any draught points, holes that shouldn't be there, rotted floorboards and any structural alterations from the original building. You can help by looking for signs of dampness.'

'Shall I start in here?'

'No, take this other thermometer into the next room. It'll save time if we move them on when we get a stable reading.'

Jessica took the instrument from him and left the room, stopping for a moment outside. Somehow there seemed to be less light in the hall than before. It was almost as if dusk were falling. That was silly, she told herself. It was still mid-morning. The clouds outside had become heavier, that was all. She moved along to the next door and twisted the handle.

It turned easily enough, but when she pushed against it, the door barely moved before meeting resistance. Jessica pushed harder and the door seemed to sink into something soft yet resilient. This time she put her shoulder to the door and gave it a short, sharp shove. It moved inwards about an inch. She put her eye to the gap, but it was too dark in the room to see anything clearly. Her gaze travelled down the crack and she could just make out the shape of something bulky lying across the bottom of the door. She dared not admit to herself what it might be.

'Chris,' she called out, keeping her voice steady. 'Could you come here for a minute, please?'

He came from the room and frowned when he saw the anxiety on her face. She pointed to the door.

'There's something blocking it.'

He tested the door, pulling it back then pushing against the unseen object. He felt the wood sink into something before meeting firm resistance. Jessica's features were not clear in the poor light, but he could see her eyes were wide.

'It feels like . . .' she said.

'A body? Don't let your imagination run away with you. It could be anything.' Nevertheless, there was a prickling sensation around his scalp.

He gave the door a hard push using the weight of his whole body and it swung inwards six inches. 'Get the torch,' he told her and she quickly disappeared into the other room. He pushed again, keeping up the momentum of the swing, and the door opened wide, one foot, two, a slithering noise accompanying its movement. He took the torch from the girl and stepped halfway into the room, keeping the beam low. Jessica watched his back as he leaned forward and peered around the door. It seemed so dark beyond him.

He looked back at her, a broad grin on his face. A curled finger beckoned her, then he disappeared from view. As she slowly crept forward she could hear his footsteps crossing the floor, then the sound of material being swished back. Dull grey light filled the room.

Jessica stepped sideways through the gap and breathed out when she saw the rolled carpet lying at an angle across the floor, one end resting against the open door.

'This kind of house can make you imagine all sorts of things, Jessica,' Bishop said, one hand still on the heavy drapes he had just pulled back from the window. There was a softness in his voice that she didn't expect from him.

'I'm sorry, Chris. You're right about the house, though: it does stir the imagination. It's so gloomy in here.'

He drew nearer to her. 'The carpet must have been standing in the corner over there. Some disturbance – perhaps when the police were here last – made it topple and block the doorway.'

She managed a weak smile. 'I'll try not to be so shaky from now on.'

'Don't worry about it. It's happened to me in the past. I've come to learn there's generally a rational explanation.'

'And the times when there isn't?'

'That means I haven't been clever enough to discover it.'

Before he could snap up the barrier between them again, she reached for his arm. 'Tell me, Chris, why were you so angry when you found Edith Metlock here?' She saw the coldness flicker behind his eyes.

'It was a surprise to me. I think you're well aware of my feelings towards such people, yet you asked her here.'

'But she's a genuine sensitive. Her reputation is beyond reproach.'

'Is there such a thing as a genuine sensitive? I've no doubt she thinks she is and her belief in the spiritual world is quite sincere. But how much of it is real and how much comes from her own subconscious? I'm sure she is clairvoyant, but then again, couldn't that just be the power of her own mind?'

'It could be, I'll admit that. Whatever it is, it seems to work.'

He smiled at her and some of the antagonism between them melted.

'Look,' he said, 'I've been pretty rude to you and your father – not to mention Mrs Metlock. I'll try to keep my opinions to myself while this investigation is going on and I promise to keep an open mind to whatever we find providing you and your father do the same.'

'But we have.'

'No. Your father seems to be obsessed with this Pryszlak and his view could be clouded by what he knows of the man and his work.'

'My father is totally objective.'

'If he was, he would have brought in a headshrinker to help me remember those forgotten minutes, not a spiritualist.'

She realized he had a point and kept quiet.

His voice was gentle when he spoke. 'I'm sorry, I didn't mean to bark at you again. I'm only trying to make it clear that there are two sides to this and I happen to be in a minority of one. If there is a connection between this house and all the recent killings in the road, then I'd like to find out what it is, too.'

'Let's work together, then, not against each other.'

'Agreed.'

She looked away from him and, for a moment, he felt she was flustered.

'Okay,' he said, 'set the thermometer up over there then let me know the reading on the other one before you move it on to the next room.'

They worked their way systematically through the upper floor of the house, recording the temperature of each room, checking for draughts and damp, Bishop making detailed drawings. They descended the stairs to the main bedrooms and followed the same routine. The rooms on that floor were much larger than those at the top of the house, but the low temperature seemed constant throughout: five degrees centigrade. The rooms themselves, although in good repair, had the musty smell of emptiness, the creeping decay of walls without the echoes of life.

Jessica stood alone in one room waiting to take an accurate reading from the thermometer she had placed in there moments before. She looked at the solitary bed, its bare springs somehow heightening the loneliness of the room. She wondered why they hadn't taken away the few remaining pieces of furniture and decided they probably meant nothing to Miss Kirkhope neither financially nor for sentimental reasons. When the house came down, then the contents would undoubtedly be crushed along with it. She moved to the window and watched the road below. An old woman shuffled by, not even giving Beechwood a passing glance. A cyclist came into view, his head down, scarf tight around his neck, pedalling steadily, vapour breaths dissolving fast in the cold air. An ordinary suburban street. Like millions of others. But behind certain walls, a difference.

Jessica turned from the window and crossed the room. She stooped to pick up the thermometer propped against a wall and her face creased into a look of consternation. The temperature had dropped from five degrees centigrade to below zero. Even as she watched, the red mercury crept down, the movement slow but visible. When it had reached ten degrees below and was still sinking she placed it back in position and hastily went to the door.

'Chris!' she called out.

'In here.'

Jessica ran to the next room. He had his back to her, scribbling notes on to the sketch he had just made.

'Chris, the temperature next door is dropping rapidly. It's unbelievable. I can actually see it going down.' She was suddenly aware how cold she felt physically.

He turned in surprise, then strode towards the thermometer in that room. 'Christ, you're right,' she heard him say. 'It's below twelve in here.'

The scream made them both jump. It came from the rooms below, screeching its way up the staircase and echoing around the landing walls.

For a frozen instant, Jessica and Bishop stared at each other, then, as one, they raced towards the stairs. Bishop reached them first and as he descended he sensed a blurring before his eyes, shadows hanging like cobwebs in front of him. Jessica saw him sweep a hand before his face as though brushing aside invisible curtains. She followed close behind, but could see no obstruction.

Bishop almost stumbled halfway down, missing a step as though avoiding something lying there. Jessica could see nothing.

He swung round the banister at the bottom of the stairs, then staggered against the opposite wall, a look of bewilderment on his face. Jessica reached him and held him steady. They ran onwards as another scream pierced through the suddenly cloying air and reached the room in which they had left Jacob and the woman. Bishop stopped in the doorway and collapsed on to his knees, his face draining of blood.

The room was filled with people. Their bodies, many naked, writhed and twisted in agony, features contorted as if they were screaming their pain, but no sounds coming from their lips. A woman, near enough to Bishop for him to reach out and touch, swayed unsteadily, her head swung back, beseeching the ceiling. Her blouse was open, the buttons torn away, heavy breasts thrusting the material apart. She wore no clothes from the waist down and her fleshy thighs trembled in some strange paroxysm. Her fingers were curled around a small glass and he could see the whiteness of her knuckles as she strained against it. The glass shattered and its few drops of liquid mingled with the sudden gush of blood from her cut hand. Bishop flinched as spots of blood spurted against his face and he pulled back when the woman fell. She landed in front of him, her back still heaving.

His eyes darted around the room, widening with each individual scene of horror. On the floor, not five feet away from him, three figures were locked in tight embrace, one on top of the other. Their naked bodies shook, but he could not tell whether it was from pain or ecstasy. He realized it was a woman underneath, her legs spread wide, arms scratching at the arms and backs of the two men above her. One had entered her and was moving his hips in unison with the man who clung to his back and who had entered him. The woman's face was pointed towards Bishop, but he could see her eyes were glazed as though heavily drugged. A heavy-set man lumbered towards them, his clothes open to display his genitals. Wild hair and beard almost obscured his face, but Bishop could see this one's eyes were sharp, obsessed. In his hand he held a long, pike-like object, its length black and tapering gradually to a fine point. He held the point against the back of the man uppermost in the tangled heap, pressing it slowly down until it punctured the skin and a tiny drop of blood oozed out. The naked man paid no heed to his injury, continuing to press into the man beneath him. The man with the pike reached upwards and closed both hands against the flat base of the weapon. Bishop opened his mouth to scream as he realized what was about to happen, but the cry stayed locked deep inside his chest. The bearded man plunged downwards and the long, black point sank from view, the pike descending into a fountain of red liquid, its length smoothly disappearing until the man's blood-stained hands were only inches away from his victim's flesh. All three bodies went rigid with shock, then continued trembling, this time the movements jerky, spasmodic, reaching separate crescendoes before falling limp, unmoving. Bishop could see the bearded man laughing, but still no sound came to him.

A young girl, probably in her early twenties, struggled with two men on the room's worn settee which stood beneath the high, bow window. They held her wrists and legs. Her skirt was pulled up around her waist and a woman knelt before her, pushing something bulky between the girl's thighs. The girl looked down at the object, her eyes wide with pleading and Bishop saw the tape sealing her lips. She arched her body and the trapped end of the object rose with her. Bishop raised a hand towards them, but it was as though he was engulfed in a sticky fluid that hindered his movements, bearing down on him with a debilitating force. He saw the woman squeeze the twin triggers of the shotgun and closed his eyes when parts of the girl's body ruptured through her clothes. Even the shotgun blast was silent.

A hand touched his shoulder and he opened his eyes again. Jessica was standing over him, her lips moving.

A man stood behind the door, an insane grin on his face. Liquid drooled from the corner of his mouth and the glass he held slipped from his fingers, landing on the floor without breaking, rolling away from him, then back in a semi-circle. The man slid down the wall, still grinning, his lips only curling down in an expression of painful horror when he reached the floor. His back was stiff against the wall when he slowly toppled sideways, the action like the movement of a second hand against a clockface. His legs kicked out, once, twice, and his chin receded into his neck as his jaw opened to its fullest extent, not even relaxing when he was dead.

A group of men and women sat around the table at the far end of the room, their hands joined across its surface. They waited patiently while one man walked around behind them carefully slitting their throats with a butcher's knife as he went, each member holding on tightly to the hand of the dying man or woman next to them until forced to let go because of their own dying. Soon none of the hands was joined as the bodies lay slumped across the table or had slipped from their chairs. The man who had done the slaying calmly ran the knife across his own up-stretched throat, his chest becoming sodden and red as he sank back to his knees; he fell forward on to his face.

Bishop tried to rise, the girl, Jessica, tugging at his arm to help. A man was watching him from the armchair in which Jacob Kulek had been sitting. His face was thin, cheeks hollow, shadowy, and his eyes seemed to protrude unnaturally from his skull as though he suffered from meningitis. The lips were thin, unformed, the line of the mouth curled at one end in an expression that could have been a smile or a sneer. His hair was black but sparse, swept back from his forehead, making the distance between his scant eyebrows and hairline seem extra-ordinarily long. His elbows rested on either arm of the chair, his hands raised steeple-shaped before him, a small glass of clear liquid held at their apex. His lips parted as though speaking, then he looked away from Bishop towards a man and woman nearby. They were coupled together, the woman holding the man's head down between her thighs while he thrust himself into her throat. They were frail with age, the skin hanging loosely over prominent bones; their hair was white and brittle.

The mallet was wielded by the bearded man, who laughed when the old man's skull cracked under the blow, his head becoming wedged between his partner's skinny legs. The bearded man knelt beside the aged couple and brought the mallet down hard on the man's buttocks, the woman beneath him suddenly struggling to free herself from his choking member. She twisted her head to one side, but the force of the blows pushed the man's pelvis against her, smothering her, pinning her neck at an awkward angle. It was impossible to know if she died from suffocation, a broken neck, or just shock.

The bearded man was laughing gleefully as he rained blows on the now still bodies. He stopped abruptly and looked towards the man sitting in the armchair. The man was speaking to him, but Bishop could not hear the words. The bearded man shuffled on his knees towards the seated figure, the mallet still grasped tightly in his hand. The glass of clear liquid was offered to him and he took it, hesitated, looked deep into the contents. Then he drank.

The sneer – or was it a grin? – on the seated man's face deepened and he looked towards Bishop once more. He picked up something that had been lying in his lap unnoticed by Bishop. It was heavy, black. A gun. The man took a long, sweeping look around the room, his bulging eyes finally coming back to rest on Bishop. His lips moved, then his mouth opened wide; the muzzle of the gun was pushed in, pointing high into the roof of his mouth. Everything around Bishop seemed to slow down, all movements losing speed, the struggles becoming graceful, a ballet of death. It took a lifetime for the man's finger to slide around the trigger and pull it back tight against the guard, the recoil blurred but still slow, the flame lighting up the inside of his mouth so that Bishop saw the hole appear, could almost follow the bullet's path as it travelled through the man's head, erupting on the other side, carrying bits of brain, mucous, blood, into the air to shatter high against the wall behind leaving a red smear of dripping substance.

Bishop stared at the running pattern and traced a trail of slow-moving blood back to the man below. But it was not the same man. The eyes still bulged, still stood out from their sockets, but it was fear that made them so. Fear of the unseen, sensed only, for the eyes were sightless. It was Kulek who now sat in the chair.

He was calling out and the sounds came creeping through to Bishop. It was as though Kulek was at the end of a long, winding tunnel, and was drawing near, his voice becoming louder and louder at his approach. The figures around Bishop became misty, ethereal, their twisting and writhing becoming even slower until they were still; and as they faded, so another body became clearer, more defined. Edith Metlock lay slumped against the wall, eyes closed, head hanging limply sideways. Kulek's cries came fully to Bishop's ears and with them he found the strength to raise himself, staggering back against Jessica who tried to support him.

He whirled around and she fell to one side, gasping sharply as she went down on one knee. Bishop had to get out, had to get away from the house and the terrible thing that had happened there. That was still happening.

He fell against the door-frame, his body swinging round at the impact so his eyes were looking down into the far end of the hall. There were more moving shapes, fading, slowly dissolving, their bodies grey in the dim light. He pulled himself upright and cried out, 'No!' when he saw the legs hanging above the stairway. They kicked out wildly, scuffing the wall, a shoe falling loose and rolling down several stairs before coming to rest. Dismembered hands clutched at the fading legs, tugging at them, pulling them downwards till they no longer kicked. The hands faded away and only a dim twitching outline of the limbs remained.

Bishop had to get away from the house. He knew the slaughter was going on all over; in the bedrooms upstairs; in the rooms on the second floor. He had to get out. He began to run towards the front door, his legs leaden, his breath drawn in short, sharp gasps. The door beneath the stairway was ajar, a long, narrow gap beckoning to him.

He stopped running and pushed his back against the opposite wall as he had once before. And, like before, the door seemed to be moving outwards as if someone were pushing it from the other side. He found he was reaching forward in repeat motion, his fingers clutching the door's edge, afraid to look, but compelled to, something down in that cellar commanding him to. He pulled the small door back and it swung wide, the blackness lurking behind it shuddering and falling away at the sudden light, dim though it was. He heard a movement. A shifting sound. Something on the stairs below. He had to see. Had to.

He approached the open doorway and looked down into the bowels of the house. The darkness at the bottom of the stairs seemed solid, a brooding night that invited him below, a living blackness that waited to devour. And from the blackness a shape began to emerge.

Bishop could not move. Even when the shape grew larger as it mounted the steps and the strange murmuring came to his ears he stood mesmerized. Even when he could see the wild-staring eyes, the long, dark hair hanging forward almost to her waist, the flow broken by huge bare breasts like boulders in a fast-flowing stream. Even when she was near the top step and curling her hair in big hands, stretching it taut across her chest like a thick rope, the words becoming clearer now as she repeated over and over again, 'All these years . . . all these years . . .'

The woman was real, not a spectral shape like the others. As she emerged from the shadows he saw her body had substance and seemed to grow in firmness rather than fade. And her murmuring, almost an incantation, told him she was not one of those already dead. He backed away, the deranged look on her face as frightening as the visions he had just witnessed. She stopped before him, her hands constantly twisting and turning the thick cord of hair stretched between them. Her big body was shivering, her plumpness no protection against the seeping coldness of the house. Her eyes rolled away from him, searching for something, and she suddenly wheeled away, shuffling down the corridor towards the room he had just left. Bishop slumped against the wall, his forehead beaded with perspiration that turned icy as soon as it escaped from his pores.

Jessica stood in the doorway of the room and held up her arms to ward off the lumbering woman, but she was grabbed roughly and pushed aside, the woman screaming in rage at the feeble obstruction. Jessica fell heavily and for a moment appeared dazed. Bishop could only watch helplessly as the big woman disappeared into the room and he felt a new dread when Jessica uttered a cry of alarm.

She turned her face towards him, pleading in her eyes. 'Help him, please help him!'

He wanted to run in the opposite direction, wanted to be free of the terrible house, away from the horrors that dwelt inside; but her pleas held him there and would not release him from the madness. He stumbled towards her.

Bishop tried to pull the girl to her feet, but she pushed his hands away and pointed into the room. 'Stop her! Help him, Chris!'

The woman was standing behind Jessica's father, leaning over him, her long dark hair curled around his neck. Her knuckles were white as she pulled in opposite directions.

Kulek's face was flushed red, his sightless eyes straining at their sockets, his tongue unwillingly beginning to protrude from his gaping mouth. A rasping, hissing sound came from his throat as the walls of his trachea were squeezed together. His thin hands were wrapped around the woman's wrists in an effort to pull them apart. Bishop ran forward and grabbed her arms.

It was hopeless; she was too strong, her grip too secure.

The old man's body was arched in the seat and he began to slide forward on to the floor, but the woman maintained her hold on him, keeping him from collapsing completely. Bishop knew that he was failing, that Kulek would not survive much longer. His grip on the woman's arms was only relieving the pressure slightly, only prolonging the blind man's agony. Jessica had joined in the struggle now and was tugging at the naked woman, trying to pull her away from her father. But the woman had the strength of the obsessed.

In desperation, Bishop released his hold on the woman, stepped swiftly around to the back of the armchair and kicked her sturdy legs away from under her. She fell almost to her knees, supported by the grip she had on Kulek's throat. Bishop kicked out again, the tip of his shoe sinking into the fleshy side of the woman's stomach. She screamed with sudden pain, her head swivelling towards Bishop, still keeping the pressure on the blind man's neck. Bishop drew a clenched fist back, then swung it with as much force as possible at the round, upturned face. He felt the small bones of her nose shatter under the impact and her lower face was instantly covered in running blood. Still she would not let go.

He hit her again, again, again. And finally her fingers uncurled, releasing the thick rope of hair. She sank to the floor, swaying there on hands and knees, groaning, shaking her gross body as if to shrug off the pain. Jessica ran to her father who was now lying on the floor on the other side of the chair, gasping for air. The injured woman began crawling forward around the armchair and, for a moment, Bishop thought she was trying to reach Kulek again. But she went by, heading for the open doorway, her movements slow, yet determined. He tried to stop her, grabbing her flowing hair and yanking it backwards. She half-turned, sweeping a sturdy arm back and knocking him sideways. Her strength frightened him: from her build, he guessed she was a powerful woman, and now her insanity was increasing that strength. She was halfway out the door when he lunged for her ankle, grabbing it and pulling her back. He was in an awkward position, his body stretched out on the floor, elbows supporting him, face exposed to the sudden kick she dealt him with her free foot.

The blow stunned him and he rolled on to his side, his hand releasing her and going to his head. She began crawling forward again and was soon completely through the doorway and disappearing down the hall. Suddenly he knew where she was making for. And he knew he had to stop her.

But before he could move, a figure had dashed past him into the hall. He pushed himself up and staggered through just in time to see Jessica raise Jacob Kulek's stout walking-stick above her head and bring it crashing down against the crawling woman's head. The sharp crack made Bishop wince, but he was relieved to see the woman collapse into a motionless heap, one arm stretched out towards the open cellar doorway. The darkness there was suddenly obliterated as the door was kicked shut. Jessica leaned against the stairway, the weapon she had used against the woman falling from limp fingers and clattering to the floor. Her eyes met Bishop's and for several moments they could only stare at each other.

NINE

All three looked up expectantly when Bishop entered Kulek's private study at the Research Institute.

'Is it Chris?' the old man asked, his head craning forward.

'Yes, father,' Jessica answered, smiling hesitantly at Bishop, unsure of his grim expression.

'What happened? Are the police still at the house?' Kulek asked.

'They've left a guard outside, that's all.' Bishop sank wearily into a hard-backed chair and rubbed his face with both hands as if to relieve the tension there. He looked across at Edith Metlock. 'Are you all right?'

'Yes, Mr Bishop,' she replied. 'Exhausted but not harmed in any way.'

'You, Jacob?'

'Yes, yes, Chris,' the blind man said a little impatiently. 'My neck feels somewhat tender, but my doctor says nothing was damaged. Some bruising, that's all. Do they know who the woman was?'

The memory of her being carried from the house on a stretcher, her body covered by a thick red blanket, only her face showing, the wide, blank eyes, the constantly moving lips, made Bishop shudder inwardly. Her hair had cascaded over the side of the stretcher, enhancing the madness in her features. Beneath the blanket, heavy straps kept her pinned down.

'A neighbour recognized her when she was taken to the ambulance,' he said. 'She was a nurse or housekeeper to an old man who lived further down the road.'

'But how did she get into Beechwood?'

'The police found a broken window at the back. She must have got in that way. A couple of them went off to see the old man while I was being questioned. Apparently the front door was wide open – it didn't take them long to find the old man's body.'

'He was dead?'

'Strangled.'

'With her hair?'

Bishop shook his head. 'They don't know yet. And from the look of her, it'll be a long time before she answers any questions.'

'If she killed the old man in the same manner she tried to kill me, they'll find strands of hair embedded in his throat.'

'Lilith,' Edith Metlock said quietly.

Kulek turned towards her and smiled kindly. 'I don't think so, Edith, not in this case. Just a demented woman.'

Bishop looked at Kulek in puzzlement. 'Who the hell is Lilith?'

'Lilith was an ancient demon,' Kulek said, the smile on his face implying that his words should not be taken too seriously. 'Some say she was the first woman, before Eve, joined back to back with Adam. They quarrelled constantly and, using a cabbalistic charm, she acquired wings and separation from Adam. She flew away.'

Bishop's voice was cold. 'And what has that got to do with this madwoman?'

'Nothing. Nothing at all. Edith was merely comparing their method of slaying. Lilith also used her long hair to strangle her victims, you see.'

Bishop shook his head in exasperation. 'I think this whole business is bizarre enough without dragging mythical demons into it.'

'I quite agree,' Kulek said. 'It was only an observation on Edith's part. Now please tell us what happened back at the house.'

'They ran me through the mill after they let you go. They were very curious to know exactly what we were doing there.'

'No, all that is not important. I had already informed the local police station that we would be there today with Miss Kirkhope's permission. All they needed to do was check.'

'They did that, all right. But they still wanted to know what a naked madwoman was doing in Beechwood. Finding the dead man in the other house didn't improve their disposition towards me.'

'I'm sure you explained everything adequately . . .'

'I tried to, but they'll be calling on you later. It was only because you – and Mrs Metlock – obviously needed medical attention that they let Jessica take you both away.'

'Chris, the house . . . what did you see?' Kulek's impatience was growing.

Bishop looked around in wonder at the other occupants of the study. 'I saw the same as Jessica and Mrs Metlock,' he said to Kulek.

'I saw nothing, Chris,' Jessica said. She was standing by the window behind her father's desk.

'Nor I, Mr Bishop,' said the medium. 'I . . . blacked out.'

'But that's crazy! You were both there in the room.'

Jessica spoke. 'I heard Edith scream, and I followed you downstairs. I tried to help you when you collapsed in the room. I knew you were seeing something – you were terrified – but, believe me, I couldn't see anything. I wish to God I had. All I know is that you seemed to be having some kind of fit, then you rushed from the room and made for the cellar. I saw the woman come from there – she was real enough.'

Bishop's head swung towards the medium. 'As a sensitive you must have had the same vision.'

'I think I may have caused the vision,' Edith Metlock said calmly. 'You see, I believe I was used by them.'

'You called up the dead?'

'No, I was receptive to them, that's all. They manifested themselves through me.'

Bishop shook his head. 'That's fine if you believe in ghosts.'

'What would you call them?'

'Vibrations. Electro-magnetic images. Jacob knows my theory on such phenomena. An electro-cardiograph shows the heart giving off electrical impulses; I believe someone under stress does the same. And those impulses are picked up later by someone like you, someone sensitive to such impulses.'

'But you saw them, not me.'

'Telepathy. You were the receiver; you transmitted those visions to me.'

Jessica cut in. 'Then why weren't Edith's thoughts transmitted to me? Why didn't I see them?'

'And why not me?' Kulek said. 'If they were only telepathic thoughts from Edith, then why didn't I see them in my mind's eye?'

'And why were you so afraid?' Jessica put in.

'Maybe I didn't actually see anything at all.' They all looked quizzically at Bishop. 'It could be that I just remembered what I'd seen before in that house. Mrs Metlock may have triggered off something in my subconscious, something so horrible I'd been trying to keep it from myself. And if any of you had experienced it, you'd have been afraid.'

'And the woman?' said Jessica. 'Why was she in the house?'

'She was hiding, for God's sake! She'd killed the old man. She knew Beechwood was empty, so she hid there.'

'But why did she try to kill my father? Why not you? Me?'

'Perhaps she just hates men of your father's age,' Bishop said in frustration. 'Men like her own employer.'

'She went straight to him. She hadn't even seen Jacob, but she went past us both to get to him.'

'She could have heard his voice from the cellar.'

'Yes, the cellar, Chris. You felt it too, didn't you?'

'Felt what?'

'Felt there was something evil in that cellar.'

Bishop rubbed a hand across his eyes. 'I just don't know. It all seems so insane now.'

'Chris, you still haven't told us what you saw or, what, as you would have it, you remembered,' Kulek said quietly.

Angry though she was over the investigator's refusal to accept the reality of what had happened inside Beechwood, Jessica wanted to comfort him when his face became pale.

It was seconds before he spoke, and the words came out dull and flat as if he were deliberately holding back his emotions, afraid he would lose control of them. He described the scene at Beechwood, the mad, perverted suicides, the cruel slayings. Jessica felt the muscles inside her stomach knot into a tight ball. When he had finished, there was a heavy silence in the room. Jacob Kulek's sightless eyes were closed, Edith Metlock's could not look away from Bishop's face. At last, the blind man opened his eyes and said, 'They tried to die in the foulest way possible. They had to.'

Bishop frowned. 'You think there was a motive behind all this?'

Kulek nodded. 'There is always a motive for suicide and murder. Even the insane have their reasons.'

'Suicides usually want to free themselves from the troubles of life.'

'Or the restrictions.'

Bishop was puzzled by Kulek's last remark – Jessica had talked of death as some kind of release before – but he felt too drained to pursue it. 'Whatever the motives were, it won't matter after tomorrow. The house will no longer be there.'

They were startled.'What do yo mean?' Kulek asked apprehensively.

'I rang Miss Kirkhope before coming here,' Bishop replied. 'I told her there was nothing in the house except a cold atmosphere and recommended she carry out her plan for demolition as soon as possible. She said, that being the case, she would bring the date forward to tomorrow.'

'How could you . . .?' Jessica said, furious.

'Chris, you don't know what you have done!' Kulek was on his feet.

'Perhaps he is right.' Jessica and her father turned to Edith Metlock in suprise. 'Perhaps the demolition of Beechwood will free their poor souls. I believe the house and everything that has happened there is holding them to this world. Now they may be free to go on.'

Jacob Kulek sank back into his chair and slowly shook his head. 'If only that were so,' was all he could say.

TEN

'Lucy died three days after her fifth birthday.'

The words were spoken without emotion, as though Bishop had cut himself off from the sadness that went with them. But below, somewhere inside where only he could touch, the pain fed upon itself, weaker now, yet still a living thing, a slow-dying disease of grief. Jessica, walking by his side through the cold London park, remained silent. The physical gap between them somehow symbolized their mutual antagonism, an antagonism that had frequently abated then reared into bitter life again in the few days she had known him. Now, hearing him speak of his daughter, she wanted that gap closed, yet she could not find it in herself to move closer.

Bishop paused to stare into the grey lake, the ducks tucked in close to its edges as if even they found its sombre expanse unwelcoming. 'Laryngotracheo-bronchitis was the indirect cause,' he said, still not looking at Jessica. 'When I was a kid, we called it croup. Her throat closed up, she couldn't breathe. It took us a long time to convince the doctor to leave his warm bed to come and see her that night – even in those days there were many who were unwilling to make house calls. It took three phone calls, the second threatening, the third begging, for him to come. Maybe it would have been better if he hadn't.'

Jessica stood beside him, watching his profile. The heavy cloth of her overcoat brushed against his arm.

'It was a bitterly cold night. The panic rush to hospital may have made it worse for her. Two hours we waited: an hour waiting for the hospital doctor to look at her, another hour waiting for them to decide what to do. They gave Lucy a tracheostomy, but by then she had pneumonia. Whether it was the shock of the operation in her weakened state, or the illness itself that killed her, we never found out. We blamed ourselves, the doctor who refused at first to come, the hospital – but most of all, we blamed God.' He gave a short, bitter laugh. 'Of course, Lynn and I believed in God then.'

'You don't any more?' She seemed surprised and Bishop turned his head towards her.

'Can you believe any Supreme Being would allow all this misery?' He nodded towards the tall buildings as though the city were the container for mankind's torments. 'Lynn was a Catholic, but I think her rejection of God was even stronger than mine. Maybe that's the way it works: the more you believe in something, the more you go against it when that belief is shattered. In that first year, I had to watch Lynn day and night. I thought she'd kill herself. My caring for her may have been the thing that pulled me through – I don't know. Then she seemed to accept it. She became calm, but it was a brooding kind of calmness, almost as if she'd given up, lost interest. In a way, it was unnerving, but at least it gave me something to work on. I could plan our lives again without the hysterics. I planned, she listened. It was something. A few weeks later she perked up, seemed to come alive again. I discovered she had been going to a spiritualist.'

Bishop looked around and indicated a bench on the opposite side of the path behind them. 'Shall we sit for a while? Is it too cold?'

Jessica shook her head. 'No, it's not too cold.'

They sat, and she pressed closer to him. He seemed distracted, almost unaware of her presence.

'Did you believe in spiritualism then?' she prompted.

'What? Oh, no, not really. I'd never thought about it before. But it was like a new religion to Lynn; it replaced her God.'

'How did she find this spiritualist?'

'A friend, probably well-meaning, told her of him. The friend had lost her husband years before and had supposedly made contact with him again through this man. Lynn swore to me he had found Lucy for her. She told me she had spoken to her. I was angry at first, but I could see the change it had made in Lynn. Suddenly she had a reason for living again. It went on for a long time and I admit my arguments against her seeing the spiritualist were only half-hearted. She was paying him for each session, of course, but not enough for me to suspect he was making a lot of money out of her.' Bishop smiled cynically. 'But isn't that how they operate? Build up a large clientele, accept small, individual "gifts"? It soon mounts up.'

'They're not all like that, Chris. There are very few that practise spiritualism just for money.' Jessica stemmed her irritation, not wanting to become involved in another argument with him.

'I'm sure they have all sorts of reasons, Jessica.' The implication was that any other reason was just as bad as that of financial gain, but she refused to rise to the bait.

'Anyway,' Bishop continued, 'Lynn finally persuaded me to go along to one of her meetings. Maybe I wanted to see or hear Lucy again. I missed her so much I was ready to grasp at anything. And for the first five minutes, the man almost had me fooled.

'He was middle-aged, spoke with a soft, Irish accent. His whole manner was soft, in fact; soft but persuasive. Like Edith Metlock, he looked like any other ordinary member of the public. He made no exaggerated claims to me, didn't even try to convince me he was genuine. It was all up to me, he said. The choice whether to believe or not was mine. It was his very casualness that almost convinced me of his sincerity.

'With few preliminaries, the seance began. It was in a darkened room, holding hands around a table – the sort of thing I expected. He asked us to join him in a short prayer to start the proceedings and, surprisingly, Lynn readily did so. There were others at the seance, Lynn's friend who had introduced her to the medium among them, and one by one, their dead friends or relatives were contacted. Frankly, I was a little scared. The atmosphere of the room seemed to be – I don't know – heavy, charged? I had to keep telling myself it was only created by the living people in the room itself.

'When Lucy's voice came through I was shocked rigid. Lynn was grasping my hand tightly, and without looking at her I knew she was crying. I also knew those tears were because she was happy. The voice was small, distant; it seemed to come from the air itself. A child's, but it could have been any child's. It was the things she said that made me believe. She was glad I'd finally come. She had missed me, but she was happy now. She'd felt no pain when she died, only a sadness, then a great joy. She had many new friends in the world she was now in and her only concern was that we, her mother and father, were unhappy. I felt my own tears coming, but suddenly, things didn't quite ring true. Lucy was only five when she died and here she was speaking in the manner of someone much older. If you really wanted to believe, you could convince yourself that that was how things were on the other side: you gained a wisdom beyond your mortal years. I wasn't quite that ready to accept, though. I was perplexed when she spoke of things that only we three, myself, Lucy and her mother, knew of. But then they made their first mistake. The voice was reminding me of how once, when Lynn was out shopping, Lucy and I were having a rough-and-tumble in the sitting-room. In the scramble, a favourite ornament of Lynn's got broken. It was a figurine – an 18th Century courtesan, I think – but only reproduction, not valuable. Lynn loved it though, so we knew we were in trouble. Only the head had come off and I spent the next half-hour gluing it back on. It fooled Lynn until she tried to dust it. The head just toppled off again. Unfortunately, Lucy and I were both in the room at the time and we couldn't help going into hysterics at the look on Lynn's face. Anyway, I owned up to it, and that was the last of the matter. Until the giggling voice in the room reminded me of it.

'Okay, seances are full of these trivial incidents related by departed loved ones. It's what makes them seem so genuine, isn't it? Little moments that no one else could possibly know of. That was fine, except they'd got it wrong. It was Lucy who had broken the statuette, not me. I had accepted the blame because Lucy thought she might have been spanked. She wouldn't have, of course, it was an accident. But that's how kids are.

'So now I was even more suspicious. The medium had heard the story second-hand from someone. Who? Lynn? Maybe she had told the story in one of her visits. Or her friend, the woman who had brought her along in the first place. If it was her, there was probably no bad intent. As I said, the Irishman was a soft, persuasive talker. He could have learned many things about us.

'I played along with them for a while, pretending to be convinced, waiting for another mistake. And they made it, all right. A stupid, almost farcical mistake. I suppose they had been lulled into a false sense of security by my act, imagining that here was another punter to be bled. A smoky substance came from somewhere behind the medium. It was near the back of the room, over his left shoulder, where Lynn and I had a clear view of it. An image began to appear in the smoke, hazy, not clearly defined. It was a face, fluctuating between sharpness and a blur. After a few seconds we recognized it as Lucy. The features were hers, the expression was hers; but there was something not quite right. I realized what it was and it was so silly I could have laughed out loud had I not been so angry. Her hair was parted on the wrong side, you see. They were projecting a photograph of Lucy on to a small screen from behind. The screen's edges were well camouflaged, and the smoke helped conceal it even more.

'I lost control when I realized how it was being done and rushed towards the smoke which was coming from a small tube in the wall. I pounded my fist against the screen. It was inside a small alcove that was covered by a panel when the lights were on and made of some kind of black Perspex. I managed to crack it with my fist.'

Bishop leaned forward, resting his elbows on his knees, studying the gravel path. 'Sometimes I wonder what would have happened if I had let it ride. Maybe Lynn wouldn't have had her breakdown.' His bitter smile returned as he remembered the immediate consequences of his action. 'As you can imagine, the seance ended in uproar. The medium was screaming at me, his brogue a little sharp by then. Lynn's friend was in hysterics, while Lynn herself was white-faced and quiet. The others were in various stages of shock and anger. I'm still not sure who their anger was directed at – me or the Irishman.

'I didn't even bother to look for the hidden microphone the child's voice had come from; I'd seen enough. The medium was coming at me looking as if his red face was about to burst open. A good hard shove took care of him, then I grabbed Lynn and got out of there. She didn't say a word for three days after. Then she cracked.

'Her last hope had been shattered, you see. It was as though Lucy had died twice.'

'Oh, God, it must have been terrible for her, Chris. For you both.' Jessica, too, was leaning forward.

'Lynn just seemed to sink further and further into herself over the next few months. I just couldn't reach her. She seemed to be blaming me. I finally got her to a psychiatrist and he explained that, to Lynn, I had almost become Lucy's murderer. In her confused mind, I had taken Lucy away from her again. I didn't believe him, I couldn't. Lynn and I had always been so close. When she suffered, I suffered; when I was happy, she was happy. To us, Lucy had somehow represented that closeness, had been a product of it. It was as if with her gone, our ties had been snapped. Lynn tried to kill herself twice before I was forced to have her committed. Once, she tried to kill me.'

Jessica shivered, not from the cold, and impulsively placed a hand on his arm. He sat back against the bench as if to shrug her hand off and she quickly withdrew it.

'She took sleeping pills the first time, tried to slash her wrists the second. I managed to get her to hospital before it was too late on both occasions; but I knew there would come a time when we wouldn't make it. After the second attempt, she really hated me. She wanted to be with Lucy and I was preventing her. I woke up one night and she was standing over me with a knife. Why she hadn't struck me while I was asleep, I don't know. Perhaps deep inside the old Lynn didn't want to kill me. When I woke, it must have acted as a trigger. I just managed to move out of the way in time. The knife went into the pillow and I had to hit her hard to make her let it go. After that, I had no choice: I had to have her taken into care. There was no way I could watch her all the time.'

He was silent for a few moments and from the way he avoided looking directly at her, Jessica wondered if he now regretted telling her all this. She wondered if he had ever told anyone else before.

'That happened six, seven years ago,' he finally said.

'And Lynn is still . . . ?' she hesitated, unwilling to use a title, afraid it might give offence.

'In the mental institution? She's in a private one – not the best, but one I can afford. The people who run it like to call it a rest home for the mentally disorientated. Kind of takes the sting out of it. Yes, she's still there, and as far as I can see, there's been little progress. The reverse, in fact. I visit her as much as I can, but now she doesn't even recognize me. She's built a protective barrier around herself, I'm told. I'm her biggest threat, so she's cutting me out.'

'It seems such an inadequate thing to say, Chris, but I'm sorry. These past years must have seemed like hell to you. Now I can understand why you hate spiritualists so much.'

Bishop surprised her by taking her hand. 'I don't hate them, Jessica. The real phoneys I detest, but I've learned that many are completely sincere, if misguided.' He shrugged and let go of her hand. 'That first one, the Irishman, was a complete amateur compared to some I've investigated. They've got it down to a fine art. Did you know there's a shop in America where you can buy spiritualistic miracles. A couple of dollars for the Mystery of the Gyrating Tables, a few more for the Joe Spook Spirit Rapper. It even has an Ectoplasm Kit. Spiritualism has become big business with the wave of interest in the occult. People are looking beyond the materialistic side of life and there are plenty of shysters around to cater for their needs. Don't get me wrong – I'm not on any crusade against them. At first I was ready to expose any group or individual I believed was operating fraudulently and I was pretty lucky most times. Their tricks were so obvious when you went along as a complete unbeliever. But other times I was stumped, impressed even. I began to develop a deeper interest in the whole topic of mysticism, keeping my acceptance at a realistic level. I found there was so much that could be explained by down-to-earth investigation. By practical, scientific reasoning, if you like. Of course, there's an awful lot that can't be explained, but we're slowly finding the answers, gradually moving towards the truth.'

'That's what my father's institute is all about.'

'I know, Jessica. That's why I wanted to speak to you. I've been pretty rough on you, Jacob and Edith Metlock. It seemed to me that events were being exaggerated, moulded into a shape that complied with your way of thinking. It was a kind of hysteria. I've seen it so many times in my investigations.'

He put a finger to her lips to still her protests. 'I believe what you said about this man Pryszlak. Perhaps he *was* on to something. Perhaps he *had* discovered that evil was a physical force in itself and was searching for a way of harnessing that force. But it all ended with his death and the deaths of his crazy henchmen. Don't you see that?'

Jessica gave a deep sigh. 'I just don't know any more. It could be that my father's conviction is swaying my own judgement. He knew the man so well. Their mental capabilities were so alike, so extraordinary. If anything, my father's blindness has enhanced his extrasensory faculties, although it's become a very private thing for him, not one he shares with others.'

'Not even with you?'

She shook her head. 'He will one day, when the time is right.' She smiled, almost whimsically. 'He likens himself to an explorer who cannot lead others until he has found the right path himself. His concern is that Pryszlak was way ahead of him on that path.'

'I've met many like Pryszlak in my investigations. Obviously not as extreme, but all with that same fanaticism that you tell me the man had. It's like a disease, Jessica, it spreads. I've almost caught small doses of it myself when I've been baffled by certain cases.'

'But you've always been content to label them as "unexplained phenomena" and put them aside.' There was no sarcasm in her voice, just a hopelessness.

'For the moment, yes. It's like UFOs: it's just a matter of time before we find the explanation for them.'

She nodded her understanding. 'All right, Chris. Perhaps it's good to have a cynic like you nosing around in this field; we may all be too dedicated to our own causes. I think your experience in that house has shaken you more than you're letting on, though. Your recommendation that it be destroyed immediately could be your way of chasing away your own ghosts.'

He had no answer for her; the truth wasn't clear even to himself. Instead, he tried to make light of it. 'It might destroy a reasonable living if I became a believer.'

She smiled and said, 'Thanks for telling me all this, Chris. I know it wasn't easy.'

Bishop grinned. 'It wasn't, but it helped. It's been good to talk to someone after all this time.' He rose from the bench and looked down at her. 'Tell your father I'm sorry, will you? I didn't enjoy bringing everything to such a sudden halt. I thought it was for the best, though. Really.'

'We owe you your fee.'

'For half a day's work? Forget it.'

He turned to go, but she stopped him by saying, 'Will I see you again?'

His confusion showed before he replied, 'I hope so.'

Jessica watched as he made his way towards the park exit that would take him in the direction of Baker Street. She reached into her shoulder-bag and took out a cigarette. She lit it and inhaled deeply. He was a strange man; intense. But now that she understood his cynicism, all her resentment towards him had evaporated. She wished she could help him in some way. She wished she could help rid her father of his obsession with Pryszlak. She wished it really was all over but, like Jacob, she somehow knew it wasn't.

A screech from one of the ducks startled her and she saw two of them were fighting greedily over a lake-sodden piece of bread thrown by an elderly woman. Jessica rose from the bench, drawing her coat tight around her to keep out the dampness of the air. She stopped to stub out the scarcely-smoked cigarette on the gravel path, then tossed the broken remains into a nearby bin. Hands tucked deep into her coat pockets, she walked slowly from the park.

The demolition company moved in, their machines battering the walls of Beechwood, the men swinging their sledgehammers with relish. The neighbours gawped, surprised at the sudden attack on the property and some, those who knew the history of the house, were pleased at the destruction. Within two days the building was reduced to rubble, an unsightly scar between the houses of Willow Road, an emptiness that was only filled when nightfall came. A rough wooden barrier was erected to prevent the curious, especially children, from entering the site, for the debris was dangerous, the ground floor not having collapsed completely into the basement area. There were small openings through which someone could fall.

The shadows beneath the rubble welcomed the night, merging with it, becoming more substantial, and the darkness in the cellar seemed to creep from the openings like a living, breathing thing.

PART TWO

Have regard for thy covenant;
for the dark places of the land are
full of the habitations of violence.

Psalms 74:20.
(R.S.V.)

ELEVEN

Detective Chief Inspector Peck groaned inwardly as the Granada slid to a smooth halt.

'Looks like Armageddon,' he remarked to his driver, who chuckled in response. Peck climbed from the car and surveyed the scene. The smell of smoke still clung to the air and large puddles filled the hollows of Willow Road, forming small, shiny ponds. Water tenders were dampening the ashes of the three fire-ravaged houses, their bright red bodywork a bulky intrusion on the drab greyness of the street. An ambulance stood by, its back door open wide as though expecting a fresh delivery at any moment. A blue-clad figure disengaged itself from an agitated throng and strode briskly towards Peck.

'Chief Inspector Peck? I was informed you were on your way.'

Peck acknowledged the uniformed man's curt salute with a casual nod of his head. 'You'd be Inspector Ross from the local shop.'

'Yes, sir. We've got a right bloody mess here.' He indicated the general background scene with a flick of his head.

'Well, I think the first thing you'd better do is clear the street of anyone not directly involved in last night's business.'

'Just about to do that. Trouble is, half of them *were* involved.'

Peck's eyebrows rose in an arch, but he said nothing.

Ross called his sergeant over. 'Get them all inside their houses, Tom. We'll take door-to-door statements from everyone. And get the Press back to the end of the road; we'll issue a statement later. I thought you posted men at each end to stop anyone getting through.'

'We did. It didn't work.'

'Okay, get on to HQ and have some barriers sent down. Tell them we need more men, too. Right, all civilians off the street. Now.'

The sergeant wheeled away and began barking orders at his men and bystanders alike. Ross turned back to Peck, who said, 'Okay, Inspector, let's get in the car and talk quietly for a few moments.'

Once inside, Peck lit a cigarette and opened a side window just enough for the smoke to escape. 'So tell me,' he said, looking distractedly at the activity outside.

The inspector placed his cap on one knee. 'The first sign of trouble was a radio message from one of our constables patrolling this road. Constable Posgate, it was, on surveillance duty with Constable Hicks.'

'Surveillance?'

'Well, not exactly. But it was more than the normal patrol. You've heard about the funny goings-on here recently?'

Peck grunted and Ross took it as affirmation.

'The residents demanded some protection. We gave them the patrol to let them know we were keeping an eye on things, but frankly, we didn't really expect anything else to happen.'

'Seems you were wrong. Go on.'

The inspector shifted uncomfortably in his seat. 'Our man reported what he thought was a scuffle or a mugging going on at the end of the road.'

'What time was this?'

'About half-eleven. They went down to sort things out and got pretty well sorted out themselves.'

'How many involved?'

'Three. Youths. Two white, one black.'

'And they gave your coppers a seeing-to?'

'They were vicious bastards, sir.'

Peck hid his smile by cupping the cigarette against his mouth.

'And it wasn't a mugging,' Ross said seriously.

'No?'

'No. It was a rape.'

'In the street?'

'Yes, sir, in the street. No attempt to drag the victim off into cover. But that's not the worst of it.'

'Surprise me.'

'The victim was a man.'

Peck looked incredulously at the inspector. 'I'm surprised,' he said.

Ross felt a grim satisfaction at shocking his superior. By the end of his report, Peck would be even more shocked.

'Skeates was the name of the man. He lives in the road – a young exec type. Apparently he was just returning home late from the pub.'

'He'll get a cab next time. What about your officers? How badly were they hurt?'

Hicks has a broken jaw. Not too many teeth left, either. By the time the backup got there, those three bastards had broken both Posgate's arms and were trying to do the same with his legs.'

Smoke escaped between Peck's clenched teeth in a thin, forceful stream. 'Spiteful bitches,' he commented.

Ross failed to appreciate the senior officer's sarcasm. 'There was nothing effeminate about those three. I know, I interviewed them when they were brought in.'

'Was there anything left of them?'

'They'd had a going over. They resisted arrest.'

'I'll bet.' Peck grinned at the inspector's rising indignation. 'All right Ross, I'm not having a go. I don't blame your lads dealing out some punishment of their own. Did you get anything out of the bastards?'

'No. Like zombies, all three. Haven't spoken a word all night.'

'The victim?'

'My men found him crawling down the street trying to get home. He claims the youths were just sitting on the pavement as if they were waiting for someone to come along. They don't live in this road, apparently. At least, he's never seen them before.'

'All right, Inspector, I'm already impressed. What else happened here last night?' Peck nodded towards the still smouldering house. 'Apart from the obvious, that is.'

'About half-past one this morning we received a report of an intruder on the premises of number . . .' Ross produced a notebook from his breast pocket and flicked it open '. . . thirty-three. The call came from a Mrs Jack Kimble. By the time my lads got there, her husband had dealt with the trouble himself.'

'Don't keep me guessing.'

'The Kimbles have a fifteen-year-old daughter. She sleeps in a room that looks on to the road itself. A man had forced himself into her bedroom.'

'Not another rape,' Peck said in disgust.

'Yes, sir. The intruder lived opposite the Kimbles. Eric Channing was his name.'

'Was?'

'Was. He no longer is.'

'This . . . what's his name – Kimble? . . . took the law into his own hands?'

'Channing had used a ladder to reach the girl's bedroom window. He didn't even bother to open it, just jumped head first through the glass and attacked the girl. While Mrs Kimble was phoning us, Mr Kimble was busy throwing the would-be rapist back out the way he had come. The fall broke Channing's neck.'

'Love they neighbour, eh? Is there anything dodgy about this Kimble? Is he known?'

'No record. He just over-reacted, that's all.'

'Let's hope the judge doesn't. What else have you got?'

'Well, as if these two incidents weren't enough, all hell broke loose around three o'clock. That's when the fires started.'

'Cause?'

'It started in one semi and took the adjoining house with it. We think flying sparks probably started the fire in the nearest house to them.'

'Yes, but *how* did it start?'

Ross took a deep breath and consulted his notebook again to check on the correct name. 'A Mr Ronald Clarkson, a retired businessman, raised the alarm. He'd been woken up by the smell of burning. It was his wife sitting in the middle of the bedroom floor. She'd used paraffin from one of those oil burners and doused herself with it. He was lucky: she'd doused the bed too. He only just got out in time.'

Peck's eyes were wide now, all complacency gone.

Ross continued, taking some enjoyment from the sight. 'By the time the fire engines got here, the whole house had gone up and there was no saving the one next door. The house opposite was well under way, but they managed to bring it under control before it destroyed the place completely. Eight engines they had here last night; it was like the blitz all over again.'

'Anyone else killed – apart from Clarkson's wife?'

'No. Fortunately, they got out in time thanks to Clarkson giving the warning.'

'Did he give any indication why she'd done it? Burnt herself?'

'He said she'd been depressed lately.'

Peck snorted his disgust. 'Depressed! Jesus Christ!'

'One other thing.'

'Oh, you're kidding.'

'No. This one's not so bad, though. Just as daybreak came, when the firemen were still fighting the blaze and I was running around like a lunatic trying to find out what the hell was going on, a man approached one of my officers and asked to be arrested.'

'It must have made a nice change. Who was it – another nutter?'

'He doesn't seem to be. His name is Brewer. He lives at number nine.'

'And?'

'He was afraid of what he might do to his family. The officer went back to the house with him and found Brewer's wife and three kids all tied up and locked inside a wardrobe.'

'And you say he's not a crackpot?'

'I've spoken with him. He appears to be a nice, ordinary bloke, thoroughly scared of what he did. He can't explain, doesn't know why he did it. But he wanted to be put away so he can't harm them. That's what he's afraid of.'

'I hope you obliged him.'

'Of course we did. He's in a cell now, but later on, when all this is straightened out, we'll get him to a hospital.'

'Do that, but after I've spoken with him. Is that the lot?'

'As far as we know. As I said, we're checking all the houses.'

'Just what kind of crazy road is this, Inspector? Suburbia's crackpot ghetto?'

'Until recently it was just another quiet residential area. We had all that business a year ago, of course.'

'The mass suicide you mean?'

'Yes, sir. The house – Beechwood it was called – was demolished only yesterday.'

'Why was that?'

'From what I can gather, the owner was fed up with the place. It hadn't been lived in for ages and apparently the agents couldn't sell it.'

'Maybe its ghosts have been taking their revenge for the destruction.'

Ross glanced sharply at Peck. 'Strangely enough, some funny business went on in there the other day. Someone called Kulek informed us he was holding a seance or something in the house. We checked that he'd got permission from the owner.'

'So it really was supposed to be haunted?' Peck shook his head, bemused.

'I don't know about that. But they found a naked woman hiding in the cellar. She was a private nurse who, it turned out, had done in her employer, an old man she'd been nursing for years in his house further down the street.'

'Yes, I heard about that. I didn't know about this seance going on, though.'

'I'm not sure it was a seance exactly. I know there was some kind of ghost expert present.'

'All right, I want to speak to this Kulek and anyone else who was with him at the house.'

'You don't think it's got anything to do with ghosts, do you?' There was a curious expression on Ross's face.

'Do me a favour, Inspector. On the other hand, I don't think it's got anything to do with the drinking water. I just think it's about time we collected all the pieces and started putting them together, don't you? Otherwise, before long there'll be nobody left to talk to; they'll either be dead or in the nuthouse.'

A sharp rap on the window at Peck's side made both men look in that direction. A gnarled old face squinted in at them. The woman knocked again, even though she had the attention of both men.

'Are you in charge here?' she rasped, looking directly at Peck.

'What can I do for you, madam?' Peck asked, winding down the window a little more.

'Where's me bleedin dog?' the old woman asked, and Peck was relieved to see the sergeant whom Ross had spoken to earlier hastily making his way towards her.

'Sorry, madam, but if . . .' Peck began to say.

'He's bleedin gone. Been away all night. Why don't you find im instead of sittin there on your arse?'

'Give the details to the sergeant; I'm sure he'll help you find your dog,' Peck said patiently. He gave a sigh of relief when the officer led the grumbling woman away by the arm. 'All this mayhem and she's worried about a bloody dog!'

Inspector Ross shook his head in wonder.

'Excuse me, sir.' The sergeant had returned to the car window.

'What is it, Tom?' Ross asked.

'Just thought you'd like to know. About the dog.'

Peck's eyes looked heavenwards.

'Er, it's probably nothing, but that old lady's complaint was the fifth one we've had this morning. It's the fifth family pet that's been reported missing. Seems like they've all run away.'

Ross could only shrug his shoulders when Peck looked blankly at him.

TWELVE

The drive through the peaceful Weald of Kent helped settle Bishop's troubled mind. A sudden, welcoming spring-like change in the weather had taken the dullness from the countryside and, although there was still a definite bite in the air, it could easily be imagined that the seasons had changed order. He had chosen to keep to the minor roads, avoiding the busy main routes that led more directly to his destination, but which would be crammed with other vehicles. He needed time to think.

The madness in Willow Road had persisted; had increased, in fact. The day before, two CID men had paid him a visit at his house in Barnes and had questioned him for almost two hours on his knowledge of Beechwood and the reasons for his investigation of the property. He had told them all he knew: of Jacob Kulek's concerns, of his own determination to prove the house was not haunted, of his discovering the naked woman hiding in the cellar. He did not tell them of the hallucination he had had there. When they left they hardly seemed satisfied and gruffly informed him that he would probably be asked for a formal statement within the next day or so; a Detective Chief Inspector Peck would be most interested in his story.

Bishop had later considered contacting Jacob Kulek and Jessica, but something stopped him. He realized he was sick of the whole business, that he wanted to keep away from it. Yet he felt the need to speak to Jessica again and he was confused by that need. The animosity that existed between them had faded with the conclusion of the investigation. The day before, in the park, all his resentment towards her beliefs had dissipated and he was able to look upon her as she really was: an attractive woman. But he resisted the attraction; he had to.

As Bishop kept a watchful eye out for road signs, he felt the pricking of tiny needles in his stomach. Time for something to eat. He glanced at his watch, knowing he wasn't far from his destination. Good, plenty of time to grab a bite. He wasn't due at the house until three-ish. The phone call had come after the two detectives had left, and the man at the other end had identified himself as Richard Braverman. Bishop had been recommended to him by a friend and he wished to engage his services as a psychic investigator to examine his home in Robertsbridge, Sussex. The new client seemed pleased that he was able to proceed with the investigation the following day. Apart from directions to the property itself, Bishop asked for no information concerning the alleged haunting; he preferred to be on the spot when he asked such questions. He was pleased with the job, wanting to be busy again. That night he had visited Lynn in the mental home and, as usual, had come away disappointed, depressed. If anything, she was becoming even more withdrawn. This time she had refused to even look at him. Her hands were still covering her eyes when he left.

The brightness of the following day had eased the pressure a little and anticipation of the work ahead had kept his mind occupied. He pulled in at the welcoming pub that had suddenly appeared on his left.

An hour later he was back on the road, his mood considerably brightened by a full stomach. When he reached the village of Robertsbridge he had to ask directions for the Braverman house and was guided to a small side road that crossed a railway line and led up a steep hill. At the top a discreet weathered sign, almost hidden in a hedge, reluctantly admitted that 'Two Circles' could be found down the small lane leading off from the main road. 'Two Circles' was the name Braverman had given him. He swung the car into the lane, no more than a rutted track, and almost enjoyed the bumpy ride down to the house; it made driving something to be worked at.

The house came into view and he suddenly understood its unusual title, for it was a converted oast-house, or oast-houses to be more accurate. There were two circular buildings joined together by a more conventional shaped structure which must have been at one time an enormous barn. The conversion was modern and solid, its unique shape pleasing to the eye. Beyond it stretched green fields, their lustre muted by winter, their boundaries marked by fringes of darker green. Bishop drove the car into a wide courtyard that ran the length of the square-shaped building, the adjoining oasts themselves seated in an area of lawn that ran downhill from the house towards the open fields, becoming coarse grass about halfway. Bishop already felt confident about exorcizing any alleged ghosts as he strode towards the main door, for large-scale structural alterations like this were often prone to strange creaks and rappings, the owners more concerned that they had aroused a resentful spirit than with the effects of joining new materials to old. He rang the large brass doorbell and waited.

No one came. He rang again.

A movement inside? But still no answer. He rang once more.

Bishop rapped on the door with his knuckles, and called out, 'Hello, anybody there?'

Only us spooks, he told himself.

He tried the handle and pushed the door inwards. It swung smoothly open.

'Hello! Mr Braverman? Anyone about?' Bishop stepped into a long balconied hallway and nodded appreciatively at his surroundings. The wood flooring was stained a rich walnut, light from the many windows bouncing off its highly polished surface and reflecting on to the dark, hessian walls. The odd pieces of furniture scattered around the spacious hallway were interesting enough to be of antique value, and a few carefully scattered rugs managed to diffuse any bareness the flooring may have presented. To his right were two double-doors leading to the circular sections of the house. He walked over to the nearest, his footsteps ringing hollowly around the walls, avoiding a rug in case he dirtied its delicate pattern, and knocked once, then pushed the door open. A huge table imitated the round shape of the room, its surface of the darkest oak. A broad beam, recessed into the curved wall, acted as a mantel to the open, log-filled and unlit fireplace. A small portrait hung just above the mantelpiece and the image it represented seemed vaguely familiar. The floor was covered with dark brown carpet, its pile deep and springy.

'Mr Braverman? Are you home?'

A noise from behind made Bishop turn. He glanced up towards the balcony. 'Mr Braverman?'

No sound, then a bump. *Someone* was up there.

'Mr Braverman, it's Chris Bishop. You rang me yesterday.'

No reply. He approached the stairs. Movement up there.

He placed a foot on the first step.

Jessica descended the stairs leading to the Institute's reception area.

'Mr. Ferrier?' she said to the small, bespectacled man waiting there. 'I'm Jessica Kulek.'

The man sprang to his feet and nervously turned the brim of the hat he was holding round in his hands like a steering-wheel. A smile briefly quivered on his face, then was gone. His raincoat was dotted with dark specks as if it had just started to rain before he'd entered the building.

'I'm afraid my father hasn't much time to spare today,' Jessica told him, not unused to nervousness in those visiting the Institute for the first time. 'We've been rather ... busy, lately, and have a backlog of work to catch up on. You said you were from the Metaphysical Research Group?'

Ferrier nodded. 'Yes, it's rather important that I see Jacob Kulek.' His voice was thin and reedy, like the man himself. 'If I could just have ten minutes of his time? No longer.'

'Can you tell me the nature of your business?'

'I'm afraid not,' the little man snapped. Then, realizing his brusqueness, he added apologetically, 'It's confidential.'

He saw a firmness stiffen her features and stepped quickly towards her, casting a nervous glance at the receptionist as he did so. The girl was speaking to someone on the phone, but still he kept his voice low.

'It concerns Boris Pryszlak,' he whispered.

Jessica was startled. 'What do you know of Pryszlak?'

'It's confidential,' Ferrier repeated. 'I can only speak to your father, Miss Kulek.'

She hesitated, uneasy. But it might be important.

'Very well. Ten minutes then, Mr Ferrier.'

Jessica led the little man up the staircase and along to her father's private study. They heard the muffled tones of Jacob Kulek's voice before they entered the room. The blind man switched off the dictating machine and looked up at them.

'Yes, Jessica?' Kulek said, knowing her knock, knowing her footsteps, knowing her presence.

'Mr Ferrier to see you. I mentioned his visit earlier.'

'Ah yes, from the Metaphysical Research Group, wasn't it?'

The little man was strangely silent and Jessica had to answer for him. 'Yes, Father. I've explained you're very busy, but Mr Ferrier says it's a matter concerning Boris Pryszlak. I thought it might be important.'

'Pryszlak? You have some information?'

Ferrier cleared his throat. 'Yes, but as I explained to Miss Kulek, it's confidential.'

'My daughter is also my personal assistant, Mr Ferrier. As well as being my eyes.'

'All the same, I'd rather . . .'

'Jessica, perhaps Mr Ferrier would like some coffee. Would you mind?'

'Father, I think . . .'

'Black coffee would be fine, Miss Kulek.' Ferrier smiled anxiously at Jessica, his eyes suddenly hidden by the light reflecting off his spectacles. Her unease persisted.

'I'll take coffee, too, Jessica.' Her father's voice was quietly firm and she knew it would be pointless to argue. She left the study and hurried along the corridor, not wanting to leave Jacob alone with the nervous little man for a minute longer than necessary. She paused when she drew level with her own office, then changed direction and went in. She picked up the telephone.

Anna opened the door and beamed at the two women standing there, her smile as warm for strangers as it was for those she knew.

'Yes, please?' she asked, giving a little bow of her head.

'We'd like to see Miss Kirkhope,' the taller of the two said, returning Anna's smile.

A regretful frown creased the housekeeper's broad face. 'Oh, I don't tink . . .'

'Please tell her it's about her brother Dominic,' the other woman said, face unsmiling, her tone abrupt.

Anna was too polite to close the door fully on the two women and when she returned moments later she found them waiting in the hallway itself. If she was surprised, she did not show it.

'Miss Kirkhope will see you much soon. You will wait in here, please.' She beckoned them to follow and showed them into the 'visitors' room. They seated themselves on the Chesterfield, the taller one smiling sweetly at Anna, the shorter one studying her surroundings, her face impassive.

'One moment please. Miss Kirkhope will arrive shortly.' Anna bowed her way from the room.

It was a full five minutes before Agnes Kirkhope entered, insisting that she and Anna finish that particular round of rummy in the kitchen before she received her unexpected guests. The Filipino housekeeper had an uncanny knack of finding black deuces to bolster otherwise unpromising hands and Miss Kirkhope was determined to win back the five pounds she had already lost that afternoon. One card away from victory, she had groaned aloud when Anna had rapped the table and splayed her hand before her mistress, the inevitable black deuce substituting for the Queen of Hearts that Miss Kirkhope held. Why hadn't she plucked a couple of useful cards from the deck when Anna had been answering the door?

Miss Kirkhope looked down at the two women, her irritation plain on her face and in her voice.

'You had something to say about Dominic,' she said without preamble.

'Did you know he was a paraphiliac?' the shorter of the two replied with even less preamble.

'A what?' Miss Kirkhope was taken aback by the coldness in the woman's tone.

'A paraphiliac,' the taller one said, smiling sweetly. 'It's someone who indulges in abnormal sexual practices.'

Miss Kirkhope's hand went involuntarily to her throat. Recovering quickly, she strode stiffly to the centre of the room and glared down at them. 'I suppose this has something to do with blackmail.' She spat the words out.

The taller woman reached into her handbag and said pleasantly, 'Oh no, Miss Kirkhope. Much worse than that.'

THIRTEEN

Bishop paused on the top step and looked around. To his right were doors leading off to rooms in the square-shaped section of the house; to his left was the balcony rail overlooking the hall below and another staircase leading upwards.

'Mr Braverman?' Bishop called again. He swore under his breath. Was the house empty? Had the noises he had heard just been the house settling? Or the wandering ghosts the owner alleged inhabited the house? One more try, then forget it. Braverman should have been here to meet him.

Light rain began to patter against the windows.

'Is there anybody home?'

Bump. Bump. Bump, bump, bump. The red rubber ball bounced down the stairs, gathering speed, then struck the facing wall. It bounced back against the stairway and lost its impetus, skipping low then rolling towards the wall again where it trickled to a stop.

Bishop craned his neck to see the floor above. It had to be kids playing a prank. 'I've come to see Mr Braverman. Can you tell me where he is?'

Nothing, except a movement. A scuffle of feet?

Bishop had had enough. He mounted the stairs two at a time, annoyance reflected in his forceful stride.

Had they attempted to kill him right away they would have succeeded; but they wanted to enjoy his dying, to relish it. So the blow to his head was too light.

The man appeared in the doorway, the double-barrel held shoulder high and pointed at Bishop's face. The man had enjoyed the game so far and grinned in anticipation at what was to follow. Bishop had stopped dead on the landing, his mouth open and alarm in his eyes; the woman stepped from another doorway, her raised arm which held the hammer already beginning its descent. Stun him, her husband had told her. Hit him just behind the ear, just hard enough to stun him. Then we can have some fun with him before he dies.

The blow knocked Bishop sideways, but he had turned to see the woman coming at him and had instinctively ducked when he saw the falling hammer, so the weapon had glanced across his scalp rather than striking solidly. He fell against the wall and felt himself spinning backwards down the stairs. The woman was too close: her legs became entangled with his and she went with him, the hammer clattering down the wooden steps ahead of them. She screamed as they tumbled and finally slid on to the landing below.

Stupid bitch! the man with the shotgun cursed silently. Trust her to do it wrong! He raised the gun again and aimed it at the struggling figures below. 'Get away from him, you silly cow! Let me get a clear shot!' he bellowed. Bishop would have to be killed outright.

The woman tried to free herself from the tangle of arms and legs and, though he was dazed, Bishop saw the twin-barrels pointing down at him. He pulled at the squirming woman just as one of the black holes exploded with light. Her chest took the full blast, tiny fragments of scattered lead tearing past her body and tugging at Bishop's clothes. She would not stop screaming as he tried to roll clear of her.

The man at the top of the stairs seemed hardly shocked, merely angry, as he lowered the shotgun then raised it again. His aim was more careful this time. Bishop saw the hammer lying propped against the bottom stair and, now on his knees, scooped it up and hurled it towards the man above. It was a wild throw and missed completely, but the man automatically ducked, giving Bishop the chance to gain his feet and run. The second blast powdered the floor behind him. He ran through a doorway leading off from the balcony, sure he could not make it to the front door below before the man had reloaded, praying there would be another staircase leading down at the back of the house. At least this way there would be some cover. He found himself in a room that contained a small bed and ran across to a facing door. The next room also had a bed and little else. Another door, then he was in a dark, narrow corridor. Stairs led down to a closed door.

He could hear footsteps close behind, the man screaming abuse at him. He ran down the stairs, slipping near the bottom, crashing into the door. He scrabbled around in the gloom searching for the handle, found it, jerked downwards. It was locked. A shadow above blocked out what little light there was.

Bishop sat on the second step and kicked out with both feet. The door sprang open, slivers of wood bursting away from the frame. He staggered through, slamming it behind him to stop any gunshot blasted from above. He was in a kitchen and there was a back door.

Footsteps were pounding down the stairs. He ran across to the back door, almost crying out in frustration when he found this, too, was locked. He hurled himself back across the room just as the door leading from the stairs into the kitchen opened. The man was halfway in when the door slammed back on him, trapping the shotgun across his chest, his head jolted back against the door frame. Bishop grabbed the exposed section of gun barrel, pushing against the door with all his strength. The man tried to free himself, but he was in an awkward position, his head turned sideways, his chest crushed by the pressure of the door against the weapon.

The dizziness was beginning to clear from Bishop's head and he concentrated on exerting as much pressure on the door as possible, maintaining his advantage, but not knowing where it would get him. They could hardly stay like that all day. The man's face was beginning to go red as he pushed back against the door; his eyes were wide, turned towards Bishop, glaring their hate. His mouth was open and curved downwards in a snarl, the snarl itself a choking sound. Bishop felt the door moving towards him, slowly pushing him back. He redoubled his efforts, digging his feet into the tiled kitchen floor, his shoulder pressed flat against the woodwork.

The quivering hand that grabbed at his hair from behind made him shriek with fright. He whirled around and saw the woman, her face and chest oozing fresh blood, swaying before him. She had come into the kitchen through another door that must open out into the hallway. The door at his back burst open and he was propelled forward into the mutilated woman. She fell to her hands and knees, the blood flowing freely and forming a deep red puddle beneath her.

Bishop swept his arm round without taking time to look at the man rushing through the door. His elbow caught the man square against the bridge of his nose, abruptly stopping his advance. The decision whether to run or stay was made for Bishop as the gun barrels were raised towards him once more. He had no choice: he had to fight, to run would be suicidal.

He pushed the gun upwards and lunged into the man. They fell back through the doorway on to the stairs beyond, their hands locked around the weapon between them. Bishop heaved himself up and the man came with him using the momentum to push Bishop backwards. They staggered into the kitchen once more and Bishop's foot slipped in the spreading pool of blood. He fell to his knees and suddenly his assailant was standing over him, his contorted face only inches away. Bishop's body was arched backwards, his hold on the shotgun now being used against him. He went back on to the floor, his legs forced sideways and out, his shoulders sinking into the sticky redness beneath him. Still he refused to let go of the gun, but he could not prevent the weapon from being turned inwards towards him.

A hand flailed weakly at his face, trying to gouge out his eyes. The woman was still alive, trying to help the man destroy him. He suddenly allowed the gun to turn, bringing it towards him but twisting his body so the twin-barrels struck the floor. The man staggered forward, falling with the gun, and Bishop let go of the warm metal with one hand and struck out, hitting him below the left ear. The man fell sideways and Bishop grabbed at the gun again, but the woman dug painfully into his eyes, forcing him to wrench himself free, to roll his body away from the sharp claws. He realized his mistake when he was halfway across the kitchen floor. The man was free to raise the gun and take a shot at him.

He could only stare as the man grinned in triumph and began to rise to his feet, knowing his quarry was trapped. His fingers had already curled around the two triggers and he was stepping forward when his foot slid in the viscous mess on the kitchen floor. His leg shot out and he staggered to keep erect, but then both feet were in the blood and he fell, going forward, slightly sideways. The gun roared, taking off the top of his head with the double blast. The kitchen ceiling became a shocking canvas of red fluid.

The woman's moan was long and agonized as she stared at the twitching form of her husband and she did not look away nor did the moan die in her throat until his body was still. Then she turned to look at Bishop and held him there sprawled on the floor with her wild-eyed, mesmerizing gaze. It was only after the thick gob of blood oozed from her lips that he realized she was dead and her eyes saw nothing. Released, he rose weakly to his feet and stumbled towards the kitchen sink, his stomach heaving in juddering movements. He was still crouched over the metal sink ten minutes later when the pattering on the window panes increased its intensity as the rain became more fierce and the skies overhead darkened.

Jessica hurried along the corridor, her heart thudding. She had just called the Metaphysical Research Group at their headquarters in Sussex: they had never heard of Ferrier. She reached her father's study and pushed against the door, twisting the handle, prepared to feel foolish if the man and her father were merely engaged in conversation, but somehow knowing that would not be the case. She cried out in alarm when she saw the thin, leather belt around Jacob Kulek's throat, the little man behind him, his hands pulling the belt tight, his body shaking with the effort. Jacob had one hand against his own throat, fingers curled around the improvised garotte as though he had become aware of his assailant's intention just before the little man had struck. His face was a deep red, turning purplish, his tongue emerging from his open mouth, his sightless eyes bulging from their sockets as though a parasite growing inside his head was pushing everything else out. A tight asthmatic wheezing sound came from his throat as he tried to suck in air through his strangulated windpipe.

Jessica ran forward, afraid that she was already too late. The little man seemed almost oblivious of her as she grabbed at his wrists and tried to force them together again to relieve the pressure on the belt. But it was no use; his strength belied his frame. She struck out at his face when she realized that her father's gasps for breath had stopped. Ferrier turned his head away to avoid the worst of her wild blows, but still he maintained the pressure, still he pulled at the leather belt, still his whole body quivered with the effort.

Jessica screamed, knowing she was losing. She pulled at the man's hair, scratched at his eyes, but it had no effect: he was like a robot, unfeeling, governed by something outside his own body. She looked around desperately for something to use against him. The silver paperknife lay gleaming on the desktop.

Frantically, Jessica grabbed it, turning on the man, the weapon raised high. She hesitated before sweeping her arm down, the intent abhorrent to her, but knowing she had no choice. The narrow blade sank into the side of Ferrier's neck, just above the shoulder bone.

His body suddenly went rigid and, for a moment, his eyes stared unbelievingly at her. Then they seemed to cloud over and with horror she saw his hands resume their pressure. The knife protruded from his neck, only half of its length sunk into his flesh, and Jessica threw herself at him, screaming with frustrated fury, beating at his exposed face, thrusting down on the knife again to sink it in further, praying the blade would find a vital artery.

The little man's body shuddered, and his knees sagged. Then he straightened as if he had regathered his strength. He let go of one end of the belt to sweep his arm around and knock the girl to one side. Jessica staggered against the bookshelves, her eyes blurring at the pain and tears of helplessness that had formed.

'Stop!' she cried out. And then a moan: 'Please stop.'

But both hands pulled at the belt once more.

She heard the footsteps running along the hall and then suddenly, mercifully, there were figures in the dooray. The two men and the woman who peered over their shoulders were members of the Institute.

'Stop him!' She implored.

They were stunned by what was happening, but one, a tall grey-bearded man, generally timid, and usually slow in action, rushed forward, lifting a chair as he went. Without losing stride, he raised it over the desktop and half-threw, half-pushed it into Ferrier's face. The rungs of the chair caught the little man across the forehead, knocking him back, sending him against the window behind, the glass shattering outwards, his body hanging there, hands outstretched to grasp at the window-frame. He seemed to study them for a moment, their actions temporarily frozen, before his fingers uncurled and he let himself fall backwards, his legs rising upwards then slithering down out of sight over the sill.

Jessica wasn't sure whether or not she really heard the sickening squelch of his head bursting open on the pavement below, for the woman was screaming hysterically and she, herself, was stumbling towards her father, who had now collapsed on to the floor. But her mind had recorded the sound, imaginary or not.

Anna had packed away the playing cards and was on her way back to the 'visitors' room to see if her mistress would require tea for herself and the guests, when the smile disappeared from her face leaving an expression of total incomprehension. Miss Kirkhope had appeared in the hallway, crawling on hands and knees, something wrong with her face, something distorting her features. Her eyes looked beseechingly at Anna, a thin, heavily veined hand reaching towards her, a weak croaking noise coming from a face that was sizzling, the skin popping and tearing.

For Anna, confusion did not turn to terror until she saw Miss Kirkhope's two women guests stroll from the room behind her crawling mistress, each holding what seemed to be nothing more than small bottles of clear liquid. They could have contained water – the fluid looked harmless enough – but the old lady's head shook in horror when the taller woman smiled and raised her bottle. Miss Kirkhope tried to scramble away, but the woman jerked the bottle in her direction, the liquid splashing out and landing in heavy splats on the old woman's back and head. Anna's hands went to her mouth as she heard the faint sizzling sound and saw what looked like small trails of curling steam rise from the wetness.

Miss Kirkhope arched her back inwards, her agonized groans spurring the housekeeper onwards a few paces. But Anna's courage failed her when she saw the shorter of the two women step forward and kick the old lady over on to her back. Anna sank to her knees and joined her hands in supplication when she saw the woman stand astride Miss Kirkhope's slumped body and slowly pour the contents of her bottle in a steady stream into the open, upturned mouth.

The gargled screams filled Anna's head before they became a low rasping sound as vocal cords were burnt away. Anna found she could not rise, not even when she felt the trickle run down between her legs and the floor around her became wet with urine. Not even when the taller woman strode towards her, still smiling, sprinkling the contents of the bottle before her like holy water. Not even when the first splattering of acid touched her skin and began to burn.

FOURTEEN

Peck looked disbelievingly across his desk at Bishop. 'Do you know how incredible all this sounds?'

Bishop nodded without apology. 'I find it hard to believe myself.'

'But why should a total stranger try to murder you?'

'Braverman had to be a part of Pryszlak's sect. They didn't all commit suicide. Some were left to carry on his work.'

'Which was killing people?'

'I don't know, Inspector. Maybe we were getting too close.'

'Too close to what?'

Jessica spoke up, and there was repressed anger in her voice. 'The reason for the mass suicide. My father knew there had to be a reason for Pryszlak and his sect to kill themselves.'

Peck sat back in his chair and regarded the girl silently for a few moments, his thumb scratching an itch at the end of his nose. She looked pale and worried, on the surface the type who would crack when things got too rough. But Peck knew better; he had dealt with too many people for too many years to be deceived by appearances. The girl was stronger than she seemed.

'But you still have no idea what this is all about,' he said.

Jessica shook her head. 'I told you Pryszlak came to my father to enlist his help a long time ago, and that my father refused.'

'You think this could be some kind of perverted revenge, then? Instructions carried out by Pryszlak's followers after his death?'

'No, it's not revenge. Why should they try to kill Chris? Why did they kill Miss Kirkhope?'

'And her housekeeper.'

'The housekeeper probably got in their way. Pryszlak's sect has no regard for human life, not even their own. This man, Ferrier, killed himself without hesitation when he saw he was trapped. The motive wasn't revenge. I think the idea was to kill anyone who had any knowledge at all of their organization.'

'There's been no attempt on your life.'

'Not yet, Inspector,' Bishop said. 'Maybe Ferrier would have turned on Jessica once he'd disposed of Jacob Kulek.'

Peck frowned and turned to Bishop. 'I still don't understand why I haven't booked you for the murder of Braverman and his wife.'

'I came to you, remember? I could easily have left that house without anyone ever knowing I'd been there. I could have wiped away any fingerprints. It would have been easy for the police to have believed that Braverman fought with his wife, shot her, then shot himself. It makes no sense for me to have murdered them and reported the crime myself.'

Peck still looked sceptical.

'And the others,' Bishop went on. 'The attempt on Jacob Kulek's life. The murder of Agnes Kirkhope and her maid. All connected with the Pryszlak business. Kulek, because he was investigating Pryszlak's activities. Agnes Kirkhope, because we had been to see her and told her of our suspicions. And, of course, her brother, Dominic, had been a sect member. It's logical, Inspector, that I should have been a victim too.'

'Nothing's logical about this business, Mr Bishop.'

'I agree. Even more illogical are the events in Willow Road. How do you explain them?'

'At the moment, I wouldn't even try. We've got people locked up and they're like zombies. Even the one man who didn't seem to be as bad as the others has deteriorated – he's now like the rest of them. A man named Brewer – he'd tied his family up and locked them in a wardrobe. But he gave himself up before he could do any harm.'

Bishop noticed the puzzled look on Jessica's face. He was concerned for her: the near-death of her father had left her in a brittle state. He had rung the Research Institute from the house in Robertsbridge, resisting the urge to flee from the blood-stained corpses lying there on the kitchen floor, worried that if an attempt had been made on his life, then the same could happen to Jacob Kulek. He had seen for himself how the madwoman in Beechwood had tried to get at Kulek. And he knew there was a connection: the portrait he had seen in the round room at Robertsbridge was of Dominic Kirkhope: he had remembered Agnes Kirkhope's photograph of her brother and although there was an age difference between the portrait and photograph, the resemblance was distinct. He had been surprised to find that Detective Chief Inspector Peck, the man who was apparently in charge of the investigation into Willow Road and its mishappenings, was at the Institute. It came as no surprise that an attempt on

Jacob Kulek's life had already been made.

'Now all I've got,' Peck was saying, 'are murders, suicides, attempted rape – homosexual and otherwise – mutilation, arson and cells full of people who don't know what time of day it is. To help me with my report to the Commissioner – and which you seem to think explains everything – I've got your information on a nutcase named Boris Pryszlak and his crackpot organization who believed in evil as a powerful, physical force. How do you think he's going to take it, Miss Kulek? He'd order me to be locked up with the other nutters.'

'I've given you no explanations, just what I know. Your job is to do something about it.'

'Any ideas exactly what?'

'I'd start by trying to find the names of all Pryszlak's associates.'

'You mean the members of his sect.'

'Yes.'

'And then?'

Jessica shrugged. 'I don't know. Keep a watch on them?'

Peck snorted.

'At least you'd find out if Braverman and Ferrier were members,' Bishop said. 'It might even lead you to the murderers of Miss Kirkhope and her housekeeper.'

Peck wished he could make up his mind about Bishop, one way or the other. He had ordered him to stay at the house in Robertsbridge until the local police arrived, and then arranged to have him escorted back to London, to Peck's office in New Scotland Yard. He had questioned the ghost-hunter – what kind of profession was that? – for a solid hour before Kulek's daughter, again under escort, had arrived from her father's hospital bedside. It was getting on for ten now and still he wasn't any nearer to the truth. It would have been easier if he could believe Bishop was either lying or totally innocent.

Peck leaned forward on his desk. 'Okay, we're not going to find out much more tonight. I'm letting you go, Bishop. I'm not convinced, but your story might just be feasible. This Pryszlak may have had friends who didn't like you and Jacob Kulek snooping around Beechwood. It could be that they regarded it as some kind of holy shrine after the mass suicide. The fact that poor old Miss Kirkhope ordered it to be demolished may have been her undoing. We'll put it down to a lunatic fringe for the moment. It still doesn't explain all the disasters in Willow Road, of course, but I can hardly blame you for that. Anyway, we'll be keeping a close eye on you.'

'Don't worry,' Bishop said wryly, 'I won't be running away.'

Peck stabbed a finger against the desktop. 'We'll be keeping an eye on you not just because I'm suspicious – and I bloody am – but for your own protection. That goes for your father, too, Miss Kulek. For protection, I mean. If his assailant was part of Pryszlak's mob, they might have another try.'

Alarm showed in Jessica's eyes.

'Sorry. Didn't mean to frighten you,' Peck said soothingly. 'It's better to be safe than sorry, that's all.' He turned to one of his officers, who had been leaning against the wall, arms folded, bemused by the whole exchange. 'Frank, get someone to show them down, will you?'

As Bishop and Jessica rose to leave, Peck looked up at them, his scowl still in evidence. 'Keep us informed of any more little trips, Mr Bishop. I'll probably want to speak to you again tomorrow. I hope your father recovers, Miss Kulek.'

Jessica nodded her thanks and they left the detective's office.

The officer returned a few seconds later, amusement on his face.

'What are you bloody grinning at?' Peck growled.

'You don't believe in all this bollocks about the power of evil, do you, guv?'

'That's not the point, Frank. *They* believe it, that's what matters. At least, the girl does. I think Bishop hasn't made his mind up yet. To tell you the truth, I don't think *I've* made my mind up, either.'

They drove away from the tall building, silent for a few moments as if Peck could still hear their conversation from his office high above them. The rain had finally stopped, leaving a dampness in the night air. Jessica pulled her coat collar tight around her neck.

'Will you take me back to the hospital, Chris?'

'I'm already headed in that direction,' he told her. 'How was he when you left?'

'Shocked, weak. He was still finding it difficult to breathe.'

'How much damage?'

'Physically, just bruising, as before. The doctor said his difficulty in breathing was more to do with the emotional shock than constriction of his windpipe. Oh God, if I'd have gone back to his study a few seconds later . . .' She left the sentence unfinished.

He wanted to reach out to her, to pat her hand, to touch her; but he felt awkward, a stranger.

'He'll be all right, Jessica. He's a strong-minded man.'

She tried to smile at him, but failed. His attention was on the road ahead, anyway. She studied his profile, noticing the lines of tension around his eyes. 'And you've been through so much, too,' she said eventually. 'It must have been a nightmare.'

'It was even more of a nightmare for Agnes Kirkhope and her housekeeper; one they didn't come out of. What manner of creature could do such a thing?' He shook his head in regret, disgust. 'I think Peck still believes I murdered Braverman and his wife.'

'He can't, Chris. It doesn't make any sense.'

'None of this does. You and I, in our different ways, deal with matters that defy logic all the time. Peck's a policeman: they like some kind of order to things. We can't blame him for his suspicion.'

'Nor his aggression.'

'Nor that.'

He pulled up at traffic lights, floodlights turning the square before them into a daylight scene. Tourists, thousands it seemed, watched the silvery fountains and craned their necks to see the sculptured naval man standing aloft on the huge rising column as though it were the crow's nest on one of his ships. As a brilliantly lit backdrop, the impressive structure of the National Gallery dominated the thriving square, while a constantly surging stream of traffic flowed round and out.

'It's so bright,' Jessica remarked distractedly. 'So alive. It could be daytime.'

The red light blinked off and the green appeared. Bishop edged the car forward into the metal throng, finding a niche and flowing with the tide. 'I wonder how many of Pryszlak's people stayed alive? And why?'

'Perhaps for a time like this.'

He had to concentrate on avoiding a taxi which was making a claim to a three-foot space just ahead of Bishop's car.

Jessica went on. 'If the police can locate them all, perhaps this can end now, before it's too late.'

He snatched a quick glimpse of her. 'What can end, Jessica? Do you and your father know what's happening?'

She hesitated before she spoke. 'We're not sure. We discussed it with Edith Metlock only yesterday –'

They both looked at each other at the same time.

'Christ!' Bishop said quietly.

Bishop turned the car into the wide tree-lined avenue, keeping in second gear and peering from left to right at the houses on either side.

'What number is it?' he asked Jessica.

'I'm sure it's sixty-four. I've never been to her home, but I've often contacted her there.'

'Even numbers on the right. Keep your eyes peeled.'

Once they had passed through London's West End they were able to make rapid progress to Edith Metlock's address in Woodford. Both were angry at themselves for having forgotten the medium, for they realized that she, as a part of the group investigating Beechwood, might also be in danger.

'Fifty-eight . . . sixty . . . sixty-two . . . There! Just ahead.' Bishop pointed towards a small bungalow, twenty feet of garden on either side separating it from its neighbours. He waited for an approaching car to pass, then drew over to that side of the road, stopping just in front of the bungalow.

'She's there,' Jessica said. 'All the lights are on.' Suddenly she felt afraid to leave the car.

Bishop slid his glasses into his top pocket and switched off the engine. 'We're probably over-reacting,' he said unconvincingly, then sensed Jessica's fear. 'Do you want to stay in the car?'

She shook her head and reached for the door-handle.

The garden gate squealed noisily as Bishop pushed it open. Light from the windows spilled on to the lawn on either side of the narrow path leading to the bungalow's porch, the clipped grass a flat green vignetting into total blackness. The porch itself was lit by an external light.

Bishop rang the doorbell and they waited for movement inside. Jessica bit down on her lower lip; her eyes were wide, almost vacant. He touched her arm, at the elbow, giving it a little shake as if to dispel her anxieties. He tried the doorbell again.

'Maybe she's asleep,' he said.

'With all the lights on?'

'She may have dozed off.'

He rattled the letter-box for added noise, then ducked to look through it.

'All the doors in the hallway are open. She must have heard us. Looks like every light is on, too.' He put his mouth to the opening and called out Edith Metlock's name. There was no reply.

'Chris, let's get the police,' Jessica said, slowly backing away from the front door.

'Not yet.' He caught her arm again and this time held it firmly. 'Let's be a little more sure there's something wrong first.'

'Can't you feel it?' Jessica looked around at the shadows surrounding the house. 'It's . . . I don't know . . . unearthly. As if . . . as if something is waiting.'

'Jessica.' His voice was soft. 'You've been through a bad time today – we both have. It's getting to you, eating away at your imagination.' And it was eating away at his, too. 'I'm going to take a look round the back. Why don't you go and sit in the car?'

Her alarm flared to a new level for a brief moment. 'I think I'll stick with you,' she said firmly.

Bishop smiled and moved off, stepping on to the lawn and glancing into a window as he passed. The curtains were drawn wide and lace netting diffused the image inside. He saw it was a small dining-room, the table bare except for a pot containing a leafy plant. There was no one in the room. They moved around the corner of the one-floor building and Bishop felt Jessica draw closer to his back as they found themselves in an area of darkness. The ground became softer beneath their feet as if they were walking through a dormant flower-bed. More light shone ahead and they passed a reeded glass window which Bishop assumed would be the bungalow's bathroom. Beyond, the light was more brilliant, throwing back the night with unimpeded force. The blinds to the kitchen were drawn upwards and Bishop blinked against the harsh neon light.

'Empty,' he told Jessica. 'There's a door over there leading out to the back garden. Let's try it.'

More light flooded outwards from the back of the house and he wondered if it was only because of the natural nervousness of a woman living alone. But Edith Metlock had not struck him as the nervous type.

He tried the kitchen door and was not surprised to find it locked. He jiggled with the handle for a few moments, then rapped on the glass. Maybe she was out and had left the lights on to discourage any would-be burglars. But every light? And the curtains open?

'Chris!'

Bishop turned to see Jessica gazing into a window nearby. He hurried over to her.

'Look,' she said. 'Over there, in the armchair.'

He found himself looking into a bedroom, again the curtains drawn wide. Through the lace netting he could see an unoccupied bed, a bedside table, the lamp on it adding more brightness to the already well-lit room, a wardrobe, a chest of drawers. And in an armchair in the far corner sat the figure of a woman. His vision was hazy through the lace, but he was sure it was Edith Metlock.

'Mrs Metlock.' He tapped at the window. 'It's Chris Bishop and Jessica Kulek.' He used his knuckles against the glass.

He thought he saw a movement, a slight turning of the head, but couldn't be sure.

'Why doesn't she answer?' Jessica said. 'Why is she just sitting there, Chris?'

The thought flashed through his mind that Edith Metlock may have had a stroke; but her body sat erect, not slumped. Was she too afraid to answer?

'I'm going to break in,' he told Jessica. He walked back to the kitchen and angled his body to see through the small glass panels that ran the length of the door. He could just see the end of the key poking from the lock on that side. He half-turned away from the door, then brought his elbow swinging back at a pane alongside the lock. The glass fell inwards and clinked to the floor. He pushed his hand through the opening, carefully avoiding any remaining shards, and twisted the key, grunting with satisfaction as the lock clicked. Turning the handle, he pushed inwards. It wouldn't open. There was less resistance when he put pressure on the top, and solid defiance when he tried the bottom. Without hesitation he kicked in one of the bottom panes, then stooped and drew back the bolt inside. The door swung open.

Jessica followed him in, keeping close, trying to see over his shoulder. Edith Metlock's eyes were closed when they entered her bedroom and they remained so even when they called her name. Her back was stiff, her face pointed towards the ceiling light. Her hands clutched at the arms of the chair.

'She's breathing,' Bishop said and, as if his voice had triggered off something in the medium, her breathing became deeper, her breasts beginning to heave with the effort. Her lips parted and air was exhaled, then noisily sucked in. Her breathing became sharper, gasping, and Jessica knelt before her, touching the medium's shoulders, gently calling her name. The panting became frantic and Jessica looked anxiously at Bishop. He felt useless, tempted to slap the medium and bring her out of her trance-like state, but afraid of what the sudden shock might do to her. Then Edith Metlock jerked forward in the seat, her gasps brought to an abrupt halt. She sat that way for long seconds, then slowly sank back into the armchair, her breath released in a long, drawn-out sigh. The medium's eyelids flickered, opened; her pupils were tiny pinpoints. Her jaw was slack, lips moving, tongue lolling within its cavity as though its muscles were limp. A low murmuring came from somewhere at the back of her throat.

'She's trying to say something, Chris. Can you understand her?'

Bishop leaned his head closer to the medium's and listened. Slowly, the words began to take form, began to shape themselves into a meaning.

'Keep . . . it away,' Edith Metlock said, her voice slurred but just coherent. 'Keep . . . it . . . away . . . The dark . . . keep it away . . .'

FIFTEEN

The home crowd was angry, its wrath rolling around the stadium in a mighty roar. The ref was a wanker: even the minority away-fans, delighted though they were at his dubious decisions in their team's favour throughout the match, had to admit it. Now even the goalkeeper was going into his book for dissent and *he* had never received a booking in fifteen years of soccer. The overwhelming anger reached fever pitch when the tiny yellow card was raised into the air and the away-fans – except for the lunatic few whose brains were in the tips of their tongues – refrained from jeering. The hostility around them had made them nervous.

The home team had been playing well all season, and the smell of the First Division was in their fans' nostrils. They had completely dominated their rival clubs in the Second Division. Their new striker, imported from Italy for an incredible sum of money (to make up the loss, the club had had to sell two players, one mid-field, the other a popular left-back, and admission prices had been raised) had contributed remarkably to their success. But after only ten minutes, the Italian had been stretcher-carried off with a leg injury. The word spread around at half-time like an uncontrolled brush fire that his leg had been broken. In two places.

The away-team had played like non-league factory workers throughout the match, their studded boots scything opponents rather than playing the ball. It had been the same on Saturday when ugly brute force at their own ground had earned them the draw. Their fear of relegation next season had turned them into eleven crude defenders, only occasional bouts of real skill reminding the crowd they were playing football and not rugby. Tonight the match was a gruelling affair and already several fights had broken out among the crowd. The policemen seated on benches placed strategically around the pitch, helmets at their feet, glanced nervously over their shoulders at the ranting mob, the surge of faces merged into a dark swaying mass behind the brilliant glare of the floodlights. The mood was ugly.

Eddie Cossins pulled his girlfriend, Vicky, closer to him. He was beginning to wonder if it had been wise to bring her tonight. She didn't even like football as a rule and he suspected her insistence on coming with him was more to do with ingratiating herself with him than interest in football itself. Five weeks was a long time to be going out with a bird. Too long, really. They started getting ideas.

'What's he booked him for, Eddie?'

He barely heard her shrill voice above the uproar even though she had stood on tiptoe and bellowed into his ear.

'Ref don't like bleedin arguments!' he yelled back.

'What's he arguing about?'

Eddie groaned. 'The ref's given the other side a penalty. Anyone could see the player took a dive. All the bleedin fouls they've done and they get a penalty. What a tosser!'

Vicky sank back inside her heavy overcoat, pulling Eddie's club scarf tighter around her neck. Stupid game, she told herself. Grown-up men kicking a bag of wind around a field. And the crowd getting upset just because their team wasn't winning. Like a load of kids. Eddie too. Look at him shouting at the referee as if he could hear him. Poor little man was only doing his job. So this was what she had to compete against. Another girl might have been easier. Oh no. Now it's raining. Jostled, pushed, crushed, touched-up by invisible hands – and now a soaking! It wasn't worth it. He could have his bloody football! He was spotty, anyway.

The crowd hushed as the away-team's skipper placed the mud-smeared ball on the penalty spot. His left foot was renowned.

On the terraces, Jack Bettney held his breath, almost afraid to watch. Twenty-five years he'd supported the club, through the good years and the lean. After a long stretch in the Second Division they were on the way up again, back to their rightful place among the leaders of the game. They had won back their old days' glory last season and this one. Nothing would stop them now. Nothing except a team full of cowboys and a bent referee. He kept the anger tight within himself.

He blinked away rainspots from his eyes and watched the enemy pace himself away from the ball. The goalkeeper danced nervously from foot to foot and finally settled down on his line, heels raised from the muddy earth. To the right, son, he'll aim it at the bottom right-hand corner, Jack Bettney told him silently. He knew the opposing captain's favourite spot. Jack could feel the tenseness around him; the apprehension passed through the mass of tightly packed bodies like an electric current. The enemy began his run, pounding up to the glistening ball like an express train. To the right, son, to the right.

Animal, sometimes known as the Beast to his friends, whooped with glee when the ball shot into the bottom left-hand corner of the net, the goalkeeper left sprawled in the mud on the other side of his goal-mouth. Animal leapt in the air using the shoulders of a fellow supporter in front to hold himself aloft. His friend's knees buckled under the seventeen stone weight, but others grabbed his arms to keep him upright. It would have been difficult to get up again in that crowd.

'Fuckin magic, fuckin magic!' Animal screeched. Hostile eyes turned to look in his direction.

He chortled as the goalkeeper dejectedly retrieved the ball from the back of the net. 'What a load of wankers!' he chanted.

'Leave it out, Animal,' one of his companions said nervously, feeling the resentment around them. 'We're not bloody at home now.'

Animal didn't give a shit and he let the home supporters around him know it. Personally, he didn't care much about the game either. It was the excitement he liked, not the excitement of the competition but, although he couldn't have expressed it himself, the raw emotion the game produced, feelings that could be demonstrated without embarrassment.

He turned to face the crowd behind him, his thick, porky arms raised, middle and index fingers stiff and parted in his favourite up-yours gesture. The rain suddenly fell as though someone had pulled the plug from the clouds above and it spilled on to his fat cheeks and open-necked shirt. He laughed, catching the torrent in his mouth. Their faces were just a watery blur, but he could feel their hate and it cheered him.

He found another pair of shoulders to leap on and this time his companion went down. Animal collapsing with him. He giggled in the darkness, thrashing out at the jostling legs around him. It was like being underground, subdued light sinking down through cracks in the earth, the surrounding legs like moving tree roots. He giggled louder at his friend's muffled cursing, maliciously pushing his gross body on hands and knees further into the throng, causing those above him to lose their balance and spill over. He liked the darkness as much as he liked being in a crowd. It was almost the same thing: you couldn't be seen. For a moment it had become too black down there, as though the crowd had joined together to form a solid crust above him, and he felt a little afraid. The darkness somehow had a gooey thickness to it.

Animal burst to the surface like a whale from the sea, throwing those nearest to him backwards, laughing at their shouts of anger. The fact that their club scarves differed from the one he wore tied around his wrist didn't bother him at all: Animal was afraid of nothing and no one.

Fans at the back resented the crowd ripple that had thrust against them and several saw the cause of it, the fat grinning face turned away from the pitch in their direction, thick bare arms, despite the weather, raised in defiance against them, the opposition scarf tied to one wrist. The rain had drenched them, their team was losing – and this fucker was taking the piss. They surged forward as one, a ripple that grew into an onrushing wave, gathering momentum, gaining force, breaking over the fat man and pounding him like a rock on the sea-shore.

Eddie and Vicky had been standing halfway between the grinning monster and the fans at the back who had started the push. The girl screamed as they were carried forward, her feet swept off the ground, her body held tightly aloft, desperately clinging to Eddie who was powerless to resist the torrent. Eddie had been used to crushes like this before, but he had never had a girl to look after. He knew these sudden rushes could be dangerous, fights inevitably breaking out in the aftermath. The thing was not to go down – you'd be kicked to death beneath all those feet. It was the poor sods at the front who took the full weight of it: they'd be crushed against the barriers. He managed to get an arm around Vicky's waist, his other arm locked tight against his body. He shouted a warning to the girl when he saw what was happening ahead of him. Bodies were going over, *going down!*

Jack Bettney felt the swell reach him. Fortunately, he was away from the path of the main stream, but even so he and the other fans around him were pushed back then sucked in with the flow. He kept his balance, well experienced nowadays in the art of surviving a football match. Silly bastards! he thought. No wonder the armchair was the best place to watch a game these days. Those nearest to him managed to steady themselves and they jigged on tiptoe to see what was happening in the other part of the crowd. A great hole had appeared and they realized many of the people had gone down, more bodies toppling over them as the surge continued.

Jack winced. There'd be a few broken bones among that lot. His woolly cap was sodden now, and rain ran off the end of his nose. He blinked and saw the ball was in the centre of the pitch again, the players deliberately oblivious of the reaction in the crowd. They probably couldn't see too much against the glare of the floodlights anyway. Jack turned his attention away from his team's centre forward who was preparing to tap the ball towards a mid-field player, and tried to see what was happening to the fallen spectators. The atmosphere in the stadium was bad tonight and he was glad he was a home supporter. The hostility towards the away-fans had been growing since the beginning of the match and the commotion over there was just the start of the trouble to come. Needle matches always infected the fans and tonight the infection was going to run wild. He could feel it.

A flickering behind and high above distracted him. He looked up at the tall metal tower set into the concrete terraces towards the back of the stadium, sixteen blinding lights at the top helping three other similarly situated towers around the ground to turn night into day on the pitch. Fifteen lights. One was spluttering, going dim, reviving briefly, sparks flying into short-lived arcs, then fading completely. Bloody rain. That shouldn't be happening, though. When was the last time they were checked? A cheer rang out from the other side of the pitch as another light abruptly popped off, then another. More sparks began to fly and soon the whole array of lights was fizzing and smoking. The section of the crowd beneath the tower began to grow anxious and started backing away from the area beneath it, pushing at those around them for room. All the lights suddenly exploded at once, glass and sparks falling with the rain on to the people below and a sharp, tangy smell was carried into the air. The gloom on that side of the stadium suddenly became denser and Jack felt the panic as a crowd wave started again, this time rippling outwards, the movement resembling a pond's surface disturbed by a stone.

Animal was on the ground kicking out with heavy boots trying to clear a space for himself. It had become darker now, almost black and, strangely, rather than fearing the blackness, he welcomed it. Someone was on top of him and he managed to get one beefy hand beneath the man's chin. He pushed up sharply and was delighted to hear above the clamour of the spectators – or had he only felt it? – something snap. The body fell limply against him and Animal felt good. He had enjoyed that. Something chuckled in the blackness of his mind and it wasn't him.

A foot came down on his cheek and he twisted his head to dislodge it. He heaved the body on top of him away, but there were others, alive and thrashing, to take the man's place. Animal managed to get an elbow beneath himself and raised his shoulders from the ground. A figure crashed down beside him – man or youth, he couldn't tell – and this time he definitely heard the crack of skull on concrete. He lifted the fan's head by the hair and shoved it down to hear the sound again. Nice one.

Eddie tried to pull Vicky closer to him, but he was pinned to someone else's back. The body beneath him squirmed to free itself, but there were others on top of Eddie. Vicky's screams could be heard clearly over the predominantly male cries of alarm and anger and he tightened his grip around her waist, determined not to let her go. He felt a blow behind his ear, then another. For fuck's sake, someone was hitting him! Twisting himself around, he spilled the two on top of him over, using his elbow to help them on their way. He rolled on to someone else and he realized it was Vicky.

Pushing himself up, not caring if he was treading on anybody, he pulled at the girl, drawing her halfway out of the scrambling heap.

Hysteria was in her eyes as she grabbed wildly at him.

'Take it easy, Vicky!' he shouted. 'You'll have me over!'

Something thudded into him from behind, causing him to lose his precarious balance. Then someone had him by the throat and was pounding a fist into his face to the accompaniment of Vicky's screams. Rage replaced the fear inside him as he struck back at his aggressor. No one was going to belt him and get away with it! And as he fought, a blackness seemed to fill him.

The girl felt the mob violence. It wasn't just the physical aggression of the crowd; it was something else, something that slowly, stealthily, smothered them all. Her head snapped upwards when she felt icy, black fingers tapping on the surface of her mind, fingers that wanted to scratch their way through and explore inside. She screamed again, fearing the dark hand more than the madness around her. Someone was pulling her up and she opened her eyes, grateful for the firm grip beneath her arms. The face was smiling, she could just make that out in the gloom. But she sensed there was no humour in the smile. It was a huge bloated face, the hair closely cropped and plastered to his scalp by the rain. His body was big, his arms bare, and he held her upright against the frenzied tide surrounding them. She knew the evil that was in the air was also in him. The cold black fingers had found easy access into this man.

Animal's smile became a grin as the voices inside told him what to do.

Something was tugging at Jack Bettney and it had nothing to do with the spectators who were clawing at each other to get clear of the crush. It was something nipping away at his thoughts. No – it was something nipping away at his will, he was sure of it. He had read somewhere about mass-hysteria, how panic or even adulation could pass through a crowd, hopping from mind to mind, touching every person present until they were enveloped in a binding cocoon of emotion. That was what was happening here! But it was something more than panic. There was a savagery about these struggling, heaving people. Not all of them, for many were under attack from others; but the earlier hostility had somehow manifested itself into an overwhelming madness. It was the madness that was tugging at him!

He began to hit out, not caring who he struck, knowing he had to get away from them, sensing he was different – *he was not with them*. They would sense it too!

Hands reached out to him, grabbing at his clothes, pulling the woolly cap from his head, reaching for his eyes. He went down and as he lay underneath the trampling feet, the darkness all around, he began to give in to the silent, pounding voices, wanting to join them if it would give him peace, agreeing to be part of them, whatever their intent. Realizing too late they were not offering him peace.

Animal was finished with the girl. Others wanted her even though her body was limp, no life left in it. He let her fall and pushed a way through the mob, making slow but firm progress, eyes fixed on the metal structure protruding from the mass of human flesh and towering over them like a soulless sentinel.

All activity below had stopped, the players, linesmen and referee staring in bewilderment at the crowd on that side of the pitch. Policemen had left their benches and were hurrying around to gather just below the section where the trouble had started. But there was no longer one place of activity, for the skirmishes had spread, joined, merged into one massive battle, everyone on that side of the stadium involved. None of the constables felt inclined to wade into the thick of it, nor did the officer in charge encourage them to do so. Suicide was not part of their duty.

Animal finally reached the base of the floodlight tower, the short journey through the press of bodies taxing even his great strength. But adrenalin was coursing through him, for he knew what he had to do and it excited him. He was pushed up against the metal, its surface slimy wet with rain; he reached inside for the junction box from which heavily protected cables emerged, soaring their way up towards the rows of burst lights above. The cover to the box would not budge, for it had been built to resist the attention of destructive fans. Animal climbed the first two cross-struts of the tower and poked his foot inside. He kicked at the box, his heavy boot scarring and denting its surface. It took long minutes for the cover to work itself loose but, for perhaps the first time in his life, Animal had patience. He kept doggedly at his task and whooped with glee when the cover finally fell away. Then he reached inside and curled his huge hand around two of the heavy cables. He began to tug, the crowd pressed tight around him, the rain drenching everyone and everything.

The cables finally came away, for Animal was strong, and the power passed through him into the wet, tightly-packed crowd, sweeping outwards with paralyzing swiftness, spreading like a deadly germ. Hundreds had been touched before the current finally blew itself out and plunged the entire stadium into total, screaming darkness.

SIXTEEN

Bishop studied Lucy's tiny face, holding the framed photograph in one hand, his other hand resting on top of the mantelpiece. His thoughts of her had become frozen moments, still-life images like the photograph he held, single frames his memory had captured. He could still hear her squeaky giggles, her panting sobs, but they were echoes, not attached to Lucy herself. He missed her and, with a slight feeling of guilt, realized he missed her more than Lynn. Perhaps it was because in reality his wife was still there: only her mind was dead. Did it amount to the same thing? Could you still love a person when they had become someone else? Something else? You could, but it wasn't easy; and he wasn't sure he was capable any more.

He replaced the photograph and sat in an armchair facing the empty grate. A new guilt was rising in him, compounding the old, and it was to do with Jessica. Perhaps it was because she was the only woman he'd had any real association with for a long, long time. Since Lynn's illness he hadn't sought female company, nor missed it. So much had been drained from him after Lucy's death and Lynn's breakdown; only resentment had been left, the remnants of his own sorrow. The resentment had become a fierce anger which had been channelled into the new work he had found for himself. But even that had begun to die, leaving only the bitterness that clung like a withered vine to a crumbling wall. Now something inside that had lain dormant for many years had begun to breathe again, lightly at first, stirring gently, unfurling, becoming steady. The old feeling had moved aside a little, making room for the new. Was it because of Jessica or because of the passage of pain-healing time? Could any attractive woman coming into his life at that point have had the same effect? He didn't have the answer, nor did he want to ponder the question. One day, Lynn might become whole again. And if she didn't . . . she was still his wife.

Restless, he heaved himself from the chair and went into the kitchen, taking a can of beer from the fridge. He pulled the tab and drank straight from the can, half its contents gone before he took it from his lips again. He returned to the armchair, his thoughts dark and brooding.

It was crazy. Everything that was happening was crazy. The madness was growing, a virulence that was spreading like an ancient, uncontrolled plague. An exaggeration? The suicides at Beechwood had been the beginning. Then the insanity that developed a year later, a madness that had soon enveloped most of those living in Willow Road. An attempted murder on himself and Jacob Kulek. The slaying of Agnes Kirkhope and her housekeeper. And then the riot at the football stadium last night. *Nearly six hundred people dead!* Hundreds electrocuted, floodlight wiring torn loose and the current directed into the rain-soaked mob. The rest – mass suicide. Any way they could find. Climbing then leaping from the floodlight towers or the girders supporting the covered stand area. Or hanging themselves with their club scarves. Belt buckles, metal combs – other concealed weapons that troublemakers always managed to smuggle in – anything that was sharp used to sever arteries. There had been a record gate for a midweek match in the small Second Division ground: twenty-eight thousand. Nearly *six hundred dead!* What kind of nightmare must it have been inside that darkened stadium? Bishop was unable to control the shudder that ran through him. The beer spilled on to his chin when he raised the can again and he realized his hand was shaking.

Others had run into the streets, most to escape the bedlam, many seeking alternative means of destroying themselves. Hands had been smashed through shop-front windows, the jagged shards used to slash wrists. Twenty youths had run into the nearby railway station and jumped as one from the platform when an express hurtled through. The nearby canal was still being dredged for the bodies of those who had chosen drowning. Tall buildings had been used to leap from, lorries or buses to leap under. Cars as weapons. The destruction had gone on through the night. *Six hundred!*

When daylight finally came, scores of them had been found wandering the streets, their faces blank, their minds seemingly empty. The word *zombie* flashed through Bishop's head, a word that had always held humorous connotations for him in the past; but now the description had a true sinister meaning. That was what these people had become. Zombies. The walking dead.

Just how many had been found in this state was not yet known; but according to the news media, there were more still not accounted for. Still wandering mindlessly? Dead but not discovered? Or had they found a place to hide? The horror of it had been with Bishop throughout the day, for he had made the connection, the obvious connection. And so had Jacob Kulek, who was now out of hospital, and Jessica – Bishop had spoken to her earlier that day. The insanity was not confined to Willow Road: it had travelled a distance of nearly a mile to the football ground.

He wondered if Edith Metlock had been touched by the same madness. When he and Jessica had found her in her home two nights before, she had mumbled something about the dark over and over again as though she were afraid that the night outside might enter the house and somehow consume her. Bishop had wanted to get her to a hospital, but Jessica had told him she had often seen mediums in this state, that Edith had become lost within herself and could only find her way back on her own. The trance would wear off; all she needed was protection until it did. They had put the medium on to her bed, Jessica covering her with a quilt, propping her head up with a pillow. While Bishop had checked every room in the house and relocked the kitchen door, Jessica had rung the hospital where her father was being kept for observation. He was fine, sleeping under mild sedation and there was no point in her coming over that late; unless there were any unforeseen developments overnight, she could come and collect him in the morning.

They had sat with Edith Metlock all night, and they had talked, occasionally breaking off to listen to the medium's sudden disturbed murmurings. It was well past three before the tension drained from Edith's face and she seemed to drift off into a deeper, peaceful sleep. By that time Jessica's eyes were closing and he finally persuaded her to lie down on the end of Edith's bed. He found a blanket to cover her with and, half-asleep, she had smiled when he touched a hand to her cheek; then she was gone, her breathing becoming deep and regular to match Edith Metlock's.

Bishop had sat in the chair previously occupied by the medium, uneasy at being left alone with the oppression that seemed to surround the house. It was just his imagination, he told himself. There was nothing out there. It was just the result of everything that had happened catching up. Eventually the oppression seemed to lift. His eyelids grew too heavy and he slept.

Gentle prodding had woken him the following morning and he had found Jessica kneeling before him, her smile a welcome sight. Edith Metlock was propped up on the bed and, although she appeared to be exhausted, she thanked them both for staying with her through the night. She seemed nervous and constantly glanced around the room as though expecting someone else to be there hiding in the shadows. She was too confused to tell them what had happened the night before – Bishop suspected she wasn't sure herself. Fortunately, because of her unsettled state, it had not occurred to Edith to ask them what had brought them to her house, and they deemed it wise not to tell her.

After a light breakfast cooked by Jessica, they had persuaded the medium to stay at Jacob Kulek's house for a few days. Edith had declined at first, but when Jessica mentioned that her father had had a slight 'accident' – she would explain later – and that it would be enormously helpful if Edith could take care of him for a few days until he was better while Jessica organized the day-to-day running of the Institute, she readily agreed. There was much she and Jacob could discuss over the next few days, Edith told them, a distant look in her eyes.

By the time they were ready to leave the house, some of the colour had returned to the medium's cheeks, although they still found her occasionally glancing around the room in a perplexed manner.

Bishop was surprised when he saw the home in which Jacob Kulek and his daughter lived. It was in a small, secluded lane just off Highgate Village and, as they turned into the narrow driveway almost hidden by trees, it was as if they were approaching a building constructed entirely of broad sheets of shining bronze, the sun reflecting from their surfaces, a dazzling contrast to the surrounding sombre winter greens.

'It's iodised glass,' Jessica had explained, amused by his reaction. 'You can see out, but you can't see in. At night, when it's lit inside, vertical blinds give us our privacy. My father can see shadows, you see. With daylight all around he can see any movement inside the house. It's the only vision he can enjoy.'

Jessica had rung the hospital again from the house and was relieved to hear Jacob was well and would be allowed home later that morning after one or two tests had been carried out. Bishop left and before he turned from the driveway into the small lane, he glanced in his rearview mirror and saw Jessica standing at the door of the house, watching him. He almost raised a hand to wave back, but stopped himself.

Once home, the drive through the rush-hour filled city having wearied him even further, he had undressed and thrown himself into bed, not waking until five that evening. A phone call to Jessica's had disappointed him, for Edith Metlock had answered. Jacob Kulek was resting, she herself was fine although still not quite clear on what had happened the previous night, and Jessica was at the Institute. He put down the receiver and stood by it for a few moments, debating whether or not to ring Jessica's office. He decided not to.

He cooked and ate a lonely dinner, then settled down to work for the rest of the evening. A publisher was interested in a new book he had planned and had already agreed on a small advance on production of a synopsis. Bishop's idea was to write a detailed study on the many occult associations that were now thriving in different parts of the world, organizations as varied as the Institute of Parapsychology and Cybernetics Inc., in Texas, to the Foundation for Research on the Nature of Man, in North Carolina. A list of all these associations and societies had been drawn up by him, but he would have to sift through and choose those he would major on, for there was no possibility of visiting every place in person and, indeed, some were behind the Iron Curtain and access to them might prove difficult. Several of these, however, sounded intriguing: the Czechoslovak Coordination Committee for Research in Telepathy, Telgnosis and Psychokinesis, and the Bioelectronics Section of the Polish Copernicus Society of Naturalists were just two he was determined to see for himself. His publisher had agreed to pay his travelling expenses as part of the advance, this later to go against his royalties, and Bishop hoped that many of the associations would receive and accommodate him as a guest; most were eager to have their work recognized. He planned an objective study on these foundations, societies, associations, institutes – whatever they termed themselves – keeping his own attitudes carefully in check until the conclusion of the book. It was only then that he would know himself what those attitudes would be. In a way, the exercise was almost self-indulgent: he wanted to discover more about the paranormal. When he had begun his strange career as a psychic investigator, he had had an intransigent prejudice against mysticism in any form and had quickly come to learn that there was a great difference in what was commonly termed the supernatural and the paranormal: one had mystical connotations while the other was an unknown science, perhaps – and, as yet, no one was *really* certain – the science of the mind. He felt sure that by studying the activities of these various groups he would have a clearer picture of the overall progress this relatively new field of science had made. The growth in public interest was incredible. The young were shying away from materialism and seeking their own higher levels, their elders seeking a refuge from the chaos around them. It seemed that for many, conventional religion had failed to provide that comfort, for prayers and paying homage did not always work. In fact, for most, it rarely worked. Where was justice, where was right? The more communications improved throughout the world, the more the injustice could be seen. When the new generations looked at religion they could only see manmade ritual, manmade hypocrisy. Even history told them the pursuit of God had meant the slaughter and suffering of millions. Many turned to new cults, fringe religions such as the Scientologists, the Moonies, the People's Temple (what was the real reason for *their* mass suicide?). Gurus had replaced messiahs. Psychiatrists had replaced priests. Parapsychologists might eventually replace both.

There was a growing belief that man's soul was hidden deep in some dark recess of his mind, not an invisible entity filling his whole being. If it was there, it could be found; the scientists needed only to know where to look and produce the instrument to trace it. And science in its study of the paranormal, was slowly, very slowly, homing in. Bishop had to smile at his own uncomplicated logic; Jacob Kulek could probably improve on the substance of his reasoning, but he felt their separate conclusions would not be that far apart. He made a mental note: Kulek's Research Institute would be a good place to start with for his book.

Bishop worked late into the night, outlining the structure of his thesis, drawing up a shortlist of associations he would include, making a note of their locations and any specific field of the paranormal they were involved in. It was well past one when he went to bed and sleep quickly claimed him. The nightmare returned and he was once again sinking into the black, brooding depths of the ocean, his lungs crushed by the pressure, his limbs stiff and useless, his body's leaden weight dragging him below. A face was waiting for him down there, a greyish blur that grew clearer as he plunged. This time it was not Lucy's. It was a man he recognized, yet did not know. The man was grinning, and withered lips called Bishop's name. His eyes seemed to bulge unnaturally from their sockets and Bishop saw there was nothing but evil in them, a cold, mesmerizing darkness that sucked him in, that drew him into a blackness that was even deeper than the ocean. The grin was a sneer and Bishop suddenly knew it was the same man he had seen in Beechwood, the man who had watched his followers kill each other and themselves before putting a gun into his own mouth. The lips parted, yellow, ill-formed teeth guarding the glistening cavern inside, the fleshy, quivering tongue resting on the entrance floor like a huge slug waiting to curl around and engulf any intruder. Bishop floated through, the jaws closing behind him with a thunderous steely clang, and he was totally blind and screaming, the soft enveloping surfce of the tongue reaching up for him and moulding itself around his feet. He tried to tug himself free but only sank further into the gripping slime and in the darkness he sensed the tongue curling round, rearing over him to descend upon his shoulders. His own panic-stricken screams deafened him as white, floating shapes came into view, rising from the tunnel that was the man's throat, their faces familiar, the images of those who had died in Beechwood. Dominic Kirkhope was with them. And so was Lynn.

Her eyes were wild, both terror and beseeching in them. Her lips formed words that were cries for help. She begged him. She pleaded. Help me.

And he couldn't; the tongue was pressing down on him, smothering his head and shoulders, choking him with its sticky juices, forcing him to fall, crushing him in a cushion of softness. Until everything exploded. And he was the bullet smashing its way through the man's brain. The man he suddenly knew was Boris Pryszlak.

He awoke still screaming, but no sounds came from his lips. It was light outside and he almost wept with relief.

The beer can was empty and Bishop placed it on the floor at his feet, then slumped back into the armchair, one elbow resting on the arm of the chair, hand across his brow as though shielding his eyes from the lamp-light. His head ached and every muscle in his body felt lifeless. He had spoken with Jessica that morning, ringing her as soon as he'd heard the news on the radio. She had been at home and told him she would stay there today to look after her father. Jacob had also heard the news of the bizarre tragedy at the football stadium and he, too, felt sure it was related to the incidents in Willow Road. He was still weak from the attack, but had made her promise to arrange a meeting for all of them later that evening, a meeting that would include Detective Chief Inspector Peck. Even if the policeman thought they were all insane, they had to try to convince him there was a connection between the Pryszlak sect and the recent events. Bishop had agreed to keep himself available that evening; she would ring him when she had fixed a suitable time.

He still hadn't heard from her and he was becoming concerned. That concern finally drove him out of the armchair into the hall. He was just reaching for the phone when it rang.

'Jessica?'

'Uh, no. Mr Bishop? Crouchley here. From Fairfields.'

Fairfields. The mental home.

'Has something happened to my wife?' Dread hit Bishop's stomach like a lead weight.

'It's important that you come over right away, Mr Bishop,' said the metallic voice.

'Is Lynn all right?'

There was a slight pause at the other end. 'We've had what you might call a slight breakthrough. I think we rather need you here. I'll explain when you arrive.'

'It'll take me twenty minutes. Can't you tell me a little more now?'

'It's better that you see for yourself.'

'Okay. On my way.'

Bishop's heart was thumping as he raced upstairs to grab his jacket. What did a 'slight breakthrough' mean? Was Lynn at last beginning to emerge from the shell she had retreated into? Would there be some warmth, no matter how faint, in her eyes when she saw him? He tugged on his jacket and raced back down the stairs, a new hope urging him on.

When the phone rang again only moments later, the house was already empty.

SEVENTEEN

Bishop had to force himself to concentrate on driving as he sped towards Twickenham, the rain splatting off the road like tiny cannon shots. Fortunately, the traffic was light and he was able to make good progress. He was filled with apprehension; there had to be good reason for Crouchley to call him out at that time of evening. If Lynn had finally . . . he refused himself the thought. Better not to expect too much.

It was not long before he reached the quiet cul-de-sac at the end of which stood the Fairfield Rest Home. He drove straight through the tall entrance gates into the wide drive. Slamming the car door, he hurried up the steps leading to the building's main door, rain speckling the driving glasses he had forgotten to remove. He whisked them off into his top pocket, ringing the doorbell with his other hand as he did so. The home was a large redbrick building which in appearance could have been anything from a small, private school to a residence for geriatrics. Only when the discreetly lettered sign mounted on the front railings had been read did the building take on a faintly daunting atmosphere. The fact that most of the interior lights seemed to be off, made it look even more grim.

Bishop heard the lock click, then the door opened slightly.

'I'm Chris Bishop. Dr Crouchley asked me to come over.'

The door opened wider and he saw the silhouette of a short, plumpish woman standing there. 'Oh, yes, we were expecting you, Mr Bishop. Won't you come in?'

He stepped into the home's reception area and turned anxiously towards the small woman as she carefully locked the door again.

'Is my wife . . .?'

'We'll take you straight up to see her, Mr Bishop,' a voice said from behind and he turned to see another woman sitting at the reception desk to one side of the hall. Her face was turned away from the small desk-lamp that did its feeble best to light up the gloomy surroundings. The figure rose and came around the desk towards him.

'I'm sorry about the poor light,' she said as if reading his mind. 'We always keep the lighting subdued after eight o'clock. We find it's restful for our patients.'

She was taller than the woman who had let him in and Bishop realized he had seen neither of them before. Perhaps they were new, the tall one certainly, for patients were never referred to as such in Fairfield – they were always 'residents'.

'What's happened to Lynn?' he asked. 'Dr Crouchley wouldn't tell me over the phone.'

The two women eyed each other and a pleased look passed between them. 'I think you'll find a marked improvement, Mr Bishop,' the taller one said. 'Would you like to follow me?'

They walked towards the broad staircase that led to the first floor of the home, the smaller woman falling in behind Bishop, hands thrust into her white medical coat. The taller woman kept up a flow of conversation as they climbed the stairs, but he hardly listened; his mind was on Lynn. The corridor on the first floor was also lit only by a small lamp on a table at the far end and he found the dimness disconcerting. He hadn't realized they kept the lights to a minimum after visiting hours; it was more depressing than subduing. A door opened as they passed, the room beyond in total darkness; the smaller woman hurried over and stretched out an arm as if to gently push someone back towards their bed. The taller woman smiled sweetly at him as though nothing had happened.

Bishop had always found the mental home slightly unnerving, which was natural enough; but at this time of night, without the usual bustle of visitors and staff, it was more than that. His mouth felt dry and he wondered if the tension was because of Lynn or because he had become a little afraid of the place. They passed more doors and he wondered what lay behind them, what was going on inside those damaged minds.

'Here we are.' The tall woman had stopped outside a room he knew Lynn shared with three other residents. The wards were kept small at Fairfield, the doctors reluctant to separate their charges from each other, although they believed in keeping the numbers to a minimum.

'Won't we disturb the others?' Bishop asked.

'They're sleeping soundly – I checked just before you arrived. Please go in, your wife is waiting for you.'

'Is Dr Crouchley with her?'

'He'll be along shortly. He wants you two to be alone for a few moments.'

Bishop's face lit up, the tension beginning to leave him. 'She's . . .?'

The white-coated woman put a finger to her lips, then smiled pleasantly, her eyes sparkling at his anticipation. She pushed open the door and motioned him to enter. He said a quiet 'Thank you' and went into the room. The door closed behind him.

Lynn's bed was in a corner by the window and a small night-light had been placed on her bedside cabinet. She was propped up on pillows, her head turned to one side as if she had dozed off while waiting for him. He tiptoed towards her, conscious of the grey, sleeping forms in the shadows around him, his eyes moist, throat still dry.

'Lynn?' he said gently when he reached her side. 'Lynn, are you awake?'

He touched her hand lying on top of the bedsheets and softly shook it. Her head slowly came round towards him and in the poor light he saw the grin on her face. His body went rigid and all the openings in his body seemed to curl inwards.

'Lynn?'

Her eyes still bore the look of insanity. Her grin reflected the madness. She began to sit up and he was aware that the others in the shadowy beds around the ward were rising also. Someone snickered.

Lynn's lips were glistening wet as she pushed back the bedclothes and began to reach for him. He had to stop himself from backing away.

'Don't get out of bed, Lynn.'

Her grin widened.

One leg slipped from the covers.

Her hand touched his shoulder.

'Lynn!' he screeched as the other hand whipped up and clawed at his face.

She was laughing and it wasn't Lynn at all: the features were the same – same mouth, same nose, same eyes – but they were distorted, twisted into an ugly grimace, someone else, something else, behind those wild eyes.

He grabbed her wrists and held her away from him, her body exploding into violent motion. Screams were mixed with her laughter as she kicked out at him, snapping her teeth like a rabid dog. He pushed her back towards the bed, unnerved by her strength, frightened by her condition. The bloody fools! Why had they dragged him here to see this? Had she fooled them, made them believe she was changing for the better? Or had just the sight of him broken down what good had been done?

She was on the bed now, her head thrashing around on the pillows, her flimsy nightdress kicked high over her thighs. She hissed and spat at him, the bubbled saliva smearing his face. He was dimly aware that other shapes were moving towards him from out of the darkness, but he was afraid to let go of his wife's wrists, afraid of those claw-like nails.

His head was jerked back as a hand grabbed his hair from behind; he twisted his neck, trying to pull himself free. But the hand grasped him tightly and another reached around and across his throat. Bishop was forced to let go of Lynn and clutch at the arm that was squeezing his neck. She was off the bed immediately, coming at him, hands flailing, her mouth snapping at him once more. They went down in a heap, the woman behind losing her grip on his throat, but still gripping his hair at the roots. He blinked away the blur in his eyes and rolled over, taking Lynn with him, the other woman scrabbling at him with her free arm.

He managed to get a foot up and kicked out at Lynn, her cry of pain a terrible sound, but knowing he had no choice. She scudded away from him and he turned on the woman still clinging. A fierce backslap of his hand stunned her and she shrieked with the shock. Even in the darkness he could see she was an old woman, her hair white and frizzed out as though filled with static.

A bare foot kicked him, striking his cheek and knocking him sideways. Two other nightgowned women were standing over him, their faces masks of grinning hate. They ran forward, kicking out, crying their triumph. A body landed on him and teeth sank into his neck. In the nightmarish confusion he knew it was Lynn. He broke her grip, but felt skin tear away and a spurt of blood run into his collar. He grabbed a foot that was pushing at his chest and twisted it forcefully, the woman above him falling back with a scream. He got a knee beneath him and pushed himself upwards, taking Lynn with him, a figure in front pounding his face with clenched fists. He struck out, hitting the woman on the forehead, sending her hurtling backwards into the shadows. He held Lynn to him, pinning her close to his body, trapping her arms. The white-haired woman was slowly creeping towards him like a ghost from the mists, arms stretched out before her holding what looked like a rolled-up bedsheet, a twisted shroud he knew was to go around his neck. He almost collapsed with relief when he saw the door behind her begin to open, the dim light from the hallway casting dark shadows into the room.

The silhouettes of the two women who had shown him in, the tall one and the short one, stood there.

'Thank God,' Bishop said, the moans, the giggles, the screams – Lynn's squirming – suddenly coming to a stop. Even the old woman bearing the twisted bedsheet paused and looked back over her shoulder.

The tall woman stepped into the room and the other one followed. The two women moved to the side, opening the door wide, and he heard the tall one say: 'Bring him along.'

They poured into the room, demented, arm-waving creatures from hell, the women dressed in plain, shapeless smocks that served as nightgowns, the men in similar garments. Bishop backed away, almost believing he had walked into a terrible dream.

Lynn broke free and suddenly the twisted bedsheet was thrown around his shoulders, then jerked tight. He was pulled forward and a screaming mass of bodies enveloped him, hands tearing at his clothes, darkened manic faces appearing before him, disappearing as others brushed them aside to see their victim. Bishop blindly hit out, their screams deafening him, his fists sinking into fleshy parts of bodies and sometimes striking hard bone. Those that fell back were immediately replaced by others and he began to go down, clutching at their robes to stop himself. A knee came up into his face and for a second he felt only white-hot shock, the numbing pain reaching him split seconds later. He went down on to his knees and a hard slap rocked his head backwards. His hands spread themselves on the floor before him and he felt the sheet around his neck tightening. Bruising feet toppled him over.

They used the sheet to drag him towards the door.

The tall woman looked down at him, the gloomy light from the hallway throwing her face into half-shadow; the pleasant smile was still there. He lay on his back staring up at her and she and her short companion took delight in his horror. She held up a hand and for a moment the clamour died, just a sigh, a moan, a giggle, coming occasionally from the shadows.

All she said was: 'It's too late, Mr Bishop. It's already begun.'

Then they were on him again and he was half-carried, half-dragged into the hall. He thought he heard Lynn laughing with them.

He managed to get his feet beneath him and forced himself erect, digging his heels into the tough cord carpet, pressing himself back against the mob, unwilling to go wherever it was they wanted to take him. He groaned aloud when he saw what lay ahead of him in the corridor.

The bodies of the mental home's staff had been tumbled out from the rooms on either side of the long corridor. Very little white showed through their bloodstained uniforms. With revulsion, he saw they had not just been murdered; mutilation had taken place. Whether or not they had been dead before . . . He shook the thoughts from his mind.

He was shoved forward and the fury inside him broke. He did not know what had happened to them all, why or how their unbalanced minds had turned to such appalling violence, but he hated them for it. Events of the past weeks told him they were not responsible – their enfeebled minds had been taken over by a greater madness. It was *that* madness he felt hate for, but they were its hosts, they were its perpetrators. They had allowed themselves to be used. They were no longer human.

The short woman stepped in front of him, her face pinched and malicious, ready to taunt. His foot came up and caught her just below her plump belly, and her ducking face met his swiftly lifted knee, choking off her piercing shriek.

Those holding him were momentarily stunned and a dagger of fear found its way through their insanity. Bishop tore an arm free and twisted himself to strike the madman holding his other arm. He felt a fleeting satisfaction as the man's nose squelched beneath his knuckles. The sheet around his neck loosened and he quickly pulled it over his head, already jumping away from the mob crowding into the corridor. The cries reached a new pitch as he shoved the man who had been holding on to his other arm back into the mob. Hands were clutching at him, trying to drag him back into their midst.

He was backing away, slapping at their hands as though they were naughty children grabbing for sweets. He almost stumbled over the outstretched legs of a male nurse and then he had turned and was running for the stairs, the sight of the dead man looking up at him, deep red holes where his eyes should have been, completely unnerving him. The residents chased after him, stumbling and giggling over the bodies of those they had already slain.

Bishop reached the top of the stairs and fell against the banister. Two figures, clad in the white starched trousers and jackets that were the Fairfield uniform, were mounting the steps, their faces hidden in the shadows. One held a long iron bar that he was rattling along the uprights of the banister and, when their heads and shoulders came into view, Bishop saw the same wild-eyed glee in their eyes that belonged to the mad men and women behind him. He staggered up the staircase leading to the second floor.

A hand curled round his ankle, bringing him down, and he grasped at the banister to stop himself from sliding to the bottom. He twisted and found it was Lynn holding on to him, a chuckling, drooling Lynn, a Lynn he no longer knew, who was enjoying the game, who wanted him dead. He had to close his eyes when he brought his foot down into the upturned face.

The metal bar crashed against the rails his fingers clung to, only inches away, and the grinning face of the male nurse peered up at him from the other side. The mob at the foot of the stairs were tripping over the fallen body of Lynn as Bishop lumbered onwards, taking the stairs three at a time, the terrible fear that his legs would turn to lead fuelling his panic. He used the rail to pivot himself around the bend in the stairs, the mob now trampling over Lynn to reach him. He reached the second floor corridor and it was dark. But not so dark that he couldn't see the white clad figures drifting down the corridor towards him, doors opening on either side and others stepping out, dim spectres in a world of blackness and screams.

He was trapped.

Except for a door on his left that had not yet opened.

He burst through and slammed it behind him, leaning back against it to prevent them from following, sucking in huge swallows of air. Keeping a shoulder against the door, he scrabbled around for a key in the lock. There was no key. Not even a bolt.

He could hear them gathering outside.

And his feet were wet.

He reached for a light switch, found nothing, but felt something brush against the back of his hand. A cord. A light. He pulled. He was in a bathroom, the white tiles stark and blinding. That was why there was no lock on the door: mad people were not allowed to lock themselves in rooms. The floor was covered in puddles and the deep, claw-footed bathtub was filled to overflowing, the water smooth and placid, its highest level reached.

A chair with two carelessly dropped towels draped over its back stood in a corner next to him. He reached for it gratefully and jammed it against the door at an angle, its back beneath the handle. It might hold them for a precious few moments, time enough to reach the high window opposite. He saw the frosted glass was reinforced with metal wire and prayed he would be able to break through, already sure the frame was set in its surround, unable to be opened naturally. He splashed across the bathroom floor, ignoring the shrill laughter from outside. And as he passed by the huge bath, he realized it had all been an evil game for them, that they meant to let him escape to the second floor, that they had directed him to this particular room. They had wanted him to see what lay beneath the unstirring water in the bath.

EIGHTEEN

The house surprised Peck. Not the kind of place he expected Jacob Kulek to live in; somehow he thought the old man would have preferred oak beams, roses running up the outside walls, or maybe something Georgian, tall and elegant. Still, his kind was unpredictable; something a little cranky about most of them. Seemed well-balanced enough until you started listening to what he was saying.

'Some shack, eh, guv?' Frank Roper, his DI said as Peck pressed the doorbell. 'All glass and chrome. I'd hate to be their window cleaner.'

Peck grunted, his thoughts now distracted. He was wondering why Kulek had insisted on seeing him, especially at this time of night. The insanity of the night before had meant an overload – and that was an understatement – for everybody: how the hell do you deal with mass murders by a mass of murderers? And what was the connection between the incidents at the football ground and Willow Road? Or, to be more specific, the house that had once been there: Beechwood. Because there was a definite link now. If Kulek hadn't asked for the meeting, then Peck, himself, would have wasted no time in interviewing the old man. It seemed he was the only person who could give some clue as to what was going on.

The door opened and Jessica Kulek's white nervous face peered out at him.

'Come in,' she said, opening the door wide.

'Sorry we're a bit late,' Peck apologized. 'As you can imagine, we've been pretty busy today.'

'That's why my father wanted to see you, Inspector. It's about what happened last night.'

'You're going to tell me there's a link. And you'd be right.'

Jessica's eyebrows arched in surprise. 'You think there is, too?'

'Let's say it's a strong possibility.'

Kulek was waiting for them in a large L-shaped lounge, the room itself, like the house, of modern design, although the furniture seemed old, possibly antique; surprisingly, the combination worked. Peck noticed everything was set out in straight lines or at right-angles to each other and he realized a blind man wouldn't want odd bits of furniture scattered at random around the room. The vertical blinds were drawn against the night.

'Good of you to come, Inspector,' Kulek said. He was standing by an armchair, one hand resting on its back, whether for support or merely guidance, Peck wasn't sure. He looked older than when the policeman had first met him, but infinitely better than when he had seen him in the hospital two days ago. His skin had taken on a dry, pale yellow cast and his stoop had become more pronounced. A silk scarf peeping over the top of his shirt-collar hid his bruised neck.

'You've met Detective Inspector Roper,' Peck said without looking at his colleague.

'Yes, indeed. And this is Edith Metlock.'

The medium smiled briefly at the two policemen.

'Won't you sit down? Can we offer you something to drink? Something stronger than tea or coffee?'

Peck relaxed his body into a sofa while Roper chose an uncomfortable hardbacked chair. 'Whisky, a little water, for me,' Peck said. 'I believe Inspector Roper will have the same.'

Roper nodded and Jessica made herself busy at the drinks cabinet.

'I thought you said Chris Bishop would be here tonight?' Peck said.

Kulek seated himself in the armchair he had been standing behind. 'My daughter has been trying to contact him for the past half-hour. He must have left his house.'

Jessica came over with the drinks. 'Chris may have decided to come over anyway. I said I would ring him as soon as I fixed the time for the meeting with you. I'm afraid you weren't easy to reach today.'

'Well, we can soon find out where he is. I've had two men watching him all day. Frank, tell Dave to radio through, will you?'

Roper placed his glass on the deep red carpet and left the room.

Kulek spoke. 'Jessica tells me there has been a man in a car parked near this house for the last two days.'

'For your protection, sir. There's been one attempt, no sense in risking another.'

An awkward silence followed Peck's statement before the detective cleared his throat and said: 'I had planned to see you first thing in the morning, Mr Kulek. I think there's a lot we have to discuss.'

'Yes, Inspector, indeed there is. But I gave you all the facts concerning Beechwood and Boris Pryszlak at our first meeting. Tonight I wanted to talk theory with you.'

'I'm always interested in theories. Provided they're sound, that is.'

'I can't promise you that. What may be sound to me might be completely irrational to you.'

'I'm prepared to listen.' Peck turned to Edith Metlock. 'Mrs Metlock, one of my detectives spoke to you the other day, after the madwoman was found in Beechwood. You were there at the seance.'

'It wasn't a seance, Inspector,' the medium said. 'At least, it wasn't planned as such.'

'You said you saw nothing yourself of this, uh, vision or hallucination – whatever you might call it – that Bishop claims to have seen.'

'No. As a medium, I seldom see or remember such things. My body is used as a receiver by the spirit world. They speak to others through me.'

'And you think this is what happened at Beechwood? The spirits of Pryszlak and his people used to speak to Chris Bishop? He was the only one who saw them, wasn't he?' Peck shifted uncomfortably in his seat, glad that Roper wasn't in the room to hear his line of questioning.

'They didn't speak to him,' Edith replied. 'He was shown what had happened there.'

'Why not you, Mr Kulek? Or your daughter, Jessica?'

'We don't know,' the old man answered. 'Perhaps it was because Chris Bishop discovered the bodies originally. Perhaps Pryszlak was mocking him with the truth of what had happened.'

'Pryszlak's dead.'

This time there was no reply.

'There could be another, more reasonable, explanation,' Peck said finally.

'Bishop had a mental block on what he stumbled across in Beechwood for nearly a year. It could be that going back into the house shocked him into seeing it all over again.'

'But he only discovered them when they were all dead,' said Jessica. 'The other day he actually saw them killing themselves and each other.'

'We only have his word that they were already dead.'

Jessica looked at her father, who said: 'Wasn't there a witness who saw him go into the house? A woman with a child who was passing by at the time?'

'Yes, I've read the report. But how do we know he hadn't already been to the house, hadn't actually been present when the suicides and executions took place. From what I've learned of this Bishop, he believes in a more scientific approach to the supernatural. Didn't you tell me Boris Pryszlak also had a scientific interest in these matters?'

'Yes, but . . .'

Peck went on. 'You see, it could be that our Mr Bishop is part of Pryszlak's secret sect himself. It could be that he was a member chosen to stay behind to carry on whatever fanatical cause they were all involved in.'

'That's nonsense!' Jessica's face was flushed red. 'Chris was also attacked two days ago!'

'He says.'

Kulek's voice was calm. 'I think you're wrong, Inspector.' His sightless eyes looked towards his daughter and Edith Metlock. 'We all think you're wrong.'

'I also got the impression that he wasn't entirely in favour of your investigations into Beechwood.'

'That's true,' said Jessica, 'but only in the beginning. His opinion is different now. He's trying to help us.'

'Is he?' Peck's tone was flat.

Roper came back into the room and sat in his chair again, retrieving the whisky glass from the floor with an undisguised look of relish. He glanced over at Peck before he drank.

'Bishop went out just after eight. Our obo followed him to a place near Twickenham, Er, Fairview . . . no, Fairfield Rest Home.'

Jessica said, 'It must be the home where his wife is a patient.'

'A mental home?'

She nodded and couldn't read the expression on Peck's face.

'Get back on the radio, Frank. Tell them to bring Bishop here. I think he could be useful to this little gathering.'

'Now?' Roper's lips were poised over the edge of his glass.

'Right away.'

The policeman replaced his glass and left the room once more.

Peck sipped at his own whisky and water and regarded Jacob Kulek over the rim of his glass. 'Okay, sir, you said you wanted to talk theory.'

The blind man's mind was still on Bishop. No, it wasn't possible. Chris Bishop was a good man, he was sure. Confused. Angry. But not of Pryszlak's kind. Jessica had finally come to like the man and she was the best judge of character he knew. Sometimes he felt her judgement was a little too good, a little too critical . . . The few men in her life had never come up to her expectations.

'Mr Kulek?' There was a note of impatience in Peck's voice.

'Sorry, Inspector. My mind was wandering.'

'You have a theory?' Peck prompted. Kulek's eyes seemed to be boring into him and he could have sworn he felt the back of his mind being searched.

'It's difficult, Inspector. You are a practical man, a down-to-earth person who does not believe in ghosts. But, I think you are probably very good at your job and therefore, you may have some imagination.'

'Thank you,' Peck said drily.

'Let me start by telling you of the strange experience Edith had two nights ago. Or perhaps she will tell you herself?' he turned to the medium.

'As a sensitive – medium, spiritualist, are words you are probably more familiar with, Inspector – as a sensitive I am more susceptible to forces, influences, that are outside out daily lives. Forces from a world that is not of our own.'

'The spirit world.'

'If it can be called that. I'm not sure any more. It may be that we have a misconception about what we term "the spirit world". There are others in my profession who are beginning to have the same doubts.'

'Are you saying there are no such things as, er, ghosts?'

Roper had re-entered the room and he gave Peck a bemused look. He nodded at his superior to indicate that his instructions were being carried out, then took his place in the chair and reached for the glass at his feet.

'Perhaps not as we have always considered them,' the medium replied. 'We have always thought of them as individual spirits, existing in another world not unlike our own, but on a higher level. Closer to God, if you like.'

'And that's all wrong?'

'I'm not saying that.' There was a trace of irritation in her voice. 'We just don't know. We have doubts. It may be that this spirit world is not as far removed from our own as we thought. And it may be that they do not exist as individuals but as a whole. As a force.'

Peck frowned and Roper gulped his drink noisily.

'Inspector, I will try and explain later,' Kulek interrupted. 'I think Edith should just tell you what happened two nights ago.'

Peck nodded his agreement.

'I live alone in a small house in Woodford,' Edith told him. 'On Tuesday evening – it was late, some time between ten and eleven, I think – I was listening to the radio. I like those phone-in programmes, you know. It's good to hear what ordinary people think of the state of the world occasionally. But the set kept crackling as if someone nearby was operating a machine without a suppressor. I tried twiddling the knobs, but the interference kept coming back. Short bursts of it, then longer. In the end it was one continuous buzz so I turned the radio off. It was then, sitting there in the silence, that I noticed the change in the atmosphere. I suppose my attention had been too fixed on that blessed radio interference for me to have noticed it before. There was nothing alarming about it – presences have often made themselves known to me in the past without invitation – so I settled back in my armchair to allow it through. It took me only a few seconds to realize it was unwelcome.'

'Hang on,' Peck interrupted. 'You've just been telling me you aren't sure there are such things as ghosts.'

'Not as we think of them, Inspector. That doesn't mean something other than what we see or feel does not exist. You can't ignore the incredible number of psychic experiences that have been recorded. I must stress that at the moment I'm confused as to just what it is that communicates through me.'

'Please go on.'

'I felt my house was being surrounded by a . . . a . . .' she searched for the word '. . . a dark shroud. Yes, as though a blackness were creeping around my home, pressing itself up against the windows. And part of it had already reached me.

Part of it was already in my mind, waiting to spread itself, waiting to absorb me. But it needed to smother me physically and something was holding it at bay.'

'Your will power?' Peck said, ignoring Roper's grin.

'Partly that, yes. But something else. I felt darkness was its ally, its travelling companion, if you like. I don't know what made me do it, but I switched on every light in the house.'

Nothing unusual in that, thought Peck. He didn't personally know of any woman living alone who wasn't afraid of the dark. Plenty of men, too, although they wouldn't admit it.

'I felt as though a pressure had been taken off me,' the medium said, and Peck could see by her expression she was reliving the experience. 'But it was still outside . . . waiting. I had to block my mind, resist the urge to let it flow through me. It was as though something were trying to devour me.' She shivered and Peck himself felt a certain coldness at the base of his neck.

'I must have gone into a trance – I can't remember any more. Except for the voices. They were calling me. Mocking me. But enticing me, also.'

'What were these voices saying? Can you remember that?'

'No. No, not the words. But I felt they wanted me to turn off all the lights. Somehow, a part of me knew if I did I would be lost to them. I think in the end I just retreated into myself, fled to a corner of my mind where they couldn't reach me.'

That would be a nice trick for me to use when the Commissioner asks me what I've uncovered so far, thought Peck, holding back a weary smile.

They sensed his cynicism, but understood it. 'Edith was in that state when Chris and I found her,' Jessica said. 'When we left you that evening, Inspector, we were suddenly afraid that something might happen to her. Chris, my father, and Mrs Kirkhope had been attacked; we'd forgotten about Edith.'

'And what did you find at Mrs Metlock's house? Apart from the good lady herself.'

'We didn't *find* anything. We sensed an atmosphere. A cold, oppressive atmosphere. I was afraid.'

Peck sighed heavily. 'Is this really getting us anywhere, Mr Kulek?'

'It might help you to understand my . . . theory.'

'Perhaps we can get on to that now?'

The blind man smiled patiently. 'Believe me, we understand how difficult this is for you. We cannot give you solid evidence, no hard facts. However, you must *not* dismiss us as cranks. It's vital that you seriously consider whatever we tell you.'

'I'm trying, Mr Kulek. You've told me very little so far.'

Kulek bowed his head in acknowledgement. 'My daughter and Chris Bishop brought Edith here – they thought she would be safer. As you know, I was in hospital but returned home later that day. It wasn't until yesterday evening that Edith began to talk of what had happened. When she had been found she was in an extreme state of shock, you see, and it took some time for her to emerge from that state. The only words she had said before then were, "Keep the dark away." It seems the darkness was somehow symbolizing whatever it was she feared. Now I'm sure it hasn't escaped your notice that everything that happened in Willow Road recently has taken place at night.'

'The woman who attacked you in Beechwood. That was in the daytime.'

'She had killed her employer the night before. I believe that was when the madness hit her. Remember she was hiding in the cellar of Beechwood; in the dark.'

'The murder of Agnes Kirkhope and her housekeeper? The further attack on you? Bishop's alleged attack? These were all during the day.'

'It's my belief that the perpetrators were disciples of Boris Pryszlak. Theirs was a different kind of madness. I think they were a physical guard left behind by Pryszlak to carry out certain duties. Protectors, if you like.'

'Why should he need protection if he's dead?'

'Not for *his* protection. They were left as a safeguard to his plan. Perhaps as a tangible force to support his ethereal force.'

Peck and Roper exchanged uncomfortable glances. 'Could you explain exactly what you mean by "ethereal force"?'

'A force not of this world, Inspector.'

'I see.'

Kulek smiled. 'Bear with me; you might see some sense to it by the time I've finished.'

Peck hoped so, but he wouldn't have laid odds on it.

'When Boris Pryszlak came to enlist my assistance some years ago, he told me he was a man who did not believe in the existence of God. For him, science was the key to mankind's salvation, not religion. Disease and deprivation were being overcome by technology, not by prayer. Our economic and social advances were achieved by science. The decision to create new life was now our own; even the gender of the newborn would one day be decided by ourselves. Death itself, if not entirely thwarted, could at least be delayed. Our superstitions, our prejudices and our fears were steadily becoming obsolescent in the face of new scientific discoveries. World wars had been virtually eradicated not because of Divine Intervention, but because we, ourselves, had created weapons too fearsome to use. Old barriers had been broken down, new barriers smashed through – by mankind's own ingenuity, not by some superior being in the heavens.

'Pryszlak claimed that one day we would even discover scientifically how we gained that ingenuity; how, in fact, we were not created by a mystical Someone, but created ourselves. We would prove by science that there was no God.'

Kulek's words were said calmly, his voice soft and even, but Peck could feel Pryszlak's madness in them. It was the cold logic of a fanatic and Peck knew these were the most dangerous kind.

The blind man went on: 'So, if there was no God, there could be no Devil. Yet, as a pragmatist, Pryszlak could not deny the existence of evil.

'Through the centuries, religious and mystical leaders had always played on the superstitions and the ignorance of their fellow men. The Church had always insisted that Satan was a reality: for them it helped to prove the existence of God. Freud had confounded the Church and demonologists alike by explaining that each of us has been through a phase of individual development corresponding to that animistic stage in primitive man, that none of us has traversed it without preserving certain traces of it which can be re-activated. Everything which now strikes us as "uncanny" fulfils those vestiges of animistic mental activity within us.'

'You're saying that somewhere in here – Peck tapped his temple ' – is a part of us that still wants to believe in all this "evil spirits" nonsense.'

'Freud said this and, in many respects, I believe he was right. In thousands of cases where ecclesiastical exorcists have tried to rid disturbed men and women of so-called diabolic possessions, rational examination has revealed a varied range of psychoses in those same people. Philosophers such as Schopenhauer advocated that evil sprang from man's fear of death, his fear of the unknown. It was man's will to survive that brought conflict to the world, and within himself. But his own iniquity had to be blamed on something – *someone* else: Satan provided the ideal psychological scapegoat. In the same way, because of the adversities inflicted on man throughout life, and because he knew his own inadequacies, man needed a god, a superior, someone who would help him, someone who, in the end, would provide the answers. Someone who would pull him through.

'Unfortunately for the Church, the age of rationality is here; perhaps one could say that education has been the greatest enemy of religion. The edges have become blurred, questions are being asked: How could atrocities be committed to achieve right? Wars, killing, executions – how could "bad" acts achieve "good"? How could men the world knew to be evil claim God was on their side? Would a civilized country ever fight a religious war again? In the late seventies, who had been the more evil, the dictatorial Shah of Persia or the religious fanatic, Ayatollah Khomeini who overthrew him? Idi Amin claimed to have conversed with God several times. Hitler claimed God was on his side. The persecution of so-called heretics throughout the centuries by the Church itself has still not been answered. This dichotomy has been challenged and Pryszlak saw it as man's recognition of his own powers, a predetermination over his own destiny. He had discovered his own Original Sin and decided it wasn't as evil as the Church had always taught him. Satan has now become a source of ridicule, of entertainment, even. A comical myth. A bogeyman. And evil came from man alone.

'Pryszlak believed it was a physical energy field within our mind and, just as we were learning to use our psi faculties – energies such as telekinesis, extrasensory perception, telepathy, telergy – so we could learn to use physically this other power.'

Kulek paused as if to allow the two policemen's thoughts to catch up on all he had said. 'I think Pryszlak developed his concept into a proven fact: he located this source of energy and used it. I believe he's using it now.'

'That's impossible,' said Peck.

'Many things in your own lifetime that you once thought impossible have been achieved by science, and knowledge in every field of technology is in escalation. Man has accomplished more in the last hundred years than in the previous thousand.'

'But for Christ's sake, Pryszlak is dead!'

'I think he had to die, Inspector. It's my belief that Boris Pryszlak and his followers have become that energy.'

Peck shook his head. 'I'm sorry, you know I can't buy all this.'

Kulek nodded. 'I didn't expect you to. I just wanted you to hear a theory I'm convinced is true. You may have cause to reflect upon it over the next few weeks.'

'What do you mean by that?'

'The madness will get worse, Inspector. It will spread like a disease. Every night there will be more who will succumb to its influence, and the more minds it takes the stronger it will grow. It will be like the raindrops on a windowpane: one small drop will run into the one below, then both into the one below that, growing in size and weight until it is a fast-flowing rivulet.'

'Why night-time? Why do you say these things only happen when it's dark?'

'I'm not sure why it should be so. If you read your Bible you'll see evil is constantly referred to as darkness. Perhaps that terminology has more significance than we thought. Death is darkness, Hell is in the dark, fearful underworld. The Devil has always been known as the Prince of Darkness. And isn't evil expressed as the darkness in one's soul?

'It could be that darkness is the physical ally to the manifestation of this energy. Perhaps the biblical concept of the constant battle between Light and Darkness is a true, scientific concept. Whatever energy light rays contain, be they from the sun or artificial, it may be that they counteract or negate the catalystic qualities of darkness.

'Pryszlak inferred much of this at our last meeting and I must admit that although I often found his ideas fascinating, this time I thought there was some madness in his thinking. Now I'm not so sure.'

Kulek's frame seemed to relax imperceptibly in his chair and Peck realized the blind man's disquieting statement was over. He looked at each individual in the room and noticed even Roper's secretive smirk had disappeared.

'You realize everything you've just told me is totally useless to my investigations, don't you?' he said bluntly to Kulek.

'Yes. It is at this moment. Soon I think you will change your mind.'

'Because more is going to happen?'

'Yes.'

'But even if what you say is true, what would be the point for Pryszlak?'

Kulek shrugged, then said, 'Power. More power than he had when he was alive. A larger following, one that will grow.'

'You mean he can still go on recruiting?'

Kulek was puzzled to find no trace of sarcasm in Peck's question. In fact, he was surprised the policeman had listened so patiently. 'Yes, others will join him. Many others.'

Peck and Roper exchanged sharp glances which were not lost on Jessica.

'Is there something you haven't told us, Inspector?' she asked.

Peck looked uncomfortable again. 'The crowd that ran amok last night – those that got away, that is – dispersed into the surrounding area. We've been picking them up throughout the day. Many have been dead when we've found them, mostly killed by their own hand. Others have been . . . mindless, wandering around lost.'

His face was grim, as though he did not like what he had to say next. 'Quite a few made straight for Willow Road. They smashed the barrier surrounding the Beechwood property. We found them standing there in the debris, just waiting like bloody vultures.'

NINETEEN

Bishop stared at the still body lying in the bath. The white, contorted features stared back.

He had spoken to Crouchley many times over the past few years, their conversations confined to Lynn's mental progress – or regress, as it turned out – and always on a professional basis. He couldn't say he ever got to like the man, his approach was a little too impersonal for Bishop; but he had respected him as a doctor and he had soon realized the man's dedication to his patients' welfare went beyond professional bounds. In the end they had turned on him.

The two women who had let Bishop in: had they been patients? He thought not; there seemed to be no insanity in them. Were they tools of Pryszlak as Braverman and his wife had been? Probably. They had taken over the home, the patients becoming their allies, and murdered those of the staff who had not succumbed to this new, deadly madness. Then they had forced Crouchley to ring him. After that, they had dragged him up here and drowned him.

Crouchley's mouth was open, the last bubbles of life-giving air having long exploded from his lungs to fight their way to the surface. His fair hair had turned dark beneath the water and now floated softly around his head like pondweed. Even though he was dead, fear still showed on his face.

They were banging on the door now, laughing and screaming Bishop's name, taunting him with the terror to come. The small wire-toughened window was on a level with his face and he saw, as he had expected, the frame was fixed into its surround. He looked around desperately for something to smash it with, but the bathroom was bare of implements. The chair may have helped, but that was the only thing keeping his pursuers out. The blows on the door had become harder, their rhythm more definite, as though the crowd had stood back to allow someone to use his boot against it. The angled chair shuddered.

A faint hope fluttered inside him when he saw the towel rail hooked over the bathroom's radiator. It was made of chrome and felt heavy enough to have some effect when he lifted it clear. The large towel that had been draped over it slid to the floor when he raised the rail to shoulder level. With one hand behind the triangular shaped hook and the other around the long metal rail itself, Bishop ran at the window and thrust it at the frosted glass, his feet almost slipping in the puddles beneath him.

The glass fractured, a jagged hole appeared; the wire reinforcing the glass held it together. Bishop drew the rail back and thrust again. Still the wire held.

The chair shook.

He thrust again.

The chair legs moved a fraction.

Again.

Another fraction.

This time the hook at the other end of the towel rail became entangled with the wire mesh and Bishop pulled inwards, twisting the hook to entangle it more, drawing the wire with its clinging fragments into the room, stretching it until it snapped, dropping the rail and pushing his fingers through the tiny holes, ignoring the sharp pain as the wire bit into his flesh, tugging frantically, hearing the sound of the chair scraping on the damp bathroom floor, feeling the cool night air breathing on his face through the opening that was growing wider, the wire and glass coming loose from its frame, feeling the draught grow stronger, sucked through as the door behind him burst open, tearing and twisting the wire and glass free, seeing there was enough room for him to squeeze through . . .

. . . feeling the hands on his shoulders . . .

They clawed at his body, dragging him to the floor, their screams shrilling in his head as they bounced from the tiled walls. He kicked out, his own cries joining theirs. They bore down on him, smothering his thrashing limbs with their own. A hand reached into his open mouth in an effort to pull his tongue from its roots and he bit hard, tasting blood before the scrabbling fingers jerked themselves free. He screamed when excruciating pain stabbed up from his groin area, manic hands squeezing him in a merciless grip. His shirt was ripped open and sharp fingernails dug into his chest, sinking into his skin and drawing short jagged lines of blood.

His wrists were being held and even through the confusion he could feel someone bending the fingers of one hand back, trying to snap them. Before they could succeed, he was lifted, his squirming body held in eager grips. Wild deranged faces were around him and, as he twisted his head to and fro, he caught a glimpse of the two women, the tall one and the short one, standing in the doorway. Their smiles were not sinister, merely pleasant.

He arched his body upwards, the circular light set in the ceiling a huge sun filling his vision, almost blinding him. Shock hit him as he was plunged downwards and water engulfed his body. He choked as it rushed into the canals of his nose and throat, forcing out air in huge explosive bubbles. The light above was broken into frantic patterns as the water's surface scattered into stormy motion and he could see the blurred silhouettes of those who leaned over the bath and held him down. The body of the dead man stirred beneath him.

The illogical thought that Crouchley was suddenly waking from the dead threw yet more panic into him even though whatever reason was left inside told him it was only the water's disturbance that made the body move. He pushed himself upwards, resisting the hands that held him back, forcing his head above the surface. He coughed water from his lungs, retching and gasping in air at the same time. His head was gripped and he was forced down again, hands tugging at his legs to jerk him back. The water splashed at his face, covering his chin, nose, eyes. Then he was below the surface again, the world suddenly going quiet, the screaming an imaginary sound in his head. His hands reached upwards for the side of the bath and fierce pain told him they were being battered, prised away from the slippery, enamel surface. A shadow loomed over him and he felt a crushing weight on his chest. Another sudden weight on his hips pinned him helplessly to the body beneath him. They were standing on him.

His breath was beginning to go, the weight on his chest forcing it out. He closed his eyes and the darkness was tinged red. His lips were closed tight but the air bubbles steadily forced their way from them. Like his body, his mind began to drown and he felt it plummet downwards. There was no redness any more, only the deep sucking blackness and now he was living his constant nightmare, his body sinking down into the depths, small white blobs that he knew were faces waiting for him below. Pryszlak wanted him. But Pryszlak was dead. Yet Pryszlak wanted him.

He was fathoms beneath the ocean now and his body was still, struggling no more, resigned to its death. The last silvery pearl of air fled his lips and began its hasty mile-long journey to the ocean's surface above. There were many, many faces waiting below for him and they grinned and called his name. Pryszlak was among them, silent, watching. Dominic Kirkhope, gloating. The man who had tried to shoot him, Braverman, and his wife, were laughing. Others, some of whom he recognized from his vision in Beechwood, were reaching up with shrivelled, water-crinkled hands.

Then there was anger in Pryszlak's face and the others were no longer grinning. Now they were howling.

Bishop felt himself rising, rushing to the surface. He was suddenly worried about the rapid change of pressure, that nitrogen bubbles would be trapped in the tissues of his body and he would suffer what every deep-sea diver dreads: decompression sickness – 'the bends'.

Then he was above the surface, spilling bath water from his mouth, wheezing in air when he could, choking as uncleared water rushed back down his throat. Strong hands held the lapels of his jacket collar and above the roaring in his ears he heard a distant voice shout, 'There's another one underneath him!'

He was dragged from the bath and allowed to fall on to the wet, tiled floor. He sucked in air, his senses spinning. Crouchley's staring face appeared before him, his limp body hanging over the side of the bath, water flowing from his mouth as though it were the end of a drainpipe.

'This one's dead,' the distant voice said.

Bishop was pounded on the back and he retched up the rest of the water inside him. He was pulled to his feet.

'Lean against me, but try and stand, mate. We'll get you out!'

Bishop tried to see who was helping him, but the room spun dizzily. He wanted to be sick.

'Get back!' A cannon roared and he saw splinters of wood fly from the wooden frame around the open doorway. White shapes scurried back into the shadows.

'Come on, Bishop, you'll have to help me. I can't carry you on my own.'

The voice was coming nearer, the words becoming more clear. The man had slid a shoulder beneath Bishop's arm and was holding him up. Bishop tried to push himself away, thinking the man was one of the maniacs, but the grip tightened.

'Hold up, pal, we're on your side. Try to walk will you? Move your legs.'

They staggered forward and Bishop felt the strength willingly flow back into his body.

'Good man,' the voice said. 'Okay, Mike, I think he's going to be all right. Keep that bloody mob back.'

They lurched into the dark hallway and began a slow, stumbling march towards the stairs. Something moved in the shadows ahead and the man in front of Bishop and his helper fired a shot into the air. The hallway was lit up for a split-second by the gunflash and he saw the mad creatures crouching there, afraid but ready to pounce.

Bishop and his two men had reached the bend in the stairs when the mob decided to attack.

They came tumbling out of the darkness like screaming banshees, pouring down the stairs in an unbroken, human stream.

Bishop fell back into the corner as his support was taken away and he saw both his helper and the other man raise their guns and fire into the crowd.

Cries of pain and fear rang through the corridors of the large house and he heard bodies falling, those behind toppling over the injured in front. Something slumped across his outstretched leg and began to writhe there. Bishop kicked the body away.

A hand tugged at his arm and he pushed himself upright, ready to fight.

'Come on, Bishop, let's keep moving.' With relief he realized the hand belonged to his helper.

'Who the hell are you?' he managed to say as they descended the next flight of stairs. It was lighter down there, but the man leading them improved matters by flicking on a switch. The hall and stairs were flooded with light.

'Never mind that now,' the man helping him said. 'Let's just get away from here first.'

A sudden thump on the stairs behind made them whirl. The male nurse who had tried earlier to attack Bishop with an iron bar stood above them. He still held the iron bar.

A blast from the gun and his white uniform became a shredded mass of red just above the knee. His leg buckled and he fell back on the stairs, the bar clattering down noisily. He clutched his leg and burbled his pain. Others were creeping round the bend in the stairs behind him, their eyes wide and fearful.

Bishop and the two men backed away to the next flight of stairs which would lead them to the ground floor. His clothes felt heavy with water, but noradrenaline was coursing through him once more, giving him the strength he needed.

The two women were waiting below. The short one was splashing liquid from a can on to the wide stairway. She stood back, placing the can at her feet, and smiled up at her companion. The taller woman struck a match and flicked it at the stairway.

The petrol ignited in a brilliant *whoosh* and the three men at the top of the stairs raised their arms against the fierce heat. The flames hungrily climbed the wooden staircase towards them and beyond they could see the two women backing away, grinning delightedly.

'We can't get down,' one of the men shouted. 'There must be another way out. They've got to have a fire escape.'

Bishop's head was still reeling, but through the confusion he heard the other man say, 'Can you make it, Bishop? We're going to try the back way.'

He nodded and all three men turned as one, ready to run towards the back of the building. A ring of white-robed people blocked their way.

The patients shuffled forward, their nightclothes tinged red from the rising flames, and Bishop saw Lynn was among them.

'Lynn! It's me, Chris!' he cried, moving ahead of the two men to plead with her. 'Come with us, Lynn, before the whole building goes up.'

For a brief moment, Bishop thought he saw a tiny flicker of recognition in Lynn's eyes, but if she had realized who he was, the memory only renewed her hatred. She tore herself away from the crowd and ran at him, arms flailing, hands outstretched, claw-like. In his weakened state he could not hold her; he fell and she toppled over him. Her hands clutched at the stairs as she slivered down towards the flames and Bishop desperately tried to grab her ankle. He touched her heel but the limb was gone before he could gain a hold. Her screams pierced all other sounds as she slid into the fire and her nightdress and hair became a blaze. Her tumbling body was lost in the inferno and her screams stopped abruptly. Something fell half out of the flames into the hallway below, a blackened, charred shape that bore no resemblance to a human body. It was quickly covered as the flames spread.

'No! No!' Bishop's cry descended into a low moan.

He was pulled away from the raging heat by the two men, his body totally limp now, his senses numbed with shock.

The patients had cowered back, the full horror of their companion's death striking fear into their disordered minds. The men with Bishop saw that whatever extreme madness had driven them to this, it had been overcome by their own natural terror of the fire. The patients began to whimper as the heat grew in strength, and smoke filled the hallway.

'Let's get going while we can, Mike,' one of the men holding Bishop said just loud enough to be heard.

'Right,' his colleague agreed, his back beginning to feel singed by the heat. With Bishop between them, their Webley .38s pointed at the figures in the crowded hallway, they cautiously moved forward.

'This way, Ted,' the man called Mike said, indicating to the right with the muzzle of his gun. 'There's a window down at the end of the corridor. Oh shit!'

The lights in the hallway had suddenly gone off. Had the fire burned through the wiring or had someone pulled the master switch? Both men thought of the two women who had started the fire.

'Let's move,' Mike said grimly.

The hallway was bathed in a red, weaving glow, dark shadows rising and dancing against the walls. The whimpering patients glared at the men who were retreating down the hall and carefully stepping over the sprawled bodies lying there. The white-gowned figures edged forward and doors on either side of the three men began to open.

The man called Ted glanced nervously from left to right. The only sound that could be heard now was the crackle and roar of the spreading fire. 'They're going to rush us again,' he said.

Figures were stepping into the hallway, hemming them in, watching silently, not yet raising their hands against them.

But the tension was rising, a huge bubble of hysteria that was swelling to breaking-point, and when it broke the retreating men knew they would be easily overwhelmed. As they backed further down into the blackness at the end of the hall, each of the three men felt something else nudging against the walls of their mind, something that seemed to be seeking access.

The fresh attack was started by one old woman who stood in the centre of the hall near the burning staircase. Her brittle legs were wide apart, her hands clenched and arms held rigidly to her sides; flames licked up at the ceiling above her. The cry started somewhere low in her abdomen and began to build, rising to her chest then up through her throat until it came out as a shrilling scream. The others had joined in with her mounting cry and when it broke, so they broke and came running towards the men.

The ceiling above the staircase and the next flight of stairs had become potent with heat; the flames below billowed upwards, old timbers eagerly giving themselves to the fire. A huge ball of flame spilled into the hallway, enveloping the white-robed figures who stood in its way, searing others who were too near.

Black smoke swirled towards the three men and they began to choke, their eyes already stung by the heat of the fireflash.

Bishop was dragged to the window, his body heaving as his lungs tried to eject swallowed smoke. He was pushed into a corner while the two men struggled to open their only means of escape. The fire spread rapidly and patients were running into open doors on either side of the hallway, many of them with nightclothes on fire.

'It's fucking locked!' Bishop heard one of the men shout.

'Shoot the bloody glass out!' his companion told him.

Both men stood back from the large single-framed window, raised one arm each to shield their eyes, and pumped bullets through the glass. The window shattered and a cold blast of air sucked in towards the flames.

Bishop was yanked away from the corner and steered towards the window. He drew in a deep breath of air and felt some reason returning as he leaned out into the night.

'There's – there's no fire escape,' he managed to gasp.

'Jump! It's only one floor up!'

He climbed on to the sill and let himself go. It seemed a long time before he hit the soft earth below.

TWENTY

Peck gazed down at the slow-moving traffic and filled his lungs with cigarette smoke. He wondered if the people scuttling around below in their tiny Dinky-toy cars had any real idea of what was going on in their city. It was impossible to keep an absolute clampdown on the bizarre events of the past few weeks; the media had made the connection between the events at the stadium and Willow Road days ago, but had reluctantly agreed to contain the full story until the authorities had come up with some rational answer to quell the mounting anxiety of the general public. It was an uncomfortable collaboration between the authorities and the media and one that would undoubtedly fail when the next major incident occurred. The newsmen could only be suppressed for so long.

He took the half-smoked cigarette from his mouth using his index finger and thumb, the palm of his hand curved around the butt. Janice was always telling him he'd never make Commissioner if he continued to smoke cigarettes with such mannerisms. Sometimes he thought his wife was serious.

Peck turned away from the window and slumped into the chair at the desk, stubbing the cigarette out against the side of his waste-paper bin and dropping the butt inside. Mannerisms? It had taken her ten years to stop him rolling his own. The knot of his tie was hanging loose over his chest, shirtsleeves rolled up to the elbows. He rubbed a hand across his face, conscious of the scratching sound his chin made, and studied the last page of the report he had just completed. Better grab a quick shave before I show this to the Deputy, he told himself. It wouldn't matter to that pompous bastard if you'd just arrested Jack the Ripper if you hadn't shaved beforehand.

As he re-read the last lines in his report his hand consciously travelled towards the back of his head, cold fingers breaking through his concentration to tell him no new hair had miraculously grown overnight. In fact, he thought, his attention now fully with his probing fingers, a few more had said their last farewells. He quickly dropped his hand lest any of his new men saw him through the glass panelling of his office. He'd rather be caught playing with himself than checking to see how his baldness was coming along. Getting old and feeling it, he silently grumbled. Still, they said baldness meant virility. He couldn't say he'd noticed lately.

He closed the report and sat back in his chair, taking another cigarette fom the pack on the desk as he did so. He flicked the Zippo and stared through the billow of smoke as it escaped his lips.

What the fuck is going on? he asked himself.

The football incident had been the biggest so far, but there had been others just as alarming. The burning down of the Fairfield Rest Home, for one. The riot in the boys' Remand Home, for another – the little bastards had turned on their wardens and then on themselves. Sixteen dead, twenty-four terribly injured. The rest? Where were the rest? The inmates of another mental home, this one run by the National Health, therefore known more accurately as a hospital for the insane, had turned on the staff first and then, as with the boys' home, themselves. Fortunately, the alarm had been raised before too much damage was done, but five were dead – two nurses, three patients – before the police had arrived in force. The mystery was why several of the staff had joined in the riot.

There had been many smaller incidents and if anything some of these were even more disquieting than the major events. Perhaps it was because they had involved perfectly normal people – at least considered to be normal before they had committed their individual acts of madness. A man had slaughtered every animal in the pet shop he owned, afterwards taking to his bed with the one fortunate creature he had spared, the showpiece of his collection: a ten-foot long South American boa constrictor. He had been found dead with the snake wrapped around his throat like a muffler. Three nuns had gone berserk in their convent, creeping through the corridors one night and attempting to smother several sleeping sisters with pillows: they had succeeded twice before they were discovered. A doctor on night duty – the inquiry discovered he had worked non-stop for two days and nights – had toured the wards of his hospital injecting patients with a lethal dose of insulin. Only the intervention of a duty-nurse had prevented more than a dozen deaths – she herself had been injected and killed when she had struggled with the doctor. A labourer, working late to finish an urgent job on a block of offices that was undergoing modernization, had knocked his foreman semi-conscious, then pinned him to the wall with a nail-gun. The gun individually shot six-inch nails with a force strong enough to pierce concrete and by the time the other workmen got to the unfortunate foreman, his arms and legs were firmly pinned. The crazed workman managed to fire a nail through his own head before they could get to him and another labourer had narrowly missed being punctured when the nail had emerged from the other side without losing any impetus. Perhaps the most bizarre of all was the butcher who had served his chopped-up wife to his customers – Today's Special, regular customers only. A section of thigh was still missing and the police were desperately trying to trace the unlucky housewife who had made the 'bargain' purchase.

There had been other crimes, other suicides, but it was not yet known if these were connected with the more bizarre incidents. And what exactly could the connection be other than the fact that each horrendous act had seemingly been carried out at night? Could the dark really have something to do with this madness as Jacob Kulek had suggested?

Peck had included the blind man's theory in the report, but had left it as a separate section, adding no personal comment himself. He had been tempted to leave it out completely and if he could have offered any reasonable theories himself, then perhaps he would have done so. What the Commissioner would make of it all he dreaded to think but he, Peck, was only a small cog in the operation now; the big boys had taken over. All he could do was provide them with every scrap of information he had. A couple of weeks ago Peck had considered Kulek to be a little crazy; now too much had happened for him to dismiss the man as such. If only they could find out more about Boris Pryszlak. His home had been a flat in a huge apartment block near Marylebone although, according to his neighbours, he was hardly ever there. The flat itself offered no information whatsoever; it was a spacious accommodation which held little comfort in the way of furniture. There were no pictures on the walls, no bookshelves, few ornaments of any kind. What items of furniture there were were expensive but functional and bore little sign of wear. It was obvious the man used the apartment only as a base, his activities – whatever they may have been – keeping him away most of the time. Even the information gathered at the time of the mass suicides in Beechwood had revealed little. If Pryszlak was head of some kind of crazy religious sect, then his organization kept an extremely low profile. They seemed to have had no specific meeting place, and there was no indication of how they gained recruits. Also there was no record of the work – scientific or otherwise – Pryszlak had become involved in. Several of the people in the house had been wealthy, Dominic Kirkhope being a prime example, and Peck felt it reasonable to assume they were sponsoring Pryszlak with his project in some way. Did they have genuine aspirations or were they just a bunch of deviates who enjoyed getting together on odd occasions for orgies? The information gathered so far on Kirkhope and some of the others indicated that their sexual preferences were somewhat bizarre. Dominic Kirkhope had once owned a farm in Hampshire which, acting on complaints from neighbouring properties, the police had investigated. It seemed the animals kept there were not being used for natural purposes. The scandal had been hushed up, for the indignant landowners in the surrounding properties did not want their tranquil existence shattered by such adverse publicity. No charges had been brought against Kirkhope and his guests, but the farm itself had changed hands soon after the police raid. Kirkhope had been watched for a while after that, but if he indulged further in such sexual malpractices, then he did so very discreetly.

The backgrounds of Braverman, his wife and Ferrier, the man who had fallen from the window at Kulek's Institute, were being checked: so far, nothing unusual had been unearthed about any of them. Braverman had been a creative director of an advertising agency, a leading figure in his field. Ferrier had been a librarian. There seemed to be no obvious social connection between either party. Could they have been followers of Pryszlak?

There was only one lead on the murders of Agnes Kirkhope and her housekeeper. Two women had been spotted strolling past the Kirkhope property by neighbours on the day of the murders. Had it not been a quiet residential area, then they probably would not have been noticed; as it was, they had been observed walking by Miss Kirkhope's house two or three times by different people. It could be that they were waiting for the right moment to strike. One woman had been tall, the other short.

Chris Bishop had said that two women, one tall, the other short, had let him into the Fairfield Rest Home. Were they the same two? It was possible. Probable in fact. Peck had almost lost all suspicions regarding the psychic investigator now. He was involved all right, but only as a potential victim, of that the detective was sure. Whoever – whatever – was behind all this was trying to get at Bishop. Why? Who the hell knew? None of it made any sense.

It had been fortunate for Bishop that Peck had ordered an obo on him. The two officers on observation duty that night had followed him to the mental home, then gone in to bring him to Kulek's house as instructed over the car radio. They had found the patients trying to drown Bishop in a bathtub. It was a good thing that the two detectives had been armed – Peck had suspected Bishop of murder at that time and was taking no chances with the lives of his own men. Without firearms, they would never have fought off the berserk residents. His men had also seen the two women at the mental home who had set light to the staircase. The home had been razed to the ground, burning almost half the patients to death, and Bishop – poor bastard – had lost his wife in the fire.

All the nursing staff had been killed, whether in the fire or before it, no one would ever know – Bishop and the two detectives had seen several staff members already dead before the fire had struck. Some of the patients had leapt from the same window Bishop and Peck's men had escaped through, and had run off into the night to be picked up later by patrol cars; others had managed to use the fire escape on the other side of the building and these, too, had been found wandering the streets later that night. But a few had disappeared completely, the body count of those living and dead carried out the following day failing to tally with the known number of residents and staff.

Peck scratched the bottom of his nose with his thumb. He briefly wondered if he should recommend that a general alert be put out, to warn the public of the menace that was roaming the streets, then discarded the thought. Why be accused of over-reacting when it was up to the boys upstairs to make such drastic decisions? Besides, the trouble was still confined to an area south of the river. No point in causing panic in the rest of the city. No, he would just hand in his report and let his superiors get on with it. The only thing was, he thought, studying green pins on the large map of London he had stuck to his office wall board, the trouble was growing outwards, the pins spreading from the centre like a green starburst. Each pin indicated a fresh incident, the common denominator being that they had happened at night and that there was some kind of evil lunacy involved. What was it Kulek had said about rainspots on a window? It did seem to be gathering momentum.

The police cells and hospital wards were full of people who had had to be taken into custody for their own protection. Not all had committed acts of violence, but every one of them had that same brainless appearance. There had to be several hundred people being held at that moment, most of them part of the football crowd. The football match incident had been put down to crowd hysteria. Crowd hysteria! Jesus, the understatement of all time. Fortunately, it had been regarded as a single major phenomenon by the public and the authorities had played down the other comparatively 'minor' incidents, never once suggesting and always refuting any connection between them. The condition of those held seemed to be deteriorating rapidly, the first ones taken into custody having become nothing more than empty shells. Dozens, particularly those from Willow Road, had somehow managed to take their own lives, for there was no way such vast numbers could be watched all the time. Many were being fed intravenously, all will to live seemingly gone. Zombies, that was the word Bishop had used when he had spoken with him earlier that week. It was a good word. Apt. That's just what they were. Many shuffled around all day, some murmuring, others silent and immobile, lost within themselves. The medics were baffled. They said it was as if part of their brains had decided to close down, the part that controlled motivation. They had a fancy name for it, but however it was termed it amounted to the same thing: they were zombies. Only one thing seemed to stir them, one thing that had them all staring at the windows of their wards, rooms or cells: the coming of night. They all welcomed the darkness. And that worried Peck more than anything, because it gave substance to Kulek's theory. '

The other matter that concerned Peck almost as much was the fact that over seven hundred people had been reported missing, most of them part of the crowd that had run amok at the football match. His chair scraped noisily against the floor as he pushed it back. He straightened his tie and began to roll down his sleeves as he walked to the window once more. He dragged on the cigarette, deep, sharp breaths, wanting to finish it before he went to see the Deputy Commissioner. *Seven hundred!* He gazed down at the slow-moving traffic once more. Where the hell could seven hundred people disappear to?

'Gorn, out of it!' Duff aimed part of a crumbled brick at the creature caught in the beam from the lamp fastened to his safety helmet. The rat scuttled from the narrow ledge running alongside the sewer channel and plopped into the foul-smelling water. It vanished into the darkness ahead.

Duff turned to his companions and said, 'Watch yourselves along here. It's part of the old network – bit dodgy.'

The man immediately behind him wrinkled his nose against the heavy nitrous smell in the sewer, cursing the bright spark at the GLC who had thought up this unpleasant little assignment for him. There was a growing concern over the decaying state of the major cities' sewer networks and inspections were being hurriedly carried out to see if what was happening in Manchester could happen elsewhere. Huge holes had appeared in the busy roads in the northern town, holes big enough for a bus to drop through, caused by the collapse of the underground walls. The danger had been coming for years, but it was something out of the public eye and therefore something that could be put off to a later date. Now the worry was that it would soon be very much in the eyes of the public as cracks and holes appeared in the streets; in their noses too, as the stench wafted upwards. Berkeley, the lucky man in his department chosen to study this section of London's sewer network, shivered in the damp air and had visions of the whole city collapsing inwards into the slimy catacombs beneath. So long as he wasn't down here when it happened he didn't give a damn.

'All right, Mr Berkeley?'

He shielded his eyes against the glare of Duff's headlamp. 'Yes, let's get on with it. You say there's a section ahead that's particularly bad?'

'Last time I had a look at it. That was about two years ago.'

Wonderful, Berkeley thought. 'Lead on,' he said.

There were three men in the inspection team: Charlie Duff, senior repairs foreman for the water authority, Geoffrey Berkeley from the ministry, Terry Colt, assistant to the foreman. They were forced to stoop as they moved along the old tunnel and Berkeley tried to touch the fungus-covered walls as little as possible. His foot slipped at one stage and his leg disappeared up to the knee into the murky waters flowing beside them.

Terry Colt grinned and reached down to grasp the man's elbow, saying jovially, 'Slippery, innit?'

'Be all right in a minute, Mr Berkeley,' Duff said, also grinning. 'Tunnel widens out up ahead. Just have a look at this brickwork.'

He reached up and prodded the ceiling with a spiked metal bar he always carried when inspecting the sewers. Loose cement and brickwork crumbled away and plopped down into the centre channel.

'I see what you mean,' said Berkeley, shining his torch upwards. 'Doesn't look too good, does it?'

Duff grunted his reply and moved further along, poking the ceiling as he went. Suddenly a small section of brickwork came away completely causing Berkeley to cry out in alarm.

Duff merely stared up at the damage, shaking his head and mumbling to himself at the same time.

'I suggest you are less forceful with your probing, Duff,' Berkeley said, his heart pounding wildly. This job was unpleasant enough without adding danger to it. 'We don't want the whole roof down on top of us, do we?'

Duff was still grumbling to himself, his torch beam weaving from side to side as he shook his head. 'All these old tunnels are the same, you know,' he finally said to Berkeley. 'It's gonna cost millions to put them right. Solid enough when they were built, but all that traffic up there over the years, all those bleedin juggernauts, all those buildings goin up . . . People who built these never dreamed they'd have to bear such a load. Never thought they'd have to carry so much shit, either.'

Berkeley wiped his slime covered hands on his overalls. 'Fortunately, that's not my problem. I only have to submit a report.'

'Oh yeah?' said Terry from behind. 'An who d'you think pays for it, then? Only comes out of our pockets, dunnit?'

'Shall we move on? It's rather uncomfortable crouching like this.' Berkeley was anxious to get the inspection over with.

Duff turned and made his way further down the tunnel, keeping his experienced eye on the ceiling, looking for breaks and signs of sagging. He saw plenty.

His assistant's voice came from the rear. 'D'you know what? If you got lost down here on your own, Mr Berkeley, you could wander around for years and never find your way out.'

Silly sod, Duff thought, but grinned to himself all the same.

'There's miles and miles of tunnels,' Terry went on. 'You could get from one end of London to the other.'

'Surely you would have to stop at the Thames?' came Berkeley's acid-toned comment.

'Oh yeah, if you could find it,' Terry answered, unabashed. 'You could drown before you did, though. You should see some of these tunnels after heavy rainfall. Some of em fill right up. Just think of it, wanderin around down here, your lamp battery runnin down, things scuttlin around in the dark. I think the rats'd get you in the end. Some big bleeders down here.'

'All right, Terry, leave it out,' said Duff, still grinning. 'It's gettin wider up here, Mr Berkeley. We'll be able to stand up soon.'

Berkeley wasn't bothered about Terry's remarks – he knew the idiot was only trying to intimidate him – but he could not help being afraid of the tunnels themselves. He felt a huge pressure bearing down on him, as though the city above were slowly sinking, pressing down on the tunnel roofs, compressing them, squeezing them flat, inch by inch. He would be forced into the slime flowing beneath him, the ceiling pushing him underneath, holding him there until he had to swallow, the filthy waters gushing down his throat, filling him . . .

'There you go!' Terry had spotted the opening ahead where their tunnel joined another.

Berkeley was grateful to step through into it and stand erect. This branch of the sewer network must have measured at least twelve feet across and the domed ceiling was high at its apex. The causeways on each side of the channel were wide enough to walk along comfortably.

'This looks fairly sound,' he commented, his voice ringing out hollowly against the damp curved walls.

'Should be all right along this stretch,' said Duff. 'It's the pipes and small conduits that give us the most problems – you'd never believe just what they get blocked up with.'

'No, I meant the brickwork here. It seems solid enough.'

Duff took the lamp from his helmet and flashed it down the tunnel, searching walls and ceiling for breaks. 'Looks okay. There's a storm weir further down. Let's just have a look at it.'

By now, Berkeley had lost all sense of direction, not knowing whether they were heading north, south, east or west. The foreman's assistant was right: it would be easy to get lost in the maze of tunnels. He heard Duff poking at the walls with his metal pike and briefly wondered what would make a man take up this kind of work for a career? Career? Wrong word. His kind didn't have careers – they had jobs. And the young man behind – surely working in a garage or a factory was better than creeping around in the dark among the city's filth. Still, Berkeley reflected, thank God someone was stupid enough to do it. He peered into smaller openings leading into the main channel as he passed, shuddering at the total blackness they presented, his beam seeming to penetrate very little of their length. He imagined one of the huge rats the foreman's assistant had spoken of lurking there, waiting to pounce on any unfortunate who would unknowingly wander into its lair. Or a giant spider, huge and malformed, glutted on the slivering dark life all around, never before seen by human eyes, its web strung completely across a tunnel, waiting for an unsuspecting victim... Or a giant slug, blind and slimy, sucking itself to the lichen-covered walls, living in perpetual darkness, greedy for the next human feast . . .

Oh my God!'

Duff swung around at the sound of Berkeley's shriek. 'What is it?' he asked, his voice a little higher-pitched than he'd intended.

The ministry man was pointing into a tunnel. 'Something moved in there!' His hand was trembling uncontrollably.

Duff lumbered back to him thinking, *silly sod*, and peered into the opening. 'You probably saw a rat,' he said reassuringly. 'Lots of em down here.'

'No, no, it was much bigger.'

'Trick of the light, probably all it was. It's the imagination that does it, every time. Takes a while to get used to things down here.'

Terry was peering over Berkeley's shoulder into the opening, a big smile on his face. 'They say the sewers are haunted by murder victims whose bodies've been dropped into them to get rid of the evidence,' he brightly informed the ministry man.

'Hold your noise, Terry,' Duff told him. 'You'll be givin me the bleedin creeps next. Look, Mr Berkeley, there's nothing down there.' The combined lights from their lamps forced back the darkness in the tunnel, revealing nothing but green-and-yellow-streaked walls. 'It must have just been your light throwin a shadow as you passed. Nothin to worry about.'

'I'm sorry. I'm sure . . .'

Duff had already turned away and was marching onwards, whistling tunelessly to himself. With a last look into the tunnel, Berkeley followed, feeling foolish, but none-the-less, still nervous. Stinking bloody job to send him on!

As Terry moved away from the opening he thought – just thought – he heard a sound from its depths. 'Frightened me bloody self now,' he muttered under his breath.

Berkeley was hurrying to catch up with Duff, finding a small comfort in the man's no-nonsense, down-to-earth attitude, when the foreman came to an abrupt stop, causing the ministry man to bump into him. Duff was pointing his lamp into the channel at their feet.

'There's something in the water,' he said.

Berkeley looked towards the centre of the wide torch beam. Something was floating lazily along, drifting with the slow-moving current, its progress hindered as it bumped against the raised side of the causeway. It looked like a large sack in the inadequate light.

'What on earth is it?' Berkeley asked curiously.

'It's a body,' said Terry, who had now joined them.

This time Duff knew his assistant wasn't joking. He knelt down on the edge of the causeway and caught the drifting shape with his metal bar as it came close. He pulled and the body turned languidly over in the water. All three men gasped when they saw the white bloated face and wide, staring eyes.

Berkeley found himself bent double against the moist wall, his stomach heaving up and down like a berserk lift. Through his dizziness, he heard Terry say, 'Christ Almighty, there's another one!'

He forced himself to look when he heard a splash. Terry had dropped into the sewer, his thigh-high boots giving him adequate protection against the foul-smelling stream that reached a point just above his knees. He was wading to another floating form on the other side of the channel.

'This one's a woman, I think!' he called back over his shoulder.

'Okay, Terry. Try and lift it on to the causeway,' Duff told him. 'We'll go back and get a team to come down and collect em. Mr Berkeley, give us a hand to pull this one out, will you?'

Berkeley shrank back against the wall. 'I . . . I don't think . . .'

'Would you believe it?' It was Terry's voice again. 'There's another one comin down.'

Duff and Berkeley followed his gaze and saw the shape floating towards them. As it approached they saw it was the body of another woman, a white shape that could have been a nightdress billowing out around her. She was on her back, glazed eyes staring up at the dripping ceiling. Fortunately for Berkeley's stomach, her features did not have the puffiness of the first person they had found.

'Grab her, Terry,' Duff ordered.

The assistant heaved the body he was holding on to the causeway, then waded towards the new one. They watched him as he caught a leg, Duff with his hand grasped around the lapel of the dead man below him, Berkeley wondering at the assistant's lack of nerves. Perhaps the boy was too thick to be bothered.

Terry leaned over the floating woman, his arms going around her waist and reaching to grip her beneath the armpits. What happened next caused the same reaction in both men watching but with different results.

As Terry's head came close to the woman's, two pale-fleshed arms slid from the water and encircled his neck. He screamed as he was pulled down, the scream broken off by a choking gurgling sound as he plunged beneath the water. The oozing fluid became a white-foamed eruption as he struggled to free himself from the deathly grip, but the creature held on to him, dragging him down in her embrace.

Berkeley's mouth dropped open in a soundless scream and he was only dimly aware of the hot excreta that had been jettisoned down his sagging legs. He staggered back against the wall again, the knuckles of both hands filling his open mouth.

Duff's initial shock was instantly followed by a paralyzing pain that began in his chest and swiftly travelled up to his neck and arms. A red, blinding mist closed the vision before him and he toppled forward into the water, his heart already given up before he could be drowned.

Berkeley watched as Terry rose from the water just once and he saw the assistant's eyes were staring into the face before him as if in disbelief. The woman hugged him tight, a lover's embrace, and her cracked and bitten lips were smiling. The boy stumbled backwards and the creature fell with him. Berkeley could see the dim glow of his lamp beneath the churning, green slime, but it grew weaker as he watched, the disturbance becoming no more than ripples, the ripples themselves fading after the last confusion of bubbles shot to the surface. Finally the light shrank to nothing.

> The water was still.
> Until she slowly emerged.
> Green slime running from her body.
> Looking at him.
> Smiling.

Berkeley's shrieks echoed around the dingy caverns, the sound multiplied into a hundred screaming voices. There was more movement further down the tunnel. Figures were stepping from black openings into the main sewer. Others were in the water, wading towards him from the direction in which he and the two workmen had come. He didn't want to look, but he couldn't help himself, the headlamp swinging in a frantic arc towards the approaching figures. A cold, wet hand closed around his ankle.

The woman was standing close to him and he jerked his foot away from the edge of the causeway. Her long damp hair hung like the tails of rats over her face and the white gown she wore was ripped almost down to her pubic area, revealing sagging breasts and a stomach that was strangely distended as though she had not eaten for a long time. He cowered before her in the darkness and wondered if she was dead.

The woman reached for him again and began to clamber on to the causeway.

'No!' He kicked out at her and scrambled away on all fours. 'Leave me alone!'

He staggered to his feet and pushed himself against the wall, scraping lichen off with his back as he moved away. She began to crawl towards him. The others were moving closer.

He fell into an opening behind him and, as he looked for a means of escape, white, shaking hands reached for him from within. He tumbled back into the main tunnel, gasping, whimpering sounds burbling from his lips. He slipped from the causeway and fell headlong into the slow-moving fluid, emerging spluttering and crying, but still running. The water, thick with soilage, clung to his legs as though mud creatures at the bottom were gripping his feet and holding him back. Lifting his knees high, he splashed down the channel, away from the dark figures that followed, away from the woman who held her arms out to hug him. He was conscious of more and more objects bumping into his legs and was afraid to look down, knowing what they were, knowing arms would reach up to drag him down if he did look. The sewer opened up into a huge chamber, the ceiling some thirty or forty feet above him and supported by sturdy iron pillars. The massive weir controlling the flow of water through the sewers stood opposite. But he did not see it. For this was where they were all waiting.

They stood around the edges of the chamber, others in the water itself. More were crammed into the many openings in the circular wall. The water at the bottom of the chamber was full of bodies, several drifting away into various outlets as he watched. His headlamp swung round from face to face and he had the eerie sensation of being in a dark underground cathedral, the black-smeared people choristers awaiting the arrival of the choirmaster. The lamp beam seemed to be growing weaker, the surrounding darkness closing in around it, slowly stifling its brightness. Hundreds of eyes watched him from the shadows and the gaseous fumes from the chamber assailed his nostrils with added force. The stench here was somehow more acrid.

He began to back away from the crowded chamber. But a damp, white hand on his shoulder told him there was nowhere to run.

TWENTY-ONE

The cat kept to the shadows, its progress along the rain-freshened street silent and unseen. The rain had stopped, otherwise the cat would still be skulking somewhere under cover. It was an animal that had no owner, one that needed no permanent home; it lived on its own cunning, its own stealth, its own speed. Humans would never pet its kind, nor welcome it into their homes, for it was a scavenger and had the looks of a scavenger. The black fur on its back was sparse, almost bare in places where the cat had come off worse in fights with others of its breed. One ear was just a mangled shape, a stub protruding from its head; the dog that had inflicted the wound could now see only from one eye. Its claws were stunted from too much running on concrete, but were still lethal when fully extended. Its pads were hard, like tough leather. The cat sniffed the damp night air and its eyes, caught in the dull glow of an overhead streetlight, were glassy yellow.

It turned into an alleyway and padded towards the dustbins hidden there in the dark doorways. The scent of other night creatures was strong in its nose. The cat recognized most of the individual smells, some friendly, others producing a new sharpness to its already acute senses. The furtive, sharp-nosed, long-tailed creatures had been there, a cowardly enemy that would always choose to run rather than fight. They were gone now. Its own kind had been there earlier, but they, too were gone.

The cat sniffed its way through the litter on the ground, then leapt on top of a dustbin, disappointed that its lid was sealed tight. The lid of the next dustbin was at a slight angle and the smell of corrupting food wafted through the narrow, new-moon gap. The cat poked its nose inquisitively into the opening, poking a paw through to tug at the loose paper and rubble at the top. The lid moved a little under the cat's insistent probing, then even more when the creature pushed first its head then its shoulders through the widening gap. The metal lid finally slid gratingly across the rim of the dustbin and landed with a loud clatter on the ground. The cat fled, alarmed by the noise of its own making.

It paused at the entrance to the alley, its one good ear pricked for unfriendly sounds, nose held high and twitching for hostile scents. The animal stiffened when it detected the slight acrid smell in the air and the sparse hairs on its back began to bristle. As its fellow creatures had been only minutes before, the cat became aware of a strange presence that somehow belonged to man, yet wasn't man. It crept over the paralyzed cat like a crawling thing, a shadow that mixed with the other shadows. The terrified creature bared its teeth and hissed. Something was moving in the middle of the glistening wet road.

The cat arched its back, every hair on its body stiff and erect, mouth wide in a hissing snarl. It spat its defiance, afraid though it was, and its eyes narrowed, full of venom. The streetlights had dimmed as though a mist had drifted across them and the pavements no longer offered any reflections in their wetness. A heavy, metallic sound came from the road's centre as the manhole cover shuddered, then began to rise. It was pushed higher, one side resting on its base, and something black began to emerge. The cat recognized the shape that came over the edge of the hole. It knew it was a human hand. Yet instinctively, it knew the hand did not belong to a human.

The cat hissed once more, then fled, for some reason heading for the lights rather than the shadows.

The three youths waited in the weather-battered shelter on the common. Two were white, one was black. They puffed on cigarettes and jiggled their knees to keep out the cold.

'I ain't stayin much longer,' the coloured boy said. 'It's too fuckin cold.' His name was Wesley and he was on probation for purse snatching.

'Shut up an wait a minute. Won't be much longer,' said one of his companions. His name was Vincent and he was on probation for half-killing his stepfather.

'I dunno, it's gettin late, Vin,' said the third youth. 'Don't think there'll be no one about.' His name was Ed – his friends thought it was short for Edward but, in fact, it was short for Edgar – and he had recently finished his villain's apprenticeship in an approved school.

'What you wanna do, then, go ome?' asked Vince of his two friends. 'Got any money for tomorrow night?'

'No, but, I'm fuckin cold,' Wesley told him again.

'You're always fuckin cold. Miss the old Caribbean, eh?'

'Ain't never been there. Born in bloody Brixton, were'n I?'

'Get out of it. In your bloody blood. You all miss your bleedin sunshine. It's what makes your hair curly.'

'Leave im alone, Vin,' said Ed, peering around the edge of the shelter into the gloom. 'He's joinin the Front, inne?'

'Do me a favour! They won't have him! He's a nig-nog imself.'

'Yeah, but I don't want no more of them comin over ere. Specially those Pakis.' Wesley protested. 'Too bloody many.'

The other two youths shrieked with glee. The thought of Wesley marching along with the National Front holding a banner saying 'KEEP BRITAIN WHITE' was too much. Wesley was too puzzled by their laughter to feel aggrieved. Soon he was laughing with them.

'Ang on, ang on,' Ed said suddenly. 'I think there's someone comin.'

'Right. Down to you Ed,' said Vin, springing to his feet. 'Me an Wes'll be over there in the bushes.'

'Why always me?' Ed protested. 'You av a go.'

Vince patted him on the cheek, the last pat a little more forceful than the rest. 'You're so pretty, that's why. They like you more than us. Think you're one of them, don't they?'

Not for the first time, Ed cursed his own blond good looks. He would much rather have had Vince's tough, pock-marked features and short ginger hair than his own almost girlish looks.

'What about Wes, then?'

'Nah, they don't trust coloureds, do they? Think they're all fuckin muggers.' He gave his black friend a playful shove. 'Right, innit, Wes?'

Wes grinned in the dark. 'They's fockin right, man,' he said, mimicking his own father's accent.

Vince and Wesley ran quietly from the shelter, both sniggering and prodding each other as they went. Ed waited silently, taking a last drag from his cigarette and listening for the approaching footsteps. The common was a favourite haunt for clandestine lovers of all varieties, that variety having increased since the surrounding working-class area had been infiltrated by middle-class residents. The cost of travelling every day from the surrounding suburbs to their jobs in London had become too much for the *nouveaux-pauvres*. The area that had become multi-racial over the years was now fast-becoming multi-class. Ed threw the half-inch butt on to the ground, then took another loose cigarette from the pocket of his denim jacket. He was about to step from the shelter into view when he realized there were two sets of footfalls. He slunk back into the shadows.

The couple walked past the shelter, arms tight around each other's waists; Ed was worried that they were going to make use of his hideaway for their own purposes, but when they moved on he realized the stink of stale urine in the shelter would put any lovers off, no matter how desperate. He cursed under his breath and dug his hands deep into his pockets. There'll be no gingers about now, not this late, he told himself. Yet he knew from previous experience that the lateness of the hour meant nothing to certain lonely men, nor did the remoteness of the locations they wandered through. Sometimes Ed wondered if they went out of their way to be attacked. Maybe they enjoyed it. Or maybe it was their own subconscious way of punishing themselves for what they were. The last, deeper thought was immediately dismissed by one more obvious to Ed's way of thinking; maybe they just got more horny at night.

He looked out into the darkness towards the spot where Vince and Wes had disappeared. The feeble glow from a nearby lamppost did little to pierce the shadows. He was about to call out to them, imagining them both giggling and playing around in the dark, when he heard more footsteps. Ed listened, making sure they belonged to one person. They did. The man came into view seconds later.

He was slightly built, about Ed's size. A heavy belted overcoat hung loosely on him, emphasizing his narrow shoulders rather than compensating for them. Definite pouf, Ed told himself, not sure if he was pleased or displeased with their luck. He knew these were easy pickings, that there was little danger from them; but something inside always made him scared of them. Perhaps that was why in the end he always used more violence against them than his companions did. The memory of when he had decided to tackle one on his own was still fresh in his mind for, instead of attacking his intended victim and relieving him of his wallet, he had let himself be used, then run off sobbing before he could even be paid. The shame of it still stung his face, and he knew his skin had become bright red in the darkness. If Vince and Wes ever found out . . .

'Got a light, John?' Ed had pushed all further thoughts away and stepped on to the pathway leading across the common.

The man came to an abrupt halt and glanced around nervously. The boy looked all right, but was he really alone? Should he walk on or . . . should he take a chance?

He took out his own cigarettes. 'Would you like one of mine?' he asked. 'They're tipped.'

'Oh, yeah. Thanks.' Ed stuck his battered cigarette back into his pocket and reached towards the proferred pack, hoping the man hadn't noticed his hand was shaking slightly.

'You can have the pack, if you like,' the man said, his face serious.

My Gawd, a right one ere, Ed thought. 'Oh, great, thanks a lot.' He pushed the pack into another pocket.

The man studied the boy's face in the glow from the cigarette-lighter. It became indistinct when he drew back, his cigarette lit. The man snapped out the small flame.

'It's rather cold tonight, isn't it,' he said cautiously. The boy was attractive in a rough sort of way. Was he genuine or just a tart? Either way, he'd want money.

'Yeah, bit nippy. Just out for a walk?'

'Yes, it's nicer when it's quiet, I hate crowds. I feel I can breathe at night.'

'It'll cost you a fiver.'

The man was slightly taken aback by the boy's sudden bluntness. He *was* a tart.

'Back at my place?' he asked, the excitement that had been triggered off at the boy's approach now accelerating.

Ed shook his head. 'No, no, it'll ave to be ere.'

'I'll pay you more.'

'No, I ain't got time. Got to be ome soon.'

The boy seemed a little afraid and the man decided not to push his luck.

'All right. Let's find somewhere nice.'

'Over there'll do.' The boy pointed towards a clump of bushes and trees and this time it was the man's turn to become a little nervous. It was so dark over there: the boy could have friends waiting.

'Let's go behind the shelter,' he suggested quickly.

'No, I don't think . . .'

But the man now had a surprisingly firm grip around Ed's shoulders. The boy allowed himself to be propelled towards the back of the wooden shelter, hoping his friends were watching. It would be just like those two bastards to leave it till the last minute.

They squelched through the mud at the side of the hut, the man warding off bushes that threatened to scratch their faces. They turned a corner and Ed found himself pressed up against the back of the hut. The man's face was looming larger in front of him, his lips only inches away, and Ed felt the revulsion rising in him. Fumbling fingers pulled at the zip of his jeans.

'No,' he said, turning his head to one side.

'Come on. Don't be coy. You want it as much as me.'

'Fuck off!' Ed screamed and pushed at the man's chest. His face had grown red-hot again and his vision had become blurred with sudden tears of rage.

The man was startled. He staggered back and stared at the youth. He began to say something but the boy rushed at him, lashing out wildly with his fists.

'Stop it, stop it!' the man screamed, falling backwards. Ed began to kick him.

'You dirty fuckin queer!'

The man tried to rise, whimpering with fright now. He had to get away, the boy was going to hurt him. And the police might hear the disturbance.

'Leave me alone! Take my money!' The man managed to reach his inside pocket. He threw his wallet at his attacker. 'Take it, take it, you bastard! Just leave me alone!'

Ed ignored the wallet and continued to rain punches and kicks down at the curled form at his feet until his arms and legs grew heavy and his anger began to subside. He stumbled back against the shelter's wall and stood there leaning on it, chest heaving and legs weak. He could hear the injured man crying out but, for some reason, he could no longer see him lying there on the ground. The night darkness had somehow become more dense.

'Vin! Wes!' he called out when he had recovered enough breath. 'Where are you, for fuck's sake?'

'Ere we are, Ed.'

The youth jumped at the close proximity of their voices. It was almost as if they were inside his head. He could just see their dark outlines as they stood at the corner of the shelter.

'You took your time, you bastards. I ad to deck im on me own. Let's get is money and split.'

'Nah, I don't think so, Ed.' It was Vince's voice. 'Let's av some fun first.' He heard Wesley giggle.

This is stupid, Ed thought. It'd be better to get away . . . but it would be nice to do something to this cunt . . . something nasty . . . he was helpless . . . there was no one around . . . something that would hurt him . . . something . . .

There were other voices inside his head now, not just his own. Something was creeping along corridors in his mind, cold fingers that probed and searched, fingers that spoke to him and laughed with him. And he was leading them on, guiding them. The coldness was all-enveloping as it suddenly lunged and caught him in its icy grip, and he was pleased to receive it, the shock turning into pleasure like the swift effects of an anaesthetizing injection. He wasn't alone any more. The voices were with him and they told him what to do.

Vince and Wes had already begun and the damp earth that was being pushed into the struggling man's mouth stifled any screams.

The filling station stood at the edge of the common, an oasis of light in the surrounding darkness. The yellow Ford Escort pulled into the forecourt and came to a smooth halt before a petrol pump. The driver turned off the engine and settled back to wait for the attendant to emerge from his office. The car's occupants did not know that the man on duty, who was, in fact, the garage manager, had popped round to the back of the building twenty minutes earlier to lock up the toilets there; he didn't want any lingering customers at that time of night. Regretfully, he had had to let his usual attendant leave earlier; the man was obviously coming down with a bad attack of flu and the manager wasn't taking the risk of catching it himself. His profit margin was small enough without his being off sick and leaving the staff to run the garage. He'd go broke within a week with their fiddles. It was normally bad policy to man a garage alone at night, for it made the station an easy mark for villains; but tonight he had no choice. He kept the door of the office overlooking the forecourt permanently locked and scrutinized every customer that came in for petrol before unlocking it. If he didn't like the look of them, he turned the OPEN sign around to CLOSED and ignored their muffled curses. It had been well after twelve when he remembered the toilets were still unlocked.

'You sure it's open, George?' the woman next to the driver said testily. 'There doesn't seem to be anyone around.'

'It says "open" at the entrance,' her husband replied. 'And look, on the cashier's door. There's another "open" sign.'

'I should give him a toot, George,' said the driver's father-in-law from the back seat.

'I'll give him a minute. He might be round the back.' There was nothing pushy about George.

His wife, Olwen, pulled the hem of her flouncy, sequined dress into a tight bunch over her knees, afraid the chiffon and layers of netting would pick up dirt from the car's interior. A large polythene bag was draped over the passenger seat to protect her meticulously made ballroom frock and fur shoulder-cape from any hidden grime. Her high coiffured hair brushed against the car roof as she stared through the windscreen, her mouth set in a firm, straight line.

'We should have won,' she announced grimly.

'Now, Olwen,' George said patiently, 'Nigel and Barbara were very good.'

'That's right, defend them. I suppose it doesn't matter that they bumped us twice on the dance floor. Never even apologized afterwards. You'd have thought there was no one else in the ballroom the way they pranced around. We should have objected. Bloody judges should have spotted it.'

'Well, we were runners-up, dear.'

'Runners-up! That's the story of your life, isn't it, George? That's all you'll ever be.'

'There's no call for that kind of talk,' Olwen's father rebuked.

'Shut up, Huw,' said Olwen's mother who sat cramped in the back with her husband. 'Olwen's quite right. She could have been ballroom champion by now, that girl.' She did not add, 'with a different partner'. There was no need to.

'Take no notice, George,' Huw said. 'Neither of them are ever satisfied.'

'Satisfied? What have I got to be satisfied with? What have you ever given me?'

'I'll give you the back of my hand in a minute.'

'Dad, don't speak to mother like that.'

'I'll speak to her however I . . .'

'You certainly won't. You see what he's like, Olwen? You see what I've had to put up with all these years?'

'Put up with? I've had your nagging . . .'

'Nagging?'

'Mum doesn't nag.'

'She nags all the time. Same way you nag poor old George.'

'Me nag George? I never nag George. Do I ever nag you George?'

'The attendant's a long time,' said George.

'Well bib him.' Exasperated, Olwen reached across George and thumped the car's horn. 'Lazy bleeder's probably sleeping under the counter.'

George ran his finger and thumb along his pencil-line moustache, smoothing down the Brylcreemed hairs, and briefly wondered what would happen if he punched Olwen on the nose. She'd punch him back, that's what would happen. And she could punch harder.

'Ah, here he comes,' he said, pointing to the figure that had emerged from the darkness at the rear of the garage.

'It's about bloody time,' said Olwen.

'Don't swear, dear, it's not very nice.'

'I'll swear if I like.'

'George is right, Olwen,' said her father. 'It's not very ladylike.'

'Leave her alone, Huw,' said her mother. 'She's had a lot of stress this evening. George didn't help by letting her fall on her bottom in the *pas redoublé*.'

'Best part of the bloody evening,' her father remarked, smiling at the memory. 'Dad!'

'Take no notice, Olwen. It's just like him to enjoy seeing his own daughter make a fool of herself.'

'Mum!'

'Oh, I didn't mean . . .'

'Five of 3-star, please.' George had wound down his window and was calling out to the approaching figure.

The man came to a halt, smiled at the occupants of the car, and looked over towards the petrol pumps. He made towards them.

'He's slow enough, isn't he?' remarked Olwen's mother. 'And what's he got that silly grin on his face for?'

'Look at the state of him,' said Olwen. 'You'd think he'd been down the mines. I wonder if the manager knows his staff walk around like that?'

'Perhaps he is the manager,' said her father, chuckling in the back, not knowing that the manager lay dead on the floor of the toilets, his skull cracked open like an egg from the repeated blows of a brick.

They watched the man as he lifted the dispensing nozzle from the rack set in the pumping unit. He came towards the car holding the hosecock alongside his head like a duelling pistol. His eyes were half-closed as though they had not yet adjusted to the contrast between the harsh overhead lighting and the darkness from which he had just emerged. He grinned at the four people watching him from the car.

'Silly bugger,' Olwen remarked.

George poked his head out of the window. 'Er, no, old chap. I did say 3-star. You've still got it switched to 4-star.' He drew back quickly when he found himself staring into the black hole of the dispensing nozzle.

In the back of the Escort, Olwen's father had a puzzled frown on his face. He had seen movement in the fringes of darkness around the service area. There were shapes moving closer. They were stepping into the lighted area, then stopping. They were waiting. Watching. Others stood behind them, still in the shadows. What the hell was going on? Why were they staring at the car? He turned to say something but stopped himself when he saw the metal nozzle from the petrol pump stretching into the car window and George, a startled expression on his face, leaning away from it. Olwen's father could only watch in dumbstruck amazement as the index finger on the hand holding the nozzle began to tighten.

The petrol gushed out, covering George's head and shoulders in a filmy fluid. Olwen began to scream when the nozzle was aimed down into her husband's lap. Her father tried to push forward and grab the long barrel of the hosecock, but it was turned in his direction and he fell back, choking on the petrol that had poured into his open mouth. Olwen's mother was screaming now, knowing she and her husband were trapped and helpless in the back of the two-door vehicle.

Olwen's screams became even louder as her dress was suddenly splashed by the foul-smelling liquid. She tried to reach for the door-handle on her side, but her fingers slid from the petrol-soaked metal.

Her father, still choking on the fuel he had swallowed, could only watch in horror as the nozzle waved around, the petrol pouring out in a solid stream and filling the car with its noxious fumes and deadly liquid. George was striking out blindly, his eyes stinging and useless. Olwen's hands were covering her face as she cried out and beat her feet against the car's floor. Her mother was trying to burrow her way down into the gap between the back of the driver's seat and her own. The flow of petrol abruptly stopped and the nozzle was withdrawn.

Olwen's father could only observe the middle portion of the man through the windows; it was enough to see him drop the nozzle and reach into his jacket pocket for something. Huw began to moan when he saw the box of matches, the sudden bright flare as one was lit, the small arc of smoke as the match was tossed into the car.

The man stood back as the Escort's interior burst into a blinding cauldron of flame, his face peeling instantly as the fire licked out at him. He did not seem to feel the pain as he reached down for the hose at his feet and drew the dispensing nozzle towards himself. His fingers curled around the trigger and squeezed.

He walked around the forecourt as far as the hose could allow, splashing petrol everywhere, becoming saturated himself, but seeming not to care. Then he turned back towards the little yellow car that had by now become a raging inferno, the sounds of its occupants no longer heard, and he aimed the jet of fuel at it. The flames rushed towards him and he stood there and screamed as he became a black charred shape. His companions turned away from the heat and light, sinking into the darkness that was itself forced back when the filling station exploded into a huge ball of fire that rose hundreds of feet into the air and lit the night sky.

The Dark drifted on, an evil, creeping blackness that had no substance, yet was full of invisible energy, an expanding shadow that existed only in other shadows, an incorporeal thing that sucked at human minds, invading and searching for the hidden repressed impulses that were of itself. There were solid, dark shapes within it and these were the forms of men and women whose will it did not just govern, but who embodied the material part of it, those who physically enacted the evil that it was, its earthly force. It had a smell, a faint acridity that tainted the air it filled, a bitter aroma that men were aware of when lightning struck the ground, or when electric cables discharged sparks into the air. It was a dark stain on the night.

The blaze was left far behind with the wailing sirens and distant shouts, and the Dark relished the blackness it crept into, its edges probing like tentacles at the shadows before it, sensing a fresh force that was somewhere near, a huge source of energy that was as yet untapped, a chained gathering of dark minds that was the very substance it needed.

It seeped across the grassland on to an open road, shying away from the orange-glowing streetlights, surging around them like a stream around rocks projecting from its bed. The shadowy figures drifted with it, several collapsing, their bodies drained, lack of food or water finally bringing them down like machines not fuelled or oiled. Some died – the others would follow later – and as they did, a part of them was released: the darkness within them was welcomed by the mass.

The long wall loomed up high and the darkness flowed over it, leaving the men and women who walked with it below, helpless and suddenly afraid. It rushed towards the sleeping inmates of Wandsworth Prison, creeping into the openings, pouncing and absorbing, the recumbent minds receptive and eager. Not all though. But these did not last long.

TWENTY-TWO

The ringing phone woke Bishop from a deep sleep. It was strange, but since Lynn's death two weeks before, his recurrent drowning nightmare had left him. Perhaps it had been purged from him by the experience in the mental home that night, living out the dream, almost taking it to death's conclusion. He pushed back the covers and switched on the bedside lamp. The small alarm clock told him it was just after two o'clock. Alertness spread through him as he heaved himself from the bed and padded down the carpeted stairs to the hall. He grabbed the phone.

'Bishop? Detective Chief Inspector Peck here.'

'What's wrong?' All drowsiness had completely left Bishop now.

Peck's voice was urgent. 'I haven't got long, so just listen and do as I tell you.' Something knotted inside Bishop's stomach.

'I want you to lock your doors, front and back,' Peck went on. 'Check all your windows, make sure they're locked, too.'

'What's going on, Peck?'

'Have you got a room you can lock yourself into?'

'Yes, but . . .'

'Then do it. Barricade yourself in.'

'What the hell are you talking about?'

'Look, I haven't got time to explain. All I can tell you is that something is going on near your part of London. Our Information Room is being flooded with emergency calls. Our biggest problem is a riot in Wandsworth Prison.'

'Jesus. Can they break out?'

'It looks like they already have.' There was a short pause at the other end of the line. 'It seems some of the prison warders themselves may have been involved. To make matters more confused, a garage on the other side of the Common has been blown up.'

'Peck, has all this got something to do with the Pryszlak business?'

'God only knows. If it has, some of these maniacs may come after you. That's why I want you to lock yourself in. I'm afraid I haven't got enough men available to send you any protection. I could be wrong anyway.'

'Thanks for the warning. Have you told Kulek and Jessica?'

'I still have a man watching their house. I've sent a radio message telling him to inform Kulek of what's happening. I've let the guard stay there, even though we can't really spare him. Unfortunately, the officer keeping an eye on you had to be called in – that's why I'm ringing you. You'll be okay if you do as I say.'

'All right. Just tell me one thing. Do you now believe Jacob Kulek's theory?'

'Do you?'

'I'm beginning to more and more.'

'Well, maybe I am too. I don't *understand* it, but there's nothing else to explain what's going on. The thing is to convince my governors. I've got to get back now. You just sit tight, understand?'

The receiver was replaced before Bishop could answer. He quickly checked the front door to make sure it was bolted as well as locked, then went out to the back. The kitchen door leading to his tiny rear garden was also locked. Next, check the windows, he thought, but instead he decided to first ring Jessica; even with police protection she was probably scared to death. He had seen her only twice since Lynn's death: once when she had come to his house after learning about the tragedy in the mental home, and then a couple of days later, at a meeting held by Peck and several of his superiors, including the deputy commissioner. Since then she had left him alone and he was grateful that she realized he needed time to get over the shock of losing Lynn, this time permanently. It disturbed him that rather than feel remorse, he felt anger at his wife's death. To him, she had begun to die years before, a long, lingering illness of the mind from which he somehow knew she would never recover; it was the manner of her death that angered him. She had been used, controlled by an unknown power along with the others at the home. Her death had been horrible, although mercifully quick, and he wanted it avenged. If Pryszlak was in some bizarre way involved, then he, Bishop, would find a way to strike back. There had to be a way.

He dialled Jessica's number, hoping she would still be awake after the policeman's message. It was several long moments before the receiver was lifted and Jessica's voice came through.

'Jessica, it's me, Chris.'

Her tone became alert as had his only minutes before when Peck had called him.

'Chris, what is it? Are you all right?'

'Didn't you get Peck's message?'

'No, what message? It's the middle of the night, Chris. We've been asleep.'

'But there's a policeman on guard outside. Hasn't he told you?'

'Nobody's told us anything. What on earth's going on? Tell me what's happened.'

Bishop was puzzled. 'Peck rang me a few moments ago. He said he'd got a message to you. There are more incidents being reported, Jessica. All on this side of the river, it seems.'

'What kind of incidents?' Her voice was calm, but it had an edge to it.

'A riot in Wandsworth Prison. Something else about an explosion in a garage nearby. Others that he didn't have time to tell me about.'

'And he thinks there's a connection . . .'

'With Pryszlak and his sect? He's not sure, but he felt he ought to warn us, anyway. Jessica, he said they might come after us again if there is a connection.'

'Oh, Chris.'

'Don't worry, you'll be all right. So far, all the trouble is over here. You've got a man outside who will contact his headquarters if anything begins to happen there.'

'But what will you do?'

'I'll barricade myself in, don't worry. We're all probably going to feel embarrassed later when we learn these are entirely separate incidents that have nothing to do with us.'

'I hope . . .' Jessica's voice broke off. 'There's someone at the door now. Our guardian policeman, no doubt. I'd better let him in before he wakes my father – if he isn't already awake, that is.'

'I'm sorry, Jessica. I just wanted to make sure . . .'

'Don't be silly, Chris. I'm glad you rang. Just hold on for a minute while I open the door.'

Bishop heard the clunk of the receiver being placed on the small table he remembered the phone rested on in the long hallway. There was silence for a few moments save for the strangely hollow sounding atmospherics in his own earpiece, then he thought he heard the distant noise of the front door being unlocked. For some reason he began to feel uneasy. Why had the detective been so slow in delivering his message? Perhaps he had taken it into his own head not to disturb the sleeping household – what they didn't know couldn't hurt them. After all, the policeman was keeping a watch on the place. The hall light being switched on by Jessica as she answered the phone could have prompted him to change his mind and inform them there and then. Yet Bishop could not imagine any of Peck's men not carrying out his instructions to the letter. He had said he'd told the officer to inform Kulek immediately.

Bishop's hand tightened around the receiver, his knuckles becoming white. 'Jessica, can you hear me?'

His listened and thought he heard the approaching footsteps at the other end.

'Jessica?'

A click, then a burring noise as the receiver was dropped on to its cradle at the other end.

Bishop slowed the car as he turned from the main Highgate High Street into the village itself. The drive across London had been swift, for there was little traffic around at that hour, although there had been much activity in the Westminster area as police vehicles and minibus 'pixies' were deployed to deal with emergencies across the river. Bishop had tried to ring Jessica back, but this time only got an engaged tone. He had also attempted to contact Peck again, but the detective had already left his office. Not sure if he wasn't exaggerating the situation, Bishop left a message and set off for Jacob Kulek's house himself, a little wary as he stepped outside his front door, almost expecting to be attacked. The street was deserted.

He found the narrow lane leading to Kulek's house and headed into it, the car's headlights casting their twin beams far ahead, pushing back the darkness. Small, elegant houses sped by and, because the lane was downhill, he could see the bright glow of the city in the distance. He applied the brakes gently and changed down to a lower gear, sure that Kulek's house lay just ahead in a turn-off to the right. He brought the car to a halt when he saw the vehicle parked opposite the entrance to the house. It was tucked well into the side of the lane, the passenger doors no more than six inches away from a high brick wall that gave privacy to a residence beyond. Bishop pulled in behind and saw that the car appeared to be empty; he wondered if the policeman might be slumped down in the driver's seat – asleep or perhaps dead. He switched off his engine, but left the headlights on. Discarding his driving glasses, he stepped from the car.

The night was cold, but he wondered if the sudden chill he felt was due to something more. He cautiously approched the other vehicle and bent down to peer into a window. It was empty.

Bishop tried the handle and, finding it unlocked, pulled the door open. The radio equipment inside told him he hadn't been mistaken – it *was* a police car. Where was the policeman himself, though? He must have gone into the house. Bishop felt somewhat foolish for having panicked so easily. Yet, with all that had happened recently, he had reason to be a little jumpy. Peck may have told his man to stay inside Kulek's house – it seemed to make sense if Peck's concern for Jessica and her father's safety had suddenly been heightened by that night's events. Why had the phone been put down on him, though? Then he cursed himself, feeling even more foolish. The line had been engaged when he had tried to ring Jessica back – she must have realized she had cut him off, then tried to reach him again! He was behaving like a frightened old woman.

He went back to his own car, switched off the headlights, and strode across the lane towards the driveway leading to Kulek's house. From the entrance he could see a light shining ahead, a long rectangular glow that had to be the glass side-panel that ran the length of the front door. At least, if Jessica and her father were asleep, the policeman would be awake and could let him in. Yet, despite all the rationalization, his anxiety still persisted. Somewhere inside him he knew things were wrong. If he could have seen the corpse of the policeman, his throat slit from ear to ear, lying in the darkness of the undergrowth only two feet away, Bishop might have turned away from the house.

His feet crunched on the gravel drive as he approached the glass-structured building, its smooth exterior as black as the night around it. The light from the side panel guided him towards the door and he hesitated when he had stepped on to the wide porch area. He was afraid to ring the doorbell.

He did not need to – the door was already opening. The light from behind threw her shape in silhouette, but her voice was strangely familiar to him.

'Welcome again, Mr Bishop. We've been waiting for you,' the tall woman said.

Jacob Kulek and Jessica were in the living-room. Both were seated and dressed in nightclothes. The short woman was holding a knife at the blind man's throat, a long butcher's knife that had dark, reddish stains on its blade. She smiled at Bishop.

'Are you all right, Jessica? Jacob? asked Bishop, standing in the doorway.

Jessica could barely tear her eyes away from the blade at her father's throat.

'We are all right for the moment, Chris,' the blind man answered. 'Unfortunately, our guard, we are told, has been murdered.'

A gentle push from behind with the small Beretta the tall woman held urged Bishop further into the room.

'Yes, Mr Bishop,' she said. 'You passed the poor policeman on your way in. I must say he was very easy to kill. But then would you suspect Miss Turner there would cut your throat if you didn't know better?'

The smile on the small woman's face broadened. 'The silly man thought I was a helpless old bag who'd had too much to drink.'

'We knew he was there, you see. We, also, have been watching this house all week. Would you please sit down, Mr Bishop? We don't want any more deaths just at the moment, do we? Later, of course, but not just yet.' The tall woman pointed to a place on the settee next to Jessica.

Bishop sat and saw the terror in Jessica's eyes. He took her hand and held it.

'Yes, very touching, Christopher. May I call you Christopher?' It was hard to imagine the tall woman was anything more than a member of the Women's Guild, the type who sold paper flowers on Poppy Day. The small gun in her hand and her next words reminded Bishop just how evil she really was. 'Have you forgotten your wife already, Christopher? Did she mean so little to you?'

He began to push himself from the seat, his rage smothering any fear, but Jessica caught his arm.

'No, Chris!' she cried out.

The pleasantness had suddenly left the tall woman's manner. 'Take notice of her, Christopher. She has been told her father will die instantly if there is any trouble from you.'

He sank back, the anger making him tremble.

'That's right,' the tall woman said soothingly, her pleasantness returned. She sat down in a straight-backed chair which stood against the wall, keeping the gun pointed in Bishop's direction. 'You're an interesting man, Christopher. We have been finding out more about you over the past few weeks. I've even read one of your books. In a strange way, your theories are not too distant from Boris Pryszlak's. Nor Jacob Kulek's here, although I gather you care more for explainable science than the unexplainable.'

'May I ask what Pryszlak was to you?' Kulek asked. 'And may I also ask that this knife be taken away. It is rather uncomfortable. Surely the gun that you hold is enough.'

'Yes, Judith, I think you can relax a little now. Why don't you sit on the arm of the chair and keep the knife pressed against Kulek's heart?'

'I don't trust the old man,' the short woman replied. 'I don't trust any of them.'

'No, dear, nor I. But I don't imagine there is much they can do in the short time they have left. I'll keep my gun pointed straight at Mr Bishop's head.'

The short woman grudgingly changed her position and Kulek felt the tip of the knife pressed against his chest a little harder than was necessary to make him aware of its presence.

'Will you now tell us of your relationship with Pryszlak?' he asked, seemingly unaffected.

'Of course. There's no reason why you shouldn't know. Judith and I – my name is Lillian, by the way, Lillian Huscroft – were introduced to Boris many years ago by Dominic Kirkhope. Dominic knew the sort of games Judith and I enjoyed – I could say his knowledge was intimate – and he knew we were reasonably wealthy. Boris needed money at that time for his experiments. He also needed people, people of his own kind. If there was an overall characteristic among the members of his specially chosen group, I suppose you could call it "moral wickedness". We were all evil, you see. But we regarded that as a virtue, not a weakness. A quality held by man, but repressed because of the distorted prejudices so-called civilized society had thrust upon us. We found our freedom with Boris. Every sinful act we committed was a step nearer to our ultimate goal.'

She gave a short laugh and looked mockingly at her three captives. 'The police in this country would be amazed how tidy their files on unsolved crimes would become if we revealed the part many of our members played in them. The hardest crime to solve is the one without apparent motive and I'm afraid our dear law enforcement officers find the concept of evil for the *sake* of evil hard to grasp.'

'I find it somewhat hard to grasp myself,' said Kulek calmly.

'That, if I may say so, is why Boris is a great innovator, while you are merely a mundane theorist. It was a pity you did not accept his offer – you may have become as great as he.'

'You said "is". Are you telling me that Pryszlak is not dead?'

'No one really dies, Jacob.'

'The policeman outside is dead,' Bishop said evenly. 'My wife is dead.'

'Their bodies are discarded shells, that's all. Your wife, I believe, is still very active. As for the policeman – it's up to him how he continues. It will depend on which were the stronger powers within him. I can assure you, the fact that he was a law enforcer does not mean his powers for "goodness" were necessarily the more dominant. Far from it.'

'What the hell are you talking about?'

'She means there are two invisible powers that control the destiny of mankind,' Kulek explained. 'If you were a religious man, you might label them the Powers of Light and the Powers of Darkness. The Bible refers to them often enough. What we've never realized or, if you like, what we've forgotten over the centuries is that they were scientific concepts, not merely religious imagery. It seems Pryszlak did find a way of tapping that power. He used his knowledge of psychism to find the key. Others have achieved it in the past, only we've never recognized the fact. They probably did not fully realize it themselves. Just think of the tyrants, the mass murderers, the *evil* geniuses of the past. How did ordinary men like Adolf Hitler gain such incredible power?'

'Excellent, Jacob,' said the tall woman. 'You really could have been helpful to Boris.'

'But what was that key?' Kulek had involuntarily leaned forward and the sharp pain from the knife prick made him move quickly back.

'Don't you know, Jacob? Ah, but of course, you are not a scientist. You know little of the powers of pure energy. Have you any idea of the immense energy in one person's brain? The electrical impulses created by chemical reaction that keeps our bodies functioning throughout our lifetimes? An energy that cannot disappear, cannot dissolve just because our bodies die? An electrical force, Jacob, that can be reached. Its potential is limitless. Have you any concept at all of its collective force?' She laughed again, enjoying the moment, and her companion smiled with her. 'Of course you haven't. None of us has! But we will. Soon!'

'Electrical energy.' Kulek's face had gone deathly white. 'It's not possible. We must be more than that.'

'We are, Jacob. But then energy itself is more than just that. It is a *physical* thing but, you see, we underestimate the term. The paranormal is perfectly normal. We just need to understand it. I believe that is one of your own doctrines.'

'Matters that today we believe are extraordinary will not be so in the future.'

'Yes, scientific progress will see to that. And the momentum of that progression is increasing. Boris was far ahead of us all, and he had the courage to take the final step to give proof of his discovery.'

'By killing himself?'

'By freeing himself.'

'There has to be more to it.'

'Oh there is, and it was very simple. For a man like Boris, that is.'

'Won't you tell us?'

'I think not. You'll find out yourselves soon enough.'

'Why are you holding us here?' said Bishop. 'What are you waiting for?'

'You'll see. It shouldn't be long now.'

'Is it anything to do with the trouble that's going on tonight on the other side of the river?'

'Yes, it is very much to do with it.'

Jessica spoke. 'What is happening there, Chris? You said on the phone there was a prison riot.'

'All I know for sure is that the police are being kept pretty busy – and not just with the riot.'

Kulek sighed heavily and said, 'It's the Dark, isn't it? It's growing more powerful.'

The two women only smiled more meaningfully. 'No more questions,' the tall one said.

Bishop was puzzled. Kulek had just referred to the dark as if it were some special entity, a force on its own. The powers of Darkness, he had said before. Was it possible that the night could harbour such adverse potency? Bishop was confused and he forced himself to push the thoughts away to concentrate on the immediate problem. He felt helpless. If he made a move towards the tall woman Kulek would be stabbed in the heart. If he tried for the short woman, he would himself be shot in the head. Their only chance would be the failure of the policeman to report in – surely he would have to report back to HQ every so often? But then with all the confusion going on over the other side of London it might go unnoticed. Beside him, Jessica trembled and he reached for her hand again.

'Stop,' the tall woman ordered. 'If you move again, I'll kill you.'

Bishop let his hand drop and tried to smile reassuringly at Jessica. 'I think the waiting is making them more nervous than us.'

'Shut your mouth,' the short woman hissed. 'Why don't we kill him now, Lillian? He's not important.'

'We'll wait. But I warn you, Christopher, if you move or speak again, I *will* shoot the girl.'

As the minutes ticked by, the tension in the room began to mount. Bishop noticed the short woman kept glancing over at the dome-covered clock resting on the sideboard and then at her companion, agitation plain on her face.

'There isn't much time,' she finally said.

'Just a little longer. Concentrate, Judith, help me bring it here.'

The tall woman's face became damp with perspiration and occasionally her eyes would half-close, the hand holding the gun wavering slightly. The short woman seemed to be undergoing a similar stress. Bishop tensed his muscles, waiting for the right moment.

Suddenly, the one called Lillian took in a sharp breath and then she was smiling again. 'Can you feel it, Judith? It's coming. It knows.'

'Yes, yes.' The short one had her eyes closed as though in a trance, but the knife was still pressed into Kulek's nightclothes.

The tall woman's expression was almost orgasmic and Bishop shifted his weight forward when her eyelids began to flutter. She knew his intentions, though, for her eyes abruptly became sharply focused on him. 'I'm warning you not to move!' The words were almost spat out.

'No!' Jessica and Bishop looked across at Kulek who had cried out. The blind man's hands were like claws around the sides of the armchair and his neck was stretched upwards, tendons standing out like stiffened rods, eyes gazing sightlessly at the ceiling. 'It's so close.'

The short woman began to laugh, her plump, round shoulders heaving spasmodically. The tall woman rose from her chair and approached Bishop, the gun only inches away from his head.

'Now you'll see,' she said, her breathing jerky, sharp. 'Now you'll see the power.'

He shuddered, the tension in the room reaching a peak, but now a stifling oppression seeming to mingle with it. Short gasps were coming from Jessica and he knew she was terribly afraid. And he, too, felt the same fear.

The figure that appeared in the doorway caused the scream that had been building up inside Jessica to finally break free.

TWENTY-THREE

Bishop grabbed the tall woman's wrist and pushed the gun away from his exposed face, at the same time driving his clenched fist hard into her midriff. Her shout became a breathless gasp as she bent double and Bishop wrenched the Beretta from her grasp. He threw her away from him as he rose and turned to face the short woman, who was still staring at the figure in the doorway. She realized Bishop's intentions and drew the knife back to give it added thrust when she plunged it into the blind man's heart. But Kulek was faster: he thrust out and she toppled from the arm of the chair, not falling completely, but unbalanced enough to reach out wildly to save herself from going down. She grasped the back of the armchair and Bishop quickly stepped closer, bringing the pistol butt down on her forehead. She let out a yelp and collapsed on to the floor, helped by Bishop hooking a foot under her knee and jerking it from beneath her. He leaned forward and took the knife away, slapping her with fist and gun as she tried to resist.

Jessica ran to her father and held him. 'I'm all right,' he told her, then turned his face towards the door, knowing someone was there even though he could not see.

Edith Metlock looked pale and frightened. Her eyes went from one figure to the next, confused and unable to take in the situation. She slumped against the doorway, her head shaking from side to side. 'I came to warn you,' she managed to say.

'Edith?' asked Kulek.

'Yes, Father, it's Edith,' Jessica said.

Bishop went to the medium. 'You couldn't have arrived at a better moment.' He took her arm and drew her into the room.

'I came to warn you,' she repeated. 'The door was open.'

'They were expecting someone – or something else.'

From the floor, her mouth still open and desperately sucking in air, the tall woman stared at the medium. Bishop kept a cautious eye on her, ready to use the gun if necessary.

'Edith,' said Kulek, 'what brought you here? How did you know we were being held by those two?'

'I didn't. I came to warn you of the Dark. It's coming for you, Jacob.'

The blind man was on his feet and Jessica led him over to the medium and Bishop. His voice was full of interest rather than fear when he spoke. 'How do you know, Edith?'

Bishop let her down on to the settee and she slumped back as though exhausted. 'Voices, Jacob. There are hundreds of voices. I was at home, asleep. They invaded my dreams.'

'They spoke to you?'

'No, no. They are just there. I can hear them now, Jacob. They are becoming louder, clearer. You must get away from here before it's too late.'

'What are they saying, Edith? Please try to stay calm and tell me exactly what they are saying.'

She leaned forward and clutched at his arm. 'I can't tell you. I hear them, but there are so many. They're so confused. But I hear your name, over and over again. He wants his revenge, Jacob. He wants to show you just what he has achieved. And I think he fears you, too.'

'Ha!' The tall woman was on her knees now, wary of her own gun that was pointed in her direction. 'He fears nothing! He *has* nothing to fear!'

'Pryszlak? Do you mean Pryszlak, Edith?' The blind man spoke more sharply.

'Yes. He's nearly here.'

'I'm going to call the police,' said Bishop.

'They can't help you, fool!' the tall woman's face was twisted into a malicious sneer. 'They can't harm him.'

'She's right,' said the medium. 'Your only chance is to run. That's all anyone can do.'

'I'm calling the police anyway, even if it's only to take these two away.'

'It's too late, don't you see?' The tall woman was rising, her eyes gleaming.

'It's here. It's outside.'

The arm that encircled Bishop's throat from behind was plump and powerful. His body was arched back as the short woman brought her knee up against the base of his spine. One hand was reaching for the knife he held.

Jessica tried to force the little woman away from him, grabbing at her hair and pulling, but it had no other effect than to overbalance the two figures and send them crashing to the floor. Bishop tried to twist himself away from the tenacious woman, unable to break the grip around his throat. He raised his elbow, then swiftly drew it back, feeling it sink into her fatness. He repeated the action, using all his strength, and felt her legs flailing out beneath him. The tightness against his throat began to slacken and he renewed his efforts. He managed to turn his body and, because she would not let go of either his neck or hand, the knife sliced across her plump breasts and blood spurted from them. She screamed.

At last he was able to pull himself free and he turned his head, expecting to see her tall companion bearing down on him. But she was gone.

Hands clawed into his face and his attention was drawn back to the squirming woman beneath him. Her chest was now a mass of red stickiness, yet still she fought on, her lips bared to reveal stained, yellow teeth. The sounds she made were like those of an enraged dog and her eyes were becoming clouded. Her struggles began to weaken as the wound sapped her strength; only her will prevented her from collapsing. He pushed her hands away and staggered to his feet, feeling no pity as he looked down on her, her hands still scrabbling feebly at empty air.

'Chris.' Jessica clung to his arm. 'Let's get away. Let's call the police from somewhere else!'

'It's too late.' Edith Metlock was looking over her shoulder at the glass walls behind. 'It's already here,' she said tonelessly.

Bishop could see their own reflections against the darkness outside. 'What the hell are you talking about?' he found himself shouting. 'There's nothing out there!'

'Chris,' Kulek said quietly. 'Please go and make sure the front door is locked, Jessica, turn on every light in the house, outside lights, too.'

Bishop could only stare wordlessly at him.

'Do as he says, Chris,' Jessica urged.

She ran from the room and he followed. The front door was ajar and before he pushed it closed, Bishop peered out into the night. He could barely see the trees that lined the narrow drive leading to the house. After slamming the door, he pushed home the bolts and turned to see Jessica flicking down all the light switches in the hall. She pushed past him to climb the stairs leading to the rooms on the upper level; Bishop followed.

'In there, Chris!' Jessica pointed at one of the doors leading off the upstairs hall as she disappeared through another. Still puzzled, Bishop obeyed and found himself in a large, L-shaped bedroom. This side of the house overlooked the city and he realized that on any other night, the view would have provided a dazzling display of lights. On this night, though, there was something odd about the shimmering glow. It was as if he were watching it through a moving lacy veil, the lights twinkling and growing faint, then emerging brightly again. It wasn't like fog, for that would have shrouded everything in its rolling grey mist; it was a shifting inky darkness punctured by the brightest of the lights, smothering those more distant, dulling their luminosity.

'Chris?' Jessica had entered the room. 'You haven't turned on the lights.'

He pointed towards the glass wall. 'What is it, Jessica?'

Instead of answering, she flicked down the light switch, then hurried over to a bedside lamp and put that on also. She left the room and he heard other doors opening. Bishop went after her and caught her arm as she emerged from one of the rooms.

'Jessica, you've got to tell me what's going on.'

'Don't you understand? It's the darkness. It's a living entity, Chris. We've got to keep it away.'

'By turning on lights?'

'That's all we can do. Don't you remember how Edith had kept it away that night we found her? She knew by instinct that that was the only way.'

'But how can darkness harm us?'

'It's what it does to people. It seems to prey on weak or evil minds, it somehow makes the badness in them dominant. Can't you see what's happening? That night at the rest home – don't you see how it used their enfeebled minds.' She saw the pain in his eyes. 'I'm sorry, Chris, but don't you see how it affected Lynn? She wanted to kill you again, and so did all the others. They were being directed, don't you see? Their minds were being used. The same happened at the football match – in Willow Road itself. Pryszlak has found a way to use the evil lying in everybody's subconscious. The stronger that evil, or the weaker the person's mind, the easier it is for . . .'

'Jessica!' Jacob Kulek was calling from the foot of the stairs.

'I'm coming, Father!' She looked earnestly up at Bishop. 'Help us, Chris. We have to try and keep it out.'

He nodded, his mind a jumble of thoughts, everything he'd seen and heard in some crazy way confirming her statement. 'You go down to your father, I'll see to the rest of the lights up here.'

Bishop checked every room, even turning on the bathroom light for, though its two outside walls were part of the rare brick segments of the structure, it had a huge glass skylight in the ceiling. He also twisted a wall spotlight around and directed it towards the skylight. When he finally descended to the ground floor, Jessica had switched on the outside lamps, flooding the grounds with their brightness.

Bishop, Jessica and Kulek stood in the main lounge again, Edith Metlock trying to stem the flow of blood from the injured woman lying on the floor with a white linen towel Jessica had found for her. The wounded woman, Judith, lay still, her eyes staring up at the ceiling and occasionally flicking towards the huge window-wall.

'What now?' Bishop asked.

'We can only wait,' Kulek replied. 'And perhaps pray.' Almost to himself he added, 'Although I'm not sure that will help any more.'

'I'm going to try and reach Peck again,' said Bishop, heading for the hallway. 'We'll need an ambulance too – for her.' He indicated the injured woman lying on the floor.

Jessica clung to her father, both of them feeling the oppression that now hung over the house. 'Is it really possible for this to happen? Could Pryszlak have really found a way of tapping this power, Father?'

'I think he has, Jessica. Those who have studied the subject have always known it existed. The question is: does Pryszlak control the power, or does it control Pryszlak? I think we shall soon find out if what the woman called Lillian said is true. Will you find my cane for me? Then you must help Edith with the injured woman.'

Jessica found Kulek's stout cane lying behind the armchair in which he had been sitting; she gave it to him then went to the medium who was still kneeling beside the recumbent figure.

'How is she?'

'I . . . I don't know. She seems to be in a state of shock. If she's in pain, she doesn't show it.'

The linen towel was no longer white. Edith held it against the long slash, her hands, along with the cloth, red from the woman's blood. 'I don't think it's too deep, but she's losing a lot of blood.'

'I'll get another towel. We'll have to open her blouse and try to cover the whole of her chest.' Jessica felt herself shudder as she gazed down. The still woman's pupils had retracted to small pinpoints and for some reason, there was a distant smile on her face. She seemed to be listening.

The medium looked up at the glass wall. She, too, could hear something.

'Edith, what is it?' Jessica shook her.

'They're all around us.'

Jessica looked towards the windows, but could only see the glow of the outside lights. They didn't seem as bright as they should have been.

Bishop returned to the room, a determined look on his face. 'Peck was still unavailable, but one of the men in his department told me the trouble seems to be shifting over to this side of the river. There's been a constant stream of emergency calls and they're pretty thin on the ground for reinforcements. His advice is to sit tight and he'll get someone out to us as soon as possible. Even telling him one of their own officers has been murdered didn't get me too far. It seems he's only one of many dead policemen tonight.' He took out the small gun that he had put into his jacket pocket earlier. 'If anyone tries to break in, I can try and hold them off with this. Have you any other guns in the house, Jacob?'

The blind man shook his head. 'I have no use for them. And I think weapons of that sort will not help us.'

'Jacob, the lights outside are dimming.' There was dread in Edith Metlock's voice.

'There must be a reduction in power somewhere,' Bishop said, walking towards the glass wall.

'No, Chris,' said Jessica. 'The lights inside the house haven't been affected.'

Kulek turned toward the sound of Bishop's voice. 'Chris, are you by the window? Please keep back from there.'

'There's nothing outside. No movement, except . . .'

'What is it? Jessica, tell me what is happening.'

'The shadows, Father. The shadows are drawing closer to the house.'

Bishop spoke. 'The lights are just a dull glow now. There's a . . . sort of . . . blackness creeping forward. It's only a few feet away from the windows. It's moving all the time.' He began to edge away from the glass wall, stopping only when he had reached the back of the settee. Suddenly, all they could see was their own reflections, the outside lamps hardly visible. The feeling of oppression had increased: it seemed to be bearing down on all of them, straining against the very house itself, pressing, crushing.

Edith Metlock slumped against the settee, her eyes closed. Jessica reached for her father but found she was too frightened to move towards him. Kulek stared out at the darkness as though he could see it and, in his mind, he could. Bishop raised the gun towards the glass wall, knowing he could not pull the trigger.

'It can't get in!' Kulek shouted, his voice raised even though there was total silence in the room. 'It has no material form!'

But the bulging inwards of the huge sheets of glass joined by thin metal strips belied his words.

'Jesus Christ, it's not possible.' Bishop couldn't believe what he was seeing. The glass was bending like the distorted mirrors in a funfair's crazy house. He put his other hand up to protect his eyes, sure that the windows would burst inwards at any moment.

The injured woman pushed herself into a sitting position, the stained linen towel falling away from her chest and blood flowing freely into her lap. She watched the windows and laughed. The cackling sound she made died when, without warning, the bulges in the glass subsided and the windows returned to their normal shape. For several moments, no one in the room dared to speak.

'Is it ov. . .?' Jessica began to say when an ear-splitting *crack* made them all jump back in alarm.

The middle section of the wall was split from top to bottom, jagged streaks running from the main crack like forked lightning. Again the sharp sound of splintering glass came to them and they watched in paralyzed horror as the section next to it began to split. They saw the thin cracks travelling in different directions, patterning a jigsaw of sharp lines on the treated glass. Soon the lines resembled a spider's web. Another *crack*, and the section on the other side of the centre piece began to break, this time two lines travelling up from the base and joining near the top, etching out a jagged mountain shape.

With explosive force, all the sections shattered inwards, showering the occupants of the room with thousands of lethal glass shards. The sound was that of a hundred pistols being fired at once. Bishop fell back over the settee, his clothes and hair covered in silver fragments. Kulek instinctively turned his body and ducked, his dressing-gown instantly covered in tiny porcupine quills of glass. The shock had sent Jessica reeling back, the long settee between her and the windows protecting most of her body; she screamed when a section of glass the size of a dinner plate scythed along the side of her raised arm as she fell. The settee served to screen Edith Metlock and the short woman completely from flying glass.

Bishop had rolled on to the floor, tumbling over the injured woman. He lay still for a few moments, waiting for the ringing in his ears to clear, then forced himself to stand. He saw Kulek groping his way towards Jessica, calling out her name.

'I'm all right, Father.' She was pushing herself up on to one elbow and Bishop winced when he saw the long, red tear in her arm. He reached her just as Kulek was leaning forward to help her up, pieces of glass falling from their bodies like brushed snow. There were many tiny cuts on Jessica's forehead, neck and hands, but the rent along her arm was the worst damage she had suffered. He held her with Kulek and all three looked across at the broken wall, cold air flowing in unhindered and chilling them.

There was nothing outside now but blackness.

They kept still, scarcely daring to breathe, waiting for something to happen. The first figure appeared, standing just beyond the area of light so his body was ill-defined, shadowy. Bishop realized he had dropped the gun.

The figure stepped over the threshold, out of the darkness, into the light. He stood there, head turned slightly sideways, eyes blinking as though the light was hurting his eyes. The man was filthy, his clothes torn and covered with grime. Even in their dazed state, they could smell his corruption.

'Who is there?' asked Kulek softly, his question directed at Jessica and Bishop. Neither could answer.

The man's head was slowly turning towards them and, even under the dirt that covered him, they could see his face was drawn and emaciated. His eyes were still half-closed, and there were no whites to them, only a dull, greyish-yellow. His movements were sluggish as he walked towards them.

Jessica began to back away, dragging her father with her, but Bishop stood his ground. There was a hollow, vacant expression on the man's face and Bishop felt revulsion when he saw the dried mucous and spittle that covered the lower half of his face. His revulsion heightened when the man grinned at him.

Bishop ran forward, afraid yet repulsed enough to want to crush the thing before him as though it were a loathsome spider. He pushed the man and to his surprise felt no resistance; it was as if he had no strength left at all, that his body had wasted into a debilitated state, a withered frame that was hardly living. The man staggered back and Bishop followed through by lifting him and throwing him back out into the darkness. He stood there, panting from fear rather than exertion, and looked out into the night. There were many more standing in the shadows, watching the house.

He backed away and, as he did so, three figures came running forward from the blackness. They leapt into the room and came to an abrupt halt as the sudden glare blinded them. There were two men and one woman: the men wore grey denims, and one of them was shoeless; the woman was dressed normally. Bishop realized these three were not in the deteriorated state the first man had been in. He quickly looked around for the lost Beretta and gratefully lunged for the pistol when he saw it lying on the floor half-under the settee. He was on one knee retrieving the weapon when Jessica shouted; he turned to see one of the men rushing at him. His intention had been to try and warn them off, but without thinking he swung the gun in the advancing man's direction and squeezed the trigger. His would-be assailant spun around and fell to the floor as the bullet spat into his shoulder. The woman fell over the sprawled figure, but the other man skirted them both and came running towards Bishop, who was still crouched low. The next bullet punctured the second man's neck.

'Chris, there are more of them outside!' warned Jessica.

He saw them hovering just beyond the area of light. 'Quick, upstairs. We haven't got a chance down here!'

Leaping over the back of the settee, he pulled Edith Metlock to her feet. 'Take your father up, Jessica. We'll follow.' He did not allow his eyes to stray from the broad wall of darkness before him, the gun held up, trembling slightly, towards it. His first two shots had been lucky, for he was not at all familiar with guns, nor was he used to maiming or killing people; but he was aware that at such close range it would be virtually impossible to miss and he would not hesitate at firing at anyone entering the room. He pulled the medium along with him and she allowed herself to be led, her hands over her ears as though the sound of breaking glass was still reverberating in them. She looked dazed and pale. Bishop felt perspiration trickling into his eyes and he hastily wiped the back of his hand over his forehead. He was surprised to see his hand smeared with blood when he brought it away; parts of his face must have been lacerated by flying glass.

'They're at the front door,' he heard Jessica call out. 'They're trying to force it open!'

He could hear the muffled thumps coming from the hallway. 'Up the stairs, quickly,' he ordered. At least they would not be able to rush him up there and he might just be able to hold them off until the police arrived. *If* they arrived.

The hand that hooked itself behind his knee and brought him down belonged to the short woman. He fell heavily, taking the medium with him, and the injured woman threw herself on top of him, oblivious of the pain she suffered. Twisting his head to avoid the sharp-edged fingers, Bishop saw the woman who had leapt into the room with the two men crawling towards him, a long sliver of glass held in her hand like a knife blade. He brought a knee up and it sank viciously into the plump side of the woman above him, causing her to topple sideways. His back still against the floor, he pointed the gun straight into the advancing woman's face. She did not seem to notice; or she did not seem to care. Panic-stricken though he was, Bishop could not pull the trigger. He twisted away as the jagged glass came rushing down at him and heard it break against the floor. The woman stared at her bloody hand, then reached for him again. He swiped away the arm that supported her weight and brought the end of the pistol down on the back of her head as she collapsed. Kicking himself free of the short woman, whose legs were still tangled with his, he pulled himself clear. A well-aimed shove sent her crumpling back against the settee and he thought she would not be able to rise again. Incredibly, he was wrong.

She flew at him with a strength that was frightening for someone in her condition and her blows sent crystals of glass that had already pierced his face deeper into the skin, making him cry out. Others were in the room now, men and women who had stepped from the cover of darkness they seemed to favour, some of them shielding their eyes from the harsh glare, others squinting their eyes against the light. Bishop felt the plump woman's body shudder as the bullet entered her groin, but it took two more to stop her struggles. As she slid away, he saw there was no fear in her eyes, only a strange look of pleasure.

He fired into the crowd that had invaded the room and, for a brief moment, their disorganized rush was halted. It gave him just enough time to gain his feet and stagger towards the door. Roughly pushing Edith Metlock through, he pumped two bullets into the nearest man, this one also dressed in grey denims which Bishop suddenly recognized as prison clothes. The man fell forward just as Bishop pulled the door closed and the wood shook as his body crashed into it on the other side.

Jessica and her father were on the stairs, the girl looking down over the balustrade at him. Her face was streaked with tears that came from absolute terror. Bishop felt the handle twisting beneath his grip and he knew he would not be able to hold the door shut for long.

'Move yourselves!' he shouted. 'Take Edith with you!'

Jessica was galvanized into action by the harsh command. She reached down over the balustrade and guided the medium around to the stairs. Bishop waited until they were out of view before he released the door-handle. It flew open and he kept firing into the room beyond until the gun made only a sharp click. It was empty, empty and useless. He turned and fled.

As he passed the glass panel that ran the length of the heavy, wooden door, it broke and a hand reached in and grabbed his arm. Another hand shot forward and pulled at his hair. It was then that all the lights in the house went out.

Even as he struggled, he realized someone had broken into another part of the house and found the main power switch. He tore himself away from the grasping hands, feeling his jacket rip and some of the hair pulled from his scalp. He collapsed on to the stairs, hearing the rush of footsteps in the darkness, the shrieks of the possessed, their cries of triumph. Hands groped at him through the banister rails as he forced himself upwards. They tore at his face and hands, ripping his clothes, trying to pin him down. A steel-like grip closed around his ankle and he was pulled back down the stairs. He groaned aloud as he held on to the balustrade, desperately trying to halt his descent back into the mob. Wild screams and laughter filled his head, then a voice, a voice that barely pierced the babble, but a voice he knew to be Jessica's. But the words made no sense.

'Close your eyes, Chris, close your eyes!'

The brilliant flash that lit up the hallway stung his vision and silver and red images danced beneath his closed eyelids for long seconds after. He felt himself released and heard the howls of anguish.

'Come on, Chris!' It was Kulek's voice this time. 'Up, up! While they are blinded!'

Bishop moved fast, even though dazzled; he knew which way was up. He reached the landing and fell against the facing wall, his vision still swimming with swirling lights. More hands grabbed him and he knew these were friendly.

'This way, into the bedroom,' he heard Kulek say.

Heavy footsteps came from the stairway as the blind man guided him into a nearby room and Jessica's fear-filled voice cried out, 'Close your eyes!' just before the brilliant flash froze everything into an eerie white stillness. Screams and the sounds of tumbling bodies came to them. Bishop felt rather than saw Jessica rush into the room and quickly close the door; he rubbed his eyes, trying to clear the dazzle from them.

'Quickly, we must barricade the door!' Kulek shook Bishop's arm.

Jessica locked the door, then hurried over to a heavy-looking dressing-table. 'Help me, Chris, Edith.' She began pulling it away from the wall it rested against.

Bishop blinked several times and gradually began to make out shapes in the room. Just enough light filtered through the long window-wall for him to see the two women struggling with the dressing-table. He joined them and soon the unit was up against the door.

'Let's get the bed!' Bishop shouted. They tipped it up and he was relieved to feel its heavy weight. It crashed against the dressing-table, reinforcing the barricade. Footsteps came running along the hallway and they heard movement in the room next to theirs. More running, then the footsteps stopped outside their door. The handle turned and Bishop leaned against the makeshift barricade, whispering to the others to do the same. The pounding that started made them all jump even though they were expecting it.

The door shook in its frame, but mercifully held.

'Who are they? Where have they come from?' Jessica was next to Bishop and he could just make out the white blur of her face in the gloom.

'Some of them are from the prison, I'm sure. They must have escaped in the riot.'

'But there are women among them, and other men. They're in a terrible state.'

'The missing people! It must be them! God knows how they got into that condition.'

'What condition?' asked Kulek, who was also pushing against the upturned bed.

'They're filthy, their clothes in rags. They look starved, too. The first one I tackled was as weak as a kitten.'

The banging against the door became louder as though those outside had found heavy objects to beat at the wood with.

Kulek's voice was grim. 'They were the first victims. Whatever it is that possesses them has no regard for their lives. It uses them and destroys them.'

'And the stronger are the more recent victims? Like the convicts?'

'It would seem so.'

The whole barricade trembled a fraction and Bishop knew the door lock had been broken. He dug his feet more firmly into the carpeted floor and pushed harder against the bed, one hand reaching round to steady the dressing-table behind it. He was vaguely aware that Edith Metlock had sunk to the floor and was swaying on her knees, head in her hands.

A crash from behind made them all turn sharply towards the long windows. Jessica covered her face, expecting the glass to shower inwards again, but as they watched, a black object sailed into view and smacked against the window again.

'They're throwing things at the window,' Bishop said breathlessly and was suddenly aware that the banging against the door had ceased. 'Keep pushing against the bed,' he told Jessica and her father as he crossed the room. In the gloom, he kicked something lying on the floor and he almost smiled when he saw it was a camera, a rectangular attachment fitted. Jessica had used the flashgun against the mob chasing him, blinding and stopping them with its brief but powerful light.

He reached the window just as another object crashed against it and he pulled away in reflex action. Fortunately the treated glass was extremely strong and, although a whitish crack appeared, the glass did not break. Cautiously, Bishop crept forward again and looked down into the grounds below. The bedroom overlooked the rear garden and he could see figures standing in the shadows of the shrubbery and trees. As he watched, a man began pulling at the brickwork of a low garden wall, then stepped out on to the lawn and raised the object of his efforts, his body leaning backwards for the throw. But the brick never came towards the window; it dropped from the man's fingers and thudded to the grass.

The man moved back, his gaze still on the window from where Bishop was watching; he sank into the shrubbery behind him and Bishop noticed that the other figures had now disappeared. The man became part of the shadows and then, like the others, was gone.

A movement by his side made Bishop turn his head; Edith Metlock was staring over the treetops at the city beyond. 'They're leaving,' she said simply. 'The voices have gone.'

Jessica and Kulek joined them at the window.

Bishop shook his head. 'Why should they suddenly go? We had no chance against them.'

There was a tiredness in Jacob Kulek's voice when he spoke and, as Bishop turned to him, he saw the tiredness was in his deeply lined face too. And, even as the blind man said the words, it occurred to Bishop that there *was* enough light to see him.

'The dawn is here,' Kulek said. 'There is a greyness in my eyes where before there was only blackness. They have fled from the morning light.'

'Thank God,' Jessica said softly as she leaned against Bishop and held on to his arm. 'Thank God it's over.'

Kulek's sightless eyes were still directed towards the approaching light, the world outside grey, almost colourless, but no longer black. 'No, it is not over. I'm afraid it has only just begun,' he said.

PART THREE

They will growl over it on that day,
*   like the roaring of the sea,*
And if one look to the land,
*   behold, darkness and distress;*
and the light is darkened by its clouds.

Isaiah 5:30.
(R.S.V.)

TWENTY-FOUR

Many were found wandering aimlessly through the streets of the city, confused, their eyes half-closed, hands acting as shields against the glare of the sun. Others cowered in darkened rooms or hid in the basements of any building they could find access to. The London Underground system was brought to a halt when shocked motormen staggered from their trains, the sight of countless bodies they had ploughed through in the black tunnels a nightmare they would never forget. A search of the sewer network was ordered – three men on inspection duty the day before had been reported missing – and the searchers did not return. Corpses were found in the streets, many with bodies wasted, clothes bedraggled. Some had taken their own lives, others had died through self-neglect. Not all were in a helpless state: a large number were bewildered, remembering the violence they had committed during the night hours, but unable to explain it. Many of these, if they managed to find their way home, were hidden by their families. Once safely inside, they insisted that the curtains be drawn against the daylight; they listened apprehensively to the reports of the previous night's mass-violence, aware they had been a part of it, but afraid to go to the police. Those close to them could only watch, frightened by what had happened, but reluctant to seek outside help, for they knew that anyone involved in the riots was being rounded up and taken away. It was midday before the wailing sirens of fire-engines ceased, but the sounds of ambulances rushing through the streets went on well into the afternoon. It was never truly estimated just how many lives had been lost or how many minds had been taken on that first night of terror, for events after that took on such major proportions and with such rapidity that it became hopeless to keep accurate accounts of human or material damage. The prime objective was to survive, not to record details.

It began all over again the following night.

And continued the night after that.

And the next.

The congregation inside the Temple of the Newly Ordained had gathered earlier that afternoon, for they knew the five o'clock curfew would not allow them to leave their homes and travel to the modern, white-painted building. They had been ordered to keep silent while they waited – Brother Martin did not want their presence inside the church to be known – but their minds were in a turmoil of excitement. They were afraid, but eager, too. Their leader had told them of what was to come and they had faith in his word. Brother Martin had the knowledge, for he had spoken with the Dark.

In a room at the far end of the church which was not really a church but rather an assembly hall with rows of benches, near the altar which was not really an altar but an elaborate lectern, sat a neatly dressed man, his features lit only by a solitary candle that stood on the table before him. The man's eyes were closed and his breathing was deep and rhythmic. He felt the tension emanating from the hall next door and smiled. It would help; the vibrations of the thought-flow would act as a guide. He was ready and they were ready. Nearly a hundred and fifty people. The Dark would make them welcome.

His eyes snapped open as a soft tap on the door roused him from his deep thoughts. One of his followers, a tall coloured man, entered the room. The coloured man was in his early thirties, his hair allowed to grow Afro-style, but his suit conservative. Brother Martin smiled at him.

'Is everything ready?' he asked.

The coloured man was too nervous to return the smile. 'Ready,' he affirmed.

'Are you afraid, Brother John?'

'Brother Martin, I'm shit-scared.'

Brother Martin laughed aloud and his follower managed to join in.

'There's nothing to fear any more, John. This moment has been a long time coming – we mustn't balk at it.'

Brother John seemed uncertain. 'I know that, I know that. But what if you're wrong?'

Brother Martin's hand snaked out and struck the coloured man across the cheek. No resistance was offered, even though Brother John was at least a foot taller than his aggressor.

'Never doubt me, Brother John! I have spoken with the Dark and I have been told what we must do.' His voice became softer and he reached out and touched the cheek that now bore the marks of his hand. 'We've enjoyed what we've gained from these people, Brother, but it's time for something more, something better. Their faith has given us wealth; now they can help us reach something that transcends material gain.' He went to the door and turned towards his companion. 'Is the potion ready?' he asked.

'Yes, Brother Martin.'

'Let your faith rest in me, Brother John.' He opened the door and stepped into the hall beyond.

'Faith, shit,' the coloured man muttered. It had been good for them once, convincing people they would find their salvation with Brother Martin, accepting their donations, travelling the country looking for more. They had trust in their leader, the man who preached that love was the giving of one's-self, the giving of one's possessions. And Brother Martin was there to receive everything they gave. Especially the women. Brother Martin would never turn away even the ugliest. It could churn a man's insides to think of some of the dogs Brother Martin had bedded. He, Brother John, had been more choosey.

The followers were grateful to be told lust was just as much a part of love as was affection: lust meant procreation and that led to more offspring to follow God's way. They loved to hear that to sin was good, for sin meant repentance, and only by repenting could they know humility, and only by feeling true humility could they reach the Almighty. Sin today, regret tomorrow – what could be better? The only problem was that Brother Martin had come to believe his own preaching.

They had both been surprised eight years ago when what had started out as a small-time confidence trick to gain a little extra cash had turned into an ongoing, lucrative profession. Those early years had been one great merry piss-take, both of them cracking up after meetings, their eyes too filled with laughter tears to count the night's take. They had both soon learned that money was not the only pleasurable benefit from their operation: the weakness of the flesh had quickly been established as a worthy sin for remorse. The more remorse he could help them feel, the more he praised the Lord he had been given to them as an instrument of sin. Privately, he would wink at John and ask: 'Who could resist the concept that to fuck illicitly is good for the soul?' But since Brother Martin, alias Marty Randall, had caught the syph three times in two years, his attitude had changed. Wasn't it only gonorrhoea that was supposed to drive you nuts? Gon today, gone tomorrow? Maybe it was just the idolization they had thrust upon Brother Martin that had made him begin to believe it all himself. Up until founding the Temple of the Newly Ordained, Randall – Brother Martin – had been small-time: now he had become something to be worshipped. It was enough to turn any mother's head. He, Brother John alias Johnny Parker, had watched with awe as Randall had begun to change over the years: his sermons had become more emotional, each one always reaching a crescendo that would leave the whole congregation on its feet, clapping and yelling, 'Amen, Brother Martin!' There were still the odd occasions when the two of them would snigger at each other and congratulate themselves on their good fortune and their flock's gullibility, but these occasions were becoming less and less frequent. Now, tonight, Brother Martin seemed to have really flipped his lid. Would he go through with it or was it just to test them all, a megalomaniac's way of proving his command over them, an experiment to be halted at the last moment? Brother John, alias Parker, hoped it was the latter.

Brother Martin strode to the lectern, his eyes quickly becoming accustomed to the brightness of the hall after the gloom in the small room next to it. A bustle of excitement greeted his entrance and the people nervously glanced at each other, afraid of what was about to happen, yet eager for this new and far-from-final experience. There were a few in the crowd who still doubted, but these were not too concerned with living anyway. Everything that was happening in the city gave credence to what Brother Martin told them. The time had come and they desired to be among the first.

Brother Martin directed their attention towards the three punch bowls that stood on a table at the head of the centre aisle. 'You see there, my dear brothers and sisters, our elixir,' his voice boomed out. 'With just one sip you will be eternal. You have seen for yourselves the chaos outside, the people who are dead yet still refuse to give up their bodies. Will you allow the torturous degenerations of the shell you inhabit, or will you follow me, cleanly, without stress? With purity!'

He allowed his eyes to glance over the congregation so that each member felt the words were meant for him or her alone. 'There are some among you who are afraid. We will help you overcome that fear. There are some among you who still doubt: we will help you overcome that doubt. There are many among you who hate the world and the terrible hardship it has caused you: and I say that is good! It's good to hate, for the world is a vile, loathsome place! Detest it, brothers, revile it, sisters! Remember the words: "Is not the day of the LORD darkness, and not light, and gloom with no brightness in it?" This *is* the day of the LORD! The brightness has gone!'

Brother Martin waved a hand and, at the signal, all the lights in the hall were flicked off by Brother John, who stood by the main switches. A moan came from the crowd as the hall was plunged into darkness, except for the poor light cast from the flickering candles strategically placed around the walls.

'Open the doors, Brother Samuel,' their leader commanded and a man standing by the temple's double-doors swung them wide. The darkness outside became part of the darkness inside. 'Concentrate, my brothers and sisters, bring the Dark to us. We must hurry.' He could see the street-lights beyond the temple grounds, the houses with every light in them turned on. The order had been given for every possible light in the capital to be left on overnight: the authorities knew the Dark's strength. Night after night it had returned, the natural darkness its ally, and each time the chaos had become greater. No one could tell who would succumb to its influence – father, mother, brother, sister. Child. Friend. Neighbour. What evil lay tethered in each of these, waiting to be freed, yearning to be cut loose. The light was the only barrier. The Dark feared light. 'The light shines in the darkness, and the darkness has not overcome it.' Gospel according to John. But *man* can overcome the light. Brother Martin chuckled to himself, the sockets of his eyes dark shadows in the candlelight.

'Come forth, drink of the liquid that will make us whole.' Brother Martin held out his arms towards the congregation.

Despite the chill sweeping in through the open doors, beads of sweat broke out on Brother John's forehead. Oh man, oh man, he's really going through with it. He really wants to kill them all. Randall really believed all this shit the people upstairs were putting out about the Dark. Jesus, didn't he know it was just jive? The word was out on the street: it was a chemical gas that couldn't activate under sunlight or any other fucking light. Nobody knew who had released it – a foreign power, terrorists? The fucking British scientists themselves? Nobody on the street knew. But the motherfuckers in power did. Only they weren't saying. Stay inside at night, keep your lights on – that's *all* they were saying. Police and troops patrolled after curfew to make sure the rule was obeyed, using powerful searchlights themselves for their own protection. And this stupid fuck Randall was disobeying the law, turning all the lights out, ordering the doors opened. What the hell would happen when he discovered the mixture in those punch bowls had no cyanide in it? What would he do when the stupid fucking sheep who followed him didn't drop dead after they'd tasted Potion 99? He'd know who to blame: it was sweet Brother John who'd been given the order to get the poison. Where the fuck did Randall expect him to find enough cyanide to kill off a hundred and fifty mothers? Brother John began to edge his way down the side aisle, away from the three containers of harmless Sainsbury's own-brand wine towards the open doorway. Time to split. Should have done it a long time ago.

The congregation were filing forward, each holding a plastic beaker they had been issued with on entering the temple. Brother Martin smiled benignly as they passed him. A woman in her early forties threw herself at him, her face soaked with tears, nose running. Helpers broke her hold on Brother Martin and gently led her away, soothing her with words she hardly heard. A man in his sixties passed before him, eyes downcast.

'I'm afraid, Brother Martin,' he said.

Brother Martin reached out with both hands and touched his follower's shoulders. 'We all are, Brother . . .' what the shit was his name? '. . . dear friend, but our fear will soon be replaced by great joy. Have faith in me. I have spoken with the Dark.' Now move on, you silly bastard, before you frighten the others.

It was important not to allow the mood of euphoria, albeit a tense euphoria, to be broken: if one panicked, then others would follow. He needed them all, wanted their strength, for he really *had* spoken with the Dark. Or at least, he had dreamt he had spoken with it. It amounted to the same thing.

The Dark wanted him, but it also wanted his people. The more life that was given to it, the stronger it would become. Brother Martin, alias Marty Randall, was happy to be the Dark's recruitment officer.

The people moved in an orderly flow to the punch bowls and then back to their seats, disguising Brother John's progress towards the doorway; the general dimness of the interior also offered concealment. However, he expected to hear

Brother Martin calling him back at any moment, and the further he moved away from his leader the more nervous he became. He licked his lips, aware his throat had become very dry. Some of the flock looked at him inquiringly and he had to nod and smile at them reassuringly. He was thankful that the light was so poor, for it meant they could not see the perspiration he felt on his face. Brother Samuel was still standing near the open doors and Brother John approached him cautiously. This man was a devout follower, a mother who would lay down his life for their leader, a honky whose brain functioned only under the guidance of someone else. Just the kind of dogshit Randall needed to keep his followers in order. The big man cocked his head to one side like a curious labrador when Brother John drew near. He didn't like black men and he particularly didn't like Brother John. The nigger always seemed to have a smirk on his face, as if he were taking the piss all the time.

Brother John leaned forward and whispered into the big man's ear. 'Brother Martin wants you to go forward, Brother Samuel, and drink with the others. He feels they need your encouragement.'

Brother Samuel cast an anxious glance over the shadowy congregation. A deep moaning noise came from some of them, while several of the women were openly wailing. He tucked his hand into his jacket pocket and closed his fingers around the gun lying there. Brother Martin had warned him it might be necessary to persuade some of the followers to carry out what was required of them. But he had also told him that he was to wait until last, just in case any were not killed by the poison, or had only pretended to drink. A bullet in the head was to be the answer to that. Why had Brother Martin changed his mind?

'He told me to stay by the door.'

'I know, Brother Samuel,' the black man said patiently, aware that his legs were beginning to feel weak. He could hear Randall's voice from the front urging the people to concentrate, to draw the Dark to them. 'He's changed his mind. He needs you up there, Brother.'

'Who'll watch the door? Who'll see no one gets out?'

'No one's leaving. They want to follow Brother Martin.'

A crafty look came into the big man's face. The nigger wasn't wearing his usual smirk. And at this close range, he could see he was sweating. Brother John was afraid. 'Then why does he need me up there if they want to follow Brother Martin?'

Oh shit. 'One or two need help, Brother Samuel. They're not all as strong as you.'

'Are you as strong as me, Brother John? Do you need help?'

The coloured man tried to keep his hands from shaking. 'No, Brother Samuel. It's the others. Now you do what the man says, Brother, and get yourself up there. He's gonna get mad if you don't.'

The big man seemed uncertain. He looked towards Brother Martin, his hand leaving the weapon inside his jacket pocket.

Brother John was cursing himself for not having left sooner. He should have vanished as soon as Randall had begun his crazy suicide talk. It had become a fascination with him after the mass self-destruction of the People's Temple sect in Guyana several years before, and kindled even further by the other group suicide that had taken place in the suburbs of London just about a year ago. During the last few weeks it had become an obsession; it was as though he had discovered the ultimate truth. Oh Jesus, he should have scooted when Randall ordered him to get cyanide. He couldn't believe the man intended to go through with it. It was no place to be when they all sat around gawking at each other, waiting to drop like flies. They wouldn't be amused and neither would Brother Martin.

'Come on, Brother Samuel, don't keep him waiting.'

Unfortunately for the coloured man, Brother Martin had been scanning the crowd for him. Brother John's faith had seemed a little shaky over the last few days. He needed help, perhaps coercion. Of late he had become a cause of concern, his enthusiasm for Brother Martin's way seemed to be waning. It might be a good idea to let him be the first to taste this nectar of the after-life.

'Brother John. I can't see you? Where are you?'

The coloured man groaned inwardly. 'Right here, Brother Martin,' he said aloud.

'Come to the front, Brother, where we can see you. Yours will be the honour of leading the way.'

'I, uh, I'm not worthy of that honour, Brother Martin. Only you can lead us.' Brother John licked his lips and glanced nervously towards the doorway.

Brother Martin laughed. 'We are all worthy! Come now, drink first.' He walked over to a punch bowl and dipped a white beaker into the dark red liquid, then proffered it towards the black man. Heads began to turn and look towards Brother John. As if guessing his intention, Brother Samuel moved his big frame into the entrance, blocking any escape.

Oooooh shit! Brother John's head screamed and he brought his knee up into the big man's groin area. Brother Samuel fell to his knees, his hands clutching at his genitals. Brother John jumped through the open doorway into the even greater darkness outside. And stopped.

It was around him like cold clammy hands, like icy treacle smearing itself over his skin. He shivered and looked wildly around, but could see only blurred pinpoints of light in the distance. He backed away from it, but it came with him as though it were stuck to his body. He felt an eerie kind of probing going on inside his head and cried out when the cold fingers touched something inside his mind. No, I don't want this! something inside him screamed, but another voice answered, yes, yes, you do!

Other hands reached around his throat, and these were real hands, the big, strong hands of Brother Samuel. The grip began to tighten as the inky blackness enveloped both men, and Brother John's thoughts tumbled over themselves to run from the unreal dark fingers that touched and ravaged his mind. He sank to the hard paving stones leading up to the temple, the big man standing before him, never letting go, and slowly he realized Brother Martin was right: this was the eternity they had been seeking. Although his body was trembling with the pain, something inside him was dancing with happiness. Oh, you *mother*, you were right, Brother Martin, Brother Marty Randall, you were *soooo* right. Even as his closed throat strained to suck in air through his lungs, his lips were parted in a rapturous smile. His red-filled vision began to cloud into a deepening blackness and soon that was all there was – total, welcoming darkness. Amen to that.

Brother Samuel dragged the limp body back into the temple and the Dark followed, flowing in greedily, spreading and seeping, dimming the already faint light from the candles. Brother Martin closed his eyes and spread his arms wide, ignoring the sudden cries of fear around him, welcoming the Dark into his church.

'We will drink the poison and join you,' he said aloud and wondered at the mocking laugh he thought he heard. It had sounded like Brother John. One by one, the candles sputtered and finally went out.

'Tell them to keep the noise down, Alex. If the Law finds out you've got a meeting going on in the back, they'll have your licence.' Sheila Bryan held the glass up to make sure she had wiped away all the smears in the bottom of the pint glass. It wasn't often the pub's glasses received such close scrutiny, but then it wasn't often a curfew was imposed. She briefly wondered if there had been such restrictions during the war. She didn't think so, but couldn't be sure; it was before her time.

'They're all right. They're not disturbin anybody.' Her husband, Alex, regarded Sheila with ill-disguised impatience. He was a hefty man, large of gut, loud of voice, and it needed a woman with similar attributes to handle him. He was just approaching forty, she had just said goodbye to her twenties; their mutual largeness somehow made them appear the same age.

'I don't know why you have anything to do with them, anyway,' Sheila said, placing the glass next to its dry companions on the bar. Ash from the cigarette dangling between her lips fell into the murky washing up water as she leaned forward and reached in for another glass.

'They've got the right idea, that's why,' Alex retorted as he dumped the tray of glasses on the draining-board next to the sink. 'They want another round.'

'Well they'll have to use those. I'm not using fresh glasses.'

'Of course they'll bleeding use these. Who's askin for new ones. I don't know what gets into you at times. We wouldn't be makin a penny if we didn't av that lot tonight. Bloody filth keepin everyone indoors.'

'The Law says it's dangerous to go out at night.'

'That's all bollocks. They've got somethin goin on, that's all, somethin they don't want anybody to see.'

'Don't be bloody daft. You've seen what's going on on the telly. Riots, fires – all those murders.'

'Yeh, because somebody's used a nerve gas on us, that's why. Bastard Lefties, that's who's done it, brought it in for their friends abroad.'

Sheila stood up from the sink and took the cigarette from her mouth with damp fingers. 'What are you talking about now?' she said, looking at her husband with disdain.

'Everyone knows the Commies are behind it. They won't tell you on the news, but just you ask anyone. It'll be New York next, maybe Washington. You wait and see. Then Paris, then Rome. All over. Won't appen in Russia, though.'

'Oh, you do talk wet, Alex. That mob next door been filling your head with ideas again?'

Alex ignored the question and began filling the glasses with their appropriate drinks. 'It makes sense when you think about it,' he said undeterred as he poured.

His wife raised her eyes towards the ceiling and resumed polishing the glasses. It *was* worrying, though, the whole town being placed under some kind of martial law. It was the sort of thing you expected to happen in foreign parts, but not England. Not London. Why should they have to keep all lights on as though they were afraid of the dark? The Dark: that was what everyone was calling it because it only happened at night-time. They said people were losing their minds with it, roaming around the streets setting fires, killing. There was no sense to it. She, herself, had seen the army trucks searching the streets in the early hours of the morning, picking up people who seemed to be wandering loose and taking them away somewhere. She'd watched them from the window upstairs one morning when she couldn't sleep. Some poor sod had just been lying in the road, covering his head with his hands. There had been blood on his fingers because he had been trying to pull up the manhole cover in the middle of the road, but it must have been too heavy, or he couldn't get a grip. He didn't say a word when they slung him into the truck, and his face had been deathly white, white as a ghost, and his eyes black and half-shut. She shivered. It was like one of those old horror films, like Quatermass.

'Where's all the fuckin light ales?'

Her attention was abruptly drawn back to her husband. 'Don't swear in the bar, Alex, I've asked you before.'

He looked back at her, then around at the empty saloon bar. 'There's no one ere, you know.'

'That's not the point. You've got to get out of the habit. It's not necessary.'

Silly cow, he said to himself. Then aloud, 'We can't av used all the light, we've only ad lunchtime trade the past couple of weeks.'

'Alex, there's plenty in the cellar if you'd like to make the effort and go down and get it.'

Alex's sigh turned into a grunt when he leaned forward and pulled at the ring set into the trapdoor behind the bar. He heaved it open and stared down at the blackness below. 'I thought we were supposed to turn on all the lights,' he said.

'I did,' his wife replied, looking over his shoulder into the square of darkness.

'Well that one's not bleedin on, is it?'

Sheila walked over to the set of light switches that lay near the doorway to a small back room they used mainly as an office, their living quarters being on the floor above. 'They're all on,' she called back to her husband. 'The bulb must have gone.'

'Oh fuck it,' her husband groaned.

'I'll get you another one, Alex. You can put it in.'

'Great,' Alex replied wearily. He wanted to get back to the meeting; he enjoyed listening to the boys and tonight, because there were no other customers, was the ideal opportunity to sit in on their discussions. Fortunately, his was a Free House, so no interfering nosey-parker could inform any brewery of the type of organizations he allowed to hold meetings in his pub. One of his mates, a publican in Shoreditch, had had to vacate when the brewery which owned the pub discovered he was letting his back rooms out for National Front meetings. That was the trouble with being a tenant-landlord – you had to dance to someone else's tune. 'Come on, Sheila,' he called out, 'let's av it!'

She returned, a cold look on her face, and handed him a torch and a new light bulb.

'Forty watt?' he said disgustedly. 'This ain't gonna be much cop, is it?'

'It's all we've got,' she replied patiently. 'And you can bring up some Babycham while you're down there.'

'Babycham? Who the ell's gonna be drinkin that tonight?'

'It's for tomorrow lunchtime. You know we're packed during the day now.'

'Yeh, they're all makin up for what they can't get in the evening.'

'Just as well they are, otherwise we'd soon go broke. Hurry up, or your mates will be screaming for their beer.'

'They're not me mates.'

'You could have fooled me. You spend enough time with them.'

'I just appen to agree with a lot of what they say. You've seen ow many blacks there is around ere. More of them than us.'

'Oh go on, get down there. You talk like a big kid at times.'

Alex hoisted his frame on to the ladder. 'You mark my words, they'll be comin in ere to drink next.' His big, round head disappeared from view.

'Heil Hitler,' Sheila commented drily and took another puff of her cigarette. With a resigned sigh she returned to polishing the glasses.

Below, Alex flashed the torch around the grimy, beer-smelling cellar. The beam soon found the naked light bulb hanging from the low ceiling. Better have a stock-take tomorrow, he told himself as he crossed the dusty stone floor. Running low on – oh *fuck*! He stepped out of the puddle and shook droplets of stale beer from his shoe. He shone the torch down and dazzled himself with the reflection off the thinly spread liquid. The cellar floor sloped towards its middle so that all spillage would run into a centre channel then into a drain. He followed the direction of the channel with the torchlight and saw rags or sacking were blocking the flow.

'That silly bastard Paddy,' he said under his breath, referring to his daytime barman. It was the little Irishman's job to stock up the bar each morning, using the dumb-waiter to carry the drinks to the floor above. He must have dropped the rags or whatever it was. 'Bloody Irish twit,' he muttered, kicking the damp bundle aside. 'He's been dipping into the till again, too. Christ, it was difficult to get honest bar staff. Alex watched the strong-smelling mixture of combined beers gurgle into the square, grill-covered drain. At least it wasn't blocked. If there was one job Alex could not abide it was unblocking drains. All that shit and slime. The drains had to be kept clear otherwise the basement would be ankle deep and stinking like a brewery within a week with all the breakages that went on down there. The delivery men didn't give a sod. Slung the crates down any old how. He thought he saw something scuttle away from the circle of light cast by the torch. 'Don't say we've got rats down ere now,' he groaned aloud.

He swung the beam around but found nothing, only retreating blackness.

Alex plodded over to the dangling light bulb, not sure if he had only imagined the dark thing scuttling away. He hadn't heard any movement. The light itself hung over the drain and the publican stretched upwards to reach it, torch held precariously with the fingers of one hand and pointing up at the ceiling. His feet were spread out on either side of the drain.

'Ouch!' Alex cried out when his fingers touched the hot glass. The bulb must have blown just before he opened up the cellar. He jerked his hands away and the torch fell from his grasp. 'Oh *fuck* it!' he shouted when it crashed to the floor and its light was extinguished. The open trapdoor at the far end of the cellar threw down a little light, but its range was not enough to reach where he stood. He dug into his pocket and pulled out a handkerchief, his other pocket bulging with the new light bulb. Alex reached up for the dead one, this time using his handkerchief for protection against the heat.

The gloom did not bother him, for he had never been afraid of the dark, not even as a kid. But the prickling at the back of his neck warned him that something was not quite right in the cellar.

Sheila rested her elbows on the bar top and stared reflectively at the locked door. A fresh cigarette dangled from her lips and her large breasts lay comfortably on the bar's wooden surface like full sacks of graded flour. She didn't know how many more nights like this she could stand. Dolling herself up, slipping into the mental gear necessary to sustain herself through the evening's jollifications or commiserations, whatever the individual customer's mood required, being nice to everybody, firm to those who took liberties. It was like showbiz in a way, only these nights there was no biz. Surely they were going to get rid of this gas, or whatever it was soon. The whole town would go to pot otherwise. Still, she supposed she should have been grateful for the small amount of evening trade she had in the back room, as much as she disliked their views. It was only because they had booked the room a month in advance that she had let Alex persuade her to allow the meeting to be held. He was one of them, even though he wouldn't admit it. They'd have to pay for the use of the room all night, of course; there was no chance of any of them leaving before tomorrow morning. They'd be nicked if they were caught out on the streets at night. Where was Alex? He was taking his time. Who was it who came on telly the other night. A cardinal or bishop, wasn't it? Told them all to pray. Hah, that was a laugh! She could just see old Alex going down on his knees to pray. Probably would if someone held a gun at his head. What were they supposed to pray for? What good were prayers against a nerve gas, as Alex said it was? It was the scientists who had to do the praying. It was down to them, all this mess. Let them come up with something. And not prayers.

'Sheila.'

She looked around. What was that?

'Sheila.'

She sighed and lumbered towards the open trapdoor. 'What're you up to, Alex. How long does it take you to send up a crate of light and Babycham?'

She peered down into the blackness.

'Haven't you put the bulb in yet?' she said, irritated.

'Sheila, come down.'

'Where are you, Alex? I can't see you.'

'Come down.'

'Do what? Me, come down there? Do me a favour, Alex.'

'Please, Sheila.'

'Are you sodding about, Alex? I'm not in the mood.'

'Come on, Sheila, come down. I've got something to show you.'

The publican's wife chortled. 'You can show me that later, in bed.'

'No, come on, Sheila, now. Come down.'

Alex's voice sounded strangely urgent.

'It's dangerous, Alex. I might fall.'

'You won't, Sheila. I'll help you. Come down.'

Oh my Gawd, Sheila said to herself. The things I do for love. 'All right, Alex,' she called down, a giggle escaping her. 'It had better be worth it!'

She gingerly lowered herself on to the metal-runged ladder, her hands firmly grasping the wooden sides. Sometimes she wondered if Alex was all there, the strokes he pulled. But he was good for a laugh, she had to give him that.

'Alex? Alex! Where are you?' She was halfway down the ladder and looking around, trying to pierce the gloom. 'I'm going up again if you don't stop hiding right this minute.'

'I'm right here, Sheila, waitin for you.'

'Well what do you want?' Sheila had decided she didn't really like this game. The cellar stank – beer dregs and something else. What? Funny smell. It was cold and dark there too. 'I'm going up, Alex. You're acting stupid, true to form.'

She waited for a reply, but there was only silence.

Sheila came down two more rungs then stopped. 'Right, that's it. This is as far as I come unless you come over here into the light.'

Alex didn't make a sound. But she heard his breathing. She suddenly felt uneasy.

'Bye, Alex.' She began to climb back up the ladder.

Alex came out of the dark, a lumbering shape that held something high above his head. Sheila just turned her head in time to see the mallet used for opening kegs of beer descending. There was no time for her to scream and no time to wonder what had come over Alex.

She fell to the floor and lay still, but the heavy wooden mallet continued to batter her head and soon it was blood that flowed down the basement's centre into the dark, noxious drain.

Alex climbed through the trapdoor minutes later, a smile of pleasure on his face. He heaved his heavy body through the opening, the bloodied mallet still held in one hand. Reaching up to the bartop with his free hand, he pulled himself to his feet. He walked to the set of switches that controlled all the downstairs lights in the public house and ran his hand over every one until both bars and back rooms were plunged into darkness. He walked back the length of the bar, careful not to fall into the even blacker hole that was the open trapdoor. Confused voices coming from one of the back rooms guided him, although guidance wasn't really necessary, for he knew his pub like the back of his hand. He hurried to rejoin the meeting. They would be pleased to see him. They would be pleased to see what he had brought along with him.

He looked to the right, studying the wide road for several long seconds before directing his gaze to the left. All clear. No police, no patrolling army vehicles. It was now or never. He ran, heading for the road leading to the big park. To where it was empty. And dark.

His gait was awkward, more of a waddle than a run, his short legs treading the hard, smooth road's surface as though it were cobblestones. The thought of jogging which several of his colleagues in the House had taken up when it had become fashionable a couple of years back made him wonder at their sanity. Moving at any speed faster than a brisk stroll *had* to be damaging to one's health. No wonder some of them had collapsed with heart attacks. He remembered the leaflets all the Members had received encouraging them to use the Parliament gym, telling them that by keeping a healthy body, they would have the stamina to serve their constituents better. Well, his stamina was in the mind, not in the body. As far as he was concerned, each leaflet should have been issued with a GOVERNMENT HEALTH WARNING. You couldn't serve your constituents very well from a wooden box six feet under the earth. And if his heart was going to collapse, he would rather it was due to the demands of a good whore than running through the park in plimsolls. He paused at the entrance, his rotund body heaving and sucking in huge, rasping lungfuls of air. He studied the broad expanse of darkness before him, afraid now, then forced himself on, the night swallowing him up as though he had never existed.

Once he was safely inside the black sanctuary, he slumped to the grass, heedless of its cold wetness, and endeavoured to recover a normal rate of breathing. The lights of the city blazed away in the distance, but they barely penetrated the fringes of the park. He was in the Kensington Gardens section, deeming it wise to keep well away from Hyde Park on the other side of the Serpentine where a police station operated. He would find it difficult to explain his presence. Even being a Labour MP for the past sixteen years would not prevent his immediate arrest. Any Member of Parliament on government business had to have an army escort after nightfall, otherwise they had to stay indoors like any other citizens. The uproar over the restrictions still raged every day in the House, but the PM and the Home Secretary were adamant. Anyone who wished to leave the capital while the emergency was on was perfectly entitled to do so, but if they remained, then they came under the government edict. Until the solution was found to this madness, conditions for living in London were severe. Never mind the solutions, backbenchers on either side had cried out, what was the problem? Just what was happening each night? Why was there, as yet, no official statement? The public were entitled to know. *The Members of Parliament themselves were entitled to know!* They had been astonished, then disbelieving, when they were told of the ethereal mass of dark substance that had strange effects on the brain, a mass that had no defined shape nor, as far as anyone could tell, material form. It was neither a gas, nor a chemical. Autopsies on the brains of victims affected by it, and who had taken their own lives, revealed nothing unusual. Why those that could be found wandering the streets by day were docile and in almost trance-like states, no one knew. Paranormal connotations were still being denied, as could be expected.

He rose to his feet, brushing the dampness from his knees. His eyes had become accustomed to the gloom and he realized the patch he was in was considerably lighter than the heavy blackness ahead. He shuffled forward, eager to be completely enveloped by the darkness. The bloody fools didn't understand the significance of it all! This was a new entity – no, not new: it was as old as the world itself. It was a power that had existed even before human life, a dark power that man had allied himself with from the beginning. Now it dwelt in man. It had always been there, the darkness where evil lurked, the darkness that bestial things crept in, the darkness waiting for man to give himself up completely to it. And now was the time.

He froze. Something was moving in the shadows ahead. No sounds. No more movement. His eyes must have been playing tricks on him.

The Dark had called to him, told him what he must do. The power of politics was nothing to the power he had been offered. It was a giant step to take, but the rewards were infinite. No hesitating now, no second thoughts. He had been chosen.

It was difficult to see anything in front of him, for the moon was behind heavy clouds. He could see lights through the trees coming from the hotels that edged the opposite side of Park Lane, but they were far away and had nothing to do with the void of blackness he stood in. Was this *the* Dark around him? Was this the force he had come in search of? Let it happen, then. Absorb me, take me in ... He stumbled over a figure sitting on the ground.

The politician fell heavily and rolled on to his back.

'Who's there?' he asked querulously when he had recovered from his surprise.

He heard a mumbling sound, but could make no sense of it. He squinted his eyes, hoping to see better. 'Who's there?' he repeated, then became a little bolder. 'Speak up!' His voice was still a whisper, though the words were spoken harshly.

He cautiously crawled forward, afraid yet curious. 'Come on, speak up. What are you doing here?'

'Waiting,' came the murmured reply. It was a man's voice.

The politician was taken aback, somehow not really expecting an answer. 'What do you mean "waiting"? Waiting for what?'

'Waiting like the others.'

'Others?' The politician looked around and suddenly became aware that what he had thought to be dark shapes of bushes and shrubs were, in fact, the figures of people, some squatting on the ground, others standing. All were silent. He grabbed the man by the shoulder.

'Do they – do you – know about the Dark?'

The man shrugged his shoulder away. 'Piss off,' he said quietly. 'Leave me alone.'

The politician stared at the shadowy figure for a while, still unable to make out his features. Finally, he crawled away and found a space of his own. He sat there for a long time, confused, then ultimately, resigned. It made sense that he would not have been the only one; others would have been chosen. At one point, when the quarter moon was able to free itself of clinging black clouds for a few seconds, he was able to look around and see how many others there were waiting with him. At least a hundred, he thought. Perhaps as many as a hundred and fifty. Why didn't they communicate? Why were they not speaking? He realized that, like him, their minds were too full of what was going to happen, opening themselves to receive the probing darkness. Willing it, demanding it. The clouds covered the moon and he was alone once more, waiting for the Dark to come.

When the first haziness of dawn edged its way over the tall buildings on the horizon, he rose wearily and stiffly to his feet. His overcoat was covered in a layer of morning dew and his body ached. He saw the others were rising, their movements slow and awkward as though the night's long wait had rusted their joints. Their white, early morning faces were expressionless, but he knew they felt the same bitter disappointment as he. One by one they drifted away, the low-flying dawn mist swirling around their feet.

He felt like weeping with frustration and shaking a fist at the vanishing shadows. Instead, he went home.

TWENTY-FIVE

Bishop sipped his scotch, then lit his third cigarette since he had been sitting in the hotel bar. He glanced at his watch. The conference had been running for over three hours already and when he had left just half an hour earlier, it seemed far away from any firm conclusions. With so many now involved he wondered if there would ever be any real agreement between them. The combination of scientists and parapsychologists, with government ministers trying to find a common ground between both factions, was hardly ideal for a conducive atmosphere. An American Research Society had expounded on Jung's collective unconscious theory – 'Just as the human body shows a common anatomy over and above all racial differences, so too the psyche possesses a common substratum transcending all differences in culture and consciousness' – and maintained that this collective unconsciousness consisted of latent dispositions towards identical reaction, patterns of thought and behaviour that were a common heritage of psychological development. Different races and separate generations had common instincts – why else the similarity between various myths and symbols? And perhaps one of man's most shared instincts was that for evil. It was argued that surely good was the more predominant instinct throughout history, despite the terrible atrocities that had taken place, and the speaker had agreed, but had gone on to add that perhaps after centuries of enforced suppression, the evil instinct had broken free of the mind's confines. It had finally evolved into a material form.

Bishop, seated in the back row of the modern auditorium, had almost smiled at the perplexed looks that passed between the Police Commissioner and the

Army Chief of Staff. If they hadn't had official reports as well as personal eyewitness evidence of the massive unexplained destruction taking place in the nation's capital each night, they would have dismissed such jargonized theories out of hand. However, when a member of the delegation from the Institute of Human Potential insisted that this new madness was the final breakthrough to sanity, their looks turned to mutual anger. It was the Home Secretary, himself, who delivered a severe rebuke to the man who went on to explain that what society considered to be the norm was not necessarily so, and that the condition of alienation, of being asleep or unconscious, of being out of one's mind, was the natural condition of man. The men and women who had been affected had all been in a trance-like state, an altered state of consciousness, an *enlightened* state. They had a mission that so-called normal people – which included everyone in the conference theatre – did not yet understand, nor appreciate. The Home Secretary warned the man and others of his group that they would be removed from the auditorium if they persisted in putting forward these non-productive and rather absurd arguments. The country was in a state of emergency and, while every opinion was valued at this juncture, frivolous speculation would not be tolerated.

Relief on the faces of the Home Secretary and several of his ministerial and law enforcement colleagues showed visibly when the general discussion took on a more medically scientific aspect, but they were soon disappointed by the statement of a prominent neurosurgeon seated in the front row of the audience. He explained how he and a special team of surgeons had performed craniotomies on several of the London victims, the dead as well as the living, in an attempt to find out if their brains had been affected physically in any way. The results had proved negative: no inflammation of the membranes or nerves, no deterioration of tissue, no blockage of cerebrospinal fluid, no bacterial infection, no blood clots or restriction of blood flow to the brain. The surgeon went on to list further defects such as chemical deficiencies that could have damaged the brain's normal functioning, and assured everyone present that none of these had been present. Other tests had been carried out, more in desperation than in hope, and these, too, had proved negative. There had been no lack of enzyme in the victims' systems – without this there would have been an accumulation of amino-acids such as phenylketonuria in the blood. Nor had there been any sudden imbalance of chromosomes in the body cells. A thorough examination had been made of the central region of the brain, particularly the regions grouped around the fluid-filled cavities called the ventricles. One of these regions, the hypothalamus, controlled hunger, thirst, temperature, sex drive and *aggression*, and a close study of the collection of structures around that area forming the limbic system – the septum, fornix, amygdala and hippocampus – which were believed to be particularly responsible for emotional responses such as fear and aggression – had revealed nothing unusual. That is, as far as they could *tell*; no matter how far science had come, the brain was still very much a mystery.

The participating audience, many of whom had become lost with the eminent doctor's medical terminology, stirred uncomfortably. The Home Secretary, anxious to have as many opinions as possible aired in the time available, asked for the view of the psychiatrist seated next to the neurosurgeon, and the two main psychoses of the emotionally disturbed were quickly and clearly explained in a voice that was loud, yet somehow soothing. In manic depressive psychosis, the patient's mood changed from deep depression to mania, which might possibly explain the victims' trance-like quietness during the day and the uncontrollable urges to commit acts of destruction at night. Yet treatment with drugs such as lithium had had no effect on these people. The other chief psychosis was schizophrenia, which generally occurred in those with a hereditary disorder in their metabolism. The symptoms were irrational thinking, disturbed emotions and a breakdown in communications with others, all of which applied to the recent victims. Phenothiazines, also used as tranquillizers, and other drugs such as fluphenazine, had been used unsuccessfully on the victims. As yet, shock treatment had not been tried, but the psychiatrist had also expressed his doubts as to the effectiveness of this method. An alternative which would undoubtedly succeed would be a lobotomy on each individual, but he did, of course, understand that this would be impractical with so many victims. He looked steadily up at the Home Secretary and his hastily appointed 'emergency' council seated on one side of a long, highly polished table on the small stage, remaining silent until the minister realized the psychiatrist had nothing more to say. It was then that a member of an organization called the Spiritual Frontiers Fellowship Rescue Group rose to his feet and informed those present that the phenomenon being witnessed in London was no more than a large gathering of discarnate beings who did not know they were dead and were possessing others in their confusion. The destructive acts of violence that the possessed were committing were caused because the lost spirits were frightened. He asked that mediums be allowed to guide the tormented souls onwards, to leave their earthly ties behind. Bishop had decided he needed a drink at that point in the proceedings.

He had crept from the conference theatre as unobtrusively as possible, pushing his way through the throng of journalists cramming the back of the auditorium. The hotel bar was empty and the lone barman seemed relieved to have some company. Bishop, however, was in no mood for conversation. He swallowed the first scotch fast, then nursed the second.

The meeting was being held in an hotel at the Birmingham Conference Centre, a huge complex of exhibition halls and conference rooms. The complex was, in fact, some miles from the town itself, in a position easily accessible from the M1 motorway. The authorities considered it too risky to use a more convenient London venue for, although the danger only presented itself at nightfall, the situation in the capital was unpredictable. It was feared that many of the various organizations invited to take part in the general debate might have declined the offer if it were held in the danger zone. And anyway, as the Army Chief of Staff had said: 'A general doesn't hold his war council on the field of battle!' When Bishop had arrived with Jacob Kulek, Jessica and Edith Metlock earlier that morning, the hotel lobby had been filled with clamorous groups of scientists, medical experts and parapsychologists. Outside had been an even larger gathering of media people, many of these too, from other parts of the world. Bishop was unsure if the conference was being held merely for cosmetic reasons to show that the government was taking some action, or out of sheer desperation because they had no solution to the problems. Probably for both reasons, he decided.

Jacob Kulek had become adviser to the special action committee formed to deal with the crisis, his Institute suddenly becoming almost another branch of the Civil Service. Just as Winston Churchill had introduced an occult bureau into the Secret Service during World War Two, so had the Home Secretary adopted what he considered was a similar, ready-made organization. The government was not convinced it was dealing with a paranormal phenomenon but, because it had not found any other answers, it was not ruling out the possibility. Hence the conference with its diverse groups of experts. At the moment, the 'trouble' in London was being contained, although the city was too vast to be effectively policed for long. New disturbances broke out every night, more victims were found cowering in the streets each morning. The sewer exits were being watched.

How long the police and troops could maintain control was anybody's guess; the night was already beginning to catch up with the mopping-up exercises of the day. And how many more victims affected or infected – still nobody was sure of the correct term – by the Dark could be kept under lock and key was another problem that was reaching crisis point. The exodus of London residents was relatively small so far, but the sudden influx of outsiders gave cause for alarm. Why would men and women flock to the city when such danger stalked the streets at night? And why were so many flouting the 'lights-on' regulations? It was almost as if some welcomed the phenomenon that had become known as the Dark. Bishop sat in the bar, pondering over the imponderable. Were they faced with a crisis that could be dealt with by scientific means, or a crisis whose cause lay in the paranormal and therefore, could only be answered by psychic means? He, himself, felt they were about to discover there was a definite link between the two.

He drained his glass and waved it at the barman for another.

'I think I need the same,' came a voice from behind him.

Bishop turned to see Jessica had entered the bar. She perched herself on the stool next to him and he ordered her a scotch.

'I saw you leave the conference theatre,' she remarked. 'I wondered if you were okay.'

He nodded. 'Just weary. The discussion doesn't seem to be getting far. Too many fingers in the pie.'

'They feel it's necessary to get as many views as possible.'

'Some of those views are a little eccentric, wouldn't you say?' Bishop passed Jessica's drink over to her. 'Water?' he asked.

She shook her head and sipped the scotch. 'Some are fanatical in their beliefs, I agree, but the others are well respected in their particular fields of psychic research.'

'Will any of it help, though? How the hell can you beat something that apparently has no material form?'

'The idea of germs being living organisms was unknown not too long ago. The Bubonic Plague itself was at first thought to be the work of the devil.'

'I thought you believed this was.'

'In a way, I do. I think our terms are wrong, though. Many think of the devil as a creature with horns and a long forked tail, or at least, a living creature who pops through the gates of hell every now and again to create havoc. It's a belief the Church has done nothing to discourage!'

'And the devil is behind all this?'

'As I said, our terms are wrong. The devil is within us, Chris, just as God is.'

Bishop sighed wearily. 'We are God, we are the devil?' There was disdain in his words.

'The power for good and the power for evil is in us. God and devil are just symbolic names for an abstraction.'

'That's some abstraction if, as you're implying, it's the root cause of everything good and everything bad that's happened in the world.'

'It's an abstraction that's fast becoming a reality.'

'Because Pryszlak has found a way of using it?'

'He's not the first.'

Bishop stared at her. 'This has never happened before.'

'How do you know? Read your Bible, Chris; it gives us plenty of indications.'

'But then why this evil power? Why hasn't someone used the power for good?'

'Many have. Jesus Christ was one.'

Bishop smiled. 'You mean all those miracles were due to a force He knew how to tap?'

'Miracles are more common than you think. Christ may have been a man who knew the process of using that power.'

'Would that make Pryszlak the anti-Christ? I mean, he went for the other extreme.'

Jessica ignored the mockery in Bishop's question. 'There have been many anti-Christs.'

The whisky on an empty stomach had begun to make Bishop slightly light-headed, but the earnestness in Jessica's eyes made him bite back his cynicism. 'Look, Jessica, if you say miracles are fairly common, why is it that no one else is using this other source in the way Pryszlak apparently is?'

'Because we're still learning. We haven't yet grasped it. When it is used, it's done unconsciously. When we learned to walk, did we think about it first, or did the realization come after? Once we were aware that we could walk, that it was physically possible, we could learn to do other things. Run, then ride, use implements, make vehicles to carry us. It's a gradual process, Chris, and only our own awareness can speed up that process.'

Bishop wondered why he was resisting the argument, for it explained much of his own thoughts regarding the paranormal. Perhaps it was because it all seemed too simple, too obvious an answer; but then, who said the answer had to be complicated? Everything came from the individual, no outside force was involved; and when each personal source was discovered, then, united with others, that collected power became massive. It did seem that the Dark affected those people who were in some way mentally disturbed, whether they were criminals, insane, or – his grip on the glass tightened – or had evil in their minds. Many of the cases he had heard of over the past few weeks concerned individuals who held some grievance against others – even mere dislike – and it seemed the madness around them had triggered off their own violence. If the Dark could seek out this evil, invade their minds and draw out that force, uniting with it, reinforcing its own strength like some giant, rapacious organism, then where would it end? As it grew stronger, would it be capable of swamping any opposing force for good in the mind, finding the evil that lurked in every living soul and using it? Was the reason for that power not having been developed more fully in the past because of the conflicting oppositions within everybody, only those rare beings who were truly good or truly evil being capable of harnessing it in their own way? And when you died, did that entity die with you or was it released into . . . into what? Bishop realized that Jessica's answer had not been simple at all: it was as complex as man's own evolution.'

'Chris, are you all right? You've gone deathly white.'

Jessica's hand was over his own, and he became aware of the crushing grip he had on the glass. He placed the scotch back on the bar, but still she kept her hand on his.

He took in a deep breath. 'Maybe it's all catching up with me.'

Misunderstanding him, she said, 'You've been through so much. We all have, but you more than most.'

He shook his head. 'I don't mean that, Jessica. Lynn's death is something I'll never really get over, but it's something I know I'll learn to accept, just as I've accepted Lucy's. The hurt will always be there, but it'll become controllable. No, what's shaken me is your explanation for the Dark. I take it Jacob shares your view?'

'It *is* his view. I agree with him.'

'Then there's no way we can overcome it.'

She was silent for a moment, then replied, 'There has to be a way.'

Bishop turned his hand over so that the palm joined with Jessica's. His fingers curled around her hand and gently squeezed; but he said nothing.

He was still awake, sitting in the uncomfortable armchair in his hotel room, facing the large picture window and wondering what fresh atrocities were breaking out in London, when the light rapping on the door disturbed his thoughts. He glanced at his watch and saw it was 10.30. The rapping came again. Crushing his half-smoked cigarette into the ashtray resting on the arm of the chair, he rose and walked over to the door. He hesitated before turning the twist-lock handle, apprehension having become a part of his life-pattern now. Jessica's voice dispelled his anxiety.

He opened the door and found himself looking into the sightless eyes of Jacob Kulek, Jessica standing just behind her father.

'May we come in, Chris?' Kulek said.

Bishop stood aside and Jessica guided her father into the room. He closed the door and turned to face them.

'I'm sorry I have not been able to speak with you during the day, Chris,' Kulek apologized. 'I'm afraid my time is governed by others nowadays.'

'It's all right, I understand. These people seem to expect a lot of you, Jacob.'

The blind man gave a small laugh, but Bishop noted there was a tiredness to it. 'The scientists and medical people on the one hand are sceptical, while most of the psychists on the other are cautious – they see this as an opportunity to prove everything they have preached over the last few decades. The irrational ones among them have, thank God, been largely ignored. The authorities are stuck somewhere in the middle of both groups, naturally leaning more towards the logical or, if you like, the scientific, point of view. I believe it is only because the scientists have not as yet provided any clues, let alone answers, that our opinions are being sought. May I sit, Chris? It's been a wearisome day.'

'Please.' Bishop turned round the armchair he had just vacated to face the room and Jessica guided her father into it. She smiled warmly at Bishop as she sat in the chair provided with the room's dressing-table. He settled on the edge of his bed and returned her smile.

'Can I order you both some coffee?' he asked.

'No, thank you. I think a large brandy might help to ease my aching bones, though.' Kulek inclined his head towards his daughter.

'Coffee will be fine for me, Chris.'

Bishop picked up the phone and ordered two coffees and one large brandy. When he replaced the receiver he said, 'Is Edith okay?'

'Tired, frightened, like all of us. Our smaller, more intimate meeting in which she was included, broke up only twenty minutes ago. The select committee had to discuss all the points raised at the conference today – the valid points, that is.'

'Who decided which were and which were not?'

'I suppose you could say moderation did. Our Home Secretary is not one for extremes, you know.'

'From what I hear, he's not one for action, either.'

'Then his decision may surprise you.'

'Oh?'

'I'm not sure he's convinced, but he has agreed to – what shall I say? – to an experiment.'

Bishop leaned forward, arms resting across his knees, interested.

Kulek pinched the sides of his nose and squeezed his eyes tightly shut for a few seconds to ease the ache in his head. His face looked drained when he raised his eyes again. 'We are going back to Beechwood. That is, what's left of Beechwood.'

Bishop was stunned. 'Why? What good could that possibly do? As you said, the place is in ruins anyway.'

Kulek patiently nodded and rested his long, thin fingers over the top of his walking cane. 'It was, and still is, a focal point in this whole affair. Every night, more and more unfortunate victims of this thing we call the Dark gather there. Some die, others are found the following morning either standing or lying helpless in the rubble. There has to be a reason for them to go there, something that draws them to it.'

'How could it help for you to go there? We tried it before, remember?'

'And something happened, Chris,' Jessica broke in.

'Jacob nearly got killed.'

'And you had a vision,' the blind man said quietly.

'You saw what went on in that house,' Jessica added. 'You saw how Pryszlak and his followers died.'

'Don't you see, Chris, there are strong vibrations around that area? Even though it is only a ruin, there will be those same energies.' Kulek fixed Bishop with his sightless gaze.

'But the danger. You . . .'

'This time we will have protection. The area will be guarded by troops, we will have powerful lighting . . .'

'You're not thinking of going back there at night?'

'Yes, that would be the only time for what we have in mind.'

'You're crazy. Jessica, you can't let him do this. The Army won't be able to protect him.'

Jessica looked at Bishop steadily. 'Chris,' she said, 'we want you to come with us.'

He shook his head. 'This is wrong, Jessica. There's no point to it. What can we do there, anyway?'

Kulek replied. 'The only thing that is left to us. We are going to make contact with the Dark. We will try to talk with Boris Pryszlak.'

The discreet knock on the door announced the arrival of the coffees and brandy.

TWENTY-SIX

It could have been daytime, the lights were so dazzling. Every house in Willow Road had been cleared of its occupants; not that there were many of them left – the road had attracted the attention of too many victims of the Dark for any residents to feel safe. Army vehicles were parked along the kerbside, all pointed in the same direction, and heavily guarded barriers had been placed across both ends of the road. Two powerful, wide-beam searchlights mounted on trucks and powered by their own generators, were directed into the open space that had once been Beechwood. Most of the rubble had been cleared to allow for an array of equipment to be set up, instruments ranging from sound and video recording machinery, to geiger-counters and other sophisticated gadgetry that Bishop had never seen before, let alone put a name to. Arc lamps, hooked into the main electricity system of the area, were placed at strategic points around the grounds. The whole scene had an unreal look and Bishop could not help feeling he had wandered on to a film set, the various cameras operated by army personnel adding to the illusion. Nearby, Jacob Kulek was having angry words with the Principal Private Secretary to the Home Office over the amount of machinery and reinforcements that were in evidence, all of which, Kulek claimed, might interfere with the energy patterns in the atmosphere and impede any mental contact that might be made with the Dark. The Private Secretary, a thin, waspish little man named Sicklemore, testily replied that they were conducting a scientific operation rather than a parlour seance and his instructions had been to gather and record all necessary data from the experiment while providing every protection possible to civilian life. He added that for decades parapsychologists had urged scientists to work hand in hand with them, so Kulek should not complain now that this was happening. The blind man had to concede the point, realizing the crisis was too grave for petty bickering. Jessica, standing by her father's side, looked relieved that the minor flare-up between the two men was over.

Bishop eased his way through the throng of technicians, police and army personnel, all of whom seemed to have some specific task to perform, and saw Edith Metlock sitting alone among the confusion in a canvas-backed chair. He went over to her and sat in the empty seat next to her.

'How do you feel?' he asked.

Her smile was faint. 'A little nervous,' she replied. 'I'm not sure this is the right way.'

'Jacob seems to think this might be the only way.'

'He's probably right.' Her mood was one of resignation.

'We've got plenty of armed protection,' he said to reassure her.

'You don't understand, Chris. I have to let this . . . this darkness enter my mind. It will be like allowing an evil spirit to invade my body, only in this case there will be several hundred demons.'

He pointed towards two men a few yards away who were talking in low tones.

'They'll be with you.'

'They're both sensitives of high repute and it's a privilege to be working with them. But our combined strength is nothing compared to the evil influences that have accumulated. I can feel their presence already and it frightens me.'

'Maybe nothing will happen.'

'In some ways, I hope you're right. It has to be stopped, though, before it's too late.'

Bishop was silent for a few moments, his head bowed as if studying the dirt at his feet. 'Edith,' he said finally, 'back in Jacob's house, when we were being held hostage by those two crazy women. Before you arrived, one of them said that Lynn, my wife, was still "active". Can you tell me what she meant?'

The medium patted his arm sympathetically. 'She probably meant that your wife's spirit was tied to those others controlled by the Dark.'

'She's still part of it?'

'I can't say. She may be. Is that why you're here tonight?'

Bishop straightened his body. 'There's a lot I've had to accept recently. I admit I'm still confused by many things, but just the thought of how they murdered Lynn . . .' With effort, he controlled his anger. 'If there's anything I can do to help smash this thing, I will. Jacob said he was unsure of what caused the manifestations in Beechwood before – you, or me, or a combination of both of us. I suppose I'm just an ingredient he wants handy to throw into the pot.'

A shadow fell over them and they looked up to see Jessica. 'Everything's nearly ready, Edith. Jacob would like you and the others to take up your positions.'

Bishop helped the medium to her feet and could not help noticing how the robustness had left her demeanour. The walked towards Jacob Kulek who was talking to a group of people which included the Police Commissioner, a youngish-looking army major, and several men and women whom Bishop knew to be scientists and metaphysicists. It's like a bloody circus, he thought grimly.

Kulek broke off his conversation when Jessica tugged at his sleeve and said something to him. He nodded, then spoke to the group around him. 'Anyone who is not necessary to this operation must leave the site. Will you please see to that, Commissioner? The very minimum of guards, the very minimum of technicians. Conditions for what we are about to attempt are poor enough without making them worse. The searchlights will have to be switched off, Major.'

'Good Lord, you're not serious?' came the immediate response.

'I'm afraid I am. The arc lamps, too, will be dimmed considerably. Edith?'

'I'm here, Jacob.'

'I'm sorry about these conditions, my dear, I hope they will not be too much of a distraction for you. Mr Enwright and Mr Schenkel, you are both ready?'

The two mediums whom Jessica had also brought over answered that they were.

'Is Chris here? Chris, I want you seated next to Edith. Could everyone please take their positions?'

Bishop was surprised: he had thought that he would be somewhere on the sidelines. Suddenly, he was even more afraid.

Six chairs forming a rough semi-circle had been placed in a flattened area of the site. To his further discomfort, Bishop realized they were in a spot close to where the main room of Beechwood would have been. Rough boards beneath his feet covered any gaps leading to the cellar below. Glancing at his watch, he

saw it was just after ten. The medium called Schenkel sat in the end seat,
Enwright next to him. Then came Edith Metlock, himself, Jacob Kulek, with
Jessica sitting slightly back from the group just behind her father.

'Please, we must have complete silence.' Kulek's voice was barely raised, but
everyone on the site heard. 'The lights, Major. Could we have them down now?'

The searchlights blinked off and the specially fitted dimmer switches of the arc
lamps were turned down. The scene that had been brightly lit became gloomy
and immediately sinister.

Kulek turned to Bishop. 'Think back to that first day, Chris. That first time
you came to Beechwood. Remember what you saw.'

But Bishop already had.

He knew what he had to do. They had told him.

The inside of the power station was like a huge cavern, a giant's lair that
roared and throbbed with the sound of the massive furnaces and turbines. He
passed between them, monster steel-plated turbines on one side, furnaces and
boilers that stretched up from the basement thirty feet below, almost touching
the ceiling over a hundred feet above, on the other. The turbines were painted a
bright yellow, each one equipped with an instrument console that kept a
watchful eye on their activity. The furnaces and boilers were deceptively cool
grey in colour, though the effort of burning a ton of oil per minute made them
dangerously hot to touch. Heavily insulated pipes ran from them combining
with the boiler pipes in the basement to carry the steam at a pressure of fifteen
hundred pounds per square inch to drive the turbine blades.

He passed a technician checking the rows of dials which monitored one of the
furnaces and he gave no acknowledgement to the waved hand. The technician
frowned, puzzled by his colleague's unkempt appearance, but his thoughts
quickly returned to the instruments before him; the loads were heavy these
nights because of the government edict that every posible light in the city should
be turned on.

The man headed for the stairs leading to the administration floors. And the
main switching room.

For two days and nights he had hidden in his basement flat, the curtains
drawn, the two rooms he occupied kept in a shadowy gloom during the day, a
total darkness during the night.

He was a squat man of twenty-eight, his face still riddled with acne that
should have disappeared years before, his hair already leaving his scalp in
disloyal batches. He lived alone, not by choice, but because no others, male or
female, had any inclination to live with him. His contempt for the human race in
general was only thinly disguised and it was a feeling he had nurtured ever since
he had realized the world was contemptuous of him. He had thought that
leaving school would mean the end of being treated like some loathsome object
by immature minds, only to find that the minds at the college he had gone on to,
although older, were still as immature. By the time he had become a chemical
engineer, the damage was entrenched within him. His parents were alive, but
hardly seen by him. They had never offered him real comfort. Their finding him
spying on his rapidly-developing sister on several occasions had earned their
early disenchantment with him. They had let him know that the thick lenses he
had to wear which made his eyes look like black buttons swimming in silvery
pools were a punishment from God. So did He also give him the spots because he
couldn't stop abusing himself? And did He make his body smell more than
others because he hated his sister, even though he spied on her? And now was He

making his hair fall out because he never stopped having dirty thoughts? Did He do all that? Well forget Him, there were other gods to worship.

He climbed the stairs to the offices, passing no one else on the way; the generating station needed little more than a complement of thirty staff and technicians to keep it functioning, a small group of people who controlled the power used by millions. Being in charge of the energy used by so many was what had attracted him to the job in the first pace. There were three ways of depriving people of their light and power in the area supervised by his particular station: one was to blow the whole plant up; two was to systematically shut down the generators and turbines, and cut the fuel supply; three was to turn off everything, apart from the furnaces, by the remote controls in the main switching room. He had no access to explosives, so blowing up the plant was out of the question. Shutting everything down and cutting the fuel supply manually would take too long and the other technicians would stop him before he'd managed one turbine. So the answer was in the control room. Cut the switches and everything would be black. Black as the night. A look of pleasure came into his eyes.

The main switching room was a large glass-fronted box projecting out into the generating hall, crammed with consoles containing dials, and a row of television screens that kept an eye on every part of the power station. The supervisors had been even more alert than usual over the past few weeks, for the danger of allowing a power failure in any area covered by their plant had been carefully explained to them. The danger within their own ranks, however, had been unforeseen.

The duty supervisor looked up in surprise as the man entered the room and was about to ask where he'd been the last couple of days when the bullet from the Beretta punctured his forehead. The other supervisors were too stunned to react quickly and he carefully shot them, each bullet finding its mark with precisioned nonchalance. He was amazed at his own accuracy considering he had never handled a gun before, but not amazed at his own calmness. The stranger, the tall lady, had shown him how to use it when she had come to his basement flat earlier that day, but it was not she who had instilled the calmness in him. The Dark had done that.

He sniggered as the bodies of his colleagues tumbled to the floor and he took time to watch their twitching limbs for a few moments. His lips glistening, made wet by the tongue that constantly flicked across them, he stepped over the bodies towards the control panels. His hand was trembling as he reached for the first switch.

Bishop blinked his eyes rapidly. Was it his imagination or was it becoming even darker? He felt the tightness in his throat as he tried to swallow. It seemed as though there were four walls around him, transparent walls through which he could see the hazy figures of others on the site, The walls grew more solid. A window to his left, curtains closed. Another window to his right, further down. Shadows moving like wispy smoke.

He resisted.

Edith's eyes were closed, muted sounds coming from her. Her head slowly sagged forward until her chin rested on her chest. The other two mediums were watching and Bishop saw their alarm. The one on the end, Schenkel, began to shiver. His eyelids fluttered and his pupils rose upwards into his head before his eyes closed completely. Enwright had not noticed what was happening to his colleague, for he was still watching Edith Metlock. Strong fingers curled around

Bishop's arm and he snapped his head around to find Kulek's sightless eyes peering intently at him.

'Chris, can you see them again?' Kulek whispered. 'I can feel there is something malevolent here. Is it them, can you see those same faces again?'

Bishop was unable to answer. It was too sudden; no sooner had the lights been dimmed than the presence was with them. As though it had been waiting.

The room was solid and figures wafted before him, floating into focus then becoming vague again, blurred images. The room seemed smaller. Sounds buzzed in his ears, voices bursting forward then disappearing abruptly, replaced by others, as though a frequency dial was being aimlessly turned across the airwaves. He looked back at Edith and saw a black substance was seeping from her lips, dribbling down her chin and on to her chest. It could have been blood, yet he knew it wasn't. He reached out a hand to touch and there was nothing there, no black stickiness on his fingers, nothing on her chin. He withdrew his hand and the substance dribbled from her lips once more. Bishop looked up and the room seemed even smaller.

Schenkel fell from his chair and lay still on the rough boards and earth covering the cellar below. No one stepped forward to help him, for they had been warned not to interfere unless something drastic occurred. Enwright glanced at his companion but ignored him. Edith Metlock moaned aloud and something dark was expelled from her mouth like a billow of smoke. The voices inside Bishop's head were laughing now and he saw that the room was shrinking, the walls and ceiling reaching in towards him. He knew he would be crushed and he tried to rise from the chair. His body had become frozen solid and he could feel the frost heavy on his eyelids, sealing them tight. His hair prickled as each one became a brittle icicle. The walls were only feet away.

A cold hand touched his and somehow warmed it. Edith had reached out to him. His other hand was being held by someone else and, although his head was frozen tight, he knew it was Jacob Kulek who gripped him. The warmth returned to his body and he felt something falling away from him, something that had threatened to smother him. The walls and ceiling had vanished, but a swirling darkness filled his vision.

The sound came from Enwright, but it was not his voice, nor the voice of any living thing. It was a high squealing sound, a tortured wailing. The medium stood, his palms pressed against his temples, his head turning from side to side as though he were trying to shake something from it. His eyes looked wildly around until they came to rest on Bishop.

The after-image of those staring eyes stayed in Bishop's vision as the dim lights went out and everything succumbed to the crushing blackness.

TWENTY-SEVEN

The hands closed around Bishop's throat and began to tighten. He could only see a black shape before him, but he knew it was the medium, Enwright, who was trying to choke the life from him. He gripped the man's wrists and pulled at them, his chin automatically tucking itself downwards, neck muscles taut, to resist the increasing pressure. Even as he struggled, Bishop was aware of the confusion around him, the shouts, the running feet, the sudden small flares as matches or lighters were lit, then the long torch beams cutting out bright sections in the night.

A dizziness made the scene even more chaotic and he knew he would soon begin to lose his senses if he did not break the choking grip, but no matter how hard he pulled at the wrists, the pressure still increased. He did the only thing possible. Releasing his own hold, he grabbed the medium's clothing and pulled the man towards him, pushing his heels hard into the boards beneath them. His chair leaned back at a precarious angle, then both men went toppling over, Bishop increasing the momentum with an added thrust of his heels. They landed heavily, Enwright's head smashing on to the boards with a loud crack, his body immediately becoming limp. Bishop had curved his back and hunched his shoulders so the impact had little effect on him. He pushed the sprawled body away and sat up, looking quickly around, then closing his eyes for a few seconds to help them adjust to the darkness more easily.

'Get those bloody searchlights on!' he heard someone shout and almost immediately a broad expanse of light lit up half the site.

'The other searchlight!' cried the same voice and Bishop could now see it was the army major who was shouting the commands. 'Get it bloodywell on!'

But something was happening at the vehicle on which the second searchlight was mounted. Bishop could just make out struggling figures and he flinched when a shot rang out. Other soldiers began to run towards the vehicle, their 7.62mm self-loading rifles held across their chests, ready for use.

More movement before him caught his eye and his saw Edith Metlock was tossing her head from side to side, her hands waving in the air as though warding something off. The other medium, Schenkel, was now on his knees, body bent forward and hands covering his face.

'Chris, help me!'

Jessica was trying to pull a man away from her father, a man who wore the dark blue uniform of a policeman. The realization struck Bishop in a flash of new dread: the Dark had penetrated the minds of some of those meant to protect them. He staggered to his feet and ran towards Jessica, but another figure reached them first. The policeman was behind Kulek and was dragging him backwards, an arm locked around his throat, Jessica in front of both men trying to wrench the arm away. The other man came up behind the policeman and dug rigid thumbs into the flesh points just under the uniformed man's jawline, digging them in deeply with a screwing motion. The policeman screamed and was forced to release Kulek; as he turned, the second man brought the heel of his hand sharply up beneath the policeman's nose, snapping his head backwards. A swift chop at the exposed windpipe sent the policeman reeling to the ground where he lay squirming and gasping for breath.

By then, Bishop had reached them and he recognized the man who had saved Kulek as Peck's DI, Roper.

'Bleedin wollies,' Roper said, barely giving the injured policeman a second glance.

Just then, Peck himself emerged from the general confusion. 'Are you okay, sir?' he asked, a hand reaching out to steady Jacob Kulek.

The blind man drew in deep breaths as Jessica held on to him. 'I'm . . . I'm learning how to resist such attacks,' he managed to say and Peck allowed a brief flicker of amusement to cross his face.

'We'd better get you out of here,' he said. 'It looks as if the power supply to half of London has been switched off. Anything can happen now.' He turned to Bishop. 'You all right? I saw that bastard ready to attack you just before the lights blew. Sorry I couldn't get to you in time.'

'I'm okay. How could the power fail?'

Peck shrugged. 'Overload, maybe.'

'Or sabotage.'

'For the moment, it doesn't matter. The main thing is to get you all somewhere safe.'

'Edith. Where is Edith?' Kulek was clutching at Jessica, frustrated by his own blindness.

'She's still in her chair, Father. She's in a trance state. I think she's trying to break free of it.'

'Quickly, take me to her before it's too late.'

'I think we ought to get away from here, sir,' Peck interjected.

'Edith first,' Kulek said firmly. 'We must take her with us.'

Jessica led him over to the agitated medium and Roper looked uneasily towards his superior.

'I don't like this, guv,' he said. 'We don't stand a chance if that searchlight fails.'

'Get over to the cars, Frank. I want all their lights on right away. Where's the bloody Commissioner? And the army major – he should have had things organized by now.'

But more gunfire told him that organization under those circumstances would prove difficult, and when the shattering of glass preceded the extinction of the remaining light, leaving the site filled only with individual torch beams, they knew it would prove virtually impossible.

'The cars, Frank, quick. Get those lights on.' Someone bumped into Peck and he roughly pushed the figure away. He reached inside his jacket for the Smith and Wesson holstered discreetly at his hip and drew it.

'Bishop! Where are you?'

'Right here.' He had been following Kulek and Jessica before the remaining light had blown and now stood midway between them and Peck.

The detective cursed the lack of moonlight. What a bloody silly night to choose! 'Can you reach Kulek?' He had to shout to make himself heard over the general clamour.

'Yes, they're not far . . . Jesus!'

Peck made his way towards the dark shape a few feet away when he, too, felt the coldness stab inside him. It blanked out his thoughts for a few moments, a numbing iciness that seemed to fill every secret crevice of his mind. He stumbled against someone.

'Bishop? What is it? Can you feel it, too?'

'Don't give in to it, Peck. Force it out!'

'What is it?' Peck was shouting, his free hand against his eyes and forehead, the gun held away from him.

'It's the Dark. It's probing your mind. You can resist, Peck, but you've got to want to.' Bishop's mind was clearing fast after the first paralyzing assault on it and he suddenly understood that the Dark could only claim those who allowed themselves to be claimed. The Dark had to be accepted before it could take, like the mythical vampire who could not cross a threshold unless invited.

He grabbed Peck and shook him. 'Fight it!' he yelled. 'It can't touch you if you fight it!'

Bishop lost his grip as Peck slid to the ground. 'Get them . . . get them out of here!' he heard the detective say.

Bishop wasted no more time: only Peck could save himself now. More shots were ringing out and the brief gunflashes lit the scene into frozen actions. The darkness around them was heavy, cloying, but his eyes were slowly adapting to it and he was able to make out shapes more clearly. He moved towards Jessica and her father, finding them crouched beside Edith Metlock, who still writhed in her chair.

'Jessica,' he said, kneeling next to her, 'we've got to leave here. It's too dangerous to stay.'

'They're torturing her, Chris. She can't bring herself out of the trance.'

Kulek was clutching the medium's shoulders. He softly called her name over and over again. Her body heaved as she began to retch, the sound dry and agonized until she slid from the chair and vomit spurted from her mouth in an arched stream. Bishop felt warm, sticky particles spatter his face and a foul stench came to his nostrils. He brushed the speckles away with the sleeve of his jacket, then reached down for the medium and pulled her into a sitting position. Lights began to spring into life from the roadway and two sets swung their beams on to the site as drivers manoeuvred their cars. Edith's eyes were wide and staring and, although she still shook, the wild writhing had stopped.

Bishop stood and dragged her up with him. She offered no resistance and he was relieved she could stand albeit only with his support. 'Jacob, hold on to Jessica. We're getting out now.'

'We made a mistake. We did not realize the madness we were dealing with, the evil that is around us.'

'You're telling me. Now come on, let's go!' There was an anger in Bishop that he did not understand, but was glad to have; it somehow threw strength into him.

He half-carried, half-dragged Edith across the site, making for the road where the lights were, urging Jessica and her father to keep close to him. The soldier who stood in his way took his time in raising the rifle and aiming it at Bishop's head.

All Bishop could see was the black silhouette against the glare from the nearest car, but he knew the soldier's intention. He started at the shot that rang out and watched the soldier's body slowly crumble.

'You going to stand there all night?' said Peck, emerging from the shadows to one side of the bright twin beams. Bishop almost cried out with relief; he never thought Peck would have been such a welcome sight. He tightened his hold on the woman, who still stared blankly ahead, and moved forward, Peck joining him and helping to support her weight.

'I thought it had me back there,' Peck said loudly. 'Couldn't move, like being doped up for an operation but not as pleasant. Scared the life out of me. Keep up with us, Miss Kulek, we'll soon be out of this!'

The site was further lit by the first searchlight coming back into action again and, as Bishop swung his head to survey the scene, he saw there were many individual struggles taking place, soldier against soldier, policeman against policeman, and a mixture of both. There were others on the site now, men and women who had not been there before, and these people cowered under the naked glare, shielding their eyes with raised arms. Where they had come from, he could not guess, but it was evident that they were victims of the Dark. Bodies of policemen or soldiers whom they had attacked lay at their feet. He couldn't be sure, but one of these recumbent figures looked like the Police Commissioner himself.

They stumbled over the rubble around the edges of the site and crossed the small concreted area that had once been Beechwood's car space. To Bishop it seemed like only yesterday that he had crossed that area for the first time, yet so much had happened since, it could well have been years ago.

Willow Road and the Beechwood ruin were a bubble of light in that broad section of the city, the glow tingeing the night sky so that it could be seen for miles around. People were stirring, looking out from their windows at the bright glow, wondering why it was lit when their streets were in total darkness. Others left their homes, or emerged from sewers and other dark places to make their way towards the light, already knowing what they would find there.

Bishop squinted his eyes against the headlights, the shouts, the screams, the crackle of gunfire spurring him on. They reached the first car and almost fell against the bonnet in their haste.

'Over here, guv,' came a familiar voice.

Policemen, uniformed as well as those in plain clothes, were all around, and Peck led the small party through them towards Roper who was standing by another car.

'Bloody murder going on back there,' the Detective Inspector said. 'I didn't think you'd make it.'

'Yes, me too,' Peck replied. 'Have you been on to HQ?'

'Yeah, they're sending all available help. They've got their own problems, though; trouble's breaking out all over again.'

Peck called a uniformed sergeant over. 'I want one more car swung round to point its lights into the site. Back as many of the others as possible up against one another to give us a circle of light around us. Let's keep any marauding maniacs away, or at least see them before they get too close.'

They ducked instinctively when a bottle shattered into the road near them. They tried to see who had thrown the missile, but were dazzled by the other car lights parked further down. Another bottle came sailing through the air and this one broke against the shoulder of a plain-clothes policeman. The man went down on one knee, then rose again, apparently not badly hurt. Shadowy figures flitted momentarily through the beams of light before disappearing into the surrounding darkness once more. Peck knew he would have to get his men organized quickly – their fear was becoming greater because of their confusion.

'Bishop, I want you and these people out of the area. My driver, Simpson, will get you over to the other side of the river.'

Bishop thought Kulek might offer some resistance to Peck's directions, but when he turned to the blind man he saw only a look of utter defeat on his face.

'Jacob?'

'It's become too strong. I did not realize.' The words were spoken to no one in particular; it was as if Kulek had retreated within himself.

'We must leave, Father. We can't do any good here,' Jessica urged him.

Peck was already opening the doors of the Granada. 'In you get,' he ordered crisply. 'Kulek and the two women in the back, you in the front, Bishop. Frank, grab a patrol car and go with them. Take a couple of wollies.'

Roper dashed off to commandeer a white Rover nearby, its driver immediately gunning the engine, relieved to be on the move. The car screeched over to the Granada as Peck slammed the door after Kulek and the two women. Other police cars were positioning themselves in the road, tyres screeching as they turned their vehicles so their headlight beams shone outwards. There were several muffled thuds as bodies of people lurking in the darker areas were struck by the fast-moving vehicles. Peck was surprised at just how many people were advancing on them, their forms frozen in the swinging lights reminding him of paralyzed foxes caught on country roads at night. Whether or not they were all victims or some had merely come to investigate the lights and commotion, there was no way of knowing; there was no choice but to treat everyone as a potential enemy. He leaned into the Granada's passenger window and spoke across Bishop to his driver.

'Back to HQ, and don't stop for anything. Just follow the patrol car.'

Bishop called after Peck as the detective made his way towards the Rover. 'What will you do?'

Peck turned and said, 'We'll get the Commissioner and the civilians out of here, then head back over the river. The Army can sort themselves out!'

He turned and shouted instructions at the driver of the patrol car before Bishop could tell him he thought he had seen the Police Commissioner either dead or unconscious on the ground. Peck banged his hand down hard on the Rover's roof and the car shot forward. Bishop was thrown back into his seat as the Granada lurched after it. They had only travelled a hundred yards when the red brakelights of the car ahead blinked on and both cars screeched to a halt. Bishop poked his head out of the passenger window and a wave of despair swept over him.

The end of the road was completely blocked by crowds of people. They moved forward, some running, others walking slowly as if by automation. He could see that many were in a bad state of deterioration, while others were alert, their actions quicker, the light not seeming to bother them as much. There was no way of knowing just how many were out there, but it seemed like hundreds, an unbroken mass of advancing bodies. As they drew nearer, he saw that many carried weapons ranging from iron bars to knives and milk bottles. One of the running men held what looked like a shotgun.

Jessica, directly behind Bishop, was leaning forward in her seat, unable to see clearly. 'What is it, Chris?'

He had no time to reply, for the driver in the car ahead had decided what to do: the Rover accelerated towards the mob and the Granada followed. If the policeman in the first car expected the crowd to jump aside and leave a path clear for him, he was mistaken: they stood their ground and the Rover plunged into them.

Jessica screamed when she saw the bodies tossed into the air, the headlights of the Granada illuminating the scene in shocking relief. Their car skidded as the driver turned the steering-wheel to avoid crashing into the back of the now stationary Rover; instead, the Granada's side smashed into the lead vehicle, throwing the patrol car's occupants forward and shaking Bishop and the others badly.

Roper's head appeared out of the white car's rear passenger window and he waved his arm in a forward motion at them. His own driver was quickly recovering from the shock of running down so many people and was starting his stalled engine once more when a man appeared near the bonnet of the Rover. He carried a shotgun and he aimed it at the windscreen.

Bishop heard the blast and saw the glass shatter leaving an irregular opaque fringe of glittering silver around the edge of the black hole it had created. Both policemen in the front of the patrol car jerked backwards, then their bodies slipped from view. Roper was already pushing his door open when eager hands grabbed at him. He raised his gun, but the weapon was forced aside as he was mobbed.

'We've got to help him!' Bishop cried as he reached for the door-handle on his side.

The driver grabbed him and pulled him back. 'No way. My orders were to get you lot out of here and that's what I'm going to do.'

'We can't just leave him!'

'We'd have no chance out there – there's too many!'

Even as he spoke, their own car was being surrounded, fists and makeshift weapons pounding on the roof. Hands reached in and tore at Bishop's arms and face; the driver had wisely kept his window closed throughout. Bishop pulled himself away from the grasping hands and struck out at them, feeling no pity for these people and what they had become, just a loathing fear. Metal scraped against metal as the Granada lunged forward once more, friction between the two cars sending a shower of sparks into the air.

Jessica watched with horror as one man refused to let go of the door on Bishop's side and was dragged along with the vehicle as it gathered speed. Slowly and deliberately, Bishop prised the man's fingers away from the door-frame until the hands fell away; Jessica felt the slight but sickening bump as the car ran over the man's trapped ankles.

Simpson headed towards the pavement which seemed less congested than the road itself. A woman leapt on to the bonnet and managed to cling there staring with manic eyes through the windscreen before the car mounted the kerb and she was tossed off. Bishop looked back, but could see nothing of Roper, just a mass of black shapes swarming over the Rover. Another blast, then a great roar as the patrol car's tank exploded; someone – probably the same man who had shot the driver and his partner – had deliberately fired into the Rover's bodywork. A great ball of flames rose into the air, killing those too close, burning others. Most of the road was lit up by the explosion, but the shadows quickly regained ground, beaten back only by the red glow from the ensuing fire.

The Granada bounced back on to the road, the main body of the crowd having been skirted, and sped on, heading for the T-junction at the end of Willow Road. The headlights caught the figure of a man as he ran forward and hurled a milk bottle at the windscreen. Both Bishop and the driver raised their arms to protect their faces as their view became a web of fractured glass. Barely slowing, the driver punched a hole through the windscreen and shouted to Bishop, 'Take my gun – smash out the glass.'

He had flipped back his jacket and Bishop could just make out the gun butt protruding from the holster at the driver's waist. The policeman loosened the restraining grip, his attention still firmly directed through the jagged hole he had created. Bishop pulled out the gun and used it to smash a larger hole in the glass. The wind rushed through the gap, but they hardly noticed it. The car tore into the street at the end of Willow Road, the tyres flattening out and desperately biting into the road's surface for grip. Bishop was thrown against the passenger door and he grabbed the frame to hold himself there until the car had regained stability. He had one last look at Willow Road through the windows opposite him before they had turned the corner completely and houses blocked his view. Lights, flames and milling people were all he had seen. Now there was blackness around them, probed only by their own headlights.

Bishop became conscious of the cold steel he held. He proffered the weapon towards the driver. 'Here's your gun.'

The policeman's eyes were screwed into narrow slits against the wind rushing at his face and he did not take them from the road ahead. 'You keep it, I've got to concentrate on driving. Don't hesitate to use it if necessary.'

Bishop was about to protest, but thought better of it. The man was right: he could hardly protect them and drive at the same time. It was fortunate that all senior policemen had been issued with guns – the whole force would have been armed if there had been enough weapons to go round – for the numbers of victims claimed by the Dark was growing day by day. Or, more appropriately, night by night.

He wound up his side window, then turned to the three passengers in the back. 'Are you okay?' he asked above the noise of the engine and the wind rushing through the interior. Their shapes were barely discernible in the darkness. Jessica's face came close to his.

'I think they're both in a state of shock, Chris.'

'No, no, I'm all right.' It was Kulek's voice. 'It was just so . . . so . . . overwhelming. The power has become so great.'

Bishop sensed the blind man's utter weariness and shared in his feeling of defeat. How did you combat something so intangible, something that had no material form, no physical nucleus? How did you destroy energy from the mind? The living people who gave themselves up to the Dark could be controlled, killed, but the killing itself allowed that energy to become stronger.

A wild skid as the driver tried to avoid a group of people in the centre of the road caused Bishop to clutch at the back of his seat. The car swerved into a narrow sidestreet, leaving the group calling after them; they may or may not have been victims, but the driver had no inclination to stop and find out. Dull glows were coming from the windows of many houses they passed as though the occupants were lighting fires or candles to create a natural light. They saw that other people were leaving their homes, leading or carrying children, and jumping into their cars, switching their headlights on.

'Looks like we're not the only ones heading for the bright lights,' the driver remarked as he swerved round a car that was just pulling out ahead of them.

There were more headlights in the distance as people followed the example of neighbours and hurried out to their own cars, not understanding what was happening, but knowing enough to realize the darkness around them was dangerous.

'It's going to be bloody chaos soon!' Simpson shouted. 'They'll all be trying to get to the other side of the river!'

'Who can blame them?' Bishop replied.

Their car was forced to stop when two cars on opposite sides of the road swung out and collided. Their speed had not allowed any serious damage, but the cries of anguish and panic could be plainly heard. Another car screeched to a halt behind the Granada.

'The silly bastards have blocked the road.' The policeman looked behind, hoping to reverse away from the situation. Yet another vehicle had pulled up behind the car blocking their exit and horns began to bellow their annoyance.

The police driver looked swiftly from left to right, searching for a way out. 'Hold on tight!' he yelled, then jammed the gearstick into reverse and struck down hard on the accelerator pedal, braking almost immediately after. The Granada shot back a few feet, crunching into the car behind and pushing it back, allowing the policeman valuable room ahead to manoeuvre. He spun the wheel round and once more mounted the kerb. Bishop sank back into his seat, his heels pressing involuntarily into the flooring as though to brake, sure there was no way the Granada could pass between the lamp-post and the low garden wall on their left. They got through only because the car itself widened the gap considerably by taking much of the garden wall with it. The tearing of metal and crumbling brickwork on the passenger side made Bishop lean towards the driver, expecting his side of the car to rip free at any moment. The policeman found his way back on to the roadway, the two crashed cars successfully passed.

'Always wanted to do that,' he said, grinning despite the tension.

'Sunday drivers,' Bishop commented, relieved to still be in one piece.

'There's a main road ahead. We should be able to make better progress.'

The driver's optimism, however, was misguided, for as they tore into the wide road, they saw that the intersection ahead which was normally controlled by traffic lights was jammed solid with vehicles.

'The sideroad – there!' Bishop pointed at the narrow turning to their left and the driver directed the car into it without hesitation. At the far end they could see a building blazing, figures standing in the road watching.

'Right!' Bishop shouted, but the driver had already seen the turning and was reducing speed. The car struck something that made a dull thud against the metalwork; neither of the two men in the front had seen whether it was a man, woman or stray animal. The driver accelerated once more, saying nothing.

The sidestreet ran into another main road and the Granada came to an abrupt halt halfway across it. To their right was the jammed intersection they had just avoided and now they could see people being dragged from the cars and attacked. Again, there was no way of knowing whether or not the attackers were Dark victims or merely angry motorists frustrated at not being able to escape the lightless area of the city. As they watched, a man, lit by the headlights, leapt on to the roof of his car while hands reached up and clawed at him, trying to drag him down. His resistance came to an abrupt halt when his legs were swept from beneath him by a stick or iron bar of some kind; he fell on to his back, then slid from the roof, fists pummelling him as he went down. Screams directed their attention to another spot in the jumble of machines: a woman was being stretched across a car bonnet, her clothes ripped from her body, arms and legs pinned down by eager hands. The rush of others towards her obscured what followed, but as the screams became more shrill, there was little doubt as to what was happening to her.

Bishop's hands tightened on the Smith and Wesson as Jessica said, 'We've got to help her, Chris, please, stop them!'

He looked towards the policeman who shook his head. 'Sorry,' Simpson said, 'we'd have no chance. There's too many.'

Bishop knew the man was right, but he was unable to sit there and let the atrocity happen. The driver sensed his mood and quickly stabbed down at the accelerator pedal. He swung the car around in a tight quarter-circle, heading away from the intersection. Anger burst from Bishop and for a brief second he considered levelling the gun at the policeman's head.

Then Edith Metlock began to laugh.

He swivelled around to look at her, the gun poised, barrel angled towards the car's roof. Kulek and Jessica had recoiled away from the medium and were staring at the dark form sitting opposite them.

The laughter did not belong to her. It was deep, nasty, a man's heavy laughter.

The driver kept his foot down, knowing it could be fatal to stop in that blacked-out area, but he experienced the same dread as the others: the coldness seeping through him, the feeling of fluttering pressure just below the back of his neck, the loosening of sphincter muscles. The laughter was unnatural.

'Edith!' Kulek said sharply, the weariness now gone from his voice. 'Edith, can you hear me?'

Oncoming cars flashed by, their lights briefly casting beams into the interior of the Granada, the drivers unaware that the way ahead would be blocked by the jam at the intersection. Edith's face was momentarily illuminated as each fleeing vehicle swept by and they could see her eyes were full of a malice that was alien to the woman herself. Her mouth was open, but her lips did not curve upwards into a smile; the laughter rattled from somewhere deep in her throat.

Kulek blindly reached out towards her, his searching hand finding her immobile face. The wind blew in through the broken windscreen and howled around the interior of the car. Still she laughed.

'Force him from you, Edith!' Kulek shouted above the noise of the wind and the car's engine. 'He cannot take you unless you allow him to!'

But the laughter had become that of many now. And the wind had stopped.

It was as though they were in a vacuum; even the noise from the engine could not be heard. Only the hollow laughter of things that were dead filled their heads, mocking them and enjoying their fear.

The driver nervously glanced back over his shoulder, unsure of what was happening, the sounds making him hunch his body over the steering-wheel as if he were warding off something physical. 'For Christ's sake, make her stop! Hit her, do something!'

Kulek began to talk to her again, his voice low and soothing; the others could not hear him, but each time the interior was lit up, Bishop could see the blind man's lips moving, and he knew Kulek was urging the medium to rid herself of the demons using her body.

'Oh, no!' It was the driver again.

Bishop turned and saw the policeman was staring at the road ahead; he was heaved towards the smashed windscreen as the brakes were slammed on. The car skidded to a halt and rocked backwards and forwards on its suspension; the three passengers in the rear were thrown against the backs of the front seats.

Because of the remaining shattered glass in the windscreen, Bishop could not see what had made the driver stop. He quickly leaned over towards the steering-wheel and peered through the gaping hole in the glass. He drew in a sharp breath.

A line of vehicles stretched across the road, those at each end jammed into shop doorways so there was no possible gap for other cars to break through. The blockage had been deliberately set up to prevent the main road being used as a means of escape to the other side of the river. They saw the wrecks of other cars that had reached that point before them, their bonnets buckled and bent because the drivers had not braked in time. Faces peered over the top of cars at the Granada, then figures leapt over the barrier and appeared from doorways on either side of the road, streaming towards them. Their cries snapped the policeman into action, but not before the first man had leapt on to the car bonnet and was curling his fingers around the jagged windscreen glass for grip. Another joined in, this one a woman, her face black with dirt and her body emaciated.

The door on Bishop's side was pulled open just as the car shot backwards away from the blockade, swinging wide with the added momentum. Bishop felt Jessica's hands on his shoulder as he nearly tumbled out on to the road. A man clung to the door, his legs stretched out behind him as he was dragged along. The woman on the bonnet was thrown off and landed in the road, her piercing scream instantly cut off as her skull cracked against the hard surface. The first man still miraculously clung to the broken window and was hauling himself forward against the gravitational pull, his free hand reaching in and clutching the steering-wheel.

'Shoot him, Bishop!' the policeman cried and, almost in a reflex action, Bishop raised the weapon and pointed it at the gaping hole in the windscreen. Instead of squeezing the trigger, he brought the gun down hard on the man's knuckles. The hand opened and glass snapped from the windscreen as the man flew away from them.

The Granada gathered speed, the driver silently praying that no other vehicle would suddenly appear behind them. Without warning he jumped on the footbrake and spun the wheel into full lock. The car did a hundred and eighty degree turn, its nose ending up pointed in the direction from which they had come. The passenger door swung shut, sending the man clinging to it skidding and bouncing across the road.

Once again the accelerator pedal was pressed and the car leapt forward. Bishop was too breathless to make any comment on the driver's skill; he checked behind to see if the others were still in one piece, but even before he could ascertain whether or not they were, the car was screeching around to their right, the driver knowing it was useless to go back the way they had come. When Bishop had righted himself again he saw they were speeding along a street that had high-rise buildings on one side, a row of shops on the other.

Somehow, he knew there was something ominous about the headlights that swung into view ahead of them.

Simpson raised an arm to shield his eyes from the glare. 'Silly bastard – he's on full beam.' He flashed his own headlights to warn the other driver, but the advancing beams were not dipped in acknowledgement. Their faces were brilliantly lit by the oncoming lights and Bishop realized the vehicle coming towards them had to be a lorry or a truck of some kind – its lights were too high above the ground for it to be a car. The policeman steered over to his right, for the other vehicle was on the wrong side of the road. The other driver matched his direction, pulling to his left.

'Jesus, he's trying to hit us!' the policeman whispered, but the wind was back in the car and no one heard his words. The glare became even more harsh, the dazzle painful. It filled their vision, drawing closer like a fiery comet dashing across a black void. Bishop could hear Jessica screaming, the policeman shouting. The laughter of the dead.

He closed his eyes and pushed himself back against his seat, bracing himself for the impact.

TWENTY-EIGHT

For Bishop, there was no sense to the next few moments, just the shock of screaming noise and whirling lights. The police driver had spun his steering-wheel to the left in an effort to thwart the oncoming vehicle, but the other driver had altered his direction just enough to clip the Granada's rear wing, sending the car into a screeching spin, the occupants violently jarred by the blow. The policeman was powerless to control the skid and the car turned completely around almost in its own space, before careering across the forecourt of a block of flats to their left. Most of the glass in the windscreen had been shaken loose and Bishop opened his eyes in time to see the entrance to the high-rise building tearing towards them; he jammed his feet hard into the footwell in front of the passenger seat and pushed both hands against the dashboard to prevent himself going through the windscreen when the car hit concrete.

Even though the driver had the brake pedal fully-pressed and was turning the wheel to avoid hitting the building head on, the impact, when it came, was tremendous. The bonnet buckled upwards as it met the corner of the entrance, the radiator cut in half and each segment pushed back into the engine in a shower of scalding steam. Bishop was thrown forward, but was saved from going through his windscreen by the position he had taken up moments before; his chest hit the dashboard and he was thrown back into his seat. The driver clung to the steering-wheel which collapsed against his weight and he found himself out of the windscreen, his face against the risen metal of the bonnet, unaware of the body that slammed past him. Edith Metlock was saved from flying over the front seats because she had been knocked to the floor when the lorry had struck the wing on her side; Jessica had already been clinging to the back of Bishop's seat when they had first been hit and her grip had tightened so that when they plunged into the building she was able to prevent herself from being propelled forward. Jacob Kulek was less fortunate.

The total silence that followed did more to rouse Bishop than any voices or body-shaking hands could have; the screams, the laughter, the screeching tyres, had all culminated in the strident cry of torn and crushed metal, and now the contrasting quietness seemed to prod him physically.

He pushed himself upright, his movements slow and deliberate, waiting for sudden pain to tell him he was injured. None came, but a general numbness gave a hint of the pain to come from the bruising he had received. He heard a whimper from behind.

'Jessica?' He twisted his body to see. Somehow the headlight on the passenger side had remained undamaged, although its twin was completely shattered, and just enough light was reflected back from the cavern of the building's entrance to enable him to make out shapes in the car's interior. 'Jessica, are you hurt?'

He half-knelt on his seat to reach her. Her face came up from the top of his seat where it lay, her eyes still closed, beginning to open. She whimpered again and shook her head slightly as if to clear it. Her eyes opened fully and she stared blankly at him.

Movement on the driver's side caught Bishop's attention; the policeman was cautiously drawing himself back from the glassless windscreen into the car. He groaned aloud as he slumped back into his seat. There was blood on his forehead and Bishop could see tiny sparkles of imbedded glass. The policeman gingerly rubbed his chest then drew in a sharp breath when his probing fingers reached his ribs.

He groaned. 'Cracked one, I think,' he said turning to Bishop. 'Maybe just bruised. You okay?'

Before he could reply, Edith Metlock's head and shoulders came into view. 'Where are we? What's happened?' she asked.

Bishop and the policeman exchanged quick glances. 'It's all right, Edith. We've had an accident,' said Bishop gently, aware of the obviousness of his statement.

'Come on,' Simpson said abruptly. 'We'd better get out of here. We're sitting ducks. Did you lose the gun?'

Bishop felt around the floor of the passenger footwell and his fingers touched cold metal. 'Got it.'

'There's a torch in the glove compartment – get that, too.' He pushed open his door, grunting with the effort.

Bishop took the torch and stepped from his side of the car knowing they were lucky not to have been seriously injured: the damage to the front of the Granada was appalling.

'Father!' Jessica's scream sent Bishop rushing to open her door. She tumbled out and pushed past him, running towards the wrecked part of the car. He realized what must have happened when he saw only Edith Metlock in the back passenger seat: Jacob Kulek had been hurled through the windscreen.

He found Jessica kneeling beside the still body of her father. Slipping the gun into his jacket pocket, he knelt and shone the torch on to Kulek's face. The blind man had the look of death on him, his eyes narrow slits through which only the whites showed, his mouth partially opened, a faint, empty smile on his lips. Bishop frowned, for he could see no outward physical signs of injury. He probed the skin beneath Kulek's jawline with two rigid fingers and was surprised to find the pulse fluttering weakly.

'He's alive,' he told Jessica and her sobs subsided. She slipped her arm beneath her father's head, raising him slightly from the paving. The blood from his skull began to flow freely.

Bishop became aware that the driver and Edith had joined them.

'Dead?' the policeman asked brutally.

He shook his head. 'Unconscious. His skull may have been fractured.' Bishop took a handkerchief from his pocket and helped Jessica place it against the wound; the cloth immediately became a soggy, red mess. But Kulek moved and a murmuring came from his parted lips.

Jessica called his name, touching his cheek with her free hand and, for a moment, his eyelids flickered as though he were going to open them.

The policeman crouched low and said urgently, 'We've got to get going, Bishop, it's too dangerous to stay here.'

Bishop stood, passing the torch over to Edith who had replaced him by Kulek's side. Although still bewildered by her surroundings, she had the presence of mind to loosen the blind man's tie and shirt collar.

'We shouldn't move him,' Bishop said to the policeman in soft tones so Jessica could not hear. 'We don't know how badly he's hurt. Fortunately, most of the glass was out of the windscreen, but he must have gone through the opening with some force. Either the top of the car or the concrete pavement must have . . .'

The policeman cut in, 'We've got no choice – we'll have to carry him. We'll need to find some other transport to get us away from here.'

'There are plenty of parked cars around, but how can you get one started?'

'That's no problem – it's just a matter of jumping the wires. I'm going . . .'

This time it was the policeman who was interrupted as the revving of an engine came to their ears. They turned and looked back in the direction from which they had come. Probing headlights lit up the street throwing elongated shadows from the many figures making towards the wreck.

'They're coming for us,' Bishop said quietly.

The sound of the lorry's engine grew to a roar as it began to gather speed, several of the walking people silently disappearing beneath its wheels as if they were unaware of the vehicle's presence, even when they were crushed. Bishop and the policeman guessed the driver's intention.

'Get back into the building!' the policeman ordered the two kneeling women. Jessica opened her mouth to protest, but quickly saw what was happening. Bishop and the driver reached down for the injured man, pushing the two women towards the swing doors just beyond the lifts in the entrance hall. They roughly pulled Kulek towards the doors, a hand each beneath his shoulders, allowing the rest of his body to drag along the floor.

The whole of the entrance became bright as the lorry drew nearer, the driver beginning to angle his vehicle towards the block of flats and the wreck in its forecourt. Jessica and Edith pushed at the yellow swingdoors; they were stiff and opened only slightly. The women used their shoulders and swung the doors wide, holding them open for the two men to drag Kulek through.

'Use the gun!' the policeman shouted. 'Try and get the bastard before he reaches us!' Bishop let go of the injured man and ran back to the entrance, drawing the Smith and Wesson from his pocket. The lights were blinding once more and he kept his eyes narrowed against the glare. With both hands curled around the butt of the gun he took careful aim, amazed at his own coolness, knowing he had to somehow divert the lorry – if it hit the entrance square on, the impetus would easily carry much of the bodywork straight through to the rear stairwell. He aimed the gun at a point just above and slightly to the right of one circle of light, to where he hoped the driver would be. The vehicle was no more than seventy yards away, going into a sharp turn that would bring it head on across the forecourt towards the entrance. Fifty yards away. Bishop squeezed the trigger.

Nothing happened. Forty yards.

He resisted the urge to run and fumbled at the safety catch. Thirty yards. Squeeze. Recoil. Three times.

One of the headlights went out. Glass shattered. The lorry came on. Bishop ran.

He threw himself at the swingdoors that Jessica and the medium held open and heard the explosion of metal against concrete behind, his fully-stretched body sliding on the tiled flooring and tipping over the few steps leading down to the building's rear exit. The two women fell away from the released doors which were slowly closing, covering their faces with their hands, more against the horrendous tearing noise than the flying wreckage. As Bishop rolled on to his back, the building itself seemed to jolt and he saw something bulky shoot from the cabin of the lorry and scrape itself along one wall of the entrance, leaving a large smear of red as it went. It smashed against the swingdoors, an arm becoming trapped between them, preventing them from closing completely. Bishop just had time to see the driver's bloody face peering at them through the reinforced glass, his neck propped up at an impossible angle, before flames billowed out and filled the entrance in a great, leaping ball of fire.

He drew his knees up and covered his head as a blast of hot air swept through the partially open doors; for a moment he thought he was alight, but the searing feeling quickly passed as the air was funnelled up the stairwell. Cautiously raising his head once more, he looked over the top of the three stairs he had fallen down and saw the flames had retreated, but the burning cabin of the lorry completely blocked the entrance. The hallway was filled with chunks of twisted metal, much of it smouldering and black, and the vehicle had struck the entrance at an angle, totally destroying the crashed Granada. Edith Metlock had fallen to one side of the swingdoors and had been protected by the solid wall facing the stairway leading to the upper floors. The police driver was half-sitting against the exit doors, the body of Kulek sprawled beside him.

Bishop put the gun back into his pocket and crouched beside Jessica whose legs were stretched out on the lower two steps. He helped her into a sitting position and when she saw the burning lorry in the entrance, she clung to him. His fingers sank into the soft hair at the back of her neck and he held her to him, her small, trembling body feeling vulnerable to his touch.

She pulled her head away from him and looked quickly around. She found her father and tore herself away. Kulek's eyes were fully open now and confusion was clear on his face, which was bathed in a flickering warm glow from the fire. His mouth opened and closed as if he were trying to speak, but no words came.

Bishop rose to his feet and pushed at the exit doors. They were locked.

The policeman looked up at him. 'Don't worry about them – we might be better off staying inside this building.'

'But the fire.'

'It won't spread. They built these blocks of flats to contain any fires. Let's get upstairs and find a phone – at least they shouldn't be affected by the power cut. We'll get some help sent to us.' He eased himself into a standing position, keeping his grip on the blind man. 'Right, let's get him up.'

Together, they managed to get Kulek on his feet. 'Jacob, can you hear me?' said Bishop.

Kulek slowly nodded, a hand trying to reach behind his head.

'It's all right. You've had a bad knock. We're going to try and get into a flat upstairs and find some help.

The old man nodded, then managed to say his daughter's name.

'I'm here, Father.' She had found another handkerchief or a piece of cloth from somewhere and was holding it against the wound on Kulek's head. Fortunately, the blood was not flowing as badly as before.

Bishop put his shoulder beneath Kulek's arm, grasping the wrist around his neck, his other arm around the blind man's waist. 'Can you walk?'

Kulek took a tentative step forward, Bishop holding him tightly. The policeman held his other arm, supporting him, and between them they managed to get the blind man up the first three steps. Edith came forward from the corner she had been crouching in.

'Lead the way,' Bishop told her. 'Upstairs to the first floor.'

They half-carried, half-dragged the weak form of Kulek up the stairs, going fast, thankful that the lorry was partially blocking the entrance to the flats, the flames preventing anyone from passing through any gaps. Neither Bishop nor the policeman had forgotten the approaching figures.

The fire from below lapped over the balcony of the first floor, so they decided to continue upwards to the second. Edith led the way down the short hallway to the open landing, a four-foot high balcony running in either direction along the length of the building. The block of flats seemed comparatively small against normal high-rise buildings. There were only three apartments to each floor and as yet they did not know how many floors there were, but Bishop guessed there were probably nine or ten. There were two flats on the landing to the left of the short hallway, one to the right. The policeman helped Bishop prop Kulek against the balcony, then hurried along to the single flat on their right. While he banged on the door, Bishop looked down into the forecourt and street below.

Smoke rising from the burning wreck stung his eyes and he quickly drew back, but not before he had seen the people standing just beyond the ring of light thrown by the flames. Their faces were turned upwards as though watching him.

'Police. Come on, open up in there!' the driver was calling through the door's letter-box.

Bishop left Jessica steadying her father with Edith helping her, and hurried over to the irate policeman.

'There's someone in there,' he said, turning to Bishop, 'but they're too scared to open the bloody door.'

'Have they said anything?'

'No, but I can hear them moving around.' He put his face to the letter-box again. 'Look, it's the police – we're not going to hurt you.' He rattled the flap when no reply came.

Bishop looked back over the balcony and did not like what he saw. The flames below seemed to have lost much of their intensity; soon they would be low enough for those waiting to get through to the stairs. And although they were only shadowy blurs, there were many more people down there than he had at first thought.

'Let's try another flat,' he said hastily to the policeman.

'Yeah, I think you're right; wasting our bloody time here.' He stooped for one more try. 'Look, if you won't let us in, at least call Emergency. Ask for the police *and* an ambulance – we've got an injured man here. My name's Simpson, driver to Detective Chief Inspector Peck. Got that? Chief Inspector Peck. Tell them I've got Jacob Kulek with me and to send immediate assistance. Please do it!'

He rose once more, shaking his head. 'Let's hope they listened.'

'Let's hope they've got a phone,' Bishop replied, leaving the policeman staring after him as he returned to the two women and Kulek.

'Shit,' Simpson said to himself, then followed Bishop, 'Let's get up to the next floor,' he said. 'These other buggers won't open their doors now they know their neighbours wouldn't.'

This time Jessica helped Bishop move her father as Edith and the policeman led the way, the medium shining the torch ahead of them in the darkened stairwell. On the next landing, Simpson went to the first door on their left and rattled the letter-box.

'Hello in there. This is the police. Open up, please.'

They leaned the injured man against the wall in the hallway, Bishop reluctant to be seen by the victims below.

'Edith, bring me the torch,' he called out softly, and the medium left the policeman to come round to them. 'Shine it on Jacob; let's see how he is.'

He looked a hundred years old, his face drawn and pale, the lines in his skin somehow more deeply etched than before. His sightless eyes blinked against the light, but there seemed to be little thought behind them. Bishop knew by the way his tall but frail body sagged that he would collapse without their support. Just how badly he was hurt, there was still no way of knowing; he had known men to be conscious even with a fractured skull. Yet, it seemed impossible that Kulek could even be semi-conscious after being tossed through the windscreen with such obvious force.

'Father, can you hear me?' Jessica anxiously bit her lips when she received no reply, and looked across at Bishop pleadingly.

'He's a strong man, Jessica. He'll be okay once we get him to a hospital. Hold him, Edith, while I see how Simpson is getting on.' Bishop really wanted to find out what was happening below without alarming the two women. Allowing the medium to slide into his position without losing grip on Kulek, he turned the corner, then peered warily over the balcony. The area of light below had become smaller, the blaze on the lorry and the Granada having become several separate, weaker fires rather than one large inferno. The ring of waiting people had drawn closer. Bishop shuddered at the thought, but it seemed as though these people knew who had been in the Granada, knew that Jacob Kulek was in the block of flats. Was it possible? Was there some telepathy between them and the Dark? This strange force possessed and directed them; did it really have an intelligence?

Someone stepped into the area of light below and looked directly up at him; it was a woman and there was something vaguely familiar about her. He reached for the spectacles he used for driving, pulling them from his breast pocket and slipping them on. For the first time that night, anger became more dominant than his fear. It was her, the tall woman, the one who had helped kill his wife. His fingers tightened around the balcony rail and for one wild moment he wanted to run back down the stairs and throttle the life from her. How had she known where to find them? Had it been what Pryszlak had wanted all this time – to trap them in an inescapable area of darkness? And why? Was it just revenge on a man who had refused to help him so many years before? Or was Jacob Kulek a threat? The questions flooded his mind, but they remained mere questions, for he had no answers at all.

'Someone's coming!'

The policeman's voice brought Bishop back to the situation behind him.

'Will you open the door please?' Simpson said, this time keeping any harsh authority from his request. 'There's nothing to be afraid of. I just want to use your telephone if you have one. Look, I'll put my identification card through the letter-box, then you can examine it under any light you've got in there.' He lifted the letter-box and slid his wallet through. 'Okay. Now please have a look at it, then let me in. We've got an injured man out here and we've got no time to waste.'

Bishop could just see a vague shape through the window next to the flat's hallway, in a room that was probably the kitchen. It moved from view and again there seemed to be movement behind the reeded glass of the hall door.

Simpson looked across at Bishop and said, 'I think we're in luck this time.'

There were noises inside, a bolt being drawn back, a door-chain being loosened. Finally the lock turned and the door opened fractionally. Bishop thought he could see a face peering out at them, but it disappeared when the policeman moved closer.

'Hello?' Simpson said. 'Don't be alarmed, no one's going to hurt you.' He reached towards the door and gave it a gentle shove. It opened a little wider and he poked his head into the gap. 'Have you got a phone?' Bishop heard him say.

The policeman pushed the door all the way open and stepped into the blackness of the hallway. For a moment, Bishop lost sight of him; then he appeared again, backing out of the doorway. He slowly turned, his eyes looking pleadingly at Bishop, who now saw the hilt of the carving knife protruding from a point just below the policeman's rib-cage. Simpson sank down the door-frame to the floor, one leg buckling awkwardly under him, the other sprawling outwards so he was propped there. His head gently lowered itself to his chest and Bishop knew he had died.

The shock had dulled Bishop's reactions, for he was not even reaching for the gun in his jacket pocket when the figure came lurching out of the blackness. He reached up automatically to ward off the thin clutching hands. The glasses he had just donned were knocked away, the lenses having prevented his eyes from being raked by sharp-nailed fingers. The creature he struggled with hissed and spat at him and he realized that it was an old woman. Her wrists felt brittle in his grasp and although she only had the feeble strength of the aged, she fought with an intensity that was frightening. She pushed him back so that his shoulders were over the balcony, her fingers curling closed then open like talons. It was Jessica who ended the battle by coming up behind the old woman, reaching both arms around the scraggy neck, and pulling her away from Bishop. He felt no remorse when he clenched his fist and struck the ranting woman's jaw as hard as he could; to him, she was no longer a human being, just a shell, a host for an energy that was pure evil. She gave a sharp cry and staggered from Jessica's grip, falling backwards over the sprawled leg of Simpson into her own hallway. Her head cracked against the wall inside and she went down in a heap, her body crumpled like a bundle of old rags.

Bishop had to draw Jessica away from the still form of the policeman and she moaned softly as she leaned against him.

'How many, Chris? How many more will it take?'

He was afraid to reply for the answer depended on how much evil existed and in how many minds. Who knew what dark thoughts a friend, neighbour or brother kept hidden? And who didn't possess such thoughts? He led her back to Edith and her father.

'Let me have the torch, Edith. I want you to wait for me here while I search the woman's flat for a phone.'

'Can't we lock ourselves in there?' said Jessica. 'We'd be safe, wouldn't we?'

'If I can call the police from there, maybe.' He hesitated before deciding to tell them the truth of the situation. 'There's a crowd down in the forecourt – I think they want us, or at least, Jacob. It wouldn't take them long to break down the door or smash the windows. We'd be trapped.'

'But why should they want my father?'

It was Edith Metlock who answered. 'Because they fear him.'

Both Bishop and Jessica looked at her in surprise, but the sounds of footsteps prevented any further questions. Someone was coming along the landing from the single flat on the other side of the hallway; a faint glow preceded the footsteps. Bishop pulled the revolver from his jacket pocket, and pointed it towards the approaching light, hoping there were still bullets left in the chamber. The man peered cautiously around the corner, holding the candle well before him. He was dazzled by the torchlight.

'What's goin on ere?' He blinked his eyes against the light.

Bishop relaxed slightly; the man seemed normal enough. 'Step out where I can see you,' he said.

'What's that – a gun?' The man raised the long, iron bar he was carrying.

'It's all right,' Bishop assured him. 'No one's going to harm you. We need some help.'

'Oh yeah? Well put the gun down first, mate.'

Bishop lowered the pistol, holding it by his side, ready to be raised if necessary.

'What appened to the old lady? I saw her run out at you from me door.'

'She killed a policeman who was with us.'

'Bloody ell. I'm not surprised though – she was always a bit crazy. What did you do with her?'

'She's unconscious.' He decided not to tell the man she was probably dead. 'Can you help us?'

'No, mate. I'm looking after meself and the family, that's all. Any bastard who comes through my front door cops this.' He brandished the iron bar in the air. 'I don't know what's goin on lately, but I ain't trustin no one.'

'My father's hurt, can't you see that?' Jessica pleaded. 'You've got to help us.'

There was a short silence, but the man had made up his mind. 'I'm sorry about that, miss, but I don't know who you are or what you are. There's too many nutters around for me to take any chances. I mean, who crashed the bleedin lorry down there, for a start? Thought the buildin was coming down.'

'We were being chased.'

'Oh yeah? Who by?'

Bishop was beginning to grow irritated by the man's doubting attitude. 'Look, we wanted to use that woman's telephone. That's what I'm going to do now.'

'You'll be lucky: she ain't got one.'

'What about you? Have you got one?'

The man was still cautious. 'Yeah, but I ain't lettin you in.'

Bishop raised the gun once more.

'I'll av you with this first, mate,' the man warned, holding the iron bar in front of him.

'Okay,' Bishop said resignedly, knowing it was pointless to argue; any man who thought he could beat a bullet with an iron bar either had to be very dim or very sure of himself. 'Will you ring the police for us? Tell them where we are and that Jacob Kulek is with us. We need help urgently.'

'They're likely to be a bit busy, aren't they?'

'I think they'll make the effort. Just remember to tell them Jacob Kulek is here.'

'Kulek. Right.'

'Tell them to get here fast – there's a mob downstairs after us.'

The man took a quick peep over the balcony. 'Oh my Gawd,' he said.

'Will you do it?' Bishop persisted.

'All right, mate, I'll get on to em. You ain't comin in though.'

'Just keep your door locked and barricade yourself in. You should be okay – it's us they want.'

The man backed away, the iron bar still pointed forward, his eyes never leaving the group in the hallway. They heard his front door close and the bolt being drawn.

'Nice to see the old blitz spirit coming back,' Bishop remarked wearily.

'You shouldn't blame him,' said Edith. 'There must be millions like him, totally confused by what's going on. He has no reason to trust us.'

'Let's hope he at least rings the police.' Bishop glanced towards the balcony and saw the glow from the fire had dimmed considerably. 'We'd better move on,' he said to the two women.

'Where can we go to?' Jessica asked. 'We can't get out.'

Bishop pointed upwards.'There's only one place to go. The roof.'

Inside the flat, the man was trying to calm his terrified family. 'It's all right, it was just some people in trouble – nothin for us to worry about.'

'What are they doin ere, Fred?' his wide-eyed wife asked, clutching her ten-year-old daughter to her. 'Were they in that crash downstairs?'

'I dunno. They wanted me to get the police.'

'Are you goin to?'

'I'll av a go, won't do no arm.'

He pushed past his wife and entered the sitting-room, walking over to the telephone resting on a sideboard. 'Keith!' he called back to his teenage son, 'get something up against the door – somethin solid.' He laid down the iron bar and leaned close to the telephone, using the candle to see the dial.

He let it ring for a full two minutes before replacing the receiver. 'Would you believe it?' he said incredulously to his wife who had followed him into the room. 'It's bloody engaged. Their lines must be jammed solid. Either that or they're out of order.'

He shook his head regretfully. 'Looks like those poor beggars out there are on their own.'

TWENTY-NINE

They had only reached the sixth or seventh floor – Bishop had lost count – when they heard footsteps on the stairs below.

He leaned against the rail, gasping for breath, trying to listen. Jacob Kulek was now over his shoulder in a fireman's lift, and with each step Bishop took, the blind man seemed to grow heavier.

'They're in the building.' He looked into the blackness below and could see nothing. The acrid smell of smoke from the burning wreck seemed to fill the stairwell even though it was apparent that the worst of the fire was over.

Edith Metlock shone the torchbeam downwards and they saw what looked like tiny white creatures sliding upwards along the stair rails; they soon recognized the shapes as the hands of ascending people, the rest of their bodies hidden by the overhanging staircases. It was an eerie sight, for the hands seemed to be disembodied, a nightmare army of marching claws.

'We'll never make it!' Jessica cried. 'They'll catch us before we reach the top!'

'No, they're moving slowly – we've still got a chance.' Bishop pushed himself upright again, adjusting the weight of the semi-conscious man on his shoulder. 'Take the gun from my pocket, Jessica. If they get too close, use it!'

They went onwards, Edith leading the way, shining the torch ahead of them. Bishop felt his legs weakening, his body slumping more and more under the load. His teeth bit into his lower lip with the effort and the muscles in his back protested their agony. They reached another floor and he fell to his knees, unable to stop himself. Kulek slid from his shoulder and Jessica just caught her father's upper body before it touched concrete. Bishop drew in sharp breaths, his chest heaving. He leaned his head against the bars of the stair rail, his face wet with perspiration.

'How far down are they?' he asked between gasps.

Edith shone the torch downwards once more. 'Three floors below us,' she said quietly.

He grabbed the rail and jerked himself to his feet. 'Help me,' he said, reaching down for Kulek.

'No.' Kulek's eyes were open and he was pushing himself into a sitting position. 'I can walk. Just get me to my feet.'

The way in which the blind man was drifting in and out of consciousness was somehow more worrying to Bishop than if he had just remained unconscious. Kulek groaned aloud and clutched at his stomach as they lifted him. His body was stiff as he forced himself upright.

'I'll be all right,' he reassured Jessica as she held on to him. A trembling hand reached for Bishop's shoulder. 'If you will just bear my weight,' he said.

Bishop slipped the blind man's arm around his own neck and they turned the bend to the next flight of stairs. They began to climb and he felt Kulek wince at every step. 'Not far, Jacob,' Bishop said. 'We're nearly at the top.'

Kulek hadn't the strength to reply.

'LEAVE HIM, BISHOP. HE'S NO USE TO YOU NOW!'

They froze on the staircase as the words spiralled upwards. It was a woman's voice, and Bishop knew it was the tall woman, the one called Lillian.

'He's dying, can't you see that?' The words were no longer shouted, echoing up from the stairwell like a hissed whisper. 'Why be hindered by a dead man. Leave him, otherwise you'll never escape us. We don't want you, Bishop; just him.'

As Bishop stared down into the blackness, he knew the Dark was all around them, carried in the night air like some invisible parasite. He could feel its coldness caressing his skin, freezing the beads of perspiration into tiny globules of ice. He saw pale blurs that were faces in the black pit below.

'Leave him. Leave him,' other voices inside his head told him. 'He's no use to you. An encumbrance. A dead weight. You'll die if you keep him with you.'

His grip tightened on the rail. He could make it without Kulek. He could get on the roof. They wouldn't be able to reach him there. He could hold them off.

A rough hand snapped his head around. 'Don't listen, Chris.' The torchlight stung his eyes as Edith Metlock spoke sharply to him. 'I can hear the voices. They want me to help them, too. Don't you see? It's the Dark – the voices are trying to confuse us. We must go on, Chris.'

'I hear them,' said Jessica. 'They want me to shoot you, Chris. They keep telling me you're leading my father into worse danger.'

'BISHOP, IT'S NOT TOO LATE – YOU CAN JOIN US!' the tall woman screamed. 'YOU CAN BE PART OF US!'

'Take the light out of my eyes, Edith,' he said, turning away from the stairwell.

Both women sighed with relief and, once more, they resumed their arduous climb. The footsteps below grew louder, became more hurried. Through sheer willpower, Bishop increased his own speed, almost lifting the injured man clear of the steps and dragging him upwards. They reached the next floor, turned the bend, began the next flight upwards. But the footsteps were drawing closer, running, scrabbling up the staircase, other sounds accompanying them, noises that could have come from frenzied animals. They were now below the floor

Bishop and the others had just left, scurrying up from the darkness like creatures climbing out from hell.

Jessica felt weak with fear. She pushed her back against the wall, her legs still climbing, but her movement slow. She held her arm out rigid, pointing the gun towards the terrible scuffling noises that were drawing closer and closer.

A light appeared at a point between her and those approaching, growing stronger, beginning to fill the darkness in the bend of the stairs. Cold air blew in from the landing as the swing-doors were pushed open, and suddenly there were voices, more lights adding to the brightness of the first.

'Who's down there?' a gruff voice demanded to know.

'Look, Harry, there's someone up there on the stairs,' another voice said.

Jessica was suddenly bathed in bright light.

'Christ, she's got a gun!' the same voice exclaimed.

Edith, who had been concealed around the bend halfway up to the next floor, quickly descended a few steps and shone her torch towards the voices.

A group of men and women stood in the entrance to that particular landing staring up at Jessica and now her. They were obviously neighbours who had banded together for safety when the power had been cut.

'Go back!' Edith called out to them. 'For your own safety, go back into your homes and lock yourselves in!'

Someone pushed past the first man in the doorway. 'You tell us what's goin on first, lady.' His flashlight was powerful and threw out a wide, undefined beam. 'What's this girl got a gun for?'

'They must've had something to do with the crash downstairs,' another voice murmured.

Bishop was close to Edith, but still out of sight of the people below. 'Shine the torch down the stairs, Edith,' he whispered. 'Show them the mob coming up.'

The medium leaned over the rail and did as he said. The figures crouching below were suddenly lit up.

'There's more of em down there!' All the lights were pointed downwards and the people on the stairs covered their eyes, moaning in pain.

'Jesus, look at that lot. They're all the way down the stairs.'

One of the men cowering under the glare began to creep upwards, keeping his head tucked down. Another man followed, moving in similar fashion.

'They're coming up!' a woman's voice screamed out.

The man carrying the flashlight stepped forward, descending a few steps and bringing a heavy boot down hard on the creeping figure, sending it reeling backwards. 'I've had enough of this,' was his only comment.

All hell seemed to break loose at that point. Other men and women who had come to a halt on the stairs suddenly surged forward, shielding their eyes from the light, shrieking their demented cries, and swamping the man who had been foolhardy enough to defy them. His friends ran forward to help and more lights appeared on the floors below and above, almost as though a signal had been given for many of the residents to venture out from their separate flats, curiosity overcoming their previous caution. Many rushed back indoors as soon as they saw the people on the stairs, while others decided enough was enough: if the Law wouldn't do anything about intruders, then they, the residents would. Perhaps they would have stood more chance in the confused and brutal battle that ensued if a number of their own neighbours had not already succumbed to the Dark as they had waited in the blackout. The residents of the tower block had no way of telling who was friend and who was foe.

The swingdoors on the floor above Bishop opened and lights were flashed through it. He grabbed Edith's arm and said, 'Get Jessica – we're going on.'

The medium did not bother to protest, for she saw his logic: the roof – if they could get on to it – was still the safest place to be. She reached Jessica and pulled her upwards, leading her around the bend in the stairs, catching up with Bishop and Kulek. They reached the next floor and the people waiting there watched them curiously.

'You'd better lock yourselves in until the police get here,' Bishop told them. 'Don't try to fight those people downstairs – there are too many.'

They looked at him as though it were he who was mad, then peered down into the confusion of sounds and flashing lights below. He didn't bother to see if they had taken his advice, but kept onwards, the cool air that was rushing in through the open doors helping to revive him. Kulek was trying to help their ascent, his legs moving haltingly over each step, his thin frame trembling with the exertion.

'We're nearly there, Jacob. Just a little further.' Bishop could almost feel the remaining dregs of strength draining from the blind man. Kulek's left arm was tightly clamped against his stomach.

Jessica cried out in relief when she saw that the stairs ran out on the floor above: they had nearly reached the top of the building. Her arm encircled her father's waist and she pulled and lifted with Bishop, urging her father on to the last flight of stairs. Edith's steps were heavy, her breathing laboured. It had been a long climb and her body was in no condition for such stern exercise. One plump hand grasped the stair rail and dragged the rest of her body forward, the movement slow, the effort exhausting. Not far, she kept telling herself, not far now, a few more steps, just a few.

The man who waited for them at the top was the caretaker of the flats. He lived, in fact, on the ground floor, but earlier that evening had gone up to the tenth floor of the building to give a warning to the elderly couple who lived there. He had warned them before – or at least, he had warned the old man. The Council did not, *absolutely* did not allow urinating in the lifts. The old man had always denied it had been him, blaming it on the kids who roamed the estate, vandalizing property, making the lives of the residents miserable. The little bastards broke windows, scribbled graffiti four-foot high on walls, and generally created pandemonium up and down the stairs. The lifts were a particular source of joy to them and the all-too-frequent breakdowns were due to the kids tampering with the buttons, blocking the closing doors, opening the doors between floors, or jumping up and down while the lifts were in motion. Certainly, they messed in the lifts, but they were not the main culprits of this misdemeanour. Oh no, the old man had a lot to answer for in this respect. Why they put elderly people at the top of these flats, God only knew. When the lifts were out, either through the misdoings of vandals, the normal and not infrequent mechanical malfunctions, or – as was the case tonight – general power failures, these old folk were stranded. Another problem – and this was the relevant one – the two lifts had been engineered to move slowly, for too swift ascents and descents scared the life out of the residents. If you were aged, and if you liked to drink a lot, and if your bladder was no longer the sturdy water carrier it used to be, then a trip up in the lift could take a lifetime. Unfortunately, the old man was well past his prime, and had a weak bladder. Other residents had complained more than once that the lift doors had opened revealing the old boy standing in a puddle of liquid. The way in which he always doffed his hat and bid them a pleasant good day or evening could never disguise the foul smell of piss as he swayed past them. The caretaker had warned him three or four times so far, ignoring the protested denials, and now he would warn the old lady as well. Either she kept reign on him, or they were out. O.U.T. No nonsense. No more pissing in the lift. Putting up with the other tenants with their carping complaints about the heating, the plumbing, the vandalism, the rent, the lifts, the refuse collectors, the noise and their neighbours, was bad enough, but having to mop up the mess left by some incontinent old imbecile was too much. Sometimes the caretaker fantasized about planting a time bomb in one corner of the tower block, setting it for one-thirty and retreating to the pub further down the road, sitting there with his pint of bitter, checking the second hand of his watch as it crept up to the thirty minute mark, chomping on his veal-and-ham pie, studying the building through the pub window, ordering a fresh pint, having a joke with the landlord as the fatal seconds ticked away; then the lovely bang, the floors of the tower block crumbling like playing cards or like those films you see of industrial chimneys being demolished, blown up at the base so the bricks tumbled down in a straight line, the structure resembling a telescope closing in on itself. All those tenants off his back once and for all, no more complaints, no more running around after them. All crushed, all dead. Lovely.

The caretaker had been halfway up when the lights went out and the lift came to a shuddering halt. He had groped around in total darkness, cursing loudly as his index finger finally found the alarm button. He hoped his silly mare of a wife would hear it in their ground-floor flat, but after ten minutes of constantly stabbing at the button and banging on the metal walls of the lift, he decided the breakdown was probably due to something other than just mechanical failure in the drive motor. Bloody power cut, he told himself.

It had been creepy sitting there in the dark, sightless and unseen. Yet it was strangely comforting, like being back inside the womb, still unborn and still untouched. *Or like being dead, nothing for companionship but nothingness.* Soon, though, he had found he was not completely alone in the darkness.

After a while, the caretaker had forced open the lift door and, feeling with his hands, had discovered he was almost on the next floor, the step-up no more than three feet. Opening the shaft door which would let him out into the hallway beyond was a little more difficult, but he persisted, summoning up the reserves of strength the voices inside his head told him he had. The strange thing was that once you knew you could do something, it became easier to do.

He had continued his journey to the top of the building, using the stairs, no longer bothered by the blackness around him. The wind had howled around him when he had pulled open the swingdoors to the tenth floor landing, but he was grinning as he walked the length of the short hallway, then round to his right to the old couple's flat. They hadn't wanted to open the door at first, and he'd had to insist, telling them it was official business. The old lady had been the first to go and for her he had made use of the broom she kept in the hall of the flat, knocking her down, then forcing the broomhandle into her throat as far as it would go, blocking it so she could not draw in air. He had taken his time with the old man who had not tried to help his wife, but had cowered in his bedroom beneath his bed. The caretaker had merely laughed as he splashed through the foul-smelling puddle that was spreading out from under the bed, and had dragged the old boy out, enjoying the croaking screams as he hauled him back down the hallway and into the kitchen where so many innocent implements of death were waiting. Unfortunately, his victim's heart had given out before he could finish the job, but at least it had been pleasurable up until that final moment. No more pissing in the lifts for the old boy any more. No more pissing.

The caretaker had sat on the floor next to the warm corpse and continued to enjoy himself, free now to do whatever he pleased, free to indulge in new, forbidden experiences. The freedom tasted good. The sound of the crashing lorry came not long after and the sky outside briefly flared orange. The caretaker selected one of the bloodied kitchen tools he had been using and walked out on to the landing. He stood at the top of the stairs and waited.

Edith Metlock sensed his presence before she saw him. She was nearly at the top of the stairs when she stopped, her mind abruptly cutting out the screams, shouts and sounds of struggle below, to direct itself toward what lay ahead. One hand still gripping the iron stair rail and one knee resting on a step, she slowly shone the torch upwards – slowly because she dreaded what the beam would reveal, an inner sense fearing the worst – and found the man's legs, his knees, his waist. He was dressed in the blue overalls of a workman and, as the torch beam came higher, she saw he was holding a stained, short-bladed chopper across his chest, the kind used in a kitchen for chopping meat; and as the beam reached higher still, she saw he was grinning, only his teeth were red, and his mouth was red, and the redness ran down his chin and she now noticed it had splashed on to his overalls. She knew he was insane, for what normal person would eat raw meat. He came down a step and she screamed.

The first swing of the small chopper missed because he was blinded by the light, but the second scythed across the arm she had put up to protect herself. The whole of her arm went numb, as though it had been struck with a hammer and not a sharp instrument; she tumbled backwards, the torch in her other hand, sending its beam careering upwards, then around the walls as she fell. Bishop used his body to block her descent, gripping the handrail tight and still maintaining his hold on Kulek. His legs nearly went from beneath him with the medium's weight, but he managed to steady them. She had collapsed sideways on the stairs, her stout legs sprawled across one step, her body against the uprights of the stair rail; mercifully, she had not released the torch. Sure she would fall no further and sure he had regained his own balance, Bishop quickly snatched the torch from her grasp and pointed it upwards again. The man was slowly walking down, his grin made even more obscene by the sticky blood around his lips and on his teeth. The weapon was held high over his head, poised to strike.

Bishop tried to back away, but encumbered by Kulek's limp body, movement was awkward. Edith clawed at the man's legs, grabbing his overalls and tugging, trying to overbalance him. It was no use; the man was too strong.

The chopper was already swinging downwards when the bullet shattered his breastbone, the blast from the .38 made even more thunderous by the concrete walls around them. The caretaker screamed and fell backwards, the chopper dropping from his hand and slithering harmlessly off Edith Metlock's sprawled body. He turned over and tried to crawl away from them, but his legs kicked out spasmodically before he reached the top step and he slid back down, bumping Jessica as he passed her on the stairs. The gun was still pointing at the empty space where the caretaker had stood when she shot him, smoke curling from the barrel, the smell of cordite heavy in the air. The noises below had ceased as though the single, reverberating blast had stopped all action. Bishop knew the silence wouldn't last.

With one hand, he helped Edith to her feet, catching a glimpse of the cut in her lower arm as he did so. It was a long wound, just below her elbow, stretching from one side to the other, apparently not too deep, for she seemed to have no trouble in using her arm. He pushed her in the direction of the landing above and followed, almost lifting Kulek with him. He gently sat the blind man down with his back against the swingdoors. The stairs ended on a small landing, separated from the short hallway leading to the other side of the building by the yellow swingdoors. The iron stair rail ran off to the left making the small landing Bishop was on a balcony overlooking the steep stairwell. At the end was a door, which he assumed was the fire exit to the stairs for anyone living in the top flats on that side of the hallway. He saw what he was looking for when he shone the torch towards the ceiling: a large trapdoor was housed there, the metal ladder leading to it running down the wall opposite the balcony railings. A wooden plank was chained and padlocked to the ladder, top and bottom, a simple device to prevent children or trespassers from climbing up to the roof.

The sounds of battle began again and he ran down the few steps to Jessica. He had to prise the gun away from her clenched fingers and forcibly drag her past the spot where the overalled man had been standing.

'See to your father, Jessica,' he said harshly, shoving her towards Kulek. He knew the killing had sent her into a state of shock and the only way to bring her out of it was to occupy her mind with other problems; after all they had been through, it would be too easy for her to crack completely. Jessica knelt beside her father and cradled him in her arms.

Bishop shone the torch on to the lower retaining chain on the ladder, tugging at it to feel its strength. He was surprised when it fell away in his hand; someone – kids probably – had already worked on one of the links, cutting through it, but leaving it in position until they had cut loose the chain near the top of the ladder. The second chain was just within reaching distance, too high for smaller children, but easy enough for the caretaker or maintenance men to get at. He gripped the chain and pulled. It held.

Bishop swore. Should they use the fire escape door and get into one of the flats beyond? No, they'd be trapped in there; a determined mob could easily force their way in. The roof had to be the best bet – an army could be held off from that position. He had to break the chain somehow, or bust the padlock; the gun he was holding would do it.

'Edith, get over by Jessica!'

The medium quickly did as she was told, realizing his intent. Bishop moved around so his body was between the three crouching figures and the target he was aiming at. He half-turned his head, keeping his eyes narrowed, praying there would not be a ricochet. The sound of shattered metal was smothered in the blast and the deflected bullet spun onwards, thudding into the wall just above the fire escape door. The chain fell to the floor and the wooden plank toppled away from the ladder, bouncing against, then resting on, the railing opposite. Bishop wasted no time; he climbed the ladder and pushed at the trapdoor. It would not budge.

He slipped the gun into his pocket and used the torch to examine the trapdoor; a small hole was set into a metal square at a point near the ladder. The caretaker obviously had a special key to allow access for himself and any authorized person.

'Edith, quickly – hold the torch!'

She reached up and took the torch from him.

'Shine it on the lock,' he told her. His ears were still ringing from the previous gunshot, but he was sure he could hear footsteps mounting the stairs once more. He jammed the .38 up against the lock, having no other choice but to hope for the best. The recoil in the confined space jerked his arm downwards and scraps of metal and wood spat into his face. He clung to the ladder, his head tucked down, almost losing his grip on the rung he was holding. Then, the gun still clenched in his fist, he pushed at the trapdoor. For one dreadful moment, he thought it would not lift, but he exerted more pressure and grunted with relief when the door shifted. He climbed another rung and pushed even harder; the trapdoor swung open and came to rest against something behind it. Bishop jumped back down on to the landing.

'Up you go, Edith,' he said, once more taking the torch from her. He watched her climb, telling her to reach inside the opening for some kind of handhold. She had obviously found something, for soon she was pulling her plump body through the gap, her injured arm hardly impeding her progress. Bishop stepped up a few rungs and handed the light back to her.

'Keep it on us,' he said, then jumped down and went to Jessica and her father. 'We're going to get him up to the roof, Jessica.'

Kulek opened his eyes at the sound of Bishop's voice. 'I can make it, Chris,' he said, his words slightly slurred but still coherent. 'Just get me to my feet, will you?'

Bishop smiled grimly at the blind man's willpower. He and Jessica lifted the thin body and Kulek bit his lower lip in an effort to contain a cry of pain; something was wrong inside, something deep in his stomach had been twisted or torn. Yet he had to go on; he could not allow those creatures of the Dark to take him. Despite the weakness he felt and the pain he suffered, a thought was pounding in his brain, a thought that was struggling to surface, to sweep through his mind and . . . and what? Even as he tried to concentrate his head swam with a nauseating dizziness. The thought was close, but the barriers seemed impenetrable.

They helped him to the ladder and Bishop told Jessica to go first. 'I'll support him from down below, you try and pull him through.'

She swiftly climbed the ladder and disappeared into the black hole above. Bishop guessed there was some kind of box room built on to the flat roof of the tower block, the kind that usually housed the lift motors and drive pulleys, or water tanks. Jessica leaned her body back through the hole and reached down.

Bishop guided Kulek's hands on to the ladder and immediately knew the blind man would never make it. Kulek clung to the metal frame but did not have the strength left to move his legs. And the footsteps closing in from behind told Bishop that time was running out.

The first man was nearly at the top of the stairs, his two companions almost halfway. In the wide angle of light from the opening above, Bishop saw that all three were in a dishevelled state, a condition that had come to be recognized as belonging to the longer-term victims, those who had been affected perhaps weeks before. Their faces were black, their hands and clothes filthy and torn; no one could be sure where these people hid during the daylight hours, but it had to be somewhere dark, some place beneath the ground where nothing clean existed. The first man lurched forward, his deeply-sunk eyes fixed on Bishop, but dead and expressionless. The festering sores and scabs that corrupted his skin became clearly visible as he drew nearer.

Bishop drew the gun and pointed it at the advancing man who ignored the weapon, fearless because inside he was already dead. Bishop squeezed the trigger and the hammer clicked against an empty chamber. In panic, he tried again, knowing the gun was empty, the bullets all used.

The man spread his arms open to take him in his embrace, his eyes mere slits against the light, and Bishop struck out with the pistol, using it as a club, the blow cracking against the bridge of the creature's nose. The man still staggered forward as though the pain meant nothing to him, blood pouring from his injury and adding to the grotesqueness of his appearance. Bishop ducked beneath the clawing arms and used his shoulder against the man's chest, sending him reeling back towards the stairs. The gun was useless to him and he let it drop when he saw the only other object on the landing that could be used as a weapon. He picked up the heavy wooden plank that had been resting against the balcony rail and hurried towards the sub-human teetering at the top of the stairs, smashing it into him and pushing with all his strength. The man toppled backwards, falling on to his fellow victims, who were almost on to the landing, all three going down, their deteriorated bodies glancing off the concrete steps as they went, the heavy board following. They did not stop until they had reached the broader bend in the stairs where the tall woman stood gazing upwards.

Bishop saw her there in the gloom and hate surged through him. Again he wanted to rush down and kill her, not as punishment for what she had become, but for what she was and always had been; instead he hoisted Jacob Kulek over his shoulder and began the strenuous climb up the ladder. Just when he thought he would never make it, his last reserves of strength almost depleted, helping hands reached down and lightened his load. Jessica and Edith pulled together, grasping the blind man by his clothes, beneath his arms – anywhere they could get a grip. Bishop made one final effort and heaved upwards, almost willing the injured man into the opening, and the two women gained firmer grips, lifting Kulek's upper body through, pulling him to one side so he could not fall back. The relief to Bishop was shortlived, for other, hostile, arms were wrapping themselves around his legs and pulling him down. His feet slipped from the rungs and he fell, the people beneath him cushioning the blow. He flailed out at the bodies trying to smother him, using his arms and feet to clear some space for himself, hearing Jessica's scream from above, the sound somehow making him even more desperate.

He felt himself lifted and then knew what they were about to do; the railings of the balcony rushed to meet him and suddenly he was looking directly down into the terrifying black depths below.

THIRTY

His body was slipping from them, going over the rail, beginning to slide forward; and the receding floors below were like a square-shaped whirlpool, its dark centre eager to suck him down. He started to scream, but his own instinctive reaction took over from his petrified mind. He grabbed at the handrail that was only inches away from his face just as they released him. His body went over the top, but he maintained his grip, falling back against the other side of the rail, feet dangling in empty air. He gasped at the pain as his shoulder socket was wrenched, his fingers almost opening at the shock. In one movement he swung round and grasped a metal upright, both hands now taking his full weight. He managed to get a foot on to the sill of the landing and there he clung, pausing for brief seconds to recover his strength and senses.

A hand smashed down against his and he looked up to see the tall woman standing over him. Bishop knew who it was even though her features were in shadows, and, despite his helpless position, the anger flared once more. A man was reaching over to grab at his hair, trying to push him down, away from the rail. Bishop twisted his head, in an attempt to break the grip, but the hand merely moved with him, pushing, forcing him away. Someone else had a foot through the metal supports and was kicking at his chest, trying to dislodge him; through the fury of the attack, Bishop was vaguely aware that this third person was a young girl, no more than a teenager. Another shadowy figure, unable to reach Bishop because of the others, stood at the rail and shouted encouragement.

Bishop felt his fingers becoming numb and he knew they could not resist the constant hammering for much longer. The tall woman changed her tactics and began to prise them open one by one. His body was well away from the rail, the girl's foot forcing him outward, the man's vicious grip on his hair pushing his head backwards. The tall woman cried out in triumph as she finally broke his hold on the rail; only his grip on the upright prevented him from plunging downwards. He knew he had only seconds left.

And then Jessica was down among them, kicking and clawing, merciless in her desperation to help Bishop. She pulled the teenager away and thrust her hard against the wall, the impact stunning the girl. Then she was on the man who held Bishop's head, tearing into him and raking his face with her fingernails. He let go of Bishop and tried to grab her, but was powerless against her fierce onslaught; he fell back, his arms covering his face. Jessica had her back towards the man who had been watching and now he moved towards her, arms outstretched.

'No!' the tall woman screeched, knowing Bishop was the more dangerous. 'Help me!'

He stopped, then leaned over the rail and began to smash his fist down against the clinging man's head. The blows stunned Bishop and he did the only thing possible: he jumped.

Using his grip on the rail and his foothold to thrust himself sideways, he snaked out a hand to grab the descending stair rail to his right. He seemed to be suspended in open space for an eternity and Edith Metlock, in the hatchway overhead, closed her eyes, unable to watch the frightening leap. His fingers curled around the slanted rail as his body slammed into the uprights and the side of the concrete steps. His other hand found purchase and he pulled himself up instantly, tumbling over the stair rail with a speed that owed much to panic. Without pausing, he raced back up the stairs, reaching up for the collar of the man Jessica had been forcing backwards and who was now near the top step. Bishop pulled hard, twisting sideways as he did so, and the man hurtled past, his body only striking concrete when it was three steps from the bottom. He screamed as he made contact, then was silent as he rolled down. He came to rest in a crumpled heap among the groaning bodies of those who had fallen earlier.

Still Bishop did not stop; he was on the landing, running past Jessica and slamming his shoulder into the other man standing next to the tall woman. They both went down, but Bishop's mind was his own and he was able to move quickly. His fist smashed down into the upturned face, knocking the man's head against the concrete. Bishop dug both hands into the man's hair, then lifted the head almost a foot off the floor and pushed it back, the sickening smack telling him the man would not be a problem for a while.

Hands closed over his eyes, digging into them, and he knew it was the tall woman who was trying to tear them from their sockets. He threw his head back and the pressure eased slightly. Then he was released and, as he staggered forward on his knees, he saw that Jessica was holding the tall woman from behind, one arm around her waist, the other around one shoulder. The tall woman was too strong, too cunning; she brought an elbow sharply back, driving it into Jessica's ribs. Jessica doubled up and the woman whirled around, aiming two swift punches to her breasts. Jessica screamed and collapsed to the floor. The tall woman's eyes were hidden in the dark shadows, but Bishop could feel the hatred in them. She rushed at him like a thing possessed, her teeth bared in a snarl that was primitive, the sound ascending to a high-pitched screeching as she closed in on him.

He rose to meet her and failed to stop her clutching his throat, her strength no longer normal, her savagery no longer her own. But he remembered her evil, the horrible deaths of Agnes Kirkhope and her housekeeper, the near-killing of Jacob Kulek, the murder of the policeman. The burning of Lynn. She was the willing tool of the unclean force that was in every man, woman and child; she was its servant and its instigator, a creature who worshipped the dark side of the mind. He pushed her back against the rail, her eyes visible now, tiny black pools in muddy brown irises, shrunken apertures to something darker and boundless inside. She squeezed his throat, spittle from her open mouth splattering his face, her own neck straining forward in an attempt to tear his flesh with her bared teeth. His whole body quivered with the fury he felt and blood rushed through him, swelling veins and arteries with their torrent. Then he was liftng her, scooping her legs up in one mighty heave, the movement fast but drawn out in time so the action was slow and dreamlike. Higher, her back on the rail, her shriek becoming that of fear, her hold on him loosening. Higher until she was tilted over the black void as he had been earlier. Higher until the balance was drawing her down. Then her body slipped from his grasp and she was screaming and flailing at the air as she plummeted, bouncing against the sides of stairs, an arm snapping, a leg torn from the hip, her back breaking even before she disappeared from sight and squelched against the concrete below.

Bishop hung over the rail, the strength finally drained from him. He could no longer think, no longer reason; the urge to sink to the floor and lie there was almost overwhelming. But the shouts below grew louder and footsteps drummed on the stone steps. He saw faces peering up at him, disappearing, hands snaking up the stair rail, the crowd now ascending as one, the battle with the tenants of the tower block over. A hand pulled him away from the railing and towards the ladder reaching up into the roof. Jessica implored him to climb to safety, her face stained with tears of anxiety and exhaustion.

'You first,' he told her.

'Hurry!' came Edith's voice from the open hatchway. The mob were on their last flight of stairs, the strongest of them coming fast, the torchlight growing strangely weaker as though the darkness of night were approaching with them.

Without further hesitation, Jessica climbed the ladder and disappeared into the hole above. Bishop leapt upwards, forcing his weary legs to climb, knowing the desperation of the hunted. He felt a hand close around his ankle and he stamped down hard with his other foot, the heel scraping down his pursuer's face, causing the man to drop to the floor. And then Bishop was rolling over the side of the opening, the hatch slamming closed behind him. Edith and Jessica fell on to the covering as fists pounded against it. Fortunately the hatch was solidly made and they knew that no more than one person at a time could climb the ladder to push against it. They lay in the gloom, the torch on its side and pointing towards the machinery that operated the lift, Edith and Jessica slumped over the hatch, Bishop on his back panting for breath and totally spent,

Kulek sprawled on one side near a wall. They listened to the muted howls of anger below, the drumming of fists against the hatch, and they were aware of the oppressive darkness that was there with them in the small box room on top of the ten-storey building. The wind tore round the corners outside as though it were an unseen force trying to enter and Edith Metlock rejected the probing she felt at the edges of her mind, refusing to hear the anguished voices that whispered their threats. She thought only of her three companions in the machine room, keeping an imagined wall of light between her and the Dark.

After a while the noise from below faded away and there was no more pressure against the hatch. Bishop breathed more evenly as he raised himself on one elbow.

'Have they gone?' he asked, not daring to hope.

'I don't think so,' the medium said. 'I don't hink they'll give up until they have Jacob.'

'But why do they want my father?' said Jessica. 'You said before that they feared him. Why should they? What can he do against them?'

'Because I'm close to the answer, Jessica.'

They swung their heads around at the sound of his weak, quavery voice. Edith picked up the torch and shone it towards where Jacob Kulek sat, his back propped up against the wall, his hands pressed down against the floor to keep his body erect. He seemed strangely shrunken, as though his body were slowly crumbling in upon itself, his cheeks collapsed inwards, eyes half-closed as though resisting sleep. Jessica quickly crawled towards him, not having the strength to rise, and Bishop followed.

Jessica took one of her father's hands and tenderly touched his cheek. The lids of his eyes briefly opened wider and he tried to smile at her. She pressed her face against his, afraid for him without knowing why; it had nothing to do with the physical danger they were in, and concern over his injuries was only part of it. He opened his mouth to speak again, but she softly placed her fingertips against his lips.

'Don't, Father. Save your strength. Help will be here soon, I'm sure of it.'

A trembling hand took hers away. 'No, Jessica . . . there will be . . . no help . . . for us this night.'

'We managed to get a message through to the police, Jacob,' Bishop said. 'They'll try to reach us.'

Kulek wearily turned to him. 'They have no . . . control over this . . . terrible thing, Chris. Only people as individuals . . . can fight against it. But it can be defeated.' Strength seemed to be returning to his words.

'How, Jacob?'

'Pryszlak . . . Pryszlak knew how to unleash the evil inside him. At the moment of death, he knew how to direct that evil. Don't you see, his death was like opening a box, releasing the contents. The content was his own psyche, and his will was strong enough – even in death – to control that psyche.'

'It isn't possible.'

'Years, Chris, years of conditioning his mind for that final moment.' Kulek sucked in a huge breath and began to cough, his body doubling over and shoulders jerking spasmodically. They lifted him upright when the seizure had passed, resting his back against the rough brickwork; they were alarmed to see the speckles of blood on his lips and chin. He breathed slowly for a few moments, then his eyes opened. 'Don't you see? He built up the power of evil around him over the years through his own practices and those of his followers, their minds communicating, joining as one, directing their separate forces so they merged;

all that remained was the barrier of life.'

'And he knew he could go on even after his own death?'

Kulek's eyes closed again. 'He knew. He was an extraordinary man, his mental development stretched far beyond that of normal men. He could use areas of the brain that we know nothing of. The mind is a mystery to us; he had unravelled some of its secrets.'

Edith Metlock spoke from the darkness on the other side of the torch beam. 'Jacob is right. They fear him because he knows the truth.'

'But I do not have the answer!' Kulek said loudly, anger and frustration in his voice.

Edith was about to say more when she suddenly looked down at the hatch beneath her and listened. 'They're still there,' she said in a whisper. 'Something is being moved – I can hear a scraping noise.'

Jessica and Bishop moved towards the hatchway and listened, fighting to keep their own breathing as soundless as possible. They did not see the thin line of blood appear at the corner of Kulek's lips, running down his chin, forming a pool around his jawline before falling in spots on to his chest. The flow thickened and then ran from his chin in a steady stream.

The scraping noise below had stopped and for a moment there was only silence. All three jumped when something crashed against the hatch. It rose several inches before slamming shut again.

'Christ, they've found something to batter against the hatch!' Bishop said, his nerves beginning their frenetic dance once more.

The crash came again and both Bishop and Jessica combined their weights with Edith's to keep the hatch closed. It slowly began to rise beneath them.

'They must have got a table or something from one of the flats to stand on. There's more than one person pushing now.' Bishop grabbed the torch from the medium and shine it quickly around the machine room, looking for a weapon of some kind, anything he could use to beat back someone climbing through. There were small windows set in the walls and a door leading out to the roof itself; the drive pulley and the lift motor were nearby, the opening to the shaft black and menacing. There were no tools lying around, nothing at all that could be used as a weapon. The hatch beneath them opened a few millimetres wider and a stout, metal bar was pushed through to keep it open. Bishop pulled at the bar, but it was jammed into the gap. Fingers curled around the edges of the hatch opening and the pressure below became even more intense. The gap widened and they heard another object being scraped through to be used as a lever by the person on the other side. They tried to prise away the fingers around the edges but they merely returned in another position. Their arms and shoulder muscles were taut with the effort of pressing down, yet they could feel the hatch rising higher each second. An arm came through the gap and Jessica screamed when the hand closed around her wrist.

It was at that point that the power came back on.

Light flooded in through the opening, blinding them with its suddenness. The lift machinery clanked into life and the pulley turned as the car resumed its interrupted journey. There were cries from below as the hatch dropped and came to rest on the objects that had been pushed through; the arm and the hands around the opening had already disappeared. They heard scuffling on the landing below, the sound of footsteps running down steps, screams as people fell in their haste to escape the dazzling lights.

The two women fell away from the hatch, both crying with relief, praying that it was finally over for them – for that night at least. Bishop cautiously swung the hatch open wider, the metal bars sliding away and bouncing off the table below before clanging down on to the concrete landing. The upper stairs were empty apart from the sprawled bodies of those who had been injured before. He could hear the others scurrying down, many moving fast, knocking aside those who had been victims for a longer period and who were totally blinded by the lights.

'They've gone,' he quietly told the two women. He shivered as the wind rushed into the machine room and turned to see the door was open wide. Jacob Kulek was no longer sitting against the wall.

The two women looked up when he dropped the hatch and rushed to the door. They, too, realized the blind man was missing.

The wind hit Bishop like a physical blow as he ran out on to the roof, tearing at his clothes and whipping at his face so that he had to half-close his eyes against its force.

The lights of the city spread out before him like a vast silver and orange constellation and, for a moment, he could only gaze at its manufactured beauty, for the first time truly understanding its potency. He panicked when he could not see Kulek; the roof was completely flat apart from the machine room and another similarly shaped building that he guessed housed the tower block's massive water-tank. Jessica and Edith joined him and all three apprehensively scanned the rooftop.

'Jacob!' Edith Metlock called out.

Jessica and Bishop followed her gaze and saw the blind man standing just ten yards away from the edge of the building; they could only make out his shape because of the lights blocked out behind him. He turned to look at them as they began to walk towards him.

'No,' he warned them, 'it's dangerous here. You must stay back.'

'Father, what are you doing?' Jessica cried against the noise of the wind, her arms reaching imploringly.

Kulek clutched at his stomach, but refused to bend to the pain. His face was just a vague whitish blur against the night sky, but they could see the blackness spreading down from his mouth on to his lower jaw. There was a thickness to his words as though the blood was filling his throat.

'They wanted me dead! They wanted to kill me before I found the answer . . . before I learned how I could use my own . . .' his words were lost as he stumbled towards the lip of the roof.

'No!' Jessica screamed, breaking away from Bishop and Edith Metlock and running towards the blind man. 'No!'

Kulek turned to look at Jessica and his words were whipped away by the wind. Then he plunged into the night.

THIRTY-ONE

Jessica brought the car to a halt and once more Bishop leaned out the window and showed the special pass card to the soldier. The sergeant examined it then ducked his head to scrutinize Edith Metlock sitting in the back. Satisfied, he signalled to another soldier standing by the red and white striped barrier, which was then dragged to one side. It had been the third time their car had been stopped since entering the area around Willow Road. The group of soldiers idly standing around an army truck watched them as they drove through, their curiosity apparent, their weapons even more apparent. The military were taking no chances with this operation, not after the total disaster of three weeks before. Many men had been lost that night, police and civilians, as well as soldiers, their brains infected or affected by whatever chemicals the scientists said the Dark contained, turning on each other, damaging the lights that had been their ultimate protection. Their defence against the hordes who poured into the area had been hampered by the confusion within their own ranks. The battle that had taken place had been horrendous and only the swift arrival of reinforcements had prevented those unaffected from being completely over-come. A nightmare action, but one brought about by their own underestimation of the unseen enemy. Tonight they would be better prepared.

Jessica swung the car out to the middle of the road, avoiding the lorry bearing the huge searchlight parked at the kerbside. They had passed many such machines on their journey, many of which had been in service for the past two weeks, others brought in for that night's particular operation. Most had been adapted so they did not throw directional and defined beams, but shed a broad and powerful area of light. Smaller lights had been fixed to roofs of houses or hung from their eaves; that area, which seemed to be the worst affected in London, had been literally flooded with lights. The curfew was still imposed throughout the city and lighting-up time had taken on a whole new meaning. Veterans of the wartime blitz thought it ironic that now it was unlawful not to show a light at night-time, whereas in the war years it had been a punishable offence to do so.

Bishop's uneasiness grew as they approached Willow Road and he looked across at Jessica to see her features were also strained, her hands clamped tightly around the steering-wheel. She felt his gaze on her and turned to give him a quick, nervous smile. Since the death of her father, they had grown close, the earlier attraction they had felt for each other developing into a strengthening bond of friendship – and something more. They were not yet lovers, but both knew that when their separate wounds had healed, their mutual stress subsided, then their intimacy of feeling would be matched by a physical intimacy. It was a desire in both of them, but one that could not – and would not – be hurriedly fulfilled.

She braked as a military vehicle carelessly turned the corner from Willow Road and swerved across their path, the driver obviously taking advantage of the empty streets. He waved an apology and sped on. Jessica took her foot off the brake and guided the car into Willow Road.

Bishop's eyes widened at the sight ahead, even though the details were not clear because of his slight short-sightedness. The road was filled with vehicles of all kinds, most of them military, others belonging to the Metropolitan Police, and also many civilian cars. Open-topped lorries bore more searchlights and armoured scout cars kept a watchful eye at each end of the road. There seemed to be uniformed figures everywhere, blue mingling with khaki, soldiers lining the pavements as though they were a guard of honour. Houses were being entered and searched for any hiding victims undiscovered in the earlier searches. He could just make out the bright red of fire tenders at the far end of the road, and the ominous white shapes of ambulances told him the authorities were prepared for the worst. But the sight that astonished Bishop most of all as Jessica eased the car past the parked vehicles and scurrying men was that of the strangely naked area halfway down. The houses on either side of the Beechwood debris had been completely demolished, leaving a wide, empty space. He had no clear view into the extended site because of the confusion of machinery and vehicles around its fringes, but he guessed what lay inside the boundary, for the intentions of that night's operation had been fully explained to him. The authorities had been forced to involve Edith Metlock and himself, albeit reluctantly, for they had unsuccessfully repeated their experiment for the past three nights and, as yet, the Dark had not returned to the site. Sicklemore, the Principal Private Secretary to the Home Office who had been fortunate to survive the disaster of three weeks before, had suggested that Bishop and Edith Metlock be called in to assist once more. There were protests, for the scientists and technicians involved claimed that the Dark had nothing to do with the paranormal, that it was merely the carrier of some unknown and, as yet, untraced chemical that in some way triggered a reaction in the hypothalamus region of the brain, creating electrical charges that manifested themselves in acts of extreme aggression. The Dark was a physical entity, a chemical catalyst, not some mystical and incorporeal leech, and therefore could be overcome by scientific means, not by spiritualistic mumbo-jumbo. Since Jacob Kulek's death, the uneasy alliance between scientist and parapsychologist had become a disdainful non-alliance. But Sicklemore had insisted. Three nights of failure and three days of the Home Secretary bellowing for results had made him desperate: Bishop and Metlock were thin straws to clutch at, but at least *something* had happened when they had last been present.

Edith Metlock stared out at the military and scientific paraphernalia from the darkness of the back seat and her heart sank into further depths of despair. Had it all been for nothing? Had Jacob died in vain? The Dark had only grown stronger after that night, nothing happening to dissipate its power. She had tried to make contact with him, but now it seemed her powers as a sensitive had left her, for nothing came to her any more, no visions, no voices. It was as though the thin veil between herself and the spirit world had become an impregnable barrier. Perhaps it was because she had lost her own beliefs.

Peck saw their car approaching and walked out into the middle of the road, waving his arm at them. He leaned in the window when Jessica brought the car to a stop.

'You'll find a space to park further down, Miss Kulek,' he said, then directed his attention towards Bishop. 'If you and Mrs Metlock could come with me?'

They stepped from the car and Jessica went on searching for a gap by the kerb in the congested street.

'How is she?' Peck asked, nodding towards the departing vehicle.

'She's come to believe her father's death was pointless. It's made it worse for her,' Bishop replied.

Peck mentally sighed. He remembered how he had found them on the tower block rooftop weeks before, almost frozen, physically exhausted. It had been dawn before he and a couple of squad cars had made their way to the high-rise building, only the persistence of one of the block's tenants alerting them to Kulek's whereabouts. The tenant had tried all night to get through to the Information Room, phoning in every hour but, because the lines had been flooded with emergency calls, his message had only been taken when daylight was approaching. Peck and his officers had been halfway to the top, checking each body on the stairs as they passed, not allowing themselves to spare time on the injured, when they had met Bishop coming down. He had looked dazed, his shoulders slumped in a weariness that was both physical and mental. He told them the two women were still on the roof, that Jacob Kulek was dead. It was only when they had all been brought down to the safety of the ground that he learned that Kulek had deliberately jumped; Edith Metlock had said that Kulek's death would provide the answer to the Dark. The medium hadn't appeared to be hysterical – she spoke softly, calmly – and Kulek's daughter seemed to see some sense in what she had told them, although the girl's grief was apparent. When Peck had walked around to the side of the building and had found Jacob Kulek's smashed body, his rage burned inside. The blind man had been badly injured when the police car had crashed – from what Peck had gathered, Kulek had been busted up inside as well as concussed. He had obviously been delirious when he had jumped, they should have seen that. Now, the medium was making him out to be the new messiah, someone whose death was for the benefit of mankind. Peck had turned away from the misshapen body, barely disguising his anger when he returned to the waiting group. The blind man had been thrown through the windscreen of a car, dragged up ten flights of stairs, chased by a mob of zombies and madmen, and then had fallen from the roof; what glory could there be in such a death? Even Bishop had seemed to listen to the medium's crackpot assertions. But now three weeks had passed and nothing had happened to diminish the power of the Dark. They had been wrong and Peck could only feel sorry for them.

'I'll take you over to the site,' he said to Bishop and Edith. 'The Private Secretary wanted to see you as soon as you arrived.'

They followed the detective, carefully stepping over the thick electric cables and avoiding the white-coated technicians who were making last-minute adjustments to various pieces of equipment. Dusk was not far away and already many of the smaller lights had been switched on. Bishop looked incredulously at Peck when he saw the newly expanded site. A huge pit had been dug out in the area that had once been Beechwood and its grounds, and seated within it were four massive light machines, each rectangular in shape, their Perspex surfaces pointed towards the sky. Similar machines, but smaller, more compact, were placed in positions around the pit. Further back, on the flattened land that Beechwood's neighbouring house had been built on, stood a prefabricated steel hut, a dark-tinted window stretching along its entire length and overlooking the site. On the opposite side stood the generator which would supply the power for all the apparatus.

'They're taking no chances this time,' Peck explained as he guided them towards the hut. 'They've got backup generators and lights, and enough guards to fight off an army. The power stations are heavily guarded too, by the way, so there's no chance of someone doing the same as that madman three weeks ago. He held out for hours before they finally got to him.'

They had just reached the squat, metal-walled building when Sicklemore emerged followed by a bespectacled man in shirt-sleeves, whom Bishop recognized as the chief scientific adviser to the government, and who, at the Birmingham Conference Centre, had openly rejected any paranormal connotations regarding the recent disasters.

'Mr Bishop, Mrs, uh, Metlock,' Sicklemore briskly acknowledged. 'Perhaps your presence tonight will bring us more luck.'

'I don't see why it should,' Bishop replied bluntly.

The Private Secretary regarded him speculatively, then said, 'Nor do I, Mr Bishop, but you seemed to last time. You remember Professor Marinker?'

The scientist gave them a grudging nod of his head.

'Perhaps you'll explain tonight's operation, Marinker?' Sicklemore said, having privately made it clear that he was no longer prepared to put up with petulance over the use of what the scientist termed as 'bloody cranks'.

'Your part is simple enough,' Marinker said gruffly. 'You just do the same as three weeks ago. I, personally, don't see why the Dark should return just because you're here – it makes no sense at all to me – but that's the decision of others.' He looked meaningfully at Sicklemore. 'Although the Dark seems to be an insubstantial thing, we have managed to detect a denser area at its centre – a nucleus, if you like. We believe the chemical which reacts on certain other chemicals present in the hypothalamus region of the brain is strongest within that centre. Our intensive tests on living victims have now made it clear that the disturbance is certainly in that region of the brain, and further tests have shown that minor radiation disperses those chemicals. Unfortunately, the radiation, slight though it is, damages brain cells to a degree where the victim can no longer function as a living person.'

Bishop shook his head, no humour in his smile. 'You mean your experiments kill them.'

Sicklemore hastily interjected. 'We have no choice but to be brutal in our tests. Those victims would not have lived long, anyway.'

Marinker continued as though there had been no interruption. 'It explains why the Dark can only exist at night, why the radiation in the sun's rays causes its disappearance. It goes to ground, if you like.'

'You said you believed it was a chemical. How could it react in such a way unless it were a living organism? Or something else?'

'I used the term loosely, Mr Bishop, to keep the conversation in layman's terms. Certain chemicals do have negative reactions to opposing properties, you know. We are sure it's the ultra-violet rays from the sun that are harmful to the chemical and further tests on victims bear this out. The tiniest exposure to ultra-violet light makes them try to hide, to cover their eyes. You've seen our light machines set beneath ground level, the others angled around the excavation. Unfortunately, the ultra-violet wavelength does not travel far, but our specially constructed machines are extremely powerful and, so that the area will be fully saturated, we will have several helicopters mounted with similar but obviously smaller lights overhead, their beams directed at the ground. Gravitation itself will give them a longer wavelength so the helicopters will be fairly high and in no danger. Of course, gamma rays or X-rays would have been even more effective, we believe, but then, that would have been highly dangerous for everyone in the immediate area, too.'

'Lasers?'

'Too defined an area. They would penetrate, but not saturate.'

'But surely too much exposure to ultra-violet rays is harmful to us.'

'You will be protected and we will be inside the hut. Those outside will wear gloves and hoods and stand behind shields. Their normal clothing will give them added protection.'

'How will we be protected?'

'Special suits with oxidized visors.'

'And if nothing happens? If we don't attract the Dark?'

'Let me speak plainly, Bishop: I don't expect you to. I think that what took place three weeks ago happened by mere chance. The fact that the victims seem to be drawn to this place each night indicates that there is a fundamental source of energy in this area; we have no idea what that source is nor have we been able to locate it specifically. But we know it's here, we're sure this thing that everyone calls the Dark will return to it. It's just a matter of time.'

'Which we don't have,' Sicklemore snapped. 'The point is this, Mr Bishop: your presence will not hinder the operation, and it might just do some good. I mean no offence, but I personally find the argument for psychic phenomena far from convincing, but at this particular moment, I'm ready to try anything if it will mean our success. In fact,' he said, turning his eye on the scientific adviser, 'I shall even indulge in a few prayers when I'm inside that hut.'

Marinker opened his mouth to speak, but thought better of it.

'Now,' Sicklemore continued, 'The light is fading fast. Can we please make our final arrangements?'

Marinker called through the hut's doorway and an agitated youngish man appeared, a sheaf of papers in his hands, a well-chewed pencil clenched between his teeth.

'Get these two kitted out, Brinkley,' Marinker said. 'Full gear, they'll be fully exposed to the light.'

Brinkley waved the papers in the air with one hand and grabbed at the pencil in his mouth, pointing it behind him into the hut. 'But I . . .' he began to protest.

'Just get on with it!' Marinker pushed past him and disappeared through the doorway. Brinkley stared after him, then turned to inspect his two charges.

'Right, I'll leave you to it,' Sicklemore said. 'Will you stay with them, Peck, see that they have all they need?'

'Yes, sir.'

'I'll see you both presently, then.' Sicklemore strode hurriedly away from them, his small, waspish figure soon swallowed up by the crowds of technicians and soldiers on the site.

'Gone to report to his superiors,' Peck said, enjoying the fact that the man he had to be servile to had to be servile to others. 'He's had his own little department set up in one of the nearby houses, with a direct line to the Home Secretary. Poor bastard's been popping in and out every half-hour all day.'

'Er, if you'll come along with me we'll find you a couple of suits to put on,' Brinkley said, eager to get back to his work. He led them through the site to the road. 'You're Bishop and Edith Metlock, I take it,' he said, forced to slow his brisk pace so the others could keep up. 'I heard what happened three weeks ago; sounds to me as if the whole operation was too hastily put together.'

Peck looked at Bishop and rolled his eyes upwards.

'Still,' the scientist went on brightly, 'that won't happen tonight. I think I can promise you we've found the answer. All very simple really, but then aren't most things if you approach them correctly?'

As Brinkley babbled on, Bishop looked around for Jessica and saw her making her way towards them along the pavement. He waved an arm and her pace quickened.

'Here we are then.' Brinkley had stopped beside a large, grey-coloured van The back section was open and they could see the shelves inside were filled with white garments. Brinkley stepped in and checked the sizes marked on the shelves. He soon returned with the appropriate uniforms. 'They're pretty loose and very light – you can slip them on over your normal clothing. Helmets are separate, but they're not at all cumbersome. There we are, the light will just bounce off you.' He gave them a cheerful grin, then frowned at the medium. 'That's a nuisance – you're wearing a skirt. Never mind, you can change in one of the houses – they're all empty.'

Jessica had joined them by now and Peck noticed how close to Bishop she stood, almost leaning against him. It gave the detective some satisfaction, for he knew the ordeal both had been through; perhaps they could at least give a little comfort to each other. He was worried about the medium, though: she seemed lost, confused.

'Are you all right, Mrs Metlock?' he asked. 'You look a little pale.'

'I . . . I don't know. I'm not sure that I can be of any help tonight.' She looked down at the pavement, avoiding their eyes. Jessica went to her.

'You must try, Edith,' she said gently. 'For my father's sake, you must try.'

There were tears in the medium's eyes when she looked up. 'But he's not there, Jessica. Don't you understand? He's gone, I can't reach him. There's nothing there any more.'

Brinkley appeared to be embarrassed. 'I'm afraid we don't have too much time. Could I, um, ask you to put the suits on now, please? I've rather a lot to cope with in the operations hut, so if you'll excuse me . . .?'

'Go ahead,' Peck told him. 'I'll bring them over when they're ready.' He turned to the medium and his voice was hard. 'I know you're frightened, Mrs Metlock, but they're only asking you to do what you've been doing professionally for years.'

'It isn't fear . . .'

'All right, maybe it's exhaustion. We're all bloody tired. I've lost some good men over the past few weeks – two of them trying to protect you – and I don't want to lose any more. Now, all this may be nonsense, I don't know – I don't have to judge – but they . . .' he waved his hand at the site in general '. . . see you as a last resort. I've seen things recently that I never thought possible, so there may be something in it. The point is, we've got to try anything, and both you and Bishop *are* our anything! So will you please help us and get into that ridiculous spaceman's outfit?'

Jessica took the medium by the arm. 'I'll help you, Edith.'

Edith Metlock looked at Bishop, her expression a mixture of helplessness and pleading, but he could only turn his head away. 'Go with Jessica, Edith,' he told her.

The two women left, Jessica leading the medium by the arm as if helping a very old, and very tired woman. Bishop struggled into the white suit, surprised at its toughness despite its flimsy appearance. The helmet itself, with its stiff, black visor, hung loosely over his back; it could be pulled forward like a hood, the visor snapped into position by two clips on either side. The arms ended in close-fitting gloves, elasticated at the wrists, the feet made to the same principle. He zipped the suit up to a point just below his chest and looked up to see Peck watching him, his face grim.

'Bishop,' the detective said, then hesitated.

Bishop raised his eyebrows questioningly.

Peck looked uncomfortable. 'Just watch yourself in there.'

They sat side by side, the huge, square lights set out before them, lifeless yet threatening. Two lonely, white-clad figures, the centre-piece in an outward spreading array of technical equipment, weaponry and manpower. They were afraid, and those around them were afraid, for the tension among them was steadily increasing, feeding upon itself and touching them all as they watched. The sun had disappeared from the sky an hour before, its sinking hidden by dark clouds that had formed on the horizon, and now the site was lit only by subdued lights. The men around the perimeter were all shielded by metal screens and they wore special glasses already positioned over their eyes, making them look sinister and emotionless; a certain number were equipped with full protective headgear and gloves. They waited as they had waited for three previous consecutive nights; but this time they sensed it was different. This time, each man would occasionally look up at the sky, removing his dark glasses to study the black rolling clouds for long moments before turning his attention back to the two figures sitting in front of the open pit. Something would make each one shiver, but not outwardly; it was more like a sudden shudder of internal organs. It passed from man to man, mind to mind, an infection whose carrier was their own thoughts. Even the scientists and operatives inside the squat steel hut, surrounded by their own technology, felt particularly uneasy that night. Marinker's mouth was dry, the palms of his hands wet. Sicklemore kept clearing his throat and tapping one foot. Brinkley could not stop blinking.

Outside, behind a screen, Peck jangled the loose change in his trouser pocket, while Jessica, who stood by the detective's side, bit on her lower lip until her teeth left deep indents. The minutes passed and all casual chatter ceased; if anyone did speak, it was in a whisper just loud enough to be heard over the steady hum of the generators. The air seemed to be growing colder. And, of course, through their protective glasses, the night looked even darker than usual.

Bishop found it difficult to think clearly. He tried to remember, as he had done before, the first day he had come to Beechwood, the terrible sight that had confronted him. But it was all vague, all misty and remote, as though it had only been a dream which could not be brought into focus. He looked over at Edith sitting two feet away, but her features were barely visible through the darkened visors they both wore. Her hands were clasped across her lap and he could see them clinging tightly to each other.

'I can't think, Edith. It's all a blur to me for some reason.'

She said nothing for a few moments, then her visor turned in his direction. 'Don't try to think of it, Chris. Leave your mind blank. If the Dark really is what we believe it to be it will seek you out. It doesn't need your guidance.'

'Can you . . . can you sense anything?'

'I see Jacob's face, but I can't feel his presence. I feel nothing, Chris, only emptiness.'

'Did he really believe . . .?'

The medium turned away. 'I don't know any more. Jacob's perception was stronger than any man's I've ever known; even stronger than Boris Pryszlak's.'

'You *knew* Pryszlak?'

The black visor made her inscrutable. 'I was once his mistress.'

For a few moments, Bishop was too stunned to speak. 'His mistress? I don't understand . . .'

'It was a long, long time ago. Twenty years, perhaps more. So long, it sometimes feels as if it never really happened, as if the woman who slept with him was someone I knew vaguely, but whose name or face I can no longer remember. Boris Pryszlak was an astonishing man, you see; his very wickedness made him attractive. Do you understand that, Chris, how a malignant thing can be attractive?'

Bishop did not answer.

'I found him fascinating. At first, I didn't see the deepness of his corruption, the depravity that was not just part of him, but *was* him, his very being. It was he who recognized my powers as a sensitive, who encouraged me to develop those powers; he thought he would be able to use me. It was Jacob who finally drew me away from Pryszlak's influence.' She smiled almost wistfully beneath the mask. 'Jacob and I were never lovers – he has always been faithful to the memory of his wife. You of all people will realize that in our world, nobody dies; they merely pass on to more enduring.'

'But why didn't Jacob tell me this at the beginning?'

'Because I asked him not to. Don't you see it wasn't important? It had nothing to do with what was happening. Boris Pryszlak's immorality was like an infectious disease – it tainted anyone close to him. For a while I wallowed in the filth he thrived on and it was only Jacob who tried to help me. Perhaps he saw I was being used, that I was a victim of evil rather than a perpetrator. Jacob once told me he had tried to lure away other followers of Pryszlak, but had come to see those people were as sick and twisted as the man they idolized, and it was my own desire to leave – to be saved, if you like – that made me different from them. Even so, Pryszlak hated Jacob for having taken away just one of his followers.'

'Yet he came to Jacob for help.'

'He needed him at that time. He wanted to combine his own extraordinary mental powers with Jacob's; that combination would have been formidable. But Jacob had no desire to become involved in the ultimate aims of such a man. Besides, he knew that involvement would mean eventual subjection. Jacob bitterly regretted not having tried to destroy Pryszlak's plans all those years ago before they had become fully formed; but then, he was a truly good man and failed to recognize the extent of Pryszlak's malignancy. Even I failed to see that and I had shared his bed for almost a year.'

Bishop drew in a deep breath. He was disturbed by Edith's revelation, but not shocked; too much had happened for his emotions to be jarred by any fresh disclosure. 'Is that why Jacob called you in at the beginning of all this – because you had some connection with Pryszlak?'

'Yes. He felt it would be easier for me to reach Pryszlak. I knew something of his mind, something of his intentions. I had never visited Beechwood before, but I felt his presence as soon as I entered the house. It was almost like walking into Pryszlak's mind, each room a different, dark cell. He used to experiment with his own telepathic powers when we were . . . together . . . using me as his receiver. He never failed to penetrate my mind with his evil thoughts. For him it was a new kind of eroticism, a fantasy of imagined deviant sexual acts yet, because of the strength of his mental powers, experienced as though physically performed.'

Bishop saw her white-clad figure shudder.

'Those thoughts are still with me, burned deep into my brain. Only Jacob could help me subdue them and now he's gone. That's why I'm so afraid, Chris.'

'I don't understand.'

'Jacob poured his strength into me. Here, when we first gathered at Beechwood and you saw the vision, I was the one who made contact, but Jacob was helping me resist Pryszlak, preventing him from dominating my mind completely. Even when you found me at my home in a trance state, Jacob, who was lying injured in hospital, was using his mental powers to keep Pryszlak from taking possession. He was my protector, the barrier between myself and the full force of Pryszlak's parasitical soul.'

'But the Dark *can* be resisted, Edith. The reaction is only against those who have some imbalance in the brain.'

'We *all* have that imbalance. We all feel hate, aggression, jealousy! As the Dark grows stronger – as Pryszlak gathers his spiritual army – it will seek out the evil inside all of us and use it to destroy! Those it can't overcome – and they will be few – will be killed by its still-living physical legions. There will be no escape for any of us!'

'Only if the Dark is what you say it is. The scientists claim otherwise; they'll destroy it with their machines.'

'And with all you've seen, all you've been through, can you believe the Dark is just a chemical reaction?'

Bishop's voice was firm. 'I don't know any more. I almost came to believe in what you and Jacob told me, but now . . .' He looked away from her, his gaze falling on the huge light machines before them. 'Now I hope you were both wrong.'

Edith's body seemed to slump further into itself. 'Perhaps we were, Chris,' she said slowly. 'Perhaps I hope so, too.'

'Bishop?' The call came from the tiny radio receiver fixed into Bishop's ear. The voice had a metallic sound to it, but he assumed it was Marinker from the control hut speaking. 'Our helicopters are in the air. Anything happened with you two out there?' The question had a cynical edge to it, but Bishop sensed the underlying tension.

'Nothing so far.' His reply was picked up by the small microphone clipped to his chest. Slight static in the receiver made the scientist's next words hard to grasp. 'I'm sorry, what was that?' Bishop asked.

'I said we've just had a report . . .' more static '. . . trouble near here. Nothing for us to worry . . .' static '. . . being dealt with. More victims on the loose, that's all.'

Another voice came through the earpiece and Bishop guessed it was Sicklemore. 'You'll let us know the moment you feel anything, um, strange happening?'

Marinker spoke again. 'The build-up from the ultra-violet rays will be gradual, Bishop, so you needn't worry about any sudden flare. Just give us some warning . . .' more static, then, 'Can you hear us all right, Mrs Metlock? We seem to be getting interference from somewhere.'

There was no reply from the medium and Bishop anxiously turned towards her. Her body was rigid in the chair, her black visor facing straight ahead.

'Mrs Metlock?' the metallic voice came again.

'Be quiet, Marinker,' Bishop said harshly. Then, more softly, 'Edith? Can you sense something?'

She continued to look ahead and her voice sounded faint. 'It's here, Chris. It's . . . oh my God!' Her body shuddered. 'Can't you feel it? It's growing. It's all around us.'

Bishop tore his eyes away and quickly looked around the site. He felt nothing and the tinted glass he stared through made everything seem darker. He quickly unclipped the visor and lifted it back over his head.

The soldiers and technicians positioned around the site glanced uneasily at each other, sensing something was finally about to happen. Jessica felt a weakness spread through her, a weakness born of dread. A perception that was akin to intuition but stronger, more certain, told her that the menace was even greater than before, that they were all more vulnerable, their resistance against the Dark a fragile thing. She clutched at Peck, afraid she would sink to the ground. He turned in surprise, beads of perspiration on his forehead despite the coldness of the night. He supported her weight, then turned his attention back to the two figures sitting near the open pit. Bishop was looking around him as though searching for something, his visor pushed up from his head.

Inside the control hut, Marinker was speaking agitatedly to his radio operator. 'Can't you cut out this bloody static? I can't hear what they're saying out there.'

'I'm trying, sir, but there's not much I can do about it. I'm afraid it's atmospherics – it's interfering with out contact with the chopper, too.'

Marinker avoided Sicklemore's eyes, afraid he would give away the alarm he was strangely feeling. He cursed himself inwardly for being stupid and hoped no one noticed his hand trembling as he stabbed at the speaker button once more, 'Bishop, is something wrong out there? Can you hear me?' A constant crackle of static was his only reply.

Bishop tore the earpiece away, the interference becoming unbearable. His eyes narrowed as he searched the site. The general gloom was because only a few lights had been switched on, but was the air becoming heavier with something more than just nightfall? He blinked, but still he could not make out any definable difference in the lighting. He began to wonder if an hallucinatory tension had built up in the minds of everyone present on the site, a muted form of mass-hysteria that was creating a false fear.

'Edith, I can't see anything.'

'It's here, Chris, it's here.'

Something swirled in the corner of Bishop's vision and he snapped his head around to see what it was. Nothing there. Another movement, to his right this time. Nothing there . . .

Edith was pushing herself back against the chair, her hands tightly gripping the seat. Her breathing was heavy, laboured.

Bishop felt the coldness on his exposed face, a prickling sensation of closing pores, tightening skin. The coldness crept through to the rest of his body. More movement, and this time he caught sight of something shadowy. It flitted across his vision like a tenuous veil, gone when focused upon. A sound, the kind the wind makes when it suddenly sweeps around the corner of a house. Gone. Silence. Lights dimming.

Bishop spoke, hoping the microphone would pick up his words. 'It's beginning,' was all he said.

But in the control hut they only heard the irritating noise of static. All eyes watched the two white-uniformed figures through the long, shaded window until Marinker said, 'Check those lights – they seem to be fading.'

A technician turned a dial and the lights grew bright again. But slowly, almost imperceptibly, the brightness dulled.

A low moaning sound came from Edith and Bishop was about to reach out to her when his movement froze. Something was touching him. Something was running a hand over his body.

He looked down at himself and saw the loose folds of the white suit becoming smooth, flattening out. But the material moved on its own; nothing pressed against it. The whiteness of the suit which had been subdued under the poor lighting now became a dark grey in colour. The coldness that was in his body began to creep into Bishop's mind, a numbing frost seeking corridors to chill, and the familiar welling up of fear encouraged its progress. He tried to speak, tried to warn the others of what was happening, but his throat was too constricted. The darkness was descending, a shadowy blackness that threatened to extinguish all light.

Bishop tried to stand, but felt a crushing weight pushing against him, the same cold hand that had explored his body and which had now grown into a giant, invisible claw holding him captive. He knew it was only his own confused mind lying to him, making him believe what was not possible, but the pressure existed as though it were real. Once more, he tried to reach Edith, and his arms were held down by his sides, too heavy to lift. He saw the medium begin to slide from the chair, her own moaning rising to a piteous wail. Then the figure began to appear.

Inside the control hut, Sicklemore was speaking urgently to Marinker, years of civil service breeding preventing his voice from rising to a shout. 'For God's sake, man, turn on the machines. Can't you see what's happening out there?'

Marinker seemed uncertain, his eyes switching from the array of controls before him to the barely visible figures outside. 'Bishop hasn't got his visor in position. I can't risk turning on the machines while he's exposed like that.'

'Don't be stupid, man! He'll use the mask as soon as the ultra-violet lights begin to come on. Do it now, that's an order!'

The figures were just dark, ethereal shapes, their forms having no clearly defined image. They drifted closer, converging on the two people by the pit, black shapes that were part of the blackness around them. They drew near, looming over Bishop and Edith, the man locked into his seat by an unseen force, the woman cowering on the ground. Bishop gasped for breath, feeling as though he were sinking into thick, slimy mud, his mouth and nostrils choked by the foul-smelling substance. He forced his arms up, slowly, tendons straining, fists clenched and trembling. He tried to grip the invisible thing that pushed against his chest and found nothing there, no shape, no substance. But the pressure still remained.

The soldiers around the site, those in the road, and those in the streets beyond the road, held their self-loading rifles and Sterling sub-machine guns at the ready, knowing the inactivity had come to an end and that the danger had finally presented itself. The policemen felt comforted to be under the protection of their weaponry. In the distance, they could hear shouts, the occasional burst of gunfire; elsewhere trouble had already started.

Jessica tried to dodge round the metal shield, wanting to reach Bishop and Edith, but Peck grabbed her wrist and held her back.

'Leave them,' he said gruffly. 'You can't help them! Look.'

She followed his gaze and saw the sudden white glow emerging from the pit. The ultra-violet lights had been switched on, their brilliant light slowly spreading upwards and out. Other lights around the site began to glimmer, growing stronger second by second. Overhead could be heard the whirring blades of helicopters and the sky itself began to glow with the spreading white light.

'Chris hasn't got his visor down!' Jessica cried, struggling to free herself once more.

'He soon will have, don't worry. Just keep still, will you, and watch!'

Jessica stopped and Peck released his grip. 'Good girl. Now keep behind the screen.'

Bishop was dazzled by the rising brightness. He closed his eyes against it and tried to reach the visor lying flat over his head. He forced his hands towards it, sucking air in wheezing gasps, the black slime clogging his throat. Suddenly the pressure on his chest was gone; his arms felt free. He snapped the visor down and opened his eyes. The glare was still strong, but the silver chloride in the photochromic glass of the visor steadily counteracted the brightness, enabling him to see around him. Edith was half-crouched, one arm on the seat of her chair, looking towards the pit, her other arm shielding her eyes even though her visor was down. Bishop thought he could see the dark shapes falling away from the light, the images disappearing as though swallowed by the brightness.

The intensity of the light grew, becoming bluish in colour, a red tinge tainting the hue as it became more powerful. Soon the whole site was flooded with the blinding glare, shadows dispersed completely because of the positioning of other lights. The glow merged with the lights from above, the Gazelles maintaining their position, careful not to infringe on the air space of their fellow helicopters.

The area was completely bathed in the peculiar blue-violet light, every shadow quenched by it; even the man-made metal screens were lit from the back with less powerful lights so that no darkness could linger behind them.

Bishop felt his mind soaring, his fear leaving him. 'They've done it!' he cried to Edith. 'It's gone, they've destroyed it!' The scientists had been right all along: the Dark *was* a material thing, a physical property that could be obliterated as any other chemical, gas or solid matter could be. Jacob, poor Jacob, hadn't realized what it was; his mind had been too steeped in the paranormal to understand that the Dark was nothing more than an unexplained phenomenon and not a spiritual entity. Their own minds had fed the exaggeration, making them see things, imagine things, that did not exist. He, Bishop, had received the telepathic thoughts of Edith when he had the 'visions' at Beechwood; she had known Pryszlak, had associated with his followers, known their cravings, their degeneracy, and he was receptive to her thoughts because he had discovered the dead and mutilated bodies. Everything else was the madness inflicted by the thing known as the Dark, and the earthly evil of those who had been followers of Pryszlak when he had been alive. The knowledge was overwhelming, for it was not just the answer to the terrible, catastrophic events that had recently passed but a reaffirmation of his beliefs over many years.

Bishop staggered towards Edith, his arms reaching out to help her. And it was as he was leaning forward over her, a hand beneath her shoulder to pull her upright, that the shadow fell across the glaring blueness of her clothing like a dark blemish on fresh-fallen snow.

He stumbled away from her and fell, going down on to his knees and staying there, the mask hiding the horror on his face. Edith was rising, looking down at the shadow spreading across her body, her arms outstretched, her legs wide. She lifted her head and screamed up at the skies.

Then the blue-violet glow began to dissolve under the swift-falling darkness.

The shapes came back with the shadows, like wisps of black smoke, twisting, spiralling above the light machines in their pit as though taunting their power. The lights could clearly be seen receding back into their source as though forced by some invisible, descending wall. The generators on one side of the site began to whine, reaching a pitch, slowing, then rising again. Technicians leapt away from them as sparks began to shower outwards. Every glow, whether it was from floodlight, searchlight or handheld torch began to fade, bulbs popping and glass shattering. The instruments inside the control hut became erratic, needles bouncing across dials like metronomes, switches shutting themselves off as though operated by invisible fingers, noises booming from receivers and transmitters. The hut was plunged into darkness as all the lights failed.

Overhead, a helicopter had pulled sharply away from the confused scene below, its broad, ultra-violet beam of light fizzling out as had the others in the companion helicopters. The pilot felt the Gazelle dip suddenly and struggled to maintain height; but the power was no longer there. It hit the helicopter which was rising from below and had inadvertently crossed the former's flight path. The roar of the explosion was deafening, the swirling ball of flame blinding. The tangled machines plunged to the ground, the red flames trailing behind like the tail of a comet. Because both Gazelles had veered away from the site their death fall took them into the troop-filled road. The screams of the soldiers were drowned in the second explosion as the machines struck the ground. Scalding metal and burning petrol splattered towards the exposed men.

The third pilot was more fortunate, for he was able to direct his machine into a clear space two streets away as it lost power. It crashed to the ground, but neither the pilot nor his companion was badly hurt. As they climbed shakily from the damaged machine, they failed to notice the people who moved in the shadows towards them.

Bishop tore the mask from his face, the site now lit only by faint light from the machines in the pit and the red glow that came from the fire in the road beyond. His cheeks were wet from tears of rage and frustration – and newfound fear. Other small fires had started, caused by dropping flames when the helicopters had first made contact, their height spreading the fallout wide. Edith Metlock was silhouetted against the feeble light in the pit, her arms still held wide, the screams still bursting from her. He tried to push himself upright, but the oppressive weight was on him again, bearing him down, crushing his limbs. The black shapes swirled towards him, growing out of the darkness, seeming to become solid as they approached. He felt something hit him and he fell to the ground, shocked rather than hurt. He raised himself on one elbow, but there was nothing near him. Another blow, glancing off his forehead, and the skin where he had been touched burned as though ice had been smeared across it. The man he knew had been Pryszlak was before him, his malicious features clear even though they were totally black. The head came forward and his breath was fetid as he revealed his black teeth in a grin that made Bishop cry out and try to cover his eyes. There were others with Pryszlak, familiar faces that had become distorted with their own corruption. The man who had tried to kill him with the shotgun. The bearded man he had seen in his visions at Beechwood. The tall woman, her eyes ablaze with triumphant hate. And her short companion, cackling derisively. Others he did not recognize. And one who could have been Lynn, but the distortion was too great to tell. They moved closer to him, touching his body, prodding him. Yet he could see through them; he could see Edith, still hear her screams; he could still see the dimming glow from the pit.

Then the glass from the lights was bursting upwards, sparks, then flames leaping from the machines as they exploded, destroyed by something that had come to know no limitations, something that could only become stronger. The glass spun in the air, the shards flashing redly as they turned and reflected the distant fire; huge sheets specially strengthened to protect the delicate but powerful filaments beneath them. He saw a piece flying towards Edith, its glistening surface the size of a door, saw it slice her body in half, and closed his eyes before her legs, standing on their own, slowly toppled over.

The hands that were smothering him clutched at his throat and it seemed that each figure had a grip, their faces swimming before him, the mass that was the mind of all of them sucking at his own mind, no longer probing, searching, instead drawing out what it desired, what it needed to exist, to propagate. Just before the blackness became total he saw that crowds had invaded the site, screeching maniacs who attacked anyone who was not of their kind. Jessica was running towards him, her face hardly visible in the darkness. The shroud descended and there was nothing more to see. He could only close his eyes against the Dark.

And then he opened them, wondering where the blinding white light came from, the light that grew from nothing and washed the area on which the house called Beechwood had once stood with its vivid radiance, scouring out every rut and crevice with its brilliant intensity, making every brick and stone shadowless, casting out the darkness.

The light that burned into his eyes even though he had closed them once more.

CHAPTER

. . . The dreams have left me; time has numbed the horror of those terrible days. Even Jessica is no longer afraid of the night. We're together now, not yet as man and wife, but that will come. We need to adjust more fully to our new existence; formal rituals can take their turn.

After two years, we still remember that night at Beechwood as though it were only yesterday. The events have been discussed, analysed, written about, but still no one can explain the phenomenon that took place. The Church tries, of course, and now the scientists are prepared to listen to us, to consider what we tell them, for it was they, the technologists, who were proved wrong, they who came to realize that evil is a spiritual power and not a biological malfunction of the brain. Jacob Kulek would have been pleased – is pleased – that a true bond has been struck between the scientist and the parapsychologist, a working relationship no longer grudging, the alliance opening new doors to our self-discovery. It's everything he worked for when he was alive, only his death achieving those aims. Jessica frequently communicates with him, and I am slowly learning to. Edith is helping, acting as my guide.

She has spoken to my daughter, Lucy, and has promised she will bring her to me soon. She tells me Lucy is very happy, and Edith, too, is content in her own death.

The Dark never returned after that night, but Jacob has warned us it has not been truly vanquished. He says that as long as there is evil in the minds of men, it will always exist. One day, I suppose it will manifest itself again.

There are many of us who are aware now. All those who were at Beechwood and saw the Light form and grow until its effulgence destroyed every dark shadow has gained this unique extra-sensory perception. Only those who could not cope with the new powers they found they possessed have suffered, for their minds have retreated from it, hidden within themselves so they can no longer function as people. The scientist, Marinker, was one such person. But they are being cared for, and have not suffered the same fate as the victims of the Dark, who were left empty and alone, their bodies becoming weak shells that no amount of medical attention could save from wasting away and eventually dying. Some who were present that night say the Light was like a ball of fire, a new sun rising from the earth itself; others claim it had no form, no visible shape, but was a tenuous gas, expanding in sudden flashes, filling the air with its charges. Several say it grew in the shape of a cross, losing its outline as the brightness became too intense. For myself, I remember seeing only the brightness, no shape, no structure, just a brilliant light that flooded my mind.

We've heard reports that the Light has been seen since, in different parts of the world where oppression is prevalent. Jessica tells me Jacob is strangely uncommunicative about this. She has also asked him what part God has played in all this, but again, Jacob will not answer the question. He has told her that our new perception is at too fragile a stage for us to know, that even in death we are still learning, no truth fully realized.

Jacob had known he was dying from internal injuries that night on the rooftop; but he also knew his own mind had to maintain control as death eclipsed his life. The Dark, with its growing power, had endeavoured to fill him as he died, to swamp his thoughts, to destroy his spiritual will; the swiftness of his death prevented that. These black, incorporeal beings knew that as the body died, so the will, the essence that is within everyone, faded too, only to be restored, reawakened, when the tenuous strands that tied it to its earthly shell were finally broken. A metamorphosis that, in our terms, took three days. But Jacob had not allowed his will to deteriorate with a slow death; he had controlled his spiritual power in his last fleeting moments, aware of and playing a wilful part in his own rebirth. As had Boris Pryszlak. Both had chosen different paths.

Jacob had found himself among an awesome realm of energies, a new dimension that was partly of this world, but ultimately a doorway to something greater, something that could be glimpsed, but not fully perceived. He had been confused, lost; and not alone. Others awaited him.

He had become part of them, joined the flow that never ceased growing, moving, yet which, again in our terms, had no reality; and eventually a part of that flow was allowed to return to its beginnings and combat an opposite energy that threatened its embryo. We are that embryo. The Dark is that opposite energy. The Light is the power we will become.

None of us who saw the Light resents the affliction it dealt us, for the blindness isn't a burden but a release from our lack of vision. Jessica is carrying our child and we both know that he – it will be a boy – will be blind, like us. The thought makes us happy, for we know he will be able to see as we do.

Fluke

To Kerry and Emma

PART ONE

ONE

The warmth from the sun beat against my eyelids, soft persuasion to open them. Noises crept into my ears then burst through to my consciousness, confusing sounds, a gabble broken by strident pitches.

Cautiously, almost unwillingly, I half opened my eyes, the sleep in them sticky, a soft moist glue. Through the blur I saw a dark furry body, big as me. It heaved rhythmically up and down, up and down, in a contented sleep. My mouth opened wide as a yawn escaped and my eyes suddenly snapped fully open. Other bodies lay around me, blacks and greys – mixtures of both – some of the coats short and straight, others tufty and curly. A flash of white leapt over me and I felt sharp teeth nip at my ear. I pulled away with a whimper. Where was I? Who was I? *What* was I?

Smells came to my nostrils, unpleasant at first and then strangely pleasing. I wrinkled my nose, breathing in the fumes, powerful odours that somehow made me secure. I wriggled my body closer to the other warm bodies, away from the energetic white pest that finally gave up and bounded towards the surrounding wire. He stood up on his hind legs, resting his paws on the top of the wiring, his rump and stubby tail waggling excitedly. A huge pallid hand reached down and he was lifted away out of sight.

I whimpered again, this time with shock. The hand – so big, so strong! And the smells emanating from it – so alien. Frightening, yet ... interesting. I tried to snuggle further into the packed lumps of sluggish fur, seeking a contact I didn't understand. Why was I surrounded by these monster animals and why did I feel so akin to them?

The sleep had left me now and my body quivered with awareness. I was in some sort of pen – it looked very large to me – the floor of which was covered in straw. The wiring around us was high, much higher than me, and my companions were dogs. I don't think I really felt fear at that moment; probably just confusion. I remember my breath coming out in short panting gasps and I think I urinated a little, just a trickle. I know I tried to burrow even further between two plump bodies, with two of which I felt some association, some common bond. Now I can guess it was because we were related, but at the time I reacted to instinct alone.

I peeped around me, keeping my head low, my jaw firmly tucked into the straw. Everything was so muted, the colours barely distinguishable apart from their varying tones, only hues of greys and muddy browns. Yet I saw the colours in my mind's eye because I had known them before ... before ...

Before?

In my bewildered state even the question, let alone the answer, evaded me.

But now colours were already beginning to filter through, a legacy left to me, a gift that separated me from my fellow creatures. The soft greys turned to light browns, the denser greys to darker browns. The blacks remained black, but deeper. The rainbows flew at me, filling my head with a dazzling variegation, blinding in its intensity. The blacks were no longer black, but blue, indigo, hundreds of shades of browns. The colours hurt my eyes and I was forced to close them. Yet the sun still stung through and the colours still exploded before me. And then the spectrum took its proper order, the colours found their correct balance; the flashes became subdued, the tones began to relate to each other. I opened my eyes and the brief monochrome world had vanished and been replaced by a rich, moving canvas where each colour belonged to itself yet interlocked and shared with its opposites. Even today, I still delight in everything I see, new, surprising colours revealing themselves without warning, seeming to be borne freshly before me only for me to realize they'd always been there but that I'd never really looked. The colours are more muted now, but still feel fresher and more interesting than they'd been in the past. I suppose it's something to do with the world being bigger to me; being closer to the ground somehow makes me closer to nature.

Having passed through this curious stage I neither understood nor appreciated, I began to be a little more adventurous in my exploration. I lifted my head from the straw and stretched my neck upwards. Faces passed by, looking down at me, funny tender smiles on them. At that time, they all looked the same to me; I couldn't tell male and female apart, nor one individual from another. Nor did I know what they were exactly. Stangely enough, I could tell the difference between the smaller giants right from the start, not just from the elders, but as individuals. Several looked down at me, laughing and making strange noises with their mouths, peering expectantly at the taller ones behind. Above these giants I could see enormous grey-brick buildings stretching far into the sky – and the sky itself seemed so blue, so deep and clear. Sky is the purest thing I've ever known, whether it's the cold azure of dawn, the striking cobalt of day, or the deepest silver-perforated blackness of night. On the darkest day, when the sky is masked by sullen clouds, the tiniest patch of blue makes my heart jump a little. It seemed then as if I were seeing sky for the first time, and in a way I was – through different eyes.

I gazed rapturously at the blue ceiling for several moments until the rays of the sun made my eyes mist over, causing me to blink rapidly. It was then I realized what I was. I wasn't shocked, for my new brain was still functioning mainly as it should and memories were still lying dormant within it. I accepted what I was; only later did I question my new beginning. But at that time, I thought it was perfectly normal to be a dog.

TWO

Is it doubt I sense in you, or something more? Maybe a little fear. All I ask is that you let your mind listen, that you forget for a moment your prejudices and beliefs; when I've finished my story you can decide for yourself. There's a lot that's not clear to me yet and I know it never will be – not in this existence anyway – but I may help you to understand your life a little more. And I may help you to be less afraid.

As I looked around, my vision so different to yours, I felt the fur at the back of my neck being tugged, and suddenly the straw bed dropped away leaving my paws waggling frantically in empty air. A huge rough hand came up from beneath and the pressure was taken off the taut skin at my neck as my bottom was given support. I didn't like the smell of the hands at all, or their hardness. Each smell was separate and mostly new to me. They didn't blend together to make one complete odour; each had its own identity and combined to represent the man. It's difficult for me to explain, but as humans identify each other by assembling in their mind's eye the various features of another person – the shape of the nose, the colour of the eyes, hair, general skin tones, the set of the lips, the build of the body – we animals find it easier to assemble through our senses the various body smells. They're much more reliable, for physical features can be disguised or may change through age, but there's no disguising your own personal scent. It's a gradual build-up from everything you've done in your time and no amount of scrubbing can erase it. The food you've eaten, the clothes you've worn, the places you've visited; that's what gives us your identity, and no visual aspect is more recognizable.

I suppose the giant (I still had no concept of man at that point) who lifted me from the pen reeked of tobacco, booze, fatty foods and the aroma I've found is ever present – sex – but at that time they were all new to me and, as I've said before, frightening, unpleasant, yet interesting. The only familiar smell was the doggy one, and my sensitive nose sought this out and clung to it for comfort. I could now see what seemed like millions and millions of two-legged animals shuffling backwards and forwards, their noises hurting my ears and baffling me. I was in a street-market, of course, and even in those early stages there was some recognition, some familiarity with the place. Rough, growling sounds came from somewhere close to my ear and I snapped my head round nervously. The lips of the creature that held me were moving and these were the source of the growling noises. I don't say I recognized the actual words then, but I understood the intent.

Another voice spoke on the other side of me and I was thrust forward into another pair of arms. The aroma was so different. I suppose the food and drink smells were still there, but the nicotine stench was absent. And there was so much more. You can smell kindness; it's like a fragrance. It's not that interesting, but it's reassuring. There wasn't too much of it, but compared to the hands I had just left, it was like suddenly being sprayed by the finest perfume. I began to lick the hands, for there were still traces of food on them. It's such a treat to lick a human hand or face; the sweat on every part of a human body still holds the food recently eaten and the saltiness gives it a special tang of its own. The taste is subtle and soon gone, but the delicate flavour, combined with the ticklish scratching of tongue against skin, is an exquisite pleasure every dog loves. It's not affection, you see (although after a while a familiar taste is more pleasurable than a strange one and almost becomes a show of love) but more an exercise for appreciative taste-buds.

While one hand hugged me against the friendly giant's chest, the other stroked my head and softly tickled me behind the ears. This sent me into raptures and I tried to nip his nose. He jerked his head away with a sound I could only interpret as a happy growl so I increased my efforts to reach that bulbous feature on his face. My tongue touched his chin and scratched against its roughness. This surprised me a little and I drew back, but the excitement overcame me again and I launched myself forward in a fresh attack. This time, firm hands restrained me.

The voices bartered to and fro and suddenly I was placed back in the pan. I immediately jumped up again, trying to reach the friendly giant, my front paws resting on the wooden top of the wiring. A white body joined me and attempted to shoulder me out of the way. I pushed back though, realizing something nice might be about to happen to me and I saw several pieces of greenish paper pass over my head to the rough red hands of my keeper. Then I was in the air again, hoisted high and hugged to the kind-smelling giant-creature's chest. I let out a little yelp of glee and tried to lick the huge face above me. I don't know if or what I suffered under the care of the other giant, but something told me it was good to get away from him; badness poured from his body. Looking down at the other bundles lying there, I felt a pang of regret; they were my brothers, my friends. Sadness swept through me as I was carried away and a vision of a much bigger dog, probably my mother, flashed into my head. I wept then and cowered into the huge creature. At the sound of my whimpers his hand began to stroke my body and soft tones came from his lips.

The crowds of two-legs were even more frightening now I was moving among them and I began to shiver with fear. Everything, everyone, was so big. I tried to snuggle my head inside a fold of the big animal's skin and he allowed me, sympathizing with my fright, quietly reassuring me. Now and again I would peep out, but the noise, the flashing colours, the bustle, would soon send my head digging back deeper inside the loose skin, the beat from the broad chest having a strange calming effect on me. Soon we had left the market-place and a new, more terrifying sound roared in my ears.

My head jerked out from its hiding place and my jaw dropped open with fresh terror at the sight of the huge monsters bearing down on us, then whisking by in a whirlwind of disturbed air, seeming to miss us only by inches. They were strange animals to me, much stranger than the animal that carried me, and fearsomely devoid of any character except power and size. Their fumes were nauseating and lacked any food or sweat smells. A worse monster was to appear: brilliantly red and four times the size of the other creatures. I just had time to notice its legs were round and whirled at a tremendous rate before I leapt from my bearer's arms, spilling droplets of urine on to the grey concrete as I dashed away from the approaching beast. Shouting noises sounded from behind me, but my legs refused to stop running as I dodged between the giants who tried to block my path. A foot stretched out in front of me, but I flew over it without even breaking my stride. I veered off course as big hands reached down to grab me, leaving the pavement, throwing myself into the river of fast-moving monsters. Screeches filled my head and dark shapes loomed over me, but I kept running, my eyes focused only on what lay ahead, the advantage of my new-found wide periphery not used, my whole being concentrated on a dark hole that lay ahead of me. And then a memory stirred: *I was something else for a moment, high off the ground, and the fear inside me then was the same as the fear inside me now. Something hurled itself at me, something white and blinding. Then the light exploded into pain*, and I was a dog again, fleeing in a straight line across the paths of screeching cars and buses.

It must have been then that things were triggered off inside me: memories, feelings, instincts – I don't know what – flickered, were aroused, but were not yet exposed, uncovered. They had been woken and had begun to live, but my canine brain was not yet ready to receive them.

I entered the shop doorway I'd been heading for and skidded along the floor in an effort to prevent myself crashing into a tall thing which held brightly coloured squarish objects. It tottered dangerously as my scurrying body struck and hands clutched at it while voices were raised in alarm. I found another hole to scoot into and whipped through it, round a corner and into a nice secure dark area. I cowered there, shivering, my jaw open and my tongue hanging down like a long streak of loose liver. My stomach heaved as I drew in short, sharp panting breaths. My sanctuary didn't last long though: hands grabbed me by the scruff of the neck and rudely tugged me from the recess. Angry growls flayed at me and I was pulled along the floor, my yelps of protest ignored. My head was cuffed several times, but I don't think I felt any pain. I reached the bright doorway and tried to dig my paws into the unhelpful shiny floor. I had no desire to be back out there among those murderous creatures.

A dark shape appeared in the doorway and familiar smells came to my nostrils. I still wasn't sure of the giant but instinct told me he was all I had. He came forward and I allowed him to lift me without protest. I sought out the steadying beat of his heart again and tried to shut out the angry sounds around me. The thumping from inside his chest had a different rhythm now, slightly faster, but I still derived great comfort from it. Tempers, if not actually soothed, were checked, and I found myself out in the open again, this time held more firmly, fingers digging into my soft body like iron rods. Fresh sweat glands had been aroused in my protector and new smells released; I was soon to learn that these were the smells of anger or distress. He carried me along the road, his voice scolding and misery dragged at my spirits.

Gradually, his heartbeat slowed to a more comforting pace and his grip lost its rigidity. A hand found the back of my ear again and began to stroke it, eventually calming my shaking body. Soon I had plucked up the courage to withdraw my nose from inside his jacket and look up at him. As he brought his head down I licked his nose and once again sniffed the smells of affection. His face changed in a strange way, and that was when I first began to recognize expressions and associate them with feelings. It was the start for me, the thing that set me apart from others of my kind. Maybe it *was* the shock of the roaring traffic that in some way had set off remembrances in me, shocked my system into a freakish awareness; or perhaps it would have happened in its own time anyway. At the time, though, I knew the big creatures that moved so fast on round legs were something to be feared – and for me, to be despised.

The man suddenly broke his stride and turned to his left, pushing open a heavy piece of wood and stepping through. The stale atmosphere engulfed me; the contrast between the bright sunshine outside and this cool, dim, smoke-filled cavern was awesome. The hubbub of sound was confined within walls and rebounded from them; the smells, the foul smoke, were contained and magnified, and, overriding all, came a powerful smell which filled every nook and cranny, pungent and bitter.

The man moved forward and set me down between his foot and a gigantic wooden wall, a wall he was able to lean over so that his body disappeared from view. I peered round his legs and studied the other animals standing about the place in groups, their commotion making a rich, interesting sound, unlike the sharper, less friendly, noises of the market. Everyone seemed to be holding clear bowls of liquid in their hands which they raised to their lips and poured into their mouths. It was fascinating. I saw others sitting around the walls with the various-coloured liquids set on a sort of platform before them. Again, something familiar stirred within me but I wasn't yet ready to pursue the thoughts.

Something wet struck my head and instinctively I flinched. Several huge pats of liquid splattered on the floor before me and I backed away against the wall. I couldn't go far, for I was surrounded by legs, rearing up like thick tree-trunks around me. But curiosity soon overcame my wariness of the wet, shiny pools. My nose twitched and I inched forward, the smell from the liquid not as unpleasant as it had originally seemed. I bobbed my nose over one pool then moved on to another. Rashly I stuck my tongue into it and lapped up the liquid. The taste was ghastly but it made me realize how thirsty I was. I quickly moved to the other puddles and licked them dry. It took about three seconds, I think, to clear that small area of drips. I gazed expectantly up at the man, but he was ignoring me, his body hunched over, head out of vision. I could hear the familiar sounds he made over the general din. I shied away as a strange hand reached down for me and patted my head. I sniffed and the smells were good; I sensed friendliness.

A roundish, yellow-brown object was shoved under my nose and against my mouth. The saltiness reached my taste-buds and released waters in them. Without further thought, I snapped at the proffered food and crunched it into gooey mash. It was crisp yet oily, full of lovely flavours; it was delicious. I swallowed three in quick succession and shuffled my hindquarters in anticipation of more, my head craning upwards, jaws half open. No more was offered me, and as the figure moved away a funny gurgling noise came from his throat. Disappointed, I studied the ground for any small crumbs that may have escaped my munching teeth. Soon, the floor around me became a very clean area. I gave a little yap at the man above me, demanding his attention. But still he ignored me, and I became a little cross. I pulled at the soft skin that hung over his hard feet (it was a little time before I realized these tall creatures wore other animal's skins and in fact *couldn't* shed their skin at will).

His hand came down and once again I was hoisted aloft. A big round face, big as my body, confronted me across a wide expanse of shiny wood. The mouth opened wide, exposing closed teeth that were subtle shades of yellow, green and blue. The smells from him made me wary but didn't alarm me at all. He reached a great fat hand towards me and I sank my teeth into the soft flesh. Although I hadn't the strength really to hurt anyone yet, the hand was jerked away in surprise then returned to give me a firm cuff on the jaw. I shouted at him and tried to nip the offending hand again, but it began to weave in circles, teasing me by suddenly tapping my nose. Now a dog's nose is a sensitive area, and I began to get really angry. I shouted at him again and he roared mockingly at me, increasing his taps to a very annoying degree. My protector seemed quite happy to let this stranger irritate me, for I sensed no nervousness in him at all. Pretty soon, my whole world was focused on that moving lump of flesh and I lunged my head forward hopefully.

This time, my pointed little teeth sank into the meat and I crunched down, hard as I could. The taste wasn't much but the satisfaction was exquisite. Even though the hand was wrenched from my grasp, I had the pleasure of seeing tiny pinpricks of blood in a neat row across three fingers, and the short howl of pain excited me even more. I yapped defiantly at the creature as he shook his stinging paw in the cold air. He made as though to lunge at me and I was whisked smartly away by my giant. Once again I found myself on the floor, small and vulnerable among the massive figures around me. Curiously, the sharp roaring sound from above had a quality to it that bespoke friendliness; I was beginning to recognize the sound of laughter from the other noises these big animals made.

Still puzzled by everything that had happened to me that day, and still trembling with the excitement of it all, I spread my legs and urinated on the floor. The puddle spread beneath me and I had to shift slightly to prevent my feet getting wet. This time, although many of the sounds that reached me were of this happy nature, there were others that alarmed me terribly. I felt a blow to my flank, sharp growls, then I was dragged by my neck across the vast cavern. The sun hit my eyes, blinding me after the gloom, and the giant crouched beside me, stern sounds coming from him, his finger waving in front of my nose. I tried to bite the finger, of course, but a hard thump across my withers told me this would be the wrong thing to do. I felt utterly miserable again and my tail dropped between my legs. The giant must have sensed my dejection, because his tone softened and once again I was riding high, snug against his chest.

As he walked, a new sensation reached me. It was a fresh sound in my inner ear and I looked up in surprise. The giant's mouth had formed a curious round circle and he was blowing air through it, making an appealing, high-pitched noise. I watched him for a few seconds then called out encouragement. Abruptly the noise ceased and he looked down. I sensed his pleasure and the noise continued. The whistling had a soothing effect on me and I settled down on his arm, my rump supported in the crook of his elbow, his fingers spread across my brisket, and my head against his heart. I began to feel drowsy.

It was just as well I felt tired, since the next stage in my traumatic journey was inside one of those mammoth red creatures. I realized now that the things were not living animals like the giant and me; but they were all the more disconcerting for it. However, my sleepiness overcame my fear and I half slept on his lap for most of the journey.

My next memory is that of a long drab grey road with equally grey drab houses on either side. I didn't know what houses – or roads, for that matter – were at that time, of course; to me, the world was full of strange shapes which had no identity of particular relevance. I learned fast, however, because I was unique; most animals accept rather than learn.

He stopped and pushed a wooden caging that reached as high as his waist. A section of it opened and he marched along a hard flat surface, surrounded by beautiful green fur. The multitoned greenness dazzled my eyes and I was aware that this fur was a living, breathing thing. One hand reached inside his skin and emerged with a thin-looking object. He put this into a tiny hole in the structure before him and gave it a quick twist. A rectangular shape, sharp-cornered, taller than both of us, and coloured a vivid brown (even deep brown can be vivid when you see things as I do), swung inwards and we entered my first real home as a dog.

THREE

I didn't stay there long.

Those early months are a confusing blur to me. I suppose my freakish brain was trying to adjust to its new existence. I remember being placed in a basket which I refused to stay in; I remember strange white flimsy things placed on the floor all around me; I remember the lonely darkness of night.

I remember being shouted at, my nose being rubbed in foul-smelling puddles – and worse, nasty, sticky stuff, the smell of which clung to my nostrils for hours afterwards. I remember torn and mangled articles waved in front of me, the giant's companion screeching hysterically. I remember an excitingly smelly place, the mingled scents of many creatures blending into a sniffer's paradise, where an ogre in a loose, white skin stabbed me with a long, thin object, pressing it into my back and holding it there while I yelped. I remember an annoying length of dried skin being fastened round my neck, occasionally joined to a longer piece which the giant held and used to drag me along or hold me back when we were out in the open. I remember my dread of the big non-animal creatures that would chase us but lose interest and speed by with snarling roars just as it seemed they would crush us to death.

If all this sounds as though I had a miserable time as a pup then it's not quite accurate. There were lovely moments of both comfort and exhilaration. I remember cosy evenings snuggled up on my keeper's lap in front of the wispy hot thing that scorched my nose when I tried to sniff it. I remember my coat being smoothed by the giant's hand, from the top of my head to the root of my tail. I remember my first introduction to the endless green fur that lived and breathed, and smelled so fragrant, so full of life itself. I ran, jumped, rolled in its softness; I chewed, sniffed, I positively wallowed in its abundance. I remember chasing the funny, sharp-eared thing who belonged to the creatures living on the other side of our wall, his fur sticking out from his body like thousands of needles, his tail ramrod straight, his mouth spitting obscenities at me. That was fun. I remember teasing my giant by grabbing one of the funny old pads he would cover his feet with, and making him run after me until he gave up in exasperation. I'd sidle up to him, place it on the ground before him, give him a happy grin, then whisk it away before he had a chance to grab it. I remember the delicious scraps of food they would feed me; the food I refused to eat at first because it was so distasteful, but when hunger pains had overcome my repugnance, I'd eaten it with relish, saliva drooling from my clamping jaws. My own blanket, which I chewed and pawed until it became a tatty old thing, but which I refused to be parted from. My favourite bone, which I hid behind a bush in the little square green path just outside our see-through wall. All these things I remember vaguely, but with nostalgic fondness.

I suppose I was a neurotic pup, but then you would be too, if you'd been through my experience. As indeed, you might.

I'm not sure just how long I stayed with the giant and his companion – I suppose it was three or four months at least. It was a doggy life for me, my human senses still dormant but ready to erupt at the slightest nudge. I'm thankful I was allowed to adapt to my new shell before the shattering knowledge burst through. The next stage wasn't far off though, and of course I was quite unprepared for it.

The reason for getting rid of me, I imagine, was because I was a pest. I know the giant liked me, even loved me in a way, for I can still remember his affection, *feel* his goodness, till this day. Those first terror-filled nights when I howled in the darkness for my brothers and sisters – my mother – he took me up to his sleeping-place. I slept on the floor beside him, much to the annoyance of his companion, and much to her even greater annoyance when she discovered the damp patches and the soft, gooey mounds scattered around the spongy floor the following morning. I think that put me on the wrong side of her from the start. The relationship between us never really developed into anything more than wariness of each other. In due fairness to her, I think the best I can say is she treated me like a dog.

Words were only sounds to me then, but I could feel the emotion in them. I sensed, without understanding that I was a substitute for something else, and it's easy enough now to realize just what. They were, as far as I can remember, a mature couple, and they were alone. I could tell, from the noises the couple made at each other, that the giant was full of shame and his mate full of scorn. I was confused enough as a pup and the atmosphere between them did nothing to help my emotional stability. Anyhow, as a substitute, I was no great success.

I don't know whether it was just one particular incident or an accumulation of disasters that led to my dismissal. All I know is that one day I found myself back among canine companions. My second home was a dogs' home.

And it was there that the breakthrough came.

FOUR

I'd been there for about a week, quite happy with my new friends, although a few were a bit rough. I was reasonably well fed (you had to fight for a fair share, though – a case of dog-eat-dog really), and quite well looked after. The big two-legged animals used to file past most days, calling down to us, making silly clucking noises, then pointing out one of us in particular. An older dog told me these creatures were called people, and it was they who governed everything; they ruled the world. When I asked what the world was, he turned away in impatient disgust and ran over to the people, sticking his nose through the wire grille in a show of homage. I soon learnt he was an old hand at the game of selection, for this wasn't his first visit to the dogs' home. I also learnt it wasn't a good thing not to be selected – eventually you would be taken away by a white-skin, and there was no mistaking the smell of death hanging over you.

The more experienced dogs told me about people: how they shed their skins at will, since it was only dead skin like the thing round my neck; how there were males and females, like us, and that they called their puppies children. If they kept repeating a sound to you, sometimes kindly, sometimes harshly, then that was probably your name. They would feed you and look after you if you were obedient. They had learned to walk on two legs a long, long time ago, and had felt superior ever since. They were a little stupid, but could be very kind.

They had the power to destroy *all* animals, even those bigger than themselves.

And it was that power, *and only that*, that made them the masters.

I discovered I was what was called a crossbreed – in other words, a mongrel. There's no class system among dogs, of course, but different breeds do have different characteristics. For instance, a labrador retriever is gentle and intelligent, whereas a greyhouse is generally skittish and somewhat neurotic; you can hardly say a word to the latter without getting a snappish reply. It's funny how the dogs knew what they were: a terrier knew it was a terrier, a spaniel it was a spaniel. However, a Scottish terrier couldn't tell it was different from an Airedale; nor would a cocker spaniel know it was different from a clumber. These differences weren't important enough to be noticed.

Another point I soon discovered was that generally the bigger the dog, the more placid he or she was. It was the little squirts who caused the most trouble. And at that time, I was a little squirt.

I'd howl for my once-a-day meal; I'd whine against the blackness of the night,

I'd torment the sillier dogs, I'd wrestle the friskier ones. I'd snap and snarl at anyone who displeased me and I'd get very angry and chase the long thing that curled from my rump (I never caught it and it was quite a while before I accepted I never would). Even the fleas irritated me, and if I saw one hopping about on a companion's back I'd lunge for it, nipping the other dog's flesh. This would usually create a fine din and pretty soon a white-skin would throw a cold-making liquid over our struggling bodies.

I was soon earmarked as a troublemaker, often finding myself separated from the rest in a cage of my own. This made me even more morose and irritable and pretty soon I felt very unloved. The people just didn't realize: I had problems!

The problems were of course buried deep inside me where a strange conflict was going on. I knew I was a dog; yet instincts, senses – call it intuition – told me I wasn't. The conflict erupted to the surface on a cold, dream-filled night.

I had been asleep on the fringe of a group of furry bodies that had closed their ranks on me – I wasn't very popular with the other canines by that time – and my head was full of strange images. I was tall, precariously balanced on two legs, my face level with those of the people; a female people was walking towards me, kindness radiating from her, nice sounds coming from her jaws. I seemed to know her, and I wagged my tail, the motion almost unbalancing me. She made a soft sound that was familiar to me and her jaws formed a curious round shape. Her head was only inches away from mine and coming closer, making contact. My tongue snaked out and licked her nose.

She pulled back, a tiny sound escaping from her. I could tell she was surprised by her sudden body smell. She became even more surprised when I started panting and wagging my tail even harder. She backed away and I followed unsteadily on my two back legs.

She began to run and now I had to drop on all fours to follow. Colours, sounds and scents cascaded into my head, and all was chaos, all was confusion. Other faces appeared before me. One was tiny, beautiful, a little female people – a child. She rubbed her head against mine, then climbed up on my back, kicking her legs against my flanks. We frolicked on the green stuff and I felt I would burst with joy. Then darkness shadowed the sky. Another face. Anger glowing from it. I disappeared and I was in a cage. In the market-place. Then I was in among other warm bodies which froze, went icy cold when the dogs opened their eyes and saw me.

Then all was total blackness.

But I was safe. I was warm. A loud, comforting thumping noise sounded close to me, almost inside me. Other, less strong sounds ticked away furiously all around. Everything, everywhere, was soft; I was encased in life-giving, life-preserving fluid. I was in my mother's womb and I was content.

Then the driving force behind me – the sudden brutal jerks of contraction. I was being forced from my safe nest, thrust down a long black tunnel into the harsh cold of the outside. I resisted. I wanted to stay. I'd known that outside before. I didn't like it. Please, please let me stay! Don't send me out. I don't want life. Death is more pleasant.

But the forces were so much stronger than me. Death had been stronger, and now life was too.

My head was pushed through first, and for a moment my small body lingered. There were others in the queue though, and they forced me through, eager in their ignorance. I shivered and my eyes refused to open: reality would find me in its own time. I felt the other glistening wet bodies around me, then a sandpaper-rough tongue cleansed the filth from me and I lay there, humble and vulnerable.

Reborn.

I screamed and the scream woke me.

My head felt as if it would explode with the new knowledge. I wasn't a dog; I was a *man*. I had existed before as a man and somehow I had become trapped inside an animal's body. A dog's body. How? And why? Mercifully the answers evaded me; if they hadn't, if they had come roaring through at that point, I think I should have become insane.

My scream had woken the other dogs and now the pen was a bedlam of excited barking. They snapped and snarled at me, but I just stood there shivering, too dazed to move. I knew myself as a man, I could see myself. I could see my wife. I could see my daughter. Images rebounded around the walls of my mind, merging, splitting, rejoining, bedevilling me into a state of complete disorientation.

Suddenly the place was flooded with light. I squeezed my eyes shut to ease the pain and opened them again when I heard men's voices. A door opened and two white-skins stepped through, grumbling and shouting at the disturbed dogs.

'It's that little bugger again,' I heard one of them say. 'He's been nothing but trouble since he got here.'

A hand reached down and grabbed me roughly. My collar was used to drag me from the pen and down a long corridor of similar cages, the dogs in these now yapping furiously, adding to the uproar. I was shoved into a dark box, a kennel separated from the others to house nuisances. As the door was locked behind me I heard one of the men say, 'I think he'll have to be put down tomorrow. Nobody's going to want a mongrel like that anyway, and he's only upsetting the others.'

I didn't hear the murmured reply, for the words had struck new terror in me. I was still confused by the awful revelation, but the brutal statement had cut right through the haze. Standing there, rigid in the dark with my mind in a fever, I began to weep. What had happened to me? And why was my new life to be so short? I slumped to the floor in despair.

Soon, other instincts began to take over; my jumbled self-pitying thoughts began to take on an order. I had been a man, there was no doubt about that. My mind was that of a man's. I could understand the words the two men had spoken, not just their general meaning, but the actual words themselves. Could I speak? I tried, but only a pathetic mewing noise came from my throat. I called out to the men, but the sound was just a dog's howl. I tried to think of my previous life, but when I concentrated, the mental pictures slid away. How had I become a dog? Had they taken my brain from my human body and transplanted it into the head of a dog? Had some madman conducted a gruesome experiment and preserved a living brain from a dying body? No, that couldn't be, for I had remembered being born in my dream, born in a litter, my mother-dog washing the slime from my body with her tongue. But had that merely been an illusion? Was I really the result of a sick operation? Yet if that had been the case, surely I would be under constant surveillance in a well-equipped laboratory somewhere, my whole body wired to machines, not cast into this gloomy wooden dungeon.

There had to be an explanation, whether logical or completely insane, and I would seek out the truth of it. The mystery saved my mind, I think, for it gave me a resolve. If you like, it gave me a destiny.

The first need was for me to calm myself. It's strange now to reflect on how coldly I began to think that night, how I held the frightening – the awesome – realization in check, but shock can do this sometimes; it can numb sensitive brain cells in a self-protective way, so that you're able to think logically and clinically.

I wouldn't force my memory to tell me all its secrets just yet – it would have been impossible anyway. I'd give it time, allow the fragments to make a whole, helping the images by searching, searching for my past.

But first I had to escape.

FIVE

The latch being lifted aroused me from my slumber. It had been a heavy sleep; empty; dreamless. I suppose my fatigued brain had decided to close down for the night, give itself a chance to recuperate from the shocks it had received.

I yawned and stretched my body. Then I became alert. This would be my chance. If they were to destroy me today, I must make my move while they were off-guard. When they came to take me to the death chamber, their own sensitivity to the execution they were about to carry out would make them wary. It's easy for humans to transmit their feelings to animals, you see, for their auras radiate emotions as strong as radio waves. Even insects can tune in to them. Even plants. The animal becomes sensitive to his executioner's impulses and reacts in different ways: some become placid, quiet, while others become jittery, hard to handle. A good vet or animal keeper knows this and endeavours to disguise his feelings in an effort to keep the victim calm; but they're not successful usually and that's when there's trouble. My hope was that this visit was social and not for the more ominous purpose.

A young girl of about eighteen or nineteen wearing the familiar white smock of the handlers looked in. She just had time to say 'Hello, boy' before I caught the whiff of sadness from her, then I was off like a shot. She didn't even try to grab me as I dashed by; she was either too startled or secretly pleased I was making a bid for freedom.

I skidded, trying to turn aside from the pound opposite and my toenails dug into the hard ground. My whole body was a scrambling mass of motion as I streaked around the half-covered yard, searching for a way out. The girl gave chase but in a half-hearted way as I scurried from corner to corner. I found a door to the outside world, but there was no way to get through it. I was filled with frustration at being a dog; if I'd been a man, it would have been easy to draw the bolt and step outside. (Of coure, I wouldn't have been in that position then.)

I turned to growl at the girl as she approached, soft, coaxing words coming from her lips. My hair bristled and I went down on my front legs, my haunches quivering with gathering strength. The girl hesitated and her sudden doubt and fear wafted over me in waves.

We faced each other, and she felt sorry for me and I felt sorry for her. Neither of us wanted to frighten the other.

A door opened in the building at the far end of the yard and a man appeared, an angry look on his face.

'What's all the fuss, Judith? I thought I told you to bring the dog from Kennel Nine.' His expression changed to one of exasperation when he saw me crouching there. He strode forward, muttering oaths under his breath. I saw my chance – he'd left the door open behind him.

I hurtled past the girl, and the man, now half-way down the yard, spread his arms and legs as though I would jump into them. I passed underneath him and he vainly scissored his legs together, howling as his ankles cracked together. I left him hopping and flew through the open doorway, finding myself in a long, gloomy corridor, doors on either side. At the end was the door to the street, huge and formidable. Shouting from behind made me scurry down the corridor's length, desperate for a way out.

One of the doors on my left was slightly ajar, and without pausing I burst through. A woman on her knees just in the process of plugging in an electric kettle in the corner of the room stared across at me, too surprised to move. She began to rise to one knee and in panic I ran beneath a desk. My nose picked up the scent of fresh air mingled with dog fumes and, looking up, I saw an open window. A hand was reaching under the desk for me now and I could hear the woman's voice calling to me in friendly tones. I sprang forward, up on to the sill, then through the window.

Terrific. I was back in the yard.

The girl Judith saw me and called out to the man who had by now entered the building, but the yapping of the other dogs succeeded in drowning her cry. I kept running, back through the door and up behind the man chasing me.

He shouted in confusion as I scurried round him, and gave chase immediately. I was sure they'd have the sense to close one of the outlets if I went through my door-window-door routine again, so I ignored the open office. I found an alternative: facing the heavy street door was a flight of stairs, broad and dark-wooded. I did a scrambled U-turn and flew up them, my little legs pumping away like piston-rods. The man began mounting the stairs behind me and his long, long legs gave him the advantage. He sprawled forward, arms reaching upwards and I felt my progress abruptly halted by an uncompromising grip on my right hind leg. I yelped in pain and tried to draw myself away and up. It was no use, I hadn't the power to escape from such a tight clutch.

The man pulled me down towards him in one strong wrench and grabbed me by the neck with his other hand. He released my leg and put his hand underneath me, lifting my body up against his chest. At least I had the satisfaction (even though it was unintentional) of peeing on him.

It was my good fortune that at that precise moment someone else decided to show up for work. Brilliant sunshine flooded into the hallway as the front door swung open and a man carrying a briefcase entered. He stared in surprise at the scene before him: the young girl and the woman from the office gazing anxiously up at the dancing, cursing man who held the struggling pup away from his body, trying desperately and failing miserably to avoid the yellow stream that jetted from it.

It was just the right time to bite my captor's hand and, with a twist of my neck, I managed to do so. My jaws weren't that strong yet, but my teeth were like needle-points. They sank into his flesh and went deep – deep as I could make them. The sudden shock of pain caused the man to squawk and release his grip on me; I suppose the combination of wetness at one end and burning fire at the other offered him no alternative. I fell to the stairs and tumbled down them, yelping with fright rather than hurt. When I reached the bottom, I staggered to my feet, gave my head a little shake, and bolted into the sunlight.

It was like bursting through a paper hoop from one dark, depressing world into a neighbouring world of brightness and hope. It must have been the taste of freedom that exalted me so, the gloom of the building I had just left contrasting with the brilliance of the sun and the exciting multifarious scents of life on the outside. I was free and the freedom lent vigour to my young limbs. I fled and wasn't pursued; nothing on this earth could have caught me anyway. The taste of life was in me and questions pounded my brain.

I ran, and ran, and ran.

SIX

I ran till I could run no more, shying away from passing cars, ignoring the entreaties from the bemused or curses from the startled, nothing on my mind but escape – freedom. I had streaked across roads, blind to the danger because of the worse fear of capture, and had found quieter refuge in the back-streets; yet still I did not decrease my pace, still my feet drummed on the concrete pavements. I fled into the courtyard of an ancient, red-bricked block of flats, its redness darkened by the grime, and came to a quivering body-heaving halt inside a dark stairwell. My tongue flapped uselessly below my lower jaw, my eyes bulged with still unshed fright, my body sagged with utter weariness. I had run for at least two miles without pause, and for a young pup that's quite a distance.

I sank to the cold stone floor and tried to let my muddled brain catch up with my still dancing nerves. I must have lain there, a boneless heap, for at least an hour or more, too exhausted to move, too fuddled to think, the previous elation dissipated with dispersed energy, when the sound of heavy footsteps made me jerk my head up, my ears twitching for more information. I hadn't realized until then how acute my hearing had become, and it took long, long seconds for the owner of the footsteps to come into view. An immense figure blocked out most of the light infiltrating the dark stairwell, and in silhouette I saw the round shape of an enormous woman. To say her bulk filled the whole of my vision, periphery and all, may sound an exaggeration, but that's how it seemed to me in my shrunken body. It was as though her grossness were about to envelop me, to roll over me so that I would come up again, flattened to her side, just another added layer to the multitude of other layers. I cringed and I grovelled, no defiant pride in me, no sense of manhood available to hinder my cowardice for I was no longer a man. But her words halted my rising fear.

'Hello, boy, what you doing there, then?' The voice was as expansive as her body, booming and raspy, but the words were full of goodness and delighted surprise. She lowered her crammed shopping-bags to the floor with a grunt, then bent her vast upper structure towards me.

'Now, where've you come from, eh? Lost are you?'

Her gravelly tones suggested London, probably East or South. I backed away from the approaching hand even though my fear had been subdued by the quality of her voice; I knew once within the grip of those big, sausage-fingered hands, no amount of struggling would free me. But the lady was patient and undemanding. And the delicious aroma from those puffy fingers was overwhelming.

I sniffed small, tentative sniffs, nose-twitching sniffs, then inhaled deep lungfuls, the juices beginning to flow in my mouth. I flicked out my tongue and almost rolled my eyes in ecstasy. What this woman must have eaten! I could taste bacon, beans, tangy meat I couldn't identify, cheese, bread, butter – oh, butter – marmalade (not so nice), onions, tomatoes, another kind of meat (beef, I think) – and more, more, more. A taste of earthiness tainted everything, almost as if she had collected potatoes fresh from the ground, but it failed to sicken me as it should; instead, it heightened the deliciousness of it all. Here was a person who believed in food, who worshipped it with her hands as well as her palate; no stainless steel instruments would delay the journey from plate to munching jaws when the trip could be accomplished faster and with a heavier load by using her own living flesh to transport the goods. I could feel my devotion growing with every lick.

Only when the fat hand had been completely licked free of all its flavour did I turn my attention fully to the rest of the woman.

Dark blue eyes grinned down at me from a wide, rusty face. Rusty? Oh yes, you'd be surprised at the colours in faces if you could only see them as I did then. Red and blue veins coursed through plump, flushed cheeks, just beneath the skin. Other colours glowed from her – yellows and oranges mostly – changing hues constantly as her blood circulated beneath the surface. Brown and grey hairs stood out from her chin like tiny porcupine quills; and over the whole countenance ran deep grooves, starting at the corners of each eye and spreading down and around the cheeks, up and over the forehead, twisting and merging, cross-hatching and fading to a gradual end. It was a wonderful face!

I saw all this in the gloom of the stairwell, remember, and with the light behind her. That's how powerful my new vision was and would have remained had not time organized and dulled it.

She clucked her tongue and gave a little laugh. 'You're a hungry little thing, aren't you? You know me, though, don't you? You know I'm a friend.'

I allowed her hand to ruffle the fur at the back of my neck. It was soothing. I sniffed fresh food from the shopping-bags and edged towards them, my nose twitching inquisitively.

'Oh, smell food, do you?'

I nodded. I was starving.

'Well, let's just see if there's anyone about that might have lost you.'

She straightened up and lumbered back towards the entrance and I trotted after her. We both stuck our heads out into the courtyard and looked around. It was deserted.

'Come on then, let's see what we can find.'

The old woman turned back into the gloom, hoisted her shopping-bags with a loud grunt and carried them down the short hallway behind the stairwell, calling encouragingly to me as she went. I padded after her and muscle movement in my rump told me my tail was wagging.

Placing the bags on the floor next to a badly worn green door, she produced a purse from her coat and rummaged through it until she found a key, cursing her failing eyesight. She opened the door with a hard shove and a practised twist of the key, reached again for her bags, and disappeared inside. I ambled cautiously up to the door and poked my nose round it. The musty smell that hit me was neither pleasant nor unpleasant; it told of old-age neglect.

'Come on, boy,' the woman called out, 'nothing to be frightened of. You're all right with Bella.'

Still I did not enter the room. My nervousness had not yet completely disappeared. She patted her knee in enticement, not an easy thing to do for one of her proportions, and without further thought I skipped towards her, my tail now causing the whole of my rump to vibrate.

'There's a good boy,' she rasped, and now I could understand words and not just feel them, I knew I really was a very good boy.

I forgot myself and tried to speak to her then; I think I wanted to tell her how kind she was and ask her if she knew why I was a dog. But of course I only barked.

'What's that, then? You hungry? Course you are! Let's see what we can find then.'

She went through a door and soon I heard the clatter of cupboards opening and closing. The deep, scratchy sound of her voice puzzled me for a few seconds, then I realized Bella was singing, an occasional word interrupting a series of monotone 'mmms' and 'laaas'.

The crackle of frying fat took my attention and the glorious smell of sausages beginning to cook sucked me into the kitchen like dust into a vacuum cleaner. I jumped up at her, resting my front paws against a broad leg, my feverishly wagging tail threatening to unbalance me. She smiled down at my excited whimpers and placed a huge hand over my head.

'Poor old thing. Won't be a minute now. I suppose you'd like them raw, wouldn't you? Well you just wait a couple of minutes and we'll share them between us. Now get down and be patient.' She gently pushed me away but the savoury smell was too much. I jumped up at the cooker and tried to see into the frying-pan.

'You'll burn yourself!' she scolded. 'Come on, let's put you out of harm's way until it's ready.' She scooped me up and lumbered over to the kitchen door where she dropped me with a soft grunt. I tried to squeeze through the narrowing gap as the door closed on me but had to withdraw when my nose was in jeopardy. I'm ashamed to say I whined and groaned and scratched at the kitchen door, my thoughts concerned only with filling my belly with those mouth-watering sausages. Questions of my bizarre existence were thrust aside, easily overwhelmed by the stronger, physical desire for food.

Finally, after what seemed an eternity of waiting, the door opened and a cheery voice called me in. I needed no second bidding; I streaked through and made a bee-line for the plate containing three powerful-smelling sausages. I yelped as the first I snapped at burnt my tongue, and the old lady chuckled at my greedy attempts to bite the sizzling meat. I'd picked one up and immediately dropped it on to the floor when it stung my mouth. I did manage to swallow a chunk but it scorched my throat painfully. Bella thought it wiser to take the sausages away from me and, annoyed, I yapped at her.

'You just be patient,' she reprimanded. 'You'll do yourself an injury with these.'

Gingerly she picked up the sausage I'd already bitten into and blew on it – long, strong puffs that defied the sizzling heat to resist it. When she was satisfied she popped the sausage into my upturned mouth. In two quick swallows it was gone and I was pleading for more. She went through the ritual again, ignoring my impatient entreaties. I appreciated the second even more, the savoury meat filling my mouth with its juices, and, I can honestly say, never had I enjoyed a meal so much in my life – lives – either as a dog or as a man.

When I had gulped down the third, the old lady turned her attention back to the frying-pan and stabbed out four more sausages with a fork, placing two each on a slice of thick bread lying on the table. She smeared them with mustard and covered them with another slice, almost tenderly, as if putting a couple of children to bed. Without bothering to cut it she opened her jaws and stuffed as much of the sausage sandwich into her mouth as possible. Her teeth clamped down and when she withdrew her hand, a huge semicircular hole had been left in the bread. I watched enviously and tried to jump up on to her lap, the sight of those huge munching jaws sending me into a frenzy of pleading. I was starving! Didn't she have any pity?

She laughed and ruffled my head, holding me at bay, keeping the sandwich well away from my snapping teeth. I was in luck, for a lump of sausage fell from the bread and I was on it in an instant. I licked my lips with pleasure as I looked up for more.

'All right, you villain. I suppose it'll do you more good than me.' Bella smiled, and with that she dropped the rest of the sandwich on to the plate on the floor.

So we feasted, me and the fat lady, happy in each other's company, both of us demolishing our piece of sausage sandwich in seconds, grinning and smacking our lips at each other when we'd done.

I was still hungry, but at least the edge had been taken off my appetite. I lapped up the water Bella gave me in a soup-bowl and licked the traces of food from her hands. I asked for more but she didn't understand. She hoisted herself to her feet and began to unpack her shopping-bag while I kept a wary eye out for any scraps that might fall to the floor. It was risky dodging between those two wonderfully stout legs, and no food fell my way, anyway, but I enjoyed the game.

Bella dropped my spotless plate into the sink and called to me to follow her. I padded after her into her front room and scrambled up on to the musty old settee as she sank into it with a groan. I jumped up at her chest, two paws placed between two massive breasts, and licked her face in gratitude. It was a pleasing face to lick. She stroked my head and back for a little while and the strokes became slower and heavier as her breathing became slower and heavier.

It was not long after Bella had lifted those great tree-trunks on to the settee and rested her head on a cushioned arm that she was fast asleep, her snoring strangely comforting to me. I curled up my own weary body between her mountainous tummy and the back of the settee and soon I was deep in slumber too.

My awakening was fairly alarming. I heard a key in the lock and was instantly alert. I tried to stand, but my legs were wedged firmly inside the crevice between the old lady and the settee. I lifted my head and began to bark as loud as I could. This startled Bella into wakefulness and she looked around for a few moments as though she didn't know where she was.

'The door, Bella.' I told her. 'There's someone coming in!'

She didn't understand, of course, and gruffly told me to hush my barking. I was too young though, too easily excited, and my barks only got louder and more challenging.

A man staggered in and fumes of alcohol assailed me. I had been into pubs a few times with my previous master and had always found the smell of alcohol unpleasant but not disturbing. However, this had the smell of sickness.

'What the bloody 'ell's that?'

The man lurched towards us. He was fairly young, about thirty, thirty-five, prematurely balding, his face vaguely containing the same features as Bella's. His clothes were untidy but not dishevelled; he wore no shirt, just a loose-fitting sweater under his jacket. Just as Bella was broad and expansive, he was small and mean. A giant, to me, of course, but a small, mean giant.

'Haven't you been in to work again?' Bella asked, still drawing her sleepy wits together.

He ignored the question and made a grab for me, a horrible sneer distorting his lips. I growled and snapped at his hand; I didn't like him at all.

'Leave the dog alone!' Bella pushed his hand away and heaved her legs on to the floor, causing me to fall back into the space she'd just vacated.

'Dog? Call that a dog?' He cuffed my head with malicious playfulness. I warned him not to do it again. 'Where'd he come from? You know you're not allowed dogs in the flats.'

'Leave him be. I found him outside – starving, he was, poor little thing.'

Bella rose, towering above me and dwarfing the weasel I supposed was her son. 'You stink,' she told him, standing between us to stop his teasing. 'What about your job? You can't keep taking time off like this.'

The weasel cursed his job then his mother. 'Where's me dinner' he asked.

'The dog's had it.'

I groaned inwardly. That should endear me to him.

'He bloody better not have!'

'I didn't know you'd be home, did I? I thought you'd gone off to work.'

'Well, I haven't, so find me something.'

I think she should have picked him up by the scruff of the neck and stuck his head in a bucket of water – she was big enough to do so – but instead she marched off into the kitchen, and soon the sounds of cupboard doors opening and closing reached our ears.

He leered down at me and I glared nervously back at him.

'Off!' he commanded, jerking his thumb away from the settee.

'Get lost,' I replied with more coolness than I actually felt.

'I said *off*!' He lunged and swept me from my comfortable perch with a strength that petrified me. I still had to learn I was only a dog, and a pretty feeble one at that. I yelped in dismay and scooted off into the kitchen, seeking protection from Bella.

'All right, boy, all right. Take no notice of him. Let's give him his dinner and he'll soon be off to sleep, don't you worry.' She busied herself preparing the weasel's meal while I kept as close to her as possible. The food odours began to arouse my palate again and suddenly I was just as hungry as before. I rested my paws against her broad flank and begged to be fed again.

'No, no. You get down now!' Her hand was more firm than before. 'You've had your dinner, it's his turn now.'

Still I persisted, but Bella ignored my whines. She began to talk to me, maybe to soothe me, or perhaps she was really talking to herself.

'Takes after his father. Never no good, but what do you do? They're flesh and blood. He could've been something, that boy, but he's wasted himself. Just like the old man, God rest him, same blood in 'em. I've done me best, God knows I've done me best. Kept him – kept 'em both – when they were out of work. They've made me old, they have, between 'em.'

The smell of cooking was making me delirious.

'He's had some nice girls too. Can't keep 'em, though. Run a mile when they find out what he's like. He'll never change. Arnold, it's nearly ready! Don't you go asleep!'

Bacon, eggs, more sausages. Oh God!

She began to butter bread at the kitchen table while I stayed rooted beneath the cooker, oblivious to the hot fat that spluttered and occasionally spat over. Bella brushed me out of the way with a leg and emptied the contents of the pan on to a plate. She put the plate on the table then clattered about for a knife and fork.

'Arnold! Your dinner's ready,' she called out. No reply. With an annoyed grunt and a determined look on her face Bella marched into the front room.

The dinner on the table beckoned to me.

It was unfortunate really that the chair previously occupied by Bella was still projecting out from the kitchen table. I clambered on to it, falling back down once but renewing my efforts with desperate eagerness, then rested my paws on the table-top. Bella could only have been out of the room for no more than a few seconds, but that's all it took for two slices of bacon and one and a half sausages to be devoured. I was saving the eggs till last.

My shriek of alarm joined Bella's shriek of dismay and the weasel's shriek of rage in a reverberating cacophony. I leapt from the chair just as the son lunged past his mother, claws outstretched to throttle me. Fortunately Bella used her massive frame to block his path and he sprawled forward over her fleshy hip, tumbling on to the floor in a loose bundle as only drunks can.

But even Bella was cross with me. I could see those muscled forearms were going to deal out some heavy punishment, so I did my best to keep the kitchen table between us. She stepped round her floundering son and advanced on me. I waited till she was half-way round the table, my front legs down, chin almost touching the floor, haunches high and quivering, then I shot beneath the table, heading for the open doorway – and straight into the arms of the weasel.

He picked me up by the neck, using two hands and squeezed as he did so, and raised himself from the floor, his demonic face only inches away from mine. My squirming body made him even more unsteady on his feet and he fell forward against the table. What was left of his dinner went flying as my back legs scrabbled for support, and his buttered bread, tomato sauce and God-knows-what-else followed suit.

'I'll kill 'im!' was all I heard before I sank my teeth into his skinny nose. (I'll bet he's still got those two rows of indents on either side of his snout today.)

'Get 'ib boff,' he cried out to his mother, and I felt huge banana hands engulf me. Bella ripped me away from him and I had the pleasure of seeing red skid-marks down the length of his nose. He clutched at it with both hands and howled, skipping on the spot in a sort of dance.

'Jesus, Jesus,' moaned Bella. 'You'll have to go now. I can't keep you now.'

She swept me out of the kitchen, shielding me with her body from her hopping son, lest he forget his pain for a moment and make a grab for me. I don't think I wanted to stay any more, so I hardly protested when the front door opened and I was dumped outside. A heavy hand descended upon me and gave me one long last stroke. 'Off you go now, go on, get away,' Bella said, not unkindly, and the door closed, leaving me alone again.

Even then, I lingered for a moment looking mournfully up at the door, but when it flew open and the weasel appeared, his nose a bloody protuberance and his body shaking with fury, I knew it wouldn't be healthy to stay any longer. So I scooted, and he scooted after me.

As an ally to speed, I think terror has it over rage; I soon left him far behind, anyway.

Blurred images again: cars, people, buildings, none of them focused, none of them very real. Only the overpowering scent from a lamp-post halted my flight. I skidded to a stop, my back legs overtaking my front legs, and executed a clumsy turnabout. I trotted back to this ambrosial column, senses keen, nose twitching inquisitively. Of all the smells that had recently come to me, this was by far the most interesting. It was dog, you see, dog in the plural. There were six or seven different personalities wafting from the base of that concrete structure – not to mention a couple of human smells – and I drank them in giddily. I had sniffed trees and lamp-posts before, but now it seemed my senses were wakening afresh, or perhaps they were just heightening. I could almost *see* the dogs that had visited this towering urinal, almost *speak* to them it was as if they'd left a recorded message for me. I could even detect the female of the species, and that, I think, has a lot to do with the dogs' interest in each other's pee: the sexual instinct, the search for a mate. The girls and boys had left their calling cards as if to say: I've been here, this is my route; if you're interested, I may pass this way again. I was too young to be disturbed by any sexual connotation at that time, the rank yet spicy odours interesting me on a different level. They were company.

When my nose had been satiated I began to sniff my way along the pavement, oblivious to the passers-by, lost in the pursuit of intriguing trails. It was not long before sounds even more intriguing reached my ears. They were just a babble at first, like the clacking of excited geese, but as I drew nearer to their source, they took on a distinctly human quality. I quickened my pace, elation beginning to rise in me, the sounds sending out attracting waves of excitement.

Reaching a broad river of road I hesitated before dashing across and, fortunately, no dragons bore down on me. The sounds were now clamorous in my ears and, turning a corner, I fell upon their origin: an enormous expanse of running, jumping, shouting, screaming, giggling, crying, playing children. I had found a school. My tail launched into its self-motorized wagging and I sprang forward, thrusting my narrow head between the railings surrounding the playground.

A group of small girls spotted me and gleefully ran over, their hands reaching through the iron bars to pat my back. They screamed in delight as I tried to nip any fingers that tried to stroke my head; my intention wasn't to bite them, but to taste their soft flesh, to savour them. Soon, a large group of both boys and girls had formed a semicircle around my protruding head, the bigger boys pushing themselves forward through the crowd. Toffees were thrust into my eager mouth and fingers hastily withdrawn when it seemed I would swallow them too. A tiny girl with sunshine hair pushed her face close to mine and my tongue made her nose and cheek glistening wet. She didn't pull away, though, she hugged my neck.

And then fickle memories returned to taunt me. I had owned one of these! I almost thought this one was mine, she was the child who had belonged to me, but different features swam into vision. The hair was the same, a bright halo around an urchin face, but my daughter's eyes had been blue and the eyes that now smiled into mine were brown. A cry of hopefulness escaped me and the girl mistook it for one of fear. She tried to soothe me over the clamour of the other children, pleading with me not to be afraid, but my mind was paralyzed with one thought. I was a man! Why was I living as a dog?

Then the paralysis wore off as the realization slipped back into its hidden crevice and once again, in essence, I was a dog. (Although the disturbing fact that I was really a man never left me in those early months, because of the conflict of also being a dog, my humanness played a very varying degree of importance.)

My tail began its flag-waving again and I gratefully accepted more sweets. The kids fussed over me and tried to discover my name by calling out possibilities and waiting to see if I reacted to any. For the life of me I couldn't remember what I'd been called before, and the boys found nothing inscribed on my collar. Rover, King, Rex, Turdface (*Turdface!* What little horror threw that one in?) – I beamed at them all. Names meant nothing to me, nor do they to any dog – they recognize particular sounds. I was just happy to be among friends.

A sharp whistle shrilled through my ears and a loud moan went up from the children. Reluctantly, and only after a few sharper blasts from the whistle, they turned away and left me, my shoulders pressed hard up against the railings in an effort to follow. Sunshine Hair stayed till last and gave my neck a long, hard squeeze before departing. I woofed at them not to go, but they stood in rows with their backs to me, occasionally sneaking a look round, their shoulders jerking in suppressed giggles. Then, row by row, they filed into a miserable grey building and the door was closed behind the last one.

I stared blankly into the empty playground, distressed that I'd lost my new friends. I grinned and straightened up as little white faces appeared at upstairs windows, but these were soon joined by the older, wizened face of a teacher whose harsh, muffled voice carried across the playground, ordering the pupils to return to their seats. A boy who was slower than the rest got his ear tweaked as encouragement. I stayed there for a few more hopeful minutes, but finally, and mournfully, I tugged my head loose from the railings.

Dogs generally have happy spirits, and most emotions are sacrificed to inquisitiveness anyway, so when an old man cycled by with a shopping-bag dangling from his handlebars, I forgot my disappointment and trotted along after him. I could see a leafy sprig protruding from a hole in the base of his shopping-bag. I think it must have been rhubarb – it had a sweet tangy smell – and it looked very appetizing. I soon caught up with him, for he was quite old and peddling very slowly, and before he had a chance to notice me I leapt up at the tantalizing sprig. I was both lucky and unlucky.

I pulled the leaf and its stalk through the hole, but the sudden action unbalanced the cyclist and he came crashing down on top of me, machine and all. The breath was knocked from me so that my yelp of pain was only a crushed squeal. I spluttered for air and tried to apologize to the old man for bringing him down, but my words emerged as a series of wheezy grunts which he didn't understand. He flailed his arms around, trying to hit me, not even *trying* to sympathize with my hunger, cursing and groaning as if he'd been tossed by a bull on to a bed of nails. And I'd managed to break his fall too!

There was no point in my staying, he wasn't in the mood to offer me any food, so I tried to struggle free of both man and machine. A few hefty clouts from him helped me considerably and I was delighted to discover the contents of the shopping-bag had scattered along the pavement. I ignored the long red stalks whose brief taste of foliage hadn't excited me tremendously and dashed at a juicy looking red apple. My jaws clamped down on it – not an easy feat, for it was a large apple – and then I scampered out of range of angry fists and abusive language. It was fortunate his feet were tangled up in the bike frame otherwise I'm sure they'd have been used to send me on my way. At a safe distance, I turned and dropped the apple on the ground before me. I had meant to apologize again for I did feel sorry I'd caused the man to fall and hurt himself, but his purple face and shaking fist convinced me he wouldn't be pacified. So, picking up my apple, I made off, looking back once to see him being lifted to his feet by two passers-by. He seemed all right as he hobbled around testing his aged legs, so I continued on my way.

I found a reasonably quiet side-street and settled down against a wall to eat my plunder. My appetite never seemed to be satiated in those early days and those 'experts' who tell you dogs need only one meal a day are talking through their hats. Certainly a dog only *needs* one meal a day to get by, but then, so does a human. How would you feel if that's all you had? And how would you feel if you had to fast for one day a week, something the 'experts' also recommend? What's the use of a glossy coat and a damp nose if you've got a gnawing stomach? I wolfed that apple down, core and all, as if it was all I'd eaten that day. The sun beat down on me and I dozed off, forgetting my problems, drowsiness forcing me to accept what was.

One of those inevitable English summer showers aroused me and I automatically looked at my wrist to see what the time was. The sight of my thin, hairy dog's legs shocked me into reality. I trotted to my feet and shook myself, then looked around; it must have been mid-afternoon and I was hungry again.

I set off down the narrow street, investigating new smells as they came to me, chasing a beetle as it scurried across my path, calling hello to a dog being led by a man on the other side of the street. The dog, a disdainful little corgi, ignored me and I just wasn't interested enough to make conversation. It slowly dawned on me as I trotted on that I needed a quiet safe place, somewhere I could rest and try to unscramble my jumbled thoughts. I needed food and I needed protection. Some kind of sympathy would have been welcome too.

But I didn't find it that day.

I pushed my rump back in the doorway to avoid the drizzling rain spattering against my nose and foreface. It had been an afternoon of wandering and wondering; the sun had been dimmed by the steady drizzle and the damp had made the people even more insulated. Earlier on, the streets had suddenly become crowded, overwhelming me with their congestion so that I could only cower miserably under a railway arch. After what seemed a long time, their numbers dwindled and I ventured forth again, but by now my spirits had caved in completely. My tail dropped between my legs and my eyes scarcely left the pavement in front of me. As the evening drew on and the light faded, my loneliness had increased to such an extent that I was tempted to go back to the dogs' home – the Return of the Prodigal, Lassie Comes Home. The thought of being put to sleep – murdered, I mean – wouldn't have deterred me. I would be good, I would play the underdog to its lowest level, and the keepers would forgive me, give me another chance to prove my worthiness to be an unworthy creature, to be just another dog. I couldn't remember where the hell the dogs' home was, though.

I gazed longingly up at lighted windows, yearning for company, drinking in the inviting smells, but the rain drove me on, searching and just not finding.

The hour was late now and, apart from the occasional swish of a passing car, the streets were cold and empty. I huddled in the doorway, and my wretched spirit huddled within me. Tiredness made my eyelids droop, only hunger keeping me awake. Questions invaded my misery.

This place wasn't familiar to me, yet I knew it was London. Was I from London? No, I wasn't from London. How did I know? I just knew. I had a memory of green fields, open space; a town, but not a big town. They had formed the greater part of my life, these fields and this town. Where were they? If only I could find them. And yet I knew this city, even if this particular district was unfamiliar. Had I worked in London? I had a sudden vision of a woman, in her late fifties, plump but not large, smiling and holding her arms out, and it seemed she held them out to me, calling a name that was soundless to my ears. Her head became that of a dog's, and was just as warm, just as affectionate, just as welcoming. My two mothers vanished from my mind and were replaced by the figure of a man, a man who appeared quite normal, handsome in a featureless way, and his environment was somehow different, not part of the scene I had just envisaged.

I hated him. Was it me?

My thoughts wearily wandered on, uncontrolled, undirected: the child again, obviously mine; the girl – young woman – certainly my wife; a house; a street, a muddy lane; a town. The name of the town almost came to me; the names of the girl and the child hovered behind a tissue-thin barrier; my own name was rising from ocean depths and about to break surface. But a car swished past and the names scattered like startled fish.

I watched the car's rear lights recede into the distance, twin reflections on the soggy road diminishing with them, suddenly reinforced by brake lights, and disappearing as the vehicle turned a corner (even that seemed familiar). I was alone again in an empty world and with an empty head. Then I saw the ghost.

Have you ever seen a ghost? Probably not. But have you ever seen a dog suddenly become alert, for no apparent reason, his ears cocked, his hair bristling? You'd undoubtedly think he's just heard something that's escaped your ears, somebody walking by the house, another dog barking somewhere far in the night: and many times you'd be right. But often, it's because he's aware of presence – a spirit. He won't always be alarmed, perhaps just disturbed; it depends largely on the nature of the ghost itself. It could be friendly or unfriendly.

Think I'm going a bit far now? Just wait till later.

The ghost drifted across the road towards me, a shadowy form, a wispy, vaporous figure. It didn't see me, or, if it did, it chose to ignore me, and as the shape drew nearer, I was able to distinguish a face, shoulders, and a part of a torso. The apparition seemed to be wearing a jacket, and I could certainly make out a shirt-collar and tie. Why wasn't it naked – why do astral bodies never seem to be naked? Don't ask me, I'm only a dog.

Now, I was disturbed, I admit it. There was nothing evil emanating from the spirit, I'm sure, but it was my first ghost both as a dog or as a man. My hair stood on end and my eyes widened. My mouth suddenly felt very dry. I was too frightened even to whine and the power to run had left me completely.

It had the saddest countenance I've ever seen, a face that had been made aware of the ills of mankind, had learned the first lesson in death. It passed by me, close enough to touch, and I could clearly see the rain drizzling through it. Then the spectre was gone, drifting off into the night, leaving me to wonder if my restless mind hadn't invented the whole thing. It hadn't, for I was to see many more of these wandering spirits, most with the same burden of sadness, unaware it was just a phase for them; but it was a long time before I discovered their meaning.

The experience drained me of what strength I had left and I fell into a deep undisturbed sleep.

SEVEN

Gentle nudging woke me.

I shifted my position and tried to ignore the prodding, but I was too cold to become comfortable again. My eyes opened of their own accord and I saw a big black dog hovering over me.

'Come on, squirt, don't let them find you napping there.'

I blinked my eyes furiously, now fully awake.

'Where did you get loose from, eh? Run away from home, or did they lose you on purpose?' The big dog grinned down at me.

I shivered and tottered to my feet. 'Who are you?' I asked, unable to stifle a yawn. I stretched stiff limbs, my front legs going down on the ground, my back pushing my rump into the air as far as it could go.

'Rumbo's what they call me. You got a name?'

I shook my head. 'I might have. I can't remember it, though.'

The dog regarded me silently for a few moments, then had a sniff around me. 'There's something funny about you,' he announced finally.

I gulped at the understatement. 'You don't seem like the other dogs I know either,' I said. And he wasn't, I could sense it immediately. He was somehow brighter, or un-doglike, or . . . more human.

'We're all different. Some are more dopey than others, that's all. But with you it's something else. You're definitely a dog, aren't you?'

I nearly blurted out my problems to him there and then, but he suddenly lost interest in that line of thought and directed my own on to a much more basic level. 'You hungry?' he asked.

Only ravenous, I thought, nodding my head sharply.

'Come on, then, let's go and find something.' He turned away and was off down the road at a brisk pace. I had to scamper to catch up with him.

He was a bony mongrel, about five or six years old, an amalgamation of several breeds. Imagine a Dalmatian without spots, just black all over, and without elegant lines, with turned-in toes, cow-hocked hindquarters, excessive angulation of the back legs (they stuck out backwards too far) and weak pasterns, then you'd have a fair impression of Rumbo. He certainly wasn't ugly – not to me anyway – but he wouldn't have won any prizes, either.

'Come on, pup!' he called over his shoulder. 'We don't want to be late for breakfast!'

I drew level with him and said breathlessly, 'Do you think we could stop for just a minute, I need to do something?'

'What? Oh yes, all right.' He stopped and I squatted on the ground before him. He turned away in disgust and trotted over to a nearby lamp-post, cocked his leg and relieved himself in a professional manner. 'You'll avoid accidents if you do it this way,' he called over, as I tried to shift a leg that was being threatened by a spreading puddle.

I smiled back feebly, grateful that the streets were fairly empty and no human could see me in this undignified pose. It was the first time I'd felt self-conscious about that sort of thing, a sign of the dog versus human instinct conflict that was going on inside me.

Rumbo came over and sniffed mine and I went over to the lamp-post and sniffed his. When we were both satisfied, we went on our way.

'Where are we going?' I asked him, but he ignored me, his step becoming faster, excitement tightening his movements. Then I caught the first whiff of food, and my attention was captured.

The roads were busier now, yet the noise and the bustle didn't seem to bother Rumbo at all. I stuck as close to him as possible, my shoulder occasionally bumping against his thigh. The roads still frightened me; the buses seemed like mobile blocks of flats and the cars like charging elephants. My supersensitive vision didn't help matters much, the blinding colours heightening my fears, but nothing seemed to bother Rumbo. He skilfully avoided pedestrians and used crossings to negotiate the dangerous roads, always waiting for a human to cross first, then trailing behind him, with me trying to become an extension of his body.

We reached a thunderous place where, even though it was still early morning, there were masses of people, hustling, bustling, hurrying – worrying. The noise was deafening, with men shouting, lorries hooting and hand-pulled barrows grinding along the concrete. Rich scents filled the air – the tang of many different fruits, the more earthy smell of vegetables, raw potatoes. If it hadn't been for the apparent chaos, I would have believed I'd found Heaven.

We were in a market, not a street-market, but a covered wholesale market, where restaurateurs, fruiterers, street-traders – anyone who sold fruit, veg or flowers – came to buy their stock; where growers and farmers brought their goods; where lorries arrived from the docks laden with food bought from exotic countries, and trucks departed, full to bursting point, bound for different parts of the country, or back to the docks where their contents would be loaded on to ships; where voices were surly as barter took place, as credit was extended – even as debts were paid.

A burly man, red-faced, bull-necked, wearing a dirty once-white smock, lumbered past us, pulling a barrow piled high with precariously balanced boxes, all packed with greenish-yellow bananas. He sang at the top of his voice, stopping only to swear amiably at a passing workmate, unaware that a hand of bananas was about to topple from the top of his load. As it did so I started forward, but Rumbo barked sharply.

'Don't you dare,' he warned me. 'They'd skin you alive in this place if they caught you stealing.'

Someone shouted and the man stopped his barrow, looked back round the stacked boxes to see the stray bananas. He cheerfully walked back to them and threw them high on to his load. He spotted us as he returned to the barrow's handles and stopped to give Rumbo a hearty pat on his back. I think the pat would have broken my spine. My new friend wagged his tail and tried to lick the man's hand.

'Hello, boy. Brought a friend with you today, 'ave you?' the market porter said, reaching out for me. I backed away; my young body was too tender for such rough treatment. The man chuckled and turned back to his barrow, resuming his tuneless tune.

I was puzzled by Rumbo's attitude: why had we come here if we couldn't sample the food?

'Come on,' he said, as if in answer, and we were off again, dodging round salesmen, porters and buyers, threading our way through the disorder, Rumbo receiving a welcome or a friendly pat now and again. Occasionally we would be shooed on, and once we had to avoid a malicious boot aimed at us, but generally my older companion seemed to be well-known and an accepted part of the scene. Rumbo must have been working at it for quite a long time, for animals – apart from rat-catching cats – aren't generally tolerated around food-markets, particularly strays.

A new overpowering smell reached my sensitive nostrils, easily defeating the tang of mixed fruit and vegetables, and much more enticing to my grumbling tummy: the smell of frying meat. I saw where Rumbo had been heading and raced ahead, leaping up at the high counter of the mobile snack-bar. It was much too high for me, and I could do no more than rest my front paws against it and look up expectantly. I couldn't see anything because of the overhanging counter, but the smell of frying wafted down over me.

Rumbo appeared quite angry when he arrived, and said through clenched teeth, 'Get down, squirt. You'll spoil everything.'

I obeyed reluctantly, not wanting to upset my new-found friend. Rumbo paced himself back so that he would be visible to the man behind the high counter and yipped a couple of times. A skinny old head peeked over the edge of the counter and broke into a yellow-toothed smile.

''Allo, Rumbo. 'Ow yer doin' today? 'Ungry belly, eh? Let's see what we can find yer.' The head disappeared from my view so I rushed to join Rumbo, excitement at the prospect of food elating me.

'Keep still, pup. Don't make a nuisance of yourself or we'll get nothing,' he scolded.

I did my best to remain calm, but when the man behind the counter turned to face us, a juicy-looking sausage held between two fingers, it was too much for me. I jumped up and down in anticipation.

'What's this, then, brought a mate along? This ain't meals-on-wheels yer know, Rumbo, I can't start feedin' all yer mates.' The man shook his head disapprovingly at Rumbo, but nevertheless dropped the sausage between us. I made a grab for it, but my companion was quicker, snarling and gobbling at the same time – not an easy thing to do. He gulped the last morsel into his throat, smacked his thin lips with his tongue and growled. 'Don't take liberties, shrimp. You'll get your turn, just be patient.' He looked up at the man who was laughing at the pair of us. 'What about something for the pup?' Rumbo asked.

'I suppose yer want something for the pup now, do yer?' the man asked. His tired old eyes crinkled and his large hooked nose became even more hooked as his grin spread wide across his thin face. He was an interesting colour actually: yellow with deep mahogany etchings patterning his features, greasy but still somehow dry skinned, the oiliness being only on the surface. 'All right then, let's 'ave a look.' He turned away again and as he was about to find me something a voice called out, 'Cuppa tea, Bert.'

One of the porters leaned his elbows against the counter and yawned. He looked down at us and clicked his tongue in greeting. 'You wanna' watch this, Bert, you'll 'ave the inspectors after you if you 'ave too many of these 'anging about.'

Bert was filling a cup with deep brown tea from the most enormous metal teapot I'd ever seen.

'Yerse,' he agreed. 'It's usually the big one on 'is own. Brought a mate today though, probably one of 'is nippers, looks like 'im, dunnit?'

'Nah,' the porter shook his head. 'The big one's a proper mongrel. The little one's a crossbreed. Got a good bit of Labrador in 'im and . . . let's see . . . a bit of terrier. Nice little thing.'

I wagged my tail for the compliment and looked eagerly up at Bert.

'All right, all right, I know what you want. 'Er's yer sausage. Eat it and then scarper, you'll 'ave me licence.'

He threw the sausage down at me and I managed to catch it in mid-air; it burnt my tongue though and I had to drop it hastily. Rumbo was on it immediately. He bit it in half and swallowed. I pounced on the other half, but Rumbo stood back, allowing me to gulp it down. My eyes watered from the heat of it and I could feel its warmth working its way down my throat.

'Sorry, squirt, but you're here only because I brought you. You've got to learn respect.' Rumbo looked up at the snack-bar man, barked his thanks and trotted away from the stall.

I glanced at the two chuckling men, said my thanks, and chased after him.

'Where we going now, Rumbo?' I shouted.

'Keep your voice down,' he reprimanded, waiting so I could catch up. 'The trick is not to be conspicuous in a place like this. That's why they don't mind me coming in, because I behave myself, keep out of their way and . . .' he looked meaningfully at me, seeing I was about to run after a rolling orange which had fallen from one of the display stands 'and I *never* take anything unless it's offered to me.'

I ignored the orange.

We left the market, accepting half a black soggy banana each on our way, and skipped along into the less cluttered streets.

'Where are we going now?' I inquired again.

'We're going to steal some food now,' he answered.

'But you just said back . . .'

'We were guests there.'

'Oh.'

We found a butcher's on a busy main road. Rumbo stopped me and peeked round the open doorway. 'We've got to be careful here, I did this place last week,' he whispered.

'Er, look, Rumbo, I don't think . . .'

He hushed me up. 'I want you to go in there over to the far corner – don't let him see you till you get there.'

'Look, I'm . . .'

'When you're there, make sure he *does* see you, then you know what to do.'

'What?'

'You know.'

'I don't know. What do you mean?'

Rumbo groaned aloud. 'Save me from stupid mutts,' he said. 'Your business, you do your business.'

'I can't. I can't go in there and do that.'

'You *can*. You're *going* to.'

'But I'm not in the mood.' The thought of the danger had put me in the mood, though.

'You'll manage,' Rumbo said smugly. He sneaked a look back inside the shop. 'Quick, now's the time! He's cutting meat on his slab. Get in there, quick!'

He bustled me in, using his powerful jaws to nip my neck as encouragement. Now, I'm sure you've never seen two dogs act this way outside a butcher's shop before, but there aren't many dogs like Rumbo and me around, just the odd few. You've seen dogs mugging kids for their ice-creams and sweets, though, and I'm sure you've caught your own dog stealing at some time or other. What you haven't seen – or perhaps noticed – is organized canine crime. Most dogs are too stupid for it, but I can assure you it does exist.

I entered the shop and slunk along under the counter where the chopping butcher couldn't see me, looking back pleadingly at my forceful partner. There was no reprieve in his dark brown eyes. Reaching the end of the counter, I cautiously looked up, the sounds of that falling chopper making my body judder with every blow. I made a dash for the corner and squatted, squeezing my bowels to make something happen. We were lucky it was still early morning and there were no customers to complicate things. After a few strained grunts, I began to have some success. Unfortunately, I'd forgotten to draw attention to myself and could have squatted there in peace for quite a long while had not Rumbo lost patience and begun yapping at me.

The butcher stayed his small meat chopper in mid-air and looked over to the doorway.

'Oh, it's you again, is it? Wait till I get hold of you,' he threatened.

He hastily placed his chopper on the counter and started making his way round towards Rambo. That's when he saw me.

Our eyes met, his wide and disbelieving, mine wide and knowing only too well what was going to happen next.

'Oiii!' he cried, and his journey round the counter took on a new pace. I half rose, but running was a problem at that particular moment. Instead, I did a sort of undignified shuffling waddle towards the open doorway. Rumbo was already up at the counter, sorting out the nicest cut for himself while the butcher's whole attention was focused on me. The red-faced butcher had picked up a broom in the course of his journey, one of those heavy jobs used for scrubbing floors as well as sweeping. He waved it in the air before him like a knight's lance, its base aimed at my backside. There was no avoiding it and my awkward predicament didn't help matters.

Thank God the broom had a multitude of bristles, strong and hard but not as strong and hard as the handle would have been. I yelped as they cracked down on my rump, the butcher extending his arm so I was sent scuttling across the floor. I skidded and rolled but was up like a rabbit, running for the open doorway, Rumbo close on my heels, at least a pound and a half of raw steak hanging from his jaws.

'Oiiiii!' was all I heard from the butcher as I flew down the street, my partner-in-crime keeping pace and chuckling at his own cleverness.

Men and women hastily stepped to one side when they saw us coming and one man foolishly tried to snatch the dangling meat from Rumbo's mouth. Rumbo was too wily for that and easily avoided the grasping hand, leaving the man sprawled on hands and knees behind him. We ran on, Rumbo keeping a measured pace beside me and much amused by my panic. Finally he called out through his clenched mouth, 'This way, squirt, into the park!'

The urge to go my own way, to get away from this thief, was great, but my appetite was greater; besides, I'd earned my share of the booty. I followed him through rusted iron gates into what seemed to me to be acres and acres of lush greenery surrounded by giant foliage, but what must actually have been a fairly small city park. Rumbo disappeared into a clump of bushes and I chased after him, flopping into a panting, eyes-rolling heap on the soft soil two feet away from the spot where he'd decided to go to earth. He looked at me in a smirky way as I heaved in great lungfuls of air, nodding his head at some inner satisfaction. 'You did all right, pup,' he said. 'With a little bit of guidance you could amount to something. You're not like the other stupid dogs.'

I didn't need to be told that, but his praise pleased me all the same. Nevertheless, I growled at him. 'I could have been hurt there. I can't run as fast as you.'

'A dog can always outrun a man. He'd never have caught you.'

'He did, though,' I retorted, wriggling my rump to make sure nothing had been seriously damaged.

Rumbo grinned, 'You'll learn to take more than that in this life, pup. Men are funny creatures.' He turned his attention to the meat lying between his front paws, nudging it with his nose then licking the juices on it. 'Come on, come and get your share.'

I rose to my feet and gave my body a shake. 'I've got some unfinished business first,' I said huffily, and slunk off further into the bushes. When I returned only moments later, Rumbo was well into the raw steak, chomping and sucking in a disgusting manner. I hurried forward lest he swallowed the lot and launched myself into the meat in an equally disgusting manner. It was a fine meal, the finest I'd had since being a dog. Perhaps the excitement of the chase, the tension of the robbery, had increased my appetite, for even Bella's sausages hadn't tasted as good.

We lay among the bushes smacking our lips with satisfaction, our mouths still full of the steak's juicy blood flavours. After a while, I turned to my new companion and asked him if he often stole food in that way.

'Steal? What's steal? A dog has to eat to live, so you take food where you find it. You can't rely on what man gives you – you'd starve if you did – so you're on the lookout all the time, ready to grab anything that comes your way.'

'Yes, but we actually went into that butcher's and stole that meat,' I insisted.

'There's no such thing as steal for us. We're only animals, you know.' He looked at me meaningfully.

I shrugged my shoulders, unwilling or too content for the moment to pursue the matter further. But all the same I wondered just how aware Rumbo was.

He suddenly jumped to his feet. 'Come on, pup, let's play!' he shouted, and was gone, streaking through the bushes out on to the open grassland. A burst of energy swept through me as though a switch had been turned on somewhere inside, and I dashed after the older dog, yapping joyfully, tail erect, eyes gleaming. We chased, we rolled, we wrestled, Rumbo teasing me mercilessly, showing off his skills of speed, manoeuvrability and strength, submitting to my wilder onslaughts and tossing me aside with the slightest shrug just when I began to feel his equal. I loved it.

The grass was wonderful to wallow in, to rub our backs against, to breathe in its heady fumes. I'd have been happy to have stayed there all day, but after ten minutes or so a surly park-keeper came and chased us away. We mocked him at first, taunting him by coming within easy reach then dodging just as he took a swipe at us. Rumbo was the more daring, actually leaping up and giving the man a gentle push in the back when his attention was on me. The park-keeper's angry curses made us roar with laughter, but Rumbo soon tired of the game and was off through the gates without a word, leaving me to chase after him.

'Wait for me, Rumbo!' I called out, and he slowed his pace to a trot, allowing me to draw alongside.

'Where are we going *now*?' I asked.

'We're going to have our breakfast now,' he replied.

Rumbo led me through a confusing number of side-streets until we reached an enormous corrugated-iron wall running the length of the pavement. We reached a break in it and Rumbo trotted through, his nose twitching for some familiar scent.

'Good,' he said to me. 'He's in his office. Now listen to me, pup: stay good and quiet. The Guvnor doesn't have much patience with dogs, so don't be a nuisance. If he talks to you, just wag your tail and play dumb. Don't get frisky. If he's in a bad mood – I'll give you the nod if he is – make yourself scarce. We can try again later. O.K.?'

I nodded, beginning to feel apprehensive about meeting this 'Guvnor'. Looking around, I saw we were in a vast yard filled with old broken-up and broken-down cars, all piled in precarious-looking heaps. Other, smaller heaps, were scattered around and I saw these were made up of rusted parts from the damaged cars. A weary-looking crane stood at one end and I realized we were in a breaker's yard.

Rumbo had made his way towards a dilapidated wooden hut which stood in the centre of the metal-torn domain and stood scratching at its door, occasionally giving out a moderate bark. The shiny blue Rover parked near the hut stood out like a sore thumb among the mangled wrecks around it, the bright morning sun making its bodywork gleam disdainfully.

The door of the hut swung open and the Guvnor stepped out.

' 'Allo Rumbo, boy!' He beamed down at my tail-wagging friend; his mood seemed good. 'You been out all night again? You're supposed to be a guard dog, you know, stop me having headaches.' He squatted in front of Rumbo and ruffled the dog's fur, slapping his flanks for extra welcome, Rumbo was good – very good; he wagged his tail and shuffled his feet, grinning up at the Guvnor all the time, but not trying to thrust himself on to him, his tongue hanging loose, occasionally flicking upwards to lick the man's face. The Guvnor was heavily built, his long leather jacket bulging tight around the shoulders. He had that fleshy-looking hardness about him, a tough nut who had become used to the good things in life – good food and good liquor. A fat cigar protruded from his mouth and it looked a part of him, like his flattened nose; he would have looked silly without either. His hair, which was just beginning to thin, covered his ears and flowed over his collar at the back. A gold-sovereign ring flaunted itself from one hand while a large diamond ring outdid it on the other. He was about fortyish and had 'Villain' written all over him.

'Who's this you got with you?' The Guvnor looked over at me, surprise on his face. 'Got a little girl friend, have you?'

I bridled at his silly mistake. Fortunately, he corrected himself. 'Oh no, I can see he's just a pal. Here boy, come on.' He extended a hand towards me but I backed away, a little afraid of him.

'Get over here, squirt,' said Rumbo quietly, warning me with annoyance in his voice.

I crept forward cautiously, very uncertain of this man, for he was a strange mixture of kindness and cruelty. Generally, when you taste them, people have both these qualities but usually one is more dominant than the other. With the Guvnor, both characteristics were equally balanced, something I now know is very common in men of his kind. I licked his fingers, ready to bolt at the least sign of aggression. He stopped me as I got carried away with his delicious flavours by clamping my jaws together with a big fist.

'What's your name then, eh?' He yanked at my collar and I tried to pull away, very fearful of him now.

'It's all right, squirt, he won't hurt you if you behave yourself,' Rumbo reassured me.

'No name? No address? Someone didn't want you very much, did they?' The Guvnor let me go, giving me a playful shove towards Rumbo. He stood up and I could sense I was instantly forgotten.

'O.K., Rumbo, let's see what the missis has sent you.' The man walked round to the boot of his Rover, unlocked it and pulled out an interesting-looking plastic bag – interesting because it bulged with what our noses told us could only be food. We danced around his ankles and he held the bag aloft out of reach. 'All right, all right, take it easy. Anyone would think you hadn't eaten for a week.' Rumbo grinned at me.

The Guvnor walked round to the back of the hut to where an old plastic bowl lay and emptied the contents of the bag into it. A meaty bone, soggy cornflakes, bits of bacon fat and half a chocolate bar fell into the bowl, a rich concoction of leftovers. There were even some cold baked beans among the scraps. As a human, my stomach would have turned over; as a dog, it was a gastronomic delight. Our noses disappeared into the mixture and for a few moments our minds were concentrated solely on filling our bellies. Rumbo got the tastier morsels, of course, but I didn't do too badly.

When the bowl was spotlessly clean, my friend wandered over to another bowl which stood beneath a dripping tap. He began to lap greedily at the water and I, my stomach fit to burst, drifted over and did the same. We slumped on the ground after that, too full to move.

'Do you eat this well every day, Rumbo?' I asked.

'No, not always. It's been a good morning. The Guvnor doesn't always bring me something – there've been times he hasn't fed me for days – and it's not always easy to steal. The shop-keepers around here are a bit wary of me now.'

The Guvnor had disappeared inside the hut and I could hear music blaring from a radio.

'Have you always belonged to the Guvnor?'

'I can't remember, to tell you the truth. He's all I've known.' Rumbo became deep in thought. Finally he said, 'No, it's no good. My mind goes fuzzy when I try to think too hard. Sometimes I remember scents when I sniff certain people. They seem familiar to me. I can't remember not knowing the Guvnor, though. He's always been there.'

'Is he good to you?'

'Most of the time. Sometimes he ties me up when he wants to make sure I stay in all night, and sometimes he kicks me hard for shouting too loudly. But I can't help it. He's got some nasty friends and I just let fly at them when they come round.'

'What do they do here?'

'Talk mostly. They stay in that hut for hours, arguing and laughing. There's a few regulars who do the work around here, mess around with those heaps of junk, and things; bring new ones in. They're never very busy.'

'What does the Guvnor do?'

'You're a bit nosy aren't you, squirt?'

'Sorry. I'm just interested, that's all.'

Rumbo eyed me suspiciously for a few moments. 'You're not like other dogs, are you? You're . . . Well, you're a bit like me. Most dogs are very stupid. You're stupid, but not in the same way. Where exactly *are* you from, pup?'

I told him all I could remember and discovered I was beginning to forget my past also. I could still remember the market where I was bought, but not much more between there and the dogs' home. It's something that's happening to me more and more; I have periods of complete lucidity, then my mind can go virtually blank – my past, my origins, a vague blur. I often forget I was a man.

I didn't voice my anxiety over my human ancestry at that time because I didn't want to alarm Rumbo in any way; I needed him so I could learn how to survive as a dog. Acceptance of circumstances comes more easily to an animal, you see, and it was that animal part of me which turned away maddening thoughts.

'You were lucky to get away from the dogs' home, pup. That's the death-house for many,' Rumbo said.

'Have you ever been inside?'

'No, not me. They'll never catch me as long as I can run.'

'Rumbo, why aren't all dogs like us? I mean, why don't they talk like us, think like us?'

He shrugged. 'They just aren't.'

'Rumbo, were you ever . . . do you ever remember being . . . er, have you always been a dog?'

His head jerked up. 'What are you talking about? Of course I've always been a dog? What else could I have been?'

'Oh, nothing.' My head sank miserably down on to my paws. 'I just wondered.'

'You're a strange pup. Don't cause me any trouble here, shrimp, otherwise I'll turn you out. And stop asking silly questions.'

'Sorry, Rumbo,' I said and quickly changed the subject. 'What does the Guvnor do?' I asked again.

Rumbo's answering glare and bared teeth killed my curiosity for the moment. I decided to take a little nap, but just before I dozed off another thought struck me.

'Why don't men understand us when we talk, Rumbo?'

His voice was drowsy with sleep when he replied. 'I don't know. Sometimes the Guvnor understands me when I talk to him, but usually he just ignores me, tells me to quit yapping. Humans are just as stupid as stupid dogs sometimes. Now leave me alone, I'm tired.'

It was then that I realized we hadn't actually been communicating with words: it had been our *minds* speaking to each other. All animals or insects – fish even – have a way of communication whether it's by sound, scent or body display, and I've come to learn that even the dumbest creature has some sort of mental link with his own species – as well as others. It goes far beyond physical communications: how do you explain individual grasshoppers grouping into a swarm of locusts, what makes soldier ants march, what suddenly makes the lemming decide it's time to jump in the sea? Instinct, communication by body secretions, the sense of race survival: they all play their part, but it goes deeper. I'm a dog, and I know.

But I didn't know then. I was a pup, and a confused one at that. I'd found a friend I could talk to through my mind, someone who was more like me than the other dogs I'd met; few had come close, but none were like old Rumbo. I gazed at him fondly through blurred eyes, then I dozed off.

EIGHT

They were good, those days with Rumbo. The first morning had been enlightening and the days that followed were an education. We spent a large part of the time foraging for food, visiting the huge market most mornings (it slowly dawned on me that this was Nine Elms, the fruit and veg. market which had been yanked cruelly from the Covent Garden area to an obscure South Thames position, so I knew I was in South London, somewhere around Vauxhall) and then visiting the shops to see what we could steal. I soon learned to be as swift and cunning as Rumbo, but I never became as audacious. He would disappear into an open doorway of a house and seconds later calmly stroll out with a packet of biscuits, or a loaf, or anything he could lay his jaws on (he once emerged with a leg of lamb between his teeth but he didn't get away with that; a coloured lady came flying out and frightened old Rumbo so much with her shrieking he dropped the meat and bolted, a thrown milk bottle shattering on the pavement behind him).

Once we came across one of those pastry vans unloading its morning delivery. It was filled with trays of sweet-smelling buns and cakes, not to mention freshly baked bread. Rumbo waited until the driver had taken a large tray of pastries into the baker's, then leapt into the open interior of the van. I held back, of course, coward that I am, and watched enviously as Rumbo jumped from the van with a lovely sugared bun glued to his mouth. He crouched beneath the vehicle wolfing his booty as the driver returned for another tray. When he went back into the shop, freshly laden, Rumbo was up inside the van again, gulping down the remains of the first bun while snatching a chocolate éclair from another tray. He did this three times, each time hiding beneath the van before the driver returned, swallowing as fast as he could, when the dope (me) decided to chance his arm. I waited until the man was well inside the shop, scrambled up into the van (no easy task for a pup) and fussily sniffed my way along the delicious racks of confectionery. Rumbo was in and out like a shot, needless to say, but me – I had to be choosy. I had just decided upon a large, succulent-looking lemon meringue tart, torn between it and the chocolate éclair oozing cream lying beside it, when a shadow fell across the open doorway.

I yelped in fright and the man yelped in surprise. His surprise turned to menace and my fright turned to more fright. I tried to explain I was starving, that I hadn't eaten for a week, but he wasn't having any of it. He lurched forward and grabbed for my collar; I backed further into the van. The man cursed and hauled himself inside, crouching so he wouldn't hit his head on the low roof. He advanced on me and I retreated as far as I could go, which wasn't far enough. It's an unpleasant feeling when you know you're going to be hurt and, I must admit, I indulged in pity for myself to the full. Why had I allowed myself to be led on by that thief Rumbo, that crook in dog's clothing? Why had I let myself be bullied into this low life of petty thieving by this sneaky mongrel?

And then there he was, good old Rumbo, on the tail-end of the van, snarling at the delivery man's back, shouting defiantly at him. He was magnificent! The man turned in alarm, bumped his head on the roof, lost his balance and fell backwards on to the trays with their squashy contents. He slipped almost to the floor of the van, only the confined space saving him, and his elbows sunk into the creamy goodies behind him.

I dodged over his sprawled legs and leapt from the van, running even as I landed. Rumbo took his time and helped himself to one more delicacy before he jumped down after me. When we stopped, about a hundred miles later, he was smacking his lips contentedly. I panted my thanks to him and he grinned in his superior way. 'Sometimes, squirt, you're as dumb as the other mutts – maybe dumber. Still, I suppose it takes time to teach a new dog old tricks.' For some reason, he thought that was very funny and repeated it to himself over and over for the rest of that day.

Another trick of Rumbo's, using me as bait, was his diversion tactic. I would gallop up to an unsuspecting, shopping-bag-laden housewife and use all my puppy charms to make her lower her burden to the ground and pet me, maybe even offer me a titbit. If she had children with her it was even easier, for she would be forced into making a fuss of me with them, or at least drag them away. When all her attention was on me – I'd be licking her face or rolling on the ground, offering my tummy to be rubbed – Rumbo would rummage through her unguarded shopping. When he found something tasty he would streak off, leaving me to make my excuses and follow at a more leisurely pace. We often got found out before he'd grabbed anything useful, but that didn't spoil the enjoyment of the game.

Taking sweets from babies was another delightful pastime. Mothers would howl and their offspring would bawl as we scooted off with our prizes. Sudden raids on kids around ice-cream vans were always rewarding, the van's jangling jingle acting as a homing beacon for us. The coming of winter, forced us to cut down on this kind of activity unfortunately, for the parks were empty and the ice-cream vans in hibernation.

Rumbo loved to taunt other dogs. He looked down on all other animals as inferiors, resenting their stupidity, especially dogs, most of whom he considered more feeble-minded than any other living creature. I don't know why he held such a prejudice against dogs; it may have been because he was ashamed of them, ashamed they didn't have his intelligence, his dignity. Oh yes, rogue that he was, Rumbo had lots of dignity. Rumbo never begged, for instance; he asked for food, or he stole it, but he never grovelled for it. Sometimes he might act out a parody of a dog begging for food or affection, but this was always for his own cynical amusement. He taught me that life took advantage of the living, and to exist – really to *exist* – you had to take advantage of life. In his opinion, dogs had let themselves become slaves to man. *He* wasn't owned by the Guvnor, he did a job of work for him by guarding the yard, thereby earning his keep, such as it was. The Guvnor understood this and their relationship was based on mutual respect. I wasn't sure the Guvnor had such finer feelings, but I kept my opinion to myself, for I was only a pupil – Rumbo was the master.

Anyway, my companion never lost a chance of telling another dog how stupid he was. Poodles were his greatest source of derision and he would laugh uncontrollably at their clipped curls. The poor old dachshund came in for a bellyful too. Rumbo didn't care whom he picked on, be it an Alsatian or a Chihuahua. However, I did once witness him go very quiet and reflective when a Dobermann passed us by.

He got himself, and often me, into some fine old scrapes, other dogs sensing our difference and ganging up on us. I suffered as a pup, but it certainly toughened me up. I learned to run a lot faster too. The funny thing was, Rumbo could have been leader of the pack easily, for he was strong as well as smart, a good combination for the dog world; but he was essentially a loner, he went where he wanted to go, unhampered by thoughts of others. I'm still not sure why he took up with me; I can only suppose he recognized our mutual freakishness.

He was a Romeo, too. He loved the ladies, did Rumbo, and there again, size or breed meant nothing to him. He would disappear for days, returning with a tired but smug grin on his face. When I asked where he'd been, he always said he'd tell me when I was old enough to know.

I always knew when he would be off, for a strangely exciting smell would suddenly fill the air and Rumbo would stiffen, sniff, and bolt out of the yard – with me vainly trying to follow. It would be a bitch in heat of course, somewhere in the neighbourhood, possibly a couple of miles away, but I was too young to know about such things. So I'd wait patiently for his return, moping around until he did, angry at being left behind. Still, Rumbo was always pretty easy to live with for the next few days.

Another great pastime of his was rat-catching. God, how he hated rats, that Rumbo! There were never many in the yard, he made sure of that, but occasionally the odd two or three would make a reconnoitre, looking for a fresh supply of food, I suppose, or perhaps a new breeding ground. Rumbo would always know when they were about, he had a sixth sense for it. His hairs would bristle and his lips curl back revealing yellow fan-like teeth, and he'd snarl a deep menacing animal snarl. It would frighten the life out of me. Then he'd creep forward, taking his time, and he'd mooch through the old junks, oblivious of me, a hunter stalking his prey, a killer closing in on his kill. At first, I'd stay in the background, the vile creatures terrifying me with their evil looks and their foul language, but eventually Rumbo's hate passed on to me, turning my fear into revulsion then detestation. Detestation led to anger, and anger overcame my nervousness. So we'd rout the rats together.

Mind you, they were brave, some of those rats, loathsome as they were. The sight of nice juicy puppy flesh may have had something to do with their fearlessness, and in those early days my life was often in jeopardy, and it's thanks to Rumbo that I'm still in one piece today. (Of course, he soon realized what wonderful rat-bait he possessed, and it wasn't long before he'd coaxed me into acting as such.) As the months went on, my meat became more stringy – thin I think you'd call me, despite our scavenging – and my legs longer, my jaws and teeth stronger. The rats no longer regarded me as dinner but as diner and treated me with much more respect.

We never really ate them. We'd tear them to pieces, we'd break their bones – but their flesh just wasn't to our taste, no matter how hungry we felt at the time.

Rumbo loved to taunt them when he had them cornered. They'd hiss and curse at him, threaten him, bare their cruel teeth, but he would only sneer, taunt them all the more. He would advance slowly, his eyes never leaving theirs, and the rats would back away, bunch up their hindquarters, their bodies tensed for the leap forward. They'd make their move and Rumbo would make his. Dog and rat would meet in mid-air and the ensuing fight would be almost too frenzied to follow with the eye. The outcome was always inevitable: a high-pitched squeal, a stiff-haired body flying through the air, and Rumbo pouncing triumphantly on his broken-necked opponent as it landed in a nerve-twitching heap. Meanwhile, I was left to deal with any of the unfortunate vermin's companions, and this I learned to do almost as ably – but never with quite as much relish – as Rumbo.

We almost came unstuck one day, however.

It was winter, and the mud in the yard was frost-hard. The yard itself was locked and deserted – it must have been a Sunday – and Rumbo and I were warm and snug on the back seat of a wrecked Morris 1100 which was acting as a sort of temporary bedsitter until more suitable accommodation came along (our previous lodgings, a spacious Zephyr, having been broken up completely and sold as scrap). Rumbo's head shot up first and mine was a close second; we'd heard a noise and that familiar rank smell was in the air. We crept silently from the battered car and followed our noses towards the odour's source, in among the jumble of wrecks, through the narrow alleyways of twisted metal, the rat scent drawing us on, the occasional scratching against metal making our ears twitch. We soon came upon them.

Or rather, he came upon us.

We had stopped before a turn in the path through the cars, aware that our prey lay just around the corner, the strong smell and the scratching noises our informant, and were tensing up for the rush when, suddenly he appeared before us.

He was the biggest rat I'd ever seen, more than half my size (and I'd grown considerably), his hair was brown and his incisors were long and wicked-looking. The creature was just as startled as us by the sudden confrontation and disappeared instantly, leaving us to blink our eyes in surprise. We rushed round the corner, but he was gone.

'Looking for me?' came a voice from somewhere high up. We looked around us in bewilderment then spotted the rat together. He was perched on the roof of a car and looking down at us contemptuously.

'Up here, you mangy-looking curs. Coming up to get me?' he said.

Now rats aren't generally given much to conversation, most of them just spit and swear or scowl a lot, but this was the talkingest rat I'd ever come across.

'I've heard about you two,' he went on. 'You've caused us a lot of problems. At least, so the ones who've managed to get away tell me.' (You can't catch 'em all.) I've been wanting to meet you both – especially you, the big one. Think you're a match for me?'

I had to admire Rumbo's nerve, for I was set to run and hide. The rat may have been smaller than me, but those teeth and claws looked as though they could do a lot of damage to tender dog-meat. However, Rumbo spoke up, not a trace of nervousness in his voice: 'Are you going to come down, mouth, or do I have to come up and get you?'

The rat actually laughed – rats don't laugh much – and settled himself into a more comfortable position. 'I'll come down, cur, but in my own time; first I want to talk.' (*Certainly* no ordinary rat this.) 'What exactly have you got against us rats, friend? I know we're loved neither by man or animal, but you have a special dislike, haven't you? Is it because we're scavengers? But then aren't you worse? Aren't all captured animals the lowest scavengers because they live off man – as parasites? Of course, you can't even dignify your existence with the word "captured" because most of you choose that way of life, don't you? Do *you* hate us because we're free, not domesticated, not . . .' he paused, grinning slyly, '. . . neutered as you are?'

Rumbo bridled at his last remark. 'I'm not neutered, rat-face, they'll never do that to me!'

'It doesn't have to be a physical thing, you know,' the rat said smugly. 'It's your mind I'm talking about.'

'I've still got a mind of my own.'

'Have you, have you?' The rat snorted. 'At least we vermin run free, no keepers for us.'

'Who the hell would want you?' Rumbo scoffed. 'You even turn on each other when things get rough.'

'That's called survival, dog. Survival.' The rat was displeased. He rose to his feet. '*You* hate us because you know we're all the same – man, animal, insect – all the same, and *you* know rats live an existence others try to hide. Isn't that so, dog?'

'No, it's not so, and *you* know that!'

There were a lot of 'you knows' flying around. Unfortunately, *I* didn't know what they were talking about.

Rumbo advanced towards the car, his coat bristling with rage. 'There's a reason for rats living the way they do, just as there's a reason for the way dogs live. And you know it!'

'Yes, and there's a reason for me to tear your throat out,' the rat spat at Rumbo.

'That'll be the day, ratface!'

They ranted at each other for another five minutes before their anger finally boiled over. And it boiled over in a strange way.

Both rat and dog went suddenly quiet as though there were nothing left to say. They glared into each other's eyes, Rumbo's brown and bulging, the rat's yellow and evil; both pairs were filled with hate. The tension between them mounted, a screaming silence, a building of venom. Then, with a squeal, the rat launched himself from the car roof.

Rumbo was ready. He leapt aside so that the vermin landed heavily on the hard earth, then struck out for the rat's neck. But the rat squirmed away and turned to meet Rumbo's charge. Teeth clashed against teeth, and claws dug into flesh.

I stood there, stunned and fearful, watching them try to tear each other to pieces. Growls, snarls and squeals came from the struggling bodies, but it was Rumbo's yelp that set me into action. I rushed forward, shouting at the top of my bark, trying to find the rage to give me the courage. There wasn't much I could do, for they were locked together in a writhing embrace, rolling over and over, flaying each other with their feet, biting, drawing blood, ripping skin. I could only lunge in whenever I caught sight of that stinking brown fur, nipping at it with bared teeth.

Quite suddenly, they drew apart, panting, beaten, but still glaring into each other's eyes. I saw that Rumbo's shoulder was badly torn and one of the rat's ears was shredded. They crouched, bodies quivering, low growling sounds at the backs of their throats. I thought perhaps they were too exhausted to carry on, but then I realized they were only regathering their strength.

They sprang at each other again and this time I sprang with them. Rumbo caught the rat by the throat and I managed to bite into one of his front legs. The taste of warm blood sickened me, but I clung to the creature with all my strength. He rolled and squirmed and snapped at us; I felt a sharp pain across my shoulders as he scythed across them with his teeth. The shock made me lose my grip of his leg and, twisting his body, the rat kicked out at me with his hind legs, sending me rolling across the frozen mud.

I rushed straight in and received a deep gash across my nose from the rodent's claws. The pain sent me back again, but I returned just as quickly. Rumbo still had the rat by the throat, endeavouring to lift him from the ground and toss him, a trick I'd seen him use to break other vermin's backs. The rat was too big, though – too heavy. At least the grip Rumbo held prevented the rat doing serious damage with those teeth; he'd cut my shoulders but could have seriously wounded me had his incisors been allowed to sink in. Such was his strength that the big rat managed to break away. He ran free, turned, and streaked back into us, twisting his head from left to right, striking at our vulnerable bodies with his vicious weapons. Rumbo cried out as he was gored along the flank. He staggered to one side and the rat, with a shout of triumph, flew at him. But in his excitement, he'd forgotten about me.

I leapt on to the rat's back, bringing him down with my weight, and biting into the top of his head, breaking a tooth against his skull. The rest was messy and unglorious: Rumbo leapt back into the fray, and between us we managed to kill the creature. The rat didn't die easily, and even to this day I have a grudging admiration for the fight he put up against two heavier opponents. When his squirming finally stopped and the last gasp left his bloody body, I felt not just exhausted but degraded too. He had had just as much right to live as we had, despicable though he was in the eyes of others, and his courage could not be denied. I think Rumbo felt the same sense of shame even though he said nothing.

He dragged the dead body out of sight beneath a car (I don't know why – a sort of burial, I suppose) and returned to lick my wounds for me.

'You did well, pup,' he said wearily between licks. His voice had a quietness to it that was unusual for him. 'He was a big brute. Different from most I've met.'

I whimpered as his tongue flicked across the gash in my nose.

'What did he mean, Rumbo, when he said we're all the same?'

'He was wrong. We're not.'

And that was all my friend had to say on the subject.

The rat incident soured me for the killing of others of the species; I'd fight them certainly, chastise them, but from then on I let them escape. Rumbo soon became aware of my reluctance to kill and grew angry with me; he still hated the creatures and slew them whenever we came in contact with them, perhaps with less relish than before, but with a cold determination.

I've no wish to dwell on our dealings with vermin, for it was an unpleasant and ugly part of my dog life, albeit a very small part; but one other incident has to be mentioned because it shows just how deep Rumbo's hate went for these unfortunate and unblessed creatures.

We came across a nest of them. It was at the far end of the yard and in a car which lay at the very bottom of a tumble of others. The vehicle's roof was crushed flat, there were no doors, and nestled among the stuffing of a torn back seat were a dozen tiny pink rats suckling from their recumbent mother. Their little bodies were still glistening and slick from their birth. The scent drew us like a magnet and we wriggled our way through the twisted junk to reach them. When I saw the babies and the alarmed parent, I prepared to retreat, to leave them in peace. But not Rumbo. He tore into them with a fury I'd never seen before.

I called out to him, pleaded with him, but he was oblivious to my cries. I ran from the place, not wanting to witness such slaughter, and flew from the yard, away from that terrible destruction.

We didn't speak for days after that; I was bewildered by Rumbo's savagery and he was puzzled by my attitude. It has, in fact, taken me a long time to come to terms with the brutality of animal life, and of course it was my very 'humanness' which hindered my progress (or regress – however you care to look at it) towards this acceptance. I think Rumbo put my sulkiness down to growing pains, for growing I certainly was. My puppy fat had almost disappeared entirely, my legs were long and strong (although my back legs were a little cow-hocked). My toenails had been kept trimmed by the constant running on hard concrete and my teeth were firm and sharp. My vision was still excellent, still vivid, unusually lucid. (Rumbo had the normal dog's eyesight: not quite as good as man's and unable to distinguish colours too well. He could see all right in the dark, though, perhaps better than me.) My appetite was extremely healthy and I had no trouble with worms, tartar on the teeth, mange, constipation, diarrhoea, irritable bladder, eczema, ear-canker, nor any other normal dog ailments. Nevertheless I did itch a lot and it was this irritation that brought Rumbo and me together again.

I had observed him scratching with more and more frequency and, I had to admit it, it had become almost a full-time occupation for me, this sucking of fur and raking of skin with hind legs. When I actually saw the little yellow monsters hopping freely over my companion's back like grasshoppers on a heath, my disgust for our condition forced me to make a comment.

'Doesn't the Guvnor ever bath us, Rumbo?'

Rumbo stopped his scratching and eyed me with surprise. 'Fleas annoying you, are they, squirt?'

'Annoying me? I feel like a walking hostel for parasites.'

Rumbo grinned. 'Well you won't like the Guvnor's method of dealing with it.'

I inquired what the method was.

'Whenever he gets fed up with my scratching or can't stand the smell any more, he ties me to a drainpipe, then turns a hose on me. I try to keep out of his way when I'm particularly rancid.'

I shivered at the thought. It was mid-winter.

'There's another way,' Rumbo went on. 'It's just as cold, but at least it's more effective.'

'Anything. Anything's better than this itching.'

'Well,' he hesitated, 'I usually reserve this for warmer times, but if you insist . . .'

I took up my usual position on his left, my head level with his flank, and we trotted out of the yard. He took me to a park, a big one this, and quite a distance from our home. The park contained a pond. And when we reached it, Rumbo told me to jump in.

'Are you kidding?' I said. 'We'll freeze to death. Besides, I don't even know if I can swim.'

Don't be daft,' Rumbo retorted. 'All dogs can swim. As for the cold, you'll find this less unpleasant than being hosed down by the Guvnor. Come on, give it a try.'

With that he plunged into the water, much to the delight of the few children and their parents who were about that wintry morning. Rumbo paddled out to the middle of the pond, swift and confident. He even ducked his head beneath the surface, something I'd never seen a dog do before. I could just imagine the panic among those fleas as they fled to the top of his head, the last refuge on a sinking island, and then their dismay as even this sunk below the waters. He swam in an arc and headed back towards me, calling out for me to join in. But I was too much of a coward.

He reached the bank and hauled himself out. Mothers dragged their offspring away, for they knew what was going to happen next. The dope (yes, me) didn't.

I was drenched with a freezing shower of water as my friend (my crafty friend) shook his whole body to rid his fur of excess moisture. I felt foolish as well as angry; I'd seen dogs do this often enough in my past life, so I shouldn't have been caught napping. Anyway, there I stood, dripping wet, as cold as if I'd plunged in myself.

'Come on, squirt, you're wet enough. You might as well go the whole way now,' Rumbo laughed.

I shivered and had to admit he was right. There was no point in not going in now. I crept towards the edge of the pond and gingerly dipped in a front paw. I pulled it out fast; the water was colder than freezing! I turned my head to tell Rumbo I'd changed my mind, I could put up with the itching for a few more months till the weather got warmer. I barely caught a glimpse of his big black body as he hurtled himself at me. With a yelp of surprise, I fell head-first into the pond, Rumbo tumbling in behind.

I came up spluttering, gasping for air, my mouth and throat, my nose, my ears, my eyes filled with choking water.

'Ooh!' I cried. 'Ooooh!' And over the sound of my splashing I could hear Rumbo laughing. I wanted to strike back at him, I wanted to drown him, but I was too busy trying to survive the cruel pond. My teeth were chattering and my breathing came in short, desperate gasps. Pretty soon – when I realized I could swim – the unpleasantness drowned instead of me and I began to enjoy this new experience. I kicked out with my back legs and paddled with my paws, just managing to keep my nose above the waterline. The effort prevented my limbs from going completely numb and I found I could use my tail as a sort of rudder.

'How d'you like, pup?' I heard Rumbo call out.

Looking about, I saw that he was back in the centre of the pond. I made towards him.

'It's g-good, Rumbo, b-but it's cold,' I replied, my anger forgotten.

'Huh! You wait till you get out!' He submerged again and came up smiling. 'Down you go, pup, put your head under or you'll never get rid of them!'

I remembered the point of the exercise and ducked my head beneath the surface. I came up coughing.

'Again, pup, again! Go right under or they'll never leave you!'

Down I went again, this time holding my breath and staying under for as long as possible. I don't know what the people on the bank thought, for it must have been a peculiar sight to see two mongrels acting like performing seals. We romped around in the water, splashing and barging into each other, thoroughly cleansing ourselves with our vigorous actions. Five minutes was enough, and by mutual consent we headed for the shore. We clambered out, deliberately drenched the human onlookers, and began a game of chase to warm ourselves up.

By the time we got home we were both laughing and giggling, feeling fresh and alive as never before – and, of course, ravenous. We found a well-wrapped packet of sandwiches that one of the Guvnor's workmen had foolishly left lying on a bench while he dismantled a broken engine, and we took them to our snug bedsitter, scoffing the lot within seconds. For once, to my surprise, we shared the food equally, Rumbo making no attempt to gobble the major portion. He grinned at me as I finished the last few crumbs and, after smacking my lips contentedly, I grinned back at him. Our differences were forgotten and Rumbo and I were friends again. There was a subtle change, however: I wasn't exactly equal to Rumbo now, but I was a little less inferior than I had been.

The pupil was beginning to catch up with the master.

NINE

So what of my feelings of being a man in a dog's body?

Well, they certainly never left me, but they didn't often play an important part in my thinking. You see, I was developing as a *dog*, and this development took up most of my time. I was always conscious of my heritage and my human instincts often took over from my canine tendencies, but my physical capabilities were those of a dog (apart from my extraordinary vision) and this governed my attitude. There were many times – nights mostly – when memories fought their way to the surface and questions, questions, questions, tussled with my mind; and there were many times when I was completely and wholly a dog, with no other thoughts but dog thoughts.

I recognized my similarity to Rumbo and I'm sure he recognized it too. The disturbing fact was that I also recognized it in the big rat. Had Rumbo? He was deliberately vague when I tackled him on our difference to others of our kind, and I was never quite sure whether he understood it or if it was just as big a mystery to him. He would shrug his shoulders and dismiss the subject with a remark such as 'Some animals are dumber than others, that's all.' But I would often find him regarding me with a thoughtful look in his eyes.

So I lived my life with Rumbo and the urge to discover the truth of my existence was held in abeyance while I learned to live that life.

Like all dogs, I was fanatically curious; nothing near me went unsniffed, nothing loose went untugged, and nothing pliable went unchewed. Rumbo would lose patience, scold me for behaving like any other stupid mutt (although he liked a good sniff and chew himself) and would generally berate me for my inquisitiveness. We had many afternoons or evenings when he did answer my questions (he had to be in a relaxed and talkative mood to do so), but when he thought too long or too deeply he would become confused and irritable. I often seemed to be about to learn something of significance – perhaps a clue to my own strange existence or a reason for our obviously more advanced development to others of our kind – when his eyes would become blank and he'd go into a long, trance-like silence. It would frighten me, for I would think I'd pushed him too far, his searching mind becoming lost within itself, unable to find the route back. On such occasions I was afraid he'd become just another dog. Then he would blink a few times, look around curiously as though surprised at his surroundings, and carry on talking, ignoring the question I'd asked. These were strange and apprehensive moments for me, so I refrained from triggering them off too frequently.

Other apprehensive moments were when we saw ghosts. It didn't happen often enough for it to become a common occurrence, but enough to be disconcerting. They would drift sadly by, a feeling more than an expression of utter loneliness about them, and some seemed to be in a state of shock, as if they had been torn brutally from their earthly bodies. Rumbo and I would freeze at the sight, but we'd never bark as other dogs might. My companion would warn them to keep away from us with a low growling, but we were of no interest to these spirits and they would drift on without even acknowledging our presence. On one occasion – it was in broad daylight – four or five ghosts, bunched tightly together, wandered through the yard like a small, drifting cloud. Rumbo had no explanation for the phenomenon and forgot about it as soon as it had passed, but it puzzled me for a long time afterwards.

The comings and goings of more mortal beings into the yard began to increase. There were normally two or three full-time overalled men working in the yard, breaking up the junks, and a steady stream of customers looking for cheap parts. Gigantic lorries (gigantic to me) would be loaded with crushed car bodies by the yard's crane, then disappear through the gates with their valuable metal. Vehicles battered beyond repair or too old and tired to run anymore were brought in and dumped unceremoniously on top of precariously balanced scrap piles. But it was a different increase in activity that aroused my curiosity.

The Guvnor began to have frequent visitors who had no interest in the yard itself, but would disappear into his office and remain there for hours on end. They arrived in twos and threes and left in the same numbers. They came from different areas, mostly from Wandsworth and Kennington, but others from Stepney, Tooting, Clapham, with a few from nearby outlying counties. I knew this because I'd listened to their conversations as they waited outside the hut for the Guvnor's arrival (he was often late). One or two would even play with me, or torment me in a friendly way. Rumbo frowned upon my childishness with these men, for they never offered food nor were they relevant to our life-style (Rumbo was choosy about offering his friendship), but I, like any other pup, wanted to be loved by everyone and anyone. I didn't know what their business with the Guvnor was (I noticed they treated him with a lot of respect), nor did I care much; I was just curious because they were outsiders and I could learn more about the other places from them – not just the surrounding area, for I knew enough about that – but other parts further away. I was looking for clues, you see, clues about myself. I felt the more I discovered – or rediscovered – about the world outside, the more chance I had of solving my own riddle.

It was on one such occasion, in fact, that I earned my permanent name. Some of the workmen in the yard had taken to calling me Horace (God knows why, but it seemed to tickle them), and it was a name I detested. They used it in a mocking way and usually – unless they were offering something (which was rare) – I ignored their calls with a nose-up dignity. Even Rumbo, in moments of sarcasm, would call me Horace rather than 'squirt'. In the end, even I was beginning to get used to it.

However, the Guvnor had never bothered to give me a name – I was never important enough to him for that – and he really didn't have much cause to refer to me anyway after our initial meeting months before. I was grateful, at least, that he hadn't picked up this awful nickname from his workmen.

So this is how I got a proper and appropriate name.

A small group of the outsiders had gathered in front of the Guvnor's office – hut – and were awaiting his arrival. Rumbo was away on one of his 'bitch-in-season' jaunts and I was wandering aimlessly around the yard, sulking at being left behind again. I trotted over to the group to see if I could overhear anything of interest (or perhaps to beg for some affection). One of the younger men saw me coming and crouched low, a hand outstretched, to welcome me. ''Ere, boy. Come on.'

I bounced towards him, pleased to be called. 'What's your name, then, eh?'

I didn't want to tell him I was called Horace so I kept quiet and licked his hand.

'Let's 'ave a look at you,' he said, pulling my collar round with his other hand. 'No name on this, is there? Let's see what we've got for you.' He stood up, reaching into his overcoat pocket and my tail began to wag when he produced a small green tube of sweets. He levered a sweet out and held it up for me to see. I went up on my hind legs immediately, mouth gaping for the treat to be dropped into. The man laughed and let the little round sweet fall and I caught it deftly on my tongue, crunching and gulping it down by the time my front legs touched ground again. I jumped up and put my muddy paws against him, asking politely for another; they had a nice minty flavour to them. He was a bit annoyed at the mud on his coat and pushed me down again, brushing at the marks left with his hand. 'Oh no, if you want another one, you've got to earn it. 'Eeyar', catch it.' He threw the mint high into the air and I jumped up to meet it on its downward journey, catching it smartly. The young man laughed and his bored companions began to take an interest. They had been lounging against the car they'd arrived in, a maroon Granada, stamping their feet to keep the circulation flowing, their coat collars turned up against the cold.

'Let's see 'im do it again, Lenny,' one of them said.

The one called Lenny tossed another sweet and again I caught it in mid-air.

'Do it a bit 'igher next time.'

Lenny tossed and I jumped. Success once more.

'You're a clever old thing, aren't you?' said Lenny.

I had to agree; I was feeling quite pleased with myself. As Lenny poised a mint on his thumb and index finger I prepared to repeat my performance.

''Old on, Lenny.' A different man spoke this time. 'Make it do somethin' more difficult.'

'Like what?'

The group of men thought hard for a few moments, then one spotted a couple of tin mugs standing on the hut's windowsill. 'Use them,' he said, pointing towards the mugs. 'The old ball-an'-cones trick.'

'Do leave off! It's only a bleedin' dog, you know,' Lenny protested.

'Gorn, see if it can do it.'

He shrugged and walked over to the mugs. The regular yard workers used these for their tea-breaks, but I don't think they would have offered any objection to these men using them for other purposes. In fact, I had noticed that the Guvnor's regular employees kept well away from the business acquaintances of their boss. Lenny placed the two mugs upside-down on an even piece of ground while I nuzzled him for more sweets. He pushed me away and one of the men took hold of my collar to hold me back.

Lenny levered out a little round mint again and, in exaggerated motions, showed it to me, then placed it under one of the mugs. I pulled against the restraining hand, eager to get at the sweet.

Then Lenny did a puzzling thing: he placed a hand on either mug and whirled them in circles around each other, never letting their lips come off the ground. He did it slowly, but even so it was confusing for a mere dog. He stopped and nodded for the other man to let go. I bounded forward and immediately knocked over the mug which held the strong scent of mint.

I couldn't understand the group's cries of amazement and Lenny's delight as I gulped down the sweet. I accepted Lenny's friendly thumps on the back with a wagging tail, pleased that I had pleased him.

'Aah, it was a fluke. The dog couldn't do it again,' one of the men said. He was grinning though.

'Oh yes it could. It's a clever old thing, this pup,' Lenny retorted.

'Let's 'ave some money on it, then.'

The others agreed enthusiastically. It's funny what a group of bored men will find to amuse themselves.

Once again I was held back while Lenny went through his hand-holding-mint ballet. 'All right. A oncer says 'e does it again.' I was no longer an 'it' to Lenny.

'Right.'

'You're on.'

'Suits.'

And suddenly four pound notes appeared on the ground. The four men looked at me expectantly.

Lenny went through his mug swirling again and one of the men told him to speed it up. He did, and I must admit he had a definite flair for this sort of thing: the movements were baffling to the naked eye. But not to the sensitive nose. I had knocked over the mug and swallowed the sweet within three seconds of being released.

'Fantastic! 'E's a bloody marvel.' Lenny was delighted as he scooped up the four pounds.

'I still say it was a fluke,' a disgruntled voice muttered.

'Put your money where your mouth is, Ronald, my son.'

The bets were placed again, this time one of the men dropped out. 'He's sniffin' it out, I reckon,' he grumbled. This stopped the action; they hadn't thought of that.

'Nah,' Lenny said after a few moments' thought. ''E couldn't smell it with the mug over the top.'

'I dunno, it's pretty strong – peppermint.'

'O.K., O.K. Let's see what else we've got.'

The men rummaged through their pockets but came out with their hands empty. 'Just a minute,' one of them said and turned towards the Granada. He opened the driver's door, reached across the front seat and delved into the glove compartment. He came out with a half-eaten bar of chocolate. 'Keep it in there for the kids,' he said self-consciously. 'Keep the wrapper on so it don't smell so much.' He handed it to Lenny.

My mouth watered at the sight and I had to be firmly held back.

'Fair enough. Let's do it again.' Lenny made sure the wrapping covered all the exposed end of the chocolate and placed it careful beneath a mug. The mug had a nasty-looking grease smear on its base.

The fourth man rejoined the betting and, once more, Lenny's lightning hands went into action. Of course I made straight for the grease-smeared mug.

The chocolate was pulled from my mouth before it could be devoured, but Lenny was more generous with his praise. 'I could make a fortune with this dog,' he told the others, breaking off a tiny square of chocolate and popping it into my mouth. ''E's got brains, 'e's not as daft as 'e looks.' I bridled at this but the thought of more chocolate kept me sweet. ''Ow'd you like to come back to Edenbridge with me, eh? Connie and the kids'll love you. I could make a bomb out of some of the locals with you.'

'That's the Guv's dog, 'e won't let you 'ave it,' the one called Ronald said.

''E might. 'E's got two.'

'Anyway, I still say it was only luck. No dog's that clever.'

Lenny raised his eyes heavenwards. 'You wanna' see 'im do it again?'

Ronald was a bit more reluctant this time and the sound of a car pulling into the yard saved him from deciding whether to risk another pound or not. A sleek Jaguar stopped behind the Granada and the Guvnor stepped out; he changed his cars with more frequency than most people checked their tyres. He wore a heavy sheepskin coat and, of course, a fat cigar jutted comfortably from his mouth. The men greeted him with a friendliness born out of respect more than liking.

'What you lot up to?' He stuck his hands deep into his coat pockets as he swaggered his way round the Jag to the group.

'Just 'avin' a game with the dog 'ere, Guv,' said Lenny.

'Yeah, it's a clever little bugger,' said one of the others.

Lenny seemed hesitant to tell the Guvnor just how clever he thought I was; plans for me were beginning to grow in his mind, I think.

'Nah, it could never do it again, never in a thousand years,' Ronald piped up.

'Do what, Ron?' the Guvnor asked affably.

'Lenny's done 'is ball-and-cones trick and the dog's guessed right every time,' another of the men said.

'Do me a favour!' the Guvnor scoffed.

'Nah, straight,' Lenny said, the thought of making some more instant cash overriding his future money-making plans.

'It must 'ave been a fluke. Dog's ain't that bright.'

'That's what I said, Guv,' Ronald chimed in.

'Yeah, and you lost your money, didn't you, my son,' Lenny grinned.

''Ow much you made so far, Lenny?'

''Er, let's see, Guv. Eight pounds in all.'

'All right. Eight more says it don't do it again.' He had style, the Guvnor.

Lenny hesitated for only a second. He chuckled and went down to the mugs again. 'Now then, boy, I'm relyin' on you. Don't let me down.' He looked at me meaningfully. For myself, I was enjoying the game; I liked pleasing this man, I liked him knowing I was no ordinary dog. I wasn't really grovelling for titbits. I was earning them.

Lenny shuffled the cups, even faster than before under the Guvnor's level gaze, but this time he'd placed the chocolate beneath the mug without the grease smear. He finished his intricate hand movements and looked up at the Guvnor. 'O.K.?' he asked.

The Guvnor nodded and Lenny looked across at me. 'O.K., boy, do your stuff.'

And at that moment Rumbo trotted into the yard.

Curiosity drew him over to the group, and when he saw me being held by the collar and the twin mugs set on the ground before me, he screwed up his brow in a puzzled frown. In an instant he had guessed a trick was being performed for the benefit of the men and I, his protégé, the mutt he had taken under his wing, the scruff in which he had tried to instil some dignity, was the star performer. Rising shame burnt my ears and I hung my head. I looked dolefully up at Rumbo, but he just stood there, his disgust apparent.

'Come on, boy,' Lenny urged. 'Get the chocolate. Come on!'

My tail drooped: I had let Rumbo down. He'd always taught me to be my own dog, never become a pet of man, never become inferior to them; and here I was, like some circus animal, performing tricks for their entertainment. I stepped towards the mugs, kicked the empty one over with a paw and trotted away in search of a dark hole in which to bury myself.

Lenny threw his hands up in the air in disgust and the Guvnor chuckled. Ronald, chortling loudly, stooped and picked up the Guvnor's winnings and handed them to him. As I disappeared round the corner of the hut, I heard the Guvnor say: 'I told you it was a fluke. Yeah – fluke. That's a good name for 'im. 'Ey, Georgie,' he called out to one of the yard workers. 'Get the pup's collar and put its name on it. Fluke! Yeah, that's good!' He was pleased with himself: the money meant nothing, but the scene had made him look good. He was making the most of it. I could still hear him chuckling as he unlocked the office door and the group of men disappeared through it.

So, I had a proper name. And like I say, it was appropriate: Fluke by name, fluke by nature.

TEN

Rumbo never mentioned that incident again. He was a little distant with me for a few days afterwards, but my final action had at least saved me some grace and, because of our need for each other (which Rumbo himself would never have admitted), we were soon back to our old relationship.

Lenny had lost interest in me, his plans for making money out of me dashed by my contrariness. Apart from a rueful grin now and again, he really didn't take much notice of me anymore when he came into the yard. The breaker called Georgie took my collar from me and returned it later. Rumbo told me there were scratch marks on the small metal nameplate and I assumed '*FLUKE*' had been inscribed there. Anyway, that was what they called me in the yard now, and so did the people who petted me in the street once they'd looked at the collar. I was thankful I was no longer known as Horace.

The winter froze on and times for Rumbo and me got leaner. We still made our daily trips to the fruit-market, but our pickings in the shopping-zones had become increasingly more hazardous. The shopkeepers now knew us by sight and would chase us away as soon as we came sniffing around: the cold weather made the housewives more guarded, less friendly. I was fast losing my puppy cuteness (I suppose I was around seven or eight months old by then), and people are less inclined to stop and stroke a gangly mongrel than a plump, furry bundle, so I had become next to useless as a decoy for Rumbo. However, the hardship made us more cunning, swifter in our attacks, and more resourceful in our methods.

A wild dash through a supermarket usually proved fruitful, provided there was a clear exit. One of us would knock stacks of cans over or generally cause a disturbance while the other would sneak in and grab the nearest edible item at hand. That was always very exciting. A romp around a school playground at lunchtime would inevitably yield a sandwich or two, or perhaps an apple or some chocolate. The pandemonium was lovely. A visit to the local street-market never failed to bring us replenishment for our greedy stomachs. The threats and curses our thieving from there caused was, nevertheless, a little alarming. Moreover, we had become too adventurous, and that led to our downfall.

One day Rumbo and I had marched boldly into a backyard, encouraged by our noses which had been enticed by delicious cooking smells. An open doorway stood before us and steam billowed out from within; we were at the back of a restaurant, at the kitchen entry. Both of us were over-confident to the point of recklessness; we had been getting away with it for too long. We ambled in.

It was a high-class restaurant, although you might never have suspected it from the state of the kitchen. I knew it was a good place because of the menu, part of which I could see steaming away on a centre table: roast duckling dripping with orange sauce. It was surrounded by other dishes, but not as mouthwatering, waiting to be carried away into the dining-room (or carried away by two hungry dogs). Apart from the chef, who had his stout back turned to us while he was busy stirring a huge cauldron of simmering soup, the kitchen was empty. Rumbo gave me a quick look, then with one bound was up on the table. I rested my front paws against the table's edge and smiled smugly. Our bellies would be full today.

Rumbo nonchalantly worked his way through the various dishes (if he had been a man, he'd have been humming) until finally he reached the duckling. He flicked out his tongue and began licking at the orange sauce. He looked back at me and I swear he rolled his eyes. My mouth was drooling by now and I was hopping from one hind foot to the other in frustration. Rumbo had a few more licks, then his jaws opened wide to grasp the entire roasted bird between them. It was at that moment the door leading to the dining-room burst open.

We stood paralyzed as a waiter in a white jacket and small black bow-tie, carrying a tray full of half-empty dishes, breezed in, calling out a new order to the chef before he was even through the door. The waiter was fairly small for a man (all tall to me, you see) and wore his jet-black hair greasily slicked down. Above his greasily slicked down moustache was a long, curving nose and, above that, two over-large, bulbous eyes which grew even larger and more bulbous when he saw us. His mouth dropped open to a point where it almost matched Rumbo's and the dishes on his tray slid down the incline he had unconsciously created, slipping over the edge in an avalanche. The terrible crash as they hit the tiled floor set the whole scene in motion again.

The chef whirled, clutching at his heart, the waiter screamed, (I think he was Italian), Rumbo grabbed the duckling, and I (what else?), wet myself.

Rumbo leapt from the table, slid on a slippery patch on the floor, lost the duckling, scrambled to retrieve it, yelped as the hot soup-ladle thrown by the chef skimmed across his back, grabbed the duckling again by the parson's nose end, and scurried for the exit.

The waiter threw the now empty tray at Rumbo, choked back a sob, gave chase, skidded on the same slippery patch, sprawled on his back, and managed to get his legs tangled up in dog and duckling.

The chef moved his hand from his heart to his mouth, roared with furious anguish, lumbered forward, slid on the tray which covered another slippery patch left by the skidding orange-sauce-covered duckling, landed heavily (he was very stout) on the little waiter's chest, and bellowed and kicked at dog, duckling, waiter and all.

I ran away.

Rumbo crept furtively into the yard above five minutes after I'd arrived there. He crawled through our own private entrance at the back of the yard behind a huge pile of wrecks – a one-foot high hole torn in the corrugated-iron fencing at its base – still grasping the now cold roast duckling between his jaws. The young bird looked a bit worse for wear: a *pièce de résistance* that hadn't resisted too well. Nevertheless, to two hungry mongrels it was still a gastronomic triumph, and after we'd sucked every bone clean (I warned Rumbo not to crunch the bones – too splintery, I told him) we had a good chortle over our success. The smirks were wiped from our faces a couple of days later, however.

A uniformed policeman arrived at the yard and asked one of the breakers if there were two black mongrel dogs on the premises. Rumbo and I edged out of sight behind a decaying Ford Anglia and looked at each other nervously. It was obvious the shop-keepers had got together and registered a complaint to the local cop-shop; perhaps the restauranteur had instigated the action. It certainly hadn't taken the police long to track us down. We peeped from behind the old car and saw the breaker pointing nervously towards the Guvnor's office. The young policeman strolled casually over to the hut, examining the various cars parked alongside it. The Guvnor was having one of his now regular meetings with his cronies.

The plod knocked at the door and the Guvnor appeared. We watched his smiling face as he dealt with the policeman's inquiries, showing a disarming charm that had never been apparent to us before. His hands made gestures of surprise, alarm and concern; he nodded his head gravely, then shook it equally as gravely. Then he was back to smiling and smarming, his cigar never once leaving the corner of his mouth during the discourse. With one last smile of assurance from the Guvnor, the young policeman turned and strolled from the yard.

The Guvnor smiled benevolently at the policeman's back until he had disappeared through the gate: then he turned his gaze towards the rest of the yard, a look of sheer thunder on those now rock-like features. He spotted our snouts protruding from the wreck and marched towards us with stiff, determined strides.

'Run, squirt, run!' Rumbo warned me.

I wasn't quick enough. The Guvnor grabbed me before I had a chance to make a break for it. He began to flail at me with a closed fist, keeping a firm grip on my collar as he did so. I'd always felt the Guvnor had a contained cruelty about him (this didn't necessarily make him a cruel man) and now it was let loose and I was its recipient. I howled in pain, and was grateful that a dog's sensitive cells are unevenly distributed over the body otherwise some of these blows would have hurt even more.

Rumbo stood and watched from a distance, anxious for me and fearful for himself.

'Come 'ere, you!' the Guvnor bellowed, but Rumbo wasn't having any. He darted even further away. 'You wait 'till I get 'old of you,' my assailant shouted. Rumbo skipped from the yard.

The Guvnor's anger had been flushed now, but his meanness still remained. He dragged me to the back of the yard, collecting a length of rope on the way, then tied me to a wreck wedged beneath a pile of other wrecks.

'Right,' he snarled as he looped the rope around the empty window-frame of the car. 'Right!' He gave me one last wallop before he marched off, muttering something about the last thing he needed was the law snooping round. 'Right,' I heard him say as he slammed the door shut.

A few minutes later the door opened again and the Guvnor's cronies filed out, climbed into their various cars and drove off. After they'd gone the Guvnor appeared, roared for Rumbo and, when nothing happened went back inside. I had the feeling we wouldn't see old Rumbo for some time.

I tugged and pulled the rope, calling for the Guvnor to come back and let me loose; it was no use, he wouldn't listen. I was frightened to pull on the rope too hard because the cars towering above me looked precariously balanced; I could never figure out how the piles of cars in the yard never toppled. My calls turned into angry shouts, then piteous whining, then sorrowful whimpers and finally, much later on when the yard was deserted, sullen silence.

It was dark when my companion decided to return. I was shivering with the cold and miserable with the loneliness.

'I told you to run,' he said, coming out of the night.

I sniffed.

'He's got a terrible temper,' Rumbo went on, sniffing round me. 'Last time he tied me up, he left me for three days without any food.'

I looked at him reproachfully.

'Still, I can always bring you bits and pieces,' he added consolingly. Suddenly he looked up. 'Oh-oh. It's beginning to rain.'

A raindrop splattered against my nose.

'Not much cover here for you, is there?' he commented. 'Pity the car door's shut – you could've climbed in.'

I studied him quietly for a few moments, then looked away.

'Hungry?' he asked. 'I don't think I could find you anything this time of night.'

My head became dotted with rain-spots.

'Pity we ate that bird all in one go. We should have saved some of that.' He shook his head wistfully.

I peered under the car I was tied to and saw there wasn't enough room to squeeze beneath it. I was becoming wetter.

'Well, squirt,' Rumbo said with false jocularity, 'no sense in both of us getting wet. Think I'll get out of the rain.' He looked at me apologetically. I regarded him disdainfully, then turned my head away again.

''Er . . . I'll see you in the morning then,' he mumbled.

I watched him shuffle away. 'Rumbo,' I said.

He looked back at me, his eyebrows raised. 'Yes?'

'Do me a favour?'

'Yes?'

'Get neutered,' I said mildly.

'Good-night,' he replied, and trotted off to our nice warm bed.

The rain began to beat a rhythmic pattern on my body now and I curled up as small as I could, hunching my neck into my shoulders. It was going to be a long night.

ELEVEN

It was not only a long night but a disturbing one too. It wasn't just the discomfort of being drenched, for my fur held the moisture and formed a snug coating, keeping the worst of the chill away; but my sleep was nagged by memories.

Something had triggered the thoughts off and I didn't know what; it hid away somewhere in my mind's periphery. I saw a town – a village? I saw a house. Faces swam before me: I saw my wife, I saw my daughter. I was in a car; the human hands on the steering-wheel before me were my own. I drove through the town. I saw the angry face of a man I knew; he was also in a car and driving away from me. For some reason I followed. It was dark. Trees, hedges, flashed by, flat and eerie in the headlights. The car in front of me pulled in, turned into a narrow lane. I followed. It stopped; I stopped. The man I knew left his car and walked towards me. In the harsh glare from my headlights I saw his hand was outstretched – he was holding something? I opened my door as the hand pointed towards me. Then everything became a crystal of brilliant, glittering light. And the light became dark; and I knew nothing more.

Rumbo dropped a half-eaten roll in front of me. I sniffed at it and pulled out the thin slice of ham squashed between its crusty covers with my teeth. I gulped the meat down, then licked the butter from the bread. Then I ate the bread.

'You were yelping in your sleep last night,' Rumbo told me.

I tried to remember my dreams and after a while the fragments became whole pieces.

'Rumbo, I haven't always been a dog,' I said.

Rumbo thought before he spoke, then he said, 'Don't be silly.'

'No, listen to me, Rumbo. Please. We're not the same, you and I, not like other dogs. You're aware of that. Don't you know why?'

Rumbo shrugged. 'We're just smarter.'

'It's more than that. We still have the feelings, the thoughts of *men*. It's not just that we're more clever than other dogs – we remember how we *were*!'

'I remember being a dog always.'

'Do you, Rumbo? Don't you ever remember walking upright. Don't you remember having hands, having fingers that you could use? Don't you remember speaking?'

'We're doing that now.'

'No, we're not – not in men's language anyway. We're thinking now, Rumbo, we're making sounds, but our words are more thoughts than those sounds. Don't you see that?'

He shrugged again and I could see the subject bothered him. 'What difference does it make? I understand you, you understand me.'

'Think, Rumbo! Use your brain! Try to remember how it was before.'

'What's the point?'

This stopped me for a moment. Then I said, 'Don't you want to know why? How?'

'No,' he replied.

'But Rumbo, there has to be a reason. There must be some purpose to this.'

'Why?'

'I don't *know* why.' There was frustration in my voice now. 'But I want to find out!'

'Listen, squirt. We're dogs. We live like dogs, we're treated like dogs. We think like dogs . . .' I shook my head at this, but he continued: '. . . and we eat like dogs. We're a little more intelligent than others, but we keep that to ourselves. . . .'

'Why don't we show them we're not like the rest?' I burst out.

'We *are* like the rest, squirt. We differ only in small ways.'

'That's not true!'

'It is true; you'll find out. We could show men how clever we are – lots of animals do. They usually end up in the circus.'

'It's not the same thing! That's only animals learning tricks.'

'Did you know they're teaching a chimpanzee to talk? Is that a trick?'

'How did *you* know that?'

Rumbo looked flustered.

'It was something you knew in the past, wasn't it, Rumbo? Not as a dog, but as a man. You read about it.'

'Read? What's read?'

'Words. Words on paper.'

'That's ridiculous, paper can't talk!'

'Nor can dogs.'

'We're talking.'

'Not in the same way as men.'

'Of course not. We're not men.'

'What are we?'

'Dogs.'

'Freaks.'

'Freaks?'

'Yes. I think we were men, then something happened and we became dogs.'

There was an odd look in Rumbo's eyes. 'I think the rain last night soaked into your brain,' he said slowly. Then he shook his body as if to shake off the conversation. 'I'm going to the park now. You could chew through the rope if you want to come.'

I slumped down on to the ground; it was obvious, as far as Rumbo was concerned, the discussion was over. 'No,' I said resignedly, 'I'll stay here till the Guvnor lets me loose. We don't want to make him any angrier.'

'Up to you,' said Rumbo and trotted off. 'I'll try and bring you something back!' he called out as he squeezed through the hole in the fence.

'Thanks,' I said to myself.

When the Guvnor turned up later that day he came over to see me. He shook his head a few times and called me a few more names. I tried to look pitiful and it must have had some effect, for he was soon untying the length of rope from my collar. He felt the dampness on my back and advised me to have a run to dry myself off. Accepting his advice, I shot out of the yard and made for the park where I knew I would find my companion. His trail was easy to follow but my progression from lamp-post to lamp-post was much more fun than just making straight for the park.

I found Rumbo sniffing round a little bitch, a skittish Yorkshire terrier, her lady owner anxiously trying to shoo my ragged friend away. Complex thoughts had gone: I couldn't understand Rumbo's interest in these silly lady dogs, but I did enjoy a good game. And this looked as though it could be a good game.

The weeks sped by – they may have been months – and I became lost in my canine world again, only occasionally being troubled by tormenting memories. Snow came, melted, was gone; winds swept in fiercely, spent their anger, and left meekly; the rain rained. The weather couldn't depress me, for I found its different moods interesting: I was experiencing things in a new way, with a different outlook; everything that happened was a *re*discovery. It was like the feeling you get after recovering from a long debilitating illness: everything is fresh and often startling; you observe with more appreciative eyes. You've known it all before, but familiarity has dulled things for you. That's the only way I can describe it.

Rumbo and I survived the worst winter could inflict comfortably enough. We had to travel further for our food, our surrounding area being a little too 'hot', but I enjoyed the excursions. We became firmer friends, since I was losing my overcharged puppy capriciousness and beginning to instigate some of our escapades rather than being led into them. Rumbo even called me Fluke now more often than squirt, for I was becoming almost as tall as him. When we weren't hunting for food or getting into mischief, Rumbo was off hunting bitches. He couldn't understand my lack of interest in the opposite sex and told me repeatedly I was old enough to feel some stirring in my loins at the scent of a ripe female body. I was puzzled myself, but really couldn't muster any inclinations whatsoever towards the female of my species; I suppose my instincts weren't yet canine enough. Apart from that small concern and the occasional sudden flashes of my past life, the times were good; but like all good times, they had to end.

And end they did one dull and drizzly day.

Rumbo and I had just returned from the fruit market and were sniffing around a new vehicle which had been brought into the yard a few days before. It was a large dark-blue Transit van, and for some reason it had been parked at the rear of the yard. The lettering on its side had been sprayed out and I'd watched one of the workers change its number-plates the previous day. Its front bumper had been removed and replaced by a much sturdier one. Parked alongside was another car – a Triumph 2000 – and the number-plates on this had also been changed. Both vehicles were screened from the rest of the yard by the piles of wrecks. It was the smell from the van which attracted us – it must have been used to transport food at some time – but my human faculties should have made me aware of what was going on. The constant meetings in the hut between the Guvnor and his flashy cronies (meetings which had become even more frequent recently); the curious affluence of the Guvnor himself; his anger at having a policeman 'snooping' around some time before: it didn't take much of a brain to figure it all out. Unfortunately, mine wasn't even much of a brain.

We heard the yard gates being unlocked and then a car was driven into the yard. Rumbo raced through the maze of junk to find out who had arrived: to our surprise it was the Guvnor himself. It was a surprise to us because he was not an early bird, usually never arriving at the yard till mid-morning. He generally left it to his employees to open up and get on with the work by themselves.

The big man ignored us as we yapped around his legs while he unlocked the door to the hut. I noticed he'd discarded his sheepskin for his old leather jacket and underneath he wore a dark-red polo-neck sweater. He was also wearing gloves, which was unusual for him. Throwing the butt of his cigar into the mud, the Guvnor entered the hut. No food for us today, then.

Rumbo and I mentally shrugged at each other and wandered off, but it wasn't long before the sound of more arrivals drew us back to the hut. A car pulled into the yard first and Lenny and another man got out, going straight into the hut, they too ignoring our wagging tails and eager expressions. Then three others arrived on foot.

A strange kind of tenseness had taken over the yard, making Rumbo and me nervous, edgy. The voices from inside the hut were muted, not the usual sounds of laughter or anger. This worried us even more.

After a short while the door opened and six men came out. The first four were now wearing dark grey smock-coats, the kind shopkeepers sometimes wear, and I saw they too were all wearing polo-necked sweaters. One man was just tugging the thick collar of his down from over his chin, suggesting that a moment before he'd been wearing it up to his ears. Lenny came out next, and although he wasn't wearing a smock he had on a polo-neck sweater. The Guvnor came out last and he still wore his leather jacket. They didn't speak as they passed, walking to the back of the yard, the nervous tension between them obvious and transferring to us, so that we became even more agitated. Lenny clucked his tongue at me and snapped his fingers in a half-hearted way, but ignored me when I bounded up to him.

We followed the six men round to the van. The back doors were opened and three of the smock-coated men climbed in, the fourth seating himself in the front. Before the Guvnor heaved his big frame into the passenger seat of the Triumph he said to the van driver: 'Right, you know what to do. Try and keep with us in the traffic, but if we get separated, you know where to meet up.' The driver nodded and the Guvnor turned away. Just before he slammed his door, he called out. 'Don't forget. You don't make your move till you see me wave my arm out the window.' The van driver thumbed up an acknowledgement.

Lenny was already in the driving seat of the Triumph and he suddenly gunned the engine. As the car crunched its way out of the yard, the big blue van following, I realized that for the first time I'd seen the Guvnor without a cigar sticking out of the corner of his mouth.

About an hour later the Triumph 2000 returned. It roared through the gates and drove straight round to the back of the yard. One of the yard's workmen ran to the gates and pushed them shut, then went back to his work as though nothing had happened.

Rumbo and I raced after the car and were just in time to see the Guvnor and Lenny clambering out. They ran round to the boot, opened it, and between them lifted out a large heavy-looking metal case. It had handles at each end and the two men used these to carry it round and into the hut. They returned to the car and pulled out four or five bulky sacks, and these too were hastily taken into the hut. The Guvnor locked the office door before they returned to the car. The men pushed us away angrily as we tried to clamber over them. There was an excited haste about them now – gone was the sullen nervousness of the morning – and this too was infecting us. A sharp whack on the nose kept me away, and Rumbo also took the hint.

'O.K., Lenny. Get shot of the motor,' the Guvnor said, taking a cigar from the inside pocket of his leather jacket. 'Don't worry about the smocks in the back – they don't matter now. You can dump it as far away as you like, but don't be drivin' around in it too long.'

'O.K., Guv,' Lenny said cheerfully. Before he turned on the ignition, the Guvnor poked another cigar through the open car window.

''Ere. You done well, boy. See you back 'ere Wednesday – not before!'

Lenny stuck the cigar into this mouth, grinned, put the car into gear, then moved off.

The front gate was just being opened for him by the same yard worker who'd closed it only minutes before when the police car screeched into the entrance, completely blocking Lenny's path. Doors flew open and suddenly there were blue uniforms everywhere. Another police car pulled up behind the first and more men in blue poured out.

Lenny was out of the Triumph in a flash, running for the back of the yard, his face white. The Guvnor, who was half-way back to his office when the police arrived, stood transfixed for a few seconds, then turned and bolted towards us. I can only guess that both he and Lenny intended to scale the corrugated-iron fence and make their getaway into the backstreets.

The latter didn't get as far as the former who, in the end, didn't get far at all. Lenny was brought down by a flying rugger tackle and was immediately engulfed in blue bodies. He screamed and cursed them but they wouldn't let him go.

Others gave chase to the Guvnor who had pounded past us now, throwing away his cigar as he went. The police shouted at him to stop, but he wasn't having any of it. He headed into the maze of wrecked cars.

Rumbo was both alarmed and angry. He didn't like these blue men: he didn't like them chasing his Guvnor. He growled at them and ordered them to stop. It did no good though – they weren't afraid of Rumbo. He jumped up at one and got a good grip on the policeman's sleeve, tugging and tearing at it with jerks of his body. The man went down and rolled over in the mud, taking Rumbo with him.

'No, Rumbo, no!' I cried out. 'Leave him alone! They'll hurt you!'

But Rumbo was too angry to listen. This was his territory, and the man they were after was the one he'd chosen to be his master. Another policeman kicked out at him, making him yelp in sudden pain and lose his grip on the uniform's sleeve. A stout wooden stick cracked across his nose and Rumbo staggered away from the sprawling policeman who immediately scrambled to his feet and joined in the chase after the Guvnor again.

'Are you all right?' I asked as I rushed over to Rumbo.

He moaned and his tail dropped between his legs. 'Get after them! Don't let them catch him!' He stumbled around shaking his head in a dazed way.

I dived into the alleyways separating the piles of damaged cars and pursued the pursuers. I could see the Guvnor ahead, climbing on to the bonnet of a car. He was grabbed from behind, but he kicked out with a vicious boot, knocking the unfortunate policeman on to his back. He scrambled up higher on to the roof of the car, then on to the bonnet of the car on top. If he crossed this pile of junk, it would take him close to the surrounding fence and he would be able to jump into the street below. The wreck he was climbing on to was unsteady, and it tottered precariously for a few sickening moments, nearly causing him to slither back down into the yard. He held tight and the car steadied itself. He began to climb again.

Two policemen began the ascent after the Guvnor while others headed in different directions in the hope of cutting him off. I couldn't just stand by and let them take the Guvnor; Rumbo had a loyalty to him and that meant I had too. I caught the seat of one of the climbing plod's trousers nicely with my teeth. I bit and pulled and he came tumbling down. He kicked out at me and beat me with his fists, but I was in a fury and hardly felt the blows.

Rumbo came in snarling and snapping, and the struggling policeman was forced to call on his companion for help. The dogs were tearing him to pieces, he screamed.

Well, we were being a bit rough, but we weren't savages (to tell the truth, it was a bit of a lark at that stage).

The second policeman jumped from the car bonnet into the mêlée and tried to separate man and dogs, flailing at us with his fists. This only made Rumbo more cross and he diverted his attention to the new assailant. More policemen were arriving by the second and I could see we'd stand no chance against such odds.

'It's no good, Rumbo!' I called out. 'There's too many!'

'Keep fighting, squirt,' he replied between mouthfuls of flesh and cloth. 'It's giving the Guvnor a chance to get away.'

It was no good. I felt a hand grasp my collar and I was yanked off my feet and thrown across the alleyway. I landed heavily against the boot of a car and fell to the ground badly winded. I gasped for breath and saw Rumbo receiving similar treatment. It took two policemen to deal with him, though.

By this time the Guvnor was on the roof of the second car and I could see him looking wildly around. He was being converged upon all sides by blue uniforms and he yelled down defiantly as the police below began to climb up after him again.

'Look out!' one of them shouted. 'He's pushing the cars over!'

The policeman scrambled for safety and I saw that the Guvnor had stepped over on to the roof of the next semi-crushed car and was using a foot as a lever against the one he'd just left. It was already dangerously balanced and it didn't take much to send it toppling. The only thing was, the car the Guvnor was perched on toppled after it.

And worse, Rumbo had dashed forward again to ward off the pursuing policeman.

He couldn't have known what hit him; that was the only merciful thing about it. One minute he was crouched low, baring his teeth at the police, the next he had disappeared beneath a tumble of crushing metal.

'Rumbo!' I screamed, and dashed forward even before the crashing cars had had time to settle. 'Rumbo! Rumbo!'

I dodged around the twisted metal, trying to see beneath it, trying to find an opening to crawl through, willing my friend to be miraculously alive, refusing to accept the inevitable.

The thin stream of dark-red blood that came from beneath the cars jolted me into the truth of the situation: there was no chance at all for Rumbo.

I howled, the kind of howl you sometimes hear on an empty night from miles away; the cry of an animal at its lowest point of misery. Then I wept.

The Guvnor was in agony, his arm trapped deep between the two wrecks. He was lucky, though: it could have been his whole body.

A hand took me by the collar and dragged me gently away from the metal tomb, and I felt sympathy flowing from the policeman as he led me towards the front of the yard. I was too upset to resist. Rumbo was dead, and for the moment so was my will. I heard one of the officers tell someone to get an ambulance quickly; there was an injured man back there. I saw two men in plainclothes bringing the metal case from the hut and nodding towards another man questioning Lenny. Lenny was angry now, talking belligerently as he was held from behind by two uniformed men.

'Who done it then?' he was asking. 'Who fingered us?'

'We've had our eyes on this place a long time, son,' the man before him replied. 'Ever since one of our boys spotted Ronnie Smiley's car in here awhile back. We all know what Ronnie gets up to, don't we, so we thought we'd wait awhile and let things run their course. Very interesting when we saw the stolen van coming in, then the car. Even more so when they didn't come out again – until this morning, that is.' He laughed at Lenny's obvious displeasure. 'Oh don't worry, it wasn't only that. We've had suspicions about this yard for a long time now. Wondered where your governor got his money from. Now we know, don't we?'

Lenny just looked away sullenly. The plainclothes policeman spotted me being led away.

'Funny thing is,' he remarked, 'the constable was only investigating a couple of thieving dogs when he spotted Smiley's car. Take after their master don't they?' He nodded at the man holding firmly on to Lenny and they pushed him towards one of the police cars at the entrance to the yard. Before Lenny departed he gave me one last penetrating look that made me shiver inside.

And it was then that I knew where I was going. It pushed its way through befuddled layers and struck me almost physically.

I twisted my neck and snapped at the hand that held me. The startled policeman quickly drew his hand away – and I was loose. I bolted for the street and once again I was running, running, running.

PART TWO

TWELVE

How do you feel now? Is your mind still closed to my story, or are you wondering? Let me go on; there's a few hours before dawn.

My journey to Edenbridge was a long one, but strangely I knew the way as if I'd travelled that route many times before. When the town had been mentioned in the yard it had evidently planted a seed in my mind, and it was a seed that suddenly grew and sprouted. I wasn't sure what the town meant to me, whether it was where my home was or if it had some other significance, but I knew it was the place to go, the place to start from. What other alternative had I anyway?

I must have run for at least an hour, narrowly avoiding being run down by uncaring traffic more than once, before I reached a piece of waste ground where I was able to grieve for my lost friend in private. Creeping under a dumped sofa, its stuffing more out than in, I sank to the ground, resting my head between my paws. I could still see that trickle of blood running from beneath the rusted metal, forming a pool in a small dip in the earth and creating a miniature whirlpool, a vortex of Rumbo's life. Animals can feel grief just as deeply as any human, perhaps more so; they have limited ways of expressing their sorrow, though and their natural optimism usually enables recovery more quickly, there's the difference. Unfortunately, I suffered both as a human *and* an animal, and it was heavy stuff.

I stayed there until long into the afternoon, afraid and bewildered once again. Only my loyal companion, hunger, roused me into movement. I forget from where I scrounged food, just as I have forgotten a great deal of that long journey, but I know I did eat and was soon moving onwards. I travelled by night through the city, preferring the empty quietness of the streets, the activity of the day making way for the quiet prowlings of night creatures. I met many prowlers – cats, other dogs, spirits (so many in the streets of the city) and strange men who flitted in and out of the shadows as though light or open spaces would harm their bodies – but I avoided communication with any of them. I had a purpose and would allow nothing to distract me from it.

Through Camberwell, through Lewisham, through Bromley I went, resting during the day, hiding in derelict houses, parks or on waste ground – anywhere away from inquisitive eyes. I ate badly, for I took few risks; I didn't want to be sent back to a home, you see, not now I had an objective. I had become timid again now that Rumbo wasn't there to spur me on, to chastise me when I cowered, to threaten me when I balked and to laugh when I surprised him.

Soon I reached open country.

It rolled out before me, green and fresh under the gentle beginnings of spring. It wasn't true countryside yet, for I was only just outside the London suburbs, but after the blacks and the greys and the browns and the reds and the garishness of everything in the city, it seemed like passing through a barrier to where nature governed, and human influence played only a minor part. I was no longer afraid to travel by daylight.

The sudden strength of growing things thrilled me. Fresh green shoots thrust their way through the earth to breathe in fresh air, bulbs and tubers were sprouting and buds were breaking open on broad-leaved trees. Everywhere things were stirring, new life was being created. A vibrancy filled the air, filled my lungs and filled my limbs with its tingling life. The greens and yellows were newer, more dazzling, and the reds and oranges glowed with fire, sending out waves of energy. Everything glistened, everything shone with wetness. Everything was firm, vigorous, even the most delicate flower. It put new life into me.

I scrambled through a hedge running alongside the road, ignoring the scratchy protest of the thorny hawthorn and prickly dogrose. Two startled wrens screeched and froze as I brushed by their small huddled forms. A group of bright yellow stars flashed before me as I wormed my way through lesser celandine, plants which are the first in the queue for spring regeneration. I burst through into a field and ran like mad through its dewy wetness, twisting and rolling on to my back until my whole coat was soaked. I sucked at the grass, drinking the pure water from them, and dug holes in the soft earth to see what I could find. Beetles scuttled away from my inquisitive nose and a mole turned a blind eye. An eight-inch-long keeled slug curled its slick grey body into a ball as I sniffed at him and I quickly spat him from my mouth after a tentative taste. Cooked snails might be a delicacy for many, but raw slug isn't even fit for a dog.

My appetite soon returned, however, and I began to explore the field in search of food. I was lucky enough to find a young rabbit nibbling at the bark of a tree and unlucky enough to be unable to catch him. I cursed his speed then wondered if I could have killed the rabbit even had I caught up with him. I'd never killed for food before.

Fortunately, I found some late winter fungus among a group of trees and devoured the upturned yellow caps and stalks with relish, somehow aware that the mushrooms were not poisonous. Was this animal instinct or had I some human knowledge of fungi? The question bothered me for only a second or so, for a sleepy wood-mouse shuffled lazily between my legs, his black little eyes searching the ground for snails. I felt no urge to eat or fight him, but I did give his reddish-brown back a playful tap with my paw. He stopped, looked up at me, then ambled on at the same pace, ignoring me totally. I watched him go then decided it was time to move on myself, the diversion pleasant enough but hardly profitable as far as self-discovery was concerned. I raced back across the field, scrambled through the hedge, and set off down the road again.

It wasn't long before I found myself back among shops and houses, but I kept on, pausing only once to steal an apple from a splendid display outside a fruiterer's. The road became more and more familiar to me now that the complications of the city streets were far behind, and I knew it was a route I must have taken many times before.

By the time I'd reached Keston my pads were very sore, but I kept going until I reached a small place called Leaves Green. There I rested through the cold night in a small wood, nervous of the country night noises, my unease finally driving me to seek shelter in somebody's front garden. I felt more comfortable being in range of human contact.

I didn't eat much the following day, but I won't bore you with the various misadventures that befell me in my search for sustenance; suffice to say, by the time I reached Westerham, I'd have bitten the leg off a cow.

It was at Westerham that a nasty experience was awaiting me. And this I must tell you about.

THIRTEEN

Church bells woke me. They had a strident Sunday morning sound that sent my thoughts racing back to other times – human times.

Awareness of my present plight dismissed the memories before they gathered pace and I stretched my aching limbs, wincing at the tenderness of my foot-pads as I pushed them against the ground. A bus shelter had been my refuge for the night, but the early morning chill had crept into my bones and seemed reluctant to leave. I yawned and my stomach grumbled for nourishment. Glancing around, I saw there were no shops in the immediate vicinity, so I trotted gingerly along the street keeping my nose high in the air, acutely receptive for the faintest waft of food smells. I soon found myself in the High Street and to my dismay realized it was indeed Sunday, for all the shops – apart from a couple of newsagents – were closed. It was a pretty dismal dog who stood shivering by the kerbside, looking first left then right, undecided, unwanted and unfed.

It was the pealing bells that gave me the idea. Small groups of people were walking briskly towards the sound, clad in Sunday best, a brightness about them that would wear off as the day wore on. Children held hands with parents or skipped along ahead of them; grannies clutched at the elbows of middle-aged offspring; sombre husbands walked stiffly alongside beaming wives. There was a fresh friendly feeling in the air, the beginning of spring enhancing the Sunday morning ritual, encouraging goodwill to all men. And maybe dogs, too.

I followed the people to their church. It was on a hill, half hidden away from the road by a screen of trees, its entrance reached by a gravelly path winding through a surrounding graveyard. A few of the people clucked their tongues at me or gave me a friendly pat as they passed by, but soon they had all disappeared into the cold, grey-stoned building. I settled down on a flat gravestone to wait.

I enjoyed the muted singing that came from the church immensely, occasionally joining in at the bits I knew. The service seemed to go on forever, and I soon became bored with the long stretches of silence between hymns so I began to explore the churchyard and was surprised at the thriving animal and insect life of this place of the dead. The unmistakable sound of the congregation rising as one body inside the church drew me away from my fascinating study of a rainbow-coloured spider's web, and I trotted back round to the enormous doorway, keeping to the damp grass which was so cool to my sore pads. I waited to one side of the porch and soon the flock came pouring out, some looking uplifted, others looking relieved now that their weekly duty was done. It was one of the uplifted members I wanted.

I soon spotted her: a little old lady, probably in her mid-sixties, round-faced, smiling constantly, knowing and known by everybody, it seemed. All lace and kindness. Perfect.

She spent several minutes chatting to the vicar, occasionally breaking off from her conversation to call hello to a passing acquaintance, giving them a little blessing with her white-gloved hand. I waited patiently until she'd ended her dialogue with the cleric then followed her as she made her way through the remaining gossiping cliques. Smiling sweetly and stopping to chat to every third or fourth person she finally drew clear of the throng and strode spritely down the gravel path. I followed, keeping a few yards behind, not ready to make my move while she still had so many distractions. We reached the road and she turned left, climbing further up the steep hill and away from the town.

'Good morning, Miss Birdle!' the people we passed called out, and she acknowledged them with a cheery wave.

Now's the time, I thought, and scampered up ahead of her. I stopped four yards ahead, turned to face her and gave her my sweetest smile.

'Woof,' I said.

Miss Birdle threw her hands up in surprise and beamed with delight. 'What a pretty dog!' she exclaimed and I wagged my rump with pride. She advanced on me and clasped my head between white-gloved hands.

'Oh, what a lovely boy!' She rubbed my back and I tried to lick her face, congratulating myself on finding another Bella. 'Yes, yes, he is!' she went on.

After a few moments of unbridled affection she bade me goodbye and strode on, waving at me as she went. I bounded after her and tried to leap into her arms, slobbering and grinning and desperately trying to fawn my way into her heart and charity. I admit it: I had no shame.

Miss Birdle gently pushed me down then patted my head. 'Off you go, now, there's a good dog,' she said in her kind way.

Sorry Rumbo, but at that point I whimpered.

Not only that, I hung my head, drooped my tail and looked cow-eyed at her. I was pathetic.

It worked, for she suddenly said, 'Oh my poor dear, you're starving, that's what it is! Look at those skinny old ribs.' My chin almost touched the ground as I hammed up my performance. 'Come along then, dear, you come with me and we'll soon put you to rights. Poor little wretch!'

I was in. I tried to lick her face again in glee, but she restrained me with a surprisingly firm hand. I needed no encouragement to follow her, although she seemed to think I did, for she constantly patted her thigh and called out 'Come along now.'

She had plenty of energy, this charming old lady, and we soon reached a rusty iron gate, behind which was a muddy path leading away from the road. Tangled undergrowth lay on either side of the narrow path and there was a constant rustling of hidden life as we made our way along it. I sniffed the scent of Miss Birdle along this well-used route, not the fresh powdery smell that followed in her wake, but a staler version of it mingled with the scents of many animals. Now and again I stopped to explore a particularly interesting odour, but her call would send me scampering onwards.

Suddenly we emerged into a clearing and a flint-walled cottage stood before us, its corners, door and window openings reinforced by cut stone. It was a beautiful scene – like walking on to a chocolate box – and in perfect character with Miss Birdle herself. Smug with my own cleverness, I trotted up to the weathered door and waited for Miss Birdle to catch up with *me*.

She pushed open the door without using a key and beckoned me to enter. In I went and was pleased to find the interior of the cottage matched the quaintness of the exterior. Ancient furniture, worn and comfortable, filled the main room in which I found myself, there being no hallway. Well-cared for ornaments were scattered about the room, one of those interesting dark-wood dressers filled with delicately painted crockery taking up a large part of one wall. I wagged my tail in approval.

'Now let's just see if you've an address on your collar, then we'll give you some food, eh?' Miss Birdle placed her handbag on a chair and leaned forward over me, reaching for the nameplate on my collar. I obligingly sat down, determined not to kill any golden geese through over-exuberance. She peered short-sightedly at the scratched lettering on the nameplate and tutted in mild annoyance at herself.

'My old eyes are getting worse,' she told me, and I smiled in sympathy. I would dearly have loved to have told her of my own peculiarly clear eyesight, of the many changing colours I could see in her face, of the blue deepness in her ageing eyes, of the sparkling colours all around us, even in her faded furniture. It was frustrating to have to keep these things to myself, and even Rumbo had been unable to understand my visual sensitivity.

She felt inside her handbag and produced a light-rimmed pair of spectacles and muttered 'That's better,' as she put them on. She still squinted through the lenses but managed to make out the name on the strip of metal.

'Fluke,' she said. 'Fluke. That's a funny name for a dog. And no address. Some people are very careless, aren't they? I haven't seen you around before, I wonder where you've come from? Bet you've run away, haven't you? Let me look at your footies . . .' She lifted a paw. 'Yes, they're sore, aren't they? You've come a long way. Been badly treated, haven't you? Thin as a rake. It isn't right.'

My hunger was making me a little impatient by now and I whimpered again, just to give her the idea.

'Yes, yes. I know what you want, don't I? Something for your tummy?' It's a pity people have to talk to animals as though they were children, but I was in a forgiving mood and willing to put up with a lot more than baby-talk. I thumped my tail on the carpet in the hope that she would take that for an affirmative to her question. 'Course you do,' she said. 'Let's get you something.'

The kitchen was tiny, and lying in a basket on the floor, fast asleep, was Victoria.

Victoria was the meanest, surliest cat I've ever come across, either before or since that time. Now these feline creatures are renowned for their tetchiness, for they believe they're a race apart from other animals and well above you lot, but this monster took the prize. She sat bolt upright, her fur bristling and her tail ramrod-straight. She hissed disgustedly at me.

'Take it easy, cat,' I said anxiously. 'I'm only passing through.'

'Now you settle down, Victoria,' said Miss Birdle, equally anxious. 'This poor doggie is starving. I'm just giving him something to eat, then we'll send him on his way.'

But it's no good trying to talk sense to a cat, they just won't listen. Victoria was out of her basket in a flash, up on to the sink and through the half-open kitchen window.

'Oh dear,' sighed Miss Birdle, 'you've upset Victoria now,' and then this nice old lady gave me a hefty kick in the ribs.

I was so shocked I thought I'd imagined it, but the pain in my side told me otherwise.

'Now let's see what we've got,' Miss Birdle said thoughtfully, her index finger in the corner of her mouth as she looked up into the cupboard she'd just opened. It was as though nothing had happened and I wondered again if anything actually had. The throb in my side assured me something had.

I kept a safe distance between us after that and watched her warily when she placed a bowl of chopped liver before me. The food was delicious but marred by my sudden nervousness of the old lady I just couldn't understand what had happened. I licked the bowl clean and said thank you, very aware of my manners now. She fondled my ears and chuckled approvingly at the empty bowl.

'You *were* hungry, weren't you?' she said. 'I'll bet you're thirsty now. Let's give you some water.' She filled the same bowl with water and placed it before me again. I lapped it up greedily.

'Now you come with me and rest those poor weary legs.' I followed her back into the main room and she patted a hairy rug in front of the unlit fire. 'Rest there, nice and comfy, and I'll just light the fire for us. It's still too cold for my old bones, you know. I like the warm.' She prattled on as she put a match to the already laid fire, her words soft and comforting. I became confident again, sure that the strange incident which had taken place in the kitchen was merely a slight lapse on her part, caused by the shock of seeing her beloved pet cat leaping through the window. Or maybe she'd slipped. I dozed off as she sat in the armchair before the fire, her words lulling me into a warm feeling of security.

I woke in time for lunch, which wasn't much, she being an old lady living on her own, but she gave me a good portion of it. The cat returned and was further put out at the sight of me gobbling down food which she felt was rightfully hers. However, Miss Birdle made a big fuss of her, running into the kitchen and returning with an opened tin of catfood. She poured some of it on to a small plate and laid it before the sour-faced mog. With a menacing look at me, Victoria began to eat in that jerky cat fashion, neatly but predatorily, so unlike the clumsy, lip-smacking manner of us dogs. My portion of Miss Birdle's lunch was soon gone and I casually sauntered over to Victoria to see how she was doing, ready to help her clean her plate, should the need arise. A spiteful hiss warned me off and I decided to sit at Miss Birdle's feet, my face upturned and carefully composed into an expression of mild begging. A few tasty morsels came my way, so my fawning was not in vain. This disgusted the cat even more, of course, but her sneers didn't bother me at all.

After Miss Birdle had cleared the table and washed up, we settled in front of the fire once again. Victoria kept an aloof distance and came over to settle on the old lady's lap only after much enticement. We all dozed, I with my head resting on my benefactor's slippered feet. I felt warm and content – and more secure than ever before. Perhaps I should stay with this kind old lady and forget my quest, which might just bring me more misery. I could be happy here; the cat would be a mild annoyance but nothing to worry about. I needed some human kindness, I needed to belong to someone. I'd lost a good friend and the world was a big and lonely place for a small mongrel dog. I could always search out my other past at some future time when I learned to live as I was. I could offer Miss Birdle companionship. I could guard her home for her. I could have a permanent meal-ticket.

These thoughts ran through my head as I dozed, and I made the decision that I would stay there for as long as possible – little suspecting what lay in store for me.

Later on, Miss Birdle stirred and began to get ready to go out. 'Never miss the afternoon service, my dear,' she told me.

I nodded approvingly, but didn't stir from my cosy position. I heard the old lady bustling around upstairs for a while, then the clomp of heaving walking shoes as she descended the stairs. She appeared in the doorway, resplendent in white gloves and a dark-blue straw hat. Her suit was pink and her high-necked blouse a bright emerald green. She looked dazzling.

'Come along, Fluke, time for you to go now,' she said.

My head shot up. What? Go?

'What? Go?' I said.

'Yes, time for you to go, Fluke. I can't keep you here, you belong to someone else. They may have looked after you badly, but you do belong to them. I could get into trouble by keeping you here, so I'm afraid you've got to leave.' She shook her head apologetically then, to my dismay, grabbed my collar and dragged my resisting body to the door. For an old lady she was quite strong, and my paws skidded along the wood floor as I tried to hold back. Victoria enjoyed every moment, for I could hear her snickering from her perch on the window-sill.

'Please let me stay,' I pleaded. 'Nobody owns me. I'm all alone.'

It was no use: I found myself outside on the doorstep. Miss Birdle closed the door behind us and marched down the path, calling me to follow. Having no choice, I followed.

At the gate she patted my head and gave me a little push away from her. 'Off you go now,' she urged. 'Home. Good boy, Fluke.'

I wouldn't budge. After a while she gave up and marched down the hill away from me, looking round twice to make sure I wasn't following her. I waited patiently until she was out of sight then pushed my way back through the gate and padded down the muddy path to the cottage. Victoria scowled through the window as she saw me coming and shouted at me to go away.

'Not likely,' I told her as I squatted on my haunches and prepared to wait for the old lady's return. 'I like it here. Why should you have it all to yourself?'

'Because I was here first,' Victoria said crossly. 'You've got no right.'

'Look, there's plenty for both of us,' said I, trying to be reasonable. 'We could be friends.' I shivered at the thought of being friends with this miserable specimen but was prepared to ingratiate myself for the sake of a nice secure home. 'I wouldn't get in your way,' I said in my best toadying voice. 'You could have first and biggest share of all the food' (until I was better acquainted with the old lady, I thought). 'You can have the best place to sleep' (until I have wormed my way into Miss Birdle's affections), 'and you can be the head of the house, I don't mind' (until I get you alone some day and show you who the real boss is). 'Now, what do you say?'

'Get lost,' said the cat.

I gave up. She would just have to lump it.

An hour later Miss Birdle returned and when she saw me sitting there she shook her head. I gave her my most appealing smile.

'You *are* a bad boy,' she scolded, but there was no anger in her voice.

She let me go into the cottage with her and I made a big fuss of licking her heavily stockinged legs. The taste was horrible, but when I decide to smarm, there are no limits. I was sorry not to have the dignity of Rumbo, but there's nothing like insecurity to make you humble.

Well, I stayed that night. And the following night. But the third night – that's when my troubles started all over again.

At nine-thirty in the evening Miss Birdle would turn me out and I would dutifully carry out my toilet; I knew that was expected of me and had no intention of fouling things up (excuse the play on words – couldn't help it). She would let me back in after a short while and coax me into a small room at the back of the cottage which she used to store all sorts of junk. Most of it was unchewable – old picture frames, a pianoforte, an ancient unconnected gas cooker, that sort of thing. There was just enough room for me to curl up beneath the piano keyboard and here I would spend the night, quite comfortable although a little frightened at first (I cried that first night but was O.K. the second). Miss Birdle would close the door on me to keep me away from Victoria who slept in the kitchen. The cat and I were still not friends and the old lady was well aware of it.

On that third night she neglected to close the door properly; the catch didn't catch and the door was left open half an inch. It probably wouldn't have bothered me, but the sound of someone creeping around during the night aroused my curiosity. I'm a light sleeper and the soft pad of feet was enough to disturb me. I crept over to the door and eased it open with my nose; the noise was coming from the kitchen. I guessed it was Victoria mooching around and would have returned to my sleeping-place had not those two agitators, hunger and thirst, begun taunting my greedy belly. A trip to the kitchen might prove profitable.

I crept stealthily from the room and made my way through the tiny hallway into the kitchen. Miss Birdle always left a small lamp burning in the hallway (because she was nervous living on her own, I suppose) and had no trouble finding the kitchen door. It, too, was open.

Pushing my nose round it, I peered into the gloom. Two slanting green eyes startled me.

'That you, Victoria?' I asked.

'Who else would it be?' came the hissed reply.

I pushed in further. 'What are you doing?'

'None of your business. Get back to your room.'

But I saw what she was doing. She had a small wood-mouse trapped between her paws. Her claws were withdrawn so she was obviously playing a fine teasing game with the unfortunate creature. His reddish-brown back was arched in paralytic fear and his tiny black eyes shone with a trance-like glaze. He must have found his way into the cottage in search of food. The absence of house-mice (undoubtedly owing to Victoria's vigilance) would have encouraged him and he must have been too stupid (or too hungry) to have been aware of the cat's presence. Anyway, he was well and truly aware of it now, and paying nature's harsh price for carelessness.

He was too scared to speak so I spoke up for him.

'What are you going to do with him?'

'None of your business,' came the curt reply.

I made my way further into the kitchen and repeated my question. This time a wheezy snarl was the reply.

It's not in an animal's nature to have much sympathy for his fellow creatures, but the plight of this defenceless little thing appealed to the other side of *my* nature; the human side.

'Let him go, Victoria,' I said quietly.

'Sure, after I've bitten his head off,' she said.

And that's what she tried to do, there and then, just to spite me. I moved fast and had Victoria's head between my jaws before she had a chance to dodge. We spun around in the kitchen, the mouse's head in the cat's mouth, and the cat's head in mine.

Victoria was forced to drop the terrified wood-mouse before she had done any real damage and I saw with satisfaction the little creature scurry away into a dark corner and no doubt down a dark hole. Victoria squealed and pulled her head from my jaws, raking my brisket as she did so. I yelped at the stinging pain and lunged for her again – very, very angry now.

Round and round that kitchen we ran, knocking chairs over, crashing against cupboards, shouting and screaming at each other, too far gone with animal rage to concern ourselves with the noise we were making and the damage we were doing. At one point I snapped my teeth round Victoria's flailing tail and the cat skidded to a forced halt, a scream of surprise escaping her. She wheeled and drew her sharp claws across my nose and I had to let her go, but her tail was now bald near the tip. I sprang forward again and she leapt upwards on to the draining-board, knocking down the pile of crockery left there to dry by Miss Birdle. It came crashing down, shattering into hundreds of pieces on the stone floor. I tried to leap on to the draining-board myself and almost succeeded, but the sight of Victoria diving head-first through a pane in the closed window amazed me so much I lost my concentration and slipped back on to the floor. I'd never seen a cat – or any animal – do *that* before!

I was still half lying there, perplexed, and a little delighted, I think, when the white-gowned figure appeared in the kitchen doorway. I froze for a second at the apparition, then realized it was only Miss Birdle. Then I froze again.

Her eyes seemed to glow in the darkness. Her white hair hung wildly down to her shoulders and the billowy nightdress she wore crackled with static. Her whole body quivered with a rising fury that threatened to dismantle her frail old body. Her mouth flapped open but coherent words refused to form; she could only make a strange gargling sound. However, she did manage to reach up a trembling hand to the light switch and flick it on. The increased light suddenly made me feel very naked lying there among the smashed crockery.

I gulped once and began to apologize, ready to blame the cat for everything, but the screech that finally escaped the old lady told me words would be wasted at that particular moment. I scooted beneath the kitchen table.

It didn't afford me much protection unfortunately, for one of those dainty slippered feet found my ribs with fierce accuracy. It found my ribs a few more times before I had the sense to remove myself. Out I shot, making for the open doorway, scared silly of this dear old thing. This dear old thing then threw a chair at me and I yelped as it bounced off my back. She came at me, arms and legs flailing, stunning me into submission, terrifying me with her strength. My collar was grabbed and I found myself being dragged back to the cluttered 'guest' room. I was thrown in and the door slammed shut behind me. From the other side of the heavy wood I heard language I'd been used to in the Guvnor's yard but hardly expected to hear in a quaint old cottage and from such a sweet old lady. I lay there trembling, fighting desperately to keep a grip on my bowels and bladder: I was in enough disgrace without *that*.

Another miserable night for me. I must be unique in knowing the full meaning of the expression 'a dog's life'. I know of no other animal who goes through so many highs and lows of emotion as the dog. Maybe we make trouble for ourselves; maybe we're over-sensitive; or maybe we're just stupid. Maybe we're too human.

I hardly slept. I kept expecting the door to swing open and the ancient demon to appear and deal out more punishment. But it didn't swing open; in fact, it didn't swing open for another three days.

I whined, I howled, I grew angry and barked; but nothing happened. I messed on the floor and cried because I knew it would get me into trouble. I starved and cursed the mouse who'd got me into this predicament. My throat grew sore because I had nothing to drink and I cursed the malicious cat who'd caused this situation. My limbs grew stiff because of lack of exercise and I cursed

Miss Birdle for her senility. How could she change from being a charming, delicate old lady one moment into a raging monster the next? All right, I know I was to blame to some extent – her cat *had* gone head-first through the window – but was that enough reason to lock me up and starve me? Self-pity sent me into a sulk that occasionally welled up into anger, then receded into a sulk again.

On the third day the door handle rattled, twisted and the door slowly opened.

I cowered beneath the pianoforte hardly daring to look up, prepared to take a beating with as little dignity as possible.

'There, there, Fluke. What's the matter then?' She stood smiling down at me, that sweet granny smile, that gentle innocence which only belongs to the very old or the very young. I snuffled and refused to be lured out.

'Come on then, Fluke. All's forgiven.'

Oh yes, I thought, until your next brainstorm.

'Come and see what I've got for you.' She left the doorway and disappeared into the kitchen, calling my name in her enticing way. A meaty smell came my way and, tail drooped between my legs, I made my way cautiously after her. I found Miss Birdle pouring a whole tin of dogfood into a bowl on the floor.

I might be unforgiving but my stomach has a mind of its own and it insisted I go forward and eat. Which I did of course without too much inner conflict, though I kept a wary eye on the old lady all the time. The food soon went and so did the water that followed, but my nervousness took a little longer to disappear. Victoria watched me all the time from her basket in the corner, flicking her tail in a slow, regular movement of cold fury. I ignored her but was actually pleased to see she'd come to no real harm by diving through the window. (I was also pleased to see the bald tip of her tail.)

I shied away when Miss Birdle reached down to me, but her calm words soothed my taut nerves and I allowed her to stroke me and soon we were friends again. And we remained friends for at least two weeks after that.

Victoria made a point of keeping out of my way and, I confess, I made a point of keeping out of hers, too. I would scamper down to the town with Miss Birdle when she went shopping and always did my best to behave myself on these occasions. The temptation to steal was almost irresistible, but resist it I did. I was reasonably well fed and the dreadful incident of my fight with Victoria was soon forgotten. Miss Birdle introduced me to all her friends (she seemed to know everybody) and I was made a great fuss of. I the afternoons I would romp in the fields behind the cottage, teasing the animals living there, inhaling the sweetness from the budding flowers, revelling in the growing warmth from the sun. Colours zoomed before me, new smells titillated my sense: life became good once more and I grew healthier. Two weeks of happiness, then that rat of a cat managed to upset everything again.

It was a sunny afternoon and Miss Birdle was in her garden at the front of the cottage tending her awakening flowerbeds. The front door was open and I trotted backwards and forwards through it, enjoying the luxury of having a home where I could come and go as I pleased. On my third or fourth trip, Victoria wandered in after me, and I should have realized something was going to happen when she slyly started a conversation with me. Being a fool and eager to make friends, I readily laid my suspicions to one side and answered her questions, settling down on the rug, prepared to have a good natter. As I said before, cats, like rats, aren't much given to conversation and I was pleased Victoria was making the effort on my behalf, thinking she had accepted me as a permanent guest and was trying to make the best of things. She asked me where I came from, if I knew any other cats, if I liked fish – all sorts of inconsequential questions. But all the time her yellow eyes were darting around the room as though looking for something. When they rested upon the huge dresser with all its fine crockery she smiled to herself. Then came the insults: What was a mangey-looking thing like me doing here, anyway? Were all dogs as stupid as me? What made me smell so? Little things like that. I blinked hard, startled by this sudden change in attitude. Had I offended her in some way?

She came closer so we were almost nose to nose, and stared intently into my eyes. 'You're a dirty, snivelling, fleabitten, worm-riddled mutt. You're a thief and a scoundrel!' Victoria looked at me with some satisfaction. 'Your mother was a jackal who coupled with a hyena. You're vulgar and nasty!'

Now there are many insults you can throw at a dog and get away with, but there's one we will not put up with, one word that really offends us. That's right – *dirty*! (We often are, of course, but we don't like to be told so.) I growled at her to be quiet.

She took no notice, of course, but ranted on, throwing insults not worth repeating here, but some quite ingenious for one of her limited vocabulary. Even so, I would probably have borne all these insults had she not finally spat in my face. I went for her, which is exactly what she had wanted all along.

Up into the dresser she went, spitting and howling. I tried to follow her, shouting at the top of my lungs, finding some nice insults of my own to call her. Victoria backed away along the dresser as I tried in vain to reach her and, as she moved her body backwards, so the ornamental plates which stood balanced upright on the first shelf came tumbling down.

A shadow fell across the doorway but the half-wit (that's right) carried on barking at the wailing cat. I only became fully aware of Miss Birdle's presence when the rake came down heavily on my back. I scooted for the front door, but the old lady had sprung wings on her heels and reached it before me. She slammed it shut and turned to face me, the rake clutched in her gnarled old hands like a lance, its iron-toothed end almost touching my nose. I looked up at her face and gulped loudly.

It had gone a deep purple, the tiny broken veins seeming to explode like starbursts across her skin, and her once kind eyes pressed against their sockets as though about to pop out and roll down her cheeks. I moved a fraction of a second before she did and the rake crashed into the floor only inches behind me. We did a quick circuit of the room while the cat looked on from her safe perch on the dresser, a huge smug smile on her face. On our third lap round, Miss Birdle spotted her and took a swipe at her indolent body with the rake (I suppose the frustration of not being able to catch me had something to do with it). It caught the cat a cracking blow and she shot off the dresser like a ball from a cannon and joined me in the arena. Unfortunately (more so for us), Miss Birdle's sweeping blow at Victoria had also dislodged more plates, together with a few hanging cups and a small antique vase. They followed the cat but of course refused to join us in our run; they lay broken and dead where they had fallen.

The anguished scream from behind told us matters had not improved: Miss Birdle was about to run amuck! Victoria chose the narrow cave formed between the back of the settee and the wall below the front window to hide in. I pushed my way in behind her, almost climbing on to her back in my haste. It was a tight squeeze but we managed to get half-way down the semi-dark corridor. We trembled there, afraid to go further because that would lead us out again.

'It's your fault!' the cat snivelled.

Before I had a chance to protest, the long handle of the rake found my rump and I was suddenly pushed forward in a most painful and undignified way. We became a confused tussle of hairy bodies as we now struggled to reach the other end of the narrow tunnel, violent pokes from the rear helping us achieve our goal. We emerged as one and the old lady dashed round to meet us.

Being the bigger target, I came in for the most abuse from the rake, but it pleases me to tell you the cat received a fair share. The chase went on for another five minutes before Victoria decided her only way out was up the chimney. So up she went and down came the soot – clouds and clouds of it. This didn't improve Miss Birdle's humour one bit, for the soot formed a fine black layer on the area around the fireplace. Now it was the old lady's habit to lay that fire every morning and light it when she settled down in the afternoon, even though the warmer weather had arrived, but for once she decided to bring her schedule forward. She lit the fire.

I gazed on in horror as the paper flamed and the wood chips caught. Forgetting about me for the moment, Miss Birdle settled down in her armchair to wait, the rake lying across her lap in readiness. We stared at the fireplace, Miss Birdle with grim patience, I with utter dismay. The room around us was now a shambles, all cosiness gone.

The flames licked higher and the smoke rose. A spluttered cough fell down with more soot and we knew the cat was still perched there in the dark, unable to climb any further. Miss Birdle's rigid lips turned up at the corners into a rigid smile as we waited, the silence broken only by the crackling of burning wood.

A knock at the door made us both jump.

Miss Birdle's head swung round and I could see the panic in her eyes. The knock came again and a muffled voice called out, 'Miss Birdle, are you in?'

The old lady burst into action. The rake was shoved behind the settee, overturned chairs were righted, and broken crockery was swept beneath the armchair. Only the soot-blackened carpet and a slight disarray of the room gave evidence that something out of the ordinary had happened. Miss Birdle paused for a few seconds, tidied up her clothing, rearranged her personality, and went to the door.

The vicar's hand was raised to knock again and he smiled apologetically down at Miss Birdle.

'So sorry to disturb you,' he said. 'It's about the flower arrangements for Saturday's fête. We can count on your wonderful assistance again this year, can we not, Miss Birdle?

The old lady smiled sweetly up at him. 'Why, of course, Mr. Shelton. Have I ever let you down?'

The change in her was remarkable; the demon castigator had reverted back to the aged angel of innocence. She simpered and fawned over the vicar and he simpered and fawned with her; and all the while the cat roasted in the chimney.

'Now how is that little stray fellow of yours?' I heard the vicar inquire.

'Oh, he's thoroughly enjoying his stay,' Miss Birdle replied, having the nerve to turn round to me and smile. 'Come here, Fluke, and say hello to the vicar.'

I suppose I was expected to run over and lick the clergyman's hand, wagging my tail to show how pleased I was to see him, but I was still in a state of shock and could only cower behind the armchair.

'Oh, he doesn't like strangers, does he?' the vicar chuckled.

I wasn't sure if he was talking to me or Miss Birdle, for his voice had taken on that simpleton's tone people usually reserve for animals. They both gazed at me affectionately.

'No, Fluke's very shy of people,' said Miss Birdle, melting butter clogging her words.

'Have the police located his owner yet?' the vicar asked.

'Constable Hollingbery told me only yesterday that nobody had reported him missing, so I suppose whoever owned Fluke didn't really want him very much.'

They both tutted in harmony and looked at me with soul-churning sympathy.

'Never mind,' the vicar said brightly. 'He has a good home now, one I'm sure he appreciates. And I'm sure he's being a very good doggie, isn't he?' The question was aimed directly at me.

Oh yes, I thought, and the pussy is being a very good pussy, albeit a well-cooked one.

'Oh dear, Miss Birdle, the room seems to be filling with smoke. Is your chimney blocked?'

Without turning a hair, the old lady gave a little laugh and said, 'No, no, it always does that when it's first lit. It takes a while before the air begins to flow properly.'

'I should have it seen to, if I were you, mustn't spoil such a charming abode with nasty smoke, must we? I'll send my handyman around tomorrow to fix it for you. Now the Woman's Guild committee meeting next Wednesday . . .' And that was when Victoria dropped from her hiding-place.

The vicar stared open-mouthed as the soot-covered, fur-smoking cat fell down into the fire, screaming and spitting with rage, leapt from the fireplace and streaked for the door. She flew past him and he could only continue to stare as the smouldering black body disappeared down the path leaving a jet-stream of trailing smoke behind. His mouth still open, the vicar turned his attention back to his elderly parishioner and raised his eyebrows.

'I *wondered* where Victoria had got to,' said Miss Birdle.

The cat never came back, at least not while I was there, and I seriously doubt she ever returned. Life in the cottage went on in its crazy normal way, the incident forgotten by my benefactor as though it had never happened. Several times in the ensuing week Miss Birdle stood at her front door and called out Victoria's name, but I guess the cat was several counties away by then (I still have bad dreams of her being out there in the night, watching me, smouldering in the dark). However, Miss Birdle soon forgot about Victoria and directed all her attention towards me, but, not surprisingly, I felt I could never really trust her. I spent my time nervously waiting for the next eruption, treading very warily and learning to subdue my undisciplined spirits. It occurred to me to leave, but I must confess the lure of good food and a comfortable bed was stronger than my fear of what might happen next. In a word, I was stupid (Rumbo had been right), and even I'm amazed at just how stupid my next mistake was.

I found a nice, chewy plastic object lying on the edge of the kitchen-sink drainer one night. The kitchen was my night-time domain now that Victoria was gone and her basket had become my bed. I often had a poke around during the night or in the early hours of the morning and this time I had been lucky in finding something to play with. Not too hard, not too soft, and crunchy when I bit down firmly. No good to eat, but pretty to look at with its pink surface and little white frills around one edge. It kept me amused for hours.

When Miss Birdle came into the kitchen next morning, she showed no sign of being amused at all. Her toothless mouth opened to let the raging soundless cry escape, and when I looked into that gummy mouth, the human part of me realized what lay chewed, twisted and splintered between my paws.

'My teefth!' Miss Birdle spluttered after her first wordless outcry. 'My falthe teefth!' And that old gleam came back into her eyes.

Stupid I am, yes, and stupid enough to amaze even myself, right. But there comes a time in even the most stupid dog's life when he knows exactly what he should do next. And I did it.

I went through that window just as the cat had (through the new window-pane, in fact), terror helping me achieve what I had been unable to do before (namely, getting on to that kitchen sink). The fact that Miss Birdle was reaching for the long carving knife which hung with its culinary companions on the wall convinced me this might be her worst brainstorm yet. I thought it unnecessary to wait and find out.

I went over her flowerbeds, scrambled through bushes and undergrowth and burst into the open fields beyond, a terrifying image of Miss Birdle in her long white nightdress chasing after me and brandishing the wicked carving knife keeping me going for quite some distance. It's certainly handy to have four legs when you're constantly running away.

I was a long way from that cottage before I collapsed into an exhausted heap, and had already resolved never to return. It was no way for a dog to live. I shuddered at the thought of the schizophrenic old lady, so charming one minute, so lethal the next. Were all her friends fooled by her antique sweetness, her enchanting old maidishness? Didn't anybody see what lurked just behind that veneer, ready to be unleashed by the slightest provocation? I presumed not, for she seemed so popular and respected by her townsfolk. *Everybody* loved Miss Birdle. And Miss Birdle loved *everybody*. Who would ever guess that the endearing old lady had the slightest streak of viciousness in her? Why should anyone think such a thing? Knowing her lovable side so well, even I had difficulty in believing her kindness could turn to such violence, but I shall never trust any sweet old ladies again. How do you explain such a twist in human nature? What made her good one moment, bad the next? It's quite simple really.

She was nuts.

FOURTEEN

Dog's life, dogsbody, dogfight, dog-eared, dog-days, dog-end, dirty dog, mad dog, lazy dog, dog-tired, sick as a dog, dog-in-the-manger, underdog – why so many abuses of our name? You don't say hedgehog's life, or rabbit's body, or frog-in-the-manger. True, you do use certain animal names to describe a particular type of person – chicken (coward), monkey (rogue), goose (silly) – but they're only individual descriptions, you never extend the range with a particular species. Only dogs come in for this abuse. You even use various species' names in a complimentary manner: an elephant never forgets (not true), happy as a lark (not true), brave as a lion (definitely not true), wise as an owl (are you kidding?). But where are the dog compliments? And yet we're cherished by you and regarded as man's best friend. We guard you, we guide you; we can hunt with you, we can play with you. You can even race some of our breed. You use us for work and we can win you prizes. We're loyal, we trust, and we love you – even the meanest of you can be adored by your dog. So why this derogatory use of our name? Why can't you be 'as free as a dog', or 'as proud as a dog', or 'as cunning as a dog'? Why should a skivvy be called a dogsbody? Why wouldn't you send *even* a dog out on a cold night? What have *we* done to deserve such blasphemy? Is it because we always seem to fall into some misfortune or other? Is it because we appear foolish? Is it because we're prone to over-excitement? Is it because we're fierce in a fight but cowardly when our master's hand is raised against us? Is it because we have dirty habits? *Is it because we're more like you than any other living creature?*

Do you recognize our misfortunes as being similar to your own, our personalities a reflection of yours but simpler? Do you pity, love and hate dogs because you see your own humanness in us? Is that why you insult our name? Are you only insulting yourselves?

'A dog's life' had true meaning for me as I lay there in the grass, panting. Was my life always to follow this unlucky pattern? It was the human part of my nature coming to the fore again, you see, for not many animals philosophize in such a way (there are exceptions). Fear and that good old human characteristic, self-pity, had aroused the semi-dormant side of my personality once more and I thought in terms of man yet still with canine influence.

I shook off my misery the way dogs do and got to my feet. I had an objective which had been neglected; now was the time to continue my search. It was a beautifully fresh day and the air was filled with different scents. I was without a patron again and still without a friend but because of it I was free; free to do as I pleased and free to go where I pleased. I had only myself to answer to!

My legs broke into an unpremeditated sprint and once again I was in full flight, only this time my compulsion to run was ahead of me and not behind. I knew the direction I should take instinctively and soon found myself back on the road and heading towards the town that had sounded so familiar.

Cars swished past at frequent intervals, causing me to shy away. I was still very frightened of these mechanical monsters even after months of living in the busy city, but somehow I knew I had once driven such a vehicle myself. In another life. I came to a heavily wooded area and decided to take a small detour, knowing it would actually cut a few miles off my journey.

The wood was a fascinating place. It hummed with hidden beings which my eyes soon began to detect, and to which (surprisingly) I was able to put names. There were beetles, gnats, hoverflies, tabanad flies, mosquitoes, wasps and bees. Speckled wood and brimstone butterflies fluttered from leaf to leaf. Dormice, wood-mice and bank-voles scuttled through the undergrowth, and grey squirrels were everywhere. A woodpecker stared curiously at me from his perch and ignored my hearty good morning. A startled roe-deer leapt away as I stumbled into its hiding-place. Thousands on thousands of aphides (you might know them as blackfly or greenfly) sucked the sap from leaves and plant stems, excreting honeydew for ants and others to feed on. Birds – songthrush, chaffinch, great tit, blue tit, jays and many, many more – flew from branch to branch or dived into the undergrowth in search of food. Earthworms appeared and disappeared at my feet. I was amazed at the teeming activity and a little in awe of it, for I had never realized so much went on in these sheltered areas. The colours almost made my eyes sore with their intensity and the constant babble of animal chatter filled my head with its raucous sound. It was exhilarating and made me feel very alive.

I spent the day exploring and thoroughly enjoyed myself, seeing things through new eyes and with a completely different mental approach, for I was now part of that world and not merely a human observer. I made a few friends here and there, although I was generally ignored by this busy population of animals, insects, birds and reptiles. Their attitudes were quite unpredictable, for I had quite a pleasant chat with a venomous adder, whereas a cute-looking red squirrel I chanced upon was extremely rude. Their appearance bore no resemblance to their nature. (My conversation with the adder was strange, for snakes, of course, have only an inner ear which picks up vibrations through the skull. It made me realize again that we were communicating through thought.) I discovered snakes are a much-maligned creature for this one was a very inoffensive sort, as have been most I've come into contact with since.

For once I forgot about my belly, and allowed myself to enjoy my surroundings, sniffing out trails left or boundaries marked by various animals through their urine and anal glands. I marked my own trail from time to time, more as a 'Fluke was here' sign than a means of finding my way back. There'd be no going back for me.

I dozed in the sun in the afternoon and when I awoke I wandered down to a stream to drink. A frog sat there eating a long pink worm, scraping the earth off the shiny body with his fingers as he swallowed. He stopped for a moment and regarded me curiously, the poor worm frantically trying to work his body back out of the frog's mouth. The frog blinked twice and resumed his eating, the worm slowly disappearing like a live string of spaghetti. The worm's tail (head?) wriggled once more before leaving the land of the living, then was gone, the frog's eyes bulging even more as he gulped convulsively.

'Nice day,' I said amiably.

He blinked again and said, 'Nice enough.'

I wondered briefly how he would taste but decided he didn't look too appetizing. I seemed to remember from somewhere that his legs might be quite tasty, though.

'Haven't seen you around here before,' he commented.

'Just passing through,' I replied.

'Passing through? What does that mean?'

'Well . . . I'm on a journey.'

'A journey to where?'

'To a town.'

'What's a town?'

'A town. Where people live.'

'People?'

'Big things, on two legs.'

He shrugged. 'Never seen them.'

'Don't people ever pass this way?'

'Never seen them,' he repeated. 'Never seen a town, either. No towns here.'

'There's a town not too far off.'

'Can't be any such thing. Never seen one.'

'No, not here in the woods, but further away.'

'There is no other place.'

'Of course there is. The world's far bigger than just this woodland!'

'What woodland?'

'Around us,' I said, indicating with my nose. 'Beyond these nearby trees.'

'There's nothing beyond those trees. I only know those.'

'Haven't you ever gone further than this glade?'

'What for?'

'To see what else there is.'

'I know all there is.'

'You don't. There's more.'

'You're mistaken.'

'You've never seen me before, have you?'

'No.'

'Well, I come from beyond the trees.'

He puzzled over this for a minute. 'Why?' he said finally. 'Why have you come from beyond the trees?'

'Because I'm passing through. I'm on a journey.'

'A journey to where?'

'To a town.'

'What's a town?'

'Where people . . . oh, forget it!'

He did, instantly. The frog wasn't really that concerned.

I stomped away, exasperated. 'You'll never turn into a handsome prince!' I shouted over my shoulder.

'What's a handsome?' he called back.

The conversation made me ponder over the animals' point of view. This amphibian obviously thought that the world was only that which he could see. It wasn't even that there was nothing beyond, for he had never even asked himself the question. And it was that way for all animals (apart from a few of us): the world consisted of only what they knew – there was nothing else.

I spent a restless and anxious night beneath an oak tree, the sound of an owl and its mate keeping me awake for most of the night. (It surprised me to discover the 'to-whit-to-whoo' was a combination of both birds – one hooted while the other twitted.) It wasn't so much their calling to each other that bothered me, but their sudden swoops down on to vulnerable voles scurrying around in the dark below, the sudden screech culminating in the victim's squeal of terror which disturbed and frightened me. I didn't have the nerve to upset the owls, since they seemed vicious and powerful creatures, nor did I have the courage to wander around in the dark looking for a new sleeping-place. However, I did eventually fall into an uneasy sleep and the following morning I went hunting for chickens with my new friend, (I thought) – a red fox.

I awoke to the sound of yapping. It was still dark – I estimated dawn was a couple of hours away yet, and the yaps came from not too far off. Lying perfectly still, I tried to detect in which direction the yaps came from, and from whom. Were there pups in this wood? Sure that the owls were now at rest, I inched my way forward away from the trees, my senses keened, and had not gone far when I came across the fox's earth in a hollow under a projecting tree-root. A musty smell of excrement and food remains hit my nostrils and then I saw four sets of eyes gleaming out at me.

'Who's there?' someone said in a half-frightened, half-aggressive, manner.

'Don't be alarmed,' I reassured them hastily. 'It's only me.'

'Are you a dog?' I was asked, and one set of eyes detached itself from the others. A fox skulked forward out of the gloom and I sensed rather than saw she was a she. A vixen.

'Well?' she said.

'Er, yes. Yes, I'm a dog,' I told her.

'What do you want here?' Her manner had become menacing now.

'I heard your pups. I was curious, that's all.'

She seemed to realize I was no threat and her attitude relaxed a little. 'What are you doing in these woods?' she asked. 'Dogs rarely come in here at night.'

'I'm on my way . . . somewhere.' Would she understand what a town was?

'To the houses where the big animals live?'

'Yes, to a town.'

'Do you belong to the farm?'

'The farm?'

'The farm on the other side of the woods. Over the meadows.'

Her world was larger than the frog's.

'No, I don't belong there. I'm from a big town, a city.'

'Oh.'

The vixen seemed to have lost interest now and turned back when a small voice called from the darkness.

'Mum, I'm hungry!' came the complaint.

'Be quiet! I'm going soon.'

'I'm hungry too,' I said, and I really was.

The vixen's head swung back to me. 'Then go and find yourself some food!'

'Er . . . I don't know how to in a forest.'

She looked at me incredulously. 'You can't feed yourself? You can't find yourself a rabbit, or a mouse, or a squirrel?'

'I've never had to before. I mean, I've killed rats and mice, but nothing bigger than that.'

She shook her head in wonder. 'How have you survived, then. Coddled by the big ones, I suppose – I've seen your kind with them. They even use you to hunt us!'

'Not me! I'm from the city. I've never hunted foxes.'

'Why should I believe you? How do I know you're not trying to trick me?' She showed me her pointed teeth in a grin that wasn't a grin but a threat.

'I'll go away if you like, I don't want to upset you. But perhaps me and your mate can go and find some food for all of us.'

'I don't have a mate any more.' She spat the words out and I could feel the anger and hurt in them.

'What happened to him?' I asked.

'Caught and killed,' was all she would say.

'Find us some food, Mum,' came the plaintive cry again.

'Well, perhaps I could help *you*,' I suggested.

'Huh!' scoffed the vixen, then her voice changed. 'There may be a way you can be used, though,' she said thoughtfully.

I stiffened to attention. 'Anything. I'm starving.'

'All right, then. You kids stay here and don't go outside! You hear?'

They heard.

'Come on, you.' The fox brushed past me.

'Where too?' I asked eagerly, following behind.

'You'll see.'

'What's your name?' I called out.

'Hush up!' she whispered fiercely, then said. 'What's a name?'

'What you're called.'

'I'm called fox. Vixen to be exact. You're called dog, aren't you?'

'No, that's what I am. Fox is what you are. I'm called Fluke.'

'That's daft. Flukes are flatworms!'

'Yes, but men call me Fluke – it's an expression.'

She shrugged off my silliness and didn't speak again till we'd walked for at least a mile and a half. Then she turned to me and said, 'We're nearly there now. You have to keep very very quiet from here on – and move very carefully.'

'Right,' I whispered, trembling with excitement.

I could see the farm stretched out before us and from the stench I guessed it was mainly a dairy farm.

'What are we going to do – kill a cow?' I asked in all seriousness, the excitement draining from me.

'Don't be daft!' the fox hissed. 'Chickens. They keep chickens here too.'

That's all right then, I thought. That could be quite interesting.

We crept towards the farm and I copied the fox's style exactly, running forward silently, stopping, listening, sniffing, then padding foward again, from bush to bush, tree to tree, then stealthily through the long grass. I noticed the wind was coming towards us, bringing lovely rich farmyard smells. We reached a huge open shed and slid easily into it. On our left were the remaining bales of last winter's barley and straw, and on our right bags of fertilizer piled high. When we emerged, I stopped at a water-trough and, resting my paws on its edge, had a good tongue-lapping drink.

'Come on!' the vixen whispered impatiently. 'No time for that. It'll be dawn soon.'

I padded after her, feeling quite refreshed now, every nerve alive and dancing. The fox and I passed through the collection yard, over the feeding-troughs, by the silage pit, then past a nearly empty but pungent manure hold. I wrinkled my nose – you can have too much of a good thing – and sped after the wily fox. We could hear the cows snoring in their enormous shed, and the smell of barley managed to cover the smell of manure (although not entirely) as we went by a giant barley bin. We were soon through the yard and I could see the dark outline of a house in the moonlight ahead of us.

The fox stopped and sniffed the air. Then she listened. After a while, her body relaxed slightly and she turned to me.

'There's one of your sort here, a big ugly brute. We must be careful not to wake him – he sleeps up near the house. Now this is what we'll do. . . .' She came closer to me and I saw she was quite attractive really in a sharp-looking way. 'The chickens are over in that direction. A thin but sharp barrier keeps them in and us out. If I can get a good grip with my teeth at the bottom of the barrier, I can pull it up so we can get underneath. I've done it before – it's just a knack. Once we get in, all hell will break loose . . .' (did she understand the concept of hell or was it only my mind translating her thoughts) '. . . and when it does, we'll only have a short time to grab a hen each and make a bolt for it.'

I'm sure her eyes must have gleamed craftily in the dark, but I was too excited – or too dumb – to notice.

'Now,' the vixen went on, 'when we run for it, we must go separate ways. That will confuse the big dog and the big thing who keeps him. The two-legged thing . . .'

'Man,' I said.

'What?'

'Man. That's what he's called.'

'Like Fluke?'

'No. That's what he is. Man,'

The vixen shrugged. 'All right. Man has got a long stick that screams. It kills too – I've seen it kill – so you must be careful. You had better run back this way through the yard because there's plenty of cover, and I'll go the other way across the fields at the back because I'm probably faster. O.K.?'

'Right,' I said keenly. Rumbo was probably turning over in his grave just then.

On we stalked, silently and breathlessly, and before long we'd reached the chicken-coop and its surrounding wire-mesh fence. It wasn't a particularly large coop – the farmer probably only kept chickens as a sideline, his profit coming from his cows – but it could have contained thirty to fifty hens. We heard an occasional flutter from inside, but it was obvious they hadn't detected our presence.

The vixen scuffled around at the base of the wire fencing and tried to get a grip on it with her teeth. She managed to do so and pulled upwards with all her strength. The wiring tore loose from its wooden base, but my companion was unable to keep her grip and it fell back down again, although it remained loose. There had been a ripping sound as the wire mesh tore loose and the noise had alerted the hens inside the hutch. We could hear them moving around inside. Soon they would be jabbering and screeching.

The fox tried again and this time she was more successful. The wiring sprang up and sank back only slightly when she released it.

'Quickly,' she whispered and shot through the opening. I tried to follow, but my body was bigger than the fox's and the wire cut into my back, trapping me half-way through. Meanwhile, the fox had climbed up a short run, lifted a small flap with her nose, and in a flash was inside the hutch. The screams and the thrashing sounds that came from inside paralyzed me. The sudden deep barking that came from somewhere near the house made me mobile again. I struggled to get free, knowing the farmer and his 'screaming stick' would soon be down there.

The small hatch to the chicken-hutch suddenly flew open and out poured the squawking poultry, feathers and bodies flying through the air like torn pillow-cases.

Now I don't know if you know this, but hens, as do many groups of animals, have their own hierarchy. It's called the 'pecking order', and the hen who has the biggest and meanest peck is the boss, the second meanest pecker is under the first, but boss over the others, and so on all the way down the line. But now it looked as though everyone was equal.

They all ran around like lunatics and the only competition was who could fly the highest.

The fox emerged, a hen as big as her own body fluttering feebly in her grasp. She ran towards the gap where I was crouched neither in nor out.

'Move yourself,' came her muffled command.

'I'm stuck!' I yelled back.

'The dog's coming, quickly!' she said, desperately pacing backwards and forwards along the side of the pen. But the dog must have been chained, for although we could hear him barking, he was still nowhere near. Then we heard the roar of the farmer as a window flew open back there at the house.

That moved me. With a terrific wrench backwards I tore myself free of the wire, scratching my back nastily as I did so. The fox, chicken and all, was through in a flash.

'You go that way!' she shouted at me, feathers spraying from her mouth.

'Right!' I agreed. And then I ran up towards the house, towards the dog, towards the farmer and his gun, while my friend flew off in the opposite direction.

I was half-way there before I stopped and said to myself, Hold on! I looked round just in time to see a fleeting black shape tearing across a field before being swallowed up by the dark line of a hedge.

I turned back as I heard the door of the house crash open and out leapt the farmer wearing vest and trousers and heavy boots. The sight of the long object he held in two hands before him nearly made me faint. The other dog was going mad now trying to get at me and I saw it was a very healthy looking mastiff. I had the feeling his stretched chain would break at any moment.

I groaned and wondered which way to run. The end of the cowshed lay to my left, outhouses to my right. Ahead was the farmer and his monster dog. There was only one way to go really, and of course the fox had taken it. I turned in my tracks and made for the open fields.

A choking kind of shout came from the farmer as he saw me and I heard him lumber out into the yard. I didn't have to look to know he was raising the gun to his shoulder. The blast told me it was a shotgun and the whistling over my ears told me the farmer wasn't a bad shot. My speed increased as my quickening heartbeat acted as a crazy metronome to my legs.

More footsteps, silence, and I waited for the second blast. I swerved as much as I could and crouched low to make myself as small a target as possible. The hens leapt into the air in horror as I passed them, no doubt thinking I had returned for second helpings.

I leapt into the air myself as my tail seemed to explode into shreds. I yelp-yelped in that rapid way dogs do when they're hurt, but kept going, relieved that I could actually keep going. The barking behind me reached a new frenzy and then I knew the mastiff had been let loose, for the sound took on a new, more excited pitch. The welcoming fields rushed forward to meet me and I scrambled under a fence and was into them, my tail on fire.

'Gorn boy!' came the shout from behind and knew the monster dog was closing up on me. The field seemed to stretch out before me in the moonlight and grow wider and longer, the hedge on the far side shrinking rather than growing. The mastiff hadn't caught up with me yet, but his heavy panting had. He'd stopped barking to save his breath and conserve his energy. He really wanted me, that dog.

I inwardly cursed myself for being so stupid and allowing myself to be used as a decoy by the fox. It made me very angry and almost caused me to turn and vent my anger on the pursuing dog. Almost, but not quite – I wasn't *that* stupid.

The mastiff seemed to be panting in my left ear now and I realized he was very close. I turned my head quickly to see just how far behind he was and immediately wished I hadn't – his grinning teeth were level with my left flank!

I swerved just as he took a snap at me and he went sailing on by, rolling over on the grass as he endeavoured to stop himself. The mastiff came racing back and I went racing on again, so he found himself running in the wrong direction once more.

Looming up ahead was the hedge and I was grateful it had stopped playing shrinking tricks on me. I dived into it and prayed I wouldn't hit a tree trunk; the mastiff plunged in right behind me. Brambles tore at us and startled birds complained of the noise, but we were through in an instant and tearing across the next field. Knowing he would soon catch up, I began my swerving tactics again. Fortunately, the mastiff wasn't too bright and he fell for my tricks every time. It was exhausting though and several times his teeth raked across my flank, but eventually even his energy seemed to be depleting. On one very successful twist he had gone at least five yards beyond me, so I stopped for a breather. The mastiff stopped too and we both faced each other across the grass, our shoulders and chests heaving with the effort.

'Look,' I panted, 'let's talk about this.'

But he had no inclination to talk at all. He was up and at me, growling as he came. So on I went.

As I ran, I picked up a scent. Foxes are usually pretty smart when it comes to covering their tracks – they'll double back, climb trees, jump into water, or mingle with sheep – but when they've got a dead chicken in their mouth, dripping blood and feathers, it's another story. She'd left a trail as strong as cat's-eyes in a road.

The mastiff got a whiff of it and momentarily lost interest in me, then we both tore off down that smelly path. Through another hedge we went, and then we were in the wood, dodging round trees and heavy clumps of bushes. Startled night creatures scurried back to their homes as we crashed past, twittering and protesting at our intrusion.

I don't think the mastiff's night vision was as good as mine – probably he was a lot older – because his progress wasn't so fast, and several times I heard him cry out when he bumped into trees. I gained some distance on him and began to feel a little more confident about getting away. Then I bumped into the fox.

The hen had hampered her flight and she must have dropped it at this point and paused to retrieve it. I bore no malice – I was too frightened at what lay behind – and would probably have ignored her had I not gone straight into her crouching body. We rolled over in a struggling heap, fox, chicken and dog, but parted immediately when the mastiff joined us. He bit out at everything within reach and, fortunately for both the vixen and me, we were able to leave him there with a mouthful of chicken, content in his catch as he shook the dead body and tried to rip it apart. The farmer would be well pleased when his guard dog returned with a mouthful of feathers and blood.

We went our separate ways, the vixen and I, she back to her cubs, me to find somewhere quiet to nurse my wounds. It was growing lighter by the minute now and I hurried to get away from the area, not sure of my directions but wanting to travel as far as possible before daybreak. I knew (how did I know?) farmers took great pains to seek out and destroy any killer dogs who plagued their livestock and this particular farmer would certainly regard me as such. My tail stung terribly now, overriding the hurt from my various other wounds, but I didn't dare stop and examine the damage. I came to a stream and swam across, enjoying the coolness on my wounds, and when I reached the other side, clambered out with reluctance. I gave myself a good shake then sped onwards, determined to get clear of the farmer's land.

The sun had risen and was gathering strength by the time I stumbled into a resting-place. I ached and I hurt, and all I could do was lay there in a dip in the ground and try to recover my strength. After a while I was able to twist my head and examine my throbbing tail. The wound wasn't half as bad as I expected; only the very tip had been damaged and much of the hair had gone from it. Victoria would have been pleased, for our tails were now a good match. The sting from the scratches on my back and flanks caused by the wire mesh and the mastiff's teeth weren't too bothersome, but irritating nonetheless. I rested my head between my paws and slept.

When I awoke, the sun was high overhead and covering my body with its warmth. My mouth and throat felt dry and my wounds were a dull throb. My stomach grumbled over the lack of food. Rousing myself, I looked around and saw I was resting in the dip of a gentle slope. A valley spread out below and other grassy hills rose up on the other side, their soft summits mounted by beech copses. I wandered down hoping to find a spring at the bottom of the hill, nibbling at certain grasses as I went. The grass – sheep's fescue it's called – wasn't too tasty, but I knew many downland animals ate it, so at least it would provide nourishment. Again, I wondered how I knew about such things: how I knew the snail I'd just pushed was a Roman snail that used calcium in the chalky downland soil to make its shell; how the bird that sang somewhere to my right was a skylark; how the butterfly that fluttered by was an Adonis blue wakened prematurely by the sudden warm weather. I had obviously taken a keen interest in the countryside in my past life and taken the trouble to learn about nature and her ways. Had I perhaps been a naturalist or a botanist? Or had it been only a hobby to me? Maybe I had been brought up in the countryside and names and habits came naturally to me. I shook my head in frustration: I had to find out *who* I had been, *what* I had been; how I had died and why I had become a dog. And I had to discover who the man was, the man in my dreams who seemed so evil, who seemed such a threat to my family. My family – the woman and the little girl – I had to find them, had to let them know I wasn't dead. Had to tell them I'd become a dog. Wasn't there someone who could help me?

There was. But I wasn't to meet him till two nights later.

FIFTEEN

Pay attention now because this is important. This is the point in my story where I heard a reason for my existence, why I was a dog. This is the part that may help you if you're prepared to accept it. I won't mind if you don't, it's up to you, but bear in mind what I asked if you at the beginning: keep your mind open.

I wandered on for two more days, finding the road again and relieved to find it. I was determined not to waste any more time, but to find my home and to find some answers.

Road signs were becoming more difficult to read; I had to gaze at them for a long time and concentrate hard. However, I found the right way and continued my journey, pleased to reach a town further on; it was much easier for me to get food when I was among people and shops. A few people took pity on me in my bedraggled state (although others chased me away as though I were something unclean) and gave me scraps. I spent the night with a family who took me in, and I think they had intentions of keeping me as a pet, but the following morning when they let me out to relieve myself, I ran off to the next town. I hated spurning this family's kindness, but nothing could deter me from my purpose now.

I was less successful in scrounging food in the next town, although I still ate adequately enough. The road was becoming more and more familiar and I knew I was nearing my home. My excitement grew.

When dusk fell I was between towns, so I left the roadside and entered a deep wood. Hungry (of course) and tired (naturally), I searched for a safe place to sleep. I don't know if you've ever spent the night in a wood alone, but it's very creepy. It's pitch-black for a start (no street lights), and there's a constant rustling and cracking of dry twigs as the night animals mooch around. My night vision's good – better than yours – but even so, it was still difficult to detect much in the darkness. Eerie glowing lights set my heart racing until I investigated and discovered a couple of glow-worms going through their meeting routine. Another blue-green glow upset me until I realized it was only honey fungus growing on a decaying tree-trunk.

I could hear bats flapping around, their high-pitched squeals making me jump, and a hedgehog trundled into me and pricked my nose with its spikes. I considered going back to the roadside, but the blinding lights and roaring engines of passing cars were even more frightening.

The woods at night are almost as busy in the daytime, except everything seems even more secretive. I adopted this secretive attitude myself and skulked around as stealthily as I could in search of a resting-place. Finally I discovered a nice soft mound of earth beneath a thick roof of foliage, just under a tree. It made a snug hiding place and I settled down for the night, a strange feeling of portentousness filling me. My instincts were right, for later that night my sleep was disturbed by the badger.

And it was the badger who explained things to me.

I had failed to fall into a comfortable sleep and lay dozing in the dark with my eyes constantly blinking open at the slightest sound. A shifting of earth behind me made me jump and twist my head round to see the cause of the disturbance. Three broad white lines appeared from a hole in the sloping ground and a twitching nose at the base of the middle stripe sniffed the air in all directions.

It stopped when it caught my scent.

'Who's there?' a voice said.

I didn't reply – I was ready to run.

The white lines widened as they emerged from the black hole. 'Funny smell,' the voice said. 'Let me see you.'

I now saw there were two shiny black eyes on either side of the middle stripe. I realized it was a badger speaking, and it was, two *black* stripes running down his white head which gave him this white-striped appearance. I backed away, aware that these creatures could be fierce if alarmed or angered.

'Is it . . . is it a . . . dog? Yes, it's a dog, isn't it?' the badger guessed.

I cleared my throat, undecided whether to stay or run.

'Don't be afraid,' the badger said. 'I won't cause you any bother unless *you* mean us harm.' He waddled his great coarse-haired body out of his sett and I saw he was at least three feet long and very tall.

'Yes, I thought I recognized the smell. We don't get many dogs in here on their own. You are on your own, aren't you? You're not night-hunting with one of those cattle farmers, are you?'

Like the fox, he didn't seem to trust the dog's association with man. I found my voice and nervously assured him I wasn't.

He seemed puzzled for a moment and I felt rather than saw him regard me curiously. Whatever was going on in his mind was interrupted as another badger shuffled from the sett. I assumed this was his sow.

'What's going on? Who's this?' came a sharp voice.

'Hush now. It's only a dog and he means us no harm,' the boar told her. 'Why are you alone in the woods, friend? Are you lost?'

I was too nervous to speak up right then and the sow piped up again: 'Chase him away! He's after the babies!'

'No, no,' I managed to say. 'No, please, I'm just passing through. I'll be on my way now. Don't get upset.' I turned to trot off into the darkness.

'Just a moment,' the boar said quickly. 'Stay awhile. I want to talk to you.'
Now I was afraid to run.

'Chase him away, chase him away! I don't like him!' the sow urged.

'Be quiet!' the boar said quietly but firmly. 'You go on about your hunting.
Leave a good trail for me to follow – I'll join you later.'

The sow knew better than to argue and huffed her way rudely past me,
emitting a vile odour from her anal glands as a comment.

'Come closer,' the boar said when his mate had gone. 'Come where I can see
you better.' His enormous body had shrunk and I realized his hair must have
become erectile on seeing me and had now returned to its normal smoothness.
'Tell me why you're here. Do you belong to a man?'

I shuffled forward, ready to flee.

'No, I don't belong to anyone. I used to, but don't any more.'

'Have you been mistreated?'

'It's a lucky dog who hasn't.'

He nodded at this. 'It would be a fortunate animal *or* man who hasn't,' he
said.

It was my turn to regard him curiously. What did *he* know of man?

The badger settled himself into a comfortable position on the ground and
invited me to do the same and, after a moment's hesitation, I did.

'Tell me about yourself. Do you have a man name?' he asked.

'Fluke,' I told him, puzzled by his knowledge. He seemed very human for a
badger. 'What's yours?'

The badger chuckled drily. 'Wild animals don't have names, we know who
we are. It's only men who give animals names.'

'How do you know about that? About men, I mean.'

He laughed aloud then. 'I used to be one,' he said.

I sat there stunned. Had I heard right? My jaw dropped open.

The badger laughed again, and the sound of a badger laughing is enough to
unnerve anyone. Fighting the urge to run I managed to stammer, 'Y-you used . .
.'

'Yes. And you were too. And so were all animals.'

'But . . . but I know *I* was. I thought I was the only one! I . . .'

He stayed my words with a grin. 'Hush now. I knew you weren't like the
others at my first whiff of you. I've met some who have been similar, but there's
something very different about you. Calm down and let me hear your story, then
I'll tell you a few things about yourself – about us.'

I tried to still my pounding heart and began to tell the badger about my life:
my first recollections in the market, my first owner, the dogs' home, the breaker's
yard, the Guvnor, Rumbo, the old lady, and my episode with sly old fox. I told
him where I was going, of my man memories and, as I went on, my nerves
settled, although an excitement remained. It was wonderful to talk in this way,
to tell someone who would listen, who understood the things I said, how I felt.
The badger remained quiet throughout, nodding his head from time to time,
shaking it in sympathy at others. When I had finished, I felt drained, drained yet
strangely elated. It seemed as though a weight had been lifted. I was no longer
alone – there was another who knew what I knew! I looked eagerly at the
badger.

'Why do you want to go to this town – this Edenbridge?' he asked before I
could question him.

'To see my family, of course! My wife, my daughter – to let them know I'm not
dead!'

He was silent for a moment, then he said, 'But you are dead.'

The shock almost stopped my racing heart. 'I'm not. How can you say that? I'm alive – not as a man, but as a dog. I'm in a dog's body!'

'No. The man you were is dead. The man your wife and daughter knew is dead. You'd only be a dog to them.'

'Why?' I howled. 'How did I become like this? Why am I a dog?'

'A dog? You could have become any one of a multitude of creatures – it depended largely on your former life.'

I shook my body in frustration and moaned, 'I don't understand.'

'Do you believe in reincarnation, Fluke?' the badger asked.

'Reincarnation? Living again as someone else, in another time? I don't know. I don't think I do.'

'You're living proof to yourself.'

'No, there must be another explanation.'

'Such as?'

'I've no idea. But why should we come back as someone or something – *else*?'

'What would be the point of just one existence on this earth?'

'What would be the point of two?' I countered.

'Or three, or four? Man has to learn, Fluke, and he could never learn in one lifetime. Many man religions advocate this, and many accept reincarnation in the form of animals. Man has to learn from all levels.'

'Learn what?'

'Acceptance.'

'Why? Why should he learn acceptance? What for?'

'So he can go on to the next stage.'

'And what's that?'

'I don't know, I haven't reached it. It's good, I believe. I feel that.'

'So how do you know this much? What makes *you* special?'

'I've been around for a long time, Fluke. I've observed, I've learned, I've lived many lives. And I think I'm here to help those like you.'

His words were soft and strangely comforting, but I fought against them. 'Look,' I said, 'I'm confused. Are you saying I have to accept being a dog?'

'You have to accept whatever life gives you – and I mean *accept*. You have to learn humility, Fluke, and that comes only with acceptance. Then will you be ready for the next level.'

'Wait a minute,' I said, taking on a new tact out of desperation. 'We *all* become animals when we die?'

He nodded. 'Nearly all. Birds, fishes, mammals, insects – there are no rules as to which species we're born into.'

'But there must be billions upon billions of living creatures in the world today. They can't all be reincarnated humans, our civilization just hasn't been going that long.'

The badger chuckled. 'Yes, you're right. There are at least a million known animal species, over three quarters of which are insects – the more advanced of us.'

'Insects are the more advanced?' I asked in a flat tone.

'That's right. But let me answer your first point. This planet of ours is very old and it's been washed clean many times so that life can start all over again, a constant cycle of evolvement which allows us to learn a little more each time. Our civilization, as you call it, has not been the first by any means.'

'And these . . . these people are still coming back, still . . . learning?'

'Oh yes. Much of our progress owes itself to race memory, not inspiration.'

'But no matter how long ago it all began, man evolved from animals, didn't he? How could animals have been reincarnated humans if they were here first?' He just laughed at that.

You can imagine the state I was in by now: half of me wanted to believe him because I needed answers (and he spoke in such a soothing, matter-of-fact way), and the other half wondered if he was demented.

'You said insects were more advanced . . .' I prompted.

'Yes, they accept their lives, which are shorter and perhaps more arduous. A female fruit-fly completes her whole lifecycle in ten days, whereas a turtle, for instance, can live for three hundred years.'

'I dread to think of what the turtle has been up to in his previous life to deserve such a long penance,' I said drily.

'Penance. Yes, that's a good way of putting it,' he said thoughtfully.

I groaned inwardly and was startled when the badger laughed out loud. 'All too much for you, is it?' he said. 'Well, that's understandable. But think about it: Why are certain creatures so repugnant to man? Why are they trodden on, mistreated or killed, or just plain reviled? Could these creatures have been so vile in their past lives that the malignancy lingers on? Is this their punishment for past crimes? The snake spends his life crawling on his belly, the spider is invariably crushed whenever he comes into contact with man. The worm is despised, the slug makes humans shudder. Even the poor old lobster is boiled alive. But their death comes as a blessing, a relief from their horrible existence. It's nature's way that their lives should be short, and man's instinct makes him want to crush these creatures. It's not just abhorrence of them, you see, but compassion also, a desire to put an end to their misery. These creatures have paid their price.

'And there are many more, Fluke, many, *many* more creatures below the earth's surface. Beings that no human ever laid eyes on; bugs who live in fires near the earth's core. What evil have they done to earn such an existence? Have you ever wondered why humans think of hell as an inferno, why its direction is always "down there"? And why do we look skywards when we speak of "Heaven"? Do we have an instinct born in us about such things?

'Why do many fear death, while others welcome it? Do we already know it's only an enforced hibernation, that we live on in another form, that our wrongdoings have to be accounted for? No wonder those who have lived peaceful lives are less afraid.'

The badger paused at that point, either to regain his breath or to give me time to catch up with him.

'How do you explain ghosts, then? I know they exist, I've seen them – I keep seeing them,' I said. 'Why haven't they been born again as animals, or have they passed that stage? Is that the level we're reaching for? If it is, I'm not so sure I want it.'

'No, no. They haven't even reached our stage of development, I'm afraid, Fluke. They're closer to our world though than their previous one – that's why it's easier for us to see them – but they're lost, you see. That's why there's such an aura of sadness about them. Confused and lost. They find their way eventually with a little help. They get born again.'

Born again. The words struck me. Was this why my vision, the colours I could see, was so incredible? Was this why I could appreciate scents – the most delicate and the most pungent – so fully? Was it because I'd been born again yet still retained vague memories? *I had past senses to compare with the new!* A newborn baby sees freshly but quickly learns to adapt his vision, to mute colours, to organize shapes – he learns *not* to accept. That's why you're nearly blind at birth; it would be too much for you otherwise. Your brain has to sort things out first, then let you in on it gradually. My own sight was now nowhere as clear or unprejudiced as it had been when I was a young pup. Nor was my hearing. My brain which had been born with the ability to appreciate my senses was now organizing them so they were acceptable to it, so they no longer dazzled it as much as before.

I shook the train of thought from my head and said, 'But why can't others remember? Why aren't they the same as me?'

'I can't answer that, Fluke. You're different and I don't know why. Perhaps you're the first of a new development. An evolvement. I've met others similar, but none quite like you. Perhaps you are only a fluke after all. I wish I knew.'

'Aren't you the same as me? Wasn't Rumbo almost? And a rat we met once, he seemed like us.'

'Yes, we're a little like you. I suppose me more so than your friend Rumbo and the rat. But you're special, Fluke. I'm special too, but in a different way, as I told you: I'm here to help. Rumbo and the rat may have been similar, but I doubt they were the same. I think perhaps you're a kind of forerunner; everything may be about to go through a change.'

'But why do I only remember fragments?' Why can't I remember it all?'

'You're not supposed to remember *anything*. Many creatures carry the characteristics of their past personalities, many may even have vague memories; but they don't think as you do, not in human terms. There's a struggle going on inside you – man versus canine – but I think it will eventually resolve itself. You'll either become a dog completely, or a balance between the two will be reached. I hope it's the latter – that could mean a development for all of us is taking place. But listen to me: you'll never be a man again physically in this life.'

Despair gripped me. What had I expected? That some day, by some miracle, I might return to my old body? That I would live a normal life again? I howled into the night and wept as never before.

Finally, and with no hope in my voice, I said to the badger, 'What do I do now? How can I live like this?'

He moved closer to me and spoke very quietly. 'You accept now. Accept you're a dog, accept you are a fluke – or perhaps not a fluke. You must live as a dog now.'

'But I have to know who I was!'

'No, it won't help you. Forget your past, your family – they're nothing to do with you now.'

'They need me!'

'There's nothing you can do!'

I rose to my feet and glowered down at him. 'You don't understand. There's someone evil near them. They need protection from him. I think he killed me!'

The badger shook his head wearily. 'It doesn't matter, Fluke. You can't help any more. You *have* to forget your past, you might regret it if you go back.'

'No!' I growled. 'Maybe this is why I can remember, why I'm different. They need my help! It stayed with me when I died! I've got to go to them!'

I ran from the badger then, afraid he would make me stay, afraid to hear more, but when I was a safe distance away, I turned and called back.

'Who are you badger? What are you?'

There was no reply. And I could no longer see him in the darkness.

SIXTEEN

Pretty heavy stuff, right? A bit frightening? Well, it scared me. But do you see the sense of it? If there is this great goal we're all reaching for – call it perfection, happiness, ultimate peace of mind, whatever you like – then it seems right that it doesn't come easily; we have to earn it. I don't know why and I'm still not sure I believe it myself (and I'm a dog who was once a man), so I don't blame you for doubting. But, like I keep saying: keep an open mind.

I found myself in Edenbridge High Street a day or so later. I'm not sure just how long it took me to get there because, as you can imagine, my mind was in a turmoil after my meeting with the badger. I had to accept that, as a man, I was dead (if I were to believe the badger revelations), and there would be no return to normality for me. But if I were dead, then how did I die? Old age? Somehow, I doubted it. My wife seemed fairly young in my memories of her, and my daughter could have been no more than five or six. Illness? Possibly. Yet why did I feel so strongly against this mysterious man? Why was he so evil to me? Had he killed me?

I felt sure this was the answer, otherwise why should I feel such hate for him? I was determined to find the truth. First, though, I had to find my family.

The High Street was fairly busy with shoppers and delivery vans and the scene was vaguely familiar to me. I must have lived here, I told myself, or why else would I have been drawn to the little town? It wouldn't click though, it just wouldn't click.

The shoppers must have been puzzled by the thoughtful-looking mongrel who paced up and down that street, peering up at passing faces, snooping into shop doorways. I ignored all enticements, for I had more serious things on my mind than playing games.

By late afternoon I was still no better off. I just couldn't remember clearly any of the shops, pubs or people, although everything appeared too frustratingly familiar! That old teaser hunger reminded me he was still around and had no intention of letting me off the hook just because *I* had problems. The shopkeepers shooed me away as soon as I put my sniffing nose through their doorways, and a sudden jaw-snapping thrust at an overloaded shopping-basket earned me a sharp smack on the snout and a lot of abuse.

Not wanting to cause a fuss (I didn't want to be picked up by the police since I needed to stay around that town until something happened to restore my memory) I left the main street and wandered on to what looked like a vast council estate. Then something did click, although it wasn't particularly helpful to me: South Londoners had been moved down to Edenbridge over the last twenty or so years, away from their slums into modern estates surrounded by good countryside. Many had taken to their new environment, while others (like Lenny, the Guvnor's man) had still yearned for their old surroundings and spent much of their time to-ing and fro-ing from the two vastly different communities.

I was conscious of all this because I'd obviously lived in the town and knew of its history, but where had I lived? On one of those estates? No, it didn't click; it didn't feel right.

I followed a couple of small boys home, much to their delight, and managed to scrounge a few scraps from their scolding but kind-hearted mother. The food wasn't much but enough to keep me going for a while, and to the boys' disappointment I scampered out of their back garden and towards the High Street again.

This time I drifted down all the side-streets on one side, then all the side-streets on the other, but nothing jarred that tiny trigger in my mind which I knew would unleash a flood of memories.

Night fell and so did my spirits. Nothing had happened. I'd felt so sure that when I reached the town it would be easy to find my home, familiar things would guide me to it, but it hadn't happened. I was still in the dark mentally, and now physically.

I wandered down to the very edge of the town, passing pubs, walking across a bridge, past a big garage, a hospital – and then the buildings ran out. There was only black countryside ahead. Utterly dejected, I entered the hospital grounds, found a quiet corner in the yard at the rear of the white single-storey building, and slept.

The smell of lovely cooking awoke me the following morning and I sniffed my way over to an open window from which it wafted. Rearing up on my hind legs, I rested my paws on the window-ledge. Unfortunately, the window was too high for me to see into the room beyond, but, sticking my nose into the air, I drank in the delicious smells, then cried out in appreciation. A huge round brown head suddenly appeared above and white teeth flashed a startled welcome at me. Reds and oranges shimmered in the woman's huge face as she grinned even more broadly.

'You hungry, fellah?' she chuckled, and I wagged my tail in anticipation. 'Now don' you go away,' she told me.

The beaming head disappeared then reappeared almost instantly, the smile now threatening to split the face in half. A thin, partly burnt slice of bacon was dangled before me.

'You get this down you, honey,' she said, dropping the hot finger of meat into my open mouth.

I spat the bacon out instantly as my throat was scorched then drooled saliva on the piping meat to cool it before wolfing it down.

'Good boy,' came the woman's voice from above, then another piece of bacon plopped on to the gravel beside me. This lasted for about as long as the first and I looked up hopefully, tongue hanging out.

'You's a greedy dog!' said the coloured (multicoloured) woman, laughing. 'O.K., I get you one more, then you scat – you get me into trouble!'

The promised third slice appeared and disappeared almost as quickly, and I looked up for more. Still chuckling, the woman waggled her index finger at me and then closed the window as a final word.

It wasn't a bad start to the day and my spirits rose as I trotted round to the hospital's main entrance. Hot food in my belly and a day of discovery ahead of me! Perhaps life (or death) wasn't so bad after all. Dogs are born optimists, as I said.

I reached the entrance and turned left, heading towards the High Street again, sure it was my only chance of finding someone or something I knew.

Without thinking, I wandered into the road and screamed with fright as a green monster roared down on me. The single-decker bus screeched to a halt as I scurried to the other side of the road, tail between my legs and hair on end, and the driver hurled abuse at me, thumping his horn angrily. I cowered in a hedge and rolled my eyes at him, and with a final threatening gesture he threw his vehicle into gear again and slowly moved off.

As the row of windows went by, accusing faces glared down at me while others shook in pity. And one small pair of eyes locked into mine and held my gaze until the progress of the bus no longer allowed them to. Even then, the little girl's head craned round and pushed itself against the glass so I was visible for as long as possible.

Only when the bus had disappeared over the hump-backed bridge did I realize just whom I had been looking at and had been returning my stare. It was my daughter, Gillian, only I called her Polly because I preferred the name! I had been right! Edenbridge was my hometown! I had found them!

But I hadn't found them. The bus was gone and no memories came flooding back. I remembered the names, the minor disagreement over my daughter's, but that was all. I waited for the visions to appear, sure they would, but they didn't.

I groaned in disappointment and longing, then set off after the bus, determined to catch it, refusing to throw away such a chance encounter. As I mounted the hump of the bridge I saw the bus at a stop in the distance. Barking in my eagerness, I increased my speed and hurtled down that High Street like a bullet from a gun. It was no use, though; the bus lurched forward and continued its journey down the long road. I watched it getting smaller and smaller and my legs grew wearier and wearier until I came to a panting halt.

It was hopeless. The bus – and my child – had got away.

Two more days of anguished searching went by – searching of the town and searching of my mind – both of which proved fruitless. I had eaten regularly at the hospital, having my breakfast and evening meal there thanks to the generosity of the coloured cook, and had spent the rest of the time looking through the town and its outer fringes, but all to no avail. Then on the third day, which must have been a Saturday judging by the amount of shoppers there were around, I struck lucky.

I had been wandering up and down the High Street, trying to make myself as inconspicuous as possible (a few people had already tried to catch me now I was becoming a familiar sight around the shops), and had glanced down the small side-turning which led to the car park at the rear of the shops. There I caught a glimpse of a small familiar figure skipping alongside the much taller figure of a woman. They disappeared around a corner but I knew instantly who they were. My heart tried to escape through my throat and my knees suddenly went wobbly.

'Carol!' I gurgled. 'Carol! Polly! Wait for me! Stay there!'

The shoppers must have thought they had a mad dog amongst them, for they all froze at the sound of my barking and stared in amazement as I staggered into the small side-turning. It was like a bad dream, for the shock had turned my legs to jelly and they refused to function properly. I took a grip of myself, realizing this was a chance I just could not afford to miss, and willed the power to flow through my quakey limbs. It did, but I had lost valuable seconds. I set off in pursuit of the two figures, mother and daughter, my wife and child, and was just in time to see them climbing into a green Renault.

'Carol! Stop! It's me!'

They turned and looked in my direction, surprise then fear showing in their faces.

'Quick, Gillian,' I heard my wife say, 'get in the car and close the door!'

'No, Carol! It's me! Don't you know me?'

I was soon across the car park and yapping around the Renault, frantic for my wife to recognize me.

They both stared down at me, their fright obvious. I didn't have the sense to calm down, my emotions were running too high. Carol rolled down the window on her side and flapped a hand at me. 'Shoo, go away! Bad dog!'

'Carol, for Christ's sake, it's me – Nigel! (Nigel? I remembered that was my previous name; I think I preferred Horace.)

'Mummy, it's the poor doggy I told you about, the one that nearly got run over,' I heard my daughter say.

Then I did a quick double-take. Was this my daughter? She seemed much older than I remembered; at least two or three years older. But the woman *was* Carol, and she had called the girl Gillian. Of course it was my daughter!

I leapt up at the side of the car and pushed my nose against the bottom of the half-open window.

'Polly, it's your daddy! Don't you remember me, Polly?' I pleaded.

Carol smacked me on the top of the head, not viciously but defensively. Then the car's engine roared into life, the gears clunked, and the vehicle began slowly to move away.

'No!' I screamed. 'Don't leave me, Carol! Please don't leave me!'

I ran alongside the car, dangerously close, but it gathered speed and soon outpaced me. I was sobbing by now, seeing them slip through my paws like this, knowing I could never match their speed, realizing they were driving from my life again. I felt like throwing myself beneath the wheels to make them stop, but common sense and my old chum, cowardice, prevented me from doing so.

'Come back, come back, come back!'

But they wouldn't.

I saw Polly's wide-eyed face as the car twisted its way round the winding road that led from the car park to the outskirts of the town, and willed her to make her mother stop the car; but it was no use, they sped away.

Many onlookers were regarding me rather nervously by now and I had the good judgement to make myself scarce before I was reported. I took off after the Renault and, as I ran, memories began to pour into me.

Soon, I remembered where I had lived.

SEVENTEEN

Marsh Green is a tiny, one-street village just outside Edenbridge. It has a church at one end and a pub at the other, one general store in the middle and a few houses on either side. There are other houses hidden away at the back of these, one of which I stood gazing at now.

I knew this was where my wife and daughter lived – where I had once lived.

My name had been Nigel Nettle (yes, I'm afraid so) and I had originally come from Tonbridge, Kent. As a boy, I'd spent a lot of time working for local farmers (hence my knowledge of the countryside and animals), but careerwise I'd turned to – of all things – plastics. I'd managed to set up a small factory in Edenbridge on the industrial estate leading to the town and had specialized in flexible packaging, branching out into other areas as the firm prospered and grew. Speaking as a dog, it all seemed very boring, but I suppose at the time the company meant a lot to me. We had moved to Marsh Green to be near the business, and I had found myself taking more and more trips up to London for business reasons (which is why the route was so familiar).

As far as I could remember, we'd been very happy: my love for Carol had never diminished with time, only grown more comfortable; Polly (Gillian) was a delight, our home was a dream, and the business was expanding rapidly. So what had happened? I had died, that's what.

How, and when (Polly seemed so much older than I remembered) I had yet to find out; but I was even more convinced my death was connected with the mysterious man who floated into view so often, yet eluded me before recognition. If he were still a threat to my family (and *that* thought still clung to me), and if he had had something to do with my death (something told me he had been the *cause* of it), then I would find a way of dealing with him. Right now, though, I just wanted to be with Carol and Polly.

It was mid-afternoon, I think, and the sun was hidden behind heavy clouds. I was at the bottom of an unmade road and staring at the detached house before me. The walls of the ground floor were constructed of red brick, while the upper floor's surface was covered with red clay tiles; the doors and window-frames were painted white. A feeling of warmth spread through me and I swallowed hard.

I had to steady myself, it was no good acting the way I had in the town; they would only become frightened again. Keep yourself under control, I told myself, act like a normal dog; there'll be plenty of time to let them know who you really are once they've got used to you.

Pushing the latch of the garden gate down with a paw, I nudged my way in and trotted up the path, keeping a firm rein on trembling body and quaking nerves. I reached the front door and scratched at its surface with a paw.

Nothing happened. I tried again and still nothing happened. I knew they were in, because the Renault stood in the open garage to my left.

I woofed, quietly at first, then louder. 'Carol!' I called out. 'It's me, Carol, open the door!'

I heard footsteps inside, footsteps coming along the hall towards me. With a great effort of will, I stopped my barking and waited. The door opened slightly and a solitary eye peered through the two-inch crack.

'Mummy, it's that dog again!' Polly cried out. The crack shrunk to an inch, the eye now regarding me with both excitement and trepidation.

More footsteps sounded down the hallway, then Carol's eye appeared over my daughter's. She looked at me in amazement.

'How did *you* get here?' she said.

'I remembered where we lived, Carol. I couldn't follow the car, but I remembered. It didn't take long!' I was finding it hard to contain myself.

'Scat! Go away now, there's a good dog,' Carol urged.

I whimpered. I didn't want to go away; I'd only just found them.

'Oh Mummy, I think he's hungry,' Polly said.

'It might be dangerous, dear. We can't take chances.'

'Please,' I wailed, giving them my most beseeching look. 'I need you. Don't turn me away.'

'Look, Mummy, I think he's crying!'

And I was. Tears rolled down my cheeks.

'That's impossible,' Carol said. 'Dogs don't cry.'

But they do. In fact, I wasn't just crying, I was blubbering.

'Let him come in, please, Mummy. I'm sure he doesn't mean us any harm,' Polly pleaded.

Carol looked doubtful. 'I don't know. It doesn't look very dangerous, but you never know with dogs. They're a bit unpredictable.'

I was really snivelling by now and looking as pitiful as I could. The hardest heart would have melted and I knew my wife's heart was by no means hard.

'All right then, let it in,' she said with a sigh.

The door flew open and I flew in, crying and laughing at the same time, kissing and licking hands and legs. They were startled at first and leapt back in alarm, but soon realized I was only being friendly. 'He's lovely, Mummy!' Polly cried, and knelt on both knees to cuddle me. Fear showed on Carol's face for a second but she relaxed as I smothered Polly's face with wet kisses. It's impossible to tell you how wonderful that moment was – even now it gives me a choking feeling – but if parts of your lives closed in episodes as in a book, then that would have been the end of a chapter. Maybe the end of the book.

My wife joined my daughter on the floor, ruffling my hair with a gentle hand, and I made the mistake of trying to take her in my arms and kiss her on the lips. She screamed in horrified glee and we became a struggling heap of squirming, giggling bodies on the hallway carpet. Polly tried to pull me off and her fingers dug into my ribs, making me shriek with laughter. The harsh tickling continued when she realized she had found my vulnerable spot. the fun stopped when the first sprinkle of water jetted from me (I tried hard but I've never been on the best of terms with my bladder) and Carol leapt to her feet, caught hold of my collar and dragged me towards the door.

I found myself outside on the path again, and to convince my wife I was really quite clean I went through the exaggerated pantomime of cocking a leg (an art in itself) and sprinkling her flowerbed. She wasn't too pleased about the flowers, but understood I was trying to prove something. I waited patiently, beaming up at her, tail wagging itself into a blur, wanting desperately to hug her and tell her I still loved her, until she invited me back into the house.

'Thank you!' I barked, and shot past her legs down the hallway.

Polly chased after me, her laughter beautiful to my ears. I skidded to a halt when I reached the kitchen and my eyes drank in the room, the memories returning like old friends from an outing: the huge old black fireplace with its iron oven, a relic of the past which we decided to preserve; the round pine table, deliberately scored and scratched with initials, noughts and crosses, I LOVE YOUs and HAPPY BIRTHDAYs, and any messages we cared to mark for posterity; the antique clock which always informed us the time was a quarter to four, but did so in such an elegant way; the blue-and-yellow vase on the window-sill that looked as if it had been made up from a jigsaw, the result of my patiently piecing it together after Polly had knocked it on to the floor in her 'just-about-walking' days. There were new items around the kitchen, of course, but these seemed alien, an intrusion upon a memory. I sighed, ready to burst into tears again, but a hand grabbed my collar and interrupted my nostalgia.

'Let's just see who you belong to,' Carol said, tugging the nameplate round into view. 'Fluke? Is that your name?'

Polly cupped a hand to her mouth and tittered.

'No address? Nobody wants you, do they?' Carol said, shaking her head.

I shook my own head in agreement.

'Can we keep him?' Polly said excitedly.

'No,' was Carol's firm reply. 'We'll take it to the police station tomorrow and see if it's been reported missing.'

'But can we keep him if no one wants him?'

'I don't know, we'll have to ask Uncle Reg.'

Uncle Reg? Who was he?

Polly seemed pleased enough with that and began to run her fingers down my back. 'Can we feed Fluke, Mummy? I'm sure he's very hungry.'

'Let's see what we've got for it, then.'

Please call me him, or he, Carol, not *it*. I prefer Fluke to *it*. I prefer *Horace* to *it*.

Carol went to a freezer, a new item in the kitchen, and looked thoughtfully into it. 'I'm sure you'd like a leg of lamb or some nice juicy steak, wouldn't you, Fluke?'

I nodded, licking my lips in anticipation, but she closed the freezer and said to Polly, 'Run down to the shop and buy a tin of dogfood. That should keep him happy until tomorrow.'

'Can I take Fluke with me, Mummy?' Polly jumped up and down at the prospect and I began to get excited at her excitement.

'All right, but make sure he doesn't run out into the main road.'

So off we set, my daughter and I, girl and dog, down the lane that led to the main road and the village's only shop. We played as we went and for a while I forgot I was Polly's father and became her companion. I stayed close to her skipping feet, occasionally jumping up to pull at her cardigan, licking her face anxiously once when she tripped and fell. I tried to lick her grazed knee clean, but she pushed me away and wagged a reprimanding finger. While she was buying my dinner in the grocery I stayed on my best behaviour, refusing to be tempted by the pile of within-easy-reach packets of potato crisps, 'all flavours'. We raced back down the lane and I let her beat me for most of the way, hiding behind a tree when she reached the garden gate. She looked around, bewildered, and called out my name; I remained hidden, snickering into the long grass at the base of the tree. I heard footsteps coming back down the lane and, when she drew level with my hiding-place, raced around the other side, scooting towards the gate. Polly caught sight of me and gave chase, but I was an easy winner.

She reached me, giggling and breathless, and threw her arms around my neck, squeezing me tight.

We went into the house – my home – and Polly told Carol everything that had happened. Half the tin of dogfood was poured on to a plate and placed on the floor, together with a dish full of water. I buried my nose in the meat and cleared the plate. Then I cleared the dish. Then I begged for more. And more I got.

Everything was rosy. I was home, I was with my family. I had food in my belly and hope in my heart. I'd find a way of letting them know who I was, and if I couldn't . . . well, did it matter *that* much? As long as I was with them, there to protect them, there to keep the mysterious stranger at bay, my true identity wasn't that important. I wasn't worried about the police station tomorrow, for there'd be no one to claim me, and I was sure I could ingratiate myself enough for them to want to keep me. Yes, everything was rosy.

And you know how things have a habit of turning nasty for me just at their rosiest.

We'd settled down for the night (I thought). Polly was upstairs in bed, Carol was relaxed on the settee, her legs tucked up beneath her as she watched television, and I lay sprawled on the floor below her, my eyes never leaving hers. Occasionally, she would look down at me and smile, and I would smile back, breathing deep sighs of contentment. Several times I tried to tell her who I was, but she didn't seem to understand, telling me to stop grizzling. I gave up in the end and succumbed to the tiredness that had crept up on me. I couldn't sleep – I was too happy for that – but I rested and studied my wife's features with adoring eyes.

She'd aged slightly, lines at the corners of her eyes and at the base of her neck where there'd been no lines before. There was a sadness about her, but it was a well-hidden inner sadness, one you had to sense rather than see; it was obvious to me why it was there.

I wondered how she had coped without me, how Polly had accepted my death. I wondered about my own acceptance of the badger's pronouncement that I certainly was dead as a man. The lounge still contained all the cosiness I remembered so well, but the atmosphere of the whole house was very different now. Part of its personality had gone, and that was me. It's people who create atmosphere, not wood or brick, nor accessories – they only create surroundings.

I had looked around for photographs, hoping to catch a glimpse of my past image, but to my surprise had found none on display. I racked my brain to remember if ever there had been any framed photographs of myself around, but as usually happens whenever I try consciously to remember, my mind became a blank. Perhaps they had been too painful a reminder to Carol and Polly and had been put away somewhere to be taken out only when they could cope.

Whether my plastics business had been sold or was still running I had no way of knowing, but I was relieved to see my family seemed under no great hardship. Various household items confirmed this: the freezer in the kitchen, the new television set here in the lounge, various odd items of furniture scattered about the house.

Carol was still as attractive as ever, despite the telltale lines; she'd never been what you might call beautiful, but her face possessed a quality that made it seem so. Her body was still an inch away from plumpness all round, as it always had been, her legs long and gracefully curved. Ironically, for the first time as a dog, I felt physical feeling stir, a hunger aroused. I wanted my wife, but she was a woman and I was a dog.

I quickly turned my thoughts towards Polly. How she'd grown! She'd lost her baby chubbiness but retained her prettiness, fair skin and darkening hair emphasizing her small, delicately featured face. I was surprised and strangely moved to see her don brown-rimmed spectacles to watch television earlier on in the evening; it seemed to make her even more vulnerable somehow. I was pleased with her; she'd grown into a gentle child, with none of the petulance or awkwardness so many of her age seemed to have. And there was a special closeness between her and her mother, perhaps a closeness born out of mutual loss.

As I had noticed before, she appeared to be about seven or eight, and I pondered over the question of how long I had been dead.

Outside, the sky had dulled as night bullied its way in, and a chill had crept into the air with it, an agitator urging the night on. Carol switched on one of those long, sleek electric fires (another new item, for we'd always insisted on open fires in the past – logs and coal and flames – but maybe that romanticism had gone with me) and settled back on the settee. Headlights suddenly brightened up the room and I heard a car crunching its way down the gravelly lane. It stopped outside and the engine purred on while gates grated their way open. Carol craned her head around and looked towards the window, then turned her attention back towards the television, tidying her hair with deft fingers and smoothing her skirt over her thighs. The car became mobile again, the glare from its lights swinging around the room and then vanishing. The engine stopped, a car door slammed, and a shadowy figure walked past the window rattling fingers against the glass as it did so.

My head jerked up and I growled menacingly, following the shadow until it had gone from view.

'Shhh, Fluke! Settle down.' Carol reached forward and patted the top of my head.

I heard a key going into its latch, then footsteps in the hallway. I was on my feet now. Carol grabbed my collar, concern showing on her face. My body stiffened as the door of the lounge began to open.

'Hello . . .' a man's voice began to say, and he entered the room, a smile on his face.

I broke loose from Carol's grip and went for him, a roar of rage and hate tearing itself from me. I recognized him.

It was the man who had killed me!

EIGHTEEN

I leapt up, my teeth seeking his throat, but the man managed to get an arm between us. It was better than nothing so I sank my teeth into that instead.

Carol was screaming, but I paid her no heed; I wouldn't let this assassin anywhere near her. He cried out at the sudden pain and grabbed at my hair with his other hand; we fell back against the door jamb and slid to the floor. My attack was ferocious for my hate was strong, and I could smell the fear in him. I relished it.

Hands grabbed me from behind and I realized Carol was trying to tug me away, obviously afraid I would kill the man. I hung on; she didn't understand the danger she was in.

For a few seconds I found myself eye-to-eye with him and his face seemed so familiar. And strangely – perhaps I imagined it – there seemed to be some recognition in his eyes too. The moment soon passed and we became a frenzied heap again. Carol had her arms around my throat and was squeezing and pulling at the same time; my victim had his free hand around my nose, fingers curled into my upper jaw, and was trying to prise my grip loose. Their combined strength had its effect: I was forced to let go.

Instantly, the man slammed me in my under-belly with a clenched fist and I yelped at the pain, choking and trying to draw in breath immediately afterwards. I went straight back into the attack, but he'd had a chance to close both hands around my jaws, clamping my mouth tightly shut. I tried to rake him with my nails, but they had little effect against the suit he was wearing.

Pushing myself into him was no use either; Carol's restraining arms around my neck held me back. I called out to her to let me go, but all that emerged from my clenched jaws was a muted growling noise.

'Hang on to it, Carol!' the man gasped. 'Let's get it out the door!'

Keeping one hand tight around my mouth, he grabbed my collar between Carol's arms and began to drag me into the hall. Carol helped by releasing one arm from my neck and grasping my tail. They propelled me forward and tears of frustration formed in my eyes. Why was Carol helping him?

As I was dragged towards the front door, I caught a glimpse of Polly at the top of the stairs, tears streaming down her face.

'Stay there!' Carol called out when she, too, saw her. 'Don't come down!'

'What are you doing with Fluke, Mummy?' she wailed. 'Where are you taking him?'

'It's all right, Gillian,' the man answered her between grunts. 'We've got to get it outside.'

'Why, why? What's he done?'

They ignored her for, realizing I was losing, I had become frantic. I squirmed my body, twisting my neck, dug my paws into the carpet. It was no use, they were too strong.

When we reached the front door he told Carol to open it, afraid to let go himself. She did and I felt the breeze rush in and ruffle my hair. With one last desperate effort I wrenched my head free and cried out, 'Carol, it's me, Nigel! I've come back to you! Don't let him do this to me!'

But of course all she heard was a mad dog barking.

I managed to tear the sleeve of the man's coat and draw blood from his wrist before being thrust out and having the door slammed in my face.

I jumped up and down outside, throwing myself at the door and howling. Carol's voice came to me through the wood; she was trying to soothe Polly. Then I heard the man's voice. The words 'mad dog' and 'attacker' reached my ears and I realized he was speaking to someone on the phone.

'No! Don't let him, Carol! Please, it's me!' I knew he was calling the police.

And sure enough, not more than five minutes later, headlights appeared at the end of the lane and a car bumped its way towards the house. I was underneath the ground floor window by now, running backwards and forwards, screaming and ranting, while Carol, Polly and the man watched me, white-faced. To my dismay, the man had his arms around both Carol's and Polly's shoulders.

The little blue-and-white Panda car lurched to a halt and doors flew open as though it had suddenly sprouted butterfly wings. Two dark figures leapt from it, one carrying a long pole with a loop attached to it. I knew what *that* was for and decided not to give them a chance to use it. I fled into the night; but not too far into it.

Later when the police had given up thrashing around in the dark in search of me, I crept back. I'd heard voices coming from the house, car doors slam, an engine start, then tyres crunching their way back down the lane. No doubt they'd be back tomorrow to give the area a thorough going over in the daylight, but for tonight I knew I'd be safe. I'd wait for the man to come out of the house and then I'd do my best to follow him – or maybe get him there and then. No, that would be foolish – it would only frighten Carol and Polly again, and Carol would probably call the police back. Besides, the man was a little too strong for me. That would be the best bet: follow him somehow – maybe I could even track his car's scent (even cars have their own distinct smell) – then attack him, the element of surprise on my side. It was a hare-brained scheme, but then I was a pretty hare-brained dog. So I settled down to wait. And I waited. And waited.

The shock of it hit me a few hours later: he wasn't coming out that night. His car was still in the drive so I knew he hadn't already left, and there would have been no reason for him to have gone with the police. He was staying the night!

How could you, Carol? All right, I'd obviously been cold in my grave at least a couple of years, but how could you with him? The man who had murdered me? How could you with anyone after all we'd shared? Had it meant so little that you'd forget so soon?

My howl filled the night and seconds later curtains moved in the bedroom window. My bedroom window!

How could such evil exist? He's killed me, then taken my wife! He'd pay – oh, I'd make him pay!

I ran from the house then, unable to bear the pain of looking at it, imagining what was going on inside, I crashed around in the dark, frightening night creatures, disturbing those who were sleeping, and finally fell limp and weeping into a hollow covered with brambles. There I stayed till dawn.

NINETEEN

Have patience now, my story's nearly done.

Do you still disbelieve all I've told you? I don't blame you – I'm not sure I believe it myself. Maybe I'm a dog who's just had hallucinations. How is it you understand me, though? You *do* understand me, don't you?

How's the pain? You'll forget it later; memories of pain are always insubstantial unless you actually *feel* the pain again. How's the fear? Are you less afraid now, or more afraid? Anyway, let me go on: you're not going anywhere, and I've got all the time in the world. Where was I? Oh yes . . .

Dawn found me, full of self-pity again, confused and disappointed. But, as I keep telling you, dogs are born optimists; I decided to be constructive about my plight. First I would find out a little more about myself – like exactly when I died – and then the circumstances of my death. The first would be easy, for I had a good idea of where I would find myself. You see, now I was in familiar surroundings, memories had started to soak through. Well, perhaps not memories, but – how can I put it? – recognitions were soaking through. I was on home ground. I knew where I was. Hopefully, memories of events would soon follow.

The second part – the circumstances of my death – was more difficult, and because I felt familiar places would begin to open memory valves, a visit to my plastics factory might help.

First, though: When did I die?

The graveyard was easy to find, since I knew the location of the dominating church (although the inside wasn't too familiar to me). What was hard to locate, was my own grave. Reading had become difficult by now and many of these gravestones were poorly marked anyway. I found mine after two hours of squinting and concentrating, and was pleased to see it was still neat and tidy in appearance. I suppose to you it would seem a macabre kind of search, but I promise you, being dead is the most natural thing in the world, and it disturbed me not in the least to be mooching around for my own epitaph.

A small white cross marked my resting-place, and neatly inscribed on it were these words: 'NIGEL CLAIREMOUNT' – I'm not kidding – 'NETTLE. BELOVED HUSBAND OF CAROL, BELOVED FATHER OF GILLIAN. BORN 1943 – DIED 1975.' I'd died at the age of thirty-two, so it seemed unlikely it was from natural causes. Below this, two more words were carved out in the stone, and these made my eyes mist up. These simply said: 'NEVER FORGOTTEN.'

Oh yes? I thought bitterly.

The plastics factory was easy to locate too. In fact, as I trotted through the town, I began to remember the shops, the little restaurants, and the pubs. How I would have loved to have gone in and ordered a pint! I realized it was now Sunday, for the High Street was quiet and in the distance I could hear church bells start their guilt-provoking ringing. It was still early morning, but the thought that the pubs would not be open for a few hours yet did not lessen their attraction; I remembered I had always enjoyed my Sunday lunchtime drink.

The sight of the one-floor factory itself, almost a mile beyond the town, stirred up old feelings, a mixture of pride, excitement and anxiety. It was small, but modern and compact, and I could see a fairly substantial extension had recently been added. A long sign, itself made of plastic and which I knew lit up at night, stretching along the face of the building, read: 'NETTLE & NEWMAN – ADVANCED PLASTICS LTD.'

Nettle & Newman, I pondered. Newman? Who was Newman...? Yes, you've guessed it. My killer had been my partner.

It all began to take shape, all began to fall into place; and the thing that hurt most of all was that he wasn't content just to take my business – he'd taken my wife too. I remembered him clearly now, his face – his person – clearly formed in my mind. We had started the business together, built it up from nothing, shared our failures, rejoiced together in our successes. He had the shrewder business brain (although he could be rash), but I had the greater knowledge – an almost instinctive knowledge – of plastics. It seems crazy now, a silly thing to be proud of, but proud I had been of that knowledge. Plastics! You can't even eat them! We had been good partners for a time, almost like brothers, respecting each other's particular flair. It was often I, though, as smart as my partner had been, who had a hunch on business matters and, as I remember, could be very stubborn if I considered a certain direction was the right or wrong one to take. I believe it was this stubbornness which began to lead to our disagreements.

The facts of the disputes hadn't swung into focus yet, but the image of heated arguments in the latter days of our partnership clung heavily to my mind. It had seemed our disagreement would lead to the breaking up of the company at one time, but then what had happened?

Obviously I'd been murdered.

Newman. Reginald Newman. Uncle Reg! That's what Carol had said to Polly when she'd asked about keeping me – 'Wait till Uncle Reg gets home'. Something like that! The creep had really crept in! Had I been aware of his intentions before I'd died? Was that why I was different? Was I like one of those unfortunate ghosts I'd seen, tied to their past existence because of some grievance, some undone thing holding them? Had I been allowed (or had my own natural stubbornness caused it?) to keep old memories in order to set things right?

I stood erect, vengeful, defiant of the odds. I would protect my own. (There's nothing worse than an idiot ennobled my revenge.)

The factory was closed for the day, but I sniffed around the outside wondering about the new extension built on to the back of the building. Business must have been good since my death.

After a while I got bored. Strange to think that an interest which had been a large part of my life should seem so uninteresting, so trivial, but I'm afraid after my initial stirring of emotions it all seemed very dull. I went off and chased some rabbits in a nearby field.

I returned to my home later on in the day and was surprised to find it empty. The car was gone from the drive and no noises came from the house. It seemed an empty shell now, just like the factory; they had both lost their meaning. Without their occupants, without my direct involvement, they were just bricks and mortar. I don't remember being conscious of this sudden impersonal attitude in me at the time, and it's only now, in times of almost complete lucidity, that I'm aware of the changes which have taken place in my personality over the years.

Starvation became my biggest concern – at least, the prevention of it – so I trotted back to the main road through the village and the ever-open grocery store. A lightning raid on the 'all-flavours' secured me a small lunch although a hasty departure from Marsh Green.

I took to the open fields when a blue-and-white patrol car slowed down and a plod stuck his head out of the window and called enticingly to me. After my attack on dear Reggie the night before, I knew the local police would be keeping a sharp lookout for me; you're not allowed to attack a member of the public unless you've been trained to do so.

A romp with a flock of longwools (sheep to you) passed a joyful hour for me until a ferocious collie appeared on the scene and chased me off. The derision from the sheep at my hasty retreat irritated me, but I saw there was no reasoning with their canine guardian: he was too subservient to man.

A cool drink in a busy little stream, a nibble at a clump of shaggy inkcaps – edible mushrooms – and a doze in the long grass filled out the rest of the afternoon.

I awoke refreshed and single-minded. I returned to the factory and began my vigil.

He showed up early next morning, much earlier than any of our – I mean his – employees. I was tucking into a young rabbit I'd found sleepy-eyed in the nearby field (sorry, but canine instinct was taking over more and more – I was quite proud of my kill, actually), when the sound of his car interrupted me. I crouched low, even though I was well hidden in the hedge dividing field from factory, and growled in a menacing, dog-like way. The sun was already strong and his feet disturbed fine sandy dust from the asphalt as he stepped from the car.

The muscles in my shoulder bunched as I readied myself to attack. I wasn't sure what I could do against a man, but hate left little room for logic. Just as I was about to launch myself forward, another car drew in from the main road and parked itself alongside Newman's. A chubby grey-suited man waved at Newman as he emerged from the car. The face was familiar, but it was only when an image of the chubby man in a white smock flashed into my mind that I remembered him to be the technical manager. A good man, a little unimaginative, but conscientious and hard-working enough to make up for it.

'Scorcher again today, Mr Newman,' he said, smiling at the foe.

'No doubt of it. Same as yesterday, I reckon,' Newman replied, pulling a briefcase from the passenger seat of his car.

'You look as if you caught some of it,' the manager replied. 'In the garden, were you, yesterday?'

'Nope. Decided to get away from it all and take Carol and Gillian down to the coast.'

'I bet they appreciated that.'

Newman gave a short laugh. 'Yes, I've spent too many weekends going over paperwork lately. No fun for the wife.'

The manager nodded as he waited for Newman to open the office entrance to the factory. 'How is she now?' I heard him say.

'Oh . . . much better. Still misses him, of course, even after all this time, but then we all do. Let's go over this week's schedule while it's still quiet . . .' Their voices took on a hollow sound as they entered the building and the door closing cut them off completely.

Wife? She's married him? I was bewildered. And hurt even more. He'd really got everything!

My fury seethed and boiled throughout the day, but I stayed well hidden as the factory buzzed into activity and became a living thing. A coldness finally took over me as I waited in the shade of the hedge: I would bide my time, wait for the right moment.

Newman emerged again around midday, jacket over his arm, tie undone. There were too many factory workers around, sitting in the shade with their backs against the building, munching sandwiches, others lounging shirtless under the full blast of the sun; I stayed hidden. He climbed into his car, wound down a window, and drove off into the main road.

I gritted my teeth with frustration. I could wait, though.

The murderer returned about an hour later, but again, there was nothing I could do – still too much activity.

I slept and evening came. The workers – many of whom I now recognized – left the building, relieved to escape its exhausting heat. The office staff, consisting of two girls and an administrator, followed shortly after, and the chubby technical manager an hour after that. Newman worked on.

A light went on when dusk began to set in and I knew it came from our – his – office. I crept from my hiding-place and padded over to the building, gazing up at the window. I stood on my hind legs and rested my front legs against the brickwork, but even though I craned my neck till the tendons stood out I could not see into the office. The fluorescent light in the ceiling was visible, but nothing else.

I dropped to all fours and did a quick tour of the building looking for any openings. There were none.

As I completed the circuit, I saw the lone car standing where he had parked it face on to the building. And as I approached, I noticed the window on the driver's side had been left open. It had been a hot day.

The thing to do was obvious: the means to do it a little more difficult. It took four painful attempts to get the front portion of my body through that opening, and then a lot of back leg scrabbling and elbow heaving to get my tender belly over the sill. I finally piled over on to the driver's seat and lay there panting, waiting for the pain from my scraped underside to recede. Then I slid through the gap between the front seats into the back and hid there in the dark cavity on the floor, my body trembling all over.

It was at least an hour before Newman decided he'd had enough work for one day and left the office. My ears pricked up at the sound of the front door being locked and I slunk low when the car door jerked open and a briefcase came flying through on to the passenger seat. The car rocked as he climbed in and I did my best to contain my eagerness to get at him. He started the engine, clicking the light switch, and reversed the car from its parking space. A hand fell over the back seat as he reversed and the temptation to bite his fingers off was almost overpowering, but I needed something more than my own strength if I were to claim retribution.

I needed his car's speed.

He swung into the main road and sped towards the town. He had to pass through Edenbridge to reach Marsh Green and, as town and village were not too far apart, I knew I hadn't too long to make my move. There was a long straight stretch of road leading from the town before it curved to the left towards Hartfield, and a smaller road to Marsh Green joining it from the right on its apex. Most cars speeded up on the clear stretch before the bend and it seemed likely he would do the same, for the road would be fairly empty at that time of night. That was where I would go into action – even if it meant being killed myself. I'd died before; it would be easy to do so again. After all, what did I have to lose? A dog's life?

The thought of what this evil man had reduced me to made the blood rush through me again, and the anger beat against my chest. A low rumbling started way down in my throat and began to rise, molten lava full of hate, seeking an opening, gushing up the hot passage of my throat and finally bursting through to the surface with a scream, an eruption of violence.

I saw the fear in his face as he looked back over his shoulder, his eyes wide and white-filled, forgetting to take his foot off the accelerator, the car speeding on unguided. I had time to see the bend was almost upon us before I lunged forward and bit into his cheek.

He went forward, trying to avoid my slashing teeth, but I went with him, catching and tearing his ear. He screeched and I screeched and the car screeched. And we all went crashing off the road together.

My body hurtled through the windscreen and suddenly I was bathed in a blinding whiteness as I skimmed along the bonnet and into the beam of the headlights. For a split second, lasting for at least a year, I felt as if I were floating in an incandescent womb; until darkness and pain hit me as one.

Then I remembered all and knew I'd been so very, very wrong.

TWENTY

Reg Newman had been a true friend. Even after my death.

The realization hit me along with the pain as I lay there stunned and breathless in the dusty lane – the small lane rutted and stone-filled, which ran directly on from the main road, used only by residents who lived further down its length. We'd been lucky: instead of running into the trees lining the sides of the bend, the car had plunged straight ahead into the lane, the rough bank at one side bringing it to a gut-wrenching halt.

The fragments joined; pieces merged, the jigsaw made a whole. I knew why the bad memories of Reg had lingered on after death, why my very death had confused and distorted those memories. I saw how the stupidities of life could warp the senses in the afterlife, unsettle a soul's peace. I lay there and let my mind welcome the memories, ashamed and relieved at the same time. I saw the images of my ex-partner had been only vague because he'd been connected with my death and part of me had wanted to forget why and how I had died. Because I had only myself to blame.

We'd had many disagreements in our partnership, but one or other of us had usually given way out of mutual respect for the other's special qualities: Reg's business acumen or my knowledge of plastics. Only this time it had been different. This time neither of us was prepared to back down.

The argument was one we were bound to reach at some time in our growth: level out or expand. I was for levelling out, maintaining our position in soft plastics, improving and diversifying only in certain areas. Reg for was expanding, going for hard plastics, investigating the qualities of polypropylene in this area. He maintained that eventually glass would be a thing of the past, that it would be replaced by the more durable plastic, first in the container market, then in most other areas where glass was now used. Polypropylene seemed to possess most of the qualities needed: clarity, strength, the ability to withstand a variety of temperatures, and it was durable to most conditions.

We were using polythylene mainly at that time for flexible packaging such as carrier-bags, frozen food pouches and containers for garden feed produce; to change from this to hard plastics would have meant a huge investment. While I agreed with my partner about the future of plastics, I argued we were not ready to venture into that field just yet. The company would need new extruders for the raw materials to be softened and moulded, the factory itself enlarged or a complete move made to a bigger site. In addition new technical staff and engineers would be required, and transport costs would rocket because of the larger delivery bulk. It would take an investment of not less than one and a half million pounds to bring it off. And that would mean bringing in new partners, even merging with another company. The business, I argued, was fine as it was; let other companies pave the way into these new areas. It would be foolish for us to take expansion risks so soon after the oil crisis anyway. If it happened again, or if there were serious delays in bringing home North Sea oil, then many companies would be left out on a limb. Now was the time to maintain our growth, reach a good economic level, and bide our time. But Reg wouldn't have it.

He blamed my ego, my unwillingness to allow strangers into the business we had built up ourselves. He blamed my failure to see beyond the specific product I was dealing with, to see it in future business terms. He blamed my stubbornness, my lack of imagination. I scoffed and blamed his greed.

We were both wrong about each other, of course, and secretly we both knew it, but you need words to sling in arguments, and words so often exaggerate.

It all came to a head when I discovered he had already begun undercover negotiations with a hard plastics company. 'Just sounding them out', he had told me when I confronted him with my discovery (I had taken a call when Reg had been out from a director of the other company who was unaware of my resistance to my partner's plans), but I wouldn't be pacified. I had a suspicion of business 'practices' even though I had a genuine respect for Reg's flair, and now I began to be afraid that things were running too fast for me, that my technical skill was no match for business politics. Anger, spurred on by this fear, poured from me.

Reg had had enough: so far as he was concerned he was acting in the company's best interests, negotiating for our growth, afraid that if we didn't expand into other areas we would eventually be swallowed up by the bigger firms. It didn't worry him that we would lose much of our independence: there was no standing still in business for him, only progression or regression. And here I was holding him back, content to let the company slide into mediocrity.

He threw the telephone at me and stormed from our office.

It caught me on the shoulder and I fell back into my chair, stunned not by the blow, but by his irrational behaviour. It took a few seconds for my temper to flare again, then I tore after him.

I was just in time to see his car roar off into the main road. I yanked open the door of my own car, fumbling angrily for my keys as I did so, and jumped in. I gunned the engine as an expression of my rage and swept from the factory yard after him.

The red tail-lights from Reg's car were two tiny points far ahead and I pushed down hard on the accelerator to make them grow larger. We sped through Edenbridge, down the long stretch of straight road that followed, and round the curving bend at the end, then on into the unlit country darkness. I flashed my lights at him, commanding him to stop, wanting to get my hands on him there and then. His car pulled into a side road which would take him across country to Southborough, where he lived, and I slowed just enough to allow me to take the turn.

I jammed on my brakes when I saw he had stopped and was waiting. My car rocked to a halt and I saw him climb from his car and stride back towards me. As he drew near, his hand stretched forward, he began to say, 'Look, we're acting like a couple of ki . . .' But I ignored the look of apology on his face, his outstretched hand which was ready to take mine in a gesture of appeasement, his words that were meant to bring us both to our senses.

I threw open my door, striking his extended hand, and leapt out, hitting him squarely on the jaw all in one motion. Then I jumped back into the car, snapped it into reverse, and raced backwards into the main road again. I looked forward just in time to see him raise himself on to one elbow, his face lit up in the glare of my headlights. I saw his lips move as though calling my name, and a look of horror sweep across his features.

Then I was in the main road and engulfed in a blinding white light. I felt the car heave and heard someone screaming and through the searing pain that followed I realized I was listening to myself. And then the pain and the light and the screaming became too much and I was dead.

I was floating away, and my car was a mangled wreck, and the cab of the truck that had hit it was buckled and smashed and the driver was climbing from it, his face white and disbelieving, and Reg was crying, trying to pull me from the wreck, calling my name, and refusing to admit what my crumpled body swore to.

And then there was a blankness; and then I was reluctantly pushing myself from my new mother's womb.

I staggered to my feet, all four of them. My head was dazed and spinning, not just with the physical blow it had received, but with the facts that had been revealed to me.

Reg was not the evil man of my dreams: he had been a friend in life and a friend in death. He'd succumbed to my wishes, kept the company small; the extension was a sign that the company was still profitable and growing in the way I had wanted, for it meant no drastic development had taken place, only improvement to existing production. Had he kept it this way out of respect for me, or had his business venture merely fallen through without my added strength? There was no question in my mind; I *knew* the former was the case. And Reg, the lifelong bachelor, the man I had teased so often about his unmarried status, the friend who had admitted quite openly there had only ever been one girl for him and I had married her, had finally taken that plunge. Not just for me, a noble act in taking care of my bereaved family, but because he had always loved Carol. He'd known her long before I had (it was he who had introduced us) and our rivalry for her had been fierce until I had won, and then he had become a close friend to both of us.

Our business partnership had often been stormy, but our friendship had rarely rocked. Not until our final conflict, that is. And that was a conflict I know he regretted bitterly. As I now did.

I looked back at the car, its engine dead but the lights still blazing. Disturbed dust swirled and eddied in their beams. Blinking my eyes against the brightness, I staggered forward, out of their glare and into the surrounding darkness. My eyes quickly became used to the sudden change in light and I saw Reg's body slumped half out of the smashed windscreen across the car bonnet. He looked lifeless.

With a gasp of fear, I ran forward and jumped up at the bonnet. One of his arms dangled down the side of the car and his face, white in the moonlight, was turned towards me. I stretched forward and licked the blood from his gashed cheek and ear, begging forgiveness for what I had done, for what I had thought. Don't be dead, I prayed. Don't die uselessly as I had.

He stirred, groaned. His eyes opened and looked directly into mine. And for a moment I swear he recognized me.

His eyes widened and a softness came into them. It was as if he could read my thoughts, as if he understood what I was trying to tell him. Maybe it was only my imagination, maybe he was just in shock, but I'm sure he smiled at me and tried to stroke me with his dangling hand. His eyes suddenly lost their sharpness as consciousness slipped from him. There was little blood on him apart from the gash in his cheek and ear caused by my teeth in our struggle inside the car; my body had broken the glass of the windscreen, he had merely followed through.

The steering wheel had prevented him going further and I checked to see it had done no serious damage to his body. It was of the collapsible kind and so he would have a massive bruise across his stomach the next day, but probably nothing more serious. His head must have struck the top of the windscreen frame as he'd gone through and this had caused his blackout. There was no smell of death on him.

Voices came from further down the lane as people left their houses to investigate the sound of the crash. I decided it was time for me to leave; there was nothing here for me any more.

I stretched forward and kissed Reg on his exposed cheek. He stirred but did not regain consciousness.

Then I dropped to all fours and padded away into the night.

TWENTY-ONE

So there you have it, old man. That's it.

Do you believe me?

Or do you think your pain is driving you mad?

Dawn is creeping up on us now, and death – for you – is creeping with it. I knew when I found you here by the roadside last night it was too late to find help for you; the cancer in your stomach had already made its claim.

How long have you walked the roads, caring for no one and no one caring for you? What did life do to make you flee from it? Well, it's over for you now; your years of wandering are done.

I wonder if you do understand all I've told you? I think your closeness to death had made our communication possible. You're in that transitive state which helps the dying receptive to many things they've closed their minds to before. Do you still think there's only blackness waiting for you? Or Hell? Heaven? If only it were that simple.

There's not much more to tell you now. I waited, hidden in the darkness, until they had pulled Reg from the car and saw he had regained consciousness again. He actually walked himself to the ambulance which had arrived by then, and I could see him twisting his head, peering into the gloom, looking for me. The people helping him must have thought he was concussed when he kept asking about the dog he'd seen.

I left the area shortly after, paying one last visit to my own grave before going. I don't quite know why I went there; perhaps in some strange way it was to pay my last respects to myself. It was the end of something for me. The end of a life, possibly.

Fresh flowers had been placed at the graveside, and I knew I had not been forgotten. The memory of the husband, the father, the friend, would dull with time, but I'd always be somewhere in a corner of their minds.

For me, it was to be different. The memories might still linger, to surface occasionally, but the emotions had changed. My emotions were fast becoming those of a dog, as though, now my search was over, a ghost had been vanquished.

The ghost was my humanness. I felt free, free as any bird in the sky. Free to live as a dog. I ran for nearly a day and, when I finally dropped, the last remnants of my old self had been purged.

That all happened at least – in your terms – two years ago. Memories and old habits still visit me from time to time and I remember myself as a man. But now they only return to me in dreams. Finding you last night, tucked away in this hedge by the roadside, dying and afraid of death, stirred those hidden feelings again. Your dying, the aura that's now around you, drew those feelings out, and with the feelings came the old memories, so clear, so sharp. Perhaps you've helped me too, old man; it would never do for me to relinquish my heritage completely. What was it the badger had said? 'You're special.' Maybe he was right. Maybe everything he told me was right. Maybe I'm meant to remember. Maybe I'm here to help those like you. Maybe.

All I know is that I forget more and more what I was and become what I am.

And by and large, I enjoy what I am. I see life now from a different level: knee-level. It's surprising the difference it makes. It's like always approaching a place from the same direction, then suddenly coming from the opposite way: the familiar changes shape, looks different somehow. It's still the same, but has taken on a new perspective. Know what I mean?

I've travelled the country, swum in the sea. Nobody's ever owned me again, but many have fed me. I've talked with, ate with, and played with so many different species my head aches trying to remember them all. I've been amazed at and chuckled over the neuroses in the animal world: I've met a pig who thought he was a horse; a cow who stuttered; a bull who was bullied by a shrew he shared a field with; a duckling who thought he was ugly (and he was); a goat who thought he was Jesus; a woodpigeon who was afraid of flying (he preferred to walk everywhere); a toad who could croak Shakespeare sonnets (and little else); an adder who kept trying to stand up; a fox who was a vegetarian; and a grouse who never stopped.

I've fought a stoat (we both broke off and ran at the same time – otherwise we'd have both been slaughtered), killed an attacking owl, battled with a rat-pack, and been chased by a swarm of bees. I've teased sheep and irritated horses; I've philosophized with a donkey on existentialism's possible influence on art, ethics and psychology. I've sung with birds and joked with hedgehogs.

And I've made love to seven different bitches.

Time's running out for you now; death's nearly here. I hope what I've told you has helped, I hope it's made some sense to your feverish brain. Can you smell that heavy sweetness in the air; it means I've got to go. It's a lady friend, you see. She lives on a farm three fields away and she's ready for me now. It's just a matter of getting her out of that shed, away from the jealous old farmer; but that shouldn't be too difficult for a smart dog like me.

One other thing before I go: I met Rumbo again the other day. I'd been sleeping under a tree when an acorn hit me on the nose; when I looked around I heard a voice call out 'Hello, squirt,' and there he was above me, grinning all over his little squirrel face. He showered me with a few more acorns, but when I called his name he looked blank, then scurried off. I knew it was him because the voice – thought pattern if you like – was the same; and who else would call me 'squirt'?

It made me feel good, although I had no desire to follow him. It was just good to know someone like Rumbo was around again.

Excuse me now, my lady friend's scent is really becoming too much to ignore. You don't need me anymore anyway, the next part you have to do on your own.

At least, I hope I've helped. Maybe we'll bump into each other again sometime.
Good-bye.
Hope you're a dog!

The tramp tried to follow the dog with his tired old eyes as it scampered away, through the broken hedge, into the fields beyond. But the effort was too much.

His body twisted with the pain and seemed to shrivel within the rags he wore as clothes. He lay on his side, his grizzled cheek resting against the damp grass. A solitary ant, not three inches from his eye, gazed at him without expression.

The tramp's lips tried to smile but the pain would not allow it. With his last remaining strength he brought a shaking hand up, and with all the concentration he could summon he placed a finger carefully over the creature's tiny body, but the ant scurried away and hid in the forest of grass. With one last painful shudder, the old man's breath left him and took his life with it.

He died. And waited.